NAUGHTY OR NICE

A Holiday Regency Anthology

BREE WOLF SYDNEY JANE BAILY TRACY SUMNER
FENNA EDGEWOOD CHARLIE LANE
JENNIFER MONROE MEREDITH BOND

Naughty or Nice: A Holiday Regency Anthology

Published by WOLF Publishing UG

Cover Art by Victoria Cooper
Edited by Chris Hall

Ebook ISBN: 978-3-98536-070-3
Paperback ISBN: 978-3-98536-102-1

WOLF Publishing - This is us:

Two sisters, two personalities.. But only one big love!

Diving into a world of dreams..

...Romance, heartfelt emotions, lovable and witty characters, some humor, and some mystery! Because we want it all! Historical Romance at its best!

Visit our website to learn all about us, our authors and books!

Sign up to our mailing list to receive first hand information on new releases, freebies and promotions as well as exclusive giveaways and sneak-peeks!

WWW.WOLF-PUBLISHING.COM

ONCE UPON AN AGGRAVATINGLY HEROIC KISS

A WHICKERTONS IN LOVE NOVELLA

BREE WOLF

Once Upon an Aggravatingly Heroic Kiss by Bree Wolf

Published by WOLF Publishing UG

About the book

ONCE UPON AN AGGRAVATINGLY HEROIC KISS

A meddlesome lady.
An honor-bound lord.
And quite a few misunderstandings.

England 1749: LADY EDITH WESTON, daughter to the EARL OF SWANSBOROUGH, is determined to see her friend wed to a man she loves. Unfortunately, Lady Adele, however, has been promised since birth and refuses to break her father's heart by going against his wishes. Edith, though, cannot accept that, and when she sees the first stirrings of love between her dearest friend and a visitor from the north that Christmas, she is determined to work a miracle.

JASPER BEAUMONT, EARL OF WHICKERTON, made the monumental mistake of promising his father upon his deathbed that he would wed within the year. Unfortunately, eleven months and far too many days have passed without a suitable bride in sight. At least, until he visits Cumberton Castle for the holidays and his path crosses that of a most intriguing young lady.

Never having been one to mind her own business, Edith does what she must to prove to her friend that one must never give up on love. A statement ringing all the more true when Edith finds her every move observed by a teasing gentleman with wicked eyes and a devilish smile...who, oddly enough, does not seem to disapprove of her meddlesome tendencies.

Impressed by Lady Edith's quick wit, Jasper watches as she directs all those around her like a gifted puppeteer, determined to ensure her friend's happiness. Only before long, he comes to wonder if perhaps...he, too, has been caught in her web, doing precisely what she wants him to.

The only question: could she possibly want him?

Prologue

Somewhere in northern England, 1749 (or a variation thereof)

The carriage rattled through a particularly deep hole in the frozen road, swaying so violently from side to side, that Lady Edith Weston, daughter to the Earl of Swansborough, was surprised to see Lord and Lady Ashbrook continue to slumber like babes rocked gently in their mothers' arms. While Lady Ashbrook's breaths came evenly, her husband uttered a slight snore every once in a while that echoed through the carriage and almost drowned out the rattling sound of the carriage's wheels.

Edith chuckled, covering her mouth with her hand as she glanced at her oldest friend, seated beside her. "Addie, would you say this is their secret?" she asked with another sideways glance at Lord and Lady Ashbrook. "Sleeping in the carriage?"

With a wide grin upon her face, Lady Adele Berkley, daughter to the Duke and Duchess of Ashbrook, rolled her eyes. "Quite frankly, I cannot remember a journey of any length when they did not fall asleep." Still, an almost adoring look came to her hazel eyes as she looked at her parents. "Somehow, they cannot seem to stay awake."

"Fortunately for us, wouldn't you agree?" Edith pointed out with an arched brow. "After all, conversation is so much easier when one is not constantly overheard by one's parents, even parents as adorable as yours."

Adele nodded. "Indeed, there are some things I would rather not have my parents know about me." Her smile dimmed and then vanished as a thoughtful gaze came to her eyes.

Edith placed a hand upon her friend's. "Is it your betrothal?" Although betrothed since she had been a babe, Adele barely knew the man she was to marry. He was the son of Lord Ashbrook's oldest friend, and the day after Adele had been born, the two fathers had thought it a marvelous idea to draw up a marriage contract, tying their two children to one another for life.

As much as Edith adored Adele's parents, she could not help but shake her head at such a foolish notion. Of course, she knew well that, among the *ton*, marriages were most often agreed upon for fairly rational reasons. However, in her heart, Edith believed that there was no better foundation for any marriage than affection.

True and honest affection.

Adele's gaze swept over the snow-covered landscape outside the window, her shoulders rising and falling with each long, heavy breath. "Do you think I shall like him?" she asked unexpectedly and then turned to look at Edith.

Shrugging, Edith wished she could reassure her friend. "I have no way of knowing," she said quite honestly. "I, myself, have seen the man no more than once or twice. Do you think he's the adventurous type? Traveling the continent, going from place to place, seeing the world?"

A small smile teased Adele's lips. "I hope he is," she replied, a faraway look coming into her eyes. Indeed, Edith knew perfectly well that Adele possessed an adventurous spirit. She might seem shy at times or act hesitantly, but deep inside she longed for new experiences. Would this unknown husband be a good match for her?

"Will you truly do this?" Edith inquired carefully. "Marry a man you hardly know?"

Adele shrugged. "I don't have much of choice, do I? My father gave his word, and I cannot dishonor him."

"Even if it robs you of happiness?"

For a brief moment, Adele closed her eyes and drew in a deep breath.

Then she straightened and met Edith's gaze. "Perhaps at the end of this house party, he will be a stranger no longer." She glanced across the carriage. "Perhaps my parents were right to do as they did. Perhaps they did choose wisely for me. In any case, this house party is a good chance for me to get to know him, would you not agree?"

Edith nodded. "It is a chance; however, we cannot be certain of the result. What if you get to know him, only to realize that you do not care for him? What then? Will you still marry him?"

Adele's shoulders slumped instantly. "Must you always point out the flaws in any endeavor?" She heaved a deep sigh. "Honestly, Edie, sometimes it is better to simply look on the bright side."

"I suppose that approach has...some...merit," Edith conceded, surprised by her friend's words. Indeed, she had always thought of herself as someone seeing rather the good than the bad. "However, I do not believe it wise to simply accept what is because one believes oneself without options."

"I am without options!" Adele exclaimed rather loudly, the sound of her agitated voice causing her parents to stir in their sleep. Fortunately, they did not wake.

"Of course, you have options," Edith insisted, disliking the notion of simply giving up and accepting one's fate.

Adele rolled her eyes at her. "That is easy for you to say. Your parents allow you to choose freely. You do not need to worry about disappointing them."

Edith looked across at the slumbering Lord and Lady Ashbrook. "Do you truly think they would be disappointed? What if you simply told them the truth? Do you think they would not help you? Do you think they would not understand?"

Adele slumped back in her seat. "I don't know. My father always speaks with such admiration and fondness for his old friend that I cannot help but think it would break his heart." She heaved a deep sigh. "Oh, I wish we could switch places," she whispered then, turned her head slightly toward Edith and cast her a mischievous smile. "However, I would not wish this situation on you, either."

Edith laughed. "I have a feeling that this Christmas season shall bring a lot of new revelations. Just you wait. I assure you everything will be all right."

Adele stared at her for a moment before she finally blinked. "You have a feeling? What does that mean?" Chuckling, she shook her head. "Honestly, Edie, sometimes you confuse me."

Edith held her friend's gaze. "There *always* is a bright side, Addie. Trust me." She squeezed her friend's hand. "I want to see you happy, and if Lord Halston's son does not make you happy, then you should not marry him." A deep smile came to her face. "Can you imagine marriage being based on affection alone? What would such a world be like?"

Both women sat back, exhaling a deep breath as their thoughts contemplated such an idea. Indeed, Adele's parents had meant no harm when they had set up the contract between her and Lord Halston's son. At the same time, Edith's parents did not allow her to choose freely who she would marry out of the goodness of their hearts. With six elder siblings advantageously married, they simply did not worry about their youngest daughter's choice, no doubt believing that everything would sort itself out.

"Do you think you will know right away?" Edith asked, turning her head from the window, and looking once more back toward her friend. "Do you think one glance can ever be enough to know?"

Adele shrugged. "I've never been in love," she stated quite matter-of-factly. "I do not know. Yet I cannot imagine seeing a stranger and..." She shrugged once more, and Edie could tell that an instant connection seemed truly impossible to her.

Edith smiled. "I think I'll know." Indeed, over the past few years, Edith had watched her siblings most attentively. She had seen them become betrothed, seen them married and become husbands and wives, and more than that, she had seen the way they had looked at their spouses, spoken to their spouses. Indeed, she felt quite confident in her ability to judge another's affections correctly. In her opinion, her eldest brother as well as two of her sisters were in love with their spouses. Although her youngest brother clearly held affection for his wife, it was not the kind of love she had seen in the other three marriages. Unfortunately, her other two sisters seemed rather indifferent to their husbands, clearly not seeking their company, most content when they could spend time apart.

For so long now, Edith had watched them all, observed those little interactions between husband and wife, and come to the conclusion that there was only one kind of marriage she would ever agree to. She wanted love, plain and simple.

For herself.

But also for Addie.

"Truly?" Adele inquired, a questioning look in her eyes. "Do you truly expect to see someone, look into his eyes and...?" Again, she shrugged. "I mean, even if he looks dashing and kind, you still do not know him. You do not know his thoughts, the way he would speak to you. How can your heart possibly...?"

Edith squeezed her friend's hand encouragingly. "Don't worry, Addie. I shall help you find your one true love."

Adele laughed. "Oh, Edie, you'll be the death of me one day! Please, do not make me hope!"

Edith cast her a wicked grin. "There should always be hope!" she exclaimed determinedly. "What would life be without hope? Never give up on it, Addie! Never!" Again, she squeezed her friend's hand. "Trust me. All will be well. I promise."

Heaving a deep breath, she sat back in her seat, allowing her eyes to drift out the window and sweep over the glistening countryside. In the distance, she could see Lord Cumberton's ancient castle appearing upon the horizon and wondered what this Christmas season would bring. She could only hope it would see Adele happy. With Lord Halston's son or another, it did not matter to her. The only thing that mattered was to ensure Addie's happiness.

And Edith vowed she would not rest until she saw it secured.

Chapter One

A WOMAN WORTH KNOWING

Jasper Beaumont, Earl of Whickerton, hated societal events of any kind. He particularly hated the ones his mother attended alongside him. The woman knew no boundaries in her attempts to see him advantageously married. And fool that he was, Jasper had given his late father a deathbed promise to marry within a year of his death.

Unfortunately, it almost was.

"You look rather uncomfortable," Andrew Abernathy, Viscount Dalton, remarked with a rather unbecoming grin upon his face. "Simply make your choice and be done with it. It shouldn't be that difficult!"

"Pray tell, why am I friends with you?" Jasper asked, turning to glare at his friend, well aware that his mother stood only a few paces away, observing the comings and goings of the Christmas house party with rapt attention as well as a calculating gleam in her eyes. To her great disappointment, neither one of her two children showed the necessary ambition to secure themselves an advantageous match, thus causing their mother one disappointment after another. While Jasper rarely cared to spend more than an hour or two in any woman's company, his younger sister Mary was almost painfully shy, often unable to utter a single word in the company of others. Most of the time, she could be spotted standing somewhere off to the side, a rather distant look in her eyes as though her mind were elsewhere.

Jasper sighed, wishing *he* were elsewhere!

"If choosing a wife is indeed that easy," Jasper remarked with a bit of an acidic tone to his voice, "then how is it you are not married yet?"

Andrew shrugged, a rather disinterested expression upon his face. "Well, I suppose I was not fool enough to make any such ridiculous promise." A wide grin came to his face. "You, however, were and must, therefore, live with the consequences." He let his gaze sweep over the entrance hall of Cumberton Castle and the arriving guests. "What of her?" he asked, nodding toward a slender young woman, her hair piled so high on top of her head that she seemed to have trouble maintaining her balance.

"Lady Lucinda?" Jasper growled with an eye roll. "You cannot be serious! Have you ever spoken to her? The only topic she loves to discuss is herself."

Andrew groaned. "I must admit, I'm growing tired of your objections," he replied curtly. "Every woman I point out you find something wrong with. Honestly, I am simply trying to help you. If you continue this way, the year will end, and you will still be unwed."

Jasper gritted his teeth. Indeed, the prospect of remaining unwed was most pleasing; however, the thought of breaking the promise he had given to his late father caused him an almost physical pain somewhere in the left side of his chest.

"I insisted my parents invite you here this Christmas season," Andrew continued, nodding toward their hosts, Lord and Lady Cumberton, as they stood receiving more guests, "to see an end come to your constant moaning and complaining. Choose a bride, marry her and be done with it. Life does not end after marriage." He exhaled rather loudly, annoyance marking his every feature.

Jasper nodded. Indeed, for many people, marriage changed little in life. He had seen it in his parents' marriage as well as in other marriages. They continued on as though the other one, their spouse, barely existed. Yet, some were different. His gaze moved over to Lord and Lady Cumberton, their hosts and Andrew's parents. They stood close, her hand upon his arm, her eyes turned up to look into his. Jasper saw affection there, something deep and all-consuming, something that made him think that for Lord and Lady Cumberton life *had* changed after marriage.

Changed for the better.

As much as Jasper hated the idea of thinking of himself as a romantic sap, he wanted what they had. He wanted to *want* to be near his wife. He wanted to miss her when she was not around. He wanted to look into her eyes and know who she was while at the same time finding himself awed by the magnificent creature at his side.

Considering Andrew's parents, Jasper wondered about his friend's outlook on marriage. "Perhaps coming here was a mistake," he remarked dryly.

Andrew scoffed. "We both know you don't have much of a choice." Then he suddenly stilled, and his eyes slowly narrowed as he looked past Jasper at something or someone beyond his shoulder. "Brace yourself," he then warned in a hissed whisper. "I believe your mother has found another target." He chuckled before adding, "Perhaps you should simply let her make this choice for you. Heaven knows she wouldn't mind!"

Before Jasper could reply, his mother suddenly stood before him, her sharp eyes meeting his before once more moving across the room toward the front entrance. "Do you see the young lady just arriving?" She jerked her chin in the direction in question. "The one with the dark brown hair and hazel eyes?" She looked back at him until he nodded. "I believe that is the daughter of the Duke of Ashbrook, Lady Adele." She heaved a rather wistful sigh. "She would be a marvelous match; do you not agree?"

Jasper heaved a deep sigh. Yes, the young lady seemed lovely, and yet he felt not a spark of interest at the sight of her.

"I beg your pardon, Lady Whickerton," Andrew interfered, and for once Jasper was grateful for his friend's company. "However, I am fairly certain that she is already betrothed."

Jasper's mother huffed out an annoyed breath. "True or not," she replied pointedly, as though Andrew had set out to ruin her plans on purpose, "nothing is set in stone until the marriage vows have been spoken."

Ignoring his mother, Jasper met his sister's gaze. Compassion rested in her eyes because like no other, she understood what it was like to have their mother interfere in her life.

"Well?" his mother prompted, a note of impatience in her voice.

Jasper turned to look at her. "Well, what?" he inquired, knowing precisely what she meant.

Her lips narrowed as she shook her head at him. "Your father would be most disappointed," she remarked chidingly. "At the very least, look at the lady. She is lovely, is she not? And a duke's daughter! What more can you ask for?"

To avoid looking at his friend and the undoubtedly self-serving grin currently plastered upon his face, Jasper moved his gaze to the young lady in question. Indeed, she had a kind face and possessed the sort of elegant beauty admired by the *ton*. Yet, once again, Jasper felt nothing. He felt nothing beyond the usual boredom that seemed to accompany him day in and out as he—

His gaze flickered to the right for only a split second, and yet it was enough.

Eyes the color of a brilliant summer sky looked into his, and...he felt *it*.

A flicker.

A spark.

Something that was definitely not boredom.

He blinked, and then he saw *her*.

Standing next to Lady Adele was a rather petite young woman with wide blue eyes and blond hair that shimmered with a red hue in the candlelight. She looked like a hundred other young ladies, and yet...

Jasper all but stared into her face, waiting for—

There it was!

An almost sly curl came to her lips as she returned his gaze with equal frankness, not once dropping her eyes in coy surrender. Indeed, a moment later, her right brow seemed to arch up in...challenge?

Jasper shook his head to clear it. Was he mistaken? Was it possible that such a woman truly existed? Bold and daring and...mysterious?

In his chest, his heart suddenly seemed to collide with his ribcage as though urging him to her side, determined to uncover her secrets. His hands clenched into fists as he stared at her, knowing he could not do as he wished. After all, he did not know her. They had never been introduced, and it would be nigh impertinent for him to—

With that sly curl still upon her lips, the young woman leaned closer to

Lady Adele and whispered something in her ear. Instantly, Lady Adele's eyes opened wide, as though in shock, and then snapped to him with lightning-speed.

Jasper felt shaken to his core. What could she possibly have said?

"She is lovely, is she not?" his mother inquired, for once a satisfied tone in her voice. "Do not worry. I shall arrange for you to be introduced," she assured him before hurrying away.

"I cannot help but think," Andrew remarked in a hushed tone beside him, "that it is not Lady Adele who has caught your attention." He chuckled. "Am I right?"

Jasper swallowed, finding it almost impossible to avert his gaze and turn to face his friend. "Do you know who she is?" he asked, ignoring Andrew's teasing grin, and casting a look over his shoulder at *her*.

Andrew paused for an agonizingly long moment before finally saying, "I believe she is the youngest daughter of the Earl of Swansborough." Again, he paused—if one could call it that for he did not continue.

"What is her name?" Jasper growled under his breath so as not to be overheard by his sister. Once or twice, their mother had managed to elicit information from her regarding his whereabouts, pastimes and whatnot.

Andrew chuckled, watching him with interest. "Indeed, this is serious! I have to say I've never seen you so—"

"Her name!" Jasper hissed, grasping his friend's arm.

Andrew smiled, completely unimpressed. "Lady Edith."

Jasper exhaled the breath he had been holding and turned to look at her once more. To his surprise, their eyes met instantly, as though she had been watching him this whole time. And this time, he was certain that both her brows rose in what he could only assume to be a challenging gesture.

A wide grin came to his face, and his heart seemed to stumble in his chest. Now, this was a woman worth knowing!

Chapter Two
THE RIGHT MAN

Bundled-up in warm cloaks, fur-lined boots, gloves, scarves and mittens, Edith and Adele stepped outside into Cumberton Castle's lush garden, currently buried under a thick blanket of snow. The soft crunch under their feet brought a smile to Edith's face, and she breathed in deeply of the fresh—and admittedly, freezing—air.

Her heart beat fast in her chest, faster than it ever had before, and it felt heavenly.

"Would you stop smiling?" Adele hissed under her breath, annoyance mingling with disbelief. "You cannot possibly mean to say that you—"

"There he is," Edith whispered as she spotted the tall, broad-shouldered gentleman, who had seemed quite taken-aback upon seeing her earlier. Indeed, the moment had caught Edith off guard as well, for she had not expected to—

"Don't stare at him!" Adele hissed once more, a tone of warning now in her voice. "It is unseemly."

Edith laughed. "I never knew you were such a stickler for propriety, dearest Addie." She clasped her friend's hands within her own. "Don't worry. Everything will be all right."

Briefly closing her eyes, Adele inhaled a deep breath. "Promise me you won't do anything...you know?"

Edith grinned. "As I dislike breaking promises, I'm afraid I cannot make such a promise." Ignoring her friend's eye roll, she glanced back at Lord Whickerton as he strolled through the gardens with their host's son as well as his own mother and sister.

Fortunately, Adele's mother, Lady Ashbrook, had been aware of the young lord's name and responded without suspicion when Edith had made casual inquiries.

Lord Whickerton's mother, the dowager countess, appeared to be another one of those match-making mamas while her daughter, Lady Mary, looked ready to faint the moment someone looked at or—Heaven forbid! —addressed her. The poor thing had the look of a deer cornered by a prowling predator, and Edith felt her heart go out to her.

She felt her heart go out to Lord Whickerton as well...but in an utterly different way.

Indeed, there was this strange flutter in her belly as their eyes met across the ice-studded bushes running between the two paths on which they were currently strolling along. Her heart paused for a brief moment, as though it, too, needed to inhale a deep breath before continuing on, and despite the ice-cold wind, Edith felt warm all over. Oh, this was a most wonderful feeling, and Edith fully intended to explore it further!

"You're staring again," Adele hissed under her breath, giving Edith's arm a quick tug to gain her attention.

Blinking, Edith gave in and turned to look at her friend; still, she could feel Lord Whickerton's eyes upon her. Indeed, it seemed this utterly new *feeling* was mutual. "I am no more looking at him than he is looking at me."

Adele cast a quick glance past Edith's shoulder at Lord Whickerton. "Be that as it way. I don't think you should reveal your...partiality toward him this openly. He might think you—" She broke off, and a frown drew down her brows. "How can you even say you care for him if you've never even spoken a word to him? Even I know my betrothed better than you know him."

Edith breathed in slowly and deeply, trying to sort through her feelings. "I don't know," she finally said with all the honesty she possessed. "I suppose there is nothing I can say for certain. All I know is how I feel when I look at him, when he looks at me." She smiled at her friend reassuringly. "But I suppose you're right. I'll have to get to know him better, to be certain."

Adele's eyes widened. "No, that's not what I meant. I—"

Edith grasped her friend's hand, looking up into her hazel eyes. "Are you truly trying to dissuade me from finding love?" she asked teasingly; yet her friend's cheeks darkened...and not from the cold.

With wide eyes, Adele shook her head. "Of course not! I would never —" She broke off, a measure of shock coming to her eyes as she stared at Edith. "I was merely..." Her eyes closed, resignation falling over her face. "Perhaps I simply wished..."

Edith squeezed her friend's hands. "I know," she whispered compassionately. "You deserve love as well, and I promise I will help you find it."

Adele lifted her head, her eyes glistening with tears. Still, a tentative smile teased her lips. "You know, when you speak like that, Edie, I truly believe anything is possible."

Edith felt her heart lighten. "That's because it is!" she insisted, tugging her friend into a quick embrace. "Never doubt that! Anything is possible. It might not always be easy or straightforward, but it is still possible."

Adele looked at her with questioning eyes. "You truly believe that, do you not?"

Edith nodded. "With all my heart. You shall see."

However, before more could be said, Edith spotted not only Adele's parents approaching from down the path but also the Duke of Halston as well as his son. The young man was tall and fair-haired, with a square jaw and a rather serious countenance. Still, Edith thought to see something kind, even shy, linger upon his face that endeared him to her instantly. Yes, her heart told her he was a good man. But was he the *right* man for Adele?

Nodding toward the approaching group, Edith slipped her arm through Adele's, knowing her friend would need support and reassurance. She watched Adele square her shoulders and inhale a deep breath, as though she were preparing herself for battle. Then Adele slowly turned upon her heels, and she finally found the man she was to marry.

Edith wished she knew what Adele was thinking, what she was feeling. She could not be certain, of course, but a slight shiver trailed through her friend's body, and Edith felt it like an echo.

And then they all stood face to face, and introductions were made. The

Lord Halston and his son spoke politely, smiles upon their faces, their words kind. Still, Edith could not shake the feeling that Adele's betrothed felt just as apprehensive about their upcoming marriage as her friend did herself. Perhaps this was a good sign.

Or perhaps not?

Remembering the utterly overwhelming surge she felt the moment her eyes had landed on Lord Whickerton, Edith could not help but notice that neither Adele nor Lord Halston's son showed any such spark lighting up their eyes. Might it still come? Not everyone fell in love at first sight, did they?

"Would you care for a stroll, Lady Adele?" the duke's son, Albert Kingston, Lord Aberley, asked with a formal bow.

Although clearly hesitant, Adele agreed, and they turned down the path, walking side by side.

Edith saw smiles come to their parents' faces as they fell a few steps behind, eagerly discussing their children's upcoming marriage. All the while, Edith strolled along, her gaze fixed upon Adele and her fiancé, wondering what their hearts were telling them at this very moment.

Straining to listen, Edith heard them exchange inquiries about their journey here before discussing the weather as well as current affairs. It was nothing personal. It was the kind of conversation one would have with a stranger; of course, that is what they were. Eventually, though, Lord Aberley asked Adele what pastimes she enjoyed.

A smile came to Adele's face as she spoke of the outdoors, of riding and hiking, enjoying the feel of the sun upon her face and the sensation of her heart beating fast in her chest from physical exertion. Edith could see that these thoughts brought her friend joy, but she could just as easily see that Lord Aberley knew not what Adele spoke of.

"I must admit," he finally said, a touch of regret in his voice, "that I never much enjoyed the outdoors."

Adele's smile vanished, replaced by a frown. "And yet you traveled the continent, did you not?"

Lord Aberley nodded. "That I did. It broadens the horizon, and as heir to my father's dukedom, it is my duty to prepare myself as best I can for such a noble position."

Edith could have groaned, recognizing his words as something he had no doubt been told many, many times throughout his life. It was not something he believed himself, not something he felt, but rather something he had come to accept as the truth.

"What books do you prefer, my lady?" Lord Aberley asked after a somewhat painful silence.

Again, Edith wanted to groan, for she knew Adele did not much care for the written word. She did not have the patience to sit still and read, her limbs always eager to move and experience things firsthand.

As much as Edith had hoped that her friend would find happiness with her betrothed—of course, that would make things easier by far—it seemed clear that that would not be the case. So, essentially, Edith had two options: she could either stand by and let things unfold, risking her friend's unhappiness, or...she could interfere.

Meddle, as her old governess used to call it.

Excusing herself, Edith left the path and headed back toward the castle, knowing beyond a shadow of a doubt that she simply could not stand by. Adele would find herself most unhappy, and so would Lord Aberley. But what to do? She mused as she climbed the few steps to the door. It was not her place, and yet...

As she stepped across the threshold, Edith once more looked over her shoulder. However, her gaze did not fall on Adele and her fiancé...but on Lord Whickerton instead.

His dark brown eyes looked into hers, and instantly, that flutter returned with full force. Edith drew in a shaky breath, delighting in the teasing smile that came to his lips. Indeed, he could be just the man for her. If only she knew!

Chapter Three

UNBECOMING OF A GENTLEMAN

"You're staring again," Andrew murmured quietly beside him, jabbing an elbow into Jasper's side.

Jasper glared at his friend. "And you are commenting upon it again," he snapped, annoyed by that look of glee upon Andrew's face. After rolling his eyes at his friend, he instantly turned back to staring at Lady Edith as she followed her friend Lady Adele and Lord Aberley down the path. Her head was pitched forward the slightest bit, as though she were straining to listen to their conversation.

Jasper grinned.

"As I said, Lady Whickerton," Andrew addressed Jasper's mother as she stood watching Lady Adele and her soon-to-be husband with a disapproving frown upon her face, "Lady Adele is promised to the Duke of Halston's son."

A noncommittal, yet displeased sound escaped his mother's lips. The look upon her face, though, suggested that she loathed admitting defeat, her mood now as dark as that of a storm cloud. That did not bode well for any of them.

Doing his utmost to ignore his mother expressing her disapproval of his sister's dress, her posture, her smile—basically her entire person—

Jasper watched Lady Edith intently. Even from this far away, he could all but see the cogs inside her head turning, and he realized he burned to know what she was thinking.

Generally, Jasper found that women, like Lady Lucinda, for example, most often thought of balls and gowns, accessories and invitations, their only concern the next event, the next moment to present themselves. Indeed, these thoughts were mind-numbingly boring, which was precisely why Jasper tended to escape their company as quickly as he possibly could.

Lady Edith, however, was not thinking of these things; of that, he was certain. Why, he did not know. However, he would have wagered his entire fortune on it. However, if she truly was not thinking of the things women generally thought about, what went on in her head instead? Jasper did not know. He did not even have the slightest inkling, and that bothered him more than he thought it would.

His heart suddenly skipped a beat when he saw Lady Edith excuse herself and then hurry back toward the castle. A thoughtful expression rested upon her features, as though she were no longer aware of her surroundings. Yet upon reaching the door, she paused and looked over her shoulder...

...and their eyes met.

Jasper could feel it all the way to his toes. It felt like a an earthquake, knocking him off his feet. It felt like a warm summer rain. It felt like the first light after the dark of night. It felt...utterly unexpected and equally overwhelming.

And then she smiled at him, and Jasper knew he had to know her. He had to find out what thoughts lived in her head, if that smile she granted him meant something.

Heaven help him, but he *wanted* it to mean something.

"Go after her," Andrew suddenly hissed in Jasper's ear. "Don't let her get away."

Jasper glanced at his friend, surprised to see Andrew's brows rise in teasing encouragement, a moment before he turned away to address Jasper's mother once more, drawing her attention and allowing Jasper to slip away.

Jasper smiled, feeling himself reminded of why, indeed, Andrew was his friend.

Quickening his steps, he reached the door only moments after it had closed behind Lady Edith. Yet when he stepped inside, there was no sign of her.

After the brilliantly bright sunshine in the gardens, the interior seemed overhung with shadows. He had to blink his eyes to clear his sight, chase away those bright spots that seemed to dance there. The corridor snaked off in various directions, and he wondered which one she could have taken. Was she headed toward her chambers? Or to a parlor, perhaps, seeking company?

Then he suddenly heard an agitated voice echoing to his ear from the right-hand corridor. Without another thought, Jasper turned toward it, his steps quickening as the voice grew louder. Indeed, it sounded familiar.

Annoyingly so.

Jasper debated turning back when he suddenly turned a corner and spotted not only Lady Edith, her feet still carrying her onward, but also Lady Lucinda, standing near a row of bay windows, lashing out at a maid, who seemed to shrink into herself with every word flung at her.

As always, it was Jasper's first instinct to escape Lady Lucinda's company. However, that would also mean giving up his pursuit of Lady Edith, and he was most unwilling to do that. So, he simply hung back a little, his eyes slightly narrowed as he watched the scene unfold from a distance.

"I am appalled by your lack of diligence," Lady Lucinda exclaimed with haughty derision, looking down upon the trembling maid. "Is it truly too much to ask to have fresh flowers on my vanity?" Her brows rose threateningly as she glared at the maid, daring her to contradict her. "I think not."

"I'm begging your pardon, my lady," the maid stammered, her eyes glued to the floor, her shoulders hunched. "I meant no disrespect. Please, I—"

"Oh, Lady Lucinda, I must apologize," Lady Edith suddenly exclaimed as her feet carried her the last few steps toward Lady Lucinda. "I am deeply sorry that you were affected by my foolishness. Please, accept my deepest apologies." Looking honestly contrite, Lady Edith stepped in front of the trembling maid, her eyes wide as she met Lady Lucinda's.

Jasper was confused, yet he watched with rapt attention as a look of incomprehension came to Lady Lucinda's face. "I beg your pardon?" Lady

Lucinda asked, giving her head a slight shake. "I do not know what you mean."

"Oh, I know I should, at least, have had a spot of tea before venturing outdoors," Lady Edith chided herself, a melodious chuckle drifting from her lips. "I suppose I was too excited. This is a beautiful place, is it not?" She allowed her gaze to sweep over their surroundings, taking in the ancient castle and all its beauty. "Of course, I was beginning to feel faint." She shook her head at her own foolishness.

Jasper could not suppress a chuckle at the sight of her acting prowess. After all, Lady Edith was not a silly debutante, was she? Of course, he did not know her, not in the least, and yet Jasper felt certain of it. Lady Edith was not a woman to act foolishly or to faint because of a missed meal.

"Fortunately, I made it back inside to the parlor," Lady Edith continued her tale, a look of exhaustion now playing across her face, "where—" She turned to look at the maid, one eyebrow arching upward in question.

"Betsy," the maid quickly supplied.

"Where Betsy found me," Lady Edith continued, smiling at Lady Lucinda. "She assisted me to my chamber and fetched me some smelling salts. Indeed, I feel much improved. However, it plagues me to think that you suffered on my account. Please, do forgive me."

Lady Lucinda inclined her head graciously. "Of course, no harm was done. I am glad to hear that you feel better."

"I certainly do." She turned to look at Betsy once more. "And I apologize for delaying you in your duties. Please, go ahead and see to Lady Lucinda's chambers."

Casting Lady Edith a grateful smile, Betsy hurried away, a look of relief and gratitude upon her face.

The moment the maid vanished from sight, Jasper stood back against the wall, his mind churning with thoughts he had never before entertained. Indeed, Lady Edith had not hesitated to come to the aid of a young maid, one she could not possibly know. Why? Would *he* have done the same? Jasper rather doubted it. Indeed, it had been kindness of heart that had led Lady Edith to interfere. He had seen it upon her face. Just as he had seen indifference and disregard upon Lady Lucinda's.

Never had Jasper seen a young lady of the *ton* act quite like this, and he felt a surprising surge of pride well up inside his chest. Yes, she was unlike any woman he had ever met.

After a few more exchanged words, Lady Lucinda took her leave. Lady Edith, however, remained, her eyes turned to the world outside beyond the windows, her back to him. She stood quietly, unmoving, as though lost in thought, and Jasper felt disinclined to disturb her. Yet he knew he could not walk away.

And so, he put one foot in front of the other, quietly moving closer as his gaze swept over her golden tresses that gave off a red glimmer wherever sunlight touched upon them.

"Do you know who these people are?" Lady Edith asked suddenly, her gaze still fixed out the window. "The ones just now arriving?"

For a moment, Jasper was uncertain who she was speaking to, but he stepped forward, nevertheless, his large strides quickly eating up the last bit of distance between them. He came to stand beside her, forcing his gaze from her lovely features to the people arriving outside the window. "I believe these are Lady Cumberton's Scottish relatives."

A soft sound of surprise left Lady Edith's lips before she finally turned to look upon him. Her blue eyes were wide and deep and utterly compelling, momentarily making Jasper forget everything around him. "Are you all right?" she asked with a slight chuckle, the smile upon her face genuine despite the teasing note to her voice. "You look rather as though you've seen a ghost."

Jasper smiled. "Perhaps that is an accurate description." Indeed, she did not seem from this world at all.

"Is that so?" she inquired with a raised brow. "Are there rattling chains attached to my leg that I am unaware of?"

Shaking his head, Jasper laughed. "Not that I can see," he finally said as his gaze swept over her once more, trying to take in every little detail about her.

"Scots, you say," Lady Edith remarked, casting another look out the window where a group of men dismounted, handing their horses off to stable boys. "I must admit, I am rather surprised."

Jasper nodded, taking another step closer to the window...and to her. "Well, Lady Cumberton is originally from Scotland, and as I understand it, she invited her relatives to join in the festivities to try and mend the rift between England and Scotland. I believe her clan is called MacKinnear."

A warm smile came to Lady Edith's face as she slowly turned her gaze from the window to him. "That is a noble gesture," she whispered almost reverently. "I will be pleased to make their acquaintance."

Jasper could not help the frown that came to his face. "You will?" To his surprise, he noted a hint of displeasure in his voice.

Her smile broadened. "You won't? Is the idea of meeting people from a faraway place not appealing to you? Do you not also long for adventure and something that might...disrupt the monotony of everyday life?"

Jasper exhaled audibly, surprised how deeply the thought of her showing interest in another unsettled him. How had he suddenly come to think of her as his in the span of only a few hours? She was a mystery to him, and no matter how long or intently he looked at her, he could not quite decipher what made her so.

A soft chuckle drifted from her lips. "Is something wrong? Do I have a smudge of dirt on my face?"

Still staring, Jasper merely shook his head, a voice deep down urging him to rein in these musings and finally focus on the moment at hand. Yet he could not bring himself to look away. She was utterly compelling, and the smile that teased her lips drew his attention in an almost magnetic way.

Lady Edith laughed, as though she had read his thoughts. "Because, quite frankly, you're staring at me."

Closing his eyes, Jasper bowed his head. "I've been told this all day," he murmured, remembering Andrew's comments.

"All day?" Lady Edith inquired, taking a step closer, a flash of curiosity upon her face. "By whom? And why?"

Jasper grinned, delighted with her direct manner. Perhaps he should simply... "You lied," he remarked, holding her gaze, his own brows arching upward in question.

Lady Edith's eyes narrowed ever so slightly, and yet nothing dark came to her face. Neither suspicion nor defensiveness. "I lied? Pray tell, what did I lie about?"

"You never felt faint, did you?" he demanded, leaning closer, his eyes searching hers. "And you most certainly did not need smelling salts, is that not so?"

Like a governess chiding her charge, Lady Edith shook her head at him, clucking her tongue in an utterly adorable way. "Does that mean you were eavesdropping, my lord? That is truly unbecoming of a gentleman. Do you not know that?"

Jasper grinned. "Why did you do it?" Slowly, his smile dimmed as her features transformed.

All lightheartedness vanished, replaced by a most serious expression as she regarded him carefully. All of a sudden, she seemed wiser than her age, something deeply thoughtful and even burdensome lingering in her blue eyes. "One should always help when one can, do you not agree, Lord Whickerton?"

Swallowing, Jasper felt himself nod. "Honestly, I never thought about it much. To my great shame," he added, running a hand through his hair as her eyes continued to look at him in that way of hers, seeing more than he would want to reveal. "But I shall from now on."

Again, a smile tugged upon the corners of her mouth, and Jasper exhaled. "I am delighted to hear it. Now, if you will excuse me?" She made to step away, but Jasper held out a hand to stop her.

"Can I see you again?" he asked almost desperately, such a pleading tone in his voice that surprised even him.

Lady Edith's smile changed. It became teasing and daring, matching the mischievous spark that briefly lit up her eyes. "I suppose you could try," she replied with a nonchalant shrug. "However, I expect to be rather busy the next few days." Casting him another challenging look, she spun upon her heel and walked away.

Staring after her, Jasper drew in a deep breath, surprised to feel a little lightheaded. Perhaps *he* was going to need smelling salts! He chuckled at the thought. Indeed, Lady Edith had a way of upending his world, and he rather like that.

He rather liked *her*.

Then he frowned. She would be rather busy? With what? Indeed, something had been on her mind. He had seen it. She had looked thoughtful, contemplative. But what? Clearly, she was up to something...if only he knew what that was.

But he would.
That, Jasper vowed.

Chapter Four

UNEXPECTED CONFIDANTS

Turning a corner, Edith was surprised when her gaze fell on Lady Mary, Lord Whickerton's sister. The young woman seemed rather tense, casting uneasy glances over her shoulder before she hurried down the corridor and then vanished from sight around another corner.

Her interest piqued; Edith followed her. Truthfully, she had not believed Lady Mary capable of secrecy. Yet, clearly, here she was, trying her very best to reach a certain destination with no one the wiser. Where was she headed? And why?

Edith had to admit that she burned to find out, for there clearly was more to Lady Mary than met the eye. Could the same be said for her brother? Perhaps it would be wise to speak to the man's sister and find out more about him.

Indeed, Lord Whickerton was a terribly fascinating man. Edith could not even say why. All she knew was that he made her feel all tingly inside. She loved the way he looked at her as if he was trying to look deeper, to truly understand who she was deep down. His smile was intoxicating, and she had delighted in the way he had stepped closer without crowding her, simply drawn to her, as though they had been friends forever and had not seen each other in a long time. Being around him had felt natural, as though he had always been missing from her life. Was that what love felt like? Edith wondered, trying her best to rein in these overwhelming emotions before they could run off with her sanity.

Perhaps Adele was correct. Perhaps she ought to proceed with more caution. But how could she when her heart did this odd little flutter every time she beheld him?

Hurrying around yet another corner, Edith pulled to a halt when she found the corridor in front of her empty. Where had Lady Mary disappeared to? She could only hope the young woman had not somehow gotten herself in trouble.

Approaching the first door on the right, Edith carefully opened it and stepped inside, her eyes falling on a snug little parlor, lovingly decorated. She was about to step back out into the hall when the sound of a sharply indrawn breath reached her ears.

"Begging your pardon, my lady."

Glancing around the door, Edith spotted a maid in the corner, dusting the portraits hung along the wall. The maid curtsied, keeping her head down in a way that made Edith wonder if she, too, had encountered Lady Lucinda. Quite clearly, the woman was a menace!

Taking a step back from her feelings of utter annoyance toward Lady Lucinda, Edith smiled at the maid. "Oh, please do not let me interrupt you." She swept her gaze over the parlor. "Indeed, you're doing a marvelous job. Everything looks quite beautiful."

A hesitant smile came to the maid's face. "Thank you, my lady."

Offering the young woman another smile, Edith then once more stepped out into the corridor, disappointed to have lost Lady Mary. Could she possibly still be close by? Perhaps she ought to try another door? If only she knew this castle better! She paused, then turned back to the maid. "Pardon me. Can you tell me what rooms are nearby?"

The maid nodded eagerly. "The library's just up ahead, my lady."

Edith was about to ask another question when her mind took her back to the moment, she had seen Lady Mary for the first time. Indeed, the young woman struck her as someone who would cherish each and every opportunity to withdraw from the world. She clearly had an overbearing mother, who no doubt forced her daughter into all kinds of uncomfortable situations. What better place to seek solace than in the library?

"Thank you," Edith mumbled, and then hurried away.

Sliding open the heavy door, she stepped over the threshold, quietly closing it behind herself. A comfortable silence engulfed her, as her eyes swept over lush carpets, beautiful stained-glass windows and intricately carved shelves, holding Lord Cumberton's treasured library. A grand fireplace occupied one wall with upholstered armchairs set in a half-circle in front of it. Unfortunately, each and every one of them was empty. Where could Lady Mary be?

Stepping around a bookcase, Edith drew to a halt when her gaze fell on a small sitting area in an alcove. It was no more than two armchairs facing one another, but it was out of the way, as though in a world all its own. The perfect place to evade one's overbearing mother, as Lady Mary's presence clearly indicated.

The moment the young woman beheld Edith, alarm came to her features. All blood seemed to drain from her face, and her mouth fell open in a rather unbecoming way.

Smiling at the other woman reassuringly, Edith stepped toward her hiding place. "Please, do not worry. I promise I will not say a word."

For a moment, Lady Mary hesitated, clearly uncertain whether to believe her. Her hands gripped the book she held tighter, pressing it to her chest. "Thank you," she finally breathed, her voice barely audible. Then she forced her grip to loosen before laying the book on Ancient Egypt on the small side table. "I…I…"

Edith stepped forward. "You don't have to explain yourself, Lady Mary, and I'm sorry if I disturbed you. Do you enjoy reading?"

Swallowing, Lady Mary nodded, the look in her eyes still reminding Edith of a startled deer. "I do," she replied after a moment. "My mother, however, considers it a waste of time." Shock showed upon her face at having spoken such bold words.

Edith chuckled. "Well, then it's a good thing that she was not the one to find you here, isn't it?"

The tension in Lady Mary's shoulders waned a little more. "And you… won't say anything? To her, I mean?" She exhaled a shaking breath, clearly not convinced that placing her trust in Edith was a good idea.

Edith took a step toward her, her hands clasped together in a solemn vow. "You have my word."

The ghost of a smile flashed over Lady Mary's face, and a deep breath rushed from her lungs. “Thank you.” Her chest rose and fell with several rapid breaths before she managed to calm herself.

“You prefer the company of books to the company of people?” Edith asked, stepping toward the other armchair to sit while gesturing for Lady Mary to reclaim her own.

Sighing, Lady Mary reached for the book she had set down earlier. “I’m afraid I do.”

“There’s nothing wrong with that, is there?”

A rather uncharacteristic scoff left Lady Mary’s lips. “My mother would strongly disagree. She often encourages me to be more outgoing and companionable...like my brother.” A deep, almost defeated sigh left her lips as she slumped back in her seat. “But I... I don’t know how to be someone I am not.” Wide, round eyes looked into Edith’s, begging her to understand.

“No one does,” Edith reassured her. “Just like your mother is the woman she is, you must be the woman you are. I see nothing wrong with that.”

Relief stood upon Lady Mary’s face, and yet she said, “She argues I will never find a match if I constantly retreat from company. Of course, I cannot fault her for that. She only wants the best for me, but I...” She shook her head helplessly. “I do not possess the talent to converse with other people. It feels like a chore to me, and even when I try, I never manage it effortlessly. It exhausts me. Sometimes I think my mother has already given up on finding me a match. I think she might believe it to be hopeless.”

“I don’t believe forcing a match will do anyone any good,” Edith replied, thinking of Adele and her betrothed. “I believe we need to be who we are, openly and honestly, in order to find someone who is a good match.” She smiled at Lady Mary. “Sometimes, patience is needed, but it will happen. You just wait and see.”

A tentative smile came to Lady Mary’s face, one that even reached her eyes, such relief in them for having found someone approving of her that it transformed her face beautifully.

“And your brother,” Edith began, curious to learn more about the man who had caught her attention, “he is quite unlike you?”

Lady Mary nodded. “I’ve never heard him stammer for words even once. He has more friends than I have acquaintances, and he never seems to dread meeting any of them."

Edith watched the other young woman carefully, trying to decipher how she truly felt about her brother. After all, a sister's opinion was priceless and quite telling. "Does that mean you have little to say to each other?"

A smile claimed Lady Mary's face. "It is true that our interests are not the same. However, we are...close. He listens, even when he doesn't care about the topic I am talking about, and...he tells me things about himself," a bit of a grin came to her face, "things not even my mother knows. Things she wishes she knew. Things I do my best to keep from her."

Edith remembered such a bond from growing up with her own sisters. Even her younger brother had occasionally confided in her, in his siblings, instead of speaking to their parents. "So, how does he feel about your mother's insistence you mingle?"

Lady Mary sighed. "He tries to interfere, but in the end she remains relentless. At the moment, however, he has more important things on his mind." Lady Mary's brown eyes looked up into Edith's, something contemplative and hesitant in them. However, it passed after a moment and she leaned forward. "Our father died not long ago, and my brother promised him on his deathbed to marry within the span of a year." She sighed compassionately. "The year is drawing to an end."

Edith felt a nervous tingle chase itself up and down her back. "And...has he already chosen a bride?"

Lady Mary shook her head, and Edith exhaled. "He has not. Truth be told, I believe the only reason he now considers marriage is his duty to the earldom as well as the promise he made our father. He has a wild spirit, and I think he wishes he could simply spread his wings and be carried elsewhere, from place to place."

Edith nodded, understanding that desire perfectly. Yet for her, it did not run contrary to marriage. Always had she hoped to find someone who shared her adventurous spirit. Could Lord Whickerton be the one? Would he make her a good husband?

Edith almost laughed at herself for having such a thought. She had met the man only a few hours ago, and here she was already contemplating marriage. Was she a fool? Never had Edith thought of herself as a fool. She was perhaps a bit impulsive, never hesitant to trust in her instincts, but not a fool. Yet marriage was the most important decision she would ever make. She should not take it lightly but consider it carefully.

She was just about to ask another question when the sound of a door opening drifted to their ears. Instantly, Lady Mary tensed, her eyes going wide as they stared into Edith's.

"She has to be somewhere," an older woman's voice muttered, annoyance marking her tone. "She said she wanted to return to the parlor. However, no one has seen her there. Unbelievable!"

Without needing confirmation, Edith knew that the woman who had spoken was none other than Lady Mary's mother.

"Mary! Are you in here?"

Slowly rising to her feet, Edith met Lady Mary's eyes and slowly shook her head, urging the young woman to remain quiet and stay where she was. Then she moved out of the alcove and stepped around the large bookcase. "I'm afraid she's not," Edith replied, the moment her eyes fell on the Dowager Countess of Whickerton. "It is only me in here, I assure you."

The dowager countess had a rather pointed nose and high forehead, brows drawn down, and her lips pressed into a perpetual snarl. Edith could not help but wonder if the woman ever smiled. "Lady... Edith?"

Edith nodded. "Yes, I arrived with Lord and Lady Ashbrook earlier today. They were kind enough to allow me to accompany them here this season. It is all so splendid, is it not?" She stepped closer, sweeping her gaze over the room in raptures. "Almost magical."

Before the dowager countess could reply, someone else stepped across the threshold: Lord Whickerton.

It seemed her voice had drawn him—perhaps he had been waiting out in the corridor or searching for his sister in another room—for the look upon his face held wonderment, delight even, as his eyes swept over her, the hint of a smile curling up the corners of his mouth. "Lady Edith," he exclaimed before his gaze moved to his mother, and a more sober expression fell over his face.

Edith felt as though they were confidants, unable to speak openly as they found themselves in the company of another, an outsider. It was a most delightful thought, and Edith struggled to maintain a straight face.

"Have you seen my sister, Lady Mary?" Lord Whickerton asked, casting a sideways glance at his mother, who seemed to be observing them rather intently.

Edith shook her head. "I'm afraid I have not. I hope she's not missing."

Lord Whickerton shook his head. "Not at all. I am certain we shall find her shortly." Still, his eyes narrowed ever so slightly, as though he could tell that she was not being truthful. Could he see it upon her face? Clearly, his mother could not. Edith saw no suspicion in her gaze. What made him different?

"I believe there is another parlor on the south side," Edith exclaimed, determined to keep Lady Mary hidden from her mother. "Perhaps it was merely a misunderstanding."

Lady Whickerton nodded. "Perhaps," she murmured, the tone in her voice suggesting that she did not believe so. "Thank you, Lady Edith." With a look at her son, she stepped from the room, more mumbled words falling from her lips, each one dripping with annoyance and disapproval.

"I believe I, too, must take my leave," Edith stated, moving to step past Lord Whickerton.

However, before she could, he moved to block her path, one hand held out, almost touching her arm. His warm brown eyes looked down into hers, before they swept past her shoulder to where Lady Mary sat quietly in the alcove. "Again, you are lying," he whispered, a rather delighted smile upon his face. "Thank you." Then he stepped away, and followed his mother down the corridor, casting her one last wicked grin over his shoulder.

Indeed, Edith could not shake the thought that he was the perfect man for her!

Chapter Five

A GENTLEMAN'S CHOICES

Jasper had never quite enjoyed balls. This one, however, had his rapt attention. Or rather, the young lady in the stunning azure gown did.

Once again, Lady Edith stood across the room with her friend, Lady Adele as well as Lord and Lady Ashbrook. Nearby, Jasper also spotted Lord Halston as well as the man's son, Lord Aberley. It was quite apparent that Lady Adele and Lord Aberley were expected to wed, and it was equally apparent that neither one of them particularly liked that fact. Only their parents seemed to be enjoying themselves, expectant expressions upon their faces, the likes of which Jasper had seen upon his own mother's countenance numerous times.

For some reason, Lady Adele's and Lord Aberley's misery bothered him. At first, he did not quite know why, as they were not acquainted. Perhaps it was simply that their situation reminded him so much of his own: parents negotiating contracts and urging their children to do as they were told. After all, it was obvious even to him that Lady Adele and Lord Aberley would not have chosen one another if they had indeed been given the choice.

"Why the grim expression?" Andrew asked, that teasing note in his voice once more. "I had expected you to be in better spirits after watching you stare at Lady Edith these past few days." He moved to look at Jasper's face. "What is the problem? She's young, beautiful and you clearly like her. She is an earl's daughter, which means your mother would not object, and as far as I can tell she's not spoken for. Go and asked her to marry you, and you'll have that deathbed promise nonsense taken care of."

Rather aghast, Jasper turned to stare at his friend. "It is not that simple," he replied sternly, uncertain *exactly* why he was objecting to his friend's plan. Yes, as annoying as it was to admit this, Andrew was right. He *was* rather taken with Lady Edith. She *was* beautiful and young, and he *did* like her. He liked her a lot. In fact, he could not stop thinking about her or looking at her. Still, this was going too fast, was it not? Was courtship not something that required time?

"Why?" Andrew had the nerve to ask.

Jasper shrugged, feeling like a complete fool. Still, he was enjoying getting to know her, watching her and trying to decipher all the many expressions that always flitted across her face. She clearly was one who knew how to keep a secret, one whose mind rarely stood still, one who executed her plans with patience and precision. But what *were* her plans? Jasper burned to know.

His gaze briefly drifted to Lady Adele and Lord Aberley as they stood up for the next dance before quickly returning to Lady Edith. Her own blue eyes were slightly narrowed as she watched the couple with rapt attention, a slight frown upon her face as though what she saw displeased her. Clearly, she had noticed their indifference to one another as well. Was her friend's situation the most prominent thing on her mind at present?

A jolt of awareness sizzled through Jasper as Lady Edith abandoned her spot and moved around the room. Slowly, she walked the edges of the ballroom, her eyes never quite leaving the dancing couple, something deeply thoughtful in her expression. Jasper almost craned his neck to keep her in sight, to see past those mingling in between.

"You do know that your shoes are not glued to the floor, don't you?" Andrew inquired with a laugh. "You *can* move!" He jerked his head in Lady Edith's direction. "Go! You clearly prefer her company to mine," he added with a feigned note of disappointment.

Glaring at his friend for a second, Jasper stepped away, his gaze fixed upon Lady Edith. He moved slowly, winding his way through the crowd as he followed in her wake. She kept her head turned sideways, still watching

Lady Adele and Lord Aberley, neither of whom seemed to be enjoying themselves.

With every step Jasper drew closer, he could feel his heart speeding up in excitement. He stepped around a group of giggling females before dodging a rather agitated matron. Another step and then another before he stood barely an arm's length away from her, his gaze sweeping over her golden tresses. Instead of pulling them back and forcing them into some kind of elaborate hairstyle, they hung down her back like waves rolling onto a beach.

About to clear his throat to catch her attention, Jasper almost flinched when Lady Edith suddenly said, "Good evening, Lord Whickerton." Then she turned, her blue eyes settling upon his, a radiant smile upon her face that once again stilled his breath.

Chuckling, Jasper shook his hand. "How did you know I was there? Do I shuffle my feet?" He glanced down and then back up, unable not to look at her.

For a moment, her blue eyes swept over his face, and he could not tell what she was thinking, not even in the least. Then, however, a bit of a chiding look came to her face. "You have been watching me, my lord. Why?"

Again, Jasper stared at her, the smile upon his face widening with delight. Who was this mysterious creature? "Is there anything you don't know? Pray tell, what is your secret?"

She grinned. "If I told you, it would be a secret no longer, would it?" A sly smile came to her face, a smile he was coming to love.

Inclining his head to her in defeat and respect, Jasper held out his hand. "May I have the next dance?"

For a moment, she hesitated, and Jasper felt his heart pause in his chest. "I thought you'd never ask," she finally replied, slipping her hand into his as though it belonged there.

As they moved onto the dance floor, they passed Lady Adele and Lord Aberley, who were now returning to their parents' side. The two women exchanged a meaningful look Jasper could not quite identify. However, the moment the next dance began, he was well aware that Lady Edith's attention no longer remained with him. Instead, she kept looking over his shoulder, her brows slightly drawn as though she were watching something most intently.

Or most likely someone.

"Is my company so tiresome?" Jasper asked lightly as the dance led them back together; yet his heart once again seemed to pause in his chest. Indeed, her opinion mattered to him. More than he would have expected.

"Not tiresome at all, my lord," she replied, yet her gaze remained fixed on something beyond his shoulder. "However, you caught me at a busy time."

"Busy? Please, enlighten me."

For a moment, her gaze moved to his, and she regarded him thoughtfully. "How do I know if I can trust you?" Her eyebrows rose challengingly. "Perhaps it would not be wise to trust a stranger with such an important secret."

Jasper could tell that she was teasing him, but was she also testing him? "How do you suggest I prove myself, my lady? Name the challenge, and I shall prove my worth."

For another few dance steps, she seemed to regard him carefully, as though weighing her options. Yet every once in a while, her gaze flitted either past his shoulder or sideways to the right or left, always directed at either the refreshment table or the tall arched windows on the eastern side.

"Well?" Jasper prompted, as he could bear the suspense no longer. Yet he could not deny that he savored each and every time her delicate hand slipped back into his own. He wished he could move closer, perhaps whisper into her ear or feel her breath upon his skin. An arm's length between them was simply too great a distance...especially for whispering secrets to one another—whatever they were.

Or for stealing a kiss.

Jasper almost flinched as that thought instantly drew his attention to her lips, a sensual curl to them that he found utterly irresistible. Again, he stared, felt the urge to move closer, to ignore each and every societal rule and kiss Lady Edith right here on the dance floor.

Another turn brought her back to him, and again she all but squinted her eyes before a dawning look of realization lit up her face. Fortunately, her distractedness stopped Jasper from doing something unwise. So, instead of stealing a kiss, he turned his head to see what she had just noticed...but failed to understand. All he saw were Lord and Lady Cumberton's guests, mingling, chatting, dancing. Nothing out of the ordinary.

"Are you by any chance acquainted with the Scots who arrived a few days past?" Lady Edith inquired suddenly, her gaze now fixed upon his face, eagerly awaiting his answer.

Jasper frowned, then tensed when a new thought occurred to him. Was she asking him this because she had taken a liking to one of them? Indeed, the thought was most painful, and he was surprised to feel red-hot jealousy shoot to his heart, squeezing it cruelly. "Why do you ask?"

The left corner of her mouth twitched. "That is none of your concern," she said sweetly, as though complimenting his dancing. "Your choices are these: assist me or not."

Jasper frowned, disliking this game while also reveling in it. "Assist you with what?"

"First, give me your answer," she insisted, her eyes looking into his, as though the rest of the world no longer existed. Jasper rather liked it. Oh, she had a way of making him forget everything else!

He inhaled a deep breath, considering her words, at the same time certain that he could not deny her. "Very well."

A radiant smile came to her face, and yet it was a look of relief that lit up her eyes, making him realize how much this plan—whatever it was!—meant to her.

"What then will you have me do, my lady?"

A contemplative expression came to her face, and once again her gaze swept from one side of the ballroom to the other as though she were considering her next steps. "Do you see that tall, dark-haired Scotsman over there?" She nodded her chin to a man beyond his shoulder.

A few more steps and Jasper was facing the direction she had indicated. "I believe I have met him before." His frown deepened. "Why?" Suspicion clung to that one word, and his hand momentarily tensed upon hers.

The smile upon her face deepened as she saw his reaction. "Are you jealous?" she asked, as though they had known each other forever, as though they were confidants, as though he had every right to be jealous.

Jasper wanted to laugh her question off but could not. His gaze held hers, and he could see that she understood his answer. "I've known you for no more than a matter of days, and yet..."

Not saying a word, Lady Edith merely nodded. Still, all of a sudden, there seemed to be a deeper understanding between them. Jasper could not put it into words, but it was there like the air he drew into his lungs.

The dance then came to an end, and the music faded away. Lady Edith took his arm, and together, they moved off the dance floor. "In five minutes," she whispered, leaning closer, "come and find me," her blue eyes looked into his, before a wicked curl came to her lips, "and bring him." Her brows rose as her eyes moved past him, indicating the tall, dark-haired Scotsman.

Jasper felt himself tense, and yet the look upon her face spoke of delight. Was it her intention to make him jealous? Or was it simply a pleasant byproduct of her original plan? Jasper did not know, and he loved and hated that fact with equal measure. She was indeed unpredictable and mysterious. Was that not precisely what he had always hoped to find in a woman?

Watching her return to her friend, Jasper heaved a deep breath, still a bit shocked at her impertinence, her way of addressing a virtual stranger in such a direct manner. However, what shocked him even more was the fact that he was more than willing to comply.

Chapter Six
MATCHMAKING

For the past few days, Edith had been racking her mind about what to do, about how to help her friend. Whenever she spotted Adele and Lord Aberley together, it became abundantly clear that they were not well matched; a fact that seemed to escape their parents entirely.

Indeed, upon returning to their chamber the day of their arrival, Edith had found her friend most distraught. Adele, too, had just returned from her stroll through the gardens with Lord Aberley, and it had made her realize that she did not care for him...and never would.

Edith had seen that with one glance. "He's a decent man, is he not?" she had asked, nonetheless.

With a heavy sigh, Adele had agreed.

"And he is handsome and well-behaved," Edith had remarked, watching her friend most carefully.

Another heavy sigh had followed. "He certainly is."

Edith had grinned a wide grin, unable to help herself. "And he bored you to tears, did he not?"

"Yes, he certain—" Adele's head had flown up, her eyes wide as she had stared at Edith.

Edith had laughed. "Oh, dearest Addie, if you could only see your face! You look positively shocked. However, it is only the truth, is it not?"

With yet another heavy sigh, Adele had flung herself onto her bed, burying her face in her pillows. "What am I to do?" she had moaned. "What am I saying? There's nothing to do!" Flipping onto her back, she looked up at Edith. "I'm doomed. I'm absolutely doomed."

Seating herself beside her friend, Edith had patted her hand reassuringly. "Now, now, now, don't be so glum. Nothing is ever as bad as that. Indeed, there's a simple solution to your problem."

Hope had blossomed in Adele's eyes against her will.

"Don't marry him!"

And hope had died an equally quick death as Adele had once more slumped back onto her bed. "But I must!"

Again, Edith had patted her friend's hand. "We shall see," she had whispered. "We shall see."

Indeed, ever since that moment, Edith had been determined to prevent Adele's betrothal from going forward. The only problem was that she had no idea what to do about it. Clearly, both Adele and Lord Aberley cared deeply for their parents and did not wish to disappoint them. Of course, Edith knew that Lord and Lady Ashbrook adored their daughter. Were they completely unaware that she did not wish to marry the man they had chosen for her? What would they do should Adele decide to tell them? Would they understand or be shocked to see this alliance prevented?

Yes, Edith could speak to them. However, she suspected Adele would be less than helpful in facing her parents, in speaking the truth, so long as she did not have another incentive.

And then, most unexpectedly, that incentive had materialized in the form of a tall, dark-haired Scotsman.

Stepping away from Lord Whickerton, Edith cast him another teasing smile over her shoulder before she returned to her friend's side. "I could do with a little refreshment. How about you?" She slipped her arm through Adele's, pulling her along without waiting for a reply.

"I suppose," Adele mumbled, her spirits subdued and the look upon her face one of resignation. Still, every so often, her down-turned gaze slid outward and across the ballroom...to linger upon the tall, dark-haired Scotsman.

Edith cheered inwardly, struggling to maintain a straight face. "Did you enjoy your dance with Lord Aberley?"

Reaching for a glass, Adele shrugged. “He is quite the proficient dancer,” she said in a tone of voice that showed she was upset with him for not, at least, granting her the opportunity to say something displeasing about him.

Beyond her friend’s shoulder, Edith’s gaze followed Lord Whickerton as he approached the Scot. She loved watching him, loved seeing the determined set of his jaw, the way he would every so often glance in her direction, his eyes lighting up in that utterly adorable way of his. He had been jealous, had he not? And he had been tempted to kiss her, was that not so?

Something deep inside Edith danced with joy. He had thought her interested in the Scotsman, and he had not liked that thought. *Interesting*, Edith thought. *Most interesting.*

“I believe I shall turn in early tonight,” Adele remarked, stifling a yawn. “Perhaps I’m still a bit fatigued from our journey.”

Edith laughed. “Nonsense. You are merely trying to escape Lord Aberley’s company.”

Adele huffed out an annoyed breath. “So, what if I am?” Her lips thinned as she looked across the ballroom at her betrothed. “This is what my life will be like from here on out, won’t it? How can you fault me for escaping from it for at least one evening?”

Edith wanted to dance on the spot when she saw Lord Whickerton approach with the Scotsman by his side. “I cannot find fault with you at all, dearest friend. However, if you leave now, you might come to regret it.”

“I rather doubt it.” Setting down her glass, Adele turned...only to pause, her entire body going still, as her eyes fell on the two approaching men. “Edie?” she gasped before managing to tear her eyes away from the man who had undoubtedly caught her attention and turn them toward her friend. “What is this? What did you—?”

And then the two men stood in front of them.

Lord Whickerton still had that scrutinizing look in his brown eyes as they moved from the man beside him to Edith, a question there that made Edith’s heart pound against her rib cage. “Ladies,” he began, and his eyes remained on hers, “allow me to introduce Cameron MacKinnear, Laird of clan MacKinnear in the Highlands.” He forced his gaze from her before letting it sweep from Mr. MacKinnear to Adele. “Mr. MacKinnear, these are Lady Edith and Lady Adele.”

Mr. MacKinnear inclined his head, and a dark lock fell into his face. "'Tis a pleasure to make yer acquaintance." A cheerful smile rested upon his face, and Edith was pleased to see that his gaze lingered upon Adele.

Who at present could not manage so much as a simple greeting!

Oh, this was most promising indeed! Edith thought with a sideways glance at Lord Whickerton. Two-fold!

"We are delighted to meet you, Mr. MacKinnear," Edith greeted him, delighting in the way Lord Whickerton's eyes narrowed as she smiled at the Scot. "Are we not, Addie?"

As though shaking off a trance, Adele bobbed her head up and down. "Y-Yes." She cleared her throat. "Yes, we are."

"If you are a Scot," Edith remarked, noting the way Mr. MacKinnear's gaze lingered upon her friend for another heartbeat or two before it turned to her, "then you must know how to dance a Scottish reel, do you not?"

The man laughed good-naturedly, and it was a lighthearted and joyous sound. "Aye, I do." Again, he briefly glanced at Adele before meeting Edith's eyes once more. "Would ye like to dance?"

Edith saw his reluctance, saw his desire to lead Adele onto the dance-floor instead of her. She also noticed Lord Whickerton tense, a muscle in his jaw suddenly twitching furiously, as though he wished to prevent her from accepting Mr. MacKinnear's invitation. Was she truly the only one who noticed? How could that be?

"You're too kind, Mr. MacKinnear," Edith told him with a glowing smile that made Lord Whickerton's muscle twitch even more. "However, I admit I am already fatigued. But perhaps you would like to instruct my friend?" she asked, turning to look at Adele.

Out of the corner of her eye, Edith noticed Lord Whickerton exhale a deep breath.

"It would be my pleasure," Adele breathed, her gaze now fixed upon Mr. MacKinnear's. All shock had disappeared, and she stepped forward and accepted the Scot's arm without a moment of hesitation. He, too, looked overjoyed with this outcome, and before long, they joined the other dancers on the dance floor, completely unaware that the next dance was, in fact, *not* a Scottish reel.

Standing shoulder to shoulder with Lord Whickerton, Edith smiled, seeing Adele's face light up as she stepped toward Mr. MacKinnear. "Why so furious, Lord Whickerton?" she asked, before turning to look at him, allowing a wide grin to show upon her face. "Still jealous?"

His eyes widened as he stared down into her face, as though she were a fairy, just sprung from the earth. Then humor overtook his face, and the smile that teased his lips sent another flutter through Edith's belly. "Are you playing matchmaker?" Lord Whickerton asked, a devilish grin marking his amusement.

Returning his smile, Edith shrugged. "I suppose I am. Quite frankly, I never thought Fate particularly knew what she was doing. It always seemed rather accidental that some people would find love while others did not."

"You are aware that Lady Adele is to be married to Lord Aberley, are you not?" he inquired, his brown eyes once more searching her face as though trying to unearth her secrets.

"That is their fathers' plan, yes," Edith conceded, casting a quick glance at the two men across the ballroom. Fortunately, they were deep in conversation with one another, completely unaware of the glowing expression upon Adele's face as she danced with Mr. MacKinnear. "Their children, however," Edith continued as she turned her attention back to Lord Whickerton, "clearly disagree."

"Are you certain?" Lord Whickerton turned to look at Lord Aberley, looking rather bored as he stood beside his father, his gaze distant, as though his mind were elsewhere. "What if Lord Aberley *does* wish to marry your friend?" Yet doubt rang loud and clear in his voice.

"He does not," Edith said with conviction.

Lord Whickerton smiled at her. He smiled at her in a way that made Edith's knees go weak. A smile that reached his eyes and whispered of secret longings in his heart. A smile that made Edith momentarily forget what she was about to say.

Heat shot to her face, and yet she delighted in these unfamiliar stirrings within her. What did they mean? Was he truly the one meant for her?

"Are you unwell?" Lord Whickerton asked; his voice, however, held no sign of concern, but rather rang with teasing delight. "You look rather...flushed."

Edith smirked at him. "I'm perfectly fine, my lord."

His grin broadened. "I'm glad to hear it."

The moment between them stretched into another and then another.

Edith felt something tugging her closer, saw him lean in ever so slightly, his sparkling brown eyes fixed upon hers. The world fell away, and for one long moment, nothing and no one existed but them.

And then Lord Whickerton's shoulders snapped back, and he cleared his throat, his face looking a little unsettled. "So," he began, his gaze slightly narrowed as though he were reaching for something to say, "you've chosen Mr. MacKinnear, is that right? For Lady Adele, I mean."

Edith grinned at seeing him so flustered. It made him look terribly endearing. "They are a much better match."

He glanced past her shoulder. "How do you know?"

"How do you not? Anyone with eyes can see that there is something between them."

Smiling, he nodded as his gaze continued to linger upon the dancing couple. Then he turned to look at her. "Nothing can dissuade you?"

Edith shook her head, a flicker of nervousness darting down her spine.

Lord Whickerton's smile broadened. "Good," was all he said...

...and it was all Edith had wanted to hear.

Chapter Seven

A SLY FOX

Over the course of the next few days, Jasper watched as Lady Edith continued to circumvent the dukes' intentions of seeing their children get better acquainted. She flitted around like a fairy, always there, but at the same time almost invisible. Again and again, she secured moments for Lady Adele and Mr. MacKinnear to dance and speak and laugh together.

Jasper had to admit that they did look rather besotted. Neither one of them had eyes for another, and Lord Aberley did not truly seem to mind that his betrothed fancied another. In fact, he seemed rather oblivious, as though his eyes were not seeing what was right in front of him, but had strayed to something else entirely, making him rather blind.

One evening, Jasper sat down to dinner once again to find that Lady Adele and Mr. MacKinnear had been seated next to one another. Indeed, it was the third evening in a row for him to notice this occurrence, and he could not help but think that Edith had something to do with it. How had she done it though?

"What makes you think it was her doing?" Andrew inquired; Jasper had no doubt he had overheard his muttering.

Thinking, Jasper moved his gaze from the young couple to Edith, herself seated down the table, her blue eyes watchful and a beautiful smile upon her face; a smile that whispered faintly of triumph. "Oh, I know it was her."

"But how—?" Andrew broke off, and as Jasper turned to look at him, he spotted a deepening frown coming to his friend's face. "Quite frankly," Andrew finally continued, his distant gaze clearing and once again focusing upon Jasper, "I saw her speak to my mother the other day, but that does not mean that Lady Edith—"

Jasper laughed. "Oh, it does!" Again, his gaze moved to her, and this time she turned to look at him.

The look in her eyes made him draw in a deep breath, and the smile she granted him was one full of shared secrets, as though she could read his thoughts and knew full well what he had just concluded.

And she did not mind.

Awed by her cunning spirit, Jasper continued to watch her. Indeed, she was a marvel, the way she spoke to people, always having a kind word to say to everyone. Sometimes it was a simple compliment on another's wardrobe. Sometimes her words were meant to be reassuring and uplifting to someone in doubt or even crisis. And sometimes it was a sweet, amusing anecdote intended to make people laugh and bring them joy. Still, whatever it was, all those she spoke to smiled at her, their eyes shining with approval, with gratitude.

With thoughts of friendship, even.

Was this her secret? Jasper wondered. Indeed, after no more than a fortnight at Cumberton Castle, Lady Edith already seemed well acquainted with about everyone, guests and servants alike. Jasper could see it in the way people looked at her, nodded to her.

And so, Jasper was not surprised at all to see not Lord Aberley seat himself in the sleigh with Lady Adele and Lady Edith but Mr. MacKinnear instead. The two women sat side by side while Mr. MacKinnear took the seat opposite them. Clearly, this arrangement was to everyone's liking, for Lady Adele and Mr. MacKinnear once again looked at one another in that terribly besotted way, almost oblivious to Lady Edith's presence.

What surprised Jasper, though, was that Lord Aberley ended up in the sleigh with Jasper, his sister and mother. He gave no reason for it, but merely took a seat next to Jasper, greeting everyone in a kind, yet somewhat tense manner. While his mother seemed quite delighted to have the duke's son seated opposite her unwed daughter, Mary instantly averted her gaze the moment Lord Aberley appeared. Her cheeks flushed a bright red, and Jasper could see how deeply uncomfortable she was.

For a moment, Jasper felt tempted to ask Lord Aberley to leave; however, that would have been beyond rude. Indeed, he had nothing against the man, for he was perfectly polite.

One horse-drawn sleigh behind the other, they made their way through the snow-covered landscape. Fortunately, Jasper's sleigh came right behind Lady Edith's, granting him a rather good view of the sleigh ahead. He saw Lady Adele and Mr. MacKinnear speak animatedly, now and then leaning closer to whisper to the other. At one point, Mr. MacKinnear even reached out and tugged a loose curl back into Lady Adele's fur-lined hood.

And all the while, Lady Edith appeared fast asleep.

Since the two ladies sat in the seats facing forward, Jasper could not see their faces. However, he had taken note of the way Lady Edith seemed to have grown smaller in her seat, her head slightly tilting to the left, as though sleep was tugging on her, and she could no longer keep it upright.

Jasper grinned, for he would bet his entire fortune that she was not truly asleep.

Indeed, she struck him as a sly fox. She knew how to read people, understood their intentions and motivations. She knew their hearts and minds and used that knowledge to see her plans realized.

Indeed, if she wanted to, she could easily build herself a reputation that saw her propelled into the highest ranks of the English *ton*. She could use her talents to deceive others, to gain favors, to manipulate, solely focused on her own advantage.

It was a thought, however, that had never occurred to Lady Edith. Jasper was certain of it. Yes, he loved her integrity, her devotion to others, her determination to see them happy. She used her gifts for the good of all, and Jasper marveled at all the many things she might still do throughout her lifetime.

He also marveled if perhaps some of her plans extended to him.

Chapter Eight

ON ANOTHER'S BEHALF

Keeping her eyes firmly closed, Edith listened as Mr. MacKinnear bid Adele goodbye, wondering why he would take his leave so quickly. Then, however, she heard approaching footsteps, a moment before Lord Aberley's voice drifted to her ears. "Did you enjoy the sleigh ride, Lady Adele?"

"Very much so, my lord," Adele replied, a touch of regret in her voice, no doubt caused by Lord Aberley's sudden appearance.

Deciding that it was time to awaken from her nap, Edith drew in a deep breath before blinking her eyes open and appearing to stifle a yawn. "Oh, goodness, did I nod off?" She rose to her feet, her eyes sweeping over her surroundings, as though she could not quite believe what had happened.

And then her gaze fell on Lord Whickerton.

The smirk upon his face told her in an instant that he knew what she had done. He knew she had not truly been asleep. He knew she had not truly awoken a moment earlier. And she suspected he also knew why she had pretended to be napping, for his gaze darted to Adele and then to Mr. MacKinnear, just now disappearing inside the castle.

Lord Aberley stepped forward and offered Adele his arm, which she accepted, but not without a look of regret upon her face. Of course, she tried her best to hide it, but Edith had seen it, nonetheless.

"May I escort you back to the castle?" Lord Whickerton asked as he stepped toward her. "Or are you too fatigued?" Edith loved that wicked grin playing over his face.

"Not at all," Edith said, playing along. She took his arm, and they followed the other two through the snow up to the castle.

Edith noticed few words were spoken between Adele and Lord Aberley. The occasional uneasy glance was cast at the other but not much was said. Indeed, they simply had little to say to each other.

Something else Edith noticed was that Lord Whickerton seemed to be slowing his steps, allowing the gap between them and Adele and Lord Aberley to grow bit by bit. "I know what you're doing," he finally whispered, winking at her as she turned her head to look at him.

"I have not the faintest inkling what you could mean, my lord," Edith replied, trying her very best to look innocent.

Edith knew that Lord Whickerton saw right through her act, and she could not say that she minded. "I concede," he finally said, "that your friend and Mr. MacKinnear are a superior match to the one planned by her father. However," he stopped and turned to look at her more fully, "are you not concerned that your interference might draw their anger?"

Edith sighed, for admittedly she had asked herself that very question. "In my experience, there are two kinds of parents," she told him. "The first were never able to truly connect with their children and, therefore, do not place their well-being, their happiness above all else." She looked past him to where Lady Mary and the dowager countess were moving along the path back toward the castle. Lady Mary walked with her head bowed down while her mother continued to speak down on her, no doubt lecturing her, correcting her, urging her to behave as she saw fit.

Lord Whickerton looked over his shoulder, and she could see him exhale deeply as his gaze fell on his mother and sister. Understanding marked his gaze the moment he turned back to her. "And the other?"

Edith smiled. "They are just the opposite."

Lord Whickerton nodded thoughtfully. "And you believe Lady Adele's parents to be the second kind of parents?"

Edith nodded.

"And what of Lord Aberley's father?"

"Truth be told, I cannot be certain," she admitted with a sigh. "I met the man barely a fortnight ago, yet I have seen moments of affection and concern. Yes, I believe that he, too, cares for his son."

Pulling her arm once more through the crook of his, Lord Whickerton led her onward. "So, you are determined to continue on this path?"

Edith looked up at him. "Do you object?" Her heart seemed to pause in her chest, waiting for his answer.

Grinning, he met her gaze. "I cannot say that I do." There was a touch of surprise in his voice, as though he ought to object, as though he had expected himself to do so.

Edith chuckled. "You sound surprised."

"I suppose I am."

"And yet what I do is not all that different from what your own mother is doing, is it? She, too, does her utmost to lead two people together." She paused, waiting to see how he would reply, if indeed he saw her in exactly the same light.

Again, Lord Whickerton drew to a halt, a frown darkening the look upon his face. He turned to look at her, his eyes sweeping over her face before he shook his head. "Yet there is one marked difference, is there not?"

With bated breath, Edith waited for him to continue.

"You do what you do to see someone you care for happy," he murmured, more to himself than to her. "My mother, on the other hand, does not care for my sister's happiness, does she?" He blinked, and his eyes focused on her once more. "Of course, that is not a surprise." He scoffed. "Of course, I've always known it. Yet..." He shook his head, as though putting that knowledge into words for the first time had suddenly made him look at it in a different way. "My mother belongs in that first category of parents, does she not?"

Edith nodded. "From what you and your sister have told me, I suppose that is a fair assessment."

Lord Whickerton heaved a deep sigh, full of disappointment and regret. "Well, then I suppose—" He broke off and then turned to look at her, his eyes widening. "You've spoken to my sister?"

Edith chuckled. "Yes. Why? Do you object? Are you perhaps worried about what she might have told me of you?"

Smiling, he shook his head. "There is no need for me to worry."

"And why is that? Are you such a good person that you need not fear another's assessment of your character?"

Throwing back his head, Lord Whickerton laughed. "Oh, no!" A warm glow came to his face. "But my sister loves me."

Edith smiled, feeling a warm glow spread through her. "I am glad to hear it. In fact, that was my assessment as well."

Lord Whickerton blinked, then shook his head, a wide grin upon his face. "Perhaps I should ask you to interfere on my sister's behalf as well."

Edith grinned. "How do you know I'm not already doing that?" The moment his disbelieving eyes turned to her, Edith released his arm and hurried the last few steps to the door. A footman held it open, thus allowing her to enter the great hall, where her eyes immediately fell on Adele and Lord Aberley. They stood rather quietly next to one another, looking forlorn.

"Lord Aberley," Edith addressed him with a smile. "I'm afraid I must steal away Lady Adele. After such a wonderful morning outdoors, I admit I'm rather fatigued. Are you not as well?" she added with a glance at her friend.

Adele nodded. "I'm afraid I am." Indeed, relief shone in her eyes at Edith's interference.

"Of course, of course," Lord Aberley assured them quickly, understanding marking his features as well as the same kind of relief that had sparked on Adele's face. "I shall leave you to it then."

"My lord!" Edith called out before he could disappear. "Have you already been to the library? It is a most magnificent place! I found peaceful solitude there the other day and can, therefore, only recommend it."

An honest smile tugged upon the corners of his mouth, and he inclined his head to her in gratitude. "Thank you, my lady. I appreciate it." Then he turned and walked away.

"Are you truly in need of rest, dear friend?" Adele asked with a chuckle, slipping her arm through Edith's. "I am rather surprised to hear that. Did you not already *nap* on the sleigh ride?"

Edith forced an innocent expression upon her face as they headed upstairs towards their chamber. "Oh, I do not know what you mean!"

Adele elbowed her playfully in the side. "Yes, I've heard that before."

"Are you truly complaining?" Edith looked at her with raised brows.

A slow smile curled up the corners of Adele's lips. "I did not say that, did I?"

Together, they burst out laughing. "Then, does this mean you appreciate the privacy I granted you?"

Adele nodded, and yet the expression upon her face fell. "Only it will not do any good, will it?" A heavy sigh left her lips, one full of disappointment. "I cannot marry him."

Edith pulled to a sudden halt, staring at her friend. "Has he asked you?"

Adele shook her head. "He has not," she admitted with regret. "However, sometimes I think..." She shook her head. "He must know of my contractual betrothal to Lord Aberley. And if he does, then why would he ever propose to me?"

Edith tugged her friend onward. "And yet the man spends all his time in your company. Why would he do that if he truly believed you lost to him?"

The smile that came to her friend's face was answer enough. "But even if he—?" Adele began hurriedly, then broke off, her teeth sinking into a lower lip. "Oh, I do not know what to think, what to hope for."

Edith affectionately squeezed her arm. "You know that's not true. You know what to hope for, what you are hoping for at this very moment. Be brave and take this risk. Trust me. It'll be worth it."

Stepping into their chamber, her friend closed the door behind them. "Even if I did, what of my father? What would this do to him? You know, he is a proud man. He always stands by his word. Could I ever truly be happy, knowing what my choice did to him?" Closing her eyes, she shook her head. "No, there is no hope."

Edith exhaled a slow breath, somewhat taken aback by her friend's lack of faith. Never before had she noticed the doubts that lived in Adele's heart. Would she truly lie down in defeat? Would she not even try to fight? To find a solution?

Well, in any case, Edith would not allow it.

That, she vowed.

Chapter Nine

A TWIST OF FATE

Jasper frowned when next he sat down to supper at the large table in the dining hall and found that Lady Adele and Mr. MacKinnear were, in fact, not seated next to one another. What had happened? Was this some sort of mistake? Or had Lady Edith given up after all?

Or...was this still part of some elaborate plan of hers?

Jasper grinned, suspecting the latter. Never would he believe that the woman ever gave up. No, this had to be part of her plan. His gaze drifted across the table to where she sat next to her friend, the two women chatting animatedly. Mr. MacKinnear, however, had been seated at the far end. While it kept him from speaking to Lady Adele, it did not keep him from stealing glances at her again and again.

Far too many for Jasper to count.

Toward the end of supper, Lord Cumberton rose to his feet at the head of the table. He looked around the circle of guests seated before him, his eyes glowing and a wide smile upon his face, and the room slowly quieted. "My dear friends," he began in his booming voice, "we count ourselves most fortunate that you have decided to celebrate this Christmas season with us." He looked across the table toward its other end, and his gaze met his wife's. A warm smile graced her features, making it apparent to every observer that a deep bond connected them.

"Many years ago," Lord Cumberton continued, "my dear wife and I met during another Christmas season. We were strangers then, but we did not remain strangers for long." Cheers erupted around the table, and Lord Cumberton's smile deepened.

"In fact, it was one particular tradition that brought us...closer." He teasingly wiggled his eyebrows, and his guests roared with laughter. "As that particular tradition managed to bring such happiness to us, we wish to uphold it." He nodded toward an arched doorway, and immediately a long procession of servants emerged, each carrying a silver platter with a small pie set in its center.

"Do you know what this is about?" Jasper whispered to Andrew, seated to his right.

His friend merely rolled his eyes in a rather annoyed fashion, clearly embarrassed by his parents' show of affection.

"All those yet unwed," Lord Cumberton explained as his servants proceeded around the table, setting down the pies in front of chosen guests, "will receive one of these delicious treats," he lifted a hand, "two of which contain a golden coin, one for a lady and one for a gentleman. And those who find them," he paused for dramatic effect, "shall be tied to one another for the rest of the evening." Murmurs went around the room, some excited, some concerned. "And by tied, I mean quite literally *tied.*" The hand he had lifted before opened, and one end of a red velvet ribbon fell out of his grasp, gently dangling from side to side.

Loud cheers erupted now, and Jasper saw several young ladies blush as their eyes darted up and down the table to the unwed gentlemen in attendance. Jasper's gaze, in turn, immediately went to Lady Edith, and he was not surprised to see that the look upon her face showed neither surprise nor excitement.

At least, not the same kind of excitement he saw upon the other ladies' faces.

Jasper frowned as Lord Cumberton invited his guests to inspect their desserts, reminding them to eat their pies with care, lest they'd lose a tooth. Of course, Jasper, too, had one such pie sitting right in front of him. However, his own attention was diverted as he glanced back and forth between Lady Edith, Lady Adele and Mr. MacKinnear.

All but holding his breath, Jasper watched and waited, his skin tingling with anticipation. Indeed, he saw not even a mild echo of what he felt upon Lady Edith's face. Instead, her blue eyes seemed calm and expectant. Was it possible that she already knew the outcome of this game?

Of course, she did! Jasper knew what would happen moments before Mr. MacKinnear discovered a gold coin in his pie. He held it up for all to see, and another round of cheers erupted around the table, followed by inquisitive looks at all the young unwed ladies. Which one of them would find the other coin?

Jasper chuckled, for there was not a single doubt in his mind that it would be Lady Adele.

However, there seemed to be in Mr. MacKinnear's. The man looked rather uncomfortable before he carefully chanced a look down the table at Lady Adele. Her lips had thinned upon Mr. MacKinnear's discovery of the coin, making it absolutely clear that neither of them was privy to Lady Edith's plan.

Jasper almost burst out laughing. He felt oddly excited, as though *he* had discovered the coin and knew that the other one was in Lady Edith's pie. Oh, he wouldn't mind being tied to her for the remainder of the evening! Not at all!

And then Lady Adele found the other coin!

At first, it was not apparent to anyone, for she did not pull it from the pie in one flourishing motion, triumphantly showing it to all those around. No, she merely stilled, her eyes widening ever so slightly as the breath seemed to catch in her throat. Then, disbelief mingling with joy upon her face, she slowly raised her head and her gaze traveled down the table to Mr. MacKinnear. Once their eyes met, that tentative smile bloomed into something powerful and utterly enchanting, and its effect upon Mr. MacKinnear was immediate.

The man looked as though he had found a pot of gold, a basket of jewels...or, Jasper supposed, the love of his life.

"Oh, look!" Lady Edith suddenly exclaimed, gently grasping her friend's wrist, and lifting her arm, thus revealing the gold coin for all to see. "She found it!" She appeared as though that discovery had come as quite a shock to her as well.

Jasper laughed, then suddenly stilled, overcome by the thought that he would never tire of this woman, would he? She was different in every way, and he would be a fool to let her slip from his grasp.

Instantly, more cheers erupted, and everyone shot to their feet, clapping their hands, their faces expectant. Lord Cumberton beckoned the two fortunate ones to his side, and slowly, Mr. MacKinnear and Lady Adele rose from their seats. Lady Adele, in particular, seemed to stagger a bit on her way; however, the moment she came to stand in front of Mr. MacKinnear, a calm serenity fell over her face. Within moments, Lord Cumberton moved their hands together and then tied the red ribbon around their wrists. No more than a minute passed, and yet it was a powerful moment, reminding Jasper of a marriage ceremony, something life-altering.

Without thinking, Jasper felt his gaze travel back to Lady Edith, drawn to the joyous look upon her face as she watched Lady Adele and Mr. MacKinnear. Tears misted her eyes, and she held her hands clasped together, the tips of her forefingers pressing to her lips, as though to hold back even more powerful emotions. He could see how deeply she cared for her friend, and it made him wish she would care for him just as much.

Or perhaps a bit more?

Suddenly, her gaze moved from the happy couple, and she blinked her eyes rapidly, clearing away the tears that threatened. A grateful smile came to her face as she looked at someone off to the side, and Jasper saw her give a quick nod.

His own gaze moved swiftly in the direction she was facing, and he found himself looking at a familiar face. At first, Jasper could not quite place it, but then he remembered the day of his arrival at Cumberton Castle. It was the young maid Lady Lucinda had berated for failing to place flowers in her chamber. The young maid to whose rescue Lady Edith had ridden. The young maid who clearly had not forgotten her kindness.

Staring, Jasper looked back and forth between the two women. Was this how she had done it? How she had ensured the coins would find their way into the right pies? Or rather the way the right pies would find their way to the right people? Indeed, it had to be!

One should always help when one can, do you not agree, Lord Whickerton? Was that not what Lady Edith had said to him? It seemed a kind deed often led to another. Those who cared and came to the aid of others never truly stood alone, did they?

Jasper had never quite considered this thought before. Too often did people in this world only see to their own advantage, never giving unless they received something in return. And while that was precisely what had happened, Jasper knew that Lady Edith had not been kind that day because she had wanted the maid to be in her debt. She had simply been kind to be kind, to help, to do the right thing. That was what made all the difference, did it not?

Chapter Ten

TWO BIRDS WITH ONE STONE

Oh, the rest of the world had to be blind, Edith thought as she stood in the parlor and watched Adele and Mr. MacKinnear. How could anyone not see the love between them?

She paused. Perhaps that was not the problem at all! Her gaze swept over the faces of Lord and Lady Ashbrook before moving to the Duke of Halston. Indeed, they looked far from happy, and why else would they look unhappy if not because they had come to realize that Adele held affections for Mr. MacKinnear and not for Lord Aberley.

Edith watched as Lord Ashbrook and Lord Halston exchanged whispered words, their faces taut as they cast the occasional glance at Adele. Lord Aberley, however, seemed far from upset by this evening's development. Indeed, he hardly even looked at Adele. Instead...

Smiling, Edith followed his gaze and found him looking at none other than Lady Mary. The young woman, in turn, did her very best *not* to look at Lord Aberley, her cheeks slightly flushed as she kept fidgeting with the hem of her sleeve.

Oh, how endearing, Edith thought, contemplating how best to proceed. Clearly, life was simple. Or rather, it should be simple, were it not for the interference of the two fathers currently eyeing Adele with a mixture of disapproval and regret.

"This was your doing, was it not?"

Edith flinched at the sound of Lord Whickerton's voice, for she had been too absorbed in the scene before her to have heard him approach. Turning to face him, she frowned upon seeing his face lit up with delight. "What was my doing?" she asked innocently, batting her eyelashes at him.

Lord Whickerton laughed. "You truly are impossible!" he murmured, and from his lips, it sounded like a compliment. "But you have a problem."

Edith nodded. "I am aware of that." She turned back around, now standing shoulder to shoulder with Lord Whickerton, and regarded the two fathers. "What would you do?" she asked him without looking up.

Beside her, she could feel him shrug. "I'm not certain anything can be done," Lord Whickerton remarked. "In my experience, parents can rarely be reasoned with once they have made up their minds." A hint of bitterness swung in his tone.

Edith considered his words for a moment. "Perhaps...this is not about reason. Perhaps it shouldn't be."

Lord Whickerton turned to face her, a frown upon his face. "What do you mean?"

"Mmmh," Edith murmured as her gaze swept from the two fathers to Adele and Mr. MacKinnear before seeking Lord Aberley and then Lord Whickerton's sister, Lady Mary. "Perhaps...a different approach would work." And with that, she left Lord Whickerton's side, moved across the room, and stopped in front of Lord Aberley.

The young man seemed rather caught off guard by her sudden appearance. "Lady...Lady Edith, good to see you. I hope you are enjoying yourself." Indeed, he did look a bit flustered, which, of course, was not surprising, as he was trying very hard not to glance at Lady Mary.

Edith smiled at him. "Oh, yes. This is a marvelous evening; would you not agree?" She moved to stand beside him so as not to obstruct his view of Lady Mary. "Did you happen to seek out the library, my lord?"

A genuine smile curled up the corners of his mouth as he looked down at her. "Yes, I did. Thank you so much for the suggestion. It is such a... beautiful place, calm and serene."

"I'm glad to hear it," Edith assured him. "I had a feeling you would appreciate its beauty." She breathed in deeply and then turned her gaze back towards the many goings-on in the room. "We are not all the same, are we?" she murmured, as though to herself. "Not everyone enjoys the outdoors, to mingle from sunrise to sundown. Some of us do prefer quiet solitude as well as the company of others who share our inclination." Without turning her head, Edith could tell that Lord Aberley was listening most intently.

His shoulders drew back with a deep breath, and for a moment, she thought to see him nod almost imperceptibly out of the corner of her eye.

"May I speak honestly, my lord?" Edith asked, chancing a quick glance at him.

"Of course," he replied after a moment of hesitation, the look on his face one of surprise. "Feel free to speak your mind."

Edith smiled, for she liked him. He was not the right man for her friend, but he was a good man. "I have to admit that I was a bit...apprehensive about your betrothal to my dearest friend," she admitted, noting the way he tensed. "After having gotten to know you, though, I find I no longer hold any reservations." She smiled at him sweetly. "Indeed, you're a good man, and I have no doubt that you two shall find happiness in marriage."

Out of the corner of her eye, she could see that Lord Aberley's frown deepened, his lips thinning. "Thank you, my lady. That is too kind of you."

"You're most welcome," she assured him. "Although I cannot speak from experience, I believe that a good marriage makes all the difference. To have someone to share one's interests, someone to speak to and confide in is priceless."

Lord Aberley inhaled a deep breath, his gaze directed across the parlor at Lady Mary. "Indeed, you are quite right, my lady." Yet the tone in his voice suggested regret and sadness.

Inwardly, Edith smiled. Of course, she felt for his misery, and yet his state of mind made her believe her plan could work, that everything would truly end well.

From across the room, Edith caught Lord Whickerton's narrowed gaze. Speculation rested in his brown eyes as they moved from Lord Aberley to her, and she smiled.

Two birds with one stone.

Chapter Eleven

A SPRIG OF MISTLETOE

The fact that Lady Adele and Mr. MacKinnear seemed more and more in love with one another each day, unfortunately, did not escape her parents.

Only a day before the cutting of the yule log, Jasper overheard a conversation between Lady Adele and her mother, Lady Ashbrook. The two women were striding down a lonely path in the gardens when their voices echoed to his ears from beyond a snow-covered hedge. Recognizing them, Jasper immediately froze, putting his finger to his lips to keep Andrew from uttering a word as well.

His friend frowned but remained quiet.

"Your father and Lord Halston have been watching you with care, my dear," Lady Ashbrook said to her daughter, a cautious but also inquisitive tone in her voice, "and I fear they did not like seeing you with the Scotsman the other night."

A shuddering breath left Lady Adele's lips. "What was I supposed to do, Mother? I found the coin. Was I not to comply with Lord Cumberton's tradition?"

"It is not that you complied," her mother replied with a heavy sigh, "but rather that it seemed to be your heart's desire to do so."

A long silence stretched between mother and daughter as Jasper stared at his friend. Andrew's forehead was wrinkled, portraying his confusion with what was being said. He looked at Jasper questioningly, but Jasper merely shook his head.

"It was," Lady Adele finally admitted on a sob.

"Oh, dear," her mother murmured a moment later, pulling her daughter into her arms—at least that was what it sounded like to Jasper. "What are we to tell your father?"

"Say nothing!" Adele exclaimed, her voice a tad shrill, filled with panic and despair. "Nothing has to change. I will...I will keep my distance from... from..." Another sob slipped from her lips. "What can I do to fix this? Please, Mother, help me!"

Seeing Lady Edith's efforts come to nothing in the face of her friend's loyalty to her father, Jasper turned away, signaling for Andrew to follow. "I have to find Lady Edith," he whispered when they had moved farther down the path. "I have to tell her what happened."

"What is going on here?" Andrew inquired, a puzzled look upon his face. "I'm afraid I don't understand."

Jasper winked at him. "Neither did I at first. Don't worry. I'll tell you later."

Unfortunately, locating Lady Edith was easier said than done. Jasper felt as though he had walked every corridor at least twice, checked every chamber three times before his feet pulled to a halt and he exhaled an exhausted breath. "Where can she be?"

Andrew chuckled. "There."

Jasper snapped around, looking through the arched doorway and into the parlor, where several guests were singing along to the pianoforte while others swayed gently to the soft notes. Lady Edith stood with her friend as well as Lady Ashbrook, a bit of a frown upon her face while Lady Adele's portrayed sheer misery.

Not hesitating, Jasper stepped inside, relieved to catch Lady Edith's eyes quickly. He gestured for her to come to him and then moved to stand a few paces from the handful of guests near the pianoforte. Their singing would surely drown out his words should anyone be nearby to overhear what was being spoken.

Lady Edith approached him without a moment's hesitation, and he smiled. "Is something the matter?" she asked before casting another look over her shoulder at her friend, the look in her eyes still betraying her confusion.

"I overheard a conversation," Jasper murmured, glancing at Andrew, who was listening with rapt attention, "between your friend and her mother."

Lady Edith's eyes narrowed, and a hint of alarm came to her features as she cast a questioning look at Andrew. "Something is wrong," she murmured. "She seems...forlorn, as though she's given up hope."

"I believe she has," Jasper replied, surprised how deeply Lady Adele's loss affected him. Perhaps he was not the shallow rogue many thought him to be!

Lady Edith was about to speak when she suddenly stilled and watched with drawn brows as Lady Ashbrook led her daughter...to a spot right beneath a sprig of mistletoe!

Jasper could not help but think that Lady Adele looked miserable, like a lamb being led to the slaughter. "Oh, no!" Lady Edith exclaimed, and Jasper's head whipped around. He took note of Lord Halston all but shoving his son in the direction of the mistletoe while murmuring something to him that made Lord Aberley look about as miserable as Lady Adele.

This was ludicrous! Jasper thought, surprised that he had never before realized how ridiculous the proceedings of the marriage mart were.

"Do something!" Lady Edith hissed to him, her hand upon his arm, as she stared across the room at Lord Aberley, slowly approaching. "You have to interfere!"

"What?" Jasper demanded as his gaze moved from the two miserable people back to Lady Edith, her blue eyes pleading. "What do you suggest I do? Knock the poor chap unconscious?"

Andrew chuckled. "This is fairly entertaining!"

Lady Edith glared at his friend, and Jasper wanted to applaud her. Then, however, she rushed off in a flurry of skirts, reaching her friend's side a split second before Lord Aberley, and in a surprisingly natural embrace followed by a turn, she maneuvered Lady Adele out of the way, taking her place...

...under the mistletoe.

Something painful slashed through Jasper.

"Perhaps, you ought to have interfered after all," Andrew chuckled beside him.

Jasper wanted to throttle his friend! Still, he could not avert his gaze and watched as Lord Aberley paused, clearly caught off guard. Lady Edith, too, feigned a look of surprise, pretending to only now become aware of the bit of green above her head.

Everything might have ended there—as there was no reason for Lord Aberley to kiss Lady Edith!—if the singing around the pianoforte had not in that moment come to an end. With their attention no longer focused, people quickly took note of the drama unfolding before them, clapping and cheering, delighted to witness a mistletoe kiss.

Cursing under his breath, Jasper raked a hand through his hair.

"She is not just any woman, is she?" Andrew inquired, his voice surprisingly earnest.

Jasper shook his head. "She is not," he growled, watching in shock as Lord Aberley moved in for a kiss.

A kiss Lady Edith did not seem to have the slightest interest of preventing! Surely, she could have thought of something if she had wanted to. After all, he had never known anyone to think more quickly on their feet than her.

Yet she did not.

Why?

Anger burned through Jasper, and belatedly, he realized his hands had balled into fists. Quite frankly, he felt an almost desperate need to stride across the room and punch Lord Aberley square in the face! Poor chap or not!

"Don't," Andrew whispered beside him. "It is not your place."

Jasper gritted his teeth as he listened to the guests' cheers and watched Lord Aberley take a reluctant step toward Lady Edith. A delicate smile lingered on her face as she turned toward the man, and to Jasper, the absence of reluctance upon her face felt like a stab to his heart. What was happening here? Was this not about helping her friend, after all? Was there more to it?

Jasper struggled to remain where he was when Lord Aberley leaned down and placed a kiss upon Lady Edith's cheek.

It was no more than a peck.

But that did not matter.

It was a kiss too many.

And Jasper felt close to erupting, to doing something utterly foolish in front of numerous witnesses.

Andrew's hand grasped his shoulder, holding him in place. "Not yet," his friend murmured, his grip determined.

After their kiss, both Lord Aberley and Lady Edith stepped back, looking a bit flustered as they tried their best to smile. Lord Aberley instantly retreated to his father's side, a dark glower upon his face, while Lady Edith cast a gracious smile around the room before moving toward the door. She stepped out into the hall but turned to look over her shoulder one last time. Her blue eyes met Jasper's, and a teasing smile curled up the corners of her lips before she was lost from his sight.

"Now," Andrew murmured, releasing his grip upon Jasper's shoulder. It was as though someone had fired a shot.

Without another thought, Jasper shot from the room, determined to catch up to Lady Edith.

Chapter Twelve

THE RIGHT INCENTIVE

Slow steps carried Edith down the hall until she could hear Lord Whickerton following behind her, his thunderous footsteps echoing to her ears. Immediately, she quickened her own steps and then slipped into a small parlor, leaving the door ajar. She could not help the smile that came to her face, nor could she prevent her heart from hammering excitedly inside her chest. She forced a slow breath down her throat, trying to remain calm. She stepped up to the window, keeping her back toward the door...

...and listened.

Truthfully, what had just happened with Lord Aberley had not been her plan. It had merely been an improvisation. Yet it had been necessary to protect Adele, to keep her friend from sealing her fate. To Edith, while not pleasurable, the kiss had meant nothing. To Adele, it would have been like a signature upon a marriage contract. Edith had seen it in her friend's eyes. She had not only seen despair and misery but also resignation. Adele was willing to sacrifice her own happiness to not disappoint her father, and Edith could not allow that to happen.

And so she had acted on instinct alone. There had been no time to think things through carefully. She had simply rushed to her friend's side, in that moment uncertain of what would happen next, of what she might do. Yet when she had turned to see Lord Aberley standing before her, Edith had a glimpse of Lord Whickerton.

The look upon his face had decided her next step.

Oh, Edith was not a deceitful person. She preferred honesty over lies and rarely kept things from others. Still, watching her siblings enter into their betrothals and then marriages over the course of the past few years had taught Edith a few things. She had learned that simply because something was the truth; it did not mean people were necessarily aware of it or ready to admit to it. Sometimes, an incentive was necessary.

The right kind of incentive, of course.

Lord Whickerton's footsteps drew closer until Edith heard him fling open the door in such a way that it thudded off the wall. "What just happened?" His words came out as a bit of a snarl, and Edith smiled, for she knew it was jealousy that fueled his anger.

Indeed, allowing Lord Aberley to kiss her proved to be a most powerful incentive.

Slowly, Edith turned to face him, aware of the wild expression in his eyes and the way his shoulders rose and fell with each rapid breath. His hands were fists at his sides, slightly trembling as he took a step toward her. "Why did you do this?" he demanded, as his eyes raked over her.

An almost giddy feeling surged through Edith, and the corners of her mouth twitched with teasing delight. "My lord, if you intend to shout like this, I'd advise you close the door." She lifted her brows challengingly, well aware of the way his eyes narrowed at the tone in her voice.

With a kick of his boot, Lord Whickerton did as she had suggested. Then he prowled toward her, his dark gaze fixed upon hers. "Why did you let him kiss you? You could've prevented it! You are not one shy for words, and yet when he turned toward you, you—" His teeth gritted together as he glared at her. "Why?"

Lifting her chin, Edith looked up into his eyes. She felt almost dwarfed by his tall stature, and yet she was not afraid. Her heart was beating strongly, still excited, still expectant. She felt that flutter in her belly again, and although Lord Whickerton stood close, so very close, he still was not close enough. "Do you truly not know?" she asked just as teasingly as before, delighting in the way his eyes narrowed even farther.

"Is this a game?" he growled as his dark gaze swept over her face. "Do you want Lord Aberley for yourself? Is that the reason for your interference?"

Edith was not surprised to hear his accusations, for she had already read them upon his face. "Even if that were the case, what does it matter to you?"

Instead of answering her, his glare darkened and that muscle in his jaw twitched angrily. "Do you make it a habit of kissing men under some mistletoe?" Bitterness rang in his voice. "Can anyone get a kiss? Or is it only betrothed men you pursue?"

Edith regarded him carefully, unable to ignore the sting of his words. "I ask again, what is it to you?"

His lips thinned, and his jaw worked as he leaned closer. Then he swallowed, and for a split second, something vulnerable sparked in his eyes. "I thought..." His gaze briefly dropped from hers. "I..."

It was all Edith wanted. "No, I do not make it a habit," she told him honestly, peeking up into his downcast eyes. "Truth be told, it was my first kiss," his eyes widened, "and...and I wish it had been yours."

For a long moment, Lord Whickerton simply stared at her, his body so still that he appeared like a sculpture, lifelike but frozen in place for all eternity. And then, like a strike of lightning, he hauled her against his chest and his mouth claimed hers.

Even though she saw his intention a split second before feeling his touch, Edith gasped. His closeness overwhelmed her, made her heart trip and stagger and her skin tingle with delight. His lips on hers were demanding, his kiss fierce, nothing compared to the emotionless peck Lord Aberley had bestowed upon her only minutes earlier.

Oh, how she loved the feel of him! The taste of his lips! The urgency in his embrace! As much as he had tried to hide his longing for her, his jealousy, she felt it now, knew that things between them would forever be different now.

Because she knew.

Because he did as well.

He kissed her again, slowly and thoroughly, before lifting his head, his eyes almost midnight black as they looked into hers.

Edith smiled. "See? All that was needed was the right incentive," she teased, delighting in the way he stilled as understanding dawned.

Rather dumbfounded, Jasper stared at the lady in his arms. Even though he had come to know her well this past fortnight, she still had the power to surprise him, to make his jaw drop and his eyes gawk at her as though she were a fairy, flitting through the air with golden wings.

Her words echoed through his head, *See? All that was needed was the right incentive*, and all of a sudden, Jasper was laughing. "I cannot believe I did not see this coming," he said, shaking his head in disbelief. "You did this intentionally, didn't you? You manipulated me into..." He stared at her in awe, realizing that he no longer felt angry. Instead, he felt almost flattered. If her manipulations always ended in such a kiss, she was more than welcome to do this every day of the year.

"Into kissing me," Lady Edith finish for him. "Yes, I admit it. Do you mind?"

Grinning, Jasper shook his head. "Do I look as though I mind?"

Placing a thoughtful finger to the corner of her mouth, she gazed up at him. "I believe not," she replied, her pale blue eyes glowing like the sky on a bright summer's day. "Yet...an incentive was needed." Her eyes searched his. "More than once, I thought...you wanted to kiss me, but then you did not. I wondered what it could be that held you back." A questioning look came to her eyes.

Jasper shook his head. "I honestly can't say. Yes, you're right. I thought about kissing you more than once, but..." He trailed off, shrugging his shoulders. Why had he not kissed her before? He did not have a clue. Then he paused, his eyes narrowing. "So...everything that happened just now, including letting Lord Aberley kiss you, was to lead to this very moment right here? You planned it all?"

Lady Edith smiled at him. "As much as I would love to take credit for this," she shook her head, "no. No, I did not plan it all like this. While the thought occurred to me to make you jealous," she grinned at him in an almost diabolical way, "I could not possibly have planned it all like this. There were too many variables outside of my control for that. No."

Jasper nodded. "So, you simply reacted? You took advantage of the situation the moment it presented itself?"

Her grin widened. "I did," was all she said, her blue eyes looking into his, as though she were waiting to see how he would react. Was she truly worried he would disapprove? After such a kiss? Perhaps, though, it was something more meaningful that made her draw in an unsteady breath. Was she perhaps apprehensive to see how he would react to her meddling ways?

"That was quick thinking," Jasper replied, delighted to see the corners of her mouth twitch as she exhaled audibly. He wondered if she had even been aware of the tension that now slowly left her body, relaxing her arms and shoulders. "You are a marvel."

A joyous smile lit up her face, and without thinking, Jasper leaned down and kissed her again. His arms wound around her, holding her tightly against him, reveling in the way her fingers twirled through his hair. He kissed her again and again, certain he would never tire of doing so.

"Feel free," he murmured against her lips, "to manipulate me like this anytime." Again, he claimed her mouth. "Yet, truth be told, it's not necessary. All you need to do is ask. Or not even ask. Just—"

Pushing up onto her toes, Lady Edith reached for him, her hands tugging down his head so their lips could meet. "This is wonderful," she murmured against his mouth. "I wondered how it would make me feel. I wondered—"

The door suddenly opened, and as they turned toward it, Jasper was surprised to see a maid—not the one who had been berated by Lady Lucinda—rush toward them. "Lady Edith, you need to hurry. Lord and Lady Ashbrook are looking for you. They're headed this way." She waved Lady Edith forward, glancing nervously back out into the corridor.

"Thank you, Sally," Lady Edith replied, and once again, Jasper was amazed at how effortlessly Lady Edith seemed to connect to others in a new place.

Without another look, Lady Edith tiptoed cross the room and then disappeared out the door, following Sally down the corridor. Rather dumbfounded, Jasper stared after her, realizing...rather belatedly...with a bit of shock...that he was falling in love with her. Was that even possible? How long had they known each other? A fortnight, perhaps?

In a daze, Jasper returned to the parlor, barely registering the stupid grin that came to Andrew's face the moment his friend beheld him. His thoughts lingered with Lady Edith and their kiss, with everything they had said to one another and—

—then he paused.

She had wanted his kiss, but...was that all? Jasper's heart constricted painfully in his chest at the thought that, for her, it had been nothing more than that. Was that possible? Indeed, the way she had looked at him, he could have sworn that...

Or was he a fool? He ought to have asked. Instead of kissing her again and again, he ought to have made it unmistakably clear that...he wanted to marry her...

...because he did, didn't he?

Running a hand over his face, Jasper felt confused. His thoughts were strangely sluggish, the way they were when he was too deep in his cups. They were spinning, going in circles, and looping around one another until they were hopelessly entangled.

"There you are!"

At his mother's sharp voice, Jasper's head snapped up. "Where have you been?" she demanded that usual look of disapproval and disappointment upon her face. "Did you not see the opportunity that presented itself to you?" She shook her head at him.

Jasper did not have the faintest inkling of what she was speaking.

"Lady Adele," his mother clarified with an eye roll at seeing his no doubt dumbfounded expression. "She—"

"Pardon me," his sister interrupted, surprising them both. After all, Mary rarely spoke, and Jasper could not recall a single time when she had dared interrupt their mother. "I'm afraid I feel a headache coming on." Her eyes blinked rapidly, as though she were struggling to hold back tears. "I shall go to my chamber and lie down." And without another word, she disappeared.

Jasper looked after her, even more confused than before, when his gaze fell on Lord Aberley, his face a mask of anguish while his father, Lord Halston, appeared rather put-out. Lady Adele and her parents, though, were nowhere to be seen. Jasper wondered what they would say to Lady Edith about what had happened here today. He wondered even more how Lady Edith would meet their questions.

Indeed, she knew how to think on her feet! Would she be able to put their concerns to rest? For she had no interest in Lord Aberley, did she?

Belatedly, Jasper realized that he could not be certain...for she had never quite answered his questions. She had wanted his kiss, but did she want Lord Aberley, a future duke, for a husband?

Chapter Thirteen
A LITTLE MAGIC

Closing the door to the small sitting room behind himself, Lord Ashbrook sat down in the upholstered armchair opposite them. Lady Ashbrook, Adele and Edith herself had found room upon the settee. Tension lingered. Lord and Lady Ashbrook's faces were taut, their eyes stern, while Adele looked like misery incarnate. Seeing her like this broke Edith's heart.

"Edith, you are aware," Lord Ashbrook began carefully, exchanging a meaningful look with his wife, "that Adele is to be married to Lord Aberley, are you not?"

Edith chuckled, putting on a look of confusion. "But of course. How could I not? Why do you ask me that, your grace?"

Again, Lord and Lady Ashbrook looked at one another before Lady Ashbrook turned to look at Edith. "Well, dear, after what happened today, we were wondering if...perhaps...you harbor affections for him." Her voice rose a fraction, giving her statement a bit of a questioning touch.

Edith allowed her eyes to widen as she kept her gaze fixed upon Lady Ashbrook. Then a second later, she let her jaw drop, her eyes blinking rapidly, as though their line of thinking thoroughly shocked her. "Oh, goodness, no!" She moved her wide-eyed gaze back and forth between Lord and Lady Ashbrook. "I...I...," she stammered for good measure, then inhaled a deep breath, briefly closing her eyes as though fighting for composure.

"Oh dear, this is all a terrible misunderstanding. You see," Edith began, allowing a tentative smile to show up on her face, "I just received news from my sister." She tugged the corners of her mouth a little higher. "I am an aunt all over again. A little baby boy. My sister and her husband are overjoyed." She glanced next to her at Adele. "I was so swept away by the news; I simply wanted to share it with my friend. I'm sorry to say I was completely unaware of...the situation." She lowered her eyes for a brief moment before looking up at Lady Ashbrook once more. "I am deeply sorry I ruined the moment."

A look of relief came to Lady Ashbrook's face as she exchanged a look with her husband. "I quite understand," she told Edith with a gentle pat of her hand. "Congratulations on your new nephew. This truly is delightful news, and I can understand how it might have blinded you to everything else."

To Edith's great relief, that concluded their questioning. The look of suspicion she had seen in their eyes disappeared as though it had never been there, and Lady Ashbrook embraced her with all the warmth Edith had always known her capable of.

"You're too kind," Edith replied and then quickly, not daring to wait another moment, she tugged Adele to her side and out of the room. Arm in arm, they hastened up the stairs to their chamber, and the moment the door closed behind them, Edith turned to her friend. "What are you doing?" She demanded, looking at Adele through narrowed eyes.

With a disheartened look upon her face, Adele shrugged, then sat down on the side of her bed with a heavy sigh. "I don't know what you mean," she replied with a downcast look.

Edith huffed out a deep breath. "Don't you dare lie to me," she snapped, seating herself on her own bed, across from Adele. "I saw the look upon your face. You gave up!" Accusation hung heavy upon her words.

Adele's eyes closed. "It's not giving up when there is no hope."

Edith grasped her friend's hand, and Adele's eyes flew open. "There's always hope." She smiled. "Lord Whickerton kissed me."

Adele's jaw dropped, and the hint of a smile teased the corners of her mouth. "He kissed you? How? Why?" Her brows drew down. "When?"

Edith laughed, delighting in seeing her friend's spirits reawakening. "Only moments after I prevented Lord Aberley from kissing you."

Adele's eyes widened. "Then you did do it on purpose!"

"Of course!" Edith exclaimed. "Don't tell your parents!"

Adele chuckled. "You're truly one of a kind. I had no idea you could lie so convincingly."

Edith shrugged. "If it serves the greater good."

Adele's gaze darkened, and she rose to her feet and began pacing around their chamber. "There is no greater good. Believe me, I've considered this from all sides." She turned to look at Edith, utter hopelessness in her eyes. "There is no way out."

"There always is a way out," Edith replied as she rose to her feet. Walking to her friend's side, she grasped Adele's hands. "Do you trust me?"

Adele frowned. "What do you mean?"

"Do you trust me?" Edith insisted, realizing that sharing her plan with Adele might prevent its successful execution.

"What do you intend to do?"

Edith shook her head. "Do you trust me?"

Adele sighed, her eyes contemplative, before she slowly nodded her head up and down. "Yes, I trust you."

Edith smiled at her warmly. "Then do as I say, and we shall see you married to the man you love without breaking your father's heart." She squeezed Adele's hands. "I promise."

A slow smile came to her friend's face as a flicker of hope sparked in her eyes. "You truly mean it," Adele breathed, surprise mingling with disbelief. "You truly think this can be done."

Edith nodded. "Now, go and put on your warmest cloak and boots."

Adele frowned. "Why?"

"Trust me," was all Edith said as she herself hastened to the armoire in the corner to do the same. Indeed, the next step of her plan was a bit tricky, for it involved a large number of people, and as Edith knew from experience, people and their behavior were difficult to predict. Still, nothing ventured, nothing gained. She had always found that to be true.

Only half an hour later, Edith and Adele were gathered in the great hall with a large number of guests all dressed for the outdoors. Once again, Lord Cumberton addressed his guests, speaking of the wonderful tradition of cutting the yule log, before he sent them all out into the cold.

Unfortunately, Lord Halston urged his son to offer Adele his arm, which she accepted graciously, the look in her eyes once more overshadowed by doubt as she looked at Edith. Edith, in turn, smiled at her reassuringly, for she had expected this to happen. Indeed, everything was going according to plan.

An icy wind blew that evening as the sun slowly began to disappear behind the horizon, their steps slowed by the snow that covered the ground inches deep. Some gentlemen held torches to light the upcoming darkness, while others carried an axe. As the light more and more disappeared and the night darkened, Edith looked up at the clear sky, her eyes drawn to the twinkling stars shining down upon them. Indeed, it was a beautiful night, perfect to work a little magic!

Walking on Adele's other side, Edith allowed her gaze to sweep over the other groups of guests, picking their way through the snow nearby. In the distance, she spotted Adele's Scot, his gaze narrowed and his jaw tense whenever he glanced in their direction. Past her right shoulder, Edith took note of Lady Mary, walking at her brother's side, as the two of them listened to a story recounted by their hosts' son. Still, Lord Whickerton's attention seemed far from focused upon his friend, for Edith could all but feel him looking at her.

The sensation almost made her stumble, her heart suddenly speeding up as though urging her to his side. Edith wished she could comply but first things first.

Tonight, she had a plan. Tonight, she needed to stay focused. Her own heart needed to be patient a little while longer.

With a tight hold on Adele's other arm, Edith began slowing their steps a little, urging their group a bit to the right until she spotted Lady Mary appear on Lord Aberley's other side. Fortunately, in that moment, there was a bit of a pause in the other group's conversation, and so Edith exclaimed, "Lady Mary, can you recommend a book on Ancient Egypt?" Edith remembered glimpsing the title of the book Lady Mary had been reading when she had come upon her in the library that day.

Lord Aberley's gaze swiveled from Edith to Lady Mary. "You're interested in Ancient Egypt? By any chance, have you read...?" And he launched into a discussion Edith had no longer any interest in following. Lady Mary, however, looked utterly delighted, the shy look in her eyes slowly replaced by one of enjoyment.

Edith smiled, well-aware of Lord Whickerton's curious gaze upon her. Still, she made it a point not to meet his eyes. Instead, she stumbled in her step, holding on tightly to Adele. Her friend slowed as well, turning to her with questioning eyes. "Are you all right?"

Edith nodded, noting that Adele's arm had slipped from Lord Aberley and that he, in turn, had failed to notice, for he was too engrossed in his conversation with Lady Mary.

Trudging onward, Edith glanced around and quickly located Cameron MacKinnear, his gaze still fixed upon Adele, who tried her best not to look at him. Edith, however, had no such qualms. As Lord Aberley and Lady Mary walked ahead—the distance between them and the rest of their group growing larger with each step—Edith smiled at the Scot, beckoning him over. The man hesitated for no more than a second before purposeful strides carried him closer.

Beside Edith, Adele drew in a shuddering breath, her gaze fixed upon the snow-covered ground.

"Mr. MacKinnear," Edith exclaimed, once again feeling Lord Whickerton's calculating and somewhat amused eyes on her, "I see you've brought your own axe." She pointed to the sharp blade protruding from the wooden handle currently resting upon the Scot's shoulder. "My friend," she tugged Adele forward, "has a truly good eye for a fitting yule log. Perhaps she can assist you."

The look in Mr. MacKinnear's eyes told her loud and clear that he knew what she was doing...and that he was grateful for it. "Aye, I'd appreciate that," he replied, stepping forward and offering Adele his arm.

Somewhat hesitant, Adele accepted, clearly fearful of seeing her hopes disappointed. Still, her cheeks glowed a rosy-red, and Edith doubted it had anything to do with the cold and everything with the dazzling man by her side.

Slowing her steps yet again, Edith smiled as she watched them walk ahead.

"You're a crafty one," Lord Whickerton's friend commented with an amused grin as he looked past his friend at her. "And here I thought only old matrons tried their hands at matchmaking."

Edith laughed. "I assure you, my lord, it is a skill that must be honed. Only years of practice enable one to do this with ease."

He chuckled before winking at her as he took his leave. "I'll see you later, old friend." He clasped Lord Whickerton's shoulder briefly and then walked away.

Drifting closer, Lord Whickerton looked at her. "May I offer you my arm?" he asked as he searched her gaze in the dim light of the torch he held.

Edith smiled and nodded, and the moment she settled her hand upon his arm, her insides did that odd *thing* again. They seemed to twist and turn and flutter, as though she were falling from a great height while at the same time floating almost weightlessly on the surface of a lake. It felt exhilarating and peaceful, too, and it make her wonder how she had not longed for this feeling every day of her life.

"Do you regret our kiss?" Lord Whickerton asked, unexpectedly, as he pulled to a halt, his jaw tense, as though his teeth were grinding together almost painfully.

Chapter Fourteen

IF...

Holding his breath, Jasper looked down into Lady Edith's face. In the dim light from the torch, her face lay in shadows, the fur-lined hood of her cloak keeping her almost hidden from his curious gaze. If only he knew what she was thinking, for as expressive as those deep blue eyes were, she knew how to keep her thoughts concealed.

"Why would you ask that?" Lady Edith inquired instead of answering him. Not that Jasper was surprised!

"Because I wish to know," he simply replied, determined to have an answer, to not allow her to sidetrack him.

Indeed, their kiss had meant everything to him, had made him believe that she, too, cared for him the same way he had come to feel for her. Yet the way she seemed to almost effortlessly manipulate those around her—even for their own good—gave him pause. Could anyone truly know her motives? Her heart? Or did every look and smile serve a purpose? Were they only the means to an end?

With most rushing ahead to witness the cutting of the yule log, Jasper found the world around them quiet. Soft snowflakes danced in the air, settling on her cloak, the light from his torch making them glisten like diamonds. Her warm breath drifted from her lips in a small cloud, and Jasper watched it—almost mesmerized—as it slowly disappeared into the night.

"What is it you fear, my lord?" Lady Edith inquired, a soft smile curving her sensuous lips.

"That you will forever evade my question," Jasper huffed out in a deep breath. Still, her smile was intoxicating, and he felt himself answer it without thinking.

Lady Edith laughed. "I admit I have that tendency." She breathed in deeply of the cold night air. "No," she finally said. "No, I do not regret it."

Jasper exhaled the breath he had been holding.

"Do you?"

Watching a slight frown come to her face, Jasper shook his head. "No, never. I—"

Something heavy crashed to the forest floor, sending vibrations out through the land, quickly followed by a loud cheer.

"I suppose they found a fitting yule log," Lady Edith exclaimed with a laugh as they turned toward the commotion. Excited voices drifted through the air, and they already glimpsed a few guests beginning to make their way back to the castle.

"May I?" Jasper asked, once again offering her his arm. "Unless you insist on waiting for your friend." He grinned at her, wiggling his brows.

Lady Edith chuckled. "I wouldn't dream of it."

At her words, he tensed involuntarily.

With her eyes upon his, Lady Edith stepped closer and accepted his arm. "I meant I wouldn't dream of waiting for them…not of accepting you."

Jasper swallowed, surprised how deeply her words affected him. "Good," was all he said as they turned to trudge back up the path they had come. Still, in his head, her words continued to echo. She had not said *accepting his arm* but *accepting him*. Did that mean anything? If he were to… propose, would she accept him?

As they walked on in silence, Jasper realized he ought to simply speak his mind. He ought to ask her and see his questions answered. And yet he did not.

What if she said no?

It was that question that echoed through his mind predominantly. Always had Jasper thought that if he ever were to propose, he would be certain of the lady's answer. With Lady Edith, however, he was not certain of anything.

A scoff almost came over his lips at the irony of his words. Indeed, had he not wished for an unpredictable woman? A lady who would keep him on his toes? Surprise him at every turn?

Indeed, fool that he was, he had.

Once back in the castle, the yule log was placed in the large hearth in the great hall while servants offered hot beverages to Lord Cumberton's guests. "I feel like an icicle," Lady Edith murmured with a slight tremble to her words as she wrapped her hands around her hot cup, breathing in the steam.

Jasper returned her teasing smile; although, he could not say that he felt the same. Far from it. Never had he felt warmer, heat almost burning beneath his skin. It was her doing, was it not? Simply being here in her presence did this to him. He could feel it every time he caught a glimpse of her, her voice drifting to his ears and those blue eyes of hers looking up into his.

She was the one! And as that thought echoed through Jasper's being, he knew he could not wait. He could not risk losing her. He needed to act.

Now!

"Lady Edith," Jasper began as he turned to her, his eyes finding hers, "I wish to speak with you. I—"

"Edie!" came a hushed voice a moment before Lady Adele appeared beside them. Her face was flushed, and although her eyes glowed with joy, the lines of her face seemed tense.

"Are you all right?" Lady Edith exclaimed, passing her cup to Jasper. "Is something wrong?"

Belatedly realizing that they weren't alone, Lady Adele cast a careful glance at Jasper.

"Would you excuse us, my lord?" Lady Edith asked him with a smile. "I promise I shall return as quickly as I can," she paused, and a shockingly knowing look came to her face, "and then you can ask your question." The smile upon her face made him believe that although he could not read her thoughts, she knew his without the shadow of a doubt.

In the next moment, the two ladies disappeared to the other side of the hall, whispered words passing between them, as Jasper remained where he was, still shocked to the core by the only woman who had ever managed that feat.

Chapter Fifteen

IN LOVE

"He asked me to marry him!" Adele exclaimed in an excited whisper. "Mr. MacKinnear, he...he..." She swallowed, tripping over her words. "What do I do? What do I—?" Her gaze flitted across the hall to the man who had conquered her heart before darting to its other end to the man who would claim her hand.

Edith wanted to sing with joy! This was it! As much as she longed to return to Lord Whickerton, she needed to secure her friend's future first.

A quick sideways glance confirmed that Lord Aberley was still deep in conversation with Lady Mary, and so Edith grasped Adele's fluttering hands. "Calm yourself or you'll faint," she urged her friend.

Closing her eyes, Adele inhaled a deep breath. Still, her knees looked ready to buckle.

"Now," Edith began, meeting her friend's gaze imploringly, "go and fetch your parents to the upstairs parlor."

Adele frowned. "Why?"

"I cannot explain now," Edith replied, squeezing Adele's hands. "Do you trust me?"

Inhaling another deep breath, Adele nodded.

"Then go! Now!"

Nodding, Adele made to dash away before she remembered to slow her steps. Edith smiled at her friend's intentional calmness. After all, it would not serve them if the entire hall took note of what was going on.

Focusing her thoughts, Edith signaled to a footman, then instructed him to escort Lord Halston to the upstairs parlor as well. All the while, she could all but feel Lord Whickerton's eyes upon her, and she longed to hasten back to him.

But not yet.

Ignoring the confused expression upon his face as she walked past him, Edith approached Lord Aberley and Lady Mary. Both were completely absorbed in their conversation, their eyes aglow in a way that brought a smile to Edith's face. "Pardon me, Lord Aberley," she addressed them, wishing her next words need not be spoken. "Your father and Lord Ashbrook bade me fetch you to the upstairs parlor. I believe it concerns your nuptials to Lady Adele."

A hard lump settled in Edith's belly as she saw not only the expression on Lord Aberley's face fall but Lady Mary's as well. Yet, their reaction was the confirmation she needed to proceed with her plan.

Lord Aberley cleared his throat, suddenly unable to meet Lady Mary's gaze. "Of course. Yes. Certainly," he murmured, too overwhelmed to even question why his father would send Edith instead of a footman.

Mumbling an excuse to Lady Mary, Lord Aberley fell into step beside her, his arms linked behind his back, his gaze fixed ahead.

"May I ask you a question, my lord?" Edith asked as they left the great hall and proceeded toward the stairs.

Lord Aberley inhaled a slow breath, his shoulders tense. "Certainly, Lady Edith."

"Do you even wish to marry my friend?"

Clearly shocked by her words, he paused mid-step, then turned to face her. His mouth opened and his lips moved, and yet no words came out.

Edith smiled at him. "I understand," she said gently, before they continued on their way. She could feel him glance at her every so often, his lips parting as though to ask a question. But he did not.

When they reached the door to the parlor, Edith turned to look at him once more. "Let me speak first," she urged, meeting his eyes imploringly.

Lord Aberley hesitated, a frown drawing down his brows. Again, he seemed on the verge of asking a question when he sighed and then simply nodded.

Pushing open the door, Edith walked inside, Lord Aberley following on her heel, and found herself facing not only Lord and Lady Ashbrook's questioning eyes but also Lord Halston's. If possible, Adele looked even paler than before.

"What is this?" Lord Halston asked as he looked past her at his son. "Why are we here?"

"Is there something the two of you wish to share with us?" Lady Ashbrook asked her daughter, and Adele turned pleading eyes to Edith.

Steeling herself for what lay ahead, Edith straightened her shoulders. "In truth, it is I who asked you all here," she looked from Adele to Lord Aberley, "because there is something that you need to know." She smiled, ignoring the hopeful expressions upon the parents' faces as they looked at their children. "Lady Adele and Lord Aberley...are in love."

At Edith's words, wide smiles came to the parents' faces while Adele began to sway on her feet, her strained eyes seeking Edith's, who did not even dare glance over her shoulder at Lord Aberley.

"However,...not with each other," Edith added the second Lord Halston opened his mouth, no doubt, in order to congratulate the happy couple.

Now, however, he froze, his eyes narrowing as he turned to look at his son. "What is the meaning of this?"

Again, Lord Aberley's mouth opened and closed without a word leaving his lips.

Looking from one father to the other, Edith smiled at them. "It actually is quite simple, your graces. While your children have found that a deep friendship connects them," again, she smiled at the two fathers, praying that neither Adele nor Lord Aberley would contradict her, "they've each lost their hearts to another." While surprise showed upon the parents' faces, Adele and Lord Aberley seemed deeply unsettled to have their innermost feelings revealed in this way. "They have come here today to ask for your blessings to marry the ones they love."

Swallowing, Edith braced herself. Even though her plan was well-thought out, it was hard to predict another's reaction. What if she had miscalculated? What if this would end badly? What if—?

"Is this true?" Lord Ashbrook asked his daughter. He stepped toward her, his eyes seeking hers.

Adele swallowed hard, her hands trembling. "It is, Father. I'm so sorry. I never wanted to disappoint you, but I…I…" She looked past her father's shoulder at her mother.

Lord Ashbrook sighed, then turned to smile at his wife, who stepped forward to stand at his side. Then he looked at Lord Halston, something silent passing between him and his old friend, before he met his daughter's gaze once more. "Am I correct to assume that it is the Scot who has won your heart?"

Edith smiled as Adele's eyes widened dangerously.

Lady Ashbrook chuckled, exchanging a smile with her husband, who then once more looked at his old friend. "What do you say, Halston?" A smile played over his lips as he arched his brows. "Friendship was enough for us, was it not?"

Inhaling a deep breath, Lord Halston glanced at his son, who stood rooted to the spot, eyes slightly widened as he observed the scene before him. "I cannot say that I have noticed any partiality toward a certain lady on my son's part," Lord Halston grumbled, a touch of disappointment in his voice.

"It is the Lady Mary," Edith supplied helpfully, certain that no words would make it past Lord Aberley's lips. "Lord Whickerton's sister. Is that not so?" she asked the duke's son.

Briefly closing his eyes, Lord Aberley sighed, then nodded. "It is," he confirmed, then took a step toward his father. "While I hold Lady Adele in the highest esteem, it is Lady Mary who has stolen my heart." He swallowed. "May I have your blessing to ask for her hand, Father?"

Edith watched as Lord Halston met his son halfway, grasping Lord Aberley's shoulders. "Yes," he said simply, a rare smile coming to his face before he glanced at his old friend. "Yes, you have our blessings," his gaze moved to Adele and then back to his son, "to marry your own choice."

Joy flooded Edith's being as she saw Adele sink into her parents' arms, sobbing helplessly as the strain of the past few weeks fell from her. Lord

Aberley, too, embraced his father, hugging him tightly before his eyes rose and met Edith's, a grateful smile upon his face.

Oh, if all things would go according to plan! Edith thought as her mind turned toward her own hopes for a happily ever after.

Chapter Sixteen

A FOOLISH MAN

Watching Lady Edith leave the great hall on Lord Aberley's arm, Jasper once again felt his insides twist painfully as all sorts of dark forebodings flooded his mind. Anger ignited in his blood, mingling with an almost blinding fear that he was on the brink of losing her to the duke's son. Had he truly misunderstood? Perhaps she had liked his kiss but was still determined to become a duchess.

After all, the lady was an enigma.

"Are you skulking in a corner again?" Andrew asked chidingly as he walked up to Jasper, his gaze returning from the arched doorway through which Lady Edith and Lord Aberley had disappeared.

"I'm not skulking," Jasper hissed, glaring at his friend before redirecting his gaze. "I'm merely...observing."

"Then stop *observing* and ask the girl to marry you," Andrew huffed impatiently. "She clearly returns your affections. What more do you want?"

Jasper's head whipped around. "She...?" He eyed his friend carefully, his throat suddenly too dry for words.

Andrew laughed. "Is it not obvious?" He shrugged. "Although I have to admit that she knows how to mask her feelings a bit more effectively than you, I've seen that smitten look on her face as well. If you don't believe me, go and ask her." He pointed at the arched doorway. "Now, Jasper, before it's too late and I'll have to live with that morose look upon your face for the rest of my days."

Jasper inhaled a deep breath, then nodded. "Very well." He grinned at Andrew. "If you insist."

Andrew chuckled. "I'm afraid I must."

"Thanks," Jasper mumbled to his friend before hastening out of the hall. Although he did not know where Lady Edith and Lord Aberley had gone, a few inquiries among the footmen gave him a reasonably good idea, and so he hastened up the stairs to the next floor, praying that he was not too late.

Pulling to a halt outside a small parlor, Jasper was tempted to press his ear to the door. He could hear faint voices speaking within, but he was unable to determine what was being said or even who was speaking. Still, simply stepping inside would display poor manners, and he could not bring himself to do so as much as he longed to find out what was happening.

And thus, Jasper was forced to pace back and forth outside the door, pausing now and then to listen, only to grumble in frustration when he could not understand a word. Was he already too late? Were Lady Edith and Lord Aberley alone in there? If so, then he should burst in, should he not?

However, before Lady Edith had left the great hall on Lord Aberley's arm, Jasper had observed her speaking to Lady Adele. The young woman had been agitated, and Lady Edith had sent her away before waving over a footman and bidding him to deliver some kind of message. Jasper was certain of it. But what and why? Was this another one of her plans he did not see coming?

Suddenly, footsteps approached the door from within, and Jasper darted down the corridor to hide around the next corner. Indeed, he felt like a fool, and yet he could not help it.

The door opened and Lady Edith stepped outside into the corridor. However, before Jasper could reveal himself, Lord Aberley followed her, calling her name.

Jasper tensed as he watched her still her feet and turn around to look at the man. "Yes, my lord?"

Lord Aberley inhaled deeply before a joyous smile came to his face.

"Thank you," he said then, almost reverently. "I don't know...how you knew, but you've made me the happiest man."

Lady Edith returned his smile affectionately. "I am truly glad to see you so happy, my lord, and I have no doubt that you will make a fine husband."

Jasper felt their words like a punch to his midsection, and he struggled to remain upright as he watched them part ways. While Lord Aberley hastened back downstairs, Lady Edith turned toward the wing, harboring the guest chambers.

For a moment, Jasper warred with himself, torn about what to do before his feet made the decision for him, rushing down the corridor after Lady Edith. No matter her choice, he needed her to tell him. He needed her to say the words because he needed to hear them.

Rounding another corner, he spotted her enter a chamber at the end of the corridor. The door fell closed behind her, but Jasper did not slow down. Large strides carried him onward, and his hand reached out to push open the door without a moment's hesitation.

Jasper all but barreled through it...and then pulled up short to avoid stepping on Lady Edith's toes because she stood just inside the room, her arms crossed over her chest and her gaze seeking his as though she had been awaiting his arrival. Jasper frowned. Had she?

Exhaling a deep breath, Jasper stilled, then swiftly kicked the door closed, his breath coming fast as he looked at her. Clearly, something had escaped his attention. Clearly—

"Well," Lady Edith addressed him with a raised brow, "are you here to stake your claim?"

Jasper all but stared into her face, slowly becoming aware of the sly twinkle in her blue eyes as she watched him with equal care. And then the air rushed from his lungs in one long breath when he realized what a fool he had been. "You did it again, didn't you?" he demanded with a laugh, shaking his head in disbelief. "You manipulated me into storming in here!" He moved closer, searching her face. "How? How could you possibly know that I...?" Again, he shook his head, completely overwhelmed and utterly amazed.

A delicate smile tickled the corners of her mouth as Lady Edith shrugged. "I see things others do not. It's a gift," she snorted, "or a curse perhaps, but I prefer to look on the bright side."

Her blue eyes seemed to glow as they looked into his, and Jasper inched closer, drawn to her like a moth to a flame. "Is there nothing that surprises you, my lady?" he whispered, wanting nothing more than to feel her in his arms again.

Her lashes fluttered downward in a surprising show of vulnerability before her eyes found his once more. "I...I did not expect to lose my heart this Christmas." As formidable as Lady Edith always seemed, Jasper realized he had not been the only one who had feared the outcome of what had developed between them. Did she truly doubt how he felt about her? It seemed impossible!

With his gaze locked upon hers, Jasper moved closer, his hands moving to touch her, brushing along her arms before he pulled her into his embrace. "I thought you were betrothed," he whispered as her breath quickened in tandem with his own.

"I know," she breathed, and a smile teased her lips.

Jasper chuckled. "You wanted me to think that?" He could not say that he was surprised!

For a moment, her teeth sank into her lower lip, and he saw that sly twinkle return to her eyes. "You're here now, are you not?" Lady Edith teased as her hands moved onto his shoulders, giving him a little tug. "Are you truly complaining?"

Smiling, Jasper closed his eyes and rested his forehead against hers. He breathed in deeply, feeling her warm breath tease his lips. "I love you," he whispered, then opened his eyes, "and I did not expect that, either."

A slight crease formed between her brows. "Do you regret it?"

A wide smile claimed Jasper's face before he dipped his head and kissed her, relishing in the feeling of her yielding lips beneath his own. Her hands snaked around his neck, and she returned his kiss with utter abandon, and his heart soared as she sank into his embrace.

"Marry me," Jasper gasped as he pulled back, staring into her eyes. "Say that you'll marry me."

A teasing chuckle left her lips. "Truly? Have you thought this through? I am who I am, and I will not change." A touch of sadness came to her eyes. "Not even for you."

Jasper paused, wondering at the vulnerability he heard in her voice. "I wish to marry you because of who you are. Why, then, would I want you to change?" He shook his head. "Never. You're precisely the woman I always hoped to find but never thought I would."

Her smile returned with full force. "Good." Then she pushed herself up onto her toes and kissed him again.

"Is that a *yes*, dearest Edie?" Jasper asked, laughing, holding her snug against his chest.

"Yes!"

As his heart swelled with joy, Jasper tightened his hold on her and pulled her off her feet, spinning her in a tight circle as they laughed together. When her feet touched the floor again, he still could not bring himself to release her, his arms still wrapping her in a snug embrace. "When you said to Lord Aberley, he would make a fine husband," Jasper murmured as he pulled back to look into her eyes, "I thought I'd lost you. I thought you'd agreed to marry him."

Edith grinned, shaking her head at him. "You're a bit of a foolish man, are you not? But do not worry, I'll teach how to tell truth and lie apart."

Chuckling, Jasper squinted at her. "Are you admitting you lied?"

"Oh, lies aren't always bad," she insisted with a compellingly wise look in her blue eyes. "Just as the world is not black and white. Nothing ever is. Everything comes in layers, in shades, in degrees. Nothing is simply good or bad."

Mesmerized, Jasper sighed. "I'm only sorry that Lady Adele will not get her own happily ever after."

"What makes you say that?"

Jasper frowned. "Is she not to marry Lord Aberley?"

Grinning, Edith shook her head.

Jasper gave a short laugh. "Then whom is the man supposed to make a fine husband? That is what you said, is it not?"

His fiancée's grin widened. "Your sister."

Utter surprise froze every muscle in Jasper's body as he stared down at his future wife. "My...My s-sister?" He felt his mouth open and then close, trying to remember if he had ever seen Mary with Lord Aberley. Had he truly missed an attachment between them?

Of course, they had spoken earlier this evening during the cutting of the yule log. In fact, they had seemed quite engrossed in...what topic had they discussed? Jasper could not recall, for he had only had eyes for Edith.

Of course, she had been the one to introduce the topic between them, had she not? How had she known? How—?

That familiar indulging smile came to her lips as Jasper stared at her, trying to understand. "I see things," Edith said with a shrug. "I cannot help it."

Jasper laughed. "Honestly, if all your scheming leads to happiness for all those involved, who would ever complain?"

"I'm glad you see it like that," she replied as she grasped his hand and pulled him to the door. "Come or we will miss the lighting of the yule log."

Chapter Seventeen
WHISPERED WORDS

The great hall glowed warm and bright, the smell of evergreens lingering in the air, as Lord and Lady Cumberton's guests gathered to watch the lighting of the yule log. Edith felt the warmth of that night in every fiber of her being because, no matter where she turned, she saw people in love. Indeed, Adele looked blissfully happy as she clung to Mr. MacKinnear's arm, the look in his eyes as he gazed down at her promising a most wonderful life. Lady Mary and Lord Aberley, too, seemed transformed. Gone were the downcast eyes and the sullen expression upon their faces. Although they were not as expressive in their affections as Adele and her Scot, Edith could see with a single glance that their world, too, had been turned upside down...

...or rather right side up—finally!

"For once," Jasper whispered in Edith's ear as he leaned down to her, "my mother could not be happier with Mary. She was altogether speechless when she learned that her shy wallflower of a daughter had managed to catch a future duke." He chuckled, shaking his head at his mother, who stood across the hall with other matrons, no doubt bragging about her daughter's success.

Edith looked up to meet his eyes. "And you?"

Jasper let his gaze travel to his sister, her cheeks rosy from the warmth in the hall or the love in her heart—possibly both. "I'm happy to see her in love, to see her happy."

Edith smiled at him, and her own heart skipped a beat as she looked into his eyes. It was an odd sensation but also one most wonderful. One she would cherish for the rest of her life!

Yet a hint of sadness overshadowed this evening; after all, once married to Mr. MacKinnear, Adele would go live with him in the Scottish Highlands, a place so far away that Edith could hardly imagine it. "I don't want a long engagement," she blurted out, turning her gaze from her friend back to her fiancé. "I want to get married as soon as possible so that Adele can attend."

Jasper chuckled. "And here I thought you could not wait to become my wife!"

"Can I not have two reasons?" Edith asked teasingly, before her voice faltered, and she felt tears pricking the backs of her eyes. "She's...my best friend. She's like a sister to me."

Understanding warmed Jasper's eyes, and he pulled her closer, his hand closing over hers as it lay upon his arm. "I know," he murmured, "and I understand. But know that no matter how many miles may separate you, nothing will ever sever the bond between you."

Blinking back tears, Edith nodded.

Indeed, that night was one that Edith would remember for the rest of her life, and as they all stood together later, offering their respective well-wishes for their lives ahead, she knew that Jasper's words would prove true. Nothing would ever come between them.

"Ye'll always be welcome to visit us in the Highlands," Mr. MacKinnear boomed in his Scottish brogue, his green eyes shining with deep affection as he looked at Adele. "I know my Addie would love nothing more."

Jasper nodded. "The same holds true for Whickerton Grove. Please, feel free to visit us any time."

Edith and Adele embraced, brushing away tears. "Thank you so much for everything, dearest Edie," Adele whispered, her voice choked. "Without you," she glanced at her fiancé, "we'd have lost each other." A shudder went through her at the thought before she shook it off and smiled at her future husband. "You are the love of my life," she told him, and her eyes returned to Edith, "but you, dearest Edie, are my hero." She chuckled, embracing Edith again. "Thank you so much. For all you've done."

Overwhelmed by her friend's words, Edith held her tightly in her arms, wondering how much longer she had to spend with Adele, before her dear friend left for Scotland. Still, today had been a good day, an exceptional day, and she always looked on the bright side, did she not?

"Did you ever tell him?" Adele asked, once again brushing away tears. She glanced at Jasper before meeting Edith's eyes again.

"Tell me what?" Jasper asked as his gaze moved back and forth between the two friends.

Edith chuckled, remembering that first moment when she had laid eyes on her fiancé. Had only a handful of weeks passed since? It almost seemed like a lifetime ago...or perhaps merely a day?

"The moment of our arrival," Adele explained, a wide grin upon her face as she lifted her eyes to look at Jasper, "Edith leaned over and whispered something into my ear."

"And what was that?" Jasper asked as he reached for Edith's hands, pulling her closer. "What did you say? For I do remember the moment Lady Adele is referring to. I remember the way you turned to Lady Adele, as though you were challenging my regard for you." He cleared his throat. "I wasn't sure what to think of it, you had already captured my interest."

Edith chuckled, delighting in the ease of their conversation. "I told her," she whispered, holding his imploring gaze, "that I would marry you one day." The way Jasper's jaw dropped made Edith's heart falter in her chest in a most delicious way.

"What?" He gawked at her. "How could you pos—?" Jasper broke off and shook his head. "No, I'm not even going to ask. Perhaps I'm simply not meant to understand." He grinned at her. "I can live with that so long as you remain by my side."

Stepping into his embrace, Edith smiled up at him. "Always," she promised, hoping with all her heart that the days ahead would be happy ones.

But, of course, they would be!

Bright side, remember?

Epilogue

Three years later at Whickerton Grove

Standing arm in arm with her husband upon a gentle hill that sloped down toward Whickerton Grove, Edith breathed in the warm summer air. A soft breeze stirred the leaves and made the tall grass sway gently from side to side as bees buzzed busily nearby and crickets chirped here and there. The sun warmed her skin, and for a brief moment, Edith closed her eyes and leaned into her husband's embrace.

"It is truly a peaceful day, is it not?" Jasper asked with a chuckle, brushing a kiss onto her temple.

Sighing, Edith nodded. "A rare thing indeed." Then she opened her eyes and looked down upon their son, Charles, not yet two years of age. He sat in the tall grass farther down the hill, grabbing fistfuls of grass and yanking it from the ground before inspecting his treasure most thoroughly. Once satisfied, he held out his open hands to show his discovery to Aiden, Adele and Cameron's little lad, who clapped his hands together excitedly. Then he reached out and plucked something from Charles' hand, holding it carefully between two fingers.

Edith narrowed her eyes. "What do you think they found? A bug of some kind?"

Squinting his eyes, Jasper shrugged. "As long as they don't eat them."

Edith slapped his shoulder playfully. "Don't put that thought in my head."

Down in the meadow, Adele and Cameron were strolling through the tall grass, occasionally casting the same curious glances at their son and Charles as Jasper and Edith. Meeting Adele's eyes, Edith waved, overjoyed to have them here in Whickerton Grove.

"Did they say how long they wished to stay?" Jasper asked with a sideways glance, his voice gentle.

Edith turned to smile up at him, excitement coursing through her veins. "Until the end of summer! We shall have picnics and catch fireflies and—"

Suddenly leaning down, Jasper captured her lips in a kiss. "I love that adventurous spark in your eyes," he murmured against her lips. "It suits you." His arms tightened upon her back, pulling her closer. "You've missed her dearly, have you not?"

A deep sigh left Edith's lips as she looked up into his warm eyes. Then she nodded. "It is hard to be this far apart, but I'm overjoyed to have her here now." She smiled. "And I will make the most of the time we've been given."

"Any regrets?" Jasper asked all of a sudden, an oddly serious note in his voice. "After all, decisions were made rather quickly that Christmas season."

Holding his gaze, Edith shook her head. "Not one." She pressed a tender kiss onto his lips. "I love you, and if I'd had a year to think everything through, I would not have chosen differently." She held his gaze, then turned to look at their son. "Promise me something."

"Anything."

Edith sighed, her eyes finding his once more. "Promise me we will encourage our children to marry for love and nothing else. I want them to know the same happiness we found."

Gently grasping her chin, Jasper leaned down to brush his lips against hers. "I promise," he whispered before kissing her. "Let's make it a family tradition."

Edith smiled. "I love the way you think, my lord."

"And I've always adored the way you..." His voice trailed off, the look upon his face suggesting that he was lost for words.

Edith frowned. "What? Nothing comes to mind?"

Chuckling, he pinched her chin. "Too much comes to mind." He kissed her gently, then looked past her down the slope at their son. "He will be happy one day, won't he? And in love?"

Edith nodded, turning in his arms to look at her precious child. "I will do what I can to make certain of that."

Jasper smiled. "Then it is guaranteed."

Edith chuckled. Then she rested her head against her husband's shoulder, enjoying the way his arms wrapped around her as they looked out over their home. Yes, a new family tradition. To marry for love: what a splendid idea!

THE END

Thank you for reading *Once Upon an Aggravatingly Heroic Kiss* by *USA Today* Bestselling author Bree Wolf!

Have you read the Whickerton saga yet? Of course, Edie will not take such a vow lightly, determined to ensure that the next generations will know the same love she found with Jasper...in her very own, meddlesome ways!

Read book 1, *Once Upon a Devilishly Enchanting Kiss*, a captivating enemies-to-lovers Regency romance!

Phineas, Viscount Barrington, has known — and teased — Lady Louisa all of his life. But when another man takes an interest in her, he suddenly realizes he's been taking her for granted...

USA TODAY BESTSELLING AUTHOR
BREE WOLF
ONCE
UPON a Devilishly
Enchanting
KISS

Also by Bree Wolf

The Whickertons in Love

The WHICKERTONS IN LOVE is a new series by USA Today bestselling author BREE WOLF set in Regency-era England, portraying the at times turbulent ways the six Whickerton siblings search for love. If you enjoy wicked viscounts, brooding lords as well as head-strong ladies, fierce in their affections and daring in their search for their perfect match, then this new series is perfect for you!

#1 Once Upon a Devilishly Enchanting Kiss

#2 Once Upon a Temptingly Ruinous Kiss

#3 Once Upon an Irritatingly Magical Kiss

#4 Once Upon a Devastatingly Sweet Kiss

#5 Once Upon an Achingly Beautiful Kiss

#6 Once Upon an Accidentally Bewitching Kiss

Prequel to the series: Once Upon A Kiss Gone Horribly Wrong

THE WHICKERTONS IN LOVE

About Bree Wolf

USA Today bestselling and award-winning author, Bree Wolf has always been a language enthusiast (though not a grammarian!) and is rarely found without a book in her hand or her fingers glued to a keyboard. Trying to find her way, she has taught English as a second language, traveled abroad and worked at a translation agency as well as a law firm in Ireland. She also spent loooong years obtaining a BA in English and Education and an MA in Specialized Translation while wishing she could simply be a writer. Although there is nothing simple about being a writer, her dreams have finally come true.

"A big thanks to my fairy godmother!"

Currently, Bree has found her new home in the historical romance genre, writing Regency novels and novellas. Enjoying the mix of fact and fiction, she occasionally feels like a puppet master (or mistress? Although that sounds weird!), forcing her characters into ever-new situations that will put their strength, their beliefs, their love to the test, hoping that in the end they will triumph and get the happily-ever-after we are all looking for.

If you're an avid reader, sign up for Bree's newsletter on www.breewolf.com as she has the tendency to simply give books away. Find out about freebies, giveaways as well as occasional advance reader copies and read before the book is even on the shelves!

Connect with Bree and stay up-to-date on new releases:

facebook.com/breewolf.novels

twitter.com/breewolf_author

instagram.com/breewolf_author

amazon.com/Bree-Wolf/e/B00FJX27Z4

bookbub.com/authors/bree-wolf

A DIAMOND FOR CHRISTMAS

PREQUEL TO THE DIAMONDS OF THE FIRST WATER SERIES

SYDNEY JANE BAILY

A Diamond for Christmas by Sydney Jane Baily

Published by WOLF Publishing UG

This is a work of fiction. Names, characters, businesses, places, brands, media, events and incidents are either the products of the author's imagination or used in a fictitious manner.

Any resemblance to actual persons, living or dead, or actual events is purely coincidental.

About the book

A DIAMOND FOR CHRISTMAS

In a Regency ***Romeo and Juliet****, heady desire blossoms between a lord and a lady from warring families.*

Lord Geoffrey Diamond is the heir to an earldom with dash-fire to spare. There is no lady in London he ought not to be able to woo and win. Except one. Lady Caroline is vexed to learn the only man who makes her tingle is prohibited. Forbidden even to dance with Diamond, she finds herself breaking all the rules in order to follow her heart.

When they take a desperate chance on happiness, will it lead to a Christmas miracle or a Christmas calamity?

Introduction to
DIAMONDS OF THE FIRST WATER

Once upon a time, an Irish family by the name of O'Diamáin emigrated to England from the north of Ireland, from County Doire to be specific. You may know the area as Derry or even Londonderry if you are thinking of it after King James I granted the city a royal charter.

Felim O'Diamáin, who was the youngest son, sailed across the Irish Sea to make his fortune, bringing his pretty wife and two young children with him. As the story goes, they stopped over on the Isle of Man for a perfectly peaceful night before landing at Ravenglass the next day and traipsing through the Lake District.

Another version swears they took the shorter but far more dangerous route north across the sea to Portpatrick, finding themselves in the southernmost part of Scotland. From there, if they indeed came that way, they headed east toward Gretna Green. Not for any quick anvil marriage, mind you, but to traverse the border to England.

No one knows for sure the veracity of either tale, nor particularly cares. Once they arrived in England, Felim did very well for himself, as did his descendants.

At some point during the twelve-year reign of George I, another O'Diamáin by the name of Liam was made an earl for his devoted service to the Crown. During those years in the early eighteenth century, King George also created a few dukes, at least one marquess, some barons, a single viscount, and other earls. But we're not interested in any of them, although some may have helped to quell the riots that ensued when Hanoverian George outmaneuvered any pesky residual Stuarts hoping to claim the English throne.

Nevertheless, our interest lies with Liam. With his new earldom came much wealth and land, specifically in Derbyshire. And naturally, a title. However, George I, being of Germanic descent, didn't find the Celtic name of O'Diamáin tripped easily off his tongue. Neither did he master Gaelic or Manx, for that matter. In any case, with a little persuasion and an extra thousand acres, Liam became William, Earl Diamond, as his male descendants have been known ever since.

Over the years, the earls have enlarged the original house to be an impressive manor, always named Oak Grove Hall, which is the translation of their long-ago home of County *Doire*.

Generations later, as the heir to the earldom and all its assets, Lord Geoffrey Diamond seeks a wife.

Chapter One

1824, Mayfair

Of all the clumsy, imbecilic things to do! And in front of a lovely lady, no less. Geoffrey had tripped over the cellist's chair leg and nearly bumped into a pretty blonde.

"Terribly sorry," he said when the musicians beside him turned as one to glower while not missing a note of the mazurka quadrille they were playing. And quite loudly in his ear, too. But he wasn't apologizing to them, rather to the vision in blue.

However, she gave him a withering look, not the warm one he'd hoped for when deciding to go in her direction. Having been introduced earlier, Geoffrey fully intended to ask for a dance.

Lifting her chin, the lady strolled past him to take another man's hand.

Still looking back at her shapely figure, Geoffrey crashed into another guest.

"Ow!" came a female voice from the vicinity of his cravat where her face was now pressed.

"Terribly sorry," he repeated, holding her by the shoulders so she wouldn't tumble backward. All he could see was the top of her head. It was a view of fiery, copper-haired coils and an aigrette of small emeralds, which anchored two peacock feathers tucked alongside her chignon.

Holding her still, he stepped back. When the lady's green gaze locked with his, Geoffrey was reminded of his family's verdant Derbyshire estate.

"No harm done, my lord," she said, offering a smile that stole his breath.

"Who *are* you?" he asked, mesmerized. At the same time, the performers enthusiastically played a crescendo.

Frowning, she asked, "Into the garden?"

That couldn't be what the red-headed young woman said, not unless she was the most forward lady at Lord and Lady Fenwick's Belgrave Square ball.

Bending low, he put his ear close to her pink-tinged, satiny lips.

"I said, 'I beg your pardon,'" she clarified.

Then he put his own mouth to the delicate shell of her ear.

"I asked your name," he explained.

She reared back and looked up at him. As the musicians now played less enthusiastically, he could hear her next words.

"You are breaking rules right and left," she told him, entirely without animosity. In fact, she seemed entertained. "You know you cannot ask me that question, not in such an informal manner."

"Of course not!" he agreed, glad she wasn't annoyed. He needed a formal introduction. *What on earth was wrong with him?*

Yet never having seen her before at any assembly, Geoffrey feared she would vanish before he could discover her identity.

"And your hands are still upon me," she reminded him, having to speak loudly over the music.

Yes, they were. And under his gloved fingers, she was warm and soft. He didn't wish to release her, but he did.

"Stay there," Geoffrey ordered. "Don't move."

Her eyes widened.

"If you wouldn't mind," he added.

Looking around wildly, he spotted their host walking in the opposite direction.

"Lord Fenwick," he exclaimed. Then he looked at the coppery goddess. "I shall return with our host at once."

Sprinting in the direction of the old viscount, Geoffrey managed to catch him before he left the room, going so far as to grab his father's friend by the arm.

"My lord, if you would be so kind as to introduce me to a female so I may ask her to dance, I would greatly appreciate it."

"Diamond," the man greeted him. "Searching for a wife at last, are you?"

At last? Geoffrey wasn't ancient! At twenty-six, he considered himself the perfect age.

"Hoping for a new bride by Christmas?" Lord Fenwick continued. "That would make your parents happy, no doubt."

"No, my lord. I mean, yes, I would like to marry, but not in haste."

"Right you are. Marry in haste, repent in leisure, as they say."

"Exactly," Geoffrey agreed. "Would you mind introducing me to a fetching lady whom I've never seen before?"

"Naturally, I shall."

Geoffrey turned, peering across the room to where he'd left her, but she was no longer there.

"She's gone!" he exclaimed, experiencing keen disappointment.

"Who is?" the viscount asked.

Geoffrey sighed. "I don't know her name, my lord. I shall go find her again."

"Don't let her get away," Lord Fenwick called after him, making other heads turn.

Geoffrey would be the laughingstock of this springtime ball.

Caroline wished the dashing, dark-haired man would come back before her mother or her aunt spied her. Alas, within a few seconds of the stranger's departure, her mother noticed she hadn't returned from speaking with a friend. Lady Chimes, with her sister beside her, came to collect her only daughter.

"Why are you standing like a fence post?" her mother asked.

"I am waiting for a handsome man," Caroline replied.

Her aunt smiled, but her mother did not.

"I am certain you shall better capture a man, handsome or otherwise, by dancing with him rather than by standing next to the musicians. Come along, Caroline. I have the very nobleman in mind for you. He was just introduced to us by our host."

Caroline was unceremoniously dragged away to meet some Lord Nit-Wit. Sadly, although the new man was also a stranger, he wasn't the one who had placed his hands upon her shoulders, making her tingle. He wasn't the one with dark hair and deep blue eyes the color of delphiniums, nor the one who smelled deliciously of sandalwood and Pears soap, the same as her family used.

He had crashed into her and then held on, and every part of her had cried out for him never to let go. It was the strangest, most delightfully overwhelming sensation she'd ever experienced.

She danced a quadrille with the young man whose name she'd instantly forgotten while wishing she'd learned the name of the man whom she would not soon forget.

And then she saw him, standing by a towering candelabra, surveying the dance floor. She had the strangest inkling he was searching for her.

Sure enough, when his blue gaze landed upon her, he smiled, and it lit up his entire face. He even took a step onto the dance floor and was nearly run over by two couples before he hurried to the side again.

He was as enthusiastic as a puppy, yet as alluring as a sable-haired wolf.

"Lady Caroline," came the voice of her partner.

She had faltered and made a misstep while making moon-eyes across the room.

"I apologize." She wanted to ask if they could stop, but it would ruin the formation for the other three couples in their group, so she persevered. As soon as the music ended, Caroline let her partner escort her back to her mother and aunt, who had come to the ball to keep them company as they often did.

A moment later, her blue-eyed stranger appeared before them. Beside him were their evening's hosts, both Lord and Lady Fenwick, who addressed her mother first.

"Lady Chimes, may we introduce the son of an acquaintance of ours?"

Lydia Chimes smiled to their hosts and to the broad-shouldered young man, letting her hazel glance slide over him. When she turned her mouth up, Caroline's mother looked like a young lady herself and had not a streak of gray in her red hair, a shade darker than her daughter's.

"Why, yes," her mother said. "If he and his family are known to you, then I am sure we would be delighted to meet him."

"Good, good," Lord Fenwick said. "Lady Chimes, this is Lord Diamond. His father is—"

"I know who his father is," Caroline's mother interrupted, and the change in her was as unexpected as it was swift. "And his mother, too."

Caroline gawked at her harsh tone, having never heard the like in public and rarely in private, either. She glanced at her aunt for an explanation, but Aunt Cordelia merely shook her head. Apparently, she knew what this was about.

Lady Fenwick frowned, obviously not enjoying any discord at her ball. However, not catching the import of Lady Chimes's words, Lord Fenwick continued, "Well, that's fine, then. Lord Geoffrey was under the impression you were both unknown to him and sought me out to make an introduction."

"We have no interest in making this man's acquaintance," her mother added with a voice as chilly as ice.

"Mother," Caroline said softly, wishing she could recant Lady Chimes's rudeness. She would not dare to gainsay her in front of others, even as she watched a puzzled expression cross over Lord Diamond's face. At least now she knew his name.

"His mother, I shall not discuss, but his father is a dishonorable man," Lady Chimes continued, "and thus, I can only assume *his son* is as well."

"My lady, I assure you—" Lord Diamond began.

"You shall not assure me of anything, young man," Caroline's mother said before addressing their hosts again. "I have been dreading such an occurrence, of coming across a Diamond whilst at an event, ever since we moved back from Bath. And now it has happened, and me without my husband by my side for strength."

Caroline managed to stop herself from rolling her eyes while her aunt raised an eyebrow of incredulity. After all, the fierce Lady Chimes was every bit as formidable as Lord Chimes. In some instances, more so.

"Frankly, Lord Fenwick, I'm dismayed this happened at *your* ball." Then her mother turned to her. "Caroline, come along. We shall leave at once."

"Please do not leave on my account," Lord Diamond said, his tone now one of bewilderment.

Caroline felt bad for him, trying to make eye contact, hoping he realized she was as confounded as he was.

"Don't leave upon *any* account," Lord Fenwick entreated. "You three ladies are most welcome to remain."

Her mother lifted her chin and looked away.

"I shall be the one to leave, of course," Lord Diamond said. "I wish I knew what this is about," he told Lady Chimes's shoulder.

Caroline could have died of mortification when her mother continued to ignore him.

Then he looked directly into Caroline's eyes again, and something undeniable passed between them. She believed it was a promise that they would meet again.

Then he turned to their hosts. "While I am befuddled by this lady's accusations, I will not remain and make her uncomfortable. Thank you for inviting me, my lord."

With that, he nodded, bowed shallowly, again to her mother's averted form, to Caroline's aunt, and to her before he strode away.

Chapter Two

Geoffrey had never heard of the blasted Chimes family before, but now he intended to know everything he could. He'd done the only gentlemanly thing he could think of in the impossibly awkward situation. Nevertheless, he vowed to see Lady Caroline again.

Even if her mother guarded the castle door like a fire-breathing dragon. A red-headed one at that. Speaking of mothers, his own was no shrinking violet.

"Mother!" he called out as soon as he arrived at his parents' townhouse on Hanover Square the following morning. If he wished, he would have inherited it and lived out his days there in later life, except he'd found a residence more in the thick of things on Piccadilly where he intended to raise a family.

Their butler, Mr. Fogerty, didn't mind when he showed himself into the drawing room to wait.

"Geoffrey," Lady Marianne Diamond greeted, sweeping in on her satin-slippered feet. "How wonderful of you to visit but how dreadfully naughty. It's frightfully early. The sun is barely up," she declared, even though it had gone half-past nine. "Fogerty, bring me a cup of chocolate as soon as you possibly can."

"Yes, my lady. And for you, my lord?" he addressed Geoffrey, who hadn't lived there for going on three years.

"Coffee," Geoffrey said. "With cream. Thank you, Fogerty."

When the man had gone, Geoffrey turned to his mother, who had seated herself upon the gold velvet sofa.

"What can you tell me of the Chimes family, and why do they hate us?"

He had her attention at the mention of the family's name.

"Hate us?" She sniffed, then sighed and looked at her nails, plainly stalling.

"Yes, you know them. I can see that."

"Don't tell me the frightful Lady Chimes has come back from Bath and brought her handsome, beleaguered husband with her? It was so pleasant knowing that family was on the other side of England. I suppose she made a scene. She is the lowest mushroom I can imagine. I don't know how Lord Chimes puts up with her."

Geoffrey narrowed his eyes. And then, thinking of his mother's wild youth, considered the most sought-after young lady at the turn of the century, a favorite at King George's court, he could guess she was involved.

"What did *you* do to them?" he asked.

"Me?" She was all blue-eyed innocence.

"Yes, you." He took a seat, determined to hear the *whys* and the *hows* of it.

"Why does everyone always think I am responsible when things go badly? Your father used to say I caused those three big stones to fall over at Stonehenge."

"No, Mother, that was due to frost and happened a long time ago. More recently, if you recall, you caused Lord Spiren to leave Lady Spiren."

Her nostrils flared. "It was not my fault the man became entirely besotted with me."

"Perhaps. Perhaps not." His mother was an unconscionable flirt.

"You are my son, and I will not be interrogated by you," Lady Diamond declared.

After the chocolate and coffee were served, Geoffrey tried again. "I only want to know why Lady Chimes wouldn't accept a simple introduction from me. Although come to think of it, she said Father had no honor, not you."

Instead of being bothered by a slight against her husband, his mother shrugged.

"Coming from a mushroom," she muttered.

"An attractive one," he said, trying to learn the truth, all fiery hair and green eyes like her beautiful daughter. "Did Father love her very much?"

"*Pish,*" his mother said, and the story came from her lips like water from a fountain. "It's the other way around. Lord Chimes adored me, but your father enticed me away from him. She's simply annoyed at being chosen second. She knows if her husband could have had me, she would have ended up some obscure baronet's wife, or worse, instead of a countess."

Geoffrey stirred his coffee. "Are you telling me on behalf of her jealous husband, she considers *my* father dishonorable? That's unlikely. After all, Lord Chimes's loss of you was her gain."

His mother sipped her chocolate. "There may have been something else."

"May have been?" Geoffrey prompted.

"Your father *may* have placed a wager with Lord Chimes and against all odds won, thereby draining the other man's coffers a little. I don't think the money mattered. It was the issue of the wager, which I never did suss out."

Geoffrey sighed. His mother liked to dance and batt her eyelashes and sing, too, whenever asked, and his father liked to laugh and occasionally to gamble. Mostly, they were both harmless since his mother never took her flirtation too far, and his father usually came out on top. *But, still!*

"Anyway," his mother asked, "why do you care if you are introduced to Lady Chimes? She's a bit long in the tooth for you, dear son of mine." Her familiar, ready laughter erupted.

He didn't feel like laughing.

"I wanted to dance with her daughter."

Lady Diamond perked up. "Don't even think it."

"Mother, you don't know the Chimes's daughter."

"True, and you don't either. Only think how she could exact revenge upon her parents' behalf. She might lead you on simply to break your heart. Or worse, lead you down the garden path to ensure a proposal. The idea of being linked through marriage to Lord and Lady Chimes is absolutely out of the question."

"I wouldn't mind," he said, thinking again how lovely Lady Caroline was and how sweet her lips.

"Not *you*! Us!" she said. "Your father and I could hardly invite them over for supper, could we? It would be excruciating."

"Liable to end in a duel if you behaved as your normal self," Geoffrey suggested.

"Preposterous," his mother said. Then added, "But entirely likely. Thus, the answer is no, no, no!"

"I wasn't asking your permission," Geoffrey reminded her. He would dance with, kiss, and marry whomever he damn well pleased.

His mother rolled her eyes. "Never mind. I don't need to do anything to stop this carriage wreck. Lord and Lady Chimes won't let you within a furlong of their precious daughter. Mark my words."

"Why won't you tell me?" Caroline demanded of her mother as soon as the ball ended, and they were in their carriage, on the way home to Upper Brook Street near Grosvenor Gate. Her parents had purchased the residence upon returning from fifteen years in Bath.

Her mother had refused to speak of the Diamonds at all. But her aunt raised a single perfectly auburn eyebrow, and Caroline knew she would find her answers the following day.

Thus, taking her maid, Caroline went directly to the home of her mother's sister at the polite hour of two o'clock. If they hadn't been out late at the ball, then she might have gone at regular visiting hours, beginning at eleven, but she knew Aunt Cordelia wouldn't have yet awakened.

As it was, her aunt, while still wearing her dressing gown and house slippers, invited Caroline upstairs to her bedchamber.

"We'll take tea in here," Cordelia told her maid, and they sat on the soft, blue velvet chairs by her aunt's window overlooking Berkeley Square. "You want to know about that dash-fire, Diamond, don't you?"

Caroline smiled. "Yes!"

"What a family!" her aunt exclaimed.

"Tell me," Caroline insisted.

"His mother was a stunner. She still is, I would warrant, although I haven't seen her in ages. She caught your father's eye, along with every man's, in her first year out in society. My sister saw it all. You know she loved your father at first sight but was too shy to tell him."

"My mother... shy?" Caroline mused.

"You become more of a tiger with age, dear girl, especially after having children. You and your two brothers are her whole life. And your father's, too, of course."

Caroline contemplated her mother as a young, unsure woman. It was hard to do.

"So, Father fell for Lady Diamond—"

"*Before* she was Lady Diamond," her aunt reminded her. "It was anyone's guess whose lady she would become. I believe for a little while, your father thought she would become *his* Lady Chimes. And then Diamond decided he wanted her for himself. I believe he secured her by compromising her. A little scandal brewed, and then suddenly, they had announced their engagement."

"Really!" Caroline's imagination took flight. After having gazed into the younger Diamond's blue eyes, she could well believe he might get her into a compromising situation with a crook of his finger.

On the other hand, what if it had been a forced marriage? "Maybe Lady Diamond really loved *my* father but had to marry Lord Diamond," Caroline considered.

Her aunt wrinkled her nose and shook her head. "I think she knew exactly what she was doing and whom she wanted. In any case, with her out of the way, your father noticed your mother. And that, as they say, was that."

"And my mother disapproves of Lord Diamond because of his rakish behavior with Lady Diamond?" Caroline asked. "That seems absurd, considering he cleared the way for Father to be with Mother."

"I think my dear sister states that she dislikes Lord Diamond but is actually still a bit green at the gills over *Lady* Diamond, although she shouldn't be. Your father was absolutely besotted with your mother from their first dance, and he's been a devoted husband ever since."

"I know," Caroline agreed with a nod. "I've seen evidence of their love many times over the years. Just the way they look at one another."

"Precisely," her aunt said.

"And does Father dislike the Diamonds, too?"

Aunt Cordelia sipped her tea. "Lord Diamond and your father both belong to White's. There was a wager. Diamond won."

"Oh dear," Caroline said. Her father hated to lose.

"Some said Diamond cheated."

"At least now I understand why Mother thinks him dishonorable." And maybe she was correct. "And thus, she'll never let me have an introduction to his son."

"It is highly unlikely," her aunt agreed.

"But did you see his lovely eyes, Auntie? And his face? And his mouth? And his hair?" Caroline couldn't contain her enthusiasm.

"Yes, and his height and the breadth of shoulders, too." Her Aunt Cordelia wore a smile. "A strapping man, to be sure. Regardless, I believe your parents stayed in Bath longer than they'd intended purposefully to keep you out of certain circles of society so you wouldn't run into that particular Diamond heir. And your trip abroad during last year's Season kept you out of harm's way."

Her aunt paused, looking unsure, but then she blurted, "Also the reason why your parents have all but promised you to Lord Mangue."

Caroline set down her teacup with a shaking hand.

"They wouldn't. They haven't!"

"I hoped you were aware," Aunt Cordelia said, "but since you hadn't mentioned it, I wasn't certain."

Shaking her head, Caroline could not credit her aunt's words.

"This isn't the eighteenth century. I do not believe my parents would force me to marry a man I don't know or love."

"But you *do* know him. I've seen you dance twice with him. At the Fenwicks' ball and the one before."

Caroline frowned. "Which man? The tall baron with those unbearably large ears, or the stocky viscount with a single eyebrow stretching across his forehead? Not that looks are the only thing, but sadly, neither man made any further impression upon me besides those unfortunate traits. Certainly not with their humor, nor clever conversation."

"Mangue is the eyebrowed viscount," her aunt confirmed. "And you don't know anything more about Diamond except his looks, either."

"But I wish to," Caroline insisted. "And I intend to. That's the difference. When Diamond stumbled into me, I vow lightning zigzagged throughout my body. His eyes held mine, and there was a kindred spirit."

"Kindred spirit or merely ardent desire for the opposite gender?"

Caroline wasn't shocked at her aunt's question. Certainly, she had felt a wave of yearning for Lord Geoffrey Diamond, but it wasn't solely due to his looks. If it were, then she would feel desire for every good-looking male whom she came across.

"Eyebrow or not, Auntie, I refuse to be forced."

Cordelia sighed. "I believe Lord Mangue is merely a secondary plan in case you don't find someone suitable by yourself. However, if you make a move toward young Diamond, perhaps accepting a dance, you are likely to find yourself engaged to Mangue with a contract signed before the last notes of the quadrille fade away."

"Will you help me? You are my favorite aunt, after all."

"Naughty girl, I am your only aunt, but you know I'll help. I am all for true love, as you know."

Her aunt had been widowed during the Battle of Waterloo when her husband, a captain and one of Wellington's officers, was mortally wounded. She'd never remarried but kept company with some very distinguished gentlemen, nonetheless.

"I do know," Caroline said, smiling fondly at her. "What's more, I hope you find it again yourself."

"You are a good girl for saying so." Aunt Cordelia's cheeks turned a little pink. "Let us focus upon you though, shall we?"

"How do you mean?" Caroline sipped her tea and pushed thoughts of Lord Mangue aside.

"Knowing you would visit me today, I scoured last night's and this morning's papers. It seems young Geoffrey Diamond—"

"Geoffrey," Caroline repeated. "That's a strong yet kind name, isn't it? Geoffrey Diamond. It suits him."

Her aunt sniffed. "I'm surprised you haven't tried out your own name with his yet."

She felt her cheeks grow warm, recalling lying in bed the night before, thinking she liked the resonance of *Lady Caroline Diamond,* repeating it more than once aloud. It had a romantic but steady character.

"Go on," she urged her aunt. "You were saying."

"Lord Diamond hasn't been much out in society until recently. His showing up at the Fenwicks' home has caused something of a stir, especially when he left so abruptly. That gave him an added layer of mystery. If he was a few years younger, I would say he only wants to dillydally, dance with pretty ladies, and perhaps kiss a few, too. Anything else, we couldn't even discuss. Yet at his age, it can only mean he's ready to find a wife."

"That seems like quite a lot to infer from a single ball," Caroline said, although she couldn't help thinking of the kissing as well as the "anything else" which they couldn't discuss.

Aunt Cordelia shrugged. "Trust me. And trust *The Times*!"

"Even if Lord Diamond is looking for a wife, and even if I wished to discover whether I wanted to be the one for him, what good does that do me when I cannot get near the man?"

"I can almost hear my late husband talking about plans of attack," her aunt said. "We need to maneuver you into close proximity. You simply must attend the next ball at which Diamond may appear, then send an introductory volley over his right flank."

They both chuckled.

Her aunt continued, "And you will need me by your side to permit this perilous mission, rather than my dear sister, who will forbid it."

Caroline's eyes widened. "You would do that?"

"As long as you promise not to do anything rash," Aunt Cordelia said. "Simply dance with the man, see if you fancy him, and then we'll worry about what comes next."

Chapter Three

Geoffrey had made it extremely clear to anyone who asked that he would attend Lady Plain de Ville's ball. He'd mentioned it to his tailor so his peers would know, to his butler and housekeeper, so the news would make it through the servant's grapevine, and lastly, to his parents. If Lady Caroline appeared, then she had been forewarned. He hoped he'd seen something in her eyes that bespoke an interest in getting to know him, despite her mother forbidding any such occurrence.

And if Lady Caroline wasn't at the ball, then he would take notice of the lovely ladies who were. He hoped one of them would be as alluring. One of them might make his heart speed up and take his breath away while causing that randy tightening in his loins that the mere sight of the red-headed beauty had produced.

When he entered the ballroom on the second floor of the grand house on Cowley Street, he knew within minutes she wasn't there. Her flame-colored hair would be easy to spot, as well as the glow he seemed to recall emanating from her.

But that was probably only in his imagination.

He greeted the hostess and then began to make his way around the room, chatting with friends, gathering well wishes to give to his parents, and being introduced to a few females with whom he thought it might be pleasant to dance.

In the midst of the Grand March, he saw her enter wearing vivid green silk that set off her fiery locks to perfection. On the other hand, he couldn't think of what color wouldn't. He easily pictured her in scarlet, in saffron, in sapphire blue, and even in black—looking equally stunning. Naturally, his brain added a vivid image of how perfectly spectacular naked as a needle against his cream-colored sheets, too.

She strolled the side of the room with the other woman he recalled from the Fenwicks' ball. He didn't know who she was, but she was definitely not the prickly mother. His luck was changing.

"Careful, my lord," came the warning voice of his partner as he missed a turn.

"My apologies," Geoffrey said and tried to keep his mind on finishing the dance with the lady at hand.

When he left the floor, however, and returned her to her chaperone, Lady Caroline was on the opposite side of the room. Worse, Lady Plain de Ville was introducing her to another man with whom she partnered for the next quadrille.

God's teeth! Geoffrey refrained from asking another lady to dance, as he wouldn't risk laying claim to Lady Caroline a second time. To that end, he approached Lady Plain de Ville.

"Will you make an introduction for me upon the dance's end? I would very much like to meet Lady Caroline," he confessed.

"Certainly," their hostess agreed. Yet she smirked. "Given your two families' histories, I shall be surprised indeed if anything comes of it."

Geoffrey was taken aback. It seemed nobility of a certain age knew about his mother and Lord Chimes or maybe about his father's wager with the man. Either way, it didn't bode well.

"I merely wish to dance with her."

"She is a lovely girl," Lady Plain de Ville said. And then they waited for the interminable quadrille to come to a conclusion.

"Shall we?" their hostess asked.

Together, they intercepted Lady Caroline and her dance partner.

Geoffrey was thrilled to see the lady's ready smile upon seeing him. If he was interpreting correctly, they shared a mutual attraction. For his part, he knew he had a large, foolish grin on his face, and he tried to quell it.

"Lady Caroline, this is Lord Diamond," Lady Plain de Ville got right to the point. "His father is the Earl Diamond. No other family name, as I recall. Most unusual to have the title and the family name be the same, but there you are."

Geoffrey barely heard her prattle. He took Lady Caroline's gloved hand and bowed over it.

"I am enchanting," he said.

As soon as the last word left his lips and he lifted his head, seeing her start to chuckle, he realized his error.

What turned him into a dunderhead around this woman? No one would ever accuse him of being a smooth rogue.

Even Lady Plain de Ville was snickering.

"Well done, my boy," she said and wandered off to tend to her other guests.

"My apologies," Geoffrey said, "but at least I didn't almost knock you over this time."

"You still have hold of my hand," she pointed out, with her perfect lips and soft voice. Not to mention sparkling eyes like sunlit dappled leaves staring into his.

"I do, don't I? And I shall release it," he promised, "as soon as you agree to grant me the honor of the next dance."

"Yes," she agreed.

However, since a dance had begun, he had to release her until a new one began. *What could they do in the meantime?*

"Shall we see if there is any punch or lemonade set out yet?"

"That would be lovely."

They left the ballroom and strolled toward the refreshments in the salon across the hall. A throng of others were already jostling by the serving table.

"I noticed your mother did not accompany you," he said, hoping it wasn't a mistake to bring up the woman who wouldn't even acknowledge him.

"My parents had tickets to the theatre. Thus, Mrs. Waycott, my mother's sister, brought me. Come to think of it, I should have taken you directly to meet her."

He couldn't help his expression of dread as they shuffled closer to the punch bowls.

"Do not worry, my lord," she said, mirth dancing across her face. "My aunt does not hold the same views as my parents."

"That's a relief," he said, handing her a full glass, which was nearly bumped from his grasp by a careless swell.

Snagging another for himself, they moved to the other corner of the room.

"After all," he added, wondering if Lady Caroline knew that both his parents seemed to have strained relationships with hers, "I am not my father, nor my mother."

"I understand," she said.

They spoke no more about it. Instead, he asked her about her life in Bath. She asked him what he'd studied at Oxford. Then, as oft happened, she asked him about his unusual family name, which he explained briefly since the hubbub was loud around them.

"Yet the king couldn't—or wouldn't—pronounce O'Diamáin," he finished. "Which gained us an extra-large land holding in 1717 in exchange for anglicizing our surname. And now, it's time for our dance," he reminded her.

Geoffrey had never enjoyed a dance more, nor a partner. He was as comfortable with Lady Caroline as if he'd known her for ages. At the same time, he relished the new sensations coursing through him—an intense awareness of wherever they touched. With heady desire sparking in his veins, he ached to be alone with her, without any idea how to make that happen.

The dance ended sooner than he could have imagined.

"Will you escort me back to my aunt?" Lady Caroline asked.

"I would be honored." But he held back. "Before I do, I wonder if you might wish to take a turn in the garden. Lady Plain de Ville is famous for her...," he trailed off.

Blast it all! He didn't know what the lady had in her garden. There might be an unusual fountain or some exotic plant, but he could hardly say such in case there wasn't any.

To his relief, Lady Caroline finished his thought. "Shrubberies," she offered, tilting her head mischievously.

"Yes, exactly."

"Lord Diamond, let me be clear. Normally, without a chaperone, I would not go beyond the boundaries of the ballroom with any man. But I shall go outside with you for one simple reason. I fear this may be a singular opportunity for us to speak privately. My mother will surely catch wind of our dance, and I believe I shall not be allowed to have another."

She was a reasonable female, which he appreciated. Yet he could not credit this was their one chance to be alone. He already liked her more than any woman he'd ever met. It was premature, irrational, and lunatic, but it was the bald truth.

"I understand," he told her, "although I cannot say I am happy to hear it. It seems unfair to set limitations upon us because of anything that occurred years ago."

"And that is why I will venture outside with you."

With a hand on the small of her back, he propelled her from the ballroom once again, toward the refreshment salon across the hall. Yet instead of entering with other revelers, they turned and walked swiftly along the hallway to the back staircase. In a flash, they were downstairs at the door to the garden, which turned out to be the tiniest plot with a few rose bushes and a single tree.

They stopped short on the stone terrace. You could even smell the mews behind the garden wall. No one would believe they were out there admiring anything except each other.

To his delight, she started to laugh at the absurdity. Geoffrey squeezed her hand and stepped onto the grass.

"It's a fine hazel tree," he said, gesturing to the single stunted plant.

"I believe it's a birch," Lady Caroline said, "and not the least bit fine."

"Let's circle it and see it from the other side," he suggested, emboldened by her acquiescence.

He'd always imagined ladies to be skittish and prudish, a far cry from the flash mollishers he visited at the best bawdy houses. Years earlier, he'd briefly escorted a lady whom he met through her brother, a fellow university student. A marquess's daughter, she had pursed her lips at everything Geoffrey said, yet still, he'd persevered for two weeks.

Unbelievably, without so much as a kiss, she had demanded a declaration of intent if not of actual love. At the tender age of twenty-one, he had not been remotely ready.

Seeing no point in forming an attachment to a female in whom he had no interest marrying, he'd gradually started a regular routine of engaging the excellent services of high fliers, usually keeping one of the experienced, polished whores for as long as six months.

When the time was ripe for taking a wife, Geoffrey had always planned on ceasing what some might consider to be libertine ways and become a dedicated husband, as his own father purported to be—despite what Lady Chimes might think of him.

It seemed only fair and right.

They circled the tree and were on the far side where the lamps inside the house no longer shone directly upon them.

Strangely, as he looked down at her under the moonlight, he felt a little unsure. While his body urged a smoldering embrace with her crushed against him, he reached out and trailed a gloved finger down her cheek.

"I'm glad you came tonight," he said.

"As am I. I admit I was curious about you. After my mother's refusal at Lord and Lady Fenwick's ball, I asked my aunt the reason."

"I asked my mother the same thing. I had never heard anything about your family before."

Stepping closer, Geoffrey took hold of her hands.

"Regardless," he added, "I appreciate how you didn't let any bitterness between our parents stop you from dancing with me."

She nodded before her gaze dropped to where their hands were clasped.

Not wanting to waste another moment at the wondrous opportunity to be alone with her, Geoffrey slowly drew Lady Caroline closer, his heart thumping at the notion of kissing the most gorgeous woman he'd ever seen.

He knew they should spend time talking frankly, but what if she was never again allowed to be anywhere near him? This could be his only chance, and a single kiss might prove them entirely unsuited. With that knowledge, he could put thoughts of this flame-haired lady aside.

Briefly wondering if he should ask permission to kiss her, or if that would mark him as a noodle-head, he heard himself say, “May I?”

Yet by then, it was too late. He was already lowering his mouth to hers. In the next second, he kissed her, and a tendril of passion unfurled inside him at her taste, blossoming into white-hot desire. They’d sipped the same punch, yet her mouth had the additional flavor of orange blossom and lavender flowers. He could both smell the delectable scents and experience them upon his tongue.

Releasing her hands, he slid his arms around her waist, enjoying her surprised gasp. With her lips parted, Geoffrey gently slid his tongue between them. To his joy, he felt her melt against him, with her hands suddenly behind his neck, hanging on.

When he stroked her tongue with his, she froze before tentatively echoing the movement. Tilting his head, he deepened the kiss, sucking her lower lip into his mouth.

Kissing Lady Caroline in the dark garden was the single most sensual, tantalizing thing he’d ever done, despite having tupped his share of lightskirts.

Hearing her small sigh of pleasure, for a moment of complete insanity, he considered going farther into the darkness, a mere few yards toward the brick wall. There, if she were willing, he could at least touch her skin.

Just the thought inflamed him, and he nibbled a hot trail down her neck, making her arch away and give him access to the curving upper swell of her breasts with a searing open-mouthed kiss.

“Dear God!”

Chapter Four

Aunt Cordelia's shocked voice was like a splash of frigid water. Lord Diamond released her so quickly, Caroline stumbled forward until he put his hands out to steady her.

At the same time, she opened her eyes as lamplight destroyed the sanctuary of their dimly lit embrace.

"You are in dreadful trouble," her aunt said. And then she added, "And so am I."

It was true. Caroline's mother would smite them both with her wrath. And who could tell what her father might do if he caught wind of it?

Next to Aunt Cordelia was their evening's hostess.

"Most unacceptable," said Lady Plain de Ville. "Shocking, in fact."

"Hardly shocking," Lord Diamond said. "It was merely a kiss."

Caroline wished he hadn't said anything. The lady's eyes widened.

"Not *merely* a kiss," pronounced their outraged hostess. "Your mouth was *not* upon her lips when we found you."

For a moment, Caroline didn't know what Lady Plain de Ville meant. Within seconds of Geoffrey touching her, she'd known nothing but excited, sizzling sensations. Her other more discerning faculties had all but shut down. And then she recalled his lips on the curve of her breast.

Looking at him, he appeared unrepentant, and she wished he wore an expression of chagrin at the very least.

Caroline decided to plead for them both. "I beg of you, my lady, not to think badly of us. We are two people who are not pledged to others. We were causing no one any harm, simply sharing a kiss, albeit perhaps a little something more than a chaste one," she added, glancing at Lord Diamond, "and therefore undoubtedly ill-advised."

Perhaps he didn't understand the dire circumstances. He made a sound of exasperation before addressing their hostess and her aunt.

"We are *not* children, and I, for one, find this snooping and spying to be beyond the pale."

Caroline wanted to clamp her hand over his mouth, but stood staring, aghast, as did her aunt and their hostess.

"We are trying to decide whether we have enough interest in one another to bother beginning a courtship," he continued. "Or at least that's what I was doing. What about you, Lady Caroline?"

Is that why they kissed? She already had quite an emphatic interest in the man, or she wouldn't have gone outside with him, but all she did was nod in agreement.

"Thus, you see, ladies, now that Lady Caroline and I have come to an understanding, we can face the rest of the obstacles of which we've been told there are at least four."

Caroline thought he summed it up well. Four parents, all determined to keep them apart.

"Aunt Cordelia, Lord Diamond and I merely wanted... that is, oh, please don't tell Mother and Father."

Her aunt fixed her with a stare that reminded her too much of her mother's, making Caroline shiver. But it was Lady Plain de Ville who brought it all to an end.

"I do not approve of my party, nor my garden, being used for such behavior. However, we shall say no more about it since we caught you before anything too egregious occurred."

"Then you will say nothing?" Aunt Cordelia asked.

"I don't want anyone to know of such reprehensible behavior, either. My home is *not* Vauxhall!" With that, the older lady turned heel and walked away, taking the oil lamp with her.

Lord Diamond gestured for her and Aunt Cordelia to go ahead of him, which they did.

"What now?" Caroline whispered to her aunt.

"I suppose I get to keep my head upon its shoulders," she jested. "As for you two, heaven help you if you decide to continue in this folly."

"I can hear you," Lord Diamond said, sounding annoyed. "Why is this folly?"

"While I am a sappy fool who allowed you to meet," her aunt snapped at him, "Lady Caroline's parents will not look kindly on any association. I had half-hoped my niece would find you lacking and speak no more of you. But mark me, Lord and Lady Chimes will not give their blessing and certainly not my niece's dowry to a Diamond."

Silence met those daunting words. By then, they were back inside and heading upstairs to the ballroom. Lady Plain de Ville had disappeared from view.

"Maybe Lord Diamond doesn't want an association," Caroline began.

"I believe I do," he muttered, and she almost laughed with relief for, more than anything, she wanted to get to know him better. When she stopped in her tracks at the top of the staircase, Lord Diamond ran into the back of her.

"Ooph," he said. "I nearly tumbled back down to my death."

"That might have been easier on you," her aunt quipped.

Caroline ignored them both. "I merely wanted to ask if we would be allowed to dance again tonight."

Aunt Cordelia sighed. "Yes, you two can have another dance, but I shall have my eyes upon you both, and if I'm lucky, a glass of rum punch in my hand."

Caroline wondered how she could win either of her parents over to her side. Dancing twice with Geoffrey Diamond had been heavenly, despite Lady Plain de Ville's disapproving stare for the rest of the evening.

Moreover, every other partner that night was inconsequential in comparison, and all she could do was hope this wouldn't be the last time she was in Lord Diamond's arms.

In the carriage, her aunt was not hopeful.

"While I believe our hostess will not mention seeing you two together, the fact that you were both at this ball will most likely reach your mother's ears. You could pretend you never even saw Diamond, I suppose, but that won't get you any closer to your goal. That is, if you truly wish to have that plummy young man court you in earnest."

"I believe I do," Caroline said, echoing Lord Diamond's earlier statement. She decided to tell her parents the following day. If she was honest with them, surely they would want her happiness as they always had before.

As circumstances happened, she didn't catch them together until dinner.

"Sit," her father said as soon as she entered the dining room.

"That was my intention." Caroline glanced at the two of them. Her mother's lips were set in a straight line, and her father was drumming upon the table as if he'd been kept waiting. Unmistakable tension shrouded the room.

Her usual place on one side, halfway between them, felt like a trap, and she fervently wished one or both of her brothers were at home to offer a diversion or at least bolster her spirits.

"I hope you are both well," she started, then hurried on. "I have something to tell you."

"If it is about Diamond, we already know," her father said.

Her gaze flew to his and then back to her mother.

"From Lady Plain de Ville?" Caroline asked. If that was the case, then they knew about the kiss. *That glorious, breathtaking, soul-shattering kiss!*

"The newspaper had a paragraph about the party," her father continued, "mostly because the Diamond heir was in attendance. Word has it he's looking for a wife."

"I see." Caroline quickly decided to change tactics and let them draw any information out of her.

"Did you dance with him?" her mother asked, her tone soft, which was more cause for alarm.

She had to tell her. After all, they'd been seen dancing, and it was nothing to be ashamed of.

"Yes," she said.

Her father's hand slammed upon the tablecloth, making her jump. Her mother flinched slightly as well. But the next harsh words came from her end of the table.

"I believe I told you not to. Do you have no recollection of my refusal to allow him to be introduced?"

"Yes," Caroline said again. "But—"

"But you thought you knew better," her father ground out.

"We merely danced."

"There is no 'merely' with a Diamond," Lord Chimes said. "They want and they take."

Her mother glanced at him, her eyes widening. Caroline wondered if his words hurt her. *Did her father wish the earl hadn't taken the woman who might have become his Lady Chimes?*

"That is nothing to do with me," Caroline insisted, using all the strength of her twenty years to stand up for herself. "I enjoyed dancing with Lord Diamond and intended to tell you tonight that we had done so. Also, I would like to see him again."

Her father nearly slammed the table again. Stopping himself by fisting his hand, he ran the other over his forehead and gestured for wine from the silent footman who watched the entire scene from his place by the wall.

"Handle your daughter," Lord Chimes said to Caroline's mother without looking at either one of them.

"*Handle me!*" Caroline exclaimed. This was so unlike her normally loving and generous parents; she could almost believe she had walked into the wrong dining room. True, her father was strict with his sons, and her mother had a strong personality, but neither had ever directed any dissatisfaction toward her.

"I ask you to recall I have two decades behind me. I have met a man who interests me enough that I wish to know him better. I am not doing anything outrageous, like trying to run away with a street-sweeper. He is an earl's only son, and I have heard nothing bad about him. Indeed, I had heard nothing about him at all before the Fenwicks' ball. Moreover, he will be an earl some day."

No point in saying he had alluring eyes, a wicked grin, and solid muscles she had felt for herself.

"There are other eligible men who are not street-sweepers, as you said so dramatically," her mother pointed out. "Last week, you didn't know of his existence. Next week, you can just as easily forget about him, too."

"I don't wish to forget about him, Mother. I want to—" she broke off, seeing her father start to seethe, his jaw clenching as he gritted his teeth.

"Sometimes, you don't get what you want," he said after a moment.

Again, seeing her mother's wounded expression, Caroline thought his choice of words was terribly poor. He might be speaking of the current Lady Diamond, for all she knew.

"And this is one of those times," her father continued. "You will *not* dance with him again. If you see him at a ball or a party, you will *not* speak to him, nor allow him to speak with you. Your mother will accompany you at all times to ensure that is the case."

"But I—"

"That is the end of it," Lord Chimes said. "Did I forget anything?" he asked his wife.

"No," Lady Chimes said softly. "I think you said it all."

Chapter Five

Geoffrey was determined to see Lady Caroline again. And not only to see her but to speak with her.

"It's not a case of wanting what I cannot have," he told his close friend, Jasper Trent, who thought himself clever with women. They sat at a table in White's dining room having finished a good meal. "I wanted her *before* I knew I couldn't have her."

"Then it's *Romeo and Juliet* all over again," Jasper said, sipping brandy. "You and the Chimes are the Capulets and the Montagues. Given that fact, we don't want to end with so much poisoning and death now, do we?"

Geoffrey rolled his eyes. "We shall not."

"What about her brothers?"

"What about them?"

"What if they come after you?" Jasper asked.

Geoffrey smiled wryly. "They'll have to stand in line behind their father and mother and my own father and mother first."

That tickled Jasper to no end, and he laughed at Geoffrey's expense. After a minute, however, he spoke again.

"Maybe you had best throw them off the scent."

"What do you mean?" Geoffrey asked, then drained his brandy, gesturing to the server for another.

"Escort some other young lady about Town. In fact, dance with everyone *except* Lady Caroline, don't even try to speak with her. Laugh and chat with the other females instead so your parents and hers suspect nothing of your heart."

"You dolt! That will make me look like a rake, especially to Lady Caroline. And how will that help me get closer to her?"

"I may be a dolt," Jasper said, "but I am a willing one who would carry your messages to her in your stead."

Geoffrey gaped at him. "You really do think I am Romeo come to life. That makes you Juliet's nurse, by the way, as she was the one who carried all the messages." He saw his friend smile again. "And you are liable to get me poisoned or stabbed after all."

Besides, Geoffrey didn't want to play games and pretend to care for other ladies. *Why bring more people into it?* He wanted to be frank. On the other hand, he could use Jasper's help in communicating with Lady Caroline if necessary.

As it turned out, at the next assembly in a grand house on St. James's Square, Lady Caroline was there with her indomitable mother. The woman's head appeared to be upon a swivel, and she didn't let her daughter out of her sight.

And thus, he needed Jasper after all.

"Dance with Lady Caroline," Geoffrey instructed from a position behind a column. "And please tell her I'll be waiting in the vestibule, next to the vase of flowers."

Jasper, who had made sure to gain an introduction to Caroline early during the evening, saluted rudely. "As you wish, sire."

After watching his friend take the coppery-haired Caroline as his partner, Geoffrey left the room just before the dancing ended. He waited for half an hour, but she never appeared. Eventually, forced to give up, he returned to the main hall and spotted her dancing with another gentleman, Lord Mangue.

Jasper intercepted him. "Your Juliet was willing, but there was no way for her to leave the room without her dear mother at her side."

"Then we shall have to find another way. Will you dance with her again later in the evening?"

Jasper grinned. "People will start to link *my* name with Lady

Caroline's."

"I shall risk it," Geoffrey said. "Find out if she goes anywhere without her mother. With another chaperone or, better yet, with her aunt. If there is such a place, find out the time and I shall go there, too."

It couldn't have worked out better. Geoffrey met Lady Caroline at Hatchards bookshop on Piccadilly with her maid two days later. Jasper told him Lady Chimes considered it to be, in Caroline's words, "a dull outing." And therefore, safe.

Upon entering the shop at number 187 between the bay windows, Geoffrey spied Lady Caroline at once by her hair. Although under a cream-colored bonnet with a yellow ribbon, enough of her glorious locks showed like a beacon. What's more, she had claimed a space in the middle of the ground floor, perhaps in order to see him easily. Dressed in a lemon-colored gown of fine cotton, with a matching short satin spencer, she was the epitome of femininity, and he would have noticed her even if she'd been in a dark corner.

Her face lit up with a smile. He nodded, seeing her maid beside her.

Now what?

Moving closer, he browsed the books on the round tables, not actually seeing anything, too aware of her nearness.

"Keep an eye on these books," he heard her say to her maid when he was a mere few yards away. "I am going to see if they have the latest Waverly novel."

"Yes, miss."

Geoffrey waited a few moments, moving toward the bookshelves that lined the walls, keeping his back to the maid. He picked out a thick volume, inspected it, and returned it before starting to hum quietly.

Sauntering along in the direction Lady Caroline had gone, he increased his pace as soon as he was out of the maid's view.

"Here," Lady Caroline said when he nearly passed her hiding place, squeezed between two bookcases.

Grasping her hand, he pulled her along behind him farther into the back of the shop.

"That was a good ruse," he commended, "gathering up so many books your maid would have to stay put."

"It wasn't a ruse," she said. "I really shall buy them or at least some of them, with my allowance, and the Waverly novel *St. Ronan's Well*, too, if I find it."

He was impressed.

"Besides," she said, "if I went home empty-handed, that would be suspicious indeed."

"You are a clever lady," he praised.

And they reached the last of the public area at the back of the shop.

"I suppose this will have to do. Perhaps next time, we can meet upstairs."

"Next time?" she murmured softly.

He sighed. "I know this is hardly ideal, but unless your aunt accompanies you to another ball—"

"She will not. My mother won't allow her to be my chaperone again."

"I see." Geoffrey couldn't imagine how they would begin any kind of meaningful association if they could only meet for a few minutes in a dusty bookstore.

"There is always Gretna Green," he said.

Lady Caroline visibly startled.

"Merely a jest," he assured her, although if he did fall in love and there was no other way, he was not entirely opposed to a Scottish border wedding.

They remained silent a moment. He didn't find it the least bit awkward, happy simply to be in her presence.

"My friend, Lord Trent, doesn't mind carrying messages between us," he said.

"That's kind of him. And he is a good dancer." Suddenly, she sighed. "This is ridiculous."

He flinched. *Was she ready to give up?*

"What can my parents do if you simply come claim me for a dance at the next ball?"

Relieved to learn not only wasn't she giving up, Lady Caroline was ready to stand up to her parents, he drew her into his arms. Instantly, a sizzling heat raced through him. His attraction to her was like nothing he'd ever experienced.

Without asking or waiting, he lowered his head and kissed her. At once, she melted against him. Having never swived with a woman he was in love with, he could easily imagine how good it would be with a beloved wife. One could take years to explore the other's needs and desires. That might be life's best adventure of all.

With her hands grasping his arms, he tilted his head and kissed her as thoroughly as he could against shelves of books that threatened to tumble down upon them. Their tongues danced briefly, and she sighed into his mouth, making his loins take distinct notice.

Wanting to plunge his hands into her hair and disturb the pins and her adorable yellow bonnet, instead Geoffrey took care not to leave her in the slightest disarray.

"My lady," came her maid's voice, and they broke apart.

Dammit all! he swore silently. "We hardly had a minute, it seems. Can you be at Vauxhall tomorrow night?"

Her eyes were a little glazed, and he was pleased to have caused her distracted expression.

"I believe so," she said. "I've been once before, and Mother said we could return. If the weather is fine, she will allow it."

"If you come, Lord Trent will find you between the Turkish Tent and where the orchestra plays. He shall tell you where I am."

"It's pointless," she began. "Wherever I go, my mother will, too."

"Don't you have a friend you can meet by chance and walk with? Maybe if Trent escorts you to the Rotunda, I can run into you."

"Maybe," she said, sounding forlorn but tugging on her spencer to make sure she was in good order.

"Tell me why you taste of orange and lavender," he asked.

"Lip balm," she said.

"You taste delicious."

That brought a smile back to her face. "What's your favorite color?" she asked in return.

"My lady?" came the maid again.

"Why?" he asked.

"I simply want to learn more about you. If I come away with a little nugget of information after each meeting, eventually, I'll know you."

"At this rate, I will need a cane before you get through my likes and dislikes."

"I must go," she said. "Tell me your answer."

Without hesitation, he said, "Your hair. That is my favorite color."

Her cheeks pinkened, and she turned to leave.

"And yours?" he asked quietly.

She glanced back at him. "Blue," she said, gesturing at her own gown. "Like your eyes."

And then she was gone.

Chapter Six

Vauxhall Pleasure Gardens were as Caroline remembered them—bustling, loud, and thrilling. And this time, she knew Geoffrey Diamond was awaiting her.

Unfortunately, her mother had taken to the idea so readily because both she and Caroline's father would enjoy the evening. Also, Lord Mangue would be there. Lady Chimes had fixed herself upon the idea that if only Caroline spent more time with the viscount, then she would find herself developing a *tendre* in no time at all.

Caroline ignored the knowledge that he would be thrown in her path that night. At the very least, if she gave Lord Mangue a modicum of attention, it would keep her mother from watching her too closely. Moreover, her best friend, Daphne, had responded to an eager request for her presence, agreeing to come since her husband was away overseeing their country estate. Daphne, whom Caroline had known in Bath, had fallen wildly in love, married young, and she and Lord Hollidge already had a dear little boy. Caroline could only hope for similar happiness.

Thus, she and her parents along with Daphne, whom they had collected at her home, stepped off the ferry boat that carried them swiftly from Westminster to the south bank of the Thames. After climbing the Vauxhall steps, as they'd been dubbed a century earlier, the four of them entered through the proprietor's house. Out the back door, they spilled into the wondrous acreage known as the Vauxhall Pleasure Gardens.

Immediately, the excitement of the spectacle took hold of Caroline. It was impossible not to feel a thrill when taking in the long walks, dining pavilions, groves and grottoes, colonnades and music, and twenty thousand oil lamps hanging from every branch and structure. Add to that the myriad entertainment and crowds of revelers, and it was impossible for one's heart not to pound a little more quickly.

After they were assigned one of the supper boxes on the left side of the garden by the Chinese Temples, she and Daphne were ready either to stroll toward the orchestra or to tour the grounds with her parents.

As if it hadn't been planned by Lady Chimes, Lord Mangue arrived, expressing delight upon seeing them.

"Well met," he said all around.

Thwarting his hope to monopolize her company, however, Lord Trent also appeared. Thus, after a few minutes of prattle with her parents, the four single people went to the area where couples danced by the so-called Gothic Orchestra, a two-story structure housing the musicians on the open-air second floor.

Lord Mangue took her in his arms without asking.

As soon as the dance ended, Lord Trent smoothly suggested he and Mangue switch partners.

"You did that expertly," Caroline told him.

"My dance steps?" Lord Trent asked innocently.

"You know what I mean," she said. Then feeling like an English spy in Paris or a Bow Street detective, she asked, "Where is Lord Diamond?"

"Down the Grand South Walk near the third Triumphal Arch," Lord Trent responded. "You know, he is a good chap. It's a pity about your parents and his."

"A pity, indeed," she agreed.

A few minutes later, when the dance ended and the orchestra took a break, Lord Trent returned her to her parents' table. Daphne and Lord Mangue arrived a moment later.

"May I escort these two lovely ladies down the Grand South Walk?" Lord Trent asked. "We'll go down one side and back up the other. As a married lady and mother, Lady Hollidge must be considered a suitable chaperone."

"As long as you don't go as far as the Firework Tower," Lord Chimes warned. "I don't want these girls anywhere near the Dark Walk."

"We shall turn on the path by the third arch," Lord Trent promised.

Caroline thought Geoffrey's plan was going exceedingly well, but Lord Mangue was not to be left out.

"Capital idea," he said, earning Caroline's mother's nod of approval. "Lord Trent and I shall keep them safe and enjoy the gardens at the same time."

Caroline's heart sank. *How would she get away from him?*

The four of them departed the Grove to promenade down the Grand South Walk toward the less busy sections of the Pleasure Gardens.

Simply knowing Lord Diamond was nearby had Caroline tingling with excitement. As they approached the third Triumphal Arch where Lord Trent had indicated Geoffrey would be, the hair on the back of her neck rose, imagining him watching from the darkness. They turned as promised to cross the width of the gardens.

A moment later, Lord Diamond sauntered toward them, hailing his friend Lord Trent and also greeting Lord Mangue.

"Do you know Lady Caroline and Lady Hollidge?" Lord Trent asked his friend, sounding sincere.

"I have had the pleasure of making Lady Caroline's acquaintance," Lord Diamond acknowledged, taking her hand and bowing over it, giving her knuckles a gentle squeeze before he released her.

"And while I have met Lord Hollidge at my club, I have not yet been introduced to his lovely wife. Good evening, Lady Hollidge." He turned his full attention upon Daphne, taking her hand and bowing over it.

Caroline almost wished Daphne were single at that moment, for then Lord Diamond could feign interest in her. If he were linked with Daphne in the public's perception, then they could be near one another more easily.

"Even though it is an odd number, my lord, if you are alone, why don't you join our happy group," Caroline offered.

"How gracious of you," Lord Diamond said.

Soon the five of them were watching the rope-dancing theatre. If only

Lord Mangue wasn't there, Caroline could speak freely in front of their respective friends. Yet despite wracking her brain, she could think of no way to put the man off.

"Are you here escorting your sister?" Lord Diamond suddenly asked Lord Mangue.

"No, why do you ask?"

Lord Diamond made a great show of appearing mortified. "I should have said nothing. I apologize."

Alarmed, Lord Mangue insisted he answer. "Tell me, Diamond."

"I would swear I saw her earlier when I arrived. She has brown hair and a single mole on her cheek, does she not?"

"She does, but my family made no mention of her coming here tonight, nor can I imagine whom she was with."

Lord Diamond gave a grimacing smile. "No matter, then. She wasn't actually with anyone. Walking along on this very path when I last saw her, and she was quite alone, so that's fine."

"Are you mad?" Lord Mangue exclaimed. "That's not fine at all. Tell me precisely where she was going."

Lord Diamond widened his eyes as if only just realizing something.

"Come to think of it, Mangue, I believe she was heading toward," he paused, looking toward the far wall at the back of Vauxhall's acreage before he whispered, "the Dark Walk."

Lord Mangue reared back as if facing a tiger.

"You probably should make sure she is well," Lord Trent advised. "Although odds are she was meeting a friend and isn't alone any longer."

"What are you saying?" Lord Mangue demanded.

"I only mean the way Lady Caroline might meet up with Lady Hollidge. What did you think I meant?"

"I cannot abandon Lady Caroline," Lord Mangue fretted. "I told her parents I would escort her."

"Please, my lord. You should go find her at once," Caroline said. "I have these two gentlemen and my good friend with me. I would never forgive myself if anything happened to your sister with no one at all to protect her."

"Yes, you're correct. I bid you good evening." He didn't even wait to say goodbye to the rest of them before hurrying away.

"Poor girl, I hope she is unharmed," Daphne said.

Caroline nodded, but when she caught Lord Diamond's eye, she nearly began to laugh.

Lord Trent shook his head. "Remarkable that you could see a girl's mole in this dusky light."

"Amazing, isn't it?" Lord Diamond said. "I do hope it was the correct lady."

Just then, the bell announced the start of the mysterious Cascade. And they moved toward it as did many other of the gardens' visitors. Somehow, Caroline found Lord Diamond directly beside her.

"Are you interested in this?" he asked.

"It is amusing, don't you think?" When she'd seen the mock waterfall and fake mechanized carriage crossing the bridge the first time, she had never seen anything like it before or since.

"I find *you* far more amusing and interesting," Lord Diamond said. "Shall we take a stroll?"

Caroline tensed. This was not the safety of Lady Plain de Ville's tiny plot of garden. This was Vauxhall where reputations were ruined on a nightly basis.

"Just to talk," he added.

Caroline hesitated. She barely knew him, but what she did know, she liked. And again, this might be one of the few, precious moments they could spend in one another's company.

She nodded.

"Lady Caroline and I are going to take a walk. We shall return here shortly."

"This show lasts about a quarter of an hour," Lord Trent reminded them.

Lord Diamond nodded. "I shall have her back here and in time for you to escort her to her parents."

"Understood," Lord Trent said.

Daphne was watching with her mouth in the shape of an *O*, and Caroline knew she would have to explain it all to her later.

When Geoffrey got Lady Caroline alone in Vauxhall, he surprised himself. The first thing he wanted to do was talk with her, not kiss her, despite wanting very much to do that as well.

"I want to know everything about you," he confessed, drawing her arm through his and continuing to move along the path, so they didn't appear scandalous. "Do you enjoy riding?"

"Very much."

"And boating?" he prompted.

"Do you mean rowing or sailing?" she asked.

"Either. Both, I suppose."

"I have sailed across the Channel to France, but I would very much enjoy an outing in a rowboat."

"I would enjoy rowing you wherever you wish. As long as it's upon water."

She laughed, a beautiful warm sound.

"What is your favorite season?" he continued.

"Spring. It brings such promise for the year, as well as flowers."

"A good answer," he said.

"And you, my lord?"

"I believe I like summer best when that spring promise has been fulfilled with sunshine and warmer weather," he said. "Is there a food you most favor?"

"I like this game," she said. "No gentleman has ever asked my opinion on even the most mundane things."

"I honestly don't think I've ever asked another female about her likes, so I cannot speak too ill of my fellow sex in that regard. Only when a man is truly taken with a woman does he care to know more."

He felt her shiver. "Are you cold?"

"No, not in the least. In answer to your previous question, I enjoy roasted chicken, and I adore sponge cake with thick, warm custard. And now, it is my turn to ask," she said. "What is your favorite taste?"

His loins tightened at once, and the answer came easily. "You, my lady."

Her gasp was nearly silent. Then she laughed. "Be serious."

"I am. When I kissed you the first time, I thought you tasted better than anything else in the world."

Lady Caroline said nothing for a moment, then spoke. "It was simply the orange blossom and lavender beeswax balm."

"Maybe at first, but only when mixed with the essence of you. I kissed your skin, too, you may recall. I thought all of you to be exquisite."

She shook her head and touched her gloved palm to her face, dropping it quickly in case she was seen.

"You speak like a lover," she said.

"Or like a man falling in love."

Chapter Seven

Geoffrey said the words spontaneously, not to intrigue or ensnare her. Yet as soon as they were out of his mouth, he considered their absolute truth. He would not confess to already loving her, yet his heart might say differently.

Lady Caroline stopped and turned to face him, even as others walked around them along the path.

"I know precisely what you mean. Strange as it may sound, I feel attracted to you beyond reason, beyond the shallow knowledge I have of you, and certainly beyond the little amount of time we have shared."

Hearing her confession, he nearly drew her close, then recalled where they were.

"I would like to kiss you again," he said frankly, "but I think it would be better to act honorably if we have any chance of winning over your parents."

"What about yours?" she asked.

He shrugged. "My parents do not control whom I marry, nor do I live with them. Thus, it is yours we must succeed in placating."

She sighed. "I believe you are correct. Shall we return to our friends?"

Thus, after being alone with a woman at Vauxhall, he returned her to Trent and Lady Hollidge without having kissed her. *It was almost unnatural!*

Ignoring Jasper's knowing look—*the devil take him!*—Geoffrey had to leave Lady Caroline in his safe hands and watch the three walk away. It was irksome and as she'd once said, it was plainly ridiculous. They were being penalized for something that had occurred before either of them were born.

It was time to speak with his father.

A short while later, Geoffrey entered his parents' house, hoping they were at home. For all he knew, he'd just left them behind in Vauxhall. His luck held. Not only were they there, they were together, both of them in the upstairs salon, wearing slippers and dressing gowns, sipping brandy and reading.

Lord and Lady Diamond were the picture of domesticity, which tickled him considering his parents' reputations as being a little wild when they were younger.

After kissing his mother's cheek and accepting his father's offer of French brandy, Geoffrey suddenly wasn't sure if he ought to speak privately with the earl. If there was something unsavory in his father's past of which his mother was unaware, he would become as tight-lipped as a clam.

Deciding to risk it, Geoffrey flopped down in a chair and poured from the decanter on the table beside him.

"I saw Lady Caroline Chimes tonight at Vauxhall."

Both his parents lowered their books.

"That was unwise," remarked his father, James Diamond, "but probably a delightful experience, nonetheless."

His mother, on the other hand, narrowed her eyes. "Not if she was with her parents. In which case, I'm sure you had a ghastly time of it."

"I didn't meet with Lord and Lady Chimes. In case you've forgotten, I am not allowed," Geoffrey said, hoping all his frustration was in his voice. "Because of the two of you."

His father started to laugh until his mother jabbed him in the ribs with her elbow.

"Why must you be so intent upon this particular girl?" she asked. "There are marriageable young ladies all over London."

"What do you mean *intent* on her?" his father asked. "What have I missed?"

"Geoffrey spotted Lady Caroline at the Fenwicks' ball. Lady Chimes gave him a public dressing down and refused an introduction."

His father looked unimpressed. "And now you're going out of your way to try to meet your elusive, impossible quarry, is that it? Is she a copper-haired beauty like her mother or a sandy-brown toad like her father?"

Geoffrey gripped his glass tighter, irritated by the earl for making light of the situation.

"I have succeeded in gaining an introduction to Lady Caroline," he said, "at Lady Plain de Ville's home. And I have come to admire her greatly, but Lord and Lady Chimes have forbidden us to keep company, not even to dance."

"You have come to admire her," her mother echoed. "I take it you've had more than a single introduction."

That was not their business. Geoffrey shrugged, making his father laugh again.

"What do you want us to do? Grant our blessing?" Lord Diamond gestured to Geoffrey to hand him the decanter so he could refill his glass.

"As if we would do that," his mother said. "Blessing, indeed!"

"Why?" Geoffrey snapped.

"That mushroom," she began, but he interrupted her.

"Why do you call Lady Chimes such a thing?"

"Because she sprung up out of nowhere and landed in the titled class with nothing more than a baronet for a father and no dowry to speak of, or so I've heard."

The earl crossed his arms and said nothing.

"Come along, Father. Surely you have an opinion."

"On Lady Chimes? No, not really. I don't know her. I saw her years ago. She's beautiful though, with that fiery hair I mentioned."

"When?" Lady Diamond demanded. "When did you see her?"

Geoffrey's father sighed. "It was probably at that ball when you and I arrived together as a couple for the first time. I thought Chimes was going to fall upon his sword. Instead, suddenly, he was dancing with her, looking pleased as Mr. Punch."

"You noticed her?" Lady Diamond asked.

"Only because of her hair, my love. Obviously, she can't hold a candle to you. If she could, then I would be with her instead."

He laughed hard at that, but by her scowl, Geoffrey's mother didn't think her husband the least bit amusing.

"I'm only teasing," the earl reminded his wife, draping his arm along the back of the sofa and around her slender shoulders. "Remember, once I saw you, I had to have you, despite how you were ill-advisedly keeping company with Chimes."

"Hardly that," she grumbled. "He and I had barely enjoyed a few dances."

"That's not how I recall it," Lord Diamond said, his tone growing serious for the first time. "I believe there was riding and a dinner party or two, as well."

"Excuse me, dear parents, but while this stroll through your memories is as fascinating as waiting for bread to rise—"

"When have you ever done that?" his mother demanded.

"Never," Geoffrey quipped. "Because it would be boring and tedious and not worth my time, precisely like this entire discussion. All I want to know is whether either of you or both of you perpetrated some wrong upon the Chimes and if I can do anything to fix it."

His parents looked at one another and then back at him.

"We have always acted with the utmost decorum," his mother said, "except for what I told you before."

"What did you tell him?" Lord Diamond asked.

"Just that you stole me from Lord Chimes and also beat him in a wager at your club."

His father nearly spat out his brandy, which expensive as it was would have been a damn shame.

"How did you know about that?"

His mother smiled with satisfaction. "We wives have our ways of knowing what goes on at those gentlemen's clubs."

The next thing Geoffrey knew, his feisty parents were arguing loudly about "interfering, nosy-poke harpies" and "depraved, pompous bucks."

Sighing, Geoffrey downed his brandy and rose to his feet. They didn't even notice. In any case, he doubted they would ever be the least bit helpful.

After Vauxhall, Caroline endured a series of frustrating experiences. Inside the new National Gallery, at number 100 Pall Mall, she was with her mother when she spied Geoffrey, as Caroline now dared to think of him. He saw her nearly at the same moment. They both pretended to look at the works by Raphael and Hogarth while surreptitiously sneaking glances at one another.

Finally, Caroline's mother caught sight of him, and they left without her getting to exchange more than a smile with him.

Then there was the night at the theatre when she and her parents had been in the same audience as the King and Queen of the Sandwich Islands. Despite the impressive six-foot king and his exotic queen, she'd noticed Geoffrey in his family's private box and soon had his attention. When the theater was darkened and the performance began, she still stared in his direction. And when the lamps were lit once more, they practically had a conversation across the expanse of the theatre with smiles and nods. She even risked the smallest of waves.

Finally, they were both at the same ball, and she prepared herself for another exasperating experience. Recalling what she'd said to Geoffrey, she wondered what her parents would do if he boldly came over and led her to the dance floor.

She sighed. It would be a disaster, and she couldn't pretend otherwise. Caroline's mother was not above grabbing her daughter by the ear and forcibly removing her. It would be humiliating. And despite being twenty, she imagined her father could and would confine her to their home for the rest of the Season.

Daphne, who was also at the ball, knew her sorrowful situation but had no suggestions. When Lord Hollidge was around her, as he was that night, her best friend was so madly in love, she only half-listened. Moreover, Daphne kept her eyes upon her husband, who gazed at her in return with equal ardor.

Geoffrey stayed on the opposite side of the room until Caroline accepted a partner. Each time she did, he would quickly ask a lady to dance and thus be nearby.

Shaking her head at him, she wished he would give up. While she wasn't jealous of each and every pretty miss whom he took for a partner, she was dreadfully envious.

And then Daphne, bless her heart, with her cheeks in full bloom from having danced with her husband, announced a dinner party at her home. By the sparkle in her friend's eyes, Caroline guessed Geoffrey would be invited, too.

"I shall send out the invitations over the next couple of days," Daphne told Lady Chimes just before the ball ended. "Naturally, we will have musicians and perhaps some other entertainment."

"We shall be pleased to come," Caroline's mother agreed.

"Oh, I am sorry, my lady. My husband and I are hosting this dinner only for unmarried people. No chaperones are needed nor allowed as there will not be even one unsupervised minute."

"It's a modern notion," Lady Chimes said, "but I understand the fun of young people gathering together without their parents. I wonder if I can request any particular bachelors. My daughter is becoming fond of Lord Mangue. Isn't that right?"

"Which one is he, Mother?" Caroline asked, hoping to dissuade her from pushing him toward her despite having danced with him again that night.

"Stop teasing! You know very well he's that sturdy, solid viscount."

With the single eyebrow, Caroline added silently. In truth, she was getting used to it, like a friendly caterpillar crawling across his forehead.

"I'm sure Lady Hollidge has a guest list in mind, Mother. We cannot start inserting our own guests into her party."

"I shall certainly add Lord Mangue to my guest list," Daphne promised, doing a better job of appeasing Caroline's mother than she could do herself.

"What a generous hostess and a respectful young lady," Lady Chimes said, piercing Caroline with a look that said she wished she were more like her friend.

Caroline didn't care. She'd been given permission to go to a dinner party, and she would be there *without* her mother. If Lord Diamond agreed to go, she would be satisfied Fortuna had turned her wheel.

Chapter Eight

Lord and Lady Hollidge's home on Grosvenor Square, shared by Daphne, her beloved Thomas, and their young son Alexander was not far from Caroline's parents' own townhouse on Upper Brook Street, practically around the corner. Regardless, her mother had their carriage brought around from the mews, and she rode with Caroline to deposit her upon Daphne's doorstep.

"Good night, Mother. I shall see you anon." For Daphne would make sure she got home in her own carriage in the wee hours after the party.

In seven minutes, she waited excitedly in the drawing room with a glass of wine in hand, waiting for Geoffrey Diamond. Not that her friend would willfully go against the wishes of Lady Chimes. However, since Daphne could claim ignorance of any ill feelings between the Chimes and the Diamonds, she had simply included him with the other eligible men.

"But why did you actually invite Lord Mangue?" Caroline asked, when she saw him enter.

"When your mother finds out Lord Diamond is here, she won't think I did it on purpose if her favorite is also attending," Daphne explained.

Caroline supposed her friend was correct, but with Lord Mangue peering at her from under his brow, she wondered how she would be able to speak freely with Geoffrey.

"The place cards on the table will undoubtedly please you," Daphne told her with a wink before she went to greet other guests.

Before Lord Mangue could move into the vacated space, Geoffrey appeared in the doorway. Caroline waved him over, unable to contain her enthusiasm.

"Good evening, Lady Caroline. You are looking especially breathtaking tonight."

She liked the term he used, having dressed in her favorite shade of green, hoping to please him.

"You are no more handsome than usual," she returned. Lowering her voice, she added, "And yet you are still the most attractive man here."

It hardly seemed possible that every other gentleman in the room paled in comparison, but they did. She especially adored the rich raven-color of his hair and how his blue eyes contrasted with his dark lashes.

Suddenly, Lord Mangue was at her elbow. "Good evening, Lady Caroline."

"Good evening, my lord. I didn't know you were acquainted with the Hollidges."

She wished Daphne hadn't thought it necessary to be cautious in this instance and to please Caroline's mother.

"I am not, except for meeting Lady Hollidge at Vauxhall. Apparently, one of the young ladies here tonight asked for me particularly to be invited. I wonder whom it could be," Lord Mangue mused with a cock of his head.

Her stomach twinged. She hoped Geoffrey didn't think she'd had anything to do with it. All she could do was nod politely.

Then Lord Mangue turned to Geoffrey, and his greeting was less pleasant. "It seems you keep cropping up wherever Lady Caroline and I happen to be."

"I don't think that's the case," Geoffrey answered lightly. "Merely a happy circumstance."

"*Happy*?" Lord Mangue frowned, causing his single eyebrow to crease in the center. "Hardly. And do you know what, Diamond?"

"No," Geoffrey said, not asking the question Lord Mangue wished him to.

"Well, I'll tell you. My sister was most definitely *not* at Vauxhall. I meant to let you know when I saw you again, but you were always on the other side of the room at the last ball."

Geoffrey shrugged. "Better to be safe than sorry, as they say."

"Lord Diamond is correct," Caroline spoke up. "Imagine if it had been your sister, and you hadn't gone to her aid. You would never have forgiven yourself. You probably should thank Lord Diamond."

"But it wasn't Lettie! That's the point," Lord Mangue fumed. "I missed out on the rest of the evening with you."

"I kept her company," Geoffrey added wickedly, causing Lord Mangue to narrow his eyes in his direction.

Caroline wished Geoffrey wouldn't tease, nor bring attention to any time they'd spent in one another's company, especially not to Lord Mangue.

"Are you sure you even saw anyone who looked like my sister?" he demanded.

"Oh, very sure, Mangue. Mole and all."

"Lord Mangue, will you come greet the other guests?" This from Daphne, who like an angel was trying to draw him away.

"You must meet everyone," Caroline insisted when he hesitated. "You wouldn't want to insult our hosts, nor miss out on meeting whichever young lady requested your presence."

He glanced at her and a smug smile appeared. "I see. Trying to throw me off the track like a red-headed vixen. I shall make the rounds and return."

"Don't hurry," Geoffrey muttered when Lord Mangue finally walked away.

It was a brief respite from the tension between the two gentlemen. By the evening's end, though, Caroline felt as though they were engaged in a tug of war with her as the rope. She sat beside Geoffrey for dinner, which had been extremely pleasant, allowing them to discuss each course with a measure of mirth, as well as learn more of their food likes and dislikes.

However, she ended up next to Lord Mangue for the concert, with no way to change seats without causing a huge disruption.

Finally, while they were having glasses of madeira during a beautiful dramatic recitation by Daphne, whose husband accompanied her softly on his violin, Geoffrey moved toward the drawing-room door.

He didn't even have to look at her for Caroline to know he wished her to follow.

After waiting an interminable two minutes which she counted in her head, she leaned toward Lord Mangue.

"I shall be back shortly."

"I'll accompany you," he offered, starting to rise.

"No," she snapped. Then more graciously, "I am only going to the water closet."

His cheeks turned red at the mere mention of such a private task, and she hurried away. The hallway seemed deserted, and Caroline had no idea which way to go.

"*Psst,*" came a sound from farther along the dimly lit hall, and she followed it.

Near the cellar door where the kitchen was housed, there was a butler's pantry for serving the drawing room and other rooms on the main floor. Its door was ajar. As she approached, Geoffrey reached out and drew her swiftly inside.

Without preamble, his arms went around her. When he molded her body to his, heat sizzled through her.

"That was torture," he ground out before kissing her.

As he slid his tongue between her lips, she slipped her hands up and around the back of his neck, flattening her breasts against him.

In response to her acquiescence, his hand roamed down her back to cup her rounded backside, tilting her hips against his. A wicked, desperate yearning unfolded deep inside her.

"Geoffrey," she said his given name against his mouth, simply because she could.

"Yes, Caroline," he replied, and she shivered at the intimacy.

Tilting her head and going up on tiptoe, she wanted to get as close to him as she could, until she could feel his arousal pressed against her.

"I want more," she confessed.

"As do I."

She knew a little of what that meant but didn't see how anything meaningful could be accomplished in a pantry. Its cold-water sink, cupboards filled with all manner of tableware, and narrow shelves with glasses and teacups did not exactly inspire passion, despite decanters of ruby-red claret standing ready.

To her amazement, Geoffrey lifted her by the waist, turned quickly, and set her upon the marble countertop over a bank of glass-front cupboards. With her dress drawn tightly, he was unable to stand between her legs. Thus, he drew her skirts up both legs until her gown and petticoat rested atop her knees, which he gently pushed apart.

As soon as he settled between her thighs, he began to kiss her again.

Caroline had accepted all his outrageous actions with wide eyes until his mouth covered hers once more. The thrill of feeling air upon her silk stockings made her giddy, even light-headed. Sinking her hands into his hair, she opened her mouth and let their kiss deepen.

His tongue explored her mouth most thoroughly, and when she tried to do the same, he sucked upon hers, causing her toes to curl with longing.

"I'm tingling everywhere," she said quietly after he drew back, and they both were dragging in long, ragged breaths.

"As am I," he confessed, sounding hoarse. "You have bewitched me."

She giggled, too loudly, and he clamped a swift hand over her mouth. *"Shh."*

She nodded. She would try to rein in her happiness, but when he took his hand away, shocking words came out.

"Touch me," she asked brazenly, because she knew enough from the books she had been forbidden to read and had read anyway that if a man touched her between her legs, it would be like nothing she'd ever experienced. And that was precisely where she was throbbing.

The fingers of his right hand trailed along the path her skirts had taken, up and over her knees, across the warm flesh of her inner thigh, making her tremble.

Holding her breath until the moment he brushed against her damp and silky core, she gasped and closed her eyes.

Immediately, his lips nuzzled the exposed column of her neck while wantonly, she tilted her hips, straining to deepen his too-delicate touch.

Knowing what she wanted, Geoffrey slid a finger between her plump folds, stroking with greater vigor directly where she pulsed.

It took almost no time at all until Caroline was clinging to his shoulders while her body throbbed and tightened. And then, for a few moments, she forgot everything—that she was an earl's daughter. That she was in a butler's pantry. That she was a lady who didn't allow a man to take liberties.

Moaning loudly, she quivered, arching and tightening until a flooding release left her entirely spent.

When his hand stopped touching her, she opened her eyes and looked directly into his vivid blue gaze.

"Dear God!" she exclaimed too loudly.

"I think that came from in there," said a voice sounding unbelievably like her mother's.

Terror shot through Caroline, replacing all the ecstasy she'd experienced mere moments before. Shoving desperately at Geoffrey, who hurriedly stepped back, she frantically pushed at her skirts.

When the door opened, she was still sliding down the face of the cabinets, but at least she didn't appear to have recently had a man nestled between her legs. Regardless, her mother watched the moment her daughter's feet touched the floor, and then Lord Mangue's face appeared. There might be others in the hallway for all Caroline knew, but the room was too small to hold them.

"What is the meaning of this?" Lady Chimes demanded.

"We were just talking," Caroline said. Her voice sounded high and strained to her own ears.

"I am to blame," Geoffrey said. "Lady Caroline was walking by, and I invited her in here to chat."

"You are a dog!" Lord Mangue said.

"Is there a dog in my house?" Daphne asked from the hallway, trying to make light of it.

"Be careful what happens here," Geoffrey warned, speaking only to Lady Chimes. "Your daughter's reputation and future are at stake."

"You should have thought of that," Caroline's mother said, anger lacing every word.

"Your cheeks are frightfully flushed," Lord Mangue pointed out.

"Yes, I was feeling unwell, looking for the water closet, as I told you."

"This is *not* a water closet," her mother pointed out.

"Is everything all right?" Daphne asked, and if not for Lord Mangue, leaning against the door, she would have opened it.

"We are fine," Lady Chimes said. "My daughter didn't feel well and wandered in here by mistake. Will you clear the hallway please, Lady Hollidge, to give her some privacy? I shall take her home at once."

"I will still marry you," Lord Mangue declared.

"Marry?" repeated Caroline and Geoffrey at the same time.

"Yes, as arranged. I know this rascal was kissing you, but that is forgivable. I have kissed a few ladies. It meant nothing."

Geoffrey turned to her. "Did you know about this? That you were promised to him?"

Caroline nodded. "I knew that—"

"I don't want you speaking to my daughter. I don't want you even to look at her." Lady Chimes spoke with a tone of icy determination. "I know you did this deliberately, exactly as your father did with your mother. Is that the only way a Diamond man can get a woman to marry him? By compromising her?"

Geoffrey went tight-lipped, clenching his jaw until Caroline thought he might grind his teeth to powder.

"She's not compromised," Lord Mangue insisted.

However, Caroline kept her gaze upon Geoffrey. "Did your father risk your mother's reputation?" *If Lord Diamond had, wouldn't Geoffrey have known better than to do the same?*

"Risk it?" her mother exclaimed. "He shredded it. And yet for that, I have the Earl of Diamond to thank." She turned to Geoffrey. "Otherwise, my dear Chimes might have been saddled with your debauched mother as a wife."

"If you were a man," Geoffrey said, "I would call you out for those words."

Caroline stepped between them. "If my mother speaks the truth, then there is nothing over which you could call her out."

She ignored Geoffrey's livid expression and turned to her mother.

"As I said, I don't feel well. I'm glad you came back to fetch me. Take me home, please."

"Move aside," Lady Chimes said to Lord Mangue, who was still hovering.

"Yes, my lady. Of course. I shall call upon you tomorrow." Opening the door, he stepped into the hallway. "There is no one visible."

Without another word, her mother walked out, knowing Caroline would follow. Her mantle was on the bench by the front door, thoughtfully put out by Daphne.

Lord Mangue accompanied them to their awaiting carriage and even assisted them inside.

"Thank you," her mother said frostily.

And then neither of them spoke another word for the brief journey home, except when Caroline asked, "What made you return?"

Lady Chimes shrugged. "Mother's intuition." Then she sighed and lapsed into silence again.

Caroline had behaved abominably, as had Geoffrey Diamond. She hadn't even looked back to see what became of him.

When they reached their own front hall, Lady Chimes dumped her cloak and hat on the hall stand and mounted the stairs. Following her, Caroline watched her mother's rigid, regal rear heading along the hallway.

Outside her own bedroom door, Caroline knew she ought to at least offer thanks.

"Mother, I—"

"Not another word," Lady Chimes said, then stopped without turning. "Not tonight. We shall talk in the morning. But you should count your blessings before you lay your head upon the pillow. You still have your reputation and a fiancé. You could have been left with absolutely nothing."

And then her mother continued toward her own room, entered, and slammed the door.

Caroline had faced the evening with such anticipation and delight. Now, she dreaded what the morning would bring.

Chapter Nine

Geoffrey stormed through his house, wanting to throw something, anything. Mostly he wanted to plant a facer directly into Mangue's sappy, concerned visage. *And why didn't the man's valet trim his ridiculous single eyebrow?* Surely someone ought to tell him he looked like a monkey.

And yet Caroline had an understanding with him!

That fact, Geoffrey could simply not fathom. Her words, "Yes, I knew," continuously crashed down upon him like a wall of crumbling bricks.

How could she possibly have said yes to Mangue? At the same time, she continued to keep furtive company with him, enjoying every clandestine meeting.

For two people meant to stay apart, they'd managed to kiss many times. *And more!*

Shaking his head, he stalked through his silent townhouse, unable to sit. He'd only pleasured her in the butler's pantry because he believed they were going to figure out a way to be together. Never would he have let himself get carried away if he had truly thought she was already spoken for.

Regardless of his father's outrageous past, Geoffrey didn't go around ruining ladies! Not even ones who all but begged to be ruined.

Why would she do such a thing if she was promised to Mangue?

Unless she was being forced.

He stopped. *Of course!* She didn't want Mangue. The man was titled and had a good fortune, but that was all that recommended him. Geoffrey had jumped to conclusions, and now it would be even harder to get close to Caroline to speak to her.

Hastening to his study, he picked up a piece of cream-colored paper. Then he dropped it. He couldn't risk putting anything in writing. Without regard for the time, he donned his jacket and left for Trent's house. If he didn't find him at home, he would track him to their club.

A half hour later, he was satisfied Jasper would get a message to Caroline.

"Simply tell her to return to Hatchards tomorrow at the same time as previously."

"Ridiculous," Jasper said. "I cannot even promise to see her tomorrow. And if I do, I highly doubt she can drop everything and go to a bookseller. You had best make it the following day."

"Very well." Frustration welled in him.

"But don't expect too much," Jasper added. "After all, I may be refused entrance."

"Why would you be?" Geoffrey realized he was running his hands through his hair like a madman.

"If your lady-friend is in disgrace and has been forced to accept an offer," Jasper said, "then maybe she won't be allowed to see any other man, including me."

In disgrace! Geoffrey felt his heart sink. If she was, it was because of him. He should have been more careful. *What a clodpate!*

"Do your best," he said. "Whatever it takes to get a message to her, I suppose, even if you have to write a missive. I cannot imagine a note from you would be suspect."

"You are in love with her," Jasper concluded.

Geoffrey nearly naysaid him on the spot. Then it dawned on him what the pain in his chest was and why his heart felt like a solid lump of brass. He wouldn't deny he loved her.

"I believe it crucial to my future happiness that I halt any marital plans being made for Lady Caroline with that dratted Mangue."

"Agreed," Jasper said. "Life is hard. For some it's short. We shouldn't squander something as precious as love."

He spoke like a man in earnest. Geoffrey stared at him.

"Are you in love?"

Jasper shrugged. "I may have my sights set on a lucky lady." Then he grinned. "But let us deal with you first, shall we?"

Caroline didn't think she could feel any more miserable, but then she heard Lord Trent's voice downstairs. Geoffrey was plainly trying to reach her despite thinking her complicit in some scheme of treachery, which she couldn't imagine.

Hardly sleeping the night before, she was torn between the wondrous sensations Geoffrey's intimate touch had elicited and the black melancholy from seeing how he looked at her after Lord Mangue arrived.

Plainly, Geoffrey thought himself betrayed, but she hoped he had come to a more sensible conclusion.

Their butler informed Lord Trent she was not accepting visitors. Caroline assumed her mother had given those instructions. She would not create an unpleasant commotion by rushing down the stairs and trying to see him against Lady Chimes's wishes.

However, as soon as he departed, Caroline descended, hoping Geoffrey's friend had at least left a note.

Her mother was in the drawing room, reading from a single sheet of paper.

At her entrance, Lady Chimes looked up, her green gaze hard as emeralds.

"I don't know what you're playing at, but I will not let you throw yourself away on Diamond."

"Throw myself away?" Caroline sputtered. "He's not a pauper or a reprobate."

Her mother pursed her lips and looked back down. "You shall not be going to Hatchards bookshop again, not until you are a happily married woman."

"Happily?" Caroline shot back. "Or merely married to anyone as long as he does not carry the name of Diamond."

"Why is Lord Trent acting as a messenger?" She waved the note she was holding. "I allowed him to dance with you in good faith and even to spend time with you at Vauxhall. Apparently, he is as unsavory as Diamond."

"Mother, please give me the letter if it was intended for me. You have no right to—"

In response, her mother turned, crumpled the page, and tossed it into the glowing hearth.

Caroline nearly darted forward to snatch it back, but she was a woman, not a child. Instead, she straightened her shoulders and lifted her chin.

"If I don't want to marry Lord Mangue, then I won't. I have your red hair, and I also have your spirit." Turning on her heel, she walked out.

With no idea when she was supposed to go to Hatchards, she couldn't meet Geoffrey. Lingering for hours in a bookseller's shop was not an option. Her other avenue of communication was Daphne. However, not wishing to bring scandal to her friend's door, she would have to tread carefully in that regard. Caroline regretted the hint of impropriety having already taken place in the Hollidge home.

Having already sent Daphne a letter of apology, Caroline would wait until she encountered her at the next assembly and hope they were still as close as sisters. Meanwhile, there was nothing she could do to further her own cause.

By dinnertime, with the delivery of the evening papers, her world had turned upside down.

Lord Chimes came from his study clutching a newspaper.

"My daughter was caught in a compromising situation at a dinner party, and I have to learn of it in *The Times*?" he demanded of his wife.

Caroline and her mother were silently seated in the drawing room, ignoring one another. She was reading the Waverly novel while her mother attempted needlepoint and doing it badly, as she always did.

At her father's words, Caroline and her mother exchanged matching wide-eyed verdant glances. Suddenly, they were on the same side of the battle, for they had both kept the truth from Lord Chimes.

That gave Caroline a small sense of satisfaction.

"I would have thought Mother might have come straight home and told you," Caroline said, sounding bored.

"What?" Lord Chimes exclaimed, rounding on his wife. "Lydia! What is our daughter saying? You *knew* about this?"

"I rescued her from Diamond's clutches," her mother said dramatically. "No one saw her, not even the hostess."

"No one except Lord Mangue," Caroline pointed out. Perhaps the man had changed his mind, and instead of marrying her, he'd decided to drag her name through the gutter as revenge.

"And Diamond," her mother said.

"Of course it was Diamond," her father spat out, sounding bitter. "I suppose he didn't like being thwarted."

Then he turned to Caroline.

"He *was* thwarted, wasn't he?"

She felt a flush of heat creep up her neck and over her face. This was a discussion she had hoped never to have with her parents.

"He *was* thwarted, Father," she insisted. *Was that the truth?* She didn't know if Geoffrey's fingers upon her counted as ruining her, but she doubted it. It must be the act of creating children that was the true destruction of a woman's virtue.

"He was thwarted!" her mother insisted. "I told you that I barged in on them. The rascal had kissed her, but that was all."

Her father sighed. Then he threw the newspaper onto the table.

"I suppose Mangue will cry off any marriage arrangement after this."

"That's convenient," Caroline said, "because I don't intend to marry the man." Furtively, she leaned forward and pulled *The Times* toward her.

"Is *your* daughter speaking to me that way?" her father asked, looking at her mother.

"Yes, dear, but she is *our* daughter after all. Would you have her be a noodle-headed namby-pamby?"

"I would have her be sensible and obedient," her father retorted. "If I go to the trouble of arranging a fine young man to marry her, I think she should be both grateful and agreeable."

"Speaking about me as if I am not in the room is intolerable," Caroline said. "If I am old enough to be married, then I am old enough to be treated as an adult and not a mischievous child. I don't find Lord Mangue to be a *fine* man, at least not fine-looking. Moreover, he has a tepid nature."

She wrinkled her nose, unable to explain why he reminded her of runny custard or tasteless blancmange while Geoffrey Diamond was like the best juicy piece of roast beef or a delicious slice of buttered toast.

"Why are you smiling then?" her father demanded.

"Merely looking forward to dinner."

"I tell you what," Lord Chimes said, "marry Mangue, if he'll still have you, and I'll add a little something extra to your dowry for your marital allowance."

"I cannot be bought," she insisted.

"It is dreadfully difficult to live a happy life without money," her mother pointed out.

"Are my own parents threatening me with penury?" Caroline asked.

There was a moment's hesitation, and then her father blinked.

"No, of course not. I was only thinking to gift you with more if you decide to be sensible."

"And if I decide to marry for love?"

"Do you fancy yourself in love with Diamond?" Lady Chimes asked. "You scarcely know him except for his dark-haired looks."

Caroline could hardly confess to how many conversations and kisses they'd actually shared. She merely shrugged.

"If he did tell *The Times* about your tryst in the pantry, then he is a blackguard," her father reminded her. "After all, it's unlikely it was Mangue unless he wants to appear a fool. Why would he blacken your name before he takes you as his wife?"

They were back to Lord Mangue. Caroline hoped he did in fact cry off because of the article in the paper, despite a ruined reputation being nothing to celebrate. Yet if Geoffrey had been the one to disclose their encounter, then she didn't want him either. Such a betrayal was the opposite of chivalry and gentlemanly behavior. It was unforgivable.

She scanned the single paragraph in the column on London's fashionable folk. While the rag-writer only vaguely referred both to her and to Geoffrey—*"Young Lady C__ who chimes like a bell and Lord D__ who knows well how to ring said bell with sparkle"*—their identities would be clear to anyone who knew the members of the *ton*.

As she came to the conclusion, she stifled a gasp. "*...were found in a pantler's closet, where the former, a diamond of the first water, was being polished by the latter, a diamond in the rough.*"

Her father had handled such a titillating public denouncement very well. Frankly, she was shocked and embarrassed to be the topic of such a scandal.

Could Geoffrey be the type of person to do such a thing out of anger?

For the first time, she wondered if he was exactly like his father after all, a flagrant rake who stole other people's sweethearts and ruined them. On the other hand, his father had married Lady Diamond, thereby restoring her to respectability.

If Caroline didn't receive and accept a marriage proposal quickly, her own reputation might be irretrievably lost.

Chapter Ten

Geoffrey paced the floor of Hatchards, but Caroline never arrived. And why would she if she was perfectly happy giving her hand to Mangue? If only he knew for certain whether she had a secret *tendre* for the man.

He wasn't going to wait for another infernal ball. Instead, he loitered outside the Chimes's home the following day, not in his own carriage emblazoned with his family's coat of arms. Rather, he was in a hired hackney.

After seeing the incriminating article in *The Times*, even his own parents demanded he offer for Lady Caroline. He didn't bother to tell them his own doubts over whether her heart was already given to Mangue, or at the very least, her hand. If they thought she might be fickle, they wouldn't condone him taking her as his wife.

From his vantage point, Geoffrey saw Lord Chimes leave the residence. Stretching out his legs, he continued his vigil. If Lady Chimes left, too, then he might attempt to breach the front door. However, she never went out.

Instead, Lord Mangue arrived around noon, and Geoffrey sat up, scowling. *Had the rogue spoken to The Times in order to lower her dowry price?* That seemed the only reasonable explanation as to why Mangue would have told the newspaper about what he saw and embellished it with what he imagined.

Deciding to take the bull by the horns, Geoffrey jumped down, paid off the driver, and crossed the road. Knocking upon the door, he asked to see Lady Caroline.

"She is not receiving visitors, my lord," came the butler's reply.

"Then I would like to speak to Lady Chimes." For Geoffrey didn't give a fig with whom he met, as long as he got his foot in the door and talked to someone.

The butler sighed. "Her ladyship is also not receiving visitors."

Crossing his arms, against all standards of politeness, he said, "That's ridiculous! I can hear voices in the drawing room."

Seeing one of the double doors was ajar, he skirted the shocked butler and hurried toward it.

Sure enough, there was Lady Chimes and Lord Mangue, while Lady Caroline was nowhere in sight.

"What is the meaning of this?" Lady Chimes demanded.

"I wish to offer for your daughter," he said at once. "May I speak with Lady Caroline?"

"Here now," Mangue said, rising to his feet. "Her parents and I already have an understanding."

"You have done enough damage already," her mother added, "with that unforgiveable tattling tale to *The Times*."

"Indeed," Mangue said.

"I didn't say a word," Geoffrey vowed. "How would it benefit me? Obviously, this man did."

"I didn't. Not a peep," Mangue protested. "It would benefit me even less. You told the newspaper, so I would cease my pursuit of Lady Caroline. Obviously, *you* did it. And the proof is that you're here now."

"I am here because only by marrying her can I salvage her reputation."

"On the contrary," Lady Chimes insisted, "if Lord Mangue marries her, it will disprove the false statements. Who would believe a sane man would marry her if she were truly ruined? Ergo, Lord Mangue will marry her and remove any whiff of tainted virtue."

"And I shall receive a larger dowry for my trouble," Lord Mangue added, causing Lady Chimes to narrow her eyes at him.

"We were discussing it," she said firmly, "but no decision can be made until I've discussed it with my husband."

"I will take Lady Caroline without any dowry at all," Geoffrey offered, as if he were bidding on horseflesh at Tattersall's.

Both of them stared at him, mouths slightly open.

"Not if you betrayed me to *The Times*," Caroline said from the doorway. "In which case, I shall have nothing to do with you."

Geoffrey felt a shard of warmth slice through him like summer sunshine, simply from seeing her. Moreover, he couldn't help smiling.

"How dare you grin at my daughter?" Lady Chimes said.

"How can I not?" he asked. "She is perfection."

"What poppycock!" Mangue muttered. "If Diamond doesn't want a dowry, he'll probably be miserly with his wife, keep her in rags, and not give her any pin money."

"Nonsense. My wife may have all my fortune," Geoffrey insisted. "I will rest it at her feet."

Instead of garnering a smile in return from Caroline, she frowned.

"I want to hear the answer. Did *you* speak with *The Times*?"

"No," he said firmly.

She looked at Mangue. "Did *you* talk to *The Times*?"

"Indubitably not," he said, sounding sincere. Even Geoffrey couldn't doubt him.

"Then I am entirely bewildered for I know it was not I nor my mother." Caroline looked at Mangue. "Only know, my lord, I think it the height of kindness that you would still offer for my hand."

"I want your hand," Geoffrey interrupted, "and not out of kindness."

They stared at one another.

Her mother bristled. "You will leave, Lord Diamond, or I will have our butler toss you out."

Geoffrey tried to imagine the Chimes's butler achieving such a feat, but it didn't matter. He wouldn't create such an ignominious scene. That was, not unless Caroline asked him to stay.

"I came to see you, Lady Caroline, to pledge my troth and to ask for your hand."

"You are out of line," Lady Chimes said, but Geoffrey didn't turn his gaze from her daughter's exquisite face.

"I will gladly help your butler get rid of this rascal," Mangue offered.

Geoffrey heard him but ignored his words, waiting only for an answer from Caroline.

She stared at him a long moment before glancing at her mother.

"Don't you dare respond to this scoundrel," Lady Chimes directed. "His behavior is beyond the pale!"

Caroline bit her lower lip, which he found not only charming but incredibly arousing.

"I don't believe I shall marry either one of you," she said finally.

While he was digesting that odd statement, she turned heel and left.

Geoffrey had to endure first one week and then two of missing Caroline. He had not simply enjoyed each of their brief, furtive encounters, he had relished them. She'd become a necessary part of his existence, even if he'd had to hide his affection and disguise his admiration. Yet she disappeared from the events on the Season's social calendar and cut off all contact.

He sent notes on three occasions, left his calling card twice, and even demanded to see her to an utterly impassive butler—all to no avail. Either she had lost interest, or her parents were keeping her on a tight rein.

And then one day, she appeared again. He was at the theatre with a young lady whose mother was a friend of his own mother. His companion was attractive, soft-spoken, and had a sweet smile, but she wasn't Caroline. It wasn't the lady's fault that he couldn't muster up the enthusiasm to even sniff her hair or do anything more than politely smile.

While he was looking out over the audience from his family's box during the intermission, having been a terrible escort and declining to go to the lobby for wine and jabbering prattle, he saw a head of glorious red hair. Paired with another equally coppery-headed female, he knew in a heartbeat it must be Caroline and her mother.

Leaning forward, he tried to see the rest of their party. He spied Lord Chimes, too, and hoped Caroline was with only her parents, but then she leaned over to speak to the man at her left and even laid her hand upon his arm. With their heads bent close, they spoke and then laughed.

Geoffrey's insides tightened as a burst of jealousy raced through him. *Dammit all!*

"Are you well, my lord?" asked the lady beside him. "You groaned and muttered."

He wanted to tell her he felt bloody awful and do the unforgivable—take her home before the evening's entertainment ended. However, his mother would give him hell if he offended her friend's daughter.

"My apologies. A touch of indigestion is all." He rolled his eyes at his ridiculous words, making himself sound like an old man with gout. Glad when the lamps dimmed, so he could no longer see Caroline and her escort, who appeared a damn sight more appealing than Mangue, Geoffrey settled back for the longest evening of his life.

He would not make the same mistake. He would remain a monk rather than be tortured by being in the company of a hapless miss who could do nothing but disappoint him through no fault of her own. She was simply the wrong woman.

Thus, the rest of the Season passed without him in attendance.

He didn't want to see Caroline, so he stayed away from the ballrooms. Despite his self-imposed banishment, he read the daily papers, dreading the appearance of an engagement announcement between her and Mangue or even with the mysterious stranger. Luckily, there were none.

Waiting did nothing to further his own pursuit of her, and while the passage of time gave tongues other scandals to wag on about, it did little to lessen Geoffrey's obsession with the red-haired goddess. Finally, it was Stir-Up Sunday, the last Sunday before the season of Advent, and he was at his parents' home for a long-held tradition.

"This has seemed an exceedingly long year," James Diamond said, rubbing his hands as he stood before the hearth in their drawing room. "Parliament has been busy. We started a new war with the Burmese, which I think shall drag on and be damnably expensive. Regrettably, it had to be done."

He took his glass of brandy from the mantel and sipped.

"On the other hand, I personally helped create a few acts that hopefully shall prove useful, and we signed a good treaty with the Dutch."

The Earl Diamond loved when they had a peaceful accord rather than a ruinous war. But Geoffrey was in no mood for good news.

"From the sublime to the ridiculous, our government stopped a war, started one, and spent a fortune on Angerstien's art collection," he said, feeling dour despite the normally festive occasion.

This custom of discussing their year on Stir-Up Sunday had begun when he'd been sent away to school. Upon his return for the long winter break, they would enjoy recapping what each had done, with the comforting knowledge that in their well-staffed kitchen the Christmas puddings were being made as they traditionally were on this day. For the next month, the liquor-soaked puddings would cure until they were brought to the table on Christmas day.

"With Angerstien's collection, we now have a public art gallery," his mother reminded him. "I think it's wonderful and worth every penny. If my loving husband wishes to commission a painting of me before I lose my looks, then I shall donate it."

"I shall do so in the new year at the earliest instant," the earl promised. "As soon as I find the best painter."

Lady Diamond narrowed her eyes. "Why the rush, husband? Are you saying I am already in danger of showing my age?"

When his father threw him a desperate look, Geoffrey merely shrugged. Let the man get himself out of it.

"Not at all, my love," Lord Diamond said. "But you cannot fault me for wanting the public to be able to enjoy your likeness on canvas as soon as humanly possible."

Marianne Diamond smiled and lifted her glass of wine in agreement.

Geoffrey ignored them. The new National Gallery, as it was known, only reminded him of seeing Caroline there before their debacle at the Hollidge dinner party. Her mother had kept him at bay.

"I sat in on the founding of the Society for the Prevention of Cruelty to Animals," his father continued to boast his list of accomplishments. "I was invited to Old Slaughter's Coffee House by the Reverend Broome himself and am proud of our members of parliament who sat with me for such a worthy cause."

"A good thing, too," Lady Diamond said. "There is no reason to strike a dog or a horse."

"No more than one would strike a woman," the earl agreed. "Poor creatures."

"Women or animals?" the countess quipped.

They laughed.

Geoffrey didn't join in and thought he ought to have stayed home this year and avoided the family tradition, especially since his biggest accomplishment was failing to gain the hand of the woman he loved. And he could hardly share that since he would garner no sympathy with his parents for the loss of a Chimes as his wife.

Nevertheless, he knew how to put a damper on their fun.

"As a nation, we hosted the King and Queen of the Sandwich Islands," he said. "Hosted them right into an early grave."

"Geoffrey!" his mother exclaimed. "How could anyone know they would catch the measles so easily? Besides, they had a wonderful time before they got sick."

"Got sick and *died*, Mother, far from home. What's more, the king was a year younger than I am."

"Still," she said, "they enjoyed the opera at Covent Garden."

"And you saw them at the Theatre Royal, didn't you?" his father asked him. "I saw the king myself, tall chap."

Geoffrey had seen King Kamehameha before he fell sick without ever getting an audience with King George. *Poor man!* But that night, Geoffrey had also seen Caroline with her parents. Again, that had been when his future still seemed as if it might have her in it. She'd looked beautiful, and he'd watched her instead of the stage. She had even discreetly waved at him in the dimly lit auditorium.

"The king and queen couldn't have done any of the entertaining things they did in London," Lady Diamond pointed out, "if they'd stayed on their little island."

"Island*s*, Mother. It's a chain of them. Never mind." Geoffrey shook his head. His mother was indeed frivolous. Apparently, she thought coming to London to see the opera and meet a bunch of noblemen had been worth their lives.

"Come now, think of something happier," Marianne Diamond insisted.

"Lord Byron died," Geoffrey said. At least the adventuresome baron had lived life to the fullest and known more than his share of passionate love, too, if all the newspaper recounts were true.

"I said *happier*," his mother reminded him. "Poor foolish man!"

She might as well have been speaking of her own son as of Byron. For Geoffrey was foolish through and through to have thought Lady Caroline genuinely cared about him.

He still wasn't sure whether she'd merely been exacting revenge on him for her parents' sake. It had seemed so when she cavalierly said she didn't wish to marry him and left the room. He remembered the moment as if it had been yesterday.

Geoffrey imagined it was why she'd allowed him to take liberties, too.

Now that Stir-Up Sunday was done and dusted, they would hurtle swiftly toward Christmas and the new year. Strange how he'd been all but certain he would have proposed to a willing wife by now.

The following day, he met Jasper at White's and endured another cheering-up similar to what his parents had attempted, although they were ignorant of the reason for his fit of the blue devils that would not abate. With Jasper, he could speak plainly.

"I haven't seen Lady Caroline for months. Yet sometimes, it seems as if I've seen her quite recently—she is still so clear before my mind's eye."

"Saw her and kissed her," Jasper added.

"And kissed her," he agreed.

Geoffrey had no wish to continue moping and feeling sorry for himself. Nevertheless, it was hard to disabuse his heart and his brain of the notion that he had found the one woman who suited him best in every regard. Even less did he have enthusiasm for hunting another, knowing she would be second best.

With his fist, he hit the linen-covered table, making Jasper jump as well as some of the other diners nearby.

"I can't stand this another minute," Geoffrey vowed. "I tell you she is mine and meant to be. She said she would not marry me, but I ought to have tried harder."

"Harder than the notes, flowers, and getting the Chimes's door slammed in your face?"

"Yes, harder. She is worth it. And I didn't ever try flowers. That seemed a tad sappy, frankly."

Jasper shrugged. "Do you have a plan?"

"Actually, yes, I do." Geoffrey could think of only one plan, clichéd as it was. "You provided it to me with your talk of *Romeo and Juliet* months ago."

Chapter Eleven

"I appreciate your help," Geoffrey told Jasper before they dropped as silently as possible over the garden wall. Landing on the coal bin had been unexpected, making a clattering sound that caused them to remain motionless, holding their breath. When no one opened the back door, they moved forward.

Although Jasper wasn't so much helping as offering friendly support, agreeing to be a lookout or a second in a duel if it came to it.

At White's, his friend had been nonchalant. "We shall go to her home tonight, and I vow you will speak with her," Jasper said as if sneaking around after dark were the most natural thing in the world for a couple of titled bucks. "Like men of derring-do."

And now Geoffrey found himself hiding behind a tree in the Chimes's back garden, feeling more foolish than daring. On the other hand, he would be happy to escape without a lead ball fired into his body, so Geoffrey supposed there was some measure of actual danger.

"I don't suppose you know which is your lady's bedchamber," Jasper asked.

"How would I know that?" Geoffrey asked. *Was his friend casting aspersions on Caroline?*

"Don't get into a high tweague, Diamond. But it would be damn useful if you knew which window."

Jasper was right. But over brandy, going there at two in the morning had seemed like a good idea and an easy one.

"Would it be better to break in the back door and roam the house?" his friend wondered aloud while staring at the upper floors.

While Geoffrey thought he might meet with better success indoors than climbing a tree or a trellis and knocking on Lord and Lady Chimes's window by mistake, it was also riskier. He could get sent to jail for breaking in like a thieving *fidlam ben*.

"If she were my daughter, I would have her room away from the street, I suppose," he guessed.

"But not at the very back of the house," Jasper added. "In case any nefarious nobleman wanted to use an apple tree to climb in her window."

Geoffrey sighed. This was a bone-headed plan. Luckily, the Chimes's had a corner home, so he could explore the side of the house as easily as the back.

"I'm going to guess that window." He pointed above them.

Jasper handed him a rock.

"If I'm wrong," Geoffrey said, "prepare to bolt like a skittish deer."

Setting his lantern upon the ground, he hefted the rock in his hand.

"I believe it's supposed to be a few small pebbles, enough to make a noise but not break the glass. Give me something smaller," he demanded.

"If you hit the house, not the glass, it will be fine," Jasper insisted.

"That won't awaken her. I need pebbles," he insisted. "Maybe I could toss coins. That would make a goodly racket."

"I don't think you should throw anything directly at the glass," Jasper said.

Dropping the rock, he searched in his pockets and withdrew some coppers.

"Perfect. Stand by, Trent."

"I am, Diamond. I am."

"Very well." He jiggled the coins a moment as if he were shaking dice.

"Let them fly," Jasper said encouragingly.

"I was about to. Stop talking."

Taking a step back, he tossed them at the window he'd chosen just as the sash lifted.

"Oh!" Caroline exclaimed as a handful of coins hit her in the face and chest. *What the devil?*

"My apologies," came Geoffrey's voice as he bent to retrieve his lantern. "Are you injured?"

As the frigid air swirled into her room, she peered into the side garden. *Was he in his cups?*

"Who is with you?" she asked, seeing another figure beside him.

"'Tis I, Lord Trent," came a cheerful voice, and to prove it, he lifted his lantern up to his face.

"A moment," she said, wondering if she were still asleep and dreaming.

Hurrying to light a lamp, she snatched up her thick wool dressing gown and wrapped it around herself. Having been awakened by voices, she had lifted the sash at precisely the wrong instant.

Returning to the window, she heard Lord Trent exclaim, "What light through yonder window breaks."

"Quiet," she pleaded. If her parents weren't already awake, they would be. And that would bring this unexpected farce to a hasty end.

On the other hand, knowing Geoffrey was mere feet away, for the first time in weeks, she felt happiness drizzle like a gentle rain upon her.

"Yes, do muzzle yourself," Geoffrey added. Then he looked up. "I need to speak with you."

"Come closer and speak softly," she said.

They both shuffled forward, but then Geoffrey waved his friend away. "Stay back, for God's sake," he ordered.

"Only trying to help," Lord Trent replied, but then he and his lantern disappeared toward the wall.

Geoffrey began again. "I am sorry to awaken you and to hit you with coins."

Her heart melted at his awkward beginning.

"After what you said about not marrying me, I had to discern the true depths of your feelings. I must know what's in your heart."

She caught her breath. Perhaps he was the terrible rogue her parents believed him to be, for it was inconceivable he could ask her to state plainly such an intimate thing. And how unwise for her to tell him that she loved him. If he knew, it would put her in a terribly vulnerable position.

In the end, all she said was, "Why?"

"Why?" he repeated. "I assume you are asking why I wish to know."

"Yes, exactly."

"Because you have moved into my heart and taken up all the space."

Then they were as twins. *How brave of him to confess that to her.*

"Your silence makes me exceedingly nervous," he said. "Moreover, I saw you with an unfamiliar man at the theatre."

She leaned a little farther out, wishing she could be down in the garden with him, but it was too dangerous to try to sneak past her parents' room and down the stairs.

Taking a deep, chilly breath, Caroline decided to tell him. Either she would be as happy as her best friend Daphne, who had long since forgiven her for sullying her pantry, or she would become as forlorn as Shakespeare's doomed Juliet, to whom Lord Trent had just alluded.

"I love you," she confessed.

When he said nothing, Caroline's heart began to pound. *What was he thinking?* That this was a turning point in their lives, or maybe he was pondering the impossibility of their situation given the animosity between their parents.

When she was about to demand he tell her his thoughts, he spoke.

"I wish someone had thought to put a strong rose trellis here or planted a sturdy tree with branches touching your window. I love you, and I swear I would be up there beside you in a twitch of a lamb's tail if I could."

Relief poured through her, and she closed her eyes with a long sigh.

"Will you marry me, Lady Caroline Chimes?"

Her eyes popped open. "If I could, Geoffrey Diamond, I would." It was as honest as she could be.

He stared up at her.

"And you don't actually long for Mangue?"

"I promise you, I do not. I was stunned when I found out that my parents had spoken to him about marrying me. I should have told you."

She wouldn't be so petty as to discuss his mercenary tendency in requesting a larger dowry, for he must be a decent man to wish to marry her despite the ugly rumors.

"I see." Another pause, and then he added, "I have already told you in front of your mother that I wish to marry you," Geoffrey reminded her. "That has not changed in all these weeks."

"Did you tell *The Times* about the butler's pantry?" she asked, needing to know.

"I swear I did not."

"I did," came Lord Trent's voice out of the darkness, proving he had been listening all along.

"What?" Geoffrey roared.

"Sshh," she admonished.

"You said you wanted to do whatever it took to break up an arrangement between Mangue and your lady," Lord Trent explained. "But I knew you to be too honorable to actually follow through."

Stunned silence met his statement, and then Geoffrey's disbelieving exclamation, "You tattled to the newspapers!"

Caroline tried to imagine what Geoffrey had told his friend of their intimate encounter and felt her cheeks heat even with the cool night air streaming against her.

"I made up a story based on the little you told me," Lord Trent said. "It helped, didn't it?"

"I would punch you if you weren't my best friend," Geoffrey growled.

"Gentlemen," she said to regain their attention. "I think it was a terrible idea, but what's done is done. My parents think only marrying Lord Mangue will erase the stain upon my reputation. For you see, if he marries me, it will plainly demonstrate that nothing really happened."

"Oh!" came Lord Trent's voice again. "I hadn't thought of that, only of driving Mangue and his extraordinary eyebrow away."

She would have laughed if it weren't all so serious.

"I don't care," Geoffrey said. "Marry me, and we'll weather any storm."

"You don't know what it might mean," she said, although like sunshine between the clouds, a shard of hope broke through the heavy doubt and melancholy that had dogged her.

Then to her amazement, Geoffrey laughed.

"Dearest Caroline," he said. "Do you forget who my parents are, and what my father has long been reputed to have done? More than anyone, I understand what this could mean. And still, I don't give a fig. We shall not be shunned, I promise you. If anything, it lifted my parents into a mythological realm of desperate, undeniable love."

Caroline considered his words. *Desperate, undeniable love*—that was a perfect description for what she felt.

"Besides," he added, "any blame has been laid at my father's feet as a bit of a rake. Even then, he is widely forgiven because he married my mother, and they've stayed together without anyone ever being able to say either has been unfaithful."

It was true that she'd only ever heard any fault being placed on Lord Diamond, except where her parents were concerned. Lady Diamond was considered an unwilling victim, and also a perfectly lovely and lucky countess who snared an earl.

"Please marry me," he said again, his tone causing a lump in her throat.

"How?" she asked even as her pulse fluttered. She might actually get to marry the only man who had ever made her shiver.

"I spoke in jest once about Gretna Green," he reminded her. "Now I believe we ought to take our chances. The alternative is to wait a year until you don't need anyone's permission."

A wretched long year of being berated, scolded, pushed, and coerced.

"I think a border wedding sounds wonderful," she agreed. "When?"

She half expected him to say, "Now," which would have put her into a panicky rub. She wanted to bathe with her favorite floral soap, pack a bag, choose the perfect gown, and tell Daphne the thrilling news.

Nevertheless, if he said it had to be that instant or wait for the reign of Queen Dick, as her father would say to mean never at all, then she would dress in the first gown she had at hand and slip outside to meet him. Or more romantically, she could drop into his awaiting arms.

Gauging the distance, Caroline hoped she didn't end up with a broken neck.

Luckily, Geoffrey needed time to plan, too.

"Can you go to Lady Hollidge's tomorrow around ten o'clock? I shall meet you there with enough funds for our journey, and we shall take flight directly."

Just eight hours! Caroline had trouble catching her breath. She was going to do something she had never considered possible—*elopement!* Some thought it a starry-eyed endeavor. Most knew it was the stuff of foolish girls and greedy, wicked men. But she was no fool, and Geoffrey was not after her money.

Yet even if she could get ready in time, which she would, her mother would question her sanity at going out visiting at such an impolite hour.

"Eleven would be better, for the sake of civility," she said.

"Very well. I will be at Lady Hollidge's home five minutes before eleven."

In the glow of his lantern, she could see his handsome grin, and her heart clenched.

"I love you," he said, surprising her.

More than ever, she wished she were in his arms instead of hanging over the casement.

"I love you, too," she told him, no longer the least bit embarrassed.

"Parting is such sweet sorrow," quipped Lord Trent, whom she'd entirely forgotten.

"Shut your gob!" Geoffrey ordered. And then the two men disappeared into the shadows.

Caroline sighed and, with frozen fingers, closed the window sash. She knew she would not sleep, nor could she ask the staff for a bath or do anything out of the ordinary until morning. Belatedly, she realized it would have been smart of her to toss a sack down to Geoffrey containing clothing, for she would not be able to leave in the morning with anything except her reticule.

In fact, knowing she would have to hide her excitement from her clever mother, she decided to take breakfast in her room and stay there until the last possible moment.

Even when her maid was delivering the requested hot chocolate and toast to her room, Caroline was still toying with the notion of wearing a second dress under her day gown, but if her mother should see her leave, it would be all too obvious.

Unless she put on her fur-trimmed redingote while still in her room.

"Bring my winter coat up here," she asked her maid. "I'm going out in an hour, and I'll get bundled up before I go downstairs."

Her maid looked at her, probably wondering why Caroline was prattling on and explaining herself. She offered the young woman a smile and sent her on her way. And then, as she was wondering which of her prettier dresses would best fit under what she was wearing, something she would be proud to be seen in even for an anvil wedding, there was a knock at her door.

She knew that knock. Only her mother's knuckles made that particular rapping sound.

Glancing around the room, she began to shove the dresses from her bed into her wardrobe, knowing it to be a hopeless task.

Her plan for a speedy escape was already in ruins.

Chapter Twelve

"Caroline, are you awake and dressed?"

"Yes, Mother." Drat! *Why hadn't she said she was feeling ill and had decided to sleep in?*

With that answer, her mother felt it her place to open the door and stroll in. And thus, Caroline was discovered with an arm full of gowns.

"What on earth are you doing?"

What was she doing? Caroline could barely come up with the simplest excuse.

"I was bored and decided to look through my dresses and see if I should consider having any altered." With that, she dumped them back on the bed.

"Your poor maid will have quite a time tidying all that up," her mother said. "If you're bored, why don't you come with me? I'm going to the new National Gallery."

"We've already been," Caroline reminded her.

"Darling, you don't go once to a museum and consider it finished. You go again and again to study the paintings and remark upon them."

"Some people go to see who is there and to be seen admiring great art," Caroline said, hoping to dissuade her mother with the intimation it was a vulgar outing.

Her mother shook her head. "That sounds rather shallow. Something Lady Diamond might do. In fact, she's probably trying to figure out how to get her own portrait onto the wall." Then her mother frowned. "Are you well?"

"Yes, why?" Caroline realized she'd gasped aloud.

"You paled suddenly."

"Did I?" She'd been startled beyond reason by her mother mentioning the name of Diamond.

"And now you look flushed. Sit down."

Caroline did as her mother said, finding a spot between the gowns just as there came a knock at the door.

"Come in," her mother answered for her.

Caroline's maid entered carrying her dark green redingote with its soft gray fur trim.

"Why have you brought that up here?" Lady Chimes demanded.

"Lady Caroline asked me to, my lady."

Both pairs of eyes stared at her, and Caroline took a step back.

"I was going out because... as I said, I was bored, and I... I thought seeing how it is cold, I would don my coat and hat while in the warmth of my room."

"Where were you going?" her mother asked.

"Merely for a walk."

"Then I shall accompany you. I can go to the museum later if you still don't wish to go. I suppose some fresh air is a good idea, as long as we don't stay out too long and risk catching a chill."

Geoffrey paced Lady Hollidge's drawing room, but after waiting an hour and a half, it was obvious Caroline was not coming.

Had she changed her mind?

"My lord, I fear something has detained her," Daphne Hollidge said, stating the obvious while bouncing her little boy on her lap.

Geoffrey feared it was not something but *someone*. He eyed the young Alexander Hollidge, knowing the boy wanted his mother's attention. The totiken had arrived about twenty minutes earlier after awakening from a nap. And when he did, he'd made enough noise while entering with his nanny that Geoffrey had been sure Caroline had at last arrived.

He could not know for certain whether it was Caroline's disinclination to elope that had stopped her or an external factor. He prayed it was the latter.

"I am sorry to have disrupted your household today and to have wasted your time," he said, wondering if he would be spending another evening tossing coins at Caroline's window to obtain an explanation.

A noise in the foyer snagged both of their attention.

"Daphne, is he still here?" came Caroline's voice, and then she appeared in the doorway.

Her hat was askew, her cheeks were pink with exertion as if she'd been running, and she never looked lovelier.

"Oh!" she exclaimed upon seeing him, and then she burst into tears.

Not caring that Lady Hollidge would bear witness, Geoffrey rushed to claim her and wrap her in his arms. She collapsed against him.

"What's happened? Are you well?"

"My mother thwarted me at every turn. I fear she suspects something since, in the middle of Hyde Park, I finally declared I needed to be alone and rushed straight here."

"I shall order a pot of tea," Lady Hollidge said. "Do sit and try to catch your breath."

Caroline's lovely gaze looked up at him. "Do we have time? Have I ruined everything?"

Geoffrey tried to calm his racing heart. She was in his arms, and she still wanted to elope with him. Everything was fine again.

"We should begin our journey. It will take three days if we don't kill the horses. You'll have plenty of time to sit, I assure you."

"I have nothing with me. I couldn't leave home with a bag."

Lady Hollidge instantly became their angel. "Take tea, please, Caroline. While you do, I shall have a trunk packed at once with everything you'll need."

"Dear Daphne. How can I ever repay you?"

"We are like sisters, are we not?" She was already heading for the door. "Catch your breath. Tea will arrive in five minutes, and I vow I will have you out the door in fifteen."

As good as her word, Lady Hollidge sent them swiftly on their way, and Caroline was a good deal calmer than when she'd stumbled in.

"My friend is so thoughtful," she said when they were passing Shoreditch Church. "She even gave me a novel and some biscuits and cake." She was digging in the carpet bag that had been pressed into her hands after a trunk was stowed on top of Geoffrey's travel coach.

"Her husband is equally kind. I hope you will enjoy their company as much as I do," she added.

Geoffrey nodded. "Gaining a wife and two friends into the bargain! And I hope, despite Lord Trent's failings, you come to like him, too. He's been a good friend to me for years."

"Maybe we shall gain yet another friend," she mused, "for he has his sights set upon Miss Holcombe, a pretty brunette."

Geoffrey was astounded. He had heard nothing about it. "How on earth do you know that?"

She smiled. "I have kept my eyes open all Season. Mostly, I was looking for you. But when you were not in sight, I noticed other people."

He laughed. "Will you sit beside me?" He patted the leather seat.

"Will you behave yourself?" she asked, tilting her head, beaming with happiness.

He could only promise he would try, but the unusual circumstance of being in a carriage alone with a beautiful woman without a chaperone was titillating beyond all measure.

Moreover, in light of what they were doing, her question gave him pause.

"You know it no longer matters what we do or do not do. We are alone, and thus you are irreparably ruined."

She wrinkled her adorable nose. "A horrid word."

"But you understand we shall be spending two or possibly three nights staying at coaching inns. Even if we have separate rooms, which you should demand of me, it shall make no difference to what others will say and conclude."

"I know," she agreed quietly. "I am ruined."

"But you shall be my wife and one day a countess. I believe when we return as a wedded couple, as long as we behave with decorum, the scourge of our disgrace will disappear."

"Eventually," she agreed.

"Soon," he corrected.

"Unless we have a child too quickly."

Geoffrey's heart sped up at the realization she was already contemplating swiving, which was practically all he could think about. He didn't like to consider himself a randy dog, but he hadn't enjoyed any female company in his bed since the night he slammed into Caroline Chimes.

"Luckily," he said, "that won't be the case. Even if we..." He trailed off when faced with her curious green gaze.

"Yes?" she prompted.

"Even if we share a room tonight, which you should insist we do not, and even if we marry in three days, the baby will be born at the right time."

"True enough." Without another word, she lifted the thick wool blanket under which she'd been keeping warm and changed her place, nestling beside him.

He put his arm around her shoulders.

"I am sorry," she said, straightening. "This is all wrong."

Geoffrey tensed. If she'd changed her mind, he would probably throw himself out of the moving carriage over a well-placed cliff if he could find one.

"I need to sit facing the way we travel."

He breathed a sigh of relief. Many people felt a stomach upset when riding backward, including his own mother.

They rearranged themselves and faced forward, snuggling under the covering.

"Much better," Caroline said. Once again, she rested her head upon his shoulder.

"I confess I barely slept last night. And then after the excitement of the morning, I believe I could doze off if you didn't think me too rude."

"Please, take a journey to the land of Nod if you can. Maybe I shall join you. My driver and footman will alert us if there is any trouble whatsoever."

As she rested her hand on his chest, his heart bloomed with love, and he thought nothing could be better than having her start snoring gently in his arms.

Until that night when she told him to obtain a single room.

As he descended from the carriage to speak to the innkeeper, she reached out and laid her hand upon his arm.

"After all," she said, "I consider myself already your wife in all but the formality."

Her trust in him shook Geoffrey. When he had secured them the best room and were now discussing going downstairs to dinner or having it brought up to their room, he couldn't help telling her what was on his mind.

"I am actually concerned for you."

"What do you mean?" She had been removing her outer coat but now stopped to look at him, her pretty lips parted in a smile.

"You are too trusting. What if you were here with a rogue? You can't tell a man you already consider yourself married. What if I tupped you and left you here?" He was working himself up into righteous outrage on her behalf.

Instead of understanding the gravity of her circumstances, Caroline laughed and finished shrugging out of her coat, which she laid over the end of the bed. Approaching him, she put her hands up to take his face between her slender fingers.

"Geoffrey Diamond, are you going to tup me tonight?"

Swallowing hard at the instant image of fornication that sprang into his brain while his staff sprang to hard arousal as well, he stared into her unfathomable green eyes and could speak only the truth.

"Probably. In fact, certainly. Yes, I intend to." He stopped babbling as she stroked her thumb over his lower lip.

"And are you going to leave me here afterward as a fallen woman? Or will we continue our journey to Scotland, so we can marry in haste and enjoy our lives at leisure?"

"That is not how the saying goes," he pointed out. "Regardless, I am never going to leave you anywhere but stay always by your side."

She nodded, went up on tiptoe, and kissed him full upon his lips.

Before he could wrap his arms around her, however, she had broken contact and slipped past him.

"I am famished," she said. "If we are going to get to swiving later, then I need to eat now."

Chapter Thirteen

Lord James Diamond decided his son was a chip off the old block. First the episode in the butler's pantry that all of London had read about, and now it seemed Geoffrey had absconded with the willing Chimes wench.

If there was any doubt, it evaporated when he witnessed Lord and Lady Chimes barging across his foyer as soon as his butler admitted them. Allowing them in was probably a mistake, but the alternative was cowardly.

And James was no coward. Caught on the staircase, he called behind him.

"Dearest wife, we have visitors." *Intruders, more like*, he added silently.

"The Fenwicks?" Marianne called back. "I hope."

"Alas, no," he sighed. "Do hurry." And he went down to greet the least likely of guests.

"I pray you know where your rapscallion son is," Lord Chimes began.

"Good evening," James replied, ignoring the man's tone. "There is a lady present, so we shall adhere to all manner of civility. Lady Chimes, would you care for a glass of wine, given the hour?" It was that between time after dinner and before supper.

"No," she said, and James could see it cost her to finish politely, "thank you. We are here because our daughter has disappeared. And we fear she is with your son."

James wasn't done with playing host despite not fearing anything. Rather, he knew with certainty because that's what he would do if he fancied a forbidden lady. And also, because he had run into his son's best friend, Lord Trent, at White's.

"It sounds as if we have trouble brewing, and that's always better handled with brandy." Yanking the bellpull, he offered once again. "What about you, Chimes? Are you thirsty?"

"I wouldn't drink with you if you were the last man on earth."

"Rather harsh," James muttered.

Luckily, Lady Diamond entered before he could make matters worse. And then she proceeded to do precisely that.

Upon taking one look at their guests, she announced, "Our offspring have eloped."

"You knew about this?" Lady Chimes asked.

"About what?" his wife asked, infuriating their guests.

"About what?" Lord Chimes repeated. "About the elopement, of course."

"Not at all," Lady Diamond said, exasperated. "I'm not clairvoyant. Yet our son has gone away unexpectedly and then, here you are. What else can I conclude? In fact, when he didn't turn up to dinner as expected, I said to my husband, our son has probably run away with that pretty, red-headed girl. Didn't I, my love?"

"You did," he agreed, then turned to the Chimes. "She honestly did. And I told her I had heard as much at my club from a gentleman with close ties to our son. And now you've confirmed it. Do you understand now?"

He was playing the devil but couldn't stop himself.

On the other hand, his wife appeared resolved to be a hostess. "Diamond, have you offered our visitors wine?"

"Yes, my love, and brandy, but they refused," he told her.

Turning her smile upon them, he didn't know how anyone could resist Marianne's charm. "How about tea, then?" she asked.

"We don't want anything," Lady Chimes insisted in clipped tones, "except our daughter."

"Well, *we* don't have her," Lady Diamond told them. And then she took a seat, and James realized she'd come to the end of her graciousness already. She did have a rather short rope and little tolerance for anything unpleasant.

"It was careless of you to let her wander away from home unsupervised, don't you think?" she added.

James wished his countess hadn't said that. Sure enough, fireworks ensued.

"Let her *wander*!" Lord Chimes spluttered.

"More like she was snatched," Lady Chimes put in, but she also took a seat.

James didn't like that insinuation one bit. "Are you stating you believe our son kidnapped your daughter?"

"Poppycock!" Marianne said.

"Caroline was perfectly content this morning," Lady Chimes insisted. "We took a walk. There was no hint of her leaving. She didn't even have luggage!"

"If they are together, and it seems likely they are," James said, "then they are in a carriage on the best road to the closest Scottish town."

"Gretna Green," Lord Chimes interrupted.

"However, if I take my best horse," James continued, "then I may be able to beat them there."

"You mean *I* might," Lord Chimes corrected. "For I intend to go after my daughter."

"Not without me," Lady Chimes insisted. "She might be frightened or in a dreadful circumstance if your dastardly son has had his way with her."

"Then I shall go, too," Marianne insisted. "If your daughter is trying to ensnare my boy, then he'll need me to see through her feminine wiles. His heart will be broken."

"Ridiculous," Lady Chimes insisted. "Your son is obviously just like his father."

"Meaning?" Marianne asked tightly.

"Not a gentleman at all. Rather, he's willing to ruin a woman to secure her hand."

"And your daughter is just like you," Marianne said, rising once more. "A grasping mushroom!"

"How dare you!" Lady Chimes exploded, jumping to her feet. "We can't all be fickle, shallow females, tempting men in order to secure an engagement."

Marianne laughed. "Well, which is it? Did my husband ruin me or did I tempt him?"

"I thought we were talking about my daughter and your son," Lord Chimes said. "I fail to see how your sordid history is important." Even he seemed disconcerted by the turn which the conversation had taken.

"I suppose we ought to stop the wedding," James said, "at least until we sort out a marriage contract and your daughter's dowry."

Lord Chimes turned red. "Not another penny from me to you," he declared.

"We don't want to negotiate a marriage arrangement," Lady Chimes said. "We want to stop them getting married. I'm going, too, but not all that way on horseback."

"Neither am I," Marianne said. "Not when we have a comfortable traveling coach."

"As do we," Lady Chimes said, with a tilt of her chin.

"Why don't you ladies go together?" James suggested. "Then when we find them, you'll both be there should either one of our offspring need comforting or support."

It sounded ridiculous, but he knew neither of the women would want to be left behind. Nor could he allow his wife to undertake such a journey alone.

"And we shall go on horseback," Lord Chimes said, glancing at James, "to intercept them."

"Will you ride straight through?" Lady Diamond asked. "How exciting and utterly exhausting!"

"We cannot stay alone in coaching inns," Lady Chimes pointed out. "Can we?"

"We cannot stay with you," Lord Chimes pointed out, "or we might as well be in the blasted carriage, and we'll never make up time enough to catch them."

"I'll send the ladies with my driver and two footmen," James proposed. "The driver is very experienced and will know where it's safe for them to stay. And all three will be fully armed."

"I shall have to go home and pack," Lady Chimes said.

"I won't wait," Lady Diamond threatened. "Every minute wasted—"

James hated to gainsay his wife. It would mean a frosty reception in the marital bed when next he reached for her. However, since they would be apart for a few nights, she might soften toward him and forgive him by the time they met up again. Thus, he suggested a compromise.

"Dearest, I think you should give Lady Chimes leave to go home with her husband and pack what she needs. The two of you can depart at first light when you collect her in our carriage. Meanwhile, I'll have my horse saddled and some provisions put in my saddlebags and be away within the half-hour."

Lord Chimes huffed. "I need to go get my best runner. Will you head out without me or wait at Hick's Hall?"

"If I see you, we'll ride together," James said, not making any promises.

Caroline had never been happier. The only blight was how she'd deceived her parents and how disappointed they would be. She might never see her father look at her with his loving smile again. Moreover, they might instruct her brothers to shun her, too.

Yet she would have her heart's desire by her side. She would be Geoffrey's wife and hopefully, one day, mother to his children. They both wanted a large family if they were so blessed. They'd had so much time to confirm their compatibility during the hours of travel, she was amazed at how perfectly they suited.

And the night before, after dinner, he'd taken her innocence gently and given her pleasure in return. After another long day of travel, with the Scottish border growing ever closer, she was looking forward to another night of passion.

"You ate your dinner rather quickly," he teased once they were alone in their chamber. Already, he was helping her to undress.

"As did you," she said, letting him pull her gown over her head, not feeling the least shyness now when she stood before him in her shift. When that last barrier was slid off her shoulders and down her breasts, her nipples stiffened.

"You are so beautiful," he said, reaching out to brush his knuckles over each peaked bud.

"There are many beautiful women in the world," she said.

"I love only one," he promised. "And if all you had to recommend you was your beauty, I would not have fallen in love with you, but if you had no beauty at all, I vow I would love you as much as I do now. Caroline Chimes, you have captured my heart and own it entirely."

Her cheeks heated. "You sound more like a poet every day."

"Indeed, you have brought out the romantic side of me. But also, the animal side." Without warning, he scooped her into his arms and deposited her upon the bed.

She yelped and then laughed. "Hurry," she beseeched. "Undress and join me."

The night before, for her sake, he'd dimmed the lamps before they removed all their clothing, making it all the more sensual when they stroked each other's bare skin while preserving a modicum of modesty for her first time.

Tonight, she could see all of him, his hard planes and his muscular figure, the dusting of hair across his chest and legs, and his manhood jutting out and up.

"We are so different," she said with wonder.

He chuckled. "And for that, I thank God."

Once beside her, he claimed her mouth under his while stroking her sensitive skin. Circling her breasts first, he caressed lower, down her stomach.

When he tore his mouth away and bent lower to suck upon first one of her pink pearls, then the other, Caroline thought the bed was tilting beneath her. Arching back, closing her eyes, she gripped his shoulders, only to feel Geoffrey's hand slide lower. Unable to help her wanton behavior, she lifted her hips to meet his skilled fingers as at last he touched her core.

As happened the previous night, it took very little time for her to reach the utmost pleasure, her body tightening almost unbearably and then releasing all at once in a joyful, exquisite blossoming sensation.

Even before her heart ceased its frantic racing, he fitted his jutting arousal to her damp channel and surged inside her. Again, her hips lifted to meet his thrust.

"I love you," he reminded her.

"I love you," she echoed.

They said nothing more as he began a slow rhythm of desirable torture.

When she was panting with exertion, trying to reach the pinnacle again, he slipped his hand between their bodies to touch where she most throbbed.

"Yes," she hissed, then shattered beneath him into a thousand pieces of ecstasy.

With a guttural groan, he continued rocking, increasing the pace until his body tensed. While she felt him shudder under her fingertips, he released the warm proof of his fulfillment deep inside her.

When Geoffrey collapsed atop her before quickly rolling to the side and hugging her to him, she decided she wouldn't mind if they had a baby by next autumn. In fact, such a happy occurrence would please her immensely.

As she drifted off to sleep, she was thinking of names for their children, names that evoked the many facets of a diamond—clarity, purity, and brilliance.

Chapter Fourteen

"Ha! Caught you." James didn't know how Chimes could have been so quick, but the earl had beaten him to the start of the Great North Road and then kept on going, albeit at a slower pace.

"I told you I had a rum prancer," Chimes said. "If I'd known you were going to ride a miserable rip like that, I would have insisted we journey separately. At the very least, I would have lent you some respectable horse flesh."

It was an idiotic insult since they both rode thoroughbreds. James dug his heels in, and his horse surged forward. For a furlong he raced Chimes, neck and neck, until they realized the futility.

"You know we'll be switching horses constantly, and thus, it's ridiculous to argue who has the best mount. We're wasting any endurance they may have at any rate."

"True," Chimes said, easing up.

James did the same. The best part about this type of exhausting, determined gait was it was nearly impossible to talk more than a short quip every once in a while. Thus, they lapsed into silence until the time came to switch out their horses in four hours at a coaching inn.

"If we keep this up and ride through the night, we may even get to Gretna before them."

"You were going to leave me behind," Lady Chimes insisted, taking the empty backward-facing seat and setting her bag beside her on the fine leather squab.

Marianne Diamond, who had climbed in first and taken her preferred place, could only shrug. Lady Chimes was correct. After telling James she wished he hadn't pushed them together, she'd kissed him goodbye at midnight and then decided to travel alone.

If Lady Chimes hadn't returned to the Diamond home at dawn as the maid and footman were packing the traveling coach, Marianne would have given a rude salute when she passed by the street upon which the Chimes lived and not bothered to collect her.

Yet before she could head out, Lady Chimes had arrived with a trunk, a leather bag, and a basket of food. And Marianne was trapped with the infernal woman for God only knew how many hours.

"Since we are as different as chalk and cheese," she said, "why don't we maintain a polite silence unless absolutely necessary?"

"Fine with me," Lady Chimes agreed, drawing needlepoint out of her bag.

Hating to do needle work herself, still, Marianne stared with fascination at what a hash the other woman was making of it and longed to point out there were more knots and holes than actual proper stitches. Not that she could do any better.

Pulling out a brand-new book, *The Inheritance* by Mrs. Ferrier, she set it on her lap, fully intending to delve in. For a moment, she thought what wicked fun it would have been to have brought Mrs. Ferrier's previous novel, simply titled *Marriage*, and left it in view of her carriage companion, to vex her.

In any case, after staring unseeingly out the window for a long while, Marianne closed her eyes, lulled by the rocking of the carriage.

"It's going to be too late," Geoffrey said, squeezing Caroline's hand as they crossed the River Sark after the sun had set. "It's called an 'irregular marriage,' but I don't fancy stumbling around Gretna Green in the darkness looking for someone to wed us."

"Nor I." Caroline shivered beside him. On the carriage floor, the hot bricks from the morning had long grown cold as marble. "It's far too brisk to do anything tonight except sit by a warm and perfectly regular fire."

"We'll stay at the King's Head. It's right on the roadside, according to reports. I don't believe it is grand by any means, but someone there can marry us in the morning."

Sadly, Geoffrey was correct. From what he could see as they drove alongside, the hostelry had a very plain, even shabby façade. However, the chimneys were smoking, indicating some heat, and lamps shone through the lower two windows.

"Doesn't seem like the type of place to send in my footman and arrange a room," he said. "We'll go in together and see if it looks up to snuff."

He helped her down.

"The thought of returning to that chilly carriage makes the King's Head look most welcoming," Caroline said.

He'd learned she wasn't fussy or persnickety. Moreover, she could tolerate a great deal of inconvenience, whether gristly steak pie, a lumpy mattress, or a noisy tavern directly below their room.

They entered through the low doorway directly into a small passage. On the right was the pub room and on the left was a closed door. In front of them, a staircase disappeared into the unlit floor above.

The only saving grace was a cat seated at the foot of the stairs, which greeted them by rubbing against Caroline's ankles.

"At least there won't be mice," Geoffrey said, and they went into the barroom.

It wasn't joyless, but it wasn't bustling with happy locals either. At one of the small tables nearest the hearth sat a couple who looked down and away as if to hide their faces. The other tables were empty save one occupied in the far corner by people with their backs to the room. Geoffrey assumed it was the nature of a place that was infamous for hurried weddings—everyone would wish to keep their identities concealed.

A barman looked up from where he was reading a newspaper and nodded by way of greeting.

Geoffrey nodded back. "Do you have a room for us, and another for my two servants?"

"Aye," said the man.

Geoffrey wanted to ask if the room was clean, but seeing how Caroline was tired and the December weather frigid, they should settle in while they could.

"Can we get a meal, too?" he asked, wondering how far hospitality would extend in the stark little place.

The man looked past to the darkness outside as if determining the time, and then he sniffed and swung his head toward an open doorway behind him, which led to the back of the house.

"Mattie!" he yelled.

"Aye," called back a female voice.

"You got any stew left and bread?"

"Aye," she answered.

The barman faced them again.

"Aye, we can feed you."

"Only if we want stew," Geoffrey quipped.

The man didn't smile. Apparently, there was not much of a sense of humor in this dour little inn.

"Which we do," Caroline asserted, beginning to pull off her gloves.

"It's quite good," Geoffrey's father said.

His father!

Geoffrey gaped at the man who rose from the table in the corner, joined by Lord Chimes.

"Father!" Caroline exclaimed.

"No trouble in here," the barman warned, standing straight.

"No trouble," James Diamond agreed affably. "Merely a family reunion."

"Two reunions," Lord Chimes said. "And I don't know yet about trouble."

"Nonsense. Come, sit with us," Geoffrey's father invited. "Bring these travelers some stew," he said to the barman.

"And red wine," Geoffrey added, feeling Caroline trembling beside him.

They crossed the small room and, surprisingly, Lord Chimes grasped his daughter's shoulders and drew her in for a hug.

"Your mother and I were worried," he told her, loudly enough for them all to hear.

Geoffrey felt like a cad for the first time since they'd fled London. Then before he could do so himself, her father drew out a chair for her.

In the next instant, to his astonishment, he found himself sitting with the two fathers as if it were the most normal thing in the world to be caught trying to elope.

"You made good time," Geoffrey said. "I imagine you didn't get any sleep."

"You are correct," his father said. "At least, not a full night. We wasted time looking for you at some of the inns along the way." With that statement, he glared at Lord Chimes.

"It's true I had hoped we would find you before you reached this godforsaken place."

"Hear now!" said the barman who was delivering their bowls of stew and a basket of bread. "That's uncalled for."

"I meant the village, sir, not your fine establishment," Lord Chimes said.

"Wine," Geoffrey croaked, making a desperate drinking motion with his hand.

"Coming up," the man said and departed.

"We looked in some of the more likely coaching inns," James Diamond continued. "And then we gave up and rode like the devil was after us. We've been here for hours." He looked pleased with himself.

"What if we hadn't come in here," Geoffrey asked.

"We've paid people in all the nearby hotels to keep an eye open for you."

"There's only two others," Lord Chimes said. Then he fixed Geoffrey with a hard stare.

"In truth, you're lucky you made it this far. If I'd found my daughter with you in one of those inns, I would have taken her directly home," Lord Chimes said.

Then he looked at Caroline. "You're awfully quiet, Daughter. What do you have to say for yourself?"

Geoffrey watched her take a deep breath, visibly sit taller, and then address her father with confidence.

"I am quite pleased to be marrying Lord Diamond no matter the how and the where of it. I hope you won't try to stop us. You cannot do so, here in Scotland."

"Only with my pistol," Lord Chimes threatened.

Geoffrey startled and saw his father straighten, too. He had no doubt whose side his father would be on should violence erupt.

"Father!" Caroline admonished. "The law is on our side."

"Speaking in jest," Lord Chimes grumbled. "Merely in jest."

"We plan to marry in the morning and head straight back to London," Geoffrey explained to the man who would be his father-in-law.

He wished he could add that he hadn't laid a finger on Caroline and had waited for her to become his lawful wife. Yet such restraint had proven impossible.

"You cannot marry," Lord Chimes said.

Geoffrey looked to his father for support but found none.

"As much as I hate to agree with Chimes on anything he says, he is correct," Lord Diamond said. "You cannot. And if we have to use force to stop you, we will."

Chapter Fifteen

"I love him," Caroline declared. She glanced at Geoffrey, and he winked, giving her strength. "As deeply as you love Mother," she said to her father. And then she addressed her would-be father-in-law. "And as assuredly as you love Lady Diamond."

The barman took that moment to deliver a carafe of ruby-red wine and two glasses. With haste born of the tension that had Caroline's nerves stretched taut, Geoffrey poured them each a full glass, and they drank a hardy sip.

"That may be, Lady Caroline," said the Earl Diamond, "but you cannot marry tomorrow morning. You cannot marry my son until his mother and your mother arrive."

Caroline's mouth dropped slightly open before she regained her composure.

"My mother is coming? Here?"

"With *my* mother?" Geoffrey asked. "Together?"

"In the same carriage," her father assured her.

"Impossible," Caroline murmured, thinking she would have to see the two women descend from the same coach to believe it.

"When they arrive, which may be by the end of tomorrow if they followed the same path as you, then we shall have one of these anvil weddings," Lord Diamond said.

Her father shook his head slowly. "It might be better to get one of the innkeepers to do it." They all turned as one to look at the barman who was blowing his nose on a rag and drinking what appeared to be a large glass of whisky.

"Or some type of *official* person, if not an actual vicar," her father continued. "Your mother will have a fit if you let a blacksmith marry you."

Caroline considered all the demands her mother might make when she arrived. The wedding could be delayed for days if not weeks.

"This is why we eloped," she protested. "We are not supposed to wait for family or worry about the officiator. Next thing, Mother will arrive and want to order a special gown."

"You should have traveled as quickly as Diamond and I did if you wanted to elope without interference," her father said, "not dillydallying up the countryside, stopping each night."

As he said the last word, his gaze turned to Geoffrey. His expression became a scowl. "I'm sure you had separate rooms for the journey."

Caroline pressed her lips together, but Geoffrey swallowed his wine in a gulp and began to cough, spluttering the wooden table with droplets. His father reached around and began to pound his back until he held up his hand.

She was glad when Geoffrey said nothing. It was better not to respond than to offer an outright lie.

"There is nothing for it," she said, changing the subject. "We shall have to wait for the ladies. Hopefully, the weather remains clear. Now, I shall eat my stew and get a good night's sleep, for I vow I have barely—" she cut herself off.

What a ninny! She nearly told both the fathers how little sleep she'd had the past two nights. *And how would she explain that?*

"Both inns were extremely loud," Geoffrey said into the awkward silence.

"A good thing this one seems perfectly quiet," her father said tightly, continuing to glare at Geoffrey.

Caroline felt the heat rush to her cheeks. She could never have imagined sitting at a table with three noblemen, one of whom was her father, with the prattle being about her sleeping or not sleeping, as the case had been.

Another mortifying moment occurred when they retired. The barman led her and Geoffrey upstairs to a room. A single room.

"I told you," Geoffrey said, "we need two."

"You said the other was for your servants," the man protested. "In any case, this is the last one, and both your trunks have been put inside by your footman."

"My son will sleep with me," Lord Diamond said, averting disaster. "Grab your case."

Hurrying to avoid the sight of their trunks resting side by side taking up all the floor space, Geoffrey hefted it into his arms. She stood aside so he could exit the small room.

"Goodnight, Lady Caroline," he said politely as if they'd never been entwined naked in each other's arms. And he disappeared from view around her father, who stood with his arms crossed in the hall.

Just like that, without even being able to give Geoffrey a kiss, she found herself alone in the room where a single lamp had been lit and three small chunks of coal were smoldering.

"I'm in the room directly beside yours," her father said as a warning more than to reassure her of her safety. Then he closed the door on her astonished face.

As it turned out, she slept like the dead after stripping off her outer garments and climbing into the soft bed in her shift. However, in the morning, two astonishing things happened.

"Did you see the snow?" she asked Geoffrey, who was seated in the room across from where they'd eaten the night before. The hearth was glowing, and he was the only one there, reading an old newspaper and drinking tea.

He rose to his feet upon her entrance.

"I couldn't miss it. There was a large gap in the window glazing in our room, and the snow started blowing in last night before we stuffed my father's handkerchief in the hole."

"It's beautiful," she exclaimed with a sigh.

"Not when it's on your counterpane," he said. "Besides, the only beauty I see is you."

With that, she walked directly into his outstretched arms, and they shared a kiss. Her body tingled when his mouth touched hers, and she couldn't help pressing close.

"A fine sight for a father to see on Christmas Eve."

Belatedly, they sprang apart. With cheeks flaming, she faced her father.

"Seeing your daughter in love should be a fine sight, indeed," she told him. Then she realized what he'd said. "Christmas Eve! Is it?"

She looked at Geoffrey. "I hadn't realized."

He appeared equally astonished. "Nor I. I suppose we had our minds on other matters, and the month slipped away."

Lord Diamond came in looking concerned. "I may head out to find the ladies. They should still be about five hours away. The snow has stopped, so I doubt they will get stuck anywhere, but I don't want to risk it."

"I'll go with you," her father said.

She felt a tingle of anticipation. She and Geoffrey would be left alone again. By the quick smile upon his handsome face, he realized the same thing, quelling it just as quickly when their fathers stopped discussing their travel plans.

"We'll trust you to remain here," Lord Diamond said.

"And unwed," her father added.

"Of course," Geoffrey answered. "I would offer to go, too, but I don't want to leave Lady Caroline alone in this place."

"Hear now!" said the barman as he brought in tea service. "That's uncalled for," he repeated his words from the night before, sounding as if he were used to having his establishment slighted. "We have no trouble in this inn."

"You have a broken window," Lord Diamond said, "giving us a chilly night."

The man's eyebrows rose, but he set down the plain wooden tea tray. "We'll put some wax paper on it if you're staying another night."

"I believe we are," Lord Diamond said.

The barman rubbed his hands. "Don't usually have our rooms all filled for two nights in a row by the same folks." And he wandered off, presumably to tell Mattie in the kitchen the good news.

"I'll have a cup of tea," her father said, "and one of those scones before we go."

Lord Diamond shrugged, but in two minutes, all four of them, including both the fathers, were tucking into scones with cream and thistle jelly.

Caroline wondered how terribly disloyal it would be if she and Geoffrey married and left as soon as the men went in search of their wives.

And then a third astonishing thing happened. The front door of the inn opened, and the two mothers blew in along with a frigid gust. Caroline could see it all through the open sitting-room doorway.

"Mother!" she exclaimed, jumping up, causing the three men to do the same.

The two ladies turned in amazement and stumbled into the room.

"Isn't this a fine how-do-you-do!" Caroline's mother exclaimed. "We're out in the brutal elements, and they're all inside here warm as toast. And eating it, too."

They all started talking at once.

"Did they marry?" Lady Diamond asked.

"How did you get here so quickly?" Lord Chimes asked.

"Did you stop them?" Lady Chimes asked.

"Are the horses in good condition?" Lord Diamond wondered.

"Would you like tea?" Caroline offered.

"Is this the best inn in the area?" Lady Diamond asked, looking around.

"Hush," Geoffrey said. That made the four parents stop and stare at him with varying degrees of annoyance. "Please, ladies, won't you sit and warm up? We'll get more tea and scones."

At the commotion, the barman wandered in. "I don't have any more rooms," he said, rubbing his hands with glee at being full up. "But I'll bring more tea and my wife's scones."

"We won't need more rooms," Lord Diamond said. "These ladies are with us."

Caroline considered that statement. They certainly would not need another room if she and Geoffrey married that very day.

"My father and Lord Diamond were about to head out and find you, thinking you still hours away."

Her mother made a face, and Lady Diamond raised a perfect eyebrow.

"It looked to me as though they were stuffing their potato traps, not the least bit worried over us," the latter said.

"How did you get here so quickly?" Lord Chimes repeated his question while he dragged more chairs to the table.

"We didn't stop the second night. The innkeeper's wife had an elbow for weather, and she said—"

"I beg your pardon," Geoffrey's father interrupted. "Did you say an elbow for weather?"

"Yes," Lady Diamond said. "Her elbow twinges when snow is imminent."

"And it was twinging," Lady Chimes agreed. "We ate our supper and continued on with fresh horses."

"But how did you find us here?" Geoffrey asked.

"Your carriage is parked directly across on the square. I hope no one steals it."

"Hear now!" said the barman, who was carrying in another tea tray, piled high with scones and jam.

"That's uncalled for," Caroline, Geoffrey, and the two fathers said at the same time as the barman.

The ladies looked at all of them as if they were lunatics.

"If we'd stayed at the last inn," Lady Diamond said once she had a cup of tea in hand, "we might have spent our Christmas Eve and Christmas Day trapped there, too."

"How brave of you," Lord Diamond said, looking fondly at his wife before taking another bite of warm scone.

"Never mind that," Caroline's mother snapped. "Are these young people married?"

Caroline's father answered. "We told them they couldn't do so until you arrived."

Her mother pursed her lips and shook her head while Lady Diamond observed her with interest. Hopefully, she wouldn't mind having Caroline for a daughter-in-law.

"Do you condone this marriage now?" her mother asked her father.

Caroline held her breath.

Chapter Sixteen

Caroline felt Geoffrey take her hand and give it a reassuring squeeze. What's more, he did it in front of everyone. Whatever her parents and his parents said, she knew they would marry, even if they had to run away again, farther into Scotland.

"We are too late for condoning," Lord Diamond pronounced.

"Or for prohibiting," her father added. "Our daughter has spent three days alone traveling with this man. They must marry. I think we all know that now."

Caroline felt a twinge in her stomach, and it had nothing to do with the miracle of snow. Mortification, embarrassment, a little shame over causing their parents to come such a long way chasing after them—*were she and Geoffrey selfish?*

She glanced up at him, and the warm sparkle in his eyes quashed all her doubts. They were in love after all.

"Very well," her mother said. "Allow Lady Diamond and I to get our feet under us, and then we shall bear witness to the marriage of our children."

Caroline was surprised to see Geoffrey's mother nodding. "Agreed," Lady Diamond said. "Do they have chocolate here, by the way? Or only tea?"

After all the hullabaloo, the actual anvil ceremony was almost humdrum. Geoffrey was pleased to have the entire authentic experience once the mothers agreed to the location. The King's Head barman said he could do the proceedings if pressed, but referred them to the best officiator, the smithy next to the road in the very center of Gretna Green.

Thus, around two o'clock, the party of six strolled from the inn across the grassy green to the blacksmith's shop. The apprentice was the first to greet them, and he went to find Mr. Lang, who appeared in his heavy apron in the open doorway.

"Will you marry them?" asked Lord Chimes, nodding toward Geoffrey and Caroline.

The man grinned to see an entire wedding party when usually he was faced with only a harried couple, looking fearfully over their shoulders.

"Aye, if you've got the coin."

Geoffrey was astonished when Caroline's father did, indeed, pay the blacksmith, handing over two guineas and earning a kiss on his cheek from his grateful daughter. They entered the hot, almost stifling workroom.

And then the man asked them their names as he and Caroline stood before him holding hands. Mr. Lang even managed to bring a little formality to the absurdly brief ceremony, mentioning God and trust and long happiness before proclaiming them man and wife.

When the blacksmith told them they could kiss, Geoffrey thought it would be the most uncomfortable thing he'd done in his whole life. Moreover, it might earn him Lord and Lady Chimes's fury. Regardless, as soon as he locked gazes with Caroline, she smiled up at him. In front of all those watching, he gave her a brief but firm kiss.

Then Mr. Lang lifted a hammer resting at the wooden base, which held an anvil, and gave the iron a mighty whack.

"The sound will tell the whole village another couple has married," the man said. Then he handed each of them a calling card. "Tell your friends of my easy, swift, affordable service."

With that, he walked away, unconcerned about their signing a register. Regardless, the apprentice provided a half-sheet of paper, a "certificate," he called it proudly, which he said they could put their names on as well as those of their witnesses. Then he, too, disappeared.

Geoffrey glanced down. "The blacksmith can write, apparently. He has signed his name." He handed this to his father.

"Simon," Lord Diamond exclaimed. He started to laugh. "My boy, heir to an earldom, has just been wed by a Simple Simon."

Lord Chimes didn't look so amused. "As long as it's legal." He peered at the card in his hand before shoving it into his pocket. "Tell our friends! Hardly."

The mothers were silent. Then each sniffed and withdrew a handkerchief, wiping their noses and dabbing at their eyes. It might be because the building was hot as Hades, but more likely, sentimentality had overcome each of them.

"Lady Chimes, please don't cry," Geoffrey said. "I have gained a second mother, and I vow never to give your daughter a moment's grief. I shall make her as happy as I am able."

The lady nodded before hugging her daughter and then taking her husband's hand.

Geoffrey's father slapped him on the shoulder, and Lady Diamond actually hugged Caroline.

"Welcome to the Diamond family."

"Thank you, my lady. I hope to be a worthy member."

Lord Chimes, who was still within earshot, let out a loud snort of derision.

Before any unpleasantness could arise, Geoffrey said, "I think it would be a good idea to cross back over into England and lodge at the closest coaching inn before dark. One that has a bit of luxury to it. The Crown and Blade, perhaps."

With everyone in agreement, they returned to the King's Head and packed up, much to the disappointment of the barman.

"For the first time, I am helping you into our carriage as my wife," Geoffrey said to Caroline, who hadn't stopped beaming since he'd kissed her at the blacksmith's.

She offered a squeak of excitement and settled in on the same side as him. The bricks had been warmed, they had a woolen blanket over their laps, and a flask of brandy. Their mothers had been joined by their fathers in the earl's coach with the horses tied up to follow.

"I am extremely glad not to be in my father's carriage," he said. "I cannot imagine how thick the silence, nor conversely how tense the conversation."

"And to think, we brought about their new friendship," she said teasingly.

He laughed. In the next instant, she'd twisted to face him and put her arms around him.

"That was a tepid kiss at Simple Simon's, dear husband. I think we can do better."

Long before sunset, they reached the Crown and Blade. A celebratory meal was ordered, and the three married couples were assigned their rooms.

"I don't care if we were given the smallest room of the three," Caroline said. "We only need room for the bed."

"You are a wanton wife," Geoffrey said, "and I would strip you now had we time. Being without you last night was torture. But our parents will be waiting in the dining room."

"I'm sure they are already drinking wine and won't notice if we're a little late. In fact, isn't it expected?"

"I believe you are the wiser of the two of us, Lady Diamond. In fact, you would be expected to change from that pretty gown into something less delicate."

"Daphne was an angel to loan it to me, but no one saw it under my redingote."

"I see it now, and you are the loveliest bride I could ever imagine."

"Thank you. But undress me quickly."

With the hearth already glowing, warming their small room, Geoffrey removed all her layers until she stood bare before him in the rosy light.

"What is my excuse for appearing downstairs in different clothing?" he asked, shedding his jacket and waistcoat before tearing off his cravat.

She sighed. "No excuse is needed. You are a new husband. And if you don't touch me this instant, you will have broken your promise to keep me always happy."

She took the two steps to the bed, which sported a thick mattress, puffy with down. Scrambling onto it, she gave him a delightful view of her rear end.

He stepped out of his trousers, nearly tripping in his haste, and joined her. First a thorough kiss, with dancing tongues and sighs of relief at having made it exactly where they wanted to be.

Then he ran his finger across her nipple which pearled, begging him to kiss it. He complied.

"Are you truly mine to love and pleasure for the rest of our lives?" He could hardly believe it.

"I am. But we must make love hastily at this moment and can do it again more languidly after dinner."

"As I said before, you are the wiser of the two of us." He covered her body, settling between her thighs.

In a short while, they reached the pinnacle of their passion together.

As they were dressing, Caroline said, "I half expected my mother to knock on the door and ask what was taking us so long."

"That would have diminished my ardor considerably," Geoffrey told her.

"I confess I am more comfortable in a thicker weave. And I am exceedingly grateful we don't have to go any farther than the dining room tonight. Will you do up the buttons, please?"

"I am already turned into a lady's maid," he teased.

"Is it every husband's dread?"

"Not this husband," Geoffrey vowed. "I am honored. Glad you didn't accept either of those young men I saw you with in the autumn, one at the theatre and the other at the park."

Furrowing her brow, Caroline considered, and then she widened her eyes.

"Oh, sweet husband. I hate to tell you this, but you were jealous of my own brothers."

Stunned, Geoffrey considered.

"Then I guess I should be glad they didn't ride to Scotland, too. They might have been less understanding than your parents."

"Truly. My eldest brother might still wish to punch you in the nose for eloping with me. I suppose they are having Christmas alone this year."

"They'll blame me for that, too."

"Probably."

"Before I get into any more trouble," Geoffrey suggested, "let's go down to dinner."

After a sumptuous Christmas repast of two soups and sixteen dishes, including doe-venison and goose, a roasted vegetable dish of parsnips, potatoes, and leeks, and poached pears and walnuts with fresh cream, their party of six sat with three empty carafes of wine on the table.

With their stomachs bulging, the Diamonds and the Chimes began to bicker.

"What was the wretched wager?" Lady Chimes demanded of her husband. "Didn't this rascal," she jerked a thumb at Lord Diamond, "try to make you claim *his* wife was the most beautiful woman in London?"

"What!" exclaimed Lady Diamond. "I never heard of such a thing. It would be vulgar, no matter its veracity."

"In fact," Lord Chimes said, already red-cheeked, "the scoundrel tried to get me to claim that *you*, my lady wife, were *not* the most beautiful woman."

Lady Chimes's mouth worked as she considered. "Are you saying you lost the wager because you wouldn't disparage me?"

"When Diamond set up the wager and said he would name the most beautiful woman in London and that I couldn't disprove it, how could I know he would name my own wife? But he was correct, I couldn't disprove it. I couldn't lie," Lord Chimes said. "You are the most beautiful woman, not just in London, but in all of England, as far as I'm concerned. Before a room full of our peers, I wouldn't gainsay him. Thus, I paid my debt."

"You thought I would name my own wife, I suppose," Lord Diamond said, looking far too delighted at having outfoxed the other man.

"Any honorable man would have done so," Lord Chimes stated, wiping the glee off the other man's face.

Lady Diamond's expression was furious as she rounded on her husband.

"In front of all the men at White's, you declared Lady Chimes to be the most beautiful woman."

"In *London*," Lord Diamond corrected. "And you were at our country home in Derbyshire." He let that sink in.

Meanwhile, Lady Chimes had moved closer to her own husband. "Then you didn't wish you had ended up with her?" She jerked her head toward Geoffrey's mother.

Lord Chimes appeared shocked. "Of course not. She's vain, fickle, and flighty."

"I say!" Lady Diamond interrupted.

"Indeed," Lord Diamond added, setting down his glass and leaning toward Lord Chimes. "You must apologize for such slander at once."

"Oh no, dear husband," Lady Diamond said. "He speaks the truth but still! He didn't have to say it so boldly."

"Indeed," said Lord Diamond again. "Apologize to my wife for stating the truth so boldly and in mixed company, too. She may be vain, fickle, and flighty, but she's perfect for me."

Lady Diamond started to laugh. "I'm glad to hear that." And then her husband draped his arm around her.

Lord and Lady Chimes stared at them as if they were in a madhouse. But then, the lady had another question for her husband.

"So, you don't hate Diamond for taking *her* away from you?"

"No, I hate him because he swindled me out of a goodly sum with his tricky wager."

"Well, do you loathe the Lady Diamond for going with him?" Lady Chimes persisted.

"Again, no. I'm glad she went with him because it opened the way for me to find you. But why do *you* hate him?" Lord Chimes demanded of his wife.

"I don't really," she confessed, "only for your sake, dearest. I thought he'd pricked your pride and was a dishonorable dog to boot."

Lady Diamond patted her husband's cheek. "He's not a dog, but he's no saint, either. After all, he did lead me down the garden path," she pointed out. "I never had a blemish upon my reputation before."

This caused Lord Diamond to break out into whoops of laughter that instantly snatched the affectionate expression from Lady Diamond's face.

Ignoring them both, Lady Chimes spoke only to her husband. "Anyway, it was *her* I hated because I thought she had won your heart before I ever had the chance."

"No, my love. From the moment I saw you, I knew you were meant to be mine."

Finally, Geoffrey spoke up. "That is precisely how I felt when I first saw Lady Caroline. That is, when I first bumped into her."

"And I, when I saw him," she admitted. "I didn't know he was meant to be mine exactly, but I felt a sizzle of interest to discover if I wanted him to be mine."

"And did you?" he asked.

"Most certainly, I did."

Not a single one of their parents was bothering to listen.

"But after our long journey together," Lady Diamond said, "we don't hate one another anymore."

Lady Chimes frowned. "Why did *you* hate me?"

"Because you so easily took my place with Lord Chimes, as if I didn't matter. Also, because you're a mushroom."

"Shall we take a stroll outside and discuss our future?" Geoffrey asked her.

"It's rather frosty out," she reminded him. "Perhaps we could stroll inside the inn instead. Or maybe we could simply retire for the night."

By her sparkling gaze, he knew they would find something interesting to do in their small but plush room. Offering her his arm, which she took, they left behind their parents, still squabbling and discussing the distant past.

He didn't care. All he cared about was having fulfilled his goal for the year, finding and marrying the most perfect woman!

Epilogue

"Are you awake?" Caroline whispered.

Geoffrey yawned and rolled over, seeing her green eyes open and her glorious red hair spread out upon the pillow. He grinned.

"We just had our first full night in bed as husband and wife," he said, as if it was a revelation she might not have realized.

She nodded. "And it's Christmas day. How did we forget?"

"I guess we had other things on our minds." He still did, and he started to reach for her.

"Luckily, I have a gift for you, something I was working on in the carriage during our journey to Gretna Green. I thought up a poem and memorized it."

"I thought you were sleeping quite a bit. I didn't realize someone could snore while dreaming up poetry."

She smacked his shoulder. "I do not snore. And I promise you, I was fashioning a poem. I haven't had a chance to write it down, but as your Christmas present, I shall recite it for you."

He drew the sheet and blanket down to expose her bare breasts.

"Go ahead." But one of his hands stroked the sensitive area at her waist, making her shiver.

She laughed. "You are being wicked and will make me forget my poetry."

"Very well. I will behave." He placed his palm on her stomach, then brushed back and forth with the pad of his thumb, which was even more distracting.

Taking a breath, she began:

"Like Romeo and Juliet, we were thwarted from the start.
Yet unlike her, I shall not end with a dagger in my heart."

Geoffrey startled at her choice of words. "Caroline, that's rather—"

"*Shh,* I'm not finished!" She cleared her throat and continued.

"At first, I wondered 'wherefore art thou Diamond?'
A name I was not allowed to love nor to dance."

"You can't dance with a name," he pointed out, feeling the hint of laughter stirring inside him. She shook her head to silence him.

"What's in a name? I asked. By any other, you would still smell like a rose."

He bit his lower lip wanting to giggle.

"And for the rest of my life, my full heart will happily prance."

"Stop, please," he begged. Her poem was so awful he knew he would be unable to hold in his laughter any longer.

"But there is much more," Caroline protested. "Don't you want to hear about my boundless love? The more I have, the more I give to you for both are infinite."

He chuckled. "You just mangled one of Shakespeare's best lines."

She blinked innocently, then she shrugged. "I couldn't possibly say it any better. I was teasing you. I really was sleeping in the carriage."

"Thank God. Your poem was dreadful."

"I'll say only this—I am glad you stumbled into me at the Fenwicks' ball."

"'They stumble that run fast,' said the Bard's Friar Lawrence."

Scrunching up her nose, Caroline shook her head. "I don't think that applies, or at least, I hope not."

He leaned over and placed a kiss on the gentle curve of her stomach.

"I think you're correct. Our story is already faring much better than Romeo and Juliet's. Let's forget about them. Besides, I don't need anything more from you. You have presented me with the most wonderful gift already. Quite simply, you gave me yourself."

Again, he kissed her stomach, and while he was deciding whether to move up or down, he added, "I am the one who must think of what to give you on this special day."

She stroked his hair, her fingers threading through it, tugging gently.

"Dearest husband, how many women can say they received a Diamond for Christmas? I need nothing else."

He began to kiss a trail along her body.

"On the other hand," she said, her breath catching in her throat when his tongue touched her, "it would be rude of me to turn down your generosity."

"Merry Christmas, Wife."

"Merry Christmas, Husband."

The End

Thank you for reading *A Diamond for Christmas* by *USA Today* Bestselling author Sydney Jane Baily!

. . .

Are you eager to meet Caroline's and Geoffrey's five diamonds?

Read *Clarity*'s story. The eldest daughter in the Diamond clan. She is breathtaking, joyful, and adventurous... and entirely unsuitable to become Lord Alex Hollidge's viscountess! Or is she?

Find out in this fun and sexy early Victorian romance!

Also by Sydney Jane Baily

Diamonds of the First Water

Four sparkling sisters and their dash-fire brother dazzle the London social Season. Enjoy the excitement of Mayfair's ballrooms and the luxury of country house parties in this romantic new series with mischief, misunderstandings, and mayhem. And of course passion!

#1 Clarity

#2 Purity

#3 Adam

#4 Radiance

#5 Brilliance

DIAMONDS OF THE FIRST WATER SERIES

About Sydney Jane Baily

USA Today bestselling author Sydney Jane Baily writes historical romance set in Victorian England, late 19th-century America, the Middle Ages, the Georgian era, and the Regency period. She believes in happy-ever-after stories with engaging characters and attention to period detail.

Born and raised in California, she has traveled the world, spending a lot of exceedingly happy time in the U.K. where her extended family resides, eating fish and chips, drinking shandies, and snacking on Maltesers and Cadbury bars. Sydney currently lives in New England with her family—human, canine, and feline.

At her website, SydneyJaneBaily.com, you can learn more about her books, read her blog, sign up for her newsletter (& get a free book), and contact her. She loves to hear from her readers. To be notified of her new releases, please follow Sydney on BookBub or Amazon. Or you can connect with her on Facebook.

facebook.com/sydney.jane.baily

bookbub.com/authors/sydney-jane-baily

amazon.com/Sydney-Jane-Baily/e/B009LAIOM6

goodreads.com/sydney_jane_baily

tiktok.com/sydneywritesromance

THE GOVERNESS GAMBLE

A DUCHESS SOCIETY SERIES NOVELLA

TRACY SUMNER

The Governess Gamble by Tracy Sumner

Published by WOLF Publishing UG

About the book

THE GOVERNESS GAMBLE

A woman from another world...

American Heiress Francine Shaw never dreamed she would become a governess! But desperate times call for desperate measures when Francine must flee to London to escape a scandal, save her reputation and... find a titled man to marry or risk losing her family.

But when her new employer turns out to be a "love 'em and leave 'em" rake, Fanny finds herself trapped in more ways than one. Stunned by the sizzling heat she finds developing between herself and the handsome and enigmatic Viscount Remington, she bravely makes him an offer he can't refuse...

He's not who she thinks he is...

As it turns out, Francine is not the only one who is hiding her true identity. Despite his devilish reputation, Chance Allerton has a tender heart of gold—and has secretly vowed to marry for nothing less than love. When he learns he has a ward just before Christmastide, he seeks the aid of the Duchess Society in the hopes of finding a governess for the child. When a beautiful, clever American hellion shows up on his doorstep instead, Chance is soon in over his head.

Francine Shaw exceeds his every expectation… and soon Chance finds himself utterly infatuated.

Can a wicked viscount learn to love? Or is this dalliance with the governess merely a Christmas tryst destined to end in heartache?

If I could but know his heart, everything would become easy.
-Marianne Dashwood, *Sense and Sensibility*

Chapter One

Where Our Heroine Becomes an Accidental Governess

A Warm Parlor in a Cold Country
Limehouse, December 1823

Of all the salons in London, he had to walk into hers.

Although he didn't notice her.

Which wasn't a surprise as she wasn't noticeable.

Francine Shaw recorded Lord Remington's brazen entrance, recognition rolling through her like a wave off the ocean she'd crossed to get to this grit-choked city. During her time in England, almost six months now, he was the only man who had sparked her interest.

A fascination that ticked upward each time she'd seen him.

A notorious libertine who didn't even know her name.

While Franny's job, according to her father, was to attract a destitute nobleman, not a rake, and unite centuries of English nobility with her family's common-yet-prosperous lineage.

Two unremarkable people in an unremarkable world.

An unremarkable marriage but a solid business venture.

Franny grimaced behind her gloved hand, recognizing the irony. She was *exactly* as expected. A covetous American in want of a title. While William Allerton, fourth or fifth Viscount Remington, she couldn't recall without consulting *Debrett's*, was exactly as expected as well. A handsome scoundrel fighting to retain his masculine liberties while protecting a legacy he feasibly hadn't wanted in the first place. She'd heard the story numerous times batted about society parlors like a ball. No one in London seemed to have the funds to maintain the burdens they'd inherited.

In America, most inherited nothing and fought for *everything*.

As the viscount crossed the room, Franny tucked herself tighter into the recessed alcove, her back butting the chilled windowpanes overlooking the Thames. She peeked around the velvet drape, perfectly content to hide during this exchange. *Damn and blast*, she vowed, her heart giving a hard kick. Lord Remington looked as delectable as ever. Stylish but not flawless. Sturdily rumpled. Dark hair in relaxed disarray. Tall and trim, with an athletic grace few men in society could claim.

She sighed softly, giving her hands a tremulous clench. Thankfully, the echoes of ships banging the dock and the shouts of stevedores unloading crates funneled inside her nook, hiding any sound she might make. Interestingly enough, at least to Franny, Mrs. Hildegard Streeter, recently married to Mr. Tobias Streeter, rogue king of the Limehouse docks or so the scandal sheets claimed, occasionally chose to conduct business from her husband's rookery warehouse.

Today that business was with Franny. In a vibrant, vile neighborhood her father would faint upon learning she'd agreed to visit.

This morning had been the most exhilarating Franny had experienced in months. Which said much about her state of boredom *and* her predisposition for trouble.

"You've got to help me," Lord Remington said, his first words spoken, the casualness of the statement detailing a startlingly close relationship with Mrs. Streeter. The viscount didn't stop until he practically bumped the desk Hildy sat behind with his lean hip, casting a twisted grin her way, charm he was renowned for.

He was taller than Franny had realized, a shade too thin perhaps. But with broad shoulders and chiseled features one didn't easily forget. Something apart from his physical gifts, however, captured her attention. Lurking beneath his careless smile was serious intent. Even, possibly, a hint of vulnerability.

Franny wasn't the only woman enthralled. He'd been known to dance not a set, yet leave the ballroom with the most beautiful woman in attendance.

Hildy, perhaps the most stunning creature in England, calmly placed her quill beside her folio, her brow winging high. Daughter of an earl who had married a smuggler-cum-architect for an improbable love the likes of which London had never seen, she had it all. Had what Franny *wanted.* Aspirations considered silly on this side of the ocean, and the one she claimed across the way.

For once, England and America were in agreement.

Wishing to be someone's once-in-a-lifetime anything was pointless—when marriage was a business. She'd been raised by a father who believed in nothing *but* business.

Love had never factored into the equation, not once.

Bringing Franny from her musing, Mrs. Streeter laughed and smoothed her hand across the desk, her elegance truly admirable when Franny recognized the defiant personality buried beneath. "Chance, you're coming to me, oh, about a year sooner than expected. But I did expect it."

Chance. Franny pressed her palm to her belly, her cheeks heating. *Chance.*

Remington choked out a groan and dropped into the chair across from Hildy. Hooking a boot certain to be Hoby on his opposite knee, he drummed a silent tune on his thigh. "Oh, *no*. No matchmaking, Hild. No Countess Society or whatever it is you've got going. I need help, but not that kind." His smile dimmed, the song on his thigh going silent. "Not yet, anyway."

"We're not matchmakers," Hildy murmured. Although in a roundabout way, they were. She and the Duchess of Markham, Georgiana Munro, had created the Duchess Society with the thought to empower women on the cusp of marriage. Review of marital contracts and placement in a union not solely benefitting the husband. In the course of business, matchmaking had occurred even if Hildy and Georgie preferred to lightly conceal this fact. Their endeavors also included investigation into prospective partners, which is why Franny was there. Men in want of a wife often lied about their circumstances. Franny's father had someone he thought would make an adequate husband. *Adequate* was all he was shooting for. A baron he wanted to ensure wasn't in worse financial trouble than he'd stated.

Remington dropped his head back, his gaze crawling to the ceiling. Franny drank him in like brandy, drawing the strong line of his stubbled jaw on her palm. He had a crook at the top of his nose from some misadventure. Her fingertips itched to sketch him. The pad of paper and pencil hidden away in her spencer's pocket fairly shouted to be released. "You've made quite an exceptional life for yourself, Hild. Queen to the rogue king, the two of you ruling Limehouse. If I hadn't seen you together, I'd likely never believe it myself."

Hildy's cheeks pinkened as they did when anyone brought up her husband, Tobias. Her love, a glow that radiated like a flame to brighten the room. "Enough flattery, Chance, out with it."

"I've got a problem," he finally said, his voice sullen. Swiping a thick strand the color of charcoal from his brow, he slid lower in the chair. "An immense one."

Hildy rearranged a folio on her desk, patience personified. "Is it Arthur?"

Remington grunted softly and yanked again at his hair. It was longer than current style dictated, the locks snaking around his slim fingers like a vine, dusting the edge of his collar. He'd apparently left his hat in his carriage because Franny could see an indentation where it had recently sat on his head. "Unbelievably, my brother has managed to remain at Cambridge for the term. I negotiated a settlement of sorts for the brawl in the Wren Library. It's been around since the 1600s, so they're fairly protective of the place. As if the crumbling roof on the estate in Hampshire wasn't enough to deal with.

"Tenants in Derbyshire are set to revolt after the way my father left things. The townhouse in Berkeley Square is not in the grandest condition, either. This title is killing me. If not for my side project, and your husband's valued partnership, I'd be in appalling financial shape like the rest of the *ton*. My dipping my toe in trade sickens them but saves *me*. For the moment."

Hildy braced her palm on the desk and rose. Strolling to the stack of crates serving as a mock sideboard, she shot Franny a fast look and brushed her index finger across her lips—*quiet*. A command Franny was exceedingly happy to follow. "You know Toby and I are more than willing to assist if you need a loan. I've known you since we were children, Chance. There aren't many friendships I value, but yours is one of them. My mother even said, if we traced our lines back far enough, we'd find we were cousins."

"Well, Cousin, my solicitors have informed me that I have a ward. A little girl. Six years old. Her father was my uncle, a distant relation three times removed or something. He left the care of her to my father, so she now falls to me along with the rest. When I've never even had a sister to look after. Only one unruly brother. I'm vastly out of my element here."

Hildy popped the tumbler to the sideboard, thankfully cutting off the sound of Franny's gasp. "A ward?"

"Hence my frantic need for a governess."

Hildy lifted the glass she'd likely intended for Remington and took a stunned sip. "You have frantic need of a *wife*."

Massaging the bridge of his nose, Remington closed his eyes. Franny couldn't determine their color from this distance. And she'd never been close enough to see. "I'm begging you. Through Christmastide. A fortnight. In the new year, I'll secure a proper arrangement."

"You've pedaled through a dozen mistresses. Ask one of them. The Duchess Society does not supply governesses. Or wives, for that matter."

"Bloody *hell*." Remington shoved from the chair and strode to her, snatching the glass from her hand and polishing off the contents. "Consider this a familial favor, Hild. One measly governess for a well-mannered urchin. How hard an ask is that for your society magicians? I'll pay as well as I'm able. And I'm a deuced congenial employer." This said, he unleashed a smile that crinkled the skin around his eyes, a smile that Franny felt to her toes and back. While his cousin seemed unaffected.

"Don't waste your charm on me, Chance Allerton." But she was grinning when she said it. It was confirmed then. No woman could resist the man. "Or should I now call you Lord Remington?"

The viscount's shoulders slumped, a weary sigh leaking forth. "You'll help me."

Hildy wiggled the glass from his hand. "I'll help you. But only through the holiday. A fortnight. Then you must find a permanent solution. I have two children, two felines, and a growing business to care for without worrying about you. And Arthur. And now this poor, orphaned girl."

Crossing the room, Remington halted by the door. "I must be off. I'm leaving to retrieve the girl. Then I'll be at the Derbyshire estate, which may or may not be overrun by irate tenants. I'm fairly certain it *won't* be by servants. I think my funds only employ three. I'll send a carriage round for the governess you locate on Friday. Is that enough time?" Knowing he'd won the battle, he leaned recklessly against the doorjamb, his good humor returning. His reputation for masterfully blending gallantry with a cagey hunger that drew women like cats to cream was well deserved. "I thank you from the bottom of my battered heart, Hildy."

"I'll figure something out, as I always do." Hildy tapped her knuckle on her bottom lip. "We'll be at Hampton Hall for the holiday, so I'll pop over and check on things next week. Lord Grimley is holding a ball, too. I'm assuming you were invited, along with everyone in Derbyshire."

Remington grumbled, his delight fading. Titled men were sought-after properties, even the impoverished ones, eliciting what amounted to female skirmishes on ballroom floors. She'd witnessed more than one from her frequent spot behind a fern or column.

Hildy settled the glass on the sideboard and turned to him. "The governess I send you, she's not to be dallied with, Chance."

A hint of temper sparked in his form. He straightened from his slouch, offended. "Message delivered, Hildy. You have my word. With the thousands of mistresses I apparently have, who needs a governess?" Then he tipped his head and was gone, his footfalls ringing off the scuffed planks outside Hildy's makeshift office. A brother's exit, almost rude but acceptable, again proving how close they were.

Franny stepped from behind the drape, her nerve endings tingling. She looked to find Mrs. Streeter gazing at her with a concerned expression.

"Not like any viscount you've ever seen, is he, Miss Shaw? Arrogance and helplessness wrapped in silk. What a captivating combination, and he probably doesn't even realize why."

"I'll do it."

Mrs. Streeter stumbled over a wrinkle in the Aubusson, the only graceless move Franny had ever seen her make. "Do *what*? You're here to review agreements my solicitors have preemptively drawn up for Baron Hillsdale. This tangle with Remington"—she slashed her hand through the air as if she held a wand—"has nothing to do with you. If not for my affection for the man and my appreciation of his dire situation, it would have nothing to do with me. But as you can see, he's like family, so..."

Franny shrugged and dragged her slippered toe across a silver thread in the carpet. "I haven't agreed to Hillsdale," she said in a tone that sounded less amenable than it should when she understood her fate perfectly. Her father had threatened to cut her off should she refuse to marry. "This governess gamble isn't the worst proposal unless you have someone else in mind. Lord Remington is desperate, and I'm educated fairly well for a woman. My father believed in tutors, even for a girl. I'm without any plans for the holiday, as Papa is on a ship bound for New York as we speak. A strike in one of his plants. I'm an American outcast, but perhaps this won't make much difference to a reprobate viscount in need of assistance. I can sketch the days away while helping with this girl. I like children. Strangely enough, although I have no siblings, I'm quite good with them."

And I want to sketch Lord Remington more than I want my next breath. But I need to be close enough to him to do it.

Mrs. Streeter groaned and slumped into the chair behind her desk. "Your father has requested we investigate details of the baron's situation, so he's certain of this association even if you're not. Hillsdale swears on his mother's health his debt is not worse than he's admitted. When what he's admitted is not good. He has a penchant for gaming hells without any talent to support his passion. The bright spot is, he seems rather timid around women. Therefore, there aren't any he's *keeping* if you get my meaning."

Franny strolled to the chair Lord Remington had vacated and casually settled into it as if she wasn't seeking a trace of his heat. His scent. The air smelled faintly of raw wood and leather. Her heart gave a frightening kick. "Then trust his information is accurate, as the baron is *very* attached to his mother."

Mrs. Streeter chewed on her lip. "I can talk to your father. Give you more time perhaps to meet someone—"

Franny interrupted with a flick of her hand. "If not Hillsdale, Papa will decide on someone else. At least the baron is young and rather attractive.

If you fancy bashful, light-haired men of small stature. You're going to factor my return to Philadelphia into the contracts. Should I choose to do that. This leaves me room to maneuver when I wouldn't have otherwise had that. It's my dowry he's after, not my person."

"At some point, the baron will want an heir, Miss Shaw. It's more than money with English society."

Franny glanced at the ceiling, searching for what the viscount had seen. Nothing but a tiny spider crack near the corner and row upon row of industrial crimson pipes running the length of the space. Mrs. Streeter's husband, Tobias, was an architect, in addition to an entrepreneur and distillery owner. A philanthropist. All this from a half-Romani who had crawled from the gutter to sit atop a kingdom. Coming from a country that valued the common man building an empire, Franny found this extremely impressive.

She could tell Mrs. Streeter she was aware of a wife's marital responsibilities. Aware, too, of what a physical relationship with a man entailed. She'd made a colossal mistake a year ago that had started her father down the path of seeking a marriage for his daughter, far from scandal. An idea orbiting wildly among affluent circles in Philadelphia. Purchasing a blue-blooded Brit was becoming fashionable when Franny had never been a fashionable girl.

She could also tell Mrs. Streeter she'd seen Viscount Remington exactly three times before today.

The first had snagged her like a hook beneath her skin. A musicale at an earl's townhouse, a name she couldn't recall on a day she could barely remember. She'd only been invited because her father and the earl were discussing an investment in railways in the north. She'd been hiding on the terrace, her small sketch pad balanced on the marble balustrade when she'd heard sounds rippling through the open window at her side. The click of a door, a heavy tread, a whispered sigh of appreciation. She'd leaned to peer inside, expecting to find a couple embracing.

Which would have brightened up a dreary evening considerably.

Instead, she'd found Viscount Remington crouched before an ornate bureau the English loved to call an escritoire. She'd watched in utter fascination as he ran his hand along the fine-grained rosewood, his lips parted in admiration. He had long, slim fingers better suited to a pianist. It'd been the first time—the first *true* instance—when she identified raw desire coursing through her body. A yearning so fierce it weakened her knees. She'd had to brace her hand on the balustrade to support herself.

This instance had brought to light her absolute foolishness in a murky parlor in Philadelphia. That had been nothing compared to this. Mere curiosity she'd ruined herself over.

When she'd looked back through the window, Viscount Remington had been gone.

He'd not once glanced at her that night. Or the other two times she'd seen him on the streets of London.

If she accepted this phony governess assignment, he'd have to.

"I'm frightened of the rapture on your face, Miss Shaw. Lord Remington is a complicated man, and his reputation is less than desirable. Women and wood are his main pleasures in life."

Franny huffed a startled laugh, her gaze seeking Mrs. Streeter's. "Wood?"

"If you follow through with this outrageous idea, you'll find out, anyway. He designs furniture."

Franny blinked, her curiosity growing. The scent of raw wood *had* invaded the space with him, which now made sense.

"A hobby that has grown to be more than a hobby. Although the *ton* has no idea, even if they're sitting in a chair he created. My husband and his partner, Xander Macauley, ship Lord Remington's pieces and act as cover for the business. It wouldn't do for a viscount to be openly involved in trade. Tobias even has a desk of Remington's in his study." For some reason, Mrs. Streeter's cheeks flushed at this declaration. "He's incredibly gifted. And conflicted because his talent isn't valued and likely never will be. His father was not kind, to start. His childhood wasn't a happy one."

Happy and childhood didn't belong in the same sentence. At least they hadn't belonged in Franny's sentence.

"Miss Shaw, let me be clear. I love Remington dearly, but I wouldn't want my sister, if I had one, to set her cap for him."

"I'm not setting my cap for anyone." The idea was ludicrous. She was plain. Bookish. She *looked* like a governess. Tightly wound as a clock, according to her companion, Ada, who had been with her since Franny's mother passed when she was three. Her ability to sketch was the only remarkable thing about Francine Shaw.

And her eyes. They were a rather dazzling shade of gold. But that was it.

Furthermore, she was plump when current fashion preferred reed-slim. Her hair was as badly behaved as she was, bursts of amber streaking through the curly, brown strands, feral unless she severely contained it. She even had a scattering of freckles across her cheeks. Her accent was a flat-voweled atrocity the English found vulgar. It was certain no man would offer for her that wasn't being paid to.

"Then there's the matter of your notoriety at the moment. Your father has been vocal about his hopes for you at every event he's attended. Public discourse the Duchess Society wouldn't advise, but it's too late. Unless he's been living under a rock, Lord Remington will recognize you the moment you step into his home. The moment you say one word."

"Simply tell him I've come from America and need employment. A pet project of the Duchess Society or some such. Distant relation of one of your husband's shipping partners. Lord Remington won't recognize me. I'm invisible to men like him."

Mrs. Streeter stilled, her lips parting in astonishment. "Miss Shaw, shy isn't unattractive. It may dim the blaze, but it doesn't expunge it. You're lovely and unique. It's a perilous combination."

Franny waved the comment away, unaccepting. "I'll tell my father I've been invited to a winter house party at the country estate of a viscount. Through your introduction, of course. The opportunity for encounters with titled men of modest means. Ada will hate it, but she hates everything about England. I can't change that. In any case, how challenging can one little girl and a cantankerous viscount be?" Franny crossed her fingers in the folds of her skirt, the lie rolling off her tongue like honey. "I'm only suggesting it because I have nothing better to do, and your cousin needs assistance."

Mrs. Streeter shook her head woefully. "Fine. I'll arrange it. Your last hurrah before marriage to the scant-statured baron. If your companion sticks to you like glue, and you avoid Remington as often as possible, perhaps nothing will go awry. Our home in Derbyshire is only a twenty-minute carriage ride away, should you need me."

Franny sat back with a smile, her plan in motion. She might like the country, she decided, future sketches of Chance Allerton swimming through her mind.

An orphan. An outcast. A tortured artist.

What could possibly go awry?

Chapter Two

Where a Fatigued Viscount Ponders Parenthood

Three Days Later at a Viscount's Shabby Estate

Chance threw his booted feet atop a desk in the Allerton family for two centuries and dropped his head to his hands. His skin smelled of nutmeg and chalk. He had a dab of what he hoped like hell was jam on his sleeve. He'd run circles around the house without a hint of pleasure surrounding the effort.

It was two hours past twilight, and he'd just gotten the girl to bed.

Katherine Elise Brierly, a six-year-old termagant and his problem for the rest of his *life*, wasn't well-mannered as he'd promised Hildy. She was the most talkative creature he'd ever had the misfortune to meet. She had opinions on every topic, many suited to a woman, not a child. How his cravat was tied. His boots polished. The ragged trim on her counterpane.

The tattered velvet drapes in her bedchamber. The water stains on the ceiling in the breakfast room.

Chance groaned and massaged his temples.

And the *questions*. How old was the estate? How big? Did he have horses? Why was his majordomo, Alfred, so crooked? Was he married? Did he plan to be? Did he have a dog? Perhaps kittens? The girl had stated unequivocally that she wanted kittens.

Chance glanced across the space, considering the drink cart without thought to make that wish happen.

Raising a child was a damned sight harder than it looked.

He'd found himself explaining things he could—his marital state, number of horses and pets—and leaving much of the rest to his housekeeper, Mrs. Walker. Who let him know right off she couldn't keep up with a child without the assistance of the governess variety. His father had, somewhere along the way, let Rose Hill's staff go due to dwindling funds, so they had the bare minimum. Although he'd not spent much time in Derbyshire growing up, Chance recalled Mrs. Walker being around *forever*. She was likely as old as this desk.

Despite it all, however, he liked it here. Miserable memories from his childhood weren't a part of this place.

Lifting his head, he gazed about at what had once been an impressive library. His father had sold off many of the volumes, leaving gaps on dusty shelves. Cobwebs. Streaked windowpanes. Faded carpets. General neglect, which his father had excelled at. With regard to dwellings and children.

But the foundation was solid. Like a sliver of wood that would make a gorgeous piece of furniture once he took it in hand, he knew, with hard work and an infusion of capital, he could restore the estate to some level of its former glory. There was a dowager's cottage at the edge of the woodland that would make an astounding workshop. He currently leased space in London from Xander Macauley, his shipping partner, which worked out well enough.

But this would be *his*.

It all came down to blunt he didn't have. Time he wasn't sure he could allocate when he had two *other* decaying properties to worry about. A brother in the middle of a dangerous rebellion. A thriving business, his passion. When aside from making furniture, he'd never had a passion. No woman he couldn't live without, that was certain.

He recalled the smile on Hildy's face the other day. He wanted what she had with Tobias Streeter. He truly did. Society assumed because he played fast and loose that he didn't wish for a wife, a family. He might be a scoundrel, but he was *not* a cad. Of all his affairs, none had ended, except for the one with that fanatical countess, with a vase being thrown at his head. He was friends with each and every chit he'd tupped. His predicament was more, well, he'd never needed anyone enough to *fight* for them. Or had never felt he could *let* himself need anyone might be the best way to describe his quandary.

Now this girl. Katherine Elise Brierly. Six-year-old hellion in muslin.

Was *she* the peculiar start to his family?

Chance drifted to sleep dreaming of off-limits governesses and talkative girls who tugged his heartstrings.

Viscount Remington's eyes were blue.

A piercing, haunting blue. She likened the color to the icy glints shimmering in the snowflakes swirling about. One caught on the bow of his top lip and melted while she watched, setting her knees trembling beneath more layers than she'd ever needed to wear in Philadelphia.

Alas, her shivers were not due to the brutal English winter.

His expression stunned, Remington halted in the entranceway, her portmanteau dangling from his fingers. The coachman who had accompanied her was seeing to the carriage and horses, arranging for her trunk to be delivered to her bedchamber. Her companion, Ada, stood to the side of the corridor in disparaging silence, which was as it should be. Ada was unhappy about arriving four hours late due to the storm and even *more* unhappy to be plotting a governess farce in this "blasted wreck of a country."

"You're American," Remington said, his gaze racing the length of her as if he searched for a mark to verify his evaluation.

Flustered, Franny gathered her woolen spencer at her neck and trundled into the house, shutting the door behind her with a creaking slam.

Her skin was chilled to the bone, but her cheeks were hot. "And you're a viscount who answers his own door."

He laughed, a husky surprise to the three souls huddled in the foyer of a medieval structure in obvious need of love. And heaping piles of money, Franny surmised as she gazed around.

The dwelling dazzled, nonetheless, make no mistake.

Although she'd come to sketch the man, the viscount's fortress would do in a pinch. From the ancient gatehouse at the end of the winding drive to the acres of winter-lush forest wrapped like a cloak around the estate. Towering chimney stacks rising from the snow-laden mist. A trench surrounding the house she thought could properly be called a moat. It was like nothing *she'd* ever seen. A castle straight out of the fairytales Ada had read to her when she was a child.

Remington gestured to the barren hallway. "The few servants I have are abed. My majordomo is as aged as the planks beneath our feet. He rarely makes it past sunset. Our housekeeper, Mrs. Walker, is much the same. I'm afraid it's left to me to escort you to your chamber. We're rather informal in the country."

Informal meaning impoverished. The funds needed to fully staff such a monstrous place were not available. Franny glanced over the viscount's shoulder, down the arched gallery, to the grand staircase spiraling to opposite wings of the house. Except for being wealthier than almost everyone in London, she could be Cinderella. Stepping away from her staid life for one night of adventure. Or two weeks, rather.

When she looked back, it was to find that the viscount's gaze had followed hers down the hall. From his scowl, it appeared that what she considered magnificent, he considered a burden.

"It needs work," he muttered, his chest lifting with his deep inhalation.

"It's lovely, my lord," she countered, her fingertips giving a familiar tingle, yearning to sketch. His vexed expression was nothing short of enchanting. "Majestic. Stately, even. We have nothing like this in Philadelphia. And in your family for centuries. How remarkable. My home is less than ten years old." She shrugged. "Everything in America is new."

Ada grunted and scrubbed her thumb over the scuffed oak paneling that was likely two hundred years old, obviously preferring new.

Remington took his time returning his attention to Franny. His thorough review revealed his effort to see the dwelling as she had. A considerate, unexpected response. His lashes were long and dark, dusting his skin as he blinked. His shirt and buckskins were damp at the hem and cuff, as if he'd recently returned from outdoors. He wore an unbuttoned gray waistcoat, his cravat untied and hanging loosely from his neck. No coat. Sleeves rolled to show an indecent amount of muscled forearm. He ran his palm over his unshaven cheek in contemplation, his jaw flexing with thoughts he kept to himself.

This was not the flippant lord the *ton* whispered about.

Hildy's words rang in her mind. *Doesn't look like any viscount you've ever seen, does he?*

No, he did not. It's why, from first glance, she'd been intrigued. Intrigued enough to lie about being a governess and wedging her foot inside his castle door.

The most appalling in a life of appalling decisions.

Franny's heart skipped a beat as she stared at him. Men never listened. No one who looked like him anyway, sly beauty and winsome charm. Franny spoke without expecting anyone to. The men who listened, listened because her dowry was big enough to solve their problems and nothing more.

"The well-mannered girl I promised Hildegard Streeter is a terror," he said when his gaze finally met hers. His eyes were the color of hydrangea petals, even more glorious in milky candlelight than they'd been in full moonlight. "She assured me in her letter that you're experienced enough to handle it. The chit has a thousand questions for which I have no answer. She wants biscuits and milk every other minute. Her threshold for boredom is the lowest I've encountered in another living soul." He cocked a broad shoulder and chewed on his lip, the one the snowflake had melted on. "I don't have sisters, and I don't know how to talk to girls."

Franny covered her mouth with the back of her hand, but too late. Her laughter rolled like a carpet between them. *Not know how to talk to girls, indeed.*

Then, there it was.

A flash of temper she would wager a hundred English shillings, or half crowns, or whatever the coin the British preferred to wager was not an emotion William Allerton, fifth Viscount Remington—she'd looked it up in *Debrett's*—often exhibited to the masses. A cross turn of his mouth she was *determined* to capture with her charcoals.

"A lot written about me in the rags is rubbish, Miss..."

"Shaw. Francine Shaw," Franny replied, certain he wouldn't know who she was. Giving a false name was more of a charade than she was willing to construct. She didn't like lying even if she was moderately gifted. Strolling down the hallway, she noted the vaulted ceiling rising three stories, the balconied floors leading off the central staircase bordered by imposing balustrades and chipped sculptures. Faded carpets, tattered velvet drapes, threadbare furnishings. Ancient stone and marble. It was shabby but glorious. "The story about an opera singer leaving the stage to kiss you in full view of a slew of patrons is slanderous drivel then?"

"*Miss*," Ada hissed, striving to dictate what a proper lady would do when she was only guessing herself. They both knew it was a waste of time. Franny was hopelessly improper in every way. In America *and* England.

Remington froze, her luggage bumping his muscular thigh. Some mysteriously masculine scent drifted from him. Spicy, perhaps citrus. This overruled only by the dour odor of spearmint. On more than one occasion, her companion's stinging fragrance had arrived before her, notice Franny had used to her advantage. "That was the Duke of Leighton, who was sitting to my right. It was *his* box. Of course, they attribute the mischief to me. His Grace has the foulest temperament in London and a *worse* reputation but somehow gets aways with everything. It's the damned duke privilege."

She'd heard about the Duke of Leighton's antics. Why, he'd recently gotten tossed in the Thames by Xander Macauley. The men traveled in a pack, Viscount Remington an oft-time contributor in their escapades. "I'm teasing," she finally said when he didn't seem to understand that she was.

Remington frowned, tiny grooves radiating from his eyes. He looked bewildered; the kind of bemused charm Franny imagined his paramours overlooked. "That must be an American pursuit. We English never, *ever* tease. Especially governesses. My tutors were dry as cedar. Smacked my knuckles with a ruler while expecting absolute obedience. The number of broken ones, rulers, that is, during those years was enough to make my father weep."

She tilted her head, imagining how she was going to draw that lank of hair on the side of his head that kicked out a bit. She'd noticed it on two occasions now. "I don't think that will be my approach."

Remington grimaced. "You haven't met the girl."

Franny grinned. She couldn't help it. She had two weeks to explore this monstrous medieval fortress and the complexities of a man she found fascinating. She'd brought enough charcoals for a hundred sketches. Plus, she loved children.

Truly, what an adventure.

Ada coughed from somewhere behind her, the scent of spearmint clinging to the air.

Catching her companion's response, Remington eyed Franny with curious intent. "Why are you so delighted?"

Franny dragged her sodden slipper across the frayed carpet, working to erase her smile. "Christmastide is just around the corner." Although there wasn't one hint of cheer about the place.

He snorted, a dimple flaring in his cheek. How maddeningly handsome he was. It was unjust.

"This fascinating position as governess?"

He shifted her portmanteau to his other hand and flexed his fingers like he was working out a cramp. "Try again."

"My un-English nature?" she said with a laugh. A foxed baronet had told her it was the most sensual of sounds after he'd cornered her behind a settee at the countess's dinner party last week. She'd eventually had to bring her heel down on his instep to get him to move away from her person, but she'd been flattered, nonetheless.

Remington tried his best but, in the end, laughed with her. His fist going to his mouth to cover it. "That must be it." Then, he shook himself from his reverie and jogged up the staircase, her gaze left with nothing to do but record his trim bottom shifting in meticulously fitted buckskins. He must have forgotten the adage, ladies first.

But then again, she was no lady.

Ada hooked her arm through Franny's and tugged her up the stairs. "Stop it. I can see those scalding glances a mile away," she whispered, thankfully so low only Franny heard. "Flirting and your feeble inability to tame your base attractions is what landed us on this horrid side of the ocean. If I have to drink another cup of tea..."

"I'm not flirting. I'm talking to my employer. And what woman doesn't have base attractions? Isn't it normal to appreciate art? A fine form? Men are surely allowed this weakness."

Ada sighed wearily. "Heaven help me, should your father find out about this scheme. Daughter of one of the wealthiest men in Pennsylvania acting as a servant. The girl who went through a governess a week herself. When he does, it's off to live with my brother and his wife in Dyberry. You'd do that to me when I changed your nappies? Wiped your nose and darned your stockings? Covered for you that time you snuck in the window after dark with blackberry brambles in your hair? Dyberry is my pension, is that it? Why, it's in the country, and you know I have allergies!"

Franny drew Ada close. She was the only mother Franny had ever known. The only parent she'd *needed*. Her father certainly hadn't been up for the job. "You're going to change my children's nappies someday. Where I go, you go. How could I live without you?"

Ada sniffed. "Are you sure, Franny darling? After all that happened last spring?"

Her breath tight, Franny paused at the top of the staircase, noting that the shabbiness continued on this floor. Not even half of the lamps were lit. Dour paintings covered the walls, their frames coated in dust. Tattered carpets in worse shape than those on the main floor. The sconce's glow struck the viscount's broad back as he continued down the hallway, in and out of shadow, unaware they weren't following.

She didn't want to think about that night ever again.

Sliding her arm from Ada's, she sucked regret back through her teeth. "It's very simple. I won't let Gerald ruin me."

Any more than he already had.

Her reputation was one thing, her happiness quite another. She would die before letting him take more from her.

Ada twisted her gloved fingers in the folds of her skirt. "The English aren't forgiving. I could tell this right off. The way they gossip at these parties we've been forced to attend, it's more of a lashing than high society back home ever thought to give. Should the scandal reach this side of the ocean, your father's money won't be enough to buy a cobbler, much less that baron he has lined up. Women aren't allowed the mistakes men are, not in this world, not in any world. I wish you'd get that through your lovely but thick head."

Franny watched the viscount halt before a door at the end of the corridor, his long body hidden in shadow. When he turned to her, his eyes glimmering in a flicker of candlelight, she made a promise.

Two weeks. To play this harmless game in a hidden locale where she might be able to take a full breath for the first time in years.

She didn't deserve more. She didn't deserve *love*.

She'd written the ending of her book during one fateful encounter.

After this impulsive respite, she would marry the baron who wanted her money—and follow society's rules.

Every last one of them.

Chapter Three

Where a Forlorn Heiress Finds a Friend

Franny guessed it might be easier to connect with a lonely child when you'd *been* a lonely child.

In some ways was still one. Or rather, a lonely woman.

Taking a deep breath, she entered the playroom as if she belonged there. She'd traveled the hallways, passing dozens of parlors and snaking warrens before finally locating the chamber. Katherine Brierly perched on the window seat, gazing at the snow falling in feathery wisps outside. She was thin, tall for her age, her disheveled hair shot through with red-gold sparks much like the crimson threads running through the threadbare carpet at her feet. Her stockings were tattered, her dress rumpled. She looked like an urchin but held the stately bearing of a queen.

Franny had been warned by the housekeeper, Mrs. Walker, that the ginger coloring matched the girl's temperament. She'd laughed when Mrs. Walker said it, eliciting a smile and an extra biscuit on her plate at breakfast. Franny had found that the English domestics were surprised when they were treated as *people*.

"Hello," Franny said as she crossed the threshold. The room smelled like the rest of the house, of dust and if not decay, disuse. There were scant books and toys on the shelves. Landscape paintings unsuited to a playroom lined the walls. The wallpaper faded and of scenes no child would want to see. Franny made a mental note to send to London for supplies the viscount could likely not afford but couldn't reject, either, once they'd arrived. Already paid for. Better to ask for forgiveness than permission, she'd always thought.

Katherine swiveled on her seat, the second-view of the child's face before she drew it into recalcitrant lines.

She was lonesome. And frightened.

Franny made a decision then and there. This girl's happiness added to the list that included her own. "We build snowmen at home," she said and moved into the chamber. "Although we don't often get enough to make a truly good one. I never had anyone to help me, so I got very skilled at making them myself."

Katherine swallowed, her apple-green eyes widening with interest. "Snowmen?"

Franny laughed and strolled into the room as if this interview wasn't of great importance. Love or hate, the battle lines drawn in moments with children, she'd found. "Not something you can do in the city, is it?" She crossed to the window and gave the chilled pane a hard tap. "This snow looks fluffy. So, it may be a challenge. Are you up to it?"

Katherine slithered from the window seat, her lips forming a half-smile. "You want to go outside? In the snow? Right now?"

Franny shrugged. "You can't build a snowman inside the house."

Katherine took a step closer, her hands twisting in her skirts. "We'll get wet."

"Probably, yes."

"Our hair messy," she challenged and drew a lazy loop around her head. "Our clothes drenched. We'll look like we've been pulled through a keyhole."

"Uh-huh."

"I don't have boots."

Franny sent a sweeping glance around the playroom. "We can locate something."

"Not very ladylike," Katherine whispered, reaching to pull her braid between her teeth. "But Americans aren't ladylike, are they?"

"We're not known for it. I'm certainly not." Through the window, Franny searched the distance, marveling at the parklands stretching as far as she could see. A rolling vista gorgeous enough to take one's breath. This estate was in need of care, true, but the terrain surrounding it was amazingly beautiful. "We'll get holly and pine to decorate while we're at it."

Katherine turned from her search of a wardrobe tucked in the corner. She had a boot in her hand that looked fifty years old. "For what?"

"Why, Christmas, of course."

The child's gaze shuttered. "The viscount won't like that."

Franny rested her hip on the window ledge, entering delicate territory. "Whyever not?"

"He doesn't like me," she said, chewing on her braid. "He prefers calm and order. Like my uncle. Then he died, and now I'm here. In another dreary household with another dreary man."

Franny traced a sketch of a bluebird on the wall, her gaze leaving Katherine. Sometimes falsehoods were hard to issue while staring into someone's eyes. "Lord Remington has great responsibility resting on his shoulders with his viscountcy. And he has no sisters, no children, so this is very new to him. *You* are new to him. But that doesn't mean he doesn't want you. He's likely to start building his family soon, and you're a part of that now."

"Are you my new governess?" Katherine's brow scrunched curiously, her braid dropping from her teeth. "You don't look like any governess I've ever seen."

Franny grinned, delighted. "I am. You may call me Miss Shaw. I'm here until Lord Remington can secure someone properly English. I'm a friend of his friend and in need of companionship during Christmastide. My father returned to America, and I truly had nowhere to go. My companion, Ada, loves the season and will help us decorate."

This could not be further from the truth. Ada had never met a length of garland she wished to hang nor a present she wished to wrap.

Katherine plopped to the floor and wrestled the boot on her foot. "You were drawing in the parlor after breakfast."

"That's my favorite hobby in the world. I've been sketching since I was your age."

"Can you teach me? I don't have anything I know how to do well."

Franny felt a surge of affection, fierce in its power. "I can."

Katherine giggled and reached for the other boot, finally looking like a little girl set to go on an adventure. "Miss Shaw, since we're becoming friends, you may call me Kat."

Chance couldn't tear his gaze from the enchanting scene outside the library window.

Katherine and his new governess, Miss Shaw, were building a lopsided snowman on the sloping lawn across the way. It was going to tumble if they put too much weight on the top portion. He'd been waiting for it to tumble. Ten minutes earlier, he'd watched them gather pine branches and holly from an overgrown thicket near the side garden, frolicking about as if it wasn't cold as a witch's teat this morn.

They had to be soaked to the skin. Clothing sodden, fingers and toes numb.

Nevertheless, they looked rapturous. The first time he'd seen this emotion from either of them.

He wanted to ignore the enchantment of the scene but couldn't.

As was often the way with life, he was toasty from a blazing hearth fire, his belly full of tea and toast—yet he was melancholy for some reason.

"You shouldn't have come without alerting me," he murmured to Lady Chapman-Holmes as she wiggled into the nook between his body and the wall. "I have the girl to think of now."

Eleanor snaked her arm through his, leaning into him. "How was I to know you'd been burdened with a child to care for? As if anyone would consider you father material. I'm staying down the way at Lady Dane's as we discussed last month. A ten-minute carriage ride. I'll see you at Grimley's ball in any case. Remington, I didn't want to unduly surprise you. I simply wanted to *see* you. One of the benefits of being a widow, I can travel alone on occasion."

Chance withdrew his arm as politely as he could. Eleanor wanted to stake her claim is what she wanted. As she'd wanted in London, to his discontent.

It was his fault, the direction his life had taken. He'd once desired her. Or women like her. Desired a different piece every night if he could manage it, in fact. And in his youth, he had. Champagne sipped from slippers. Or navels. Tangled sheets one moment and awkward silence the next. Interactions lasting only as long as his release.

Truly, he'd only been passionate about designing furniture.

He glanced back to the girls romping in the snow.

Something was happening, a mysterious yearning. He rubbed his chest, his breath catching. His existence was changing in the seconds being counted off on the mantel clock behind him. He felt powerless and *powerful*. On the precipice.

Lady Chapman-Holmes was situated in his old life.

When he suspected he was preparing for his new.

"What are they doing?" she asked, her tone scathing. "I assume the little one is the urchin you're now guardian of."

Enjoying life, he thought dully, suddenly determined to follow Miss Shaw's improper lead. At breakfast, she'd chatted with every servant who had stumbled into the morning parlor. Which due to his meager finances, amounted to four. Chance was charmed by her nonchalant playfulness. The joy she took in the blueberry jam she claimed was the best she'd had since leaving Philadelphia. The delicate teacup she claimed must have been in his family for years. Mrs. Walker's grandson, the scullery maid's brother. She asked about them all.

She was unlike any woman he'd ever met in that she didn't seem bothered by what people thought of her. When he'd been raised by an indifferent man who believed in basing his entire *being* on what people thought of him. Chance recalled being hugged exactly once by Viscount Remington. At his mother's funeral.

His father had never made any dwelling feel like *home*.

In the two days his temporary governess had been in residence at Rose Hill, there were changes he could only attribute to her. Feminine touches. The dank hallways smelled faintly of lemon and linseed oil. The paneling in the foyer glistened. The scent of biscuits—nutmeg and cinnamon—wafted down the gallery and into the space he'd set up as his workshop. More sconces were lit on the corridors he traveled. The drapes were open in rooms once deserted, letting in sunlight and life.

When he noticed Miss Shaw and her charge gathering up their pine branches and sad bits of holly to return to the house, he shoved off the window ledge. "You must go," he said and propelled Lady Chapman-Holmes across the parlor with a hand at her lower back.

Suddenly, he didn't want his old life to meet his new.

But the collision was inevitable.

Miss Shaw was opening the door as his majordomo was nowhere in sight, her bonnet a soggy mess hanging half off her head, her hair curling wildly about her face. She had insanely beautiful hair, so thick pins could scarcely contain it. A mass of mahogany and auburn, he'd been tempted since the moment they met to tunnel his fingers through. And her eyes... they were a remarkable shade so light they looked almost gold. He'd glanced at them twice across his breakfast table to confirm the assessment.

Lastly, and he hated to contemplate the notion with a former lover standing by his side, but his governess had the most delectable body of any chit in England. In Europe. In America. A voluptuous, petite package he longed to unwrap. Almost perfect from the little he'd seen of it.

Curve upon curve upon curve.

While he stood there lost in lusty reflection, Katherine barreled in behind Miss Shaw, her arms full of branches. "Franny," she called before she saw him. Because if the child had seen him first, her joy would have shriveled like the branches in her arms were soon going to. "We'll place these greens on every hearth in the house. It'll look like Christmastide then!"

Franny. He rolled the name across his tongue like a fine Bordeaux.

His governess spun in a circle, her merriment illuminating the foyer like a thousand candles. Happiness this house had not seen in years. Happiness he'd *never* seen.

Chance knew it was a ridiculous flight of fancy, but part of his heart raced away from him at that moment. A gut punch he felt to his toes. Greedy, he wanted to snatch her joy and light his soul with it.

Eleanor glanced at him, noting his stillness, her lips pursing into a severe pout. He couldn't stop her before she leaned in and busked his cheek, lingering in a manner that spoke of extreme familiarity.

Franny and Katherine quietened, believing they were intruding.

"My lord," Franny murmured, her cheeks coloring. Her wisp of a stunning smile dying. Her gaze darted between him and Eleanor. "Come, Kat, let's go organize our decorations. Excuse us, please."

Then she was down the gallery and up the stairs, Katherine-who-apparently-preferred-to-be-called Kat's footfalls tapping against marble as she raced alongside her.

Eleanor turned to him in a fury. "Why is that uncouth title-chaser in your home, Remington? She didn't even wait for an introduction! Common behavior one expects from a person raised in the Colonies, I suppose."

He pulled his gaze back from where it had danced along behind Miss Shaw. "We don't refer to them as the Colonies any longer, Eleanor."

Lady Chapman-Holmes gathered four centuries of exceptional breeding and stared down her nose at him, a mere viscount, number five. "As if I wouldn't know that woman, my lord. Francine Shaw, daughter of Archibald Shaw, the American investor. He's in London to talk railroads and marriage of his only child to the highest title he can purchase. Rumor is, he's drawing up agreements with Baron Hillsdale this very minute. You know Hillsdale's financial situation is abysmal, his father and brothers wastrels. She's been thrust into every event this season that would have her." She hummed, a grating sound that made him wish he'd never met her. Made him wish he could blow out a candle and ask for a different life.

"The Duchess Society sent her. I see. Your friendship with Hildegard Templeton... no, now it's Streeter. Dear God, she *married* that smuggler. She'd rather draw up those agreements with a viscount, wouldn't she? A smart business move on her part. But she is a shrewd woman."

Chance swallowed hard, stunned to his core. He'd rarely allowed himself to be played for a fool. That his childhood friend would do this to him—and Miss Shaw, with her innocent smiles and winsome nature—brought an ache to his heart he hadn't felt since his father turned his back on him years ago for refusing to give up his plan to manage a business *and* a viscountcy.

Why would the Duchess Society propel Miss Shaw across his path if it was anything *but* a trap?

Nevertheless, he realized his situation.

And Miss Shaw's. And Katherine's.

So, the lie came easily.

"I know who she is. There wasn't time to secure a proper governess, and Miss Shaw is a personal friend of Mrs. Streeter's who has experience with children, which I obviously do not. It's only until the new year. Her companion is in residence as well. Hildy and Tobias are on the way for the holiday. If you recall, they have a residence not a twenty-minute ride away. Nothing inappropriate in the event you thought to share this news. With Miss Shaw's expected marriage to Hillsdale, an untruth could be damaging." Chance crossed to the front door and yanked it open, his patience depleted. *Christ*, he was glad her carriage was waiting on the drive. "It's for the child, Eleanor. Her happiness as she settles into a new life is of utmost importance to me, believe it or not. If you make this afternoon anything else"—he bared his teeth, taking his anger out on her—"I'll consider it a personal affront. Do we understand each other?"

Lady Chapman-Holmes stalked past him, tying her bonnet string with trembling fingers. "I honestly don't know what I saw in you, Remington. You're as arrogant and thoughtless as they say."

"Likewise," Chance murmured dispassionately and shut the door behind her with a click.

A frigid gust swirled through the foyer, chilling him to the bone. Leaning against the jamb, he knocked his head against the aged oak, betrayal enveloping him like a cloak.

Hildy Streeter and Francine Shaw were like all the rest.

Clawing their way to the top without consideration of who they trampled on the way up.

Chapter Four

Where Light is Shed on a Misunderstanding

She couldn't sleep.

A thunderstorm had rolled in after sunset, snow turning to rain that pelted the windowpanes in steady, disturbing thumps. Franny had never liked storms. That night in Gerald's parlor, a downpour had hammered the sparkling new shingles of his home. A deluge that washed down her face as she stumbled from the house and into a waiting conveyance.

She didn't often conjure that incident, or tried not to, but when it rained like this, she couldn't help herself.

Clutching her portfolio to her chest, she searched for the library Mrs. Walker had shown her, a space that wasn't in quite as dismal a state as most of Rose Hill. Although in need of loving care, she was enchanted by the estate. Absolutely enchanted. Turrets and moats, portraits a hundred years old, room after room, stories this place would tell. Humming softly, she turned down a corridor, her footpads muted on the runner, then came to a swift halt.

Candlelight spilled like mist from an open door.

With a tightly drawn breath, she advanced. Despite the risk. There was likely only one person still awake.

But Franny could be honest with herself if no one else.

She was attracted to Lord Remington.

And had been from the moment she'd seen him crouched before that escritoire. The way he'd studied her over the breakfast table this morning, his eyes near the color of the vast sea she'd crossed to get to him, suggested he felt something as well, however slight.

However for men, attraction was rarely significant.

For women, it could be deadly.

She should know.

Franny paused in the doorway. It wasn't the library but rather a deserted chamber the viscount appeared to be using as his workshop. There were tools scattered atop a length of stained linen being used to protect the floors. Aged planks she wasn't sure needed protecting. Remington was on his haunches beside a partially constructed desk, working sandpaper over a rounded wooden block in his hand. Of most interest to her were the sketches he'd crudely tacked to the walls. Paintings had been removed to allow for this, dull squares stamped over faded wallpaper.

Knowing no way to make a delicate entrance, she wandered inside, crossing to the drawings. They were unrefined but workable diagrams, mostly of desks in some version of creation. She'd begun to see pieces scattered about the house that she assumed were his. The style bold and unmistakable, lodged somewhere between elegant and contemporary. For a moment, the sound of the rain striking the windowpanes was the only sound flowing between them.

"Miss Shaw," Remington said after a charged pause, his voice wavering slightly. It was then she noted the brandy bottle by his hip, the half-empty glass beside it. "You've found me. What a surprise."

She turned from her study of his schematics, unclear what he'd meant by the statement. Unclear about the heat behind his words. Gone was the profligate he presented to society. This man was a simmering cauldron, the ruthlessness he tried to hide shimmering like firelight around him. Perhaps he found it easier to sell the simpler version of himself.

She did that every day.

He gave the wood in his hand, what looked to be a table leg, a vigorous buff. "You've made changes during your short time in residence. Managing this house less like a governess and more like a woman who has managed her own. Decorations on the banisters and hearths. The parlors open to light, drapes beaten of dust, the scent of decay vanquished. You're friendly with the servants even."

"You mean I actually talk to them. I ask their names and about their families. You should try it. Everyone wants to be valued in this way."

"I wasn't raised to converse with domestics. Including governesses."

Franny settled back against the wall, clutching the portfolio to her chest. "You're angry with me."

Katherine was sleeping like a child who'd had a wonderful day. They'd decorated the house, brightening up what *was* a dismal residence. Had she done something untoward with the girl? Was it interrupting his meeting with the woman who was rumored to be his mistress?

She didn't want to contemplate the fury that had sizzled through her when Lady Chapman-Holmes's lips grazed his cheek. The seductive smile on her face speaking of ownership.

She'd wanted to do a very uncouth thing and sock the woman in her patrician nose.

Franny's desire to sketch the man was overruling common sense. And what little breeding she had.

Remington went to his knee to steady himself and, placing the wood aside, lifted the glass to his lips. "When you create a hinge for a gate leg, you have to round the teeth's edges so the hinge swings freely. But not too freely. You bullnose the corners. It's a negotiation with the wood." He sipped, his gaze finding hers across the distance. "Like life, a negotiation between what one wants and what one *gets*."

She drew a delicate breath, helplessly drinking him in. Competing shafts of light fought for his attention. The wall sconce above battling the candle at his side. His jaw was stubbled in grain so dark he looked like a pirate. His overlong hair tickled the crisp fold of his collar. His shirttail hit his hip; tattered trousers covered his long legs. Working clothes. Nothing he'd wear in the city. The muscles in his shoulders flexed as he stared at her staring at him, controlled displeasure.

"What have I done?" she finally asked, fine to be the one who buckled. Women were used to removing pride from the equation.

The viscount released a bitter huff, setting the glass to the floor with a clink. "You look at me like I'm cream, and you're a starving cat when you're engaged to Hillsdale? I begin to feel sorry for a reprehensible bloke I don't *like*."

Franny's exhalation left her lungs in a rush. So that was it. "I'm not engaged," she whispered. "The agreements are not signed."

"Are you sure about that, Miss Shaw?"

"I have to agree," she said, temper sparking her words. "I'm *not* engaged."

"You're also not a governess."

She swallowed, desperately wishing for a sip of brandy. "For the next two weeks, I am."

"Perhaps," he murmured and refilled his glass. Then he gazed at her through the curtain of inky hair falling across his brow.

Scooting the glass toward her, he nodded. *Have some.*

She wasn't going to deny the offer. Perhaps an English woman would, but an American one would not.

"Why did you do it?" Remington asked as she stepped closer, placing her portfolio on the floor and reaching for the glass. She had to go to her knees, putting them on equal, intimate footing. His scent, leather and something peppery, crept in to tease her senses. As if she needed more to snag her awareness. "To secure a destitute viscount? Couple notches higher than a baron, true. Although deception isn't typically the Duchess Society's style. Isn't Hildy's style, I should say. I've known her since we were in leading strings."

Franny was taking a sip when he made his claim. She coughed and scrubbed her wrist across her lips, the liquor burning a path down her throat. "Is that what you think? Hildegard Streeter had *nothing* to do with this. She was against the idea. Believe me." Franny would never forgive herself should her bit of whimsy damage his relationship with his friend. "I was there, in the corner of the room when you burst in. I volunteered for this."

He rocked back on his heels, giving her a thoroughly carnal review. She was dressed informally as well. *Too* informally. A sleeping gown covering every inch of her, but without the undergarments in place to contain her generous curves. Her hair braided and hanging over one shoulder, stray strands she could never control dusting her brow and cheek.

She looked a fright, she was sure.

He lifted the bottle to his lips, his gaze inscrutable. "Not possible. I would have noticed you."

"We've attended at least two of the same events in the past six months. Maybe three. Occupied the same parlor four days ago, and you had no idea I was there. I can prove it. Mrs. Streeter, she called you Chance."

He scowled, the arrogant cur not liking to lose even so much as a silly argument. "You must have been hiding. I would have seen you." He dragged the bottle across his bottom lip. Her belly clenched, a perilous signal to her growing attraction. *Oh*, he was beautiful in the light. "The enchantress has teeth, I see." With a wicked expression she couldn't decipher, he snatched her portfolio from the floor, untied the leather bind, and began flipping through the sheets. As if he had the right to.

"I saw you once before, at the earl's musicale," Franny blurted, breathless and panicked, aroused and bewildered. When he saw her sketches, the jig was up. "You were running your hand over an escritoire. I was on the veranda. I noticed you through the window. I wanted to sketch you, that's why I told Hildy I would come. Truthfully, I forced her hand." He continued to flip through the sheets, blinking rapidly, engrossed, while she babbled.

Her fascination was laid out in bold strokes her art instructor had stated were too extreme a representation for a female. There weren't many sketches of Viscount Remington yet, but the number was increasing. Rose Hill had proven to be inspirational, creatively. She could only thank the gods she'd not included anything risqué. Those were stuffed in the bottom of her portmanteau—derived from imagination only.

Although the trip up the staircase that first night, following along and watching his taut bottom flex had helped.

"You're quite gifted." He closed the portfolio and presented it to her with a sheepish, slated twist of his lips. He had a scar bleeding into the top one that she longed to press her tongue to. An image she'd never in her life envisioned.

Recognizing her absurd cravings, she grabbed her artwork and brought them back to her chest like a shield. "It's nothing. A hobby."

"It's attraction, Miss Shaw. We all feel it from time to time. Some more than others. It's rarely convenient. Although I've never seen it displayed in such an authoritative manner. Not personally. Tons of it on exhibit in museums, of course."

"I wanted to sketch you. That's all it was. All it *is*. It's what artists *do*."

Remington grinned, the bounder. Spreading his fingers wide across the floor for balance, he leaned in like a feral cat. *Damn and blast*, she wanted his hands on her. "If this an extreme case of infatuation, I find myself unduly flattered. Hell's teeth, you set up a novel deception simply to capture my face in charcoal. I believe this is the most any woman has ever done to establish contact with me. One not looking to be a viscountess, that is. There was a determined chit that shall go unnamed who climbed a tree to get into my bedchamber last year. *That* was noteworthy. I found I couldn't turn her away after such tremendous effort, in case you're wondering."

Franny rose to her feet with a growl, jealousy and embarrassment eating a hole in her belly. "It's *art*. I don't want any part of your blasted title! I truly don't want any part of *anyone's* title. Those are my father's dreams. I may have to fulfill them due to my own transgressions, which aren't a topic for discussion, but that's not your concern."

"Ah, yes, your young baron. Can I say, I'm more than happy to examine this dilemma of yours." He made a lazy X over his heart with his crossed fingers. "Our discussion will stay in my sparse parlor-cum-workshop, between friends. Or between governess and employer. We're still playing those roles, correct?"

"*What* dilemma?"

He was smirking, though he covered his mouth to hide it. She preferred this, even if it vexed her, to his anger. "Lust, sweetheart. Yours for me. Americans seem less concerned about hiding what they feel, which is unusual for an Englishman. We're not the most expressive of souls. And when we are, usually it's the man who has to break the proverbial ice." He flicked his hand between them, signaling there was an *us*. "This is bloody refreshing."

She spun on her heel, returning to his wall of sketches. "You're laughing at me, like the rest. The *ton* thinks I'm foolish and inappropriate. Vulgar. Why should you be any different? When it was my father who dragged me to this godforsaken country. My art is all that is mine alone."

She felt him move behind her, invading her space but without touching her. His brandy-laced breath slipped past her annoyance, melting her already fragile resistance. "I need you. Through Christmastide. Katherine likes you, and she was happy today. I saw it." His husky plea streaked in her ear, warming something inside her that had been cold for months. For years. Forever. "I'm not making fun of you. That isn't what this is. I'm an outsider in society myself. I always have been. Even if society doesn't realize it. They don't know the man, just the blessed title."

Franny lifted her hand to trace the imprecise marks of his drawing. Her fingers shook, and she pressed her knuckles to the wall to quell the reaction.

He reached to steady her, his arm aligning itself alongside hers as if he was showing her how to discharge a rifle. "It's a writing table." Taking her hand, he drew her fingertip along the parts as he rattled them off, his voice oozing the same liquid charisma she bet he used when he charmed someone out of their gown. "This is the pen tray. The leather skiver, twin tooled in gold. A brass keyhole lining to the frieze. Tapper legs, capped and footed with gilt capitols and mounts. It will be the most gorgeous piece in England when I'm done. I'll have one in Carlton House, you watch. Prinny, or the King now, I suppose I should say, will beg for it. The one love of my life, this work. Like your art, I understand. I *do*."

"I can do better representations for you," she murmured, struggling to lead him off course. He was half-foxed, and she was smitten. She knew enough from her past mistake to realize this was a lethal combination. Yet, she let herself stand there, mere inches separating their bodies, awareness as thick as London's fog encasing them in sensual heat. "I could try."

Remington straightened, his hand falling from hers as he stepped back. "They're my designs, each and every one. But my drawings aren't good. It's a problem. Nevertheless, when I've tried to describe what I *want* to an illustrator, it's been off. I can't find anyone who can capture my vision."

The challenge was there, the need to solve it undefined and reckless. To please him in this way. "What do I get in return if I do this for you? If I'm able to capture your vision on paper?" She turned to find his intent gaze focused on her, unwavering. Absurdly, she loved that he was intelligent *and* uncompromising. "Consider it repayment for misleading you, even if my intentions were genuine."

"There must be a trade." He tapped his chin in thought. "How about this? I'll sit for your sketches."

Her hand clenched around her portfolio. She struggled for a clever response when she wasn't a clever woman. Her witty retorts always arrived an hour too late.

His lips tilted, a small dent that could possibly be called a dimple pinging his cheek. That lank of hair jutting out, calling her hand to smooth it. "Can I ask about clothing, as much of the portraits I've seen feature men who are... how shall I delicately say this? Unclothed. I feel I should call you Franny if you're set to see me in the buff."

Her cheeks burned while lascivious images assaulted her mind. "Your normal attire"—she flicked her hand toward him, brow to toe—"will be adequate." Although she longed to know. If she asked him to disrobe, would he *do* it? "But you can call me Franny. I don't mind."

"Then you may call me Chance." He shrugged, humming beneath his breath. "I had a high fever as a babe, for days, but I survived. My mother felt it was a remarkable piece of luck as she'd lost a child to something similar. She called me her lucky chance. But she died before I truly got to know her." He frowned when he finished the explanation, as if he'd not considered what he was disclosing. Or to whom.

Hoping to break the intimate moment, Franny carefully removed one of his drawings from the wall. "Can I take this? I'd like to create a more detailed illustration. Anything is better than a blank page, as they say."

Remington stepped in, his gaze searching. First the sketch in her hand, then a lingering assessment starting at the hem of her sleeping gown and concluding just past her chest. After a charged moment where it seemed he was deciding what to do, he reached to tuck a strand of hair behind her ear. He dawdled, caressing her cheek. His blue eyes were shot through with flecks of gold, she noted at this distance, truly dazzling in the candlelight. His jaw muscle flexed as his lips pressed tight, his own ideas running loose.

Kiss me, she thought wildly.

With a muted sigh, he shook himself free, his gaze dropping to his drawing. "Add a finial here," he tapped the parchment. "And here. The legs need to be more elegant. More in line with the design of the desktop. Not too delicate. See what you can come up with. As you said, it's easier to edit than create."

Then he crossed to the door, and she had the feeling she was chasing a fox from his lair. He paused in the threshold, candlelight shining in his eyes. "Thank you for agreeing to this, for any reason you agreed. I want Katherine to be happy, and somehow, I'm going to find a way to make sure that happens."

Then he was gone.

And all she could think was, *I want him back*.

He'd almost kissed her.

In fact, Chance had wanted many things in that moment.

It stunned him to realize who his phony governess was. Francine Shaw. Heiress to a mad American fortune. One of the so-called title-chasers flooding the city. Now that it had been pointed out to him, he recalled reading about her in the *Gazette's* gossip column.

Nothing the author had stated matched the woman, however.

She was an intriguing mix of daring and naivete. Embarrassment and hunger crossing her face in swift intervals. Her expression *begging* him to kiss her. The look of unconcealed longing sending an aroused rush through him.

What would it be like to seduce someone who wanted you but didn't *want* to want you?

Chance knew what a melting glance meant. The skip in breathing, a fierce pulse tapping at the base of a woman's neck. Francine Shaw was lovely in an understated, absolutely compelling manner. Gorgeous eyes near the color of the calla lilies that bloomed outside his Mayfair bedchamber in spring. A mix of hazel and gold. Too, her bloody hair was indescribable.

What he would pay to see *that* glory spread across his sheets.

And her body. A goddess in conspicuously unattractive clothing. He'd about choked when she strolled into the library, every curve she possessed on display in that hideous dressing gown.

Incredibly, Chance questioned if he ought to use his title as a bargaining chip. Because his intriguing governess was far too interesting a package for that fop Hillsdale.

After all, she'd done the near impossible.

She'd ignited his senses for the first time in *ages*. Maybe it was the scent of lilacs and a hint of lemon that drifted like snowflakes around her. Or her accent, flat as the moors, but charming in its unfussiness. He'd pay a thousand pounds to hear her whisper in his ear as she came around him. Thinking this at an inopportune time, he'd been forced to stalk from the room like a man possessed before she noticed his cock threatening to bust his bone buttons.

How had he missed her at the Earl of Devlin's musicale?

Odd, as he'd never been attracted to an *American* before.

It was too bad really. Timing and circumstance not meeting in the middle. Her needing a title and him needing blunt to keep the viscountcy afloat. But he'd promised himself he'd never marry without love after growing up in a home without it. Head and heart needed to be in alignment for him to promise his future to anyone.

The lonely little boy he'd been demanded it.

Sighing, he gazed across the lawn from his perch on the veranda wall, his breath fogging the air, his fingers frozen from the chill. The rain had stopped a half hour ago, leaving a damp, leaden mist to color the world a snowy white. He was coming to quite appreciate Derbyshire. For all the reasons his father had hated it. It was remote. Untamed. The air crisp and clean. The land stretching to the horizon calling to him in a possessive, elemental way. *His* land. Custody he'd never felt about anything outside his furniture.

He'd told Francine Shaw about his nickname. He'd talked about his mother, the only person who had shown him love that he could recall.

Something he never, ever did.

The story of his family wasn't an uplifting tale, and he rarely found the need to share it.

Her serene presence, the mix of goodness and heat shimmering in her eyes, unlocked something in him. And the other...

Her illustrations had aroused him more than he'd thought a mere sketch could. Sent a ragged claw of need straight through him. They'd been drawings in various phases of completion. Mostly of his face. His hands. He lifted one and stared at it, spread his fingers, wondering what she saw that he didn't.

The man in those sketches had a regal, confident bearing—when Chance was uncertain. About life and his place in it. His ruse was nearly as great as hers. He played the charming viscount while struggling to locate the person beneath. A burden deposited on his shoulders at the ripe age of nineteen. When he'd had another passion altogether.

He worried over his relief when he'd realized Francine Shaw hadn't played him for a fool. She had her own troubles. Transgressions, she'd called them. Who knew what bit of mischief had had her running to England. Anyway, what did he care if his temporary governess was after his title? Like a thousand and one inane chits before her.

But he did care.

He blew a frosty breath into the sky, wishing for another glass of brandy.

This realization was disconcerting indeed.

Chapter Five

Where a Forlorn Viscount Opens His Heart. A Little.

Kat had been staring at him for the past ten minutes from her spot on the faded Aubusson. She had a ragdoll of unknown origin clutched in her fist. She'd wandered in with a biscuit and the toy, settling herself on the floor without a word.

Strangely, he found the sound of her frayed breathing comforting. She had a stuffy nose from yesterday's activities in the snow, but he figured the fun had been worth it.

Chance placed the quill aside and leaned back in his chair. He was in his study, a chamber that had housed the resident viscount for generations. Although, he'd changed enough about the room to drive out the ghost of his father. Mostly. Starting with a desk of his own design. New curtains. Wallpaper. The little he could afford had gone into this space to help eradicate the memories.

Now, he would channel his meager funds into the nursery. The girl needed a better one than she currently had. Here and in London. He was set to sell two desks next week, which would provide blunt through the summer. He hoped. Tobias Streeter had offered a loan if he fell short, but he was hesitant to take an offer that indebted him to anyone.

"You're a viscount," Kat murmured while he sat there formulating what he could possibly say to start a conversation with a child. "Is that higher than a king? The last uncle I stayed with was the second son of a baron. He was ancient and smelled like peas. But he gave me gumdrops on occasion."

Chance rolled his lips in to hold back his laughter. "Much lower than a king. And I'm not your uncle. I'm your cousin through my mother's side of the family. *Your* mother was her second cousin, I believe. That would make me your third."

Kat gave an inelegant shrug, smoothing her hand down the doll's snarled ginger yarn hair. "I don't remember her."

Chance traced his finger over a blemish in the wood that he particularly loved. He'd chosen this piece for the desktop because of the mark. He'd always thought beauty lay in imperfection. "I don't remember mine very well, either."

Kat glanced up at this, seemingly startled to find they had anything in common. "You don't?"

Chance shook his head, wondering at speaking twice in two days of a woman he rarely recalled except in his dreams. It was being here, at Rose Hill. Where he'd lived with his mother until her death. Then at the tender age of five, he'd been shipped to the city to reside with a father who clearly hadn't wanted children. "She was lovely. I have her eyes and not much else. She was kind. Patient. She liked gardening and spent much of her time in the conservatory. Which is now in shambles."

Kat thought hard about this, twisting her doll's braid around her finger. "Can I be the next viscount? I can fix it up."

Chance's heart gave a hard thump. "That will go to my son. The eldest. Even if I have a daughter first. But you will be their older sister."

She sighed longingly. "No girls as viscount. That's not fair."

Chance gave his teacup a spin. "No, it isn't."

"Franny says women must work twice as hard in this world to make up for the inaccuracies."

He laughed, charmed. "Inequities."

Kat rose, the doll dangling from her fingers. She crossed to the desk and with confidence born of youth, circled his diagram into view. Her nose wrinkled with her frown. “Your desk looks crooked. One leg is shorter than the other. Franny is a much better artist. Maybe you should ask her.”

“Actually, she’s working on a drawing for me. Perhaps two even.”

Kat’s bright green eyes flicked to his. She chewed on her lip, debating, then blurted out, “She said you sent for gifts. For Christmastide. For me.”

He recovered quickly. It was not the first time a woman had stunned him with the notion that he’d overlooked a special occasion. “I think rather than tell you, I’ll let it be a surprise. Aren’t surprises better?” he asked, wondering what he could find in the village at short notice.

Kat grinned and shifted from foot to foot. “I like surprises.”

He was reaching before he had time to ponder the decision. His hand covered hers. It was small, her skin warm and… quite perfect. She turned, linking her fingers with his.

He hadn’t held hands with anyone since his mother’s passing.

A foreign emotion traveled through him, settling firmly in his chest.

Of course, his errant governess arrived to find man and child beaming at each other across a desk, unspoken promises floating between them.

Franny cleared her throat, hesitating in the doorway.

Light from the sconces washed over her, igniting sparks in her glorious hair and across her freckled cheeks. She had an ink smear on the sleeve of another atrocious gown. He’d never known a woman in more desperate need of a modiste. Hideous clothing, however, couldn’t hide her beauty. Too, he liked that she didn’t seem to care for such things as gowns and fripperies. A folio was clutched in her hand and the expression on her face —tentative excitement—led him to believe she’d come with sketches to share.

Her companion stepped behind her. Ada’s shrewd gaze instantly found Chance’s, her scowl growing. The woman was no fool and recognized his attraction. Probably because it sat out there like a lazy cat snoozing in the sun. Then she looked to Franny, recognizing her charge faced the same dilemma. Sighing, she jabbed Franny in the side with a murmured oath.

“Excuse us,” Franny said and stumbled into the room. “Ada is going to take Kat down for her lunch. Then a nap.”

Kat groaned and wiggled her hand from his. He missed the feeling of contentment immediately. “I don’t want to. We’re having fun.”

Chance felt a smile lift his lips. *Fun?* Perhaps this child-rearing business was easier than he'd thought. Straightforward conversation. Touches. Promises of gifts. Was that all there was to it? It wasn't much different a set-up than with his mistresses. Young or old, women were women.

Franny's soft snicker snapped him out of his musing. Her golden eyes fixed on him; her lips parted in amusement. Somehow, she knew what he was thinking. This insight brought comfort and panic. He'd gotten used to feeling alone in a ballroom. Isolated in a city packed with distractions. Lonely in a bed with rumpled sheets, the warm body of someone he didn't love lying beside him.

To have Francine Shaw see him was exhilarating and *terrifying*.

"Go on," he urged when he was sure his voice wasn't going to shake, shooing Kat from the room. "Young ladies need their beauty sleep. We'll talk more at dinner. You can tell me about the decorations you've placed all over the house."

Groaning, she clutched the threadbare ragdoll to her chest and trudged across the room. Ada gave him a piercing glare—*look but don't touch*—then escorted Kat from the room. He vowed then and there that the girl would have a new doll for Christmas.

Franny watched them go before turning to him.

Nervous. She was definitely nervous. Deciding to take pity on them both, Chance tossed her a lifeline. When he'd never felt like seducing someone more—or acting on the impulse less. "I've heard I'm to provide gifts for Christmas. I'm glad Kat informed me before it was too late."

Instead of flushing with mortification, Franny laughed, and stepped into the room. "They're arriving tomorrow. I know you have enough to worry over." She flicked her hand around the space, a benevolent gesture meant to encompass his wealth of responsibilities. "This is part and parcel of what I agreed to. Take care of the child."

"Responsibilities as in, low on funds to purchase gifts. My dire situation is fodder for gossip, I realize. Most of the mamas throwing their daughters my way have introduced the topic of finances first, before beauty or skill with the pianoforte. My father wasn't an able fiscal manager. In fact, he was a profligate gambler, unconcerned with the inconvenience he was leaving me to handle. Estates and no funds. A brother in need of guidance. For myself, I don't care so much, I make enough to survive with the furniture, but the staff, the tenants..."

He dragged his hand through his hair, his breath shortening as it did when he thought of the lives attached to the viscountcy's payroll. When he thought of Arthur. His brother was fragile in ways he'd never been. "Some servants have worked on the estates, three including the townhouse in Mayfair, for most of their lives."

Her chagrin arrived, flushing her cheeks a rosy hue. Yet she didn't deny the assertion. He was destitute, and everyone in London knew it.

Chance sprawled in his chair, stacking his hands over his belly. Her gaze followed the movement, lingering on his chest, then rising to his face. Her eyes were a golden explosion, heaps of emotion contained in their fiery depths. He had to work to hear her soft exhalation. *Christ*, he wanted that sound skating across his skin while he sank inside her. More than he wanted his next breath. Indeed, his attraction was astonishing. He could see no way he'd been in the same room with her and not *felt* it. He must have confused the vibration for something else, not knowing what he was feeling.

He swallowed hard, his throat dry. What had they been discussing?

"Presents," she murmured. Again, knowing where his mind had gone.

"Is a doll arriving in the shipment?"

She nodded. "Of course. What little girl doesn't want a new doll? And sweets, as the English call them, when we simply say candy. Books. Boots. A dress."

"You're the most efficient member of my staff, Miss Shaw. Thank you. The last thing I want to do is disappoint her." He shrugged, discomfited. Scrubbed the back of his neck with his hand. "Although I don't know how to please her, either. My brother is the only person I've tried to accommodate, and that hasn't worked out so well."

Franny took three steps until her hip hit the edge of his desk.

Because she'd done the same without concealing it, Chance let his gaze travel the length of her. Following Ada's unspoken advice, he wouldn't touch, but he would *look* all he pleased. Trap visions of her lush curves in his mind, the swell of her breast pressing against her bodice, and use them. Later, in his massive medieval bed. Where he'd stroke himself to completion while fantasizing of the sweetly guileless American who had stumbled into his life.

"Is this the way you look at every woman?" she asked breathlessly. "If it is, I understand."

He wrenched forward in his chair, his hands going to the desk to brace himself. "Excuse me?"

She leaned in, palming the wood as he had, her hands settling on each side of his. Her gown dipped at the neck, allowing a slender view of the rounded slopes of her breasts. He dragged his gaze to hers with extreme effort while his cock hardened beneath buckskin. His fingertips tingled, his body tensing in anticipation. "I understand why half of London is desperate to get to you. Climbing inside second-story windows for even one moment basking in the intensity of your regard. I've heard of a man undressing you with his eyes, but I've never experienced it." She licked her lips, and he felt his breath sucked from his lungs. "Until now. It's quite... extraordinary."

Touch her, Chance, round this desk and touch her.

Seduce her, you're bloody good at it.

But he sat, immobile, aroused beyond measure. Dazed. A thousand responses flowing through his mind, not one worthy of her. Glowing with the rush of finding a treasure no one in England had discovered, he stumbled into the moment, unsure. Franny Shaw was the most delightful piece he'd ever encountered. She actually said what she meant. She was honest. Beautiful. Kind. Giving. Unique.

And... *no. One. Knew.*

There had to be something wrong with her. There *must* be something wrong with her. No chit could be this perfect.

The colossal difference in their upbringing unfurled like a carpet between them as they stared, lost to the sensual fog enveloping them. She'd not been taught that one didn't discuss seduction in such a forthright manner. One didn't admit attraction unless the reputations involved were irretrievably tainted, and so far, only *his* was.

She hadn't been taught that you hid everything from everyone to protect yourself. He didn't have enough courage to display himself thusly.

"I think you'd better go," he whispered, his voice ragged. If she continued to gaze at him like this, her desire his for the taking, he was going to drag her to the door, lock it, and shove her against it. He *loved* tupping standing up.

And he would make sure she left unable to ever, *ever* forget him.

"I have sketches of the desk. Two versions. As you requested, I placed the—"

"Leave them," he growled and grabbed the folio from her hand. "I thank you in advance. I desperately need assistance. I do. However, either you're leaving this room right now, or I'm coming around the desk to kiss the blessed breath from you. Push you against the wall and show you what the heat of my regard *really* feels like. My desire to erase every thought from your mind is blindingly compelling. Draw the air from your lungs into mine. Send you into a molten puddle at my feet, one I'll happily follow. It's your choice, of course. Completely. Your. Choice. But I'm shaky. And close to making it for you."

She hesitated, damn her. Lifted her hand to her lips and gave them the lightest caress. His body lit as he scrubbed his hand across his own. Raw *want* pierced him, weakening his resolve to do the right blasted thing for once.

He was rising, done, ready to test this attraction between them when she released a quivering sigh he would take to his grave, turned, and fled through the open doorway.

Leaving a provoked viscount to sift through the remnants of his yearning.

Chapter Six

Where a Curious Heiress Ponders the Rules of Attraction

The village seamstress jabbed her with a needle without Franny feeling a thing. Which was her own fault. She'd never been able to stand still during fittings with her modiste, which could account for her gown's shortcomings.

This fidgeting, however, was due to Viscount Remington.

Since the incident in his study, she'd been walking around in a fever dream. Her skin sensitized to the slightest caress of muslin or lace. Her breath teasing lips that were bruised from her touch and sadly, *only* her touch.

Damn and blast, she thought hotly. He'd taken something from her without her even realizing she was relinquishing it. And he hadn't even let her sketch him as he'd promised.

Although, he'd occupied her dreams for two nights, his body covering hers, the fantasy bleeding into a mix of heat and sensual urgency, her frustration staggering when she woke to an empty bed and cool sheets.

Strangely enough, they were working together. Or working *apart* might be the better way to describe it.

They were passing her sketches back and forth, in ways that limited the chance they'd find themselves alone in the same room again. She'd gotten used to deciphering his scribbled modifications in the margins, the sheets left during the night on a desk she'd appropriated in a library that regrettably contained few books. She returned the revised drafts to his workshop each morning.

They were getting close to the design of the desk he wanted in Carlton House. Theirs was a partnership unlike any she'd envisaged she would have.

Ada knew something had happened between them. Franny couldn't get much past her. Consequently, her companion had not let Franny out of her sight.

Until the Duchess Society stepped back into the picture.

Hildy Streeter had stopped by the evening prior to check on a situation she'd not agreed to, and upon seeing the gown Franny had selected to wear to Lord Grimley's ball, quickly located a seamstress who could modify one of hers. She was taller than Franny, her curves less plentiful, but with a skilled craftsman, it would do. Georgiana Munro, the Duchess of Markham, Hildy's partner in the Duchess Society, had also arrived and was currently trying to arrange Franny's hair into something resembling a chignon. Ada wasn't skilled, and Remington had no maid on staff who was.

"I shouldn't be going." Franny stilled lest the needle make another strike, but her toe tapped a furious rhythm on the carpet. "Lord Grimley and I haven't been introduced. My father hasn't done business with him even. No one is expecting me. I'm an American version of a wallflower. Worse. I promise you that I add nothing to the event."

Hildy seethed in ladylike decorum from her spot on the threadbare settee jammed in the corner of Franny's bedchamber. The hulking furniture did not fit the space. Like most of the rooms at Rose Hill, this one was a jumble of masculine embellishment and blatant neglect. "Being recognized by Lady Chapman-Holmes of all people made the decision, Miss Shaw. *Everyone* in Derbyshire is expecting you. Lord Remington stated publicly that I knew about this governess arrangement, almost as if I was your chaperone. So, you'll accompany me and prove it. There are rules to uphold. The baron agreed to the latest set of contracts, and we've forwarded them to your father's local solicitor. Hillsdale was unsettled by the rumor of you being in the residence of a notorious rake, even if properly accompanied, so he arranged for transport he cannot afford, and he'll also be in attendance."

"Can't blame him, considering the viscount's horrid reputation," the duchess mumbled around the hair clip jammed between her teeth. "Dogs like to fight over their bones, don't they? Maybe Remington assuming care of a child will polish off a few of his rough edges. It won't make the hungry mamas harass him any less, that's certain, but perhaps he'll forgo a mistress for a bit. That would help."

"Bother," Franny whispered, her heart giving a jarring thud. The thought of Chance Allerton and his sizzling glances, and Baron Hillsdale and his tepid ones, occupying the same space made her want to crawl beneath her ratty counterpane and hide until spring. While the thought of the viscount's many mistresses made her want to break something.

"Have you talked to him?" This question was thrown over Franny's head by the duchess—who had asked to be called Georgie—to her partner in crime, Hildy. They'd held multiple hushed conversations while she stood there fuming. "Close friends, aren't you?"

"Chance? We're distant cousins, actually." Hildy smoothed her hand over her gently rounded stomach with a clever smile. She was expecting in a few months, and her excitement was surpassed only by her husband's. All of London was commenting on Tobias Streeter's transformation from rookery brawler to lovesick husband. "Oh, he's avoiding me."

The women looked to her as if Franny knew the reason behind this.

Franny's lips parted, a terse exhalation slipping free. "He's working." And riding his midnight-black bay across the frozen landscape each morning like he was fleeing from something. Or someone. "A new desk design. It's actually quite lovely. Gorgeous finials and these tapered, very elegant legs. Rosewood, I think he said he's going to use. I—" Halting, she realized she'd said too much. In a tone that spoke of familiarity well above a governess's lot.

"Oh, dear," Georgie murmured, giving a lock of Franny's hair a yank. "I was afraid of this."

While Hildy simply watched, waiting. Patient but expectant. She was going to make a magnificent mother if she used these dead stares on her children when they'd done something wrong. It was worse than a ruler across the knuckles, which her father had employed many times.

"I'm helping him," Franny finally said. Then stronger. "He doesn't have an artist who understands his vision."

"His vision," Hildy whispered into the hand she'd bought to her lips. "His *vision*. I'm going to kill him. How about *that* for a vision, Chance Allerton?"

Franny gave the seamstress, Mrs. Smithe, who was also a midwife in the village, a chagrined grimace. "Perhaps it's good enough? I like the fit." She wasn't going to mention that Lord Remington had begun tacking her sketches up alongside his own on his workshop wall.

Mrs. Smithe sucked her cheek between her teeth, running her hand over the altered waist of a gown that was the loveliest Franny had ever worn. She'd never cared much about clothing or had anyone special to dress for. "If you don't eat a thing this evening, not so much as one biscuit, it might work. I wouldn't exhale too hard, either. Dancing is questionable. You are slightly more endowed"—she wagged her hands to describe a fuller figure, then nodded to Hildy—"than the missus. Keep a shawl handy just in case you split a seam."

Franny's cheeks flushed. She was *healthy*, according to Ada, who had a vile, defensive hatred of slender figures. "Thank you for the advice. I appreciate your prompt assistance."

Mrs. Smithe whistled and gathered up her basket of materials, stabbing needles in the velvet cushion strapped to her wrist. Crimson thread matching Franny's gown dangled from her sleeve and her bodice. "Dear heart, you paid me London wages for Derbyshire work. I'm not even the best seamstress in the village. But it'll do. And so will I. My stitches are straight and strong, don't you worry. But don't go and cough, not even once."

Georgie covered a burst of laughter with the hairbrush and escorted Mrs. Smithe into the hallway.

Once they were alone, Franny rounded on Hildy. "There's no reason to hurt him. I'm helping Lord Remington, true, but we're barely speaking if that makes you feel better. It's the most distant business relationship imaginable. He's not coming to dinner or breakfast while Kat and I are there."

Her hand going to her lower back, Hildy stretched with a muted groan, her gaze taking no prisoners. Franny could see how she'd captured the most cunning man in London. She was a fierce competitor. "He's avoiding me, avoiding you. Why is that, do you think?"

Knowing exactly why that was, Franny decided it was a perfect time to test the gown's seams, circling the room, trailing her fingers across dusty shelves, making a mental note to have someone clean the room. This house would take a year of hard labor to get in order. With a sinking heart, she realized Remington would soon marry, and it would be his viscountess making sure that happened.

"My husband did something similar after we kissed the first time. He made quite a show of running, Miss Shaw. I know what men trying to escape a realization look like."

Franny did a slow rotation on the balls of her feet. "We didn't kiss." She hadn't kissed anyone since that disaster in Philadelphia. She'd wanted to kiss Lord Remington, of course. What woman wouldn't? He was the most handsome man in England. Tall, dark, and...

Hildy snorted, an inelegant sound from an elegant woman. "You should see the dreamy expression on your face. Whatever happened was enough to have the viscount making a respectful fool of himself. When I told him you were off-limits. About to be married to Hillsdale. The man is a menace. A bounder. A scoundrel. I presented a challenge he can't deny. Unless..." Hildy sat up, her feet hitting the floor with a *thump*. "You want to marry Hillsdale, don't you?"

Franny gave a half-hearted shrug. "Truthfully, I don't want to marry anyone. If not for my father and his threats, I'd live my life as a sketching spinster. But I want freedom, financial and personal, and it seems marriage is my only way to get it. I'm purchasing a husband if I may be bold, so I have control I wouldn't otherwise have." She picked up a vase with a chipped edge and ran her thumb over the imperfection. She'd always thought imperfections made a piece. She didn't want to tell Hildy about the scandal that had brought her here. It didn't really matter except in the depths of her heart. "Look at the vexed expression on *your* face. You believe in love. Matchmakers often do. It's not surprising. But it's not reality, either. I've never known anyone to marry for anything but business. My parents included. My mother's dowry backed his first company. He didn't come from money, believe it or not. Baron Hillsdale's children won't have a storied birthright, but they won't be destitute, either."

"We're not matchmakers, but I believe in love. I'm in the midst of living it. I want what I have with Tobias for every woman who crosses the Duchess Society's threshold. Every woman in England. There's no greater joy than marrying the *one* person you can't live without. I would have gone anywhere with Toby, marriage or no. Followed him to the ends of the earth and back. He had me from the first moment, the first word. I can't explain it. I only know it's what I felt." She smiled softly, her hand settling on her stomach in a protective gesture. "What I *feel*. I also understand this isn't practical for most."

Franny placed the vase back on the shelf, turning the chipped side to the front. "There's truly no reason to delay. My father and I agree this is the best choice for me." Acting on an infatuation with the most infamous rake in London wasn't a wager she could safely make.

But she would have liked a kiss.

She glanced over her shoulder, a sense of urgency driving her toward something. "So, you'll continue to help me? Until we have the papers signed?"

Hildy slumped to the settee, grooves of exhaustion streaking from the corners of her eyes. "Of course. That's what I was hired to do, but I won't be happy about it."

I won't either, Franny thought woefully.

Chapter Seven

Where a Forlorn Viscount Ponders the Rules of Attraction

Chance hated balls. They made him feel like he was standing outside his body, watching the proceedings from an ambiguous vantage point. As if his clothing was two sizes too small or his skin covered in hives.

As if he was playing a role and doing a bloody pitiable job of it.

Although this event was smaller than most, sold as a winter celebration in case the melted snow mucked across the marble floor, the pine branches tacked to every ready surface, it wasn't a clear reminder of the season.

Winter simply meant it was too frigid to open the veranda doors to invite even the suggestion of fresh air. So here he stood, the scent of sweat mixing unpleasantly with lemon verbena and pine. Every starving mama in the room giving him a jaundiced eye because he'd yet to sign so much as one dance card. He dragged the toe of his Wellington, not boots meant for dancing, mind you, through a layer of chalk on the floor. In use so one didn't go careening across marble, landing on one's bum. An occurrence which would have made the festivities a bit more interesting at least.

"You're going to have to dance with someone, mate. Your role as a nobleman, innit? Give the unattached ladies some hope for the future? Their mother's stares are starting to torch my skin," Xander Macauley said, shoving a beverage that Chance prayed was stronger than champagne in his hand. "Glad they don't want anything to do with me."

Macauley was Tobias Streeter's partner, London's finest smuggler since Streeter had stepped down when he'd gotten married and started a family. Both men had grown up in the slums and now ruled parts of the city most had never visited or *wanted* to visit. Macauley owned a shipping company, a distillery, and half a dozen other incredibly profitable ventures. Rumor was, a gaming hell was next. Chance's partnership with Streeter, Macauley & Company had earned him enough blunt to keep from being so desperate he would have signed every dance card in the building during the first ten minutes of his arrival.

And as friends, they'd protected his identity. No one in the *ton* knew Washburn Furnishings was his. Washburn had been his mother's maiden name.

Although he couldn't avoid marriage to some dazzlingly wealthy blue-blooded chit forever. Even with his love promise. Only this morning, he'd found a rather substantial leak in the roof at Rose Hill. In a back parlor. One that could potentially bleed him dry to repair. His chest ached when he thought about the care the estate needed. A life that now included a little girl.

Lifting his gaze to the gilt-edged ceiling, Chance tossed back half the drink—scotch, thank God—in one punch.

"There you go, Remington, grease the wheels for the night you're set to have. No need for sobriety for this." Macauley leaned his broad shoulder on the column Chance had chosen to hide behind, elegance in nonchalant repose.

Chance grimaced and finished off the scotch, welcoming the path it burned down his throat. What did Macauley know about it? He had enough blunt to fund a country's takeover and absolutely no expectation that he'd marry anyone above an opera singer or possibly an actress. He could fall in love with his *mistress* and make it come out all right. As long as he didn't try to climb higher, he was fine.

"Quit frowning, mate. Your night has just gotten a lot more interesting."

Chance swiveled to face the ballroom, his gaze sweeping the revolving couples, then climbing the spiral staircase at the opposite end of the hall. He blinked, momentarily blinded by a thousand candles' glow. Awareness shot down his spine before he recognized her, landing regrettably in his nether region. A response he struggled to hide with an arm dropped low.

His cock never played fair. Not once in his life.

This is what he'd feared but hadn't needed to see. Her beauty on display. Franny Shaw after someone with knowledge of English fashion got their hands on her. Her hair, for once contained in a stylish coiffure, sparking in the light until it glowed. And the gown. Layer upon layer of crimson silk leaving absolutely *nothing* to the imagination. She looked like she'd been sewn into the bloody thing. He nearly groaned as his gaze ate her up, feet to brow and back again. Like a gift he yearned to unwrap with his *teeth*.

Hildy had arranged this. Dangling the chit before him when she *knew*—oh, he wasn't fooling anyone—he was attracted. Frankly, his pulse started throbbing when she entered a room. He exhaled sharply, trying to ignore the way her breasts shifted as she descended the stairs into the ballroom.

She had the most gorgeous figure he'd ever set eyes on.

And unlike the others, her mind and heart were quite remarkable, too.

Macauley grinned, jamming his elbow into Chance's ribs. "*Ah*, the look on your face might make this dull-as-shite country jaunt noteworthy, as your posh set likes to say. Noteworthy as hell. I'm suddenly glad I accepted Streeter's offer. Your governess is a far sight prettier than I'd heard." He whistled softly between his teeth. "That is one delectable piece. Without the silly English prattle to deal with."

Chance slammed his glass on the tray of a passing footman, causing the servant to balance it with both hands before it tumbled to the floor. "Stay away, understood? She isn't like the ones you keep."

Macauley chuckled but there was a brutal edge racing beneath it. "She's not like the ones you keep, either."

Unfortunately, this was true.

"Hold up," Macauley whispered and took hold of his arm. He nodded to the bloke elbowing his way through the crowd to get to her. "Her betrothed, am I right? Even I occasionally take a look at the gossip rags. You don't need to get there panting like a horse out of the gate."

Chance yanked his arm free as Hillsdale arrived at the bottom of the staircase—just as Franny was set to officially enter the madness. He could have sworn the baron glanced back with a triumphant smirk. "They haven't signed any agreements."

"Hold on, I need another drink if we're discussing marital contracts," Macauley groused, going in search while Chance stood there, tucked behind a column, pondering the sentiment that had his belly tied in a quivering knot.

Franny went through the motions; he'd give her that. Smiled at the baron. Made a feminine show of offering her dance card, which Hillsdale signed twice with a flourish. When everyone knew two signified intent. She took a glass of champagne and sipped carefully. Only Chance noted her stiff posture, overly precise. The uncomfortable stretch of her lower back. The charcoal stain on the tip of her glove. The wrinkle on her bodice.

No one in this bloody country had any idea she was *real* beneath the posturing.

The most unique woman in the room.

Somehow, it had settled in his mind that Hillsdale was marrying her for her money. And he'd accepted this. But when the baron gazed down her bodice, his face getting the look only an aroused man's did, Chance realized he was entering virgin territory.

He'd never been jealous of any woman. Not once, ever.

"Drink this," Macauley muttered and bounced a tumbler off Chance's clenched fist. "We're not brawling tonight, at least until his babe is born. Streeter made me promise. No more. He'll be here any second with a wife glued to his side, a chit who has little tolerance for our antics. That gives us six months or so to exercise our wisdom. Hildy told me I had it in me to be better if I'd only try. Fetching simple, innit? But for me, nothing about women seems simple."

Chance took the glass and sipped, his gaze fastened on Miss Shaw, who had begun to waltz with the baron. Her step was sure, almost athletic, impressive for a girl he imagined hadn't grown up waltzing. Chance had learned from a pitiless French instructor when he was twelve, at his father's command.

It had been harrowing and unpleasant, like much of his childhood.

Finally, on a swift turn, Franny caught his gaze. Her cheeks were rosy from exertion, but the bloom on them increased when she looked at him. Her silky smile reminded him of a gold- and-pink dusted dawn, brightening everything it touched. A buoyant sense of wonder stole through him. It was seconds that they stared, no more, but it was enough to confirm that Chance wasn't the only entranced soul.

Somehow, this knowledge bound him to her with invisible threads of need.

It was easy, *so* easy, to imagine what he'd do to her if given the opportunity. He'd start by unfastening the buttons of her bodice. Sliding the silken bundle from her shoulders to pile at her feet. Chemise ties loosened. Lace swept aside. Breasts straining for attention. Nipples pebbling as he tugged them between his lips. He wanted to mark her, change her. Turn them inside out. Situate himself between her thighs and stay there until she screamed.

He was *very* good at persuading without saying a word.

And he wanted to persuade Francine Shaw more than any woman of his acquaintance.

Without tearing his gaze from her, he asked, "Macauley, can you get something here by Christmas?"

"Three days until the day, mate. Gonna cost you. But I control half of the shipping channels in London, so anything can be bought. And I do mean damn near anything." He slipped a cheroot from his waistcoat pocket and wiggled it between his lips. "As your friend, because blunt is tight, I suppose it's gonna cost *me*. For the girl, I'm guessing? I can secure any toy you wish to put your hands on."

Chance rubbed the glass back and forth across his lips. He could ask Macauley for this favor when he wouldn't ask Tobias Streeter. Because Hildy's husband was in love and at the stage where he wanted everyone *else* to be. Macauley didn't believe in love. In fact, he often compared the emotion to an infection. He'd never suspect Chance was doing anything aside from trying to get into a chit's drawers. "Her presents are hidden at the bottom of my wardrobe. Doll, new clothes, sweets. Even a puzzle of a duck in a lake or some such. She's swimming in gifts. What I need is for the governess."

Macauley grunted, the unlit cheroot bobbing between his lips. "Ah, there it lies. This entire city is collapsing around me. Love, marriage, children. It's ghastly. I may have to move to the continent."

"This is nothing romantic. Just art supplies. I can give you a small list."

Macauley blew a breath though his teeth, removed the cheroot, and tossed his scotch back. "Hildy will bash you over the head with her umbrella should she find out. The Shaw chit is one of hers now, you know that. The bloody Duchess Society. The American is in knee deep, God help her."

Chance couldn't stop himself from asking, a blunder he blamed on the scotch, "Have you ever felt something you didn't want to, Mac? Even once? Like you stumbled across a treasure in the most unexpected place?"

"Under someone's skirt, you mean? Sure, lots of treasure to be found there." But his gaze immediately skipped across the ballroom, defying his indifference. Chance followed it only to find the Duke of Leighton's sister, Lady Philippa, standing by the window, plotting her escape. Blond, beautiful, and animated in a way that drew a man's attention, she was dangerous. A reckless chit who pretended not to be. The worst kind. Too *everything* for Xander Macauley, a blackguard who would never be allowed near her.

It would be irony of a sort if *that* was the chit who brought him down.

Leighton and Macauley were friends, of sorts. If you counted being thrown in the Thames as friendship, which had happened last year. Leighton the one doused, Macauley the one standing on the riverside laughing. But Macauley going after Lady Philippa would ruin everything. The man couldn't be that foolish.

Chance peered into his glass, wishing for more alcohol. "I guess your silence means no."

"Send me the list of supplies you need," Macauley growled and strode away, headed to the drink cart in the corner.

Leaving Chance to watch his bogus governess twirl in the arms of her betrothed.

Franny was starving. Lightheaded, her stomach growling incessantly.

She wasn't used to going hours without a bite to eat.

But she'd followed the modiste's advice, and her borrowed gown had held.

After being escorted back to Rose Hill by Tobias Streeter and his contingent, she headed directly for the kitchen—and the plate of lemon scones she'd spied before leaving. Shrugging from her coat only to find Chance Allerton sprawled on the bottom step of his grand staircase like an expectant father.

He'd been at the ball, studying her from the perimeter of the dance floor much like he was now. Emotion she couldn't discern lighting his vivid blue eyes. She'd heard the whispers about him. He'd refused to waltz, angering every ravenous mother in attendance, then rudely disappeared. There were numerous theories about where he'd gotten off to. A new mistress, a card game in a back parlor, a brawl with his hoodlum friends, but near the truth of possibly being sick of occupying a room swarming with sycophants.

Franny hated to admit it, but she'd felt a burst of relief at seeing Lady Chapman-Holmes in the crowd after Remington left. He wasn't with his old mistress. However, he could have been attending a *new* one.

She was jealous... but no one needed to know.

He glanced up as she halted at the staircase. Close enough to catch the scent of bergamot clinging to his skin, the faint hint of scotch riding the air. His hair was a gorgeous disaster, disheveled from handling. His cravat untied, the ends dangling down his chest. His jacket tossed over the banister, shirt undone enough to expose his collarbone. Sleeves rolled to his elbows, exposing muscular forearms that almost no man in the *ton* could claim. He'd gone from masterfully attired to lord of a country manor in a blink.

She didn't have to try hard to imagine him with no clothing whatsoever. Another of her secrets. She had a vibrant imagination where he was concerned.

"Katherine is asleep in the nursery. Your companion is with her, on a settee that looks to be barely holding her. I think, despite her frightening demeanor, she's actually good with children."

"She's very good with children. She's simply not good with men."

Chance's brow rose, waiting for her to say more, so she didn't.

Finally, he scrubbed his hand over his mouth, tilting his head, thinking. "You're going to marry him, then. It looked quite official on the ballroom floor. Hillsdale had a look of complete ownership on his face. Should I offer congratulations?"

A wave of lightheadedness hit her, and Franny swayed, reaching for the newel post. Her bonnet tumbled to the floor. Chance was on his feet instantly, grasping her shoulders. She shook her head, embarrassed, trying to sidestep his bruising hold. Yanking her coat from her arms, he tossed it over the banister alongside his.

"I haven't eaten. This dress. It's Hildy's, and the modiste implied my ample curves would bust the seams if I consumed so much as even one biscuit."

With a harsh oath, his hand trailed down her arm, leaving fire in its wake. Clasping her fingers, he led her down the hallway, thankfully toward the kitchen. He linked his with hers, the first time she'd held hands with a man in her life. "Your body is a bloody fantasy, don't let anyone tell you differently."

She stumbled along behind him, her breath caught in her chest. *Fantasy*. She'd never been anyone's fantasy.

Well past midnight, the kitchen was deserted when they entered it. Only the scent of grilled meat and stewed cabbage remained. Lighting a candle, then a wall sconce, Chance pulled out a chair from a scuffed table the scullery staff used for meals. "Turn," he ordered after she sat. Too hungry to argue, she swiveled, presenting her back.

From the first touch, she couldn't have said a rational word had her life depended on it.

He was efficient. Obviously well acquainted with the intricacies of women's attire. Easily undoing the top two buttons of her gown, allowing her to breathe without constraint. He wore no gloves, and his calloused fingertips sent trails of heat whispering through her.

The man worked with his hands, and it showed.

He paused, a sigh slipping free, his body towering over her. She was thankful she couldn't gaze into his face from this position. "If you were truly my governess, I wouldn't be this familiar. Not that I should, in any case. But we're friends more than the other, I suppose. Employer and such.

I wanted you to know." Stepping back, he swore beneath his breath, his hands dropping from her. "I'm not, that is, I've never taken advantage of someone vulnerable."

Her heart skipped a beat because a man had once taken advantage of her vulnerability. "You've never had to. They come to you." She glanced over her shoulder, letting him know she appreciated his honesty. And that she was teasing.

Startled, he blinked and stepped back, bumping into the cupboard. Lips curving in self-mockery, he began assembling the items to make tea. *Tea*. Her fascination blossomed in the cozy confines of his decaying estate's kitchen—as she watched an honorable viscount trying desperately to *prove* he was honorable.

No one had believed him before, she guessed.

In less than a minute, he delivered a plate piled high with cheese, ham, and the lemon scones she'd spied earlier, followed soon by a cup of tea, steam lifting free to tickle her nose. Then he sprawled in the opposite chair, his own cup cradled in his broad palms. The tip of his boot edged her ankle, and they shifted in their seats to adjust, gazes downcast.

She took a sip of excellently brewed tea and dug into the ham. "You're quite handy in the kitchen, my lord," she murmured, chewing as delicately as a ravenous person could.

"Destitution requires a man to prepare his own meals. My funds only allow for service at breakfast and lunch." He sipped, his cobalt gaze striking hers over the rim of his cup. "You've never had a viscount wait on you before? Is that what I'm hearing?"

"I've never had *any* man wait on me."

Her words registered in a way she hadn't intended. The chemical charge that traveled between them whenever they were in the same space crackled like lightning. His pupils expanded, a muscle in his jaw starting to tick. Seconds passed while they breathed softly in the winter twilight.

Finally, in tense silence, he reached for a scone. Then turned it in his hand like he didn't know what to do with it.

"You don't like Hillsdale." Dusting a crumb from her bottom lip, she tried to ignore the way his gaze tracked the movement. But her body clenched, seeing everything her mind sought to repel.

He shook his head, biting into the scone. His hair glimmered, amber threads sparking in the candlelight. Grainy stubble dotted his cheeks, giving him the look of a swashbuckler. Both elegant and ferocious. And beautiful, even if she wished he wasn't. "No, more like I feel you're selling yourself to the lowest bidder."

"I don't have the luxury to be selective. My father will disown me. He's threatened, and I believe him. We're not close. We never have been. A woman alone, without funds, can't survive in this world." Glancing at her plate, she decided to be honest. Flickering candlelight and the gentle rumblings of a slumbering house made it seem as if they were the only two people in England. "I made a mistake a year ago that limits my negotiating power."

He looked up, arrested. Swallowing, he placed his cup on the table. "A mistake."

She traced a crack in the plate with her pinkie, avoiding his gaze. "The kind that men can make every day, but a woman never can. Not even a hint of one. He was cruel, and I was foolish. Other than that, it's in the past."

He sat back, his chair squealing in protest. Such a broad body housed in a threadbare piece. He must have hated it when he designed the most gorgeous furniture. "So that's why you're running." His words were edged with anger. She wasn't sure where they were directed.

Her temper sparked when she had no reason to be incensed. "I'm *not* running. I would have stayed despite the scandal. It only ruined my chances of a proper marriage in Philadelphia. High society, they call it there. Nothing so graceful as the *ton*. An entanglement I never desired anyway. I could have lived as a spinster without issue. I want to, in fact."

His lips parted, closed, then parted again. He fiddled with his cup before grabbing another scone. She'd never known a man to consider *her* opinion before imposing his own. "What about love?"

The sip of tea she'd taken went down too fast. She coughed and dropped a slice of cheese to her plate. "*Love?*"

"You don't believe in it?"

She coughed again, struggling to take a full breath. "Yes, of course. Well... perhaps." She dusted a crumb from her plate. Shrugging, she knocked her knees together beneath the table. "I'm not sure."

He tilted his head, a charming habit she'd noticed he made when he was thinking. "I've seen it, you see. Living proof. Tobias Streeter and Hildy, a woman I believed would never get twisted up, are in deep, sickening love. From the first moment, too. The Duke of Markham and his duchess, Georgiana, the same. Have you taken a look at those two? They went sneaking off tonight to a back parlor or something. They can't keep their hands off each other, and they have *children*."

Franny pretended extreme interest in the border of lilies circling her plate. She couldn't look into Chance Allerton's indigo eyes and talk about *this*. "I find this a little hard to believe coming from the biggest rake in London. Lord tup-'em-and-leave-'em."

"That moniker is absurd. And untrue. My relationships are entered into with full knowledge regarding my expectations. *And* hers. Breaking someone's heart, if that's possible, isn't my goal. I only want the moment of solace the connection brings."

She sniffed. *Men*. With women, it was never that simple.

"Listen here, sweetheart, I *could* believe in it," he said, his voice rising. "More than you seem to be able to."

Her smile was unexpected and undeniable. *Sweetheart*. She couldn't stop herself from lifting her gaze. He had a scowl on his face and was staring at his scone like it held answers to life's questions. "What about marriage then?"

"What about it?" he growled, taking an angry bite.

She pointed. "Your leaking roof. Your housekeeper's bad tooth. The vicar's home in the village that needs renovations. You have to marry. You need funds. Blunt, as the English say. Are you telling me you require *love* before you'll do it? I've been in this country six months, my father talking nothing *but* marriage, and I've never heard love mentioned once. Except by Hildy Streeter, and I agree, she's too over the moon for her husband to pay any attention to."

"Thanks for the reminder of the dismal state of my affairs." With a grunt, Chance rose from his chair and began riffling through the cupboard. Locating a dusty liquor bottle on the back shelf, he turned with a grin that sent her stomach to her knees. He was unfairly, unjustly handsome, the bounder. "I'm not following my parent's example. I bloody refuse. They hated each other and made life miserable for anyone around them." Pouring a measure into his empty teacup, he lifted a brow. "I can't guarantee the quality, but it's likely to warm the soul."

She finished her tea, then held out her cup. Her hand was trembling. Perhaps not enough for him to notice. The brandy *was* abysmal, but it did the job as it trailed down her throat.

"You could be right. Maybe fancying a chit is enough."

Her heart gave a leaden thump. Franny didn't actually want to talk Viscount Remington into marrying someone who—she could admit in the depths of her mind—wasn't *her*. "Fancy," she said with a false laugh. "Such an English way of putting it. So delicate."

"When it's not delicate," he murmured, his eyes glowing. "Not at all."

Franny slid her cup to the table, her mind whirling with lewd images. A mysterious thread in his tone was lighting a fire inside her. She shifted to find a position that relieved the pulse settling fast and hard between her thighs.

He sighed, his eyes closing. "You're supposed to hide what you're feeling right now, Francine Shaw."

"Why?" she whispered.

"Because it tempts a man beyond measure, sweetheart." He leaned in, letting her see the same on his face. His cheeks were flushed, his breaths coming in shallow bursts. "Passion is different from love. Don't confuse them. I never have."

She slid closer until her bottom was on the edge of her seat, helpless to deny her attraction. She'd never been a good liar. The scent of raw wood drifted to her, mixing with the pleasing kitchen aromas. He'd apparently been working before she arrived.

"Is that what you did before?"

She licked her lips, a band tightening around her chest. "I never felt this for him. For anyone, I think I'm realizing. Never experienced... *passion*."

He flattened his hand to the table, his knuckles paling. It provoked her to see his reaction, even if she wasn't sure what she was doing to cause it. "Do you want to tell me about it?"

Someday, she thought but didn't say it.

That life seemed like another now. Another time and place. This room, this estate, this *man* was all she wanted at the moment. In mere days, she was leaving for a new one.

Her now was *his*.

Chapter Eight

Where a Viscount Learns Lessons in Love

With an oath, he was out of his chair, sending it to the floor with a bang.

He dropped to his knees before her, studying her stunned expression like he would a diagram of one of his designs. His hand went to cradle her cheek. Her skin was soft, creamy, glowing in the candlelight. Her lips parted, inviting him to touch her. He didn't understand why he wanted her with such intensity. Stronger than he recalled yearning for another human being. "I'm going to kiss you, sweetheart. Senseless, if I can manage it. Stop me now if that's not what you want."

She reached and, instead of pushing him away, wrapped her hand around his wrist and held him to her. "I haven't agreed to any agreements. This is *my* life. Until I leave Derbyshire, it's my life. You're only taking what I want to give. There is no betrayal or confusion on my part."

He closed in until his lips brushed hers. She tasted of tea and lilies, lemon and life. "Your choice then."

She hummed a *yes* and slanted her head, seizing his lips when he would have moved in gradually. Awkward, eager, remarkable. Her hunger palpable, wrapping him in gossamer strands of longing.

She was untried but not.

Tangling her hand in his hair, she slid forward, sending his body rocking back. Her breasts were full and warm against his chest. Her bountiful body within reach for the first time. Weakened, he parted his lips, engaging her tongue in play. Showing her. *This. And this.* She moaned, the ragged vibration trailing from his mouth directly to his hardening cock.

Without hesitation, she followed his guidance until they found a faultless fit. That moment when a kiss climbs a mountain, soars away from the people initiating it, and into the heavens. Two becoming one.

Take, his mind shouted. *Take her*.

Show her how wonderful it can be.

Her hairpins were easily removed until her glorious strands filled his fist. His other hand going to her waist, fingers curling around her hip in possession, bringing her off the chair and against him.

On their knees, they worshiped. She was on a quest to destroy—even if she didn't know it. She handled him greedily, exploring. Smiling against his lips when he groaned low in his throat at her aggression.

The sensation was dizzying. Of being seduced. Coerced. Splendidly manipulated. When that had always been *his* role. This witty, kind, intelligent American hellion was diminishing his prior experiences until they were muted images and nothing more.

She was making him forget everything but her.

The ground shifted beneath his feet, around his heart, in ways he wasn't ready to allow. Because something about this—about *her*—felt *right*.

Which scared the shite out of him.

Taking her face in his hands, he wrenched back, their breath pelting each other's cheeks. "We'd better stop, Franny. I'm losing my list of reasons for *not* taking you upstairs and discovering your incredible body on a medieval bed the size of a small village."

She smirked, a cagey bit of feminine persuasion that had his cock threatening to make choices for him. Dusting her thumb across his lower lip, she added a nibble to seal the deal. "Do you want to stop? I don't."

Rising, he yanked her up and stepped between her legs. His hand cupped the back of her head, bringing her lips to his. The kiss immediately tumbled into that magnificent spot it would never leave—not as long as they continued.

For years. Forever.

The intimate, lush space they'd created. The *us*.

Dazed, he roped his arm around her waist and lifted her to the balls of her feet. His shaft met the molten valley between her thighs in a grinding, elemental, age-old dance. She clutched his shoulder, hand curving around the nape of his neck, urging him closer. Mating with clothing rumpled but in place.

He wasn't unfastening more buttons on her gown, he *wasn't*. Even if he wanted to more than he wanted to get his desk into bloody Carlton House.

Losing patience, his skin starting to tingle, he walked her back until she hit the wall, his lips sliding down her jaw as he pressed his hips to hers. He would *die* for her body. Throw himself before her and *beg* for... one... taste. Imagining her naked, and that's what he was doing, brought him closer to doom. Sparks lit behind his lids as she wiggled against him, his cock finding a delightful temporary home nestled between her thighs.

He had the sensation. The I-could-come-soon buzz from nothing more than a kiss. Grabbing her hips, he let her feel everything she was doing to him, unable to hide his need. Unable to do a damned thing but want her.

Her head dropped back, a sigh ripping free. "*Remington.*"

"Chance, remember?" he murmured, his breath a tender burn over her skin. "Remington was my father."

She pulled back enough to stare into his eyes. Hers were wide and such a vibrant golden hue it took his breath. "Only your friends call you Chance."

He touched his brow to hers, willing his heart to slow. "How good"—he swallowed, a loud click in the night—"a friend do you want to be, Franny Shaw?"

She gazed at him, candlelight creating magic. Bathing them in gilded awareness. Desire and inevitability converged, a blistering shroud. "I want to sketch you in that medieval bed the size of a small village. You promised I could, after all." She caught the edge of his mouth with her tongue, seeking admission. Rough, unsteady, and devastating. "*After*," she whispered, her voice cracking with desire.

Chance's hand closed into a fist at her hip. Drawing her skirt up, he tried valiantly not to imagine what lay beneath.

Although he was losing the battle.

He wanted her to leave this night believing she couldn't live without him. "You know what you're asking?"

For the space of a second, she looked uncertain. More understanding than he wished she had flashing across her face. Then the passion they generated floated back in, erasing her unease. "I know. And since you're being a gentleman and asking, I'm saying yes."

"I'm asking," he murmured hoarsely, took her hand, and dragged her from the room.

Franny thought to tell him she had experience. A little.

To ease his concern. Because he glanced back twice as he hauled her along the darkened corridors, indecision marking his features. A slight frown dancing in and out of candlelight. His features starkly stunning, reminding her why she'd wanted to capture them on paper. Indecision even as his shaft jutted beneath the fine wool of his trousers, proof of his yearning. There was simply no way to conceal it, especially when it had been pressed like a stone against her hip.

Franny smiled tenderly. She was going to touch him. *Soon.*

And then she would fill a thousand canvases with his image.

She would discover what she'd missed before. When she'd let curiosity and a half-attraction mistakenly lead her to a man's bed. A man she'd assumed *liked* if not loved her. A man who had been her friend. A man who had falsely said no one else would want her.

But *this* man wanted her. So, she was letting him take her.

They stumbled down passageways, taking turns until she lost her way. Up a narrow, winding servant's stairwell. Curving, curving. Where she finally stopped him, taking the higher step and his lips in a bruising kiss because she couldn't *not*. A persistent pulse began to beat between her thighs, a rush of blood through her head. For the first time, she believed she was going to experience pleasure with someone, not merely her forlorn touch in the darkness of her bedchamber.

Chance moaned in silent, unwitting agreement, lingering, his touch trailing from her waist to her shoulders. Along every curve, and she possessed a few. Back to her breasts, where he filled his hands, his thumbs snaking over her nipples.

What he could locate beneath layers—layers she wanted *gone*.

Their harsh exhalations filled the confined space, echoes reverberating as she yanked his cravat free and let it flutter to the stairs.

Pulling himself from the kiss, he crouched to retrieve the strip of silk, then continued up, his fingers linked with hers. "We're not tupping on the staircase, my eager girl." He glanced over his shoulder, his gaze molten. "And yes, it's possible. Not comfortable perhaps... but possible. Maybe someday, I'll show you. Now, we need a bed."

Then conversely, he made the trip to his chamber a challenging journey.

Stopping her at the top of the stairs, at each doorway they passed, a meandering, passionate exploration that carried them in circles down the hallway. As if he couldn't go two steps without touching her. Working the buttons on the back of her gown until it hung off her shoulders. His cravat lost. A button on his shirt tumbling away from them and across the faded runner.

When they made it to his bedchamber, it was madness. She didn't even stop to examine his personal space for the clues she desperately wanted to grasp about him.

Wrapping her in his arms, he kicked the door closed and murmured words she didn't comprehend against her neck. His breath was sweet and hot, scorching her to her bones. He moved away only long enough to awkwardly remove his boots while she toed off her slippers. Then they challenged each other with snickering, gasping pleas and gazes that singed the air. Clothing became a puddle at their feet. Shirt, trousers, drawers. Gloves, gown, chemise, stays, stockings.

When they were done, they stood, panting, gazes roaming. There had not been time to look at the man she'd chosen to initiate her before. He hadn't allowed it. And she'd been too apprehensive to ask. Fumbling in the dark, pain, then him leaving the bed to put on his trousers.

Chance Allerton allowed her curiosity free rein.

After a languid journey along the muscle and sinew of his finely toned body, she met his gaze. He had the physique of an active man. Unlike anyone she'd yet seen in the *ton*.

His throat worked, his lids fluttering, his breath slipping out in a rush. "You're the most stunning woman I've ever seen. And *bloody hell*, I really thought I knew what to expect."

She started to argue, tell him he was mistaken. That *he* was the beautiful one. But he shook his head, backing her into the bed before she could. Where she went down. And he crawled over her.

She stopped him, hand on his chest.

He looked up, through a swing of tangled, damp dark-as-midnight hair. "Is this too fast?" His shoulders rose and fell. "Stop me. Tell me no."

She giggled, trailing her finger down his chest to his belly. His muscles quivered beneath her palm. His cock was jammed between them, against her thigh, hard and hot. It twitched with his effort to hold himself back. She wanted to wrap her hands around it but wasn't sure if she should. "I merely wanted a moment to look. I'm going to capture you on paper, like I've wished to for *months*. I'm as enthralled with your body as you are with mine. I want to remember."

His smile was glorious, softening his features, a sweetness that made her heart stutter. His eyes shimmered in the dim light, inviting her in. "There's no bloody way that could be true, sweetheart. My adoration is fierce. More than I've felt in my life. Yours can't compare, though I'm thankful for it."

Then, he took her under. Weight pressing her into the mattress. Braced on his forearms, he kissed her hungrily, his hand finding her breast, his thumb her hardened peak. Circling, palming, until she lost reason entirely, her head rolling to the side. She arched into him, seeking more. Perhaps she even whispered it. Her body was melting, racing away from her and toward him.

With a muffled groan, he caressed his way down her body.

Sensation exploded as his lips circled her nipple, rolling it gently between his teeth. "Shall I make you come like a proper Englishman, my American jewel? Very thorough but at a dignified pace. The English disposition is good for something, I suppose."

He notched himself between her legs, working his hips from side to side. Deliberately, until her vision blurred. Dear heaven, she'd never imagined this was a whole-body experience. Skin slick from exertion, bodies grinding like they were polishing stone. Lifting her leg high on his hip, he leaned over her, working one breast, then the other with his lips and fingers.

"I have one question." He blew a purposeful breath over the now-sizzling nub, making her gasp. His hand snaked between their bodies, fingers dancing south. Between her thighs, parting her folds, he slid a finger gently inside. Stroking tenderly as she sighed, hips lifting. Deeper, then deeper still. "Would you like to crest the first time with my cock inside you or my tongue?"

Grasping the counterpane as he began to pump his hand, she whispered hoarsely, "Cock first, tongue after. If I'm allowed both. Then sketching, like you promised."

She realized he'd halted, his movement stilling. Soaring from the passionate sea he'd tossed her into, she opened her eyes to find his expression filled with disbelief. A howling gust of wind rattled the windowpanes as they stared. His lips parted, but it was a minute before any words came out.

"Where did you come from, Francine Shaw? You're my dream come to life. Such. A. *Dream*. I fear if I touch you, you'll disappear, a misty yearning deep in my soul evaporating into the night."

She raised to her elbow and reached for his shaft, wrapping her hand around him. Hard, smooth, sleek. He was beautiful, ravenous, cheeks flushed, skin moist. He moaned softly, his lids quivering. "Stay."

"I'm not going anywhere, Chance."

With a sigh, he tore into her. The kiss feral, then he was gone, sliding down her body for real this time. Caressing her ribs, her belly, the side of her breast. While pumping his finger in long, sluggish strokes inside her, seeking to drive her mad.

Although she'd asked for the other first, he moved between her legs, nipping her hipbone, his bristly cheeks grazing her thighs, his mouth delving between her moist folds until she arched and moaned, turning into someone she didn't recognize. He took the pebbled bit of hidden flesh between his lips and sucked, groaning into her skin, his own pleasure breaking the surface. His tongue and finger worked in tandem, in a coordinated, furious pace. She cried out. There was no way to contain her rapture, the sound and scent of them infusing the air.

A rush of sensation crept from the base of her spine, threatening to consume her. Curling her toes, her fingers going into fists, her body arching.

In moments, she was coated in dew, heat, arousal. Wrapped up and around him. Mindless, starved for pleasure. For him.

"*Now*," she said and lifted her hips, needing, wanting. Begging. She wanted him to take her to that place. Now. Now. *Now*.

"Look at me," he murmured against her thigh, his tongue drawing a maddening, lazy circle. "A sketch for your collection. Or maybe we'll make art right here. I'll trace on your bare skin with my fingertips and solve for the complexities of the design with my tongue."

She followed orders—and knew she'd never forget the sight of Chance Allerton stretched across the bed, his muscled arms wrapped around her legs, his dark head resting between her thighs. She should have been embarrassed. When all she felt was a nagging sense of rightness and humbly fragile ownership.

She didn't want him to do this with another woman. *Ever*. That wish was clear.

The wind whipped against the windows, howling, drowning out their staggered breaths.

Growling faintly, he nipped her thigh, her belly, levering on his forearms and rising over her. His fingers leaving her only to nudge his shaft into place at her entrance. "You are delectable. I hardly know how to contain my avarice. An unfamiliar occurrence. A gift delivered to my doorstep that I'm bloody accepting even if I shouldn't."

She arched her hips, seeking. "Quit talking," she rasped against his neck when he lowered himself over her. His delicious weight sinking them into the mattress. "Start doing."

Laughing, he grasped her arm and pinned it over her head, sampling the hard nipple thrust against his cheek by the movement. "What a little bulldog you are. My gorgeous American bulldog."

"I know what I want." She angled his mouth back to hers. "Why act like I don't? I don't understand that about this country. Every desire hidden beneath a thousand layers of dread."

"Why, indeed." Sighing raggedly, he accepted her offer, kissing her while he nudged his shaft between her slick folds, then with a jolt, sliding inside her. A gradual possession. Measured. Determined. Filling her, changing her. Rocking movements that she caught on to quickly.

It was the most natural of unnatural performances. Addictive from the start. She closed her eyes to the glory, skin tingling, air trapped in her lungs. Positioning her bent leg against his hip, he shifted and eased deeper into her, the push and pull lighting a fire inside her.

More *and* less as he stroked. Waging a war. To go faster, to linger. To speed up, to slow. He got her close to a summit, her brusque entreaties filling the silence, the creak of the bed marking their tempo, then he paused, murmuring profane suggestions in her ear. Every one of them—bending her over his desk, having her ride him, filling her again and again—increased the delight she chased. Until she was bound to him, a quivering, helpless mass of nerve endings.

She caught his shoulder, his jaw. Fingers tangling in his hair. Nails digging into the band of muscle around his forearms. Urging him, biting him, hips lifting, bumping in a synchronized cadence.

It was brutal, magnificent elegance.

Sensation gathered, and this time, he let it build. Rocking from tip to base, fully owning her. Entrenched as far as possible one moment, almost sliding out the next. His arms trembled where he held himself over her. Dropping his brow to her shoulder, he took gasping breaths and murmured lost bits of nothing in her ear.

"Close," he said, the word wrenched from him. "*Close*. Come with me."

She shook her head wildly, unable to reply. Unable to do more than move with him, hold him, possess him as he possessed her. Swearing beneath his breath, his hand slipped between their bodies, grazing the swollen nub just above where he penetrated her.

Circling, pressing, demanding her release.

It was enough. Too much. *Everything.*

He knew exactly how to touch her, exactly what she needed.

Finally, splendidly, her climax ripped through her. Dimming her vision, snatching her breath. Her hands flew to the counterpane, fisting, body bowing. Her cry was savage, and he seized her lips, swallowing the sound lest it rouse the household.

He tangled himself around her, grinding, moist skin and fury, his release claiming him. They gasped and panted, bumped and shifted, sighs, groans, murmurs filling the dark night. Drawing forth every last bit of pleasure.

Finally, his weight settled upon her in surrender.

It was the most animalistic experience of her life. Incredible and tumultuous. She felt turned inside out, like a piece of clothing ripped from one's body.

She was ruined. In the best way possible.

"Remy," she murmured against his temple, a bead of sweat streaking down his jaw to her cheek.

He took her with him when he rolled away, tucking her against his side. His lips dusted her brow, a haphazard caress. His chest rose and fell in a mad rhythm. "Remy," he repeated in a sleepy, sated murmur. Stretching, he sighed in gratifying contentment and hugged her close.

She sought to ask him if lovemaking was always like this.

Life-altering. Crushing. So, so beautiful.

Adorable, troublesome man, exhaustion claimed him before she could.

Chapter Nine

Where a Recalcitrant Viscount Broods

"Why are you so grouchy?"

Chance bit into an apple he'd pilfered from the kitchen during his foray for food and art supplies an hour ago, chewing slowly. He was trying to come to grips with the sentiments swirling through him—and the effort was affecting his mood. He'd never been much for Christmas, and here it was, dawn of a new one. And his emotions were tangled in knots. "Is that the American term for vexed? Who says I'm grouchy?"

Franny smiled, a winsome, knowing curve of her lips and licked her thumb, then swiped it across a stroke she'd drawn on the page.

Chance's belly quivered, his fingers curling around the fruit. Discomfited, he glanced to the window. They had at least two hours before daybreak, when she'd need to return to her chamber. Katherine would be up soon after, excited about the holiday, and her governess couldn't be found sketching the master of the house in his drawers. The artist in a ripped chemise and nothing else. Her hair untamed, flowing down her shoulders and back in a crimson-threaded bounty. Her nipples, which he'd found were the shade of a dusky sunset, straining against silk and calling to him to suck them. The bed behind them an utter disaster. The room smelling marvelously of carnal delight.

He'd bottle the scent if he could. Lifting his hand to his nose, he drew her—*them*—in.

"You should be happy," she said cheerfully and drew a swift set of lines, glancing at him once to make sure she was capturing him correctly. "I did what you asked. Now you do what *I* ask. Getting you on paper is why I ended up here, you know. This was the deal. Consider this my Christmas present. I want to capture that little crook on your nose. The scar on your lip. That lank of hair that juts out no matter how hard you try to contain it."

He sank back against the settee, vanquished. Trying very diligently to avoid looking at the dark thatch of hair between her thighs. Flattered to his soul that she'd studied him so well. And feeling a bit clever that he had her a *true* present shoved in his cupboard across the way. She *had* done what he asked. The second time. When he'd awoken to find her circling his nipple with her fingernail. Climbed atop him without a hint of apprehension, in fact. Worked his shaft inside her with only the slightest clumsiness. How his thumb had ended up between her lips, he couldn't say. Just the tip, a gentle suck and nip. He'd about come then and there.

Since when did he like *that*?

Breasts bouncing, calling him Remy in that breathy voice. In crisis mode, he'd flipped her over and resorted to some fancy finger work to make sure she came before he did.

"Quit fidgeting, my lord."

"I said I would pose. I'm posing."

Pose. Bloody hell, was he in deep trouble with this chit.

Her gaze flicked up, taking him in. She was resting against an armchair enough of a distance away to keep him from easily touching her. With his toe if he stretched perhaps. Her eyes were a painfully vivid shade of gold. Her cheeks ruddy from stubble-burn, lips plump from abuse. He let his attention meander down her body. Amazing breasts, slender, graceful feet

—and everything in between made for pleasure. Made for *him*. She really was unfairly endowed.

Duly appreciative, he wanted her with an intensity he'd never imagined. Not since his boyhood had he been less in control.

With her soft smiles and tender touches, she made his world shrink until it was merely them filling it. When he'd always occupied the largest, loneliest of worlds.

The difference between lust and love circled, bringing a leaden ache to his chest. A tightness to his breathing. A clamminess to his skin.

How to tell, he wondered? How to tell?

Because he feared this was happiness he was suffering from, or more confusing, contentment. Of that, he was fairly bloody sure. Bits of the wall he'd built around his heart tumbled when she was near, the barricade getting lower and lower. Like she'd taken a pickax to it.

"Are you still planning to marry him?" he asked without strategy. The thought of her with another man made him want to put his fist through a wall. His emotions were under siege, like he was preparing for a round at Gentleman Jackson's. Seconds from being punched in the face. Or the gut. When he'd never been covetous of a woman. Never trotted himself out like that, vulnerable and unsure.

And there had been many women. An unwarranted number he couldn't now recall.

Her charcoal skidded across her sheet, but she didn't look up. "Are you offering another solution?"

He took a vicious bite of the apple, his gaze roving to the ceiling. Spiderwebs and cracks. Faded wallpaper. Leaky roof. Rose Hill was tumbling down around him. He needed funds. Franny Shaw was wealthy. She understood his vision, was becoming a helpmate. He'd never met a woman who shared his passion for design or one who even *had* a passion outside him. She was an artist, talented and incredible.

And *bloody hell*, did he want her. Insanely. Criminally.

But he'd promised himself long, long ago. Promised that boy. No marriage without love.

"I didn't think so," she murmured.

"I don't have all the answers, you know."

She hummed a raw, jittery sound. "You don't seem to have any."

He dropped his head back to the settee with a sigh. "I knew this was going to happen if I touched you. But I couldn't *not* touch you. And you didn't say no when you bloody well could have! I would have gone crawling back to my bedchamber and pleasured myself all night while thinking about you, yes, but at least we'd be safe."

She rose, crouching before him in that diaphanous chemise that provided absolutely no protection against his hunger. He glanced at the sketchpad, his chest tightening. A reflection of a man in the midst of indecision stared back at him. How honestly she saw him took his breath away.

"There was a man. In Philadelphia. A family friend. He didn't force me. I don't want you to think it was any choice but my own. My mistake, the way I term it. A mistake that became known because he let it be known, necessitating my leaving America. Anyway, he was cruel after. And during, now that I have..." Her smile was splendid despite the conversation. "Now that I have another experience to compare. He made me feel no one else would want me, so I took his offer. I was naïve, and he was heartless. It happens to women every day. I realize my foolishness isn't novel."

Chance cradled her jaw, drawing her lips to his. She went willingly. The kiss was tender and much less than he wanted to share. And much more. "He was a *fool*. You're my fantasy, my dream. I wish I'd been your first everything."

Touching her brow to his, she whispered, "I could help you with your designs more easily if you talked to me. This passing notes back-and-forth nonsense isn't aiding the process."

Chance dusted his lips beneath her ear. "Our current state of undress is why I resorted to this nonsense."

Sitting back, she drew a languid circle on his belly with her charcoal.

He grabbed the pencil and tossed it aside, rolling her over on the carpet. Where they kissed, touched, moaned. Grappled for control before submitting.

He was going to make her come again before dawn.

Then she laughed, belly-deep and authentic, and he hesitated, startled. He'd never laughed in bed. Teased. Talked. He felt as if he'd plunged into a lake with no bottom. Braced on his arms over her, he stared into her face, questioning the thoughts circling his mind, his heart. She had a tiny birthmark on her temple he'd never noticed. Freckles on her nose. Flecks of amber in her eyes. His fingers trembled where he held her. "If I asked, would you say yes?"

Her cheeks paled, her hand falling from the nape of his neck to the floor. "But you said, you told me… you won't marry without love. Does that mean, are you saying—"

He popped his palm over her mouth before she could finish the question. A question he wasn't prepared to answer.

She sat up, breaking his hold. Her dejected expression breaking his heart. "No, then. I'd say no."

"Hillsdale? He gets a yes? When I get a no?" He gestured to the room they'd torn up in their passion, knowing he was being a jackass but unable to help himself. The fate of millions of asinine fools before him.

Franny scrambled to her feet, a woman on a rampage.

Chance's lips parted on a sigh. He'd never seen her angry—not truly—and a depraved part of him was aroused. Cheeks flushed, glorious breasts rising and falling beneath that twist of rumpled silk. Hips perfect for his hands to mold as he brought her against his body. *God*, he wanted to sink into her, make them forget about all this life shite.

Couldn't they simply get back to the basics?

"I can marry him knowing my father's money is all he's after. It's business. But not you, Remy."

"It isn't the money. We're friends. Or something lost in the chasm in-between that I can't for the life of me define. I only know that I'm trailing after you like a hungry hound, desperate for attention. But despite all that, despite my desire and my yearning, bloody hell if the blunt wouldn't help." He shoved to his feet, getting irritated himself. The viscountcy was not of his choosing, but he was trying to make the best of being saddled with it. Stalking across the room in search of his trousers, he found them in a wad under the bed, next to one of his boots.

"Have you seen this place?" he groused, jamming a leg into his pants and hopping around trying to secure the other. "My father left it in ruins. Left my family in ruins. My brother, Arthur, someday I'll tell you about his trials and my desperate effort to keep him on the straight and narrow. You want me to let Mrs. Walker's tooth fall out? The church roof to cave in? Oh, yes, they need a new one of those. I've got not only this estate and every member of the staff under my jurisdiction, but an entire village to worry over."

A gust of sour amusement left her lips. She was dancing about herself to get into her rig, a harder task than his. "Then find someone you don't fancy in *any* way to marry. You won't have questions in your eyes when you look at them. No woman wants to see those while in the midst of the act, my lord. Advice for your next encounter." She yanked her gown to her neck, the bodice gaping provocatively. To him at least. She had no hope to secure the thing without his assistance. "Don't judge the decisions I'm making, and I won't judge the ones *you're* making. The opera singer you engage in the new year will be your business and yours alone!"

He found his shirt draped across the escritoire and tunneled his arm in the sleeve. "How about this, sweetheart? You marry that pathetic example of baron manhood, but we continue to work together. We'll negotiate on a desk design some smog-filled morn in the near future, then I'll drag you upstairs for a quick tup. Because I won't be able to keep my damned hands off you if we're ever, *ever* in the same room."

Franny unsuccessfully fiddled with the buttons at the nape of her neck, her furious words lost. Although her caustic tone was clear. Holding her gown closed, she snatched up her sketchpad and charcoal, searching the room for the rest of her attire.

Chance sighed through his teeth and pointed. On the chair before the hearth. When he'd gone down for her art supplies, he'd found their clothing strewn about the house and collected everything in a tidy pile. Even her hairpins. He didn't want Mrs. Walker to find his cravat on the stairs and wonder what the hell had gone on the evening prior. Although he wouldn't be surprised if Franny's shouts of ecstasy had traveled down the corridor and directly to her.

"Don't go," he blurted when she turned her back on him, realizing it was too late. Realizing they needed a bit of distance to think this through.

Last night was the most incredible of my life.

Nine words that whispered through his mind.

Nine words he couldn't release.

So, with a lingering glance filled with everything he'd lived his life without thus far, Franny was gone.

Leaving her stockings and one slipper but taking part of his heart.

Franny hobbled down the hallway to her bedchamber, through narrows bands of light and shadow. The rosewood paneling shone from a recent polishing she'd asked Mrs. Walker to organize. She wasn't going to cry, she thought and sniffled into the wadded coat pressed to her chest.

There was no need.

This wasn't like that last time, with Gerald Humbard III. Son of one of her father's business partners. Chance Allerton was turning her away out of panic, not callousness. The viscount was scared. She'd noted the emotion shimmering plainly in his cobalt eyes.

Only, she didn't know if she had the strength to fight him.

Thank goodness, she didn't encounter any of the pathetically modest staff currently employed at Rose Hill on her slog of shame. She opened her bedchamber door with a sigh that turned into a gasp the second she looked in the room.

Ada, mother of her heart, sat curled on the settee. A cup of tea in her hand, a wretched pout on her face. "Oh, my cheeky girl, have you flipped the wheels off the carriage this time."

Franny closed the door with a dull click and let the clothing she held tumble to the threadbare carpet. There was no way in Hades she could hide from the one person who, aside from a wayward viscount coming to know her well, knew her *best*. "I did possibly accede to another dreadful impulse."

"He won't marry you," Ada murmured and took a choked sip of tea. Like England, something she loathed. "Although I've seen the way he gazes at you. The way you gaze right back. Like two candles melting in the sun. Both when you think no one else is looking. But lust only creates trouble, dear heart. Never solves any in my humble experience. Your desire to sketch the man, don't argue because I know the way your mind works, has tossed us in the drink this time." She grunted and tapped the teacup's chipped rim against her teeth. "I suppose we must thank the heavens he's poor as a church mouse and can only employ three people who might have seen you. If your father should hear of this, we're doomed. I'll be living with my brother and his horrid wife before spring. Do you know what they're going to make me do with their children?"

Franny crossed to her vanity. The reflection displayed in the gilded mirror was a creature she didn't recognize. Rosy cheeks. Swollen lips. Eyes alight with feminine power. And, oh God, her hair. She tugged her hand through tangled strands that would have impressed Medusa. "He asked, actually."

In his roundabout, tiptoe fashion.

Franny knew it was absurd—but Chance Allerton's carefully veiled vulnerability made her want to pitch herself over the cliff into love with him. Foolish girl.

Ada's cup hit the table with a click. "He did *what*?"

Franny turned, clutching her gaping bodice. Plunking her bottom on the vanity's marble edge, she shrugged. "It was half-hearted. Hasty. Not insincere so much as rummaging for a solution to a tangle he's found himself mired in. Like a pig stuck in mud. It wasn't pretty or romantic."

"You said yes, of course." At Franny's silence, Ada's face paled and she slumped, head dropping to her hands. "A *viscount* who looks at you like he wants to eat you in one bite and go back for seconds. A man, a genuine one, obstinate and arrogant, but a *man*. When the lout your father has lined up is a boy. Please, dear girl, please tell me you said yes."

Franny shook her head. She wasn't selling herself to Viscount Remington. Baron Hillsdale, yes, *fine*. Baroness of naught, signed, sealed, and delivered. She'd never expected to have a *choice*. Her father had told her bluntly from the time she'd begun to attract masculine attention that she didn't.

But she would not, could not, start a life with a man who didn't want her when she suspected she was in love with *him*.

"You still plan to marry Hillsdale? After *this*?" She gestured to Franny's disastrous state.

A furious fire, unusual for her, sparked deep in Franny's belly. Like any woman, she could be a force when jammed into a corner. "We're purchasing each other. My money will be all Hillsdale's got any say over. The rest is mine to govern. I'll take my control where I can."

"As if life works that way." Ada released a scathing huff through her fingers. "What about the girl? If you decide to skip outta here before daybreak, which I think you should. What about that poor child?"

Franny pinched the bridge of her nose, tears stinging her eyes. *Kat*.

"You could take her to Hampton Hall until the new year. Mrs. Streeter invited us because she knew this silly farce of yours was going to blow like a faulty kettle. Her husband's estate is a twenty-minute carriage ride away. Inherited of a sort from Streeter's father, a viscount who didn't acknowledge him until the ancient sot was drawing his last. Unusual set of circumstances for a part-Romani bastard. Society can't decide whether to accept the man or not, and then he goes and marries an earl's daughter, making it an impossible situation. The English are a confounding lot. I swear to the ground they are."

"Lord Remington will come after me if I take Kat."

Ada lifted her head, her gaze narrowing in contemplation. Franny knew that look well, too well. The cleverness behind it had helped her avoid more than one scrape in her lifetime. "Not if we make it seem like it's a holiday invite you'd already accepted. A confused set of missives. Won't be the first time he's read about a woman's departure on a sheet of foolscap shoved beneath his door."

Franny pushed off the vanity, almost losing hold of her gaping gown. "I'm not setting up a race for the viscount to run like my prize mount. This isn't Epsom."

Ada beamed, smug and decided. Dusted her hands together as if she'd made a decision. "All's fair in love, isn't it? This lonely pile made even lonelier without women and children. A man thinks he wants his peace until he has it. The scorching glances the lord of the manor has been giving you could be close to love if you'd kick him across the ravine and into it. That you figured it out sooner can't be held against him. Men are senseless creatures."

Franny took a turn about the chamber, swiping her fingers across layers of dust on shelves, cracks in aged wallpaper, rips in an Aubusson rug that had once cost a fortune. Rose Hill made her want to weep. She would've happily sunk every penny of her dowry into the care and management of this estate, fallen in love with it right along with its owner. Become a mother to Kat.

The fact that she could so easily picture a life with them in this very house was unnerving.

Like most men, Chance Remington was a ninnyhammer when it came to affairs of the heart. Franny dragged her bare toe across a ripple in the carpet, glancing to the window and the shades of blue and pink coloring a dawning horizon. A little push wasn't deceitful if the man in question was racing in that direction anyway, was it?

He *could* love her back. He'd stared into her eyes while he trembled, his broad body curving protectively around hers. His release frenzied... but his gaze calm. Sure. *Adoring*.

"I'll do it," Franny said, never considering that those were the exact words she'd spoken to Hildy Streeter to get her into this mess.

Chapter Ten

Where a Dejected Viscount Comes Calling

Franny had taken Kat's Christmas presents when she fled.

Which was fair as she'd purchased them.

He'd been determined the little girl would have her bloody gifts. But his absconding governess was one step ahead of him, never realizing she had gifts, too. Those damn art supplies Xander Macauley, true to his word, had delivered the night before. Chance had wrapped them in a length of tartan, one in his family for generations. Remnants of the lone, black Scottish mark on his mother's side and even included a crimson length of twine around the bundle that now looked ridiculous.

Or hopeful, depending upon one's perspective.

After Franny had bolted from his bedchamber the night before, in frustration, he'd finished sanding a desktop, then ridden his horse, Talbot, through the snow-capped fields until they were both panting from the effort. When he returned to Rose Hill at daybreak, his decision had been firmly in place. His mind calm. His body sated, thanks to a certain tenacious termagant's loving attention.

He'd only needed a few moments to search his heart, breathe deeply of the crisp winter air. And think.

Then he'd known.

Love. This was love he was feeling, blind and unrelenting.

For the woman *and* the girl.

He was giving in. Gladly giving *up* a life he didn't want for a new one he did.

He'd never felt the like, a sudden rush of emotion weakening his knees when a woman crossed within viewing distance. Her unique scent enough to have his heart skipping a beat. And... an *American*. This fact delighted him for many reasons it shouldn't. Her unsuitability made her perfect for *him*. He couldn't dictate the future, but he wanted Franny Shaw in his life. Wanted her laughter, her wit, her kindness raining down upon him.

Finally, he could picture someone when the word *viscountess* whispered through his mind. *Mine* traveling greedily behind it.

Perhaps the biggest surprise of all, he wanted to be a father to Kat. He wanted to fill Rose Hill with laughter and joy. Hers, to start. Then, the others to come.

With this certainty pillowing him like mist, he'd gone in search of his girls to find he had none in residence. Back to a lonely, creaking, dusty manor in the middle of Derbyshire. The dying pine branches attached to every available surface a reminder of his idiocy.

The answer was obvious. Franny deserved a sincere proposal.

Without questions in his eyes this time.

In a bit of a funk, he'd traipsed to his bedchamber, ignoring his disaster of a bed and the sensual aroma clinging to the air like a chill, and dug around in the side table, extracting his signet ring. It was temporary, of course. Until he had funds—*hers,* ironically—to purchase something more personal. However, he did quite like the scripted R circled by roses, modeled after the estate that had been in the Remington family for centuries. The small ruby he predicted would look stunning against her creamy skin.

She was extraordinary enough to appreciate it.

So here he stood on Tobias Streeter's country portico on Christmas morning, a gift for the woman who had led him on a merry chase to the very spot tucked awkwardly under his arm. Snow swirled inside the collar of his woolen coat, dusting his cheeks and brow. Chance rapped on the door of Hampton Hall once more, feeling the reverberation through the thick oaken slab. It was bloody freezing, and he was nervous.

Which made him annoyed and *more* nervous.

His situation worsened when the door was opened not by an aging majordomo, but Tobias Streeter himself, his canny grin saying things Chance didn't want to hear.

Macauley strode up behind his business partner, clapping his hands. "Before noon, I told you! The men in this circle are falling like diseased birds. You, the Duke of Markham, now Lord tup-'em-and-leave-'em. And for what? Bleeding *marriage*. Which I'm sick to stones of hearing about. Have to get rid of every mistress you've ever had, Remington, you understand that, right? The Duchess Society won't allow you to keep them. On a short leash forever, mate."

Tobias snaked his timepiece from his fob and flipped opened the silver case. "Shite on a shingle. Another ten minutes, and I would have won. And he won't miss the women. I've tried to tell you, Mac. If he found the right one, he'll only want her."

Skeptical, Macauley snorted around the cheroot dangling from his lips. "You owe me another ten, Street. He brought the bloody present. Didn't even try to save his dignity by sneaking in the domestics' entrance. Hands full of his embarrassment. Gads." He gestured to the tartan with a devilish smile. "Nice trimmings, mate. The American is going to slice that heart of yours into tiny pieces and wrap it up with that length of plaid."

While Tobias dug around in his trouser pocket for the wager he'd lost, Chance brushed past them, elbowing Macauley in the gut along the way.

Macauley rubbed his belly, the cheroot bobbing. "Is that what I get for delivering the best art supplies money can buy? German, those charcoals, not the pathetic English gear. And the drawing pad is *Italian* if you cared to notice. I called in a marker, a right fine one with a distributor of some very illegal but lucrative items, to get these on the quick. I've smuggled for the man for ten years now, and he's always owed *me*. Some show of friendship, this abuse, innit? And all to help another man walk the plank. I must be mad."

"Where is she?" Chance glanced around the deserted foyer, the sound of muted conversation and a child's laughter traveling down the corridor.

He would thank his friend and thank him well, once he'd accomplished his mission.

Now that he knew he was sunk, he felt a dire need to share the news with the woman in question. *Immediately*.

Then Franny Shaw, God *love* her, did something that made everything *right*.

Made everything *perfect*.

In a fury, a blur of cream and gold, the scent of lilacs snaking into his soul, she was hugging him, his bundle of German and Italian regrets jammed between them.

His arm closed around her, bringing her as close as possible with the package between them.

Tears stung his eyes, lay thick in his throat.

She was a miracle he'd somehow stumbled upon. A rose in a field of weeds. The most exceptional person of his acquaintance. She and Kat the start of his family. Franny didn't care how her affection appeared to his friends. To society. She didn't mind that he was poor. That he'd fumbled the task of proposing the first time around, trying lamely to tell her he might love her. That he said silly things and acted like an arse half the time. She wasn't asking him to plead, grovel, beg. Or holding a grudge and causing him to apologize endlessly.

All things he would have done.

She only cared about him *showing up*.

He rather thought he could do that more often. Perhaps be an outstanding husband to match her brilliance if he worked hard enough. Aside from his furniture, he'd rarely been good at much of anything.

"You came," she whispered against his lips. Glancing down, she noticed the blunt end of a charcoal pencil sticking out of the tartan. "With presents. Oh, Remy, you darling, darling man! I didn't want to set up the race, such a foolish game, but I did, silly Ada, and you came."

"*Remy*," Macauley whispered in disgust as Tobias Streeter dragged him across the gallery, away from the embracing couple. "This is almost as tragic as you and Hildy."

"What race?" Chance asked, dipping his nose into her silken strands and breathing deeply for the first time in hours. Days. Years. Helplessly lost, his body beginning to react, he started calculating. One hour of gift-giving with the group, a brief luncheon, forty-five minutes tops, then when Kat went down for her nap, he would take Franny to the closest bedchamber or a linen closet even and—

"I recognize that look. *Later*," she whispered. "I'll leave my balcony door unlatched. I'm on the first floor, you can make it up, I'm sure. There's a very sturdy oak outside." She giggled and began to plunder the package, unfolding the tartan, sighing in delight at the offering. "This is the finest set of charcoals I've ever seen. German, *my*."

He stepped back, still holding the gift, as if he was watching a scene in a play. Sunlight, a rare, mid-winter burst, pierced the windows at her back, glazing her in radiance. Her eyes were a potent, golden hue, her hair shot through with amber. She was simply the best he could wish for in a life of broken promises, others and his own.

He wanted her in a multitude of ways with a fierceness that shook him. Curiously, most of them having nothing to do with his cock.

Wife. If she said yes, she would be his wife.

"We'll have to live here for a bit. Derbyshire, Rose Hill," he murmured instead of asking. A coward to the end. At least, this way, he could gain her initial response. "The city when we have to. House of Lords and all that bother."

"I'll go where you go," she returned, flipping through pages of a sketchpad that was, even he would admit, the most superb he'd seen outside an artist's salon. Macauley knew his smuggled products. "And Ada, of course. She'll learn to like you. Give her time. She and Kat are getting on so well. I'm overjoyed they seem to like each other."

"There's an easel on the way, too. Another week perhaps. A few more odds and ends." He shifted from boot to boot, looking for a place to set the bundle. His signet ring was burning a hole in his waistcoat pocket. "There's a parlor on the western side of the house that gets light throughout most of the day. Would make a decent studio of sorts. If you'd like." He settled her gift atop a mahogany sideboard, shoving aside the length of pine and holly serving as holiday décor. A pencil rolled free and bounced across the floor. He bent to pick it up, his back to her. "I even have a friend, a well-respected artist, who teaches classes. Only men, to date. I've already contacted him about working with you. I think he would, covertly because the world is not designed for women, once he sees your work."

"Chance. *Remy*. Look at me."

Setting the charcoal aside, he followed her directive. She'd come up behind him with a furtiveness that surprised him. The beat of his heart was drowning out the sounds of a holiday gathering rippling through the house, snatching his ability to take a full breath. "Do you have something to ask me?"

Her lips were curled at the edges. Delight and a hint of mischief transforming her face. For some reason, the latter gave him the courage to spill his secrets. Machiavellian tendencies, he understood. Could work with. That she wasn't the typical proper English miss perfected the moment. "The viscountess part won't be fun. I can guarantee that much," he mumbled and tunneled in his pocket. The signet ring was warm from its press against his chest.

Taking a breath, he presented it to her. A promise. A future. Like Macaulay had said, his heart for the taking. Possibly to be cut into slivers. "It's all I had time for. I'll find you the most glorious in London when we return."

Her smile grew to incredible proportions. She had the loveliest one he'd ever encountered. She slipped it on her ring finger, when he wore it on his pinkie, and the fit wasn't horrible. Not horrible at all. "I love it." She wagged her hand, catching a ray of sunlight on the ruby. "I want it. I want *you*. I have, I think, from the first moment. Caressing that escritoire at the earl's fete. I could only imagine your hands running all over *me*."

"You will then?" He gave the ruby a light tap, trying to control what was happening—*hardening*—behind his trouser close. The future promise of her body closing around his was becoming the loudest thing in his head. "Marry me? Help me raise Kat. Have more children if we're lucky."

She wound her arms around him, tunneling her fingers through his hair and bringing his lips to hers. "Yes." She nipped his bottom lip, then backed way, causing him to follow. "Although, you're missing three words every girl likes to hear."

He pressed his brow to hers, roping his arm around her waist and settling her against him. Letting her feel what she was doing to him. "Francine Shaw, if I adored you *less*, I'd be able to say more. Say it better. I love you quite madly and without hope of recovery. I only know I want you more than I've ever wanted anything in this life."

"Yes, then," she whispered and pulled him into another sinking kiss. "I will marry you. Because I love you, too. Madly. If the easel arrives by Thursday, that is. If not, all bets are off."

He laughed, his heart breaking. But for the first time, in a good way. "Happy Christmas, my sweet viscountess."

Epilogue

Where a fantastically happy couple make big decisions

Ten Months Later
Derbyshire

Franny took a step back, tilting her head and squinting. "I think the darker shade works. Kat wanted a color close to a bluebell. This is close to a bluebell, isn't it?"

Chance lowered the paintbrush, catching his bottom lip between his teeth. "Hmm..."

Her stomach clenched, heat traveling directly to its chosen spot between her thighs.

Her gaze roved the length of her husband and back. Light hit him just so, perfect for sketching if she'd had her supplies handy. He was dressed for the country in a pair of form-fitting buckskins and a worn linen shirt that clung deliciously to his shoulders and back. Wellingtons polished to a high gloss. He'd been working around the estate the past year, and his body had gotten more muscular if that was possible.

Her need grew with every moment she spent with him. Her love. They were trying for a baby. Still newlyweds, in a sense. Chance had returned from London this morning, so they'd not been able to try for *five* nights. The longest they'd ever gone. "I suppose it works," he said, so earnest it made her heart ache. "But we could try the lighter, too. Or maybe use it on the window frames."

Their adopted daughter, Kat, wanted a blue bedchamber for her seventh birthday. They'd decided to redecorate as a surprise while she spent the day shopping in the village with Ada. Chance had picked the task over the quick romp they both desperately desired, which made Franny love him more. He placed his family's happiness above everything else. Above his own. Adoration he freely showed his girls every day.

"Wait until she finds out about the kitten. I can't wait to give him to her."

"You're spoiling her, Remy."

Shrugging happily, he tapped the windowpane with his brush. His gaze tracked a man galloping a black bay across the fields. "Why is Xander Macauley here again?"

Franny came to stand beside him, snaking her arm through his and leaning into his side. He turned slightly to kiss the crown of her head. He smelled wonderful. Leather and the crisp scent of wood, scents that were Chance's own. His furniture was selling like mad, although the *ton* still had no idea Viscount Remington had a side business. He'd yet to have a desk placed in Carlton House, though the king had expressed interest in having one at Windsor Castle, which Franny assured Chance was even better. "He's having woman troubles, or so he implied. Who was the last one? An actress?"

"Opera singer. Italian, I believe," Chance murmured, drawing his wife close and nuzzling the side of her neck. "Coincidental timing, isn't it? When the Duke of Leighton, his new duchess, and sisters are arriving tomorrow. And Arthur, finally, has agreed to stay until the summer."

Franny watched Macauley halt his mount and slide from the saddle, a towering beast of a man. She liked him. He was genuine in a sea of pretenders. Rough around the edges, cynical, demanding. But he'd been a good friend. A sound business partner to her husband. He had love in his eyes waiting to be unleashed. "What does Leighton coming to pay a visit have to do with Xander Macauley?"

Chance chuckled, a sly ripple of sound. He and Macauley were constantly trying to one-up each other. Wagers on billiards, hunting, hazard. Fisticuffs on the lawn. Fencing in the ballroom. Pushes and shoves and outright brawls. It seemed almost brotherly in nature. "He's got his eye on Lady Philippa, though he wishes like hell he didn't. I'm going to seat her right next to him at dinner and watch him squirm."

Franny's lips parted, a gasp shooting free. This *was* news. "Pippa? Leighton's little sister?" She eyed Macauley as he led the horse toward a stable they'd just outfitted with a new roof.

The *ton* would accept Macauley pilfering their ducal coffers about as well as they'd accepted Franny plundering this viscountcy. Society didn't call her the American Enchantress with great affection. "Will the Duchess Society clean him up? Straighten him out? Leighton would never let him marry her as his reputation stands."

Chance tossed the brush into the bucket by his feet and swept her into his arms, his lips seizing hers. *My*, the man could kiss. "Oh, my naïve darling. Desire isn't love. He'll never tell a soul, make an offer, or a move. But he watches her whenever she's in the room. Every *time* she's in the room. I can't believe Leighton hasn't seen it. But when he does, he'll knock Macauley flat on his arse."

"Let's seat them next to each other, let's do. I want to watch what happens."

"That's my girl," he said and kissed his way down her jaw. "Later, after Kat is in bed, you could meet me at my workshop at the edge of the woodland. You can scream as loudly as you'd like. And you know, I'll do anything you ask."

She sighed, her head dropping back. "I did terribly like that one thing you tried the other night. With your fingers *and* your tongue."

"Done," he whispered against her neck.

"I'm happy, Chance." Dipping her head, she burrowed against his chest. "You've made me happy for the first time. I never want to leave you, even for one night. I'm going to London next time. Five days apart was too much."

Chance pulled back until she could see his face. He liked to look into her eyes when he told her he loved her. "Francine Allerton, you're the light of my existence. You and Kat. And now that orange scrap of a kitten. I give thanks every night that you came into my life. You know that, don't you? I feel *lucky*. To the ends of the earth lucky."

She pressed her cheek against the warmth of his chest, his heart beating beneath her ear. "So, you'll sit for me this weekend? I want to try out the oils this time. I've been practicing."

Chance brought her close with a kiss. "My darling viscountess, I'm your subject for life."

THE END

Thank you for reading *The Governess Gamble* by award-winning author Tracy Sumner!

Interested in reading about Hildy and her sizzling love story with the king of the London underworld, Tobias Streeter? Check out their steamy, banter-filled tale in *The Brazen Bluestocking*. Your Duchess Society membership awaits!

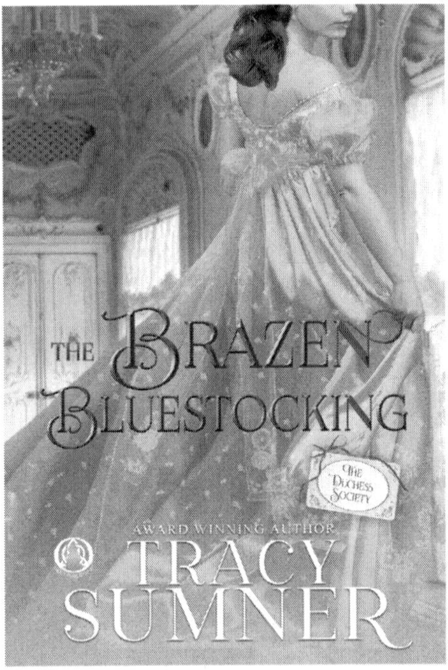
THE BRAZEN BLUESTOCKING
THE DUCHESS SOCIETY
AWARD WINNING AUTHOR
TRACY SUMNER

Also by Tracy Sumner

The Duchess Society Series

The DUCHESS SOCIETY is a steamy new Regency-era series. Come along for a scandalous ride with the incorrigible ladies of the Duchess Society as they tame the wicked rogues of London! Second chance, marriage of convenience, enemies to lovers, forbidden love, passion, scandal, ROMANCE.

If you enjoy depraved dukes, erstwhile earls and sexy scoundrels, untamed bluestockings and rebellious society misses, the DUCHESS SOCIETY is the series for you!

#1 The Brazen Bluestocking

#2 The Scandalous Vixen

#3 The Wicked Wallflower

About Tracy Sumner

USA Today bestselling and award-winning author Tracy Sumner's storytelling career began when she picked up a historical romance on a college beach trip, and she fondly blames LaVyrle Spencer for her obsession with the genre. She's a recipient of the National Reader's Choice, and her novels have been translated into Dutch, German, Portuguese and Spanish. She lived in New York, Paris and Taipei before finding her way back to the Lowcountry of South Carolina.

When not writing sizzling love stories about feisty heroines and their temperamental-but-entirely-lovable heroes, Tracy enjoys reading, snowboarding, college football (Go Tigers!), yoga, and travel. She loves to hear from romance readers!

Connect with Tracy: www.tracy-sumner.com

facebook.com/Tracysumnerauthor
twitter.com/sumnertrac
instagram.com/tracysumnerromance
bookbub.com/profile/tracy-sumner
amazon.com/Tracy-Sumner/e/B000APFV3G

THE COUNTESS'S CHRISTMAS GROOM

PREQUEL TO THE BLAKELEY MANOR SERIES

FENNA EDGEWOOD

The Countess's Christmas Groom by Fenna Edgewood

Published by WOLF Publishing UG

About the book

THE COUNTESS'S CHRISTMAS GROOM

A countess with a wounded heart...

When the recently widowed Lady Katherine Colworth returns to her childhood home for a Christmas house party, she is prepared for many things. Vicious rumors. Slanderous lies. Gossip abounds that she was responsible for her cruel husband's death. What she is not prepared to face, however, is falling in love.

A young man who is much more than he seems...

Ashley Spencer has been conscripted from the stables to the manor as a temporary footman. When he spies the Countess of Colworth, he admires her beauty, little knowing he is about to be forced into a web of lies and intrigue that will lead him straight to her bed.

A love that defies differences... and can overcome any danger.

This Christmas, two very unlikely individuals are about to realize they are one another's ideal match. And once mutual desire has been sparked, they will never be parted, no matter the price they must face.

Chapter One

December, 1816

"Is this what we've come to? Ogling footmen?"

Briar nudged her sister, and Katherine jumped.

"I was not," she said automatically. "What are you babbling about?"

"Isn't he a little young?" Briar went on, ignoring her. "I mean, he *is* handsome."

Katherine sighed. "I was staring into space. Thinking. Not looking at anyone in particular."

"Of course you would say that," Briar said, patting her elder sister's arm placatingly. "But there is nothing wrong with looking." She winked mischievously. "I may even look with you. After all, he is standing right beneath the mistletoe."

"Don't be ridiculous," Katherine said crankily. But she stole a glance at the footman her sister was talking about.

He was handsome, she conceded. Viking-gold hair, with just the slightest wave to it. Eyes the color of a stormy sea. And a strong jaw with the most wonderfully pronounced cleft chin. She had always liked a cleft chin in a man.

And though it was an absolute cliché to even think so, he had very nice calves as well. Very muscular. In fact, he was quite filled out everywhere, from head to toe. That livery he wore was almost threatening to pop open at the seams in some places. Most noticeably, his broad shoulders and upper arms.

Katherine felt a warm tingle move through her. One she had not felt in many years. She shook herself quickly.

But he was far too young. And she was *not* looking. She might never look again. She peeled her eyes away determinedly.

"It truly is all right to look, you know, Kat," Briar whispered. "I was only joking about him being too young. He's at least my age."

"Really, Briar. As if that were any better. You're no more than a child yourself." Katherine sniffed. "As if I would ever consider another man again. Besides, he is a servant."

"What's wrong with servants?" Briar asked, crossing her arms stubbornly. "He's a striking-looking young man. Servant or not. What does it matter if he's an aristocrat? It's not as if gentlemen have any claim to being gentler or nobler than any other class of men. After all..."

Katherine knew all this better than anyone. Which Briar must have remembered, for she trailed off and looked uncomfortable.

"I think I will go back to my room," Katherine announced. "I've made my promised appearance. What more can he ask of me?"

Briar gasped. "You wouldn't dare!" She shook her head. "You've been here less than five minutes, Kat. That is hardly enough to..."

"To what?" Kat snapped. "Redeem my reputation?"

Briar's look was pitying. "Well, I believe that is what he has in mind, yes. Is there really anything wrong with that? Kat, he only wants the best for you."

"What's best for the precious family," Kat muttered rebelliously.

"I mean, I suppose that is true," Briar mused. "But you are a part of our family." She edged closer and lifted her head so she could speak into her taller sister's ear, then whispered embarrassingly loud for Kat's liking, "Because he loves you, you know! We all do."

"Shush," Kat begged. "Someone is going to hear you."

Briar shrugged casually. "Let them. They're our guests, aren't they? Let them hear that we love our sister." She raised her voice slightly louder. "And that she is decidedly *not* a murderess."

"Oh, for God's sake, Briar," Kat spluttered. "Now I really am going back up."

She whirled away, her silken skirt spinning around her ankles, only to injure the tip of her nose colliding against a firm and familiar male chest.

"Oh good, it's you, Edmund," Briar said brightly. "Kat was trying to run away."

"Run away?" Edmund, the Duke of Dareford and the head of the noble Blakeley family, or what was left of it, frowned down at his older sister. "Nonsense. Haven't you only just arrived?"

Being the older sibling had not done her much good once Edmund had outpaced her in height at the early age of ten. Being a man was so unfair. He had the height *and* the title. She doubted many people even realized Katherine was the elder of the two by a year.

"Arrived. Survived. Already regret coming. Good evening to you both," Kat said through gritted teeth.

"Come now, Kat," Edmund said, his frown deepening. "You must greet our guests. There are some kind people here who are very eager to see you again."

"Let go of me, Dare," Kat hissed, feeling her back go up, exactly like her nickname's namesake, and adopting the name her brother hated.

He immediately unhanded her, his face creasing in worry. "I'm terribly sorry, Kat. I didn't mean to... I apologize if I grasped you too firmly. I did not mean to stir up anything unpleasant."

She sighed. "No, it is not that." She reached down and squeezed his hand briefly. "But thank you."

She put a hand to her hair, smoothing back a strand, thinking quickly. She knew Edmund had put a great deal of effort into planning the Christmas house party, orchestrating it carefully in a conscious effort to bring Kat out again amongst the best people, and to show that her siblings—the Blakeleys—were prepared to stand by their sister, through anything, thick or thin. Even the house had been thoroughly transformed for the festivities. It was so covered with garlands and ribbon and boughs of spruce and holly for Christmas that Kat had hardly recognized it when she arrived. And Edmund did not usually hold with excess!

It was a lovely gesture, in fact. Part of her was truly moved.

The other part of her wished to run and hide in her room, preferably under the bed, like a child.

She steeled herself. "Very well, Edmund. Who did you have in mind? Guide me."

She let herself be swept farther into the room, the Viking-esque footman with the muscular calves quickly and completely forgotten.

Serving rum punch to the *haut ton* was not Ash Spencer's idea of a good time.

Yet here he was, in too-tight livery, silk stockings, and a damned powdered wig that itched like the devil, carrying a tray around a room like a prize pig on display.

All because the butler had decided Blakeley Manor was in need of extra help over the Christmas season and that Ash would do, for he "matched."

Matched in height, that is. He was roughly of a height with the other young men who served in the manor, being six feet one in his stockinged feet.

His older brother, Wren, who worked at Blakeley Manor as a gardener, had the good luck of being too tall. Unless the butler became more desperate, Ash supposed, and conscripted Wren, too. Oh, Wren would be most displeased if that occurred.

"Stop scratching," the man in question hissed as he walked by. "You look like a sap."

"Yes, Mr. Taplow, sir. Sorry, sir," Ash mumbled, straightening.

The butler, Mr. Taplow, wasn't an entirely bad sort. He could be a great deal worse.

The underbutler, on the other hand, Mr. Morris, was a right pain in the rear, who took his duties far beyond reason, and had a poor reputation below stairs, especially with the maids.

A sharp elbow suddenly collided with Ash's ribs, and before he could help it, he winced and jostled the tray, cringing as he watched some of the pre-poured punch slosh onto it.

"Don't drop the tray, Spencer. Wouldn't like to see you dishonor us all."

It was Harry Howard, the first footman, smiling slyly. Funny how downstairs, they were called by their surnames but above the toffs preferred to call all the young men by their Christian names.

"Of course not," Ash replied. "Wouldn't dream of it."

Howard seemed afraid Ash was eyeing his position. But in truth, all Ash was eyeing was the door. He was longing to get back outside. He'd rather spend his days mucking out horse stalls than stuck inside, sweltering in this wig.

"You hold yourself in high regard, don't you, Spencer?" Howard hissed. "Don't get any ideas just because you've been brought inside for the holidays. You'll be back in the barn where you belong soon. With the animals."

Ash said nothing, simply looked straight ahead toward a cluster of ladies chatting merrily with a group of elegantly dressed gentlemen.

"That's right, Spencer," Howard whispered, sidling up even closer. "Drink your fill of these beauties while you can. A good deal better than staring at a mare, I'd expect. 'Course, they'd never look twice at someone of your..." He gave Ash a withering look. "Low caliber."

Ash tried not to smile. His birth was nothing to be ashamed of, and in fact, he was well aware he was uncommonly fair of face for a man. Had his two older sisters not enjoyed dressing him up as a girl until he was far too old for it? His older brother still liked to tease him by calling him "pretty."

The truth was, Ash was a handsome, well-formed young man of twenty-five who received more than his fair share of appreciative glances from women—no matter whether they were maids or ladies.

Howard had surely noticed this. He seemed to have pretensions of being a dandy. Clearly, he did not take kindly to having to share the spotlight with Ash, who before this he had never even met.

"What's that, Howard?" It was Frederick—an easy-going lad of nineteen, one of the regular footmen. Frederick was a good fellow. Enthusiastic, eager to please, and always ready to help Ash learn the ropes. His only flaw was being altogether too easily led and impressed by Howard.

"I was just telling our Mr. Spencer here that he should keep his aspirations to the fillies out in the Blakeley stables," Howard said coolly.

"Howard here says he could have any lady in the room," Frederick whispered, making sure to keep his voice low as guests moved past them.

"I could and I have," Howard boasted arrogantly, brushing an invisible fleck of dust from his livery coat. "Any time there is a house party, I'm sure to find a welcome bed to warm. I wonder who the lucky lady will be this time."

"Perhaps Lady Fulford," Ash said politely.

Frederick burst out laughing.

Lady Fulford was pushing eighty and walked stooped over with a cane.

"Or perhaps Lady Whitby," Ash continued, nodding his head to where the gray-haired, shrewish lady in question stood berating her husband loudly and hitting his chest with her fan. "Be careful that she does not hit you too hard with that fan, Howard."

Howard's face had grown red as Frederick laughed himself silly.

"Hush up, you arse," he hissed. "Of course, I meant the *young* ladies." He puffed up like a hen. "Lady Briar is absolutely begging for me. I don't mind telling you both. You should see how she looks at me."

He made a rude gesture, and Ash frowned.

"Oh, of course," Ash said, rolling his eyes. "Lady Briar. The most eligible daughter of the house. Yes, that's very likely. I can easily see her taking up with a footman. Especially one of such a high caliber as yourself. Because she doesn't have any better prospects, being the beautiful younger sister of a duke."

He shook his head. Fool. As if Mr. Taplow would ever condone any of his footmen sneaking into guests' rooms during a house party. Howard wouldn't have made it this long at Blakeley Manor if anything he claimed was true.

"As if you'd know anything about it," Howard sneered. "You probably prefer horses. Or perhaps the stable boys are more to your taste."

"I prefer women, thank you," Ash said, refusing to be riled. "Though of course, I would never judge if you snuck into a gentleman's room, Howard. To each their own, I say."

"As if I would ever—" Howard started furiously. But he was cut off as a dark-haired woman approached and lifted a drink off Ash's tray, nodded without smiling, then moved farther across the room.

Frederick gave a low whistle.

"Perhaps I'll bed that raven-haired minx tonight," Howard bragged, his eyes following the lady. "Lady Briar's a bit inexperienced for my tastes, but her sister..."

Ash followed both footmen's eyes across the room to where Lady Colworth née Lady Katherine Blakeley stood, sipping from the glass of punch.

She was a tall, slender, dark-haired woman of perhaps thirty and had been widowed the year before. He knew she had been married to a distant and much older cousin, an earl.

Ash watched as Lady Colworth glided across the room. She was wearing a dark red silk dress that hugged her every curve to perfection and, frankly, left him convinced that Lady Briar's claim to beauty was nothing compared to her older sister's.

"She's very beautiful," Ash said, unable to disagree with Howard for once.

Then when Howard shot him a sly look, he immediately wished he had not.

"But Howard," Frederick said, his eyes widening nervously, "she may have murdered her last husband. Isn't that what everyone says?"

"Nonsense." Howard waved a hand. "The earl was old. She was probably too much for him. But me, on the other hand." He smiled lecherously. "I'll show her too much."

Ash was growing rapidly disgusted with the subject of conversation.

"Don't listen to him, Frederick," Ash advised the younger footman. "He's an arse. You can't believe half the things he says. Do you really think Mr. Taplow would have let Howard remain if anything he said was true? Or that the duke would keep a footman who accosted his female guests?"

He shook his head as Howard glared. "I'll make a pass about the room," Ash continued. "Perhaps when I return, you'll both be talking with more sense."

"Shut up, Spencer," Howard said, seething at being taken down a peg in front of Frederick, who was looking back and forth between the two footmen, clearly uncertain as to who to believe. "You're new here, so I'll overlook your insolence this once. He thinks he's better than us, he does, Frederick. Well, go on then, Spencer. Carry your tray." He made the last sound like a command.

Ash ignored him and walked away, nodding as he passed Mr. Morris, who was heading the opposite way, straight toward Howard and Frederick. He hoped the underbutler would bring Howard into line.

He made his way around the room until the tray he carried was empty. Then he returned quickly to the kitchen for a new tray, this one of small dainty eatables.

When he came back upstairs, he noticed Mr. Morris was still with Howard and Frederick. The head footman and the underbutler seemed quite engrossed in their conversation.

Morris caught Ash's eye and beckoned to him. Ash did so with a sinking feeling.

"Yes, sir?"

Morris's expression was icy cold. Ash's sinking feeling intensified.

"We live to serve, Mr. Spencer," Mr. Morris said, slowly. "Our duty is our service. Would you not agree that is so?"

"Yes, sir," Ash agreed. "Of course."

"We do not overstep. We do not aspire. We do not interfere in the life of the family we serve, nor with their guests."

"Of course not, sir," Ash said.

He had a bad feeling about where this was going and stole a look at Howard. The first footman was smirking.

"And yet Howard here tells me," Mr. Morris said icily. "That you have done far more than overstep. You have formed a liaison. An absolutely illicit liaison. With the Countess of Colworth, no less."

Ash choked on air. "I've... what?"

Howard stepped forward, a smug expression on his handsome face. Ash wanted to punch it right off.

"There's no use in denying it, Spencer. I've just been telling Mr. Morris how you were shamelessly bragging about your exploits with Lady Colworth. Haven't I, Frederick?" He turned to the younger footman who was busily shooting Ash a guilty, pleading look.

"I... well yes, that's right, Howard," Frederick said nervously.

Ash snorted with frustration.

"That's nonsense, sir," he said, trying to keep his temper in check. "As if Lady Colworth would ever take up with a footman."

"Well, that's what I said, Spencer," Mr. Morris replied. "And yet these two claim they have witnessed you going into her room at all hours of the night. Summons you, she does, apparently. Like her lap dog." He tried to look sufficiently self-righteous, but Ash could see the underbutler was titillated by the prospect of one of his footmen being summoned to the bed of one of the ladies of the house.

"Oh, they claim that, do they?" Ash said grimly, glaring at Howard and Frederick.

"Don't deny it, Mr. Spencer," Morris commanded. "For you know, if there is one thing which could lower my opinion of you even more at this point, it is a lie. There is nothing," he stressed, "which I hate more than a liar. A cowardly liar unable to even admit to his sins."

"I'm sure he has arranged a clandestine meeting with her this very evening, sir," Howard said eagerly.

"You must be joking," Ash said through gritted teeth. "This charade has gone on long enough. If you don't believe me, go ask the countess yourself."

"I would never approach a lady with such a question. You're a temporary footman, aren't you?" Mr. Morris demanded. "And you'll be back at the stables after all this Christmas nonsense. I'll make sure of it."

Only Mr. Morris could dismiss an entire historic Christian tradition as "nonsense," Ash thought, almost amused.

"You'll be the head groom's problem then. Not mine and not poor Mr. Taplow's. In the meantime, if Lady Colworth wishes to... use you... Just know I will be watching you." He lifted his chin piously.

"Of course, if you would prefer to deny it all, Spencer," Howard said helpfully, "then... what was it you said would happen again, Mr. Morris?"

"Then he'd be no better than a bald-faced liar and a coward," Mr. Morris snarled. "And all three of you would be up before Mr. Taplow. As it stands, I won't concern him with this tawdriness... yet."

Morris looked over at the clock across the room. "I must go."

He stalked off, his back squared, as if hastening away to deal with more important matters, leaving Ash open-mouthed and furious behind him.

The urge to punch Howard right in his lying face, even in front of a room full of guests, had never been stronger. Ash even thought he might have to include Frederick.

He curled his free hand into a fist and turned to the other footmen.

"What the bloody hell, Howard?" he hissed angrily. "Are you absolutely mad?"

Frederick at least had the decency to look apologetic.

Howard shifted nervously, his eyes darting down to Ash's fist.

"It was a joke, Spencer," he said at last. "Just a bit of fun." He looked down at the floor. "I may," he conceded, "have taken the joke a bit too far."

"A bit of fun?" Ash spat. "You would jeopardize all our positions for a bit of fun?"

Howard backed against the wall quickly.

"We're sorry, Ash," Frederick said, hastily. "Aren't we, Howard? We didn't mean it to go so far."

Howard tried hard to look sufficiently repentant. "No, of course not. It was just a bit of fun. I'm... well, I'm sorry, Spencer. Dash it, will you accept an honest apology?"

Ash raised his eyebrows. This was... unexpected. He inspected Howard. The other footman's face was sheepish. That was not precisely new. Perhaps he really was sorry, though.

Howard seemed to understand his reluctance. He glanced around, then lowered his voice. "In truth, I'm a trifle foxed, if you must know..."

"Bloody hell," Ash muttered. "Of course, you are. That explains it." He cleared his throat. "Well, then. Let's get on with things. Enough already."

He turned back toward the room, his eye quickly honing in on where Lady Colworth stood by her younger sister. The two women were chattering animatedly and clearly had no idea what ridiculous lies were currently being spouted about the elder's virtue.

"God, she's a stunning woman in that dress. Why, half the men here must be imagining ripping it off her right now," the first footman whispered admiringly.

Ash glared at Howard. "Good Lord, Howard. You really just can't turn it off, can you? You daft git. Next time stay away from... well, whatever you pilfered." And from one of the duke's party trays, no doubt. Ash rolled his eyes.

Still... All this talk of bedding women. He quickly looked away from the lovely Lady Colworth, feeling oddly guilty.

He was a man of flesh and blood just like the next, but he did not hold with discussing women in this way. It was distasteful. Not to mention if his sisters got wind of this conversation, he would be limping for weeks. And he could only imagine the expression on Wren's face if he learned of the situation his younger brother had been involved in.

But what could Ash do?

For his family's sake, he'd have to have to hope Morris let the matter lie. He had no other choice.

Chapter Two

"Ash, come with me. Mr. Morris wants us to tidy things upstairs," Howard commanded. But his tone was not as haughty as it had been earlier in the evening. So Ash complied, following the footman up the side stairs.

"Where are we going?" he asked, yawning. On second thought, he was not sure he would go down to the servants' party that night. Bed was beginning to seem a most welcome place.

"Oh, just upstairs to clear away some of the trays and dishes left behind by guests. You know how they like to clutter up their room. Cook will have Morris's head if we don't get her crockery back where it belongs." Howard sounded rather cheerful at the prospect of finding stray crockery. Ash would have expected him to be itching to return downstairs.

Ash smiled. "Well, aren't you the helpful one? And here I thought Cook had it in for you."

"Oh, you know," Howard said vaguely. "She likes to fuss. I'm like a son to her, really."

That was rather optimistic of the other footman, Ash thought. The cook had shattered a teapot against a wall while aiming at Howard's head a few days before. The story had made the rounds amongst the servants quickly.

"Well, I'm glad you're out of her black books," was all Ash said, deciding to be diplomatic.

Howard pushed open the door leading to the hall. Along this wing lay most of the guest bedrooms. Ash had only a vague idea of the layout of these upper floors.

Howard glanced about. "Morris wanted us to be sure not to disturb any of the guests," he explained. "But many are still dancing down below. Best to get this done quickly. Here, you start with that room—" He gestured to a door across the hall, lavishly gilded with flowery carved trim. "And I'll start down here."

Ash stared at the door, transfixed by the richness of the decorations. Even the bedchamber doors were as luxurious as a pharaoh's tomb.

"Well?" Howard hissed. "What are you waiting for? Go on then."

"Very well," Ash said, a little startled by Howard's impatience. Perhaps Morris had given Howard another scolding. Certainly, the other footman seemed especially eager to please. "Don't worry, Howard," he added lightly. "We'll find the crockery. Chin up."

Howard gave a smile that seemed forced but nodded and started down the hall.

"You must be very quiet," Howard added. "Some of the rooms are still occupied."

Ash gave a light rap, then pushed the door open and slipped inside.

He had expected total darkness, but the room glowed with a dim light. The door closed behind him, and he stood motionless, looking at the low fire in the grate, hardly daring to breathe. It had only taken him a moment to realize that he'd been tricked.

A woman was stirring in the bed across the room.

And not just any woman.

Even from where he stood by the door, he recognized her from the dark hair spilled across the fine white pillowcase. She must have slipped away and retired early, unlike most of the duke's other rowdier guests.

Lady Colworth.

He took a deep breath and tried to calm his racing heart. It would be all right. He'd wait here awhile, right by the door, and then in a few minutes, he'd sneak back out and return downstairs.

Lady Colworth could continue to sleep peacefully, never knowing Ash had ever been in her room at all.

For several moments, he was actually convinced it would work.

Then he heard a soft scuffing noise as a candle was lit, and the room burst into light.

Out of the darkness appeared the face of a woman, beautiful finely chiseled features, soft red lips, dark hair falling gently around her shoulders.

She made an appealing sight. Her expression was anything but appealing, however.

"What the blazes are you doing in my room?"

Oh, God.

Ash froze. He could not speak. He could not utter the profuse and sincere apology he wished to make. He could do nothing but stand there, wide-eyed, frozen, staring at the dark-haired beauty who was looking back at him as if he were something she longed to crush beneath her shoe.

The split-second passed. She spoke again. This time, her voice was shaking with anger.

"Get out of my room. Now."

And he did. He scurried out.

Outside in the hall, he sank back against the wall, glancing over to the servants' stairs.

The door was open. Not one, but two faces peered out at him, like the bloody Peeping Toms they were. Howard. And Morris.

Ash gnashed his teeth and strode toward the door just as Morris turned away.

Howard jumped in front of him as he entered the stairwell. "Stop, stop," he urged, putting his hands on Ash's chest.

"Get your hands off me, or you'll be sorry," Ash growled. "Mr. Morris! Sir!" He could explain. He could apologize. And then he could throttle Howard in the stairwell.

"It's all right." Howard was still talking. And pushing his hands against Ash's chest. He must have suddenly seen the look in Ash's eyes because he dropped them quickly and took a step back. "He's not angry, you dunce. He's impressed!"

Ash stared. "What the devil are you on about?"

"He won't tell Taplow," Howard promised. "He can't. We'd all be sacked if he did. Sneaking around the bedchambers of the duke's own sister." He grinned roguishly. Ash glared, and the grin fell away. "Well," Howard continued, "it's done now. Be a good sport and don't be a gobble-cock about it. No harm done."

"No harm done!" Ash burst out. Then he stopped. He shook his head. "You are unbelievable. Do you know that, Howard? And now I'm going to..."

But Howard was too fast. The footman turned with the speed of a young colt and dashed down the stairs.

Morris was impressed. Howard had gotten away scot-free.

And only Ash stood alone in the stairwell, his conscience heavy with the knowledge that he had been caught by the countess on a foolish prank not even of his own making.

Of course, it did not matter whose fault it was now. It would not matter in the morning when the countess would demand to speak to Mr. Taplow, and then the butler would come and tell Ash to pack his things and be gone from Blakeley Manor forever.

Chapter Three

"Kat, you've been glaring all morning. Is the tea really so offensive?" Briar inquired, taking a seat next to her sister.

The pretty, airy morning room which would normally have been a quiet place of refuge for Katherine was instead full to the brim with chattering ladies. That was what came of hosting a Christmas house party. Places that would normally be only for family were suddenly opened up. There was no privacy any longer!

How was she supposed to think? During the night, she believed she had come to a conclusion about what she would do next regarding the footman who had intruded into her room.

She would go to Edmund in the morning and have the man dismissed. Perhaps even brought up before a magistrate. For who knew what the young man might have been intending?

But in the morning, things no longer felt as clear cut.

After all, he had not really done anything, had he? In fact, he had seemed quite content simply to stand there in the dark. It was rather strange, really. He had seemed quite terrified when she lit the candle.

And his back had been to her. He had not even been looking in the direction of the bed. Perhaps he had entered the wrong room and had been about to sneak back out into the hall.

But then, she vacillated again. No, he had entered her room. Her sanctum! God only knows what might have occurred if she had not frightened him off. Edmund would be furious if he learned of the incident, that was certain. The young man would be out on the road without a letter of reference quicker than he could count to three.

Briar cleared her throat delicately.

Kat grimaced. "There are too many people in here."

"It is a house party, Katherine," Briar whispered. "Emphasis on the word 'party'."

"I have never been one for parties, and you know that well," Katherine grumbled.

"I know you always hated attending functions," Briar agreed. "We are such opposites in that way. I quite enjoy them. The hustle and bustle, the buzz of excitement. So many interesting people to get to know."

"Yes, well, you inherited all our family's best qualities, didn't you? Especially the warmth and kindness. Those passed me by entirely," Katherine said drily.

But she gave her sister an affectionate glance. Tender-hearted and generous of nature, Briar Blakeley was a lover of humanity. Perhaps this was what came of being the youngest of the siblings. She had been such a well-loved baby and then a little girl. It had taught her, perhaps, that the world was all sunshine and roses.

Well, she would soon unlearn much of that, more's the pity, Katherine thought bleakly.

While Kat would reach her thirty-second birthday in a few months, Briar was just nineteen.

She was a mature girl, though. Not one of those flighty, simpering, silly debutantes. She was more than beautiful and more than eligible. She would make a good match. Edmund could be counted on to ensure it. A truly good match—meaning to a decent, *good* man, not simply one who was handsome or dashing. Or captivatingly charismatic.

No, Briar would not follow in her older sister's misplaced footsteps. Kat and her two brothers would make certain of that.

"Why do you keep staring so intently into the hallway each time the door opens?" Briar whispered next, leaning so close to Katherine that she could feel her sister's breath on her neck.

"Stop hovering," Katherine hissed back. "Why are you watching my every move? That should be the real question."

"Are you looking for that handsome footman from last night?" Briar teased. "Is he out there?"

Kat's face must have given something away for Briar gasped. "You are!"

"I am not," Katherine said, now well and truly annoyed. "I hadn't even noticed the fellow until you pointed him out." That much was true. "Perhaps it is you who has fallen under his thrall. From what I have seen, he is hardly even a decent footman. Hardly seems competent."

"Really?" Briar looked thoughtful. "But then, he is not a regular footman at all, you know."

"What on earth do you mean?" Katherine frowned. "Not regular? Is he irregular? Do we keep irregular footmen?"

Briar giggled. "I only meant that because of all the guests, I believe Edmund allowed Mr. Taplow to conscript some extra help. I believe the young man we are discussing usually works in the stables." She tapped a finger to her lips. "That would explain why his name escapes me. I like to know the names of all the servants who attend us," she explained to her sister, who was looking at her with suspicion. "To be polite, Kat. Not for any other reason. Goodness, you are crotchety this morning!"

"Oh, of course." Katherine blushed, chagrined. "So, he is a stable hand? Well, that would explain his... awkwardness. With his duties inside the house, I mean."

But even a stable hand could not use the excuse that he had somehow stumbled into her room by accident! And in the dead of night, too!

No stable hand would be that stupid. Would they?

"I haven't noticed any awkwardness on his part," Briar mused. "But you could be right. In any case, he is not simply a stable hand. I believe he is officially a groom, and he is supposed to be utterly incredible with horses. Edmund has called him a 'wonder.' And you know Edmund is not one for superfluous compliments."

"No, he is not," Kat agreed. "But what does that even mean when speaking of a groom?"

She gave a shrug so unspeakably snotty that she cringed at herself. How had she come to this? She had been like Briar once, hadn't she? If not an absolutely lover of people, then at least able to appreciate life. Now look at her! As sullen and cantankerous as... well, as Lady Whitby.

Kat gave a little shudder, then tried to focus on what Briar was saying.

"He is a genius with animals, I suppose. He has tamed beasts that Edmund says the head groom had all but given up on. I know Edmund had a colt he wished to have broken, but the poor thing had suffered an accident and was quite wild. They thought he, the colt I mean, would have to be shot. But this young man—oh, for the life of me, why can't I remember his name!"

Briar clapped her hands together suddenly—so loudly that Kat jumped.

"Don't do that," she complained.

"Sorry. It has just come to me." Briar beamed.

"Yes, well, what is it?" She would not admit she was truly curious by this point.

"Ashley. Ashley Spencer. I believe the other servants call him Ash. It is a very nice name, don't you think?"

Kat rolled her eyes. "Who cares what a servant's name is?"

"Well, that's not very nice," Briar said reprovingly. "But I suppose you have learned some not very nice ways, having been away from us for so long."

She immediately looked remorseful and clapped a hand over her own mouth. "Oh, dear. I'm sorry, Katherine. I only meant that... well, you know I never liked... I mean, none of us did, but still... Oh dear, I cannot seem to take my foot out of my mouth."

"It is all right," Kat said quietly. "You are right. Colworth was a boor when it came down to it." Once the beautiful kid-leather gloves were off, the man beneath was nothing like his surface had proclaimed.

Kat glanced around the room.

Was it her imagination, or were half the women looking in her direction? She had certainly done a terrible job of helping Briar to play hostess so far. But it was rather awkward when she was constantly wondering if their guests were looking at her as a peer—or condemning her in their minds silently as the woman who had gotten away with murdering her own husband.

Did they really think she would be so unwise?

If only they knew what sort of man he had truly been. Would any of them blame her for not mourning his loss if they knew the full story?

"It is all right, Briar," Kat said again. She cleared her throat awkwardly. "You are right about me, too, I suppose. I have no social grace these days."

"I'm sure I am not," Briar disagreed. "You are just who you always are, always have been. Our beloved sister." She snuck a glance at Katherine, who pretended not to notice. "Only, perhaps one less happy than we remember."

"Yes, well..."

"Oh! The groom! Ashley Spencer. I was in the middle of telling you about him."

"Spencer? Good lad." It was Edmund. He had approached, as was his disarming habit, without warning. Half the ladies in the morning room were preening and smiling up at him as he came to stand next to his seated sisters. There was a calm smile on his handsome face.

While Briar glowed like her namesake, the wild rose, with her mane of dark copper hair and gold-dusted complexion, Edmund was almost a twin of his older sister. Tall and lanky with a strong angular jaw, elegant Roman nose, and far too much confidence and grace than a man who was already a duke deserved.

He was altogether the perfect man, Katherine thought, looking up at her brother. A wonderful brother—loyal to a fault. A kind and generous master to his servants. An ideal duke—gracious, intelligent, and noble.

Now if only that scallywag of a younger brother of theirs, Leigh, could be brought equally to heel. A viscount, Lord Blakeley had not even done them the honor of making an appearance at the Christmas house party yet, though Kat had no doubt he would show up sometime. Probably with a hellhound hot on his heels.

"Ashley Spencer, yes," Briar said, beaming up at her elder brother. "The groom. Haven't you said before that Mr. Spencer is a wonder? I was just telling Kat what a miracle he worked with that poor colt."

"It's true." Edmund nodded. "Not that I'm certain why Katherine would care about one of our grooms."

"I don't care," Kat said automatically.

But as she listened to Briar and Edmund sing this young groom's praises, an idea struck her. A very unusual idea—at least, unusual for her.

But the more she thought about it, the more she could not unthink it. The idea seemed fitting, suitable, and fair.

"Is he a wonder with people as well?" she interrupted, eliciting expressions of surprise from her siblings.

"I really could not say," Edmund said slowly. "He is extremely gentle with animals. They adore him. I suspect such qualities would transfer to working with people. Why? Did you have something particular in mind?"

"Oh, it was just a question," Kat said, waving a hand and doing her best to look bored again. "Truly, I have no idea why Briar has been obsessing over the young man." She rose to her feet. "If you'll excuse me, there is something I must see to."

"Well really, Kat," Briar exclaimed, sounding a little offended. "Oh well, Edmund. You must come and greet Lady Lynch with me. Such a lovely woman. Come and ask her about her seven children. She adores talking about them."

Kat glided out of the room, her mind fixated on the idea. It would spare the young man. Allow him to keep his position. If he agreed, that was.

Well, why should he not? He must be desperate to keep his position, mustn't he?

She walked down the hall, thinking such thoughts and keeping one eye out for the footman.

Ashley Spencer. Yes, she supposed it was a rather nice name for a man.

But the only footman she passed was a dark-haired one who always seemed to have a smirk on his face.

Just now he was standing just inside the drawing room doors, apparently doing absolutely nothing. Edmund must be paying a fortune for footmen to stand about looking pretty.

She frowned and watched him cower as he noticed her.

Then from directly behind her, she heard the sound of someone clearing their throat.

Somehow, she knew who it would be before she even finished turning around.

"Oh. It is you," she drawled. "Well? What is it? What do you want?"

The blond Viking gazed down at her from his lofty height, an imploring expression in his eyes.

She knew they had an audience. The dark-haired footman was still lingering nearby, close enough to observe, but probably not close enough to hear what was said. What a shameless eavesdropper!

Ash was perplexed.

In the morning, Mr. Taplow had not come.

Instead, Ash awoke, tired and stiff from the still unfamiliar bed in the small room he shared with three other footmen, but very much still there.

Perhaps Lady Colworth was a late sleeper. She would rise in a few hours, and then she would summon the butler and have Ash dismissed.

Or worse! She would summon her brother, the duke, and have Ash before a magistrate.

God, think of what she might say! She might easily assume Ash had been in her room to... well, to ravish her.

Ash groaned and lowered his head into his hands.

How could he have let such a thing happen?

He forced himself to rise and began to pull on his livery.

No matter that the fault originated with Howard, the lady deserved an apology from his own lips. She must have been terrified!

He would seek her out. Apologize. Then, let her do what she liked with him.

But the morning passed by in quite an ordinary way.

As he went about his duties, not once did he manage to catch sight of the countess. No one came to berate him or to tell him he had been dismissed.

By mid-morning, he was in a state of unbearable misery. Whether the lady recalled his presence or not, he was desperate to make his apology. Like a Catholic in need of confession, he felt he could not go on without explaining to the lady and begging her forgiveness.

And then his opportunity appeared, emerging from the morning room just as he was passing by, having delivered a tea tray to a guest's room.

The countess did not notice him at first, but he strode after her. And finally, when he had approached to a few feet away, he cleared his throat.

She turned to face him, slowly.

God, but she was beautiful. Her features were like sculpted marble. Her lips so dark and red and perfectly formed. And her form, well, her form was absolute perfection. She was a tall willow tree, with just the right amount of suppleness.

If only the lie Howard told had been the truth. Ash would be a happy man indeed.

But it was not.

"Oh. It is you." Her voice sounded chill and off-putting to his ears. "Well? What is it? What do you want?"

"My lady," he started. "I am sure you have no desire to see me, but I must speak with you. I must apologize for my conduct..."

"I should have thought you would be counting your blessings at *not* having run into me yet today," the countess interrupted. "After all, you have not been dismissed."

The word "yet" hung in the air, unspoken.

Ash's jaw clenched. "Yes, I know you are right," he said carefully. "The very fact that I still remain at Blakeley Manor is proof of your benevolence, but I..."

She lifted her head and laughed, causing him to lose track of what he had been about to say.

"I am sorry. Do go on," she said, twirling a finger. "I am not sure I have ever been described as benevolent before. Well, I suppose next you will have a perfectly logical explanation for what you were doing in my room."

She took a step toward him, her eyes narrowing. "Or I suppose I might jump to the obvious conclusion and assume your intentions were ungentlemanly. Even nefarious."

Ash's eyes widened. "No, my lady. I swear, they were not. Not what you are thinking, I mean. I promise you that I had no evil purpose. It was..." He paused, suddenly conflicted.

He had not considered how telling her the truth might affect others besides himself. What of Howard or Frederick? What of Mr. Morris?

"It was a foolish prank, you might say," he went on. "And I am very ashamed for my part in it."

She grimaced. "Ah, a dare. Yes, I see. Why am I not surprised? I suppose I might have expected as much. Half the guests seem to fear me. Why would that not be true of the servants as well?"

Her face suddenly looked sad. Ash felt a strong urge to put her mind at rest.

"It was not the sort of dare you seem to be thinking, my lady," he assured her.

How could he explain things in a way that would not implicate Howard? Bloody stupid Howard. God knew he deserved whatever he got. Yet Ash thought of Frederick and wound up saying, "We were speaking of beautiful women. And one of the footmen... well, he dared me to go into the bedchamber of the most beautiful woman at Blakeley Manor."

That was something like the truth.

He watched her eyes widen in surprise as she took in the praise.

"I... see," the countess said slowly. Her eyes flickered past him. "And I suppose that is one of the fellows you were trying to impress?" she asked in a lower voice.

Ash glanced over to where her eyes had darted and caught sight of Howard lurking just inside of the open drawing room doors.

"Not impress," Ash said with a groan. "That would suggest I cared about Howard's opinion."

"He is a bully, then?" Lady Colworth frowned. "I have known my fair share of those."

"Something like that," Ash said with a sigh. "In any case, my lady, I am most profoundly sorry for frightening you and violating your private space. Regardless of whether any harm was intended or not, I am ashamed for the part I played."

"He is quite the eavesdropper, is he not?" Lady Colworth whispered, ignoring Ash and stealing another glance toward Howard. "I wonder..."

"Yes, my lady?" Ash asked politely. This was it. Now she would issue his dismissal. He would accept it with humility. He would resist placing any blame on Howard or Mr. Morris. What would be the point? He had entered her room. The blame was his.

The countess was looking at Ash.

Truly looking at him for the first time, or so it seemed to him. Her eyes were a deep brown, nearly black. But while they were beautiful, it was the intensity he saw there which struck him. Her dark eyes burned with a profound fire. He saw both pain and a fierceness, with a ferocity that startled him, seeing such a thing in a woman.

Lady Colworth was not simply beautiful. She was wounded. And being both wounded and lovely, she fascinated him all the more. He felt the same sympathy rising in him toward her that he had felt so many times for wild creatures.

She seemed to be similarly disarmed as she looked at Ash, for her cheeks had turned pale, and she was biting her lip.

"I wonder," she whispered again, this time more to herself. "I had meant to ask you..."

"Yes?" he said, tentatively.

She took a step closer to Ash. Then another.

Chapter Four

What was she thinking? Why did she not simply ask him the question?

No, not simply ask. *Demand.* He would do as she said if he wished to keep his position.

But then, she could not break her gaze from his eyes. They were a stormy blue, fierce and unforgiving, and yet... there was a gentleness, somehow an exception from the rest of him which was hard and strong.

Kat was tall for a woman. Nearly as tall as Edmund. This footman was at least half a head taller. He fairly towered over her.

Suddenly, it seemed the perfect height.

He was young. So young. And so perfect. Beautifully masculine.

He called to her, like a siren, reminding her of what she had lost, what she had given up, what she had never before had.

And abruptly, she remembered her initial reaction to seeing him in her room.

When she had woken in the night and he had stepped into the pool of light, she had drawn in her breath so sharply she had been certain he would hear.

He had been a vision, like something that had stepped out of her most intimate dreams, handsome and lush.

She looked up at him now, at the muscles of his solid, angled jaw, at his lips, so perfectly curving and full. How many girls had been kissed by this young man already? How many girls had tasted that mouth, so soft and firm?

In the dark of her room, lit up golden and beautiful by the candlelight, the truth was that she had not wanted to send him away.

He thought her the most beautiful woman at Blakeley Manor, did he? It had been a long time since she had been truly complimented by a man. Since she had felt seen and desired.

She glanced toward the other footman who still skulked, his back toward them. She knew he was lingering on purpose. Howard, like most bullies, clearly had no intention of taking responsibility for his role in events. He would allow Mr. Spencer to apologize—and to take all the blame.

And if Katherine demanded her brother dismiss Mr. Spencer, this other fellow would glory in it, she somehow knew. He would take great delight in his fellow's downfall. And he would spread word through the house of how the fearsome Lady Colworth had acted with such ruthlessness.

They expected no less from her, after all, that she should prove them all right and behave with coldness and cruelty.

Well, if they would speak of her wickedness and believed her so irredeemable, she thought, cold tears pricking the corners of her eyes, then she may as well do just what she liked and follow this urge all the way to her ruin.

She looked up at Ashley Spencer and met his stormy blue eyes with determination in her own.

And then her hands were on his chest, her fingers were lacing through the cords of his livery jacket, and she was pulling him toward her.

She did not even have to think. She simply lifted her chin upwards and kissed him.

He tasted wonderful. If this was sin, she could not repent of her indulgence. She immediately craved more. She felt his lips on hers like a shock of ice water, all the way through to her very bones.

She traced his lips with her tongue before she could help it, lightly at first, following the edges and peaks, her heart racing with the daring of it.

He was not hesitating to return the kiss. His lips had sealed to hers, pressing gently but firmly, opening to her tongue as she searched his skin, tasted him, stroked along his edges.

Somewhere along the way, his hands had grasped her waist, pulled her to him tightly, as if it were the most natural thing in the world for him to do.

His grip on her was so strong and sure, she felt dizzy. What would it be like to be possessed by such a man, fully? Her heart was pounding, the blood rushing through her veins as she felt his hands through her dress like burning coals against her skin.

If only they were truly on her skin, with nothing between them.

She tasted the salt of his lips, and the urge for more was becoming a pain, less pleasurable, more torturous.

His hands slid over the silk of her dress, cupping her more closely to him, as if he had the right to do so. As if she was his.

She could not allow it. She had already gone too far.

If anyone else were to see them, it would certainly mean his position. For his sake, at the very least, she must stop this.

She pushed away, almost roughly, just barely registering the look of disappointment that came over his face.

She ran her hands over her dress, unnecessarily smoothing down the front of her skirt, as if she might erase creases as easily as unwanted desires.

"There was another matter I wished to speak with you about, Mr. Spencer," she said, refusing to meet his eyes again. "Considering the present state of things, I do not think you will do me the discourtesy of refusing. I understand you are a temporary footman, yes? And your normal place is in the stables?" She just caught his nod. "Very well then. Please meet me at the stables this afternoon at two o'clock. I will tell you at that time what you will be doing to make up for your... mistake."

She lifted her head haughtily and, steeling her features, lowered her voice and added, "Please do not misunderstand me. It will not be more of this."

Then she brushed past him and went up to her room.

Ash had expected to fall head over heels someday.

But certainly not while standing in the hall of someone else's house, wearing someone else's clothing, being watched by another man.

And certainly not with a countess.

"Very well, my lady," Ash murmured as she swept by.

He felt hazy. As if he had had too much to drink.

He looked after her, still half-disbelieving what had occurred.

She had kissed him.

He had kissed her back. With almost embarrassing eagerness.

Worse, he had taken the most presumptuous liberties with her person, wrapping his hands around her slender waist and pulling her so tightly toward him she must have felt... Well, she must have felt just how much of an effect she was having.

She was incredible. Soft and shapely, sweetly curved yet firm.

And her smell! God, she had smelled incredible, too. Like fancy soaps, the kind that came from Paris or Venice or somewhere equally foreign and tantalizing. Floral and clean with a hint of spice. Her skirts had pressed against his legs, light but enticing, rustling, flowing silk. Everything about her seemed rare and expensive and beautiful.

He shook his head ruefully. No matter how proud the Spencers might be, a countess was clearly not for the likes of him.

A hand clapped his arm, and he turned to see Howard, looking almost as shocked as he felt.

"I thought I was just spinning a story." The head footman sounded awed. "But I had the truth of it, after all. You and Lady Colworth!"

"It isn't what you think," Ash said immediately. "You still have the wrong idea."

"No, I can see that," Howard said almost admiringly. "She really cares for you, doesn't she? Why, when she kissed you..." He shook his head in amazement. "I've never seen the like. A lady kissing a footman, right in the hall. Why, she didn't even care who saw her!"

Ash felt a surge of pride mixed with loyalty. "She's a lady. She may do as she likes, I suppose."

Then he thought of the countess's pained expression. "You must not speak of this to anyone, Howard. Do you understand?"

"Yes, I suppose," Howard said. His cheeky grin returned. "Well, she seems to like to do as she wishes with you." He hit Ash on the arm. "You lucky dog."

"It isn't like that," Ash said again. But why? Had Lady Colworth not saved his skin for this very reason? Had she not kissed him simply for show? To help him one-up Howard? "I respect her."

"Respect her all you like. You've certainly gained my respect," Howard teased. "Morris won't credit it when I tell him. I know he saw right through us last night. He expected she'd catch you in her room and make the most dreadful fuss. Then Mr. Taplow would dismiss us both. But you've sure shown him, haven't you, Spencer?"

"I haven't shown him anything and neither will you. Don't tell him," Ash said. He caught on an idea. "The countess wouldn't like it if you did, Howard. And if anyone could have us both dismissed, it's her."

Howard gave him a quizzical look, then nodded. "Very well. You're a strange one, Ashley Spencer. I wouldn't be able to stop bragging if a woman like that had just kissed me."

"That isn't my way," Ash said honestly. "And she has already been through a great deal. This was simply a mistake. As I've said, you have the wrong idea completely, Howard. She acted impulsively, and I'm sure she is already regretting it. In the meantime, I would not wish her reputation to be... well." He shrugged meaningfully.

"Ah, I see," Howard said, nodding sagely. "Well, her reputation is damaged already beyond repair, regardless of what her brother may believe. But I understand. You're being a man about it. And what's more, I see you care for her as well. You don't fool me, Ashley Spencer. You're more than half in love with her, aren't you?" His grin faded. "Well, I doubt she really murdered her husband. You're likely safe."

"Yes, thanks." Ash made a wry face as he recalled the rumors. "I suspect you're right."

Safe as houses. If one could call falling head over heels in love with a lady like Lady Colworth "safe."

Chapter Five

The truth was that Lady Colworth's husband had been killed. But she had not murdered him.

No one would dare to ask her what the truth really was. Not even her own siblings. They skirted around the topic—even Briar, who was usually so daring.

And so, Kat had come to the conclusion that they all believed she had done it. They believed their sister was a murderess.

And they loved her anyway.

She was not sure which was worse.

Part of her longed to tell someone the truth of the matter. Sometimes she felt as burdened by what had truly happened as if she had killed Colworth.

But to do so would be most unwise.

A little hand tugged her coat sleeve, and she glanced down, instantly smiling.

Her son could always bring a smile to her face.

"Where are we going?" Oliver asked. "It is cold out, Mother."

"Yes, it often is in December, my love," she agreed, squeezing his hand. "But you need to get outside more." She bit her lip. "It is not good to be shut in so much. I know you love your books, but you also need to see people, Oliver," she finished gently.

"People are so dull. Books can take me anywhere," Oliver replied. "I go lots of places. Without ever having to leave my room." He frowned. "And it is always warm. And there are pastries."

"Yes, well, nothing can compare to the smell of December. Not even freshly baked pastries. The snow is fresh, and the air is crisp and clean. Take a deep breath, Oliver," she insisted, still smiling. She watched as he wrinkled his little nose and inhaled. "Do you smell that? The freshness of winter. It will make returning to the house—and to your books—so much the sweeter. You will be cold and red-cheeked and full of fresh air."

"So, this is just a walk we are taking?" Oliver asked nervously. "I was worried that..."

"We are going to the stables," Kat said softly. "We are almost there."

She kept his hand in hers, even when he came to an abrupt halt.

"The stables? Why?" He was already shaking his head. "No, Mother."

"It is not what you think," she vowed. She held up a hand. "I promise, Oliver. No one is going to make you get on a horse. Or go near one if you do not want to. I simply wish for you to meet someone."

A young groom. One she had already sampled herself. Oh, perhaps this was a dreadful idea. She was muddling things terribly.

But Briar had claimed Ashley Spencer was a genius with horses. That he could tame even the wild, broken ones.

What of people? Was there a chance he could do the same?

She looked at Oliver and sighed. He was her entire heart. A smaller, male version of herself. Dark-haired and brown-eyed, slight of build but already tall for his age. He had pretty, delicate features. She wondered how they would shift as he went through the change to manhood. She suspected he would be a handsome young man, much like his uncles.

His father had also been fine-looking, though with very different features. At one time, Kat had believed the Earl of Colworth extremely attractive. She had been drawn to him as a young girl. This older man who called to her with his charismatic charm. Eventually she had gone. Like a moth to a flame.

Well, her mother had tried to warn her, had she not? But nothing could stop her and so she drew nearer and nearer to the flame until, finally, she had been well and truly scorched.

By then, her parents were presumed dead. They had gone missing while traveling on one of her mother's expeditions.

And Colworth... He had been there. When she had felt so alone.

When she had wound up compromised, her brother had been furious. But it had all seemed to work out. Everything could be resolved by her marriage to the man she wished to marry anyhow.

Or so she had naively thought.

Oliver was looking past her. "Is that him?" He was looking ahead at the corral just outside of the stables.

A man was within, riding a black horse around in a circle.

Kat's heart skipped a beat. It was him. The footman. He looked very different now, however.

He rode very well. He sat upon the horse as if it was his own.

As he brought the horse around again, he glimpsed them and lifted a hand.

Oliver waved back.

"He rides well," he commented.

"Oh, so you know enough about horses to know that, do you?" Kat asked, amused.

"I have nothing against horses," Oliver muttered. "They are beautiful creatures. I simply have no wish ever to ride one again."

"Well, no one is going to make you, my darling," Kat assured him gently. "Come along and meet Mr. Spencer."

They walked over to the fence just as the groom jumped down and handed the reins off to a stable boy.

He strode over to them with an easy confidence, as if this was his true domain.

"You seem very at home here," Kat said, speaking her thoughts. "More so than inside the manor."

"Yes, well, that's because I am," he said, grinning in a careless way that sent her heart fluttering uncontrollably. "I mean, Your Grace."

"That is for duchesses," Kat corrected, trying not to smile at his slip. "It is simply 'my lady'."

"Ah, yes, I see. My apologies, my lady," the young man said.

"And what shall we call you?" Kat asked, suddenly realizing she was not certain. "Inside, I suppose you are Spencer?"

"Since the footmen are called by their Christian names, your family and the guests call me Ashley. That is, when they bother to learn our names. Half just say, 'Come here, boy.'" Mr. Spencer mimicked the tone of a cranky guest, and Oliver looked shocked.

"That is very rude," Oliver noted. "They should not do that."

"I believe we shall call you Mr. Spencer," Kat said decidedly. "That is more polite, is it not, Oliver?"

The boy nodded.

"That is," she said, hesitating, "if that is all right with you, Mr. Spencer?"

"Honestly, I wouldn't mind your using my Christian name," the young man said, still grinning.

She knew he was simply trying to be reassuring, but at the same time there was a subtle—and perhaps unintended—invitation.

She felt herself blushing.

"What is wrong with your face, Mother?" Oliver asked. "You are turning very red. Are you overly warm? I am quite the opposite."

"If you are cold, you must come inside the stables," Mr. Spencer said hastily, glancing at Kat, then away again. "There is something there I wish to show you, anyway." He hopped over the fence and waved for them to follow.

"Very well, but as long as you know I have no wish to ride a horse today, Mr. Spencer," Oliver said politely but firmly, walking along beside him. "I do not know what my mother has told you but..."

"She has told me nothing about you at all," the young groom said quickly as Kat followed the pair. "In fact—" Kat felt the young man steal another glance at her and kept her eyes fixed firmly down on the trodden snow. "I did not even know she was your mother until you appeared beside her today! Just think of that. Where have you been hiding yourself, my lord?"

"Oh, you may call me Oliver," Oliver said hurriedly. "I think that will do very well." He looked thoughtful. "I suppose you haven't seen me because I have been spending most of my time in my room since we arrived. And the library."

"You enjoy books, do you?" Mr. Spencer asked. "My younger sister is very fond of reading. She reads aloud to us whenever we are all together."

"All of you? How many of you are there?" Oliver asked with interest.

"There are four of us. My older brother, Wren, works here as a gardener. My older sister Laurel is the housekeeper."

"The housekeeper of Blakeley Manor?" Kat exclaimed, surprised. "But she cannot be much older than you."

"She is about your age, I suppose," he said agreeably. "She is twenty-eight. I suppose that is young when you think of most housekeepers. But she is very good at what she does."

"My mother is thirty-one," Oliver offered. "That's *much* older."

Kat cringed.

What on earth was happening to her? As if she had ever cared about her age until now!

"That is not so old, believe me," Mr. Spencer said, laughing. "When you are my age, you will not think so. Why, your mother is Wren's age. And he's not so old."

"I am glad you do not think so," Kat muttered behind them. She was not sure if he heard.

"And you have more siblings?" Oliver asked, still interested.

"I have one more. Marigold is my other sister. She is two years younger than I am."

"And just how old are you, may I ask?" Kat said, before she could help herself.

Perhaps, Kat, you should have asked him that before *you kissed him!* She felt herself blushing again and frowned so he would not take it as provocation.

But "I am twenty-five, my lady," was all he said.

She gave a tight nod, for all the world as if she were as old and cranky as Lady Whitby.

"And what does Marigold do?" Oliver ventured.

"Oh, she has done a great many things," Mr. Spencer said vaguely. "She is here right now, working at the manor."

"All your siblings are here? At Blakeley Manor? You are very lucky to have so many," Oliver said longingly. "I have no brothers or sisters."

"Well, perhaps you will one day," the young man said.

The words were spoken innocently enough. Kat knew he was simply trying to be friendly, but a second later he shot her a look of horror, as if realizing his comment might have been overly forward.

"My apologies, my lady," he said quickly. "I did not mean to overstep."

Kat forced herself to give a small smile. "It is fine. However, I doubt that will be possible, for Oliver's father is dead."

She saw the footman open his mouth as if to object. Then he closed it again and nodded. "As you say."

"Well, Master Oliver, you say you have no wish to ride a horse," the groom said. "But perhaps you would not mind visiting one?"

"Certainly. I do *like* horses," Oliver assured him quickly. "They are noble and beautiful animals."

"I quite agree."

"Yes, well, you must if you enjoy working with them so much," Oliver said.

"They are beautiful. And majestic. And noble. But what many people don't realize is that they're also incredibly intelligent. They will remember you, always. If you mistreat them, they will always recall it. But if you befriend them, you will have a friend for life," Ash explained.

"You make them sound rather like dogs," Oliver said.

"Dogs are wonderful animals as well," Ash agreed. "Horses and dogs share many qualities. And they often get along."

"A horse can be friends with a dog?" Oliver asked incredulously.

Kat sighed to herself. Clearly her son needed to spend more time outside of books.

Ash laughed. "Of course they can. Now, come here, please."

He led Oliver over to a stall and put a finger to his lips. "Let us be quiet now. I think they are sleeping."

"Who?" Oliver whispered.

"The most beautiful thing you have ever seen," Ash whispered back. "Come and look."

Oliver's face lit up with anticipation. He was a boy who could appreciate beauty. Not all children had the mindset or patience to do so. Kat loved that about her son.

Kat peeked over the top of the stall as Oliver did the same, standing up on his tippy-toes.

A mare and foal lay sleeping together in the stall. The foal could not have been more than a few days old. It lay pressed up closely against its mother. The mare's head was nuzzled over her baby's back protectively.

And no wonder! Her baby was a beautiful thing. A lovely sorrel, its soft reddish coat gleaming under the lantern light. There was a blaze of white between the foal's eyes, stretching down to nearly the tip of its nose.

The foal was such a pretty creature that Kat felt a surge of the old thrill she used to get as a child from horses. She had always felt a kinship with them. Perhaps that was part of her determination to get Oliver to love horses as well. Her refusal to give up on him. He would learn to ride in time. He would not give in to the fear his father had filled him with. She would not allow it. To live a life apart from such beautiful animals would be a tragedy for a boy like Oliver, who was so kind and gentle and appreciative of beauty in living things.

"How lovely," she heard Oliver murmur beside her.

"Aren't they?" Ash said softly, "A perfect Christmas picture. Mother and newborn child."

"Some might say that was a little blasphemous," Kat murmured, but she could not help smiling. "What are they? Thoroughbreds?"

"You know your horses," Ash replied, smiling. "The mother is a thoroughbred, yes, but there is wild blood in the foal. Did you know your brother had brought over a mustang stallion from America?"

Kat shook her head.

"Well, he did. A glorious beauty of a horse he is, too. That stallion is this little fellow's father."

"So, he is part American?" Oliver asked brightly.

Ash laughed. "I suppose that's so."

Kat ruffled Oliver's hair. "Oliver used to enjoy horses very much," she said quietly, looking at Ash.

"What changed?" the young man asked.

Kat bit her lip, hesitating, but then Oliver replied for her.

"My father," Oliver said, his face knitting up in a scowl of pain.

"Do you want to watch the foal a little longer, Master Oliver?" Ash asked abruptly. "Perhaps I will just step over here with your mother and show her the stallion."

Oliver nodded without looking at either of them. "Very well."

If he knew they would be talking about him, he did not seem to mind.

Kat followed Ash down the row of stalls.

"In truth, I believe the stallion has been taken out by your brother," Ash said softly. "I would be happy to show him to you another time."

Kat nodded. "It is no matter."

"Lady Colworth," Ash said, stopping. "Why exactly have you introduced your son to me today? You said you had an assignment for me. What do you have in mind?"

Kat frowned. "You are rather blunt."

Ash grinned and leaned against a wooden pillar. "I suppose I am. But I think it is a fair question."

Kat looked away, thinking. "I am not sure what I am hoping for precisely." She sighed. "My sister spoke highly of you to me. She said my brother believed you had a rare touch with animals. I suppose..." She chewed her lip. "I suppose I am hoping you might have the same magic with a child."

"Well, I would not call it *magic*." Ash gave a little laugh. "There is nothing special to it, really. Simply kindness and patience. I suppose I have more when it comes to animals than some do. Though I believe we all should."

He looked at her closely. "Is your boy in special need of such magic, as you call it?"

Kat did not answer right away.

"What happened to him, my lady?" the groom persisted. "There is something..." He shook his head.

"What?" she demanded, suddenly worried he had figured it out. But that was impossible.

"Nothing. It is not my place to speculate," he replied firmly.

"Oh, now you know your place," she grumbled, rolling her eyes.

She crossed her arms over her chest and took up a similar place to his, leaning back against the pillar opposite him.

"I married in haste," she said softly. "Marry in haste, repent at leisure. Is that not what they say?"

Ash looked at her with steady eyes but said nothing.

"I had plenty of time to repent," Kat went on. "My husband had been an acquaintance of my father. He was much older than I and had been married once before. He was also a distant cousin. I suppose, growing up, I rather idolized him a bit. We did not see him often, but when we did, I perceived nothing disagreeable about him. Indeed, he had a kind of charisma which drew me. And he was pleasing in appearance, I suppose. At least, I used to think so."

She gave a short laugh. "I don't know why I am telling you all this. We should go back."

"No," he commanded. But his tone was gentle. "Please, go on. I want to hear. I do. I assume this is coming back to your son."

"It is, yes." She smiled sadly. "Poor Oliver. He is such a good boy. Very gentle."

"Yes, I can already see that."

"My husband did not approve of such tender qualities in boys." She swallowed. "He tried to rid Oliver of those traits. First with cruel words. In time, he tried to beat them out of him. He would try, at least, and... I would stand between him and my son."

"Good God," she heard him breathe.

"So, that he would strike me instead," she went on, ignoring him. "I managed to keep the brunt of it from Oliver, in that way, for years. I thought I had protected him. I tried to."

She shot a beseeching look at Ash. "I really tried."

She bit her lip. She was not the crying sort. Never had been. Instead, she shook her head, feeling furious with her own loose tongue. "Why am I telling you this?"

"Perhaps it is the horse magic?" Ash murmured, a slight twinkle in his eyes. Then his face sobered. "Please. Go on, my lady. I am listening. You may trust me."

"Yes, I feel I may, though I do not know why," she groused. "Well, we wished for Oliver to learn to ride, of course. But Colworth had such high expectations. He pushed too hard and very early. Oliver was only five when he was put on a horse. He tried to be brave, but I could see he was terrified."

She hated remembering all this.

"From there, it went downhill. It became a battle of wills. Me, trying to get my husband to be reasonable. Him, becoming more and more frustrated and determined. And angry. Oliver could pick up on all this, of course. And one day—" She paused, looking down. Her hands were trembling. She clenched them. "I came across Colworth and Oliver in the stable. He was... whipping Oliver. With a horse whip. Oliver was not even making a sound. He simply cowered. Biting his lip so hard it was bleeding down his chin."

"The bloody bastard," Ash growled. "God, what a thing to do to a child. Why, if I knew a man like that, I'd..." He shook his head. "Well, he is gone. Thank God for both your sakes."

"Yes," Kat said weakly. "He is gone."

She put a hand to her forehead. "I've said too much, but I suppose you can fill in the rest." She certainly had no plans to finish the story. "Oliver did *not* learn to ride, as I am sure you have realized by now."

"He is afraid of horses. As he was afraid of his father," Ash murmured. She watched him shake his head sadly. "Such a pity. Horses are such gentle creatures." His lips quirked. "Well, most of the time. Of course, there are exceptions. But mostly, that is when a horse is more afraid of humans."

"Yes, I agree with you. I believe Oliver... Well, I would like to see him form a friendship with a horse. I think it could be so very good for him." She looked pleadingly at the groom. "And I had hoped you might consider taking Oliver on, as it were. Perhaps starting very small. He could help you with your duties. Simply being near horses again might be good for him. He needs... He needs a gentle hand," she finished lamely.

So did she, she was almost tempted to say. She blushed. *Ridiculous, Kat. You are a fool.*

"I understand completely, Lady Colworth," Ash said. "And of course, I would be happy to spend time with your son."

"You would?" She glanced up at him.

"Of course I would. He seems like a good lad. Perfect for what you describe." He paused. "I will not force him to ride, of course. I do not think you would wish me to."

"No." Kat shook her head resolutely. "Decidedly not. I am hoping he will express the desire on his own. There is no rush."

"Good." Ash smiled. "Well, let's go and put it to him, shall we?"

His smile faded as he looked at her closely. "Or I can, if you need a moment?"

"Yes, I'll be there soon," Kat said, forcing a smile. She felt as if the pillar was well and truly holding her up right now, and if she stepped away from it, she might just keel over.

With anxiety or relief, she was not quite sure.

She watched as he stepped toward her, feeling the urge to retreat.

He was just a young man, she told herself. A very tall, very strong, and oddly imposing young man.

He stopped when he was a foot or so away and looked down at her seriously. "I will not forget all that you have told me today, Lady Colworth. Nor what you did for your son. I wonder..." He stopped.

"What is it?" she demanded. "What were you going to say?"

"Well," he said, looking at her with clear, kind eyes. "Only that it sounds as if you dealt with the worst of your bastard husband's wrath by far. Perhaps Oliver is not the only one in need of... healing."

And then he stepped down the row and away.

Kat grimaced. Perhaps he was right. But she could not find a solution for herself as easily as she could Oliver.

Yet as she watched Ash Spencer stride confidently away, she wondered if the answer might not be staring her in the face after all.

Chapter Six

"I like him very much indeed," Oliver said, bouncing energetically on the striped-silk sofa beside his Aunt Briar.

"Oh, you do, do you?" Briar asked, smoothing his ruffled hair and looking entertained. "And this is your new tutor, is it? I did not realize you had brought one with you, Kat."

"Something like that," Kat began.

"No, not a tutor," Oliver interrupted, wrinkling his nose. "I mean Ash, of course."

"Ash?" Briar looked puzzled a moment, then her face brightened. Positively gleamed.

Kat cringed inside.

"Mr. Ash Spencer from the stables, you mean?" Briar exclaimed. "The groom? How delightful. You must tell me everything, Oliver."

As was the way with small children, Oliver's talkativeness immediately depleted. He shrugged. "There is not much to tell. I go there almost every day, and he teaches me things. About horses mostly."

"Mostly?" Briar raised her eyebrows. "I wonder what else he has to teach." She cast a significant glance at Kat who pointedly ignored her.

Briar touched her nephew's cheek gently. "You were put off horses for a while, were you not, Oliver? I believe your mother mentioned something of the sort."

Oliver colored, then nodded quickly. "I was afraid of them, but not any longer. They are magnificent animals. And so gentle. Why, the little sorrel I have been helping Ash with is the sweetest creature imaginable." His eyes widened. "You must come and meet him, Aunt Briar. Perhaps tomorrow." The little boy sat up straighter. "And then you may watch me ride."

"Ride!" Kat exclaimed. She clutched her skirt with both hands, almost unable to believe what she had heard. "You are riding already, Oliver?"

Her son nodded, suddenly looking a little nervous. "Well, not really truly riding. And not for long. Ash holds the bridle and leads me around the corral."

"That is marvelous," Kat said quickly. "That is a huge achievement in such a short amount of time. I am so proud of you, Oliver."

"A wonder with horses and a wonder with boys. Mr. Spencer must be commended," Briar murmured. "Kat, you must be sure to give him your thanks personally."

"Yes, well, how else would I do it but 'personally'?" Kat muttered, rolling her eyes.

"Would you like me to go with you?" Briar asked sweetly, her smile wicked.

"I would not," Kat declared. "I am sure I can remember."

But inside, she was oddly envious of her son. He had been spending time with Ash Spencer for nearly two weeks now. What had begun as an hour every second day had somehow turned into two hours, and then she had lost track entirely.

Oliver could not stop speaking about the groom. He admired the young man immensely.

Kat was glad, of course. Why would she not be?

But it also saddened her. Oliver had taken to Ash so easily. Bonded with him straight away. He spoke of his fine qualities—his gentleness with the animals, his sense of humor, his patience.

If only Oliver might have had all that with his own father.

Instead of only horrid memories. Memories no child should have of their own parent.

"You are a million miles away, Kat," Briar said softly, surprising her as she sank down beside her. “Oliver has just slipped out. He said something about a book on horses he wished to get from the library.” She smiled. “To show Mr. Spencer, of course.”

“Ah, I see,” Kat murmured. She knew what was coming next.

“The more Oliver says, the more my respect for Mr. Spencer grows,” Briar said, watching her sister closely. “He is not only handsome but a kind man, too.”

“Young,” Kat said automatically. “A kind, *young* man.”

Briar scoffed. “Kat, what does it matter how old he is? It is not as if you were old yourself! You are a young widow. Is there not a term for it? Merry widow? Be *merry* for heaven’s sake. After all, he is simply a man. Do you think you are not still easily capable of attracting a man like that?”

Kat glared. “We have skipped quickly from respecting Mr. Spencer to matchmaking!”

“Is that so very terrible?” Briar asked. “We all wish to see you happy. And Oliver, too, of course.”

“I highly doubt our brother would agree with you,” Kat scoffed. “His sister forming an attachment with a servant? I think not. Besides, there is nothing between Mr. Spencer and I. Just because I had an inkling that he would be able to assist Oliver with his fear of horses does not mean there is anything... romantic at foot.”

Not since that kiss in the hall, in any case. Could Briar have learned of it?

As if reading her mind, Briar’s face took on a serene expression. “Oh? Isn’t there?”

She rose to her feet, surprising Kat who had been expecting more of an interrogation.

“Kat, all I know is,” Briar said, smoothly, “the more I learn about the Spencer family, the more impressed I am. There could be much worse things than having a man like Ash Spencer in your life, you know.”

Kat narrowed her eyes suspiciously. “And just what have you been learning about the Spencer family?”

“Oh, this and that, you know,” Briar said. “I am the mistress of Blakeley Manor, you know. I hear what I hear.”

Kat looked at the bloom in her sister’s cheeks. Was it just her imagination, or was she glowing more than the normal amount?

Or perhaps it was simply because Briar had learned of a certain incident involving one of her temporary footmen and her sister.

"In any case, I must go," Briar said, reaching the door. "Think on what I have said at least, won't you? And I think Edmund might surprise you if you gave him a chance. You'll never know until you try."

Kat shook her head and opened her mouth to protest, but Briar had already slipped out.

Although she told herself her younger sister was hopelessly naïve and optimistic, Kat found herself outside a few minutes later, padding through the snow in the direction of the stables.

There was nothing Ash liked more than a challenge. Breaking a horse was the best kind of challenge in his view.

Most men believed that breaking a horse meant crushing its spirit so that it would blindly obey. In that case, the horse became a thoughtless, spiritless creature. Yes, it could be haltered, ridden. But it obeyed out of fear. And in Ash's view, that was a cruel and tragic thing to do to any animal.

Fortunately, the duke did not hold with such methods. Nor did the men he had staffing his stables. When Ash was assigned a mount, he could go his own way. Take his time and be as gentle as he liked.

Of course, this did not mean there was still no battle of wills between man and animal in the process. But the battle was based upon mutual respect, not simply one forcing the other to bend to his will.

The animal he was with right now was something of a rescued creature. Like the newborn foal, this colt was a mustang-thoroughbred mix.

The duke had bought the colt from an acquaintance who had not anticipated the challenge such a breed would present to his groom. After six months of so-called "training" they had given up and had been contemplating shooting the poor beast. Fortunately, the duke had been visiting and persuaded the man to sell the colt to him.

Thus, here Ash was, with a beauty of an animal circling him in the corral with a foaming mouth, doing its best to evade him as a group of onlookers stood watching the entire performance.

That was all very well, as far as Ash was concerned. He was prepared for the long haul, and if the duke's guests found entertainment in this, let them.

Gradually, the colt—Blaze was his name—would learn that Ash had no intention of breaking him with cruel force. He would not use pain to gain obedience.

He could be patient.

He stood, calmly, holding the bridle in his hands, just a little outstretched, as Blaze showed him his flank. What a beautiful flank it was, too. A shining dark chestnut.

But then, Ash did not think it was the colt's flank which had drawn the crowd along the sides of the enclosure. Nor was he blind to the fact that his audience was made up of primarily female guests from the manor.

There had been two women at first, both quietly watching with interest. He had greeted them courteously, then ignored them.

Then one had left. She had returned, joined by a group of three more. Then one of those had gone back to the house... and returned with a second posse.

After that, Ash had given up counting.

He had also given up believing he would get the bridle anywhere near Blaze's head today.

But that was all right, for the colt was learning something else instead. To tolerate a group of chattering people observing him. Ash would not wish to try to train with a crowd every day, but for one day, he could be patient. Tomorrow, he would be sure to lead Blaze somewhere else, out of the way of the path that the guests from the manor tended to take for daily strolls.

He glanced down, wondering what kind of sight he made. It was a warm day for winter. The sun had just dropped below the horizon, but Ash had been working hard and was not cold in the least. He had long ago discarded his overcoat and stood in his shirt and trousers. The shirt was somewhat ripped down the front. He had caught it on a nail in the stable and forgotten about it. Now he was being gawked at by a group of elegant ladies.

He glanced back up to see another woman had just taken her place amongst the onlookers. She was dark-haired and wearing a lovely scarlet cape with the ermine-trimmed hood pulled up.

But the hood did not do enough to mask her features and Ash's heart skipped a beat as he recognized Lady Colworth.

Kat had never seen a man dressed so scandalously. Why, could Edmund not keep his servants in clothes that were not ripped to tatters and did not expose so much... well, bare flesh? It was a disgrace! And Mr. Spencer was certainly not helping matters, having rolled his sleeves up to expose those firm, muscular forearms.

She supposed she should simply be grateful there were no rips in his trousers! With that shocking thought she tossed her head in annoyance.

It was obvious why all these women were gathered here like ninnies. To view the pretty colt—ha! She would eat her hood if that was the truth. No, Edmund and Briar had unwittingly put on an extra Christmas exhibition for all their lady guests, and the ladies were drinking it in.

Kat expected the temperature could plummet and still they would stand there, gaping, like chickens with their heads cut off. All for the spectacle of Ash Spencer standing in his shirt sleeves with a wild animal racing around him.

You might as well just dangle a sprig of mistletoe over top and let them have their way with him. Well, someone had to put an end to the exhibition, or Mr. Spencer would never be able to get any work done.

It was obvious the colt was not about to take to the bridle today, not with all these women chattering and giggling and "accidentally" showing glimpses of ankle all along the sides of the enclosure. Why, it was a wonder the horse had not bolted back to his stall. That was surely what Kat herself would have done.

"What a sight, eh, Katherine?" An elbow that was not Briar's poked her sharply in the side, and she looked down in shock to see Susan, Lady Fulford.

The elderly woman had remarkably sharp eyes, Kat noticed. Beady, black, and full of cleverness. Just like a raven.

"Yes. I mean, no. I mean, what do *you* mean, Lady Fulford?"

The old woman chuckled. "I think you know very well what I mean. I came out for a brisk walk but did not expect the fresh air to be quite so very bracing. My, my, what a handsome young man."

"I suppose he is rather charming in a rustic kind of way," Kat said, trying to be diplomatic. Lady Fulford had been a family friend for decades. She was a marvelous mixture. Mostly intimidatingly cross, but then she could also be unexpectedly kind.

Lady Fulford cackled. "Charming. I should say so. And I understand your son has been under his tutelage."

"Well, in a way, yes," Kat said, surprised to learn that Lady Fulford knew of Oliver's visits to the stable. "He has been helping Oliver to become more settled around horses."

Lady Fulford gave her a shrewd look. "Picked up his unsettlement from his father, did he?"

"Well, yes, in fact. In a way." Kat was startled. "How did you know?"

Lady Fulford's expression became downright sympathetic. "Oh, Katherine, my dear. Why did you go and marry such a dreadful, nasty man? Did your mother never try to warn you what a piece of work he was?"

In fact, Kat's mother might have done so. When Kat was quite young, she vaguely remembered her mother expressing her dislike of her husband's cousin. But Katherine had not recalled it enough to view it as a warning.

"She may have. Once or twice. But then, she was gone. And we were alone. Colworth was... there. He was very charming," Kat said lamely.

"To marry so quickly after losing both your parents," Lady Fulford said with a sigh. "You were too young, poor thing. And there was no one to caution you. To try to stop you. I suppose I should have tried."

"Should you?" Kat asked cautiously. "I did not know you felt this way, Lady Fulford. No one ever..."

"Speaks their mind?" the old lady finished, breaking into a cackle once more. "I should have spoken it much more loudly if I thought it would do any good at the time. Would it have, I wonder?" She gave Kat a considering look.

"No," Kat said with honesty. "Probably not. Edmund tried to stop me as best he could. But I was desperate for Colworth. I thought he was to be my happiness. He was everything to me then." She sighed.

"If only he had been a better father than he was husband," Lady Fulford complained. "Some men are, you know. Wonderful fathers, terrible husbands. And sometimes, more rarely I should say, it is the other way around."

Then she surprised Kat completely. "We all know you didn't kill the man, Katherine." She scowled and waved a hand dismissively. "At least, those of us who matter. Now, perhaps you could do us all the courtesy of showing some backbone and begin to act like an innocent woman."

Kat nearly choked. "Wha-what do you mean?"

"I mean, get on with things! Live your life. Stop skulking about like a widow with a secret. You are not really mourning the terrible man, are you? You can't be! So? What is stopping you?" Lady Fulford grinned, showing a mouth full of remarkably healthy teeth for such an elderly woman. She lowered her voice. "Take another man, dearie." She inclined her head toward the corral. "There's a bonny one for you. Why not start with a young one? They are so wonderfully moldable."

"Oh, for heaven's sake," Kat exclaimed. "You cannot really think I am interested in a lover..."

But Lady Fulford simply raised a shushing hand. "Good evening, Lady Colworth. You may protest all you like, but you think on what I have said."

How familiar! Just like Briar. How many times was Kat to be instructed to give someone else's words consideration? Could she not trust her own mind? Her own judgement? She had survived this long, had she not?

She watched Lady Fulford toddle away back toward the big house, humming a Christmas carol to herself, and envied the old woman's equanimity.

She looked back at the corral. Most of the women were still there. Ash Spencer was doing an excellent job of pretending not to notice them, but surely, he did.

She felt a surge of possessiveness. How dare they? How dare they come and gape at him as if he were a performing monkey. How dare they look at him with such... such... well, with such unspeakable desire in their eyes.

Shocking herself thoroughly, she found herself climbing up onto the second rung of the enclosure and cupping her hands to her mouth.

"Mr. Spencer," she called none too graciously. "Are you quite finished with that horse? I should like a word with you, if you please."

Ash looked startled, then nodded. "Of course, my lady. I will see you inside."

He turned away from the ladies, whistling so that the colt would follow.

Kat half-expected the other women to groan with disappointment. She marched past them all, feeling a smug sense of satisfaction at spoiling their fun. She knew it was a little nasty of her, and Briar would probably disapprove. But really, he was her groom. Her son's groom, that was. She would speak with him if she wished to.

"I hope you did not mind my interrupting—well, whatever that was," she said as she stepped inside and over to where Ash was guiding the colt back into its stall.

"It was supposed to be bridle training." Ash grinned. "But you are right. I am not sure what it wound up being. As they are your guests, perhaps you can enlighten me."

"They are not my guests. They are my brother's," she countered, not sure what she was playing at.

She made the mistake of lifting her chin and meeting his eyes, then wished she had not.

He was watching her so intently, his eyes combing every inch of her as he stood, leaning beside the colt's now-closed stall. He was still breathing hard from the cold and exertion, and she watched in fascination as his chest rose and fell, the powerful swells of muscle heaving, his warm amber skin a beautiful contrast against the white of his simple cotton shirt.

She could smell him, too. Sheer, unadulterated maleness. It tinged her nostrils, left her heady and weak.

His gaze. His scent. His deep, rich voice. And oh, gracious, that grin. So playful, yet a gesture that made a secret part of her wish to drop her gown to the floor without another word.

"No wonder all those women were gadding about," she muttered angrily.

"What was that now?" Ash asked, his brow wrinkling.

"You are too handsome," she complained, plowing ahead, feeling all her armor, her pretension suddenly falling away like melting snow from a roof. What in God's name was she doing?

He grinned wider, then tried to look bashful. It was infuriating. Adorable. Infuriatingly adorable.

"Am I?" he asked innocently.

"Yes," she said, nodding. She took a small step toward him. Breathed in his scent more deeply. "You are."

She shook her head, tried to clear it. "You are also very good with my son," she said, starting again. "Which is why I have come to thank you. For your assistance with him."

"Oh, that is why you are here, is it?" he asked softly.

"Of course it is," she said. "Why else would a lady come to visit a groom in a stable?"

"You are very beautiful as well, you know." He took a step toward her, never breaking his gaze from her eyes. "Perhaps tomorrow *you* should stand in the corral with a bridle, and the gentlemen will flock to see the lovely Lady Colworth."

"Nonsense," she snapped dismissively. "Ridiculous."

But she was pleased. He thought her beautiful, did he? Lovely?

"You are most welcome for the assistance with your son," Ash said, his voice deep and soft. He took another step forward.

They were perhaps less than a foot apart now. She could feel the warmth radiating off his body and had the mad wish to reach a hand out and touch that bare flesh, part the cotton shirt a little more...

"He is a good lad. I enjoy my time with him. But I must thank you in turn."

"You... must?" Kat managed, her eyes darting back and forth between his eyes, his lips, his bare skin. "Whatever for?"

"Well, you saved me," he said, smiling. "I hated being a footman, and now Mr. Taplow believes I have more pressing duties in the stables, so has set me free. He claims he may need me for one of the last dinners, but so far, I have been able to avoid the manor ever since. I have you to thank for that."

"You prefer animals to people that much then?" Kat felt oddly disappointed. As if his saying so was a personal affront to her.

"Not to all people, of course," Ash corrected. "It depends on the person." He grinned again, and she felt herself melting like a wax candle.

He had not even touched her. And yet, even just standing there, being simply himself, he was reminding her of all the things she had become so accustomed to ignore. Parts of herself. Deep, lonely parts. Desires she had once had. Now they were rising again, demanding to be remembered, demanding to be satisfied.

She shook her head, muddled.

"I like being around *you*, Lady Colworth," he said, disarming her completely. He shook his head, and she saw a look pass over his face—a quizzical look, almost as if he were as confused by what he was feeling as she was. "There is something... almost familiar about you."

"Familiar?" she whispered. "How is that possible?"

His lips quirked upwards. "It's not."

And then he took her hand.

Reached out for it, impulsively, his warm fingers cradling her smaller one in his larger palm. He held her hand as if it were a fragile thing, then ran his thumb over the top of it. As the rough pad of his thumb moved over the smooth surface of her skin, gentle as a feather, Kat gasped.

She could feel the touch straight through her, like a bolt of lightning to her bones, leaving her hot and tingling from head to toe.

And shaking like a leaf.

Ash noticed.

"You're trembling," he said with concern, and he let go of her hand, reaching his arms out as if to grasp her by the shoulders.

Kat practically fell into them.

Chapter Seven

There were snowflakes collecting in her dark hair like sparkling diamonds. Most of the snow had melted, making the heavy coil of waves and spirals gleam darker in the shadowy lantern light. Her lips were ruby red, her cheeks tinged a soft pink.

She looked uncanny. Like an ethereal being, too beautiful to be a human woman at all. The melting snow ran in rivulets down her crimson cloak to the floor.

Ash longed to sweep the cloak from her shoulders, revealing the tall form, the perfect slender curves hidden beneath.

She stood there, her chin held at its characteristic stubborn angle, her lips pursed as if she were displeased.

But he knew she was not. She was something. Uncomfortable perhaps. Even nervous. But he did not displease her.

No, it was something else.

Her gaze kept shifting, roaming over him in a way that gave him goose-bumps. And then he realized she was trembling.

He said so and instinctively raised his arms to steady her.

She fell toward him, her hands raised to his chest, and he caught her—not by her shoulders as he had so chastely intended, but lower, his hands sliding beneath her cape, around her slim, curving waist.

Her body was soft under his fingers. He could feel the warmth of her skin through the layers of her wool dress.

He swallowed, feeling a sharp stirring of desire as his body reacted to her closeness.

She was looking at him, her eyes wide as if with shock, her lips slightly parted. And then her teeth caught the lush curve of her lower lip, gently gnawing as if she were contemplating the same thing as Ash, and he could not stand it any longer.

He leaned forward and kissed her. Kissed her as if it was the only thing she had come there to do. As if it were the only thing they were meant to be doing.

His mind was empty of all thoughts save her. Of this moment. Her warm, soft lips brushing against his for this second, blissful time.

He could kiss her forever and never have his fill of her, he thought, and he slid his tongue tentatively between her lips, stoking the kiss from a gentle spark to a roaring fire.

His hands tightened on her waist as he heard her moan, and he pushed his tongue in farther, tasting her, teasing her, refusing to surrender his hold on her, suddenly determined to stoke the blaze until she was as on fire for him as he was for her.

His hands slid over her waist, lightly caressing. Then he lifted a hand to the nape of her neck, moved his mouth to her cheek, the corner of her mouth, the edge of her earlobe, kissing ceaselessly, his lips never leaving her skin, hearing her whimper as his teeth grazed the tender skin of her neck, just a little.

His hand brushed against her breast as he made to lower it to her waist and he froze, nearly melting with lust at the unexpected contact. It had been accidental. Would she stop him now?

She moaned again, a low, desperate sound, and he thought not. He brushed his hand, deliberately, lightly over her breast again and felt her nipple pucker through the fabric of the gown.

Her hand, which had been resting against his chest, clutched him now, almost painfully, and she gasped his name, "Ash."

"Yes?" he whispered against her ear, filled with delight at her responsiveness. "What is it? Shall I stop?"

He felt her shake her head against him. "Don't stop. Go on. Don't stop."

He caught her lips with his firmly and raised both his hands to her breasts, then cupping them, lifting them, running his palms over the top of them until he could feel the small buds of her nipples hardening into pebbles. Then he brushed his fingers over their tips and relished the sound as she cried out.

"Shhh," he said, laughing. He could not help himself. He was so happy. So very damned aroused and so very damned happy. "Someone will hear."

"I can't help it," she whispered, her voice sounding choked and breathless. "It feels so..." She gave a little hiccup. "It feels so good, Ash. You feel so good."

He sensed her trembling resuming, but a different kind, and quickly lowered his hands to her waist, holding her gently against him.

"What is it? What is wrong?" he asked gently.

"It is only... I don't do this sort of thing," she whispered, against his chest not even lifting her head to look up at him. "Perhaps you think I do. But I don't."

"Neither do I," he said with surprise. "Perhaps you thought I did, too."

He kissed the top of her head then. She was tall for a woman, but he could do so easily. He could smell her and the fresh aroma of the melted snow. She was pure and clean and lovely, and he wanted her for his own. So badly.

"This is different," he said carefully. "I think you feel it, too... Katherine."

It felt strange to use her Christian name.

She looked up at him then. "Kat," she said shyly. She shook her head. "Not Katherine, please. It is what my husband used to call me."

His grip on her tightened slightly. He did not like her to have to think of that man. She always looked sad when she did.

"I understand," he said. "Kat, then." He smiled and was lowering his head to kiss her again, when he heard the sound of a man clearing his throat.

Ash had not even heard the approaching footsteps. The man must have walked toward them very quietly. He frowned and looked up, feeling Kat turn to see.

"Morris," he exclaimed. "What are you doing here?"

"I could ask you the same question," Morris said, his white teeth gleaming. He tapped his nose. "I expect I already know." He looked at Kat. "Good evening, my lady."

"Good evening," she said rather coldly.

She had not stepped away from Ash. Not yet. He was rather surprised. But then, he could not see her giving into the urge to do so. It would be a retreat.

"I am Mr. Morris, the underbutler," Morris said, seeing she did not recognize him.

"Ah, yes," she said, nodding. "And you were looking for Mr. Spencer?"

"In a sense," Morris said, shrugging as if he were in no hurry. "You know, my lady, I believe we may have a common acquaintance."

"Oh?" Ash saw her arch a brow. She was thoroughly annoyed now, he could tell. Morris was being overly familiar. She did not like it.

She felt exposed. Ash understood. He felt much the same way.

"Yes, Mr. Walter Colworth of Colworth Abbey. I believe you know the family."

She did not answer, but Ash felt her tense.

"Your late husband's younger brother, I believe," Mr. Morris went on when she did not reply. "I served at Colworth Abbey up until... well, just recently, in fact. A duke's household is, of course, a grand step up. But I must say, I miss my former master at times."

"Do you?" Kat's voice was chilly.

"Of course." Morris sounded surprised, but Ash had the impression this was feigned. "A fair man. A noble gentleman. Why, much like your own husband, I suppose. They must have had many traits in common, those two."

Kat did not reply. She turned to Ash. "I really must go."

He nodded, trying to convey what he wished to say with his eyes but feeling it was a hopeless case.

"Ride out with me tomorrow," she whispered so quietly he did not think Morris had heard.

Then she stepped away.

"Good evening to you," she said, stepping past Morris.

And then she was gone.

"Were you really looking for me, Morris?" Ash asked as soon as her footsteps had faded away. He felt absurdly bereft. "What on earth for? Surely Mr. Taplow has told you I am no longer serving in the manor."

"He has," Morris said, looking all about the stable thoughtfully. "I simply thought I would stop in and see how you were faring."

"How considerate of you," Ash said politely. He was not going to take whatever bait Morris was trying to hold out. He would not react to what Morris had seen or believed he had seen at all.

If Morris wished to stir up more gossip in the big house, well, Ash felt confident—fairly confident, that is—that Lady Colworth could handle him.

Even so, Morris was smiling at him in a queer way he did not like.

"What is it?" he demanded.

"You know she killed her husband, don't you?" Morris asked, shaking his head as if astonished by Ash's lack of insight. "Aren't you at all... afraid?"

"Afraid? Why should I be?" Ash asked shortly.

"What if she did the same to you?" Morris asked.

Ash took a step toward him, towering over the shorter man. "That's a very nasty thing to say, Morris. Besides, I do not believe the lady did any such thing, and I seriously doubt you do either. From all I have heard, her husband was not a pleasant man."

"Oh?" Morris raised his eyebrows. "I had no idea. Where did you hear that from?"

"Never you mind," Ash said shortly. "I have to finish up here. Was there something else you needed, Morris?"

"You should show more deference, Spencer," Morris snapped, sounding annoyed.

"I would have, when I was a footman and you were my superior," Ash said, smiling a little. "But out here, I am only responsible to the head groom. And to the duke, of course. And you are simply the underbutler, visiting from the manor. Rather in the way, in fact." He nodded brusquely, wanting to be away from this man. "Goodnight to you, Morris. Tell the boys I wish them well."

She must be going mad, Kat decided, as she walked back to the house. She had heard of women who reached a point in their lives where they burst into crisis. Taking up with footmen and throwing wild parties, even traveling abroad, and abandoning their own families. Of course, those women were usually much older than Kat was now.

And Kat had no husband left to rebel against. She was already her own woman.

So, what is this all about? she asked herself firmly. Why could she not leave well enough alone?

It was easier not to love. Then no one could hurt you. But it was too late for her. She loved Oliver desperately. She loved her family. She had even made the cruel mistake of loving Colworth.

Was her heart really trying to take another leap?

Something told her Ash Spencer would be different. He was so very young. He had no demons of his own as she did. He was pure. He had not yet been tainted by life's darkness.

Which is why you should leave him alone, Kat, she scolded herself.

Yet she had no intention of changing her plans to go riding with him the next day.

Chapter Eight

When Kat went down to the stables the next afternoon, Oliver was already inside. She supposed she should not have been surprised. He had been spending almost all his free time there, quickly transferring his affections from the library.

"He's becoming very close to Seren," Ash said, his voice close in her ear. He had come up behind her so quietly she had not heard him.

She turned, smiling. "Seren?"

"The little foal," he explained. He nodded toward the stall where Oliver's head just peeked over. "Master Oliver named him. It means 'star' in Welsh, apparently. He is grooming him right now. Did you wish to see him?"

I wished to see you, she nearly said but merely shook her head. "I wished to go for a ride." She bit her lip. "I suppose this is not a good time for it."

"You wish to ride and you require a squire," Ash said, grinning. "Of course I can go. Just let me tell one of the other grooms to keep an eye on Oliver. They all enjoy his company, don't worry," he reassured her over his shoulder as he strode away.

She watched him speak quickly to another man who was mucking out stalls at the end of the row, then clap him on the shoulder.

"There, that's all very well," Ash said, returning to her. "Henry will keep an eye on him. Master Oliver can take Seren out for a little walk around the corral later on." He raised his eyebrows. "Did you wish to speak with him before we go?"

"No," Kat decided. "I won't distract him. He is happy right now."

"He is always happy here," Ash agreed. "It's been a very good thing for him. You had the right idea."

"Yes, well," Kat said, blushing a little at his praise. "It was just a thought."

The day was cloudy and a light dust of snow was falling, but to Kat the rush of air in her face was bracing. She leaned into the wind as her mare followed behind Ash's own mount, tracing the familiar country road she had ridden along so many times throughout her childhood.

Gradually, they slowed to a gentle trot, riding beside one another in companionable silence along the darkening, snowy lane.

Kat was enjoying the quiet. It was not burdensome. Not with Ash beside her. She felt rather at peace. She snuck a look at his profile and was startled to see he was already looking at her.

He smiled, realizing he had been caught. "So, why do they say you murdered your husband?"

Kat's brows shot up. "Really? Is that what we are going to discuss this afternoon?"

"Well, I have to admit I am curious," he said, grinning. "Even though I don't believe a word of it, of course."

"Of course not," Kat said grimly. "You don't think I'm capable of murder?"

"Oh, I think you are," Ash said calmly. "Under the right circumstances, most people are. You would kill to save your son, would you not?"

"Of all the bizarre topics of conversation," Kat muttered, rolling her eyes.

"But your husband..." Ash frowned. "I don't believe you did. Simply because the horrible truth is I believe you were too afraid of him to do so. I don't know what is worse."

"Would it have been better had I murdered him?" Kat demanded, a little shocked.

"Perhaps," Ash replied, his eyes honest. "If he was hurting you. And Oliver. Yes."

"I..." Kat started. She stopped. He was merely being flippant.

"But why do people believe you did? That is what I was really asking. Why are they so... well, malicious?" Ash asked, genuine curiosity on his face... and also something else.

"Are you feeling sorry for me, Ash Spencer? For me? A countess? A peer of the realm?" Kat demanded, haughty yet teasing.

He threw back his head and laughed. "Peers of the realm can be just as miserable as the next man—or woman. Or so I have found."

"Oh, you have found that, have you? In your long, long life?" She narrowed her eyes.

Ash met her gaze steadily, his face surprisingly somber. "Yes, I have. I am young, but you do not know what I have experienced."

He said it very matter-of-factly with no intent to be offensive.

"No, but I would like to," she found herself saying boldly.

He smiled. "I would like that, as well."

She looked away. "I suppose the rumors exist because it became common knowledge that we were... unhappy." She shook her head. "Rather more than unhappy. I tried to run away from him."

"You did?" Ash exclaimed.

"Yes. I took Oliver with me."

"What happened?"

"I'm sure you can imagine what happened," she said slowly. It was an awful memory. The memory of her failure. "He came after us. With his brother. They found us and forced us back." She paused. "Well, that is not quite true. It was Oliver he wanted. But he knew I would never leave him, so it was much the same thing. I was trapped. I returned with them."

Her spirits utterly broken.

"And your brother? He could do nothing? A duke?" Ash said.

Kat gave a rueful laugh. "He tried. He tried everything. Oh, he was beside himself that he could not help. Poor Edmund. But no, he could not. A man has a legal right to his own children. And to his wife. Colworth could have done much worse, in truth. He might have separated me from Oliver altogether."

"Good God," Ash muttered.

"Soon after that, he had an accident. In the stables, in fact." Kat hesitated. She would not go into details. "He died. I was freed. It was all too convenient for some, I suppose. I did not seem unhappy enough over his death, I am told. The rumors began."

"Convenient!" Ash cried darkly. "Yes, very convenient that a woman had been freed from such a fate. I suppose they would have preferred the status quo. You remaining with him in misery."

Kat shrugged. "In any case, I find I am rather beyond caring what anyone thinks. I care about Oliver. Not much else."

"Not even yourself? What of your own dreams?" Ash asked. She could feel his eyes on her.

She shifted nervously. "Why all this talk of me? What of yourself? What do you dream of?"

"Well, that is easy. More days like this," he responded, not taking his eyes off her. "More time with you."

She felt her cheeks reddening. "I..." she began, but then she looked down with a frown.

"What is it?" Ash asked, looking at the mare. "Something wrong with Caramel?"

"Her gait changed," Kat explained, leaning over. "I think she may have lost a shoe."

Ash drew his mount to a halt and jumped down to take a look. "Yes, you're right. She must have dropped it back there."

"Shall we go back? I don't wish for her to strain herself," Kat said with concern, patting the mare's neck.

Ash grimaced. "I suppose we must."

"Perhaps we might try this again tomorrow?" Kat offered shyly.

She saw his eyes light up, and her heart gave a little pitter-patter of happiness.

"Yes, I would like that very much," he replied swiftly.

They were not far from the stable, but rode back slowly for the sake of Kat's mare.

As they reached the outskirts of the enclosures, Kat saw with surprise that there was a carriage pulled off to the side of the stable.

"Not one of ours," she heard Ash murmur. "That's strange."

The sound of raised voices floated across the yard.

Ash frowned. "That's Henry shouting. What's going on in there?"

They were making their way around the corrals when they saw two men rush out, carrying something between them.

"Oh, my God," Kat said a hand to her throat. "That's Oliver."

Henry, the other groom, rushed out behind them, shouting and trying to tug the boy free.

One of the men carrying Oliver let go of him and struck Henry. He sprawled backwards to the ground.

Kat heard Ash give an angry growl, and he spurred his horse forward, skirting around the pen.

But by the time they reached the place that Henry lay and where the carriage had been, it was too late. The conveyance was rolling down the lane.

Ash was already nudging his horse forward, looking back at Kat.

"Don't you dare leave me here," she cried, sliding down off her mare. She cast a quick look at Henry, who had already risen and was brushing himself off. He quickly came forward to take the reins from her.

"Come up behind me," Ash commanded. "It'll be quicker. He can easily bear us both." He reached an arm down and Kat grasped it quickly, gasping a little as he pulled her up to sit behind him.

"Go, go," she urged. "They have him, Ash. Please." She was choking on her words, filled with panic.

"Go and get the duke, Henry," Ash called back as he whirled the mount. "Tell him what has happened!"

Henry nodded and broke into a run, pulling the mare behind him.

And then Ash spurred the horse into a gallop, and they were flying down the road as quickly as the stallion could take them, careening through the snow and into the dark.

"It's Walter," she called over his shoulder. Her face was pressed tightly against the wool of Ash's coat. The warmth and scratchiness of it was vaguely reassuring. He was there. Solid and strong. They would get Oliver back together.

Wouldn't they?

"His uncle?" Ash called back. "What right does he have to do such a thing?"

Kat gulped down a sob. "None whatsoever. But he believes he does. It runs in the family." The Colworth belief that they had the right to do whatever they pleased. "He believes Oliver should belong to him now. That I am not fit... to..." She did not finish.

Ash made a sound of disgust that was not quite a word, and involuntarily, she squeezed her arms around his waist more tightly in appreciation.

"We'll get him back," he promised. "They are not far ahead, and they will be slow."

He patted a hand inside his coat, and for a moment, she was puzzled. Then she understood.

"You have a pistol?" she exclaimed. "Do you always carry one?"

"Yes," he said shortly. "Especially since your brother has had thefts. We got back the horses, but the thieves were armed. So now Henry and I and the others go armed most days, too. I'm just glad I remembered it today."

"So am I," she said weakly, not sure that she was.

"Do you think they will be armed?" Ash asked tightly.

She thought a moment, then nodded her head against him. "Yes. You are right. I am sure of it. Walter is just as ruthless as Colworth was."

"He didn't seem to expect much resistance. Stealing the boy away in broad daylight. And he knew just where to find him, too," Ash mused.

Then she felt him stiffen. "Morris. That bastard."

"Really? The underbutler? You think so?"

"I would bet on it. You must tell your brother when you return. There! There they are!" His voice rose with excitement and he urged the stallion harder.

Kat's heart leaped as she caught sight of the carriage.

"How many men do you think there are? Just the two we saw?" she asked, with concern. "Plus, the driver? How can we do this? How can we stop them?"

Ash said nothing for a moment. "I have an idea. You'll need to take the reins when I pull alongside."

They were coming up behind the carriage now. She wondered if they had hurt Oliver. He must be terrified.

She was furious. Furious for him and for herself. How dare Walter try something like this?

If they had not happened to stumble across them when they did, what then? Where would Walter have taken her son? Would he have kept him in England? Somewhere Edmund could have tracked him down? Or would he have smuggled Oliver somewhere abroad where she would never see him again?

She felt sick at the thought.

"In another moment, I am going to jump onto the carriage," Ash said suddenly. "You try to keep Bolt steady."

"Bolt? Is that his name? Keep a bolt steady?" She gave a little laugh, hearing the panic in her voice.

"You can do it, Kat, I know you can. It will be all right," Ash said steadily. "Ready, now."

And then Bolt had caught up completely. They were alongside the carriage. Ash shifted his legs, stood in the stirrups, and then—he was gone.

Kat gasped, grasping the reins, and sliding herself forward.

The carriage seemed to be going at a breakneck speed.

If she did not keep up now, they would outpace her, and she would have no chance of seeing what became of Oliver and Ash.

She looked over to see Ash clinging to the back of the carriage for a split second. Then he had the door open and was throwing himself inside.

A few seconds passed. A different form appeared in the door frame. A man she did not recognize.

Kat had just enough time to pull on the reins to avoid narrowly being hit by the flying body of the man as he was thrown out into the snow.

The door of the carriage hung open a moment, then a familiar hand yanked it shut.

Ash had never seen a man look so surprised.

"You must be Mr. Walter Colworth," he said, panting as he sat down on the carriage seat across from him. "Oliver, are you all right?"

Oliver was staring at him with eyes wide as saucers. The boy nodded quickly.

"Good. We're going to get you home," Ash said, smiling encouragingly.

"We?" Oliver squeaked.

"Your mother and I," Ash said. "She is just outside."

"She is?" Oliver looked surprised, then pleased. "Of course, she would be."

"Yes, she is very brave, isn't she?" Ash could not help but saying. He glanced at the man beside Oliver. "But I suppose you already knew that about your sister-in-law."

"I don't know what you mean," Walter Colworth said coldly. "Who the devil are you supposed to be?"

"Ash Spencer, one of the duke's grooms. Of course, I suppose your sister-in-law had to be very brave, putting up with your brother." He longed to say more, but not before Oliver.

"How dare you?" the other man sneered. "Is this how the servants talk in the Duke of Dareford's house? Pathetic."

Ash laughed. "The duke should be along soon, and you can make your complaints to him yourself. I doubt he'll be receptive, however. Why don't you ask your driver to pull over? I would have thought you'd be interested in going back for that gorilla of a manservant we left back in the snow."

"Duncan can fend for himself," Walter Colworth replied testily. "He is loyal."

Ash whistled. "Interesting way to repay his loyalty. In any case, do stop the carriage, will you? Lady Colworth is an excellent rider, and Bolt can keep on like this for a long time, but your own horses must be feeling the strain most unpleasantly."

"Oh yes, because you are a groom. I suppose you would know." The man shook his head. "Absolutely not. Oliver is coming with me."

"I am not," Oliver cried hotly. "Ash won't let you take me."

"That's right," Ash said. "I'm sorry to say your uncle is not a very reasonable man, Oliver. I am determined to return you to your mother. And if reasoning won't work, well..." He opened his coat just enough to give Walter Colworth a glimpse of the pistol he carried. "Then I'll be forced to use other tactics."

"You wouldn't—" Walter began.

"Stop the carriage now, you imbecile," Ash snapped. "You've lost your manservant. There's no one else to do your bidding. Do you really think the boy or I will listen to you? Or we can continue on until the duke catches up with us. By which time, I promise you will have more than one black eye."

He leaned forward threateningly and took pleasure in seeing the other man flinch.

"Only a coward steals a child from his mother," Ash said softly. "So, you must be the worst sort of craven, Walter Colworth."

He leaned even closer and dropped his voice so the boy would not hear. "I already know your brother was one. Do you really need to be the bastard he was, or can't you make your own way in the world?"

The other man snarled in anger and lurched forward.

"Close your eyes, Oliver," Ash instructed just in time.

When Walter Colworth sank back down on his seat, he was shrieking and clutching his right eye.

"I think I've been more than patient," Ash declared. He glanced at Oliver. "And I think your uncle—the nicer one, I mean—will forgive me if I make this a little easier on you and your mother."

He nodded to himself, then moved forward.

Kat saw the carriage door open again.

Then—"Not again!" she had just enough time to exclaim as a second man's body was tossed out of the carriage and into the snow-filled ditch beside the road.

She glanced back.

"Walter!"

Well, at least it was not Ash or Oliver.

She moved Bolt back closer to the carriage. Ash must have managed to communicate with the driver for it had begun to slow.

"Thank heavens," she muttered in relief.

There was the sound of many pounding hoofs behind her.

She turned back to see Edmund, Briar, and a group of the duke's men approaching on horseback.

Just ahead of her and Bolt, the Colworth carriage was rolling to a halt.

It had been an awful nightmare, but it was over.

Chapter Nine

"Come to me. Tonight."

She had said those words to him, had she not? He had not imagined them. They had been real.

Ash had been shaking himself ever since. All through the stiff and formal *thank yous* he had received from the Duke of Dareford, all through the much less stiff and formal thanks he had received from Lady Briar Blakeley. Kat herself had hurried Oliver into the safety of the manor house after making her hasty request.

He had gone back to the stables, seen to Bolt, helped Henry, and eaten his dinner in the cottage he shared with his brother, Wren.

Now he was strolling outside, under the stars, on his way to a rendezvous with a countess.

His countess.

Of course, if he had told Wren any of this, his brother would have yanked Ash back by his collar. And then, Ash would have sat him down and simply forced him to understand.

He could try to stay away from Lady Colworth, but there was hardly any point. He was in far too deep for that.

Besides, he had to see her. Had to be there for her. Had to be there if she needed him.

Had to.

Why?

Well, he would save the why for when he saw her.

He had a fairly well-thought-out speech prepared.

But nothing could have prepared him for what greeted him when he stepped into Lady Colworth's bedchamber.

There was a fire burning in the grate, casting a warm light over the room and illuminating the very large copper tub that sat nearby, filled nearly to the brim with hot, steaming water.

There was no one in the tub. Yet.

He heard a sound and turned to see Kat stepping softly toward him across the carpet.

She was clothed, but her feet were bare. His mind latched on to that, and he felt a shiver of anticipation go through him.

He had seen her in scarlet, in crimson, in black. They seemed to be her preferred colors.

But tonight, she wore a gown of midnight blue. It was a rich, shimmering silk and had been tailored to her slender figure perfectly. The bodice was cut low, highlighting the shape of her breasts, while a braided silver sash emphasized her slim waist. With her sable hair and dark eyes, she looked stunning.

He caught a whiff of her scent, reminding him of fresh flowers mixed with an ocean breeze, and wondered where along her body she had applied the perfume. Her neck? Just behind her ears? In that delicate crevice between her lovely breasts?

He stood like a statue, simply taking her in.

"Would you like a drink?" she asked quickly, putting a hand to her hair. She seemed nervous. Her eyes darted to his. "What is it? Why are you looking at me that way?"

"Why?" He stared incredulously, then grinned. "Because you've the beauty of Helen of Troy, that's why."

Kat poured two drinks at the side table and took a sip from one, before placing it back on the table. "I thought scholars believed she was fair-haired."

"More fools they," Ash said solemnly, shaking his head. "Everyone knows dark-haired women are more beautiful."

She gave him the flicker of a smile.

"How is Oliver?" he asked. "And whatever happened with the bastard who tried to take him?"

"The bastard is with the magistrate. Though I doubt he will stay there long, even with Edmund to keep him at bay, for he has his own powerful connections. As for, Oliver... Oliver is fine. Grateful, a little shaken, but he is safe." She clutched the edge of the table with both hands, and he saw she was still anxious.

"He is safe, Kat," he reassured her. "Your brother must be on high alert now."

She grimaced. "Yes. He does not wish us to leave Blakeley Manor. Ever. Even after the house party wraps up."

"I don't blame him," Ash said softly. "Is it normally just the two of you? Back home?"

"Well." She shrugged. "We have servants, of course. Faithful ones." He watched her scowl. "At least, I thought so. Most were Colworth's first, of course."

She sighed and rubbed her temple. "In any case, we need not talk of this."

"No? What would you like to talk about then?" Ash asked gently. He nodded toward the tub. "Who is the bath for, Kat?"

She looked up, eyes wide and appealing. "You saved him," she said slowly. "You saved him, Ash. Without a second thought. You practically flew into that carriage. It was all over so fast. And yet—I might have lost him. If it were not for you—" She caught a hand to her throat. "If you had not been there..."

He could not bear it. He stepped toward her, put a hand over the hand that lay across her throat, and gently tugged it down, wrapping her smaller one in his two larger.

"But I was. I was there."

He smiled. "And now you wish for me to bathe?"

She blushed so quickly and prettily that he laughed.

"No, I—That is... well, I thought," she stumbled.

He knew, of course. Knew what she had planned. Knew what she wanted.

But he was also damned if that was all he would settle for tonight.

No, by the time he left the room, he was determined she would be his, body and soul. He was not interested in a one-night tryst.

And he did not think that was truly all she wished for either.

And so—"A hot bath would be rather nice," he confessed, beginning to shrug out of his coat. He lay it neatly over a chair and began tugging loose the simple necktie he wore.

Kat was looking much more flustered. "What are you doing?" she asked faintly.

"Isn't this what you wanted?" He was still smiling, still at ease. "Calling me up to your room?"

"Well." He watched her swallow hard as he dropped the necktie over the coat and stood in his shirt sleeves before her. "Yes, of course, in a way. Though you are moving rather fast."

He smirked. "The water is getting cold, Kat. You'd better hurry up yourself."

"Me?" she squeaked. "Oh, no."

"Oh, yes," he insisted. "I'm not getting in that huge tub all alone."

"I couldn't possibly. I've already bathed. Yesterday, in fact." She caught the piercing look he was giving her, tilted her head back, and heaved a sigh of surrender. "Oh, very well."

She moved back to the side table and picking up her glass, drained it quickly. "Liquid courage," she explained.

Ash quirked his eyebrows playfully, then lifted his shirt over his head.

"Oh, my," he heard her gasp as he emerged.

Ash had not been with many women. Very few, in fact, though he was not about to announce that. But he was confident in his form. He had been called handsome enough times to believe it was probably true. And he could see for himself that he possessed a tautly muscled upper body, a chest that was broad and smooth-skinned, and he was equally proportioned in other ways. He had a natural strength, which had been enhanced by his work in the stables. He appreciated his own strength, especially now, for Kat's sake. He enjoyed feeling as if he could keep a woman and a child safe. Safe in his arms.

"Yes?" he asked politely. "Cat got your tongue?"

"No puns," she muttered, still looking at him with stark appreciation.

He took a step toward her, and she took one step back, her bottom hitting the table and jostling the bottles of liquid with a clinking sound.

"Most would say I should not have come here tonight, Countess," Ash said conversationally. "For I do believe you summoned me here to seduce me."

"Seduce you!"

God, her smell was driving him wild. And that was only her perfume. He longed to discover the scent and taste of her hidden places.

He lowered his mouth to her ear. "But I must tell you, my lady. You'll have a hard time of it."

"Oh, really?" She sounded more like her obstinate self then, and he grinned.

"Yes, for you see, I mean to seduce *you*."

Among other things, he thought.

He stepped back from her, his hands moving to the fold of his trousers. He undid the fall front, then put his hands to his hips, and pushed down until the trousers dropped to the floor.

He did not meet her eye but rather walked over to the copper tub, briefly dipped a hand in the water, then stepped in.

"Coming?" he asked innocently. "Don't worry, the water is still hot."

"Oh, you devil," she whispered, but there was a smile playing around her lips.

He looked like a young Greek god, lounging there in the water.

She was not sure she had ever seen another person so beautiful. His wheat-colored hair, his sea-blue eyes, his warm, amber-tinged skin. He had the grin of a scoundrel, yet he had proven he possessed the heart of a saint.

It physically hurt to look at him. It did something to her heart, her chest, leaving her feeling squeezed and empty and raw.

And yet, he also made her feel safe. So much less alone.

Even, dare she think it, happy?

But he was only here for tonight.

What more could this be?

Was that why looking at him hurt so badly? Because she knew after this, she would have to leave? Leave before her heart was anymore entwined with Ash Spencer?

"You look sad, Kat," he said. She focused her eyes on his, seeing his face turning troubled. "What is it?"

She could not speak, simply shook her head. She tried to smile, failed.

"Come to me. Come to me now," he commanded. "Forget about your clothes. Your dress. Just come. Please."

He sounded so beseeching, and he had half knelt in the tub, reaching out his hand for her to take it. She obeyed.

Walked over to him and lifted up a blue silk-covered leg and simply stepped in, feeling the water immediately seep up the skirt, pulling and tugging her down into it.

She lowered herself carefully to her knees, shivering in delight as the heat embraced her.

And then Ash's hands gripped her waist, ever so gently but insistently, tugging her toward him, until she was lying across his chest in a soaking wet, blue silk gown.

She leaned against him and closed her eyes, feeling his hand caressing her hair, while his other held her by the waist protectively.

Nothing had ever felt so wonderful, so safe, so entirely right as Ash Spencer's arms did around her.

His skin was blissfully warm, and her head rose and fell slightly with each rise and fall of his chest as he breathed in and out. He smelled sweet and clean, of hay and horses and saddle leather.

She wanted nothing so much as to stay with him this way forever.

She was falling in love with Ash Spencer.

She had known she was becoming infatuated, but this—she was damn near blinded by her attraction to him. She had believed him a boy, and he had proven himself a man. How else would he prove her wrong if she let him?

She could not stay around to find out. For her sake and Oliver's, she must make this night their first and their last.

And then he shocked all thoughts right out of her mind.

"You are thinking about saying goodbye already," he said, his voice deep and mellow. His chest rumbled slightly as he spoke, and she jumped.

"How did you—" she began.

His hand ran over her hair gently. "Of course you are. You see no way for us to be together," he said softly. "Except like this. A stolen night in your room." He gave a little laugh. "And yet, I suspect you do not simply want my body."

"I don't," Kat said, sitting up, shocked. "I mean, I do, of course..." She blushed. "But—"

"You like me, Katherine," he said simply, looking into her eyes. "And I like you. Very, very much. Every moment we spend together..." He shook his head. "Well. It feels right."

"Yes," she said, agreeing through her confusion. "It does feel right. I feel..." She swallowed hard. "Happy with you," she said, her voice falling to a whisper.

He reached out a finger to trace her lips. "That doesn't sound like a terrible thing."

"No," she agreed. "But... we are so different."

He smiled. "We come from such different places, you mean," he said. "You, a countess, the daughter of a duke. Me, a groom, a servant."

"I don't care that you're a servant," she whispered, keeping her gaze fixed on his eyes. And as she said the words, she knew they were true. She never really had.

She certainly was not the sort to care what anyone else thought of her. Or of her choices. After all, defiance and rebellion rather ran in the family. The Blakeleys had never been the conventional sort.

Most of the ton believed she had killed Colworth, after all. What would they care if she took up with a servant?

Was that what he was about to propose, she wondered? That she keep him as her lover?

"And I don't care that you are a countess," he replied, his eyes twinkling. "I only care that you are you." He pressed his forehead against hers. "After all, even day and night can get past their differences for the sake of the dawn and the twilight. Perhaps so might we. Hold tight to me for a moment, Kat. For I'm about to say something which I have no doubt will scare you."

"I doubt anything you say could scare me, Ash Spencer," Kat said honestly, but she placed her hands flat against his chest and looked up at him steadily. "What is it?"

"I want to hold you like this forever," he whispered, and for once, it was his gaze that was unsteady, his face tremulous.

She ran a hand over his cheek, offering her reassurance, but said nothing, only listened.

"I believe I forgot to inform you, Kat, that we Spencers are a stubborn and a foolish lot. Once our minds are set on something, we never give in. We are incredibly practical people, yet hopelessly naïve and idealistic, too. Completely contradictory. I believed in fairies until... oh, wait, I still believe in fairies."

Kat giggled. "I believe Oliver still does as well. You sound like a wonderful bunch. I should like to meet the others. Your brother and your sisters." She remembered then, and her smile wavered.

"I should like that, too," he said, continuing. "But wait, let me finish. We also believe in the enduring power of love. Though none of us really believe we'll ever find it for ourselves. Our parents had it, you see, and that rather left all of us children with a high standard to follow. But we believe in it, that's the main thing."

"That love conquers all?" Kat asked, wrinkling her nose as if she were astonished—though really, she was enjoying the turn the conversation was taking.

"Absolutely. Fight any man who tried to say it didn't," Ash said with mock seriousness. "We believe in all sorts of other absurd things. Why not love?"

"Why not love?" Kat whispered back, looking at him.

"And that," he declared, "is why I'm asking you to marry me. Now. Tonight. In a bathtub." He grinned sheepishly. "The proposal, mind you, not the actual wedding."

Kat's eyebrows shot up. Her heart began to pump rapidly, and she suddenly felt light-headed.

Ash leaned forward, bumping her forehead lightly with his, like a goat. She giggled and cupped his cheek.

Was this really happening?

"I love you, Kat," he said, not taking his eyes from her, his face a mere inch from hers. "Let me keep you and Oliver safe, always."

Was she dreaming?

This beautiful man, the bathtub, the sweet words.

"Am I dreaming?" she repeated. "Ash, I..." She looked at him, trying to think of the reasons she had to say no, could not possibly say yes.

For she was meant to be a lonely widow forever, wasn't she? Scorned and pitied? Never trusting another man. Always afraid he would turn out to be like Colworth. Never willing to risk that, for her sake and Oliver's.

But Ash Spencer had caught her off-guard. He had captured her heart before she had known she'd surrendered. She trusted him implicitly, without him ever asking. And what was more, so did Oliver.

In every way that truly mattered, he would make a wonderful husband. A good father.

Excitement was rising in her.

Her lips moved toward his, afraid to risk words.

"Kiss me," she begged, and she did not have to ask him twice.

His kiss surprised her with its heat, scorching in its intensity and hunger. He had missed her, she realized. And she had missed him, too.

Yet this was Ash—and so the kiss was tender, too.

And in their joining of lips, so intimate, both of them so reverent as they moved to possess one another. Kat realized with a jolt that she was already saying her vows, not with words, but with her lips. A sheer, forceful yes, over and over and over.

Ash was saying them with his hands, too. He tasted her with his lips, slid his tongue between to fill her mouth, and then his hands slid down her back to caress the soft roundness of her hips, drifted lower still, turning her and cupping her until she was taut against his naked body. She gasped against his mouth as the heat of his arousal pressed through the wet silk of her gown. He was hard, throbbing and erect, and already hot between her thighs. She felt a surge of her own wet heat and moaned, feeling suddenly desperate to be as bare as he was.

She pulled away and saw him looking down at her hungrily. "May I?" he asked hoarsely, raising his hands to the shoulders of her dress.

When she nodded, he tugged, none too gently, and the dress half-ripped, half-slid from her shoulders, baring her from neck to waist.

She glimpsed the stark appreciation in his eyes. His hands were hot against her flesh, cupping her breasts and thumbing her nipples to hard peaks so quickly she was left gasping and breathless, trembling against him as her thighs pressed around his length so tightly, worried she would hurt him.

"God," he murmured, moving his mouth back to hers. "I want you so badly, Kat."

And then his hands left her breasts and were around her waist, gently pushing the remainder of silk down her thighs and off into the water, freeing her completely as his fingers slid between her legs and into the soft, wet down, stroking the delicate, sensitive folds of her sex while she gasped and writhed against him. His fingertips were rough but expert, gently parting the slick pleats and rubbing where she was most sensitive, that half-hidden tip. His thumb touched it, lightly then harder. She was lost, gripping his shoulders, naked breasts thrusting up eagerly into his mouth as he strummed her like a harp, her hips rising, spreading, begging for more.

And then she felt him there, nudging against her, pushing inside of her.

She was molten liquid when he filled her, his first thrust sending her shattering against his hand. She gasped and arched tightly, pressing her body against his chest as he licked and nibbled her breasts, her shoulders, the nape of her neck.

She took in more and more of him while his hands grasped her hips firmly in his, thrusting deeper, his strokes long and deep and even. Kat was pushed up against the edge once more and finally joined him in his rapture, burying her face in the warm reassuring heat of his neck as they both exploded together, arms wrapped tightly around one another, this first time.

They left the tub, eventually. Sluicing each other off first with a receptacle that had been left for that purpose, then drying one another in the large towels that had been warming by the fire, and collapsing beside one another in Kat's bed.

Only when her head was finally nestled in the crook of his shoulder, did Ash finally speak again.

"You didn't answer," he noted.

"Didn't I?" Kat murmured, lifting her head slightly to look at him with a mischievous smile.

"Was that your answer?" he asked, half-disbelief, half-excitement filling his boyish face. "Truly?"

"It was," she said a little shyly. "I have no idea what my family will think about any of this, but yes, I would like to be your wife, Ash Spencer."

She shrieked as he suddenly rose up and began to smother her with kisses.

"Of course," he said after they had settled, "I must…"

Kat sighed. "There is about to be a caveat. I so dislike caveats."

He kissed her head. "I do as well, but I suspect you know what I am going to say."

"You cannot marry me yet. You must prove your worth as a man and make your fortune before you return in ten long years and finally take my hand in marriage," Kat droned. "Like Odysseus and Penelope."

"Ten years?" Ash sounded aghast. "I was thinking two at the most."

"Two, ten, what does it matter?" Kat said, suddenly grumpy. "What will you do? Join the army? Become a pirate?"

She turned onto her stomach, and he ran a hand gently over her back.

"My uncle is a merchant. He owns a vessel that sails to India. He has always said there would be a place for my brother or I on the ship if we should want it."

"And so why did you not take it before this?" Kat asked, curious.

"Because he's a right bastard, that's why," Ash said with a grin. His face sobered. "He won't be a pleasant man to work under. And I will be away for long stretches. Away from you and Oliver and…"

"And your horses," Kat said softly.

"Yes, them, too." Ash sighed. "But I am sure your family would prefer you not simply marry a groom who has very little to his name. Nothing, in fact."

"You were not expecting to marry," Kat said with understanding. "Are you sure this is what *you* really want?"

"I am absolutely certain, and I desire it—you, Kat—more than anything," he said resolutely. "Can you make this sacrifice with me? Can our love stand the test of time and distance?"

"Mine can," Kat said promptly. Her face softened, and she reached out a hand to stroke his cheek. "And I trust you, Ash. With my heart and my future."

He brought her hand to his lips and kissed it, then pulled her back against him.

Kat closed her eyes.

Was this what she had to look forward to? Nights of kisses and laughter and love-making? Of soft conversation murmured in the dark?

She could bear Ash's absence for long periods with a future like that to look ahead to.

A future where Ash's arms would always be tightly around her, holding her close, keeping her and Oliver safe.

It was too good to be true, she thought, drowsily. It was the best Christmas gift she had ever received. And the best part of all was how utterly, utterly unexpected it had been.

The touch of his lips against her damp hair was the last thing she remembered as she drifted off to sleep.

Chapter Ten

"The duke would like to see you, Mr. Spencer."

A kitchen boy had brought the message to the stables. Ash had been expecting something of the sort.

Now he stood in the hall just outside the Duke of Dareford's study. The door was closed and he could hear raised voices from within.

But when the door burst open, he was surprised to see not Kat but Lady Briar Blakeley emerging.

In spite of whatever conflict had been taking place inside the study, she wore her usual sunny expression and paused when she saw him.

"Oh, good day, Mr. Spencer. I hope my brother and I have not kept you waiting long."

Ash smiled. "Not at all. Thank you, Lady Briar." He dropped his voice a little. "Did you give him a run for his money?"

"Well, he did not win if that is what you are asking," Lady Briar replied with a grin. "I understand we are soon to be family, Mr. Spencer. I cannot think of a nicer Christmas present than learning my sister has found such happiness."

"And I cannot think of a nicer future sister-in-law," Ash said, smiling and giving a courtly bow.

"Yes, well, I hope you still think so later on," Lady Briar said a little cryptically but with a wink.

Ash had just opened his mouth to ask what she meant when the study door opened a second time, and Lady Briar swept away with a hurried, "I must go."

"Mr. Spencer." The Duke of Dareford stood in the doorframe.

He was a tall, dark-haired man. A larger, masculine version of Kat in many ways. Ash knew the duke was a year younger than his sister, but perhaps the mantle of duke added to the impression he gave of being older than his years.

He was certainly looking very imposing and serious right now.

Ash straightened up and came toward him. "Your Grace."

The two men went into the room where the duke gestured to two leather armchairs near a window overlooking the snow-covered grounds.

"Thank you for coming," the duke said politely, as if Ash were a guest and not simply one of his servants.

"Of course. I take it there is no need to beat around the bush, and your sister has already spoken with you," Ash said straightforwardly.

"She has, yes. What a blessing stubborn sisters are." The duke smiled slightly.

He met Ash's eyes. "I am not here to try to dissuade you if you are worried about that."

"I'm not," Ash said frankly. "I hadn't taken you for that sort of man, to be honest."

"Good. Because I am not," the duke said, leaning forward. "I don't know how much you know about my parents, Mr. Spencer. But one thing they were not was conventional. They lived rather wild lives, and their deaths were by no means undramatic either."

He waved a hand. "But that is a story for another time. One thing they taught their children was that life is short. It is better to live well than not to live at all." He paused, and Ash had the feeling he was being sized up carefully. "Kat has not been living well, as I think you already know. She made a tragic choice in her first marriage. If our parents had been around, I don't believe she would ever have gone through with it. Grief can lead us to make poor decisions."

"It can," Ash said, thinking of others in his family to whom the axiom applied, such as his older brother.

"I do not believe you are a poor choice for Kat, however," the duke said plainly. "I want her to be happy. Can you make her happy, Mr. Spencer?"

"I will certainly do everything in my power to do so, Your Grace," Ash said. "And not only her, but Oliver, too. I have enjoyed coming to know the boy."

"He desperately needs a father. A *good* father," the duke stressed. He leaned back in his chair and ran a hand over his face. "Has Kat told you how Colworth died?"

Ash shook his head. "Only that Oliver was there when it occurred."

The duke's expression was bleak. "Yes. He was." He shook his head. "Well, Mr. Spencer, let us get down to it. Kat tells me you have the ambition of being a sailor."

"Well, I would not say I have always had the ambition, but I *have* ambition, Your Grace," Ash stumbled. "I know you would not like to think of anyone marrying your sister for her wealth or..."

"And so, you feel you must prove yourself to me?" the duke interjected. "Or perhaps prove yourself to her and to me? Prove that you have no mercenary motives. And prove that you can be independent and provide some measure of income. Though, of course, Kat requires nothing. She has everything she needs in a material way, as does Oliver. You know all this."

"Of course," Ash said politely, not sure where this was going. "But at least this way, I will not feel like one of her dependents."

"You will not feel like one, but you will be one," the duke said matter-of-factly. He looked at Ash carefully. "I am not trying to give offense. But I must ask, is that such a bad thing?"

"I am not sure I follow, Your Grace," Ash said slowly.

"Kat needs a husband, and Oliver needs a father far more than they need you to go off to sea, Mr. Spencer. On some quest to prove yourself worthy, they may lose you to any number of dangers while you are traveling. Is it really such a necessity for you to do so?"

Ash was flabbergasted. "You... do not wish for me to go?"

The duke shook his head.

"Yet... you have no objection to me marrying Kat? With nothing?"

The duke nodded.

"I must say I am surprised," Ash said. Damned shocked would be more like it.

"If it is about the money," the duke said, "which neither Kat nor I, nor any of our siblings, give a damn about frankly, then you must decide how much you care, Mr. Spencer. For truly, I do not. I care that you treat my sister well. That you treat Oliver well. But I do not object to your suit on material grounds."

"So, we are free to marry then?" Ash asked weakly.

"You are as far as I am concerned." The duke grinned. "If Kat does not object, of course." His face turned serious. "Have you spoken to Oliver yet?"

"So, you'll be coming to live with us? At Woodcroft? For always?"

Oliver, unsurprisingly, had been located near the stables. He had Seren, the little sorrel, out of his stall and had been brushing the foal down with the care and fastidiousness of a professional groom.

"It does. If that is all right with you," Ash said.

Oliver was already nodding enthusiastically. Then his face fell.

"What is it?" Ash asked gently, stealing a glance at where Kat stood, watching the proceedings nearby.

"I'll have to leave Seren, I suppose," Oliver said gloomily.

"Ah, Seren." Ash scratched his nose to hide a smile. He did not blame the boy one bit for being just as concerned about the horse as about the man his mother would soon be marrying. "Perhaps," he said cautiously, "your uncle would bring Seren for a visit?" He glanced at Kat who was nodding.

"And we will visit Blakeley Manor more regularly than we have been doing, Oliver," Kat promised. "Woodcroft is not so very far away. You will see Seren again. And while he is still too young to leave his mother, I suspect that if we talk to Uncle Edmund, he will let you have Seren for your very own in a year or two. Would you like that?"

"Oh, yes. And I would take very, very good care of him," Oliver assured them. His face fell. "Perhaps Seren would not like to leave his mother, though. I know I would not."

Kat bit her lip as Ash smiled.

"Well, that is some time away," he said diplomatically. "We will talk to Seren about it, when the time comes. In the meantime, you can continue to be very good friends."

"We'll leave you to finish up with Seren now, shall we?" Kat said, slipping her hand into Ash's. "Come and find us when you are done, and we'll walk back to the house together?"

Ash drifted down the row; Kat's hand squeezed tightly in his.

"You never told me what it was that finally put Oliver so entirely off horses, you know," Ash said quietly as they strolled down the row of stalls.

Kat halted abruptly. "You mean, how Colworth died."

"Yes. Your brother asked me if I knew." Ash looked at her. "You do not have to tell me, Kat," he said quietly. "I don't care either way. No matter what the secret is."

"But there is one. That much you can tell." She closed her eyes. "I am sure Oliver will tell you himself one day, but for now, the simple answer is that Colworth was killed by a horse. Oliver believes he is the one truly to blame, for they had been struggling. Colworth was, quite literally, trying to force Oliver into the saddle, and Oliver was resisting. Oliver fell onto the straw, and he kicked at his father—who could blame him? Colworth was an athletic man, but he must have stumbled, and he went down. The horse was spooked, and it kicked out. Colworth was struck in the head."

"How awful for Oliver," Ash murmured.

"Not for Colworth?" Kat asked, her face grim.

Ash shook his head. "It is a sad thing to think about any man, but from all I have learned about Oliver's father—and seen of him, in his brother—this was not a man whose passing I feel compelled to regret. No matter how it came about," he added. "And from what you have said, it certainly does not sound as if it were Oliver's fault but his father's own doing. For being so ruthless with the boy."

Kat's face was sad. "We were hardly a family at all until Colworth died," she whispered. "Poor Oliver. We are only just starting to come back to ourselves, he and I."

"I would never treat him in such a way, Kat," Ash swore. "Only with gentleness. I hope you know that. Moreover, he is your son, not mine. I trust you know I will not interfere in the choices you make for his rearing."

She stepped toward him, lifted her lips to his, and kissed him briefly. "Yes. I know. But it is good to hear it." She smiled then. "Of course, it may not be only Oliver for long, you know."

Ash's eyes widened. "What are you saying? After last night? Can you really tell...?"

"No, no," she said hastily, with a laugh. "I only meant that, well, our family will likely grow in time. I think Oliver would make a wonderful brother, don't you?"

"I do," Ash said.

He looked at her, suddenly struck dumb by the thought of this woman carrying their child.

She was so lovely with her dark hair piled up in a crown of gleaming curls, and her slim figure clad in a scarlet wool riding dress. But more than that, she was so damnably happy. She glowed. And if he could see himself in a mirror, Ash knew he would see much the same thing. He loved her, and he felt lit up from inside with his love.

He bent and pressed his mouth to her lips, smothering them with an ardent kiss.

"I love you, you know," he said softly. "I love you and Oliver, every part of you, for all that you are, for where you have been, all you have gone through. I will always be here for you both, no matter what."

His heart was so full. Could he really be this lucky? How had it all began?

Oh, yes! He had nearly forgotten entirely. With a stupid jest!

"We need to pay a visit to the servants' quarters," he said suddenly, tugging at her arm.

"Right now?" Kat asked, looking surprised. "But Mr. Morris has already been dismissed if that is what you are worried about."

"Not Morris, Howard," Ash said, grinning. "We need to go and thank Howard."

THE END

Thank you for reading *The Countess's Christmas Groom* by Fenna Edgewood!

Keep your eyes peeled for the next book in this steamy, class-crossing series! Briar Blakeley is bold and beautiful, but she has never met a man quite as stubborn and provoking as the handsome gardener Wren Spencer. When Briar steps straight into danger, the gardener-turned-bodyguard sweeps into her rescue, making for a very appealing first impression. Too bad for Briar, Wren has absolutely no intention of ever letting another woman anywhere near his heart...

Read *Lady Briar Weds the Scot*!

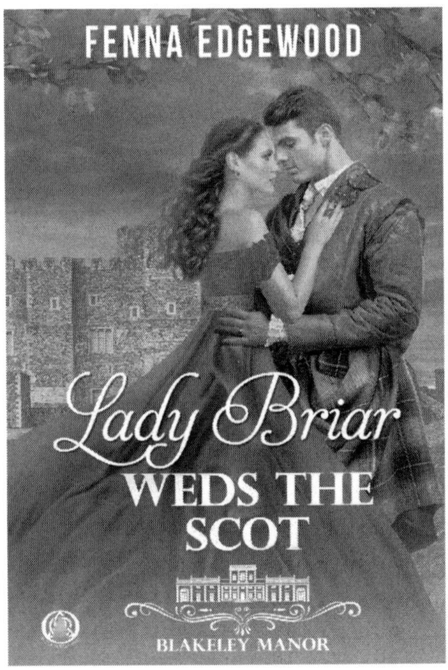

Also by Fenna Edgewood

The Blakely Manor Series

Two families, from very different worlds, are about to converge at Blakeley Manor...

Upstairs...

The Blakeley family is famed for their infinite fortune—and their infinite eccentricities. As the Blakeley siblings reunite to host a Christmas house party, they are plunged into scandal as each one forges a passionate new alliance that crosses the boundaries of all propriety.

Downstairs...

Four very different siblings–a lady's maid, a housekeeper, a gardener, and a groom–are tied together, not only by the love and loyalty they share but by dangerous secrets that could cost them not only their employment...but also their hearts.

In this steamy, cross-classing series from bestselling Regency romance author Fenna Edgewood, mismatched hearts fall the hardest at Blakeley Manor and the journey to love is unforgettable!

#1 Lady Briar Weds the Scot

#2 Kiss Me, My Duke

More to follow!

About Fenna Edgewood

USA Today bestselling author Fenna Edgewood writes swoon-worthy, humorous stories of love, family, and adventure. In other words, the most important things in life! She is an award-winning retired academic who has studied English literature for most of her life. After a twenty-five-year hiatus from writing romance as a twelve-year-old, she has returned to the genre with a bang. Fenna has lived and traveled across North America, most notably above the Arctic Circle. She now resides back on the Prairies with her husband and two tiny tots (who are adorable but generally terrible research assistants).

Connect with Fenna:

https://fennaedgewood.com

facebook.com/fennaedgewoodbooks

instagram.com/fennaedgewood

bookbub.com/authors/fenna-edgewood

amazon.com/stores/Fenna-Edgewood/author/B0929KJV52

A VERY DARING CHRISTMAS

A NOVELLA TO THE DEBUTANTE DARES SERIES

CHARLIE LANE

A Very Daring Christmas by Charlie Lane

Published by WOLF Publishing UG

About the book

A VERY DARING CHRISTMAS

Ladies are meant for ballrooms. But Lady Phillipa Hampton would rather have the open skies of Scotland where she can paint to her heart's content. She'd still be there now if she hadn't kissed her grandmother's silver-eyed steward last summer. And been caught. She was exiled back to London, but Grandmama's Christmas trip to Town offers Pippa an opportunity—prove she cares nothing for Bram Shaw and win her way back to the land she loves.

Stewards aren't meant for ladies, and Bram Shaw knows it. But he doesn't like it. Not when his heart belongs to the artistic and daring Lady Phillipa, whose grandmother is a dowager duchess. And Bram's employer. When Christmas brings him close to the woman whose kiss he can't forget, he must hide his affection or lose his position in the dowager's household. But adding another lost job to his long list will lose him the inheritance he's been working years to secure.

The dowager holds two hearts in her hands, and the crafty old woman pits the former lovers against one another. Whoever finds her the most interesting Christmas gift wins a return to Scotland. She'll take a companion or a steward, but not both.

Crowded London streets, eccentric shop keeps, violent-minded maids, and chaotic coffeehouses. Pippa and Bram will brave it all to find the elusive perfect gift to win their hearts desires.

But a single kiss can change everything, and sometimes the perfect gift isn't bought with coin but love.

Prologue

A page from Lady Philippa Hampton's diary, May 1, 1819
Clarebourn Castle, Scotland

I return to London tomorrow. I've not cried yet. You'll notice the lack of tear stains on your pages. But I do not doubt I will shed tears aplenty when the wheels begin to roll beneath me in the morning.

It is safe to pronounce the dowager duchess's comportment lessons a resounding failure. They were supposed to save me. The dowager (Grandmama, as she insists I call her) was the most revered duchess of her generation. She should have been able to transform a girl like me—timid and fearful in crowds, silent around strangers—into at least a passable debutante. But...

I kissed Bram Shaw. That's how it started, at least. A kiss when he pulled me off the roof of the folly. It's much harder to get down from such spaces than to get up. But oh, the view was worth it.

When the dowager caught us (a different kiss entirely, our... fifth? Seventh?) the kissing had begun to resemble something much more... daring.

And inadvisable.

If she had not caught us... who knows how far I would have gone?

But she did catch us, and Bram apologized and melted away into the shadows. That wrecked me for some reason. Felt like I'd fallen on a pitchfork. Speared right through.

The taste of him lingers, makes me want to cry. I will miss him in London. I'll miss his laugh and his stories of his family. I'll miss his mind, too.

But also his lips. And the muscle of his arm.

Bah. You see, it is no wonder I failed.

In crowds I'm lost, but when alone, or with people who make me feel comfortable, I'm rather daring indeed. Another reason I so need Grandmama's lessons.

And Grandmama, instead of realizing the kiss is a sign of how much I truly need her lessons, evicted me from the one place I've ever truly felt at home. Every view, a painting ready to happen. No crowds to make me shrink. Air I can breathe fully.

But I kissed Bram Shaw.

And now, I must pay the price. Kisses, unless they come with marriage or complete secrecy, are ever expensive.

I suppose I must finally make my debut in the *ton*. I need not tell you how ill that makes me. London is full of people, crowded to every edge.

I'll wrap myself up tight with the rules I've learned from Grandmama and lock up the woman who kissed a steward. Neither my fears nor my... desires will help me win my goal. At least, I have the entire trip back to London to plot and plan. How to get out of a season. How to get back to Scotland.

Chapter One

December 1819, five days until Christmas
London, England

The sky spread pale pink and yawning at the radiating point where the sun disappeared below the London skyline. A deep indigo chased it into the earth, bringing with it the promise of a blanket of stars. And hope for Pippa.

Pressed against the chilling glass of a second-floor window of her brother-in-law the Duke of Collingford's palatial home, Pippa shivered and dropped her paintbrush on the table to pull her shawl tighter about her shoulders.

She closed her eyes, remembering the Scottish sunsets. Pinks blazing, not pale. Indescribable purples bleeding into the darkest celestial blues. When she opened her eyes to the painting drying before her, she saw only a muted memory.

But soon, memory would not have to suffice. She would see, once more, a Scottish sunset with her own eyes. Winter spent at a drafty, secluded Scottish estate would seep deeper into her bones, but she did not care. She'd rather live a season of every year bundled tight in layers of shawls than join a single Season in London with the crowds, with the strangers who would expect her to be clever and quick, the *ton* who would be disappointed when she was not.

A fierce clatter of hooves on the street.

She jerked her attention to the window. At the end of the street, beyond the square, a team of horses pulled a glossy, black traveling coach toward the house. She knew, though she could not yet see it, that the duke's family crest would be emblazoned on the side. The Dowager Duchess of Collingford had arrived from Scotland for a family Christmas, and she held, though she did not know it, Pippa's future in her hands.

Pippa clutched her shawl even tighter, her heart a frantic bird, its wings beating against the bars of her rib cage. She had to find her sister. She turned and let her feet fly as her heart wished to do—into the hall, down the stairs, and to her sister's sitting room. She slid through the door, grasping the frame to stop her momentum.

Tabitha rose from her chair with a start, dropping her book to the table beside her. "Has the dowager arrived?"

"Yes." Pippa gasped for breath. "And you'd best call her Grandmama, as she's demanded, or we'll all get a lecture."

"She's Arthur's grandmother, not ours," Tabitha grumbled. "But pleasing my husband means pleasing his grandmother. Grandmama it is." Tabitha strode for the door with a roll of her eyes, and Pippa linked their arms as she passed into the hallway.

"Are you nervous?" Tabitha asked.

The question beaded the perspiration across Pippa's skin. *Grandmama,* she'd have to say, *I'd like to be your permanent companion in Scotland. I've never had a season, I am aware, but I do not wish for one, so all is well. I know you found me in a... scandalous state with your steward, but that is in the past. He could not get a kiss or otherwise from me to save his life.*

Bit of a lie, that last part, but needs must.

After that little speech, Grandmama would turn gorgon, and Pippa would have to fight with a sword, mirror, and any other weapon at her disposal, no matter how unlikely.

Tabitha's hand crept into Pippa's, a curling ivy vine of comfort. "Are you sure this is what you wish?"

"Entirely. Scotland is my home." She'd felt it the first time she'd set foot on the drive before Castle Clarebourn. The colors had erupted, and her fingers had itched for her paintbrush. The only sounds had been those of birds, bees, and wind. No crowds there. No strangers. No suitors. She'd had to learn Grandmama's lessons, read the etiquette books, wrap herself round with rules and *should nots*, but there had also been more room for her to be herself, to paint all morning and read all afternoon. To make friends with playful stewards.

"There are other options to help you escape the bustle of city life. You do not have to rely upon Grandmama and Scotland."

Other estates belonging to their father and the duke. None of them where she most wanted to be. None offered quite the same protection as a secluded Scottish castle inhabited by a grumpy dowager. She'd be a much better companion than a debutante.

"No, Tabby. Only Scotland will do."

Tabitha squeezed Pippa's hand. "Let me tell Arthur to speak with his grandmother, then. He can ensure her compliance."

"I must fight my own battles." She always did, being a solitary sort. "And I will not ask your husband to do something that might cause a rift between him and his grandmother." His marriage to Tabitha had come close enough to doing that already. Pippa would not turn a hairline fracture into a gaping crack.

Tabitha's face screwed up. "Arthur's grandmother is a crafty dragon."

"She's different in Scotland. Freer. Not entirely, of course. But her edges are not so sharp there. That's how I feel there, too." Softer, freer, happier.

Tabitha paced away from Pippa, toward the stairs, with a swish of velvet emerald skirts the exact color of the lawn in summer that stretched out before Castle Clarebourn. She spun around, her arms winging wide until they dropped like stones to her side. "You should not have gone to her in Scotland last summer to begin with. You do not need lessons in deportment, propriety, or any other *womanly* pursuit. You are fine as you are. I told Papa that, but he admires the duchess so that he rather thought the whole absurd project an honor. And Arthur merely told me to let you do as you pleased." A frustrated huff as she grasped Pippa's hand.

Frustration vexed Pippa, too. "You know why I went. I hoped to end my fear. Ballrooms, drawing rooms, even crowded parks and streets... too many people and my chest feels like it's caving in on itself. My voice dries up when anyone speaks with me. Without help, I'd never survive a season.

And no one is more regarded for her social power and influence than your husband's grandmother." She ripped her hand from her sister's hold and picked at a fingernail, scratching the skin as her stomach tumbled end over end. "Learning at Grandmama's knee did nothing to improve my faults or ease my fears as I'd hoped it would. Any Season I suffer through will be nothing but a disaster. I will go back to Scotland."

"Why did you return to London at all, then? You've refused to answer that question since you appeared suddenly on our doorstep last May." Tabitha placed a hand on the stair railing and tapped a finger. She pointed the other down the stairs and toward the front door where the coach no doubt waited. "You should be only now arriving with Grandmama. *That* had always been the plan. Why stray from the plan if you loved it so much there?"

Because of Mr. Bram Shaw, steward. Tall, strong, handsome, and entirely unacceptable. According to Grandmama. Pippa's gaze skittered away, seeking the hallway shadows to hide in.

Grandmama had sent Pippa home to keep her far, far away from the steward.

Pippa had to change her mind.

"Once more, you refuse to answer that question," Tabitha said.

Pippa ducked her head, pulled her shawl tighter about her. "It matters not why I left Scotland early—"

Tabitha snorted.

"What matters is that I will return there. And never leave again if I can help it." Pippa grinned.

"Stubborn." Tabitha dragged in a breath, took a single step downward. "Well, then. Let us go greet the woman who can make that happen." She held out her arm, bent at the elbow.

Pippa linked her arm through her sister's offered wing once more, and they descended together. "Thank you."

"Grandmama expects you to make your bow next season. How will you convince her otherwise without relying on Arthur's authority as a duke? Hm. Perhaps if we tell Grandmama she can have sole responsibility for finding you a suitable husband, she'll be quite amenable to taking you back with her if that's the case."

A smart idea. At six and twenty, Pippa should have made her bows and married years ago. But her mother's death just after she'd turned seventeen, more than a year's heart-heavy mourning, their father's increasing illness, and then investments so bad their coffers ran dry all conspired to keep the Hampton girls of marriageable age, all three of them, firmly on the shelf. Until Tabitha's marriage to the duke last year had made their come outs possible. Sarah, at two and twenty, had rushed head long into her first season. Pippa had sought lessons on proper behavior from the dowager, hoping to learn how to fit in without trembling herself to bits and pieces.

"I would not mind marrying," Pippa admitted, "if the opportunity presents itself." She could meet a gentleman in the quiet of the castle, fall in love in shadowed silence, the soft dust of almost yellow sunbeams settling about them as they kissed. He'd have dark hair and foggy eyes, a scruffy jaw and a wicked sense of humor. Lips soft as heather against her own, large hands gripping her waist, making her feel small and fluttery.

Bram Shaw, always lurking about in her brain.

Bah. She shook him out and focused. Letting Grandmama find her a husband would mean going into public, and that meant revealing all her flaws.

"I would like to marry, Tabby, but I will not let Grandmama drag me to Edinburgh balls and parties. It would just be more of what I cannot stand here. I'll find another argument to make stick."

The front door rose before them, open, and beyond it the coach, still and waiting like a giant spider spinning a web.

Tabitha sighed and dragged Pippa out the door. "As you wish."

The duke, Arthur, and his mother, Helena, stood side by side, and next to them were Pippa's younger sisters, Sarah and twelve-year-old Maggie. They talked with one another as they waited, but Pippa did not hear their chatter.

The coach shook, groaned, then the door opened, becoming a gapping maw, an entrance to a dark forest.

Grandmama's voice, a high, sharp bell's peal, rose from the forest depths. "Mr. Shaw! A hand if you please."

Pippa's nerves tangled like tortured vines in a wood, pricking every inch of her skin with thorns. Mr. Shaw... here? Impossible. Why would Grandmama bring *him*?

A figure jolted around the side of the coach, all muscle and tangled, too-long hair just brushing the top of his cravat, a hint of scruffy shadow on his cheek, his jaw, and trailing down his neck. She couldn't see his eyes in the gathering navy darkness, but she knew their color—the gray and silver of shadows, of morning fog, of glinting, precious metal.

Mr. Shaw.

He'd asked her to call him Bram. She had. Before they'd been caught and he'd slunk away, silent.

Mr. Shaw dashed into the coach. He leapt up and inside with muscular grace, his jacket stretching across a broad back, and his trousers straining against thick thighs.

Pippa's stomach fluttered, and her skin warmed and softened, as if the sun had broken through the clouds above. Yet the sky still hid it, diffusing its rays through thick clouds that promised snow. She shivered but resisted rubbing her hands up and down her arms. She pulled the red shawl tighter.

Mr. Shaw appeared once more, jumped down, and she squeezed her eyes shut so she did not notice his muscles moving, bunching, enticing. When she heard the slap of his boots on the ground, she opened her eyes. He handed the dowager out and held her steady until she could do so herself. A good bit past seventy, Grandmama still stood straight and strong, regal. But she needed help now and then and increasingly more often.

Pippa should be the one to help her.

She resisted shifting from foot to foot but could not help but dart a glance at the steward. His arms crossed over his chest, stretching wool thin against planes and hills of muscle and stealing Pippa's breath in an entirely different way than the crowds did. He caught her staring, lifted a corner of his chiseled mouth. Then he jumped toward the back of the coach and began unloading without another glimpse at the girl whose lips he'd once kissed so, so softly.

What she'd felt for him, got caught doing with him, had stolen her safe haven, yet she could not bring herself to regret it. It had been so soft, and his hands on her jaw so firm and sure. Her body had come alive in the most marvelous way. She'd not trade the encounter, her first and only of that nature, for the world, not for—

Scotland?

No. She'd give up anything for Scotland. Which meant if she were going to convince Grandmama to take her back, she'd first have to convince her she felt nothing at all for Mr. Bram Shaw.

Very well, then. An unexpected complication, but she could lock up her emotions, her body's wanton reactions to a man who did not want her. The rules Grandmama had taught her had not helped with her fears, her social discomfort, but it could help with this. When any naughty impulse pressed against the inside of her skin, she'd chain it down with rules, continue to be pleasant, proper, and nice.

She squeezed her eyes tight and pictured another her—the naughty her—shocking with a too-low bodice, wild red hair, and a come-hither, lust-heavy glow in her eyes. The woman purred. Pippa glared and pointed to an imaginary trunk. *In you go*, she told the other her, who pouted. Pippa narrowed her gaze and pointed again. *Fine*, the other her said, hiking her skirts purposefully over her knees and sinking into the trunk. Pippa wiggled. Felt wrong, that, to lock herself away. Perhaps she'd imagine the trunk bigger on the inside, an entire parlor complete with steamy tea and scones. And a few books about famous Scottish painters. Yes. Naughty Her could purr quite comfortably in there.

Out here, proper Pippa would ignore Bram Shaw, wash away the hazy, heated memory of their time together, and win her way back to Scotland.

Chapter Two

The dowager's trunks weren't heavy enough to banish the lust coursing through Bram's body. Just knowing the traveling coach brought him, mile by mile, closer to Pippa—Lady Philippa, he must remember to call her—had made the journey... uncomfortable.

The last time he'd seen her, he'd kissed her, crushed his own heart with the softness of her lips, smoothed his palms over her every curve, discovered the silken texture of her curls, explored the heated space between her legs, and almost lost his position as steward.

Not part of the plan, that.

He'd liked the look of her from the first. A bit quiet but with an upturned nose that hinted at a playful soul. He'd sought her out after that, curious to see if he could bring out the daring in her. But it was on her seventy-sixth day at Castle Clarebourn, when he caught her sketching on top of the roof of the folly, that his heart had lurched in his chest. After that, his bollocks took over for his brain. He'd rushed it. Mucked it up. Got caught wooing her. So, he'd left his gran's red shawl in her traveling coach, to keep her warm, and watched her roll away from him. No matter it had been summer and hot as his Uncle Peter's armpit.

But he had a plan now. Would stick to it. And it wouldn't work if he lost his position as the duchess's steward.

No matter he could still taste her if he licked his lips.

No matter he carried a purloined watercolor, painted by her hand and shockingly naughty in nature, in his waistcoat pocket from dawn to dusk.

No matter he woke most mornings from dreams of creamy legs tangled round his waist and a longing in his chest only Pippa could satisfy.

No matter.

Because the dowager would rip his bollocks off if she knew the thrust of his thoughts, the beat of his heart, and the content of his pocket and his dreams. Before she fired him.

He hefted another trunk, and his muscles screamed like banshees. What was in there? The crown jewels? Rocks that had tumbled off the walls of the dowager's Scottish castle? His own stubborn heart and, oh yes, his bollocks, too?

He released the trunk into the capable arms of two waiting footmen and strode back to the coach. He bent to heft another trunk on his shoulder and attempted not to look at the line of people greeting the dowager—a golden-haired man who could only be the Duke of Collingford, an older woman who resembled him enough to be his mother, four handsome redheads of varying ages.

Pippa stood among them, and he tried not to stare. No need to give his heart away so publicly, especially when it could ruin them both.

The dowager swept down the queue her family made on the street, stopping, nodding, sharing a word or two if absolutely necessary. She stopped before a redhead similar in age to Pippa. Perhaps a bit younger. Probably the Sarah that Pippa had spoken of often.

The dowager sniffed. "You should have come to Scotland with your sister for some polishing. To think you've gone about society without a hint of formal training."

Sarah's brightness did not falter. She cocked her head to the side and grinned. "I'm already shiny enough, don't you think? No polishing required."

Oh, Bram liked that one. Reminded him a bit of Cousin Flora, bold as you please the both of them.

The dowager made a sound low in her throat and turned to her grandson. "These girls are in danger. And so are you."

The duke scowled and took the dowager's arm, guiding her indoors.

"Grandmama, Sarah performed quite well this last season. I am not worried, and neither should you be."

The rest of the party turned and followed. Bram hefted a trunk onto his shoulder and fell in line, right behind Sarah.

Bram grunted loud enough to get the girl's attention.

She looked over her shoulder at him, still marching forward. "Yes?"

"You're plenty shiny. No polish necessary."

She grinned. "Are you flirting with me?"

God no. He shifted the trunk a bit higher, using different muscles to rest the weary ones. "No. Just... no." Damnation What sort of uncomfortable hell had he wandered into all in an attempt to make sure a chit didn't feel bad about herself?

She laughed, turned back around. "I'm teasing. Thank you."

The trunk bit into his shoulder as he stepped into the foyer, and his knees almost buckled under its weight. He stood awkwardly near the stairs. Where had those footmen gotten to? He had no idea where to go in this place, neither where to rest the trunk or his own head. Ha. The trunk would have posher accommodations than he would. The trunk was more *ton* than he, probably had better parentage than Bram's own—a British solicitor and his Scottish wife.

The dowager snapped her gaze toward the stairs. "Mr. Shaw!"

Relief swamped him. "Aye?"

"Instruct the footmen to unpack the rest," the dowager said. "Come along."

"As it pleases you, Captain."

The dowager narrowed her eyes but did not correct him. She pointed at the trunk. "Put it down, please."

He lowered it carefully to the floor with a grunt, and the dowager made her way up the stairs on Arthur's arm.

Bram put a foot on the first step to follow.

"Not fair." That voice, right behind him. If a flower's unfurling petals had a sound, it would be Pippa's voice. She stood too close, her clean scent consuming him. "By all rights, she should have skewered you for not 'Your Gracing' her in public. Captain? She lets you get away with much."

But not with everything. Not with seducing a lady and debutante in training.

He turned to face her, leaning into her petal-warmth. "Lovely to see you again, Lady Philippa."

Her lips parted with a jolly upward tilt, as if her words might tumble out with joy. Then her gaze skittered upward behind him, and she ruthlessly slammed those tilted corners down.

He peeked over his shoulder. The dowager glared at them from the landing. He turned back around.

Pippa had taken several steps away from him, put an entire room between them. "We should not converse, Mr. Shaw. I do not know what I was thinking. A momentary lapse of judgement." Her morning blue eyes wavered to an evening shade. Just for a moment—the shade of longing, of sweet memories.

He wanted to reply with something flirty, something to draw her out and make her laugh. Had she hardened toward him since Scotland? He didn't like that. Not that he could do anything about it. Not yet.

He should kiss her. Kisses always told the truth where words easily lied.

He couldn't. The dowager stood above them, her family bustled about, and footmen enough to fill a small church stretched their legs from coach to stairs and back. He'd only gotten to London and into this house on pretense. The patently ridiculous story that the kiss had meant nothing, had been a mere lark.

If he let his feelings slip now, he could lose his chance to woo her for good.

He turned for the stairs. "I am sure we will see one another later, Lady Philippa." A promise. "Good afternoon."

"Wait!"

He stopped but did not turn around. "Yes, my lady?"

"Our last meeting... it will not prove a difficulty between us?"

She meant the kiss. And he counted at least five sets of interested ears nearby. "Our last meeting? I don't remember."

Silence hummed right up against the tense muscles of his back.

Then, "Yes. Excellent." Winter frost on those petals. "It was of no significance. No reason for you—or me—to remember it."

Hell. His blood ran cold. The kiss had complicated his damned life, made him want to have her when having her would lose him everything else. He spoke through gritted teeth. "Precisely. Good day, my lady."

"Good day." She strode around him and ran up the stairs. When she reached the top where the hallway branched into two directions, she pulled her shawl—his shawl—close, cuddling into it as if seeking solace. Then she swept to the left and out of sight.

He trudged up the steps and cut to the right, trotting after the dowager and her grandson like some damned lapdog when he felt hungry as a wolf for Lady Philippa Hampton, duke's sister-in-law, marquess's daughter, soon-to-be debutante. *Pippa.*

He identified the dowager's rooms by the line of footmen exiting it, and he set about organizing her trunks as she liked them in an adjoining sitting room until the duke took his leave.

Disappointment simmered, but he tucked it away. He had to stay the course. He had to behave when all he wished to do was throw caution to the wind.

"You should show more respect, Mr. Shaw." The dowager strode stiff-backed into the room.

"So you've told me."

"If you were not so disgustingly handsome, I'd fire you on the spot."

"I'd like to think I'm more than an aesthetically pleasing face and figure. I'm excellent at my job, Your Grace."

The dowager strolled farther into the sitting room. "You know, you are quite lucky. It's deuced difficult to find a steward simultaneously so talented and so delightful to look upon. I'm old and do not wish to deprive myself of the small pleasure of having someone so handsome, so often about." She sighed and sank into a chair. "Are you cross with me about Lady Philippa? You know well that I stopped that disaster before it started."

"I'm not cross, Your Grace." He tried not to be.

She sighed, her usually cane-stiff spine melting a bit, cracks appearing in the coolly confident mask she always wore. "You're the only one, then. They do not understand. If I am hard on them, it is because I must be. Or they will perish in the heat of the furnace that is the *ton*. Lady Sarah and Lady Maggie have natural... vivacity. I do not wish to dig it up and discard it, but to trim it back a little, make it appealing to others so they may prosper in life, so they may find husbands."

Perhaps they did not wish husbands who wanted well-pruned women.

Best to keep that observation to himself. He knelt beside her as if she were a trunk that needed unpacking. "As I see it, Captain, you love your family too much." He winked. "Don't worry. I won't tell a one of them. My Aunt Matilda always says that the form love takes is not always a happy one."

She chuckled. "You know what to say to lift an old woman's spirits. Another reason to keep you about despite obvious reasons not to. Tell me and be truthful now. Do you find yourself tempted once more?"

He'd have to lie, wouldn't he? He rocked to his heels and stood, turning away from her. "I suffer no such temptation. Your lessons remain true. Lady Philippa is above me. I cannot provide for her as a man from the *ton* could. And"—he spun around, waved his hand in the air, put his best devil-may-care mask on—"'twas a lark. You know us younger sons. Nothing but nonsense day and night."

"And that is why I brought you. There is no need to deny myself a crucial element of my own comfort for a tragedy that will never happen. Because you are an intelligent lad, Mr. Shaw, though led, as all lads are at times, by your nether regions instead of your brain. Lady Philippa is a duchess's sister, a marquess's daughter. You are a solicitor's second son, a steward, though a good one. And not for her."

"Yes, Your Grace."

"And there is that house of yours to consider."

Bram's toes curled into the floor. "Blàr." His birthright.

She nodded.

Bram's inheritance hung on a stipulation made by a dead man. His great-great-grandfather had married into money, and the money had come with a nice big house in the Scottish hills. And that house had been willed, by sheer power of tradition, to the second child of each generation. As long as that child proved his worth, proved he wasn't a layabout, and met the standards set by his elders.

He'd lose his position if he pursued Pippa for all the world to see.

"I've no plans of losing my position, Your Grace. You rely on me too much."

"Excellent." She yawned. "I'll nap. You're dismissed."

Bram left, numb steps taking him toward the coach to make sure everything had been unpacked properly.

Caution. He must proceed with the utmost caution. His parents would not forgive another failure. Blàr was too important an inheritance to waste on a man who would ruin it in a year. He'd receive it only if he proved himself capable. And he had not, as yet, proved that.

Cambridge. The whisky distillery. The road-side inn. A brief attempt to be a rector. Pointless, that. He was too naughty for such a stolid role.

In true youngest-son fashion, he'd failed them all.

And each failure had cost him Blàr Hall. He couldn't lose Blàr. He'd wiggled his way into the dowager's employ to learn the ins and outs of running an estate and to be close to his own future home. Blàr's lands neighbored Castle Clarebourn's.

He closed his eyes as he jolted down the steps, letting each footstep shake his bones and placing his hand over the now-crinkled and creased painting nestled against his heart.

There was no shaking Pippa from his soul, and he wouldn't have to. She wore his shawl, and he had a plan. First, he'd win Blàr, and then he'd woo Pippa until she agreed to be his wife.

Chapter Three

Four days before Christmas

Pippa had let herself be run away from Scotland, but she would not run away now. Behind that solid oak door—Grandmama and Mr. Shaw.

She'd barely slept last night. Ignoring her attraction for the steward was proving more difficult in practice than in theory. She'd thought it would be easy. Dance attendance on Grandmama and win a spot in the coach when it returned to Scotland. But since his surprise arrival, ignoring Mr. Shaw had become a crucial part of the plan. If she showed even a hint of partiality for the man, Grandmama would sniff it out like a bloodhound.

"You hate him, you hate him, you hate him," she whispered to herself, bunching her fingers at her side, then stretching them out again, and giving them a good shake. "You hate him."

Naughty Her peeked out of her parlor trunk, elegant blue and white teacup hiding her sultry smile. *You don't*, she whispered.

She didn't. Not even a little bit. But they all had to think she did, and he had wounded her a bit, gave her a glimpse of passion, then let her be sent away. She would focus on that—the wound still a bit raw right over her heart. And on the rules—discuss weather, never be alone with a man, never touch a man unless dancing, never look as if you might even wish to touch him. Keep your voice low and spine straight. What were the others? No matter. Those were the ones that mattered most with Bram Shaw behind that door.

She pushed through into the room. "Good morning, Grandmama."

The dowager sat stiff on the edge of a chair near the fire. She gripped a cane before her, hand over hand, point down like a sword stabbed into the soil. "You always were an early riser. Have a seat and tell me how you've been. Any proposals on the horizon?"

Pippa obliged her, scanning the rest of the room with the barest flick of her eyes to the left and the right. Mr. Shaw sat nearby, his nose burrowed in a book. Just in case the dowager saw her looking, Pippa curled her lip, hoping to approximate a hateful sneer. She rather feared it looked more like a wistful smile.

"No proposals," Pippa said, "I've barely met a bachelor since returning to town."

"You arrived too near the end of the season. By next year's end, you'll be well wed."

"You know that may not be possible." Pippa spoke softly, studying the lace of her white morning gown.

The dowager stared into the flames. "Because you've kissed a man out of wedlock or because of what happened in Edinburgh?"

Pippa's body might as well have torn in two. Half of her hid a flinch, and the other half jerked toward Mr. Shaw, incapable of deciding which disaster to rest her attention on. The kiss or Edinburgh. The small deception had been meant to save her from the numbingly tedious round of social calls Grandmama had forced Pippa into. But pretending to faint had resulted in Grandmama thinking Pippa in possession of a *condition*, as she'd put it. Crowds made her skin itch and her temper rise, her heart race a bit and her lungs tighten. But she'd never swooned.

And she suspected that if she ever did swoon, it would be in Mr. Shaw's arms, not in the belly of a faceless crowd.

Pippa turned away from Mr. Shaw as if scorched by the fire roaring before her. "I... I do not see why a single kiss need disqualify me from marriage. No, I speak of the crowds, of my... dislike of them."

The dowager seemed to have lost herself to the dancing flames. They made her thin face with its pattern of fine wrinkles—the lace of years etched onto her skin—glow.

Pippa sprung into the warm silence between them. "I do not wish to have a season. Grandmama, I wish to return to Scotland with you. To be your companion. It is the only life I desire."

The only thing alive on Grandmama's face were the shadows of flames from the fire. She turned slowly until she faced Mr. Shaw.

"I know your reservations, Grandmama," Pippa said, loud enough for a certain steward to hear, "but you need not worry. There is no temptation greater than peace of mind and soul that motivates me. I would do nothing to threaten that."

"A reluctant debutante. Hm." Grandmama tapped her index finger on the top of her cane. "You would do well on the marriage mart, my dear. With your connections. Your striking looks. A sad-eyed waif. *Hmph*. Men love those."

"I'm not sad!" So much for keeping her voice low. She swallowed her volume and continued, "I'm quite certain I know what I want. I merely need you to believe me."

The dowager shifted to look at Pippa, and her gaze somehow sharpened, becoming a knife for ritual, to skin a young girl alive. She stuck an arm straight out to the side and snapped her fingers. "Mr. Shaw, come here now."

Bram placed his book on a table as he stood and sauntered toward them, his straight white teeth peeking out from a half smile. "Yes?"

Standing between them, he seemed an ominous beast of a man. Pippa felt the urge to stand so that she would not feel so small sitting below him, her own height collapsed and shadowed.

"Do stop looming," the dowager barked. "Pull over a chair."

He did so and sat, crossing one ankle over his other knee.

"Do you think I need a companion," Grandmama asked.

He twisted his mouth to one side, then the other. "You might like to have another female around, I suppose."

"And she's a sharp one, too brazen. But I know her true nature. You do, too." A snort. "And she amuses me. Any thoughts on that, Mr. Shaw?"

"None whatsoever." He flicked a lock of hair out of his face, and it stood straight up before falling back down, curling around the edge of his brow.

The dowager clucked. "Quite right."

Pippa stood like a fire had sparked to life under her rear. That sparse conversational exchange sounded like victory, and she'd take it before it developed any further. "Then it's settled. And while I would have liked to have been a part of the conversation to determine my future, since it's taken a direction I approve of, I'll ignore my feelings of neglect. I'll be ready to travel when you are."

The dowager poked her finger into the arm of the chair three times, punctuating three simple words. "Sit back down."

Pippa sat back down.

Bram snorted.

Pippa glared. He'd somehow transformed from a kind, funny man who made her want to fold his hand in her own to a scoffing nuisance who made her want to stomp her foot. He'd forgotten the heat they'd made in the Scottish shadows, forgotten her, and did not care whether she came or went. She pressed a hand to her belly and rubbed. It roiled with some chaotic emotion. Her skin stretched tight and dry like an unused canvas, and her eyes pinged with lightning pain.

"I'm not entirely sure it's settled," the dowager said. "Though I did enjoy having you about, Lady Philippa. And you need not marry, necessarily. With a family of four girls, at least one is destined for spinsterhood. As long as the others marry well, it's good to keep one girl to care for the rest, to be a companion for the aging and an aunt for the mewling babes. No, not a bad idea at all. With your aversion to society, well..." She looked from Pippa to Bram and back again. "And yet."

Blast! Blast, blast, *blast*! She still did not believe. How could she not see the utter disregard writ on every inch of Bram's body and face? Pippa did. It shamed her.

She stood once more and clasped her hands behind her back. "If it is the"—she swallowed to make room in her desert throat for the single word that refused to come out—"kiss that worries you, do not let it. You called our attraction a folly, and I know now you were right. I've had time to reflect on the lessons I learned from you, and I see now the mistake I made."

The dowager spoke slowly, deliberately. "Excellent. Still. I do worry. A spinster is one thing, a ruined lady is quite another. If you came with me, Mr. Shaw would have to go."

Bram sat up straight. "Go?" Bram stood and turned so that he faced only Grandmama.

Grandmama tilted her head, studied his blank face. "Yes. Go. As in you will no longer be in my employ."

His cheeks burned wine red, and he scratched a hand through his hair. "No."

"And what do you think about that, girl?" the dowager asked.

Pippa walked around the dowager's chair and knelt on the other side, wrapping her fingers around the chair's arm. "I do not like to see Mr. Shaw displaced as he is a hard-working, intelligent fellow. But... if it is a requirement for my return, then..." She succeeded in not cringing. She had to clutch to her hurt heart in order to suggest such a thing. And still it felt like utter betrayal.

The dowager threw her head back and laughed, a long cackling sound, entirely *un*duchess-like. "You'd throw him to the wolves, then?"

Pippa's gaze faltered, dropped. "Perhaps"—Pippa cut her gaze toward her shoulder, her skin acutely aware Mr. Shaw stood on the other side of the chair, glaring at her—"you should find him a new position before taking me on. He is good at what he does. It will not be difficult." She did not wish to hurt him, but she would not back down.

"*Hm*. Then everyone is happy." The dowager set a soft bony finger against the side of Pippa's chin and nudged until Philippa's gaze met hers. "Are they not?"

Pippa nodded.

"Not I." Mr. Shaw's two words dropped heavy and cold.

The dowager ripped her gaze from Pippa to face her steward.

Mr. Shaw stroked a hand through his hair, his face devoid of expression. "You said just yesterday, Your Grace, that you cannot do without me. But one word from Lady Philippa, and you're ready to toss me to the wind?" A slight Scottish brogue had slipped into the cadence of his speech, and each word seemed to harden his jaw to pure marble. His eye twitched.

Pippa stood her ground.

"Hmm. Perhaps the two of you are correct when you say you no longer care for one another."

"I don't care for chits who threaten my livelihood," Mr. Shaw growled. His gaze shifted, dug hooks into Pippa's skin. "Pippa. Don't."

He'd used her name, the one only those who truly knew her used —Pippa.

It shocked the blood in her veins into sparkling movement, despite its threatening tone. She liked *Pippa* on his lips. She should not, but heaven help her, she did. Even when—especially when, she could not deny—he growled it like that.

She squashed the liking. "I don't require payment," Pippa said. "Just let me return with you, and you will have a companion with no fee. Unlike... unlike Mr. Shaw who is paid, and handsomely, I am sure, for his services as steward."

Grandmama's mouth firmed, thinned. "And what will you do if I do not replace Mr. Shaw? How will you manage being around one you so despise every day?" She nodded toward Bram.

Bram? She'd never even thought of him as that before. Wasn't proper. Not even a little bit. But that rule must have slipped from her skin when he'd called her Pippa because she could not seem to think of him in any other way now.

"Ignore him," Pippa answered.

Bram's jaw tightened.

Grandmama chuckled. "You two are itching to tear one another apart, and not in the delicious type of way, either. Hm." She glanced to the flames, opening and closing her hand around the top of her cane. "Well, then. If you're determined to go at one another, have at it. A competition. The winner determines the future. Either I get a companion and a new steward or I keep my current steward and you"—her eyes cut toward Pippa —"stay here and have your season, find a husband, and marry well, leaving one of your other sisters to care for me in my dotage. Or a paid companion. I care not."

Hope surged through Pippa. "What sort of competition?"

Bram scoffed, throwing his hands in the air. "I'm not going to compete for a position I already have."

"You will," Grandmama said. "Hmm. But what? Something cheerful, in keeping with the festive season. Ah. Yes. I have it. If you bring me the best Christmas gift, Mr. Shaw, you get to keep your position as my steward. If Lady Philippa, however, brings me the best gift, she takes your place. As it were."

"Claptrap," Bram spat.

"On Christmas morning," the dowager continued, "the two of you will set your presents before my skirts, and I'll decide. Then, we'll stay for the Viscount Wix's New Year's Eve ball where you will practice for your true debut next Season, Lady Philippa. Or, we will leave for Scotland. Without Mr. Shaw."

Pippa breathed in, feeling her lungs expand, then out, draining them completely. She glanced at Bram.

He kept his peace, silver eyes hard as bullets.

"For the sake of fairness, I'll give both of you a hundred pounds," the dowager said.

"A hundred pounds?" Bram's eyes went round as saucers.

"Yes. Is that not enough? How much could a little trinket of a gift cost?"

"What kind of gift were you thinking of?" Pippa inquired, finding it impossible to keep the disbelief from her tone. A hundred pounds was an astounding sum for a single gift. Many lived off a hundred pounds in a year. During her family's worst years of penury, a hundred pounds would have seemed a feast of riches.

"That's for you to decide, my dears. Now"—she glanced toward the window—"the morning is halfway through, and so your time is, technically, fewer than three days. If either of you predict a difficult go of it, you'd better get to it."

Pippa stood frozen on one side of the chair and Bram on the other, statues but for their blinking astonishment.

The dowager waved a hand. "Shoo!"

On numb legs, Pippa strode toward the door, a silent presence moving swiftly behind her. She didn't have to look back to know who it was.

"Good luck, Mr. Shaw," Grandmama called. "And you, Lady Philippa."

Pippa exited the room and made her way upstairs, her mind busy with adding, multiplying, and estimating. How many shawls could she get for a hundred pounds? Rings? Necklaces? Works of art? Snuff boxes? And what would Grandmama like best? She'd figure it out. She'd do whatever it took, pay whatever price, and win any competition to return to the only place she'd ever felt truly happy.

Bram paced to the door after it shut, shock rocking his steps though he knew he should remain composed. He stared at the closed door for a moment, then swung around, lifted his arms out to the side, a brief silent query before he dropped them. "What the hell was that about?"

"Language, Mr. Shaw," the dowager cautioned. "Remember, I'm considering replacing you."

"You've used worse in front of me, and I've not sacked you."

"Because you can't. That's not how the employee, employer relationship works. Unless it's different in Scotland." She sniffed. "It's not so far as I've seen. And you're only half Scottish, anyway."

He stumbled across the room to find a chair as far from the dowager and the stifling fire as he could get. Pippa wanted to return to Scotland. Excellent! He wanted her nearer. Would make it easier to bide his time, to plan, to get the house and then woo the girl. But she appeared to be willing to shove him under a mail coach to achieve her ends. Far from ideal, that. He dropped his head into his hand and massaged his fingers into his temple, soothing the pounding that had started there.

Being booted from his position by the lady he loved rubbed the inside of his skin raw.

Yet that lady had been magnificent, storming after what she wanted even if it meant trampling him. He admired that determination, lost as he was in his own pit of indecision. He'd had to hide a smile even as his gut had hardened into a knot.

A notion pushed through the confusion and the pain. "You still have not answered my question."

The dowager lifted her cane, let it fall with a thud of the tip against the floor. "Perhaps if you phrase it in a more polite fashion."

"Why this farce of a competition? You have several reasons to want her *here*. In London."

"Farce is right, Mr. Shaw. Either she won't win, or she will. Either way, she won't return to Scotland."

The pounding in his head increased. "You've lost me, Your Grace."

She chuckled, the sound broken by the hiss and crackle of the fire.

Bram continued massaging his temple, eyes closed, reviewing the entire conversation before Pippa had left the room. His head popped up, his arm dropping to the side of the chair. "What did she mean about her dislike of crowds?"

"Listening, were you?"

"Cowering from an answer, are you?"

The dowager pulled up tall, her jaw dropping. "I should have terminated your employment long ago. You've never been as respectful as you should be."

"Ah, but I'm nice to look at, remember."

Her eyes were glassy brown marbles as she held his gaze. "And at times, your personality flaws overwhelm your good looks." She snapped her attention back to the fire. "Lady Philippa becomes distressed in crowds. She fainted in Edinburgh."

Bram rose slowly, cracking his knuckles. He'd never seen her distressed, but he'd only ever seen her at the castle, mostly secluded and almost always traipsing alone across some field or soaking in a patch of sunlight, sketchbook in her lap.

The dowager turned to him, her gaze fixed on his angry hands. "Sit back down if you please."

"You sent Lady Philippa shopping, Your Grace. Where there are sure to be crowds." His words dropped like ice shards.

"Yes. It's the perfection of the plan. She must face her fears in order to win what she desires, and hopefully, in the facing of them, she'll vanquish them. Once she realizes she can brave Bond Street without any threat to herself, she'll realize how silly she's been. She can then turn her attention to cultivating the appropriate excitement for her come out instead of these ridiculous dreams of running away to Scotland."

He set heavy steps toward the door. "Your plan is not perfect, Your Grace. It is cruel."

"It will get the job done. And then I shall not have to fire you. You should thank me, Mr. Shaw."

He opened the door. "Thank you, Your Grace." Because now he knew Pippa wanted what he did—her in Scotland.

The damned thing was, she didn't care whether he was there.

He could either find the perfect gift and keep his position, keep his family's good regard. Or he could forfeit the competition so that Pippa got what she desired.

He shrugged the choice off like an unnecessary garment on a sweltering day. A more important fact lay before him. If the dowager spoke true, Pippa would venture to Bond Street—a crowded Hell that could leave her vulnerable.

She had need of him, and that mattered more than any position, any house. Today, he just needed to keep Pippa safe. He'd worry about the rest later.

Chapter Four

Bram pulled his beaver hat low and shrugged deeper into his greatcoat. The hackney smelled of something vile, and he pulled his scarf up to mask the scent. No matter. Putrid odors were a small price to pay to keep the woman who held his heart safe.

He leaned forward and braced his elbows on his knees, pushing his fingers through his hair. Damn. A determined lass, despite the pain being in such crowds might bring her. Did he admire her for that or want to shake her?

He leaned back into the squabs. Definitely admired. Not that she seemed to admire him any longer. Presented a problem, that. Not one he couldn't hurdle over, but one he'd have to approach carefully. She disliked him. She thought they were in competition with one another, that he stood in the way of everything she desired. She did not know he wished only to protect her, to spend time with her, and make her remember how soft their kisses had been, how their hearts had raced together toward a logical and unavoidable conclusion.

Yet if he did that... what would happen to Blàr?

He had two options, as he saw it. He could find her, tell her the truth, and accept whatever reaction came his way. Or he could hide in the shadows, watch, pounce only when she needed him. The first option made him want to mess the hackney floor with his breakfast. Not much fun telling a woman trying to get you sacked that you loved her.

No, before he told her the truth of his heart, he'd have to win her trust back. He'd earned it well enough, though slowly to be sure, in Scotland. Showing her about the estate, helping her mount her horse, playing card games while the dowager read on rainy evenings. They'd marked one another one hour at a time, one look and all-too-brief touch after another, each moment knitting a bond between them.

Had it already snapped?

He'd hide, watch, and wait for when she needed him. There. Decision made.

He peered out the window. Gray buildings, brown mud, and mostly uninspired architecture. He'd been raised in London, but he'd never felt more home than when visiting Blàr. Here, even the few people walking the streets looked gray amid their sooty surroundings, sad shopfronts, and the Collingford crest on a shiny black coach.

"Stop!" he cried, banging on the roof.

The hack slowed and stopped, and he jumped out, throwing the driver some coins. He looked down the street in every direction. He shoved his hands in his pockets. Packed, the streets were. And muddier now that he was on a level with them. The thin crowd looked fashionable with their fur-lined winter wear. But he spied sharp-eyed brutes with quick fingers and narrow alleys where buildings cast shadows, turning day to night.

And the intrepid Pippa was alone. Surely, her maid attended her, though, so not entirely alone. But this was London. And if Pippa disliked crowds, she'd certainly not be happy in this crush.

There, across the street from the Collingford coach—a jewelry store. He'd bet the hundred pounds the dowager had given him to buy her a gift that's where Pippa went. She, too, had a hundred pounds, after all, and what better way to spend it than on jewelry?

He pulled his coat collar high enough to hide his jawline as he entered the glittering shop. Sunlight filtered through the glass windows, sparking the multi-faceted gems scattered about on tables in gold and silver casings. Not much room to hide here. He pressed against a wall beside a large cabinet of some sort and scanned the room for Pippa.

There. No mistaking her with all that red hair, the hood of her red cloak pushed back from her head. Her face glowed sickly pale in the sun-drenched candlelight, and her lips thinned into a tight line. She pointed with a shaking finger to something glittering laying on a bed of blue velvet and turned so he could see her delicate profile and, even from here, the freckles scattered across her cheeks and nose. Damn, she was lovely.

"Sir?"

Bram startled and turned to the voice. And found a man's chest directly in front of him.

"Sir?" The voice rumbled.

Bram raised his gaze to see the other man smiling politely down at him.

"Sir," the man said, "may I help you? I am Mr. Clarkson, the owner of this esteemed establishment. Are you in search of something particular?"

He was in search of anonymity, of secrecy. And a curiously tall gentleman offered a particularly useful hiding place. Bram must keep the man near indefinitely. He cleared his throat and leaned close enough so he could speak quietly, and the man could still hear. "I need a... a watch?"

"A watch. Yes, sir. We have several." He stepped to the side. "I'll just bring you—"

"No!" Bram reached out, caught the jeweler's hand. "No. It's a rather particular sort of watch. I'm not sure you'll have it. Let me... erm... describe it."

The man's eyes narrowed. "As it pleases you, sir."

He made sure to speak slowly, drawing out each word, planting unnecessary pauses between them. "I'm not quite sure. What I'm looking for. Something remarkable. Old and valuable. Lots of, um, gems. Diamonds. No, rubies. Gold, of course. An inscription..." His gaze drifted around the man's form, settled on the pale shivering woman across the shop. "Ignore all that. Something simple and elegant. With all the colors of the dawn in it." Like his painting.

The man looked over his shoulder and right toward Pippa, then he turned back to Bram, his grin wider, more authentic than before. "I see, sir, I see."

"Pardon?" What did the man see?

"The lady you're looking at. Across the room. You know one another, yes? She is remarkable. May I suggest a ring instead of a watch?"

"*Shh*. Keep your voice low, man." He ripped his gaze from where it most wished to settle and met the jeweler's eyes. "No rings."

Mr. Clarkson turned to the side and shoved his elbow into Bram's ribs multiple times. "A prepared suitor is a happy suitor. I'll bring some out." He inched toward the back of the shop.

"No," Bram growled, still trying to keep his tone low. He clapped a hand around the man's wrist, keeping him in place, a shield between himself and Pippa.

Mr. Clarkson's eyes widened as they dropped to Bram's manacle hold. "I say, sir. Unhand me!" His voice rose high and shrill, spreading panic throughout the shop.

Pippa's head turned in every direction, her gaze wide and wary.

The jeweler yanked his arm from Bram's grasp, wrinkled his nose at Bram, and strutted away.

Shite. Bram had brought too much attention to himself. He tried to press his body into the corner made by wall and cabinet.

"You!"

Shite. He knew that voice. Pippa. Anger had never sounded quite so sweet. He turned from his corner and tried to straighten his clothes. He'd been caught. No hiding now. Time for a change of strategy.

Across the room, Pippa burst into movement, bustling around tables and the overly tall jeweler Mr. Clarkson, her gaze tethered to Bram's the entire time. She stopped a scant inch from his nose and pointed a finger at him, the pale fear from earlier washed away by the heightened red of rage.

"You," she said, her voice calm and sharp, like a winter's morning, "are spying on me."

"I'm not."

"Then explain your presence here, Mr. Shaw."

"I'm browsing."

She whipped her accusing finger away and crossed her arms over her chest. "Ha! Mr. Clarkson, do please have this man removed from the premises."

Mr. Clarkson looked at Bram, then at Pippa, then back and forth again and again until Bram feared for his neck.

Bram rocked back on his heels. "Do not listen to the lady. I'm here to spend good money."

"He's no gentleman, Mr. Clarkson. I know he looks fine as any other Mayfair gent, but you must trust me on this. Remove him at once."

Mr. Clarkson took a step backward and away from them. Then another. Then, with a tiny squeak of boot against floor, he turned and ran.

Pippa never rolled her gaze away from Bram, and it burned. He wanted to reach out to her and smooth the lines between her winged brows. He wanted to feel her soft form against him, and her softer lips pressed to his jaw, and he wanted... he wanted... dammit all, he merely wanted her. In her velvet red spencer, fitted tightly across her bosom, her long skirts hiding what must be equally long legs. Her fear forgotten in her outrage, she broke him down to his basest parts—lust and need, to have her, to protect her.

He swallowed and blinked out of the trap his adoration had sprung on him.

"There," she said, "you're blinking. A sign of guilt. You *are* spying."

"I'm not. I'm protecting."

"Protecting your position."

"I'm protecting you, you impossible woman. Though it's quite clear you do not wish it."

"I do not need it." Her eyes glinted sharper than any of the jewels surrounding them.

He could toss out knife-sharp glares, too. "That's not what I have come to understand. Edinburgh?"

"Ah. *Hm*. Well." She tugged at a tassel on her cloak.

He stepped nearer, lowered his voice. "London is dangerous. But if you are truly well, I will leave you be."

A mist of whispers wove round them.

He leaned away from her, looked left, then right. They had attracted a crowd. Every patron in the shop gathered, their expressions running from disapproval to obvious glee. Some hid their faces behind hands, whispering to their neighbors. There could be no more than ten, though. Perhaps ten was not enough for Pippa to panic.

Pippa glanced around, too, the attractive flush of anger and determination draining from her cheeks. She tapped a staccato rhythm on the floor with one foot, then she spun on her heel and pushed through the crowd.

He followed her, and knowing he should not touch her, he tucked her arm into his own and pulled her away from the gawking customers, speaking loudly, "Perhaps, Sister, we should choose a gift for Grandmama together. No more competition, aye?"

She strode tall and regal beside him, the only crack in her composure a slight tremble of her jaw.

When they reached the back of the shop, he dropped her arm and turned to prop his hip on a tall counter there. He glanced about as if patiently waiting for Mr. Clarkson. Really, he checked the status of the crows. They had dispersed, their whispers no longer thinning the shop's air.

"Better?" he asked.

She heaved in a breath, peeked sideways. "Much. Thank you."

"Care to tell me what that's all about? Edinburgh?"

"Not particularly. I'm... I'm here to purchase a gift. So, I assume, are you."

He shook his head. "I'm not lying. I saw your coach and wanted to make sure you are well."

She held her arms out wide. "As you see, I am quite well."

He snorted, raised a brow.

"I would have been quite well had you not caused a scene."

"You were trembling before I roused the masses."

"I wasn't trembling. I was... fidgeting."

"Whatever you call it, you were not entirely calm."

"I do not like crowds is all. But I can manage for a day. Because once I win this competition, I'll never have to deal with such discomfort again."

He crossed his arms over his chest. She'd been halfway to becoming a jagged bundle of raw nerves moments earlier, and she wished him to believe that, once she stepped foot onto that crowded London street, she'd be fine?

Ha.

He scratched his chin.

"What are you thinking?" she asked, leaning away from him, skepticism and suspicion bracketing her mouth.

"How do you know I'm thinking?"

She made a circle in the air around his face with a single pointed finger. "That has gone all craggy like a cairn. I remember that look."

"I am thinking." He was thinking that she'd become ragged and raw, but that she'd also recovered quickly. "Why do crowds scare you?"

"They do not scare me," she snapped.

"Oh?"

"I'm not used to them if you must know. They make me feel... small. Vulnerable. As I said. I do not like them."

"Mere dislike doesn't cause a woman as tough as you to faint, Lady Philippa."

Her eyes widened, flooding him with blue. "Faint. Ah. Yes. Edinburgh. Well..." She lifted a shoulder, let it fall, trained her eyes on something glittering in a nearby case. "That looks promising." She bolted.

He followed, slow and steady, until he reached her side.

Her attention snapped back to him. "I am going to win this competition and earn my way to Scotland."

"Where you'll never have to suffer crowds again."

"Or the *ton*," she mumbled, bending at the waist to peer more closely at a glittering something. "Or suitors."

"Well, we're surrounded by those, I think. I'll keep close. Just in case you swoon and need strong arms to catch you."

She froze, straightened slowly. Her mouth pressed thin as a piece of parchment. Thinner. "You mean to sabotage me."

He reached for her but felt the eyes of every patron burning into them. So, he dropped his arms heavy and useless—forlorn, really—to his sides and leaned close enough to catch her warmth through all the layers that separated their skin. Bram knew from the dusk-dark drawing room at Castle Clarebourn that her skin was like velvet and dotted with delicate freckles. He'd kissed as many as he'd been able to after dragging her gown's arm down her shoulder. He steadied the impulses of his hardening body by staring so deeply into her morning blue eyes that he could not see the coming afternoon before him, and she could not look away, either.

Bram spoke without thinking. "I do not intend to win this competition."

Her chest rose and fell on sharp, quick breaths. "Ha. Only a man intent on sabotage would say such a thing."

His gaze dipped to her lips, then back up. "No. I want... I want you..." He wanted her to remember and to want in return. He wanted her secrets,

Edinburgh and all. But perhaps that required a secret from him first. To earn her trust. "I want you to be happy."

The absolute blasted truth.

Perhaps his parents would not think it a failure if he lost his position to the dowager's granddaughter. They'd see his transfer to a position as steward at another estate as a change of scenery, a sign of his success that another family would hire him based on the dowager's recommendation.

Then he'd get Blàr. Then he'd be next door to the woman whose arms burned through layers of clothing—gowns, pelisses, gloves—to brand him hers.

An optimistic view to steady the mad beating of his heart. Helping her win this day might help him in the future to win her.

"I see." Pippa took a startled step back. She cleared her throat, drew a line between them with the little half boot peeking out from under her skirts. "If you are indeed offering a protective escort, then, well"—she cleared her throat once more—"I will not say no." Her head swung with a rapid pivot to the side. "Isn't that right, Lucy?"

"Lucy?" Bram echoed, lost as a fish in a field.

A young woman with an upturned nose and blond ringlets tossed daggers at him with her toffee-colored eyes. "I suppose so, my lady."

The maid. *Dammit*. He'd forgotten about the maid. Had she been there the whole time? No wonder she looked ready to throw him beneath coach wheels and horse hooves at the first chance she got. He'd not touched Pippa, but he'd had every intention of doing so. He deserved a good flogging.

"Will we purchase anything here?" Lucy asked.

Pippa peeked up at Bram. "What do you think? Will jewelry charm Grandmama sufficiently?"

"She has too much of the shiny stuff already," Bram said.

"Hm. Excellent point." She turned abruptly and searched the shop. "Where is Mr. Clarkson?"

"Right here, my lady!" He popped out from the back. "How may I help?"

"Thank you for your time, but we must be off."

His nose wrinkled. "No watch?"

"I'm afraid not," Pippa said, folding her hands before her.

Mr. Clarkson's mouth drooped. "No rings?" he asked Bram.

"Not yet." Bram strode for the door, unwilling to see what confusion might lay on Pippa's face. "The head jeweler here, Mr. Paul Storr?"

Mr. Clarkson bowed. "Yes, sir, what of him?"

"Give him my name—Mr. Bram Shaw—and tell him the lady here needs a very special piece of jewelry made for her grandmother. We may return tomorrow if we find no suitable gift today."

"Yes, Mr. Shaw. I'll tell him."

Bram pulled his collar high and popped his hands into his pockets.

Philippa hustled up beside him, frowning. "You know the owner?"

"I apprenticed under him for a few months some time ago. Excellent fellow."

"Did you like it?"

"While it was a mystery to me, yes. But once I learned the mechanics of the business, my interest waned. It often happens. I enjoy the learning and not the doing. It's why I love running an estate. I'm always learning." He opened the door for her and held it as she and her maid passed through.

She deserved whatever help he could give her, whether it be opening a door or winning the game the dowager thought they were all playing.

If the dowager proved right, and Pippa could vanquish her fear, he'd help her do that, too. Her world would expand, then, her possibilities multiply. She could have a season without worry.

When he wanted her in Scotland with him.

He'd help her anyway—even if it meant losing her.

Chapter Five

Three days till Christmas

Yesterday's shopping excursion still sat under Pippa's skin, and it seemed the crush of people at the Pantheon Bazaar had doubled. Her ribs cinched tighter, pressing, surely, into her lungs. A child ran past, his arm sweeping across her back. She pressed her eyes tightly closed to breathe through the unexpected contact and found before her, a rising memory from Scotland.

Bram's hands on her back, lower, pressing her belly against his until two bodies had become one. When he had touched her, the world had melted away, the too-rapid beating of her heart had slowed, and calm had stroked up and down her skin. He'd felt as much like home as Scotland had. If only she could turn to his arms now to keep the frantic world at bay, to calm her rapid pulse.

Yesterday, Bram had stayed close by them, a faithful shadow stalking them into each shop. His every look had sizzled into her skin, making her want to run right into his arms. He had exceptional ones, thick with muscle yet limber. Arms to keep a woman safe, and that's what he had been there for. Not to win the competition. Shocker, that. She had no strong arms to run to this day. They'd left the house early to avoid him. She couldn't let him, innocent as his intentions were. She must focus on finding the perfect gift.

Pippa locked arms with Lucy and focused on a growing list of gift ideas as they moved into the streaming mass of shoppers. Surely, she'd find something here. The Bazaar boasted novelty items as well as luxury ones. Perhaps Grandmama would like something a little more creative, unexpected. Another day of shopping yawned before her, and without the distraction of his tingling gaze, she *would* find victory.

A tingle tripped up the back of her neck. Then another. It could only mean one thing. *Blast.*

She leaned close to Lucy and hissed, "Is Mr. Shaw following us again?" She didn't dare look left or right and let him know she knew he was there, felt him without seeing him.

Lucy reached into her pocket, dropped a piece of linen she pulled from it, and stopped. "Oh! Sorry, my lady, I dropped my handkerchief." She stole a glance behind her as she knelt to retrieve it. She stood and re-hooked her arm with Philippa's. "Yes, my lady. He's following."

"Good."

Lucy snorted.

"And what does that mean?"

"And what, pray tell, does 'good' mean? That's what I'd like to know."

It had been a gut reaction, a slip of the tongue. "Well… it means… just… good."

Lucy rolled her eyes. "You're still sweet on him."

She was. "Am not. Besides, my feelings are neither here nor there. He has offered to help and has bowed out of the competition entirely."

Lucy snorted. "That's likely what he wishes you to think. The dowager might've liked that watch. Did Mr. Shaw talk you out of it? Sabotage, I say. Outrageous we're letting him follow us about. Unless"—she bounced on her toes and clapped her hands, shaking Pippa—"we're leading him to his *doom*."

"Doom?"

Lucy waved her free arm about, indicating everything about them. "You know. Push him in front of a coach and four. Lead him down a dark alley and pay some rogues to—" She mimicked the thrust of a knife to the gut.

"We're not going to have the man killed." Pippa shivered, the red gleam of Bram's blood pooling on the street in her imagination. Naughty Her wailed in widowed misery from the elegant confines of her trunk. Pippa sat on it. Imaginatively, of course, not having a trunk to sit on in the street. But she did turn and scan the crowd, looking for him. There—not too far behind them.

He winked.

And her stomach tumbled until she pressed it into a reluctant calm by thinking of Grandmama's lectures. A debutante is innocent and aloof. She could do that. She stopped walking and waited for him to meet them.

When he did, he tipped his hat, winked again. "Good morning, ladies. I'll pretend you didn't try to leave me behind." A shiver to his words and he hunched into his great coat. The sliver of skin visible above his cravat pricked with gooseflesh.

"You are not wearing a scarf," Pippa said.

"I was in a rush this morning."

"Perhaps you'll freeze to death," Lucy mumbled.

Pippa ignored the comment, preoccupied with the corded strength of Bram's throat. She couldn't see it, of course. Cravat and all. But her fingers remembered the contours of it. "We must warm you up, Mr. Shaw. Follow me."

"*Hmph*." He shrugged deeper into his greatcoat. "I'm warm enough."

"No arguments." Pippa headed for a shop on the right side of the street, and a moment later, she and Lucy stepped over the threshold and stood in the open doorway.

Warming his neck would assuage her guilt. He'd asked about Edinburgh yesterday, and while she'd not lied, she'd not told the truth, either. The evasion soured her stomach.

A shoulder bumped into her, and she shrank against Lucy. When her attention was riveted on something, she did not feel the pressure of the bodies all around. But when a jostling shoulder woke her up... She looked around her, and everywhere people, none of whom she knew. Some laughed and chatted, others marched forward with blank eyes and scowls.

Her pulse skipped, and behind her the cold of the crowded street whistled. Until a wall of warmth pulsed at her back.

"What sort of gift do you think to procure at a hat shop?" Bram asked.

She could feel his words rumbling through her body and thundering through the air.

He offered protection from the outside, from the unknown, and she wanted to lean back and into him, gird herself all around with a Bram-shaped fortress. She could, too, since they were so close. She stepped forward instead, swallowed up in the rush of cold air between their bodies.

"We're here to procure you a scarf," she said, "to warm that neck of yours." And to protect the female population of London—and herself—from such a masculine assault. Truly, it should not be legal for a man to walk about with a throat so strong it could wrangle girls right into his arms, and a jaw so sharp it could cut their virtue to ribbons. Even when shrouded in a cravat.

"A scarf?" he asked. "In a hat shop?"

"They have accessories, you nodcock," Lucy said as she strode past them and toward a straw bonnet entirely inappropriate for the winter months.

Bram chuckled. "I want to dislike her, since she's intent on disliking me, but I can't. Aye, I think I admire her. Reminds me of my Great-Aunt Susan. Quick as a cat to scratch at a fellow. A challenge worth the work, though."

Lucy scowled. "Your charm will not work on me, sir."

A shopgirl approached, and Pippa told her exactly what she wished while Bram strolled around the shop, flicking tassels like a cat and sliding a finger up and down over the curves of hats. Heat pulsed low in her belly. Surprising that a man's finger against silk and straw could cause such confusion in a woman's body.

He looked up at her, his lips shaping into a tease. "Thank you for bringing me here, Lady Philippa. I've been thinking lately of taking a wife, and a hat might be an excellent gift for her." He scratched his cheek and tilted his head.

Pippa crossed the shop to stand shoulder to shoulder with him, studying a red bonnet festooned with white feathers. "Have you secured Blàr Hall, then?" He'd spoken of it a time or two during her stay in Scotland. She'd sat once on the boundary between Castle Clarebourn and Blàr and painted the prospect, then painted a couple into the scene who resided there only on paper. And in her imagination. And a little bit inside her heart, too.

His well-formed lips lost their happy shape, and his gray eyes shuddered with shadows. “No. Not yet.” He resumed his smile. “But I will.”

“I believe that.” She reached for a small cap made of the finest lace and handed it to him. “You will have to buy your future wife this. All married ladies wear them.”

He eyed it, his lip curling in disgust. “I’ve seen my mother wear one of these.” His eyes lifted from the cap to the top of her head, rested on her own green, silk bonnet decorated with red flowers. “Will you wear one when married?”

She scrunched her nose. “I do not like the things. Too confining. If I were to marry, I’d leave them off, I think... at least when no one is looking.” Naughty Her approved of the idea. *Hm.* Perhaps this conversation was not aloof and innocent enough.

He tossed the cap back on a shelf.

“You’ll not purchase it, then?”

“No. My wife will have no need of it. But I do need a gift for her. It’s a tradition in my family. When the men choose wives, we give them something meaningful.”

“How lovely. What did your father give your mother?”

“A shawl. Used to belong to my gran. She knitted it. My ma admired it. My pa gave it to her. With Gran’s permission of course.”

“That’s quite sweet.” She tried to imagine Bram standing, shawl in hand before some lovely Scottish lass, but the image drowned in red, and her gut threatened to revolt.

“Aye.”

“Will”—she swallowed, finding the words did not fit her tongue so well as they should—“will you gift your... your wife a new hat or an old shawl?”

“Since she will have no need of those silly little caps, the shawl might be safer. I think she likes it, anyway.”

He knew the woman already, then. Pippa turned away from him, focused on a noxious brown bonnet that looked how she felt. “Something to keep her warm when you aren’t to hand.”

“Aye.” He strode off.

She followed, each hurried footstep a question she had for the man walking just out of reach. "How soon will you take a wife?"

"As soon as I have Blàr."

"And when will that be?"

"I cannot be sure anymore."

She almost ran to keep up with his long strides. "Will... will my winning the contest impede your plans?"

He stopped.

She ran into him, bounced off his back.

He turned slowly, his face a landscape of mixed emotion. "Aye."

She picked at a string at her wrist, unable to meet his gaze. "I am sorry. It is not enough. I should back out of the challenge. I know I should. But I am not sure how to get back to Scotland. Perhaps we could convince her we remain so uninterested in one another that living on the same estate would pose no trouble."

"Impossible." The single word a conflagration.

She burned up so quickly on the inside, her heart, her lungs, her very bones lay in ashes just beneath her skin, from singed to incinerated in half a breath.

Not quite understanding why, she wrenched her gaze away from his and toward a feathered concoction. "An absurd hat." Miracle her words came out without a cloud of smoke.

She laughed and shook her head. What an odd game. His single word—impossible—felt just like their kiss had. Soft and promising much.

That, however, had led to nothing but heartbreak. Exile.

She must remember that. Something like disappointment curled in her belly. She pressed her eyes closed against the heaviness, then popped them back open, hoping to sound lighthearted. "Come. We must warm your neck."

He clasped his hands behind his back and walked away from her. "Thank you for the thought, Lady Philippa, but I do not need a scarf. I am plenty warm."

"I insist. You are protecting me. Let me protect you."

He threw her a quick glance, dark brow raised, face clear and thoughtful. "A partnership of giving and taking?"

"If you wish to think of it as such."

"I accept."

"Excellent! Anyway, it is the season for giving." The season for giving the perfect gift to Grandmama. Yet here she stood, wasting precious time finding that gift with useless flirtations. She should forget the scarf, dart back into the streets, and find the perfumery, find the perfect scent to box for Grandmama, to delight her, to persuade her.

"My lady!" The shop girl appeared, two small, flat boxes in hand. "Here you are. Just as requested." She pulled off the lid of one, revealing a soft, green cashmere. The other box held a wool confection of a similar green.

"The cashmere, I think," Philippa said. She pulled the scarf from its box and turned to Bram. "May I?" When had Naughty Her escaped her trunk and dragged the past into the present?

She'd once wrapped a cravat around his naked neck, pulled it from his pocket after he'd spent a hot day working outside in the sun. She'd held his gaze the entire time, his gray eyes almost a physical touch across her skin. She'd tied it loosely, inexpertly, fingers and knuckles brushing against his stubbled jaw, drawing her closer. Before she'd come to her senses and jolted away from him.

She did so now, too. Taking a step back, she held out the scarf and offered a weak smile. "Apologies. You should do it." Dressing a man, even in an outer garment like a scarf, would cause tongues to wag, would rile one of the rules written on her skin.

He stepped closer, dipped low. "I'd rather you tie me up, Pippa."

The words tied *her* up. She swallowed, feeling the heat in his eyes burning down her throat, and wiggled the length of cashmere. "You are competent enough to don your own scarf. I have faith in you."

He took it and wound it quickly, efficiently, hiding himself away.

Pippa sighed in relief.

Naughty Her pouted, imagined stepping close, winding the scarf, tightening her grip on both ends, and pulling him closer, lower. For a kiss.

Pippa locked the trunk tighter and followed the shopgirl to pay. A retreat? Most certainly. Most necessary, too. She could retreat no farther when she bellied up to a counter at the back of the shop.

A large, warm body settled beside her, and she didn't even jump. She knew without looking who stood there.

"I'll get it," he said. "I'm a beefwit for leaving without warmer clothing this morning. You'll not pay for my inattention."

"Not at all." She reached into her reticule and tossed some coin on the counter.

"Do you see anything here you'd like to purchase for the dowager?" His gaze roved over the shop behind her, and each inch furrowed his brow farther. "Many have entered since we did. It's quite the crush. Would you like to leave?"

Was it a crush? She could barely register the rest of the shop with him so near. The world had shrunk once more to him and her, and she could not even remember how many people crowded about the room. Miracle, that. Made her feel bold.

The concern in his face, his tone, swamped that boldness in guilt. She hated a crush, yes, but... "Mr. Shaw."

"Hm?"

"I feel I must admit something terrible to you."

His eyes lowering to her felt like hot coals burning to her very soul.

Best to get it over quickly.

She took a deep breath, leaned close, and brought her voice low, like the stroke of a man's fingers over his woman's skin, revealing the truth with an exhale. "I only pretended to swoon in Edinburgh." Now she held her breath, refusing to look away from those smokey coal eyes. It had been a childish thing to do, and her shame made her squirm, but she could not let him operate under a lie any longer.

He crossed his arms over his chest. "You are not afraid of crowds."

"I told the truth—I dislike them immensely. But I will not lose consciousness in them. You see, I am in no danger."

"Why did you pretend to swoon?"

"A gentleman was speaking with me. The fourth in half an hour's time. And he was just as boring as the rest. But then his sister and her coterie and their beaus joined us. They made me feel small, the men and women, so confident in their places. And the way they peered at me... looking for fault. I felt like a bug, pinned. My heart thumped, and I wanted no more of it. I wanted to be back at the castle with—" *With him.* "I took the coward's way out, I'm afraid."

His face cut like stone for longer than she liked, but then the smallest smile breathed life into him, and he chuckled.

"Minx," he said.

"Worse, likely. I don't wish to sit lifeless all day in drawing rooms. It's stifling. I wish to sit in the sun and paint the clouds, walk until my legs ache under a bluer than blue sky. I wish to go for days without seeing a single soul."

"Not a single one?" His gaze cut straight through her, and her breath caught in the cage of her chest. Her blood rushed like an autumn wind through her veins, and her heart thumped uncontrollably. Like in Edinburgh. But this time, it was not from feeling like a bug pinned. This time, the foggy eyes looking at her as if she alone existed in the world riled all her senses, boiled her to a pink need.

And opened her trunk. From the deep black inside, a husky feminine chuckle in Pippa's own voice.

Bother.

She lifted her heel to step back and away from Bram, but he spoke, turning her to stone.

His voice dove deep as a loch. "You're a marvel, lass. I'm proud of you for knowing what you want and taking it." The deepness held a current of sadness, a slice of somber that swamped her.

"You do not sound proud." She wrapped her hands around one another, clutching them tight to keep from reaching for him.

He blinked, and her lungs filled with air once more. He wrapped his hands up like a prizefighter with the ends of his scarf. "I am. If I sing a note of sadness, it's because I can't stop thinking of our stolen moments in Scotland. And you never think of them a bit." He tilted his head and held her gaze. Waiting?

If he wished a response, he might have to wait forever. Her head had been cleaned entirely out by his statement.

"Lady Philippa!" Lucy pushed between them, bouncing them away from one another.

Bram turned his back to them, dragging his hat from his head and running fingers through his hair. His shoulders seemed tense wings of stone, and she could not look away, could not stifle the inexplicable mystery of his statement. If she understood him correctly, he remembered kissing her and wanted to kiss her again.

She should be all confusion. She wanted Scotland. And if she got it, Bram would lose his position. But she did not want him to lose his position. She did not want to endanger his chance to secure Blàr Hall. She did not want him so far from her. He would take a position elsewhere, after all, and who knew where elsewhere was.

A muddle.

The feelings he aroused in her were not muddled at all. They felt bold and true and lit her up like the North Star in a pitch-black sky. If she were to paint a portrait of herself, she'd use up all her yellow to get the glow just right. The brilliant light of her feelings for the man illuminated a single question: how could she have both Scotland and Bram?

Was such a thing possible?

Lucy waved her hand in front of Pippa's face. "My lady!"

Pippa straightened her shoulders and found a polite smile. "Yes, Lucy?" Yet no matter how polite her expressions, she could not rip her eyes from the taut fabric stretched between the granite wings of Bram's broad shoulders.

Lucy bounced on her toes and turned Pippa's shoulder to guide her away from Bram and out of the shop. "Quick! Let's give him the slip."

"Why would we want to do that?"

"Why would we *not* want to, my lady? He has the scarf. His neck is warmer than it was before. We have no need of him. Eric and John are with the coach if we need help."

"Where are we off to next, ladies?" Bram, warm and suddenly by her side, looked terribly handsome with the green cashmere round his neck.

"Damn." Lucy uttered the curse looking directly into his eyes. She hooked her arm through Pippa's and pulled her down the street.

Bram followed, becoming their silent sentinel once more.

No matter how many shops they visited, Pippa never lost the feeling of him near, safe and solid. No matter how many potential gifts she considered, she could not choose. And when she returned to her bedchamber that afternoon, exhausted, she could not shake Bram's words.

I can't stop thinking of our stolen moments in Scotland. And you never think of them a bit.

A misconception.

She'd cried in the coach as it had rumbled back toward London that day. Not only because it rumbled back toward the nameless, bustling, suffocating crowds, but it took her farther away from him.

She could tell him that, but what purpose would it serve? A debutante and a steward had kissed and never should have. They never could again.

If she won her way back to Scotland, he would have to leave.

The rules—society's and Grandmama's—cut into her already tormented flesh. What if she cut her bindings all at once? Could she let go of everything she should be and just be who she was?

Chapter Six

Two days till Christmas

Morning dawned too soon, and stayed too gray, and Lucy dragged Pippa out onto the street much too early.

Pippa covered a yawn and tried to cover a truth that had come to her in the night when she'd woken from a dream.

More than that. A memory.

Bram's hands on every inch of her bare skin, his breath warming her freckles. His hands pulling the shoulder of her gown down to reveal more skin for his delight. Her delight, too. She'd tangled her hands in his hair and thrown her head back as he'd pressed his lips against the top swell of her breast, reached nimble fingers below the bodice, and flicked her puckered nipple. He'd pressed his hardness into the apex of her legs, and she'd pressed back, giddy and yearning for something she knew only he could provide. But never to be given. Interrupted by the squeak of a door and Grandmama's gasp.

A horrid moment of discovery because it had ripped her away from Bram. Not Scotland, but *him.* And in the darkness of the night, she'd faced that truth. Faced another one, too. Two days left till Christmas, she had no gift, and her heart was spilling open like an unwrapped present, no way to close it again.

"Two days left, Lady Philippa," Lucy said, her hands fisted on her hips like an army general. "I'm convinced the only reason we've not yet discovered the perfect gift is because of *him*." She rubbed her hands together. For warmth or glee, Pippa could not tell. "But today, we'll outsmart him. The dowager had him up all night with the horses for some reason. He'll be too tired to wake so soon. To the coach! We'll sneak away and find a shop in some hidden corner of London where he'll never follow us or find us." She pulled Pippa toward the black and red conveyance hulking like a beast at the end of the street.

"Good morning, ladies."

Lucy jumped, clutched Pippa closer, and fair ran them both toward the coach. "Blast! Quick, my lady!"

Pippa shook away the maid's manacle hold and turned toward the man striding their way, looking hazy and sleeping in the gray morning light, a slightly wicked grin picking up the corners of his lips.

"Good morning," Pippa said.

He stopped before her, picked up her hand, and kissed the air over the knuckles before dropping it. "Pippa."

Barely anything improper there, but oh how her stomach fluttered. It felt... lovely, incandescently *nice*.

"I have an idea," he said.

"We don't need it." Lucy had resumed her militaristic stance.

"I worked in tobacco several years back. It's a nasty trade. Was glad to leave it behind. But because of it, I know a tobacconist nearby. You might find a curio or snuff, or some other item of note for the dowager in his shop. He has an eye for the new and interesting, so he always has something odd about."

Lucy grunted. "Sounds much too scandalous."

"Sound perfect," Pippa said. "Grandmama loves trying new and radical things." Not that she let anyone younger than herself do the same. "Cheroots, perhaps?"

Bram shrugged. "Can't hurt to try. You ladies take the coach, and I'll get a hack." He winked. "We'll keep it proper." He gave the coach driver the address, then lunged into the street, dodging horses, coaches, and other pedestrians, comfortable in the crowd.

Lucy snorted. "Not very gentlemanly. Come! Now is the time to bolt."

"We're following Mr. Shaw." Pippa entered the coach and sat.

With a sigh fit for Drury Lane, Lucy nestled in across from her. "You're still sweet as a biscuit on that man."

Philippa's cloak burned too warm; her stays cinched too tight. Heaven help her, she *was* sweet as honey on him. And he... well, until yesterday she'd thought he felt nothing at all for her. But now, she questioned that assumption. He said he had feelings for her, but if so, why let her leave Scotland? And were his feelings of the biscuit sort or were they, like her own, pure sugar?

A question that preoccupied her until the coach rolled to a halt, and there was Bram, waiting to help them down.

"In here." He nodded at a shop and led the way.

Pippa moved to follow, but Lucy stalled her. "There's a bookshop down the street. Let's try it. Any help he offers is sure to be a waste of time."

"I trust him, Lucy." Hopefully, her maid heard her utter conviction.

Lucy sighed, stomped to the shop, and flung open the door.

Pippa followed her through and scrunched her nose. "I do dislike the smell of tobacco."

The shop buzzed with a heady warmth that clogged the throat and made the eyes water. A sickly sweet smell rolled through the heat—impossible for that time of year, surely—roiling her stomach.

Lucy inhaled and closed her eyes, wafting the air closer to her face. "I adore it." The cut-throat angle of her lips disappeared for a gentle moment as she savored the scent, but it returned when she snapped her eyes open. "Where *is* he?"

Excellent question. The shop echoed blessedly empty, and she ambled over to a nearby shelf and poked at a golden snuff box. Would Grandmama like it? Did she take snuff? She certainly smoked a cheroot now and then. Once Pippa had discovered the woman puffing away while milking a cow, her skirts hiked almost to her knees as she perched on a small stool beneath the bovine.

Lucy stabbed her fists into her hips. "He's *up to something*."

"He's not. Besides, you cannot know that if you cannot see him."

"I know that precisely because I cannot see him. Don't you—"

Rumbling voices from the back of the shop, words tumbling forth louder and more distinct.

"You do not know its value, you swine!" A male voice, high and angry.

"Swine? Why you!" Another male voice, this one low as a rug on the floor and angrier still.

Crash. The sound of broken glass and clattering shelves. Then two bodies fell through a door at the back of the shop and onto the floor in a flurry of fists and tangled winter clothing. The two men jumped to their feet, and one threw the other toward the front of the shop. He crashed into a table, and snuff boxes flew through the air, raining down on Pippa's and Lucy's heads.

Pippa bolted for the door, shock jolting her feet into action.

"No!" Lucy caught her arm and pulled her farther into the shop. "Look." She ducked low and pointed toward the back.

Pippa looked, throwing an arm over her head to protect it from further flying tobacco accessories.

A stubbled face peeked out from the doorway the two men had just flown out of. Bram. Catching sight of them, he launched into the fray, roped a sinewy arm around her shoulders, and dragged her toward his refuge.

They ducked behind tables—the brawl continuing behind them—and slid through the open door into a narrow, many-shelved room flickering with pale candlelight. A low table stood at its center, and a tall man, pressed into a stoop by the low ceiling, stood beside it. Gray streaked his flower-yellow hair, and angry eyes flickered behind spectacles.

Pippa closed the door behind them, her heart beating in her ears.

Lucy smoothed her skirts, then fisted her hands on her hips. "My word. What an insupportable ruckus." She tilted her head, screwed her mouth to one side. "Which fellow do you think won? The short one had the round one's arm twisted up like a snake. Maybe I should peek out and see."

Bram's arm slipped off Pippa's shoulder, leaving an arctic chill behind. "Your maid has a violent streak." He peered into her face, pushed back her bonnet for a deeper inspection. "You're bleeding!" His strong fingers swept across her head, wiping against her temple, probing under her bonnet and into her scalp above her hairline.

"Now that you mention it," she said in a soft, shaking voice, "my head hurts like the devil. Must have been one of the flying snuff boxes."

"Collins and Graspy, the fools," the graying giant said. "If they threw more shillings instead of fists, they'd get what they want. But I can't say I trust either of them with my Casanova box now. *Hmph.*"

"Casanova box?" Pippa peered around Bram's burly, looming form.

He pulled her gently back to center and grumbled, "Stay still. It'll likely bleed like you're dying. But you're not." He pulled a handkerchief from a pocket and pressed it into her hair.

"Good. I'd hate to be felled by a snuff box." She leaned into his investigative embrace, enjoying it, wishing for more. "But what is the Casanova box?"

"I think Her Grace will like it," Bram mumbled, his attention and his handkerchief on her hair line. "Knew Caldwell here would have something interesting."

The man touched her so naturally, as if a thousand and two rules did not say he should not, could not do so. Each time he touched her, one of the rules written on her skin slipped away, a disintegrating ribbon. Each time a rule disappeared, Naughty Her popped the trunk open a bit more. Blue eyes glowed from the sliver of darkness between trunk's top and bottom.

Pippa squirmed. "Wha—what is the Casanova box?"

"This." The man, Caldwell, held something high Pippa could not quite see.

She pushed away Bram's ministrations. She did need a closer look, but what a shame that he let her go so easily. Just as he had in Scotland. He'd put her in a coach and watched it roll away. She should not have let him. She should have broken every rule and demanded to know how he could kiss her, touch her, and then go silent as the grave. This time she would demand answers and, still heated from her midnight dream, perhaps more kisses, too.

Chapter Seven

Bram clenched his hands into fists so tightly, he pierced the skin of his palm. It was either that or drag Pippa back to him, toss her over his shoulder, then toss her into the coach, and take her back to the duke's house, apply a poultice to her head, and call a doctor.

But she needed a gift, and he wanted her to win as much as he wanted to win her.

"It's beautiful!" she gasped behind him, and he forced his hands to uncurl and turned his body back toward the trio. The damned snuffbox *was* beautiful, and likely the dowager would be amused. Highly. Especially if what Caldwell said about its origins was true.

The snuffbox Caldwell held out to Pippa and her maid was green and gold and edged in silky dark wood.

Pippa took it gently and turned it over in her hands, inspecting every inch. "Why is it called the Casanova box?"

"See?" Caldwell traced the edging of dark wood. "Made from Casanova's footstool."

The maid gasped and clapped her hand over her mouth. "No!"

"My," Pippa said, her eyes widening. "*The* Casanova?"

"Shouldn't talk about him in front of such fine ladies as yourselves," Caldwell said. "But it is a selling point of the box, you see."

"What is its price?" Pippa asked.

Caldwell took the box back and placed it in a larger box lined with velvet. "It is, as you can imagine, quite the valuable artifact."

Bram snorted. He wasn't even sure the damned thing was authentic, but the dowager would like the story, the possibility. He wanted Pippa to have it. If anything was going to win a place in Scotland as the dowager's companion, it was that snuffbox.

"Two hundred and fifty pounds," the shopkeeper said.

Pippa's face fell.

"Bollocks!" the maid hissed.

Bram narrowed his eyes. "Sounds a bit low for such a *precious* object." The price revealed the box's inauthenticity. It was a fake. He'd worked one summer with an antiquities collector, thought he would show a knack for collecting the old and valuable. No such luck. He had realized he was allergic to dust, though. He did remember one thing from those dusty days—rare items from renowned figures captured spectacular sums. Sums even the dowager might balk at.

No footstool had been dismembered for this box's creation, and if it had, it certainly had not belonged to the infamous Casanova.

Caldwell snapped the box closed and stored it on a shelf. "It's a steal, it is. But if you do not wish to pay such a sum, I know two fellows who do." His eyes flashed to the door, which still rumbled with sounds of the destruction of the man's shop.

"Should you do something about them?" Bram asked.

Caldwell shrugged. "It happens quite often. They break it down, then pay me large sums to fix it." He grinned. "Let them do their most expensive."

"Hm. I see. She'll take the box," Bram said. "But not at the asked price."

Caldwell tried to pull up to his full height, bumped his head on the ceiling, and stooped back down once more, scowling. "I won't be cheated just because we're old friends, Shaw."

"I won't be cheated because you found a lovely trinket and let your imagination get the best of you."

"What are you insinuating?" Each word a slow drop of burning tar to the floor between them. The man meant to fight.

So did Bram. "Nothing if you give us the box for what you bought it plus... oh, I'm feeling generous, it being Christmas and all. An additional fifty pounds."

Caldwell stepped toward Bram.

Soft, slender fingers wrapped around Bram's forearm, and Pippa whispered in his ear, "I do not need it, and we must pay a fair sum. If I cannot, then I will find a different gift."

Bram's gaze never left Caldwell's. They were locked in battle. "What I have suggested is a fair price. More than. What is it to be, Caldwell? Will you sell that box today, or no?"

Caldwell blinked. Caldwell broke. "For my shop's reputation, you may have the box for eighty pounds, two pence."

"Sold," Bram said, laying a hand over Pippa's where it still rested on his arm.

Lucy scowled. "It's a trick, my lady. You saw that exchange same as I did. Something is not right. Do not break like a lump of *sugar*."

Bram scowled at the woman. "If a man drove you to such distrust tell me, and I'll put a fist in his face. I'm not playing a game, Miss Lucy. I'm merely getting your mistress a fair price for an item she desires."

"*Hmph*." Lucy crossed her arms and turned away, her back a rigid spear setting the lines of battle.

Caldwell echoed Lucy's sound of derision and took the box from the back room. Lucy followed him, leaving Bram a moment alone with Pippa. The last time they'd been alone, they had kissed. *Bloody hell*, he ached to do so again, to use the silent space around them for the best of reasons, tasting her, holding her, loving her.

Pippa leaned closer to Bram. "Thank you. I am sorry Lucy is so cross with you. She is sweet on the stable master at Castle Clarebourn. Was terribly distraught to leave him." She dropped her gaze. "She wants back as badly as I do."

Even through the sweet haze of tobacco, he smelled her—mint and tea and the slight scent of paint and paper.

He reached up, ran the pad of his thumb along her plump lower lip and felt his groin tighten with desire. So soft. Her lips parted; her eyes lit with memories.

A little kiss wouldn't hurt his plans, would it? He'd simply start step two —woo the lady—a little sooner than intended.

He swept his thumb once more over her lip, a pleasurable torture. One little kiss. No. Such thinking had ruined his plans once before. He'd learned his lesson. He stepped back and guided her from the room.

They stepped over two men lying next to one another on the ground, huffing and puffing.

"Coward," one wheezed.

"Beefwit," the other groaned.

"Morons, the both of you," Bram said, striding to the counter.

Pippa settled at his side. She looked up at him, her brow a red, fuzzy squiggle of confusion over storm-blue eyes. He liked that she had eyes as changeable as the sky. He could read her moods like he read the weather sweeping through each day and season. He'd discomposed her, confounded her.

Good. Such emotions could be turned into others right quick with the alchemical pressure of lips to lips.

Caldwell dropped the box on the counter. "Eighty pounds and two pence." He ground each word between blunt teeth. "I'm sure I won't have enough to get the children a present or two this year. Not now."

Bram raised a brow. "How many do you have?"

Caldwell raised a quizzical brow. "Of what?"

"I thought so." The swindler.

Pippa dropped her banknote on the counter, and Caldwell wrapped the box and tied it with twine, then handed it over.

Bram scooped the box from the counter, handed it to Pippa, and wove his arm through hers. "Lovely seeing you again, Caldwell."

Caldwell crossed stiff arms over a hollowed chest. "Don't hurry back, Shaw."

Bram squeezed Pippa to his side. "Come. I can return you home now."

Pippa's face popped up, revealing wide, startled eyes. "Home? But—"

Lucy's head appeared between them. She swung a scowl at Bram and then at Pippa. "Apart, you two! I'm chaperone, and I'll do my duty." She squeezed her arms into the small space between Bram and Pippa, then pressed them out wide, pushing them apart.

"Blast, she's strong," Bram said.

Pippa grunted. "Terribly so."

"It's because," Lucy said finally, standing fully between them with a satisfied smile, "I carry the packages, my lady." She turned her back to Bram. "I'll return Lady Philippa home."

"A moment if you please, Miss Lucy."

The maid swung toward Bram, wielding a pointed finger like the sharpest saber, ready to do her worst. "No moments, Mr. Shaw. Not a one."

"I just wished to say, Miss Lucy, that Alec, who works in Her Grace's stables..."

"I know Alec." Her cheeks pinked, and not with anger this time. "Is he well? Has he mentioned me?"

"That's what I wanted to say. He sent his regards. Hopes you're happy. Hopes the London men are keeping their distance." Alec had not said all that, but he'd been grouchier than normal the last months, and Bram could do that kind of math.

Lucy lost at least an inch of height, melting into the floor, her muscles and bones sliding downward as the corners of her mouth tilted up.

Not that it lasted long. She snapped to attention, unsheathing her finger once more, shaking it at him. "You'll not trick me!"

Bram sighed. How the hell would he get Pippa alone if he could not shake the maid? Frustration firing his steps, he lumbered outside. On the street, the cold bit him like a rabid dog.

"Hell and damnation," he spit. Looked like rain. Steel-gray clouds rolled heavy above. The excursion would not last much longer. But Pippa had her Casanova box, and unless he did not know the dowager, she would soon have Scotland, too.

The bell over the shop door tinkled like the first drops of rain upon a rooftop.

"Bram?" Pippa's voice low and sultry, the voice he wanted to hear every damned day of his life.

He turned. "Where's Miss Lucy?"

The smile that twisted up into her cheeks could be described with only one word—naughty. "I may have suggested that Alec might appreciate a late Christmas gift—some tobacco. She can give it to him when we return." She clutched the box to her chest. "And I have hope—now—that we might." The naughty smile slipped into something bright and true that made him feel a worthy man, not a failure.

"You distracted her."

A nod. "That way, we both get what we want."

What he wished to have at that moment couldn't be taken on a street in broad daylight. It required dark and shadows and a very large, very comfortable bed.

"Good." Good? He should ask *why*. But time ticked by too quickly. He grabbed her arm and pulled her into a nearby alley. Not too far in, just until the chatter and clatter dissipated, and the shadows turned two bodies into one.

He wanted to kiss her so badly his groin stirred and tightened, and his heart ached with need. Pippa's distraction of her maid suggested he did not stir in vain.

The alley offered silent solace, the illusion of alone despite the crowd just beyond the sliver of an opening between two walls.

He pressed her back to the cold brick, his body facing hers, his weight propped up by the forearm he had braced into the wall above her head. In the darkness, her eyes turned midnight and star-studded. In the heat of his body, her breath came faster and faster, ragged and ready. In the crackling space between them, her voice unfurled, small and bold.

"Bram?"

"Bed," he said.

"Bed?" she whispered.

"You said we could both get what we want, and how can I get what I want if there's no bed?"

"Ah." Her head shifted so that her chin pointed toward her shoulder. "I see." A glinting peek up at him, like a winking star. "You are tired." She stepped to the side, toward the bright street. "You should return home." The corner of her mouth quivered, a rabbit ready to bolt.

"I'm not tired at all. Except from pretending not to want you."

"You've been pretending not to want me?" She slid back toward him. "Terribly bad at it, you are."

"*Hmph*." He grabbed her about the waist, his arm curving perfectly into the nest between hip and breast, and he pulled her back into the Pippa-shaped space between him and the wall. "Shall I tell you exactly what I wish, Pippa?" His voice growled deep, low, and feral.

"A bed?" Her body melted into his arm so that his strength alone kept her upright.

"You. And to start where we left off in Scotland. *Before* we were interrupted." He kissed her, and it was no gentle rising morning song but a crescendo of lips and teeth and wanting. A continuation.

Her arms snaked up and around his neck, and she crashed her body against his, writhing as if she could not get close enough to him. He helped her, pressing his palms into her back, pressing her into him.

"Pippa," he moaned, parting her lips and slipping his tongue inside. Their first kiss had been soft as morning dew, and if it had been allowed to continue, it may have grown inquisitive, exploratory.

This kiss skipped over those steps entirely, racing headlong into ruination. Blessed, perfect ruination.

She ruined him as thoroughly as he did her. She snagged his bottom lip between her teeth and scattered heated wind-swept kisses up his jaw, almost coming back to his mouth as if to a home.

"Bram," she sighed, his name a whispered plea.

She remembered Scotland. He had no doubt now. This was not the kiss of a woman starting something new. It was the kiss of a woman picking up where lust denied too long had left off.

Chapter Eight

Bram Shaw was devouring Lady Philippa Hampton, and the world spun on an axis of utter perfection.

Naughty Her had left the trunk long ago, blasted it to smithereens. Now no space remained between Pippa and that part of herself, needy and demanding, that pressed her heating core against the leg Bram had slipped between her legs. Every rule she'd ever tattooed into her very skin drained away now like ink washed clean by the rain.

Rain.

She gasped and wrenched away from Bram's sweet, firm mouth. "It's raining!"

He stared at her, hellish flames leaping in his eyes, sky-born drops pinging his shoulders and soaking his hair.

"Where's your hat?" She looked down. Ah, there. She bent her knees to retrieve it because she must have been the one to knock it off in her desperate haste to touch as much of him as she could as quickly as possible. She did not get far, her fingertips stretching, the hat so far out of reach.

Bram hauled her back up and crashed his lips to hers once more.

Who cared for a hat, really? What woman would choose headgear over heated kisses?

His hands wrapped around her hips, digging. It should have felt painful, but sparks of desire ignited her belly, low, low, low. In a place she only felt after fitful dreams that left her hair tangled and her hands caressing, searching for some feeling, some release she could not quite know or understand in the exact place she knew—because Tabitha had told her—that a man would join with her one day.

Join—a word that evoked more than bodies.

She opened her mouth so he could seek deeper. She arched her back to press her hips into the hard, warm center of him.

Very hard.

Very warm.

It made her feel loose, shivering, and frantic, as if she might shiver apart, becoming a volley of the very rain drops that bounced off his coat. She massaged his neck with longing fingers, diving beneath the scarf and cursing the cravat. Cursed her gloves, too, for that matter.

How long had they been apart? Six months? Too long. During that time, she'd felt a bone-deep ache but had not known why. She knew now. She'd ached for *him*.

Now as she writhed against him, needing closer in order to burrow into his very soul, he gathered her to him like wildflowers from a meadow, fragile and rare, and she scratched her nails over his jaw, curling them under the warm edge of his cravat. She dragged herself away from his lips to taste the rain-drenched scruff of his cheek, lower to where his ragged pulse beat against the delicate skin of his neck.

From there... nowhere else to go.

She groaned. "A cravat is a horrid thing, don't you think?"

"The devil's own invention, Pip."

She laughed, a hiccup of a sound much like the nickname he'd bounced off her. "Pip?"

He gathered her into his arms, and their clothes, soaked by the downpour, melted them together. She shivered.

"We must get you warm," he mumbled against her ear.

"Doing a fine job of warming me already." She opened her neck to him.

"Away from her! Now."

They jerked apart.

Standing at the mouth of the opening, an avenging angel with a sodden bonnet, Lucy glared, her ire evident even in the alley's shadows.

Pippa wrapped her arms around her ribs and ran through the puddles to reach her maid. "'Tis nothing, Lucy. He was..." She searched the unforgiving sky above for an answer but found only the sting of rain drops in her eyes.

"He was kissing you senseless, my lady!" Lucy stomped a foot, splashing water across their hems. "This is absurd. We must return to the coach this very moment. Where is the Casanova box?"

Where had the box gone to? She'd had it before the alley and presumably when she'd entered the alley.

Behind her, the slow splash of boots marching inexorably toward her. "Here." A package appeared over her shoulder as Bram's warmth soaked into her back. "The packaging's soaked through, but the box should be fine."

She took the box with shaking fingers and a body still more aware of him than she was of anything else in existence.

Lucy snatched it away. "I'll take that. Who knows where you'll drop it next!" She turned and flounced off.

Pippa ran after her, catching up and dashing with her down the street and toward the coach. The streets echoed empty, pedestrians and shoppers having retreated indoors to avoid the chilling downpour.

Now, without Bram's body all around her, without his heat pouring into her, she realized—the dead of winter was no time to be caught in a rainstorm.

Reaching the coach, she swung herself up and inside, Lucy bouncing in after her. Pippa stuck her head out, laughing as more rain hit and sluiced off the edge of her bonnet. "Bram! Come along!"

He stood several paces away, watching, holding his drenched hat between both hands.

"Please do, Bram. Come along!"

He grinned, strode toward her.

Lucy leaned over, hissed low and sharp in Pippa's ear. "Cut him, my lady. It's the only way to send a defiant message."

Did her maid mean the cut direct or something more deadly? Difficult to tell. "Defiant message about what? He's helped me with the gift." He'd kissed her and brought her to life. "A cut direct is decidedly not the message I wish to send the man. And I'm certainly not"—she looked left and right just in case the coach held eavesdropping ears—"*cutting* him. With a *knife*."

Lucy drooped into the squabs with a pouty lower lip just as the coach heaved to one side under a heavy weight. A breath later, Bram appeared. Pippa scuttled to the other side of the coach and sat next to Lucy while Bram lowered himself into the center of the backward-facing bench.

He pushed his hands through his slick wet hair, sending trails of water slicing down his neck and onto his shoulders. "We'll ruin your brother-in-law's fine upholstery." His voice, deep and gruff and tingling with a rich brogue. Pippa shivered, then she could not stop shivering.

"We must get you home," Lucy and Bram said together.

"*Hmph*." Lucy tossed her attention out the window, crossing her arms over her chest.

"Glad you can be sensible about one thing, Miss Lucy," Bram said. A grin flickered at the corners of his lips like a glowworm. "We are in agreement. Lady Philippa must warm herself."

True. Her teeth chattered. Yet, she did not wish this day to end. She'd surprised herself so many times, she wished to see how many other shocks she could suffer from her own actions, see what else Naughty Her was capable of.

She shook her head. "No. I will not return home yet. I know a place where we may sit and speak freely with one another. Few people will notice our presence there, and those who do, will not care. It's run by a man who will keep our secrets." Her need to brave every fear, experience every drop of rain, and every explosive kiss bloomed like a garden inside her.

"And what is this haven?" Bram asked. "And where is it?"

Pippa grasped a corner of her skirts and wrung them out. "A coffee-house. In Cheapside."

Lucy tugged on Philippa's arm. "My lady, no. We can't go there."

"Yes, we can, and we will." She stuck her head out the window. "Graves, to Frederick's!" The coach groaned into motion as she returned to the slightly warmer coach interior, wiping rain from her face and swiping fear from her heart. "We can get warm and dry. Lillian and Devon keep spare clothes there. We will borrow them."

"We have our own clothing at the duke's house," Lucy ground out.

Yes, Lucy's plan held more sense than Pippa's, and yet Pippa did not want sense. She wanted rain-soaked winter days, kisses and shadows, and the heat pooling low in her belly. She wanted to push the begging core of her body against the tight muscle of Bram's thigh. She could not yet see how these things fit in with her plans to become Grandmama's companion and leave London for good, but if she ran from Bram now, she may never figure it out.

He must have felt her gaze on him for his head turned slowly, tilting at the same time, and his foggy eyes flashed with lightning as their gazes collided. The fog obscured any hint of his thoughts, and she dropped her own gaze to her lap where her fingers curled in indecision.

"Pippa." His soft voice, just a hint of a Scottish lilt, rumbled across the space between them.

She did not lift her eyes. She could not. She might jump across the coach and right into his lap if she did. She looked out the window instead. The world passed by gray and wet.

"The coffeehouse is an unusual one, allows women. So, we need not worry," Pippa said.

"Not why I'm worried," Lucy grumbled.

Bram chuckled, and they settled into a tense silence until the coach slowed and lurched to a stop.

Pippa still looked out the window, and she craned her neck to see the sign swinging above a bright blue door. Frederick's stood snug between other townhomes in a lovely part of Cheapside. Lucy exited with the help of a footman, but Pippa stood in the coach door, frozen like a block of ice. Since winter hung all around them like a shroud, she might not melt anytime soon.

A large, warm hand nestled against the small of her back. "All well? It will be quite crowded inside."

She swallowed, found her voice amid the haywire beating of her heart. "It will."

But that was not entirely what gave her pause. The door seemed a portal. If she were to paint it, she'd use a celestial blue and outline it with the lightest primrose, so it gave off a sort of glow. That way, anyone who entered it would know passing through might change one's life, change one's very nature.

"We do not have to go," Bram said, his hand on her back, sweeping in slow, warm circles, igniting her every nerve. "Miss Lucy would prefer to return to the duke's house."

She shook her head, her now shapeless bonnet shaking droplets like a wet dog. "No." She turned until she could see him behind her. "I am not often brave, but today I wish to be."

"Very well. Tell me how I can help." He squeezed past her to jump to the ground below. It still rained, and he held a hand out to her, rain drops plastering his longish hair to his forehead and sweeping in loving curves down the planes of his face.

Oh, to be a raindrop seeping into his warm skin.

She shivered. She would do anything for another kiss.

Placing her hand in his, she stepped down into late morning. Noon's high sun hid somewhere behind thick, low clouds.

The mental trunk she'd shoved the naughtiest bit of herself scattered in pieces about the floor of her mind, the lock a pile of dust. She'd secured that part of herself away in order to hide her feelings for Bram and win her way back to Scotland. Now, she had the box. She'd won the competition even if by default. Everything she wanted—hers. And now that Naughty Her had broken loose, she didn't see why they couldn't continue what had been so rudely interrupted in Scotland and in the alley. What she'd dreamed about last night, and what she now could not deny she wanted almost as much as Scotland itself.

Chapter Nine

Bram followed Pippa inside the coffeehouse, keeping his gaze trained on her back. He had hope. That kiss, just like the first they'd shared, could *not* mean nothing. But was it a kiss born of gratitude and excitement, destined for a short life? Or was it a kiss that promised more, years more, a lifetime more?

Patience. Like a woodsman approaching a wild animal, he'd hold his hand out and wait and see. If she truly wished to be brave, she'd approach him soon enough.

Pippa's gaze darted about the room, and with each counted human body, she seemed to shrink into herself a bit more, a flower not blooming. "Lord Devon and Lillian do not appear to be here. It's for the best." She strode toward a tall counter next to a giant black cauldron.

The man behind the counter, the owner of a thick tangle of black hair and even darker eyes, grinned wide. "Lady Philippa! Good to see you. Lord Devon and his missus are not here."

"I see that, Mr. Logan. Could we have three coffees, please?"

"Right away, my lady."

As the man busied himself with cups and such, Bram turned from the counter and peered out into the room. At its center was a long wooden table occupied by several graying gentlemen, all impeccably dressed and in varying states of anger.

"What are they discussing?" he asked. "Seems... important."

"Oh, quite," Mr. Logan replied. "Lord Devon calls 'em his philosophers. They've been on the question of extraterrestrial life all day long."

"Extra... terre... my apologies. I cannot say it, and I've no idea what you mean."

"People who live in space," Mr. Logan explained. "On other planets. The two on the right side of the table believe they exist. Apparently, an astronomer fellow has written about it. But the two on the left side of the table call it blasphemy. I stay out of their conversations, myself."

A coffee can flew across the room and shattered on a wall as a fuming philosopher slammed to his feet.

"Get's a touch violent. If you plan on staying for a bit, you might want to sit upstairs." He placed three cans of coffee before them, then eyed their sodden state. "There's a bedroom upstairs. Last door on the right. I'm sure Lord Devon will not mind if his family borrows what they need."

Pippa nodded, wrapping her hands around one of the mugs. "I was hoping to do so."

"My thanks," Bram said, sweeping his cup off the counter.

Lucy took her cup but bared her teeth. "We should leave. There are too many people here, Lady Philippa. It will never do."

Pippa shook her head and turned toward the stairs. No need for words with such decisive movements. He liked to see her confident as she'd been in Scotland, leaving her drooping London self behind.

He followed as the voices at the central table rose high and angry.

"Preposterous!" one of the philosophers yelled. "What would they live on? Are you saying the moon's terrain supports farming as ours does? Ha!"

"I'll get the water bucket if you're not quiet!" Mr. Logan's voice, merry but stern, quieted the rousing philosophers.

"Your sister's brother-in-law truly runs this establishment," Bram asked.

"Mm hm." Each step Pippa took up the staircase swung her hips like a clock pendulum, winding Bram up, wrecking his determination to be a patient man.

He focused on cold practicalities. A duchess's grandson running a coffeehouse. He'd not believe it if he wasn't seeing it. If she could stand for this, she would not long bemoan Pippa's marriage to him. Marriage. He couldn't say that word just yet... could he?

They reached the second floor and spread out in the intimate, dark space.

"Cozy up here, it is." Lucy's scowled.

The space looked like it used to be living quarters—a spacious hallway with two doorways leading into small rooms on either side. All doors had been removed from their frames except for one in the far-right corner.

Lucy peeked into it. "The bedroom. Come along, my lady. We'll borrow a gown and have you dry in no time."

Pippa minded her maid, and the door clicked closed, separating him from the only woman he wanted to kiss for the rest of his life. A part of him wanted to rip the door from the hinges to decimate any barrier between them, but he chained it and peered into all the doorless rooms instead. All were equipped with small tables and chairs on top of large, fashionable rugs and cozy, roaring fireplaces. Paintings hung on the wall, and each room housed a bookshelf filled with books and periodicals of all sorts.

Bram placed his coffee on a table in the hallway and sat, stretching his long legs out.

Drip, drip, drip. He'd soak the rug at this rate. *Damn.*

The door to the bedroom creaked open, and Pippa stepped out wearing a simple wool gown of soft pink, her hair falling in a slick wave down her back. A scant inch too small, the dress hugged her curves. What a delight it would be to remove.

Pippa, all shy smiles and tentative steps, swayed toward him. "Lucy wished me to stay before the fire and dry my hair. But you must..." She chewed her bottom lip, let her gaze roam everywhere but him. "You must divest yourself of your wet clothing as well."

He stood. *Drip, drip, drip.* "Yes. Thank you." *Damn.* Why had the air between them grown thick with unsaid words and unacted desires? So much unsaid and undone turned his tongue awkward and his movements choppy.

Lucy exited the bedroom to let him enter, and he shut the door, yanking at his cravat as he strode for the fire.

Lucy seemed a fortress wall surrounding Pippa, so sleek and smooth there were no jutting parts to help him climb. But he must get to Pippa somehow, find out more, feed his hope further like a growing fire in a cold grate. He peeled off his jacket and waistcoat and dug from an inner pocket of the latter a small, now damp paper.

The colors ran a bit, hurting his heart. He traced the fuzzy outline of trees and sky, green bleeding into blue. "Hell." He'd ruined it. He placed the watercolor painting with the delicately traced PH in the lower right corner on a low table near the fire to dry out. Too close. He pulled the table farther away, safe from sparks but still within the warm circumference of the flames' heat.

Leaving the painting to dry, he hung the garments over the back of the chairs that held Pippa's gown and—he swallowed hard—her shift. It had not survived the soaking, and it lay over a chair back like a flattened ghost. Which meant she currently wore nothing but stays and that wool gown. The thought of the stays digging into her fine skin lit a fire in his feet to throw her over his shoulder and run her all the way back to the duke's house where she could have a warm bath and the proper undergarments to protect that skin.

Would freckles roam across those places he'd not yet seen?

Patience.

Entirely nude, he rummaged through a wardrobe, donned the slightly too-tight clothes he found there, gave his hair a tousle before the fire to shake the excess rain from it, then rejoined Pippa and Miss Lucy in the hallway.

Pippa sat at the table with the coffee cans, and Miss Lucy stood at a window in an empty room at the front of the house, looking out at the street below. A tension hung between them, tight as a wire.

"What's happened?" Bram asked, sitting next to Pippa.

She sipped her drink, eyes closing with a flutter as the warm liquid slid down her throat. "She's quite put out with me and wishes to return home, but I have told her she can return without me if she wishes." She swallowed another sip of coffee. "I am quite safe here. With you."

"I agree with Miss Lucy. You should go home. Those philosophers are a rowdy bunch."

The noise from below heightened, as if his words had sung the ruckus back into being.

Pippa shivered. She may be able to survive the crowds without swooning, but she did not like them. They cut her deep, that much was clear.

"When we arrived," she said, "there were ten altogether down below. We are safe up here." The last said with force, as if to convince herself.

He laid a hand on top of hers, a shell to protect her. Her hand felt small, fragile, and cold, so he picked it up and chafed it between both his hands, rubbing warmth into the delicate digits. "You're always safe with me, Pip."

He hooked his foot around the front leg of her chair and pulled until she sat right next to him, their bodies pressing together. His arm stole around her shoulders, pulling her even closer.

"You are all that is sweetness," he whispered, forgetting his promise of patience.

She looked up at him, her chest rising and falling with the same rapidity of his own. "There is nothing sweet about the way you make me feel."

He cupped a hand over her cheek, soft and downy and glowing under his touch. Her lips parted, a heavenly fraction of a sliver that promised delight and decimated his determination to go slow, to give instead of take. He trailed his hand around to the back of her head, supporting as she went languid, bones melting into golden pools. He dipped, and—

"This is foolish!" Lucy stomped into the hallway, her face twisted with frustration. "That sky is hard as steel, and that rain will turn worse soon. *Snow*. I know it. The coach is right outside, and you two are much too cozy inside. We should go. Now, my lady."

Pippa scooted her chair away from Bram, wood screeching against wood as she held the edges of the seat and bounced back to her original position.

"Lucy makes an excellent point, Pip," Bram said, his arms still full of the ghost of Pippa's warmth, his lips still aching for hers.

Pippa straightened, frowned. "I will stay till I've finished my coffee, Lucy."

Lucy's hands hit her hips and stuck. "More and more people are crowding inside downstairs because of the weather. And those philosophers are more akin to mad men. You cannot stay here."

Pippa wrapped her fingers tight around the edges of her seat. "I'm staying."

"You only want to stay because of him." A knife-sharp glare thrown in Bram's direction.

Pippa stood slowly, unfolding her body until she stood strong and powerful before them. "I stay for myself."

Lucy's face rushed red, then paled. She turned to the stairs. "If that is what you wish. But I am leaving. I do not like this place, and you"—her eyes, full daggers now, sliced Bram to ribbons—"are courting ruination. I hope you are ready, Mr. Shaw, to pay the price. You didn't seem to be in Scotland." She trudged down the stairs and out the door, leaving nothing but the sound of a tinkling bell. They were alone. As they should not be. He did not regret it, did not call Lucy back, or bundle Pippa into a hack.

Patience be damned.

Bram once more hooked his foot around the leg of Pippa's chair and pulled her inexorably closer.

Chapter Ten

Pippa gripped the edges of her chair as it slid across the small space between herself and Bram. It seemed the man could not be satisfied unless he was touching her. But when her chair finally bumped into his, and he wrapped her close once more, she melted into him. She, as well, could find no satisfaction in the cool air when his arms were so conveniently nearby.

Though she leaned into him and closed her eyes, she could not forget Lucy's form disappearing down the stairs, nor her final words to Bram.

You didn't seem to be in Scotland.

A pointed accusation. He'd kissed her, got caught, then let her leave.

"She's right," Pippa said. "This, us, it's utter scandal."

"Not if we're engaged."

She jerked upright to peer into his face.

Nothing there but the seriousness of a death sentence. Or marriage vows.

She inhaled and reached for her coffee, sipped it down despite the now lukewarm heat of it. "We are not engaged, Bram Shaw, and I find myself rather... confused. Six months ago, you watched me return to London without a single objection. And now you're dragging me toward you like I'm a rag doll, kissing me like a kept woman."

"More like a wife, if you ask me, as I only want to keep you in the matrimonial sense."

Her arms flew wide. "There! That is the closest to a marriage proposal I've ever received. And from you! Your second in less than a minute. What has changed?"

He took a gulp of his coffee. "I… had a plan. Secure Blàr Hall. Then secure… you. If I followed you back to London, I would have lost my position. Lose my position, lose the house. Then I'd have nothing to give to you."

She opened her mouth to speak, found she couldn't.

"I had to concoct a different plan after you were sent packing. So, I convinced the dowager you were a fling, earned my way to London with that lie."

"You could have told me. Or wrote a letter," she grumbled.

"I thought of it often. I worried I'd be caught, the letters read, my plans ruined. Again." His lips curled into a wolf's grin, possessive, lethal, the grin of a hunter who knew what he was after and how to get it. "Once I have Blàr Hall, we'll both be in Scotland. A steward may not be able to court a marquess's daughter, but he can court a dowager's companion. Can you wait for me?" He cupped her face, nudged it so she faced him, his eyes soft with fog. He tangled their fingers together, squeezed. "I can't *not* love you, Pippa. Not that I've tried very hard."

He loved her. She stretched her torso and neck to nuzzle her nose against his scruffy cheek. He filled her with warmth and courage, and before she'd left Scotland, she'd searched for him every morning and thought of him every night. Was that love? Filled with fear and worry for so long, she hardly knew what other emotions felt like. This one felt cozy and right and safe. Safe enough to be herself, no trunks or rules necessary. She'd been so busy learning the rules that would keep her safe, she'd not had time to consider love. Love had seemed one of those wild dangers that rules would tame and save her from.

But perhaps love would help her save herself.

Was this love?

She wanted him like the hard winter ground wants water.

He unwrapped his arm from her shoulders, placed both elbows on the table, and steepled his hands before him. "I know I seem a failure, but—"

"A failure? What do you mean?" How could anyone look at the man sitting next to her and brand him a failure? How could he look in the mirror and think it of himself? With the exception of Lucy, he set everyone at ease, including Grandmama. A rare gift, that.

"I've tried my hand at many tasks and not been a fit for any of them. Except for steward, and I'll soon leave that position, too. I give up when I don't like what I'm after. You... you don't give up. Get sent back to London, you devise a plan to return to the castle. I've watched you face your fears for the last three days, and damn if it hasn't humbled me. The dowager's right. You deserve better."

He was no failure, and she had to convince him of it. If she was determined, she'd plant that determination in him, taking him up as her next task until he realized he was marvelous in every way.

"Bram—"

"I don't care, though, Pip. I'm not good enough for you, but I want you, anyway. And in this one thing, I won't even think of failing."

He wouldn't have to.

Slowly, she stood, then sat again. In his lap. She hooked her arms around his neck, smiled when his breath hitched. She rubbed at the rigid muscles in his neck, soothing, branding. "Do you know, I have been saying all this time that what I want is Scotland, but I begin to think I misunderstood my own heart. What it wanted was you, and Scotland was where you were." She shrugged, blushed.

His hands, large and warm and strong clamped about her waist. "And... if I'm not in Scotland?"

"We'll figure it out." Words with more confidence than she felt. She needed the surety of his body, so she bracketed her hands around his face, leaned forward, and fell into a kiss of heather and velvet, of coffee and snow, of shadows and *just right*.

The softness of it did not last, their desire swirling into violent heat. He stood, their teeth clashing. He held her like a babe in his arms and carried her toward the bedroom.

He set her down before the door, removed his hands from her body, fisted them till bone shone white against red, winter-chapped skin, then straightened them. "If we go in there, you choose me, lass. Us. Wherever on God's green earth that might be. Be sure. I want Scotland as you do, but—"

She reached out and curled strong fingers around his lapel. She pulled at him, and he let the insignificant tug sway him forward. The tug, the sway, felt like power and control, two things she lost in a crowd of strangers. Two things he gave her without question.

She went up on tiptoe, met him lip to lip and whispered across his ragged breathing, "I choose us."

She kissed him, devoured him, hungry enough to consume every inch of him. She walked backwards, pulling his body with her until her back hit the closed door. "I want you braced over me as you were in the alley."

"Enjoyed that, did you?" He did as she asked, bracing his forearm above her head. She turned into silver liquid as he wrapped his free arm around her.

She sighed when he slipped his tongue into her mouth, and she met him stroke for stroke. Her hand ran up his arms, over his shoulders, and clasped behind his neck. Silky hair, the linen cravat warmed by his skin. Too much sensation and not enough skin. Her hands moved, knotting in the front of his cravat and tugging. His hands joined hers, helping. And soon his throat was bare. Thank goodness for simple knots.

He grabbed her to him and rolled so that his back pressed against the wall. She kissed every inch of his face, and he licked up the column of her throat, then nibbled at her ear.

She purred, then groaned, the wanton finally in control, and said, "More. I need. More."

He laughed, a lusty bark of joy and disbelief. "Greedy."

"Yes. The bed." The bed behind the closed door was the exact worst place a single woman could go with a man who made her squirm and beg. The bedroom offered nothing but ruin.

She welcomed it.

He apparently did, too. In seconds, the door was open, and he was laying her gently on the bed. She scrambled to sit up, to face him as he put a knee and hand on the mattress and prowled toward her. Their bodies clashed together, and her arms clinched around him as he fell onto the bed, covering her.

They seemed to meld together, like two pieces of iron heated until molten and joining to make a new shape, an entirely new thing, lumps of steel honed into a sharp-edged sword, smooth and glistening in the firelight.

He rolled to the side and nudged one leg between hers, pushing his knee gently, then more insistently, into her needy core. She arched her back and pressed against him.

A repeat of their interlude in the alley.

There, however, she could not peel the waistcoat from his shoulders, tug the shirt hem from his trousers, and sneak her hand beneath the linen to trace the lines and planes of muscle there. Now she could. And she did.

His muscles clenched, tightened at her touch, and he ripped his shirt off, throwing it who knew where. Why would she look for its landing place when better sights awaited her? Broad shoulders and massive chest bronzed by years spent outdoors.

She curled her fingers beneath the waist of his trousers, and he hissed.

"From hairline to waist, you're all over sun-kissed," she said. No surprise there. She'd seen his chest bared to the sky before, had painted the sight in secret.

"Aye. Often. When working alongside others who are enjoying the same comfort."

Comfortable indeed, silk skin with a fine dusting of dark hair stretched taut over muscle honed by labor.

He rolled her to her belly. His fingers found the tapes at her nape and pulled until they dangled down her shoulders. Then the tapes lower on her back gave way to his efforts, and he pulled the edges of her gown apart until cold air whispered across her skin. Then he whispered across, pressing hot kisses against her neck, her spine, dotting her back with his lips and words. "Bonnie. Pip. Brave. Pip. My. Pip."

Six kisses, six points of conflagration.

As he raised the hem of her skirts, the air hit her legs, raising prickles up and down their length. He skimmed a hand over the valley of the arch of her foot, dipped in at her ankle, and stretched a path up her calf, over the back of her knee, and up her inner thigh. Lingering there, his fingers grazing the most sensitive part of her.

She had no fear. Tabitha had told her all about what lay between a man and a woman in the marriage bed, and in surprising detail, too. Surely few other ladies of the *ton* received such an education.

And Bram had cupped *just there* before. The night they were caught.

He stilled behind her.

She gazed over her shoulder to find him studying his hand upon her skin thoughtfully. "Bram?"

"We should wait."

"I find I don't particularly want to. I've spent six months pining. I've become a tangle of frustration, no matter how I've tried to deny it. I want to finish what we began when we were discovered."

"Finish it. Yes. I remember exactly where I was."

"Me, too." Two words that sounded pleading.

His hand began to move again. It flexed on her inner thigh, flirted with the tingling center of her. Then he pulled his hand away from and curved it up over her backside, stopping there to caress. She squeezed her eyes shut as the waves rocking a gentle rhythm across her body stole all thought, carried it out to sea. His hand traveled the length of her back and tiptoed down her ribs to her front. Gently he eased her onto her back, then pressed his lips to hers.

"Sit up, lass."

She did, and he rolled the borrowed gown up her body and over her head. His foggy eyes cleared to gleaming silver, and he dragged one leg over her body to straddle her, his hands finding a perfect fit at the side of her breasts. Then he dropped his head and kissed them, too.

Completely improper. Completely perfect. Her head grew too heavy to hold up, and she dropped it back, moaning, as he pulled her breasts above the edge of her stays to lick her puckered nipples.

She bucked beneath his attentions, and her hands found his head, tangled in his hair, pressed him urgently to her breasts. Somehow, her back met the mattress, and she used the soft surface to arch her hips up against him.

He'd done more touching than she had. He had more experience, knew what to do. Yet her hands now itched to roam, so roam they did, fingernails tracing down the line of his back, counting ribs, and palms enjoying the muscled fullness of his backside.

Too bad it was covered with a fine wool.

It didn't have to be. Her fingers met in front, between their bodies, and she returned to the work he'd stopped minutes (Years? Ages?) ago. The buttons of his fly proved easy to undo, and she pushed the fabric down his hips, pausing at the jutting hip bones she revealed. Fascinating and somehow arousing. She pushed lower and found her fascination fixed elsewhere. She stroked her fingers up and down his shaft, a subtle exploration.

His throat worked. His chest tightened. He dropped a kiss on top of the pulse at her neck. "Keep doing that, lass." He kissed his way up her neck, nipped her earlobe, and sipped from her lips once more, his hands massaging, and his fingers tracing circles, tighter and tighter till his thumb flicked her nipple.

She arched with a cry.

"Too much? Should I continue?" he asked, his voice low as the wind at her ear.

She wished to join with a man like him, kind and steady, rough and soft. "Continue." She laid her hand atop his and urged him onward, deeper, to show she meant the command.

His hand wandered between her legs. His fingers worked in circles, making her frantic to move, so she did however she could, running her hands up and down the length of his shaft, then curling her arms around his body, stroking her fingers up into his hair, and lifting him to her lips. She sang his name inside the hollow of his mouth, and he gave it back to her, his fingers moving faster and faster around and over her bud, then dipping inside her. He replaced his finger with the head of his shaft and slid in easy, and then he moved, his body lightning quick, a flash in the night sky of the bedroom.

"No turning back now," he said.

She nodded, urged him on with a lift of her hips.

He entered slowly, achingly gentle with each thrust, until he lay buried fully. He nipped at her lips, whispering nonsense words between kisses, and she laughed, a heady joy-filled sound, as he began to move—in and out—rocking with her in a haze of lust and laughter.

Laughter could not last in the heated need he stoked in her body. He braced himself on the bed with one arm and slipped his other hand between them, continuing the concentric play he'd performed earlier, winding her like a coil, a curling tendril, a clock timed for... what?

The rhythmic moving of his body inside hers stretched her too tight at times, but the pleasure his fingers manifested at her bud loosened the discomfort. Her breath came fast, as if she'd been running, as if she'd ran from London to Edinburgh and back again, her skin slicked cold and hot with sweat. As the pressure built inside her, she wrapped him tightly in her arms, held on so she did not get swept away in the wave when it came.

But she could not stop it, did not want to, and when it hit, her body broke into all the grains of sand along a beach. Her fingernails dug into his back as she lifted her hips to meet his final thrusts, then he exploded, too. If she was the sand, her gentle wolf was the slowly lapping waves along the edges of consciousness.

He collapsed atop her, slid his arms under her, and rolled, taking her with him.

He should have made a terrible mattress, but he did not. She laid her ear against his chest to hear the rapid *thump* of his heart and snuggled as deep as a hard male body allowed.

His hand lifted to her head, stroking down her skull, her neck, and back, untangling her hair with each pass. "I love you."

A murmur to make her heart swell.

The words welled up from her heart and into her throat, so big, she could hardly speak them into the air. Would they scatter and dissipate, blown about by the warm breath between their bodies?

But she could not deny this man, who spoke his truth so bravely, her own truth.

She pressed her forehead to his jaw. "I. Love. You." The words so soft she barely heard them.

He must have, though, for his arms tightened about her, squeezing her, shaking her from side to side until she laughed.

She kissed his pulse. "What gift will you give me?"

"Gift?"

"The traditional bride gift of the Shaw men."

"Ah, yes. Already gave you that."

She bolted upright. "No, you have not."

He stroked his fingers down her spine, then back up. "You wore it when I arrived. The shawl."

She blinked. "The red one? Grandmama... gave me..." But she did not know who had given it to her, did she?

"Not the dowager. Me." He ran a hand through his hair. "Because even then, I meant to make you mine."

Feeling as if the knitted wool settled around her shoulders, warm and soft, Pippa settled back down onto his chest. "I love it. And I love you." She counted his heartbeats up to twenty before adding, "Do you think Grandmama will forgive us?"

"Unlikely. But we'll face her ire together. What about your father? The duke? Surely, they can tame the gorgon."

"My father admires Grandmama deeply. He will likely take her lead. Arthur will support us, but... I dislike the damage it may to do his relationship with his grandmother if he defies her for me." She hid her face in his chest. "And your family... will this ruin everything for you?"

His body stilled. His heart under her cheek bumped a bit faster.

She pressed her palm against the thumping, trying to calm it. "Whatever happens, I'll go with you. If you find a position on a boat, I'll learn to love the sea. If you find one in London, I'll reside here, too."

"I'll find a position in Scotland. Somewhere remote. Where you can paint." His voice rumbled from his chest to hers, and she clung to him more tightly. The door vibrated as something slammed against it from the other side. A knock, but heavier, harder.

Bram and Pippa bolted to their feet, gathering clothing and dressing in a frenzy of arms and legs and frantic hearts.

The door shook again. *Bang, bang, bang.*

"Lord Devon?" Bram asked, buttoning his fall.

"I don't know." Pippa tried to tame her hair.

Bram crept toward the door as it shook with three more knocks. "Yes?"

"Come. Out. Now."

Pippa stopped breathing. "Grandmama."

"Shite." He reached out, opened the door with a fast swing inward to reveal the monster in the hall.

Chapter Eleven

The dowager stood straight as an oak, her cane upright and rigid before her, likely the blunt instrument of doom she'd used to shake their door down. Her eyes were impossible to read in the dim candlelight, and the raucous conversation echoing from below seemed not to touch her.

"Good evening," she said.

Pippa moved first, backing farther into the bedroom, a clear retreat. Her hands trembled in the periphery of Bram's vision as she lifted them to her unbound hair.

Bram set a shoulder on the doorframe and crossed his arms over his chest, his legs at his ankles. "Good evening, Captain. What brings you here?"

Bram thought, for a moment, she had not heard. Then her head tilted, her mouth opened a breath, and she paused before she spoke. "You think charming roguery can save you? From a single silly kiss, perhaps. But this? Nothing can save a man like you from complete folly. Nor, especially, a girl like her." She nodded toward the room, toward Pippa's silhouette in the snow-flurry of the window.

Bram straightened, blocking the dowager's view of Pippa, love-rumpled and vulnerable backdropped against the falling flakes. "'Tis no folly, Your Grace. 'Tis lo—"

"Do not dare call it love, boy. When it's merely lust. Young people look with their eyes and leap with their loins. It has nothing to do with the heart." The dowager's frail frame vibrated. She swept around and found a chair, settling herself in it with only the slightest tremor of bone and muscle. "The heart is won slowly, day after painstaking day as man and woman work together to heal one another and to help each other accomplish their goals. That is not won after six months' acquaintance, a kiss in a barn, and a tumble in a coffeehouse."

Bram strode toward the older woman. He did not wish to hurt her. The tremble of her hands atop her cane spoke of some past pain catapulted into the present. But he was not a weak man, lectured into submission.

He pulled a nearby chair before her and sat. "Sometimes souls know one another, Your Grace. I'm sorry you never discovered that. And you need not worry. We plan to wed."

She snorted. "I set out to fix her, and you ruined her. Call you that love? Call you that *souls knowing*? Bah."

Anger bristled down Bram's back. "I will not—"

"I can speak for myself." Pippa's voice rang calm and clear behind him.

He turned to find her in the doorway, her hair braided and hanging in an orderly line down her back. Whatever nerves had jangled her were banished now. In her steady hands, she held a small square of bright paper. Her painting.

"*Hmph.*" The dowager swung her face away from them. "Speak, then. Do. Tell me why you've ruined yourself with a nameless steward."

"A man whom you admire, Your Grace."

The title startled Bram. She'd only ever called the dowager Grandmama. She'd been ordered to do so. But such a title came with time, affection, and trust, not marriage to a duke's family. His Pippa had steel in her spine, and he glowed with pride. He'd best become used to the feeling. Everything she did made his chest expand, made his palms itch to applaud.

Pippa's soft steps brought her beside him, and she rested her hand on the back of his chair, brushing against his back. "I admire him, too. Very much."

A movement over his shoulder, and something fluttered into his lap.

The painting. Dry now. A landscape at sunset, a man, bared to the waist and silhouetted against the sky. He folded it and hid it away near his heart.

"You kept it?" Pippa asked.

"You gave it to me." The smallest grin. "Was rather naughty of you. It..." His voice broke like waves over rocks at high tide, and he swallowed to control it. "It is not a passing fling I feel. I admire you, too. Your talent and your mind, your kindness and your mischief. Your fears. And your daring."

"Ha." Her gaze jerked away from him. "Daring? Me? I'm a mouse."

They did not touch, but the air around them felt like a thousand fervent caresses, a kaleidoscope of butterflies, wings fluttering to push their bodies together. "You're a damned tempest, and that's a fact. A summer storm with an artist's soul, my Pip."

Her hand crept from the back of the chair to his shoulder, and he felt in that small caress a promise.

The dowager stood, leaning heavy on her cane.

Bram moved to support her, but she waved him away. "Do not pretend you wish to help when you only wish to hurt." She looked for many moon-quiet moments at the floor, then slowly raised her gaze to Pippa. "You wish to travel to Scotland. To escape the crowds. Has nothing changed for you over the last three days?"

Pippa smiled, a small affair that crouched at one corner of her lips. "Much has changed. I am sorry I let you think otherwise, but I am not afraid. Not of crowds. I am afraid of being confined by those who make them up, though. And I refuse to be any longer."

The dowager raised her cane an inch, then dropped the point into the floor. "Then no impediment to a good marriage remains."

"No." Pippa's voice granite.

The dowager waved it away anyway, as if it were a feather instead. "If we can keep the matter of the steward quiet—"

Pippa's hand moved to Bram's shoulder. "I will not stay quiet."

The dowager's head shook side to side as if it would never stop. "You think me cruel. But I know what is best for you. For both of you. I know what will lead to the greatest happiness." Her lip curled, a sneer as she slipped her gaze toward Bram. "I know how to keep you quiet."

Bram crossed a still-wet boot over his knee. The wool of his trousers gave way to the wet, chilling his skin. "I think you underestimate my verbosity, Your Grace."

"And you underestimate my influence, Mr. Shaw. Imagine how your family will feel when you bring a ruined woman home."

"They will adore Pippa, as I do."

"You've already lost your position with me. That means you've lost Blàr Hall as well. But you must think of others for once, too, Mr. Shaw. A man like your father relies on the goodwill and patronage of women like me. He's good at what he does, but there are many others like him. I can find another. And I can convince every other seventy-year-old widowed member of the aristocracy to follow suit."

Bram's boot hit the floor, and he pressed to his feet, each inch a losing fight with his self-control. "You threaten my father, my family?" The words grit between his teeth.

"Your Grace." Pippa rushed forward. "You cannot. His father has done nothing. Bram has been nothing but kind and protective and—"

"A charming wolf who has blinded you with a cunning act."

Pippa shook her head. "You don't mean that. You *like* him."

The dowager shuffled forward until she stood before Bram. Her inconsiderable height should have put her at a disadvantage, but under her world-toppling gaze, he felt small.

"I like no one who threatens my family," she said, her words smooth as the surface of a lake turned to ice.

"I am no threat," he returned. But doubt poked through, a worm in an apple rotten to the core. He did not believe he had ruined Pippa. What they had shared had been in love and freely given, and no ruin could come of that. But what of his family? The family he loved and exasperated. The family he wanted to believe in him despite his many failures. If the dowager rescinded her patronage because of his actions, he'd ruin *them*.

A crossroads stretched before him with both ways twisting and ugly, offering no shade, no water, no place to rest.

"What a horrible thing to do." Pippa pushed him back toward his chair. "You are asking him to make an insupportable choice. If he chooses me, he ruins his family. If he chooses to remain silent and stay away from me, his family is safe, but... what of *him*?"

Ah, his Pip. His maiden in shining armor wielding a sword and shield in battle for him. He let the pride spill through him and merge with his very bones.

"He'll be fine after a time," the dowager said. "It appears mean now, but you'll both see I'm—"

"No." They likely heard Pippa's declaration even down below. The philosophical roar silenced so that only her voice echoed through the winter night. She raised her chin high. "He should not have to make such a choice, and I will not allow it." Her hands fisted at her sides. Slowly, she turned to him.

She placed a hand on his heart, curled her fingers into the muscle there. "Bram, I cannot let you choose, so I will." A tear, silent as winter and cold as ice, slid down her cheek. "Go home to your family. And forget about me."

She tried to withdraw her hand, but he clutched it, refused to let it go. "No. There's another way. I'll find it."

She dropped her forehead to his chest with a sigh that rocked the rafters, blew the snow from the roof. Then, as if the sigh had shaken something else loose inside her, she clutched her hands in hard fists and raised a gaze sharp and blinding to him. "You will. I know it." And she would not stand idly by, either. She slipped from his grasp, turned to the stairs, and disappeared into the chaos below.

The dowager followed, stopping only to say without a single glance his way, "You will hate me now. Possibly forever. But I am right, and one day you will recognize that. She made the right choice. One you would not have had the strength to make." Then she, too, disappeared.

Bram collapsed onto the chair, his chest an echo of the snow-dark afternoon sky—empty and howling.

But hope flickered there, too, a dim star, far off, but giving off enough light to brighten his way home. Pippa believed he could fix this, and he would.

Chapter Twelve

Pippa looked out the coach window at the swirling snow. It seemed to pick up the conveyance and bear it toward a dark and unknown future, not the duke's home, where the horses logically trotted toward. Whether toward a warm townhouse or the unknown, Pippa traveled through a snowstorm with an icicle as a companion.

She did not mind that the dowager offered no conversational companionship. She used the time to ponder a solution. Surely Grandmama did not mean to foist her upon the *ton* after she had given herself to another man. The question itched inside her, would not let her go.

"Grandmama," she said, softly cracking the winter air around them like a thin layer of ice upon a bucket of water.

Grandma did not turn toward her.

"I know you are angry with me. And, likely, rightly so. What I did was beyond the pale. But... a debut is not what is best for me. I have lain with Bram Shaw, and now I must marry him. I want to marry him." Sound logic, and logic she liked at that.

A sniff. "A steward. A solicitor's son."

"A man I love."

"The best thing a woman can do for herself, Lady Philippa," the dowager said, "is to align herself with someone who can protect her. Love has nothing to do with it."

"But will not a man who loves you seek to protect you even more fiercely?"

"Ha." The dowager squirmed. Her jaw worked, as if she could not choose the words to pass between her teeth. "I loved a man once. Not my husband. I only tell you because I know you were wondering. The man I loved did nothing to protect me from my husband. He was not unkind, my husband, but he was also not considerate. He killed me each day with a thousand tiny pricks of disregard. The man I loved knew, yet..." She shrugged.

"Perhaps you should have married him instead."

"And be destitute? We are women, Pippa. What power have we to make lives of our own? We must align ourselves with those who have the ability to create safe lives. Mr. Shaw is a clever fellow, a charming one, handsome. I see the appeal. He reminds me of the man I loved. Who did not love me. Mr. Shaw will not climb higher in society by marrying you. Does he know that?"

"He knows I wish to live an obscure life far from London society. Yet he still wishes to marry me."

The dowager snorted. "He says that now. You will discover he does not mean it later."

Pippa considered, but not a single moment in her interactions with Bram suggested that was true. She shook her head. "You have him wrong. You are painting him with the brush of your own past."

"I merely want what is best for you, Lady Philippa. What is best for your sisters and for all my family. You are young. You do not understand, and you let your passions carry you away."

And why not when they'd carried her right into Bram's arms?

"If there is no babe in your belly, you will make your come out next season. You will attend every event, dance with every eligible gentleman, and prove to yourself that you can exist in your rightful sphere. That you are not afraid."

She shook her head. "I'm not afraid." She proved that even now by speaking her mind to this blade of a woman. "I merely do not wish to. Even if you ruin Bram's family and we cannot wed, even if he or I do not find a solution to this farce, I will not be anyone's puppet." She would not hide herself ever again.

In fact, she'd step away from her preferred solitary path. She'd thought she would be strongest alone, happiest. When Tabitha had offered to help her, she'd spurned it. Knowing the duke would support her, she'd refused to ask for it. Her family—Tabitha and Arthur, Sarah, Maggie, and their father, the duke's brother and mother—were a crowd she'd shied away from as surely as she'd avoided ballroom crushes. No more. She'd gather this crowd about her and fight for happiness, fight for herself.

Chapter Thirteen

Bram pushed through the townhouse door and shivered off the cold. No good. It had seeped into his bones, and he might never rid himself of the chill.

But somewhere, someone laughed, high and happy, and even from the front door, he felt the caress of a fire in a room down the hall. *Home*. How long had it been since he'd last paid a visit? Two years, at least. And how much had he missed this place, these people? More than he'd ever cared to admit.

He shrugged out of the still-soaked coat from the earlier drenching rain, and he unwound the damp, green scarf. Pippa's scarf. The one she'd bought for him. He dropped it on the round table in the middle of the entry and placed a hand over it, unable to let it go.

"Bram!"

He looked up.

A young girl barreled down the hallway in stocking feet. "Bram!"

"Elise!" He rushed toward her and caught in her in a hug, holding her so tight, her legs dangled in the air.

She laughed. "Put me down, Brother!"

He set her on her feet, and she wrapped her arms around him for another hug before looking up at him, gray eyes alight with curiosity. "You said in your last letter you would not return until Christmas Eve. It is not Christmas Eve. No matter." She took his hand and tugged him down the hall. "We've all missed you terribly."

They would not feel so kindly for him when they discovered his news. He'd lost his heart, lost his position, ruined a girl, and she'd saved his family from ruin. He inhaled a breath that rattled his chest.

"And I you, Lise."

She pulled him into a room where a fire roared. "Look who's home!"

Six heads turned at once—Mama and Papa, his younger brothers, Timothy, Liam, and Grant, and his remaining younger sister, Belinda. They stood at once, too, rushing him, crowding him, slapping him on the back and shaking his hand, hugging him and bussing his cheek with warm kisses. Their bright smiles sank stones in his belly.

"Papa." Bram choked back a tremor threatening to spill water from his eyes. "I need to speak with you."

His father's face grew curious, then stern. He preceded Bram into the hallway, then ushered him into his nearby study. His mother slipped into the room behind Bram. She shut the door, but the soft click echoed in the small, cozy space. A fire roared here, too, illuminating the worried creases between his parents' eyes.

Bram sat. "Sit, the both of you. You'll not like what I have to say. But I'd best say it quick."

His mother sat near him, slipped her hand into his, and squeezed. "What is it, darling?"

"I'm so very sorry. I've failed once again. But"—he heaved a sigh, raked his hands through his hair—"in a highly spectacular fashion."

His father scowled, his entirely white brows bulling low over eyes gray like Bram's. "Have you upset the dowager?"

"Ha! Mightily so. She's sacked me. And, I'm afraid, she's threatening to ruin you, Father, your business, your entire life. If I attempt to marry the woman I love."

"What?" his father roared.

"Love?" his mother whispered.

His father erupted into a violent pacing, rocking the room with his back and forth. He bellowed. What the content of his yells were, however,

Bram could not say. His mother had caught his gaze and held it just as surely as she did his hand.

"Love?" she whispered again. She leaned close. Her yellow hair, heavily streaked with silver white strands was pulled neatly into a bun at the nape of her neck, and her eyes glinted hazel behind gold-rimmed glasses. Her lips had curved into the softest of smiles. "You've fallen in love?"

"Aye, Mama. A marquess's daughter. A duke's sister-in-law. High above me, I know, but—"

Her free hand darted out, pushed a wet lock of hair off his forehead. "No. Not above you at all. Does she love you back?"

He nodded, the surety of his answer burning bright within him.

His mother's soft grin split open wide, her face shining.

"I do not know what to do, Ma. The dowager does not approve, and she threatens to rescind her business and her support, to ruin our reputation if we marry. Pippa—that's her name, Lady Philippa Hampton—wouldn't let it happen. And I can't, either."

"But what about you, Bram?"

"I'll figure it out."

She placed her hand on his heart, the corners of her mouth lilting downward and making a thin line of her lips. "My boy. Always such a big heart." She pulled away from him, her hands settling on her own lap, her face light as a cloud. "You need not worry about us. You may not know it, but you've provided more than enough for us over the years." She stood and made a path for the desk.

Bram scratched the back of his neck. "I'm absolutely positive I've done nothing of the sort."

His mother caught his father's shoulders and pinned him with the look they all knew meant, *Remain silent and listen.*

"Malcolm." There were at least six inches of difference in their heights, and she went up on toe to kiss his chin.

He blinked at her. "You heard the boy."

"I did. And I'd like you to retrieve Bram's Christmas gift."

"So we can burn it?"

"So we can give it to him now."

"Melody!"

"Malcolm."

His father stood tall and bellowed loud. He had eyes like marble and the confidence of a king. But he bowed only to his wife.

He crossed his arms over his chest. "Why?"

"Will we be ruined if the dowager rescinds her business?"

He opened his mouth. Snapped it closed. "She's quite a large account."

"But will we be ruined? What about Mr. Caldwell? Lord Mercer? Will you lose their business?"

The tobacconist? The antiquities collector? Both men he'd worked with for short periods of time.

His father glanced at Bram, a quick, feathery look. "No."

"And the others? Mr. Storr? Will we lose him or any of them?"

The jeweler Bram had briefly apprenticed under?

"No." His father huffed, his muscles melted, and he dropped a kiss on the top of his wife's head and strode for the door. "I'll return." He lifted a hand. "Sorry for the volume, my boy. Glad you're home. Circumstances... not perfect. But you always have known how to shake things up." He chuckled as the door clicked closed behind him.

Bram's mother returned to his side.

"I'm lost," Bram admitted, unfolding his palms to the ceiling. "Why were you speaking of Mr. Storr and Mr. Caldwell? All those men... I worked with them."

"Yes, and after you left, they remember your father's name well. You speak of family often, apparently. Your father has helped them all through various legal troubles through the years. They will not part with his services, no matter what an aging dowager says or does. They are loyal. As you are. You are free, you see. You came running over here, no doubt. You're dripping wet. Something we must remedy soon. But your fears are for naught. Do not sacrifice your happiness for us. You've already given us so much."

"I... I'm quite unprepared for this turn of events. I thought the two of you would scold at the very least. I've been so shiftless, and you have not been satisfied."

"You are the one unsatisfied, bouncing from position to apprenticeship like a child's ball. But not for the past two years. You've never stayed longer in a role. And now"—she gripped his hands again, her joy breaking free

—"you've fallen in love and wish to marry." She sat back once more. "I knew it was the right time."

"Right time for what?"

His father burst back into the room, waving a brown leather folio high. "I've got it, Melody!" He tossed the folio at them, and it slid across the satiny surface of a table. "Go ahead, boy, take it."

"What is it?" His hand trembled, reaching out, and it was not from the cold.

His mother spoke as his fingers met warm leather. "Blàr Hall."

Chapter Fourteen

Christmas morning, 1819

Christmas morning dawned white and yellow, and Pippa ignored the faint light shining through her window. She rolled onto her belly, pulled her pillow over her head, and gathered her courage. Today, she would tell her sister and brother-in-law everything. They would help her tell Father. And perhaps Grandmama's iron-clad control over this crowd of people would come to an end. She'd waited, hoping Grandmama would change her mind. She did not wish to drive a wedge between the woman who claimed she only wanted what was best for everyone and the family she ruled. Attempted to. Because Tabitha and Arthur had defied her. And today Pippa would defy her, too.

Pippa sat up straight, brushed her hair back calmly from her face. Everyone would be below, gathered round a fire in a parlor perfectly decorated with greenery and ribbon. And if she did not dress and join them, Tabitha would climb the steps and seek her out. Tabitha tired easily these days, looked rather peaked in the mornings.

So, Pippa dressed in the deepest green and pulled Bram's shawl around her shoulders, sinking deep. She'd not heard from him since the coffeehouse. If he did not contact her soon, she'd try to find him.

The parlor door stood open, and the flames from the fire within danced a merry jig upon the hallway walls.

Voices floated from the room, and a male form slipped into the hall and quickly clicked the door closed. Even in flame-flooded shadows, she knew his form. Bram. She flew to him, her shawl flying off one shoulder and puddling on the ground behind her as she flung her arms around him.

"*Oof.*" His arms, warm and strong and unexpected, wrapped around her, squeezed her tight.

She popped up on tiptoe and kissed him, caring not for who might see. She poured her heart into her lips and crushed his lapels in her hands as she dragged him down, closer, closer.

He laughed. "Pippa." Another laugh, his hands warming her shoulders. "Pip." He tried to set distance between them.

She pulled him tight. "Kiss me."

He groaned and did as she requested, then pulled away once more with a shake of his head. "Not here." He laced their fingers together.

She ran down the hall, stopping only to retrieve her shawl, and tugging him along behind her. She did not stop until they reached her room, and she slammed the door closed so hard it shook the walls.

He curved his arm around her waist and swung her around, pressed her back against the door, and dipped his head until his lips hovered just over hers. "Happy Christmas, Pip." He kissed her with a grin.

She deepened it, arching against his body, hard and warm and *hers*. She pulled away, panting. "Why are you here?"

"To claim you." A growl that earned him another kiss, this one hard and fast.

"You were with the others?"

He nodded, swallowed, the foggy lust dissolving from his eyes. He took a single step back and rolled his shoulders as his arms dropped away from her. "Can we speak without mauling one another?"

"I don't know why we should."

"You brazen thing. Come." He found the old armchair near the fireplace and sat in it. He patted his knee.

She sat on him, curling up in his lap and nuzzling his neck.

He curled one arm around her shoulders and, with the other, stroked his fingers up and down her leg, from knee to toes and back. "I was with the others. Your entire family and some of mine, actually. I was speaking with your father and the duke. I have asked them permission to marry you."

"But your parents—"

"Are not likely to be overly harmed by the dowager's retribution." He tiptoed his fingers up her shin. "Can you believe it... I'm not a failure after all. While I've left many a position behind me, I've not collected enemies. Many of the businesses I apprenticed with have since taken legal counsel of some sort from my father. Neither my father nor my family rely on the good will of the dowager and her cronies."

"I knew you were no failure. No one who runs such a large estate as Castle Clarebourn, so well as you, could be a failure. I am glad you have proof, though, to quiet your own fears. I know well how important that is." She kissed his jaw. "And my father? Did he approve?"

"Aye. And the duke. As long as I stay in London for the Christmas season in order to prove to them my worth."

She bristled.

"An acceptable request, my Pip. They've not known me until today. I'm happy to accede."

"I suppose."

"And Grandmama?"

"Furious."

"Naturally." Grandmama might never accept a steward into the family. But she did not doubt her sister and the duke would call Bram their brother. She was proud to be part of their crowd.

She pressed her palm against his heart. "And Blàr?"

"Is mine. Ours." He cupped her knee and stroked his palm down her leg, circling her ankle at the bottom.

Her body tightened and tingled with each new touch and caress, and she pressed as close as she could. Still not enough. The pulse between her legs ached, more urgent with every breath. Her brain had quite forgotten how to function.

"There are... specifics," she said softly and somehow roughly at the same time, "I need about each of these items. Unanswered questions." She lifted her face from his neck and met his silver gaze, warm with lust and the surety of a future together. "Can we answer them later?"

He dropped his forehead onto hers. "As much as I'd like to accept what must surely be an invitation into the sleep-rumpled bed behind you, I must decline. Our families are downstairs."

"I find I do not care." She snipped at his earlobe.

"My, but you're naughty."

"I am." She felt proud to say it. "I dare anyone to suggest otherwise."

He groaned and stood, lifting her like a mere kitten.

She clung tightly to his neck. "Bram! What are you doing? Sit back down!"

He strode for the door. "If you're naughty, I'll have to be nice. I wish to introduce you to my family and start the process of charming yours." He left her bedchamber and set her on her feet.

She pouted. Or pretended to. In truth, her limbs rushed quick with blood. She offered her arm, and he wove his through it. As they walked, she rested her head on his shoulder.

"What an unexpected Christmas gift. You." How perfectly thrilling.

"When the duke exclaimed you would wed whomever you wished, the dowager cursed everyone with red hair and took to her rooms. My father called for brandy to toast the occasion."

"Brandy? It's barely nine in the morning."

Bram shrugged. "Your father accepted, and when I slipped from the room, they were happily ensconced in a corner, bottle and tumblers in hand."

"I wish I'd seen it."

"I slipped out unnoticed to warn you."

"I'm glad you did. It was nice to have you for a moment to myself."

At the bottom of the staircase, he stopped, stroked his knuckles down her cheek, his eyes impossibly soft. "Will you have me to yourself the *rest* of your moments, too?"

"Whether they're here, Scotland, or Timbuktu, Bram Shaw, I want them all."

They kissed all the way down the hallway and only parted at the parlor door.

Bram squeezed her hand and turned the handle. "It's quite a crowd in there. Are you ready? Sure you won't swoon?"

She pushed the door open and, in front of every gaze that swung their way, kissed Bram full on the lips, a daring display.

A cacophony of noise answered her affection—laughter, applause, and gasps from every gaze that had swung their way.

It felt nice as a warm shawl in winter and as naughty as a chemise pooled forgotten on the floor. And she did swoon, just a little, into the arms of the man she loved.

Epilogue

May 3, 1820

Bram wiped sweat from his brow and marched through the halls of his home in mostly bare feet. He'd removed his boots, muddy from an afternoon walk, and whistled as he sought his wife. She spent her afternoons in a room open to the sun, sketching.

But when he discovered her, just where he thought she would be, she was not bent over a smudged bit of paper but over a letter.

He greeted her by sliding his hand around her neck and kissing the tip of her ear. "Pip."

She swatted him away, but when he caught her hand and raised it to his lips, she let him keep it.

And he let her remain furrowed over the epistle until she dropped it, and it fluttered to the tabletop.

"From...?" he queried.

"Tabby." She straightened and turned to face him. "She says Sarah is running them all a fine race this season. She was caught *kissing* a man." Her brow furrowed again.

He wanted to kiss her concern away, but he only squatted before her and took both her hands in his. "Is there to be a wedding?"

"No. Lillian caught the kiss, and the man ran."

"Bounder," Bram growled.

Pippa shook her head. "Sarah has always had enough imagination for three girls, but I never expected her to go quite in this direction."

"The kissing direction?"

"The daring direction."

"Don't see why you wouldn't expect it. She's had nothing but daring women to look up to, after all. Are you worried?"

Pippa stood, tugged Bram to his feet, and wrapped her arms around him. "A bit. But if she is being true to herself, I cannot scold."

"Shall we visit?"

Pippa's face brightened. "We've not yet been settled half a year, but it is Sarah's first season. Do you mind?"

"Would you mind? The crowds?"

"For Sarah, I'd brave anything."

"Let's go, then." He kissed the tip of her nose. "But"—he studied the clock—"it's almost two. What will we do about our weekly visitor?"

Pippa left him to tug on the bell pull in the corner of the room. "Today or after we leave?"

"Oh, today we'll drown her in tea and suffer her sniffs. But when we leave?"

The door swung open, a maid marched through, followed by the sweeping figure of the dowager, cane always at the ready.

"Can you not," she said, "use a proper room for tea?"

Pippa swept to her side and escorted her to a seat. "I like this one, Grandmama. All the sun."

Sniff.

Behind his back, where only Pippa could see, Bram lifted a single finger. *One*.

Pippa shot him a wide-eyed glare. *Stop,* it said. She knew he would not, not if it made her laugh later and scold him with her delicious pink tongue.

"Tea?" Pippa asked, pouring the steaming stuff into a cup.

The dowager took it and held it primly on her lap. "Mr. Shaw. You are not appropriately attired."

"But am I still handsome to look upon?"

Sniff.

Bram lifted two fingers behind his back.

Pippa laughed and bussed his cheek, then poured herself and Bram a cup. They joined the dowager, making a small steam-filled circle of silence.

The dowager never said why she came. She simply did. Every Wednesday since Pippa and Bram had moved into Blàr Hall four months ago. Likely, loneliness set her steps their way. And Bram had never been able to resist a lonely creature, even one like the dowager.

He swung his gaze to his wife—her lovely profile, her bright red curls, her naughty smile.

"Go ahead, then." The dowager sniffed once more.

Bram raised three fingers and tapped them on the arm of his chair.

"Go ahead what, Grandmama?"

"Go ahead and kiss proper! Hold her hand. Make *eyes* at one another. I know you wish to."

"Aye," Bram admitted. "I do. But I won't insult you. I know you dislike it."

"Bah." The dowager tossed her gaze across the room. Her thin lips, tightly pressed, trembled, and her hands, laid one over the other on top of her cane, shook. She gripped them tightly around the golden handle of it. "I am an old fool. A cruel old fool. Yet you two have given me a gift despite it all."

Pippa rose and sliced through the circle, sailing to her knees at the dowager's side. "What do you mean? Are you well?"

She had a point. The dowager never disparaged herself.

"Quite, as well as a woman my age can be." *Sniff.*

But Bram could not bring himself to make four fingers. Saddest sniff he'd ever heard. "A gift?"

The dowager waved an arm at them. "You escaped. I lived my entire life doing as others pleased and never daring, until it was too late, to do as I pleased." Her gaze dropped to her lap. "I apologize for trying to hurt you."

Pippa took the dowager's hands and squeezed.

The dowager shook her off, and Pippa returned to her seat, sipped her tea, tried to hide her smiles.

"Now." The dowager's voice rang clearer than before, purged from all dangerous bravado. "I know you have a letter from that duchess sister of yours, and I know it says more than mine does. Information if you please."

Pippa leaned forward and got that naughty glint in her eye. Usually, it appeared when she stripped him bare in their bedroom, but sometimes he saw it when she gossiped, dared, or teased.

He adored it. It was her truest state. It made her perfect for a man like him, who was much too nice to cranky dowagers and pretty, future debutantes that society said he should not touch.

He stood and walked around the room, letting the women's chatter settle joy into his bones. He stopped before the fireplace where a low fire growled lively and warm, and he slid his fingertips over the top of a small green and dark wood snuff box. They'd kept it for themselves, in the end. No one better than Casanova to remind them to be daring and always in love.

THE END

Thank you for reading *A Very Daring Christmas* by Charlie Lane!

See how Pippa's sister won the duke's heart with a dare, a kiss, and a perfect memory in *Daring the Duke*, book 1 in the *Debutante Dares Series*.

CHARLIE LANE
THE DEBUTANTE DARES
DARING THE DUKE

Also by Charlie Lane

The Debutante Dares Series

These debutantes don't fit the mold, so they'll break it. And dare the *ton*'s most eligible bachelors not to fall in love.

#1 Daring the Duke

#2 A Dare too Far

#3 Kiss or Dare

#4 Don't You Dare, My Dear

#5 Only Rakes Would Dare

#6 Daring Done Right

THE DEBUTANTE DARES SERIES

About Charlie

USA Today bestselling author Charlie Lane traded in academic databases and scholarly journals for writing steamy Regency romcoms like the ones she's always loved to read. Her favorite authors are Jane Austen (who else?), Toni Morrison, and William Blake, and when she's not writing humorous conversations, dramatic confrontations, or sexy times, she's flying high in the air as a circus-obsessed acrobat.

Connect with Charlie: www.charlielaneauthor.com

facebook.com/CharlieLaneRomance
instagram.com/charlielaneromance
bookbub.com/authors/charlie-lane
amazon.com/Charlie-Lane/e/B089G8541W

GENTLEMAN OF CHRISTMAS PAST

PREQUEL TO THE SISTERHOOD OF SECRETS SERIES

JENNIFER MONROE

Gentleman of Christmas Past by Jennifer Monroe

Published by WOLF Publishing UG

This is a work of fiction. Names, characters, businesses, places, brands, media, events and incidents are either the products of the author's imagination or used in a fictitious manner.

Any resemblance to actual persons, living or dead, or actual events is purely coincidental.

About the book

GENTLEMAN OF CHRISTMAS PAST

Miss Agnes Fitzsimmons will do whatever it takes to catch the eye of one Mr. Phillip Rutley. Even if it means bribing a courier to deliver letters to him herself. Tall and handsome, Phillip is everything Agnes's heart desires for Christmas. But looming financial burdens are keeping him from asking that one important question.

Will he ever propose marriage?

Phillip Rutley has always thought Agnes the loveliest woman he had ever met. The more time they spend together only makes his feelings for her stronger. Smart, witty, and beautiful, she is everything he could ever want in a wife. But with bankruptcy looming over him, Phillip postpones not only asking for her hand but also turning over his heart to her as well.

They each have one wish for Christmas.

As Christmas Eve draws closer, Phillip searches for a way to provide everything they will need for a comfortable life together. And for Agnes, she must also draw on her own strengths so they both can have the happily ever after they deserve.

Chapter One

Chatsworth, England November 1777

Five times Miss Agnes Fitzimmons had intercepted the courier. Today would be her sixth. As she waited, she pushed a stray strand of chestnut hair back under her bonnet. Leaning against the trunk of a tree beside the country road, she took a moment to gaze over the sweeping faded green hills dotted with tiny white cottages. A gentle, chilled breeze rustled the skirts of her green and yellow pelisse, one far finer than anything a young woman like herself could have owned if her life had not changed as it had.

Winter had arrived; the bitterly cold weather said as much. Yet, it did not deter Agnes from her mission as she pulled her coat tighter for extra warmth.

Beside her stood Amy, her lady's maid. A lady's maid! Who would have thought that she, Agnes Fitzimmons, would ever have a lady's maid? Yet, here stood Amy, wringing her gloved hands in the skirts of her maid's livery. And on the verge of tears.

A confidante and friend, Amy had been hired on as Agnes's personal maid four years earlier, when Agnes was but fourteen and Amy twenty. She had golden curls beneath her mobcap, a round face, and was a head taller than Agnes. If the maid did not have plans to leave to get married and thereafter move to Wales, she would have remained as Agnes's lady's maid after Agnes was ready to make her debut into society. Not noble society, certainly, but the gentry had their place. Which was beneath the aristocracy but certainly above where she had come.

Agnes placed a gentle hand on the maid's arm. "You've nothing to fear, Amy. Everything will work out as it should. You'll see."

"With all due respect, miss," Amy whispered with a fervent glance at the waiting carriage and the driver who might overhear, "but there's everything to fear. Whether or not you know it, Stephen's much more observant than you believe. What if he tells Mr. Porter? I know I'll be leaving soon, but I need my wages until then."

Agnes stifled a laugh as she glanced at the older driver, who stood beside the carriage picking at his nails. Stephen might have the sight of an eagle, legs so long he nearly sat doubled in his driver's seat, and less hair than a bald monkey beneath his black hat, but his hearing was worse than that of an earthworm. "I've paid him to keep quiet, so don't worry," she said with a wink. "Plus, he believes we're here at Mr. Porter's request."

Mr. Thomas Porter had taken Agnes off the streets of London and welcomed her into his home as his ward four years earlier. Not only had he provided her with the basic necessities of a stable home, food, and clothing, he also had given her extensive education and training on how to be a lady. And most importantly, he had given her hope. Something she never possessed living alone on the streets and fending for herself.

Every summer since Mr. Porter had taken Agnes on as his ward, the two would leave London to stay at his country estate in Chatsworth. Those were the days Agnes loved the most. London had its own beauty—once one left the dirty and poor areas from where she had come—but nothing compared to the fresh air and cool breezes of the countryside.

This year, however, they would not return to London. At the age of five and sixty, Mr. Porter's health was failing. Therefore, he was conducting the majority of his local business through the use of a courier. Thus, Agnes's reason for waiting beneath the silver birch tree beside the entrance to

Meadow Estate. This particular courier was bringing letters to and from one Mr. Phillip Rutley.

Mr. Rutley was a handsome man three years Agnes's elder, and she had found an instant attraction to him when they had met the previous summer. As he was an acquaintance of her guardian, however, she had put off mentioning her interest in him and welcomed men of Mr. Porter's choosing.

Yet, each was worse than the one before. Most were more interested in dandying themselves up than paying her any attention. If she was to marry any man, he would find her more interesting than himself. After her recent parting of ways with Lord Ezra Colburn, she had diverted her attention back to Mr. Rutley.

Amy continued her hand wringing. "I don't know, miss. I think he's pretending to be deaf. He's crafty, Stephen is."

Agnes sighed. "I'll prove it to you." She cleared her throat and raised her voice to a near shout. "Why, yes, I would love to drink a mug of ale unchaperoned with a gentleman."

Amy gasped and clutched Agnes's arm. "You shouldn't say things like that, miss!"

Agnes, however, was clutching her sides with laughter. "You see? He's oblivious to anything happening around him. You really shouldn't be so worried." Indeed, Stephen did not even glance up at her short tirade.

"You're terrible, Miss Agnes," Amy said. "It's a good thing I'm leaving soon, or you'd have me turning gray earlier than I should!"

After giving the maid a hug, Agnes took hold of her arms. "Don't worry. If Mr. Porter casts you to the streets before you're married, I've friends who can help you."

This had both women laughing, for Mr. Porter might reprimand her, but not Amy. Not when Amy had done nothing wrong. He was strict but fair, and although Agnes had changed much since becoming his ward, her mischievous ways remained in one form or another. After all, four years might be able to correct fourteen years of street living, but it would never be able to eradicate it.

And she suspected her early life lessons would always remain. Even if they were buried well beneath the surface of decorum and politeness.

A small trail of dust coming down the drive caught Agnes's attention, and she flicked a coin into the air with practiced ease. William Yates, a young man in his mid-twenties with blond hair the color of beach sand beneath a brown hat and the courier for whom she had been waiting, rode up and stopped beside her.

"I don't know why you're doing this," he said as he leaned over and handed her the letter he carried. "I feel like I'm taking part in some sort of crime."

A whispered "Agreed!" came from Amy, followed by a clearing of her throat when Agnes raised a single eyebrow in her direction.

Turning her attention back to the courier, Agnes said, "I don't understand why you must complain when I'm only making your work easier." She held the coin in the tips of her fingers and turned it this way and that. Unlike Amy, and perhaps because of her own upbringing, the cold did not force Agnes to wear gloves. Even if she should. "Shall I keep it? At least then, you mightn't be seen as an accomplice in this so-called crime."

They had exchanged similar banter the last few times she had waited for him, and with a hearty laugh, he handed her the letter. With a quick bite on the coin, he flipped it into the air and placed it into his coat pocket. Then he touched his hat and dipped his head before trotting away.

"Now, that wasn't so bad, was it?" Agnes asked, clutching the letter in her hand. "I meant it when I said I'm saving the man work. He carries a letter from my house to here—that's what? Two hundred feet? He not only earns what Mr. Porter gives him, but he also receives a bit more for less work. If you ask me, he's paid far too much!"

They returned to the waiting carriage, and Agnes said to Stephen, "Courtly Manor, please."

"Yes, miss," Stephen said with a wide grin as he opened the door for her. No, the driver would say nothing about this little escapade. He liked her too much.

Once the women were settled onto the plush bench, Stephen closed the door. Agnes glanced at the letter in her hand, and curiosity filled her. What could be inside? Although she intercepted the correspondences Mr. Porter sent to Mr. Rutley, she never opened them. Their contents were not what held her interest but were, instead, an excuse to see Mr. Rutley. Prying into someone else's affairs was not something she enjoyed. But that did not mean her interest did not remain piqued.

Half an hour later, the carriage trundled up the drive to Courtly Manor and came to a stop. A white-painted, three-story house with black window frames and ivy creeping up its facade, Courtly Manor was a lovely estate Agnes admired. Far too large for a single man, it was better suited to a large family. Why should she not dream that she was the wife of that family?

Beside the drive stood an oak tree, one which Agnes had noticed on her previous journeys here. Mr. Rutley had informed her that it was well over a hundred years old. She walked up to it and placed a hand against the gnarly trunk. In the middle of the rough bark was a smooth surface where a large limb had been removed. Although many would see it as nothing but an ancient tree, Agnes saw it as much more. There was a wonderful history surrounding it. Or so she believed.

"I wonder how many secrets have been shared here," she said before glancing at the maid. "Do you not feel something special about this tree? I know I do."

Amy smiled and placed her hand against the bark. "I suppose you can say it's regal in its way. What kinds of stories would it tell if it could talk? I imagine it has many. Many stories and many secrets."

Agnes nodded and leaned in close to the tree. "I'll tell you a secret," she whispered. "I refused to allow Lord Ezra to continue calling on me because I knew he loved the *idea* of me becoming his bride, but he loves no one but himself."

Amy gasped beside her. "I didn't know that, Miss Agnes! I thought he made the decision not to call. Isn't that what you said?"

"I did," Agnes said with a sigh. "But only because I didn't want to shame him. It's best we ended his calls. Oh, I enjoyed his company well enough and perhaps could have come to care for him after a fashion. But the truth is, I adore someone else."

"Are you saying that you've already developed feelings for Mr. Rutley? You don't love him already, do you?" The shock was clear in the maid's tone.

"Feelings for him, yes. Love? Of course not. Not in such a short time. But I shall marry him one day." Agnes cringed and turned to face Amy. "But you must keep that to yourself."

The look of concern disappeared, replaced with a smile. "Don't worry, miss. I won't tell a soul. But I'm so very pleased for you, I am."

"Thank you. Now, I've a letter to deliver."

They began the short trek back to the front door, but a man's cry from the side of the house made them stop and turn. A fellow in patched trousers held his hands out in front of him in an attempt to stop the powerful wave from crashing into him. And what a force she was.

A rotund woman, her honey-blonde hair tied up with a kerchief, held a pan above her head in a menacing fashion as she barreled after the man. "You didn't mean to kiss her, did you? Well, I'll just go and tell the magistrates I didn't mean to wallop you! It's just about as believable. Now, don't you ever come back here, or I'll have you fertilizin' the potatoes in my garden!"

During her years growing up in London, Agnes had seen women such as this—tough, sharp-tongued, and fearing no one. And few chanced getting in her way.

The object of the woman's rage turned and ran away so quickly, Agnes could not help but clutch at her sides in laughter. Interfering might not be appropriate, but she did not mind being a spectator.

"Oh, miss!" the woman said with a gasp as she dropped into a quick curtsy, the pan falling to the ground with a loud *clang!* "I'm ever so sorry you had to see that!"

Agnes wiped away a tear of laughter as she reached down to retrieve the pan. "No need to apologize," she said. "May I ask what happened?"

"That cad thought he could steal a kiss from one of the housemaids," the woman said. She glowered in the direction the man had run. "He won't be comin' back here again, not if I've got anything to say 'bout it. And trust me, I get my way when my way needs to be got." She said that with a firm nod. "Pardon my actions, miss. I know they can upset the sensibilities of delicate young ladies such as yourself."

Delicate? Agnes mused. Oh, but she loved this mysterious woman already. "As I said, no need for apologies. What is your name?"

"I'm Mrs. Shepherd," she said, drawing herself up to her full height, which was not all that tall. "The cook here at Courtly Manor."

"But you're so young!" Agnes said in surprise. "You can't be any older than I."

Mrs. Shepherd's cheeks reddened as she laughed. "Unless you're older than eight and twenty, which I'm doubtin' you are, then we're nowhere near the same age."

"Well, I suppose you may have a *few* years on me," Agnes said. "I'm Miss Agnes Fitzimmons, and I think what you did is splendid."

The cook smiled so widely the corners of her mouth nearly touched her ears.

"It's been a pleasure making your acquaintance, but I must be on my way," Agnes said with a glance down at the letter she carried. "But I do hope we'll have the opportunity to speak again at another time."

"I'd like that, miss," the cook said. "I best be gettin' back inside and check on Molly. She can make a mess out of frying an egg." Bobbing another curtsy, she returned to the house.

"'Speak again at another time'?" Amy said. "You truly believe you'll be living here one day, don't you?"

Agnes placed a foot on the portico and nodded. "I'll marry him," she said. "And Mrs. Shepherd will cook us wonderful meals. There is something special about that woman. I can see us having many chats in the kitchen."

Amy smiled. "You think that about everyone, miss. That they're all so wonderful. But why?"

As she reached up to knock on the door, Agnes paused. "It's all about hope, Amy. Everyone needs hope in their lives. And it's my hope that Mr. Rutley will be in mine."

Just as the words left her mouth, the door opened, and Mr. Phillip Rutley stood in front of her. With dark hair, a chiseled jaw, and deep-blue eyes, he was as handsome as he had been the last time she had called. No, handsomer!

"Miss Fitzimmons," he said as he smiled down at her. "What a pleasant surprise. To what do I owe this honor?"

With her heart racing and the pounding behind her ears, Agnes struggled to understand what he had said. Did she hear the word honor? Yes, that particular word had been a part of what he had said. But honor what? Did he honor her? Or did he make a request of her? Yes, that had to be it. He had made a request. What could he possibly request of her?

As he tilted his head, she feared she just might collapse. Therefore, she blurted the first words that came to mind.

"Yes, I would be honored to share in a cup of tea with you."

Chapter Two

Mr. Phillip Rutley's world was falling apart. Financial ruin had him searching for any feasible way of setting to rights everything he had lost. He had worked too hard building his tiny empire to go bankrupt now! How could so many tragedies happen all at once to one person?

His mine had stopped producing. As if a sluice had been placed in front of a stream, the tin dried up. Harland Curtis, the mine's foreman, had been as surprised as Phillip at the sudden disappearance of the lucrative vein they had found two months earlier.

One of his shipping vessels had sunk off the Irish coast when its dolt of a captain brought it too close to the rocky shores of Cork. Granted, Phillip had mourned the loss of the crew, for the ship could be replaced, but he also mourned the loss of the money he gave to help the grieving families left behind.

Then there were the cattle. Every head had to be slaughtered when a goodly number of them contracted some strange cattle plague. The illness spread through the herd faster than a wildfire during a drought.

"You've no choice, sir," Tom Rollins, his tenant farmer, had said. "If that many have it, they'll all likely have it. And you don't wanna be drinkin' that milk or eatin' that meat. You're best to just get rid of them all and start anew."

As if he had the funds to purchase new animals. Perhaps he should take the money out of Rollins's hide!

But no, Rollins was not at fault any more than Curtis had been.

Yet in all that destruction, Phillip saw a glimmer of hope in a young woman named Miss Agnes Fitzimmons, who currently stood beneath the large oak tree in his front garden.

Miss Fitzimmons was a sight to behold. She had dark brown hair, a perfect nose, high cheekbones, and a smile any man could appreciate. No, any man would appreciate *her*. She was lovely, witty, and had a sparkle about her that could light up any room.

The problem had been, she was romantically entangled with Lord Ezra Colburn, the wealthy younger brother of the Duke of Elmhurst. How could Phillip possibly compete with not only the man's wealth, but his noble blood as well?

Then a rumor arrived by way of a chambermaid that the two had parted ways. This news left Phillip overjoyed, of course. His joy was only increased with each call to deliver letters from the house of her guardian.

Each time she called, their conversations became more in-depth and personal. They took numerous strolls around the grounds, each longer than the last. Each time she left his home, the same feeling clung to him. Loneliness. Yet with her return, she brought him happiness once more.

He may have been pleased Miss Fitzimmons had been entrusted with such a responsibility, but even he had to admit it was odd. Why would Mr. Porter send his ward—and a female—rather than a courier? Yet Phillip had not objected. Only a fool would complain about the arrival of a beautiful young woman on his doorstep.

At least while it was his doorstep. These correspondences pertained to a possible agreement between Phillip and Mr. Porter, one that would determine Phillip's future and that of Courtly Manor.

Yet it would be a future he would not have with one Miss Agnes Fitzimmons. If only there was a way to include her in this transaction...

Shaking his head to clear his thoughts, he watched through the window of the parlor as the two women disappeared around the house. Now, that was strange. Why would they feel the need to use the servants' entrance? She had always knocked on the front door.

It was not long before a young man appeared from the side of the house Miss Fitzimmons had gone, running as if the devil was on his tail. Moments later, Miss Fitzimmons and her lady's maid also appeared, walking rather than running.

Curious as to what had occurred beside the house, Phillip left the parlor and headed to the foyer. Henton, his butler, had been given a free day. Phillip knew full well the man was seeking a new situation, and he had Phillip's blessing. After all, a man had to make a living. Word had gotten out that the estate was in trouble, but his staff knew firsthand.

Approaching the front door, Phillip drew in a deep breath and opened the door to find Miss Fitzimmons with her hand lifted toward the knocker. And what a sight she was to behold. Was it possible the young woman had become lovelier since the last time he saw her?

"Miss Fitzimmons," Phillip said, smiling, "what a pleasant surprise. To what do I owe this honor?"

Miss Fitzimmons gave him a blank stare, reminding him of the look of a man he had seen stunned by a blow to the jaw during a boxing match the previous year. If he had not already spoken to her on several occasions, he would have thought her feeble-minded. Would she not speak?

"Yes, I would be honored to drink tea with you."

Phillip chuckled when she covered her mouth in shock. Perhaps not everything in his life was turned upside down after all. He had not offered her tea, and she clearly was aware he had not, but if she wished to drink with him, he would take advantage of her nonsensical behavior before her lady's maid stepped in and played the dutiful chaperone.

"Then by all means, come in from the cold." He moved aside to allow the two women to enter. "I had promised you tea during your last call, did I not?" he added to ease her embarrassment.

"Y-yes, you did," she replied. She stopped to hand him the letter. "The reason I'm calling."

Thanking her, Phillip took the folded parchment and slid a finger beneath the seal just as Mrs. Shepherd entered the foyer, whistling an off-key tune he did not recognize.

She came to a sudden stop and gasped as she dropped into a feeble curtsy. "Apologies, sir," she said. Then she smiled at Miss Fitzimmons. "It's good to see you again, miss."

"And you, Mrs. Shepherd," Miss Fitzimmons replied. Her smile was somehow... secretive. "I take it you've been well?"

"What's this?" Phillip asked, amused. "I was not aware the two of you knew one another."

Miss Fitzimmons nodded. "Oh, yes. We've been acquainted for several years now. Mr. Porter wished to hire her on as the cook at Meadow Estate, but she was adamant that she wished to remain here."

Phillip laughed. "You never told me you had been propositioned, Mrs. Shepherd." The cook's plump cheeks went a deep crimson. "Since Henton is away, will you please bring us a tea tray?"

"I'd be happy to, sir," Mrs. Shepherd said. "'A good cuppa tea can solve any problem.' My mum always said that. It's also how she and my da spent their courtin' days, drinkin' tea together."

Phillip cleared his throat, and Mrs. Shepherd's blush crept up to her ears. She gave a quick curtsy and hurried out of the room.

"Mrs. Shepherd will talk for hours if you allow her," he said.

"Oh, she's absolutely wonderful," Miss Fitzimmons said with a laugh that Phillip found he adored. "I would think you'll wish to keep her here forever. At least, I would hope so."

A strange, but pleasant feeling came over Phillip at hearing her words. Was she suggesting that there was a chance of them having a future together?

Bah! He was overthinking the situation.

Or was he? Did his mother not say that as Christmas drew nearer, good things happened? Yet, he was not a child anymore but rather a grown man. Such wishful thinking was a waste of time.

He took Miss Fitzimmons's coat, making no mention of the missing Henton. Leading the women into the drawing room, he offered them the couch.

"If you don't mind, sir," the maid said, her eyes downcast, "I've brought some mending to see to. Might I sit over in that chair?" She pointed to an armchair that sat alone in front of the window.

"Yes, of course," Phillip replied, pleased at the relative privacy they would be gifted. "As long as Miss Fitzimmons does not mind."

"Not at all," Miss Fitzimmons said. "Amy takes great pride in her work." She glanced around the room. "I cannot help but admire your home, Mr. Rutley. It really is lovely."

"Thank you for saying so." He glanced down at the letter still unread in his hands and mumbled, "Let's hope I'll be able to keep it."

"I beg your pardon?" Miss Fitzimmons asked, her brow furrowed.

Phillip cleared his throat. "I'm curious, Miss Fitzimmons," he replied, choosing not to repeat, or expand upon, that utterance. She had no reason to know of his financial difficulties. "Why does Mr. Porter send you to deliver his letters? Does he not trust the courier?"

The maid coughed, but it was clearly to cover a snicker.

Miss Fitzimmons went to respond, then paused and looked toward the door. When it opened, Mrs. Shepherd entered, carrying a silver tray laden with all the necessities for tea.

Phillip could not stop his brows from rising. Her hearing was very good, far better than his. He had not even heard the cook returning.

Mrs. Shepherd set the tray on the table. "Would you like me to pour for you, sir?"

"No, thank you," Phillip replied. "I'll see to it. You may go."

The cook bobbed another curtsy, smiled at Miss Fitzimmons again, and then left the room.

"Now, you were saying, Miss Fitzimmons?" he asked as he poured the tea.

The corners of her mouth twitched. "I was saying nothing, Mr. Rutley. But to answer your question, I find personal joy in delivering the letters."

He handed a teacup to Miss Fitzimmons. "Is that so? And will you tell me why?"

"Because doing so gives me the opportunity to see you, and I try to take advantage of any opportunities that may come my way," she said in a matter-of-fact tone that not only surprised him but also had her lady's maid gasping in shock. The relative privacy was not as private as he had first thought.

Miss Fitzimmons's eyes twinkled, sending his heart into strange palpitations. "The question I find myself asking is, do you feel the same?"

Phillip stared at her, dumbfounded. How could one possibly explain the enjoyment he received by simply being in her company? That because of the various rumors that surrounded him, their friendly conversations could never mature into something more serious? Not until he was able to put his life into order, that is.

Grasping for words, he said, "I, too, cherish the moments you are here. When I learned you and Lord Ezra parted ways, I considered calling on you but never found the right time." That was a bit of a lie, but the truth was far too embarrassing.

She gave him a playful smile. "Are you saying you plan to call on me formally?"

Phillip was pleased. Never had he encountered a woman so forthright and honest! It was like a ray of sunshine breaking through a dense fog. Was this coquettish behavior common in Miss Fitzimmons? If so, time spent with her would be enjoyable, to be sure!

Wetting his lips, Phillip said, "I had hoped the weather would hold so we could eat alfresco, but with this cold that has settled in, it's unlikely. That does not mean we cannot enjoy a meal together indoors. Would you care to join me?"

Placing her teacup onto its saucer, she gave him a small smile. "I would be honored."

"Wonderful!" he said, excited at the prospect. He would have Mrs. Shepherd provide a wonderful lunch. "I'll see you then." His eyes went wide, and he shook his head. "I didn't mean to sound as if I thought you were leaving... that is, what I meant to say was that I want you to remain here with me."

Close your mouth, Rutley! You're making an utter fool of yourself!

Miss Fitzimmons pressed a hand to her breast. "Are you saying you mean to keep me here with you forever, Mr. Rutley?" Her tone sounded shocked, but that tiny lift to her lips confused him.

"Heavens, no!" he blurted out. Then she laughed outright, and he realized she was teasing him. "I must say, Miss Fitzimmons, you've a wonderful wit about you."

A mischievous grin crossed his lips. Two could play at this game. "Regarding this lunch, does two days from today work with your schedule? Once I've impressed you with my ability to entertain, we can decide on meeting another day. I'd like to take you to see the stream that flows through the property before it becomes too cold for such walks. It's one of my favorite places, you see. I spend a great deal of time there meditating on life in general." He grinned at her. "Now, you may choose to reject going to the stream with me, but you've no choice in accepting my invitation to lunch. I simply won't allow it. Therefore, you may as well get it over with and accept now."

The lovely melody of her laughter filled the room. Oh yes, he would enjoy being with this woman if only to hear that lovely melody for the rest of his life.

"I would love to," she replied. Then she winked. "Since you've forbidden me from declining."

They engaged in conversation over various topics. Miss Fitzimmons was learned in many areas. She was also unafraid to give her opinion on all sorts of matters, and he found that was what he liked that about her most thus far.

"The cost of war should not be measured in shillings but rather in lives," she said. "Only then can one weigh each decision without prejudice."

Phillip had never considered such a notion. And from a woman! Many of his friends spoke about their wives as if they were nothing more than decorations for their homes. Although he would never admit such a thing to any man, he found conversation with Miss Fitzimmons far more agreeable than time spent with his peers.

Their conversation turned once again, and Phillip found himself mesmerized by her every word, movement, and her smile. Yes, he could spend the rest of his life in her company.

Miss Fitzimmons looked up at the clock and gasped. "I cannot believe we've been here for over an hour! Amy, we really should be heading home. Did you not say you have several chores you must see to before the dinner bell?"

"Yes, miss," the maid replied.

Miss Fitzimmons stood. "I thank you for the tea, Mr. Rutley, and the wonderful conversation. I look forward to seeing you again. And the visit to the stream."

Phillip could not have been more pleased as they donned their coats, and he walked them to the waiting carriage. Before handing Miss Fitzimmons into the vehicle, he said, "I must admit, our conversations in the past have been engaging, but today was far better. I do enjoy your company."

"And I've found yours delightful as well," she said. "I'll see you in two days."

Once the carriage was gone, he returned to the drawing room. How quickly had his good fortune changed! He never believed a beauty such as Miss Fitzimmons would ever look his way, yet now he learned she had gone out of her way to see him. Phillip Rutley of all people!

Yet those feelings of elation plummeted as his gaze fell on the unopened letter. Knowing he could no longer postpone the inevitable, he unfolded the parchment and began to read.

Mr. Porter was never one to mince his words, although they were always kind. The last line of the letter was not what Phillip hoped to read.

And though I do wish you the best, I'm afraid that I cannot help you in this matter.

The paper floated to the floor from Phillip's numb fingers. Mr. Porter had been his last hope in saving Courtly Manor. Now, he would lose everything.

Including Miss Agnes Fitzimmons.

Chapter Three

Agnes alighted from the carriage at her home of Meadow Estate. Made of red brick with tall birch trees flanking each side, it was a lovely home. Carefully trimmed rose bushes that bloomed in the summer sat beneath the white-painted window frames. Meadow Estate was not as large as the other estates owned by her guardian, Mr. Thomas Porter, but it was spacious enough for two people and a full staff of servants. A far cry from the meager alleyways and crates in which Agnes had often slept as a child.

Closing her eyes, Agnes brought to mind the first time she arrived at this house. Mr. Porter had taken her on as his ward only six months before, and her visit to Chatsworth had been her first outside of London.

"You own *two* houses?" Agnes had asked, her voice reflecting the awe that filled her. She did not even have *one*! But what fourteen-year-old did? "I can't believe it."

Mr. Porter chuckled. "Oh, Agnes, I own many homes. I even own a small inn if you can believe that."

Agnes gaped at him. "I do. I do believe you." She glanced at the house again.

Two houses. No, more than two! Zooks!

"But what're we doing here, Mr. Porter? I like living in London."

In your house there, that is, she amended silently.

The London house had so many rooms, Agnes could not remember all their names. And now that she could read, she had been fond of spending time in the library. Granted, most of the books there were beyond her ability, but in the short time she had been taking lessons, she could pick out more than half the words on a page.

"I like to take time for leisure," her guardian replied as he placed a hand on her shoulder. "You'll continue your French lessons, and I've hired a woman to instruct you in proper etiquette while we're here. Mrs. Gouldsmith comes highly recommended."

"More lessons?" Agnes asked, knowing she sounded sulky but did not care. "Will they never end?"

Mr. Porter stopped at the front door, his hand on the handle, and turned to look at her. "Not until the day I deem you ready."

Sighing, Agnes opened her eyes and gazed once again at the lovely country home she had come to love. Her life had changed much over the years. That wide-eyed girl she had been was nearly a stranger now. She never imagined she could be so different in a mere four years.

"Miss Agnes," the butler said in greeting as she entered the house, "I trust your visit to the village was pleasant?"

"Quite," she replied as she allowed the butler to take her wrap. "Where is Mr. Porter?"

Before Garland could reply, voices rose from the direction of her guardian's study, answering her question for him.

"You're a fool, Walcott!" Mr. Porter was saying as Agnes drew near the room. "You of all people should know that Drake Street will gladly praise your name whilst plucking your money right out of your hand. They should change the name to Rake Street as disparaging is the establishment they keep there."

"It's a tavern, Porter, not some den of iniquity!"

"It most certainly is not!" Mr. Porter shouted. "I knew your father very well and had a great deal of respect for him. Hell, I even knew you when you were running around your family estate in your short pants. I may not have a title attached to my name, but even I know what goes on there. Don't lose your fortune—and your new bride—because of your willingness to make poor decisions."

A loud snort of derision filled the room before Lord Walcott said, "I don't have to take this from anyone, least of all from someone like you! I'm an earl, for blasted sake! At least show me a bit of respect!"

The tall man, whom Agnes liked—except when he had consumed far too much alcohol, which he had done often as of late—stormed out of the study, nearly barreling over Agnes in his rush to leave. His dark hair was mussed, as if he had not combed it in days, and his brown eyes flashed with anger.

"Good afternoon, my lord," she murmured, giving him a light curtsy.

He gave her a quick nod and moved past her but said nothing. A whiff of brandy followed in his wake. Yes, he was likely drunk already. So sad, that.

Agnes turned to find Mr. Porter looking at her. "We must speak," he said rather bluntly. "Come in and sit down."

Agnes swallowed hard. Did he know she had been intercepting the letters? Likely not, but if not that, what could he possibly want to speak to her about?

As she lowered herself into the chair he indicated, Mr. Porter began coughing so violently, he had to grip the desk to steady himself.

Agnes leapt from the seat and began rubbing his back. "Would you like a glass of water?" she asked. Her guardian's health had deteriorated over the last six months or so, and Agnes feared for him.

"Air would be far more useful if you have it," he said with a wink. The fit seemed to have subsided, but his breathing still came in gasps.

With a laugh, Agnes returned to her seat. That was how Mr. Porter was, no matter the circumstances. To him, humor was as much a necessity as water—and air.

"Is all well with Lord Walcott?" she asked.

"He's young and reckless," her guardian said as he moved to drop into the chair behind the desk. "Just like you were when I found you. You've become a proper young lady since then. But I'm not surprised. I recognized her inside that street urchin you once were the moment I set eyes on you."

Agnes beamed at the compliment, followed by a twinge of guilt. Proper young ladies did not lie. Nor did they bribe couriers to allow her to intercept letters.

"There is no simple way to say this, Agnes. I fear my time on this earth is soon coming to an end."

"But—"

Mr. Porter held up a hand to forestall her, and she swallowed back the argument she meant to make. But the knot in her throat remained.

"Don't worry. I'm not dying tomorrow. Doctor Stapleton believes I have a bit more time left than that." He chuckled, but Agnes did not see the humor in any such discussion. He'd been old when he had found her in that shop four years earlier, when he had saved her from a beating by the proprietor after she had tried to hide a block of scented soap inside the pocket of her dress.

Some would have thought stealing soap a waste of time. Food was much more worth the risk. And to a point, that was true. Agnes, however, thought beyond her immediate needs. For too long she had lived day by day, if not hour by hour. If she had soap, perhaps she could have a proper wash. And if she had a proper wash, maybe she could find employment so she would no longer have to steal to live. After all, proprietors frowned on unkempt and dirty employees. But they scowled at and beat thieves.

Despite her unconventional plans, however, Mr. Porter had rescued her from not only a beating but also from a life of poverty. And for that, she was forever grateful.

Knowing he was dying made her heart clench. He had been kind to her in the years she had acted as his ward. She received training on how to be a lady, was given whatever she needed and wanted, and not once had he asked for anything in return.

"Nevertheless," he continued, "I've begun preparations for when that day does come. I've been able to amass a small fortune, and I must leave it to someone. Do you have a guess as to who that someone is?"

Agnes nodded. "Your cousin James." She had met the man only twice and did not like him. He had nothing but cruel words for everyone to whom he spoke. Even Mr. Porter. And if anyone was cruel to Mr. Porter, she did not like him. "Unless you have another cousin?"

Mr. Porter shook his head. "When my Margaret died," he was referring to his daughter who had died at a young age, "I thought Jane and I would have more children. But... well, that did not happen, did it?"

Agnes gave a sad shake of her head. Mrs. Porter, whom Agnes had never met, had taken her own life after the death of their daughter. From her understanding, the poor woman had been unable to endure the grief, and Mr. Porter never remarried.

Because he was left a widower and childless, he had chosen to take on Agnes as his ward. Why her, she never understood, for her guardian never explained whenever she took up the need to ask. Perhaps it was the circumstances in which he had found her or that recognition of her innate abilities, but he had not considered taking on a ward until he found her. Or so he had explained when she had inquired of him.

"But then you came into my life," he said as he leaned back into his chair with his fingers steepled in front of him. "In four short but wonderful years, you became the lady I knew you could be. I've come to see you not as a ward, but rather as a daughter."

Unbidden, a tear rolled down Agnes's cheek. "Thank you, Mr. Porter. You're the only father I've ever known. I cannot thank you for everything you have done for me. And I'm not speaking of the dresses or the various lessons you've afforded me, although I do appreciate them. More than you can ever know. No, I mean your willingness to love me as your own. I'll never forget the kindness you've shown me."

"Agnes," he said, running a hand through his silver hair, "because I view you as my daughter, upon my death, I'm bequeathing everything to you."

Her jaw dropped. "To me? I don't understand."

Mr. Porter rose and walked around the desk to place a hand on her shoulder. "It's because I love you like a daughter. No one is more deserving than you. I wouldn't have it any other way."

Tears flowed down her cheeks as she rose and embraced him. "And I love you like the father I never had." Then that twinge of guilt made her pull away. "I must confess something. Mr. Phillip Rutley—"

Mr. Porter laughed. "Do you mean how you've been intercepting the courier in order to deliver my letters yourself?" he asked. "I'm already aware of this."

"You are?"

"Of course. I found it odd when you wanted to go into the village every time I sent for a courier to deliver a letter for Mr. Rutley. That and I was able to convince Yates to confess."

"But why did he not say so today?" Agnes asked, unable to believe that her carefully laid plans had been so easily thwarted.

"Because I asked him to keep it between us," Mr. Porter replied. "It was well worth it to him, too, since he was paid thrice to carry a letter from the house to the end of the drive. Keeping secrets can be a lucrative business, I suppose."

"I'm sorry for lying to you," Agnes said. "I promise never to do it again."

"I know you're sorry. Now, in regard to Rutley. I've no reason to disapprove of him, but you must keep your wits about you. You're a highly intelligent young woman, so I trust you'll be prudent with your decisions concerning him."

Promising she would, Agnes soon went to her room and lay upon her bed. Mr. Porter had done so much for her, and she would do everything she could to honor him.

And as her thoughts drifted to Mr. Phillip Rutley, she let out a sigh. In two days, they would spend time together again in his home. A place where she may just one day live. They had the chance for a wonderful future together.

A memory came to Agnes's mind. The year before Mr. Porter had taken her in his as his ward, Agnes and two girls with whom she was acquainted had been discussing Christmas. One of the girls, Frances by name, swore a miracle took place every Christmas since the first.

"All we have to do," she insisted, "is make a wish, and 'cause it's Christmas, it's got a better chance for comin' true."

Despite the fact that belief in such dreams belonged to the young, Agnes closed her eyes and whispered a wish. If all worked out as she hoped, by Christmas, Mr. Rutley would make a promise to be in her life for many years to come.

Chapter Four

Pushing aside the open letter, Phillip leaned back in his chair and sighed. He had written to all the most prominent men in and around Chatsworth, requesting an audience to discuss an investment possibility. In all fairness, they had all responded but in the same manner.

My schedule is far too full to agree to a meeting at this time.

Well, that was not true. Not all had rejected him outright. One man had taken an interest, although it was short-lived. In the end, Mr. Thomas Porter had also denied Phillip's request to meet.

What was strange was the fact that, today, he would be meeting the man's ward for lunch. Warm weather had once again returned, and therefore, he chose to have the picnic lunch he had first intended. Perhaps it was an omen of good things to come.

Despite Phillip's optimism about the weather, he continued to struggle with what he considered Mr. Porter's inconsistencies. Mr. Porter trusted Phillip to spend time with his ward and yet refused to do business with him. With that type of trust, did he and Miss Fitzimmons even stand a chance at a possible relationship?

What young woman wanted a man nearly bankrupt and on the verge of losing his most viable asset—Courtly Manor? Once Miss Fitzimmons learned of his financial standing, she would turn and run. And he would not blame her.

The humiliation at the possibility of losing his home had plagued him with nightmares, terrible dreams in which the villagers gathered in the middle of Chatsworth to mock him as his possessions were sold to the highest bidder.

This would not happen today, nor tomorrow, however. Phillip had enough money to survive another three, possibly four, months. Then the end would come.

"Sir?"

Phillip looked up at Henton, who stood at the door, his light-brown hair parted in the middle and brushed down. "Yes?"

"Miss Fitzimmons's carriage is coming up the drive. You asked me to keep a lookout for it."

"Thank you. I'll meet her out front." He shrugged on his coat and made his way to the portico, where he waited for the driver to place a step.

When the door opened, Phillip smiled. Miss Fitzimmons's dress robe *à l'anglaise* reflected the simple taste of the era. The wide overskirt was cream-colored with brown trim and opened in the front to show a white underskirt. No bows, no flowers, no lace, just simplicity. And she could not have been lovelier. Her beautiful face was shaded by a large bonnet covered in the same fabric as her dress.

Phillip could only stare at her, his mouth and throat as dry as cotton wool.

"Good afternoon, Mr. Rutley," she said with that twinkle in her eye he had come to admire greatly. "I must make an admission. I've been looking forward to this outing since the day you invited me."

He bowed. "As have I." He offered her his arm, which she took without hesitation. "Mrs. Shepherd prepared a wonderful selection of food for us. We'll eat beneath a marquee I had raised. It is a lovely day, don't you think?"

"I've fared worse weather," she said in her sweet voice. "But yes, I find the weather—and company—more than acceptable." Her beauty increased when her cheeks turned pink.

Phillip smiled as he led her to the marquee that had been set up beneath the lovely oak tree. Beneath the cover sat three chairs and a table.

Miss Fitzimmons smiled. "I see you prepared a place for Amy."

"I expected you would arrive with a chaperone. Whether she be your lady's maid or some other companion remained to be seen." He turned to the maid. "I hope you feel comfortable sitting with us."

Miss Fitzimmons placed a hand on Phillip's arm. It was strange, but he swore he could feel heat emitting through the fabric of his coat and her gloves. "If you don't mind, I'd rather Amy move her chair over there and read." Phillip nodded, pleased by this decision. "Of course."

He picked up one of the chairs and moved it to a place just outside the marquee. Then she sat, opened up her book, and began reading.

"It looks like it will be just the two of us, then," Phillip said as he pulled out one of the chairs for Miss Fitzimmons. Then he poured her a glass of wine before taking the chair across from her. In his glass, he poured water provided in a tall, clear decanter. He was not opposed to drinking for moral reasons, nor would he shame anyone for indulging from time to time, but he preferred to keep his wits about him.

"Are you hungry?" he asked as he removed the dome cover from a large platter in the middle of the table.

Miss Fitzimmons shook her head. "No, the wine is plenty for now."

As Phillip took a sip of his water, he took the liberty of admiring her lovely face over the rim of his glass. Stunning. Yes, that was the correct term. She was a stunning woman. That was how he would have described her from the first time he had laid eyes on her the previous summer. And every moment since.

But when she honored him with that special playful smile of hers, he found himself longing to be in her company. As much as he possibly could.

"You seem to be far away," she said. "What are you thinking about?"

For a moment, he had no response. Could he be truthful and remain honorable? No, likely not. Not with some of the thoughts that were going through his mind. Such as holding her in his arms and kissing her...

"Work," he replied.

Miss Fitzimmons laughed. "You know, I've a special gift of which few are aware. I have the ability to tell when someone is lying. And you are doing just that. Now, what was truly on your mind?"

Phillip drew in a deep breath. "I was considering how, from the first time I saw you, I thought you beautiful, and since then, my admiration for you has only grown stronger."

She smiled and took another polite sip of her wine.

He nearly groaned. *She must think me a terrible cad!*

"Since you've chosen to be honest with me, Mr. Rutley, I'd like to make a confession to you."

Taken aback, Phillip said, "A confession? What can you possibly confess to me?"

"The letters you received from Mr. Porter? Well, he was unaware that I've been playing his messenger."

Phillip frowned. "That makes no sense. If he doesn't know, how did you come to have them in your possession?"

"I simply stopped the courier after he had collected the letters from Mr. Porter, paid him a small sum, and he gave me the letters. Then I delivered them myself." She shrugged. "It really wasn't all that difficult."

"But why? Why would you do that?"

Miss Fitzimmons sighed as she placed her glass on the table. "When we spoke those few times last summer, I enjoyed your company very much. I just knew I had to find a way to see you again. When I learned that Mr. Porter was sending you regular correspondences, I assumed it was the only way to see you without being seen as improper. Each time I made my delivery, we spoke a bit more, and I found I could not wait to play courier again."

Her tone was so matter-of-fact, Phillip nearly laughed. What a delightful young woman she was!

"I, too, found myself hoping you would be the one to come to my door, Miss Fitzimmons. I must be honest, if Yates had been standing at my front door today rather than you, I would have been greatly disappointed."

Miss Fitzimmons blushed as she turned her glass in her hand. "May I ask you a question?"

"Of course. Anything."

"If you are so eager to see me, why not simply call on me at Meadow Estate?"

The question was fair, and Phillip wished to be honest. Yet doing so would surely make Miss Fitzimmons leave. And that, he did not want.

"I've been working on certain... issues with my business prospects," he explained. "Plus, there was Lord Ezra. I must admit, when I learned he was a suitor, I was downhearted. I hope you don't mind me saying so, but when I learned the two of you parted ways, I must admit that I was pleased. Yet if you rejected a man of his standing, what does that say about the odds of me winning you over?"

He paused. Had he revealed too much? Would she believe him weak for expressing himself so openly?

To his surprise—and dare he say, pleasure—Miss Fitzimmons placed a gloved hand atop his and said, "Lord Ezra is in the past. I'm now here with you. Not because of standing but rather because of the simple fact that I like you and wish to be in your company."

Phillip considered her words. Admitting aloud that he failed at business was something he was unwilling to do. A man stood or fell based on how many agreements he made or how many contracts he signed. "I want nothing more than to spend time with you. But..." He sighed. "There are matters in my life, personal matters too complicated to share with you at this time. Not that I feel you're unable to understand them but rather because they are issues that have complicated my life as a whole."

Slowly, she removed her hand from his, and Phillip cursed himself inwardly. *You fool! She's no dimwit. You've now gone and driven her away! You blasted, blasted fool!*

Miss Fitzimmons smiled. "I've come to realize that life is complicated for everyone, even for those who deny that fact. Yet if we push ahead, we can succeed. Mr. Porter taught me that there is always hope. No matter what happens today, tomorrow, or even next year, Mr. Rutley, you must never lose hope."

How could such a young woman be both beautiful and wise? Phillip had never considered women ignorant, not in general, but few possessed the intelligence and wit of Miss Fitzimmons.

He smiled at her. It was as if all his worries had gone. Oh, he was not witless enough to believe they had disappeared for good, but at least he had a reprieve—even if only for a short while.

"I'll not lose hope. Miss Fitzimmons, in the few weeks we've become better acquainted, we've learned much about each other. Yet you've not told me how you came to be a ward to Mr. Porter."

Miss Fitzimmons took a sip of her wine before responding. "As it is,

Mr. Porter is a distant cousin of my mother. Well, I suppose that makes him my distant cousin, as well." She shook her head. "Regardless, Mother was unable to take care of me, so Mr. Porter took on the responsibility."

"Do you still speak to your mother?" Phillip asked.

Miss Fitzimmons shook her head. "She died in the interim." Then she smiled. "But we're not here to discuss those who've died, are we? Now, you told me your parents left for America two years ago. Why did you not join them? It seems a journey to America would be quite an adventure."

"I have no desire to see foreign lands," he replied. "Life here in England is adventurous enough for me."

Over the next hour, they discussed a variety of topics as they feasted on the selection of dried meats and cheeses Mrs. Shepherd had provided for their meal. By the time Miss Fitzimmons rose from her chair to leave, Phillip felt much closer to her. And he found himself not wanting her to go.

"You've not drunk any of the wine," Miss Fitzimmons said. "I thought it was quite good. Do you not like it?"

Phillip glanced at the bottle. "I've never been interested in drinking. I may take a few polite sips from time to time, but drinking alcohol creates too many problems."

Miss Fitzimmons nodded sadly. "Overindulgence certainly can be problematic. I've seen its effects far too often. You're very wise to make such a decision. Few men with whom I'm acquainted recognize its effects before it is far too late, and they are stumbling over their words. Or their feet."

Phillip laughed as he rose from his chair. "You're correct in that assessment. I know you must leave soon, but would you care to take a short stroll around the gardens with me?"

"I would love to," she replied, smiling broadly.

He pulled out her chair and offered his arm, which she took without hesitation. The maid followed closely behind.

They made their way to the cobbled path that marked the beginning of the gardens, past an outbuilding where the gardener kept his various tools.

As they approached one of the many barren flowerbeds, Phillip stopped to pick a single pink rose from one of the many well-maintained bushes. How had it survived when all the others had succumbed to the cold? Another omen perhaps?

"This rose has endured where all others have failed," he said, turning it by its stem. "Like you, it's unique and worthy of the admiration of anyone who sees it." With a smile, he turned to Miss Fitzimmons. "I think it only fitting a young woman as lovely as you should have this," he said, offering her the flower. "Even it cannot match your beauty."

Miss Fitzimmons put the flower to her nose and inhaled deeply. "I do like roses," she said with a smile. "I save the best specimens to dry so I can enjoy them long after they are removed from their vase. I hope to collect a dozen over the coming summer. Perhaps each time I call, I'll receive one to add to my collection."

"Miss Fitzimmons, if everything works out as I hope, you'll have a thousand of them."

And he could not have been more truthful. If he had it his way, she would have everything her heart desired.

All he wanted in return was her at his side.

Chapter Five

The High Street in Chatsworth teemed with people on Saturday afternoon. Some, like Agnes, strolled at a leisurely pace, taking time to stop at every window to see what new items the shops carried since their last visit to the village. Others hurried to finish errands for themselves or for their employers with no time for browsing.

Although only two days had passed since she and Phillip had picnicked together, she longed to see him again. The words he spoke to her that day, that he wished to give her a thousand roses, consumed her every waking moment. And several of her dreams. The thought that he was willing to make her happy made her heart soar, her thoughts muddle, and her breath catch.

She had no doubt as to what he had implied. He was promising her a future together. With him.

Yet two problems tugged at the back of her mind. As to her first, to what extent did he care for her? It was one thing to promise a thousand flowers and quite another to believe there was a chance for love. Men in general struggled to express themselves, especially when it came to matters of the heart. They were so silly believing that speaking of love was weak.

Agnes had promised herself she would not marry for anything but love. That had been her reason for breaking off any further entanglements with

Lord Ezra. He cared more for accumulating wealth than he ever would for another person. She refused to play a subservient role to an aspiring empire.

Her second cause for concern pertained to whatever "issues" with which Mr. Rutley was dealing. She had heard the rumors about him struggling financially, but if that were true, why would Mr. Porter engage in business with him? If she had learned anything about her guardian, it was that he was a competent businessman.

Amy walked beside Agnes as they passed the various shops, stopping in front of the local bookshop. Mistrels was a newer establishment, but it had proven to be a wonderful resource for all sorts of reading material. Mr. Porter allowed her to purchase as many books as she wanted to add to his already expansive library.

That did not mean she would purchase every book offered, of course. If her previous life taught her anything, it showed her that no one was happier simply because they had more things. Including books.

Gray skies filled with clouds said cold would soon replace the unseasonably warm temperatures they had been enjoying. Agnes was accustomed to the ebbs and flows of English weather, and she adapted easily. Anyone who was forced to endure her previous life learned to acclimate to the ever-changing weather. What choice did she have? Agnes smiled as a boy of perhaps seven approached her. He wore a grin that lacked a front tooth as he stopped before her. With unkempt blond hair, trousers that were far too short and full of patches, and dirt on his cheeks, it was clear the lad lived a hard life. Much too hard for a boy his age.

"'Scuse me, miss, but would ye wanna buy a top?" he asked. In his grimy hand lay a finely crafted wooden top. "Me da makes 'em. If ye've a son, he'd like it, I bet. Boys like tops. I know I do."

Agnes took the top and studied it. "Your father is a very good craftsman," she said. "But I'm afraid I've no children seeing as I'm not yet married." She returned the top to his hand. "But I do thank you for offering it to me."

The boy frowned. "Don't all ladies become mothers?" he asked. "I'll bet ye'll 'ave lots of kids. But what then? What'll ye do when ye've got yer son, and he ain't got this grand toy? Don't ye think he'll be sad?"

Amy gasped, but Agnes found herself laughing at the boy's cleverness.

"Why, I hadn't considered that! Perhaps you're right." She held out her hand, and the boy returned the top to her.

Agnes sighed. Although she had considered the prospect of perhaps one day marrying Mr. Rutley, she had not thought about the inevitable children that would follow. She had always wanted a daughter, perhaps a few, but a boy would be nice, too.

The door to the bookstore opened, and Mr. Mistrel, the proprietor, poked his head out. "Adam, you leave those ladies alone, you hear me?"

The boy's cheeks reddened, and Agnes could not help but feel sorry for him. "Young Adam and I were just completing a business transaction, Mr. Mistrel." She turned her attention back to the boy. "Now, how much do I owe you?"

Adam named an amount, and Agnes frowned, insisting it was far too much to pay for a toy. It really was not, but her experience said one did not simply pay outright a named price. They spent several minutes haggling. Indeed, the boy seemed to enjoy that as much as the coin she had placed in his hand once they arrived at an agreed-upon amount.

"Thank you, miss!" Adam said, his smile nearly splitting his face in half. With a bow, he skipped away. By that time, Mr. Mistrel had returned to his patrons.

Agnes and Amy resumed their walk.

"You're going to marry him, aren't you?" Amy asked.

Agnes laughed. "Adam? He may be a bit too young for me. Don't you think so?"

Amy gave Agnes an exasperated sigh. "Of course not. I mean Mr. Rutley. Forgive my forwardness, but I can see it on your face. After what he said about the roses, I'd say he wants to marry you, too." She blushed. "I wasn't trying to listen, miss, but sometimes I can't help it."

Agnes laughed. "Is that not what you're meant to do, Amy? Otherwise, you never know what sordid discussion Mr. Rutley and I may be having!"

When they arrived at Drake Street, Agnes grabbed hold of Amy's hand and pulled her into a nearby alleyway. "Do you think me mad for wanting to marry him? I feel as though I know everything about him yet know nothing. But I also feel as if we're meant to be together."

"You're not mad, Miss Agnes," the maid said. "You've always said you want to marry for love, but are you saying that because of the gift of a rose, you're now in love with him?"

Agnes frowned. "Well, no, of course not. It was a wonderful gesture, and my feelings for him are growing. But I cannot say it's love just yet. I don't even know if I understand what love is."

Amy gave a shy smile, her cheeks now crimson to her ears. "When I first met Guy, I knew I loved him. Trust me, when it hits you, you'll know whether it's love."

"Thank you," Agnes said, embracing the maid. "Let's go through here. It's a faster way to the dressmaker's shop, and I heard Mrs. Thompson has a new seamstress who is fantastic with a needle and thread. I think her name is... oh, what was it? Oh, yes, Mrs. Newberry."

Amy gasped. "We can't go through here, miss! It's dangerous. Don't you know there's a tavern where men not only drink until they can't stand upright, but they also gamble away every bit of money they have?"

Agnes laughed as she snaked an arm through that of the maid. "Have you forgotten the young girl from the streets of London you met four years ago? I may not act like her now, but I've retained my ability to walk safely through a darkened alleyway."

"I suppose," Amy replied, worrying her bottom lip and giving a frightened look at the narrow passage. "But you're cultured and all now. It's because of that, I don't think it's a good idea for us to be caught here."

Agnes ignored her and continued down the alleyway. It snaked like a winding river, the tall buildings on either side acting as its banks. Halfway down was a tavern, but as Amy had mentioned, it was rumored that much more than drinking went on in the establishment. So terrible was its reputation, that some had begun calling the alleyway Rake Street.

The tavern catered to men from all levels of society. From what she heard, the proprietor—and the handful of prostitutes who frequented the place—saw not the man but rather the money gained through him.

Including one Lord Walcott who, at the moment, bounded down the steps with a woman who was not his wife calling after him.

"Henry, darling, why'd you wanna leave me? There's nothing wrong with a gentleman having a lady friend."

Agnes clenched her fist. Five years older than she, Lord and Lady Walcott were a lovely couple married less than two years. She and Lady

Walcott had become fast friends, and Agnes had been invited over for tea several times whenever she was in Chatsworth.

She was uncertain if it was her willingness to keep a secret, the fact she was not of the aristocracy, or both, but on one of those occasions when Agnes was the only guest, the countess had confided her worries about her husband and his propensity for gambling.

He waved a dismissive hand at the woman calling after him—at least he had the decency to keep away from women of loose morals—and came stumbling toward Agnes and Amy.

Upon seeing Agnes, his eyes widened, and he came to an abrupt halt. "What are you doing here?"

Agnes pursed her lips. "I could ask the same of you, my lord."

Lord Walcott snorted. "I'm an earl, girl. You've no right to speak to me in such a disparaging manner!"

The liquor on his breath clogged her senses, and she took a step toward him, ignoring the urgent tug on her arm from the maid.

"I consider you a friend and a gentleman, not a man who leaves his wife at home worrying, so he can parade about in this degrading establishment. Have you no decency?"

"How dare you!" the earl growled, rearing his head back in obvious affront.

Placing her hands on her hips, Agnes glared up at him. She could not have cared less if he was an earl or Prince George. His behavior was appalling, and she would not hold her tongue!

"I just did!" she snapped. "You've a wonderful wife who loves you. If you wish to ruin a marriage of which very few can dream, all over games of chance and cheap brandy, that is your decision. But I suggest you consider her before deciding."

He gaped at her, clearly stunned by her candidness. Perhaps he would cut out that tongue she chose not to hold...

Well, she only told the truth!

Agnes placed an arm through that of Amy and added, "Come, Amy, we've more important matters to attend to. Let him ruin his life if he so chooses." And with that, they walked away.

"What have you done?" Amy whispered after glancing over her shoulder for the tenth time.

"Hopefully, I saved a marriage," Agnes replied firmly.

"But what if he tells Mr. Porter? What'll you do then?"

Agnes stopped and turned to the maid. "And what will he tell Mr. Porter? That I found him stumbling out of the tavern with a prostitute calling after him, as if she had some right to him? Oh, Amy, don't you see? Often the truth we need is not the truth we want to hear. Lord Walcott wanted the latter but needed the former."

The sound of footsteps made her turn. Expecting to find Lord Walcott coming after her, she was surprised when she saw it was Lord Ezra.

Lord Ezra had dark hair and matching eyes and wore a scowl that conveyed what he had tried to hide from Agnes when he called on her in the past. That he was a man consumed with jealousy because his brother was a duke and not he. Now that the Duke of Elmhurst had a son, any chance of Lord Ezra taking over the title had decreased considerably.

"Good afternoon, Miss Agnes," he hissed. Indeed, he would no longer have a kind word for her. Not that she cared. "So, are the rumors true? Has Phillip Rutley been calling on you?"

Agnes straightened her back and looked him straight in the eye. "That is none of your business. Now, Amy and I have several errands to run, so I'll wish you a good day."

As she turned to leave, however, he called out to her. "Wait! I suspected you were taken with him. Is he the reason you left me in the lurch? Did you choose him over me?"

"Again," Agnes said in a clear, firm voice, "that is my business and not yours. I've no reason to explain myself to you or anyone else."

"Perhaps so," he said, an unpleasant grin crossing his face. "But I'm curious. Why become involved with a man who is nearly bankrupt? I may never become a duke, but at least my financial future is solid."

"Mr. Rutley is not—" she began indignantly, but he spoke over her.

"Were you aware that he had the audacity to write to my brother and ask for an audience? As if a duke would entertain the likes of *him.*" Lord Ezra took a step closer, narrowing his eyes.

Instinctively, Agnes slid a hand into the pocket sewn into her dress and wrapped her fingers around the small pen knife she always carried with her. There were some things from her past of which she was unwilling to let go.

"I read the letter he sent my brother," Lord Ezra continued. "He needs investors because every enterprise in which he's been involved has disintegrated. Apparently, he's become desperate. All men of worth have refused to even hear what he has to say... well, except Mr. Porter. But then again, I suppose I cannot count him as a man of worth."

Anger flared in Agnes. How dare this man speak of her guardian in such a disparaging way! Her hand tightened on the knife, and she nearly pulled it out before she caught herself.

No, she could not revert to her old ways. She had come too far to be the lady she was today. With great effort, she released her grip and allowed her hand to drop to her side.

"Thank you for sharing what everyone already knows, my lord," she said in a sickly-sweet tone. "Do you also wish to tell me that Christmas is celebrated in December? Or perhaps that the leaves fall from the trees in the autumn? Come, Amy, I would prefer to find better company."

As she and Amy hurried away, she could hear Lord Ezra shouting after them, "I'll never forget what you did to me! One day, I'll be vindicated!"

Upon exiting the alleyway, Agnes felt safe once more. Yet now, a new concern came over her. Was what Lord Ezra said true? Were the troubles Mr. Rutley mentioned have to do with his finances? And was it Mr. Porter who was now helping him?

Well, there was only one way to learn the truth—to ask the very man the rumors were about.

Chapter Six

Nearly a week had passed since Agnes last saw Mr. Rutley. He was due to call on her early this afternoon, and she and Amy had spent the better part of the morning preparing. She had chosen a walking dress of the lightest pink with rows of printed pink vines and green leaves. On the stiff bodice was a simple lace bow. Made of Chinese silk, she still marveled at the fact that something so lovely could be a part of her wardrobe.

Forgoing a hat, Agnes had asked Amy to style her hair into a proper chignon. That had taken hours of using a hot rod to form perfect curls, which Amy then pinned into rows on top of Agnes's head. On most days, it all seemed too laborious, but today, she wanted to look her best.

For Mr. Rutley.

Although her heart pounded in anticipation at the idea of seeing him again, a tiny cloud of doubt continued to hang over her. Was what Lord Ezra said true? Were the troubles Mr. Rutley was having financial in nature? And if so, what did that mean for their future?

She cared little for the money, of course. After all, most of her life she had lived without it. Mr. Rutley, however, likely never had to endure a life of poverty. What would he do if he were forced to live in a tiny cottage tending farm animals rather than enjoying the comfort of his lovely home of Courtly Manor?

Agnes had considered asking Mr. Porter, thus ending any speculation, both about Mr. Rutley's troubles and Mr. Porter's involvement in those troubles. Yet she thought it best if she asked Mr. Rutley first. Just because the two were doing business together did not mean that Mr. Porter knew every aspect of Mr. Rutley's financial situation. Plus, Agnes preferred to be upfront and honest with people. When it counted.

"There," Amy said, sliding the final hairpin through an unruly curl. "I think you're ready, miss. Oh! Let me get your shawl."

Agnes watched through the reflection in the mirror as Amy hurried to the wardrobe. "I'll miss you when you leave next year," she said. "To whom shall I talk when you're gone?"

Amy laughed as she placed the wrap around Agnes's shoulders. "You'll find a new lady's maid, I'm sure. And if you settle here in Chatsworth with Mr. Rutley, you'll make more proper friends. Ones from your own station."

Agnes nearly snorted. Her own station? Just over four years ago, she sat on the lowest rung of society, even lower than Amy. Who was she to give herself airs?

Then there was the consideration of a romance ending in marriage. If she and Mr. Rutley did eventually marry, they would likely remain in the village. Mr. Rutley had ties to the community and, as far as she knew, he had never lived anywhere else. What reasons would he have to live elsewhere? Unless he purchased a home in London like Mr. Porter owned.

No, Chatsworth was the best place for both of them. She preferred her time in the country. The air was clean, the birds sang, the flowers bloomed. Yes, it was far better than London.

"No one can ever replace you, Amy," Agnes said, turning to look up at the maid. "But I've never had trouble making friends before, so why would I have now? Perhaps Lady Walcott and I will grow closer."

Amy's brows rose in surprise. "After what you told her husband outside that tavern on Drake Street? I doubt you'll ever receive even a smile from her again!"

Agnes nodded her agreement. She had not wanted to chastise an earl in public as she had, but someone had to say something. This time she did snort. If Lord Walcott was unwilling to pay heed to Mr. Porter, why would he listen to the likes of her? But it was well worth the risk if he changed his ways and walked a straighter path.

"Well, at least I'll have Mrs. Shepherd," Agnes said. When Amy groaned, Agnes frowned at her. "She seems a very lovely woman. Why can I not be friends with her?"

The lady's maid sighed as she helped slide a glove over Agnes's hand. "Now, don't give me that. You know what Mr. Porter says about that sort of thing."

Agnes laughed. How could she forget? Too many times he had caught her laughing and chatting with the household staff—and even the grooms and gardeners!—that he had threatened to take away all her new dresses and make her parade around town in her petticoats! It was one thing to wear clothing made from burlap sacks and quite another to wear one's underclothes in public. After that, she had been much more careful.

Not that she stopped talking to the servants altogether. She soon found ways to enjoy their company while not getting caught!

But in the end, Agnes realized that Mr. Porter was right. She was no longer of the lower class. Now, she was a member of the gentry, and young ladies of the gentry had certain expectations. The changes did not come easily, but she wanted to please her guardian. After all, he had saved her from an uncertain future. Or a possible hanging if the proprietor of that shop had chosen to have the Bow Street Runners come for her.

Yes, she was lucky, indeed.

"No, I've not forgotten," Agnes replied with a sigh. "But it's not as if I plan to take Mrs. Shepherd to the theater with me in London. There is something special about that woman. I can tell we'll be fast friends. At least I'll be able to speak to her in the kitchen every day. After all, we must discuss the menu, do we not?"

Amy frowned. "You keep talking like you're ready to move into Courtly Manor tomorrow. You do know that you must get married first, don't you?"

Agnes feigned indignation but then hugged the maid. "Oh, yes, I'm quite aware." She stood and studied her reflection. "Well, I suppose we should go to the drawing room to wait. He should be calling soon."

They were unable to reach the drawing room, however, because Mr. Rutley was already waiting in the foyer, speaking to Garland. When Mr.

Rutley turned to look up at her, any speck of doubt fled. She *would* marry this man.

It was much more than speculation, much more than a feeling. As true as grass was green and the sky was blue, she knew for certain this was the man with whom she would spend the rest of her life.

He smiled up at her as he offered her a hand to help her from the bottom step. "Miss Fitzimmons, I apologize for my tardiness. I was in the middle of an important meeting that went longer than I had anticipated."

"As long as you've come," Agnes said, although he was not late. If anything, he was at least five minutes early.

She turned to the butler. "Mr. Rutley and I plan to stroll through the gardens. Will you see tea is ready for us upon our return?"

"Yes, miss," Garland replied with a bow. Then he went to do her bidding.

"My apologies, Mr. Rutley. I should have asked if you would like to take a stroll. If you would prefer, we can go straight to the drawing room."

His smile warmed her heart. "As long as I'm in your company, where we are makes little difference to me."

Agnes thought her cheeks would burn down the house! He always had such lovely words for her. She could listen to him every hour of every day.

Meadow Estate offered one of the most beautiful gardens in the area, even now, when most of it was barren for the winter. Mr. Porter employed several gardeners who were masters at their craft. Every tree was carefully pruned, most to look like spheres atop their trunks.

How Agnes longed for the summer months when the rectangular flowerbeds that lay on either side of a stone path displayed every flower imaginable. Pink sweet briars, purple columbines, pink peonies, yellow mignonette, white Syringa, pinks, and sweet williams. Several lilac bushes filled with their fragrant purple flowers grew along a back wall, and the plum tree had tiny blush-colored flowers that Agnes loved.

Yet even with the flowers gone and dark brown soil greeting her gaze, it was still lovely, for Mr. Rutley walked at her side.

"You seem deep in thought," Mr. Rutley said. "Is there anything I can do to help?"

"Oh no, I'm well," she said with a smile.

"The weather does not bother you, does it?" he asked. A small cloud vapor escaped his lips, and she marveled in it.

"Not at all," she replied.

"You mentioned the same before. How is it you're immune to the cold? I find it a nuisance."

Agnes laughed. "It's a secret," she said with a wink. "If you're lucky, I may reveal it to you. But today I must keep it to myself."

"Then I await that day with earnest," he said, offering his arm, which she took. They strolled a bit farther, and he caught her by surprise by saying, "No, something is bothering you. I know you said you cannot say, but you must tell me. I promise to never mention what you say to anyone. In fact, if you ask me to, I'll forget it the moment you speak the words."

They stopped at a bench and Agnes sat. She had been considering how to broach the subject of the rumors she had heard. "I would like to ask you a question, Mr. Rutley. But I don't wish to offend you."

He sat in the place beside her and took her hand. "Nothing you say can ever offend me, Miss Fitzimmons, I assure you. Ask what you will, and I'll answer what I'm able."

There was comfort in his grasp, and she drew in a calming breath. Four years earlier, she would not have struggled to broach certain topics, not as she did now. This "being cultured" had proven to be more difficult than she would have thought. Now, discussing one's financial situation was considered ill-mannered. But she had to know the truth, and the only way she could do that was to ask her question.

"I've come to learn that you're having trouble with your estate."

He removed his hand from hers, and she found she missed it instantly. "Trouble?" he asked, laughing. "My estate is just fine. Things have never been better. Where did you hear such rubbish?"

Agnes studied his face. She had always been a good judge of character, and what she saw now saddened her. He was not being truthful. Agnes was certain of it. Yet one did not simply come right out and accuse another of lying. Or so she had learned. My, but society made things difficult sometimes!

Perhaps she understood why he chose to answer as he did. "You've no reason to keep the truth from me, Mr. Rutley. I'm not like other women. I'll not judge you."

Mr. Rutley turned as if studying the horizon. All was quiet except the gentle chirp of the birds around them. Would he refuse? Was he angry with her for asking? Maybe she should have used the advice given her and not asked at all.

Finally, he stood and turned his back to her. "My estate is facing bankruptcy," he said, his voice sounding as if a hot iron had been run over it. "Anything that could have gone wrong has done so, and I'm close to losing Courtly Manor. I'm afraid the end is near for me. That's the truth."

"What will you do?" Agnes asked. "Is it too late to save your home?"

Mr. Rutley shook his head. "I own several mines. Most are barren, but one is ready to be worked. I've already got miners and tools ready to begin. But I've nothing to pay their wages. I can't expect them to wait to be paid. They have families to feed, children and wives who count on them to supply what they need. It's the reason I contacted Mr. Porter. I was hoping to secure a loan, using my house as collateral. But that is just the start of my problems..."

As he continued to explain, Agnes began to understand his dilemma. Because of his failed ventures and a heavy mortgage he carried on Courtly Manor, no bank would offer him another a loan. Even the mines that had potential for earnings could not be run if the workers could not be paid.

"I can't have the bank taking my house. I would never see it again. Therefore, I asked Mr. Porter to purchase my current loans, putting me in his debt rather than that of the bank, and extending a small amount of credit beyond that. I also plan to sell one of the smaller mines for its land, so I am able to make up the difference between what he's willing to give me and what I need. Once that first mine is producing, I'll take the profit to open a second mine, and so on, from there. I'm hoping Mr. Porter will be more lenient with my repayments until the mines are fully operational. He's a man I can trust to keep his word and not call in my loan too early. I figure the entire process will take approximately five years." He shrugged, sighing heavily. "But he refused my request, and now I'm left with no way to pay my debts."

Agnes felt terrible for him. He was ready to make a small fortune, but he lacked the funds to get it started.

But Mr. Porter did not.

"Mr. Rutley—"

"There is no reason to explain," he said with a dejected sigh. "I understand my worth, and I don't blame you for wanting nothing to do with me."

It was about time she was honest with him. She took his hand in hers. "Mr. Rutley, I want everything to do with you. The truth is, I've come to care for you very deeply."

A smile spread across his face. "My situation does not frighten you?"

Agnes shook her head. "Not in the least."

"Oh, Miss Fitzimmons, you've no idea how much this means to me! I've also come to care about you but was too afraid to say so given the turmoil that is my life. To be honest, I thought you would run away if you ever learned about that which I'm currently dealing." He touched her cheek with the back of his hand. "And the thought of you leaving terrifies me more than anything. A world without you in it is not worth living."

Agnes's heart began to soar, and to her surprise, he leaned in and kissed her! Everything else disappeared around them, and only they two remained. Never had she experienced anything so wonderful in her life!

Unfortunately, the kiss came to an end.

"That was beautiful," she whispered.

Mr. Rutley raised her hand to his lips and kissed her knuckles. "My sweet Miss Fitzimmons, you have given me hope this day. I'll not fail you, I swear. Once everything is secure, I'll marry you."

A gasp escaped her lips, and a thrill filled her soul. "You will?"

"Of course. But only until I'm certain I'll not lose Courtly Manor. I'll not have my bride worrying about the home in which she lives. You do wish to live there, do you not?"

Agnes was so overcome with joy that all she could do was nod her response.

"I must go," he said, smiling down at her. "I've several more letters to write if I'm to secure a loan or gain investors. It's as you said, Miss Fitzimmons, I cannot give up hope. And I shan't." He kissed her cheek. "You've taught me much this day, and one day I'll thank you properly."

Standing in shock, Agnes watched him hurry away. Had they just confessed their love for one another? In so many words, they had! And was that a proposal?

And did he just kiss her?

One glance at Amy and her crimson cheeks said that he had.

Well, if they were to marry, Mr. Rutley needed a loan. And she knew just the right person to see he received one. And he had no reason to deny the request.

Her future depended on it.

Chapter Seven

Agnes had very few keepsakes from her previous life, but among them was a penknife she always carried. She was no longer a girl who feared for her life but rather a young woman, a member of polite society. A ward of a man of the gentry. And perhaps a woman in love. She was unsure what the future held for her and Mr. Rutley, but they would be together. That much was certain. She felt it.

Standing before the vanity table, she turned the knife in her hand. She had used it on several occasions as a way to threaten those who dared try to hurt her. A thief who had tried to rob her of a coin she had received for sweeping a stoop. Men who had tried to have their way with her.

Now however, she could allow her guard to drop. Mr. Porter had been kind to her, had provided her with a life she never thought possible.

But Mr. Rutley would protect her.

With a smile, she placed the knife in the ornate carved box she had received as a gift from Mr. Porter the first month she was in his care.

"A place to keep your valuables," he had said.

Beside it, she placed the wooden top she had bought off the young boy a week earlier. One day, she would have children, and a son would surely enjoy such a toy.

Closing the lid, she left the room in search of Mr. Porter. As expected, he was in his study. He had locked himself away, as he often did, and Agnes had left him to his work for the past two days. But it had also been two days since she last saw Mr. Rutley, and she had hoped to discuss his situation.

Standing in the doorway of the study, her heart warmed as she watched Mr. Porter hunched over a piece of parchment. Her thoughts returned to their London home and her first week as his ward. She had been in his care for no more than three days when she walked into his study there to find him very much as he was now, reading a letter.

Agnes, being the nosy girl she was, asked, "Whatcha doin'? You lookin' to sell me?"

Mr. Porter had looked up and laughed. "Nothing escapes your notice, Agnes Fitzimmons, does it? Do you not know it's improper to ask a man's business?"

Agnes lowered her gaze, and tears filled her eyes. "No, sir, I didn't know. What'll you do now? Throw me out to the streets again?"

For the three days she had been in his care, she was terrified he would get rid of her. After all, if her parents did not want her, why would he? She was no good to anyone, not important enough to take care of. And he would realize it soon enough.

But he stood and walked over to her. "Agnes, if I wanted to 'throw you to the streets' as you put it, you would no longer be available for me to sell. I've been offered three sheep for you. How could I pass up such a wonderful trade?"

He winked, and she could not help but giggle. He was teasing her!

"You should've asked for four," she said with a sniff. "I'm worth at least that."

He grinned. "I don't suspect anyone could offer me enough sheep that would make trading you worth my while."

Agnes shook the memory from her mind and stepped into the room. Mr. Porter held up a hand, indicating she was to wait to speak. Which she did, patiently, as she considered how to broach the subject of Mr. Rutley and his financial needs. The fireplace roared to life, and Agnes stood in front of it and watched the dancing flames.

"I cannot believe this," he said as he set the letter aside and walked around the desk. "I finally got what I wanted."

"Oh?" Agnes asked. "And what is that?"

"The five sheep in exchange for you," he said with all seriousness.

But Agnes knew better by now and laughed. Mr. Porter went into a coughing fit, and she led him to one of the walnut armchairs covered in Brussels tapestry.

Once the fit had subsided, he continued, "Now, what is bothering you?"

How he always knew her mood before she even began to speak was beyond Agnes. She had tried to mask her worries, yet here he was, knowing exactly how she was feeling. After all her training, Mrs. Gouldsmith would have been disappointed at Agnes's inability to hide her feelings. Then again, Mr. Porter knew her far too well by now.

Agnes had learned from a very young age that forthrightness was much more effective than skirting what one wants. Someone who was hungry could not waste time. "I've come on behalf of Mr. Rutley."

Mr. Porter's eyebrows rose. "He sent you?"

"Not at all," Agnes replied, lowering herself onto the matching settee. "Mr. Rutley confided in me about his financial situation, and I want to help. If you were to purchase the loans on Courtly Manor outright, with a little extra he can use toward his mines, he will not lose his home. He can use what the mines produce to pay you, but only when he's made enough profits to begin those payments. I realize this is asking much, but he needs the help, Mr. Porter. If he's able to open one of his mines, he'll be able to use those earnings to finance the opening of another. Then another. He'll be successful, I'm sure of it."

Mr. Porter began to cough again, this time grimacing in pain. Agnes waited patiently for the fit to subside once more.

"I've no doubt Mr. Rutley will do quite well in life, Agnes," Mr. Porter said, his voice much hoarser now than it was before. "But I cannot help him."

Agnes shook her head. "If you believe he'll prosper, why do you refuse to help?" When he frowned at her, she dropped her gaze. "I don't mean to question your judgment, but I'm confused. Mr. Rutley and I—"

"Speak far too loudly in the garden for your own good," Mr. Porter said. "Especially when you're near an open window that allows me the fresh air I need."

Agnes's cheeks heated. He had heard everything! Surely, he did not see Mr. Rutley kiss her, did he?

"My refusal to help him in the past is only reemphasized by what I overheard."

"But I understood you're already aware of the troubles he faces," Agnes said.

"I am, but I'm speaking of the fact he wishes to marry you."

For a moment, time stood still. Mr. Porter was concerned about she and Mr. Rutley marrying? How could that stop him from helping? None of this made any sense.

With a sigh, Mr. Porter crossed one leg over the other and cupped his hands over a knee. "Agnes, men suffer from a terrible dilemma known as pride. Some more so than others. I refused to help because doing so will hurt his pride. What if he's unable to repay me? I don't need another house I won't enjoy. I have plenty. He would have to put a great deal of trust in me. I have never gone back on my word and never plan to do so, but that is a great amount of trust to put in one man in my current condition. It makes little financial sense for me. I know he's desperate, and that is what drives this strange request, but I cannot put you and your future at risk."

Agnes considered all he had told her. Reluctantly, she had to admit what he said made sense. Except for one thing.

"You said you're aware that he's facing bankruptcy, correct?"

Mr. Porter nodded. "I am."

"And that he wishes to marry me?"

He nodded again.

"Then why would you allow me to marry a man in such financial straits?"

Mr. Porter laughed so hard, he erupted into another fit of coughing. This time, Agnes rose and hurried to pour him a glass of water.

He took several sips before the fit subsided.

"Thank you," he said.

"You've taught me there is always hope," Agnes said. "You saw in me what I was unable to see, which is why I stand here today. I've become something no one, not even I, could have ever expected—a proper young lady."

Mr. Porter smiled. "Ever the wise one, you are. I did see potential in you, and I do believe there is hope for Rutley."

"But I wasn't able to make those changes on my own. I needed your help in so many ways, but financial was one of the most important. Mr. Rutley is someone who is in need of a little help. For all you've done for me, I'll be forever thankful. But I must ask, will you not consider helping him, too? I'll beg if I must."

Mr. Porter rose from his chair and went to the window looking out over the garden. With his hands behind his back, he stood tall and regal despite his illness. This, Agnes knew, meant he was in deep deliberation.

"I knew this day would come," he said finally. "The day when you were no longer that young girl who needed me. I told myself that four years was a very long time, but it came far too quickly. Soon, you'll leave me and join your husband. Whomever he will be."

Tears brimmed Agnes's eyes as she joined him at the window. "That young girl I once was remains," she said. "I'm who I am today because of you, and I promise I'll always be in your life. Just as you will always be in mine."

Mr. Porter turned and smiled down at her, and for the first time since they met, his eyes were red. "I want you to be happy, Agnes. I want you to be even happier than you've made me."

Agnes embraced him, forever thankful for the loving home he had provided her. "You've done that for me."

"No, I only helped you do it for yourself," he said. "But I'll agree to help Rutley."

She smiled broadly. "I'm so pleased—"

"With one condition," he interrupted.

"Of course. What is it?"

"That you allow the courier to deliver the letter."

Agnes laughed and threw her arms around Mr. Porter, pulling him even tighter than before.

Later that evening during dinner, a twinge of sadness swept over her. Mr. Porter was right. Soon, she would be married and starting her own family. Her days with him were coming to an end. But she knew that for all he had taught her, the love and hope he had given, no matter what the future held, he would always remain with her.

Chapter Eight

The hope on to which Phillip had held was beginning to wane. Three days had passed since he had last seen Miss Fitzimmons, when they had shared their feelings for one another. And he had revealed the turmoil his estate was in. Yet the way she had responded, her belief in him, had forced him to search for a solution.

Although he had made inquiries, many were shying away from investing in mines. The business was too risky, they said. Unless a vein was already found. Unfortunately, his had been as empty as a dry well. But he knew in his soul that his mines had hidden treasures yet to be discovered.

Yet his soul was not worth a whole lot when it came to investors.

Outside of Chatsworth, he had made friends only socially, polite greetings at one party or another, but none were any he felt comfortable approaching with business propositions.

That left only one option—to sell a majority of his mines, which was something he would rather not do. Yet if he one day wished to marry Miss Fitzimmons, he would have to do what he could to save Courtly Manor.

Heaving a sigh, he rose from his desk just as Henton entered the room.

"Sir, a letter arrived for you."

Phillip smiled when he saw Mr. Porter's seal. "Is she still here?"

"No, sir," the butler replied. "He left."

He? Why had Miss Fitzimmons not delivered it? Then a sinking feeling came to the pit of his stomach. Had Mr. Porter learned about her deception and refused to allow her to come?

No, that was silly. Even if he did learn she was paying the courier to allow her to deliver the letters, she was never alone with him.

Sliding a finger beneath the seal, he unfolded the parchment, recognizing the shaky script of Mr. Porter.

And his eyes widen with every word.

"He's agreed," Phillip mumbled. "I'm to see him at once." He folded the letter and left it on the desk. "Henton, you'll not have to search for new employment. Good fortune is coming our way!"

"Most excellent news, sir," the butler said. "Will you be riding or taking the carriage?"

"I think the carriage will be better," Phillip replied. "I'm far too excited to ride."

Pacing the room, a thousand thoughts filled his mind. Although he would owe Mr. Porter a great deal of money, the debt would be paid off very soon. He had already found a buyer for one of the parcels of land, which would allow him to purchase blasting powder once the first mine was reopened. If luck was with him, they would strike copper after the first blast.

He came to an abrupt stop. "Dear God," he whispered, "by next spring I'll have all the mines running at full capacity."

As he thought of this and the money he would make, an image of Miss Fitzimmons came to mind. Now he could offer her a secure future. They would live here at Courtly Manor and spend each and every day together. No longer would the Rutley name be associated with ruin.

Less than an hour later, Phillip alighted from the carriage and was standing at the front door to Meadow Estate. The butler answered the door and led Phillip to Mr. Porter's study.

The silver-haired man had become quite thin as of late, but the smile he wore remained the same.

"Mr. Rutley, thank you for coming on such short notice," Mr. Porter said. "Please, have a seat."

"Thank you so much for agreeing to see me, Mr. Porter. You'll see your money returned sooner than you think. And with interest, of course."

The older man clasped his hands on the desk. "I've come to learn that you've an interest in Miss Fitzimmons. Is this true?"

The question caught Phillip off guard. Surely, the man was not upset? "It's true, sir. I find I enjoy her company very much."

"And has the subject of marriage been broached?"

Phillip smiled. Mr. Porter was not a man to beat about the bush, and he admired him for that. "It has. However, I told her I must secure my estate before we marry. That is if you give your permission."

Mr. Porter nodded. "I only wish for Agnes to be happy, and if marrying you makes her thus, I've no reason to impede it. I do have one question to ask concerning our agreement."

Phillip readjusted himself in the seat. He was not ignorant enough to think there would be no questions. "Of course."

"You do understand, if you're unable to pay off your loan, I'll own Courtly Manor, do you not? For the next five years, you'll attempt to make payments to me, with added interest. Because I do this for Agnes as much as you, I'll even agree to lower the amount of interest than what the banks would charge to make it more feasible for you to repay."

Phillip nodded. "I understand the terms, Mr. Porter. I don't mean any offense, but it was I who created them. And there will be no attempt made —I *will* pay off the loan and within the agreed upon time."

Mr. Porter waved a hand. "I've no doubt you will. But understand this. For all practical purposes, I'll become your father-in-law. The father of your bride to whom you'll owe a great deal of money. Who may take possession of your home if you're unable to pay. Men will whisper behind your back. Rumors will rise. Have you considered how that may affect you?"

Letting out a deep breath, Phillip shook his head. What Mr. Porter said was true. Men could gossip as well—if not better—than any woman. And to enter into a marriage where he was indebted to his fiancée's father did not sit well with him. Yet, he would move past that issue. He had to.

"I'll not allow the opinions of others to bother me, Mr. Porter. This will be a successful venture, one that will tie their wagging tongues and send them into fits of jealousy."

Mr. Porter nodded. "Then I would like to proceed with this agreement. Are you acquainted with my solicitor, Cornelius Lampton?"

"I imagine we all are, sir," Phillip replied, "given he's the only solicitor in Chatsworth. Or rather, the only one who represents those with money."

"Indeed," Mr. Porter said. "He's prepared the necessary documents and is awaiting your signature." He opened a desk drawer and pulled out a bundle of notes. "In good faith, I'll advance you the difference between the amount you owe on the loans you currently hold and the total of the loan I'll be giving you."

Phillip eyed the notes, doing all he could to keep his excitement in check. "Thank you, Mr. Porter. I'll meet with Mr. Lampton today and leave for the mines tomorrow. I'll have the first one up and running as soon as I can."

As he took the notes in hand, however, a twinge of sadness washed over Phillip. After all the years of his family owning Courtly Manor, this was the only thing to show for it. Everything else had been mortgaged and borrowed away. But at least he still had something.

Mr. Porter rose and stretched out a hand. "Good luck to you, Rutley. Agnes is in the drawing room if you wish to speak to her. I'm sure she'll be happy to see you."

"I would like that, sir. And thank you again."

Slipping the notes into his inside pocket, Phillip made his way to the drawing room, where he found Miss Fitzimmons and her lady's maid waiting for him.

Miss Fitzimmons rose from the couch, wearing a sunny day dress printed with white flowers. Oh, but she was beautiful!

"It appears you've come to an agreement," she said, smiling.

"We did," Phillip replied.

"I'm so glad!" Miss Fitzimmons said. "I told Mr. Porter his investment would be safe with you."

Phillip frowned as a jolt of annoyance ran through him. Had Miss Fitzimmons convinced her guardian to invest? And here Phillip thought it had been his hard work, the making of an offer that was too good to pass up, that had brought around Mr. Porter. Not because of any influence Miss Fitzimmons had on her guardian.

"Is everything all right?" she asked, her brows knitted with worry. "You're not upset with me, are you?"

He had to force down his pride. "No, of course not. Thank you for helping me. I'm to go to the solicitor, and tomorrow I'll leave for Staffordshire to open the first mine. We'll begin work immediately."

"I'm so happy for you," Miss Fitzimmons said. "You see? There is hope."

Phillip pushed back the sudden urge to kiss her and cleared his throat. "Mr. Porter asked about my intentions with you and says he'll give his permission when I ask for your hand in marriage."

"Then, let's hope that day comes quicker than we think," she said, grinning. "Will you send word once you've returned to Chatsworth?"

Promising he would, he bowed to her and left the house. As he settled into the carriage, he considered all that had happened. He was off to sign the proper documents that would see his life returned to him. Within weeks, he would be seeing a profit. Small profits, to be sure, but profits, nonetheless.

Yet as the carriage moved forward, Phillip could not help but wonder what would have happened if Miss Fitzimmons had not intervened on his behalf.

Patting the place where the notes lay in his coat, he realized it did not matter. What did was a secure future for him and the woman for whom he cared deeply.

Chapter Nine

Two weeks had passed since Phillip secured the agreement with Mr. Porter, and never had he felt more alive. He was a complete contrast to the early December grass surrounding his home. He had taken a large portion of the funds to secure the last necessary items to begin the excavation—blasting powder, extra tools, and wages set aside for the workers. They were as excited as he was, given the fact they had been out of work for far too long.

What was planned as a single day trip turned into five. The materials he needed had been more difficult to come by than he had expected, especially the blasting power, but now he and the workers were more than ready to begin their excavation.

Initially, Phillip had hoped to oversee the workers himself, but it was suggested to him that he hire a foreman to see to the supervising. The fact he owned a mine was one thing, but knowing how to run it was quite another. His money was better spent on Harland Curtis, a man with more than twenty years of experience. It was with great confidence that he left the foreman in charge of everything.

As promised, when he returned to Chatsworth, he sent word to Miss Fitzimmons with an invitation to dinner that evening. He had missed her terribly, but his time away had been well worth the separation.

For now, he walked along High Street, his head held high. No longer did he feel like a lesser man. He might not be of noble blood, might not have come from titled stock, but he would be wealthier than them once the mines began producing. Soon, everyone would see the progress he had made, and those dalcops who had refused to invest with him would regret not doing so.

The wintry sun attempted to break through gray clouds high in the sky. A chilly breeze blew around Phillip as he came to a sudden stop upon seeing one Lord Ezra Colburn. The brother of a duke, Lord Ezra had been a suitor to Miss Fitzimmons. From what he had heard, they had been well on their way to courtship when it came to an abrupt end. What had happened there? She had not been very forthcoming about what had caused their abrupt separation.

Lord Ezra wore his customary dark clothing as he spoke to the local butcher. Well, not spoke to as much as shouted at, given he was pointing an accusatory finger at the poor man. Whatever they were discussing, Lord Ezra was clearly upset.

Although he had spoken to the younger brother of the Duke of Elmhurst only on a handful of occasions, Phillip wanted nothing to do with him. Out of all those with sufficient funds to aid him in his endeavors, Phillip had chosen not to approach this particular man. He was nothing more than a great arrogant snake not to be trusted.

Rather than endure even a single moment with Lord Ezra, Phillip turned to cross the road but then heard his name.

Drat! He had been seen!

"Rutley," Lord Ezra repeated as he walked up to Phillip, "I've been meaning to speak with you."

Phillip stifled a sigh. He may not like the man, but he was the younger brother of a duke. One did not simply ignore a man of such high standing. "Good afternoon, my lord. What can I do to help you today?"

"You? Help me?" Lord Ezra said with a mocking laugh. "I don't accept aid of any kind from those of the lower classes. I've no need of the few coins you have to offer. No, I only wish to congratulate you on getting your mines up and running."

Phillip raised his eyebrows. "I appreciate it, my lord. But how did you learn of this?"

Lord Ezra chuckled. "Why, Miss Fitzimmons told me the good news when she called over to my house a few days ago. I merely wanted to congratulate you in person."

Confusion raced through Phillip. "Why would she tell you that?"

And why would she call on him after they were no longer on speaking terms?

"Why would she not?" Lord Ezra tilted his head, frowning. "We may no longer be seeing one another, but we've remained friends." The inkling of a sneer touched his lips when he leaned in and whispered, "Don't worry. I'll not tell you the things we used to do."

Phillip held his clenched fist at his side to keep from striking Lord Ezra. "Miss Fitzimmons is a respectable woman. I would suggest you keep whatever disparaging remarks you wish to say about her to yourself."

Lord Ezra gave him a derisive sniff that sounded much like Phillip's mother when she was alive. "Of course she is. Why do you think she still writes to me? Or why she calls on Walcott when his wife is away." He clasped Phillip on the shoulder. "Why do you think I rid myself of her despite her beauty? She'll always be a friend, but a respectable woman? Well, you'll see for yourself soon enough."

"She does nothing that can tarnish her good name," Phillip said, shrugging off Lord Ezra's hand and taking a step back. "Never speak about her in such a contemptuous manner again, or so help me!"

"Then ask her yourself. See who is lying." Lord Ezra shrugged. "Or don't. Either way, it does not change the fact that it was she who told me."

"And what exactly did she tell you?" Phillip asked, his jaw clenched so tightly, he thought it would break.

"That Mr. Porter only agreed to fund your little mine because of her." Lord Ezra threw his head back and laughed. "To think a man needs a woman to help him with matters of business. You should pray no one else learns the part she played in this scheme of yours, or you'll be laughed out of the village."

Phillip's stomach churned as he hurried across the street without so much as a farewell to Lord Ezra. Was what he said about Miss Fitzimmons true? Had she confided in *that man* the part she played in helping to bring him Mr. Porter's money?

No, it could not be. She would never do anything to jeopardize his reputation, he was sure of it.

But how else would Lord Ezra have known?

Glancing around him, Phillip felt as if everyone was staring. Oh, they spared a smile or a nod of the head for him, but inwardly, he knew they were laughing at him. Mocking him. Despising him.

With an unsettled feeling, he returned to his carriage. Home was much safer a place to be, where those around him did not show their contempt for him. He was no better than the dirt on their shoes to them.

Miss Fitzimmons was not due to arrive for at least another hour, so he spent his time after dressing for dinner in the library, attempting to read. Yet the words on the page made no sense, no matter how many times he read them. The idea that Miss Fitzimmons had spoken to Lord Ezra about him fanned the flames of his anger.

He paced back and forth in front of the roaring fireplace, contemplating this strange new development. With each pass, his anger grew stronger.

Then a thought occurred to him. Did Miss Fitzimmons still have feelings for Lord Ezra? Yet if she did, why would she bother with Phillip at all?

"Sir?"

Phillip turned to find Henton standing in the doorway. He glanced at the mantel clock. Had an hour passed already? He had been so lost in his thoughts that he had completely lost track of time.

"Yes, what is it?"

"Miss Fitzimmons has arrived."

The moment Miss Fitzimmons walked into the room, all worry evaporated. Or at least it receded to the back of his mind. He had always thought her the loveliest woman he had ever seen, but now he was certain of it. She wore a polonaise gown with a close-fitting bodice. The overskirt was the color of the summer sky with three puffed sections down the back and a slit down the front revealing a white ruffled petticoat.

Her hair had been curled and pinned up into a perfect chignon. Several light-blue gems peeked between the curls, and a gold chain with tiny pendants with the same stones was draped across the back of her hair. From her ears dangled the same style pendants as her hair ornaments.

Never had he seen anything so beautiful in all his life. Not the gems, nor the dress, for they only added to the beauty of the young lady who wore them.

"Good evening, Mr. Rutley," she said with a curtsy. "This is Mrs. Burton, my chaperone. You remember Amy, my lady's maid? Well, she was called away, so Mr. Porter retained Mrs. Burton to accompany me today." She spoke of the dumpy woman at her side. Perhaps in her mid-fifties, Mrs. Burton was as wide as she was tall, with three chins poking out from above her brown and gold gown that had too much lace and too many bows.

Yet Phillip paid the chaperone little attention, for an image of Lord Ezra's mocking laugh concealed everything else around him. Perhaps he, Phillip, was worthy of mocking.

Don't be a fool, he chastised himself silently. *Lord Ezra is just jealous that you won the girl!*

He looked at the chaperone. "Please, step out into the hallway for a moment. I must speak to Miss Fitzimmons alone about an important matter."

Mrs. Burton gave him an indignant look. "I'll do no such thing, sir. I was hired to keep everyone in check. She is not allowed to be out of my sight."

"Perhaps you can sit in the window seat instead, Mrs. Burton," Miss Fitzimmons said. "Then Mr. Rutley and I can have a private conversation, but you'll be able to see we don't misbehave." A tiny smile played in the corner of her lips.

"Well, I suppose that will be acceptable," the older woman said before bobbing a quick curtsy and doing as Miss Fitzimmons bade.

"Is there a problem, Mr. Rutley?" Miss Fitzimmons asked in a quiet tone.

Drawing in a calming breath, Phillip took her hands in his. "I must ask a question, and you must be honest in its answering. Do you still have feelings for Lord Ezra?"

"Lord Ezra?" Miss Fitzimmons repeated, frowning. "No, of course not."

"Did you call on him when I was away? If old feelings have risen, you must tell me!"

Miss Fitzimmons gasped and pulled her hand away. "Mr. Rutley, what has come over you? How could you even *think* I would be so inappropriate?

Have I done something to upset you? For I've never been alone with Lord Ezra. Ever. And certainly not this past week.

Phillip's heart began to race, and his mind became muddled. "How does Lord Ezra know about the agreement between Mr. Porter and me? He says you went to his home while I was away." Her face had gone crimson with anger, and a terrible sickness filled Phillip's stomach. What was he doing? "Miss Fitzimmons, you must understand—"

"No," she said, her voice shaking with anger. "You must understand. Lord Ezra has filled your head with lies, and you've believed him."

Phillip felt as if he had become entangled in a trap of his own making but did not know how to escape. "But... but how did Lord Ezra know about my mine?"

Miss Fitzimmons shook her head in disgust. "I assume, since there is only one solicitor in the village, Lord Ezra and you likely have used him at one time or another. And as you just recently used his services, he was likely the source of this information. I, personally, care nothing about how he uses his time, but apparently you do."

Phillip felt an utter dolt. "I'm sorry. It's just that I went into the village earlier, and Lord Ezra approached me. I should have known better than to pay him any heed." Guilt tugged at his heart. "The comments he made about you... what he alluded to about another man... just know that I didn't believe him." Of course, he spoke of Lord Walcott, but mentioning his name would only make matters worse. He shook his head. "I should have known better than to trust anything he has to say. I allowed fear to get the best of me, which makes me a fool."

"It's not that you believed the nonsense he fed you that bothers me," Miss Fitzimmons said. "Or it's not what bothers me the most. Rather it's that you confronted me in such an accusatory manner. And the fact you would even consider that I would go to his house, or any man's house while you were away hurts me deeply." She gave a sad shake to her head. "I'm not feeling well. Mrs. Burton, we're leaving. Good evening to you, Mr. Rutley."

As he watched her leave, Phillip found himself unable to ask her to stay, for he was far too busy cursing himself inwardly. How could he have been so off the mark?

"I'm truly sorry, Miss Fitzimmons," he managed to call after her. "My actions were inexcusable. Please, let us discuss this further."

But she was gone.

Phillip found himself sitting alone at the dining table. He had believed securing this agreement would seal their future together. Instead, his overreaction had caused a rift to create a divide between them. One that he feared would separate their lives forever.

Chapter Ten

Agnes was unsure what to do as the carriage trundled down the road. It had been four days since she last saw Mr. Rutley, and the words he had spoken to her had crushed her heart. Not only had he apologized that same day, but he also had sent a written apology every day since.

Although she was still upset—and rightfully so—she understood how he could have come to the conclusions he had. Lord Ezra was nothing short of a master of manipulation. He had a way of twisting words, his and those of others, to the point no one was safe. The problem was, few saw through his pleasant facade to see the evil man beneath.

Still, Agnes found Mr. Rutley's lack of faith in her concerning. She had seen the warning signs of it before, but their last encounter had been her first view of it in full fruition. What worried her most was, would it happen again? And if so, how terrible would it be?

Then there had been his reaction when she revealed it had been she who had convinced Mr. Porter to help them. He had scowled at her, and she could read quite well the sentiment behind it. Jealousy. Jealousy that she could do what he had been unable to do.

Was Mr. Rutley a jealous man? Would he make her life miserable with his incessant accusations if they were to marry? Or was this nothing more than the terrible stress he had been under as of late? Her mind told her it was nothing more than her imagination. At the very worst, it was a hit on the pride about which Mr. Porter had warned her.

Agnes struggled between believing she was overreacting, and whether she had identified something in him she wished to ignore. She prayed it was the former.

Now, she was uncertain what to feel. Or what to do. She had to ask someone who knew him, a person who might have heard a word or two around the house or a whisper of gossip.

Mrs. Shepherd.

In the letter Mr. Rutley had sent the day before, he had informed Agnes that he would be away for two days to visit the mine. This would allow her a moment to speak to the cook in private.

"Are you sure this's what you want to do, miss?" Amy asked from her place across from Agnes. "What if Mr. Rutley changes his mind and returns early?"

Agnes sighed. "I don't wish to lie to anyone, but I learned long ago there are times of exception. We're going under the pretense of acquiring a recipe from her."

Amy gave a small nod but still looked unsure.

"You always look out for me, Amy. Truly, I've been blessed to have a friend like you."

"I feel the same, miss," Amy said. "And I'm glad to be in your service for another year."

"Not as glad as I. Now when we arrive, I want you to remain in the carriage. Since Mr. Rutley won't be in residence, there will be no need for you to accompany me inside. Plus, Mrs. Shepherd may not be as forthcoming if you're there."

When they arrived at Courtly Manor, Henton, the butler, answered the door. "I'm sorry, miss, but Mr. Rutley's not in at the moment."

Agnes smiled. "Yes, he told me he would be away. But I'm not here to see him. I'd like to speak to Mrs. Shepherd if I may." When the butler's eyes nearly covered his face, she quickly added, "I asked her about a recipe for those wonderful muffins she made for our picnic, and I'm here to collect it."

"Ah, I see," Henton said as if the secrets of the universe had been revealed. "Yes, of course. Please, follow me."

Worried the butler would wish to remain and listen, Agnes said, "I'm sure you have plenty to do without having to worry about me. If you'll direct me to the kitchen, I can go on my own."

Henton frowned. "I don't mind, miss. It will only take a few moments—"

"I really must insist," Agnes said, using the same tone she had heard Lady Walcott use with her servants. "I'm quite capable of moving about a house without guidance. Unless you believe me incapable..." She allowed the words to hang in the air. Oh, why had she not thought to go to the servants' entrance? That would have saved her all this balderdash.

To her relief, the butler bowed and said, "As you wish, miss."

"That's what I'm tellin' ya, Susan," Mrs. Shepherd was saying when Agnes and Amy arrived at the door to the kitchen several minutes later. "Men have different brains than us. Don't ask me why the Good Lord made 'em that way, but He did. If he wants another kiss, tell 'im he's gotta wait. If not, that's all he'll ever want from you."

The young maid at her side nodded. "But how's come you know so much about men, and you ain't been married, Mrs. Shepherd."

The cook stopped stirring the pot in front of her and turned to stare at the girl. "That's my business and none of yours. Now, get back to work."

Susan turned, her eyes growing wide at the sudden appearance of Agnes.

Agnes motioned for the maid to remain silent, and the girl nodded and left the room. Once Susan was gone, Agnes stepped into the kitchen.

"No more talkin' about kissing," Mrs. Shepherd said with exasperation as she slammed the spoon into the pot and spun around. Upon seeing Agnes, she let out a small shriek and covered her mouth. "Oh, Miss Fitzimmons! I'm sorry. I didn't realize it was you."

Agnes laughed. "You've done nothing for which you must apologize."

The cook was dusting off her apron as if Agnes was some sort of royalty. "I must look a fright," she said, pushing back a strand of blonde hair.

"Not at all," Agnes said. "You look just fine."

Mrs. Shepherd grinned. "Is there somethin' you're needin', miss?"

"I was curious about something and hoped you could be of help. How long have you been employed here?"

"Four years, miss."

"And do you enjoy your job?"

The cook nodded. "Oh yes, miss, very much so." Then she gasped. "I've not done somethin' wrong, have I?"

Agnes walked over and placed a kettle on one of the plates on the stove. "No, you've done nothing wrong, Mrs. Shepherd. Would you allow me to join you for a cup of tea?"

"With me?" the cook asked in clear shock. "Well, yeah, of course." Shooing Agnes away, Mrs. Shepherd set to preparing a tea tray. Once the tea was ready, she poured Agnes a cup and handed it to her.

"I'd like to confide something to you," Agnes said.

"Of course, miss. I can keep all sorts of secrets."

Agnes smiled. She had no doubt this woman was a wonderful secret-keeper. "Mr. Rutley and I will soon be engaged."

Pleasure washed over Mrs. Shepherd's face. "How wonderful! You'll need to tell me your favorite dishes, so I'll know what you like. Is that why you're here?"

Taking a small sip of her tea, Agnes smiled and set the teacup on the counter. "Partly. But I was also wondering if you can tell me a little more about Mr. Rutley. How does he treat his staff here? If anyone knows anything about a man, his servants do. I've heard nothing but good things, of course, but one never knows."

"He pays fairly and hardly ever complains." Mrs. Rutley glanced around the room as if searching for a spy. "But between you and me, he's been late payin' our wages on account of the money troubles. Now I don't mean to speak poorly of him, but that's just a fact."

"Yes," Agnes said. "He's mentioned these problems, but I can assure you, that will soon come to an end. Besides that, has he ever been... I don't know, overly harsh with any of the staff? Or perhaps with any of his friends? And what about jealousy? Have you seen him act in a jealous manner?"

The cook placed a hand on her hip and frowned. "Miss Fitzimmons, I don't mean to be forward, but why are you here, really? A lady doesn't come and drink tea with servants, especially the cook. Is somethin' worryin' you?"

For a moment, Agnes considered lying. But her heart told her that Mrs. Shepherd was a woman she could trust. "I believe I'll be living in this house in the near future and for many years thereafter. At times, I'll need a friend, a confidante if you will. Someone I can trust to keep my secrets."

"Well, you can trust me, miss," Mrs. Shepherd said with wide eyes. "I mean, you didn't tell Mr. Rutley about me chasin' off that ignorant delivery boy. And not many ladies in your position would have done that for the likes of a cook." She shook her head. "But don't you have someone better for that position, miss? Like your lady's maid? She'd better for keeping secrets for a lady than someone like me."

"I know what I ask is unusual but, you see, those in service are as much friends to me as they are employees. At least those deserving of such a title. But that is a story for another time. For now, I would like your help."

"I'll do what I can," Mrs. Shepherd said.

As they drank tea together, Agnes confided what had happened between Mr. Rutley and her, including his dislike for her interference in the agreement between Mr. Porter and him, and his apparent jealous behavior concerning Lord Ezra. Of course, she left out some details, but she painted enough of a picture for the woman to see what had happened.

By the time Agnes finished, she let out a heavy sigh. "That is my dilemma. I worry that his jealousy will emerge again, but I can also see why he would be upset."

Mrs. Shepherd clicked her tongue. "It's nothin' more than man's pride. Men got smaller brains than us, you know."

Agnes could not help but laugh. "I've heard that before." She did not mention it had been Mrs. Shepherd who had said it. "So, do you think I'm being overcautious? That his pride was hurt, and he was not jealous?"

"Oh, I'm sure of it, miss. I've never seen him outright angry or actin' jealous. He's smitten with you, that much is sure. You're just worried because you're gettin' married. It's just the mind playin' tricks on you. You see, when that other man said those things to you, I bet Mr. Rutley thought he'd lose you. If he didn't care, he wouldn't've gotten so upset. I bet he feels horrible."

Agnes nodded. "His letters indicate as much."

Mrs. Shepherd placed her hands on her hips. "Just make sure he apologizes. Outright. None of this giving of gifts to make you forget and never sayin' he's sorry idiocy. He has to say he's sorry outright."

"Thank you, Mrs. Shepherd. I do feel better now that I've spoken with you. I'll wait to talk to him before making any final decisions about my future."

"You know, I do hope he mends this," Mrs. Shepherd said, smiling broadly. "I like the idea of havin' you here. Now if you ever need anything else, I'll always be here for you. Even if you decide to marry someone else."

Agnes embraced the cook. "I'll remember that. I'd best go. Amy is waiting for me in the carriage. And if anyone asks, you shared a recipe with me for muffins."

"I'll tell him it was the secret Christmas muffins I make every year!" Mrs. Shepherd said, beaming. "It'll be here soon enough. I absolutely love Christmas. Such wonderful food, the greenery, the mistletoe. Oh, just everything!"

Mrs. Shepherd spoke of the joys of Christmas. It was apparent the merry cook could go on and on if allowed, so Agnes politely excused herself and returned to the carriage. She was ready to discuss the issue with Mr. Rutley the moment he returned from Devon. They would then be able to put this matter behind them.

Chapter Eleven

Happiness should have filled Phillip's heart. The miners found the first veins of copper after only one blast and were making great progress toward excavating the ore. This was cause for celebration, yet Phillip felt as dreary as the gray storm clouds above him as he stood at the mouth of the mine. He had spent three hours with a pickax in his hands beside his workers before Harland Curtis convinced him, again, his place was outside.

"Ye've no business dirtyin' yer hands, sir," Harland had told him as he ran a hand through his scruffy blond hair before replacing his dust-covered hat. He was a sturdy man with large arms, accustomed to working with a pickax and spending time underground. "Yer too important. I'm here to see things're done properly, and ye've gotta trust I'm doing what's right. Plus, the men do their best work when allowed their head. With ye down there, they're lookin' too much at how they're swingin' their pickax than what they're hittin'. All 'cause they're tryin' to impress ye. Let'm alone to do what's to be done."

And Harland could not have been more right. He, Phillip, had no business doing the work the others had been doing for years.

Plus, his hands had never hurt as much as they did after that single day below ground.

Several of the miners' wives made sure water was ready whenever it was needed. A horse and cart transported tools and other necessities. An old man sat on a crude wooden stool, telling stories of years gone past to anyone willing to listen. His audience consisted mostly of children.

Phillip had prohibited any of the children from entering the mine. Unlike other mine owners, he refused to put youngsters into such a precarious position. Would having more hands help speed up the process? Most definitely. But that did not mean it was worth it in the end. They could help with smaller tasks, but mining was for men.

The miners and their families came from the local village of Tradswith, and Phillip had worked with many of them before. Seeing their smiles and hearing their stories of hope at the possibility of having full stomachs eased his mind. But only just a little.

He had been a fool for listening to Lord Ezra and an even bigger fool for the way he had treated Miss Fitzimmons. His jealousy had usurped his common sense, and he was paying the price. Now that his letters had gone unanswered, he feared she would never speak to him again. And rightfully so.

"Sir?" said Elden Curtis, a young miner of eighteen—and son of the foreman—a thick layer of dirt covering his otherwise blond hair. "Take a look at this beauty."

In his hand, he held a stone that had been rinsed in one of the many water troughs for this very use. And within that stone shone the telltale greenish-blue hues of copper.

"'Tis the very first bits, sir," Elden said, his smile nearly touching both ears. "They think we'll hit a main vein soon. We might need to blast one more time, though."

Phillip took the stone from the young man and admired it. The vein in this sample was the largest thus far. "Excellent, Elden," he said. "And where is Harland?"

"He's inside, sir. You know my da. Has to get his hands dirty with the others if he wants to earn their respect."

Phillip nodded. Strange how that rationale did not work the same for him. But Harland was an excellent foreman whom the miners respected. Not once did any of them complain. And one day, young Elden would take

Harland's place. Phillip had no doubt the younger Curtis would be as strong a leader as his father.

"There you are, Elden," a girl of perhaps sixteen said as she approached. With dark brown hair and round cheeks, she had a kind countenance about her. "I brought you some food." She handed Elden a hunk of bread and some dried meat, her cheeks turning pink.

"Thank you," Elden said. "Anna, this is Mr. Rutley, the man I told you about."

The girl dropped into a curtsy. "Oh, Mr. Rutley! Apologies, sir, for not knowin' who you are."

Phillips smiled. "It's a pleasure to meet you, Anna. I take it you and young Elden know each other well?"

Two sets of red cheeks confirmed he was correct.

"I should be going," Anna said. "We'll speak later?"

Elden nodded. "When I'm done for the evening." He watched her as she walked away before letting out a deep sigh. "She's the best thing that's ever happened to me. And once I've saved up enough from my work here, I'm gonna marry her. I almost lost her, though. Can't do that again."

"Oh?" Phillip asked. "How so?"

Tearing off a piece of bread, Elden said, "Me being silly. I saw her in the village talking to a lad I didn't know and got so angry, I walked up and yelled at her. Then I found out he was her cousin visiting from York and felt like an ignoramus. Apologizing wasn't easy, I tell you, but I did. And I promised not to do it again." He shook his head. "I bet you think I'm a fool now, don't you, Mr. Rutley?"

Phillip placed a hand on the boy's shoulder. "Not at all. I think you were wise to admit you made a mistake and righted the situation. But I'm glad Anna forgave you. Women can be fickle creatures."

Elden snorted. "You got that right, sir. But they're well worth it." He was watching Anna serving several other men as he said this.

Once Elden was gone, Phillip walked around the area. He, too, had made a mistake and prayed Miss Fitzimmons, much like Anna, would forgive him.

Leaning against a boulder, he closed his eyes. How could he expect Miss Fitzimmons to forgive him if he was not willing to forgive himself?

"'Scuse me, sir," Harland Curtis said, and Phillip opened his eyes. "This just came."

Phillip frowned as the foreman handed him a letter. "Who would be writing to me? Only a handful of people know I'm even here." Taking the letter, he opened it and began to read. Hope filled him as Agnes's words rang in his head.

I would like to speak to you upon your return.

"'Tis good news, I hope, sir," Harland said, wiping sweat from his brow with a soiled handkerchief.

"I'm not certain, but it seems promising," Phillip said. "As a lady once told me, 'There is always hope.'"

Harland gave him a sympathetic nod. "Aye, she's right there. And ain't that all we live for? Hope of a better future? Well, I best be getting back. I've taken a long enough break."

Phillip stared at the stone Elden had given him and smiled. Then he looked up at those milling about the area surrounding the mouth of the mine. This time, however, he noticed the joy on the people's faces. People who barely had enough to feed themselves showed far more gratefulness than he.

When he returned to the inn, Phillip turned the copper ore in his hand. He could own a thousand mines and have more wealth than most for miles. Yet without Miss Fitzimmons, none of it meant anything. Once he returned to Chatsworth, he would call on her, praying she would accept his apology.

And like Elden with Anna, Phillip would do his best to never fail Miss Fitzimmons again.

As he slid beneath the covers of his bed, Phillip knew what to do. He needed to consider a special place where he could share with her his apology. Somewhere pleasant. A drawing room was much too drab and ordinary.

And as he drifted off to sleep, a wonderful idea came to mind. *Oh, yes, I'll earn her favor in any way I can!*

Chapter Twelve

With great anticipation, Agnes reread the letter she had received from Mr. Rutley the previous day. He not only wished to speak to her, but he also wanted to take her on an outing. It was to last no more than an hour, according to him, but that was more than enough time to allow them to discuss what had happened between them.

With Amy's help, she had spent a good portion of the morning preparing for the outing. Her pink- and green-striped traveling dress had white ruffles on the neckline and the loose, elbow-length sleeves. Around her neck, she wore a pearl collar necklace with a pearl bow pendant that tied at the nape of her neck with a ribbon.

"Oh, Miss Agnes, you're so beautiful," Amy gasped. "Mr. Rutley better realize you're the best he can get."

Agnes laughed. "Is that so? He can do no better? There are daughters of earls and such looking to marry a wealthy man. Well, maybe not daughters of earls, but at least daughters of baronets or knights. Perhaps even a baron or two."

"Maybe, but they aren't you, miss. Now, don't forget your gloves again."

Once her gloves were on, the two women headed for the drawing room. When they reached the foyer, Mr. Porter was speaking to Garland. She hated how sallow his skin had become. Hopefully Dr. Stapleton would soon find a cure for whatever ailed him.

"Well, don't you look lovely, my dear?" Mr. Porter asked when he caught sight of Agnes. "Have you any idea where he's taking you?"

Agnes shook her head. "His letter didn't say anything beyond an outing."

"So, it's to be a surprise then?" her guardian asked. "How wonderful. I do hope you have a nice time. Oh, and I meant to tell you, I heard from Lord Walcott."

Agnes's heart nearly came to a stop at this. Had he informed Mr. Porter about their chance encounter in the alleyway outside of the despicable tavern? Worse still, did he mention her harsh words to him?

"He'll be hosting a party in two weeks, and you and I are invited. He's allowed us to bring one guest. Do you believe Mr. Rutley would enjoy attending with us?"

Agnes bit at her lip. She was not even sure whether she and Mr. Rutley would be speaking in a fortnight.

No, she had to remain optimistic that all would right itself. "Indeed, he would be very pleased."

A knock on the door made them start, and when Mr. Porter opened it, Mr. Rutley stood on the other side. He was so handsome in his blue coat trimmed in gold. A white cravat was tied around his neck and hung over his chest in a flurry of white ruffles. *And, my, but he had—huh?—a fine-turned calf in those white stockings!*

Despite his smile, however, Agnes saw something in his eyes. Was it regret?

"Good morning, Mr. Porter. Miss Fitzimmons." Mr. Rutley bowed. "Thank you for allowing me to take Miss Fitzimmons out on such short notice."

"Not at all, Rutley," Mr. Porter said. "Agnes told me you've been away. How are the mines faring?"

"Very well. In fact, far better than I expected."

"I'm very pleased to hear that," Mr. Porter said. "Well, I have work to do. But you have a fine time."

Agnes smiled. "I'm sure we shall."

When Mr. Porter was gone, Agnes turned to Mr. Rutley. "We must speak."

"I know," he replied. "But may I take you somewhere first?"

Those deep-blue eyes pleaded with her, and Agnes could not help but nod her agreement. They could first go to this place and then discuss what was troubling her after. What harm could it do?

Once they were settled into the carriage, Mr. Rutley said, "We'll not be going far. I expect us to be there in less than ten minutes."

"Won't you at least give me a hint?"

He grinned at her. "I just did."

Although she wanted to be excited about this surprise, Agnes found herself annoyed. What they had to discuss was far too important. After all, it could decide their future together. She could not agree to marry a man who was prone to jealousy at every turn.

Before Mr. Porter found her, Agnes had known too many women who lived terrible lives with husbands who came short of locking them away to keep other men from looking at them. She would *not* live that way. Life in the streets was far more appealing than being a prisoner. Even if the prison was luxurious.

So lost in thought was she that when the carriage came to a stop, Agnes was surprised to find them at Courtly Manor.

"Your estate?" Agnes asked, frowning.

"Trust me," he said as he opened the carriage door. Once he had helped Agnes to alight, he offered her his arm.

Rather than going inside the house, however, he walked around to the back gardens. For a moment, she wondered if he would pick another rose for her, but they passed those particular bushes and walked to a back gate that led out to a field.

If this had been any other day, any other visit, Agnes would have enjoyed this stroll. But they had far too much to discuss to be dawdling away their time in such a manner. She did not suffer patience well, and hers was wearing thin.

"Mr. Rutley, strolls can be enjoyable, but I believe it would be best if we had our talk before we eat. I realize I said the weather does not affect me, but the cold wind and dropping temperature can be uncomfortable."

"We're not going for a stroll," he said. "I've something very important to show you. We're nearly there. Please, just allow me to show you this one thing, and then we'll return to the house and warm up beside the fire. I promise."

They continued through the dry grass. It really was disappointing this was not another day, for she would have gotten great satisfaction from such a walk.

But not today.

After walking in silence for several minutes, a small stream came into view. It was narrow enough even she could step over it, and it was deep enough to cover her hand perhaps and no more.

Mr. Rutley took her hand in his. "Do you recall when we met last summer?"

Agnes nodded. "Of course. We were at the home of Lord Bancroft. His returning-from-London party, if I remember correctly." The baron held parties twice a year—one before everyone left for London for the Season and one when everyone returned. Everyone who was anyone made certain they attended both.

"Indeed, we were. Well, I came out here the following day. I stood at this very spot, looking toward where I knew the Duke of Elmhurst lives. Did you know his brother spends a great deal of time there?"

Agnes pursed her lips. So, this was why he had asked her here? To use his jealousy to annoy her further? "I do," she replied, not caring that her tone was sharp.

"Have you been to Hardwick Hall?"

"I have. I was invited to dinner, and although I had a lovely time there and found the duke and duchess a lovely couple, Lord Ezra hoped to impress me with the invitation. If that is what worries you, I'm afraid you still understand nothing about me."

Mr. Rutley shook his head. "That is not my point, I assure you. Lord Ezra might be able to offer you fine jewelry and a grand wardrobe, but he cannot care for you like I did then. As I do now." He sighed, leaving a trail of cold vapor. "These last few days, I've thought a great deal about us. That estate." He motioned toward Hardwick Hall. "I once believed I could not compete with those within it. But I've come to realize there is no need. For you see in people what I've been too blind to see. It's not a person's titles or the land he owns but rather who he is. His integrity outweighs any wealth or possession he could ever have. Thank you for showing me that."

Agnes looked at Hardwick Hall, understanding now why he had brought her here. His words were comforting, yet she wanted—no, she needed—to hear more.

A look of concern crossed his face, and he sighed. "I've no idea why I allowed Lord Ezra to infuriate me. I should not have paid him the slightest heed. There is no excuse for how I behaved." He took both her hands in his and turned to face her. "But I can promise you one thing, Miss Fitzimmons. If you say you forgive me, from this moment on, I'll never act so foolishly again."

The doubt that had clung to her like a frost on a window began to dissipate. How could she not give him a second chance to prove himself?

He took a stone from a small bag at his waist. It had a blue-green tinge to it. "The greatest treasures are often the ones that are hardest to reach. But with perseverance, we can find them. I've not only found copper in that old mine, but I've found an even greater treasure in you, Miss Fitzimmons. And I'll not lose you."

Agnes's breath caught in her throat. Never had anyone spoken such romantic words to her!

"If you'll forgive me and believe all I've told you," he continued, "I'm left with only one last request. Will you marry me?"

With her head spinning and her heart near to bursting, Agnes squeezed his hands. "I do forgive you," she said, the words sounding breathy to her ears. "Every moment we've spent together, my feelings for you have grown. Today, I see a man who recognizes he made a mistake and has set out to make it right. A man who thought all was lost and yet pushed ahead despite the obstacles. It's for all those reasons and more, Mr. Rutley, that I accept your proposal. After all, you're the man I love."

Mr. Rutley gathered her into his arms and kissed her. Yet it was not just any kiss. It was filled with a hunger that matched that of Agnes. When it ended, he pulled her in tighter.

"When can we marry?" she asked.

He smiled down at her. "We must wait a few months. I want enough money to allow us to take a small honeymoon." Then he added, "Agnes."

The sound of her name on his tongue made her shiver with pleasure. It was like a soft caress. A warm embrace. A loving kiss.

"I would like that… Phillip."

They stood together beside that stream, speaking of their future together and of the mines that would provide for them. Agnes could not have been happier.

When the conversation came to an end, Agnes mentioned the invitation to Lord Walcott's party, to which Mr. Rutley readily agreed.

As they made their way back, however, a pinch of doubt nipped at the back of her mind. Had he truly changed? Would he be able to keep his jealousy at bay?

But did you not go from the young street urchin you once were to the proper young woman you are today, Agnes Fitzimmons? she chastised herself. If she was able to make such great improvements, surely he would be able to do so, as well.

Chapter Thirteen

Phillip could not believe how true his dreams were becoming. Not only had Agnes—oh, how using such an informal address was pleasing!—but she had forgiven his moment of great foolishness. That in itself was well worth celebrating, for he was unworthy of her forgiveness. But he would keep his promise. Jealousy had no place in his life, so he would simply not allow it to enter. It was as simple as that.

He would be the loving husband she needed. After all, she had confessed her love for him. Granted, he had not returned in kind, but he did care for her deeply. Love would come in time; he was certain of it.

In the meantime, he had other things to consider. Such as the invitation to Lord Walcott's party the following week. It could not have come at a more opportune time. Many men of prominence would be in attendance, providing him another chance to approach them about his business propositions.

If he could take on other investors, he would be able to open the other mines before planned. This time he would be approaching these gentlemen in person rather than through written correspondence, making it more likely they'll listen to his ideas than rejecting him outright.

Then, there was the wedding. He had written to his parents, who were now living in America, telling them of the wonderful news. Only a select few would be invited to the reception, and then he wanted to take Agnes to the seaside for their honeymoon.

For the first time in years, Phillip had no worries. His intended was to arrive in just under an hour, and they planned to drink tea and read together in the library. Although he was not all that fond of reading, Agnes was. And that compelled him to join her. If she wished to spend an hour staring at a wall, he would stand at her side and do the same. That was how much he wanted to please her.

The door opened, and Henton barged into the room. Very unlike him, that! "Sir, there's someone here to see you. And she's quite upset."

The sound of a woman's sob made Phillip bolt from his chair. Was that Agnes? What could have possibly happened that had her weeping? "Well, send her in, you fool!"

"Yes, sir." The butler disappeared for a moment and returned with not Agnes but rather Anna, the girl on whom young Elden Curtis had his eye.

Phillip hurried to her side. "Anna? What's wrong?"

"It's the mine, sir," she said between sniffles. "The mine's collapsed, sir."

"Dear God!" Phillip breathed. "When did this happen?"

Anna hiccupped. "Last… last night, sir."

"Last night? And I'm just hearing about it? Why didn't Harland come tell me? Why send you?"

The girl covered her face and began to sob even harder.

"Here, sit." Phillip looked up at the butler. "Pour her a sherry, Henton. Now, Anna, tell me what happened."

"A group of men, they went down to look at the back, to see if it was holdin'," Anna said between sniffles. The back in a mine was the ceiling, which never made sense to Phillip, but there it was. "Elden, he'd been thinkin' they needed some beams put in 'cause the walls were shiftin' while they was workin'. Then there was a loud rumblin' sound, and the ground moved under my feet. Some of the men came out coughing, but not all. Me Elden's dead." She began sobbing again.

Phillip rubbed his temples to ease the sudden pounding in his head. "How many, Anna?"

"At least eight total, sir. Harland, too. That's why I offered to come tell you. The others're tryin' to dig 'em out, but they say it's gonna take days to reach 'em. They don't think any of 'em who went in deep survived."

Bile rose in Phillip's throat. Poor Elden, who adored the young woman sitting beside him now. Harland, a fine foreman, who was a hard worker and always had the miners' safety at heart. He had met every man who worked that mine and considered them all friends.

"I'm so terribly sorry this happened," Phillip whispered. "You must be tired. Henton will see you have something to eat." He turned to the butler. "Take her to the kitchen and see Mrs. Shepherd gives her whatever she can."

"Yes, sir. Come with me, miss."

Anna's sobs filled the corridor as Phillip tried to comprehend what he had just learned. Harland Curtis may have been in charge of the miners, but the ultimate responsibility fell on Phillip. And he had failed every one of those killed. Why had he not considered mandating beams be put up in the mine? He had been involved in mining long enough to know that every precaution should be put into place to ensure the safety of those working so hard to see the mine prosper.

What was worse, he would have no more money to put into reopening the mine once it was cleared again. Every farthing he had left would go to the families for whom the miners provided, and he had little to give.

He would lose Courtly Manor.

A knock on the door made him look up to find Agnes and her lady's maid entering the room.

"Phillip?" she asked as she hurried to his side. "What's happened?"

"The mine in Tradswith collapsed," he said. That could not be his voice. Not that thin, hollow sound that came to his ears. "A little over half a dozen men are dead, including a young man whose fiancée came to deliver the news."

Agnes gasped. "Where is she?"

"I sent her to the kitchen to have a bit of food."

"I'll go to her," Agnes said, her voice firm. "Amy, you'll come with me. And hurry."

Phillip barely noticed her withdrawing. His head felt like it was filled with cotton wool. The room moved around him as if the foundation was shifting. Would Courtly Manor sink into the ground like the earth above that ill-fated mine?

"Is there anything I can do, sir?"

Phillip had not realized the butler had returned. "No, thank you." He could not sit here waiting for the world to collapse around him, so he walked through the corridors filled with fog until he reached the kitchen.

Then he stopped and observed a most wondrous sight. Agnes was unlike other young women of the gentry he had encountered, for she did not seem to care that the woman who wept into her shoulder wore a dressed stained with dirt. Instead, she held her as if she were a best friend, a sister, rubbing her back and whispering that all would be well. That everything happened for a reason.

If only Phillip had that kind of strength.

Watching became uncomfortable, so he made his way to the study. There, he dropped into the chair behind the desk and buried his head in his hands. The little ore they had excavated thus far would go to auction today, but whatever he made off that sale would barely be enough to pay the workers and give to the families of those who died. He would have nothing left. Which meant he would lose Courtly Manor.

And he would have nothing to offer Miss Agnes for marriage. No luxury. No home. No future.

He knew she would not care, but Phillip did. What kind of man marries a woman knowing he would lose everything before their first year together? The best thing now was for him to cancel the engagement. But he would wait to do so. Right now, his main concern was for the miners.

Phillip was uncertain how long he sat at his desk in utter despondency before a soft voice made him look up.

"Are you all right, Phillip?" Agnes asked.

He nodded, albeit dejectedly, as he stood. "I'll be fine. My concern is for Anna. How is she?"

"Devastated," Agnes replied. "But more under control at the moment."

Phillip nodded, yet as he looked at the woman about whom he cared so much, he found he could not help but be truthful. "Agnes, you understand that this disaster has secured my ruin, do you not? I have no way to pay my debt to Mr. Porter, which means I'll lose my home. We must delay the wedding for now. If not indefinitely."

To his surprise, she walked around the desk and placed a hand on his cheek. "Oh, my dear Phillip, don't you see that my love for you is not tied to mines you may own? Or estates, for that matter?"

Removing her hand, he said, “I don’t doubt you believe so. But when I have nothing, you’ll think differently.”

Her smile warmed his heart. “I know lives were lost, and I don’t mean to trivialize such a tragedy. But when it comes to us, this is just another stumbling block. One you’ll overcome. As you have before, so shall you again.”

Although her words were meant to bring him hope, he did not believe them. Surely, it was too late. For all of them.

But he could not hurt her, not just yet. “Thank you, Agnes. I’ll find a new solution.” He hated that his words sounded hollow.

She stood on the tips of her toes and kissed him. “I’ll check on Anna. Don’t despair. Good things will come your way. I’m certain of it.”

Once she was gone, Phillip returned to his seat. He wanted so much to believe her, but this catastrophe would only make others all the more wary of investing in his mines. They would see him as he saw himself—a negligent businessman with no right owning a mine.

Drawing in a deep breath, Phillip took out a piece of parchment and dipped the nib of his pen in the ink. It was time to write to Mr. Porter and tell him about his misfortune. And what he thought would be best for Agnes.

Chapter Fourteen

Phillip had reread the letter he had received from Meadow Estate several times. It was not from Mr. Porter as he had expected but rather from Agnes. In it, she reminded him of his need to continue to fight for what he wanted. That he could not give up no matter what obstacles got in his way. That he had no choice in the matter.

How could anyone show such support? And not just anyone, but the woman he adored? Yet, how could she believe in him when he did not believe in himself?

Despite his misgivings, he had honored her request by writing letters to every man with the means to invest within a ten-mile radius. Unfortunately, his efforts did not pay off. Nearly all rejected him outright. Except the man before him now.

Mr. Noah Kenton was a wiry man with beady eyes, a pointed nose to make a quill's nib jealous, and gray hair that he swept over a balding pate. Yet Phillip cared nothing for the man's looks. He had agreed to listen to Phillip's proposal. Nothing else mattered.

Phillip shivered and glanced out the window from his chair in front of Mr. Kenton's desk. Large flakes of snow continued to float to the ground—appropriate weather given the fact that Christmas was less than a week away. He said a silent prayer that the Christmas miracles he had believed in as a child would come to pass today.

Not pulling his coat tighter around him was difficult. The room was as quiet as his host's unlit fireplace. Mr. Kenton preferred to wear a heavy wool coat and a thick woolen muffler around his neck than to do what he deemed as "waste valuable fuel."

Mr. Kenton strummed his fingers on the desk and sighed. "I don't believe I'll be investing with you, Rutley. It's nothing personal, I assure you, but I simply don't invest in mines. It's far too speculative, and I prefer to put my money toward investments with returns that are more assured."

"May I ask, then, why you asked me here today?" Phillip asked. "I mean no disrespect, but surely this could have been done in writing."

Mr. Kenton nodded. "It could have, yes. You see, many years ago, I invested in several mines. I lost a fortune in those investments. My story is not unique. I know many men of means who have lost as much, if not more than I. You seem a sensible young man who is willing to listen to a bit of advice." He scowled. "Unlike my son, who is coming of age next month and is a complete fool." He sighed. "I suggest you don't seek new investors nor spend another farthing in mining. It will ruin you. Have you no other sources of income? A shipping vessel or a farm, perhaps?"

Phillip tried to push away his disappointment. "Sadly, I've lost money on ventures in both areas. But I believe my luck will change with these mines. The ore is there, I'm sure of it."

"Sure, are you?" Mr. Kenton chuckled wryly. "There is no surety in anything, but especially not in mining. No, I'm sorry, but I cannot help you."

With a sigh, Phillip stood. "Thank you for seeing me."

The older man smiled. "If you find yourself looking for an investor in a more sensible area, please let me know."

A sense of defeat overwhelmed Phillip as he walked out of Mr. Kenton's home. Who was left to approach? The butcher? The tobacconist? Neither would have the funds to invest in anything but his own business.

The fresh snow crunched under his boots as he walked to the waiting carriage. His driver, Lewis Tibbons, leaped from the seat and opened the door. "Might I have a word with you, sir?"

Tibbons was in his mid-twenties with dark blond hair who always wore a friendly smile. "I assume this has to do with the position you were looking into with Lord Dowding," he said with a heavy sigh.

As strange as it was, Phillip had been childhood friends with the newly named Earl of Dowding. And as he was in need of a driver he could trust, Phillip had granted Tibbons permission to apply for the situation. As far as Phillip was concerned, Tibbons was very good at his job and deserved the opportunity to work for an earl. Even if it meant he, Phillip, would have to dish out the necessary funds to advertise for the man's replacement.

"Yes, sir," Tibbons replied. "If it's all right with you, sir, Poltis—that'd be his lordship's butler and the man who interviewed me for the position—asks that I can start right away. So, I'll be givin' you my notice now that I'll be leaving in two days."

"I'm pleased you got the position," Phillip said with all honesty. "I'm disappointed to see you go, but this will be a wonderful opportunity for you."

"Thank you, sir."

The return journey to Courtly Manor was uneventful, and soon the carriage was trundling up the drive. Miss Fitzimmons was due to arrive in an hour, and Phillip had planned a special outing for them.

"See to what we discussed this morning," he told Tibbons, who nodded before pulling the carriage toward the carriage house.

Pushing down his disappointment with the outcome of his meeting, he sat behind the desk. Taking the quill in hand, he crossed off Mr. Kenton's name from the list he had made previously.

It was the last.

Despair clung to him like a shirt after a plunge in a pond. He so wanted to marry Agnes, to provide her with the wonderful life she deserved. But unless the Almighty intervened, his prospects looked slim.

"Miss Fitzimmons's carriage is pulling into the drive, sir," Henton announced.

Smiling, Phillip returned the now-worthless list to the desk drawer and stood. Agnes could bring him from the depths of hopelessness by the mere mention of her name. That list did not matter! He would find a way so they could be together. One way or another.

Hurrying to the front door, he stepped out onto the portico just as her driver was opening the door to the carriage. As Agnes alighted, the last of his worries disappeared. She wore a white, fur-lined, hooded cloak and a fur muffler, and her cheeks were pink from the cold. Nothing in this world was more beautiful than she. And he could not wait to tell her so.

A thick blanket of snow lay all around Chatsworth as Agnes journeyed to Courtly Manor. A fair number of people had braved the weather, all smiling and waving as they passed one another along the road. She had looked forward to this day all week, for Phillip had promised her a wonderful surprise.

She paused. "Phillip," she said in a low whisper so Amy could not hear. It was so nice to test out the use of his Christian name on her tongue. It felt right.

What could Phillip possibly have planned? And why was it a surprise? Could it be he wished to celebrate finding an investor? Oh, but she hoped so!

The carriage came to a stop, and the driver opened the door. Waiting on the portico was the man she loved. He looked resplendent in his black overcoat lined with gold buttons.

Agnes raised the hem of her skirt as she alighted from the vehicle. "I'm so glad I chose to wear my riding boots. I had Amy add a fur lining to make them warmer." She glanced down at the footwear. "I must admit they're a bit snug now, but at least I'll be warm. I do hope we'll not be walking anywhere. Well, it does not matter. I do like the snow!" She twirled about twice before her foot slid on a patch of ice. Luckily, he was there to catch her before she fell.

"Are you hurt?" Phillip asked, his hands remaining on her waist as he looked her up and down, concern etching his handsome features.

"No," she replied, her breath coming in short gasps. Not from fright but rather from the closeness they were sharing. In his arms was just where she wanted to be. "No, I'm fine. But is the snow not wonderful?"

And will you kiss me?

Much to her disappointment, he released her. "I do like when it snows, yes," he replied. "And it's perfect for our outing today."

Agnes went to ask what he meant, but the sound of tinkling bells made her turn. Her eyes widened when an open sleigh emerged from the carriage house, pulled by a single black horse. The finely crafted vehicle had two runners, and offered two red velvet-covered seats, each wide enough for two people and both facing forward. High boards surrounded the sleigh so the snow would not fly up at them.

Mr. Porter had taken Agnes out on a sleigh once, and she had enjoyed it immensely. Now, however, she would be with Phillip, which made such an adventure all the better.

"Well?" Phillip asked. "What do you think?"

"Oh, this is a brilliant surprise," she said, grinning. "I don't know how I can ever thank you."

"Your being here with me is thanks enough," he said, making her cheeks burn. "Allow me to help you up."

Amy sat in the seat at the back, while Agnes and Phillip took the front. Henton laid several thick furs over their laps as he climbed into the driver's perch.

Phillip adjusted the furs on his and Agnes's laps. "Are you warm enough?" he asked.

Agnes nodded but did not mention that his nearness caused enough warmness to make the furs unnecessary. No, it was likely enough to heat the entire house!

The driver flicked the reins, and the horse moved forward. The bells tinkled merrily with the movement of the sleigh and in time with the plodding of the horse.

With a sigh, Agnes laid her head on Phillip's shoulder. "Never could I have imagined anything so romantic. A sleigh ride, falling snow... and you beside me." She glanced up and laughed. "Why did you not wear a hat?" she asked, brushing the flakes of snow from his dark hair.

"I'm afraid I forgot," he said, smiling. "And neither Henton nor Tibbons would embarrass me by reminding me to don one." This had them both laughing.

Agnes's heart raced as Phillip grasped her hand beneath the thick covers. Was it possible to feel both protected and loved at the same time? Clearly, it was, for that was how she felt at this very moment. Today proved she and Phillip belonged together no matter what the future held.

They remained holding one another's hands as the horse kicked up snow, and the sleigh glided over the open field covered in snow, creating a cold breeze that caused the tiny hairs to tickle Agnes's forehead. The air was crisp and clear, and she reveled in the feel of Phillip beside her. Neither spoke, but there was no need. Sometimes silence was as beautiful as any romantic poem found in a book, and Agnes wished for this outing to never end.

Yet, it did. As they rode up in front of Courtly Manor, the butler was there waiting to help them alight.

"I asked Henton to have chocolate brought to the parlor for us," Phillip said as the sleigh came to a stop. "But first, I've something I would like to tell you."

The seriousness of his tone sent a shiver down Agnes's spine. "Amy, you run along to the parlor. We'll be right there."

Amy gave a small nod and did as Agnes bade.

"Go on."

Phillip sighed. "This morning's meeting did not go well," he said. "Nor have any of the other inquiries I've made. I do wish to keep the hope alive as you've requested, but the days ahead don't look promising. Regardless, I want you to know that I haven't given up. I'll do whatever I can to secure our future. I promise."

Her heart beat with love and admiration for this man! Despite his many difficulties, he fought for them, fought for their love, and she could not have asked for anything more.

"It's strange," he said. "When I was a child, my mother told me that Christmas was a time when great things happen to those who believe in miracles. And I truly did believe. But as an adult, trusting in such ideals is far more difficult."

Agnes considered his words. "When I was young, I had friends in London. One day I'll tell you about them and about my life there, but not today. Regardless, during those times of Christmas past, we would wish for a better life. But I never stopped believing in Christmas miracles, Phillip. And so, this year, I wished for you to be forever in my life, and I've no doubt I'll be granted that wish."

He squeezed her hand and smiled, warming her heart. "These past few Christmases have not been ones I would look upon with fondness, but perhaps that is the problem."

Agnes frowned. "What do you mean?"

"My worries have been about the past. Every year, I've not considered what good the future may bring." He snorted. "I should assume the marker of the 'Gentleman of Christmas Past' given my propensity to mourn what has already happened rather than anticipating what could come." He turned toward her and brought her gloved hand to his lips. "A future with you, Miss Agnes Fitzimmons. One in which I'll be successful no matter what comes my way."

He leaned close to her, and Agnes thought her heart would burst from her chest it was pounding so hard. "Don't you see, my dear Agnes? My future is already better because I've met you. My life is now forever changed."

As snow floated down around them, their lips met in a soft kiss. The poor girl from London could never have imagined such a setting, nor a man with whom she could share it. Phillip had every right to surrender to his troubles, to declare bankruptcy, and admit defeat. Yet he remained strong and as unwavering as the love they had for one another.

When the kiss ended, Phillip helped Agnes alight from the sleigh. Then he took both her hands in his. "This Christmas will be different. One way or another, my life will change. The past is behind me, Agnes, and it's because of you. Now, let's go inside. It's far too cold to remain out here!"

And as they warmed up beside the roaring fire, drinking their chocolate, their conversation was not on the past but rather on the future. A future Agnes knew would come to pass.

Chapter Fifteen

Christmas eve had arrived. Agnes sat in a carriage with Mr. Porter and Phillip as they traveled to the home of Lord Walcott. They had not seen one another since their wonderful sleigh ride.

Phillip made every attempt to hide his worries over the mine collapse, and he had yet to receive word from any potential investors. Yet his smile assured Agnes he had not given up hope. In fact, his perseverance only made him handsomer.

She had selected an olive-green gown with gold embroidered leaves and vines. Amy had spent more than an hour piling her long, chestnut hair high atop her head using pomade and a gray shade of powder.

Where some women were known to keep their hair styled for weeks on end, Agnes would have it washed, dried, and brushed out by tomorrow evening. She found the scent of most pomades overbearing and could only stand them for so long. If it were up to her, she would have preferred to leave her hair its natural color, but fashion dictated what she should and should not do. It was all silly, really.

"Did you contact Langard as I suggested?" Mr. Porter asked.

"Indeed, I did, sir," Phillip replied. "Unfortunately, he has no interest in investing in mines at this time. He sees them as too risky. And after what happened in Tradswith, I cannot blame him."

"What about Lord Walcott?"

Phillip sighed. "He replied very much the same. Though I'll not give up hope."

"Right you are," Mr. Porter said. "One must keep marching ahead, even when tragedy strikes."

Although Agnes admired his tenacity, she felt terrible for Phillip and wished there was something she could do to help him. Anything. But he had exhausted the circle of those in and around Chatsworth with the funds to make such an investment. She knew little about mining, but surely someone out there would see that Phillip had a mine worth excavating. Had he not shown her that copper had been found?

So caught up on her thoughts was she that it came as a surprise when they stopped in front of the home of Lord Walcott. Foxly Manor was a lovely, three-story estate made of rust-colored bricks covered in ivy.

The foyer was impressive with a polished dark oak table and two matching side tables. A large painting of a fox hunt hung beneath the staircase along the right-hand wall. Lady Walcott, a lovely but frail woman with auburn hair powdered with the same pale pink as the fabric of her gown, stood talking to the Duke and Duchess of Elmhurst. Agnes had never had the opportunity to speak to the latter, but she would recognize them anywhere.

Soon, the call came for the guests to enter the ballroom by rank. That meant Agnes would be among the last, but that did not bother her. She knew her place in life. Four years earlier, she would never have imagined being a guest in the home of an earl!

By the time their name was called, the other guests had lost interest, or so it appeared by the din in the ballroom. As Agnes passed by Lord Walcott, he gave her a small nod but otherwise did not look at her.

So, you're still angry with me, are you? She thought. Well, she still did not regret the tongue lashing she had given him. Lady Walcott was far too wonderful to endure the carrying-on of an ill-mannered husband.

Once in the room, Mr. Porter excused himself and walked over to a group of men. Phillip looked around the room, disappointment evident in his eyes.

Agnes offered him a small smile. "Don't give up," she said. "Something good will happen. I'm sure of it."

Phillip took a glass of wine from a passing footman and handed it to Agnes. "I'll never give up," he said. "You'll never let me." He said this with a wink, causing her to laugh. "It's difficult seeing no one new tonight, but I'll find a way to see my dreams realized."

Agnes placed a hand on his arm. "I have no doubt you'll be successful."

Smiling, he said, "It appears Mr. Porter needs me. Will you be all right here alone? I'll return soon."

With a nod, Agnes watched him join her guardian and two other men. Perhaps they had some interest in investing in the mines.

Not wanting to stand in the middle of the ballroom alone, Agnes made her way to the far wall. As she passed other guests, she returned polite smiles, but a hand grasped her by the arm. Agnes turned to face the Duchess of Elmhurst. Not only was her title impressive but so was the woman's beauty. She had midnight black hair, high cheekbones, and wore a green dress of the latest fashion from Paris that accentuated her thin waist and ample bosom.

"Miss Fitzimmons, may I have a word with you, please?" Beside the duchess stood Lady Walcott and the Marchioness of Barrington. Lady Barrington was a petite woman with dark hair and eyes and a nervous habit of smoothing her skirts every little while.

Agnes began to drop into the deepest curtsy she could muster, but the duchess clicked her tongue.

"There's no need for that, Miss Fitzimmons. We've all been introduced, and someone may step on you in the process."

All three women laughed, but Agnes could do nothing more than stare. She had no idea these women had the ability to make jokes. She had always considered them far too serious.

"Is there something I can do for you, Your Grace?" Agnes asked.

The woman gave her a warm smile. "Not exactly. I just wanted to say that I'm pleased you and Lord Ezra went your separate ways. That was a very wise decision on your part."

"I appreciate you saying so," Agnes said, dumbfounded. And, she had to admit, confused. It was a bold statement to make about the brother of her husband. Then again, she was a duchess and could say what she pleased.

"Of course, you're already acquainted with Lady Walcott," the duchess said. "But have you met Lady Barrington yet?"

The marchioness gave Agnes a faint smile that did little to hide a mysterious pain. Agnes hoped whatever it was could be healed. "Miss Fitzimmons and I have indeed met, but we are not well acquainted, Your Grace."

"No? Then allow me to better acquaint you," the duchess replied. "Miss Fitzimmons is the ward of Mr. Porter."

As the lady continued to speak, Agnes took a nervous sip of her wine. Why had they stopped her? Surely, they were not planning to include her in... well, whatever women of their station discussed at these parties. It was one thing to be allowed to stand in their presence and quite another to be *with* them.

"I must admit," Lady Walcott said, "I'm pleased you came, Miss Fitzimmons. I do enjoy your company. I must have you over for tea again soon."

"That would be lovely," Agnes replied, unsure if she had overstayed her welcome.

Maybe you're being overly cautious, she told herself. Perhaps they were simply being kind to her.

The duchess frowned. "That won't do at all. No, she must join us at Hardwick House for our weekly Thursday meetings." She turned to Agnes. "If you would like to, of course. It's nothing spectacular, just a few of us ladies getting together to share in a bit of gossip and tea."

For a moment, Agnes thought of the streets of London from whence she came. Now she would be drinking tea as a true guest of a duchess! If she had not learned to be a refined young lady, she would have been jumping up and down with excitement and shouting at the top of her lungs about her luck.

"I would be honored, Your Grace," she said instead with a bob of a curtsy.

Agnes stole a glance at Phillip. When he looked her way, he gave a small shake of his head. So, they had not asked him over to discuss the possibility of an investment.

"If you'll excuse me, Your Grace, my ladies," Agnes said. "I would like to see what sort of refreshments are being served. May I bring you anything?"

"You're not a servant, Miss Fitzimmons," the duchess said kindly. "But thank you for offering all the same."

Relieved, Agnes walked away from the ladies, glancing around the room. Surely, there was someone Phillip had not yet asked. Her eyes fell on the duke. No, if there was anyone she could not approach, he would be at the top of that list.

"Miss Fitzimmons."

The voice was low and sharp, and Agnes turned to face Lord Walcott. His eyes were narrowed, and Agnes readied herself for the tongue lashing that was sure to come.

"Good evening, my lord," she said, forcing a smile. "Thank you for the invitation. It's a very fine party. But I imagine you're not here to discuss this gathering but rather our last encounter."

The earl nodded. "Mr. Porter warned me about you, but I refused to listen. After all, what proper lady openly shares her opinions? I thought he was jesting but when I spoke to you... or rather when you gave me your very scathing opinion, I must admit I was angry." He sighed and shook his head. "Yet, it's when we're presented with the truth that the flames of our anger are at their hottest."

For a moment, he turned to look in the direction of where his wife stood. "When I returned home that evening, my wife was waiting for me, worry covering her beautiful features. And for the first time, I realized I could lose her. Not that she would leave me but that there was a chance for a separation that went far deeper. If you understand my meaning."

"I do."

"Therefore, I've decided to stay away from that place. And I've got you to thank for opening my eyes to the truth. I'm in your debt."

Agnes stared at him in shock. "You owe me nothing, my lord. I only did what I felt was right. Lady Walcott is a kind soul and deserves the best in life. And that was all that concerned me at the time."

He snorted. "You did for me what my closest friends would not, Miss Fitzimmons. You told the truth despite the possible consequences. Now, I must consider you a close friend. I hope you can see me as yours."

"Of course," Agnes said, so stunned she was unable to say more.

Who would have thought this life possible for the likes of you? And yet here you are.

"If there is anything I can do for you," he said, "anything at all, all you need to do is ask."

Agnes was prepared to tell him there was nothing, but then an idea came to mind. "You're close to most of the nobility in and around Chatsworth, are you not?" She bit down on her tongue. Of course he was!

"I am."

"Then you may regret offering to help," Agnes whispered. "For what I request is great." She went on to explain about Phillip's unanswered letters. "I'm not asking you to convince them to invest. I would never make such a request. But if you would have your peers just listen to him, even for a few minutes, I believe they might change their minds."

"I refused because I've no interest in investing in anymore mines. Did the others refuse or did they ignore his request for an audience?"

"A bit of both," Agnes said. "I learned that Lord Ezra destroyed the letter that was meant for His Grace. But I cannot simply walk up to him and begin discussing the possibility of investing in mines. I'm a mere woman. He would laugh me out of the village."

Lord Walcott sighed. "I'm telling you this in the strictest of confidence. Her Grace and I don't trust Lord Ezra in the slightest. His brother is unaware of that fact. Each time we try to broach the subject, His Grace refuses to listen. But even if I'm able to set up a meeting, I cannot make any promises he'll agree to invest."

"That's all I ask," Agnes said. She grasped his arm as he turned to leave. "Thank you again."

"It is I who should thank you," he said with a warm smile.

When the earl was gone, Agnes let out a heavy sigh. She had done all she could. Now it was in Phillip's hands. And she had every confidence he would be successful.

The words Mr. Porter had told her the first day they met came to her mind.

There is always hope.

Chapter Sixteen

Here it was Christmas Eve, and Phillip's Christmas miracle had yet to come to pass. Judging by those in attendance at Lord Walcott's party—not one of them had replied to Phillip's many inquiries—it would not likely happen tonight, either.

Holly, ivy, and fir branches festooned the ballroom of Foxly Manor as the revelers enjoyed mulled wine or eggnog and admired the painstakingly designed Christmas cakes depicting an entire village complete with tiny figures. Many of the ladies gathered around in appreciation for one of the marzipan-covered sculptures in particular that depicted a yule candle. It was even lit!

Phillip took a polite sip of his wine as he listened to Mr. Porter and Lord St. John reminisce about a hunting party in which they participated several years earlier. The baron was a slim man with a stern gaze that gave him a permanent angry look. But once one became better acquainted with him, Phillip learned St. John was not as malevolent as he appeared.

Although Agnes's guardian rarely left the house, Phillip was pleased to see his health had improved enough to allow him an enjoyable evening. Perhaps that had been Mr. Porter's Christmas wish.

"Mr. Rutley?"

Phillip turned to find Lord Walcott joining him. "Good evening, my lord. This is such a lovely party. Thank you for allowing me to attend."

The earl waved a dismissive hand. "I was curious if you're still seeking investors for your mines."

Phillip could do nothing to hide his surprise. "I am."

"I was just speaking to a friend, and I've arranged a meeting with several of my peers to discuss your ideas."

For a moment, Phillip could only stare. Surely, he had heard wrong. After all, the earl had refused outright to invest. Yet Phillip was not one to look a gift horse in the mouth.

"I don't know what to say, my lord. But thank you."

Lord Walcott gave a nod. "Don't thank me just yet, Rutley. I make no promises any of us shall invest. I only offer the opportunity to present your ideas."

Phillip nodded. "Of course. I understand. When shall we meet?"

"Why not now?" Lord Walcott asked. "The others are waiting in the parlor. Unless you prefer to remain here to listen to the music and drink wine?"

Phillip thought his heart would burst from his chest. Was he ready to talk now?

Of course he was! He knew every number, every aspect of his business proposition, had known for months now. "No, no, of course. Now is the perfect time."

Phillip searched the room for Agnes, but she seemed immersed in conversation. He would wait to tell her the good news later. And good news he would have!

Half a dozen men, including the Duke of Elmhurst, were in the parlor when Phillip and Lord Walcott arrived. Phillip barely took notice of the crimson fabric trimmed in gold thread that covered the seat cushions or the mauve and white walls.

"Good evening, gentlemen," Lord Walcott said, and the room fell quiet. "You're all acquainted with Mr. Phillip Rutley, I'm sure."

All the air in Phillip's lungs was gone. These were men of the highest regard, all wealthy and titled. Such a meeting of men of their status was rare, so this was his only chance to make a good impression. And to convince them to invest in his mines.

No, to invest in *him*.

"Mr. Rutley has a potential investment opportunity he would like to present to us, and I believe we should hear him out." The earl gave Phillip an expectant look. "When you're ready."

Swallowing hard, Phillip tried to make the room stop spinning around him. Words would not come! They were gathering in his throat, and he would choke on them if he did not speak them soon.

The duke frowned. "Well?"

This was it. All was lost. He would stand here like a complete fool, using up his last chance.

Then an image of Agnes appeared in his mind. Her smile, that twinkle she always had in her eyes, untangled the words in his throat.

"Gentlemen," he began, and he was pleased his voice did not shake, "your time is valuable and thus why I'll make this short. I have numerous mines ready to be worked. They have not been open for years because they originally produced tin. When that dried up, it was believed the mines were worthless. But we've found signs of copper in four of them, one in which we've already encountered a vein, and another four show promises of coal."

Lord Walcott was the first to speak. "Mr. Rutley, may I ask why you don't have your own resources to fund such a venture?"

Now was the time to speak the truth. And so he did. Phillip explained all that had happened in the past few years, all the bad luck he had endured—the loss of his shipping vessel and the sickness that had killed all his cattle. "This is why I stand before you tonight. I... no, *we* have a chance to make a great deal of money, and it waits just beneath the ground. But until I have the money to begin the work, I can do nothing."

The duke set his glass on the table beside him and rubbed his chin. "My brother told me that one of your mines collapsed recently. Is this true?"

Phillip swallowed hard. "It is, Your Grace."

"What makes you so sure the others won't do the same?"

"I won't offend you by giving you such an assurance," Phillip said. "But every mine has risks. Even the miners know this."

Lord Cramer, a large man with a tall white wig, snorted. "And I'm sure their families will see it that way."

"I've seen that their families were compensated, my lord."

"How?" asked Lord Montgomery, a man in his middle years with the curls of his powdered wig touching his shoulders. "If you've no money, how could you possibly compensate them?"

Phillip sighed. "I used all I had to see them cared for, my lord. And I make no apologies for doing so."

"That was an admirable thing to do, Rutley," Lord Templeton said, his tall, thin frame looking odd beside that of Lord Cramer.

After several more questions, the room fell silent, and Phillip found himself holding his breath. Had he given them enough information? Were his answers satisfactory?

"I've heard enough," Lord Walcott said. "The price of ore has been moving upward as of late. I cannot speak for everyone, but I'll invest. And as the first, I would like a larger percentage."

Lord Barrington nearly choked on his brandy. "Now, see here, Walcott. There's no need for greed among friends." He turned to Phillip. "I want a percentage equal to that of Walcott."

The duke laughed, drawing the attention of the room. "Then it must be split four ways, for I don't wish to miss out on this marvelous opportunity."

By the time the meeting came to an end, all six men had given their promise of investment, all on equal terms. Soon, Phillip stood alone in the room, trying to comprehend what had just taken place. They were to meet here again after Twelfth Night to set up the contracts for the eight mines in which they would invest.

His home would be saved. Staff would be kept. And most importantly, he and Agnes would marry.

"Phillip?"

He turned to find that very woman standing in the doorway.

"What are you doing here alone?" she asked.

He hurried to her, unable to keep from smiling. "Oh, Agnes, you'll never believe what just happened!" He gave her a quick summarization of what had just taken place. "We'll be meeting again after Twelfth Night to begin the process. But do you understand what this means? All my mines will be put into production! Courtly Manor is saved! But best of all, we can now marry, and our future is set."

And although he knew it was improper, Phillip did not care. He gathered Agnes in his arms and embraced her.

"I'm so pleased," she whispered in his ear. "I had every confidence in you."

In that moment, a new feeling surged through Phillip, a feeling far better than happiness. "It was your belief in me that got me through this. And it's that same belief that makes me realize that I love you." He leaned forward, kissed her soft lips, and sighed. "Now we both have our Christmas wish."

"Tonight, you secured our future," Agnes said, causing his confidence to soar. "No longer are you the Gentleman of Christmas Past."

He nodded. How right she was! And it was a wonderful feeling.

They hurried from the room lest they be caught alone. Agnes returned to the ballroom first, and Phillip joined her. Later, as the laughter in the room echoed around them, Mr. Porter came and spoke with them. The conversation flowed, and Phillip could not keep his mind off one thing. Or rather one person. Miss Agnes Fitzimmons, whose name would soon be Rutley, and who would share with him the wonderful years ahead of them.

Epilogue

Agnes had never been happier. Not only had Phillip been able to secure all the investments, but the mines were also already thriving. Although Phillip was away for many days at a time, she knew what he was doing was for the greater good for everyone concerned.

Yet more than wealth had increased since the Christmas Eve party at Foxly Manor. Men who had gone without work now had a means to feed their families. All eight mines were fitted with support beams to make them safer. But best of all, Agnes and Phillip's love for one another had reached exponential heights.

And it was because of that love that Agnes exited Courtly Manor and made her way to the large oak tree where Phillip waited beside the local vicar. The banns had been read, and the reception was planned, but this moment was theirs.

Agnes wore a pale-rose gown with a white ruffled petticoat. Her hair was piled high and dotted with pink daisies and pink glass-studded hairpins. Never had she felt so beautiful. And judging by the smile Phillip wore, he believed the same.

"You look lovely," he confirmed in a whisper as she took her place at his side.

Her cheeks heated. "Thank you. And I must say, you look quite dashing yourself."

And he did. He wore a crimson coat trimmed with white lace and matching breeches, white silk stockings, and a white ruffled cravat. But it was his smile and confident look that held her captive, for he had never looked more handsome.

As the vicar spoke, Agnes thought about all that she and Phillip had endured. He had been a man facing bankruptcy and she a woman from an impoverished background. Mr. Porter had been right in his assertion. All one needed was hope. But something else was needed to be happy.

Love.

For it was the love Phillip had for her, and she for him, that brought them together. It was their love that helped them overcome the obstacles that came their way. The love that had seen their Christmas wishes granted. And it was his love she affirmed under the great oak tree that day.

The love they would share for the many years to come.

THE END

Thank you for reading *Gentleman of Christmas Past* by Jennifer Monroe!

The students of Mrs. Rutley's School for Young Women create a secret bond and find love in the continuing series *Sisterhood of Secrets* beginning with Julia's story, *Duke of Madness*.

JENNIFER MONROE
SISTERHOOD OF SECRETS
BOOK ONE
DUKE of MADNESS

Also by Jennifer Monroe

The Sisterhood of Secrets

There is far more for the women at Miss Rutley's Finishing School than an education, for their secretive headmistress will assure her pupils find the happiness they each deserve.

#1 Duke of Madness

#2 Baron of Rake Street

#3 Marquess of Magic

#4 Earl of Deception

#5 Knight of Destiny

#6 Captain of Second Chances

About Jennifer Monroe

USA Today bestselling author Jennifer Monroe writes clean Regency romances you can't resist. Her stories are filled with first loves and second chances, dashing dukes, and strong heroines. Each turn of the page promises an adventure in love and many late nights of reading.

With over twenty books published, her nine-part series, The Secrets of Scarlett Hall, which tells the stories of the Lambert Children, remain a favorite with her readers.

Connect with Jennifer:

www.jennifermonroeromance.com

facebook.com/JenniferMonroeAuthor

instagram.com/authorjennifermonroe

bookbub.com/authors/jennifer-monroe

amazon.com/Jennifer-Monroe/e/B07F1MRXDN

CHRISTMAS INTRIGUE

PREQUEL TO THE ROYALS & REBELS SERIES

MEREDITH BOND

Christmas Intrigue by Meredith Bond

Published by WOLF Publishing UG

About the book

CHRISTMAS INTRIGUE

Alexander, Markgraf Kottenfurst, is extremely suspicious when he is invited to a Christmas house party in England. His brother, the prince of Aachen-Düren, a tiny principality near Brussels, insists that he go as this could be an incredible opportunity for their country. But after Alexander arrives, no one is willing to even discuss the reason he was invited.

Prudence Torrington's father really doesn't want her to attend the Christmas house party. The bubbly, always cheerful young woman will be the first to admit that she does have a tendency to get into trouble but she always has the best of intentions. Her father tries to explain that this isn't merely a party, there will be other members of Parliament there to carry out sensitive negotiations with a foreign dignitary. Prudence swears she will be good and her father relents.

Is it a recipe for disaster? Not even close. It's a Christmas intrigue leading to something neither Alexander nor Prudence could possibly expect.

Prologue

December, 1791

Lady Prudence Torrington did her best to hold back a giggle. It absolutely would *not* do to laugh now. If she did, she knew exactly what her parents, who were standing directly in front of her, would do.

As one, they would turn toward her. Her father would glare, and her mother would look as if she were going to cry or perhaps scream with frustration. In fact, it was pretty much a miracle that they weren't looking at her in that way even now.

No, instead, Prudence held back her laughter and firmly pressed from her mind the idea that she felt as if she were watching a tennis match—which is what had made her want to laugh in the first place. But this was no laughing matter, she reminded herself as she looked back and forth between her parents. They had been standing in her father's book-lined study arguing for nearly a quarter of an hour, and they did not seem to be any closer to a decision—would Pru go to Lord and Lady Humesbury's Christmas house party or not?

"How many times do I have to tell you, this is not just a party. The Markgraf Kottenfurst will be there to negotiate a treaty between Aachen-

Düren and England. This is important business," Lord Torrington told his wife once again, frustration clear in his voice.

"And I cannot stress enough the fact that it would be cruelty to leave the girl behind, all alone on Christmas!" Lady Torrington said. She was beginning to sound thoroughly exasperated. "We don't know what sort of trouble she might get up to if there is no one here to keep close tabs on her."

Pru refrained from pointing out that she was nearly twenty years old and perfectly capable of staying by herself—not that she would really be alone, considering they had nearly thirty people working in and around the house. She also did not mention that she was very capable of not getting into trouble because... well, she wasn't entirely certain that was true.

It wasn't that she went out and sought trouble all the time. Sometimes it just came to her. If she opened the door to it and allowed it in, well, that *was* something she needed to work on. She would be the first to admit she wasn't always good at spotting trouble before it came barging through her door, but she had to say she'd gotten a lot better over the past few years. And who knew, perhaps if she really did try... oh, who was she kidding? She loved trouble. It was what made life fun and interesting.

"I am certain I can avoid getting into mischief—" Pru started.

Both of her parents immediately turned on her, each with That Look.

"You, stay out of this," her mother said, pointing a finger at her.

"Why is she even in the room?" her father asked no one in particular.

"Because this concerns me," Pru pointed out.

"That's irrelevant." Lord Torrington took two steps away toward one wall of dark wood paneling, turned, and strode back. "It is true that we don't know what sort of trouble she'd get into here..." he said, clearly thinking this through.

"If she were with us, we would be able to keep an eye on her," Lady Torrington said with a significant lift of her eyebrows.

Her father narrowed his eyes at her. "Do you really think you can control the girl?"

"If she doesn't behave herself, she will spend the entire party locked in her room," her mother said without hesitation.

Pru opened her mouth to protest but received such a look from her mother that she immediately closed it again.

Lady Torrington gave her the slightest nod.

Pru's father turned toward her. "If I allow you to come—"

"I promise to be on my best behavior," Pru said immediately before he even had a chance to finish his thought.

"You'd better or else you will be spending the entire time in your room. Do you understand me, Miss?" Her father's voice was so filled with anger and threats, Pru couldn't help the slight shiver of fear that slipped up her spine.

She nodded, deliberately not saying a word.

"You called for me?" Alexander, Markgraf Kottenfurst asked, coming into his brother's office after a brief knock on the door.

"Yes." Prince Heinrich of Aachen-Düren, Rich to his family and good friends, looked up from the papers in front of him. "Have a seat." He began looking through a stack of papers on his right, found the one he was looking for, and pulled it out. He spent a moment in silence reading it before looking up at Alexander, who waited patiently.

Rich frowned at the paper and then at Alexander. "You have been requested to attend a house party in England at the home of Lord and Lady Humesbury over the Christmas holiday."

"Requested... Do you mean invited?" Alexander asked, not sure what his brother meant.

"Yes, but this isn't a social invitation. They are proposing a treaty between our countries."

Alexander sat forward in his chair. "Really? What could possibly prompt one of the most powerful countries in the world to want a treaty with us? I mean... no disrespect, you know I love Aachen-Düren with all my heart and have devoted my life to furthering our interests and protecting it, but... England?"

"Yes, I know. That was precisely my thinking as well. What could England want with us? We are... tiny. Barely a dot on the map of Europe compared with other principalities in the Austrian Empire."

"But we are not part of the Austrian Empire," Alexander pointed out. "Perhaps that is why they're interested. We have managed to maintain our independence. Even Brussels hasn't been able to do that, although God knows they tried."

Rich gave a dry laugh. "Do you call that failed revolt they had last year an attempt? The United States of Belgium, really? They couldn't even agree on a single thing beyond that ridiculous name."

"I agree. It is no wonder they fell to the Austrians again, but the point is, *we* are not under the rule of the Empire."

"Because we're so small and insignificant that even *they* couldn't be bothered to worry about us," Rich pointed out.

"Precisely. But maybe we can use that to our advantage. Maybe that is precisely why England is interested."

Rich stroked his fingers down his chin. If one looked hard enough, you could see the blond stubble there. "Yes. You should go," he said decisively. "It is interesting, however..."

When he didn't continue, Alexander prompted him. "In what way?"

"They asked for you by name." He looked down at the letter again. "They don't say we should send an ambassador or a trusted advisor or anything vague like that. They specifically say I should send *you*." He looked up and pierced Alexander with his blue eyes. "Why do you think that is?"

Alexander took in a deep breath but shook his head. "I have absolutely no idea. How could they have heard of me?"

"I don't know. Do you have contacts from the *Ecole Militaire* who they might have spoken with?"

"Well, you know I am constantly in contact with my friends from school. It is how I keep abreast of what the French are doing so I can advise you," Alexander pointed out.

"Yes, I know. But how do the *English* know this?" Rich leaned forward, keeping his eyes on his brother.

Alexander could only shake his head. "Perhaps they have their own spies or contacts within the French military? Or the government?"

Rich sat back, clearly satisfied with this answer, much to Alexander's relief. He certainly didn't want his brother thinking he was doing anything clandestine without the knowledge of his prince. "Yes, that must be it," Rich said finally. "They must have their own spies in Paris. Your name must have come up at some time. It is how they would have thought to even suggest such a treaty, right?"

Alexander spread his hands wide. "It's the only thing I can think of."

Rich nodded. "Of course. Of course." A smile grew on his narrow face. "Well, it looks like you are going to England for Christmas."

Alexander smiled right back, but there was a hint of sadness in his gut at the thought. "I'm going to miss being here with you and Mother. We are a smaller family this year..." he said, alluding to the death of their father just a little more than nine months earlier. It had been a horrid tragedy when the prince had gone riding just after a few particularly rainy days. In the fickle nature of March weather, the wet ground had turned to ice. After taking a blind jump, his horse had lost its footing, and the prince had gone down.

He had been killed outright with a broken neck.

Rich ran a hand down his face. "I know. It will be a sad holiday without our father. I hope that your Christmas will be more joyous, and I will be happy knowing that you are working hard for Aachen-Düren. You will, of course, write regularly to tell me of your progress with these negotiations."

"Naturally," Alexander said as he stood.

The prince came to his feet as well and reached out a hand. "Represent us proudly and come back safe and sound."

"I shall do so, Your Highness." He bowed low after gripping the hand of his closest friend.

Chapter One

Alexander watched with some amusement as his carriage drove up and then past the front door to Lord Humesbury's home. The entire line of maids and footmen watched in confusion as the carriage drove past. The butler and housekeeper, who stood at attention as the carriage approached, both stepped forward in confusion as it continued. Another couple, who Alexander assumed were his host and hostess, looked at each other, clearly wondering what was going on—until one of the clever footmen spotted him riding up on horseback.

A boy ran forward to grab the bridle as Alexander brought his horse to a halt just in front of all the people standing, waiting for him. As he dismounted, everyone bowed and curtsied in such perfect unison he wondered if they'd practiced. He nodded in response and then strode forward to meet Lord and Lady Humesbury.

"Welcome, Markgraf Kottenfurst, welcome!" the marquess said as he stepped forward, his hand extended and a broad smile on his face.

"Thank you, my lord." Alexander took his hand and then turned to Lady Humesbury, who was standing a step behind her husband. He gave her a short bow. "Lady Humesbury, it is an honor. Thank you so much for your invitation."

"Oh, Markgraf, the honor is ours. Welcome to our humble home," she said. Her smile rivaled that of her husband's.

Alexander looked up at the "humble" home and estimated at least forty bedrooms. He just gave her a smile.

There was another man standing to the left of the marquess.

"*Willkommen, Markgraf Kottenfürst, ich bin Übersetzer, wenn Sie meine Dienste benötigen*," the man said when he noticed Alexander's attention on him.

Alexander gave a little laugh and then turned to his host. "That was extremely thoughtful of you to provide a translator. I am fluent in English, although I must apologize in advance for my accent."

Lord Humesbury's cheeks turned a little pink. "Oh no, not at all. We, er, we weren't certain how comfortable you were with the language so thought it best..."

"Of course. No, I appreciate the gesture. Actually, having someone around who can translate the, er, subtleties of our languages might be very helpful when we begin our negotiations."

"Precisely what I was thinking!" the man exclaimed happily.

"But please, my lord, do come in out of the cold," Lady Humesbury said, turning and indicating the door, which was immediately opened by a footman.

"Yes, you all must be quite cold standing out here as well. Thank you, thank you for this wonderful welcome," Alexander said, falling into step with Lady Humesbury, who had begun to go inside.

He followed her into a grand, round entry way with white marble floors, stately rose marble columns, and a beautiful, curved staircase ascending into upper reaches. He glanced upward toward a glass rosette skylight that filled the entry with natural light. He imagined, when the sun was out and hit the window just right, the floor would be covered in rainbows from the light refracting through the glass. Sadly, the English winter seemed to consist of overcast days—he had yet to see the sun, and he'd been in the country for nearly a week since landing at Dover.

"This is my housekeeper, Mrs. Britworth," Lady Humesbury said, as the older woman who had been standing in front of the maids came forward. "She will show you to your room so you may rest from your journey. Should you need anything at all, please don't hesitate to call on her."

"Thank you. My valet and luggage were in the coach. Personally, I cannot stand being cooped up inside a carriage on long journeys," he told his hostess.

"Of course, I completely understand. It can be so tiresome, especially for an active young man such as yourself."

"Indeed," he agreed.

"I'm certain your man is being welcomed by the staff and will be up to your rooms shortly, my lord," the housekeeper added.

"Ah, good. He does not speak any English, I am afraid, but I am sure he will learn what he needs while we're here. I caught him studying a phrase book on the boat while we were crossing the channel."

"Oh," the housekeeper laughed. "Well, maybe we'll make better use of that translator since you won't be needing him so much."

"Yes, an excellent idea," he told her.

"Right this way, my lord." The housekeeper started up the stairs.

He gave Lady Humesbury a nod and started after her.

He wondered if he'd been given the master suite when she showed him the magnificent rooms where he would be staying. There was a private sitting room done in attractive deep blues and white, a bedroom with matching colors, and even a room in which to bathe, which was entirely white.

"Would you like for us to fill the tub for you, my lord, or just bring in a small basin of warm water for your washing?" the housekeeper asked as he inspected his surroundings.

He leaned toward her confidentially. "Is this his lordship's chambers?"

"Oh, no," she giggled. "But it is our best guest room, naturally."

"So Lord Humesbury's rooms are even more grand than this?"

She looked around and gave a little nod. "Nearly so. He and her ladyship share a private sitting room, but each have their own bed chambers."

"And a room for the bath, like this?" he asked, indicating the bathroom.

"His lordship has one," the woman told him. "If you'd be interested, my lord, I'd be happy to give you a tour of the house—although it won't, of course, include the private rooms."

"Of course! Yes, I would like that. It is a beautiful house. I would like to see it."

"Very good. Just let me know when it would be convenient for you."

"Thank you."

His valet entered just then, directing a footman who was carrying in his trunk. He immediately started telling Alexander how pleased he was with the service.

"There are so many footmen and maids, all waiting for me to tell them what to do. It is a very well-run house," Hans told him in German.

Alexander laughed. "Now you simply need to learn enough English so you can tell them what you want."

"Ja! I am working on that. I am learning. I think I have ordered hot water to be brought—" he stopped speaking when he caught sight of the bathtub in the smaller bathing room. "Oh."

"Indeed." Alexander just laughed. "I believe I shall take a bath. I stink from the journey."

"There is even a fireplace here," Hans called out from inside the room. "And it is lit, so you will be warm while you bathe."

Alexander gave him a broad smile. "I think we are going to enjoy our stay here, eh, Hans?"

"Indeed, my lord!"

"And I'm getting some ideas about how I want to modernize my drafty little castle."

The man sighed with happiness.

"I may be a military man and used to billeting in the worst conditions, but that doesn't mean I can't enjoy a little luxury, now does it?"

"Not at all, my lord, not at all!"

Prudence sat forward in the Torrington traveling coach, watching out the window. She turned to her father sitting next to her, reading his book. How he could read in a moving carriage was beyond her comprehension. She would be sick beyond belief if she did anything other than stare out the window.

"No," her father said before she'd even opened her mouth to say anything.

"You don't know what I was going to say!" she whispered loudly, taking a glance at her mother sleeping on the opposite seat.

"All right, then. Nearly," he told her.

"Really? We're nearly there?" she asked, perking up immediately.

He finally lifted his eyes from his book and glanced out the window. How he could tell where they were was beyond her. All she saw were fields, and they all looked the same. "Yes, really. Perhaps another fifteen, twenty minutes."

She sighed with relief. They'd been traveling for two days. Two days of torture. Two days of sitting still, not doing anything. If she could have ridden her father's horse, she would have been happier, but he'd sent it ahead with a groom from their stables. She couldn't imagine why he didn't want to ride, why he'd want to sit in a coach all day.

She gave a little shrug and turned back to the window.

It was closer to thirty minutes, but finally their carriage pulled up outside of the Humesbury's country home. Pru all but tumbled out of the coach when the footman opened the door. She had to resist the urge to go running back and forth to get the feeling back into her legs and her blood moving again. Goodness, but she hated long journeys!

Instead, as she was extremely conscious of her mother's eyes boring into her back as the lady calmly and elegantly climbed down from the coach with assistance. Pru stood quietly with her hands clasped in a lady-like way in front of her.

Her mother gave her an approving look while she strode forward in Lord Torrington's wake as he approached the door. It opened before he'd even had a chance to knock.

"Good afternoon, my lord," the footman said, bowing to them into the entrance hall.

Pru followed her parents into the house, admiring the beautiful marble and the magnificent staircase. It was so pretty; she could hardly contain herself.

She wandered forward, placing a hand on one of the marble pillars and looking up as it soared toward the ceiling. It was supporting the upper floor and the gently winding staircase.

"Prudence!" her mother whispered furiously.

But Pru was too enthralled watching an elegant lady float down the stairs. How did she do that?

"Prudence, come here this minute!" her mother whispered.

"Oh, are you Lady Humesbury?" Pru asked the smiling woman as she paused near the bottom of the stair.

"I am," she answered, with a curious tilt of her head.

"You have the most beautiful home! And it is absolutely perfect for Christmas. Why, I can just imagine long ropes of pine branches circling these magnificent columns. And that stair! It's just begging for greenery to be wrapped around the balustrade." Pru tilted her head, thinking and imagining the scene. "Perhaps holly with the bright red berries still attached to bring some more color in."

The woman laughed. "My, what a wonderful thought. I have to admit, I'd not considered decorating the entrance hall, but I think you're right. It would be spectacular just the way you describe it."

"My lady, I must apologize for my daughter," Lord Torrington said, coming forward. Somehow, he managed to both smile politely at their hostess and give Pru a furious look, so she would know just how much trouble she was in the minute they were alone.

"Oh, no! Not at all. She has a wonderful imagination and some excellent ideas," the lady said.

She came forward a little as she reached her hands out to Lady Torrington. "Anne, how wonderful it is to see you again. It's been ages!"

"Too long," Pru's mother agreed.

"I am so happy you could make it." She turned back to Pru. "And you must be Prudence. How lovely. Welcome."

Prudence curtsied. "Thank you, Lady Humesbury. It was so kind of you to extend your invitation to me. I am honored to be able to join you."

The woman bowed her head graciously. Her father's eyes went wide in surprise before narrowing with suspicion. He probably didn't even know she was capable of being so polite. Well, she would show him! She'd been practicing that little speech in her mind for the past four hours.

"Humesbury is out checking the stables, making sure everything is in readiness for all our guests and their equipages," Lady Humesbury told them.

"Are we the first to arrive?" Lord Torrington asked in some surprise.

"Oh, no, no. The Bunburys arrived yesterday, the Mintons this morning, and the Markgraf Kottenfurst, our guest of honor, arrived only an hour ago."

"Ah, he's come. Good, good," Pru's father said, rubbing his hands together.

"Of course. Was there any doubt?" the lady asked.

"No, no. Well, you never know how long these channel crossings will take, you know," he said.

"I'm sure he planned for any such delays. He arrived in perfect time and was even kind enough to send word ahead, so we were all prepared to meet him."

"How very thoughtful," Lady Torrington said.

"Indeed. But you must be exhausted from your own travels. Here is Mrs. Britworth. She will show you to your rooms so you may freshen up. And Lady Prudence, I will make a point to ask my gardeners to collect the pine and holly branches to decorate the columns and staircase."

"Oh, there is no need to go to any trouble—" Lady Torrington started.

"Thank you, my lady. If you do, it truly will look magnificent," Pru said, interrupting her mother.

Lady Torrington grabbed Pru by her arm and began dragging her toward the stair. "Come, Prudence."

Pru managed to escape her mother's grasp to give Lady Humesbury another curtsy before running after her mother. At a hiss from her father, she slowed to a sedate walk. She could hear their hostess laughing behind her.

The housekeeper showed them their rooms. They were given two interconnecting bedchambers and a third room for Lord Torrington. Pru's was small with just enough room for a single bed against one wall. But there was a dressing table and a comfortable wing-back chair set in front of the merrily burning fire.

Her mother opened the connecting door to allow Pru into the other room. It was much larger, with an enormous bed hung with deep-red curtains. On the far side was another door through which Pru could see her mother's maid in what appeared to be a dressing room.

"What was that?" her mother asked once they'd been left alone.

"What was what?" Pru asked, turning toward her mother from her inspection of the mirror above the fireplace in her mother's room.

"Giving the woman advice on how to decorate her home? Never have I been so embarrassed!" Lady Torrington told her.

"Of course you have. Do you remember when I—"

"Prudence!" Her mother stopped her.

"I'm sorry, but I just couldn't help myself. It was so beautiful! And you must admit my suggestions were—"

"It doesn't matter whether your suggestions were good or well-intentioned or whatever they were. The point is that you do not tell people how to decorate their homes," her father said, interrupting.

"Not even—"

"Never," her mother said quickly.

"Oh. But—"

"Prudence!" her mother nearly screeched.

"All right."

"You said you would behave yourself," her mother reminded her.

"I can't see that telling someone that they have a beautiful home is impolite. In fact, I would think just the opposite," Pru argued.

Her mother sighed and closed her eyes as if praying for patience. "It is not impolite. Telling someone how to decorate it, however, is."

"Hmm." But she had good ideas! And so many of them. And Lady Humesbury didn't seem to mind at all. But Pru knew she couldn't say any of those things to her mother without upsetting her even more. And seeing how she truly did not want to spend the entire party in her room, she wisely kept her mouth shut.

"Now, please, *please*, Prudence, hold your tongue. Do not give advice when it is not asked for and behave yourself," her mother practically pleaded.

"Very well, Mother. I will do my best."

Her father snorted at that. "I give her twelve hours, at most twenty-four."

"Papa, you have no faith in me!" Pru protested.

"None! I know you, girl, I know you too well," her father said with a sad shake of his head.

"Well, I am going to prove you wrong. I told you so before, and I will say it again. I *can* behave and I will." Pru stamped a foot for emphasis.

He just laughed. Pointing to her foot, he said, "See? Already acting like a child."

She wanted so much to stick out her tongue at him, but she resisted and instead turned around and went back into her own room.

"You keep a close eye on her," she heard her father tell her mother.

"Oh, believe me, I will!" Lady Torrington responded with vehemence.

"Nothing, absolutely nothing may distract from my mission here. It is too important!"

"Do not worry, my lord. Prudence will be on her best behavior for the entire two weeks." The last part was said loud enough for Pru to hear her perfectly well.

She got the message.

Chapter Two

"Please excuse my ignorance, but what do we call you?" a pretty girl, her round face surrounded by blonde ringlets, asked Alexander that evening when he joined the other guests for dinner.

He widened his eyes at Lady Humesbury, who'd just introduced them. Already he'd forgotten the girl's name! He didn't know what convention dictated here. He highly doubted the English called each other by their given names, but what else could she mean?

He must have looked confused by her question because she clarified immediately, "Are you called Your Highness? Your Majesty? My lord?"

"Oh!" Alexander laughed. "No, no. I am next in line to the throne, yes, but I am not a prince. My title is markgraf... it is rather like your marquess," he explained.

"Oh, so you're called 'my lord'?"

He shrugged. "Yes, you may call me that. And you?"

The girl giggled. "Me? I don't have a title. My father is a viscount, so I'm just plain old Miss Sidwell."

"Certainly that would be beautiful, young Miss Sidwell? You are neither plain nor old," he said, smiling at her.

The girl giggled again and, this time, blushed as well.

Lady Humesbury also laughed. "I think it is safe for me to leave the two of you to talk. I need to see to my other guests. If you will excuse me."

Alexander had never been one to flirt with the girls, but perhaps it was something that came naturally rather than was learned. Miss Sidwell certainly seemed to be enjoying his company.

"And what is it you do for fun, Miss Sidwell?" he asked, unsure what else to speak to the girl about.

"Oh, I, er, I play the pianoforte, I paint, and I enjoy doing my embroidery," the girl answered.

"You do not hunt or ride?" he asked.

"No," she giggled, although he wasn't quite sure what she found amusing. "Not for fun, certainly. I know you gentlemen enjoy such pursuits, but ladies like more calm, quiet activities, you know."

"Well, not all ladies. My mother, for instance, enjoys hunting a great deal... or, at least..." She did before Father had died while hunting. He couldn't imagine how painful that must have been for his mother to watch her husband take a jump and then not... Alexander swallowed hard. No, he was not going to think of his father's death. He was here to work. He had to remember this.

"At least what?" the girl asked in complete innocence of the turmoil bubbling through him.

He forced a smile onto his lips. "Nothing. Nothing at all. If you would please excuse me."

He turned away from the girl and located Lord Humesbury among the gentlemen. He made a direct line for his host.

"I do beg your pardon, my lord," Alexander said as he approached the man.

"Ah, Kottenfurst, please let me introduce you to the Earl Torrington." He indicated the gentleman to his right. He was as tall as Alexander but slender with dark hair, a narrow face, and slanted eyebrows that made him look as if he were worrying over something. He was also the man who had written to invite Alexander to this gathering, so he was precisely the person he'd most wanted to meet.

Alexander put out a hand. "My lord, I am very happy to meet you. I have been quite eager to do so, in fact."

The other man gave Alexander's hand a brief shake as he said, "Really?

Probably because mine is the only name you knew aside from Humesbury's before you came?" he asked with a little laugh.

"Er, well, yes. You were the one to write and invite me. I appreciate—"

The rest of what he would have said was waved away by the gentleman. "No, no. It is we who are honored that you were able to come." He turned to a younger man standing on his other side and said, "Lord Kottenfurst came all the way from the Continent, you know." They then turned back to Alexander. "Oh, let me introduce you to Mr. Frank Sidwell, Lord Bunbury's son."

Alexander nodded to the man. He was probably Alexander's own age, maybe a year or two younger. "Sidwell? I believe I was just speaking with your sister, Miss Sidwell?"

"Yes, that's right. Was she making your eyes cross with her inane chatter? I know I can hardly stand to talk to the girl for more than a few minutes at a time," Sidwell said with a laugh.

Alexander was confused as to why a man would demean his sister in such a way to a stranger, then figured he was joking. He gave a smile. "No, I found her to be quite pleasant, actually."

"Of course you did. She's a very nice girl," Lord Humesbury said quickly.

Alexander turned back to Lord Torrington. "Sir, who else here will be taking part in our discussions?"

"Eh? Oh, well, Humesbury, of course. He is head of the Foreign Service Committee in Parliament. And then there's Bunbury, another member of the committee, and Lord Minton—the blond fellow over there speaking with my wife—and Lord Perbury, who is in the Foreign Office itself."

"I see. I look forward to meeting all these gentlemen," Alexander said, looking around the room as if he could identify the men to whom he had not yet been introduced.

"Of course, and so you shall. In fact, come along and allow me—"

"And when will we begin our negotiations?" Alexander asked, interrupting him inadvertently.

"Oh, don't worry about that, my boy. Come, let me introduce you." He put a hand on Alexander's back and directed him toward a man a little bit older than Alexander—perhaps in his mid-thirties—who was speaking with an older lady with light brown hair and large green eyes. "My dear, here is the Markgraf Kottenfurst. Markgraf, my wife, Lady Torrington, and Lord Minton."

Alexander bowed to the lady and gave the gentleman a nod. "How do you do?"

After half an hour, Alexander felt as if his head was spinning with meeting so many new people. He knew this was all part of an ordinary day for an ambassador, but he'd never planned on doing such work. He was a military man. He could only hope he would be able to negotiate intelligently with these men, who were certainly all much more experienced in such matters than he.

He supposed this was how his brother felt on a daily basis since he'd inherited the throne so suddenly. He couldn't imagine what that would be like. Well, he would simply do his best. It was all he could hope for: that these gentlemen would not try to trick him into anything, that they would negotiate in good faith, for they certainly had to know he was inexperienced.

A worry nagged at him that it was precisely because of his ignorance that they'd asked for him, not one of Rich's more experienced advisors, to attend this gathering. It was, of course, too late to think of bringing along such assistance—why hadn't he or Rich thought of that earlier? Because they were both just trying to figure things out as they went along, naturally.

Alexander could only shake his head at his naiveté. On the other hand, they had not invited anyone but him, which brought him around once again to worrying they would not have the best of intentions in these negotiations.

"You are looking entirely too serious, my lord," Lady Humesbury said, leaning toward him as he sat to her right in a place of honor at the dining table.

"I do beg your pardon, my lady," he answered her quickly.

"No, do not. It's perfectly all right. This must be quite overwhelming for you to arrive in England and immediately have to deal with so many strangers."

"I am afraid it rather is," he admitted.

"This isn't your first time out of your country, now, is it?" she asked as a footman placed a bowl of soup in front of Alexander.

"No, my lady. I spent the last five years studying in France at the *Ecole Militaire,* and I have traveled around the Continent as well."

"Oh. Is that normal for someone from a German principality to study at a French military school?" she asked politely.

"Not very normal, but my mother was French, so I have ties to the nobility there."

"Oh, I see. I imagine you speak French fluently?"

"Yes, French, Spanish, German, of course, and English. Do you speak any other languages, my lady?"

As he made small talk with his hostess, he wondered whether their negotiations would begin that evening or if Lord Torrington would wait until the following day to get to work.

Pru watched the Markgraf Kottenfurst have a serious conversation with their hostess. He seemed to be attempting to smile, but she wasn't sure his face was used to contorting in that way. It looked strained, she thought with an internal laugh. He was handsome enough with his broad shoulders, blond hair, and deep blue eyes. But it was his sharp cheek bones and strong jaw that really made him attractive, she figured.

As she ate her soup, she looked around the table. Almost everyone was engaged in some sort of serious conversation. There was almost no laughter, few smiles. People were being polite—too polite.

She caught her father watching her and immediately lowered her gaze to her bowl before turning to the gentleman to her right. "Mr. Sidwell, are you planning on doing anything special this holiday?" she asked, certain that was the right sort of question a young lady asked a gentleman. She couldn't quite tell if he was muscular or just a little pudgy. He was a hefty person, but again, that could have been because he didn't have the height to balance the size of his body.

He blinked at her for a moment before giving her a polite smile. "Why, I have come to this party, the same as you."

"Er, yes, of course. Is there anything in particular you hope to do here? Do you enjoy decorating for the holiday? Visiting the less fortunate? Dancing, riding?" She tried to think of anything else a young man might enjoy during the holidays.

"I will be happy to engage in all the pursuits offered by our host and hostess. Is there anything you have in mind?" he asked.

"Oh, yes! I am greatly looking forward to collecting greenery and decorating. Although I cannot decide which I like more, decorating or meeting people when we bring them their Christmas boxes filled with wonderful things to eat. I do so enjoy meeting people."

"Really? I wouldn't have thought that of you," he said, dipping his spoon into his bowl meticulously.

"Why would you say that?" she asked, curious as to how he could possibly know anything about her since they only just met less than an hour ago.

"My mother mentioned that you are nearly twenty or have already attained your twentieth year, and yet you haven't been presented. My sister, who has only just turned eighteen, made her debut last Season. I assumed you haven't made your come-out because you were shy."

Pru slowly put her glass of wine back down before she succumbed to the temptation to throw its contents into her companion's face. That would most certainly get her sent to her room for the remainder of their stay here, although it would also certainly *not* have been the sort of infraction her parents were expecting from her. Instead, she smiled at Mr. Sidwell and said, "No, I quite like meeting people. It is my mother who is loath to lose her youngest child, and so she has been putting off my debut." It was a complete lie, but a good one if she did say so herself.

"I understand," he said, nodding. "How very frustrating for you. Francis was so eager to make her debut, I'm sure you feel the same."

"And what of you? Do you enjoy the Season?"

"I do, a great deal. But I have also been working with my father's steward the past few years to learn how to manage our estates."

"Your father isn't very old. Is he unwell?"

He looked at her curiously. "No, he is perfectly healthy."

"Oh, then you are merely anticipating his demise?"

The man gave an awkward, uncomfortable laugh. "Not at all. I am learning to manage the estates so my father has one less thing to worry about while he works on weightier matters in Parliament."

"I see. How very good of you to be able to help him in that way," she said, giving herself a mental pat on the back for providing what she was sure was the correct response. She was getting very good at this if she did say so herself.

The time when the ladies left the gentlemen to their port and cigars couldn't come soon enough, but when it did, Pru almost wished herself back by Mr. Stuffy Sidwell's side. He was boring and bordering offensive, but that was better than the annoying tittering of his sister and Miss Charlotte Browning. The two young women were giggling with their heads together the minute the drawing-room door had closed behind them.

Pru wandered closer to see what they were laughing at—she always loved a good joke.

"I know! And the way his deep blue eyes crinkle when he smiles. It's absolutely adorable," Miss Sidwell was saying.

"I like the way his hair falls over his forehead," Miss Browning was saying.

"Oh, girls, really," Lady Minton said, much to Pru's relief. Surely, she would stop this ridiculous fawning. Pru was certain it was the markgraf who the girls were talking about, and it was just silly. "Surely, you can't help but admire the man's muscular stature and those calves!" the slightly older woman said before bursting in a peel of giggles.

Pru had to stop her mouth from dropping open. "Really?" She couldn't help herself from commenting. "Lady Minton, you are a married woman," Pru protested.

The woman looked at her, her eyes twinkling with mischief that normally Pru would have approved of whole-heartedly. "Married, not dead or blind," she said before laughing again.

Prudence looked over at her mother for her reaction. She was frowning at the woman, much to Pru's relief.

"Miss Sidwell, I hear you made your debut last Season," Lady Torrington said, turning the conversation. "Did you enjoy yourself?"

In other words, did you get any proposals, Pru translated in her mind.

The girl sobered quickly. "I did, my lady."

"She received two very respectable proposals," her mother said. "But we didn't feel the gentlemen were quite right for a sensitive girl. We'll see if she can't find someone more suited to her temperament next Season."

Lady Torrington nodded her understanding saying, "I expect to be bringing Pru out next Season. You must tell me who to be on the lookout for and perhaps if there are any gentlemen we should stay away from. I haven't been in society for a few years now."

"Of course, my lady, I would be more than happy to share my knowledge with you," Lady Bunbury said.

Pru really wasn't so sure she wanted to be a part of that conversation. She knew herself and would probably make note of the gentlemen she shouldn't be interested in and immediately develop a tendre for each one of them.

Chapter Three

Alexander sighed with relief when the ladies left the room. Finally, they could get down to some business. It was all well and good to be polite and get to know the other guests, but he was here for a reason and eager to get to it.

He took a swallow of the excellent port he'd been offered and then leaned forward toward Lord Torrington, who had moved to sit opposite him. "My lord, if you could tell me precisely what you and your colleagues have in mind regarding Aachen-Düren," he began.

The older man raised his eyebrows and then gave him an indulgent smile. "I would be happy to do so, and will, when we begin our talks. However, I, along with most of us here, have been traveling all day and simply want to relax among this excellent company."

Lord Humesbury laughed and patted Alexander's back. He'd moved into his wife's place at the end of the table. "Our young guest here is eager to get to work."

"Too eager," Lord Perbury agreed.

"We are here not only to work, Markgraf, but to enjoy ourselves. It is Christmas!" Lord Bunbury said, giving Alexander a broad smile. "What are *your* traditions at Christmas? How do you celebrate there in Aachen-Düren?"

Alexander felt like they were being condescending, and he didn't like it. He didn't think there was anything he could or should say. He certainly didn't want to offend these men in any way. He was here representing his country and to establish political ties that could benefit Aachen-Düren in a great many ways. Just that fact that he'd been invited at all was a great honor. He had to remember this.

On the other hand, that these negotiations were only going to be between Aachen-Düren and England meant, clearly, these men thought they would be able to bend him to their will. He was in the weaker position here. Aachen-Düren would stand to benefit a great deal more from any sort of treaty than England would. If he didn't agree to whatever their terms were, he was sure they would simply move on to some other German principality, the Belgians or someone else. Aachen-Düren was in an excellent position, politically, but they weren't the only one.

No, he had to play his cards here very carefully. And if these men wanted to relax and drink their liquor, he had no choice but to do so as well. He pulled his lips up into a smile. "I believe we have similar traditions to you. On St. Nicholas Day, we fill children's stockings with little presents. We bring in greenery on Christmas eve. And enjoy a glass or two of *glühwein*. My brother and I have enjoyed a *feuerzangenbowle*, but only at a party such as this," he told them, thinking back to Christmas the previous year when he'd been with Rich and a group of other young men.

The other men looked confused.

"I've heard of glühwein," Lord Perbury said. "It's that spiced wine that you drink warm, isn't that right?"

"Yes," Alexander smiled at him. "Warming and delicious."

"But what is feuerganz..." the gentleman began laughing. "I can't even pronounce it!"

Alexander laughed, too. "Feuerzangenbowle. It means, er, fire... *ach*! What do you call those?" He jumped up and picked up the implement from next to the fireplace.

"Tongs," Mr. Sidwell said, helping him out.

"Yes! Tongs. Fire-tongs punch," Alexander said, sitting down again.

"What is it?" Lord Humesbury asked.

"Well, you have a punch bowl filled with wine, cinnamon, and some other spices. I do not know what exactly. It's placed over a fire to keep it warm. Over the top of the bowl, you balance a block of sugar that has been soaked in rum and then set it alight. The sugar melts into the punch. It is..." he smiled, remembering the last time he'd had it. "It is very potent."

"And this is a Christmas tradition you share with... your family?" Lord Minton asked.

"Oh no! No, it's something men have in a setting much like this," he explained.

"Ah, that makes sense," Lord Torrington said, nodding.

"And you do this every year?" Mr. Sidwell asked.

"Well, my brother and I have for the past few years." Alexander began laughing again. "We got so incredibly drunk on it... well, let us just say it is not for the weak of heart."

"The Queen brings a tree into her home at Christmas. Do you do the same?" Lord Lunsdale asked. He was an older, dour looking man with thick gray eyebrows and thinning hair.

"Yes. You simply bring in the branches, no? We bring in the entire tree and decorate it with ribbons and baubles," Alexander told them.

"That must be very pretty," Lord Humesbury commented as he refilled Alexander's glass.

"It is. It is quite lovely," Alexander agreed. "I am looking forward to joining you in your traditions this year, however."

"Well, we are much simpler in what we do," Lord Torrington said.

"Yes. I believe Lady Humesbury is organizing an outing tomorrow for us to go collect greenery, and then the ladies will arrange it just so, I'm sure," their host said. "And we've got a few other amusements planned for the next few weeks."

He patted Alexander's shoulder again. "Have no fear, even though we won't have this flaming, er, sugar drink, we'll have a good time."

"I am certain of that, my lord. I just wonder about the negotiations," Alexander admitted.

The man *tsked* and shook his head. "Don't worry, don't worry. All in good time."

The ladies were still having their tea when the gentlemen rejoined them. Alexander watched as Lord Bunbury went straight to his wife and daughter, while his son kept clear of the rest of his family, staying on the other side of the room with Lord Perbury.

The two men had begun a conversation over their drinks regarding agriculture. Alexander didn't understand much of what they said and had no desire to learn more. But they seemed happy to continue their discussion.

He had just turned to see who he might engage in conversation with when three young women approached him.

"Miss Sidwell," he greeted the only one of the three he knew. "I hope you had a pleasant dinner?"

"I did, thank you, my lord. May I present Lady Minton and Miss Browning?" the young lady said, indicating the two women next to her.

Lady Minton was a taller lady with reddish-blonde hair and a rather sharp nose. He bowed to her first, taking her hand and placing a slight kiss on the back of it. The woman giggled at his attention. "It is a pleasure to make your acquaintance, madam."

He turned to Miss Browning and then remembered who she was. "You are Lady Minton's sister, are you not?" he asked after kissing the back of her hand.

She giggled like her sister had but also bobbed him a curtsy. "Yes, I am."

"I will be bringing Charlotte out this coming Season. Will you be in London at that time?" Lady Minton asked.

"Alas, I have no plans to be," he told them as if he were saddened by the fact. In truth, he hoped to be extremely busy as the new Minister of Defense, which made him very happy, indeed. Why would he want to attend parties, dance, and have to make polite conversation to such mindless women as these when he could be overseeing the growth of his country? They didn't have much of a military, being an extremely small principality, but it never hurt to be prepared should they need to defend their borders from the many larger countries surrounding them.

"Oh, but you will be missing out on so much fun," Miss Browning said, reaching out to tap his arm.

He fought to stand his ground and not retreat from the overly bold young lady. Instead, he smiled at her but shook his head. "I am certain you will have great success there."

"And I will be there, too, Lord Kottenfurst. Surely you wouldn't want to miss sharing a dance with me?" Miss Sidwell asked with a little giggle.

Alexander actually managed to contain his burst of laughter at this silly girl. It merely came out as a little chuckle, for which he was relieved. "But I will have the wonderful opportunity to dance with you, Miss Sidwell, at the Epiphany Eve Ball our generous hosts are planning."

"Oh, well, of course," she said with a slight lift of a shoulder. "But just imagine how many times we could dance if you were in London during the Season," she said with a coy little look at him from under her eyelashes. She really was trying extremely hard to flirt with him. He wondered if it were all show for her friends or if she truly was trying to catch his eye.

In either case, he was rather dismayed by such behavior. "I suppose we shall just have to make do with the opportunities we are presented with," he said. As he did so, he caught a glimpse over Lady Minton's shoulder of a girl sitting in a chair on the other side of the room.

She was probably about the same age as the young women in front of him. Yet, she sat there simply watching him speak with these women, and if he wasn't mistaken, she was laughing at him. Since the backs of the women he was speaking to were toward her, and she was facing him, there could be no other possibility. But what was it that she was finding so amusing? He simply couldn't fathom.

He had an overwhelming desire to go over there and confront the girl. Actually, he wouldn't mind that at all. He was certain he hadn't met her yet, and she was most definitely the prettiest girl in attendance. Her deep, rich mahogany-colored hair was drawn up so there was a pretty cascade of curls down her neck. Her laughing lips were a deep pink and produced the most adorable dimples in her cheeks. She had a strong jaw line, but it wasn't masculine. No, there was absolutely nothing but feminine beauty and grace about her.

"I do beg your pardon, ladies," he said, recalling himself to the three women who were still chattering at him like magpies. He carefully stepped around the girls and headed in the direction of the young lady.

He'd only made it half-way across the room, however, when another lady swooped in and confronted the girl. With a word, the woman had wiped the girl's smile from her face and had gotten her to stand and move toward the door. Once there, the girl stopped and looked back at him for one last hint of a smile before she slipped from the room.

Alexander was enchanted.

Chapter Four

Prudence closed her eyes and took in a deep breath. She'd just about made it out of her bedroom that morning before her mother stopped her. Even now, she was standing just in front of the door, itching to escape—and her mother was probably very well aware of it.

"Prudence Elizabeth Torrington, are you listening to me?" her mother's voice cut through the pleasant thoughts Pru was attempting to conjure in her mind.

"Yes, Mother, I am listening. I promise not to do anything untoward, as you say. I will behave myself," Pru said, trying her hardest to maintain her good temper. "I was doing so last night when you sent me from the drawing room. It was so embarrassing to have to leave early like a child sent back to the nursery."

"Well, if you learned how to behave like an adult, I wouldn't have to do that now, would I?"

"How was I not behaving like an adult? I was sitting quietly in a chair, doing nothing but watching everyone around me," Pru argued.

"You were laughing, and when you laugh, I know you are either up to no good or about to be," her mother told her.

"I was laughing at the Markgraf Kottenfurst. He was ambushed by Miss

Sidwell, Miss Browning, and Lady Minton the moment he and the other gentlemen entered the room," Pru told her mother.

"I am well aware of that. You leave that man alone! You know what your father said."

"I can't even speak with him?" Pru asked, rather aghast.

"It would best if you did not," her mother said with a sniff.

"But that would be rude and certainly remarked upon," Pru pointed out.

Her mother looked like she would growl if it were within her nature. "Very well, you may speak with him but only to be polite."

"Thank you. Now, I really am very hungry. May I be excused to go down to breakfast?"

"Stay out—"

"Of trouble, yes, yes." Pru slipped out the door, finally. "I know!"

"And just how do you propose to do that?" the markgraf himself asked. He was standing just behind her making her jump in surprise.

"Oh! I didn't see you there," Pru said, putting a hand to her suddenly pounding heart.

"I do beg your pardon, I could not help but overhear as I was coming out of my room," he said, giving her a smile. They continued walking down the hall side by side. "I do not believe we have met," he said, giving her a smile.

He might very well be a dangerous man to be near, Pru thought looking at the white teeth in his broad, smiling mouth. He was a great deal taller than Pru expected. Broader too. And he smelled good! Like soap and... something else, perhaps sandalwood? It was very nice.

"Oh, I'm Lady Prudence Torrington," she said, sticking out her hand without a thought.

He laughed as he took it. "Lady Prudence Torrington," he repeated back. "I am honored to meet you. I am—"

"Lord Kottenfurst," she said with a nod.

He looked at her in surprise.

"What? That is who are you, isn't it?" she asked quickly.

"Yes, it is. But you are the first person I have met here who has pronounced my name correctly. Everyone else, I believe, say it the way it is spelled—Kottenffffurst," he said enunciating the *f*. "But you said it right. Kottenvurst."

"Oh! I have to admit, I once learned a little German, so I know how some letters are pronounced," she said, starting down the stairs. She rarely admitted to anyone that she actually studied and read anything other than novels.

"*Jawohl? Kannst du Deutsch sprechen?*" he asked.

"Oh, no," she laughed. "I learned only a very little bit."

"But you understood what I said," he pointed out.

She giggled. "I have been discovered! But truly, I would be too embarrassed to even attempt to speak German with you. Perhaps I might be able to understand a sentence here and there, but that is all, truly."

"But even that is good," he said, opening the door to the breakfast room for her.

She was disappointed to see Lord and Lady Minton there, Lord Perbury, and their host, Lord Humesbury. She had to admit she'd rather been hoping to be able to continue her conversation with this charming man on her own.

"We shall discuss later why you laughed at me last night, ja?" he whispered to her before striding forward to greet the other occupants of the room.

A shiver of anticipation slid down Pru's spine.

Lady Prudence was even more fascinating than Alexander had expected. He looked forward to getting to know her better, but for now, he turned his mind back to work.

"Good morning, my lords, ladies," he said, bowing to the room in general.

"Ah, good morning, Kottenfurst," Lord Humesbury said jovially. "Grab a plate and join us."

Alexander looked over the selection put out on the side table and then helped himself to ham, eggs, and some vegetables. *These English certainly enjoyed their breakfast,* he thought.

As he sat down next to her, he noticed that Lady Prudence was merely nibbling at a piece of toast with jam as she sipped at a cup of tea. "Surely, Lady Prudence, you will eat more than that?" he asked her.

"But then how am I to keep my slender form? No, thank you. I'm happy with my toast."

Alexander had indeed been admiring her lovely figure, but he didn't think it polite to say so. Instead, he merely turned to Lord Humesbury. "My lord, will we be meeting later this morning, do you think, or this afternoon?"

"Meeting?" the gentleman asked, turning to look at him. His attention had been directed to his teacup as he'd refilled it. He then turned and handed the pot to a waiting footman. "This needs refreshing. Do you drink tea, my lord?" he asked Alexander.

"Er, no, thank you, but if you have any coffee that would be appreciated," Alexander said. "Meeting, sir, to begin our negotiations."

Lord Humesbury just burst out laughing. Alexander smiled in confusion. "My dear boy, I do appreciate your enthusiasm. You are quite relentless, aren't you?"

"Sir? That is the reason why we are all here—well, except for the ladies, of course," he said, giving a nod to Lady Minton who was holding a quiet conversation with Lady Prudence.

"Kottenfurst, it is Christmas, that is the main reason why we are here—to relax, enjoy the company of others, get to know each other, and celebrate the holiday," Lord Humesbury told him. "We will deal with business next week, perhaps."

Perhaps? Next week *perhaps*? Alexander began to seethe. He wasn't here to get to know these people. He hadn't traveled a thousand miles to relax. He was here to work. To see good things come to his country. To further the prominence of Aachen-Düren on the map of Europe. He wasn't here to make friends.

He felt a gentle pressure on his arm and turned his gaze to Lady Prudence next to him. "I'm certain what Lord Humesbury means is that while you all have gathered to hold these very important negotiations, it doesn't hurt to take a few days to get to know each other first. Christmas provides an excellent excuse to do that. Once that is past, it will be so much easier to discuss your common interests."

"That was very well put, Lady Prudence," Lord Perbury said.

She turned and gave him a little smile and a nod before returning to her nibbling.

Alexander calmed. That was actually a brilliant observation, and he was rather ashamed he hadn't thought of it himself. "Thank you, Lady Prudence. I do believe I understand now. I am afraid I was trained to lead men into battle, to take action. I am not a diplomat or a politician. I see I have a good deal to learn."

"It is merely a matter of understanding people, my lord," she said with a shrug.

"Yes. I will watch and learn," he told her.

"And in the meantime, I do believe Lady Humesbury is organizing an outing for this morning to collect greenery to bring into the house. Will you join us?" their host asked, looking around the table, clearly addressing his question to everyone present.

"I am greatly looking forward to it," Lady Minton said. "I do so love getting out when I'm in the countryside. There is nothing like a good brisk walk in the cold air."

"Will you be going, Lady Prudence?" Alexander asked.

"I wouldn't miss it! I love hunting down a good branch of holly," she said with a broad smile that made her dimples appear.

"Is it an elusive beast to find, this branch of holly?" Alexander asked with a laugh.

"Oh indeed, sir! While you may find a holly bush lurking in the wild, to find just the right branch, then capture it, requires skill and patience." Her forest green eyes twinkled at him merrily.

"Well then, I do look forward to joining you in this quest," Alexander told her.

"Do you enjoy hunting, Kottenfurst?" Lord Humesbury asked while laughing at his conversation with Lady Prudence.

"I do, actually. We hunt a great deal in Aachen-Düren—at least, my family does," Alexander answered.

"Excellent! Then we will definitely arrange some sport. I happen to love winter hunting." Lord Humesbury gave Alexander a pointed look. "Now see, this is why it is wonderful to have guests for Christmas. Otherwise, I wouldn't have such an opportunity."

Prudence donned her sturdiest boots and warmest clothes for their outing a little later that morning. She was looking forward to getting outside and to spending more time with Lord Kottenfurst. She would never have thought a serious man, such as he seemed to be, could engage in a ridiculous conversation like they'd had at breakfast. She wondered if it was an anomaly or if he did have a sense of humor.

From watching him the night before, she had been certain he wouldn't know a joke if it slapped him in the face. Then when he'd looked so hurt and angry at their host telling him that they wouldn't be getting to work any time soon, she couldn't resist trying to make him feel better. Truly, she could never have turned away from someone who had an expression like his.

But his joking with her... her heart had nearly melted in joy. He not only had a sense of humor, it was a wicked one! She was indeed looking forward to spending more time with the gentleman. She could only hope her parents didn't find out.

That thought plagued her, so she decided perhaps it would be best if she struck out on her own. She'd let the other women coo and fawn over the Markgraf Kottenfurst. She would prepare for a very merry Christmas. A slight giggle tried to escape from her lips, but she caught it before anyone else heard.

Dropping to the back of the group, Pru sought out one of the footmen who had accompanied them. There were four of them, each carrying various implements, tools, and baskets which the guests would need to gather the greenery. This particular fellow had a long pole in his hand with a sharp little scythe attached to the top of it.

"Do you suppose I could steal you away to assist me?" she asked the footman.

He looked at her, and his eyes widened. "I'm sorry, Miss. My orders were to stay with the group."

"Oh, well, then do you suppose I could borrow your tool?" she asked, indicating the pole.

"I, er, I suppose." He handed it over reluctantly.

"Thank you. I promise I will only use it to cut down mistletoe."

"I think that's all you could possibly use it for," he answered, looking a little confused.

Pru didn't think that was strictly true, but she kept her mouth shut and just nodded. She then quickly ducked off down another garden path, taking the pole with her. Alone, she moved a great deal faster than the others. She quickly made her way to the edge of the forest that bordered one end of the formal gardens. There she wandered happily, looking about for the telltale clumps of mistletoe that grew up among the branches of the trees.

Happily, she found a cluster of trees which all had some. She raised the pole toward one of the lowest, beautiful round balls of mistletoe and began to saw at the part attached to the tree. It was a lot harder than she'd imagined, and she didn't have very good leverage standing just beneath it.

"Do you need some help?"

A man's voice from behind her made her jump. She hadn't heard anyone approach because she'd been concentrating so hard on her sawing.

"I beg your pardon, I didn't mean to startle you," Lord Kottenfurst said, coming up next to her.

"Oh, it's all right," she said, still feeling her heart pounding in her chest.

"That looks ridiculously difficult," he commented, looking up.

"It is! It's much harder than I thought it would be," she agreed.

"Well, perhaps I can assist you, but first I did want to ask you about last night." He leaned up against the tree she'd been attacking.

"Last night?" Pru asked as innocently as possible.

"Yes." He narrowed his eyes at her. "If I am not mistaken, you were laughing at me."

Her mouth dropped open. "I would nev—"

"You would and you were," he accused her. "And clearly, I was not the only one who saw this. Was that your mother who sent you from the room?"

Pru could feel her face heat with embarrassment. She hated being treated like a child, and the fact that her mother did so in public was beyond anything. "She doesn't trust me," Pru admitted.

"Trust you?"

"To... to..." No, she couldn't do it. She couldn't admit that her mother didn't think she could behave appropriately. "To not get as much rest as she believes I need. That is why she sent me upstairs early. I, er, hadn't slept well the night before. We stayed at a posting house that was filled with loud revelers, and I hadn't been able to sleep through the noise."

"Oh, I see." He stood up and away from the tree. "And the laughter? Are you going to tell me that you were not laughing at me?"

"Oh, no! I was, most definitely," Pru admitted. That she didn't mind doing in the least.

The look of shock on his face almost made her burst out laughing. "Why? What was I doing that was so amusing?"

"Oh, nothing. You just looked so pleased with yourself and the attention those women were giving you. You were flirting a great deal," she told him, not being able to hold back her giggles.

His mouth dropped open a little. "I do believe they were flirting with me, not the other way around, I will have you know."

"Uh-hmmm..." she said dubiously.

"And I would dare you to find a man who is not flattered when receiving such attention," he added.

"True, but still... you *did* look funny."

He sighed. "I shall endeavor not to do so in the future. Now, I believe it would be much easier to cut the mistletoe down from a higher elevation." And with that, he jumped up, grabbed on to the lowest branch of the tree, and swung himself up so that he was straddling it.

Pru was much more impressed than she would ever admit to the man who clearly had no lack of confidence.

Chapter Five

Later that afternoon, Pru sat with the other ladies, carefully cutting the mistletoe and assembling it into pretty little arrangements with a red ribbon.

"Did I see you returning to the house with Lord Kottenfurst, Lady Prudence?" Miss Sidwell asked, barely looking up from the rope of pine branches she was assembling.

Pru lifted her eyes, immediately noticing her mother's attention on her. "Er, yes. He was so kind as to help me cut the mistletoe down from the tree. It was too high for me to reach."

"He is tall, isn't he?" Lady Minton said with a giggle.

"He actually needed to climb into the tree to reach it," Pru told them, still very impressed with his physical prowess beyond her better judgement.

Three heads all snapped up to look at her.

"He did?" Miss Browning asked a little breathlessly.

"He's quite athletic," Lady Minton pointed out.

"He is so handsome," Miss Sidwell cried.

The other women all looked at her before beginning to laugh hysterically.

"Well, he is!" Miss Sidwell said defending herself.

"Yes, he is, but you young ladies also need to remember why he is here," Pru's mother reminded them sternly.

Pru was still annoyed with herself for thinking the same way as these silly young women. She was not some giggly, brainless girl. She didn't *want* to like this man. She *shouldn't* like him—not if she knew what was good for her. If she liked him, she would do things that would get her into trouble. Honestly, she was just trying to keep her head down and not spend the entirety of this party locked in her room. The Markgraf Kottenfurst was making this extremely difficult.

Yes, she would hate him for that... Hate him for being so annoyingly handsome and kind, she thought with an inward groan.

All the girls stopped laughing and tried to look serious. Most didn't quite succeed.

"Lady Torrington is right," Lady Humesbury said. "He is here to negotiate a treaty."

"But there's no reason why he shouldn't enjoy a little flirtation while the gentlemen are *not* working," Lady Minton said.

"Yes," Miss Sidwell agreed, looking between the two older ladies for approval.

"Lord Humesbury said this morning at breakfast that he wanted Lord Kottenfurst to relax and enjoy the holiday before they began their work," Pru told them all but really directed her comment to her mother.

"Did he? Well then, we need to make sure the markgraf does just that," Miss Browning agreed.

"That's what I'm doing," Pru said with a smile as she held up her finished ball of mistletoe.

The other girls gasped before bursting into giggles.

"Oh, Lady Prudence, you're awful! I do hope you will be hanging those *everywhere*. You never know when you might find yourself standing under one when a certain handsome gentleman is nearby," Lady Minton said, giving Pru an approving look.

"That was exactly my thinking, my lady."

Pru's mother just sighed and shook her head sadly. Prudence wasn't actually causing trouble. *I'm just providing an opportunity for others to find it themselves,* she thought with a giggle.

Christmas, it turned out, was a quiet day. After church in the morning, the guests all scattered to their respective bedchambers or engaged in a quiet activity in various public rooms.

Alexander requested writing materials and sat down to write his brother a letter. Somehow, he needed to explain why there were no developments in the negotiations he was there to conduct. It was rather awkward having to tell his prince that he was being forced to relax and wile away his time doing inane things such as climb trees for a pretty, young woman. Well, perhaps it would be best to leave out that last bit. Rich didn't need to know how he'd shown off his athletic abilities for Lady Prudence. And he most certainly didn't need to tell him about how beautiful and engaging the young lady was. No. That, he thought, he'd do best to keep to himself.

The evening, it turned out, was a great deal livelier than he expected. After an excellent dinner complete with a Christmas pudding with enough brandy in it to make everyone much merrier, they all retired to the drawing room together—men and women.

He figured it was just as well since he wouldn't be allowed to question the other gentlemen regarding anything to do with the negotiations, anyway. If he couldn't work with the men, he would much rather spend his time with the ladies.

Miss Browning sat down at the pianoforte to entertain them all with some lovely music, but she had hardly gotten through the beginning of her third piece when some footmen came in with a few large bowls. One was filled with wine and the other with another liquid with small black dots floating in it. Alexander was intrigued.

The bowl with the wine was placed on the sideboard and the other on a table that was moved into the middle of the room.

"Ah-ha!" Lord Humesbury said, rubbing his hands together in anticipation. His wife just laughed and called for the attention of everyone.

"Ladies and gentlemen, on the sideboard we have glühwein in honor of our guest from Aachen-Düren," she began.

"What is that?" Miss Sidwell asked.

"It is wine with spices added," Alexander explained simply. "It is delicious. I am sure you will enjoy it."

"And it's drunk warm?" she asked, noticing the small lamp that was being placed underneath the bowl.

"Yes, it is," Lady Humesbury answered for him. "And here"—she indicated the other punch bowl which was being set alight even as they watched—"is a game of snapdragon for those fearless enough." She gave a laugh as all the younger guests became excited at the prospect of this game.

Lady Prudence laughed and began to clap in her excitement, and Mr. Sidwell was advancing on the center table in long strides.

"What is this game?" Alexander asked, coming up next to Lady Prudence.

She beamed at him. "Do you not play this in Aachen-Düren? Or perhaps you do but call it something else."

"This, my lord, is a game where you must be very fast or you will burn your fingers," Lady Humesbury said.

"Or your tongue," her husband added with a laugh.

They all gathered around the burning punch bowl.

"In the bowl is brandy," Lady Prudence explained.

Alexander nodded. "And the small black things?"

"Raisins," Mr. Sidwell answered.

"You must pick up a raisin and pop it into your mouth before you burn yourself," Lady Humesbury said.

Alexander raised his eyebrows. This sounded downright dangerous.

Lady Prudence laughed at his reaction. "Are you too scared to give it a try?" she taunted.

"No, but I certainly have not had enough wine to do so quite yet." With a laugh, he turned and was about to get a glass of glühwein when a footman approached him with a tray of glasses already filled.

"Here you are, sir. The recipe came from your man, Hans, so I'm sure it will be to your liking," the footman told him before passing around drinks to the others standing around the flaming punch bowl.

"Ah, excellent." He raised his glass to the others. "A very happy Christmas to you all."

"Happy Christmas!"

"Merry Christmas." They all answered before taking a sip of the wine.

It was perfect. He could always count on Hans.

"Oh, that is good!" Lady Prudence said widening her eyes.

"Indeed," Mr. Sidwell agreed. "Now, you must try the snapdragon."

"You go first, Mr. Sidwell, and I will watch and learn," Alexander told him.

The young man laughed and then downed his wine in one gulp. "Very well."

He rubbed his hands together and was about to reach toward the bowl when Lady Prudence began chanting.

Here he comes with flaming bowl,
Don't he mean to take his toll,
Snip! Snap! Dragon!
Take care you don't take too much,
Be not greedy in your clutch,
Snip! Snap! Dragon!
With his blue and lapping tongue
Many of you will be stung,
Snip! Snap! Dragon!
For he snaps at all that comes
Snatching at his feast of plums,
Snip! Snap! Dragon!
But Old Christmas makes him come,
Though he looks so fee! fa! fum!
Snip! Snap! Dragon!
Don't 'ee fear him but be bold—
Out he goes his flames are cold,
Snip! Snap! Dragon!

Alexander laughed and applauded. And then, much to his surprise, Mr. Sidwell reached into the flaming bowl and plucked out a raisin. Before he could get it to his mouth, however, he dropped it with a howl and a shake of his fingers.

They all laughed, and after a moment, Mr. Sidwell joined in as well.

"Do you want to give it a try, my lady?" Lady Prudence asked their hostess.

"I used to be pretty good at this game," she said. She balled her hands up into fists, released them, and shot her hand into the bowl. "Oh, no!" she said, pulling it straight out again. "It's too hot!" she laughed. "You try, my lord," she said, turning to her husband.

Lord Humesbury rubbed his hands together and reached into the bowl, but like Mr. Sidwell, he dropped his raisin before he could get it to his mouth. As they were all laughing, he said, "All right, Lady Prudence, you've been laughing at us. It's your turn."

"Me?" she said. With a broad smile on her face, she slid her eyes left and right to Mr. Sidwell on her left and Alexander on her right. "Very—" before she even finished her sentence, her hand dipped into the bowl and back, popping the raisin into her mouth. She took in a loud breath, cooling her tongue before showing them all the raisin between her teeth, then closing her mouth on it.

"Oh, well done! Well done!" Mr. Sidwell said, applauding her.

"All right, Lord Kottenfurst. You've watched and laughed, now it is your turn," Lady Prudence said, turning to him.

"Indeed. Speed seems to be the trick here," Alexander answered. He took in a deep breath, focused his eyes on one particular raisin burning closest to him and reached out. He grabbed it, feeling the burning in his fingers. He ignored the pain and popped the sweet into his mouth as quickly as he could.

"Oh ho! Well done! Well done!" Lord Humesbury burst out even as Alexander's tongue burned with the heat.

They all applauded him. He laughed after swallowing the raisin. "I knew my military training was good for something. We were taught to withstand pain. You never know if you are injured when you will be able to get to a médicale," he explained. "Er, what do you say? Surgeon."

"Oh, well, that's not fair at all," Lady Prudence said with a laugh.

"All is fair in such games," Alexander said with a shrug and a laugh.

Lady Humesbury called over Miss Browning, Lord Perbury, and some others, so Alexander ceded his place to them to try their luck.

After helping himself to some more wine, he stood out of the way in front of the fireplace to watch. Others had returned to the pianoforte with Lady Minton taking Miss Browning's place and playing some lively tunes while her husband sang along in a pleasing baritone.

"Oh, Lord Kottenfurst, you need to be a bit more careful about where you stand," Miss Sidwell said, coming over. She stopped very close to him and looked up. He followed her gaze and noticed a pretty ball of mistletoe tied together with a bright red velvet ribbon just above his head.

He'd just turned his head back toward her when the girl stood up on her tiptoes and aimed her lips for his. He managed to turn his head at the last second, so they landed on his cheek.

She gave an embarrassed giggle and then ran off toward the pianoforte, giving him a sly glance over her shoulder.

Alexander stepped away from the dangerous greenery above his head.

Lord Bunbury was watching and laughing. "You do need to be more careful about that, my lord. I imagine every young lady here would like to catch you, thus."

Alexander gave an embarrassed laugh. "I am well warned, sir."

Clearly, Mr. Sidwell had been watching as well, for he called out to Lady Prudence and asked her to come over to where he was standing just to right of the fireplace. He pointed to the Egyptian bust sitting on the mantel. Someone had tied a red ribbon around its neck and encircled the base with greenery.

"Lady Prudence, are you responsible for these lovely decorations?" he asked when she came over.

"No, your sister did—" She didn't have a chance to finish her sentence before she was pulled under the mistletoe. She was so caught off-guard that Mr. Sidwell managed to land his kiss right on her lips before she even had a chance to deflect him.

Lord Bunbury burst out laughing. "That's my boy! Well done! Get 'em when they're not ready."

Lady Prudence's cheeks turned bright pink, but she laughed in good humor. "Well, I suppose this is my own fault for putting it up."

Lady Bunbury came over and dragged her husband under the mistletoe saying, "Oh, you think that's funny, do you?" She gave him a loud kiss on his cheek, making him burst out laughing once again. In response, he grabbed her about her waist and gave her a proper kiss on the lips.

"Oh, you!" she said laughing, giving his chest a slap as she pulled from his arms.

Alexander was just wishing he could grab Lady Prudence for a kiss for himself when her mother came over and took hold of her arm. "Prudence, you look exhausted, I believe it's time for you to retire for the evening."

"But—" Lady Prudence started.

Her mother just gave her a look, and she closed her lips around whatever else she was going to say.

"Oh, Lady Torrington, let the girl have some fun," Lord Bunbury said, defending the girl. Alexander applauded him silently in his mind. He wished he could have said as much but didn't feel it was his right to do so.

"My lord," Lady Torrington started.

"Now, now, my lady, it's Christmas and time for good cheer, is it not?" Lady Bunbury said. She took Lady Torrington's arm and started to lead her away. Lady Torrington was still holding on to her daughter's arm, so she took Lady Prudence with her, much to Alexander's chagrin.

Chapter Six

It was entirely much too early the following morning that Alexander found himself riding out with the men to go hunting. After a night of drinking, he would have thought the English gentlemen would want to sleep in or, at the very least, have a relaxing morning following individual pursuits. Lord Humesbury had said that they'd go hunting the day after Christmas, however, and here they were, no one looking particularly pleased except for their host who had a very satisfied expression on his face.

Lord Humesbury's estate wasn't much larger than Kottenfurst but a great deal less of it was left in its original wooded state. Still, the man was extremely proud of the hunting he was able to offer.

"Do you hunt very much in Aachen-Düren?" Lord Torrington asked as they rode out.

"Yes. Especially in my family, we enjoy it a great deal."

"What is it you hunt?" Lord Perbury asked, coming alongside him.

"Deer, the same as you at this time of year," Alexander told him. "But we do not exclusively use guns," he said, nodding to the men accompanying them, their saddles loaded with arms.

"Don't tell me you hunt with bow and arrows?" Mr. Sidwell asked, turning around in his saddle to look at Alexander.

"Yes, we do. We bring some guns as well to put the animal out of its misery if it is wounded and not killed straight off," Alexander told him. "We are not barbarians," he added under his breath.

"No one thought you were," Lord Torrington said quietly.

Alexander hadn't meant to be heard. The man must have excellent hearing.

Well, if he had to be here, at the very least Alexander could learn something more about these men with whom he'd be negotiating.

"Do you too spend every Season in London, Lord Torrington?" Alexander asked.

"I do. It's when Parliament is in session," his lordship said.

Alexander nodded and turned to Lord Perbury on his other side. "And you, my lord? I suppose you do as well to attend Parliament?"

"Indeed. Although in truth, I live in London pretty much year-round," the man answered with an easy smile.

"Do you not have an estate which you must oversee?" Alexander asked.

"I have an excellent steward in my younger brother." He leaned over toward Alexander and added, "He's got a vested interest in it doing well. He's my heir."

"Until you marry," Alexander pointed out.

"And what of you? You are your brother's heir, aren't you?" he asked.

"I am until he marries and has children." Alexander gave him a smile. "I am actually looking forward to that day."

"Really? You have no desire for the throne?" Lord Torrington asked.

"Not really. I have seen how much work it is to be the prince," Alexander admitted.

"What role would you prefer?" Lord Torrington asked.

"Aren't you already head of the security forces?" Lord Perbury asked.

"Not officially. My brother left our father's man in place when the prince died. I am currently simply an advisor to the prince," Alexander admitted. He wasn't at all certain saying as much was a good idea, especially since the two men passed a look between them behind Alexander's back when they thought he wasn't looking.

"Lord Perbury, you are also a part of the Foreign Committee?" Alexander asked, trying to redirect the conversation away from himself.

"Er, no. I do work for the Foreign Minister, however," the man answered.

"Oh? In what way?" Alexander asked, intrigued.

The man smiled. "A good deal of diplomacy work. Traveling and speaking with people."

Alexander got the distinct impression that if he asked for particulars he wouldn't be given any more than he just had.

"Considering you are not a part of your brother's government in an official capacity opens you up to a great many more opportunities," Lord Perbury commented.

Alexander looked over at the man. He had a perfectly bland, pleasant expression on his face, but somehow, Alexander got the impression there was a lot more going on inside his mind. Alexander took a cue from him and relaxed his eyebrows that he'd raised at the man's words. He then placed a polite smile on his lips and nodded, saying, "Indeed," in an even tone.

Lord Perbury nodded approvingly.

"Perhaps we can discuss such things later?" Alexander asked.

"Oh, most definitely. I expect it will all be a part of our negotiations when we get down to them," Lord Torrington said, much to Alexander's surprise.

He turned toward the other man. Clearly, there had been a good deal of discussions already going on among the Englishmen. Now, his curiosity was piqued even more. "And when do you think that might be? Lord Humesbury keeps telling me to relax and enjoy my holiday, but I am finding it rather difficult knowing that work is waiting for me."

"Ah, Lord Humesbury does like his holidays. You, I can see, are much more a man of action," Lord Perbury said.

"I am," Alexander agreed. "This waiting is..." He stopped himself from admitting too much. "Well, it is quite lovely to spend time with the ladies, enjoy a bit of a ride and some hunting, but it is not what I came here to do." He tried very hard to keep his emotions from showing. It wasn't easy. He had to forcibly calm his racing pulse by taking in a deep breath.

"I understand," Lord Perbury admitted, for the first time showing some of his own true emotions. "I'm champing at the bit myself, eager to get to work. I think you and I are a great deal alike, Kottenfurst."

Alexander nodded but deliberately stayed quiet.

"Yes, I think our talks are going to go very well, indeed," Perbury added almost to himself.

The women spent the morning putting together boxes to give to the poorer tenants on the Humesbury's land. The younger ones laughed and teased each other over the attention Lord Kottenfurst had given to each one of them the previous evening after Pru had retired for the evening.

"It was such a shame you couldn't stay," Lady Minton told her. "His lordship has a very pleasant singing voice."

Pru turned her lips up into a smile and nodded her head. For some reason, she just couldn't find her voice with her stomach churning the way it was. How ridiculous she was. She didn't even like the man!

He was very full of himself and clearly enjoyed showing off for women—first climbing trees for her and then singing for Lady Minton. Really! No, she would not think of him and what her mother had forced her to miss. She was much better off in her own bed with her book. She only wished she'd had something more interesting to read than the dry history of Yorkshire, which was all she'd been able to find of interest in Lord Humesbury's library.

Immediately following a light luncheon, all the ladies went to dress for their outing to deliver the boxes they'd assembled.

Pru was the first one down. She was waiting in the front hall, debating whether she should wait with her coat on or off when Lady Humesbury and Lady Bunbury joined her. "Are you ready to go?" her hostess asked, greeting her.

"Oh, I am, my lady," Pru said, immediately pulling on her coat. "Delivering boxes is my absolute favorite part of Christmas."

"Really?" Lady Bunbury asked curiously. "Why is that?"

"Well, for some of my father's tenants, it's the only time I get to see them and their entire families. There are always new additions to greet and little ones who've grown so much."

"Do you not see them at church every week? Or at other times during the year?" Lady Humesbury asked.

"Oh yes, of course, but on Christmas I get to see everyone all together and in their own homes," Pru said.

"We do usually take stock of how they are living," Pru's mother added as she came forward pulling on her own coat. She'd clearly caught the end of what Pru had been saying.

"We do the same and make sure that everyone has a good roof at the very least," Lady Humesbury said.

Pru looked around for the other younger ladies but didn't see them.

"Miss Sidwell and Miss Browning won't be joining us," Lady Humesbury told her.

"Nor Lady Minton," Lady Bunbury added.

"How very odd." Pru shrugged. She couldn't imagine why anyone would want to miss meeting the tenants and handing out boxes.

"I believe they are not fond of the cold weather," Lady Humesbury said, leading the way out to their waiting carriage. Another loaded with the boxes they would be delivering followed behind. They drove to the home of the farthest tenant where they would begin.

The cottage was small but seemed to be well-built, Pru thought. The thatching on the roof seemed to be new as well.

"Happy Christmas!" Lady Humesbury called out as she knocked on the door.

It was opened by a man who looked to be in his early thirties. His ruddy cheeks and broad smile were welcoming as he stepped back to allow them to enter his home. Three children came running up as the women filled the small space.

"Merry Christmas," the lady of the house said, coming from a small kitchen area and wiping her hands on an apron tied around her waist.

"We bring you good tidings and a box of treats for your holiday," Lady Humesbury said, handing over the box she'd brought in.

The children all looked toward the box, their eyes wide in anticipation of the treats it might contain. Pru stepped closer to a far wall and hissed to get the attention of the youngest who stood behind her two older brothers. The little girl, her round cheeks ruddy like her father's, turned around.

Pru squatted down and motioned for her to come over. The little girl was shy but sidled closer. Pulling a small yarn doll from a pocket she'd hidden under her skirts, Pru offered it to the girl. The child took it reverently, running a finger down the little head and body. Her next older brother immediately snatched the toy from the girl's hands.

"What's this?" he asked no one in particular.

"That is for your sister. This one is for you," Pru said, holding out a similarly made little horse. The boy shoved the doll back at his sister and took the horse, his eyes wide.

"Really?" he asked.

Pru giggled. "Really. And here's one for you, too," she said, handing another horse to the eldest boy.

"Thank you," he said, giving her a small bow.

"You are very welcome. Enjoy them." Pru stood up and tousled the hair of the middle child. She felt her mother's stare before she saw it. For one more moment, she enjoyed the happiness of the children with their new simple little toys before looking up to her mother's glare. She gave her mother a smile, knowing full well it wouldn't make any difference. She was in trouble... again.

Her mother's gaze moved meaningfully toward the door. She then slowly made her way in that direction, as did Pru.

"Just what do you think you're doing?" she hissed quietly when they met.

"I made little toys for the children," Pru told her and pulled out another little doll from her pocket to show her mother.

"Did you ask Lady Humesbury if you could give presents to the children?" her mother asked.

Pru widened her eyes. "Should I have?"

Lady Torrington sighed heavily and looked like she wanted to give Pru a good shake.

"They are harmless little—" Pru started. "Surely, she wouldn't mind."

"But you didn't ask her. Prudence, this is *not* your home, and these are not your father's tenants. We don't know the traditions of Humesbury or the circumstances here, do we?"

"But they are just—" She stopped speaking at her mother's glare and tightened lips. "Yes, Mother. I mean, no, Mother," Pru whispered back.

"Not another word. Not another toy given out, do you understand me?"

"I've got a pocket full—"

"Do you understand me?" her mother repeated more slowly.

"Yes, my lady."

Her mother turned back toward the other women who were just saying their goodbyes.

They headed off to the next cottage and then the next. It was incredibly difficult to see so many children and know that she couldn't make one of them happy with her simple little toys. At the fourth home, Pru managed to "accidentally" drop one on a chair when no one was looking. She was about to do the same at another home but found her mother watching her closely, so she removed an empty hand from her pocket, showing it to her mother. After that, her mother kept her close by making it impossible for her to leave any more little gifts for the children they met.

She supposed she'd just have to ask one of the housemaids to distribute them to any children she knew. She had about ten more little dolls and eight little horses she'd made in preparation for the holiday.

When they arrived back at the Humesbury's home, her mother put an arm around Pru as if she were supporting her and said loudly, "Oh, you poor dear, you must have caught something when you were out collecting greenery." She put a hand to Pru's forehead, shaking her head sadly. "You are warm. To bed with you, young lady. What a shame."

"Oh, Lady Prudence," Lady Humesbury said solicitously. "Are you not feeling well? I will have my maid make up a mustard bath for your feet immediately."

"You are too kind, my lady," Pru said quickly.

"Indeed, Margaret, you must go to no trouble at all. Pru has such a fragile disposition. I'm sure that with a few days rest she will be fit as a fiddle," Lady Torrington said. "I'll just see her to her bed."

"Of course. I am so sorry, Lady Prudence," their hostess said, watching them go.

Lady Torrington kept a tight hold on her arm, and Pru knew she would only make things worse for herself if she were to say anything.

"Until further notice," her mother growled out as soon as they had entered Pru's room. "You will stay here and think about your actions, and then I will decide when you are to rejoin the festivities."

"All I did was give children toys," she said as her mother was about to leave the room. "I truly don't see what was wrong with that."

Her mother sighed and came over to her, placing a hand on her shoulder. "Think about this, Prudence. You are an intelligent girl. You didn't ask Lady Humesbury permission."

"No, but—"

"You didn't tell Lady Humesbury that you wanted to do to so, either, did you?" her mother said, interrupting her.

"No—"

"So the fact that you, a stranger, a guest of the Humesbury's, were giving out toys, no matter how small and insignificant—and Lady Humesbury was not—how does that make her look in the eyes of her tenants? Think about it, Prudence. I'm certain I taught you better than this."

With that her mother left her room.

Chapter Seven

Pru had more than enough time to think about her mother's words, although she didn't do so immediately. First, she huffed, and sat, and read. Then after a fitful night's sleep, she paced her small room feeling anxious and confined. She'd always had a touch of claustrophobia. She was an active person. Locking her into a room so small was...

Well, it did give her time to think as she paced.

Really, what was so bad about making children happy? The joy on those little faces at receiving something so small and simple as the little yarn dolls and horses was beyond wonderful. But then Pru began to go over what her mother had said about Lady Humesbury.

Prudence hadn't even thought of asking permission to give out the toys. Hadn't considered it. She'd only thought of her own happiness in giving them out and that of the children receiving them, but what of Lady Humesbury?

If the tenants knew that Pru had given the toys and believed that Lady Humesbury hadn't—and it would have been so easy for the lady to add them into the Christmas boxes—what *would* her tenants think of her? Pru rested her head against the wall. At best they would consider her thoughtless, at worst that she was cruel or didn't like children or didn't want them to be happy.

Pru groaned.

She hadn't considered how her actions would reflect on their hostess. She hadn't thought of anyone but herself—and the children—but honestly, mostly herself. It pained her to think that she'd been so selfish. She didn't want to be selfish. She simply wanted to make people happy, to bring a little joy to others. But she never stopped to think about the consequences.

A scraping noise startled her out of her reverie. Was someone there? She ran to her window and looked out. It was a windy day, the trees were blowing, and it looked like a storm was coming. Even as she watched, a branch from the tree outside her window scraped against the glass.

Her room was situated right on a corner of the house facing the garden. Someone long ago had planted a tree in the corner, probably thinking it would merely be a pretty, ornamental thing. Now it had grown tall, right up against the building.

She opened the window and leaned out, basking in the cold, fresh air. She hadn't even realized how stifling it was in her room. She looked down into the garden. It looked pretty even though her room was only on the second floor. She then turned and looked up to see how high the tree went. It had grown right up to the third floor, nearly to the top of the house. She was impressed at its temerity.

She looked over at the branches closest to her window. They looked strong. Certainly, the closer they got to the trunk, the thicker they became. Possibly even as thick as the ones the Markgraf Kottenfurst had climbed when they'd been cutting mistletoe. She quickly dismissed that thought. Thinking of him only made her even more frustrated at being locked in her room.

But that tree did look strong...

Alexander stretched out his stride, moving as quickly as he could down the garden pathway, grateful for the nearly full moon lighting his path. The need to move, to get out of that stifling drawing room had been overwhelming. The feel of the cold—

Crack!

The sound came from his right, somewhere ahead of him. He scanned through the darkness to see where it might have come from. It was immediately followed by a squeak that sounded almost human.

There was another creak, a rustle, and the sound of whispering in the quiet of the night that had him break into a run toward the tree just at the corner of the building. He paused, looking up.

"Lady Prudence, is that you?" The words burst from him as his heart leapt in his chest.

"*Shhhhh*!" the girl hissed.

The sound was followed by another ominous crack.

He watched in amazement as she slid off the unstable branch to dangle from it by her hands. She reached with her foot toward the branch just below her, not quite reaching it.

"Move your hands closer to the tree," he instructed, cursing for not having the right words in English. Then he remembered that she knew some German. "*Baumstamm! Bewege deine Hände am Ast entlang zum Stamm des Baumes.*"

"What? I don't understand," she said, her voice quivering with fear.

"To your left," he said hurriedly as they heard another crack. That branch was going to break before she made it to the one below.

She slid her hands closer to the trunk. It brought her just that much lower, so her foot could now reach the branch below, and it also gave her something to hold on to as she eased herself onto it.

Alexander breathed a sigh of relief.

"Thank you," she whispered.

"What are you doing climbing a tree at night, anyway?" he asked, looking up at her as she moved to sit on the branch while still clinging to the trunk.

"Escaping from my room," she said quietly. "I don't suppose you could help me down?"

There was only one more branch between her and the ground, but it was rather high.

"Can you lower yourself to the next branch? I can catch you from there," he told her.

She looked carefully at how far she would need to go and then nodded. "Yes."

And then carefully shifted herself, so she could reach out once again with her slippered foot onto the last branch. Once she was seated on it, she scooted out a little way from the trunk, then swung herself down so she was hanging from it, holding on with her hands.

Alexander was able to catch hold of her hips and lower her. She slid down his body, ending with her mouth less than an inch from his. He didn't know if her feet were touching the ground yet, but he just held her there, his breath mingling with hers, staring into her beautiful green eyes.

Her breath stopped as her lips parted ever so slightly. It was too much to ask of a man. He moved his head forward and pressed his lips to hers, gently at first and then more possessively, reaching out his tongue to taste her sweetness. She was as delicious as he'd thought she would be. Warm and soft. She kissed him back tentatively at first, then slowly allowing him to explore and doing a little of her own. He breathed in her taste, her scent of lemons, and an earthiness she must have picked up from the tree. It made him want to do so much more than merely kiss her. But his horrid mind remembered she was a sweet innocent while his body just wanted to explore the woman pressed so intimately against him.

He suppressed a groan of frustration as he lowered her to her feet and stepped away from temptation. "I apologize," he started.

"No, um, thank you for catching me," she said a little breathlessly.

The cold air that rushed between them cleared his mind. "You said you were escaping from your room?"

"Oh, er, yes. My mother locked me in. I was being punished."

"For what?"

"I gave some children toys when we went to deliver Christmas boxes to the tenants," she explained, but Alexander was confused.

"You were punished for giving children toys?" he repeated.

"Yes. Well, not so much for giving them toys, but for undermining Lady Humesbury's position with her tenants. You see, I hadn't asked permission first. They were just little yarn dolls and horses, and I didn't think to ask."

"Oh. And your mother felt that you should have asked Lady Humesbury if you could give the toys to the children?"

"Yes. I should have. Because I didn't, it made her look bad, as if she didn't care about the children. I didn't mean it to look that way. I just wanted to make the children happy, but…" she paused. "My mother didn't see it that way."

"And so, she punished you by locking you in your room all day."

"Yes."

"She told everyone you were not feeling well," he told her. "I asked if I could visit, but she would not allow me to do so."

"You did?" Her head shot up, so she was looking directly into his eyes once again. She was so beautiful. Her skin glowed in the moonlight.

He could only swallow and nod, forcibly keeping his arms at his side so he didn't reach out and pull her against him again.

"That was kind of you," she whispered.

"I missed you."

She took a small step toward him. "I was thinking of you—"

"Markgraf?" a woman's voice called out from behind him. "Lord Kottenfurst?"

Lady Prudence's eyes went wide before she darted away behind the tree, crouching down out of sight.

Alexander cleared his throat. "Yes?"

"Oh! There you are!" Miss Sidwell and Miss Browning came down the path toward him.

"You disappeared, and we wondered what happened to you," Miss Browning said with a giggle.

Alexander forced a smile onto his lips. "I just needed a breath of fresh air."

"But it's so cold out here," Miss Sidwell said, pulling her shawl tighter around her arms. "Aren't you cold?" She stepped up very close to him, forcing him to take a step back.

"No, actually. But your gown is much less warm than my coat. You should go back inside," he told them both.

"You must come with us," Miss Browning said, moving to take his arm.

He extracted it from her grasp gently. "Thank you. Yes, I will, er, in a few moments. You go ahead, and I promise I shall be right behind you."

"Are you sure? We could go back together?" Miss Sidwell suggested coyly.

"Thank you. But I do want to finish my walk. I shall be in directly."

"I am cold," Miss Browning complained to her friend.

"Oh, very well. We will see you inside in just a few minutes?" Miss Sidwell asked.

"Yes, absolutely," he assured her.

The two girls turned around and walked quickly back toward the French doors from the drawing room, the ones he'd slipped out of—he'd thought—unnoticed.

As soon as they were back inside, he hissed to Lady Prudence, "They are gone."

She stood up and came toward him. "You really should go back inside."

"As should you!" He noticed that she didn't even have a shawl on, only a light pelisse.

"Hmmm, that's going to be a little bit tricky," she said, looking back up at the tree.

"You cannot go back that way!" he protested.

She turned toward him with a chuckle. "No, I don't think I can."

"Come along, we will sneak you in through the back stairs."

She gasped. "You know where they are?"

"Er, yes. I did a little exploring on my own the other day."

He led her to a side door where there was a small set of stairs the servants used and a door going to the kitchen and pantries. "I will distract anyone from going up these stairs for a few minutes to give you time to get up to your room."

"And hopefully I won't meet anyone coming down," she whispered, giving him a smile. "Thank you." She gave him a quick kiss on his cheek, much to his delight, before lightly running up the stair. He only wished she'd aimed for his lips instead.

Chapter Eight

Pru couldn't believe how bold she'd been! Her heart was still pounding in her chest. She'd kissed him.

Kissed him!

And it had been wonderful. No, it had been better than wonderful. It had been heavenly. Oh, the way he'd felt when he'd helped her down from the tree. And his scent—he wore some sort of cologne that was rich and masculine. And of course...

She'd reached her room and automatically tried to open the door, but it was locked! Of course! How scatterbrained could she be? Her mother had actually locked her into the room. Since she'd gone out the window, the door was still—

"Prudence! What are you doing out of your room?" her mother's voice ran down the hall like a fox chasing its prey.

Pru spun around. "I, er," She took in a deep breath. "I wanted to find you... to apologize. I've been thinking and, as always, you were right." She advanced toward her mother who'd paused a few feet away, crossing her arms in front of her. Pru swallowed hard. "I didn't think about the consequences of my action. I was so focused on making the children we met happy that I didn't give a thought to Lady Humesbury and how my action might reflect on her. I was just coming to apologize to you and to her."

Well, most of what she'd said was true, anyway.

Her mother gave a short nod. "I appreciate that you've given this so much thought." She released her arms and came forward. "That is indeed the reason why I felt compelled to lock you into your room. I knew that, given time, you would see the error of your ways."

"Yes, Mother, you were right. And I will absolutely do my utmost to try to think of others when I do something like that," Pru said. She had no idea whether she would or, indeed, *could* consider every possible ramification of her actions before she did something, but she would certainly try. She hated being confined.

Pru moved out of her mother's way when she started toward the door. "How did you get out?" her mother asked, narrowing her eyes at Pru. She tried the door, and it was still locked.

"I, er, through the connecting door to our rooms," Pru lied.

"Ah." Her mother unlocked the door and allowed Pru back into her room, not that she had any great desire to spend even more time in there, but she didn't think she had a choice.

"Well, since you have given your wrongs so much constructive thought, I don't see why you shouldn't rejoin the party again tomorrow," her mother continued.

"Thank you, Mother. And I will apologize to Lady Humesbury—"

"No, there is no need for that. She is still unaware of what you were doing. I think it might be best if she were kept in ignorance," her mother said, interrupting her.

"Oh, all right."

Her mother nodded, then came forward and gave Pru a kiss on her cheek. "You're a good girl, Prudence. Impetuous at times, but you have a good heart."

With that, she left the room through the main door, much to Pru's relief. She knew if her mother tried to go through their connecting doors that she would have found it locked as well.

Alexander spent the following morning writing to his brother. He was embarrassed to tell him that he'd still made no headway on their negotiations. The men simply refused to begin work until their fun was had. At least he'd gained some insight while they'd been out hunting, and he relayed that information to his prince. The rest, the real work, he wrote, would have to wait until his counterparts deemed it to be the right time, and he simply did not see any way around this.

He joined others of the party in the drawing room that afternoon. He sat with a book, some of the ladies had their sewing and were chatting quietly. Lady Prudence had somehow convinced her mother to allow her out of her room and was also sitting with a book.

He looked up from the page he hadn't read, despite the fact that it had sat open in front of his eyes for the past five minutes. Lady Prudence was also not reading. She had been looking at him. Her gaze quickly shifted from him to past his shoulder. He worked to suppress the smile that threatened to burst onto his lips. She'd been watching him.

Her eyes shifted back to him, and their gazes met. He gave a little lift of his eyebrows as if asking what she was thinking. Her beautiful lips turned up into a smile that filled him with a happiness he wouldn't have even imagined possible a week ago.

He watched as she stood, carefully closing and putting her book down. She walked to the window behind him. He quickly did the same, meeting her there.

She looked up at him with a smile and then turned and announced to the room at large. "It's such a lovely day, I think I'll go for a walk. Would anyone care to join me?"

"But it's so cold," Miss Sidwell whined.

"Yes, but the sun is out," Lady Prudence said. She then spun to face their hostess. "Unless you have something else planned, Lady Humesbury. Would you mind very much?"

The lady smiled at Lady Prudence, and Alexander noticed Lady Torrington giving her daughter an approving nod. "No, Prudence, I have nothing planned for this afternoon. In fact, I think it a wonderful idea for you young people to go out and enjoy a little exercise."

"I will be happy to join you," Alexander said.

Immediately Miss Browning jumped to her feet. "As would I." She turned and gave her friend a meaningful look.

"Oh, very well. I will come along," Miss Sidwell said reluctantly.

"I think it sounds like a bang-up idea," her brother said, also standing.

Lady Prudence nodded and then gave Alexander an apologetic look and the slightest shrug of her shoulders, which nearly made him laugh. Turning back to the others, she said, "Shall we meet in the hall in ten minutes?"

"I'll need more time than that to change," Miss Sidwell said.

"You don't need to change. Just put on some good walking boots," Pru said.

Miss Sidwell frowned at her. "I'll be as quick as I can." She then strode from the room with the others following, returning to their rooms to fetch warm clothes and proper footwear.

Twenty minutes later, they all headed out, walking toward the forest with Lady Prudence in lead.

"I thought we were just going to walk in the garden," Miss Sidwell said with a touch of a whine to her voice.

Lady Prudence stopped and turned around. "You are more than welcome to do so, Miss Sidwell, if that would suit you better. I was thinking of a walk through the wood." Lady Prudence gave Miss Sidwell such a hopeful look Alexander almost burst out laughing. It was abundantly clear—at least to him—that Lady Prudence would be so much happier if the other young lady did decide to stay closer to the house.

Perhaps Miss Sidwell picked up on what wasn't said because she gave a smile and began walking toward the forest. "No, I'm very happy to go walking in the wood. It's quite a lovely day for it, don't you think, Miss Browning?"

Her friend ran to catch up saying, "Indeed, I do. A bit nippy, but with the sun, it's quite lovely."

The two young women took the lead, and Lady Prudence seemed to be quite happy to follow them.

"What does it mean, *nippy*?" Alexander asked her quietly in German.

She smiled up at him. "Chilly, cold but not very cold," she responded in English.

"Are you warm enough, Lady Prudence?" Mr. Sidwell asked, coming up and inserting himself in between them.

She frowned at him momentarily, then answered him politely, "Yes, I'm quite comfortable. Are you?"

"Indeed, I'm perfectly fine. I just overheard you say you were cold." He moved to walk more closely to her and then took hold of her hand and threaded it through his arm.

"Oh, no, you misunderstood. I was just translating for Markgraf Kottenfurst," she said, pulling her hand away.

He looked from her to Alexander and back again. "I didn't know you spoke German."

"Just a bit," she admitted. She spoke around the man to Alexander. "*Ist er nervig, denkst du?*"

Alexander held back his laughter with great difficulty, clearing his throat so it wouldn't burst out of him. She thought the man annoying, but truly, it wasn't kind to speak of people right in front of them. "*Ja, aber Sie sollten höflich sein auch wenn du es nicht willst,*" he said, telling her to be polite even if she would rather not.

She gave a little *hmph*. And then with a sigh, asked, "Are you enjoying the party, Mr. Sidwell?"

The fellow seemed very happy she was speaking with him. He gave her a bright smile. "I am, indeed. And you, Lady Prudence?"

"Oh, yes. Christmas is quite my favorite time of year," she told him.

"You do not prefer the spring or the summer when it is warm?" Alexander asked.

She gave him a smile. "I do enjoy those seasons as well, but I don't mind the cold, and I do so love Christmas with all its pretty greenery and giving of gifts to children."

"You are a very generous person," Mr. Sidwell said, taking the words right from Alexander's mouth before he had a chance to speak them.

"No, not at all. I am quite selfish, actually. It is for my own amusement that I give presents. I do so love to watch them laugh and play," she said quite seriously, as if he had hit a painful nerve.

Alexander suspected she was still thinking about her mother's punishment. He wished he could have taken her in his arms and assured her that it wasn't selfish of her at all to want to make children happy, even if it had made their hostess look bad. Sadly, with Mr. Sidwell walking in between them, she couldn't even see the sympathetic look on his face.

They entered the wood proper and were forced to walk two-by-two. Lady Prudence was very clever and managed to fall behind Mr. Sidwell so she could walk next to Alexander. "And what of you, my lord? Are you enjoying the party?" she asked as an excuse to walk next to him—or so he assumed.

He smiled at her. "I am now."

"But you weren't earlier? I don't know... last night or the day before? Did you enjoy hunting with the other men?" she asked.

"Last night was particularly enjoyable," he answered quietly. In a normal volume, he followed that quickly with, "The hunting was quite good. Don't you agree, Mr. Sidwell?"

"Er, yes," the fellow answered with only a slight glance back at them.

"He brought down a good-sized deer," Alexander told Lady Prudence.

"Did he?" She sounded quite impressed.

"Well, with the markgraf's help. It required a bit more than one shot to kill it," Mr. Sidwell admitted.

Alexander had to give the man credit. He hadn't embroiled the truth even though Alexander had given him the perfect opportunity to do so.

There was a squeal from up ahead, making the three of them quicken their pace.

"Look! Oh, do come and see," Miss Sidwell called back to them.

They came around a bend in the path and found the two women approaching a beautiful little gazebo. The trees all around had probably once been cleared away, but it obviously hadn't been looked after for some time. It was strewn with dried leaves and dirt, and a new young tree was growing up right beside it, so its branches poked into the center.

"How pretty," Lady Prudence exclaimed. "I love the dilapidated look. It gives it such character."

"How ridiculous you are, Lady Prudence," Miss Sidwell said with a laugh. "I'm certain it would be much prettier with a new coat of paint and a little cleaning up." She walked up the three little stairs into the center and tried to break off a branch from the little tree.

"Please don't hurt the tree," Lady Prudence exclaimed, running up to her. "It's perfectly fine just the way it is."

"Oh, pooh!" Miss Sidwell said, ignoring her and snapping off the thin branch.

"Miss Sidwell, I must agree with Lady Prudence. It quite gives the gazebo a *je ne sais quoi*, a secret beauty," Alexander said.

"Oh," the girl breathed, turning toward him and stepping much too close. "I didn't know you knew French, too."

He smiled at her. "I went to school in France. Do you think we could leave the tree, please?"

She giggled and batted her eyelashes at him. "Well, since you asked so nicely, I suppose we could."

"Why do you suppose they built this here, so deep in the woods?" Miss Browning asked, coming closer to Alexander and fluttering her eyelashes at him as well.

"I'm certain it was so anyone could enjoy the beauty of the forest," Mr. Sidwell said.

"Or perhaps to take refuge if it were to rain," Lady Prudence suggested.

"Ah yes, a good thought," he agreed.

"Or maybe it was a place for secret assignations," Alexander suggested, looking at Lady Prudence. He wiggled his eyebrows at her, making her laugh.

"It certainly is romantic. Don't you think so?" Miss Sidwell asked, putting a hand on Alexander's arm.

He stepped away to look out the other side. "Indeed. Sadly, it is just a bit too far into the wood to find easily at night when one would want to be romantic."

"I don't know, if you had a lantern with you..." Miss Browning began.

"I suppose it is possible. Should we come out here tonight, Miss Browning, and test it out?" Mr. Sidwell asked.

She burst into giggles. "Oh, Mr. Sidwell, what inappropriate ideas you have!"

Alexander thought it an excellent one, and judging by Lady Prudence's expression, she thought so, too.

Chapter Nine

It was much too great a temptation. Even as Pru snuck from the house, she went over in her mind exactly how much trouble she would get into if her mother found out.

"Pru, I seriously hope you like the inside of that room," she whispered to herself even as she made her way across the grounds toward the wood. Luckily, the moon was still full enough that she didn't yet need to unsheathe her lantern. Hopefully, no one from the house would see her. "You are going to be spending at least the rest of the party inside your room should Mother find out. And honestly, I wouldn't put it past her to lock me in my room at home for the next few weeks as well," she muttered to herself.

So, why was she doing this? Why was she taking such a chance?

Because the opportunity had presented itself, and she simply could not resist. It was terrible; she knew this. It didn't make anyone happy except maybe herself, so she didn't even have that excuse. This was risk for risk's sake and nothing else.

Oh, but it was fun! she thought with a shiver of delight as she stepped beyond the first line of trees.

It was ever so much darker in the copse. And the only sound she could hear was that of her own footsteps on the dried leaves and twigs underfoot.

She opened her light so she could see to follow the path. It absolutely would not do to get lost now.

A noise to her right made her jump. She stopped and listened. There was another slight sound of something perhaps burrowing into some undergrowth, and then silence descended once again. Pru began to breathe, then laugh at herself for being such a ninny.

She continued for perhaps another minute before she heard something again. This time, it definitely sounded like footsteps coming up quickly behind her. She turned and held up her lantern. Another bobbing light was coming toward her.

"Who's there?" she called out. "Mr. Sidwell, is that you?" It had been his idea after all to come out here at night. She wouldn't be surprised if he had done so as well.

"Would you prefer it to be him?" a man's voice called back. Pru knew that accent and smiled.

"Not at all, Lord Kottenfurst. I'm just surprised you were so bold as to venture out," she responded as he came closer so she could see his face.

"I saw you slip out, so I followed. It just took me a moment to get a lantern. Otherwise, I would have joined you sooner," he told her. He had a broad smile on his face.

"Well, if you'd joined me sooner, you wouldn't have needed a lantern at all. You could have simply shared mine," she pointed out with a laugh before turning and continuing on the path toward the gazebo.

He sighed heavily. "Why did I not think of that?"

She laughed but didn't stop. The gazebo looked a great deal spookier with the shadows of the trees all around it. She stepped into it, moving her light all around to take it in.

The markgraf took her lantern and hung it from a hook in the center of the ceiling she hadn't even noticed.

"Oh, that's nice," she said, looking up at him.

"It is. It is very nice. Now we both have our hands free, so we can do this." He reached out and pulled her to him. Slowly, he lowered his head and pressed his lips to hers. He was warm and tasted of the sweet and spicy glühwein he'd had after dinner.

Pru relaxed into his kiss, enjoying the heat and pleasant tingles it sent running straight through her. Sadly, after a few moments, he pulled his head back.

"You do not think Mr. Sidwell will make good on his threat to come out tonight, do you?" he asked.

"I certainly hope not. If we are caught, we'll both be in serious trouble," she told him.

"I suppose your mother will confine you to your room again," he said with a sigh.

"Er, no, it would be worse than that, my lord." Pru didn't know how much he knew of English customs and rules of society.

"Worse?"

"If we are caught here alone like this, you might have to marry me," she told him straight out, not seeing any way of saying it more delicately.

"Oh! Er, yes, I suppose I would." He took a step back, leaving Pru in the cold.

"I'm sorry. It is the way things work." She wrapped her arms around her body.

"Of course. I... I knew that. It is the same in Aachen-Düren. It is why I have been very careful, always, when I am with a young lady. In France, they are a little more understanding of such things, but still there would be questions raised."

"Well, I should hope so!"

He gave a little laugh and took a small turn about the gazebo. "It was not such a difficult walk out here even in the dark of the night."

"No. Quite simple, actually."

He stood by the tree that had been reaching into the gazebo before Miss Sidwell had broken off its branch that afternoon. He put a hand on the broken branch. "I did not come here to meet young ladies. In fact, I was quite surprised anyone was here aside from the gentlemen I was to meet."

"You came for work," she agreed. "My father told me you were going to engage in some negotiations or something."

"Yes. The invitation was rather vague, but that is what I understood. I am not much of a diplomat, but I was eager to prove to my prince that I could be more than just a military man," he admitted.

"And have you been able to do so?" Pru asked.

He turned toward her with a sad little smile on his lips. "I have not been able to do anything. The gentlemen refuse to even begin discussions as yet."

"Still? I remember the day before Christmas when Lord Humesbury said he wanted to enjoy the holiday before you got down to business. That was days ago."

"Yes. And still, we do nothing but senseless entertainments." He sounded frustrated, and Pru didn't blame him.

"Perhaps you could suggest to them once again..."

He shook his head. "I do not want to push too hard. It would make me look overeager, which could lessen my standing in the discussions."

"Oh. I'm afraid I don't know anything about such things."

He gave a little laugh. "Neither do I. My brother has written telling me to be patient."

"So, you are stuck until the other men do something."

"Yes. But it is not all bad." He came over toward her again. "I get to be with you."

"Even if doing so could risk your freedom?" she asked, trying to ignore the stab of pain to her heart. It was clear he did not want to risk getting caught with her. On the other hand, he hadn't left after she'd told him of the consequences.

"It is not just my freedom that I worry about if we are caught, Lady Prudence," he said. He reached out and caressed his gloved hand down her cheek, cupping her chin and making her look up at him. "I haven't yet done what I came to this house party to do, and I worry that if we were caught, your father would not look upon me so kindly, nor be so willing to have a treaty between our countries."

"Oh, yes. I understand. You think my father would be angry and would extend his feelings into his work, which would have a negative impact not only on you but your country."

"Precisely."

She thought about it for a moment and then gave a little laugh. "Actually, I wonder whether he might be more favorably inclined toward you—were you to take me off his hands. I'm afraid I am nothing but trouble for him."

"I cannot believe that," the markgraf said quickly. "You are a delight."

She smiled up at him. "You haven't known me for very long. Just look at where I am, risking everything just to see what it would be like to visit this gazebo at night."

"You are very brave."

"I am very foolish," she said with a laugh. "And I should not prolong my absence. Do you have your lantern still?"

"I do," he indicated the floor where he'd put it down by the steps.

"Then I will bid you a good night," Pru said, reaching for her lantern.

He beat her to it, taking it down from the hook above their heads. Before handing it to her, though, he reached down for one more delicious kiss.

When she finally was able to step away, she gave a little laugh. "That will keep me warm as I walk back. Thank you."

His quiet chuckle followed her down the stairs as she began her way back.

Chapter Ten

On the evening of the first day of the new year, Lady Humesbury requested the gentlemen join the ladies as they left the table after dinner. When everyone gave her a curious look, she merely shared a smile with her husband as they led everyone back to the drawing room.

The room had been rearranged to leave the center empty, and the pianoforte had been moved forward. Immediately upon seeing this, Pru began to laugh and clap her hands. "Is there to be dancing this evening?" she asked, turning a bright smile onto her hostess.

"Very clever, Lady Prudence," Lady Humesbury said. "Yes, there is." She turned to everyone else. "His lordship and I thought it would be a good idea to give everyone a chance to practice their dance steps before the ball on Twelfth Night."

Pru's father began to chuckle. "Excellent, then I get to have some entertainment with my brandy." He immediately headed toward the sideboard where drinks and glasses were laid out.

"Oh, not so fast, my lord," Lady Humesbury said, catching hold of his arm and forcing him to stop. "No one is exempt from dancing."

"Oh no, Papa, you can't miss out on the fun!" Pru cried. She turned to her mother. “Mother, you must convince him to dance. You’ve done it before, and you are both excellent dancers.”

Lady Torrington gave an embarrassed little laugh. “Well, we haven’t danced in public in years, Prudence.”

“Posh-tosh, this isn’t public, Anne. This is merely in the company of good friends,” Lady Humesbury said. “We shall *all* be dancing.”

“But then, who shall play the music?” Miss Sidwell asked.

“It turns out the interpreter we hired for Lord Kottenfurst, who we haven’t had to use at all thanks to his lordship’s excellent command of English—”

“But my valet has enjoyed his services a great deal, I might add,” the markgraf cut in.

“Indeed, I have heard as much,” Lady Humesbury agreed. “He is apparently an accomplished musician as well as being fluent in German. He shall play for us. Ah, here he is now.”

The gentleman in question, a tall slender man with thinning blond hair came into the room. He colored a touch as everyone turned to look at him. He bowed, then strode to the pianoforte and sat ready to play.

“Now, everyone, please, we shall start with a cotillion,” Lady Humesbury announced.

Mr. Sidwell, who was standing to Pru’s left, immediately turned to her. “May I have this first dance, Lady Prudence?”

“I would be honored, sir,” Pru said with a little curtsy.

They joined one of the lines of couples. She was especially pleased when Lord Kottenfurst lined up next to Mr. Sidwell, partnering with Miss Browning. That meant she would be dancing with him as well when they exchanged partners for some of the steps. She gave him a smile, and he winked back.

As the partners came together in the first movements of the dance, she admitted to Mr. Sidwell, “You will please have to excuse me. It has been ages since I’ve danced.”

They moved apart, but when they came together again, he smiled at her and said, “No worries, Lady Prudence.”

“Just watch out for your toes,” she said with a giggle.

He laughed and nodded before chasséing around Miss Browning as the markgraf did the same around her.

"Do you enjoy dancing, Lady Prudence," the markgraf asked as he passed her by.

She laughed, quickly saying, "I do, my lord. And you?"

He nodded and moved back to his position next to Mr. Sidwell.

Thank goodness Pru had had years of lessons, so the steps came back to her quickly. It wasn't, however, easy to hold a conversation while dancing since you were constantly on the move.

At the end of the dance, everyone was laughing and having a good time. Pru and the others applauded their pianist. Before they all broke from their formation on the floor Lord Kottenfurst stepped forward and called out to Lady Humesbury, who was standing a couple away, "My lady, do you dance the waltz?"

She spun toward him, a look of curiosity covering her face. "The waltz, my lord? I have heard of it, but have never seen it performed. Do you know it?"

"Of course. We dance it now in Aachen-Düren, and I have danced it in France as well," he said.

"Would you be willing to demonstrate?" she asked.

"I would be more than happy to do so. I will need a partner, naturally." He looked around the room at the ladies, but no one spoke up.

Pru wondered if her mother would be angry if she volunteered. She didn't even wait for her own answer. Since no one else seemed to be stepping forward, she did. "I would like to learn, my lord." She looked to her mother, who was frowning. Pru gave her a hopeful smile before turning back to the markgraf.

"Thank you for being the brave one, Lady Prudence," Lady Humesbury said with a little laugh. She then turned to the pianist. "Do you know a waltz, Mr. Jones?"

"Yes, of course," the man said. He gave the markgraf a nod as if to say, *Whenever you are ready*.

Everyone else stepped back to watch, and Pru stepped closer to his lordship who was smiling at her. He gave the pianist a nod. As the music began, he said loud enough for everyone to hear, "We begin with a bow." He executed a very fine one.

She curtsied in return.

He then came up beside her and reached for her hands in front and in back of her. She took his right hand with her left in front of her and his left with her right behind. He nodded and said, "And then we promenade."

They proceeded to take four steps forward and then stopped.

"Now, I keep my hand at your waist and you put yours to mine," he said, turning toward her.

She did as he said. It put them very close together. Pru's heart was pounding in her chest, and she knew it had very little to do with the exertion of the dance. As if he could sense her excitement, he smiled down at her. He gave her a nod, raising his free hand above their heads. He indicated that she do the same. Grasping her fingers, he told her, "Now we turn about. Just follow my lead." He proceeded to dance about in a circle. She nearly stepped on his toes a few times but quickly understood his sequence of steps.

"Excellent. And then we go back to our promenade." They moved into their previous position. After two steps forward, he paused and turned her about so that she spun and landed in the same position as before. They moved back to the face-to-face part of the dance. As they completed their circle, he stopped and turned back to Lady Humesbury. "And so, it continues. That is the waltz," he told their hostess before turning back to Pru and bowing. "Thank you, Lady Prudence, for a delightful dance."

Pru curtsied. "Thank you, my lord," she whispered, her voice not quite working right for some reason.

"Well, that was fascinating," Lady Minton said, clapping her hands together. The others quickly followed, joining in the applause.

"Do not even consider that I will dance such a thing with you in public," her husband told her.

"But Minton," she began to protest.

Pru started to laugh as did some others.

"No, I must agree, that is too fast for me," Lady Bunbury agreed.

"Too close," agreed Miss Sidwell.

"Why, it's positively scandalous," Miss Browning added. "Did you see how close they stood with their arms around each other!"

"Staring into each other's eyes," Mr. Sidwell said, not sounding very happy at all.

"Yes, I believe there is a consensus," Lord Humesbury said. "We shall stick with our country dances and quadrilles."

Pru was a little disappointed. She'd found the dance exhilarating, but she had been dancing with Markgraf Kottenfurst. She wasn't too certain she would enjoy it nearly as much with another gentleman.

They all danced another country dance much to Alexander's disappointment. A country dance was fine, but it definitely lacked a great deal when compared with the waltz. He'd been so thrilled when Lady Prudence had volunteered to dance with him. He'd been certain she wouldn't be able to resist such a temptation, and he was rewarded with her bravery. Her mother hadn't looked very pleased, but aside from a slight pursing of her lips, the lady hadn't actually said anything. He was grateful for that as well.

Alexander made sure to dance with Miss Sidwell and then Lady Minton—the youngest of the married ladies present. The older couples quit after the second dance and after his fourth, Alexander was ready for a break as well.

He was standing and watching while enjoying a glass of cool white wine when he sensed Lord Torrington come up next to him. "They have so much energy, these young ladies, do they not?"

Alexander gave a little chuckle. "Indeed. More than one would think."

"All the young ladies in attendance are quite lovely, do you not agree?" the gentleman said quietly.

Alexander looked about at them and could not in all honesty disagree.

"All three are quite eligible, you know," his lordship said in an off-hand way.

Alexander turned toward him, wondering what he was getting at. "My lord?"

Lord Torrington smiled. "Marriage. I presume you shall be looking about you for a wife before long. An English girl from a good family—"

"My lord, are you suggesting that I might be interested in marrying one of these girls?" Alexander asked, beginning to feel his ire rise. The days, nearly weeks of these men putting off their discussions was running through his mind. Humesbury had said it was so they could all relax and enjoy the holiday, but had there actually been an ulterior motive? Had these men wanted him to spend time with the eligible young ladies of the party? Had they wanted to do so in order to lure him into marriage?

Lady Prudence's comments from the other night at the gazebo also pricked his memory. She'd told him straight out that her father would insist they marry were they caught—and that her father would be more than happy to be rid of her. Had he been set up? If he'd stayed a little longer, would someone have "accidentally" discovered them? But no, she'd left first. She'd been the careful one to ensure they weren't caught. So if it had been a set-up, at least she hadn't been aware of it either.

But still...

"I don't see any reason why you wouldn't," Lord Torrington said, his smile staying fixed on his face, although his eyes began to look a little wary.

"Is that why you invited me? Is that why you have put off our negotiations? Are you trying to trick me into marrying one of these ladies?" Alexander asked quickly, moving into full-blown anger.

"Please, my lord, keep your voice down," Lord Torrington said quietly, his eyes darting from side to side as if making sure no one heard their argument.

"No, no, I do not believe I will. I have been used! Duped! You are trying to play me," Alexander said, raising his voice.

"No, no! Not at all, my lord. Honestly, it was merely an innocent suggestion," Lord Torrington said, finally backing off.

The music stopped, and everyone was turning toward them.

"If that is the case, then why have you consistently postponed our negotiations? Why have we not even begun to discuss the real reason why I came here, after over a week?"

"We just... we thought it would be more pleasant..."

"Oh, yes, more pleasant—to ply me with alcohol, games, and beautiful women. Well, I will stand for it no longer. Tomorrow, we get to work. First thing tomorrow morning, I will be in the study ready to begin our discussions. If I am not joined by all the gentlemen participating, I will be gone by afternoon. Is that understood?" Alexander was nearly shouting by the time he finished, and to accent his words, he slammed his glass down on the table behind him and then strode from the room.

Chapter Eleven

Silence reigned in the room for a good minute after the markgraf left. All the men, except for Mr. Sidwell, immediately converged in one corner. Miss Sidwell, Miss Browning, and her sister moved together to discuss what had just occurred. And oddly enough, Pru felt a lump form at the base of her throat.

She swallowed it down hard, then found her mother bearing down on her with a frown on her face. Pru just could not deal with her mother's misplaced ire just now. She looked toward the door and wondered if she could escape before it was too late. She had just started in that direction when her mother's voice stopped her.

"Prudence," Lady Torrington said, forcing Pru to stop and wait for her mother to join her. "For once, this is not your fault," she said quietly the moment she reached her daughter's side.

Pru's mouth nearly fell open.

"This one is entirely on your father. Clearly, he said something to insult the markgraf, and it will be upon his head to make this right."

"I assume they'll go into their talks tomorrow. It's the only way I see for anything to be to his lordship's liking."

"Indeed. But I just wanted you to know that even though I did not approve of you dancing that indecent waltz, I do not believe you did anything wrong. In fact, possibly just the opposite. It seems that you were playing into your father's scheme, unbeknownst to any of us."

"Do you really think I and the other young ladies were actually invited here to tempt the markgraf into a marriage?"

"I honestly don't know. Frankly, I wouldn't put it past these men," she said, not even trying to hide the disgust in her voice.

Pru didn't know what to say to this. The lump in her throat had somehow sunk to her belly where it churned up the contents there. "I'm afraid I'm feeling a little ill. Do you think I may be excused for the evening?"

Lady Torrington looked at her with concern. "Of course, my dear. I'm sure everyone will be dispersing to their rooms shortly. You won't be missed."

"Thank you. Good night." Pru did her best to move at a normal pace and not simply burst into a run as she desperately wanted to do.

She made it to her room without incident—she lost neither her dinner nor the tears that were now threatening to spill out of her eyes.

She went directly to the windowsill and stared out at the tree. It had been her escape when her mother had punished her... and it had led her directly into the arms of the Markgraf Kottenfurst. Every time she looked at it, all she could think of was the way she had slid down his hard body, the way he had kissed her even before her feet had touched the ground.

Had it all been set up somehow? Had any of it been real? Could something like that have been planned for or intentional in any way?

Her feelings for his lordship... she'd thought they were real. She'd even toyed with the idea that she might be falling in love with the man, wondered if he might feel the same.

She tried to remember his reaction when she'd told him that they would be forced to marry if caught at the gazebo. He'd moved away from her then. So, no.

He couldn't be in love with her.

If he were, he would have said it was fine. That he wouldn't mind if they were caught—but he didn't. He'd moved away.

Oh, why was she such a pea-goose? Was there ever anyone so gullible as she?

She'd danced a waltz with the man. Stood face-to-face with him with her hand on his waist—in front of the entire company—and he'd smiled. The heat had warmed her straight to her toes. She'd been so happy. So sure of herself when really, she had no basis for doing so.

He didn't care about her. He was just entertaining himself while waiting for his work to begin. What were a few stolen kisses to a man like him?

Nothing.

It had all meant absolutely—

A knock on her door interrupted her musings.

In curiosity, she got up, dashing the tears from her cheeks. "Yes?" she asked, opening her door.

The most handsome, welcome face stared back at her, his eyebrows furrowed.

"Lord Kottenfurst!" the words burst from her mouth in a whisper.

"I know I should not be here. It is inappropriate. I... I simply wanted to apologize." With those words, he turned on his heel and walked away, leaving Pru staring after him.

The overwhelming desire to stop him, to run after him, to find out what he meant, had her trembling. Voices coming up the stairs, however, stopped her. She could recognize the giggles of Miss Sidwell and Miss Browning before their faces even appeared at the end of the hallway.

Pru ducked back into her room before they could see her.

Standing with her back to her door, a tiny spark of hope lit in her heart.

Alexander was especially pleased to see he wasn't the first one in the study the following morning. Lord Bunbury and Lord Torrington had arrived first and were deep in some discussion when Alexander came into the room.

"Ah, good morning, my lord," Lord Torrington said, greeting him with a smile. "Do help yourself to a cup of tea or coffee and join us."

Alexander poured himself a cup of coffee. As he was doing so, the other men came in. Soon, they were all seated around the table. Alexander looked around, not knowing who was going to lead the meeting.

Lord Bunbury started. "We, er, we want to begin by apologizing for the delay in getting this meeting started. We truly had no intention of deceiving you or distracting you in any way."

"It is true, my lord, what I said the day after you arrived. We merely wanted to give you a chance to relax and enjoy your holiday before we got down to work," Lord Humesbury added.

"And I apologize if my comment last night regarding marriage offended you in any way," Lord Torrington added. "You certainly should feel no compunction to choose an English bride—or any one of the eligible young ladies who are here. There are many lovely young ladies if you choose to come during the Season in London, and I'm certain you have some excellent choices in your own country."

Alexander noticed Lord Perbury frowning at the man and had a momentary urge to laugh at Lord Torrington's awkward speech.

"I do beg your pardon," Lord Torrington said, suddenly realizing his position. "I have a daughter of marriageable age. It is on my mind. You cannot blame a father for having such thoughts!"

The men all broke into laughter with Alexander, glad that it wasn't only him who found the gentleman's discomfort funny.

"All right. I'm glad we got that out of the way. Now on to business," Lord Bunbury said, recalling everyone's attention. He turned to Alexander. "The reason we asked you here was to discuss a treaty that we believe will be mutually beneficial to both our countries."

The viscount proceeded to outline an excellent scheme wherein British troops would be stationed in Aachen-Düren, given barracks in which to live, and supplies such as food and ammunition. In return, the British would protect the borders of the country from invaders.

"We would be in place should there be any unpleasantness from your south or east," he said, referring to both France and the Austrian Empire, both of which were more than eager to take over such a critically positioned territory. "It will be to both our advantages to have English troops stationed in Aachen-Düren. You get the protection you need, and we will have a presence on the Continent should we need one."

Alexander sat back as he listened to their proposal. When they were finished, he simply shook his head saying, "I cannot see why we would not want to establish such a treaty. As you say, it is in both of our interests. Aachen-Düren is wealthy enough to be able to afford the cost of maintaining a subset of your army, and it is certainly to our advantage to do so." He couldn't help but wonder what they weren't telling him. There had to be more than this simple exchange.

"Excellent! Excellent. We have all the paperwork drawn up. It merely needs the signature of your Prince Heinrich. Will it need to be approved by your Parliament as well, do you know?"

"Yes, I am certain it will, but truly, I cannot see there would be any objections. As you say, this is most certainly in our interest," Alexander told them. He then sat forward and looked around the table. "Now, tell me what you have *not* yet said. I know there is more. This simple treaty could have been taken care of much more quickly and easily in almost any other manner than this."

"It was imperative we discuss this with you in person, my lord," Lord Minton began.

Alexander just gave him a disbelieving look. "Please, I am not so naive. What is it that you really want from me? And when I say *me*, I do not mean Aachen-Düren because anyone from my government could have come to negotiate this simple treaty. You specifically asked for me. I want to know why."

The gentlemen all turned to look at Lord Perbury, who gave Alexander a small smile. "My lord, we are curious about your feelings toward France and what is happening there just now."

"Aaah." Alexander steepled his fingers. "You are naturally concerned about the stability of the French government."

"How could we not be?" Lord Humesbury said.

"I understand you attended the *Ecole Militaire* in France. You must have a number of contacts both within the government and military," Perbury said.

Alexander nodded, thinking back to his time at school. It wasn't very long ago that he'd graduated. Naturally, he'd kept in contact with his friends from there—a number of whom were now in places of importance and power. "You are correct, my lord. I have a good many friends and acquaintances in such positions. You would like me to, perhaps, intentionally keep up those connections, I gather?"

Lord Perbury smiled. "We are beginning a new organization where such connections could be very... beneficial. It is to be called the Carlton Group and will consist of gentlemen such as yourself who have friends in high places."

"I see. And these gentlemen will share whatever information they might glean from those connections with...?" Alexander asked with a slight smile.

"The head of the Carlton Group who is, as you might have surmised, a person of power within the British government," Lord Perbury replied.

"I see," Alexander nodded. So, they were beginning a new spy agency, and they wanted him to join them. Interesting.

"You understand us so well," Lord Bunbury said with a little laugh.

"I would be a fool not to do so," Alexander agreed, giving the man a smile.

"Now you see why we wanted to get to know you a little better before we began these discussions, my lord," Lord Torrington added.

Alexander nodded. Yes, it did all make sense now. You didn't simply ask a stranger to become a spy for you. Now that they had all become friends, it was much easier.

"So? What do you think?" Minton asked.

"Personally, I do not have any problems with this. As you say, I have the connections, and it would be easy enough to maintain them. I will, of course, need to discuss this with my brother, the prince, and ensure he has no problems with my involvement," Alexander said.

"Of course. We do not expect an answer right away," Lord Perbury added.

There was a knock on the door, followed by the entrance of a footman. "I beg your pardon, my lords, Lady Humesbury has asked me to inform you that a light luncheon has been served in the breakfast room."

"Luncheon? Is it that time already?" Lord Torrington asked, pulled out a watch from his pocket. He lifted his eyebrows at what he saw there, making Alexander assume it was quite a bit later than expected.

At the mention of food, his stomach agreed with Lord Torrington's assessment.

"Well, I believe we are finished here," Lord Humesbury said. Looking around the table, he asked, "Does anyone else have anything he'd like to add?"

There was silence.

"I would just like to once again thank the markgraf for his patience for the time we took getting to these discussions," Lord Minton said.

"Hear, hear," Lord Bunbury agreed.

There was a general consensus and Alexander smiled. "Well, I'm just glad we finally got to talk."

"And we have given you a great deal to discuss with your brother upon your return," Lord Perbury said, standing.

"Yes, indeed." Alexander followed him out into the hall. "It quite makes me eager to get home again, I must say."

"When do you plan on leaving? Not before the ball, I hope?" Lord Humesbury asked.

"I do not know that I can stay for the ball. My mission was to have these discussions and return immediately. I would write to my brother, but in all honesty, I could get there just as quickly as the post, if not faster, and this is a conversation I would rather have in person."

"Of course," Lord Torrington said.

"Naturally," Lord Bunbury agreed at the same time.

"I will have to—" A noise to his right made him stop and turn his head. Lady Prudence was standing just outside the breakfast room, her hand on the door handle, staring wide-eyed at him.

She must have overheard. He watched as she turned to retreat up the stairs toward her room, but Miss Browning and Lady Minton were coming down just at that moment.

She turned again, strode to the foyer, and straight out the front door with no coat on, merely a thin shawl draped over her arms.

Realizing the men were all still watching him, he turned and gave them a smile. "Er, let me think on it, Lord Humesbury." He was about to go after her when another footman approached bearing a silver tray.

"I do beg your pardon, my lord, this just arrived for you." He held out the tray to Alexander. On it was a letter in his brother's hand.

"Thank you." He took it, turning back to the other men. "I will let you know shortly." He pocketed the letter and went after Lady Prudence.

Chapter Twelve

He saw her in the distance heading toward the wood and went running after her. He'd nearly caught up when he called out, "Do you not think it is much too cold to be outside without a coat?"

She didn't even glance back, responding, "I'm a little overheated at the moment, my lord. I'll be fine."

He fell into step next to her. "I am concerned you will become sick."

She stopped walking and turned to him. "Don't you have your packing to do, Lord Kottenfurst?"

"I do not know. I have not yet decided—" he stopped speaking when he noticed her eyes begin to shine with unshed tears. He took her hand in his. It was freezing. He pulled it closer to his mouth and breathed onto her fingers to warm them. "Lady Prudence... Prudence, if I may?"

"I don't see why when you are about to leave, and I shall, in all likelihood, never see you again." She pulled her hand from his and turned away.

"You knew this was merely a..." He faltered for a word.

"A what? A dalliance? A game? A moment's mistake?" she offered.

"Not a mistake. A moment's pleasure is closer to what I was thinking," he said honestly.

"Yes well, that's wonderful for you. Have a good journey home, my lord." She turned and resumed walking.

He closed his eyes and sighed. He knew what she was feeling; he was feeling it too. They had grown close, perhaps too close. He'd taken liberties with her, which had been a mistake. He'd allowed his heart to overrule his head. But now it was his mind that was in control again, and he knew what had to be done, no matter how painful.

"Lady Prudence," he said, catching up with her again. "Please, allow me to apologize. I did not mean to hurt you. It is just that..."

When he paused again, she spun around to face him again. "You seem to be at quite a loss for words this afternoon, my lord."

"I am. This not an easy conversation to have in a foreign language," he admitted.

"Perhaps it would be easier if we simply didn't have it, then, because my German isn't strong enough either." She turned back toward the wood.

He grabbed her arm before she started walking again. "Prudence, I am sorry. I was wrong to... to kiss you. I was wrong to give you any sort of hope that there could be more between us."

Her gaze dropped to the ground.

He swallowed and forced himself to continue, "I have always believed that honesty was best. I have greatly enjoyed our time together. Truly. Speaking with you, spending time with you, it has all been wonderful, but..." He held up his hand before she could interrupt him again. "But I am working on becoming a diplomat. I am second in line to the throne of Aachen-Düren and must have a wife who will add to my prestige, not... not undermine it with silly antics. You said yourself your father considers you a liability. One he is eager to get rid of."

Her gaze flew up to his, a frown forming above her beautiful eyes.

"You are a very sweet girl, but not the sort I need to marry. If I were not in this position, I might consider... but I am not. I do not wish to sound full of myself, but I have an important position in my country. I must marry well and..."

"Not some girl who climbs trees and gets into trouble giving toys to children," she finished for him.

"Not someone who acts without thought and does not consider the consequences of her behavior," he answered.

She winced, and he wished it could have been any other way.

"I am sorry," he said again. This time he did turn around and leave her because there was truly nothing more he could say.

Pru considered going on to the gazebo, where she'd originally been headed when the Markgraf Kottenfurst caught up with her. But he was right. It was ridiculously cold out, and she was not dressed for this weather.

She turned and walked as quickly as she could to the side of the house and the door he had shown her that led to the back stairs. The last thing she wanted was to walk behind him back into the house.

When she reached her room, she stirred to life the coals in her fireplace and then sat herself down in front of the fire. She was not only freezing but frozen. Frozen with the brutal honesty the markgraf had shared with her. Frozen with her own churning emotions. Frozen with the foolishness of her own actions.

The saddest part was there weren't even any tears. Not one. Her heart was broken, and she felt hollow inside knowing she was entirely to blame for this. Everything he had said was correct. She couldn't argue with one word of it. So she just sat there, staring into the fire. Numb.

Alexander couldn't stomach the idea of going into the breakfast room and being polite with the others. He then remembered the letter from his brother sitting in his pocket and went into the drawing room to read it. He sat in the window seat for both the light and relative privacy.

Dearest Brother,

I thought I would wait to share my happy news with you upon your return, but as I do not know when that might be, I decided to write.

I have decided to marry. I am stupidly in love.

I know, I know, a prince should marry to further the interests of his country not for his heart, but in this instance, I think I may do both. I think I might have mentioned I invited a few representatives from nearby principalities and states to come present information to me regarding noblewomen of marriageable age.

Alexander paused his reading. He didn't think his brother had ever told him that he'd done this. He wasn't surprised; it was absolutely the right thing to do. Still, it was interesting he had not mentioned it in any of his earlier letters.

Well, the representative Wetzlar Hessen did not come with a likeness of their princess as most of the ambassadors did, but with the girl herself! Alexander, she is lovely. She is beautiful and funny and just a delight to be with. I sent an offer of marriage to her father after merely three days in her presence, and I have just now received his blessings.

I wanted you to be the first person to know, aside from Mother who, as you can imagine, has had a strong hand in all this. Of course, by the time you receive this letter, it will probably be known throughout Aachen-Düren, but I wanted to be the one to tell you personally. I know this will affect you, but I hope you'll be happy for me.

As for you—you have spoken highly of the young ladies at your English house party, and of one in particular, Lady Prudence. I have spoken with my advisors, and they agree with me that it would greatly benefit our little country were you to ally yourself with either this girl or one of the others if any of them have taken your fancy. Do not think you need to marry a girl from Aachen-Düren. It would be much better if you could see yourself, instead, with an English noblewoman. Mother approves as well—as you can imagine, we have discussed it at length.

I must admit your description of Lady Prudence, in particular, caught my attention and had me laughing so hard I received strange looks from others in the room when I was reading your letter. She sounds absolutely perfect for you, my dear friend. She will soften you and bring joy to your life. You are much too serious, Alexander, and you need someone lighthearted and, yes, even a little rash. I fully approve of this girl. If you have any feelings of affection for her, I strongly suggest you consider marrying her.

It is with love and joy that I pen this letter,

Rich

Alexander put the letter down to stare out the window. Rich wanted him to marry Prudence? His brother, his prince, thought he should marry a girl who was fun and silly, regardless of his position.

He looked down at the letter once again. Too serious? He was too serious?

Well, maybe... perhaps... but no! Rich had not seen him climbing trees

—which he'd done merely to impress Prudence with his physical prowess. Or play that ridiculous game Snapdragon to prove to her that he was no coward. His brother didn't know that he'd demonstrated the waltz for this company. All in the hopes of getting Prudence into his arms once again even if it was in public.

Alexander dropped his head into his hands. What a fool he was! Why had he done all these things? Of course, Prudence was hurt. He'd done so much to prove himself to her and then... then he had spurned her for what made her uniquely Prudence.

He looked at the letter once again. Of course, his brother hadn't even taken into consideration the position Alexander held. He was too much in love himself, clearly. No, Alexander was right in all that he'd told Prudence. She may be fun and wonderful to be with, but he did need someone who knew how to behave properly in public, who knew better than to embarrass others, and who thought about the consequences of her actions. No, he was right in all that he'd told her.

He refolded his brother's letter and tucked it back into his pocket. No, in this instance he was right, and Rich was not, no matter what his advisors said. Perhaps he should marry an English girl, but Prudence Torrington was *not* the one he should marry.

"That girl absolutely drives me to distraction!" Lady Torrington's voice carried across the room as she and Lady Minton entered. They were clearly carrying on a conversation they'd begun in another room.

They sat on one of the sofas, not even noticing him sitting in the window.

"She is so concerned with everyone else's well-being that she doesn't give a thought to how she is going to present herself to society," Lady Torrington continued.

"That is good, and it's bad," Lady Minton commented.

"Well, it *is* good. I don't know what I will do when she marries. Everyone on the estate listens to her much sooner than they do me!" She gave a little laugh. "She makes certain everyone is happy. She knows all the children, who is interested in whom—she takes a personal interest in *everyone*."

"Everyone but herself," Lady Minton said with a little laugh.

"Yes! How is she ever to find and attract a proper husband if she doesn't want to go to parties? If she doesn't take the time to care for her complexion, her dress, her conversation? Of course, I ensure that her wardrobe is up-to-date, and she is a fine conversationalist when she puts her mind to it. But she would much rather ask about a person's life—and she truly listens and takes an interest—than engage in ordinary polite conversation." The lady sighed heavily. "I just don't know what I'm going to do with her!"

"But you must present her this year, my lady. She is already twenty, is she not?" Lady Minton asked.

"She is. His lordship and I have been putting off the inevitable, I know."

"Surely Lord Torrington is just as eager as you to see her settled well," Lady Minton asked.

"Oh, no! He is the one who has insisted that I keep her from making her debut. He would never admit as much to her, but I think he will miss her even more than I when she marries."

Lady Humesbury came in just then. She went toward to her friends but, unlike the other ladies, noticed Alexander sitting in the window. She gave him a smile, which quickly turned into a frown. "My lord, I hear you are thinking of leaving us early," she called across the room.

He stood and came toward her. "I do beg your pardon, my lady. Ladies," he said bowing toward Lady Torrington and Lady Minton. "I'm afraid I didn't announce my presence as I was just reading a letter from my brother."

"I hope all is well?" Lady Torrington asked.

"Indeed, very well. He has written to inform me of his impending nuptials."

"Why, that is excellent news!" Lady Minton exclaimed.

"Or is it?" Lady Humesbury asked with a questioning smile. "If he marries and has children, you will no longer be the heir to his throne, is that right?"

"It is, but to be honest, that only makes me happier for him. I have no desire to rule Aachen-Düren. I am quite happy in my role as advisor and will greatly look forward to being the beloved uncle to his children."

"That is good of you. And what does this say to your leaving us?" Lady Humesbury persisted.

"I believe it means I do not need to rush back as I had originally thought," Alexander answered. He actually hadn't given it any thought but simply allowed his instincts to dictate his words. "He is clearly distracted at the moment with his new bride-to-be."

"And therefore, he might not even hear your report of your negotiations for some time were you to return immediately?" Lady Torrington suggested.

"Precisely, my lady. I may as well stay another few days and enjoy myself," he told them.

Chapter Thirteen

"Prudence, are you ready to go down to dinner?" Lady Torrington asked, coming into her daughter's room that evening. She stopped just inside the connecting door to their rooms and exclaimed, "You're not even dressed! What is this?"

Pru had hardly moved all afternoon and was still sitting on the floor in front of the fire. "What? Dressed?" she asked dazedly. "What is the time?"

"It is past time for you to get dressed for dinner!" her mother said, sounding even more exasperated than usual.

"Oh no, I'm sorry, Mother. I don't think I will go down for dinner this evening," Pru said, leaning back again against the chair next to her and turning back toward the fire.

Her mother came and sat in the chair. "What is it? What's happened?"

"Haven't you heard? Lord Kottenfurst is leaving early."

"I *have* spoken with him," her mother said hesitantly. "What did he say to you?"

"He said he was leaving. I didn't even question him any further when he told me I was not the sort of girl he should marry," she told the fireplace. "He needs to marry someone who will not embarrass him. Someone who thinks about the consequences of their actions, who will be the appropriate wife for an ambassador or a diplomat, not some foolish chit like me."

"You've fallen in love with him!" her mother exclaimed.

Pru nodded, feeling the tears that hadn't come all afternoon begin to flow down her cheeks. She dropped her face into her hands, too embarrassed to allow her mother see her distress.

Much to her surprise, her mother lowered herself onto the floor and took Pru into her arms and held her, hushing her tears and whispering it would be all right.

When she could, Pru managed, "No, Mother, it won't be, and I don't quite know what I'm going to do."

"Well, I know what you're going to do," her mother said, pushing her away.

Prudence sniffed and looked up.

"First, you are going to dry your eyes, put on a pretty gown, and go down to dinner. You'll pretend as if there is nothing wrong because that's what a poised young lady does. We hide our feelings and continue on, no matter what."

Pru took a tremulous breath, knowing her mother was right. She didn't like it, but it *was* the right thing to do. She was just about to say as much when her mother continued.

"And the second thing you are going to do is to show that markgraf how very, very wrong he was in his estimation of you. He has decided to stay for the ball, and you, my love, are going to make him very sorry indeed that he has spurned you. You are going to show him how very noble and proper you can be. You know how to behave correctly despite the fact that, yes, sometimes you can be impulsive. But you, my darling, have a heart of gold. You are going to show that man what he has lost."

"I am? I do?" Prudence had never heard her mother praise her in such a way before. She'd never said such kind things to her.

"Yes, you do," her mother said, wiping away the tears still lingering on Pru's cheeks. "I am very proud of you and so is your father. We don't want to lose you to some gentleman, Pru, but we know it will happen, eventually. And whether it is the markgraf or someone else, we know you will make someone exceedingly happy. Now, prove yourself the capable lady and get yourself dressed for dinner—and you'd better do so quickly, for we are already late. Where is your maid?"

"I think she might have peeked in on me a while ago but left again when she saw me sitting here," Pru told her.

"What? And she didn't come and tell me?"

"I guess she didn't know to do so," Pru said, defending the girl who had been assigned to her by Lady Humesbury.

"Well, I will send in my woman, and she will have you dressed and presentable in a trice. Now help me up. I am too old to be sitting on the floor in this way," her mother said with a laugh.

Pru giggled and helped her mother to her feet.

The next two days were the hardest for Prudence. The first day was the worst; the second was only slightly more manageable. She did her best to look and behave as normal. She tried hard to laugh and be light-hearted, but everything within her just screamed for her to escape from company and curl up into a little ball on her bed.

Of course, she did no such thing. She smiled and chatted, and if Lord Kottenfurst made his way toward her, she would go in the opposite direction, making excuses to whoever she was speaking with at the time. It was like playing a game of tag and the markgraf was "it."

She simply kept telling herself that it was only two days. Two days that she had to deal with this. Two days that she had to see him and be reminded of all the wonderful, happy times they'd had together. Two days of wondering who he would choose to marry. What boring, beautiful girl who could smile and make polite conversation and do absolutely nothing interesting, nothing remarkable, would he choose to spend the rest of his life with? Well, she hoped he would be happy with his little piece of perfection.

On the afternoon of the ball, Lady Torrington joined Pru in her room where she was hiding from the world. "Come, Prudence, it is time for you to prepare for the ball," her mother said, coming into her room.

"What? Now? It's only..." She peered at the clock on the mantel above the fireplace. "Four o'clock! There are three hours before dinner."

"Yes, hardly enough time at all if you are going to make that man sorry he decided to spurn you."

A knock on the door immediately followed her words. She opened it to allow two footmen into the room. They carried a half-full tub of steaming water and were followed by three maids each with another bucket, which they poured into the tub as soon as the men had set it down in front of the fireplace. A fourth maid, the one who had been assisting Pru dress, came in with a towel. Lady Torrington's maid came through the connecting door, her hands filled with soap and containers of goodness only who knew what.

"Come along now, there isn't time to dawdle," her mother said, closing the door behind the extra people.

Pru jumped to her feet. She loved a bath. There was nothing so soothing as sitting in the warm water relaxing. On the other hand, considering the serious look on the face of her mother's maid, she had a feeling she wouldn't get very much time to just sit and relax.

An hour later, after being scrubbed from head to toe, her hair was nearly dry. She'd sat in front of the fire while the maid had combed it repeatedly, rubbed it with a towel, and combed it through again. After that, she spent another hour as her hair was carefully curled, braided, twisted, and pinned into place. Never had she had such a complicated coiffure. Never had her hair looked so good!

"Now for your face," her mother's maid said, coming forward with a handful of pots and potions.

"My face? What's wrong with my face?" Pru asked, looking up at her with some trepidation.

"Nothing at all, my lady. You have excellent skin and beautiful features just like your mother. But I am going to transform you from pretty to stunningly beautiful," the woman said with a calculating look.

Pru was shocked when she did just that. Cream, powder, and color applied and some time later, Pru hardly recognized herself.

"And now for your gown," the maid said as her mother's dresser went back to tending to her own mistress, who was in need of the same treatment.

She took out a white dress that Pru didn't recognize. It certainly wasn't the same one she'd brought with her for the ball. "Where did that come from?" she asked the woman.

The maid just blinked at her for a moment before smiling. "It's your gown. We merely took away some of the lace and added pearls." She held up the gown so she could see it as well. "It looks ever so much more elegant, don't you think? Oh, and just wait till you see. We lowered the neckline as well and changed the sleeves."

"When did you do all this?" Pru asked, astounded.

"These past two days. It was actually quite enjoyable, but we probably needed to measure it to you. Your mother wanted it to be a surprise, though." The girl brought the dress over to Pru and lifted it carefully over her head. Once all the tapes and buttons were fastened, she and Pru went into her mother's room where there was a standing mirror so she could see herself in full.

She was... beautiful!

The gown was indeed a little low, displaying a great deal more flesh than Pru had ever dared. But the bodice was lovely with its smattering of pearls, tucks, and shaping. The sleeves were adorable little puffs of white lace, and with her full-length white gloves, she looked elegant indeed.

"Very good, Prudence. You look very—"

"My goodness!" her father said, interrupting her mother. "What has happened to my little girl? Who is this beautiful woman who has taken her place?" he asked, coming over and giving her a kiss on her forehead. He took hold of her hands and stepped back to admire her once again. "You are going to have all the gentlemen at this ball panting and the women dripping with envy."

"Papa!" Pru said, bursting into giggles.

"Really, my lord, that is not at all appropriate. True, but not an appropriate thing to tell your daughter," her mother said, smiling at them.

"You, too, look absolutely beautiful, my dear," he said, giving her a peck on her cheek.

She gave him an indulgent smile. "And you are quite handsome as well. I do like that waistcoat."

It was deep blue with gold embroidery in a paisley pattern. "Indeed, Papa. It is quite magnificent."

"I wonder if we will be the best dressed family in attendance," he said, opening the door so Pru and her mother could precede him into the hall.

They might not have been, but after they reached the drawing room, her mother whispered to her that she was definitely the prettiest young lady that evening. She made Pru giggle, but secretly, Pru rather had to agree. Although, Miss Sidwell was also looking particularly fine in her white half-gown over a very pretty pale pink dress.

Prudence told her so.

"Thank you, Lady Prudence, you are looking exceptionally well this evening, too," Miss Sidwell said.

Her brother joined them. His eyes didn't even meet Pru's but stayed firmly fixed on her bosom as he said, "I couldn't agree more, Lady Prudence. That is a very fetching dress."

Pru unfurled her fan, simply holding it in front of her, forcing the man's eyes upward. She smiled. "Thank you so much, Mr. Sidwell."

The Markgraf Kottenfurst entered the room, looking resplendent in his military uniform complete with gold braid on the shoulders. His sharply cutaway coat was a deep blue that made the blue of his eyes stand out, with a wide, bright-red lapel, large gold buttons, and a red sash going across his chest with numerous medals pinned to it as well as the cross representing his title dangling over his heart. He wore a white waistcoat and trousers that molded to his calves, showing off the fine shape of them. In short, he drew the eye of every woman in attendance and even that of a few of the gentlemen.

Lady Humesbury was the first bold enough to greet him. "My, don't you look wonderful," she gushed.

He smiled at her. "It was my understanding that full dress was required for this evening?"

"Yes, indeed. As you see, everyone is in their finest," she said, indicating the company.

He nodded. "We are an impressive group, are we not?"

She laughed. "I do believe so."

The other guests the Humesburys had invited for the ball began to arrive after dinner, and very soon, the ballroom was well populated with anyone who could claim connection to the gentry in the area.

Pru took in a deep breath as she looked around the room. This was her first formal ball, odd as that was at her advanced age. Her mother came over to stand next to her after greeting a friend who she hadn't seen for some time. "Well?"

Pru looked at her mother. “Well, what?”

“What do you think? Do you feel ready for this evening? And quite possibly a Season in London this spring?”

“I do,” Pru said hesitantly at first. Her eyes strayed through the company and then back to her mother. “I do,” she said again, more firmly this time.

A silence descended on the room for a moment as the orchestra completed their tuning and prepared to start the first dance.

Chapter Fourteen

"I beg your pardon, Lady Prudence, but would you do me the honor?" Markgraf Kottenfurst asked as he approached them.

Pru held her breath for a moment to steady her heart. Did she really want to dance with this man? Honestly, she couldn't imagine anything more painful. To be so near to him? To have to speak politely with him? To have to touch—she glanced to her mother who gave her the slightest nod.

In that small gesture, Pru understood her mother to say not only did she have no other choice but to accept his invitation to dance—if she didn't, she would have to refuse every other invitation the entire evening—but she *could* do this. Her mother believed in her. She knew that Pru could be polite and be strong in the face of the man who had told her straight out no less than two days ago that he didn't consider her worthy.

Pru lifted her chin and gave the markgraf a polite smile as she held out her hand to him. "Why, thank you, my lord."

"That's my girl," she heard her mother whisper with approval as she allowed the markgraf to lead her to the dance floor.

They danced the first few steps of the dance in silence. Pru knew she should say something polite, but her mind had somehow gone completely blank. She could think of nothing but how handsome this man was and how much he had hurt her.

"I would like to apologize," he said as they clasped hands to promenade up the line of other dancers.

"There is no need, my lord."

"There is. I have seen how hurt you have been these past few days," he told her.

"You, you have?" She'd thought she'd done very well at hiding her feelings.

"Yes. You have done admirably in hiding it, in trying to behave normally, but I could see it in your eyes when you thought no one was looking."

She turned and looked up at him in surprise. He had seen her hurt? He had seen through the façade she had put up?

"And so, once again, I apologize," he said before rejoining the line of men. "I should not have told you... I should not have said what I said," he remarked when they took hands once again.

Did that mean he wished he hadn't been honest with her, or he didn't mean what he'd said, Pru wondered as she took the hand of the gentleman to the markgraf's right.

The smile the markgraf gave the woman he was dancing with sent a sharp jab of pain into Pru's stomach. He hadn't smiled at her in days. She was sure of it.

When he took Pru's hand again, she said, "You had an opinion, you shared it with me." She was quite proud of herself for the light tone she managed to give her words, as if she couldn't care less for his opinion.

"It was not an opinion, it was a statement of fact," he said. He then scowled as he moved back into line with the other men. When they stepped together again, he quickly said, "I did not mean that in the way it sounded."

"And just how did you mean it?" she asked, attempting to keep a hold of her anger when they met once more and clasped hands.

"I meant that, well, you cannot deny that you do... you are..." he floundered.

"A silly, thoughtless girl?" she offered before they moved apart again.

"No!" he said forcefully when he could.

"But that is what you told me." She was beginning to have serious difficulties maintaining her polite façade.

"I know and I apologize for that. You are a very thoughtful person. You try to make people happy," he said, sounding as if that wasn't the end of his sentence.

"Without thought for the consequences of my action," she finished for him. She couldn't keep the bitterness from her voice.

"You said that yourself," he pointed out.

"My lord, are you trying to make a point here or merely hurt me further?" she asked, glaring at him.

He closed his eyes for a moment, looking disturbed. "I am doing this very badly. My words... they are not what I mean to say."

"Then say what you mean."

"I am trying, but this dance does not make it easy!" he said, clearly extremely frustrated. He grabbed her hand and dropped to his knee, forcing all the other dancers to stop and stare at him. "Lady Prudence, I love you and I want you to marry me."

Pru's mouth dropped open. "What?" The word came out as a whisper.

"I was wrong. Or rather, I wasn't wrong in what I said. You *are*... spontaneous, you are impulsive sometimes. But you make people happy. You make *me* happy. I need to be sillier and more brash like you. I am too serious and... and you complete me." He took in a deep breath and looked up at her pleadingly. "I know it won't be easy being married to a boring stick, but I need you to make me less serious, less boring. I need you to bring color and joy to my life. *Ich liebe dich, mein Herz. Heirate mich*."

Pru didn't know very much German, but she had a good feeling she finally understood what he was saying. She gave a little giggle and then a nod. She realized tears were streaming down her cheeks when he stood again and wiped them away with a finger. "I love you, too," she said.

He pulled her into a hug as the people all around them began to applaud and laugh.

Alexander couldn't believe his boldness. Never in his life had he done anything so private in public. He'd been raised to behave with perfect circumspection his entire life. He was a member of the royal family; they did not put on such displays in the public eye. But he'd finally grown so frustrated with the movements of the dance, and his horrid choice of words keeping him from saying what was truly in his heart, that he'd just thrown all caution and sense to the wind.

He was glad that he had, for he was now the happiest man alive. He had his Prudence. She was his and would be for the rest of his life.

He was suddenly aware of the crowd around them applauding. He let Prudence go but kept hold of her hand and started to lead her from the dance floor. He was inundated with congratulations and pats on the back as he headed straight toward her father, who was standing with Lords Humesbury and Bunbury.

"Well, you certainly know how to start a ball," Lord Humesbury said with a laugh as they approached. "Everyone will be talking about this for years to come!"

Alexander just shook his head. "I am so sorry, my lord. I didn't mean, well, I hadn't planned to do that."

"Overcome with emotion?"

"Yes," he admitted. He turned to Lord Torrington. "My lord, I'm certain I should have come to you first to ask your permission," he started.

The man laughed and patted his shoulder. "Quite all right, my boy. I give you my permission—after the fact."

"Thank you, my lord."

"Although," Lord Torrington turned toward his daughter, giving her a sad smile, "I will sorely miss my little Prudence. She is the light of my life, my joy, and well, honestly, I don't quite know how we'll manage without her."

Prudence looked confused. "I am? You don't?"

He laughed. "Yes, my dear, you are. You do so much on the estate, managing the staff, keeping the tenants and their families happy. Your mother never had the knack you do for such work."

"Oh." Pru looked a little shocked. "I, er, I suppose I could teach her."

"No, I don't think you can. It is all you, your happy personality. That can't be learned."

"But we can change," Alexander pointed out. "If it hadn't been for Lord Humesbury insisting we not begin our talks right away as I had wanted, I would not have had the time to get to know Prudence. I have to admit at first I thought it ridiculous to waste time like that. I had come here to engage in talks, and they were being pushed aside to have fun. I… I simply did not understand the point of this. But if you had not done that, my lord, I would not have gotten to know all of you. That knowledge made it possible for us to hold our talks as friends rather than strangers, as people with a common purpose who understood each other rather than merely as representatives of our respective countries."

"Ah, now you see," Lord Humesbury said with a chuckle. "You have indeed learned something."

"I feel as if I learned a great deal thanks to both you and Prudence. You have both taught me that work is not everything. That sometimes it is more important to play and be happy." He turned to Prudence who was looking up at him with such joy. "If I had not had the time to get to know you, how would I ever have learned what a very special person you are? I would never have seen your strength and your intelligence. I never would have realized how happy I could be." He gave a shake of his head. "Seeing you these past few days trying so hard to pretend to be happy when I had hurt you. I realized just how strong you are. I never want to see you sad, never again," he told her. He turned back to her father. "I swear I will make sure she is happy for the rest of her life."

"I believe you will," her father told him seriously.

"This has certainly been a very intriguing Christmas," Alexander said.

"It has been a *merry* Christmas, and we will have a merry life together," Prudence said with a laugh.

He laughed and didn't doubt her for one minute.

THE END

Thank you for reading *Christmas Intrigue*!

. . .

This story is just the beginning! Please keep an eye out for the *Royals & Rebels series* where you'll meet Alexander and Pru's son, Klaus, and even more importantly, Prince Rich's children, Nikolas and Isa, as they are forced to stay one step ahead of whoever is trying to kill them. There are false identities, a Regency road trip, and a mystery that will require the cleverness of the Carlton Group's most secret spy to solve.

Read book 1, *In Lieu of a Princess, now!*

Also by Meredith Bond

The Royals & Rebels Series

This new, exciting, and sweet Royals & Rebels series tells the stories of Prince Nikolaus, his sister Princess Louisa, and their accidental ally Lucinda North as they each discover romance, adventure—and clues as to who wants the prince and princess dead.

#1 In Lieu of a Princess

#2 Princess on the Run

#3 A Prince Among Spies

About Meredith Bond

USA Today bestselling author Meredith Bond's books straddle that beautiful line between historical romance and fantasy. An award-winning author, she writes sweet, fun, traditional Regency romances, medieval Arthurian romances, and Regency romances with a touch of magic. Known for her characters "who slip readily into one's heart," Meredith loves to take her readers on a journey they won't soon forget.

Connect with Meredith:

https://meredithbond.com

facebook.com/meredithbondauthor
twitter.com/merrybond
instagram.com/meredith_bond
bookbub.com/authors/meredith-bond
amazon.com/Meredith-Bond/e/B001KI1SNE

Printed in Great Britain
by Amazon

13024471R10440

SAS

STORIES OF HEROES VIII

DAVID MONNERY

DOUG ARMSTRONG

DAVID MONNERY

BLITZ EDITIONS

This edition published in 1997

Published by Blitz Editions
an imprint of Bookmart Limited
Registered Number 2372865
Trading at Bookmart Limited
Desford Road, Enderby
Leicester, LE9 5AD

A CIP catalogue record for this book
is available from the British Library

ISBN 1 85605 379 2

Typeset by Hewer Text Composition Services, Edinburgh
Printed in Great Britain by
Clays Ltd, St Ives plc

SOLDIER W: SAS

GUATEMALA – JOURNEY INTO EVIL

1

Tomás Xicay reached out a hand to shake his sister by the shoulder, then hesitated for several seconds, reluctant to disturb the rare serenity of her face. In the thin wash of moonlight seeping down through the forest canopy she looked almost a child once more, and seeing her like that he felt threatened by an avalanche of memories. Emelia was now a woman of twenty-two, but she had been only eight, and he fourteen, when both had been orphaned by their mother's murder, and Tomás doubted whether he would ever shake the sense of paternal love and obligation which he still felt for his sister.

He smiled to himself and shook Emelia's shoulder. Her eyes opened at once, and her head lifted off the Spanish grammar she had been using as a pillow. The condition of the book's cover, streaked with layers of dirt and warped by damp, suggested that this was far from the first time that it had been pressed into such service.

'It's time,' he whispered.

'Right.' She pulled herself into a sitting position, conscious of the activity in the shadows around her. She felt hungry, but that was nothing unusual.

As if in response to the feeling, Tomás handed her a peanut-butter cracker. 'There's only two more left,' he said.

'I can't wait for breakfast,' she replied wryly, easing herself on to her haunches and nibbling at the cracker.

He grinned, ruffled her hair, and moved on to check out the rest of the unit. 'Ready?' he asked each *compañero* and *compañera*. Some grunted assent, some offered a nervous 'yes', some gave him only a grim smile.

Two minutes later the column of thirteen was on the move, threading its way down through the trees. Each '*compa*' concentrated on keeping the correct distance behind whomever he or she was following, short enough not to lose contact in the dark, long enough to maximize the number of survivors if the unit walked into an ambush. All around them the forest lay in virtual silence – there was no breeze to stir the branches, and most of the wildlife was holding its breath while the humans went by. Only the bats seemed indifferent to the guerrillas' passage, and every now and then Emelia could hear the dry rustle of wings or see a dark shape glide across a small patch of moonlit sky. She loved times like this, when the natural world seemed to reach out and embrace her with its wonders.

Fifty metres further down the trail, Tomás was thinking about what awaited them in the small town of Tubiala, some six kilometres and ninety minutes away. He had every confidence in the Old Man's abilities as a tactician and a strategist, but his own experience over the past five years had prepared him to expect the unexpected, which could be anything from a sprained ankle to the loss of half a unit.

The threat of sudden death was hardly inviting, but what Tomás dreaded far more was that his sister should be taken alive, and should suffer before death in the terrible way that their mother had suffered. Sometimes this fear would wake him with a dreadful start in the forest, and he would only just stop himself crying out. At such moments he would want to take Emelia back across the mountains and into Mexico, away from this land which had already brought their family such pain. But the sunrise always brought hope to set against the fear, and in any case he knew she would never agree to leave. This land was their home, to live or die for.

The unit marched on, down the long, forested slope to where the trail joined one of the many icy streams that tumbled down from the Cuchumatanes mountains. Stretches of their path were now open to the sky, but the moon had already set behind the peaks across the valley, and the darkness was deepening by the minute. For the next few hours they would be as invisible as any group of fighters could hope to be.

It was shortly after eleven when Tomás rounded a bend in the trail and saw Tubiala spread out in the valley below. There were only a handful of dim lights still burning in the small town, but the yellow glow from the illuminated military camp on the nearby rise seemed to suffuse the whole valley. He allowed the column to close up, so that each man and woman would have the chance to bring together the maps in their minds with the reality below.

After a final exchange of encouraging smiles and embraces the column moved off downhill again. The first small group to split off from the main body comprised Geraldo and Alicia, who had been entrusted with the unit's only heavy weapon, an old but still efficient Israeli mortar which had been captured from the Army a couple of years earlier. Their task was to target the military camp, but to open fire only in the event of a general alarm being raised.

The next to leave were Carlos and Fernando, whose

job was to cover the road winding west down the valley towards Champul. They were followed by Elena and Rosa, who had drawn guard duty on the road east, which joined Tubiala to the garrison town of San Juan Cotzal. That left seven *compas* for the Hotel Tezulutlán, two to cover each entrance and three to go in for Muñoz. Tomás had chosen José and Jorge to accompany him on the latter mission.

The seven waited just above the town for ten minutes, giving the road-watchers time to reach their positions, and then slipped between the first houses and on to the steep dirt track which led down towards the church. A dog barked away to their right, and another replied to the left, but there was no sign of life in the houses, and no movement on the streets.

They edged along the side of the small, whitewashed church, and Tomás gingerly edged an eye round its corner to check out the small square which lay at the heart of the town. It was empty, but beyond it, a few metres down the San Juan Cotzal road, he could see two figures sitting on either side of a kerosene lamp outside the front door of the hotel. They seemed to be playing a game of some sort.

So far, so good, Tomás told himself. If there were soldiers outside the hotel, then Muñoz was most probably inside. Tomás wondered whether it was arrogance or simple stupidity which had brought the major to the conclusion that he could leave the safety of the military camp with impunity. According to their informant, the man received almost daily deliveries of luxury items from his family in the capital, and had turned the upper floor of the town's only hotel into a sort of court-in-exile. He hardly ever set foot in the military camp, preferring to summon his subordinates to the hotel for their instructions. And only the sadistic thrill of a punitive action was capable of luring him out into either the town or the countryside which surrounded it.

Hopefully, Tomás thought, Muñoz will shortly be receiving an overdue lesson in humility. A last lesson.

He turned back to the others, gave them the hand signal for 'things as expected', and led them silently around the perimeter of the dark square. On the far side he chose Emelia and Cristobal, the unit's two best marksmen, for the task of watching the two sentries, and then led the other four through a space full of empty market stalls and down a narrow alley to the back of the Tezulutlán. There he paused, straining his ears for any unexpected sounds.

There was only silence. Tomás led the way in through the back door, and Jorge followed, with José bringing up the rear. The three men crept through the darkened kitchen, past two young boys asleep on the mats beneath the stove, and into the corridor which housed the reception desk. Light from the sentries' kerosene lamp glowed in the window beside the hotel's front door, revealing two more under-age employees curled up on the floor. As Tomás turned up the stairs he heard the two guards outside suddenly convulse with laughter at some private joke.

The carpet on the stairs was worn almost to extinction, but enough of it remained to muffle the sound of their footfalls. Tomás carefully lifted his eyes to the level of the upper floor, and found an empty corridor lit by a kerosene lamp. All he could hear was the sound of his own heart beating like a drum.

He signalled to the other two to wait, and stealthily advanced down the corridor to where the lamp was hanging from a piece of bent wire. He reached up, lifted the glass, and blew out the flame.

In the darkness he could see a faint light shining out from under one of the doors – the one which they had been told Muñoz used for a bedroom. And suddenly he could hear the sounds of sobbing coming from inside the room.

He tiptoed towards the door, gesturing to the others to follow. With his ear up against the wood he could hear a low male groaning intermingled with the sobbing. As Jorge unsheathed his machete, Tomás took his army revolver in one hand and started turning the doorknob with the other. He slowly eased the door open half an inch, and applied an eye to the room beyond.

The first thing he noticed was two wide and frightened eyes staring straight up at him. The girl was lying on the floor, half-wrapped in a blanket, but apparently naked. She made no sound, but quickly turned her head to the bed behind her, where another girl, barely into puberty, was rocking to and fro astride a naked man. She was sobbing steadily, the tears running down her half-developed breasts and on to his glistening chest, while he groaned with pleasure, eyes closed and hands tightly gripping her haunches.

As Tomás slowly pushed the door back the second girl also caught sight of him, and the motion of her body faltered, but only for a second. Two more thrusts of her small body kept Muñoz in blissful ignorance, until Tomás was over the bed and lifting her off, and then the major's eyes opened, only to find three men standing over him and Jorge's machete poised beside his erect penis.

The latter wilted, but before Muñoz could offer so much as a whimper José had stuffed a pair of convenient underpants into his mouth. Meanwhile Tomás was trying to talk to the two girls. The one who had been lying on the floor was trying to both dress and comfort the other girl, who was still sobbing with a quiet intensity which almost broke his heart. The elder girl explained that both of them came from a village down the valley which the Army had visited the previous week.

Tomás asked her if they wanted to go home or come into the mountains with the *compas*. They wanted to go home. They knew the Army would visit their village again, but they couldn't just leave their families without giving them warning. If the villagers were expecting trouble then all but the eldest could be sent into the mountains, at least for a time. Tomás didn't argue with her, but he did insist that Jorge escort them out of the hotel and through the town's backstreets to the Champul road.

Having forced a shirt over Muñoz's head, pulled a pair of trousers up his legs, and tied his hands behind his back, José was now looking around the room, an angry expression on his face. A portable television sat on a small table next to a pile of glossy American sex magazines. There were empty wine bottles everywhere, and there seemed to be enough items of food scattered across the floor to feed most mountain villages for a week.

'Ready?' Tomás asked, picking up the major's belt with its holstered handgun and fastening it around his own waist.

José nodded, and grabbed Muñoz by one of his pinioned arms. 'Any sound and your life is over,' he whispered in Spanish, and two eyes stared blankly back at him. The man was in shock, Tomás realized – he couldn't believe that this was happening to him. In a matter of minutes Muñoz's future had turned from bright to non-existent.

They walked down the stairs, the major none too steadily. The soldiers outside were still playing their game, oblivious to events within, but the sleeping staff had been awakened, by either the noise or some instinct of solidarity. They watched wide-eyed as the prisoner was led through the lobby and kitchen and out by the back door.

A few minutes more, and all the *compas* were withdrawing from their positions around the sleeping town, slipping back up the hillside towards the spot where Geraldo and Alicia waited beside the mortar. Once gathered, the unit began its return journey, moving uphill as fast as the terrain allowed, the higher reaches of the Cuchumatanes looming above them like a huge rampart beneath a swiftly clearing sky. In the middle of the column, like an animal incapable of understanding the terrible depth of its unhappiness, Major Alfonso Lujan Muñoz stumbled along, a continuous soft mewling emanating from his gagged mouth.

Five days later, Colonel Luis Serrano, Operations Director of G-2 Military Intelligence, was standing at the window of his study, staring out at the garden. It was a beautiful dry-season afternoon, with hardly a trace of smog to besmirch the clear blue sky, and for once the brilliant colours of the various flowering plants seemed to justify all his wife's battles with a never-ending series of new gardeners. She was away at the moment, visiting her sister at the Lake Atitlán villa, but their only daughter was with him, supposedly studying for upcoming examinations. From where Serrano stood, he could see her hard at work on an even tan, lying face down on a towel beside the pool, the top of her bikini untied.

Behind him, in the shadowed study, the tape continued to roll.

'Do you remember the man Miguel Ustantil, who you ordered arrested in July last year?'

'Yes.'

'Why was he arrested?'

'He was a troublemaker.'

'Can you be more specific?'

The interrogator's voice was so calm, Serrano thought, almost Buddha-like. There was no anger, or at least none on the surface. It was as if he had accepted everything on the general level, and was only now concerned with getting the details right. But was he really 'El Espíritu', 'The Ghost'?

'Did you personally supervise the flaying of his facial skin?'

'Yes.'

Why had the idiot admitted it all? Serrano asked himself. He had been over Muñoz's service record, and found nothing to indicate such a level of stupidity. He wondered what the bastards had done to turn the man to jelly and make him sound like an I-speak-your-weight machine. Whatever it was, it had left no marks on the body, and the *subversivos'* choice of dumping ground – on the steps of the Swedish Embassy – had not given Serrano's men the chance to add any.

In PR terms the whole thing had been a disaster. Copies of the tape had been delivered simultaneously to a dozen or so embassies and all the prominent human rights groups, leaving G-2 with very few options in the matter of damage limitation. Serrano's superiors had not been amused.

He found himself wondering once more if it really could be El Espíritu. The man was supposed to have died over ten years ago, though admittedly his body had never been properly identified. Even so . . . The most reliable witnesses had estimated his age at over sixty in 1980, and the average life expectancy of the most docile Indians was not much more than fifty. It was hard to believe . . .

But the tape certainly bore the man's mark. It wasn't just a catalogue of Muñoz's overzealous interrogations and punishments – in several of the incidents under discussion the man asking the questions was very careful to draw out why the Army had become involved, and exactly which interests – or, to be more precise, the interests of which landowners – they were seeking to promote.

But then again . . .

Serrano smiled to himself. The foreign press were not interested in *why* – they were too busy wallowing in hacked-off hands and breasts and gouged-out eyes. None of them got the point, which was that keeping a primitive people under control necessitated the use of primitive methods.

It was possible, of course, to go too far . . .

'Why did you take the six men back to San Benito?'

'To show the villagers of the region what lay in store for them if they made trouble.'

'You had them stripped naked, and each man was held erect while you pointed out the various wounds on their bodies – the wire burns and cigarette burns, the severed ears, the split tongues, the hands with no nails and the feet with no soles . . .'

'Yes.'

'And then?'

'They were executed.'

'How?'

'They were burnt.'

'You had your men pour gasoline over them and set fire to them?'

'Yes.'

That was Muñoz's last word on the tape, and for all Serrano knew his last on this earth. Guerrilla voices read brief extracts from the Geneva Convention and some UN-sponsored accord on human rights – the pompous bastards! – before the voice of the questioner pronounced sentence. There was an eerie gap of several seconds, and then the sound of a single gunshot. Serrano had heard the tape through twice before, and was expecting it, but the report still made him jump.

In the garden outside, his daughter had turned over, and was treating her bare breasts to the afternoon sunshine. Behind her the Indian gardener was absent-mindedly scratching his behind as he directed the hose at the scarlet bougainvillaea.

Serrano decided he needed to know more about the history of 'The Ghost'.

The following day, shortly one o'clock, Chris Martinson was sitting in Antigua's Restaurant Dona Luisa, waiting for his lunch to arrive. The place was as crowded as usual, with a clientele about equally divided between locals and gringo tourists, but Chris had managed to get the seat he wanted, on the terrace overlooking the interior courtyard. On the previous day a bird he had not recognized had paid an all-too-brief visit to the ornamental palm below, and he was hoping for a repeat performance.

He turned to one of the two newspapers he had just bought in the square, the one printed in Spanish, and started reading the lead story.

According to the Guatemalan *Daily Planet* an elaborate hoax had recently been played on those members of the international press corps who liked to defame the nation's security forces. *Subversivos* responsible for the murder of Army Major Alfonso Lujan Muñoz had fabricated a tape purporting to contain an interrogation of the young major, and a counterfeit admission of guilt in regard to certain crimes, all of which were known to have been committed by the *subversivos* themselves. Unfortunately for the perpetrators of this vicious hoax, voice identification experts had been able to establish that the speaker on the tape was not in fact Major Muñoz.

'And there goes another flying pig,' Chris murmured to himself. He reached for the *Daily News*, the English-language newspaper for tourists and Guatemala's resident British and American community, and looked for another account of the affair. He expected to find at least a different slant – the *Daily News*, for reasons which no one seemed able to fathom, was allowed a unique latitude when it came to criticizing the authorities.

Sure enough, the writer managed to pour scorn on the official version of the story without directly contradicting it. 'We can only wonder,' he wrote, 'that after forty years of incessant defeat the *subversivos* should still have the leisure time, the technology, and the system of communications necessary, to mount such an elaborate hoax.'

Chris smiled to himself, and cleared a space for the arriving chicken sandwich and papaya *licuardo*. The trouble with Guatemala was that most of the time it was hard to believe the evidence of your own ears and eyes. The accounts of atrocities committed by both sides were probably exaggerated, but he had no reason to believe that they were imaginary. And yet the country was so eye-achingly beautiful, and not just in the matter of landscape. Costa

Rica, which Chris had visited several years earlier, had beautiful countryside, but compared with Guatemala it seemed somehow bland, two-dimensional.

It was the people who made Guatemala magical, the Mayan Indians, though how they did it was hard to say. They certainly looked picturesque in their colourful traditional costumes, and their religious ceremonies seemed like a fascinating glimpse into an earlier world, but it was more than that. Something to do with the depth of their commitment to the reality of community, perhaps. An American whom Chris met had argued that Westerners here somehow just locked on to the missing piece of their own social jigsaw – a sense of belonging. Here among the Mayans, he claimed, it had somehow miraculously survived.

Chris wasn't sure he agreed, but he had yet to hear a better explanation. Every gringo he had talked to since his arrival had felt the same sense of magic. The only people who didn't, or so it seemed, were the Ladinos, the Spanish-speaking non-Indians who made up thirty per cent of the population and one hundred per cent of the ruling elite.

Certainly the family Chris was staying with as part of his language course had little good to say about the Indians or their culture. Their ambitions were all directed towards total submersion in the wonders of the West. Exciting memories of visiting the McDonald's in Guatemala City vied with distress at there not being one in Antigua.

Chris finished the milk shake and paid his bill, walked downstairs and emerged from the dark corridor into the brilliance of the sunlit street. Antigua was a beautiful town, with its grids of cobbled streets, its mostly one-storey buildings painted in a pleasing variety of pastel shades, and its myriad colonial churches and monasteries. And all of it nestling beneath the three volcanoes: the towering Agua to the south, and Acatenango and the ever-smoking Fuego, 'Fire', to the south-west.

Chris looked at his watch and found he still had fifteen minutes before his afternoon class was due to begin. The bookshop he had noticed the previous day was just across the street, and finding a convenient gap in the one-way traffic he walked over. He was examining the window display when a reflected movement caught his eye. A man had started to cross the street behind him but then apparently changed his mind. He was now standing on the opposite pavement, staring at Chris's back. Then, as if suddenly aware that Chris was watching his reflection he abruptly turned away, and stood gazing down the street.

Chris went into the shop and, after a minute or so of browsing among the natural history books, sneaked a look out of the window. The man was nowhere to be seen.

He decided he was being paranoid.

Five minutes later, walking across the main square, he stopped to tie his shoelaces and noticed the same man, some thirty metres behind him, staring vacantly into space.

Lieutenant Arturo Vincenzo ran a hand through his luxuriant black hair and scratched the back of his neck. 'So how did they manage it?' he asked his cousin. 'How did they get the body all the way from the Cuchumatanes to the front door of the Swedish Embassy without anyone seeing anything?'

Captain Jorge Alvaro shrugged and took a slug from the

bottle of Gallo beer. 'El Espíritu works in mysterious ways,' he said sardonically.

The two men were in a bar on Zona 1's Calle 14, just around the corner from the Policia Nacional building, where Vincenzo's Department of Criminal Investigation had its headquarters. Alvaro worked for G-2, and the cousins' meetings were as often dictated by mutual business as they were by familial ties. This time, though, Vincenzo was simply indulging his curiosity – the DCI had not been invited to share in the Army's latest public relations disaster.

The early evening hour ensured that the bar was almost empty, but Vincenzo kept his voice down in any case. 'He is not in our files under that name,' he said. 'But . . .'

'He is not known under any other name,' Arturo growled. 'Do you want another beer?'

'Sure.'

Alvaro lifted a bottle and raised two fingers at the boy behind the bar.

'When was he last heard of?'

'Nineteen eighty-three. Maybe. We first heard of the bastard around 1979, but by 1983 it was looking less and less likely that only one man was involved. If there was, then he must have had a fucking time machine – his name was coming up in the Atitlán area, the Cuchumatanes, even way out in the Petén, and pretty much at the same time.' He picked up the fresh bottle and poured it into the empty glass, shaking his head as he did so. 'There's no way it could have been the same man.'

'If there's one thing those Indians can do, it's walk.'

Alvaro grunted. 'They can't fly, though, can they?'

Vincenzo grinned. 'Thank Christ for that.' He took

another slug of beer. 'Weren't there any eyewitness descriptions of him or them?'

'Hundreds of them – that was the problem. Most of them were unwilling witnesses, and no doubt most of them lied with their last breath. So El Espíritu was tall, short, dark, fair, blue-eyed, black-eyed – you name it. Absolutely fucking useless. The only semi-reliable description we had came from two English soldiers.'

'What? How did that happen?'

'Remember in 1980, when that guerrilla group took over the Tikal ruins for several days?'

'Vaguely.'

'They took about twenty tourists hostage, most of them English. The whole business lasted four days, I think. The guerrilla leader . . .'

'El Espíritu.'

'So he claimed. He would only negotiate through foreign intermediaries, and, like I said, most of the tourists were English, so they sent in a couple of their soldiers from Belize, men from that group which had handled the Iranian Embassy siege in London a few months earlier . . .'

'The SAS.'

'Yeah, that was them. Anyway . . .'

'There's one of them here now,' Vincenzo interjected. 'In Antigua.'

Alvaro was surprised. 'Doing what?'

'That's what we wanted to know. He picked up a tail at the airport – the usual routine – and on his first night here he had dinner with the British Military Attaché, which isn't routine for tourists. So we kept the tail on him and had the London Embassy check him out. He's still on active service with the British Army, the SAS Regiment, but not for much longer. And he is currently on leave, improving his Spanish at one of the schools in Antigua.'

'Your people have checked that out?'

Vincenzo looked hurt. 'Of course. He's doing just what he's supposed to be doing.'

'How old is he?' Alvaro asked.

'Thirty-two.'

'Then he couldn't have been one of the men at Tikal.'

Vincenzo smiled. 'Now *that* would have been a coincidence.'

Alvaro shrugged and gulped down the rest of his beer. 'I have to get back,' he said as he got to his feet.

'I thought you were finished for the day.'

'I just remembered something.'

Alvaro walked briskly across the street to where the big Mercedes with smoked-glass windows was parked, and drove it slowly back to G-2 headquarters, his brain mulling over the idea which his cousin had unwittingly presented to him. The two English officers, whoever they were, had not only seen El Espíritu, but presumably had also heard him speak. And perhaps, in the spirit of co-operation between armed forces, one or both of the Englishmen could be persuaded to identify the voice on the tape.

Less than a mile to the north, Tomás Xicay was one of five Indians sitting in the back of an open truck, but the only one among them who was keeping an impatient watch out for their driver. Logic told him he was in no danger of apprehension – there was no Army major's body hidden in *this* truck – but he couldn't help feeling vulnerable. Beyond the cathedral, which loomed into the sky above the market, lay the city's main square and across that stood the Palacio

Nacional, which housed, among other things, the offices of the dreaded G-2.

Guatemala City was not easy on the nerves, and Tomás found himself wondering for the tenth time in as many minutes why he had chosen to stay the extra couple of days once their mission had been accomplished. To see his uncle was the obvious answer, but his uncle had hardly been at home, and his aunt had been turned into a nervous wreck by his mere presence in the house. There would be no next time, Tomás decided. Or at least not until the war was won.

It was getting dark now, and even a couple of his fellow-travellers were beginning to stir with impatience, muttering to each other in Cakchiquel. This wasn't a language Tomás was fluent in, but the gist of the conversation was clear enough – where the fuck was the driver?

Tomás rearranged his legs on the wooden floor. Judging from detritus scattered across it, the truck had arrived at the Central Market that morning loaded with squash, but now, like the many others waiting nearby, it was empty save for those taking passengers back into the Western Highlands.

On the nearest truck three Indian women were wearing the traditional skirts of San Pedro La Laguna and conversing in his native language, Tzutujil. Tomás had grown up in Santiago Atitlán, another large village on the shores of Lake Atitlán, and thought perhaps he recognized one of the women. But he made no attempt at contact – it had been almost ten years since he had lived in his home village, and he had no desire to draw attention to himself.

The driver arrived at last, wearing the smile of several beers on his face. But his driving skills seemed unimpaired, and soon the truck was threading its way out of the capital and on to the Pan-American Highway. As it climbed the first of many winding inclines the last slice of setting sun was briefly visible between distant volcanoes, and then night descended, reducing the world to those stretches of tarmac, verge and cliff face which fell within the glare of the truck's headlights.

Staring out into the darkness Tomás found himself studying a mental picture of his father.

Miguel Mendoza Xicay had been tall for an Indian, five feet nine inches by the American count, and he had worn his hair long, the way he believed their Mayan ancestors had always done. He had not been an educated man – how could he with no school in the village of his childhood? – and it seemed likely that he had been too good-hearted to understand the realities of life in Guatemala. The family had access to a little land on the slopes of the volcano behind the village, and they had grown beans, coffee, corn and various fruits. The prices they received were always derisory, and no money could ever be saved, but the family only rarely went hungry, and there was usually the additional cash the children earned from making and selling handicrafts to help them through the worst times.

Then the Army had come, and established a camp only a couple of kilometres outside the town. The amount of land available to the townspeople shrank as Indian deeds went mysteriously missing and other claimants appeared with deeds which the local Spanish-speaking authorities fell over themselves to approve. The local people protested and the most vocal swiftly disappeared, never to be seen again, either dead or alive. Rumour had it that most of them had been thrown from helicopters, still conscious, into the smoking maw of San Pedro.

Through all these troubles Miguel Xicay had tenaciously clung to the hope that somehow the Army's behaviour was an aberration, that if the authorities only knew what was really happening then they would step in and put a stop to it. No one expected life to be fair, and no one expected the rich Landinos to behave like true Christians, but he found it hard to believe that such a campaign of brutality and murder could be sponsored by a government.

It was no accident that the man whom Tomás's father most admired was the local priest, an American named Stanley Rother. The father had arrived in Santiago Atitlán in the mid-sixties, and like Miguel Xicay he had watched the escalating brutality with a mixture of horror and disbelief. When the Army called a meeting of all the village leaders he had listened with mounting rage as the local commander blamed all the killings, the rapes, the tortured corpses, on the communist *subversivos*, and furthermore demanded that the villagers report any suspicious behaviour to the Army.

He had got slowly to his feet, and in a silence pregnant with dread, told the Army commander that no one was fooled, that everyone knew it was the soldiers who raped and killed and tortured, and that they must stop these acts against man and God.

The next morning Stanley Rother had been shredded by automatic gunfire in the doorway of his church.

Tomás's father had gone out that evening to talk with his friends, and had never been seen alive again. His body had been found on the volcano slopes a week later, minus tongue, eyes and hands. The twelve-year-old Tomás had not been meant to see it, but he had, and he was not sorry. He had needed to imprint it on his brain like a scar, because only then could he be sure never to forget.

And nor would he, he thought, as the truck laboured its way up another slope. Not that he needed that one dreadful memory any more. In the thirteen years which had passed since that day he had lost a mother, two brothers, many friends – and all of them still lived inside him.

His father especially so.

I knew him and still he is there in me . . .

Tomás's hand moved involuntarily towards the pocket where he kept the dog-eared copy of Neruda's poem. It was too dark to read, but that didn't matter – he knew all the pages, all the lines, off by heart.

'*I, who knew him, saw him go down*,' the inner voice recited. '*Till he existed only in what he was leaving – streets he could scarcely be aware of, houses he never would inhabit. I come back to see him and every day I wait . . .*'

2

Luis Serrano leaned back in his leather swivel chair, fingers intertwined behind his head, and ran his tongue along his upper lip, tasting the trace of brandy which still clung to his moustache. Through two walls he could hear the TV football match his son and friends were watching, and the faint rat-a-tat of fireworks in the distant Plaza Mayor was audible above that. Presumably the Indians were dragging one of their Jesus statues around the square, choking themselves on incense as they went.

Serrano leaned forward once more, and absent-mindedly tapped the report with his right index finger. He now felt reasonably certain that the El Espíritu who had been such an irritant in the early eighties, and the *subversivo* on the tape from Quiche, were one and the same man.

It was not a good time for his reappearance. The Americans wanted a negotiated settlement with the *subversivos*, and the Government's ability to impose one that was lacking in any specific commitments – one that avoided any discussion at all of the land issue – rested on the Army keeping a strong upper hand in the rural areas. The last thing anyone needed was the public resurrection of some old Indian hero, and more humiliations like the Muñoz business.

Serrano reached for his Zippo lighter – a gift from a former American military attaché – and the packet of Marlboro Lights. Alvaro's idea of asking the English soldier to identify the voice was a good one, as far as it went. The previous day he had read through the records of the business in Tikal fifteen years before, and there was no doubt that both of the Englishmen had enjoyed several face-to-face conversations with the leader of the terrorists. If anyone could definitively identify the bastard, then they could.

He had ordered G-2's man in the London embassy to run a check on the pair of them. The older one – James Docherty – had retired from the Army, and was apparently no longer living in England, but his younger companion was still on active service. It had taken some time, and not a little money – always assuming the agent's expenses sheet could be believed – to ascertain that Darren Wilkinson was still serving in 22 SAS Regiment. His current rank was sergeant, he was attached to the Regiment's Training Wing, and he was stationed at the Stirling Lines barracks near Hereford, some 120 miles west of London.

Serrano watched the smoke from his cigarette curl away, remembering the woman in London on his second and last visit. She had been one of the English secretaries at the embassy, with bright-red hair and pale skin. So exotic. So aggressive in bed.

He sighed and forced his mind back to the matter in hand. Mention of the Training Wing reminded him of something . . . ah yes, that business in Colombia which the SAS had been involved in a few years earlier. He had heard about it from the American Military Attaché at an embassy party. The Colombian Government, busy setting up an anti-narcotics unit, had asked the British Government to send them a couple of advisers. When one of the advisers and a local politician had been kidnapped by drug barons half an army of SAS soldiers had dropped out of the sky to rescue them. Or so the story went.

It didn't really matter how true the last part was, Serrano thought. The point was that Britain had been prepared to send advisers to Colombia to help in the fight against drug trafficking. Might they not be equally willing to send one man to help in the fight against the *subversivos*?

This man Wilkinson could take part as an observer in the sweep which was planned for the following week. And when they captured or killed this El Espíritu then the Englishman would be on the spot to identify the miserable little shit.

And he would also, Serrano realized with satisfaction, be a neutral witness to the old boy's death. No one would believe an Army report that El Espíritu had been killed, but an Englishman . . . His testimony could lay this particular 'ghost' once and for all, and prevent a host of other claimants to the name springing up in the dead man's place.

Yes, Serrano thought. He liked it. He liked it a lot.

Would the British agree? They still had a reliable enough government from all reports, though maybe not quite so reliable as in the woman Thatcher's time. In any event the SAS was unlikely to be a haven for communist sympathizers.

But Serrano had to admit that Guatemala's reputation in the world had suffered in recent years. All those little creeps from Amnesty International and Americas Watch, living their safe little lives in the rich man's world and bleating on about human rights abuses everywhere else.

How could he sugar the pill? What could Guatemala offer the British?

Another Belize treaty? The last president to sign one had almost been tried on treason charges, and the idea of sticking his neck out that far was not particularly appealing. It would be better, he decided, to go through the Americans. They had a keener appreciation of what was really at stake in Central America, and they could hardly refuse to help when their own beloved peace negotiations were on the line. 'We are so close to a breakthrough,' Serrano murmured out loud in rehearsal, 'and this one terrorist could undermine everything we have all worked for.'

It sounded convincing enough for the US State Department. The Americans could then bribe or threaten the British, whichever they deemed more appropriate. Serrano picked up the phone to call the Foreign Ministry, trying in vain to remember the name of the current Foreign Minister.

The request for diplomatic assistance was delivered to the State Department by Guatemala's Washington ambassador early the following afternoon. After receiving his visitor, Sam Udovich, Acting Head of the Central America desk, stared out at the falling snow and slowly consumed a strawberry cheese croissant before reaching for the internal phone.

'Clemens,' a voice answered.

'Brent, hi. The Guatemalan Ambassador's just been darkening my office door.'

'And what do the death squads want today?'

Udovich told him.

Clemens listened in silence, and then laughed. 'They want some Brit soldier to look over a line-up of corpses and pick out the guilty man?' he asked incredulously.

'That's one way of putting it,' Udovich agreed. 'It *is* in our interests that they get this guy.'

'That's what Ollie North said.'

'He was right,' Udovich said drily.

Clemens sighed audibly.

'Look,' Udovich went on patiently, 'I'd take it as a personal favour if you could get the Brits to get with the programme on this one.' And if you can, went the first unspoken message, then I owe you one. And if you can't or won't, went the second, then don't come to me for a favour anytime soon.

'I'll ask them,' Clemens said.

'Just so long as you don't leave them in any doubt about how important we think this is.'

'How important *you* think this is.'

Udovich snorted. 'It's not going to cost the Brits any money, for Christ's sake. And that's all they seem to care about these days.'

'I'll ask them,' Clemens repeated. 'If that's all . . .'

'One more thing. I think their intelligence boys should run a check on this guy Wilkinson, just in case. The Guatemalans want someone they can rely on – you understand me?'

'Yeah,' Clemens said. 'I get the message.'

'And they want him vetted?' the Prime Minister asked rhetorically. He shook his head, looking saddened by the impertinence of the American request.

'Just informally,' Martin Clarke said assuagingly. He was the junior minister at the Foreign Office responsible for formulating a reply to Washington's request.

The Prime Minister shook his head again, and then squeezed the bridge of his nose between thumb and forefinger, as if the shaking had given him a headache. He blinked and looked round the table. 'Any comments?' he asked.

For a moment no one seemed to have any.

'What's the current state of play in Guatemala?' asked the young man with the flashy tie who was representing MI5.

'Business as usual,' Clarke answered drily.

'Not quite,' the silver-haired man from MI6 disagreed. 'The Government claims to have won the war against the guerrillas, but the fact that they're willing to negotiate a settlement suggests a rather different story.'

'The negotiations are just a sop to the Americans,' Clarke insisted.

'That's not what our people think,' said the MI6 man. 'They reckon the number of guerrillas in the mountains is at least holding steady, and may even be growing.'

'Does it matter?' asked Bill Warren, the Junior Defence Minister. 'We're only being asked for one adviser for a couple of weeks. I'm more interested in what sort of favour we can expect in return.'

'Such as?' the Prime Minister asked. 'I don't think we'll get any better guarantees on Belize. No, I think we'd be better off treating this as nothing more than a favour to Washington.' He paused for a moment and looked up, as if seeking divine guidance. 'But the further we can distance the Government from the whole business, the better I'll like it,' he added. 'If this SAS soldier gets caught up in some ghastly atrocity then all the human rights people will be screaming blue murder at me. I think this should be a strictly military affair – a matter of shared courtesy between armed forces. With a high security rating. "Need to know" only.'

He turned to the two junior ministers. 'Bill, you liaise

with Five in making sure Sergeant Wilkinson has a clean bill of health. Martin, you get in touch with the SAS CO and tell him what's required. And let the Americans know we'll be happy to oblige them.'

The PM took the bridge of his nose in the familiar pincer grip and blinked twice. 'Now let's get on to something important.'

Lieutenant-Colonel Barney Davies, the Commanding Officer of 22 SAS, had just re-entered his office, having returned for the *Daily Mirror* he had left behind, when the phone rang. He stared at it in exasperation for several seconds, and then reluctantly picked it up. 'Davies,' he said, more mildly than he felt. He had an important evening ahead, and hoped to God this call was not going to foul it up.

'Good evening, Lieutenant-Colonel,' a familiar voice said. 'My name's Martin Clarke. Foreign Office. I don't believe we've met.'

'No, I don't think so,' Davies said warily. He'd seen the bastard on TV enough times. In fact the Junior Minister had been on *Question Time* only the previous week, wearing a striped shirt so loud that it seemed to affect the broadcast signal.

'We've had a request from the Americans,' Clarke began, and went on to outline exactly who and what had been asked for.

Barney Davies listened patiently, liking the whole business less with each passing sentence. It wasn't immediately apparent from Clarke's spiel, however, whether Whitehall was asking or telling the SAS to co-operate. 'So, you'd like me to ask Sergeant Wilkinson if he's willing to go?' Davies suggested optimistically.

Clarke picked up on the tone, and made good the omission. 'Sergeant Wilkinson is a serving NCO in Her Majesty's Armed Forces. It has been decided that he should serve his country accordingly in this particular matter. As his Commanding Officer, you are naturally being notified. If you wish, I can get you written orders from the Ministry of Defence . . .'

'That will not be necessary. I will notify him, and see to the appropriate briefing . . .'

'Good. I'll see that everything we have is on your fax tomorrow morning. Wilkinson is booked on the 10 a.m. flight to Miami this Sunday,' he added, 'connecting with Guatemala City that afternoon.'

'That's . . .' Davies started to say, but Clarke had hung up. The SAS CO stood for a moment holding the dead receiver, then slammed it down with what he considered appropriate violence. Then he sat seething in his chair for several moments, staring out through the office window.

Across the frosty parade ground the last of the sunlight was silhouetting the distant peaks of the Black Mountains.

'Bastard politicians,' he eventually murmured, and picked up the phone again.

Having ascertained from the Duty Officer that 'Razor' Wilkinson was on twenty-four hours' leave, the CO left the room for the second time in fifteen minutes, wishing that he hadn't answered Clarke's call. The American request wouldn't have gone away, but at least he and Razor would have had one more evening in blissful ignorance of its existence. Though come to think of it, the bastard would probably have called him at home.

Davies climbed into his BMW, turned on the ignition and

pressed in the cassette. Billie Holiday's voice filled the car with its smoky sadness.

He drove out through the sentry post and started working his way through the rush-hour traffic towards his cottage on Hereford's western outskirts. 'Look on the bright side,' he told himself. A couple of years ago he would have felt much less happy about sending Wilkinson into a situation like this one. The man had always been a fine soldier, as sharp as he was brave, but until recently his leadership potential had been undermined by a stubborn refusal to grow up emotionally. Bosnia – and the wife he had found there – had seen him come of age, and Razor now seemed as complete a soldier as the SAS had to offer.

So why, Davies asked himself bitterly, put him at risk for a bunch of psychotic generals? What possible British interest could be served by identifying a guerrilla leader for people whose only claim to fame was that they had invented the death squad?

In fact, the more he thought about it the angrier Davies became. A mission like this should be offered to someone, not simply ordered. This guerrilla leader posed no more threat to the integrity of the United Kingdom than Eric Cantona, and probably considerably less. And though Davies didn't know much about Guatemala, he was willing to bet that anyone faced with choosing between Army and guerrillas on moral grounds wouldn't have an easy time of it.

He gripped the wheel a little tighter, and wondered, for only about the third time in a military career which spanned nearly thirty years, whether he should refuse a direct order. It would make no difference to Razor – he would simply receive the order from someone else – but the gesture might be worthwhile. After all, he only had another three months in the CO's chair – what could they do to him?

Davies sighed. Who was he kidding? They could make his life hell, and just when he was happier than he had been for years. All the cushy jobs and consultancies which a retired lieutenant-colonel could expect to be offered would just melt away. All he would ever hear would be the sound of doors closing in his face.

He turned off the main road and thought about Jean. Did he have the right to risk whatever future they might have together by making grand gestures?

She would expect nothing less of him, he decided.

But there was also Razor's future to consider. He had almost ten years to go before retirement from active service at forty-five, and a refusal to accept this mission – always assuming the bastards didn't go for a court martial – would certainly stop the lad's career in its tracks.

Davies felt his temper rising again. The man was a national hero, for God's sake, whether the nation knew it or not. He had been one of eight SAS men landed on the Argentine mainland during the Falklands War, and one of six who had returned alive. Between them the two four-man patrols had provided early warning of enemy air attacks which could otherwise have wrecked the San Carlos landings, and destroyed three Exocet missiles which might well have claimed three British ships and God knows how many lives.

There had never been any public recognition of their contribution, and now it seemed to Davies as if insult was being added to injury.

He guided the car down the swampy lane to his cottage.

Once inside, he poured himself a generous malt whisky, put on Miles's *Porgy and Bess* with the volume turned down low, and looked up Razor's home number in his book.

It was Mrs Wilkinson who answered. Davies had first met Hajrija on the occasion of her arrival in Britain two years earlier, when she was accompanying an SAS team returning from their investigation of alleged renegade activities by a regimental comrade. The welcoming committee from the MoD had asked her what she was doing on British soil, and her future husband had told him that she wanted to see if England was 'really full of pricks like you'.

Davies smiled inwardly at the memory as he asked to speak to Razor.

'He's in Birmingham,' Hajrija told him. 'Seeing his mother and his football team. The two great loves of his life,' she added with a laugh.

Razor had always been close to his mother, Davies remembered. 'Can you give me her number?' he asked.

'Yes, but he won't be there. He's meeting friends before the match.'

Hajrija's English was almost as good as Razor's, Davies thought. Maybe even better. 'I'll call his mother and leave a message,' he said.

She gave him the number. 'What's it about?' she asked with her usual directness.

'Sorry, I can't tell you,' Davies said.

'That doesn't sound good.'

Davies didn't deny it. 'When is he due back?'

'He's driving back in the morning. I think he has a class at twelve.'

'Thanks.' He hung up, feeling worse for hearing the

anxiety in Hajrija's voice. He took a sip of malt, and punched out the Birmingham number she had given him.

The drive from Villa Park to the house his mother and stepfather had recently bought in Edgbaston took Razor Wilkinson about forty-five minutes. It was the first time he had seen Tottenham since November, and the first game they had lost since . . . November. Someone up there had obviously decided he was too damn happy these days. Bastard.

Razor pulled the car in behind his mum's Escort and noticed with pleasure that the downstairs lights were still on. He let himself in, and found her watching the opening credits of *Newsnight*.

'Jack's gone to bed,' she said. 'He's got an early start tomorrow.'

And he's probably also being tactful, Razor thought. One of the things he liked most about his new stepfather was that the man understood how close the bond was between mother and son. Since Razor's babyhood it had just been the two of them – the classic one-parent family of Tory demonology. And Razor had known a lot of kids with two parents who would have happily swapped them for the relationship he had with one.

He sat down and grinned at her.

'They lost,' she said.

'Yeah, but they looked good.'

She smiled at him. 'I remember you sulking for days when they lost.'

'I was only about six.'

'Twenty-six, more like. Hajrija phoned,' she added. 'Your boss wants to talk to you. Urgently.'

'The CO?'

'Lieutenant-Colonel Davies. He wanted you to call him as soon as you got in. The number's by the phone in the hall.'

Razor left her with Peter Snow and walked out into the hall, wondering what could be so urgent that it couldn't wait until the morning. If Hajrija had passed on the message, then she had to be all right.

He keyed the number, listened to eight rings, and was about to give up when a somewhat breathless Davies answered.

'Wilkinson, boss,' Razor replied. He could hear a woman's voice in the background, which both surprised and vaguely pleased him. He had always felt an instinctive liking for Barney Davies, and it was fairly common knowledge around the Regimental mess that the man's marriage break-up had turned him into a social recluse. Maybe he was coming out of his shell at last.

Or, then again, it might be a hooker. Or his mother.

'Something's come up,' the CO was saying. 'Remember the week you and Docherty spent in Guatemala in 1980?'

'Christ, not very well. I'd only been badged a few months. Why, what's happened?'

Davies told Razor exactly what Clarke had told him, and did his best to keep his doubts to himself. Before airing them, he wanted Razor's reaction. 'Would you be able to recognize this man?' he asked, hoping the answer would be no.

'Yeah, I don't see why not. We spent quite a lot of time with him. Even taught him how to play Cheat.'

'Did you like him?'

'I wouldn't say that. He was holding English hostages, and threatening to kill them.' He paused. 'Docherty sort of liked him, though,' he said.

Davies grunted. 'Somehow that doesn't surprise me.'

'What about Chris Martinson?' Razor asked.

'What about him?' Davies asked, surprised.

'He's in Guatemala.'

'He is? I had no idea. What the hell's he doing there?'

'There's a town there where you can do Spanish courses and live with a family while you're doing them. He's hoping for a field job with one of the charities when his term ends, and he wanted to bring his Spanish up to scratch.' Razor grunted. 'And no doubt he's doing some bird-watching while he's there.'

'How long has he been gone?'

'Two weeks, two and a half . . . I'm not sure. I think he's due back at the end of next week. He had a lot of leave piled up.'

'Ah,' Davies said, wondering how he could make use of the coincidence. 'Look,' he said, 'sleep on this, and I'll see you in my office when you get here in the morning.'

'OK, boss,' Razor said, wondering why the CO sounded so anxious. Maybe he'd forgotten to drop in at Boots on the way home to pick up some condoms. Or maybe he knew more about the situation in Guatemala than Razor did. Which wouldn't be difficult. He couldn't remember reading or seeing a single news item about the place in the past fifteen years.

He did remember the ruins where the negotiations had taken place. The two of them had driven there by jeep along the jungle road from Belize, stayed in a one-room inn which deserved a minus-five-star rating, and met with the terrorist leader on a square of grass surrounded by soaring stone temples. Tikal had been the name of the place. There had been monkeys in the trees, and huge red parrots zooming round in formation like dive-bombers, and those birds with the huge multicoloured beaks whose name he couldn't remember. Around dawn the mist had lingered in the trees, and one morning he and Docherty had climbed to the top of one of the temples and seen the tops of the others sticking out through the roof of mist like strange islands in a strange ocean.

He was only twenty-one then, not much more than a kid, and he supposed he hadn't really appreciated it.

'You OK?' his mother asked from the living-room doorway.

'Yeah, fine. It's just one more job that no one else can do.'

The moon had been gone for several minutes, and the luminous haze above the distant ridge-top was visibly fading. Tomás Xicay could almost feel the sighs of relief as true darkness enveloped the clearing where the *compas* were taking a ten-minute rest-stop. There was nothing but shadows around him, and the rustle of movement, and the whisper of conversation.

A hand came down on his shoulder. 'Is everything OK, Tomás?'

'*Sí, Commandante,*' he told the Old Man. He was tireder than tired, but then which of them wasn't? Except maybe the Old Man himself, who always seemed utterly indefatigable.

'Only a few weeks,' the Old Man said wryly, and moved on to encourage someone else.

Tomás smiled to himself in the dark. When, two months earlier, their current strategy had been agreed, that had been the crucial phrase. 'We must get them on the run, if only for a few weeks,' the Old Man had told the group leaders gathered that night on the hill outside Chichicastenango. 'Show the Army and the Americans that we are still alive, and that they are not immune to retribution.'

What would happen after those 'few weeks' no one knew for certain, but there was no doubt that the sort of aggressive tactics they had decided on would have a limited lifespan, because surprise always carried a diminishing return, and without it they would always be outgunned. And they knew that the longer they pursued these tactics the more certain it was that most of them would be killed.

As the column got back underway Tomás found himself wondering whether the Old Man ever had any doubts, and if so who it was he shared them with. Tomás at least had his sister, though being the man of the family he naturally tried to shield her from his more negative feelings. On his return from the city she had been quick to notice that something had upset him, and he had told her it was just seeing their relations, and the family memories they brought back. That had been true, but it was not the whole truth. During his days in the city he had seen their struggle in a different light, and it had disturbed him.

This column of *compas*, striding through the night forest, seemed so full of strength and rightness, so powerful . . . but there were only forty-four of them, and only the trees and the darkness shielded them, and not 150 kilometres away two million people were getting on with their daily lives oblivious to the guerrillas' very existence. In the city it was hard to believe that the Government could ever be toppled, that anything could shift the dead-weight of all that had gone before. It all seemed so permanent, so solid. Five hundred years' worth. And when Tomás thought about how much his people had suffered to keep their world alive, he found it hard to imagine the world of the Ladinos and the Yankees proving any less stubborn.

Still, no matter how much he might doubt their eventual triumph, he never doubted the need to continue with their struggle. What, after all, was the alternative? To accept the way things were? The poem in Tomás's pocket had the words for that: '. . . *it seems to me that it cannot be, that in this way, we are going nowhere. To survive so has no glory.*'

It had been the Old Man who had introduced him to the poetry of Pablo Neruda, a few months after their first meeting in the Mexican refugee camp. By then they had become firm friends – or perhaps more like father and son – but at the beginning Tomás had found it hard to take the older man seriously. His stories had seemed so outlandish, so much like comic-book adventures, that Tomás had taken him for the camp storyteller, more of an entertainer than a fighter.

In one story the Old Man had been taking some explosives to the guerrillas in the mountains, when he was stopped at an army roadblock. The soldiers were in a good mood that day, and only gave him a few bruises and burns before telling him he could continue on his way for no more than the price of his sack of beans. Unfortunately this was where he had hidden the explosives, so for an hour or more the Old Man pleaded and whined for the sack's return. Eventually the lieutenant in charge of the roadblock grew so sick of this incessant lament that he hurled the bag at the Old Man and told him to get lost. His one great achievement in life, the storyteller told his listeners, was not to recoil at the prospect of an explosion as the sack landed at his feet.

And then there was his favourite escape story. He had

been staying with comrades in Guatemala City, and alone in the house when the sound of vehicles approaching at high speed had alerted him. He had walked out into the front yard, picked up a broom and started sweeping, just as the lorries came hurtling down the street. They had screeched to a halt and disgorged running soldiers, all of whom raced straight past the Old Man into the house and started breaking furniture. The lieutenant in charge, who had been sent to arrest a notorious guerrilla leader, told him: 'Get the fuck out of here, old man!' He had accordingly shuffled off down the street.

Both these stories, Tomás had later found out, were true in every detail. The man he had taken for the camp story-teller was probably the most successful guerrilla leader in the history of Guatemala's forty-year civil war. And if anyone could 'get them on the run for a few weeks', then it was him.

3

Barney Davies dropped Jean off at the hospital where she worked, and reached his office before eight, feeling torn between post-coital bliss and pre-mission anxiety. The smile which bubbled up from the one kept fading into the frown caused by the other.

The briefings on the current situation in Guatemala, which had already been faxed from Whitehall, didn't do much for the smile. There was a lot of talk about that country's return to civilian democracy, a few pious generalities about increased respect for human rights, and a lot of waffle about the importance of maintaining stability throughout Central America. According to the Foreign Office mandarins, the existence of a Mayan Indian rebellion in the Mexican state of Chiapas made it all the more imperative that the alleged progress towards an acceptable peace in Guatemala be sustained.

Reading between the lines, Davies was not convinced. After finishing the report he stared morosely out of the window for several minutes, and then ordered a second cup of tea and his first rock cake of the day.

One way of reducing the risks involved in sending Razor into the lion's den, he had decided, was to send him in with company. The two men had got to know each other during the Bosnian business, and the mere fact that Razor had known that Chris Martinson was in Guatemala suggested at least a minimal level of continuing contact.

What the Guatemalans would think of it, Davies had no idea. Nor did he much care.

The tea arrived, together with a surprisingly friable rock cake.

The seventy-mile drive from Birmingham, most of it on motorways, took Razor about as many minutes. Driving was something he had always done well, and usually faster than this. But as Hajrija had tactfully pointed out, if all the other drivers had his judgement and reflexes then he could get away with driving like a lunatic. Until then . . .

He was getting older in more ways than one, Razor thought. Ten, fifteen years earlier, and the prospect of a mission like this would have had his body churning out adrenalin by the pint. His heart would have been leaping at the thought of getting away from Hereford and into action, away from routine and into the unknown. One voice in his brain was still singing this song, but only one, and it sounded more like an echo of his youth than a part of the man he now was. Other voices were dolefully reminding him that these overseas outings only ever looked good in prospect and retrospect, and were rarely anything other than terrifying at the time. This particular mission, so far as he could tell, looked about as inviting as a fortnight in Mogadishu. And on top of everything else he would be away from Hajrija for longer than he cared to think about.

By the time he reached Stirling Lines Razor was having trouble keeping in contact with the adventurer within.

Barney Davies greeted him with a wide smile and ordered

cups of tea on the intercom. Razor glanced at the photograph frame on the CO's desk, half expecting to find a new face inside it, but it still contained the familiar picture of his children. In the dim distant past another photograph had featured a wife.

'What exactly do they want me to do?' Razor asked, once the tea's arrival had signalled the start of business.

'As far as I know, simply identify the man who calls himself "El Espíritu", or "The Ghost".' Presumably he'll be in custody by then, though how they intend to catch him without knowing what he looks like seems a moot point.'

'And then?' Razor asked.

'You come home.'

Razor grunted. 'So we have no guarantee that . . .' He paused. 'Well, that they don't just take him out and have him shot on my say-so.'

'I wouldn't have thought they'd want that sort of publicity,' Davies said carefully.

Razor looked up, feeling the weight of doubt suddenly bearing down on him. 'Which might just mean that they'll wait until I'm on the plane home.'

Davies shrugged. 'Maybe. The US State Department told the Foreign Office that if the Guatemalan Army had a hundred suspects they would probably shoot the lot, just to make sure of getting the right man.'

'Bastards,' Razor murmured, leaving Davies unsure whether he meant the State Department, Foreign Office or Guatemalan Army. Probably all three, he decided.

'Look,' the CO said, deciding to lay some cards on the table. 'I don't like this any more than you do. The Guatemalans are leaning on the Yanks, and they're leaning on us, and it's you who'll pick up the tab . . .'

'Come back, Docherty, all is forgiven,' Razor muttered.

Davies uttered a silent prayer of thanks that Jamie Docherty was now living in Chile, and far removed from this mess. 'It seems to me,' he said, 'that there's two ways we can go with this. Either you can refuse outright to go . . .' He looked Razor straight in the eye. 'And if you do I'll back you all the way.'

'Thanks, boss, but . . .'

'Or you can go out there and play it by ear. When it comes to the crunch you'll have to decide for yourself whether you want to identify this man or not. By then you should have a much better idea of who and what you're dealing with. On both sides of the fence.'

'You mean, when the moment comes I just look through the guy with an innocent expression on my face,' Razor said, amused. 'I like it.'

'Not necessarily. We know the man kidnapped a whole tour party, and God knows what else he's got up to in the last fifteen years. He's no innocent, whatever else he is.'

'He must be pretty old by now,' Razor said. 'He looked like a pensioner in 1980.'

'Anyway,' Davies went on, 'I'm not sending you out there alone.'

'I was going . . .'

'Chris Martinson can keep you company.'

'Oh, great. But I was thinking about someone else. The wife has always wanted to see Guatemala for some reason, and . . .'

'I don't think . . .'

'Only as a tourist, of course. She can do her own thing while I bond with the Guatemalan Army. She could maybe open the odd fête, if the Guatemalans ask her.'

Davies grinned in spite of himself. 'I don't know . . .'

'Maybe it's only an old Yugoslav custom, but she thinks men on diplomatic missions often take their wives along, with all expenses paid by the grateful hosts.'

The CO laughed. 'I can't wait to hear what the Foreign Office will say,' he said, reaching for the phone.

It took five minutes for the secretary to locate Martin Clarke, but far less time for Davies to lose his temper. 'If you are not prepared to ask the Guatemalans to accept a two-man team then you can go and look for help somewhere else,' he told Clarke. 'I am not prepared to send a single soldier, no matter how experienced, into a potential combat situation without any reliable backup.'

'I am not interested in debating the issue,' Clarke said.

'Then just get on with arranging what I asked for,' Davies said, and slammed down the phone.

Razor raised his eyebrows.

'He'll call back in a few minutes,' Davies said, with a confidence which he only half felt. It was kind of exhilarating, though, telling one of Her Majesty's Ministers where to get off.

And it worked. Clarke was back on the line in less than five minutes, sounding chagrined but humble. The Guatemalans didn't quite understand the necessity, he said, but they were happy to provide hospitality for as many Britons as came.

'Good,' Davies said. 'Please inform them that Sergeant Wilkinson will also be bringing his wife, who is eager to visit their beautiful country. They will need accommodation, and so will Sergeant Martinson. He is already in Guatemala, in Antigua.' He read out the address. 'If the relevant authorities can liaise with Martinson, he can meet the Wilkinsons at the airport on Sunday. Oh, and we'll need a ticket for Mrs Wilkinson on the same flight as her husband.'

'Anything else?' Clarke asked coldly.

'No, I don't think so,' Davies said, and put the phone down. He looked across at Razor, who was grinning at him, and looking not much more than half his thirty-six years. Davies smiled back, determined not to offer any outward display of the sudden sense of foreboding in his heart.

The news that the British had agreed to send their soldier reached Guatemala City soon after dawn, and an eager Alvaro was waiting to inform Serrano of the good tidings when the latter arrived at the G-2 offices in the Palacio Nacional.

'Good,' Serrano said, stirring sugar into the coffee which had just been brought to his desk.

'He will join up with the man in Antigua, the one we knew about,' Alvaro added. 'And he is bringing his wife.'

Serrano was pleased. 'Excellent,' he said. 'That must mean that no pressure has been put on him. If he is bringing his wife he must be happy to come. He will be a good witness.'

'I thought of putting them in the Pan-American Hotel,' Alvaro said. 'Tourists seem to like it.'

'They like it because it is comfortable, but not so luxurious that the streets outside make them feel guilty,' Serrano said. 'A good choice,' he added.

'Thank you, sir.'

Serrano sipped appreciatively at the dark coffee. 'Has there been any progress in the business of finding El Espíritu?' he asked, knowing full well that if there had been he would have been the first to know.

'Nothing definite yet, but the net is being drawn in.'

Serrano allowed himself a thin smile. 'Let's hope the little shit is in it.'

The sun was sinking behind the twin peaks of Fuego and Acatenango as Chris approached his lodgings. Like most of the houses in Antigua, the Martínez family residence wasn't much to look at from the outside, offering just a bare wall painted pastel yellow, with two small windows protected by wrought-iron grilles. But once through the gate the visitor found himself in an exquisite courtyard, decorated with palms and flowering pink bougainvillaea, and surrounded by cool, shuttered rooms.

From one of these rooms Chris could hear two voices which had become increasingly familiar over the past two and a half weeks; they belonged to Clara and Romero, the leading characters in the family's favourite soap opera. *Costa del Oro* was supposedly made in Colombia, though Chris had never noticed anything which reminded him of his own trip to that country. The programme was basically an Hispanic *Baywatch*, with even flimsier swimsuits, acting and story-lines. The Martínez family adored it.

He was waved into the only empty seat, next to sixteen-year-old Maria, whose life seemed to revolve around flirting with whoever was at hand, and whom Chris found worryingly attractive. This evening, though, she was too engrossed in the TV show to nestle up to him.

Chris watched it too, feeling pleased that he understood more or less everything that was being said, right down to the occasional – and probably unintentional – ironic nuances. His time in Antigua had certainly delivered the goods as far as his Spanish was concerned, and he had even grown rather fond of his hosts. In many ways they reminded him of an English family – only the names of the soap operas had been changed.

The day's episode ended with a cliff-hanger which made Chris nostalgic for the subtlety of *Neighbours*, and left the Martínezes in temporary shock. Señora Martínez recovered first, and headed for the kitchen, announcing over her shoulder that dinner would be in half an hour.

'There has been a call for you,' Maria told Chris, fixing her deep-black eyes on him.

'From who?' Chris asked.

'Your embassy in Guatemala City,' Señor Martínez told him. 'They want you to call them back. Please, use our telephone.'

Chris did so, and was put through to the Military Attaché, Ben Manley, with whom he had once served in the Green Howards. Manley relayed the new orders from Hereford, half sarcastically adding that it sounded 'like fun'.

'Doesn't it just,' Chris agreed wryly.

For the next couple of hours he put the whole business to the back of his mind, and concentrated on enjoying his dinner. After he had helped with the dishes – something which still astonished the whole family – he announced he was going for a walk, and then dealt Maria a crushing blow by refusing to ask for her company. He needed to do some thinking, he told her. She gave him a persecuted look.

Once outside, Chris began wandering aimlessly through Antigua's network of streets, feeling dismayed by the news. He told himself it would be good to see Razor and Hajrija, and that there seemed every likelihood he would now get to see parts of the country which were well off the tourist track. Who knew? – he might even find the twitcher's holy grail, a quetzal in the wild.

It wasn't enough. He felt almost cheated, and realized that although he still had two months of his final term to serve, he had begun to think and feel as if the SAS was already behind him.

He had been a good soldier – he was certain of that – but being a soldier, and an SAS soldier at that, had always been a means to an end for him, not an end in itself. It had given him the scope to stretch himself, and to see the wild parts of the world in a way which the tourist or even the seasoned traveller never could. There was no adventure-holiday company yet which offered a week-long hike out of Colombia, across mountains and through jungle, with the forces of a drug cartel and the national army on your tail.

But after Bosnia things hadn't been the same. Maybe it had been the mission itself, or maybe he had just outgrown one way of looking at himself and the world. Damien Robson had died there, making Joss Wynwood and himself the only remaining survivors of the Colombian mission. That was chilling enough, but not the main reason for his change of heart. In Bosnia he and Razor – both of whom had chosen medicine as their first SAS specialization – had spent as much time looking after people as they had fighting. There had been the women from the Serb brothel, the children injured in the shelling of Zavik. He and Docherty had been round Sarajevo's City Hospital, and witnessed the incredible dedication of people working in near-impossible conditions.

Back in England he had decided that there were other ways to travel and to serve than with the SAS. He had been quite happy to serve out the remainder of his three-year term. The work was rarely boring and there were always new opportunities to learn. Some of these – like the helicopter pilot's course he had recently begun – would provide him with skills that were bound to be useful in the sort of Third World situations where he expected to find his civilian future.

What he had not anticipated was that anyone would ask him to take up arms again, much less send him out on loan to an army notorious for its murderous cruelty.

The MI5 report was waiting on Martin Clarke's desk when he arrived back that evening from a day-trip to Brussels. Placing the miniature hamper of Belgian chocolates to one side – he had forgotten Valentine's Day the previous year, and decided to shop in advance this time – he took the file across to the armchair by the window and started to read.

Darren James Wilkinson was born on 6 February 1958, which made him almost thirty-seven. And, as Clarke's wife Sarah would have told him, an Aquarius. He had been raised in Islington and Walthamstow by his hospital nurse mother, and attended the local comprehensives. The name Highbury Grove rang a bell. Wasn't that the school Rhodes Boyson had been headmaster of? God help the pupils, Clarke thought.

Wilkinson had clearly shown no aptitude for study. He had left school in the summer of 1974, and spent the next eighteen months moving from job to job. He had been out of the country several times during that period, mostly as a travelling football supporter, but there had also been two three-month stints as a barman in Marbella. He had joined the Army soon after his eighteenth birthday. After four years' service with the Welsh Guards he had applied to join the SAS, and satisfied all the entrance requirements with flying colours.

No doubt his experiences as a football hooligan had come in handy, Clarke thought sourly.

But he had to admit that the man had an excellent service record. His first important job had been the one in Guatemala, and though he had obviously played a subordinate role, he had been commended for his performance. Two years later there had been the business in Argentina, which Clarke already knew about. The only new information in this regard concerned Wilkinson's subsequent arrest, along with fellow-trooper Stewart Nevis, on a charge of being drunk and disorderly in the Chilean town of Puerto Natales. The two men had apparently defaced a local statue and given the locals an impromptu concert at two in the morning.

'Once a football hooligan, always a football hooligan,' Clarke murmured to himself.

Still, Wilkinson had been promoted to corporal almost immediately, and raised to the rank of sergeant five years later, when he joined the staff of the Regiment's Training Wing. From then until the Bosnia mission early in 1993 he had hardly been out of the UK.

Clarke had never been privy to the details of the affair in Bosnia, and after reading the report's account he could see why his superiors had not been eager to publicize the matter. The SAS team had been sent in to investigate rumours that one of their own colleagues was running a private war in the Bosnian mountains, and if necessary to extract him by force. Instead of doing so, they had rescued about fifty women from a Serb prison, done everything but assist their renegade colleague in his private war, and then ignored direct orders to bring the man out, escorting a truckload of wounded children to safety instead.

The report attributed this wilful insubordination to the team commander, the now-retired Sergeant James Docherty, but as far as Clarke could see no action had been taken against either him or any of the others. The SAS had simply closed ranks around the matter, as if the Regiment was a law unto itself. Which it probably was, Clarke thought. He was still smarting from the way its Commanding Officer had addressed him a few days earlier.

What had Wilkinson's contribution to the affair been? Clarke wondered. Had he argued with Docherty, simply followed orders, or even encouraged him? There was no way of knowing. But it was Wilkinson who had married the Bosnian woman that the SAS team brought out with them; Wilkinson who had called the MoD official at RAF Brize Norton 'a prick'.

Clarke sighed and stared out at the London night. There didn't seem much doubt that the man was prone to insubordination. But at least he hadn't been in any trouble since the Bosnian business. According to the report he had suffered from persistent nightmares for a while, but a few visits to the Regiment's 'psychiatric counsellor' had apparently put him back together again. Anyway, he was the one the Guatemalans wanted. They could damn well keep him in order.

Ten minutes later Clarke began telling his contact in the US State Department that there were few finer examples of British soldiering at its brilliant best than Sergeant Darren Wilkinson of 22 SAS.

* * *

A solitary bird suddenly began to sing, and after what seemed only a momentary pause, another thousand joined in. Emelia Xicay lay flat on her stomach in the tall grass above the road and listened. For a few minutes the nerves which always preceded an action were banished, and she smiled with unalloyed pleasure. At times like this she always felt truly blessed – this, just as much as the horrors and the sadnesses, was her birthright as a Mayan Indian. Here in the mist she felt herself enveloped by the damp richness of the earth and trees, carried along by the song of the birds. She belonged in the natural world, the way so few foreigners seemed to do.

At such times she felt almost sorry for the Ladinos, who seemed to have no such sense. But not all of them, she reminded herself sternly. Tomás said some understood life and the earth the same way their own people did. He had Ladino friends, and she would too, once she could speak to them fluently in their own language.

She thought about the city, and wondered if she would ever see it. Tomás had told her about it, of course, and so had Francisco, but she suspected that both brother and lover had censored their accounts, as if they was trying to protect her from all the many evils which befell their people there.

She hadn't thought about Francisco for several days, she realized. It was almost a year now since his death in the army ambush.

She turned her mind back to the city. She didn't want to live there, just to see it. The biggest towns she had ever visited were Santa Cruz del Quiche in Guatemala and San Cristobal de las Casas in Mexico. They had lived just outside the latter for a while, and Emelia had sold woven bracelets to the tourists in the town's main square with several other refugee children. She could remember lifting up her wares to the smoked-glass windows of the big buses, the pale white hands reaching down with money.

The men on the road below were speaking to each other in low voices, and Emelia thought she caught Tomás's Tzutujil accent among them. The first hint of light was showing in the mist away to her left, above the deep and hidden valley which carried the road up from Cunen.

He should be leaving about now, if he was leaving at all. According to the reports of the *compas* assigned to the task of watching over him, Morales was a creature of rigid habits, and so far there had been no sign that the fate of Major Muñoz had persuaded him to deviate from any of his normal routines. Each Friday morning he left the command HQ in Cunen and drove across these mountains to the subordinate outpost at El Desengaño, where he gathered intelligence of the previous week's operations and planned those for the following week. There seemed no practical reason for this journey by road – radio communication would have served just as well, or a helicopter could have covered the same distance in a tenth of the time – but Morales liked to impose himself in person, and from all accounts he loved to drive, and to be seen driving, his new Cherokee Chief station wagon.

And in any case, the Old Man had said, what did Morales have to worry about? His friends in the neighbouring command would have told him the guerrillas were cowering in the forest, somewhere inside the closing ring of troops thirty kilometres to the west. True, they hadn't actually been seen for several days, but there was no way they could have broken out.

Emelia hoped the Old Man was right. He usually was.

It was getting steadily lighter now, and holes were beginning to appear in the mist, drifting holes, like floating windows. On the road below she could now see the seven *compañeros* in their costumes, and the glass cabinet lying on its side. At the foot of the grassy bank Jorge was setting light to the second of two censers packed with incense. Smoke from the first was already wafting up to reinforce the mist, and carrying the sweet, acrid smell to Emelia's nostrils.

With both censers burning, the group below settled into stillness, like a film frozen on a single frame, waiting to be restarted. Emelia lay there with the rifle, watching the mist slowly clear, hearing the chorus of birdsong gradually abate, feeling the cold edge drawn from the air by the rising sun. Ten minutes went by, and twenty, and thirty, and then she could hear the sound of vehicles. As it grew steadily louder the tableau on the road below sprang back into life. She swallowed nervously, and tried not to grip the rifle too tightly.

As he guided the Cherokee Chief up the steep incline, Captain Juan García Morales was thinking about what to do with his new-found wealth. He had just inherited around 200,000 quetzals from a great-uncle, and those closest to him could not agree as to how he should invest it. His wife wanted him to buy property in Florida, but his father was advising Lake Atitlán. Morales instinctively preferred the Florida option, but he had to admit that his father was rarely wrong when it came to such matters. 'You get yourself a shoreline on the most beautiful lake in the world,' he had told his son, 'and in five years the value will multiply tenfold or more. Once we have the Indian business finally settled you won't be able to see that lake for investors.'

He was probably right. After all, Lake Atitlán had continued to draw tourists no matter how bad things got. And if they could move the Indians back from the shoreline, and simply bus them in to work in the hotels and sell the stuff the tourists loved so much, then the sky was probably the limit. The place could become another Acapulco.

Morales steered the car round a bend in the slope, and drove through a small but stubborn patch of mist, emerging just above a sheer drop of several hundred metres. He could feel the nervousness of the soldiers beside and behind him, and rather enjoyed the sensation. In the rear-view mirror he was watching for the following jeep to materialize out of the mist when figures loomed out of another patch almost directly in front of him.

As he applied the brakes Morales instinctively reached for his holstered automatic, and then brought his hand away empty. It was only a bunch of Indian holy men – *cofradías*, they were called; he was always running into them on the roads, carrying their holy dummies to one of their countless festivals. And this bunch of idiots had managed to drop their dummy – he could see it, a child's version of the Virgin Mary, lying face down on the road, next to the overturned cabinet in which they had been carrying it.

One of the old men was walking towards the Cherokee, probably to apologize for getting in the Army's way. Morales took note of the ridiculous costume – the knee-length shorts and the rag wound round the man's head – and wondered why the tourists found this anything other than pathetic.

The weather-beaten face of the old man was smiling apologetically at him as he approached the car window. And then, as if by magic, a revolver was boring into Morales's ear.

'If you want to live another second,' the old man said in perfect Spanish, 'tell your men to leave the jeep without their weapons.'

Razor closed the guidebook and tried stuffing it into the pocket on the back of the seat in front of him. This was not easy, as the slim pocket already contained his Walkman, two airline magazines, instructions on how to behave if the airliner suddenly plummeted 30,000 feet into the Atlantic, a Ruth Rendell mystery and a half-empty quarter-bottle of Sauvignon Blanc.

He had learnt one thing from Hajrija's guidebook – the rest of Guatemala had little in common with the bit he had visited in 1980. The ruins of Tikal were situated in the thinly populated northern half of the country, a mostly flat area of jungles and swamps, but most of the country's people lived either on the Pacific coastal plain or in the vast swath of mountains, plateaux and valleys which formed the country's backbone. It sounded like Chris Martinson's descriptions of Colombia, and like nothing Razor had ever seen.

In the window seat next to him Hajrija was happily giggling at *Blackadder*, which was showing on the tiny screen. Razor reckoned he'd already seen the episode about half a dozen times, and watching the final scenes without the benefit of headphones, he found he could lip-read the dialogue.

He sneaked a glance at Hajrija's happy face, and wondered yet again at his luck in not only finding but also holding on to her. Her lustrous black hair was pulled loosely back in a ponytail, making her look younger than usual, and her high cheekbones were faintly glistening in the sunlight. The first time he had seen her, standing in the corridor of the Sarajevo Holiday Inn, those cheekbones had jutted from a face made gaunt by stress and an inadequate diet.

The credits started to roll, and she took off the headphones. 'The English are completely crazy,' she said, readjusting her hair.

'It's all we have left,' Razor said. He retrieved the guidebook from the crowded pocket. 'What first made you want to go to Guatemala?' he asked.

She lifted both shoulders in the familiar shrug. 'I don't remember,' she said. 'You know how it is – some countries just seem appealing. Some don't. Maybe I saw some pictures when I was a child, or a programme on TV. I can't remember. But I always wanted to see Lake Atitlán. I mean, how many big lakes are there with volcanoes all around them? And I grew up in mountains. The air is so clear in places like that, and the colours. I love it. I want to see Peru as well, and Kashmir.'

She was switching channels as she spoke, in search of further entertainment. 'Are you going to watch a movie?' she asked.

'Don't think so.'

'Are you OK?' she asked, turning towards him, feeling slightly worried. He didn't seem his usual ebullient self.

'Fine. I just don't like watching things on a screen the size of a postage stamp.'

'You should have your eyes tested,' she said.

He nodded and grinned.

Satisfied, she put the headphones back on and left him

to the guidebook. Razor squeezed it back into the pocket and sat back with his eyes closed, thinking how strange it was to be heading out on a job like this with her beside him. Still, this whole trip had a strange feeling to it. For one thing the CO had driven them to Gatwick in person, which had to be a first. And for most of the journey Razor had had the feeling Davies was biting his tongue rather than saying what was on his mind. His last words had been: 'Remember, if you feel the need to press the ejector button, just do it. And we'll just have to deal with the political fall-out.'

That was all very well, Razor thought, but he preferred Jamie Docherty's epigram: 'When the shit hits the fan, it's too late to turn the fan off.'

What the hell. He looked at his watch, and saw that the Tottenham versus Blackburn game was an hour away from kick-off. Just his luck, he thought – the day they played the League leaders and he had to miss it. If there was ever a nuclear war, Razor was convinced it would come with Tottenham one point short of their first League title since the Middle Ages.

He closed his eyes again, and let the hum of the jet engines lull him into sleep.

Chris Martinson and Ben Manley sat in the coffee bar which overlooked the arrival hall at Guatemala City's Aurora International Airport, and watched a plane-load of American tourists and returning Ladino families pluck their luggage from the carousel.

'Is this guy a friend or just a brother-in-arms?' Manley asked.

'A friend, I suppose,' Chris said. He had always been something of a loner, and since Eddie Wilshaw's death in

Colombia he had got used to the idea of not having friends, but over the past couple of years he had felt closer to Razor than anyone else, male or female.

'Well, that should help,' Manley said. 'But these Guatemalan Army guys, they're not half as bad as the press they get. Most of the officers come from good families, and most of them have been trained in the States. There are a few psychos, like there are in any army, ours included.'

'What about G-2?' Chris asked.

'They had a bad reputation in the eighties, and I suppose it's still not good. But you won't have to deal with them. We've been promised this is a strictly army affair.'

Chris sipped at his coffee, wondering who Manley was trying to kid. There didn't seem much left of the wide-eyed innocent Chris had first known in the Green Howards. Manley was a fellow East Anglian and another bird-watcher, and they had spent a lot of time together in those days, both in England and Germany. But their career paths had diverged, and Manley seemed to have acquired the blinkers necessary for following his. He hadn't changed, simply narrowed his focus.

Maybe he had himself, Chris thought, but he didn't think so. 'What's the social life like around here?' he asked.

'Restricted. Just the other embassies, really. Most of the locals you meet are too rich to notice you. There's only the junior officers, really, and some of them are OK. They know where the action is, anyway.'

'And the women?' Chris asked.

'Difficult. This is a Catholic country, so any female over fourteen is either a wife, a Virgin Mary or a tart. The only real exceptions are students, and you have to be pretty careful what you're getting into with them as well.'

'What about the Indians?'

Manley snorted. 'Another world altogether. It's like apartheid,' he added, without any apparent moral judgement. 'The two worlds just don't mix.'

Except when it comes to hiring servants, Chris thought to himself, just as a growing roar outside announced the arrival of another flight.

'That'll be the Miami flight,' Manley said, getting to his feet. 'We'd better get down there.'

Razor and Hajrija were still on the plane when a smiling young man in a uniform arrived to escort them through the entry formalities. These consisted of a single brief conversation between their young man and another uniform in a booth, who thereupon attacked both their passports with a fiercesome-looking stamp. Their bags, which included two SAS uniforms and two Browning High Power 9mm semi-automatics with extra magazines, had already reached the arrival hall, where Chris Martinson and another man were standing guard over it.

'Look what the wind blew in,' Chris said.

'It's good to see you too,' Razor said. 'I was wondering who was going to carry the luggage.'

Manley thanked the Guatemalan and led the other three across the cavernous hall and out through the exit. On the other side of the road Hertz and Budget car rental offices sat beneath a huge hoarding advertising Lucky Strike cigarettes. 'I love exotic countries,' Razor said, as Manley opened up the embassy limousine.

The Wilkinsons slumped into the back seat. 'The hotel's good,' Chris said from the front, just as a huge roar sounded to their left and two Chinook military helicopters loomed above the row of offices and lifted away out of sight. They reminded Razor of *Apocalypse Now*. Nice omen, he thought.

A few moments later they were passing under an old stone aqueduct and entering the city. At the first major intersection a large building announced itself as Chuck E Cheese's Centre Mall, and behind it were ranged several residential high-rises. It all looked like the Lea Bridge Road translated into Spanish, Razor decided.

Things improved as Manley turned the car down a broad, tree-lined boulevard. There were donkey rides for children in the wide central reservation, and one local entrepreneur was doing a roaring trade in Batman T-shirts. Most of the buildings lining the road seemed to be either hotels or offices, and all of them flew the sky-blue and white national flag.

'There's a logic to their flag,' Manley told them. 'The blue on either side symbolizes the Pacific and Atlantic, and the white in between is the peace the conquistadors brought to the land. Hence the quetzal holding the olive branch.'

Irony, blindness, or plain conceit? Chris wondered. Probably a combination of the last two.

'One of the more endearing things about this place,' Manley was saying, 'is the number of rich crazies it seems to produce. People with more money than sense. Look at this church on the left . . .'

They all stared out at the bizarre building, which seemed to have been constructed as a monument to several different architectural traditions. It looked like a cross between the Kremlin, Westminster Abbey and a Venetian palace.

'There's a copy of the Eiffel Tower a couple of streets over,' Manley went on, 'and in one of the parks there's a relief map of the country the size of a tennis court. This is a strange town.'

'I see what you mean,' Razor said, as they drove past a huge statue of two fighting bulls. 'What's that?' he asked, as they passed a large, castle-like building, complete with battlements and armed guards.

'Police headquarters.'

'Figures.'

They passed under a railway bridge and across a wide open space between parks before burrowing into a narrower street festooned with advertisements.

'This is the oldest part of the city,' Manley said.

It looked more interesting, but not a lot more welcoming. There didn't seem to be many people on the streets, and most of those seemed to be hurrying along, heads bowed down, as if keen to reach home before something bad happened. There was something distinctly shabby about the capital of Guatemala, Razor thought. And perhaps sinister as well.

'Most of the guidebooks tell tourists not to waste any time here,' Hajrija said, as if sharing his thoughts.

The hotel, though, was as good as Chris claimed. A small corridor led into a covered courtyard, whose walls were lined with samples of the woven designs of different Mayan tribes. Razor and Hajrija sat down at one of the tables and looked at them while Manley and Chris checked them in.

Having done his job, the embassy man left, and a hotel employee showed them to their rooms. The doors were numbered, and on the wall beside each one there was a small painting of a Mayan god. 'That's Ixchel, the Goddess of Medicine,' Hajrija said, looking at the one by their door.

Razor was impressed.

'Some people sleep on planes, some read,' she told him.

'I'm going to have a stroll around the main square,' Chris announced. 'You two probably want to get some rest.'

'Yeah . . .' Razor began.

'We'll come,' Hajrija said. 'I need to stretch my legs after all that sitting.'

'How far is it?' Razor asked hopefully.

'Just round the corner,' Chris said.

Five minutes later they were crossing the road which surrounded the square, and entering an expanse the size of two football pitches. At the end away to their right a large, twin-towered, cream-coloured church seemed to glow against the darkening sky, while directly ahead of them a much larger building of similar vintage was already brooding in the twilight shadows. More noteworthy than either, the square itself was packed with people, some selling a variety of wares but most simply taking the early-evening air. The majority were in Western dress, but there was also a significant number of people wearing traditional Indian costume. After the half-empty streets of their drive from the airport this much life seemed almost intoxicating.

The three of them wandered through the throng in the general direction of the church, past women cooking corn-cobs on small charcoal braziers, men hawking bursts of candyfloss that were displayed like trophies on large wooden crosses, and more women sitting with little piles of herbs arranged on cotton sheets. Children sucked lollipops, chewed on tortillas and drank from the elegant glass Coca-Cola bottles which Razor remembered from his childhood. A tide of noise, of conversation and laughter and children crying, rolled over them. A series of overlapping smells rose and faded in their nostrils.

A rapid-fire succession of deafening explosions almost

made them jump out of their skins, but there was only excitement on the faces all around, and the clouds of smoke billowing into the air above the western end of the square came from nothing more threatening than fireworks. The threesome grinned sheepishly at each other, and joined the crowd in its drift towards the scene of the action.

Another salvo of firecrackers rent the air, noisier than any of them had ever heard, and almost immediately two rockets screamed into the sky, exploding with equally deafening effect some fifty metres above the crowd. The sticks fell back to earth, causing those at risk below to scatter with screeches of mock alarm.

A procession was now emerging through the whirling smoke which covered the road. First came an altar boy, swinging a large tin brazier of smoking frankincense, and then twenty or so males, some looking no older than adolescents, carrying a huge, flower-decked bier on their shoulders. Above the flowers, swaying with the motion of the bier, loomed a half-size model of the crucified Christ. The cross was gold, the figure black.

Behind the bier came a band, all brass and drums.

'I wonder where they're going,' Razor wondered out loud.

'I'd guess the church,' Chris said. He had seen a similar, albeit smaller, procession in Antigua the previous weekend. 'They usually start and finish where the statues live.'

'It's wonderful,' Hajrija said, her eyes shining.

'Yeah,' Razor agreed. It was, although he was damned if he knew why. The music and the smoke and the costumes and the swaying Christ – a world unto itself, a foreign world.

Then his eyes caught the soldiers on the other side of

the road, standing in a group of four by the entrance to the large building. They were all wearing smartly pressed uniforms and polished leather boots. Each was cradling a dull black Uzi. None looked older than sixteen.

'What is that building?' he asked Hajrija.

'The National Palace,' she said. 'The guidebook says it was built in the 1930s as a gift to the people.'

Razor grunted. The expressions on the faces of the boy-soldiers seemed a potent mixture of envy, fear and contempt. And as if to emphasize the divide, at that moment the sounds of celebration were drowned out by the rising roar of a military transport plane, flying low across the square like a huge black bird.

'Someone's telling us all something,' Chris murmured.

The band played on, the black Christ continued its homeward journey, and the rockets reclaimed the sky from the enemy. The three of them walked back across the rapidly darkening square towards their hotel, saying little.

Once back in their room, Razor decided to take a shower, and a few moments later Hajrija joined him. There was a smile on her face, but something else in her eyes, and they clung to each other in the streaming hot water, both aroused and disturbed by what they had witnessed. And as the fierceness of this feeling slowly transmuted into the more familiar blend of love and lust, they joined together with a passionate urgency which recalled their first night together in Zavik, more than two years before.

Later, with Hajrija asleep in his arms, Razor found himself remembering the favourite book of his youth, Tolkien's *Lord of the Rings*, and wondering whether the two of them had fallen into a land of fantasy, where a sense of wonder and of evil had survived in undiluted form.

4

At ten o'clock the following morning the promised escort arrived at the Pan-American Hotel. The young officer, clean-shaven with deep-brown eyes and a friendly smile, introduced himself to the two SAS men as Lieutenant Ricardo Velázquez Gómez. 'But call me Ricky,' he added, taking each of their right hands between both of his own.

Razor wondered whether to insist on their speaking the local language, but decided that the lieutenant's English was probably better than his own Spanish. 'Where exactly are we going?' he asked as they left the hotel and walked across the road to where a black limousine with smoked-glass windows was gently purring. The driver, who was in plain clothes, eyed the SAS uniforms with interest.

'We are going to the home of Colonel Serrano in Zona 14,' Gómez said. 'He is in charge of this business and he thought it would be a more comfortable place for getting acquainted . . . more informal, yes?'

'Fine by us,' Razor said, and followed Chris into the back seat.

The limousine moved away smoothly, with both SAS men conscious of the stares pursuing them from the pavements. Gómez turned round in the front seat and gave them another friendly smile. 'I have worked with the American Special

Forces,' he said. 'Delta Force and the Rangers. I have good friends there, you know. But even some of my American friends tell me the SAS is the best. So I am pleased to be your liaison.'

Razor grinned. 'Pleasure's mutual,' he said.

'I have read about the Princes Gate. And Las Malvinas . . . the Falklands, I mean.' He grinned. 'And the operation in Gibraltar. I would like to hear your opinion of these things when we have some time. If it is allowed.'

'It's allowed,' Razor admitted.

'Are you stationed here in Guatemala City?' Chris asked.

'Yes. It is the best place to be. Not for this,' Gómez added, taking in the seedy-looking streets of the market district with a wave of his arm. 'You will see – where we are going it is a very nice place, very civilized.'

As the limousine droned down the wide avenue, past the castellated police headquarters and the statue of the fighting bulls, the smoked glass displayed the Guatemalan capital in a sinister twilight. If the authorities spent their lives looking through windows like this, Chris thought, then no wonder paranoia was rampant.

At the Chuck E Cheese intersection they turned left, away from the direction of the airport, and quickly found themselves slowing for a control booth.

'Is this a restricted area?' Razor asked Gómez, once the young officer had cleared them through.

'No, it is only a precaution against terrorism,' Gómez replied. 'There are many embassies in this area, and the terrorists like to make big news, get on CNN. And the BBC, of course.'

The SAS men were not convinced. It felt more like a

private estate than an ordinary district of the city. The streets were virtually empty of either pedestrians or traffic, and what could be seen of the houses behind the high, stucco walls and wrought-iron gates suggested money – lots of it. And the razor wire which adorned the tops of the walls made clear the intention to hang on to every last penny. Above the gleaming coils the heads of luxuriant palms basked in the morning sun, and large white satellite dishes reached up for their signals.

It was no wonder the bastards had built their little enclave so close to the airport, Razor thought. If the revolution came they wouldn't have so far to run.

'There is the Swiss Embassy,' Gómez said, pointing out a villa on their left. Through the tall gates they could see a swimming pool surrounded by flowering bougainvillaea, a gardener hard at work. 'It is nice, yes?' Gómez said. 'One day maybe I buy for my family,' he added with a boyish grin.

Another fifty metres, and the limousine turned in towards another pair of gates. Gómez left the car to use the intercom, and was no sooner back in his seat than the gates swung wide. They followed a curving drive through a stand of royal palms and came to a halt outside one of the most beautiful houses either SAS man had ever seen. Set on a slight slope, the one-storey, white-stucco villa seemed to exist on several levels, as if it were a series of rooms caught in the act of cascading downhill. Wrought-ironwork adorned the windows, and gorgeous flowering plants clung to the walls. In front of the house water rippled from an intricately carved stone fountain.

Two men were waiting on the front steps, both of them in army uniform. Gómez introduced the more thickset of the two as Colonel Cabrera. He was probably not much more than thirty-five, with neatly parted black hair and a short moustache. He was darker-skinned than either Gómez or Serrano, taller than the average Guatemalan, and looked as though he spent considerable time and energy keeping his body in trim. His welcome was jovial enough, but his eyes seemed uncertain, as if he needed a clearer statement of the visitors' status.

Behind Cabrera stood their host, the thinner Colonel Serrano. The two men might hold the same rank, but it didn't take the SAS men long to realize which of them was in charge. There was nothing overt – Cabrera didn't defer and Serrano didn't patronize – but there was still no room for doubt. Cabrera was just a soldier, which in this country might well mean no more than a well-connected bully in uniform. Serrano, his black eyes like burn-holes in a gaunt face, was obviously one of the men who took the real decisions. Intelligence most likely, despite the Guatemalan Government's promise that this would be a strictly military affair.

Lines like that were hard to draw any more, Razor thought. He and Chris had been shepherded into a spacious living room, where several comfortable sofas and armchairs were arranged around a woven rug.

'I took the liberty of ordering coffee,' Serrano said.

'Thank you,' Razor said, thinking about the football magazine which had been left lying, a little too artfully, on the coffee table. He had the strong sense that they were already being manipulated.

'My son loves football,' Serrano said in English. 'He still talks about your Gary Lineker in the World Cup.'

'Yeah, great player,' Razor agreed, manfully resisting the temptation to get drawn in.

A maid arrived with the coffee, but Serrano saw to the pouring and distribution himself, rather in the manner of someone orchestrating a children's tea party. The coffee was deliciously strong.

'How was your flight?' Serrano asked Razor.

'Fine. I slept most of the way.'

'And you have been enjoying your time in Antigua?' he asked Chris.

'Very much.'

'Well, if there is anything else we can arrange for you, any sights you would like to see, please inform Lieutenant Gómez. I'm sure he will be able to fit it into the schedule somehow.'

'Thank you.'

Serrano waved away the gratitude. 'We appreciate your help in this matter, believe me. It may not seem an important matter to people outside our country, but these are crucial times here, and any set-back to the peace negotiations could be serious, not only for us but for the whole region. You are aware of the current situation in Mexico?'

'We've got a rough idea,' Razor conceded.

Serrano leaned forward in his seat. 'The so-called Zapatistas are basically left-wing agitators from Mexico City who are using the Indians' grievances to further their own aims. And they have strong links with terrorists in this country who seek the same ends. At the moment their main anxiety is that my government will reach an accord with the Indian groups and, as you English say, pull the carpet out from under their feet.'

Razor took a sip of coffee. Gómez had listened to Serrano's pitch with dog-like devotion, but Cabrera seemed bored by the whole business. 'How does our man fit into all this?' Razor asked.

Serrano smiled ruefully. 'Until recently we thought this man was long since dead, but after he claimed responsibility for several recent outrages a full investigation was mounted, and it now seems that he has spent several years across the border in Chiapas, plotting with the Zapatistas. His group wants no accommodation with the Government, no peace, so he is an outlaw even among the other guerrilla factions, who do want peace.' Serrano looked sadly at the two Englishmen. 'This country has been at war for far too long,' he said. 'That is why we are a poor country, despite all the advantages we have.'

Razor nodded, not so much to signal his agreement as to accept that there was no point in challenging his host's version of Guatemalan reality. This was going to be one of those jobs which couldn't end too soon. 'So what exactly do you have in mind?' he asked.

Serrano smiled. 'Well, first, I would like to play you a tape of the man who claims to be El Espíritu.'

He got up and walked across to the expensive sound system in the corner, turned it on, and depressed the play button on the cassette deck.

A calm, philosophical voice floated across the room. The man was asking a series of questions in Spanish, with little clicks in between them to indicate where the answers had been edited out. In the background Chris could hear the faint chirp of a bird. It sounded like a great kiskadee.

Razor listened, conscious that the three Guatemalans were watching him closely. The voice might well belong to the man from Tikal: it held that same distinctive blend of humour and great sadness which he remembered. It probably was him. But Razor didn't feel like betting anyone's life on it.

'It could be,' he admitted. He shrugged. 'Fifteen years is a long time to remember a voice.'

Serrano sat down again. He didn't seem disappointed. 'Easier to remember a face,' he agreed. 'And that is what we hope to arrange.'

'How exactly?' Razor asked.

'We are mounting a surgical operation. A company from Colonel Cabrera's Kaibil Battalion . . . you may have heard of them – they are our special forces. They are on stand-by in Uspantan, in Quiche province, close to the scene of the latest outrage. When we receive the necessary intelligence, which should be within the next few days, the Kaibiles will be going in to pluck out this terrorist gang, and we are hoping you will go along for the ride, as the Americans say. If you are on the spot there will be less chance of mistaken identity, and less time wasted. Yes?'

It was more or less what the SAS men had been expecting. 'You understand that while we are in your country we have to act under specific "rules of engagement",' Razor said. 'We can only use our own weapons in self-defence. We cannot actively assist your troops, even in a matter of law enforcement.'

'Understood,' Serrano agreed.

'But we will expect to be issued with the necessary weapons of self-defence,' Razor persisted, determined to leave no doubts in the man's mind.

'Of course. You have your handguns – your regiment uses Browning High Powers, I believe – and we can supply you with Uzis and whatever else you consider appropriate. That can all be dealt with in Uspantan. I suggest Wednesday morning for the flight – that will give you two whole days to recover from your journey yesterday, and to see some of the city. Lieutenant Gómez has some plans for you, I know.'

'Sounds fine,' Razor said, getting to his feet. He had a strong urge to remove himself from the lounge, the villa, and probably the country as well. Colonel Serrano's expectations sounded reasonable enough, but then the German generals had thought much the same of Hitler's, at least in the beginning. Razor had only finished rereading *The Rommel Papers* a month or so before, and was more sensitive than usual to the perils of soldiers wearing political blinkers.

Serrano seemed content enough, and gave each Englishman a friendly pat on the shoulder as Gómez shepherded them back out to the limousine. Cabrera, who had not uttered a single word since the initial greetings, shook their hands again, as if to seal a non-existent relationship.

In the Pan-American Hotel Hajrija awoke to find Razor already gone. She felt slightly bilious, but nothing worse, and once again thanked her lucky stars that so far she had been spared the horrors of acute morning sickness.

In the shower she found herself smiling at the memory of their lovemaking the night before. The two of them were so good together, and at first she had assumed that he was simply a wonderful lover. Certainly her other experiences in bed had not been half as satisfying. But according to him, neither had his. It seemed that they were only wonderful for each other.

She supposed Razor would be happy when she eventually told him about the baby. For two months now they had been letting nature take its course – not so much trying for a baby as making no effort to prevent one. Abandoning the idea of a defensive midfield anchor in front of the back four, as Razor had so poetically put it.

Her pregnancy had been confirmed on the day he had gone to Birmingham, and the mission had been agreed on before she had had a proper chance to tell him. She had waited several days for a suitable moment before realizing that one was unlikely to appear before this business was over. She knew he was less than enthusiastic about this particular job, and she had no intention of giving him something else to worry about. If she had thought for a moment that the news would make him more careful, then she would have told him. But he was a happy man these days, and in Hajrija's experience happy men – or at least those over thirty – tended not to throw their lives away.

He wasn't the only one who was happy, she thought, smiling at herself as she checked her make-up in the mirror. After the horrors of the war in her country she supposed anything would have looked pretty good, but the two years in England had been more than just a relative blessing. She had picked up her journalistic studies once more, and through a series of articles had built up a reputation as a freelance expert on the affairs of her homeland. She had made friends, both among English people and members of the expatriate Bosnian community. She had a husband whom she loved and who loved her, and a baby on the way. It was all a far cry from waking up to the sound of falling shells, and wondering not only whether she would live to see another day, but whether she really cared one way or the other.

In England she had rarely felt homesick for Bosnia, and it seemed strange that the feeling should have been so strong on her first evening in Guatemala. It might have something to do with being pregnant, she thought, as the grinning bellboy took her down in the hotel lift, but on further reflection she doubted it. There had been something about the Plaza Mayor which had evoked her own country, something beyond the superficial Third World similarities. A feeling of warmth, perhaps. Or community. The word 'solidarity' crossed her mind, like an echo from the Yugoslav past. All these words were clichés. None of them offered an adequate expression of what she had felt.

In the empty dining room she pursued the thought, eating her way through a large plateful of fresh fruit and slowly sipping a cup of milky coffee. It had to have something to do with belief, she decided. Not in God so much as in some sort of wider purpose. Some connectedness. Or something. She suddenly felt determined that the child growing inside her should know other worlds than the ever-so-practical world of the English, who only seemed to indulge their sense of wonder in gardening gloves. Or, in her husband's case, in watching Jürgen Klinsmann.

She smiled to herself, finished the coffee and checked her watch. Razor had said he would either call or return by one o'clock, which left her more than two hours to explore. The guidebook said the area was generally safe in daylight, though not apparently for women on their own. But it probably hadn't been written with female veterans of the Bosnian Army's elite Anti-Sniper Unit in mind. Either way, the Plaza Mayor was bound to be safe.

She left the hotel and retraced their steps of the day before, emerging into the square opposite the flat bulk of the Palacio National. The sky was blue, the sun shining, but there were far fewer people about, and nearly all of them were Ladinos. The Indians were presumably back on their farms, or back in the houses where they lived as servants. Those groups of enchanting young girls with their beautiful woven blouses and skirts and mischievous smiles might even be in school.

Hajrija wandered around the square, not feeling in the slightest bit threatened, but experiencing an absurdly acute sense of loss. There was nothing here to evoke the homeland she loved. On the contrary, the vacant expressions on the faces of the adolescent soldiers were all too reminiscent of that homeland she had been only too glad to escape.

Back in the villa, Serrano poured Cabrera a shot of *aguardiente* and put another cassette in the tape deck. He had already heard the new tape but the Kaibil commander had not. And unlike Serrano, he had personal connections with the Morales family.

The two men listened to the now-familiar voice of the man who called himself El Espíritu, the quiet intensity of the questions and the nightmarish passivity of the answers, the obligatory propaganda, the echoing shot.

'If I ever get my hands on that fucker . . .' Cabrera said emotionally.

'With any luck you will,' Serrano told him. 'Now what did you think of the two Englishmen?'

Cabrera shrugged. 'I expect they are good at what they do.'

'But not much class, eh?'

'They are not officers,' Cabrera said, as if that decided the matter once and for all.

'A good thing too,' Serrano said, pulling the packet of Marlboro Lights from his left breast pocket. 'Officers would be more likely to worry about the whys; these two will just get on with the job.' He flicked the Zippo lighter open. 'Though I did detect some hostility from the younger one.' He smiled wryly. 'But then he's been here for several weeks.'

'Let him be hostile,' Cabrera said. 'The older one made it clear that they don't want to be considered combat personnel, which suits me fine. The realities of our war might be too much for their sensitive stomachs.' He smiled. 'We'll find this bastard, get them to identify him, and then send them home with some souvenirs.'

'OK,' Serrano agreed, 'but as long as they're with you, you'll have to keep a tight rein on your boys – we don't want to solve one PR problem by creating another . . .'

'You want results, don't you?'

'Of course I want results,' Serrano said coldly, 'and I don't expect your Kaibiles to behave like mother's boys. But nothing too gratuitous, not this time. If you want to make examples then wait until after the Englishmen have gone.'

The limousine had just passed under the now-familiar railway bridge and entered the narrower streets of Zona 1. 'How far are we from the hotel?' Razor asked Gómez.

'About two kilometres, perhaps,' the lieutenant said, surprised.

'We'll walk from here. Get some exercise. It's straight down this road, right?'

'But . . .'

'We'll meet you back at the hotel, OK?' Razor tapped the driver on the shoulder and told him in Spanish to stop the car. The driver looked at Gómez, who nodded.

'This area is not a hundred per cent safe,' Gómez said, but Razor and Chris were already climbing out.

'We can probably take care of ourselves,' Razor told him with a grin, and closed the door. The limousine drew away slowly, as if it were dragging the weight of Gómez's reluctance.

On both sides of the street locals were staring at the two men in their strange uniforms.

'They can't wait to get their hands on our berets,' Razor guessed.

'Who could?' Chris agreed, as the two men started ploughing a furrow up the pavement. 'I take it your sudden desire for exercise was a polite fiction.'

'It was claustrophobia. Lieutenant Gómez seems a nice enough lad, but I don't think I'm ever going to feel we're seeing too little of each other. And it'll probably be a damn sight easier to get some time alone here in the city than it will in the great Guatemalan outdoors.'

'And it's harder to bug a street than a limousine or a hotel room,' Chris observed.

'True. Now what did you make of Sooty and Sweep back there?'

Chris grimaced. 'I'll lay you odds Sooty's from G-2. Sweep just seemed like your average Ladino army officer – not very bright, probably a sadist . . .'

'Didn't you like him?'

'What was there to like?'

Razor grinned. 'Well, I guess we're not here to judge a Mr Human Rights contest. They did have their story off pat – one renegade guerrilla putting the peace at risk. And it could be true. According to the FO the negotiations between the Government and the guerrillas are at a crucial stage.'

Chris was silent for a few moments, as they weaved their way through the traffic on 14 Calle. 'I don't know,' he said, as they regained the safety of the pavement, 'maybe the Government wants to kill this guy because he's the strongest card in the guerrillas' hands. They're not going to tell us that, are they? They know we'd much rather believe we're helping a peace process than simply targeting one of their enemies. I mean, fuck it, if I lived in this country I'm not at all sure which side I'd be on. It sure as hell wouldn't be an easy decision.'

Razor sighed. He realized he had been hoping that the job would look more straightforward from close up, not less.

They found Lieutenant Gómez chatting happily with Hajrija at one of the tables in the hotel's covered courtyard. She had already accepted his invitation to take an afternoon tour of the city's sights, and after their hasty departure from the limousine Razor and Chris hadn't the heart to object. And in any case, what else did they have to do?

The limo's first port of call was Minerva Park, and the famous relief map which Ben Manley had mentioned. The horizontal scale was 1:10,000, which reduced Guatemala to the size of a square some fifty metres across. The vertical scale, however, was 1:2000, which exaggerated the mountainous nature of the terrain to an almost ludicrous degree. A *Lord of the Rings* landscape, Razor thought, staring down from one of the two observation towers, and remembering his thoughts of the night before. He asked Gómez to point out the town of Uspantan, and discovered that it was about a hundred kilometres north of the capital, nestling beneath the eastern end of a knife-edged range of mountains called the Cuchumatanes.

Gómez then took them to lunch. The steak-house didn't look much from the outside, but their reception within was almost ecstatic, and the food turned out to be excellent. 'This is the restaurant of my wife's family,' the lieutenant explained, after the owner had insisted on shaking all their hands.

After lunch Gómez suggested the zoo, but was overruled in favour of a drive out of the city. Chris wanted a clearer view of the mountains and volcanoes which rimmed the city, but which only ever appeared peeking above roofs or framed between distant buildings. In addition, Razor was becoming uncomfortably aware of the looks the blacked-out limousine was attracting. Everywhere they went people would catch sight of it and falter in their stride, waiting for the relief of knowing that it had not come for them.

The outskirts of the city proved uglier than the centre. The buildings grew less prosperous, a matter of breeze-blocks and corrugated iron, with rusty steel rods poking optimistically through their roofs. The wide highways were choked with traffic, and to judge from the look and smell of the air, any concern over car emissions had yet to reach Guatemala. Bus after crowded bus went by, each pursued by the black cloud of its own exhaust.

And then suddenly the limousine was pulling out across a wide bridge over a deep ravine, and they could see the city stretching away across the plateau behind them. Ahead of them a land of mountains and valleys receded into the distance, but for the moment their eyes were drawn down into the ravine, where another city, this one arranged in ragged rows of tumbledown shacks, clung to the steep slopes. There was rubbish everywhere, and a smell wafting up from the depths which seemed composed of equal parts of sewage and rotting vegetation.

'Too many people come to the city,' Gómez explained. 'There is no room for them all. But they will not go back to their villages.'

'Why not?' Chris asked.

Gómez shrugged. 'Who knows? I think they expect a miracle.'

They drove another ten kilometres down the Pan-American Highway, before using one of the observation point lay-bys to turn around. The countryside was certainly beautiful, but it was hard to shake the visual memory of the city in the ravine. Even Gómez seemed slightly subdued, though he seemed fully recovered by the time they got back to the hotel. It was now five o'clock, and he cheerfully insisted on their all eating dinner that evening at his home. Razor declined, pleading tiredness, but both Gómez and Hajrija looked so disappointed that he suggested the following evening instead. This proposal was greeted with a huge smile from the lieutenant. He would collect them at six the following evening, though of course he would be checking with them again before then.

When he was gone, Hajrija turned on Razor with an air of amused exasperation. 'What's wrong with you English?' she demanded. 'Don't you like meeting people?'

The three of them ate in the hotel restaurant that evening, at one end of a table laid for about twenty. Without any conscious decision being made, they avoided talking about either Guatemala or the job the two men were about to embark on. Chris asked the others if they had heard from Jamie Docherty, and Hajrija told him about the recent postcard from Chile. 'The beach at Valparaiso,' she said. 'It looked just like the Mediterranean. He said things were going well, but there weren't any details. Isabel has a job with a publisher, but we don't know what he's doing, if anything.'

'Maybe he's writing his memoirs,' Razor suggested.

'If he isn't he should be,' Chris said.

'I could play myself in the movie,' Razor decided.

'We all could,' Chris agreed.

She looked at them both with amusement, then suddenly remembered something. 'I had a letter from Nena,' she told Chris. 'Nothing's changed in Zavik. Which I suppose is good news.'

Chris grunted his agreement. When the three of them had left the Bosnian mountain town with Docherty, Damien Robson (the 'Dame'), six wounded children and one wounded old man, Hajrija's friend Nena had stayed behind, along with her estranged husband Reeve and their two children. In the meantime the town had obviously managed to sustain itself as an oasis of peace in a desert of ethnic madness.

'Another beer?' Razor asked the other two. Remembering those weeks, and the months that had followed, he still sometimes felt like pinching himself. He had journeyed into the horror of Bosnia's war and come back to England happier than he had ever been in his life, a metamorphosis whose only price tag had been several months of recurrent nightmares. According to the SAS shrink they had been his way of expressing the guilt that survivors of tragedies often felt, a questioning of one's right to the life and happiness which so many others had been denied.

And this was the first time the three of them had been

outside England together since those days, Razor realized, as the waiter finally noticed his outstretched arm. Maybe that was one reason for the uneasiness he was feeling. Maybe Guatemala was as innocent as Disneyland.

'A penny for 'em,' Chris said, looking at him.

'He's probably thinking about Tottenham,' Hajrija said crushingly.

'Christ!' Razor exploded, 'I still don't know what happened yesterday.' He pushed back his seat and stood up. 'Order the beers. I'll be back in a minute,' he said.

'Where are you going?' Hajrija shouted after him, but he had already disappeared through the doorway which led to the lobby.

'He's gone to ring the Embassy,' Chris told her.

'The British Embassy will have the football results?'

'Someone there will have heard them on the World Service.'

'The World Service,' she echoed. 'You know, we used to listen to that in Sarajevo, when we were on sniper watch. It was kind of strange, listening to Dave Lee Travis while you waited for a clear shot.'

Chris looked at her. It was sometimes hard to believe that Razor's wife was the same person as the young combat veteran he and Docherty had first met in a seedy hotel near Sarajevo station. He suddenly had an idea. 'What are you going to do when we head up-country?' he asked.

'Do some travelling around, I guess.'

'Well, why don't you spend some time with my family in Antigua – I mean the people I've been staying with. I was booked in until this Saturday, so I doubt they'll have found anyone else. I can call them and ask.'

She thought about it for a second, and then nodded.

'And if you two aren't back by the weekend I can go on to Panajachel. That's where . . .'

A whoop in the distance interrupted her.

'They won,' Chris said unnecessarily.

The following morning Lieutenant Gómez arrived while they were having breakfast. Their departure for Uspantan was still scheduled for early the next day, and his family was excited at the prospect of meeting them all that evening. He approved of Hajrija's plan to stay in Antigua for a few days – 'It is much safer for a woman alone there than here,' he said apologetically – and didn't seem offended when they declined his offer of another day in the limousine. He had one cup of coffee and left again, promising to pick them up at six o'clock.

Chris announced his intention of going off in search of the Botanical Garden, partly out of a genuine desire to see it, and partly because he sensed that the other two would like to spend at least some of their last free day with no more than each other for company. He returned in time to take a shower before meeting Gómez in the entrance, and the two of them waited fifteen minutes for the others to come down.

'Sorry,' Razor said, when they finally did so. 'Our siesta got out of hand,' he added mysteriously.

Gómez didn't seem to notice – he was too busy keeping up a non-stop flow of nervous conversation. This evening was important to him, the two Englishmen belatedly realized.

Instead of the limousine, Gómez had his own Toyota waiting outside. He drove well enough, though his habit of looking over his shoulder to converse with those in the back was somewhat alarming. After about twenty minutes they pulled into the parking lot of a modern-looking apartment block.

They were in Zona 10, Chris noted from a street sign, a step down from the luxury of Zona 14, but several steps up from just about anywhere else.

The apartment itself was clean, tidy and decorated throughout in a safe modern style. Lita Gómez was an attractive Ladina with a mass of dark curls, dark eyes, full mouth and a body teetering on the edge of plumpness. She wore a bright-green dress, high-heeled shoes of the same colour, and large gold earrings. Her English wasn't as good as her husband's, but good enough to make herself understood. At first she also seemed nervous, but her natural ebullience quickly won out, and within ten minutes she and Hajrija were talking like long-lost friends.

The two boys, one ten and the other eight, were obviously miffed at having to miss watching TV, but they nevertheless joined in the conversation with their father and the two SAS men, and in the process displayed a patience and politeness which many an English parent would have died for. Both wanted to be soldiers when they grew up, a fact which obviously both pleased and worried their father. Razor found himself liking the man more in his home than he had in the limousine.

The dinner was delicious, but seemed little more Guatemalan than the décor. The conversation moved easily enough from travel to TV, fashion to music, food to sports. Lita was enthralled by the story of how Razor and Hajrija had met, and her husband, to Chris's complete surprise, turned out to have a library of books on bird-watching almost as large as his own. The two boys insisted on showing Razor their collection of World Cup bubblegum cards. The thorny subject of politics surfaced only once, and then only in connection with President Clinton's abortive attempt to end the American baseball strike.

All in all it was a thoroughly enjoyable evening, and leaving the brightly lit family apartment for the dark and vaguely sinister streets of the city felt almost traumatic. Sitting in the back of the Toyota with Hajrija, Razor had a picture of a society living in rigid, self-contained compartments. As long as you stayed in your compartment, he thought, then things could be OK. The Ladinos, or at least some of them, had their wealth and their dreams of an American consumerist world. The Indians had something else, something which he didn't suppose he would ever understand. And whether or not that something made up, or more than made up, for their downtrodden situation he couldn't begin to know.

The problem was the compartments themselves. Ricardo Gómez and El Espíritu might both be reasonable human beings in their own little spaces, but that was only half the story. When people lived in such ignorance of each other, then opening doors became a dangerous business. In such situations the first reaction was usually shock, and the second was often cruelty.

Razor thought about Gómez sitting in the driver's seat in front of him, and caught him smiling in the rear-view mirror, presumably with pleasure at how well the evening had gone. Earlier he had watched him reading bedtime stories to his two boys, and noted how much enjoyment all three had derived from this simple ritual.

Once in the mountains, Razor asked himself, would this Gómez and his comrades all metamorphose into something else, Guatemalan Jekylls into Hydes, family men into the torturers for which their army was notorious?

5

There was a brisk rap on the door. '*Es cuarto para las dos,*' a voice said softly.

'OK,' Razor half shouted in reply, and groaned as the footsteps outside receded. 'Shit, I'm getting too old for this,' he muttered.

'Another day in paradise,' Chris said from the bunk above.

Their small barracks room was far from pitch-dark: the faintest of natural lights was seeping in through the small window and a brighter electric glow was outlining the ill-fitting door.

'If they've got the lights on out there, we might as well have ours on in here,' Chris said, lowering himself to the floor and reaching for the switch.

The two men, both already dressed in their jungle combat fatigues, sat side by side on the lower bunk lacing up their boots, and then took turns with the small hand mirror and make-up kit.

'I must have been a beautician in an earlier life,' Razor remarked, admiring his own handiwork.

'Frankenstein's, I should think.'

Razor laughed, and ran one last check on the Mini-Uzi 9mm sub-machine-gun. The SAS did not normally carry

Uzis, but the gun's worldwide popularity with terrorists and counter-terrorists alike had made familiarization a necessary part of their training. Razor didn't find the Uzi as user-friendly as the Heckler & Koch MP5, but there was no doubting its simple reliability. And with any luck, this time around he wouldn't have to do anything other than carry it.

It was one minute to two. 'Ready?' he asked Chris, who nodded. The two men pulled the unusually lightweight bergens over their shoulders, donned their floppy jungle camouflage hats, and let themselves out into the corridor.

The eighty-strong assault company of Kaibiles had already evacuated the barracks, which Razor supposed was a good sign. He had watched them do their physical training on the base's football pitch the previous afternoon and been provisionally impressed. They were fit, and they looked tough, not to say downright mean. They had the weapons – Uzis, recoilless rifles, mortars – and tactical air support when it was needed. Whether they could fight was something else.

It was considerably darker outside, though no obvious attempt was being made to conceal their departure from any watchers in either the nearby town or the surrounding hills. Maybe Colonel Cabrera had decided that the sound of the trucks would be enough in itself to torpedo any hopes of the company sneaking away unobserved. Maybe he was right.

Lieutenant Gómez, his smile a little more nervous than usual, was waiting to guide them into the second of the four trucks. The SAS men squeezed in beside the grinning Kaibiles, and a few moments later the driver put the truck in gear and pulled slowly away, passing under the sentry tower which loomed above the gate and rolling down the road towards the town. Through the open back of the truck they could see the bright headlights of the two following vehicles and the faint silhouette of the sentry tower against a moonless sky.

The trucks rumbled down Uspantan's cobbled streets, and swung left around the square, past the pale cathedral and up another steep street of silent houses. There was a brief glimpse of cornfields clinging to steep valley sides before a forest engulfed the road in darkness. Two hours, Cabrera had told them. Razor sat back and closed his eyes.

They had left Guatemala City soon after eight on the morning of the previous day. The Chinook CH-47D had lifted off from the military side of Aurora Airport, rising up through thick mist to reveal the flat crest of a distant volcano floating serenely on the layer of low cloud, and then headed north across a landscape of hills and valleys which seemed to have been first modelled in papier mâché, then draped in earth and trees. Mist swirled in the valley bottoms, and verdant mountains rose in the distance through layers of fluffy white cloud. Ribbons of winding road connected small towns, each of them laid out on the familiar grid pattern, each with a shining white church at its centre. Uspantan had been the last of these, and the Chinook had flown low over the central square before touching down at the base above the town.

Colonel Cabrera had been there to meet them, along with his number two, whom he introduced as Major Romeo Valdez Osorio. The major was clean-shaven, and as fair-skinned for a Guatemalan Hispanic as the colonel was dark. He had wavy, chestnut-brown hair, serious blue eyes, and seemed to be in his early thirties. His hands, Razor noticed, were beautifully manicured. His greeting had been polite but guarded.

Cabrera had seemed a different proposition from the man they had met in Serrano's villa. Perhaps he had found those circumstances inhibiting, because here, back in his natural habitat, he was all wide smiles and expansive gestures, and full of enthusiasm for the job in hand. At the dinner table he and the other officers had plied the two SAS men with questions about the Falklands War, a subject in which they were surprisingly well versed. They had little sympathy for their Latin American comrades-in-arms – as one officer put it: 'The Argentines should stick to football.'

Now, sitting in the heaving truck, Razor wondered where Cabrera and Osorio were. Probably in the truck's cab, he guessed. It had to be more comfortable than the back.

Any trace of a paved road had long since vanished, and every now and then the rear wheels would live up to their name, rearing up like the proverbial bucking bronco, and crashing the company back down on their tail-bones with jarring effect. Bloody torture, Razor thought, and smiled grimly to himself in the dark. That was probably not a diplomatic phrase to use in this part of the world.

Next to him Chris seemed to be sleeping through it all, which had to rate as some kind of miracle. Razor thought about his wife, who would soon be starting her second day in Antigua, and wished to God he was there with her.

The journey ground on, the trucks fighting their way up the dirt track into the Cuchumatanes. It was a quarter to four when they reached their destination, and disgorged the troops on to the road. Jumping down gratefully, the two Englishmen found themselves surrounded by dense forest, and a silence broken only by the shuffling of human feet.

The only light came from the starfields twinkling above the canopy of trees.

Ten metres away they could see Cabrera and Osorio examining a map by torchlight with a small man in civilian clothes. As if aware of their eyes on him, the man glanced in their direction, and they could see his Indian features reflected in the yellow light. His expression seemed almost unnaturally neutral, as if life had burned the emotion out of him.

Razor found himself thinking about all the Westerns he had watched as a kid. The Indian scout who helped the white men had usually come to a bad end.

The first of the Kaibiles filed off down an invisible path. Gómez inserted himself and the two Englishmen somewhere in the middle of the departing column, and for the next hour and a half they trekked up and down hills, through trees and across bare slopes, seeing little more than the man directly in front of them. Razor was impressed by the disciplined silence of the Guatemalan soldiers, and by how at home they seemed in the wilderness. Whatever else the Kaibiles might be, they were not parade-ground soldiers.

There was still no sign of light in the eastern sky when the column arrived at the location selected for the ambush. The SAS men had been shown a small-scale map of the immediate area – a thickly wooded narrow valley which carried a path allegedly used by the guerrillas – but for the moment they had to take the geography on trust. Along with Gómez they were allocated to the reserve platoon, which was under orders to seek concealment high on the valley side, some fifty metres above the units charged with initially engaging the enemy. Whether this was to keep them out of harm's way or to prevent them from witnessing any over-exuberance on the part of the Kaibiles, it was impossible to say. Maybe a bit of both.

The soldiers in the reserve platoon were soon at work digging themselves in, and Razor could imagine the surprised looks he and Chris were getting, as they sat there with their backs against a tree. Eventually Gómez could restrain himself no longer. 'We must dig too,' he said. 'If you like, I do all the digging.'

'We'll dig our own scrape,' Razor told him. 'When there's enough light to choose the best spot.'

'Ah, I see,' Gómez said, and sat down again.

Razor smiled at him absent-mindedly, his mind going back to the last time he had encountered this problem, on a snow-covered slope above the Serb-held village of Vogosca. He and Hajrija – who had then been no more than a beautiful dream – had been ordered to establish a forward observation post above the town. They had spent the last fifteen minutes of darkness cutting tiles of frozen snow for roofing over the yet-to-be-located hide. There was no snow here, but it was cold enough now that they had stopped walking. Ten minutes later the sky was showing its first hint of light, and over the next twenty minutes the two men watched the valley slowly swim into focus. It was only about fifty metres wide at the bottom, and in several places the trees grew right down to the edge of the stream. There were two clearings, both apparently man-made. The larger one, though now overgrown with weeds, had once been cultivated; the smaller contained the ruins of what must have been the cultivator's shack. From what they could see the path seemed to wind down from the narrow pass some three hundred metres to their left and then hug the side of the stream as it descended the valley.

Cabrera would presumably have his forward units on two sides of the larger clearing, deployed to catch the guerrillas in a lethal crossfire without risk to themselves.

When they were satisfied as to the best point for observation, Razor and Chris swiftly dug out a simple scrape in the shelter of a large bush, covered it with the rain ponchos from their bergens, and added a few pieces of foliage for artistic effect. Once ensconced, they tossed a coin for first watch, and Razor won. Despite the cold and damp he was asleep almost immediately.

Chris took out his binoculars and conducted a more thorough investigation of the terrain above and below them. The Kaibil platoons were hidden in the expected places, but well hidden nevertheless. If the guerrillas came down that path, as they were presumably expected to do, there would certainly be a few bodies for Razor to examine.

Chris turned his field-glasses up the valley to where the path climbed over the pass, almost dreading the thought of catching the approach of distant figures. But there were no humans in sight, only a single large bird – a black vulture, he thought – lazily circling in the air currents above the pass. Anticipating carrion, perhaps.

The day swiftly brightened, and as the sun burned off the clouds the landscape assumed that high-altitude clarity which Chris had first known and loved in the Colombian Andes. It would be a gorgeous day for hiking, he thought, fixing the binoculars on the distant snow-covered peaks which now lay framed in the 'V' of the pass to his left. Unless you were a guerrilla, of course, in which case such clarity could easily prove fatal. They would be much more likely to move by night, Chris thought.

So what made Cabrera expect otherwise? Information

received, no doubt. But received how? If force had been used then the information was probably worthless.

'Whatever,' Chris murmured to himself, just as a bird started singing 'pur-wheee' somewhere close by. He started searching with the binoculars for the unknown vocalist, and soon found it – a small bird crouching on a branch some twenty metres away. As he watched, the bird suddenly leapt into flight, displaying white patches in blunt-tipped wings. Chris jotted down the particulars in his notebook and reached into the bergen for his well-thumbed copy of *Birds of Costa Rica*, wishing someone would hurry up and produce a volume for Guatemala. After a short search he found the bird – a pauraque.

Over the next couple of hours he saw and heard several more of them, albeit with diminishing frequency. The presence of so many humans, no matter how silent their presence, was gradually scaring the birds away. The guerrillas might have reasons for marching in broad daylight, Chris thought, but even the most basic nature awareness would alert them to the unnaturalness of the silence which now pervaded this particular valley.

The morning wore on, and at noon a yawning Razor took charge of the binoculars. For the next ten minutes or so he swept the valley and its surrounds, and reached the same conclusion as his partner – for this ambush to prove successful the guerrillas would need to demonstrate incompetence above and beyond the expected. And nothing in Razor's recollections of El Espíritu suggested any such level of stupidity.

So today was unlikely to see an end of it. In fact the whole business could drag on for weeks, which wasn't a very appealing prospect. 'Join the Army and stare at the same line of trees for eight hours on end,' he said to himself.

For the next few hours he alternated keeping watch through the binoculars with playing one of his favourite mental games, which involved remembering the plots of famous Hollywood films and then bringing them up to date. Jamie Docherty had invented the game, and there was no doubting its efficiency when it came to consuming stretches of otherwise dead time. Razor spent much of the afternoon recalling the twists and turns of *Casablanca* before trying, unsuccessfully, to relocate the action in a modern context. Bogart, Bergman and her unbearable goody-goody husband were easy enough, but police chief Louis was a real problem. Razor couldn't find a current equivalent of the semi-independent Vichy regime in Morocco, and the more he thought about it the more crucial the balance of power between Louis and his Nazi colleague was to the plot. Without it everything else fell apart.

'Here's looking at you, kid,' he murmured, and picked up the binoculars again. He checked the pass, shifted his sights along the opposite side of the valley, and found a guerrilla looking at him through a similar pair of long-distance lenses.

The man was dressed in olive-green fatigues and a matching baseball cap. He stared at Razor for a few seconds, then took the glasses away from his eyes, and seemed almost to smile before disappearing abruptly into the foliage. Razor tried to find him again, but failed, and almost began to wonder if he had imagined the sighting.

So much for the ambush, he thought. The next question was whether to report what he had just seen. If he did, he would be actively interfering in someone else's war, and probably condemning the smiling guerrilla to death and worse. If he didn't, he could hardly be accused of helping the guerrillas to evade the ambush – they had obviously managed that much on their own.

Unless he saw any sign that the guerrillas were planning their own ambush, Razor decided, he would let the Kaibiles find their own targets.

Some four hundred metres to the north-west, just behind the ridge which separated the site of the intended ambush from the next valley, Tomás was running through the trees, listening for sounds of the chase that must be underway. There was no doubting that the soldier had seen him: Tomás had been wondering who the man was, and had probably kept the glasses on him for too long, creating that sixth-sense awareness of being watched which had led to his own discovery.

The man was probably an American or an Israeli, though he had hardly seemed big enough for one of the former, and much too pale-skinned for one of the latter. Not that it mattered who the bastard was – no gringos who sold their services to the Kaibiles could expect any mercy from the *compas*.

A minute passed, and Tomás could still detect no signs of a pursuit above the sounds of his own passage. He risked halting his flight for a few seconds, crouching down beside a tree and listening intently while he recovered his breath. There was nothing – no sounds of running feet, no shouts, no baying dogs, no distant drone of helicopters. It was as if the foreigner with the field-glasses had dropped dead with shock at the sight of him.

Tomás started running again, hardly daring to believe his own luck.

When Razor woke Chris at six the sun was almost gone, the valley below already shrouded in darkness. Lieutenant Gómez's presence made it impossible for Razor to share the news of his sighting with his SAS partner, but that didn't seem too much of a problem. He had seen no signs of searchlights among the Kaibiles' equipment, and assumed they would soon receive word that Cabrera was calling it a day. And a pretty futile one at that.

Another half an hour went by, drawing the night down across the sky. Razor was just wondering how to find out what the hell the Kaibil CO was doing when a scream sounded across the valley, pulling silence after it like a shroud.

'What the fuck?' Chris growled.

In the darkness the voices of the nearby Kaibiles were animated, almost exultant.

Another scream rang out, quieter this time, almost animal-like. Maybe it was an animal. Maybe . . .

A single shot resounded.

'Ricardo,' Razor said coldly. 'What the fuck's going on down there?'

Gómez spread his hands. 'I do not know,' he replied.

'I think we ought to find out,' Razor said, getting to his feet and staring down into the murk of the valley.

'No, I will go,' Gómez said, a pleading tone in his voice.

Razor looked at him, and then at Chris. 'OK,' he agreed.

The liaison officer disappeared down the slope.

'I wish to God we had a nightscope,' Razor muttered.

'We might not like what we see,' Chris said.

'No.'

They had been waiting almost a quarter of an hour when Gómez reappeared. 'We are returning to the base at Uspantan,' he said, as if that answered all their questions.

'And the screaming and the shot?'

'Oh, one of the men walked into a snake that was hanging from a branch. He panicked, but his comrade shot the snake.' Gómez spewed out the words in a rush, as if eager to get rid of them. And even in the darkness it was obvious that he was strenuously avoiding eye contact.

Two hours later, as they waited on the road for the trucks to return and collect the company, the two Englishmen looked in vain for any sign of the Indian guide.

Hajrija watched Maria Martínez stir three sugars into her coffee and wondered how the girl managed to keep her figure. It was partly sheer youth, she supposed, and partly the non-stop outpouring of nervous energy. Maria was presumably working on the theory that the more she said the more Hajrija would understand, because she had hardly stopped talking in the two hours they had been out together. She was talking now.

'*Más despacio*,' Hajrija told her. More slowly.

Maria grinned and tried again, mixing in some mime for good measure. Eventually Hajrija understood that she was talking about the ruined nunnery which they had just visited, and the small cells where particularly devout nuns had permanently incarcerated themselves, all the better to realize the glory of God.

'All the life,' Maria added indignantly in English, as if the nuns had done it just to spite her. 'No music, no dancing, no sex,' she said, picking up the chocolate croissant. 'No life,' she concluded, biting into it.

Hajrija smiled. It was hard for her to sympathize with the nuns' self-denial, even when it was being attacked in the name of self-indulgence. Looking at the convent cells, her first thought had been of lives without children.

She wished now she had told Razor about the baby.

He woke up in the barracks room shortly after seven in the morning, and reached out lazily for a wife who wasn't there. He groaned inwardly and lay there for a while, mulling over the difficult situation he and Chris were in. No clever means of extrication occurred to him.

The trucks had arrived back at the Uspantan base soon after midnight, and the deflated soldiers had been sent straight to their barracks. Razor and Chris had been invited to a post-mortem with drinks, but on impulse Razor had pleaded tiredness. He knew it would be futile to ask about the Indian guide – would, in fact, simply alienate Cabrera – but he was weary enough not to trust his own sense of discretion, particularly with a drink in his hand. In the morning, he had reasoned, he would probably find it easier to keep a cool head.

And, lying there on the bunk, he supposed he did feel more resigned. The anger was still there, but its focus seemed to have shifted, away from bastards like Cabrera and Osorio, and more towards the bastards in Washington and London who had agreed to help them.

There was a stirring in the bunk above, a groan, and the sudden appearance of the familiar face and spiky hair.

'Just realized where you are?' Razor asked.

'Dead right.'

'I don't know what you're complaining about – governments seem to be queuing up to pay for your bird-watching expeditions these days.'

'Not to mention your family holidays,' Chris retorted.

'Some holiday.'

Chris lowered himself out of the upper bunk and down to the floor. 'So let's go out on the sun terrace and order breakfast.'

'They never have Weetabix at these posh resorts,' Razor said, reaching for his trousers.

A couple of minutes later they were walking across the grassy parade ground, enjoying their first taste of another gorgeous day. The blue sky hung above the amphitheatre of mountains, and the sun lit the white church which rose from the centre of the town below. For the twenty seconds it took to reach the canteen, it was possible to believe that those who lived in Guatemala had been blessed.

Once inside, they were served tortilla, rice and refried beans by a smiling adolescent boy. The meal tasted better than it looked, which wasn't difficult. The accompanying coffee tasted worse, which was.

'And these are the privileged troops,' Chris murmured, just as Gómez spotted them from the doorway. The lieutenant hoped they had slept well, that the breakfast wasn't too bad – a rueful smile, here – and that they would accompany him to the colonel's office.

This was in the small building next door, and looked very much a temporary affair. The Kaibiles, Razor realized, would be shifted around the country to where they were most needed at any given time. Such a *modus operandi* would not only make military sense, but also deeply affect the character of the regiment. The life of eternal nomads would both strengthen the regiment's morale and prevent it from forming any human ties with the people of a particular locality. They were like a praetorian guard, Razor thought, with the families of Zona 14 standing in for an emperor.

Colonel Cabrera was sitting behind his desk, talking to the standing Major Osorio. He greeted the SAS men with a smile, asked the same questions as Gómez concerning their sleep and breakfast, and apologized for what he called 'yesterday's fiasco'. Their source of information had proved untrustworthy.

'So we understood,' Razor said coldly.

Cabrera chose to ignore the tone. 'The next operation will be more successful,' he promised, 'but it may be a couple of days, perhaps more, before we can move again. Is there anything you need or want?'

Razor looked at Chris, who shook his head. 'No thanks. I assume it's safe for us to take a look at the town?'

Cabrera looked surprised for a moment, but quickly recovered. 'Of course. It is perhaps more sensible to visit in the daylight. Uspantan is a safe town, but there are criminals everywhere. In the daylight they hide. And I'm sure Lieutenant Gómez can find you somewhere good to eat lunch.'

Gómez looked doubtful, but agreed nevertheless.

Walking round Uspantan proved a depressing business. The smiles which had characterized each meeting of eyes in Guatemala's Plaza Mayor, and the sense of joy which had been so much a part of that evening, were both conspicuous by their absence. As the three men strolled around the streets only the children offered anything other than a cold stare in response to their greetings. Gómez clearly found it hard to understand, and became both angry and apologetic.

'Don't worry about it,' Razor told him, wondering as he did so at how little Gómez understood of his own country. Uspantan was the Falls Road without the graffiti – sullen, resentful, an occupied town.

The largest hotel was apparently owned by a Ladino, but the only staff on display were Indians. They served up a typical *comida* lunch, which Gómez insisted on paying for. Outside the hotel he hopefully asked the SAS men if they had seen enough.

But Razor had spotted a Guatel office on the other side of the square. 'I'd like to call Hajrija,' he told the liaison officer.

'It will be quicker from the base.'

'Can't we do it from over there?' Razor asked. 'I don't like taking up a military line for a personal call,' he added ingenuously.

Gómez failed to come up with a better reason for refusal. 'Yes, you can call from there,' he agreed.

The three men walked across to the tiny office, and began negotiating with the man in charge. Half an hour and several breakdowns later the man achieved what only twenty minutes earlier he had described as impossible, connecting Razor with the Antigua number which Chris had supplied.

He listened to it ring, inwardly praying that she would be there. She was, and for ten minutes they chatted about nothing in particular, simply happy to hear each other's voice. She was going to Panajachel on the following day, she said, and gave him the name of the hotel at which she was planning to stay. Not trusting the phone, he told her nothing about how their mission was going, save to say that there was no sign of it soon being over.

After hanging up, he paid the operator in quetzals and walked slowly across to where the others were sitting on a bench, feeling surprised, and even a little ashamed, at how much he missed her.

Having spent much of the previous night returning by a deliberately circuitous route to the *compa* camp, Tomás slept through most of the daylight hours. The sun was barely above the horizon when Emelia woke him, and the distant mountains were turning purple in the fading light.

'There's an operations meeting,' Emelia told him.

Tomás rubbed his eyes, yawned, and kicked aside the thin blanket. 'I'm on my way,' he said.

He left her opening the Spanish primer, and walked up to the ancient ruins, where the rest of the *subcomandantes* had already gathered. The large chunks of broken stone had once been part of an ancient fort, from which their ancestors had tried in vain to defy the Spanish invaders. The latter and their descendants had long since forgotten the place, but the Mayan Indians had not, and the continuity which it represented always gave Tomás a feeling of strength. Sometimes he thought he could almost smell the incense which had been burned here half a millennium before.

He found a space in the rough circle and sat down.

'OK, Tomás,' the Old Man said, 'tell the others what you saw yesterday morning.'

'Kaibiles,' Tomás said tersely, looking round at the other seven faces in the circle. 'About company strength – roughly a hundred men. They were concealed in the trees, so I couldn't get an accurate count. Just below the pass, in the valley of the Chitac. You know, the old Jimón farm.' He smiled. 'They were waiting for some guerrillas to march over the pass singing revolutionary songs.'

'I think we know who they were waiting for,' the Old Man said softly.

'Yes,' Alicia agreed, 'but why there?'

'One of our people was with them,' Tomás said. 'I didn't recognize him.'

'Shit,' Gerardo muttered, sounding sad rather than angry. They all knew the many kinds of pressure the Army could exert. 'He probably just took them somewhere that would seem convincing,' he added.

'Maybe,' the Old Man said. 'But the important thing is that the Kaibiles know we are in the area . . .'

'They could be guessing,' someone suggested hopefully.

'They could be, but I doubt it. And there's something else,' he added, looking at Tomás. 'There were two gringos with them.'

'*Norteamericanos*,' Gerardo spat out contemptuously.

'Maybe,' Tomás said. 'One of them could have been a *norteamericano* – he had the short hair that looks like a brush – but the other . . . I don't know. But that is not the important thing. The second man, he saw me – we found each other with our field-glasses at exactly the same moment, and I don't think he can have told anyone. There was no alarm, no one followed me, and when I was sure of that I went back. They were still deployed for the ambush.'

There was a silence while the others took this in.

'Maybe he took you for one of the Kaibiles,' Rosa said at last.

'That is not funny,' Tomás said indignantly.

'But possible,' the Old Man admitted. 'There is no way we can know, so we must leave it as a mystery for the moment. What we need to decide now is where we go from here. And as I see it we have only two choices – retreat or engagement. We cannot just go to ground in this area.'

'But can we take on the Kaibiles?' Alicia asked doubtfully.

'Not on ground of their choosing, no. But on ground that we have chosen – perhaps that could be a different story.' The Old Man let his eyes drift around the circle. 'We knew when we started this that the risks would grow greater with each day that passed.'

6

Soon after ten o'clock on Sunday morning, with the base canteen coffee still rumbling in their stomachs, Razor and Chris climbed into the jeep which Gómez had requisitioned for their trip to Chul, the nearest of the so-called 'model villages'. Two Kaibil soldiers were accompanying them, one at the wheel and one perched precariously on the back.

Gómez had suggested the trip the previous evening, and the SAS men had decided that anything would be better than a whole day spent either sitting round the base or wandering round a hostile town. Razor had also told himself, without much conviction, that it was only fair to see the other side of the argument. If the Army really was doing something positive in the area, that would at least be some compensation for all the rest. And it might make him feel better about being in the position he was in.

Chul was about fifteen kilometres from Uspantan, but the drive, down one broad valley by paved road and up a long and narrow one by dirt track, took the best part of an hour. The village nestled in a flat fold of the foothills of the Cuchumatanes and at first sight looked remarkably like an Alpine village, with neat rows of wooden houses and well-kept fields surrounded by forested slopes. But there was something very un-Guatemalan about it, Chris thought, as the jeep descended the winding approach road. Chul looked more like a model than a real village.

A flat, triangular space with one set of football posts occupied the village centre. While Gómez went looking for the local *comandante*, the two Englishmen wandered out on to the thick grass, gazing around them. The whitewashed church was the only adobe building; all the houses were timber-built, as was the tall and apparently unmanned watch-tower. The streets were unpaved, a mess of mud and pebbles, but new lights had been installed.

The classic Third World sense of priorities, Chris thought. Electricity brought radios and TVs, the lure of the city and a world built around money and the hunger for things. It made the rural areas dependent on the city. A decent water supply and sewage system on the other hand . . . well, they might improve the health of the local people, but they would also encourage a dangerous sense of independence.

There was at least a standpipe in the village. Three women were gathered round it now, chatting with each other as they filled up identical green and white striped plastic jars. They didn't seem bothered by the Kaibiles or the gringos, which Razor and Chris assumed had to be a good sign.

An Army officer emerged from one of the nearby houses, trailing Gómez in his wake. He was young, and wore old-fashioned circular-rimmed glasses which reminded Razor of Julie Christie's husband in *Doctor Zhivago*. There was no fanaticism in this man's eyes, though – only a sort of harassed cheerfulness. He introduced himself as Major Francisco Gramajo, shook their hands, asked the usual question about how they liked Guatemala, and took them on a tour of a building which served as both the medical centre and food distribution outlet. The villagers, he explained, received both medical help and supplies free of charge. All the men had to do in return was spend so much time each week undertaking communal duties, like road repairs, reconstruction and stints with the Civil Patrols.

He then took them on a walk round the village, greeting by name each person who crossed their path. The villagers' response was polite enough, if somewhat lacking in enthusiasm.

'What happened to the old village?' Chris asked him, having glimpsed traces of several former buildings.

'It was burned by the *subversivos*,' Gramajo explained. 'Seven, eight years ago now. The people who lived here ran away, and there was no village here for several years. Then the Government brought in new settlers, and they replanted the land' – he gestured towards the cornfields in the distance – 'and of course the Army was given the primary responsibility for their safety. But not all – the new settlers were only too happy to form Civil Patrols and make certain there was no chance of the *subversivos* returning. And, as you can see, it is working. The villagers here have a good life – enough land, food, medicine.' He glanced at them, as if expecting agreement.

'Looks good,' Razor said diplomatically.

'It is,' Gómez agreed with a satisfied smile.

They went back to Gramajo's office in the Army headquarters building, where a *comida* lunch was waiting, along with half a crate of ice-cold Gallo beer. The Indian women who served them seemed pleasant enough, but there was no disguising the reserve in their eyes. None of the four men sitting at the table had any idea what these women were thinking, Razor thought. Chul seemed benign enough on the surface, but it was another occupied town. And who knew how much of the apparent placidity had been deliberately staged for their benefit. Gómez seemed as innocent of deception as ever, but then it could just as well have been staged for his benefit too.

On the drive back to Uspantan Razor decided that there was no way for a foreigner to be certain of where right and wrong lay in Guatemala – the place was too surreal, too Alice-in-Wonderlandish. In the last resort there was nothing to rely on but his own instincts, and he supposed he should have known that all along.

'Fuck it,' he muttered to himself, and decided to give his brain a rest, at least for the duration of the ride back to the base. Whatever else Guatemala might be, it was certainly beautiful, and he let his eyes feast on the landscape, each shade and line so vibrant in the clear mountain air.

In the adjoining seat, Chris was thinking about his partner while his eyes scanned the trees and sky for birds. He had few doubts concerning their mission in Guatemala – as far as he was concerned, it simply stank of political opportunism. But he was only along for the ride, whereas Razor was actually required to give these people something. Chris could understand why that might involve a degree of wishful thinking. No one wanted to believe they were helping the bad guys.

Having that wishful thinking slowly dissolve was no doubt a painful process – it was certainly painful to watch. But as far as Chris could see there was nothing they could do about their situation, or at least not until Razor got the chance to identify either prisoners or corpses. When that time came he could simply refuse to pick out the man the Guatemalan Army wanted, and at least keep his conscience clear on one account. Of course, a new problem might then arise – the Army could demand their continued presence until such time as Razor did identify someone as El Espíritu.

It was a no-win situation all right. Chris found himself wondering what Jamie Docherty would have done, and decided the Scot would have been just as stuck as they were.

They reached the end of the dirt track and turned west along the paved road, just as a bus rattled through in the opposite direction, trailing the usual toxic cloud of exhaust. They were only a few miles from Uspantan when Chris spotted a turkey vulture hanging almost motionless above the valley. He turned his field-glasses on the bird, which seemed to stare straight back at him before wheeling to match the speed of the jeep, and fly a course almost directly above their own. Chris pointed it out to Razor, who stared up at the vulture with an ironic smile. Its shadow, Chris realized, could be seen on the road ahead, as if they were following in its wake.

On the outskirts of Uspantan the vulture peeled away and headed back down the valley, as if it had successfully completed its task of escorting them through its territory. They drove through the town and up the steep hill to the military base, stopped for the obligatory security check at the gate, and finally pulled up outside the main barracks.

'Siesta time,' Chris suggested, before Gómez could suggest anything else.

'Sounds good . . .' Razor began, but the distant scream cut him off.

It was a muffled scream, but there was no mistaking the

agony which had fuelled it. And as Razor caught Gómez's reluctant eye, it sounded again.

Razor looked down at the ground for a moment, then abruptly turned on his heel and started across the grass in the direction of Colonel Cabrera's office. Chris hurried after him. 'Señor Wilkinson,' Gómez pleaded. 'Señores.'

Reaching the headquarters building, Razor ignored the tentative requests of the duty sentries and walked straight in. He didn't bother to knock on Cabrera's door either, simply swinging it open and marching inside. The colonel and his number two were in almost the same positions – one sitting, one standing – as they had been the day before. Watching Cabrera's face, Razor saw sudden fear give way to anger and anger to an empty smile. 'Señores,' he said brightly, 'what can . . . ?'

'There is someone being tortured on this base,' Razor said flatly.

'That is not . . .' Cabrera started to say, when the faint but unmistakable sound of another scream drifted in through the open door.

'We were assured by your Government,' Razor went on relentlessly, 'that this operation would be conducted with due respect for accepted standards of human rights. We will not be a party to inhumane treatment of prisoners, and I demand that whatever is going on here be stopped immediately.'

Cabrera half rose out of his chair, his face reddening.

Osorio's face had gone white. 'You demand?!' he hissed. 'This is not your country. You . . .'

'Major,' Cabrera said warningly, before Osorio could add anything else. The younger man's anger seemed to have defused his own, or at least given him time to conceal it.

'It is you who asked us for help,' Razor said coldly. He was shaking inside.

'Yes, yes,' Cabrera agreed. 'Please . . . you must understand, this is a war situation, we have to interrogate people, and sometimes . . . well, when their comrades' lives are at stake, then the interrogators get carried away. I am not excusing this, simply trying to explain it. We will attend to the matter. Major,' he said, nodding at Osorio, who gave the two Englishmen one last angry look and stalked out. 'He will see to it,' Cabrera said. 'I apologize for his words. He is a patriot, you understand, and young. He finds it hard to accept direction from outsiders.' Cabrera smiled. 'I'm sure that you would not like Guatemalans telling your English officers how to behave in your Northern Ireland.'

'No,' Razor agreed. He felt certain of Cabrera's insincerity, and no less angry, but there was nothing else to say. 'Thank you, Colonel,' he ground out.

'It is my pleasure.'

The two Englishmen withdrew from the office past an ashen Gómez, and the last thing they heard was Cabrera telling the lieutenant to close the door. 'Maybe he brought us back too soon,' Chris wondered out loud.

Razor said nothing.

They walked back across the parade ground, hearing no screams.

'For all I know, they've just put a sock in the poor bastard's mouth,' Razor said bitterly.

Chris shrugged. 'You couldn't have done any more. If they want to torture someone, it won't be hard to find somewhere out of earshot.'

'Yeah, I know.'

Back in their room the two men stretched out on their

bunks, Razor with his novel, Chris with his Walkman. He started off with U2's *Joshua Tree*, but soon exchanged it for R.E.M.'s *Monster* – some of the lines on the former just seemed a bit too close to home. '*A heart of darkness, a firezone . . . his blood still cries from the ground . . . where bullets rape the night of the merciful . . .*' It was easier to get lost in the sheer exuberance of Peter Buck's power-chords.

The afternoon dragged by, and they went for an early supper in the deserted canteen. It was there that Gómez found them. He greeted them with a smile, but there was distress in his eyes. The world was not working the way it should, with conflict replacing the harmony he loved, and himself caught in the middle. He sat down beside them but didn't say anything for a moment, as if he was building up the courage to do so. 'It is Sunday night,' he said eventually, 'and Colonel Cabrera has told me to ask you if you would like some female company.'

Razor and Chris looked at each other. 'Thank the colonel,' Razor told the Guatemalan, 'but no.'

'I understand,' Gómez said quickly, getting to his feet. 'You have happy marriage.'

'Yeah,' said Razor tersely.

They watched him leave the canteen, both feeling sorry for him.

'This is turning into a fucking mess,' Razor said. 'And the temptation to just pack it in and go home is getting stronger every day.'

Chris looked at him. 'What makes you think they'd let us go?'

* * *

Sixty-five kilometres to the south, Hajrija was sitting in the aptly named Sunset Café, watching the last throes of the day. Across Lake Atitlán the three volcanoes were starkly silhouetted against a deep-red sky, offering a vista which seemed almost too postcard-perfect to be true.

All around, fellow tourists were picking at bowls of nachos and drinking Cuba Libres, cold Gallos, even milk shakes. Between taking snaps they fended off the beautiful little Indian girls who were trying to sell them miniature dolls, parrot necklaces, purses and friendship bracelets. Hajrija already had two pocketfuls of souvenirs, all purchased for the princely sum of a dollar.

She had left Antigua late that morning on a special tourist bus. It had cost ten times the ludicrously cheap fare on the local buses, but a visit to the Mayan site of Iximche had been included in the price, and for that reason she had not resented paying the extra. The site had been interesting enough, but watching the crowded local buses on the road she had come to regret not taking one. It would have been more like travelling in Guatemala, less like travelling through it. And the wonderful views, culminating in that first breathtaking panorama of the lake as the road wound down from Sololá, would not have been any less spectacular.

The bus had arrived in Panajachel soon after noon, and after getting a room at the hotel Chris had recommended she set out to explore the 'village', most of which was now given over to the various functions of tourism. A lovely old church survived at the end furthest from the lake, but the kilometre-long road which ran down to the shore was lined with tour companies, restaurants and stall upon stall selling the brilliantly coloured Mayan Indian artefacts in dizzying profusion. There was too much, really, and it was all a little too touristy. Or it seemed that way until she saw the lake.

Hajrija had no trouble believing that Atitlán was the most beautiful lake in the world. The deep blue-green waters were a perfect complement to the pure blue sky, and the clouds which perched like haloes above the volcanoes seemed to have been placed there by either God or an exceptional artist. She had stood gazing at it all for a long time, simply drinking it in, and wishing Razor was there to share it with her.

She was marvelling still, as the light faded from the sky. At the other tables everyone was speaking in hushed murmurs, as if they were in church. Only the little Indian girls seemed immune, and they presumably witnessed this scene every day of their lives.

As the first pinpricks of light glimmered in the darkening firmament Hajrija ordered another Cuba Libre, and thanked whatever lucky stars had brought her to Guatemala.

The transferred call from Uspantan reached Colonel Serrano's home in the middle of the family dinner. He excused himself with some relief – one more argument between his wife and daughter about the latter's lifestyle and he would seriously consider eating in the Palacio Nacional canteen.

In his study he listened patiently to Osorio's angry account of the altercation with the Englishmen, then gave him a verbal rap on the knuckles. 'Colonel Cabrera acted correctly,' he told the younger man coldly. 'We need the co-operation of the Englishmen, and that means we must take account of their sensitivities, no matter how misplaced they might be.'

Osorio said he understood that, but . . .

Serrano wished him goodnight and replaced the receiver, but made no immediate move to reclaim his seat at the head of the dining-room table. There was something seriously wrong with Osorio, he thought, despite the young man's impeccable breeding. Or maybe because of it. The man seemed to have no centre: one minute he was turning to Evangelism, the next to pleasures which Serrano found dangerously perverse.

But he did understand Osorio's anger at the Englishmen's behaviour. The hypocrisy of it! When the English had colonized North America, the Indians had been virtually wiped out. In Australia they had left the native inhabitants to rot in the desert. In South Africa they and the Dutch had invented apartheid.

Serrano reached for his cigarettes, remembered he was officially in the middle of dinner, and put them back. If Guatemala had killed all its Indians the way the *norteamericanos* had killed theirs, then who would the Anglos in Hollywood have to do all their cooking and cleaning?

Razor and Chris were woken in the small hours by Gómez, presented with Colonel Cabrera's compliments, and asked to be ready for departure in fifteen minutes. They cursed their way through the routines of dressing, weapons-checking and make-up, and emerged into the cold mountain air with a minute to spare. The same four trucks were waiting in line on the parade ground, exhausts spewing yellow smoke into the glow from the headlights.

Once again the two SAS men were gestured into the second truck, and within minutes the convoy was making its way down the hill and through the town.

'They have found a guerrilla unit,' Gómez explained in English.

'Where?' Razor asked, thinking as he did so that two days ago Gómez would probably have used 'we', not 'they'.

'In the mountains,' Gómez said vaguely. 'Not very far from the place we try the ambush. Maybe two hours in the truck, then an hour on foot.'

'How were they found?' Chris asked, but Gómez didn't know.

The trucks rumbled on, bouncing the twenty-odd men up and down like a team of synchronized kangaroo-impersonators.

'Why the hell don't they use choppers?' Chris wondered out loud.

'Too noisy, maybe?'

'This is quiet?'

'Weather conditions then. These mountains always seem to be draped in clouds in the early morning – must make landings difficult.'

It was almost four o'clock when the convoy reached its destination, the front yard of what looked, in the dark, like a deserted estate. The company formed themselves into a column and moved off, heading across abandoned fields. Visibility was not much more than a hundred metres, confirming Razor's hypothesis.

They marched for the hour Gómez had promised, and then for the best part of another. Most of the route lay uphill through forest, though sometimes they had to traverse bare and stony slopes. The temperature seemed to drop steadily as the altitude increased and dawn grew nearer. The mist seemed to thicken, though bare patches would still present themselves, allowing views of the long column stretching away to both front and rear. But for most of the time there was no real sense of the surrounding terrain: it was like marching through a cloud. Whoever their guide was, he probably deserved a medal.

Even on a bad day, Razor thought, the Brecon Beacons would have a hard job competing with this. He cheered himself up with the thought that the chances of their being ambushed by the guerrillas had to be pretty remote.

That optimism began to fray at the edges when the company reached its deployment point. 'There is an old fort halfway up this hill,' Colonel Cabrera explained to them, 'and we have reason to believe that a unit of *subversivos* is hiding out there now.'

'What reason?' Razor asked bluntly.

'There are several indications.' He counted them off on his fingers. 'One, we have satellite intelligence which points in this general direction. Two, there are reports of theft from a nearby village. Three, smoke was spotted early yesterday evening by a routine reconnaissance flight. Four, an informant has told us that this place is frequently used by the *subversivos*.' He shrugged. 'It looks promising, yes?'

'Uh-huh,' Razor said noncommittally. 'Can I see the map?'

Cabrera looked slightly surprised by the request, but passed both map and torch to the SAS man. The old fort had been marked with a red cross, and two lines of approach pencilled in. Other lines, drawn in a rough circle around the mountain, apparently represented a perimeter ring. Razor checked the scale. The ring had to be at least two kilometres long, which was a lot of ground for, say, half the company to cover. And the contour lines showed that the slopes of the mountain were streaked with deep ravines, any one of which could offer an escape route for encircled guerrillas.

'Are you going to wait for the mist to clear?' he asked Cabrera.

The hovering Osorio gave the two Englishmen a pitying look. 'We would lose the element of surprise,' the colonel replied.

A few minutes later the two SAS men joined the rear of the right-hand column and began the ascent of the steep mountain path. It was now almost six o'clock, and the mist, though no thinner, was perceptibly lighter. As they climbed up through it, feeling like disoriented divers searching blindly for the surface, Razor began to feel his sixth sense twitch with foreboding.

A couple of hundred metres above them Emelia Xicay stared over the lip of the trench which she and Jorge had dug the previous evening. Visibility was less than thirty metres, but she had a perfectly adequate view of the path below, which narrowed to a metre or so as it wound between the steep outcrop and precipitous drop. The Kaibiles would have no choice but to climb this section of the path in single file, in full view of the two trenches and their four *compa* rifles. Always assuming they came.

For the moment she could hear nothing but the slight breeze in the trees behind her. Even the birds had fallen silent, as if they knew what was coming. She imagined the soldiers further down the mountain, slowly climbing the path. It had been Kaibiles who had killed her mother, and the thought of falling into their hands made her shiver.

She looked round at Jorge, whose face betrayed the fear she felt, and they grinned at each other almost sheepishly. How good it would be to talk, she thought. The previous evening the four of them had played tapes on José's boom box and sang along as they dug the trenches, lit a fire and cooked a meal, talked and laughed . . . They had done all the things a *compa* unit could never usually do, and it had felt like a small piece of heaven, a small piece of ordinary life.

How much more of their lives would they have to spend in silence, in hiding?

She looked at her watch. In an hour or so the sun would begin to burn away the mist, and then they would have to abort the ambush, because there was no way they could hope to escape from the mountain in the full light of day. If the Kaibiles didn't find them then the helicopter gunships would.

The path zigzagged across the forested slopes, easy in some places, difficult in others. The mist was slowly suffused with daylight, but refused to lift from the deep ravines or the treetops. As always, Chris moved forward with one eye alert for danger, the other searching for birds in the trees. Behind him, at the rear of the column, Razor was asking himself why guerrillas would light a fire on a mountain. There were only two reasons he could think of. Either they were too drunk to care or they wanted to attract attention. And from what he remembered of the old man at Tikal the former seemed unlikely.

They passed a point which Razor remembered from the map, where the path took an abrupt turn and began following the contour across the slope. In a couple of hundred metres it would turn again, and resume climbing through a series of steep hairpin bends, eventually reaching the high valley and its ancient fort.

Abruptly, Chris stopped, and turned to face Razor. 'Listen,' he whispered.

Razor listened, but all he could hear was the soft footfalls of the Kaibiles receding into the distance.

'No birds,' Chris whispered.

Razor looked at him. 'We've scared them away.'

'They've been singing all around us since we started climbing – haven't you noticed?'

Razor hadn't, but he got the point. 'I think we've gone far enough,' he said.

The two men retraced a few of their steps. Where the path dipped into the ravine to cross the stream, they took up positions which would protect them from all but the luckiest of stray bullets, and waited. Less than a minute later the mountain above them exploded with gunfire.

It had been agreed in advance that they would allow twenty men to pass the rock at the beginning of the single-file stretch before opening fire. As luck would have it there was a long gap between the nineteenth and twentieth Kaibiles, and for several nerve-racking seconds Emelia waited for one of the other three to jump the gun. But then the twentieth man stepped into view, and the sound of all four rifles firing simultaneously was like an explosion.

Each of the four *compas* had been allocated five of the targets, and being the best shot Emelia had been given the leading group. The first man was easy, and he seemed to be tumbling backwards into the mist before she heard the shot. The second was just as straightforward: apparently paralysed by the shock of his comrade's sudden demise, he stood stock-still long enough for her to put more than the one necessary bullet through his upper torso.

Then it got difficult. Her other three targets were moving, two trying to move up, one to head back. She took out the latter first, coolly knocking him back into the abyss. She felt completely cool, unhurried, dispassionate. The voice which said 'they killed my mother' sounded calm as a litany in the back of her mind – there was no anger in it, only justice. The fourth man went down on the path, tripping the fifth, who was still struggling to his feet when she sent a bullet through his left ear.

Beside her she heard Jorge's gun jam, and the curse that followed. Three of his five were down, but two more were fighting their way past their fallen comrades. She took out the second, but the first reached the safety of the overhanging rock which marked the upper end of the single-file stretch. If he felt either brave or stupid enough there was now nothing to stop him coming up after them.

Or maybe he didn't think it would be necessary. It seemed only seconds later that a grenade arced into view, clattered against the cliff face just beneath them and exploded in almost the same instant, sending up a cloud of rock fragments.

'Time to go,' she told Jorge, who was still struggling with his jammed rifle.

He nodded.

She took one last elated look at the body-strewn path and ducked back along the lateral trench which they had dug for this moment. She wriggled through the gap between the two boulders and emerged a couple of metres above the path, pausing for a second to make sure it was still empty.

It was. She leapt down, making sure she bent at the knees as she landed – this was hardly the time for a sprained ankle. Confident that Jorge was behind, she started sprinting down the slope in front of her, heading for the shelter of the mist and the trees.

She had only gone twenty metres when gunfire exploded behind her, and she whipped round to see Jorge collapsing on the path. She ran back up the slope, and was five metres from the fallen *compa* when the Kaibil loomed up between the rocks above him. She fired once from the hip, and it was the luckiest shot of her life, taking him right between the eyes. The Kaibil's feet seemed to keep moving forward and he slithered over the drop and on to the path, coming to rest with his head in his lap like a broken doll.

Emelia turned back to Jorge, despair in her heart. Blood was pouring from a huge wound in his neck. She leaned the rifle against him and reached for a cloth to stem the wound, her ears straining for the sound of more Kaibiles. He smiled at her, and before she realized what he was doing, he had fixed one finger on the rifle's trigger and manoeuvred the end of its barrel into his mouth.

'No,' she cried, but he pulled the trigger.

There was no time to feel or think or do anything. Sensing movement on the path below, she tried in vain to prise the rifle from his grip, crossed herself, and took off down the slope for the second time. This time she reached the shelter of the trees, but as she did so the first bullet ripped through the foliage above her head. She turned, sinking to one knee, and took aim just as the Kaibil jumped down from the rocks. He landed on both feet, and was bouncing back up when the bullet tore away the side of his head. Another figure appeared behind him, but ducked back after sending another shot into the trees.

At almost the same instant she pulled the trigger on an empty chamber.

Resisting the temptation to abandon the heavy gun – getting hold of them had probably cost *compa* lives – she resumed her descent of the slope, expecting more bullets to follow. But for the moment none did.

The ravine seemed further than she remembered, and the dreadful thought that she had somehow got the direction wrong began to take root in her head. Then suddenly the ravine was almost at her feet, like a river of mist flowing down the mountainside. She plunged in, and started moving downhill as fast as the uneven ground would allow.

All the gunfire had now died away, and she wondered if the other two had also managed to reach their ravine. Even if they had, there was still the rest of the day to survive inside the inevitable ring. But the positions had been well prepared – all they had to do was reach them.

And the four of them had killed at least fifteen Kaibiles. This was a victory to sing about, she thought, just as the arms reached out and plucked the rifle from her grasp.

Her heart sank like a stone. Not only death, she thought, but all the rest as well. There were two of them, and they were even joking about it.

But not in Spanish, she realized. She looked closer, and saw that one of them had the hair like a brush which her brother had described. Beneath the paint on their faces they were gringos.

'*Vas*,' the other man was saying. '*Tu vas*. Go.'

She couldn't believe her ears, but the man was waving

her on like the traffic policemen she remembered from San Cristobal. Were they planning to shoot her in the back?

'*Vas. Rápidamente.*'

She did as she was told, looking back at the two strange soldiers, who turned away from her and started climbing out of the ravine, still clutching her empty rifle.

Razor was still thinking about the girl when one of Cabrera's NCOs came to collect them, with the news that there was a body to look at. For a moment he had thought he was meeting Hajrija for the second time – the same long, dark hair, same dark eyes, same slim figure in an olive drab uniform. This girl had been smaller, and her face, on closer inspection, rounder than his wife's, but even so it had been a shock.

And they had done the right thing in letting her go, he told himself, as the two of them followed the Kaibil up the steep path. The mist was lifting now, almost abruptly, as if its work of concealment was done. Two Kaibiles went past in the opposite direction, bearing a body of a comrade between them.

They climbed to the beginning of the single-file stretch and looked up at the rampart above. Half an hour ago, Razor guessed, the latter would have been close to invisible – the guerrillas had chosen their killing ground with skill. And killing ground it was: half a dozen bodies were still crumpled on the narrow path, and at least as many again could be seen at the foot of the precipice some twenty metres below.

The girl's gun had been empty, and she had been alone, but it was hard to believe one rifle could have done all this.

Colonel Cabrera was waiting by the body. The young guerrilla had taken what was probably a fatal shot to the neck, and had apparently decided to speed things along by taking his own life. There was a gaping hole where the back of his head had been, and brains were splattered across the rock behind him. Yet the expression on his face was almost serene.

It wasn't hard to guess why the man had killed himself. Razor imagined that being taken prisoner by the Kaibiles was about as life-enhancing as capture by bad-tempered nineteenth-century Apaches. And on this particular day, probably even less so. There was rage in the air all around him, rage that someone would be required to suffer for. He felt glad they had let the girl go.

'Do you recognize him?' Cabrera asked impatiently.

'No,' Razor said. 'The man I met in Tikal would be about forty years older than this.'

The colonel snorted in disgust. The Kaibiles weren't used to failure, Razor guessed. For the first time he understood how humiliating the mere existence of the old guerrilla leader must be for Cabrera and his men.

'How many of them were there?' he asked.

Cabrera shrugged. 'Maybe twenty – it's hard to tell. This fucking mist,' he said, looking round at the sunlit slope.

Behind him, Chris was lowering himself down from the ledge above, having just been to take a look at the guerrillas' firing position. By his reckoning there had been four of them, but it didn't seem very politic to say so.

'They still have to get off the mountain,' Razor commented.

The colonel gave him a withering look. 'They will be long gone now. Back to their holes in the earth.

The fucking mist,' he said again, as if that explained everything.

The return journey began mournfully, with half the remaining company strength detailed to carry the dead, and matters continued to deteriorate. They were less than halfway to their destination when a series of distant explosions echoed up the valley. It didn't take a genius to guess the source, and the remains of the four trucks were still smouldering when they reached the abandoned estate. The bodies of the two men left on guard were perched up against the old door of the estate office.

The Kaibiles settled down to wait for the summoned Chinooks, simmering with collective rage.

'Round two to your pensioner,' Chris murmured to Razor. 'At this rate we could be here for ever.'

'This bunch can lose battle after battle,' Razor said. 'My old man can't afford to lose one.'

7

Hajrija spent the Monday morning wandering round the streets of Panajachel, looking at all the beautiful things for sale and enjoying the sunshine. She didn't know whether it was the place, the baby growing inside her, or the long hours of sleep she was getting, but she felt almost unnaturally healthy, and capable of walking for hours without feeling at all tired.

Perhaps it had something to do with being on her own. Thinking back, she realized she hadn't had more than a few hours to herself since her early student days in pre-war Sarajevo, which were now more than five years in the past. College had given way to a life in which she was constantly on call, first as a hospital nurse, and then as a member of the Anti-Sniper Unit. In the latter role all trace of privacy had vanished – the unit had fought together, lived together, slept together, like a bunch of sexless children on a particularly grim holiday. Since arriving in England she had lived with Razor, and not knowing anyone else had initially been more dependent on his company than was probably healthy.

She didn't regret a moment of those five years, but she had to admit that it felt good to be on her own for a few days. Taking stock, working out where she was in her life, checking that the happiness she had grown accustomed to was real.

It seemed like it was. And the baby made it more so. My daughter, she told herself – she was already sure it was a girl. She hoped Razor wouldn't be disappointed, and didn't really think he would be. Despite his devotion to a predominantly male profession, he was a man who genuinely liked women. And these days it wasn't so hard for girls to play football.

Life was good, she thought. The continuing tragedy of her homeland, and her enduring sense of guilt for leaving, might still cast a shadow over everything else, but it was a shadow that had lately grown faint, as if it was unable to hold back the joy of her new life. The blue skies of Guatemala were threatening to dispel it completely.

That afternoon she took a boat across the lake to Santiago Atitlán, a large village nestling between volcanoes on the southern shore. From the rickety wooden landing-stage she walked up another street lined with woven goods for sale, and populated by predatory children with the faces of angels. By the time she reached the top of the hill, and the bedlam of the food market, she felt in need of silence and a place to sit.

It was a need easily satisfied, for passing through a gap between buildings, she found herself in a wide and virtually empty square. There was a raised fountain at its centre, and on the far side a beautiful white church, complete with bell tower, colonnaded entrance and a turquoise balcony. She sat on the fountain's steps, gazing at the church and the volcano which loomed behind it.

'Another perfect day,' she thought, just as a mobile sales force of six-year-olds erupted into the square.

*   *   *

It was late afternoon when the two Chinooks arrived back at the Uspantan base, and for most of the rest of that day the two SAS men kept to themselves, only venturing from the privacy of their room for a quick meal in the canteen.

Gómez also seemed keen to lower his profile. White-faced and silent for most of the morning and afternoon, he failed to even appear during the evening. At breakfast the following morning the two Englishmen looked for the lieutenant in vain, before deciding that they would walk down into the town without him. The guards on the gate were loath to let them go without either authorization or a chaperone, but a call to the colonel's office provided them with the former.

In the town their reception seemed subtly different, the faces a little more friendly, which led Razor to wonder whether news of their good deed on the mountain had already reached Uspantan. He hoped to hell it had not, because he certainly didn't fancy having to explain their quixotic gesture to Colonel Cabrera and Major Osorio.

They walked right through the town and out on to the valley road, enjoying the air and the exercise. About half a kilometre down, they found a path leading up into the hills and took it, climbing steadily up the partly wooded slopes for an hour or so, until the town and base were both spread out below, shrunken by the majesty of their surroundings. Razor was reminded again of Tolkien, and almost imagined he could detect a brooding cloud of uncertainty hanging above the military base.

But Mordor had been an ugly land, and this was far from that. He remembered something Jamie Docherty had said in Bosnia: the more beautiful a country, the more ugliness it seemed to bring out in people's souls. And he remembered his own answer: 'So how come there are so few saints in Birmingham?'

'What are you grinning about?' Chris asked.

Razor told him.

The East Anglian smiled, but only for a moment. 'Makes me wonder why it brings out the ugliness in some people's souls and not others,' he said.

On the way back through the town they stopped at the Guatel office, and after half an hour of trying the operator managed to connect Razor with Hajrija's hotel in Panajachel. She was out, so he left a message saying he would call again at six that evening.

Back at the base several of the Kaibiles were enjoying a kick-around on the parade ground, and Razor asked if he could join in. Chris looked at him as if he was mad, and disappeared in the direction of their room.

The Kaibiles were only too pleased to show the gringo how football should be played, and he had to admit that they did a pretty job of it. They certainly took no prisoners on the field, and at the end of an hour Razor felt like he'd been on a pitch with a dozen Ladino Vinny Joneses. Nursing his bruised shins in their room, he decided better them than Indian heads.

At five-thirty they set out for the town again, this time in the company of a quiet Lieutenant Gómez, who strolled round the darkening square with Chris as Razor talked on the phone. It seemed an age of waiting while the hotel receptionist went to find Hajrija, but then she was there, her voice full of everything he was missing.

'And how is my lover?' she asked.

'OK, considering.'

'Considering what?'

She sounded anxious. 'Considering I haven't seen you for a whole seven days,' he said, determined not to worry her.

'I know. I count them too.'

'But you're having a good time, right?' He could tell from her voice that she was, and discovered, almost to his own surprise, that he felt no resentment of the fact that she could do so without him.

'Yes, I am,' she admitted. 'But I wish you were having it with me.'

'So do I,' he said from the heart.

'Is it really bad?' she asked.

'I guess not. We're eating OK, sleeping OK. The place is beautiful. And we haven't been in any danger,' he added, with only slight exaggeration.

'How much longer – do you know?'

'Nope.'

'I have to change my hotel,' she told him, 'after tonight this one is full of tour parties. But I have a reservation in another.'

He wrote down the number she gave him, little realizing how important it would be.

They talked for another five minutes, and reluctantly said their goodbyes. Razor walked back across the square to join the others, just as a Chinook skimmed noisily above the town *en route* to the base. He remembered Chris wondering whether the plane above the square in Guatemala City had been a simple reminder of who held the real power, and the absurd thought crossed his mind that this helicopter had been sent to cast a shadow across his happiness with Hajrija.

* * *

As the sun sank beneath the rim of mountains to the west Tomás and the Old Man finished saying their goodbyes and started off down the trail. They had about twenty kilometres to walk before morning.

Tomás was sad to be leaving the *compa* camp. The victory over the Kaibiles had engendered a euphoric mood among the guerrillas, all of whom had seen enough in the way of hard times to really appreciate a few days of celebration. The sight of smiles on one another's faces for a few days would go a long way towards sustaining them all though the difficult months to come.

The comrades were still talking about Emelia's marksmanship and her incredible encounter with the strange gringos. Everyone had a different theory as to who they were and why they were with the Kaibiles, ranging from Jorge's belief that they were mentally retarded Americans to Alicia's that they were human rights monitors sent by the UN to observe the Army's behaviour. But there was nothing on the radio to substantiate the latter theory, and Emelia herself pooh-poohed the former. They hadn't spoken like Americans, she said, and they hadn't seemed stupid.

There was a down side to the euphoria, of course – an almost dangerous leap in confidence. Tomás privately considered the UN theory a typical example of wishful thinking, and he wasn't at all sure that the Old Man's decision to visit his sister's family's village – 'while the bastards are still running around like headless chickens' – was a wise one. At the very least, he had argued, the Old Man should take someone with him.

The Old Man had agreed, and chosen Tomás. Which, Emelia had said with a laugh, served him right.

Heading down the hill, the Old Man in front of him

setting a pace which belied his seventy-odd years, Tomás found himself wondering again about his sister's reaction to killing half a dozen men. Or more to the point, her lack of reaction. It was strange, the way he felt about this: he didn't want her to suffer for doing her duty, but neither did he want her to walk away completely unscathed. A death should never be taken lightly, not even the death of a Kaibil.

It was around ten in the evening, at the close of a long and boring Wednesday, when Gómez came to inform Razor and Chris that Colonel Cabrera wanted to see them in his office.

'Any idea what about?' Razor asked.

'None,' Gómez said. He had been monosyllabic all day, as if the lengthening separation from Guatemala City and his family was weakening his ability to string sentences together.

The three men walked across the floodlit parade ground in silence. A mixture of murmured conversation, angry shouts and raucous laughter floated across from the Kaibil barracks. In the space between the lights a thin crescent moon could be seen rising up behind the whale-like humps of the mountains.

Cabrera was standing behind his desk, leaning forward over the map which was spread across it. 'We may have found him,' he said, looking up at the Englishmen. He pointed at the map. 'Tziaca – a small village about twenty kilometres north-east of here, on the other side of the Cuchumatanes. We have word that two guerrillas arrived there this morning, one of them an old man.'

'Is this source reliable?' Razor asked. He hardly needed to add that the last two had not been.

'We think so. He has a lot to lose if he's lying to us.'

'So did that man the other day, but it didn't stop him.'

Cabrera nodded. 'Some of these men are fanatics. But . . . what can I say? There is never one hundred per cent certainty in these matters.'

'What makes you think the two men are still there now?' Chris asked.

'They may not be. But the older man's sister is ill, maybe dying, so there is a good chance they have taken a risk and stayed. And perhaps they are feeling a little full of themselves too, after their good fortune on the mountain. Anyway, we can lose nothing by taking a look.'

'OK,' Razor agreed.

'Good. This time, I do not intend to use the roads. Instead, a small group of eight men – including myself and both of you – will be inserted by helicopter around ten kilometres south of Tziaca. We will then move across country and establish an observation point outside the village before it wakes. If the two men are there we shall simply arrest them. If there are more *subversivos*, then I shall call in the rest of the company, which will be on stand-by here in the Chinooks.' He looked at the two SAS men in turn. 'How does that sound?'

Razor examined the map, wondering why Cabrera was being so accommodating. Fear of a third failure, perhaps. 'What's the terrain like around this village?' he asked.

'It's a small valley. The flat ground and the lower slopes have been cleared, but the upper slopes are forested. The only track runs north, down into this valley' – he pointed it out with his pen – 'but the obvious escape route is south.

There is a path that leads up into these mountains, which are heavily forested and full of hidden valleys which these people know like the back of their hand. That's why I can't risk an airborne assault,' he added. 'Give them a few minutes' warning and everyone in the village will disappear into thin air.'

'Do you have anyone who knows the village well?'

'Someone who used to live there.'

'Then it sounds like a good plan,' Razor said. Maybe the Kaibiles would make it third time lucky, he thought without enthusiasm. Still, at least that would get Chris and himself out of this damn country. 'When do we leave?' he asked.

Cabrera looked at his watch. 'In twenty-seven minutes.'

The SAS men went to make their preparations.

'Another fiasco, do you reckon?' Chris asked, as they sat side by side on the lower bunk checking the Uzis and Brownings.

A wide grin split Razor's darkened face. 'Fuck knows. I quite enjoyed the last two.' He sighed. 'But I can't say as I fancy spending the next ten years going on op after op with this bunch of incompetent psychos. Sooner or later someone will put a bullet in me.'

'Those bastards in London can't expect us to stay here for ever, can they?'

Razor shrugged. 'They've probably forgotten they sent us by now.'

'The CO won't have.'

'Yeah, let's send him a postcard next time we pass a souvenir shop.'

Chris turned to look at him. 'This is really getting to you, isn't it?'

'Isn't it getting to you?'

'I suppose so. I guess I've been assuming that since we don't have any real options, there's not much point in worrying about things.' He sighed. 'But yeah, I guess just about anywhere else would be an improvement.'

The helicopter was a Bell 212, otherwise known as the UH1N variant of the Huey Iroquois. Razor was pleased to see it wasn't one of the more common UH1Hs, which lacked an all-weather capability. A night flight through Guatemala's misty mountains was going to be pretty hairy as it was.

The two-man crew seemed cheerful enough, if not overly so. In Razor's experience most British military pilots were certifiable, and if these two Guatemalans were anything to go by then the condition was generic rather than national.

He and Chris joined a Kaibil NCO, four privates and an Indian civilian in the passenger space. The Kaibil soldiers all grinned at them, though not perhaps with quite the same enthusiasm as on their first meeting. They reminded Chris of his mother's dog after a scolding – eager to please, but still not quite certain what it had done wrong.

The Indian did not grin at them, but simply nodded his acknowledgement of their presence. He was wearing a straw hat, woven shirt, loose trousers and battered leather sandals. He seemed outwardly calm, but Razor thought he detected anger simmering beneath the surface. Or maybe not. Maybe he just expected Indians in this country to be angry.

Outside on the landing-pad Colonel Cabrera was giving an earnest Major Osorio his final instructions. The Chinooks he had mentioned had not yet arrived, but were no doubt on their way.

The colonel climbed aboard the Huey, the rotor drone

hit a higher note, and the helicopter lifted off into the night sky. For the next few minutes they flew up through thick mist, and then the view dramatically cleared, and for the rest of the flight they were treated to the dark shapes of mountains and a starry sky. The landing was one of the softest the two Englishmen had experienced, and the group of eight jumped down into a mountain meadow.

Cutting off the helicopter's engine only emphasized how loud it had been, and it was hard to believe that anyone in this part of the mountains had not been alerted to their presence. But the distance such sounds carried had been well researched by the Americans, first in Vietnam and then elsewhere, and these days all any competent commander needed to do was factor in terrain type, altitude, humidity and all the other variables, then read off the exact distance at which any particular model of plane or helicopter would be audible. If Cabrera hadn't done as much, then this probably would turn into another fiasco.

And this time, Razor thought, they would also be outnumbered, at least for the half hour required for the Chinooks to put in an appearance. And on this side of the mountains there seemed to be no mist to hide in either.

Who dares wins, he thought. Who dares needs his fucking head examined.

They set off, the Indian in the lead, along a fairly well worn track. The crescent moon, high in the sky by this time, offered enough light to make the walking infinitely easier than it had been on the two previous operations. Much of the ground had been cleared of trees, and every once in a while they saw evidence of former occupation. At one rest-stop, beside a stream noisy enough to cover the sound of conversation, Chris asked the Indian who lived on this land.

'No one,' he said laconically.

'And before?'

He looked around, as if uncertain whether he should be speaking to these gringos. 'There was a *finca* here,' he said, 'a coffee plantation. The owner was killed . . .' He shrugged.

'Who by?' Chris asked.

'The guerrillas, of course,' the Indian said, his face a mask.

They walked on, reaching the vicinity of the village soon after two-thirty. The Indian led them round in a wide arc to a position high on the hillside, from which a watch could be kept over the whole valley. A binocular scan of the village, whose nearest dwellings were some three hundred metres away, revealed no movement. The village was either sleeping or empty.

The first proof of the former came around three-thirty, when a baby started to cry. This noise was followed by others: something being dropped, a muffled shout, the scrape of something on the ground. Then a light briefly flared, and another. Through an open doorway Razor could see what looked like hanging torches, while silhouetted figures moved to and fro. Then a fire was lit, and another, and soon several thin columns of smoke were smudging the night sky.

Two young women emerged from the house Razor was watching, and while one began washing something in a container – corn, it looked like – the other began scrubbing a grindstone. Soon both were at work grinding the corn, while a scrawny dog watched them, his tail wagging furiously.

A man now emerged, and began working more noisily on another grindstone, sharpening first a hoe, then a machete, and finally an axe. He was not alone. As Razor shifted the binoculars he caught sight of at least four other males engaged in the same activity, and shutting his eyes for a moment, he could imagine the various sounds that were emanating from the village coalescing into a strange symphony.

Soon the women were rolling the ground corn into balls for the tortillas, pans were heating on the fires, and the smell of cooking was wafting up from the village.

There was something so elemental about the scene. The sounds and sights and smells of a community waking up. The process was utterly banal, probably varied hardly a whit from day to day, and yet Razor felt almost humbled by it. It all seemed so real, whatever the hell that meant.

The sky above the watchers was showing the first hint of dawn. The families sat round in circles eating the tortillas, and drinking a steaming liquid from either clay jars or plastic cups. The dogs had already been fed what looked like scraps, but waited in hope regardless.

Then, as if propelled by inner clocks, everyone but the eldest women and those with babies, gathered their farming implements and set out through the village, calling to their neighbours as they passed. Soon there were more than a hundred men, women and children making their way through the dawn twilight in the direction of the fields.

So far there had been no sign of any strangers, let alone men wearing the olive-green uniforms of the guerrillas, and as the light gradually brightened Razor began to entertain a growing hope that their quarry had already escaped.

The few women who stayed behind were busying themselves with a variety of tasks, attending to their babies, rolling more tortilla balls, sweeping out the houses. Most of the latter were low, two-storey affairs, with the ground floor reserved for living and the upper floor for storing corn. The walls were constructed from cane, the roofs from large palm leaves, and everything seemed tied together by plant fibres.

These people don't need any lessons in recycling, Razor thought wryly, just as something moving on the edge of his field of vision caused him to shift his view through the binoculars.

Two men and a young woman had emerged from one of the larger dwellings at the far end of the village. One of the men was young – in his twenties, Razor guessed – with a compact body and a face which looked friendly even though it held a frown. He was the guerrilla with whom Razor had shared a long-distance sighting the previous week.

The other man was much older. Razor had last seen him fifteen years before, walking away across the dew-soaked grass in Tikal's Plaza of the Lost World.

Both men were wearing olive-green uniforms, but neither seemed to be armed. They sat down side by side on a well-worn log while the woman poured them something from the tin kettle on the fire.

'Is it him?' Cabrera's voice hissed in his ear.

'I can't tell from this distance,' Razor lied. He found it hard to believe he was going to give this old man up to the tender mercies of the Kaibiles.

Cabrera looked disappointed, but gestured the two Englishmen to follow him down into the gully which lay just behind their observation point. 'Where do you think we should go from here?' he asked.

He was still covering himself against the possibility of another fiasco, Razor thought.

'Flush them out,' Chris suggested. 'From what I can see there's only the one obvious path leading up into the mountains – if you send a few of your lads up the track from the valley then these two will make a run for it up that path. We can be waiting for them.'

'And that'll reduce the risk of any civilian casualties,' Razor added.

Cabrera looked unimpressed for a moment, but then his face brightened. 'Flush them out,' he repeated, 'I like it. Flushing is what you do with shit, yes?'

The colonel grinned at them, and Razor knew in that instant that he could not finger the old guerrilla and live with himself. Sooner or later the Guatemalans would give him a suitable corpse to identify, and then he would be able to say yes, but there was no way he was giving up a living prisoner to the Kaibiles.

'Three men on the track, and the other five of us waiting on the path,' Cabrera was saying, apparently to himself. 'The three on the track can take some hostages in the fields, just in case these two decide to fight it out in the village.'

He went to give the orders, leaving Razor and Chris looking at each other. 'Ve vas only obeying orders,' Chris said with a mock-German accent.

'Maybe we can limit the damage,' Razor said quietly. 'Cabrera must have some notion of PR.'

'Yeah, he thinks it stands for pillage and rape.'

Razor smiled in spite of himself.

Cabrera returned with two of the Kaibiles and the Indian, who once more led the way. They had only about five hundred metres to travel as the crow flew, but the actual journey, which involved crossing a high ridge and then circling back down across a wide forested slope, was about four times as long. Cabrera constantly urged greater speed, for fear that the two men would escape while they were *en route*.

They reached the path at a point about half a kilometre above the village, and started looking for an ambush-friendly location. The trees, most of which seemed to be either pines or beeches, were far from densely packed, so they cautiously followed the direction of the village, looking for a sudden change in elevation which would offer concealment. They found it at the top of a small waterfall, where rough steps had been cut and kept by generations of village-dwellers. A man coming up them would see nothing of what was waiting at the top until it was too late.

The five men took advantage of what cover the vegetation offered and settled down to wait. Razor could not see the village from his position, but he could see the rest of the valley stretching into a distant green haze. His mind replayed the scenes of the village waking up: the child fondling the dog's ear, a woman squatting beside a fire with a flat pan full of tortillas, the man running his finger down the sharpened axe blade. And he thought about the SAS, and the rigours of the selection process they were all so proud of, and how they had been trained to endure conditions that would kill mere mortals.

Such conceit. In these mountains life was an endurance course from the cradle to the grave, and the penalty for failure was death.

He wished he was in the East Stand at White Hart Lane, twelve years old again, praying at the shrine of the great god Chivers for something as straightforward as a last-minute winner.

The sun appeared above the ridge away to their left. Half

an hour went by, then another fifteen minutes, and Razor could almost feel Cabrera's frustration reaching out across the ten metres that separated them. But there had been no word on the walkie-talkie from the other group, so there was no reason to think anything had gone wrong.

Maybe it had taken the three Kaibiles longer than expected to reach the track, Razor thought. Maybe they had stopped for a picnic, or defected to the guerrillas . . .

The sound of panting emerged from the auditory background of the waterfall, growing louder with each few seconds. A head came into view, an old man's head, with a deeply lined face and eyes that time and the wind had almost closed. He reached the top step and looked around, but either his eyesight was bad or the ambush was better concealed than Razor thought, because he showed no alarm. He was apparently unarmed.

The younger man was. His rifle appeared before he did, clambering over the rim and taking a deep breath.

'Drop the rifle,' Cabrera said. 'You are surrounded.'

As if on cue the two Kaibil privates stepped out on either side of the two guerrillas, their sub-machine-guns raised.

Slowly, reluctantly, the two men raised their hands above their heads. The young one was looking angrily at the Indian guide, but there was no anger in the Old Man's expression, just a resigned twist of amusement.

One of the Kaibiles yanked the pistol from the younger man's belt, picked up the rifle, and retreated a few steps.

Razor became aware of Cabrera's expectant look, and took a mental deep breath. He had to sound convincing . . .

'We meet again, Englishman,' the Old Man said conversationally, pulling the rug out from under his own feet.

'So it seems,' Razor said, his heart sinking.

'It is *him*,' Cabrera exclaimed triumphantly. He looked at Razor, and the look said: 'You knew, and you weren't going to tell me.' He walked forward until he was only a metre or so from the Old Man, looked him over from head to toe, and burst out laughing. 'Keeping you alive is going to be the real challenge,' he said.

He walked away, still shaking his head with amusement, and stood for several moments looking down at the village from the top of the waterfall. Then he spun abruptly round. 'Call in the company,' he told the Kaibil with the radio equipment.

'What for?' Razor growled. 'Those people haven't done anything.'

Cabrera stared at him for what seemed a long time before deigning to reply. 'They have harboured terrorists,' he said coldly, 'but that is no concern of yours. You have done your job – and now you can go home. Galvez,' he said, addressing the other Kaibil, 'you will escort our guests back to the helicopter.'

Razor stood his ground. 'For every village you destroy there will be another fifty guerrillas in the mountains.'

'And how do you work that out?' Cabrera asked, as if he was humouring a child.

'That's what has happened in every war like this for the last fifty years.' He glared at the Kaibil colonel. 'And the British Government was assured that this operation would be conducted with due . . .'

'Fuck the British Government,' Cabrera said contemptuously. 'That operation is over,' he added. '*Finito*.'

'You're nothing but a fucking butcher,' Razor told him.

Cabrera's face reddened with rage. 'No one kills seventeen of my men and gets away with it,' he hissed. 'If I had my way

I'd kill every Indian man, woman and child in this fucking province. And then I'd move on to the next one.' He turned on the hapless private. 'Send the message,' he ordered.

Razor looked at the ground, mental pictures of the villages above Zavik crowding his mind. The pile of charred remains inside the ruined church, the villagers crucified on the wall of the barn. Hajrija's Bosnia, someone else's Guatemala. He could either walk away or . . . or what? There was only one way to stop Cabrera – anything less drastic would probably end with Chris and him being thrown out of the Huey on the way home. It was all or nothing.

But where, he wondered, could they run to?

Sometimes you just had to make it up as you went along.

The Kaibil had the radio set up for transmission – there didn't seem to be time for mapping out possible consequences. Razor took a deep breath, and looked across at Chris. Finding what he hoped was acquiescence in his partner's eyes, he took a great leap into the unknown, bringing up the stubby barrel of the Uzi and pulling the trigger in one smooth motion.

Colonel Cabrera's mouth was still opening when the first bullet crashed through his front teeth and out through the back of his head, toppling him, straight as a plank, back over the lip of the waterfall. There were several thuds as his body bounced down the fall, ending with a large splash as it landed in the small pool below.

The two Kaibil soldiers were still staring after him, their faces drawn in identical lines of astonishment, as if their colonel had been suddenly summoned to the underworld by some supernatural force.

The two guerrillas looked no less surprised, though

something like a smile was breaking out on the Old Man's weathered face.

Chris shook his head. 'Another fine mess you've got me into,' he muttered.

Razor looked at him, a sudden sinking feeling in his stomach. Hajrija, he thought. How was he going to reach her?

8

The waterfall sounded louder in the silence.

'This is the third time in five years I've suddenly found myself *persona non grata* in someone else's country,' Chris observed.

'You must be doing something right then,' Razor said absent-mindedly. His mind was racing through the problems created by Cabrera's sudden demise, looking for solutions, establishing priorities. One, how were they going to deal with the three Kaibiles in the village below? Two, how were they going to get out of the immediate area? Three, how were they going to get out of the goddamn country? Four, how was Hajrija going to get out of the goddamn country?

If they were going to find answers for three and four they would need help from the guerrillas.

For their part, Tomás and the Old Man were still recovering from the double shock. One moment they had been happily on their way home to a triumphant unit, the next confronting certain torture and death. And then, before this terrible sentence had even begun to sink in, they had been granted a sudden reprieve by the mystery gringos.

It was the Old Man who recovered first. 'How many Kaibiles are there in the village?' he asked.

'Three,' Razor told him. 'And there's another eighty waiting on the helipad at Uspantan.'

'The three down there will have heard the shot,' Chris added.

'Are they in contact with Uspantan?' Tomás asked.

It sounded to Razor as if they were discussing a game. 'No,' he said. He walked across to the Kaibil with the walkie-talkie, who was standing almost rigid with fear, and relieved him of his recoilless rifle. 'I want you to talk to your sergeant,' he told the man. 'Tell him you have captured the guerrillas – sorry, *subversivos* – but that Colonel Cabrera has been wounded. Get them up here, pronto.'

The Kaibil took a deep breath and nodded.

'No heroics,' Razor told him.

The man did well, considering. Razor herded him across to join the other Kaibil, who had been disarmed by Chris, and told both men to lie face down in the grass.

'What about chummy here?' Chris asked, indicating the Indian guide, who was sitting with his head in his hands.

The Old Man spoke to him in a language the Englishman could not understand, eliciting a long reply which seemed half defiant, half resigned. 'They have his sister in the city,' the Old Man eventually translated. 'He says his sister will die now, which makes him sad, but he is glad you shot the Kaibil colonel.'

Christ almighty, Razor thought.

'Speaking of the devil, we'd better get his body back up here,' Chris said.

'Yeah, but what do we do with this guy?' Razor asked, looking at the guide.

'We will take him with us,' the Old Man said.

'OK.'

'I will help you,' Tomás told Chris. The two men disappeared down the steps, leaving Razor and the Old Man to watch the prisoners.

'The eighty men at Uspantan, they will come eventually,' the Old Man said. 'We have to warn the village.'

'Yeah.' Razor breathed out noisily, possibilities jostling each other in his mind.

Chris and Tomás reappeared, hauling Cabrera's corpse by the ankles, and dragged it another twenty metres further up the path. They then transferred the two Kaibil prisoners and the guide to the same location.

'I'll look after them,' the Old Man volunteered.

The other three took up their ambush positions, each grateful for the chance to get their thoughts back in some sort of order.

Razor was already struggling to suppress an insidious sense of panic. He was pretty certain that he and Chris could simply walk their way out of the country. They couldn't be much more than a hundred kilometres from the border, and the terrain in between was wild enough to hide an army. The two of them knew how to live off the land. Three nights and they would be in Mexico. But Hajrija was in a town fifty kilometres to the south. There was no way he or Chris could travel on the roads or survive in the towns without help. Both of them were too tall, and Chris was too fair-haired. And every policeman and soldier in Guatemala would be looking for them.

Razor hoped the guerrillas were feeling grateful.

Ten metres away Chris was wondering why he felt so calm. Because his subconscious had been expecting it, was the answer that came to mind. They had been on a collision course with their Guatemalan hosts since day one, and here was the collision. In some strange way he felt they had vindicated themselves. No doubt the men in London would see things differently, but this was the way his SAS was supposed to operate. They might not always fight on the side of the angels, but they weren't supposed to serve as auxiliaries to the scum of the earth.

And they could get out of this, no problem. Three or four days' bird-watching in the mountains – he might get to see a quetzal after all – and then . . .

Chris suddenly came to the realization that Razor had reached several minutes earlier. 'Christ,' he murmured softly to himself, just as the sound of voices drifted up from the path below. 'How much further?' one of the Kaibiles was loudly complaining in Spanish.

They clambered unwittingly over the top step, just as the two *compas* had done, and were still getting their breath back when Razor's voice told them to lay down their guns.

One man started to do so, another stood stock-still, the third's finger clenched on a trigger, sending a spray of bullets into the trees.

A bullet from Tomás's rifle knocked him backwards into the other two, his SMG firing a death-rattle at the sky. The two survivors, one with eyes tightly closed, tried not to move a muscle.

Razor and Tomás stood guard while Chris collected their guns, and the survivors were then escorted, dragging the corpse behind them, up to where Cabrera and the prisoners were laid out in the grass.

'I will go down to the village and tell them what has happened,' Tomás announced, and was half out of sight before the others had finished nodding their agreement.

Razor removed his floppy jungle hat and ran a hand through his hair. 'We need your help,' he told the Old Man, who raised an eyebrow in wry disbelief. Razor explained about Hajrija, who she was and where she was. 'The Army knows she's here, and the moment they find out what happened to Cabrera they'll go looking for her. I have to warn her, at least give her a chance to get somewhere public, so that people will know if she gets taken . . .'

The Old Man thought about it. 'It will depend on how long the Kaibiles in Uspantan wait before coming to see what has happened. Was there no discussion of contingencies?'

'I'm sure there was, but not while we were around.'

'Well, the nearest telephone is nearly twenty kilometres away,' the Old Man said. 'In Pasmolón, at the bottom of the valley. It is a three-hour journey . . . I don't think you would get there in time, and maybe not at all – it is an open road.'

'How about their radio?' Chris suggested.

'Ah, of course.' The Old Man's eyes lit up. 'Tomás is our expert in these things,' he said, 'but I see no reason why he cannot call our people. Then they can get a message through to Panajachel.'

'Great,' Razor said, wondering how long it would be before Tomás came back. 'Don't you know the frequencies?' he asked the Old Man, who shook his head.

'My memory is not so good,' he said. 'But Tomás will not be long. Do you know what message you wish to send?' he asked.

'Christ, no.' Razor ran a hand through his hair again. Think, he told himself, think.

'Could your people get her from Panajachel to our embassy in Guatemala City?' Chris interjected.

The Old Man considered the question. 'Maybe, but I wouldn't advise it. If they want her that badly they'll just go in after her, and, forgive me for saying so, but your Government will not be very popular when this news comes out. It won't be hard to fake some sort of protest mob.'

And she was still a Bosnian national, Razor thought. If the embassy wanted to hand her over they had the perfect excuse.

'I think it would be best just to move your wife to a safe place,' the Old Man said. 'And to move ourselves to one too,' he added. 'Once we have done that we can decide on what the next step should be.'

Razor could think of nothing better. There was no way he could spirit Hajrija away to complete safety, no matter how desperately he wanted to. 'Right,' he agreed. 'Thanks,' he added awkwardly.

'I think we should be thanking you,' the Old Man said, 'and when we have a few minutes to spare I shall be most interested to hear why you decided to help us. And why you were with the Kaibiles in the first place.'

'Yeah, well . . .'

Chris was looking at their four prisoners, two of whom had their faces turned in his direction. They looked like scared boys now, but men in fear of imminent death often did. 'What are we going to do with them?' he asked.

'They are Kaibiles,' the Old Man said, 'and no doubt all of them are guilty of the torture and rape and murder of our people.' He grimaced. 'But no, we do not shoot men in cold blood, not without a trial, and in this instance . . . I think, with your agreement, we should simply deprive them of their clothes and let them go. Without boots it will take them some five hours to reach Pasmolón, and the gunships will be here long before then.'

'There is another option,' Chris said, speaking to Razor. 'I'm not saying I'm in favour, but . . .' He shrugged. 'If we kill these four then there's no way the Army will know whether we've flipped or simply been captured by the guerrillas. In which case they might give us the benefit of the doubt and not go after Hajrija.'

'Shit,' Razor murmured, and looked at the sky. 'No,' he decided. 'I think the bastards will go looking for Hajrija anyway, and even if we knew for certain that they wouldn't . . .'

The Old Man looked from one man to the other, a rueful smile on his face. 'So it is decided,' he said.

A few moments later Tomás returned with the news that the village was in the throes of evacuation.

'Where will they all go?' Chris asked.

Tomás waved an arm. 'Into the mountains. They will return when the Army has gone, and rebuild the houses. They have done it before.'

'Tomás, we need your help with the radio,' the Old Man interjected, and explained what was needed.

'Come,' Tomás said to Razor, picking up the set. 'We must do this where the Kaibil scum cannot hear us.

The two men walked back to the top of the steps, from where they could see the village below. People seemed to be scurrying in every direction, all with their arms full.

Tomás examined the radio, and pronounced himself satisfied. 'I have seen these before,' he said. 'They are easy. And it is always good to get another radio,' he added, as if to himself. 'Now, tell me the message you wish to send.'

Razor went through it.

Tomás nodded, extended the antenna and turned the tuning button until the digital display showed the correct frequency. He then pressed the 'talk' button on the handset and said in Spanish: 'Emergency. Emergency. The jaguar has woken from its dream.'

'Tomás,' a female voice answered almost immediately. 'What has happened? Is the Old Man all right?'

'Yes, he's fine. We have had a run-in with the Kaibiles, but there is no time to tell you the whole story. The two gringos Emelia saw, you remember? They helped us . . .' He smiled at Razor, who smiled back weakly, and listened to Tomás's end of the conversation.

'I will explain that later . . . I am coming to that . . . One of them has a wife who is staying in Panajachel, at the Cacique Inn Hotel, and she is now in danger . . . I want you to get hold of the Santa Catarina unit, and ask them to collect her and keep her in a safe place . . . I was coming to that. There people are to tell her that Hoddle says it's OK . . . Hoddle . . . No, I don't know what it means. That's probably the point . . . We should be back sometime before midnight . . . OK.'

Tomás turned to Razor. 'We have done all we can.'

'Yeah,' Razor said. 'Thanks.' The village below seemed empty now, like a ghost village.

They walked back up the path to find the prisoners and corpses had been stripped of their clothes and footwear.

'On your feet,' Chris told them, and they obeyed reluctantly, two of them holding their hands over their genitals like footballers defending against a free kick. 'Now get out of here,' Chris told them. Hardly daring to believe their luck, the four men took a few tentative steps forward, then burst into a helter-skelter run down the path.

'What about the villagers?' Razor asked.

'They won't be taking the road,' Tomás said. 'And in any case, those bastards are nothing without their guns.'

'Time to go,' the Old Man said, looking at his watch.

Razor looked at his own: it was only just past nine o'clock. A lot had happened since dawn.

The Indian guide was waiting, his arms full of uniforms, his shoulders crossed with laced-together boots. The two SAS men and two *compas* carried their own weapons and those of the enemy. The five of them started up the slope, leaving Cabrera and his sergeant face up to the sky, a sumptuous meal for the vultures already circling overhead.

They had been walking for twenty minutes when Razor remembered the Huey.

It was not as serious an oversight as it might have been. The naked Kaibiles wasted time searching the empty village for clothes that might have been left behind, and their progress grew noticeably slower as the rough terrain took its toll on their bare feet. Still, it was only three and a half hours after their release that the four men reached the waiting Huey, stumbling into the clearing like escapees from a nudist camp. The two pilots, who had been happily playing cards all morning, managed to restrain themselves from laughing – Kaibiles, naked or not, were not noted for a self-deprecating sense of humour.

The raw details of what had happened were conveyed over the radio link during the flight back to Uspantan, and Major Osorio was waiting on the tarmac when the Huey touched down. The three men were ordered straight to Colonel Cabrera's office, where they were obliged to begin delivering a detailed report while still awaiting their replacement uniforms.

Osorio had no difficulty believing their story. He had never liked or trusted the Englishmen, and the incident of the interrogation had only served to confirm their unreliability. Listening to the four soldiers, he took a perverse pleasure in having been proved right. But this satisfaction faded somewhat when the need to inform G-2 of these developments thrust itself to the front of his mind. Colonel Serrano did not suffer failure gladly.

Still, it was Cabrera's failure, not his own. Admittedly he had devised that morning's operational plan with Cabrera, but no one else knew that. Unless, of course, the colonel had left anything in writing. Another ten minutes was wasted while Osorio made sure he had not. It was almost twenty to two when the two Chinooks lifted themselves ponderously into the sky above the base, and headed up across the mountains towards the village of Tziaca. During the flight Osorio rehearsed what he would say to Serrano when the time came.

The village was empty, of course. While most of the company began torching the houses, the four men who had been in Cabrera's party that morning led Osorio and a platoon of Kaibiles up the path behind the village. As they clambered cautiously up the last steps beside the waterfall, their eyes caught sight of the large birds perched on the bodies thirty metres up the path. When they walked forward the vultures flapped their wings in annoyance, and then took to the air, hovering in hope overhead.

The faces were still just about recognizable.

They carried the two bodies back down to the village, the vultures shadowing their journey. As the two bodies were loaded into one of the Chinooks Cabrera's head lolled sideways, and the ruined eyes seemed to reach out for one last look at the scene of their undoing. Osorio turned away in distaste and wondered what to do next.

Find them, he told himself.

He unfolded his map and spread it across the cockpit floor of the Huey, inviting the pilots to look at it with him. It didn't take a genius to work out which way they must have gone.

He looked at his watch. 'A little more than six hours,' he said. Those Indians could walk all right, but they had the Englishmen to consider. 'Let's say eight kilometres an hour. That's a maximum of fifty kilometres.' He drew an appropriate arc on the map. 'Start on this line and then follow concentric arcs back in this direction. Don't try and engage them. If you make contact, call in and hang with them. We'll join you in the Chinooks.'

The pilots nodded. They didn't seem very optimistic, Osorio thought.

Moments later he watched the Huey take off through the cloud of smoke which now hung above the burning village.

It was slightly after four o'clock when Colonel Serrano finally became aware of the morning's events on the path above Tziaca. His first instinct was to rage at Osorio – Cabrera being no longer available – but he knew in his heart that neither officer was really to blame. He should save his anger for the two Englishmen – them and all the other gringo bastards.

He listened as Osorio outlined the current state of play, and approved the measures the major had already taken:

the setting in motion of the manhunt, the general tightening of security throughout Quiche, Huehuetenango and Alta Verapaz.

How dare they, Serrano thought as he hung up. His blood boiled at the arrogance of these people. He reached for a Pall Mall to calm himself, and stood at the window for several minutes, taking deep drags on the cigarette as he stared vacantly out across the inner courtyard of the Palacio Nacional.

One dead colonel of the Kaibiles was not the end of the world, he decided eventually. He hadn't even liked Cabrera very much – the man had been too transparently ambitious. Probably trying to compensate for the Indian ancestry implicit in his dark complexion.

Serrano flicked a wrist, as if he was dispatching Cabrera's spirit into the next world. He needed to concentrate on two imperatives: first, limiting any potential damage, and second, turning the situation to his own advantage.

The first thing was to keep the matter quiet, at least for the time it took to net the two Englishmen. It was conceivable that they would need help from the English authorities in recapturing the renegades, but that wouldn't be a problem – the government in London would be as keen to keep this business out of the public eye as he was. And it would be enjoyable to pass on the news to them, Serrano decided, if only to hear the bastards squirm.

Of course, once the men were caught all bets would be off. Then their fate could serve as an example to all the foreigners who tried to interfere in the nation's affairs. They had shot a Guatemalan officer in the performance of his duty, shot him down like a dog. They would be tried and then executed, all according to the law, offering both proof of Guatemala's devotion to legality and an example of what happened to those who took up arms against the state.

But first they had to catch the bastards. Or persuade them to give themselves up. The wife, Serrano thought. He reached for the phone which connected him with the Department of Criminal Investigation offices a kilometre to the south.

She had committed no crime, but in the circumstances no one could object to the police pulling her in for questioning.

He was put through to Vincenzo. 'The wife of the Englishman,' he asked without preamble. 'Is she still under surveillance?'

'Not around the clock,' the DCI man said, sounding surprised. 'She is staying in Panajachel . . .'

'Pick her up,' Serrano said. 'Immediately. And bring her to the Palacio Nacional.' He hung up while Vincenzo was still speaking, and lit another cigarette from the previous one.

The Americans would be upset by all this, he thought. Upset with the English, but maybe also feeling a little responsible themselves. There were possibilities here.

The party of five had been walking for several hours, sometimes through forest but mostly across lightly wooded slopes. In these foothills the signs of human habitation were few and far between: traces of a path, an abandoned farmstead, a hamlet in a valley far below. The mountains marched to their left, climbing into a perfect blue sky.

The two Englishmen had not slept for twenty-eight hours, and were beginning to feel the pace. In another two hours it would be dark, Razor calculated, and then maybe they could take a rest. On the path behind him Chris had just seen his third sharp-shinned hawk of the day, its primary feathers splaying like human fingers as it soared.

They were halfway across a long, bare slope when the distant drone of a helicopter insinuated itself into their consciousness. A few stunted bushes offered the only cover, and these were a hundred metres away.

Everyone froze, their eyes searching unsuccessfully for the approaching craft. Their ears told them there was only one, and a small one at that.

'Recon,' Razor murmured, trying to get his tired brain to work.

The Old Man was pulling maroon Kaibil berets out of each trouser pocket. 'We'll have to bluff it,' he said, throwing them to the SAS men. 'Your uniforms look like theirs. We'll play dead. You call them in, get them within range.'

Before the Englishmen could reply, the three Indians were splayed corpse-like in the grass. Seconds later the Huey loomed up over the ridge about half a kilometre in front of them.

There was no way it could miss them.

Razor and Chris jammed the maroon berets on their heads and started waving wildly. Both men felt more than a little foolish. There was no way a stunt like this could work. The helicopter had seen them now, and was slowing as it approached. As the two men redoubled their efforts, they found they were laughing, and started to jump up and down, shouting abuse at the helicopter.

It was veering to their left now, but still getting closer, and they could see the two crewmen sitting next to each other in the cockpit. Neither of them seemed to be making the head movements that usually went with talking.

The range dropped to about two hundred metres, still fifty in excess of the Uzi's effective range. Razor imperiously gestured for the pilot to land.

It inched closer, like a predator uncertain of its prey. There was a movement in the cockpit, maybe a microphone being picked up.

Maybe 170 metres.

'Now,' Razor decided, and both men swung the Uzis into position, took aim, opened fire.

The helicopter jerked away, like a horse's head responding to a pull on the bridle, and at almost the same moment both crewmen jerked back in their seats.

The Huey hung suspended in mid-air for a long moment, then seemed to drop like a championship diver, twisting to strike the ground head first. The hillside exploded in flame.

The first rap on the door was so light that Hajrija dismissed it as the wind. The second got her up off the bed on which she had been reading the Mayan 'Bible', the *Popul Vuh*.

The girl was dressed in a mostly red traditional costume, and her wares were hung round both neck and wrists. She looked slightly older than most of her fellow-hawkers.

So now they were making house calls, Hajrija thought, and was just opening her mouth to send the unwelcome visitor on her way when the girl ducked under her arm and into the room. 'Hey,' Hajrija said, more than a little annoyed. She now saw that the girl was older than she had thought, more like sixteen than thirteen.

She was fishing a piece of paper from the waist of her skirt and holding it out for Hajrija.

Another hard luck story, Hajrija thought. In Antigua

several young men had approached her with requests for help with their education costs, offering beautifully printed references from some unknown college as proof of their genuineness.

She took the piece of paper and gave it a cursory look. The words 'FOLO ROSA' were printed in large untidy letters. 'TRUBAL YOU. HODAL SAY OKEY,' it went on.

'I Rosa,' the girl said. She pointed at the door, which was still open. '*Vamos*,' she added hopefully.

Hajrija looked at the letter again. 'FOLO' was follow. 'TRUBAL' must be trouble. Who was 'HODAL'?

What the hell was this?

Hoddle, she thought. Razor's hero. Almost the first thing he had shown her in England was his video clip of Hoddle's goal against Nottingham Forest. What a romantic.

But if this was from Razor . . .

A car door slammed, and she realized she had just heard it arrive in the hotel's small parking lot.

The girl was tugging at her sleeve. 'With me,' she said, 'with me.'

Hoddle said it was OK. She grabbed the travel pouch with her money and passport from the other bed and followed Rosa out of the door. The girl made a locking mime with her arm, causing the parrot necklaces on her wrist to jingle.

Hajrija locked the door, and the two of them advanced cautiously down the first-floor veranda towards the stairs. From the bend in the latter they could see two men walking around the edge of the brightly lit blue swimming pool, heading in their direction.

Rosa tugged on Hajrija's sleeve again, pulling her down the last flight of steps and then into the shadows beneath them. Seconds later they listened to the two men mount the stairway.

Again the tug, and Hajrija was following the girl through the dark hotel garden, past the empty car and out through the gates. They turned left down the road that led to the lake, making the most of the deepest shadow they could find, ears straining for sounds of a car behind them.

The thought crossed Hajrija's mind that this was some elaborate plot to rob her, and was quickly dismissed.

They reached the rickety jetty which she had visited the night before. A crescent moon was rising in the east, but was yet to cast its light on the lake, which stretched away like a sheet of dark glass towards the looming volcanoes. A small boat was being held against the jetty by a squatting Indian. He and Rosa started talking in one of the native languages, and even though Hajrija didn't understand a word, she knew the news wasn't good.

'No boat,' Rosa told her, accompanying the information with the familiar tug on the arm.

They left the man crouching on the jetty, and turned back up the road towards the hotel. Before Hajrija could question the wisdom of this direction Rosa had pulled her off through a hedge and started across what looked like an overgrown sports field. Away in the distance they could see the lights of vehicles descending the switchback road from Sololá.

They clambered across several fences in the dark, and emerged in the backyard of a family house. A man looked up from the back steps, and when Rosa said something to him he simply gestured them on with a wave of his cigarette.

At the end of a dark lane they reached the bottom of the Sololá road, just as an Army truck full of soldiers rumbled past them and into Panajachel. Surely, Hajrija thought, this couldn't all be on her account. What could Razor have done – mounted a coup all on his own?

Rosa held them there in the shadows until the highway was clear, then scuttled across, nimbly scaled the fence on the other side, and set out across what seemed like a row of backyards. For the next fifteen minutes they worked their way around the outskirts of the large village, the cliffs which lay behind it looming to their left, the lights and sounds of evening life stretching off towards the distant lake on their right.

Hajrija guessed that they were now close to the old part of the village, and a few minutes later she gained a glimpse of the church she had visited on her first evening there. The house they were making for turned out to be in one of the small streets nearby.

Their arrival produced a storm of conversation, in which anxiety and excitement seemed present in roughly equal quantities. There were two men, two women and an ever-changing gallery of children in the small back room, and all but one of the men was wearing traditional dress. After both mime and Spanish had been tried with a similar lack of success the man in modern clothes was dispatched in search of someone who spoke English, leaving those left behind to smile at each other.

The man who eventually arrived told her his name was Mariano. He spoke good English, and swiftly translated the news which had arrived from the north. Her husband, he explained, had gone with the *compañeros*, and the Army was looking for her to use as a hostage. Panajachel was now full of soldiers, in the hotels and on the roads and out on the lake. But she would be safe in this house, at least for one night.

At this point one of the women came across to Hajrija and carefully loosened her hair from under the woven headscarf she had bought that morning. 'Look at this,' she seemed to say to the others, before suggesting something which had everyone clapping with amusement and excitement.

The bad news reached the Foreign Ministry, via the British Embassy in Guatemala City, soon after midnight GMT. Martin Clarke was in his Westminster flat, having just persuaded his research assistant that they could finish their work on Atlantic fisheries law in bed, when the call from the duty officer came through. His irritation at being disturbed – it had taken four months to get the green light from this latest research assistant – was only made worse by the nature of the news.

He gathered together the clothes which he had so recently scattered, dressed, and walked swiftly through the wet streets to the Foreign Office. The Embassy report was waiting on his desk, short but to the point. The two SAS troopers sent to Guatemala to assist in an anti-terrorist operation had apparently gone off their heads, first killing the Guatemalan colonel in charge of the operation, and then defecting to the terrorists.

Clarke sat back in his chair, massaging his forehead with his fingers, and feeling the dull ache in his unrequited balls. The Guatemalans would be hopping mad, he thought. The Americans would be furious. He was furious. How the hell was Britain supposed to sell its army as the international community's mercenaries of choice when something like this happened?

If this news spread, every government in Latin America would be crying out for the blood of these men, and if they didn't get it then few of them would be falling over themselves to buy British for years to come. And if these two men *were* sacrificed then every liberal inside and outside the House would be dubbing the Government the friend of the torturers. Whichever way it went, the political outlook seemed bleak.

The fucking SAS, he thought. He would cheerfully have the whole damn lot disbanded. Who could afford a regiment that was a law unto itself? How many times, after all, did London embassies get taken over by terrorists?

Calm down, he told himself. There was no certainty as yet that this news would get out. The Guatemalans might be willing to trade silence for co-operation, since this was not likely to be very good publicity for them either. And as for the two SAS men – well, if they had gone berserk then that was their problem. The Government had no power to save them, even if it wished to. The rule of law was the rule of law.

Clarke reached for the phone, thinking that there was at least some compensation in the news – he would enjoy sharing it with the SAS CO who had treated him so rudely less than two weeks before.

Barney Davies shivered as he listened to Clarke's account of the previous day's events. He had left Jean in bed and come out to the living-room phone, but had neglected to collect his dressing-gown on the way. Whisky, he thought, pulling the phone cord after him, balancing the receiver between ear and shoulder, and reaching for the bottle.

'What do you mean, we're accepting their story?' was his first response.

'Because we have no reason as yet to doubt it. They

have the colonel's dead body and several eyewitnesses to Wilkinson shooting him in cold blood.'

Davies took a gulp of the malt and told himself to keep his temper under control. 'The reason I have to doubt it,' he said calmly, 'is my knowledge of these two men. Guatemalan Army witnesses are hardly likely to be reliable. And if, *if*, Wilkinson did shoot the colonel then he would have had a damn good reason.'

'What possible reason could he have had?'

'I don't know. These people are animals,' he added, and wished he hadn't.

'That would be your diplomatic reply, would it?' Clarke asked scathingly.

'No, it would not. Can you fax me all the information you have?' Davies asked.

'Of course. But I'm not sure what we can do for these two men, Lieutenant-Colonel.'

Davies bit his tongue – this was not the time to push Clarke, who sounded as angry as he was. 'What about Wilkinson's wife?' he asked. 'Do we know where she is?'

'No.'

'Is the embassy looking for her?'

'She is not an English national,' Clarke said coldly, 'so the answer is probably no. I will talk to you again in the morning.' Then he hung up.

Davies stood in the middle of his darkened living room, a naked man clutching a glass of whisky. 'Shit,' he muttered.

9

Less than two hours of daylight remained after the downing of the Huey, but it felt like six. If the helicopter crew had managed to get off a sighting report then the two Chinooks would be on their way, carrying eighty Kaibiles hungry to avenge their colonel. The five men marched on, climbing ever higher into the mountains, ears pricked for the swelling drone of rotor blades.

But at last the sun sank behind the mountains on their left, throwing the slopes the party was traversing into deepening shadow. They had apparently been granted a twelve-hour respite from discovery and probable death.

Another hour brought them to a wooded valley high on the eastern flank of the Cuchumatanes, and here they found the fourteen-strong unit which Tomás and the Old Man had left two days earlier. As they walked into the lightless camp the two SAS men were conscious of the curious looks they were getting from the guerrillas, though one *compañera* seemed much more interested in hugging the returning Tomás than noticing them. It was the young woman from the ravine, Chris realized.

He noticed that there were a lot of women in the camp. Almost as many women as men, in fact. And they were wearing the same olive-green uniforms.

'Will they have any news of my wife?' Razor asked the Old Man.

'No, the message went to our base camp, not here. This is just a transit camp we use sometimes. And this is only a quarter of our company,' he added. You will see the rest – and get some news, I hope – when we reach the base camp.'

'And when will that be?'

'It is a seven-hour march, so we shall leave at around eleven. Until then, you should get some sleep.'

The SAS men needed no second bidding. Oblivious to the stares of the guerrillas, they found a flat piece of ground to lie down on, and were soon sleeping the sleep of the just.

According to Razor's watch it was just after ten-thirty when a hand gently shook his shoulder, and the lovely face of the girl who had welcomed Tomás home smiled down at him. El Jefe wants to see you,' she said in Spanish, speaking slowly as if she wanted to be certain of getting it right.

'OK,' Razor said.

'She's nice,' Chris observed, watching her walk away. A waxing crescent moon had risen while they were asleep, and visibility had increased dramatically.

'Down, boy,' Razor replied. 'I think she belongs to someone else. And I don't think we can afford to piss anyone off for the next couple of days.'

'I just said she was nice.'

'Right,' Razor said sardonically, getting to his feet and looking round. The sky was strewn with clouds, but there were large stretches of open sky, black and sequinned with stars. 'Do you remember those ads on TV about joining the

Army and seeing the world? Well, I'm afraid it looks like they were true.'

Chris grinned at him. 'Let's go and ask El Jefe to send us home.'

It wasn't just the Old Man who wanted to see them – it was the whole unit. Not surprisingly, they all wanted to know what the two Englishmen had been doing with the Kaibiles.

Razor started the story at the beginning, conscious of all the pale faces gathered around him. Almost immediately several people began whispering, and for a moment he thought they must be hostile. But then he realized: the whisperers were translating his Spanish into another language, or even several of them.

He told the assembled guerrillas what their orders had been, and the doubts they had harboured, and how they had left the decision as to whether they would identify the Old Man until the time came. He talked about seeing Tomás through the binoculars at the site of the abortive ambush – this brought a laugh – and their encounter with Emelia in the ravine after the guerrillas' highly successful ambush.

'We watched the village for about four hours that morning,' Razor said, 'and I decided I was not going to identify you. But . . .'

'I identified myself,' the Old Man said, ruefully shaking his head.

'Yeah.'

'And why did you kill the Kaibil colonel?'

Razor shrugged. 'It was him or the village. Not a difficult choice.'

The Old Man looked at him, seemed about to say something, and just smiled instead. 'Is everyone satisfied?'

he asked the company. There seemed to be general assent. 'So we will help them on their way to the border?'

A woman said something in one of the native languages which made everyone laugh.

'Alicia says it would make more sense to keep you with us.'

'We are grateful for your help,' Razor said diplomatically, thinking that a man could do a lot worse with his life than join these people.

Ten minutes later the unit was setting off once more. They were heading south-west, crossing over from the eastern to the western side of the main Cuchumatanes range, Tomás had told the two Englishmen. On a night like this, he had added, it would be cold but beautiful.

They began by climbing in single file out of one high valley and into another. In Guatemala they always seemed to be climbing, Chris thought. The country was like an inverted egg-timer – when you got to the top they turned it upside down and you found yourself at the bottom again, facing yet another ascent.

But he wasn't complaining. He felt the way he had during the second half of the Bosnian mission, both heightened and torn. A heady mix of excitement and elation had accompanied him on every wilderness journey from boyhood on, and a loud echo of this was still leaping through his veins. But now it had a permanent accompaniment, almost a counterbalance. As long as he was in the SAS, this sense of elation would be tangled up in death.

He thought about the crew of the Huey, remembering their faces. He had shared a joke with one of them on the tarmac at Uspantan. They might not have been married, might not have had children, but at the very least they would have had parents, siblings, friends.

And their lives had been so easy to take. A burst on a trigger and they were gone. Just a few seconds to wonder what they would be missing, to grasp for the crucifix which had dangled in front of them on the Huey's windscreen.

Chris did not regret killing them; the choice had been clear – the lives of the helicopter crew or the lives of the five men they were seeking. But he did feel as if he had faced more than enough choices like that for a single lifetime. He wanted a chance to choose between life and death, not between one person's death and another's.

This was the last mission, he thought, and almost burst out laughing. After this one, the chances of the SAS sending him or Razor on another seemed pretty slim. Always assuming they survived.

A few paces behind him, Razor was worrying more about Hajrija's survival than his own. He cursed himself for putting her into such danger, even as he knew in his heart that there was nothing else he could have done, and nothing she would rather he had done.

So why worry? he asked himself. Because he loved her, that was why, and he couldn't bear the thought of her falling into the bastards' hands. Couldn't bear the thought of losing her.

He had never felt like this before, or at least not since he was a little boy. Then he had been frightened when his mum was late coming home, and his mind would run through all the terrible things that could have happened to her and how he would be left alone and have to go and live with his loony grandmother in her dark flat in Hoxton.

And he wondered how he could have served with so

many men who had wives and never have realized how much harder it was to risk your life when someone else needed you to come home.

'Let me get this straight,' the Prime Minister said wearily. It was just after eight in the morning, and the day was already sliding downhill. 'Two members of the SAS . . .'

'The two advisers we sent to Guatemala,' Martin Clarke added helpfully.

'The two advisers the Ministry of Defence sent to Guatemala,' the PM corrected him. 'You're seriously telling me that they've joined up with communist guerrillas? It doesn't make sense. I know the SAS have a reputation for going their own way, but that's ridiculous.'

'I know. But I don't think there's much doubt they shot a Guatemalan Army colonel. And once they had done they may have decided that the communists were their only hope of getting out of the country.'

'But why did they shoot him, for God's sake?' The PM sighed, and picked up the few remaining crumbs of pastry on his breakfast plate.

'The Guatemalans say they don't understand it either. But they do want our help.'

The PM seemed not to hear the last sentence. 'Have the media got hold of this yet?'

'No. The Guatemalans say there will be no need to publicize the matter if it is resolved quickly . . .'

'Meaning?'

'Meaning, if they catch our men soon then they'll keep quiet. Which is why . . .'

'They are threatening us with publicity? Surely they'll come out of it looking even worse . . .'

Clarke shook his head. 'With all the bad press they've had over the last fifteen years they're probably immune by now.'

The PM allowed himself a grim smile. 'You know, I can't even remember why we agreed to this scheme in the first place.'

'The Americans asked us. And needless to say, they're not very happy at the way things have turned out either.'

'Neither am I.' The PM rubbed an eye. 'So what do they want – the Guatemalans, I mean – what sort of help do they have in mind?'

'Ah. Their ambassador thinks the SAS must have routine procedures laid down for eventualities like this – you know, some sort of handbook which tells them what to do when they get stuck behind enemy lines. Will they head for the border or the coast or the embassy? That sort of thing. Will they try and steal a plane? Can either of them fly a plane, come to that?'

'Everything I've ever heard about the SAS suggests that they make it up as they go along.'

'Possibly, but it would be good to give the Guatemalans something. We can hardly claim not to know whether either of these men can pilot a plane, for example.'

The PM considered this. 'I suppose you're right,' he said hesitantly.

'I doubt if the SAS CO will co-operate,' Clarke said.

'He won't if you tell him it's for the Guatemalans. So don't tell him that. Say it's for the diplomats. Tell him we're working through channels and we need to have some idea of what his men are likely to do next.'

* * *

Barney Davies called the British Embassy in Guatemala City at 7 a.m. GMT, and spoke to a very tired-sounding military attaché. Ben Manley was not exactly sympathetic. He had apparently known Chris Martinson for years, and was both surprised and disappointed by what had happened. He admitted that it could be difficult working with the more gung-ho members of the Guatemalan Army, but that was part of the job – you didn't always get to work with people you liked.

Davies asked him about Hajrija Wilkinson, and was told that the embassy had no idea where she was. When asked whether they were looking for her, Manley first claimed, probably with some justice, that they lacked the human resources to search a country for one missing person, and then spoiled the effect by adding that they had no reason to believe she was in any danger.

Swallowing his anger – it would be better spent on other targets – Davies asked for some geographical details, particularly the last-known location of Sergeants Wilkinson and Martinson. Manley provided these willingly enough, and after getting off the phone the CO pulled out his trusty *Times Atlas*. For once, though, he found it wanting. The smallest-scale map of Guatemala was about eighty-five miles to the inch, which left the unmarked Tziaca about an eighth of an inch from Uspantan. His ruler told him that at the moment of decision the two men had been only about sixty kilometres from the nearest border, but the map gave him only the vaguest idea of what those sixty kilometres would look like on the ground.

He sent his adjutant in search of a better map, ordered two cups of tea and two rock cakes, and read once more through the faxes from the Foreign Office, feeling decidedly at a loss as to what he or the Regiment could do to help their fugitive comrades.

He was on the point of calling Martin Clarke when the junior minister called him. For diplomatic moves to be effective, Clarke told the SAS CO, the Foreign Office would need some idea of what Wilkinson and his partner were likely to do next.

'I have no idea,' Davies said, feeling instantly suspicious.

'None at all? Surely there are contingency plans for such circumstances?'

'I don't recall any of my men ever encountering circumstances remotely similar to these,' Davies said drily.

'Well, do you think they will try to get across the border?' Clarke asked patiently.

'That sounds a fair bet.'

'Can either of them fly a plane?'

'I . . .' Davies hesitated, wondering what possible need the Foreign Office could have for information like that. The Guatemalan authorities on the other hand . . . 'No, I'm pretty certain they can't,' he lied. If his suspicions were justified, then there was always the chance the Guatemalans might not bother to guard their airfields quite so assiduously. 'I'll have to go through our files,' he said helpfully. 'We're in the middle of computerization,' he added, being somewhat economical with the truth. 'So it may take some time.'

'As soon as you can,' Clarke said crisply, and hung up.

Davies took a bite out of a rock cake and reflected that British politics was like a garden pond. The longer you went without changing the water, the more scum you could see on the surface.

His two men had been sent to do a dirty job at the insistence of the Foreign Office, and he was damned if he was going to let Whitehall wash its collective hands of them.

Hajrija was woken soon after four in the morning, and while the rest of the household readied themselves for the day, two of the women worked on her. They were both in their twenties, Hajrija guessed, and their names were Lorena and Martina.

First they rubbed the paste on to her face and neck, her arms and feet. She didn't know what it was, and she wasn't at all sure she wanted to know. It didn't exactly smell bad, but it had a slightly acrid, earthy aroma. It reminded her of the herbal potions her late grandmother had concocted after day-long expeditions into the forests above Zavik. Still, whatever it was, it worked. Her skin not only grew several shades darker, but also took on a distinctly reddish tinge.

They moved on to the hair, which was the right colour to start with. The two women parted it, flattened it and braided it, giggling as they worked. Every now and then other members of the family would walk through the small room and make suggestions, compliment the stylists, or simply smile.

They were just about finished when the clothes arrived. There was a long, wraparound skirt, a long, sleeveless *huipil* tunic, and a shoulder cape, each of them beautifully woven and embroidered in the same style as that worn by the women of the house. Hajrija put them on, feeling somewhat humbled by the process. She had read enough to know that the Mayan women spent months, sometimes even years, weaving clothes that were made to last a lifetime, and she wondered where this costume had come from. She thought perhaps she could see disapproval in the eyes of the older women, but could think of no way of allaying it. She was sure it would be a mistake to offer money.

She wished her interpreter, Mariano, would put in another appearance, and allow her to express her gratitude more clearly, but when the time came to leave there was still no sign of him.

Outside it was still half dark and the dawn air, though clear, seemed damp. There were seven females in the party, ranging in age from Rosa to a woman Hajrija hadn't seen before, who had to be over fifty. She was carrying a live but apparently sleepy duck under one arm.

As the party started down the street the one weakness in Hajrija's disguise became only too apparent – she was about four inches taller than her companions. Trying to walk with her knees bent she felt even more conspicuous.

But for the moment there was no sign of the Army or the police, only similar groups of women, all laden with wares for sale, all heading in the same direction.

The bus station turned out to be little more than a large garage with two buses, both of which were already warming up. The drivers were on their respective roofs, tying down merchandise, and the crowd milled around below, chatting and holding on to the numerous live animals. Hajrija suddenly noticed the two soldiers standing to one side, and felt her heart in her mouth as one of them looked straight at her, tapped his comrade on the shoulder, and started in her direction.

He walked straight past. Casually she turned her head, and found the soldiers looking at the passports of an arriving gringo couple, both of whom had long, dark hair. They were German, she decided, though she wasn't sure why she thought so.

The driver was getting down from the roof now, and fighting his way through the throng to the door. The women accompanying Hajrija bustled forward, almost lifting her off her feet in the process, and in no time they were all funnelling aboard the bus and into seats near the back. She was given a window seat, and the eldest of the women sat down next to her, an increasingly wakeful duck in her lap.

The bus more than filled up, the minutes dragged by, and after spending what seemed an eternity adjusting his rear-view mirror the driver ground down on the clutch and squealed the vehicle into gear. Several seconds later the bus jerked forward. Emerging triumphantly from the dark cloud of its own exhaust, it began rumbling through the streets of the still largely comatose village.

They were soon out of the village, climbing the steep and twisting road to Sololá, and Hajrija was just daring to hope that there were no checkpoints when one came into view on the road ahead. The soldiers had set up a block on one of the bends, parking their vehicle in one of the lay-bys normally reserved for travellers who wanted to sit and enjoy the view across Lake Atitlán.

There were two cars ahead of them, and while they waited Hajrija became aware of the tension building in the bus, and of the various looks being cast in her direction. They all knew, she realized with a shock. Probably every Indian in Panajachel knew she was being smuggled out of the village on this bus.

And yet she felt more secure in that knowledge, not less so. Which said volumes about Guatemala; this was not just a divided country – it was two worlds, both of which happened to occupy the same geographical space.

The bus inched forward, and one soldier climbed aboard. While he checked the driver's papers another soldier started fighting his way down the aisle, which was already jam-packed with baggage and bodies. He stopped at the Germans, and laboriously went through each passport, comparing faces with photos as if determined to find a mismatch.

Failing in this task, he reluctantly handed back the passports and continued down the aisle. Acutely conscious of her height, Hajrija tried to crouch as low in her seat as possible, turning her eyes towards the window and the gorgeous panorama of lake and volcanoes.

There was a tug on her sleeve, and she turned to find her neighbour offering her the duck. Hajrija took it clumsily, then got a better hold, and concentrated on keeping her mouth closed – the white teeth were a giveaway – and her cheeks slightly inflated.

She could feel the soldier looming above them, and was expecting the blow to fall at any moment when the duck finally realized that there was a whole lake on the other side of the window. It quacked and struggled in her hands, failed to get free, and sent an avenging stream of warm shit into her lap. Hajrija half leapt from her seat with surprise, and heard the laughter explode around her. Even the soldier was laughing, holding his nose in mock dismay. He left the bus shaking his head, as if he could hardly believe it.

A minute more and they were on their way again. Hajrija's neighbour helped her wipe away most of the mess and took back the unrepentant duck. The tension in the bus evaporated as the two worlds drew away from each other again, and to her surprise Hajrija found herself relaxing like everyone else.

They passed the Sololá cemetery with its multicoloured gravestones, rumbled through the cobbled streets of the town and out on to the road which led up to the Pan-American Highway. The sun was bathing the fields now, and there were numerous groups of women walking along the side of the road, some with large bunches of wood balanced on their heads. At the Los Encuentros junction there was another checkpoint, and for a long half hour they waited in the queue for inspection. Through the window she could see other buses waiting with trucks, pick-ups, bicycles and a single Guatemala City cab, which seemed to be carrying two tourists. Everyone seemed to be heading for Chichicastenango.

Many of the drivers had abandoned their vehicles for the line of stalls selling food and drink, and the smell wafting over from the cooking fires reminded Hajrija that she had hardly eaten anything since noon the previous day.

Eventually their turn came, and this time there was no need for the duck to perform. A single soldier climbed briefly aboard, checked the Germans' passports, took one cursory glance at the rest of the passengers, and climbed down again.

An hour later the bus drew to a halt in the small town of Chichicastenango, and began disgorging its human and animal cargo. Hajrija's friends hurried her across the street and down an alley lined with stalls selling tourist goods. This fed into the town square, which possessed two whitewashed churches staring at each other across a huge market. Hajrija caught sight of a few stalls selling food and cooking utensils but the overwhelming impression was of tourist wares –

a multi-hued riot of clothes, fabrics, bags, patchwork quilts, wooden and jade carvings, purses, jewellery, rugs, brassware and wall hangings.

Hajrija's group reached the foot of the semicircular steps which led up to the front door of the larger of the two churches. Skirting round a group of women who were sitting on the steps tying gladioli into bunches, they walked up and in through the open entrance.

It was not much later than eight-thirty in the morning but already the church was alive with activity. Along each side wall, tables had been arranged, and down the centre of the nave a line of stone slabs had been laid. Both tables and slabs were covered with candles – hundreds, even thousands, of them – and the smoke from their burning was mixing with the thicker smoke of incense, drifting dreamlike in the rays of sunshine slanting in through the high windows.

Hajrija became aware that Rosa was tugging impatiently at her sleeve, and allowed herself to be led forward to where a young woman was sitting alone in one of the pews. Rosa pushed Hajrija in beside her, gave her a goodbye smile, and retreated back up the nave.

'You speak English?' the woman asked in a whisper. She was wearing a different costume, one in which green was the predominant colour.

'Yes,' Hajrija whispered back.

'I am Lara. We wait here for ten minutes, maybe twenty.'

'OK,' Hajrija said softly. She already felt reluctant to leave the church – there was something so safe about the womb-like semi-darkness, the curling smoke, the murmur of prayer. There was what looked like a whole family gathered round the nearest slab, and the father was lighting a row of thin pink candles, while the mother watched with hopeful eyes, a baby cradled in her arms.

The infant's head was encased from the nostrils up in a cloth cap, reminding Hajrija that the Mayan Indians traditionally covered their babies' eyes for the first year of their lives. She couldn't remember why they did it, but was struck for the first time at how much trust such an arrangement would engender in a child.

Maybe that was what made these people so unusual, she thought: they trusted each other. And maybe that was why she had come with Rosa the previous evening and why she had come to Chichicastenango that morning and why she was now sitting in a church pew with one complete stranger and probably waiting for another.

She couldn't understand a word most of them said, but she trusted them with her life.

When Chris Martinson awoke the sun was an orange flash through the trees, the light still almost full. He looked across at Razor, still gently snoring in the Gore-tex bag, and decided that at least one of them should have some idea of the lie of the land.

The base camp was spread across a thickly forested fold in a west-facing mountain slope. The tree canopy offered one line of defence against prying eyes, and the well-camouflaged dug-out 'accommodations' another. These in turn were widely spread, and not, Chris suspected, from any desire for privacy. Someone knew about heat signatures, and had done his best to hide the camp from American satellite observation.

He walked slowly up the hill, hoping to find an observation point which looked out over the forest canopy. He passed a man and a woman cleaning their rifles; they stared at him for a moment before raising their hands in silent greeting.

Twenty metres further up the slope he suddenly heard what sounded like someone laughing. He stopped in his tracks, listening intently, and a few seconds later the laugh sounded again. Chris started walking as quietly as he could manage towards it, his eyes searching the trees above.

He was so busy looking upwards that he almost walked into her. She stepped backwards, saying something he didn't understand. It was the woman from the ravine, he realized.

The bird laughed again, jerking both their heads towards it.

She looked at him, then pointed a finger in the direction of the invisible bird and said a word which sounded to Chris like '*ixsharu*'. 'We call it a laughing falcon,' he whispered in Spanish.

They advanced together this time, and soon Chris could see it through his binoculars, perched on a branch of a deciduous tree which he didn't recognize. The bird's bushy white crest seemed to glow in the gathering dusk, and the dark face mask looked almost owl-like.

Chris offered the binoculars to the woman, who let out almost a purr of pleasure when she caught sight of the bird. For several minutes they passed them to and fro, until the bird either grew tired of being watched or suddenly became aware of their presence, and with one last laugh flapped awkwardly up through the branches and out of sight.

She looked up at him, both pleasure and surprise in her expression. 'You know birds?' she asked doubtfully.

Everything she had ever learned about the gringo world suggested a distrust of nature.

'Yes, I do. I watch them wherever I go.'

'I watch wherever I go.'

They smiled at each other. 'I have a book with me,' Chris said, 'with pictures of birds that live in Costa Rica. And many of them live here in Guatemala too. Would you like to see it?'

'Pictures of birds?' she echoed, her eyes lighting up. 'Please, yes.' They started back down through the trees together. 'I am Emelia Xicay,' she said. 'My brother Tomás walk with you from Tziaca.'

'I am Chris Martinson,' he said.

They found Razor in the act of waking up. 'I dreamed I was Doctor Who,' he said, and then noticed Emelia. 'But your dream was obviously better than mine,' he told Chris, who was delving into his bag for *Birds of Costa Rica*.

Emelia took the proffered book with both hands, almost as if she was receiving a religious object. Then she squatted down and began slowly turning the pages, holding her eyes close in the declining light, a finger working its way through each gallery of birds. Chris and Razor watched her, both wondering the same thing – how could this be the woman who had piled a mountain path high with Kaibil dead in not much more than a minute?

'This is beautiful,' she said, in a voice which suggested the word itself was utterly inadequate.

Chris was only prevented from giving her the book on the spot by the appearance of her brother. 'Emelia,' he said, surprised to find her there.

'Tomás, look at this,' she said.

He did so, and made a mental note to find her something

like it the next time he was in the city. Though where the money would come from . . .

'Yes it is,' he agreed, and turned to tell the Englishmen that the Old Man wanted to see them.

They left Emelia fighting a losing battle with the light and walked diagonally down through the forest for some three hundred metres. The Old Man was sitting with his back against a tree, thoughtfully smoking a cigarette, a book in his lap. From the camouflaged dug-out nearby came the unmistakable drone of a generator.

'Sounds good, doesn't it,' he said as they approached. 'If Jorge can fix it properly, and we can find enough fuel, I shall retire up here and watch football on TV.' His face screwed up in self-amusement, and then abruptly grew serious again. 'Sit down,' he told them, indicating the neatly stacked cut logs which obviously served as seating for guerrilla conferences. 'Your wife is safe,' he told Razor without further preamble.

Razor closed his eyes and clenched a fist. 'Where?' he asked.

'She's in Chichicastenango at the moment. About forty-five kilometres south of here. But I'm afraid it looks like she'll have to stay there for several days, maybe even weeks.'

Razor waited for the explanation, saying nothing.

'The people who got her out of Panajachel are Cakchiquel, and though they go to the market in Chichicastenango they do not know the Quiche lands or speak Quiche. It is one of the curses of our struggle, that we are united in everything but language. Men like Tomás here, who speak Spanish and more than one of our native languages, are very rare.' He sighed. 'So, the people who are looking after your wife would find it difficult at the best of times to bring her north to us, and these are not the best of times.' He grinned suddenly. 'Depending on your point of view, that is. Your action in killing the Kaibil colonel has not gone unnoticed, my friends. In fact, it has been like throwing a very big stone into a lake, and the ripples are still spreading. The authorities know that your wife has gone into hiding, and they know she must try to reach a border or an embassy or us. And as part of making sure she doesn't reach us, the Army is searching every town and blocking every road between Atitlán and the Cuchumatanes. If she stays where she is I think she will be safe, but if she tries to move . . .' He shrugged. 'Better she stays.'

Razor looked doubtful. 'So what do we do – just wait?'

'No. I think you two should start for Mexico tonight. Two of our *compañeros* will go with you and . . .' He stopped, noticing the look on Razor's face. 'Once you two are in Mexico they will not need your wife for leverage,' he said.

'Just for revenge,' Razor said. 'I'm sorry, I know what you say makes sense, but I can't leave her behind. I can't. I won't. If this Chichi-place is only forty-five kilometres away then all I need is a good map. I can get there across country in two nights.'

'We can,' Chris corrected him.

'No way,' Razor said. 'You should either head for Mexico or stay here, because if both of us are taken then there'll be no one to call in the cavalry.'

'And which cavalry is that then?'

'You know what I mean. People disappear in this country, and I kind of like the idea that someone will know to look for me.'

'Yeah, OK.'

'But I will go with you,' Tomás said unexpectedly. He owed the Englishmen his life, he thought. And he owed them for Emelia's too. But most of all he felt a fascination with this strange gringo, this soldier who had decided on the spur of the moment to risk everything for a village he had never seen before, and who danced like a madman to lure a helicopter to its destruction.

He turned to the Old Man. 'If the unit can spare me,' he added, by way of asking permission.

The Old Man looked at him, and seemed to guess what was in his heart. 'We can spare you,' he said, 'but not permanently. Be careful.'

10

The sky was clear as the two men began their journey, their path down the mountain illuminated by a piercing moon. Far below them coils of mist shone like silver snakes in the dark folds of the foothills.

Razor's initial sense of relief at discovering Hajrija was safe had worn off, and anxiety was gnawing away at the edges of his mind. The authorities might not have found her in Panajachel, but if the Old Man's sources were accurate, they were not going to stop looking. At this very moment they might be battering down the door of the house in which she was hiding.

He asked himself for the hundredth time how he could have put her in such danger. He should never have let her come to Guatemala with them. Such bloody arrogance. And now here he was heading out to rescue her like a knight in fucking armour. Was this another mistake? More overconfidence? For the first time in his professional life Razor felt besieged by self-doubt.

He knew that his effectiveness in situations like this had often come from an almost ludicrous surfeit of confidence. They all laughed at the Regimental motto, but in his case it had been almost prophetic. Every time he had dared, he had won. The trouble was, in order to make the dare effective you had to be prepared to lose, and he only had to think about it for five seconds to know that he wasn't prepared to lose Hajrija.

If Cabrera had given him another five seconds to consider the consequences he might still be alive.

Still, Razor had confidence in his companion. Tomás reminded him a little of Trooper Damien Robson, who had been part of the Bosnian team. 'The Dame' had carried himself with the same air of self-containment, and performed with the same quiet efficiency, as the Guatemalan. He had also, as Razor remembered from one conversation in Bosnia, been as protective of his sisters as Tomás seemed to be of Emelia. Razor found himself hoping that his new companion would have a longer life than the Dame.

It took them an hour and a half to reach the road which wound its way through the foothills, and another hour of easier walking before they came to their first major water obstacle. Nature had provided the first few stepping-stones, humankind a few more, and even in the thickening mist they had no trouble crossing the tumbling river.

'Another hour and we will have a short rest,' Tomás told him on the far bank. Two days ago he would have expected an argument, but that was before he discovered that these gringos could walk like Indians.

The going was uphill now, and soon they found themselves emerging from the mist, the fuzzy white arc of the moon growing sharper with each climbing stride. It took almost an hour to reach the next ridge-line, and here they stopped, sitting on some convenient rocks at the top of a pass, staring down at the lakes of mist on either side.

Tomás took a small stack of tortillas from his pack and

passed half across. 'Why did you become a soldier?' he asked, hoping the answer would give him the chance to ask the question which really interested him.

Razor shrugged. 'I just drifted into it. Couldn't think of anything else to do, I suppose. And I enjoyed the life.'

Tomás took a swig of water from the canteen and wiped his lips with the back of his hand. 'Can I ask you a personal question?' he asked.

'No harm in asking, as my mum used to say.'

'To be in an Army that is for the government – does that not sometimes, well, trouble you?'

'No . . . well, it never used to. The British Government is not like the one here. And most of the time we think of our Army as defending us against foreigners of one sort or another, from outside Britain. Your Army seems more interested in fighting its own people.'

'We are not their people.'

'Yeah, I know . . .'

'I understand what you say,' Tomás went on, 'but for me it is important to know what we are fighting *for*, and – forgive me – but when you are sent here to help this government of butchers and torturers I cannot help wondering what it is *you* think you are fighting for.'

Razor could see his point. To say he was just obeying orders didn't sound like much of a reason. 'I guess I have to believe that my government has the interests of the British people at heart, and that sending us here was part of promoting those interests.'

Put like that, he thought, it sounded lamer than lame. He made a mental note not to apply for a job in Army Recruitment.

Tomás was smiling at him though. 'I think your heart

told you what you wish to fight for on the day you kill the Kaibil colonel. It is justice.'

Razor grimaced. 'That was one moment. And a personal thing.' He didn't really want to think about why. Or what the British Army really was for these days. It was something of a stretch to see it as an instrument of justice.

Tomás took the hint, and even felt a little sorry for the Englishman. Clarity of purpose was something he had always felt grateful for, even when the cost had seemed so high.

They resumed their journey, hiking down into the misty valley and up towards another moonlit crest. It was midnight when they reached it, and over half the night's projected forty kilometres were behind them. Another long slope, this time heavily forested, led them down into another valley, and to another bridge of stones across a rushing river. For some reason the mist was much thinner here, and Razor could see the shapes of buildings looming in front of them.

Ruined buildings. The façade of a small adobe church was still standing among the weeds, its walls scorched by the fire that had apparently destroyed it. Twenty metres away a jumble of concrete blocks was all that remained of another building.

'What happened here?' Razor asked, although he had already guessed the answer.

'The Army came,' Tomás said shortly. 'See here,' he added, pointing at the ground in front of the church, where a large number of flower petals had been recently strewn. 'They are marigolds – the death flower. They have been left here to honour those who were killed.'

The two men walked on, the ghostly ruins fading behind

them. Razor told Tomás about the model village the Army had shown him and Chris in the mountains near Uspantan.

'I know the place,' Tomás said.

'What happened there?' Razor asked.

Tomás told him the story in clipped sentences, as if any extravagance of language would somehow mitigate the crimes which had been committed there. 'The Army came to the area,' he began, and Razor could feel the terrible weight of those few words. Groups of soldiers had started coming to the village looking for *subversivos*, and soon people began to disappear, their mutilated bodies turning up by the side of the road. Eventually the soldiers came in force, truckloads of them, with machine-guns. All the villagers were herded into the space in front of the church, and then the men were crammed into the small village hall, from where they could hear the women being first raped and then shot. After that the only sound for a while was the weeping of the children, and then the soldiers had cut out the little ones' stomachs one by one, opening the door of the hall so the men could see what was happening. The soldiers screamed that these children were the seeds of future *subversivos*, and that this was the only way to cleanse the country of such sickness. Then they took out the stunned men and slit their throats. The bodies had all been piled into the well to rot so that no one could live in the village again.

'That is what happened there,' Tomás said.

In the silence that followed Razor felt the mist like a cloak of sadness. How could such things happen? How could men behave like that? He remembered the same questions filling his mind in the villages above Zavik, but in Bosnia it had not been difficult for him and the others to justify their participation in the war. After all, the suits in Whitehall had not sent them in to help the Serb irregulars with their ethnic cleansing.

But hadn't that just been a matter of luck? If British interests had required victory for the Serbs then there was a good chance he and the others would have ended up fighting alongside them. It occurred to Razor that until now he had never really needed to ask himself the question which Tomás had asked, but that this period of grace was over, and that when he got back to England – he gave a wry smile in the dark – he would need to devote some thought to what exactly it was that he was fighting for.

For the moment, at least, he had no doubts. He was fighting for his own life and that of his wife. The fact that once again he seemed to be on the side of the angels was just a bonus.

It was now more than twenty-four hours since Lara had brought Hajrija to the house on the town's outskirts, and she was beginning to feel the strain of confinement. The old couple who lived there could not have been more welcoming – when she arrived both had embraced her like a long-lost favourite daughter – but their English was even more sparse than Hajrija's Spanish, and verbal communication was more or less impossible. So far, Lara had not returned.

On the previous day Hajrija had helped out with the cleaning, finished the small mountain of sewing jobs which had been waiting for the couple's daughter, and gone to bed early. Since waking up that morning she had spent most of her time pacing to and fro, trying to keep her mind occupied. She had already made up several stories about a big ginger cat named Hoddle that she would one day read to her daughter, and now she was telling the unborn baby about herself and Razor, how they had met, and where they both came from. She was just describing the house in Zavik where she had grown up, when there was a light rap on the door.

It was Lara. 'I have news,' she said. 'Your husband, he come and fetch you.'

'Not alone!?'

'No, no, he will be lost. One of the *compañeros* bring him. They hope to be here Monday morning. Before the sun comes.'

'What day is it today?'

Lara laughed. 'Saturday, of course.'

Hajrija felt joy bubbling up inside her at the prospect.

'I go,' Lara said, getting up. 'The soldiers are everywhere today, like swarm of hornets.'

Once the *compañera* had left Hajrija discovered that her joy had evaporated, and that new anxieties were busy tying a thick knot in her stomach.

Both men were woken in the late afternoon by the sound of the two Chinooks. They came no nearer than half a kilometre, dark shapes against the deep-blue eastern sky, headed for the towering bulk of the Cuchumatanes.

Sated with sleep, the two men waited in their covered hide for the light to fade before continuing their journey. This time there was chilli with the tortillas, but only water to drink. Razor would have killed for a cup of tea, but lighting a fire would have been akin to signing a suicide note.

'When will we reach Chichi-whatsit?' he asked.

'Chi-chi-cas-ten-ango,' Tomás said slowly, as if he was

teaching a small child, and then grinned. 'Tomorrow night, I hope. If things go well we can get your wife out of the town before dawn on the next day.'

Razor brought a picture of Hajrija to his mind, the water from the shower running down her laughing face, the love in her eyes, and the now familiar wave of panic threatened to engulf him. Think about something else, he told himself. Anything else. 'So why did you become a soldier?' he asked Tomás.

'I decided to fight for my people,' Tomás said simply.

'I understand that. But there are lots of your people who don't choose to do that. Why did you?'

'Ah, I see what you mean. I suppose most of us in the mountains have just come to a point where we can take no more, where we have no choice but to fight if we wish to consider ourselves human.'

'Are your parents alive?'

'No. The Army killed them both. My father, he was a good man who could not understand what was happening in our village. He just could not believe that the authorities would let things go on the way they were if they knew what was happening.' Tomás smiled sadly. 'Of course they knew exactly what was happening, and one day my father did not come home.' He sighed, and idly drew a circle in the dust.

'My mother understood,' he said quietly, 'but she went looking for justice. Not because she expected to find it, but because she wanted others to see that it could not be found in the way things are. At least, that is how I think she worked it out.' He gave Razor a rueful smile, but there was no disguising the pain in his eyes. 'She was kidnapped by the Army and raped by many men, and tortured. They cut off her ears and her nose and her breasts and they left her dying on a hillside, with soldiers there to make sure no one could try to lessen her pain.'

He stopped talking, and Razor could think of no way to soften the silence. 'What happened to you after your mother died?' he asked eventually.

'My two older brothers left to join the guerrillas after that, but I was only fourteen years old, and Emelia was only nine. We went to live with my uncle – the husband of my father's sister – in a village not far from here. It is about twenty kilometres in that direction.' He gestured towards the west.

'My uncle was an important man in the *cofradías*. Do you know what they are? They are a little like priests, a little like politicians, a little like community elders. They are the men entrusted with preserving the old traditions, of keeping our way of life alive. I learnt a lot from my uncle before he was killed,' he added. 'But that's another story – I think it is dark enough for us to leave now.'

The land grew no flatter, but as the evening wore on the two men saw increasing signs of human habitation: well-worn paths, areas of cleared forest, the wink of yellow lights in a far-off village. Even the rivers seemed tamer, lacking the same eagerness to reach the distant ocean.

Around nine o'clock they breasted a small ridge and saw a village almost immediately beneath them. Several of the houses were lit and, much to Razor's surprise, the sound of voices floated up into the night, singing voices, with an accordion for company. Razor could make no sense of the words, but there was no mistaking the joy with which they were being sung.

He felt close to tears, and wondered how a few happy

voices and an out-of-tune accordion could move him so much, when the tragedies recounted by Tomás had left him with only cold rage and a sense of hopelessness. But maybe that was obvious – in a heart of darkness nothing is more moving than a light being held aloft.

'We have friends here,' Tomás said, and led the way down the slope, stopping every few metres to look and listen. They were within fifty metres of the first house when two figures suddenly appeared in front of them. Tomás said something in the local language, and the men hurried forward to embrace him.

He introduced Razor, and they shook his hand with enthusiasm, all the while staring up at him with the wonder of men greeting a well-meaning traveller from outer space. Razor smiled back, and then took a back seat as Tomás listened to what the men had to tell him. In the village the accordion had fallen silent, but the voices were still filling the night air with their bitter-sweet beauty.

A few minutes later the two villagers were heading back towards the houses. 'An army patrol went up the next valley this afternoon,' Tomás told Razor, 'but my friends don't know where it was going. Otherwise they say all the activity has been north of here.' His teeth flashed white in the darkness. 'The army told one of the villagers they're looking for a couple of crazy gringo criminals. American drug-runners.'

In his study Colonel Serrano pored over the small-scale military map, mentally measuring distances in time. If the woman had been in Panajachel, the two men north-west of Uspantan . . . But how did they get her out of Panajachel? He looked again at the surveillance photos which had been taken in Antigua. She was wearing blue jeans, a white T-shirt and a beige jacket. Dark glasses perched on top of the swept-back hair. A good suntan for someone who had only just arrived . . .

So it wasn't a suntan. Señora Wilkinson had naturally dark skin and black hair. They had disguised her as an Indian, Serrano realized, and probably taken her out on a bus.

His finger followed the road out of Panajachel, through Sololá, north to Los Encuentros and then, after a slight hesitation, north again to Chichicastenango. The mumbo-jumbo town. Crawling with holy idiots and *subversivos*. If the tourists didn't spend so much of their money there the Army would have long since razed the place to the ground.

Serrano let his finger rest on the town for a second, then exchanged it for a fist, smiling as he did so.

It was almost three in the morning and the mist in the narrow valley seemed to be growing thicker by the minute. But not evenly – it was a bit like his mum's custard, Razor thought, thicker in some places than others. Sometimes the river below the path was visible, and occasionally even the steep rocky wall which lay beyond the cascading water swam into view, but for long periods now Razor's field of vision had included no more than the blurry figure of his companion and a few metres of rocks and grass on either side of the path.

Given the noise the river was making, the two men were lucky to hear the advancing patrol. Later they were unable to agree on exactly what it was they had heard – Tomás claimed that someone had laughed, Razor that the man had cursed – but whatever it was it stopped both men in their tracks as if they had hit an invisible wall.

The noise had sounded so close, but all they could hear was the river, and all they could see was the wall of grey. Both men made the same mental calculations, and simultaneously gestured each other off the path in the direction of the water. The grass and rocks were slippery, the descent decidedly uneven, and they half scrambled, half fell the twenty metres or so, ending up crouching precariously a few feet above the swirling black water.

No more sounds had emerged out of the mist, and they were just beginning to wonder if nature had played a trick on their ears when the first in a line of dim, shadowy figures came into view on the path above. Both men froze again, inwardly praying that the view looking down was dimmer than the view looking up. The temptation to bring the Uzis into the firing position was almost irresistible, but any movement might well be fatal.

The figures filed past above them, like a long line of armed ghosts. Ten men, Razor counted. Fifteen, twenty, twenty-three. And then they were gone.

The two men waited another minute to be sure, then climbed back up to the path. Tomás wiped his brow in mock relief and turned to go, just as the figure stumbled out of the mist in front of them. The man's rifle seemed to almost leap from his hands as he tried to bring it round, and Tomás's Uzi stitched a line across his chest, throwing both man and weapon into the air.

Someone shouted on the path behind them, but the two men were already running. Razor glanced down at the dead soldier as he leapt over him, and saw that the zip on the man's trousers was undone. He had obviously dropped off the back of the line for a piss. Which had been bad luck, both for him and for them.

They ran on, listening for the sounds of pursuit, but for several minutes they could hear nothing more lethal than their own footfalls and breathing above the monotonous rush of the river below. Then a sub-machine-gun opened up in the distance, much too far behind them to do any damage.

They kept running, willing themselves on. After another half a kilometre the path wound up and out of the narrowing valley, and crossed a small high meadow where swirls of mist alternated with patches of stars, before descending once more into the realms of opacity. The two men slowed their pace to conserve energy, both knowing that when the dawn came and the mist lifted the enemy would be filling the sky with reconnaissance flights.

At the bottom of the next valley they took to the river. According to Tomás the Army never used tracker dogs, but Razor was afraid the bastards might make an exception in their case. After a couple of kilometres they left the river for one of its tributary streams, heading up a forested hillside toward its source. By the time they left the water, their feet half-numbed by the cold, first light was only an hour away, and it was time to dig in for the coming day. Tomás reckoned they were now no more than twelve kilometres from Chichicastenango.

The two men dug a rectangular scrape in a dry dip, and embellished the tarpaulin cover with artistically draped foliage. Unless someone literally dropped in to see them they would be safe until nightfall.

They slept in shifts as a precaution, but there was no need. Helicopters were audible for most of the day, but the hunt for them seemed concentrated about ten kilometres to the north: either someone had reported a false sighting or no one in authority had been able to believe they could have travelled as far as they had. Not a single patrol disturbed the serenity of their forested hillside.

At around five they shared the usual scant meal and talked about the night to come. He would take them to a hill above Chichicastenango, Tomás said, and then he would go down on his own to fetch Hajrija in the hour before dawn. Razor felt like protesting about the arrangement, but unfortunately it made sense – his height would be a give-away on the streets of the town.

'Do you know the place well?' he asked.

Tomás nodded. 'We used to go there when we lived with my uncle. His *cofradía* conducted many ceremonies in the Church of San Tomás.' He smiled. 'There are many tourists now, and perhaps it is not what it was, but that is a good thing as well as a bad thing. The less land my people have the more they need the money from the tourists.'

'But you come from near Lake Atitlán, right?'

'Santiago Atitlán. It is on the south shore of the lake.'

'So why are you fighting with the Old Man in the Cuchumatanes? Are there no guerrilla units around the lake?'

'Yes, there are: the people who organized your wife's escape from Panajachel are part of one unit. It is just chance that Emelia and I are in the north. I met the Old Man in a refugee camp in Mexico and we have been together ever since. It is many years now.'

'And how many more, do you think?'

'Until the Old Man dies . . . I do not know.'

'He looks indestructible. But can you win? Or can there

be some sort of peace? What about this agreement which the Government wants to sign with you?'

Tomás snorted. 'Their agreement is a waste of paper. The issue here is land, and their agreement doesn't even mention it. When we are strong enough to make them talk about land, then there will be a chance of peace. But I am afraid that will take a long time. Five years . . . maybe ten.' He smiled ruefully. 'It is hard to think about it sometimes. We have each other, and we know our cause is just, and our hearts are full, but all of us sometimes long for a normal life. A husband or a wife, children, enough land to grow food on, an end to living in fear. Of course one day we would like proper schools and clinics and a life that is easier, but the simple things must come first. No one should live every day of their lives in fear.'

The dusk was deepening in the forest. 'It's time to go,' Tomás said.

Hajrija sat awkwardly in the confined space, trying not to worry about the staleness of the air or the complete lack of light. She had been in hiding for two hours now, ever since a breathless Lara had arrived with news that the Army had begun a house-to-house search of the town. The old couple had taken it calmly, lifting up the rug in the corner of their main room to reveal the dug-out hole beneath.

She had gone in willingly enough, and the sound of the soldiers searching the house above her had confirmed the soundness of the arrangement, but now, three hours after their departure, she was beginning to feel more than a little disoriented by the experience. Hajrija had always thought the movies exaggerated the horrors of solitary confinement, but the sharpening edge of hysteria in her own mind suggested they had not.

And the more she thought about it, the clearer it became that the real surprise was how long it had taken her to realize the seriousness of the situation. But then again, she thought, smiling grimly to herself in the darkness, it wasn't so hard to work out why it had taken her so long. When all you met was kindness, it was hard to take evil and its consequences seriously.

Two platoon-strength units of guerrillas had left on the same night as Tomás and Razor, leaving the base camp more than half empty. For the next two days and nights Chris had helped out with the maintenance chores, taken his turn on sentry duty, and enjoyed several walks in the forest with Emelia, book and binoculars. They had neither seen nor heard another laughing falcon, but on one foray up the mountain they had surprised a Montezuma quail crouching in the grass, its boldly patterned black and white face peering out at them with almost comic alarm.

The camp's social life was concentrated in the evenings, when groups of *compas* would gather around the butane stoves on which dinner had been cooked, and then there would be talking, storytelling, and sometimes singing, deep into the night.

There would also be a great deal of flirting. Some of the *compas* were obviously partnered off, but there was no way for Chris to know how permanent the relationships were. He wondered if strict Catholic precepts in this regard had ever been adopted by the Mayans, and if so, whether the pressures of life in the mountains had led to a loosening of what was deemed acceptable.

That evening he asked Emelia.

She thought about it for a moment. 'At the beginning,' she said, 'when more than a few women came to the mountains to fight, I think it was hard for all those who had been brought up to believe sex outside marriage was wrong. And not just for the women – I think some of the men had a hard time accepting women who gave them what they said they wanted! But over the years, well, we are human beings and being in love and having sexual relations are part of being human.

'Of course, it is not the same as in a village or even the city. We cannot ever pretend we are living a carefree life – quite the opposite, in fact – and just as we must always be on our guard against the enemy, so we must be twice as careful in how we deal with each other. We cannot afford jealousies and resentments in the camp, so we must be serious in love as we are in all other things. But I think that is good.

'It is hard to see someone you love die,' she said, and the slight change of tone in her voice made Chris aware that this was something she knew from first experience.

'But of course the struggle goes on,' she added.

'Did you lose someone?' Chris asked.

'Yes, I lost someone. His name was Francisco. He was killed on an operation. A year ago now.' She stared out across the rapidly darkening vista, defiance in the set of her lips, loss in her eyes. 'It seems a long time, but it isn't.'

That explained why the men rarely flirted with her, Chris thought.

'And of course we cannot have pregnant women in the mountains,' she went on, as if determined to move the conversation away from the personal level. 'If an accident happens then the *compañera* must return to her village or the city until the baby is born, and then she must leave the child with a relative if she wishes to return to combat.'

She turned her face to his in the gloom, wondering if he could understand what she was saying.

By some unfortunate quirk the mountain bowl which held Chichicastenango was free of any concealing mist. Looking down through the pines from their position on the hill Razor could see the sleeping town spread out beneath, the two white churches standing sentry at either end of the main square.

At least the moon would soon be down, he thought, turning to look for Tomás. His companion was crouching in front of the strange stone idol which resided on the hill, and which he claimed was thousands of years old. Pascual Abaj was its name, and according to Tomás it was the local representative of the Mayan earth god, whose name Razor had already forgotten. Scattered in front of the idol were a variety of offerings left by visitors in either hope or gratitude: several bunches of flowers, a small bottle of local brandy, two packets of cigarettes and a can of Coca-Cola.

Tomás got to his feet, feeling strengthened by his communion with Pascual Abaj, and looked at his watch. 'I must go soon,' he said.

'I know,' Razor replied, looking again at the map Tomás had drawn for him. He could think of nothing more to ask. With any luck his friend would return with Hajrija before dawn, and he would have no need to use it.

The two men shook hands almost formally, and then embraced. There was an almost serene expression in the guerrilla's eyes, Razor noticed. In his own he imagined there was only anxiety. 'Good luck, mate,' he murmured, but Tomás was already disappearing down through the trees, his mind focused on what lay ahead.

They had been observing the town for four hours, and there had been little activity in that time. One three-truck convoy had passed through on its way to the north, the noise of its passage down the cobbled streets enough to wake the dead, but there had been no sign of any motorized patrols within the town itself. There might be foot patrols, but none had been visible from the top of their hill. With any luck most of the local military were still scouring the countryside, but Tomás knew he could take nothing for granted.

He reached the foot of the trees just as the moon disappeared behind the mountains to his left, casting the town into deeper shadow. Keeping low, he crept round the edge of a cornfield and through the backyard of a tumbledown shack. On the other side he reached the small road which led along the rim of a ravine and into the town. A dog barked in the yard he had just passed, as if it had only belatedly realized its responsibilities.

Tomás started up the road, one hand on the butt of the handgun that was tucked into his belt. It would have been nice to have the Uzi, but there was no way of carrying the sub-machine-gun as a concealed weapon, and there was always the chance he would need to pass himself off as just another Indian.

The road turned away from the ravine and a possible escape route. Now there were houses on either side of a steeply sloping street – a death trap if an Army patrol turned one of the corners in front of him. Tomás kept close to the buildings, listening for the sound of an approaching enemy.

At the crossroads he put an eye to the corner wall, and looked down the street which led into the main square. Almost directly ahead of him the church of his saintly namesake thrust its plain white façade towards the heavens, and he felt the weight of the memories, both his own and his people's, which the sight evoked.

He cautiously advanced to the corner of the square, and crouched down in the shelter of an empty stall only metres away from the church steps. The smell of incense still lingered in the air, and in his mind Tomás could hear the fireworks and see the Virgin Mary held aloft on a sun-filled afternoon.

The town seemed locked in silence, and for a moment he let his mind wander, north towards Emelia in the mountains, south towards the Englishman on the hill. Watching Razor try to make sense of Guatemala, Tomás had realized how narrow his own experience was. Emelia was right – it was important to learn about other worlds, and even to visit them if possible. Their way of life was not so fragile that it need fear contact with others.

After the war, he told himself. Nothing lasted for ever.

He looked at his watch – it was half-past four. He had been in the same place now for ten minutes, and heard nothing. Slipping out of his hiding place, he started out for the opposite corner of the square, turning right, then left, then right again, through the labyrinth of empty stalls.

He was two-thirds of the way across when the spotlights came on, and for a second he stood half blinded in the glare, before his survival instinct kicked in, and sent him scrambling into the shelter of a stall.

It was only then, crouching in the dark, that he realized no gun had been fired. They wanted him alive.

'If you surrender yourself, you will be well treated,' a voice shouted. Its owner could hardly keep the amusement out of his voice.

Tomás could hear soldiers all around him now, talking, shuffling their cramped legs – they had no need to be silent any more. From every side of the square he seemed to hear a hum of expectancy.

I am a dead man, he thought. There is no way out of this, none at all. I made what is mine. Including this death.

Razor would have seen the light flooding the square, known that it had all gone wrong. Tomás idly wondered what the Englishman would do next. It was no longer his concern. He had just joined the end of a line which stretched back hundreds of years, a line of deaths which brought pain to the living, that pain which life dulled to an ache and new death resharpened. He felt the pain his death would bring to his sister, but also a sense almost of relief, almost of vindication. He had stayed true, he had not faltered.

He got slowly to his feet, and stepped out once more into the light. He was sure they wouldn't shoot him – the death they had planned would take weeks, even months.

'Lay down your gun,' the same voice shouted from the shadows.

As Tomás looked up at the cross atop the church and smiled to himself, the voice in the darkness was shouting something else, but Tomás didn't hear what it was. With great care he slid the barrel of the gun into his mouth and pulled the trigger.

11

On the hill above Chichicastenango, Razor had seen the square below suddenly drenched in light, and had sought in vain for an optimistic explanation. Now, hearing the single shot echo out across the town, he feared the worst.

He fought back the urge to follow the other man down. If Tomás was still alive and free then he would return. If he was captured or dead then there was nothing Razor could do.

It was now after five o'clock, and it would begin to get light within the hour. Razor studied the road which ran alongside the ravine through his binoculars and found no sign of either Tomás or the enemy moving in his direction.

He couldn't sit on this hill for ever, but for the moment at least he seemed to be safe.

The minutes went by, slowly eroding what Razor's instinct told him was already a forlorn hope. The birds began singing in the pines around him, and light filtered over the eastern wall of the valley. Pascual Abaj stared back at him with supreme indifference, and not for the first time Razor considered liberating the small bottle of brandy which had been placed before the stone idol as an offering.

He decided it would probably be a bad career move to anger the local deity.

Tourists came up this hill, Tomás had said. Gringo tourists. And what came up had to go down. If he could somehow attach himself to a group, Razor decided, then he should have no trouble entering the town unobserved. Always assuming there wasn't some bastard down there counting the tourists out and counting them in again. Finding the house where Hajrija was being hidden might be more problematic, but he could worry about that when the time came.

After all, what other choices did he have? Surrender? Heading back north with his tail between his legs? A call to International Rescue?

He walked across the brow of the hill to the side furthest from the town, used his hands to dig a hole under a bush for the two Uzis and packs, and then returned to the stone idol, wondering how long he would have to wait. Tomás had told him that it was the market which brought most of the tourist buses, and the market was only held on Thursdays and Sundays. Today was Monday, which didn't bode well.

A few minutes later he saw an Indian girl toiling up the path towards him. She was surprised to find him at the top, but lost no time in trying to sell him some of the potential idol-offerings she was carrying. Buoyed up by her presence – she obviously expected tourists that day – he bought a bunch of flowers and laid them out in front of Pascual Abaj.

An hour went by, and another. She cast the occasional curious look in his direction, but generally seemed content to whittle away at a piece of wood, and Razor began to think she had climbed the hill more in hope than expectation. He was starting to consider brazenly entering the town on his own when three women and two men appeared on the path below.

As their conversation became audible it became apparent that at least some of the party were English. This raised other questions in Razor's mind. Should he give them a message for the embassy? And if so, what should it say?

No, he decided. It was too complicated, and if they were to look like innocent tourists then they had to be innocent tourists. If he wanted to ring the embassy he could do it himself.

On reaching the summit the fivesome greeted him with nods and then inspected Pascual Abaj, laughing at the gifts of cigarettes and brandy. One of them suggested taking a photograph and selling it to a tobacco company for an advertising hoarding. Razor let them get used to his silent presence and then, while one couple was engaged in bargaining with the Indian girl, he approached the other three and asked if they could recommend a hotel in the town. He had intended to come just for the day, he explained, thinking the famous market would be open seven days a week.

The man, who looked all of nineteen, studied him pityingly, as if no true traveller could have made such a mistake. 'Our hotel is OK,' one of the women told him, 'though the waiters are a bit creepy – they all wear traditional costume.' She walked across to where they could see the town spread out below, and showed him where it was.

Razor asked her about herself and where she was from and where they were all going, and by the time they started back down the hill he was almost one of the family.

'I think there was trouble in the night,' the girl told him.

'We heard what sounded like a gunshot and this morning the square was sealed off.'

It didn't seem to have upset them very much. They stopped to buy and consume Cokes at a shop on the ravine road, while an Indian boy watched from the doorway, anxious to make sure no one escaped with an empty bottle. No soldiers appeared on this road, and none were visible as they entered the town. 'The hotel's down there,' the girl said, pointing out a large, white building with black-shuttered windows about a hundred metres down the street. 'We're going to a café. See you later, maybe,' she added almost wistfully.

Razor reached the hotel without mishap, and went straight to the desk to ask for a room. The receptionist, a plump Ladina with a big smile, asked for his passport.

He reached for his pocket and stopped himself. 'I've left it in the car,' he improvised.

'We have to see it,' she said, her smile still fixed in place.

'I'll get it,' he said, turning away, and found himself staring down the barrel of the gun in Major Romeo Osorio's hand.

Hajrija had spent much of the night awake, waiting for the desperately desired knock on the door, but around four o'clock the old woman had appeared and she had allowed herself to drift off into sleep. The shot had jerked her back to consciousness, and for a moment she thought herself back in Sarajevo, sleeping on the floor of an abandoned high-rise while her partner scoured the buildings on the other side of the Miljacka for signs of a Serb sniper.

The terrible truth had then dawned, and she had braced herself for more distant gunfire. When none came the need to find out what had happened was almost irresistible. She knew it would be a fatal error, endangering not only herself but also her hosts and potential rescuers, but it still cost every shred of her self-discipline not to go rushing out into the night.

What if he's dead? she asked herself over and over. What if he was dead without even knowing he had a daughter?

When the day finally dawned the old woman had gone out in search of information. She came back an hour later looking upset, but still managed a comforting smile for Hajrija. Several minutes of desperate mime failed to clarify what had actually happened, and the next few hours were the longest of Hajrija's life. When Lara finally appeared shortly before eleven she felt as if she had been waiting for days.

Lara also looked upset, but wasted no time in explaining why. 'The news is bad,' she said, 'but not the worst for you. The *compañero* who accompanied your husband is dead. He was surrounded in the market and he took his own life . . .'

'Oh no . . .'

'Your husband was taken by the Army about an hour ago, in a hotel in the town. We think Tomás – the *compañero* – must have left him outside the town, and when Tomás did not come back . . .' She shrugged.

Hajrija felt panic threatening to overwhelm her. 'What can I do?' she said. 'Where have they taken him?'

'Be calm,' Lara said, taking both of Hajrija's hands in her own. 'He is a foreigner, and not just a tourist, and they will think two times before they treat him badly. And while they do this thinking we must tell your government what happens.'

'I understand,' Hajrija said, and took a deep breath. 'I am sorry, I . . . you are right, we must phone the embassy in Guatemala City . . .'

'We try already. The line is busy, and one minute after we try the soldiers appear at the public phone we use. They listen to all calls that leave the town.'

'Then what can we do?'

'I hope you have answer.'

'We cannot call England direct?'

'Yes, but it take half an hour to connect – the soldiers will arrive in two minutes.'

Hajrija ran a hand through her hair, anguish on her face. 'I don't know what . . .' she began, and then an idea struck her. 'How about Chile?' she asked. 'Can you call Chile?'

'Chile?' Lara asked, surprised. 'Yes, but . . .'

'We have a friend in Chile. If you pass him a message, he will call England from there.'

'Does he speak Spanish?'

'Yes, and his wife too. She is Argentinian.'

'You have the number?'

Hajrija experienced a sudden sinking feeling, and then an equally strong surge of relief when she realized that the Dochertys' number was in the small address book she had brought with postcards in mind.

Postcards! she thought, reaching into the travel pouch for the book. 'Just tell him Razor has been . . .' She searched her mind for the English slang which her husband was so fond of. 'Banged up,' she said triumphantly. 'Tell him Razor has been banged up in Chichicastenango. Tell him to call Barney, who will know what to do. And tell him the bird-watcher and Razor's wife are not together.'

'Is this all?' Lara asked, her ballpoint poised.

'Yes, yes, I think so,' Hajrija said. She wondered how 'banged up' would translate into Spanish, and whether Docherty would be able to translate it back again. She thought about the man or woman who would be chosen to make the call, and how they would wait to be connected, listening all the while for the sound of soldiers' boots. And she thought about the man who had already died for them that day.

In his office in the Palacio Nacional, Colonel Serrano listened to Major Osorio's report and blew smoke at the ceiling, a satisfied smile on his face.

'Do you want him brought to you?' Osorio asked.

'No,' Serrano said instinctively. He wanted at least a modicum of distance between the Englishman and his embassy, not to mention the foreign press.

'So where?' Osorio asked.

'Let me think about it,' Serrano said. 'Wait there, and I'll talk to you in a few minutes.'

He placed the receiver face up on the desk and walked across to the window. Another bunch of tourists were being shepherded around the courtyard below, camcorders whirring.

Before taking a decision on where to take the Englishman, Serrano realized, he needed to take another – on what they were going to do with him. No doubt the Kaibiles had first claim – the man had murdered their colonel, after all. But the man had been arrested in a hotel lobby, in front of both local and foreign witnesses, and if the Kaibiles decided to dismember him piece by piece then there would be repercussions. Manageable ones, no doubt, but repercussions all the same.

And Wilkinson might have other uses than the simple indulgence of a few men's pleasures. A military trial and execution could offer dramatic and much-needed proof of the regime's commitment to the rule of law.

Serrano smiled to himself at the elegance of the thought, but decided that for the moment he would keep his options open. The first priority was to discover the whereabouts of the other two fugitives, the soldier Martinson and the wife.

He walked back to the desk and picked up the phone. 'Osorio? Take him to the San Pedro facility for questioning. Use Goicouria. We need to know where his partner is, and his wife.'

He listened for a moment.

'You may. But don't leave any physical evidence. No burns or amputations. This may be one body we will need to put on public display.'

In the third-floor apartment in Santiago de Chile, Jamie Docherty put down the phone, a bemused expression on his face.

'Who was it, Daddy?' eight-year-old Marie asked him.

'I've no idea,' he said absent-mindedly, his mind busy going back over what the woman had said. She had spoken Spanish, but Docherty had received the definite impression that it was not her first language.

'Was it a man or a woman?' Marie asked.

'A woman. Let me think for a moment, sweetheart.'

Docherty borrowed one of the coloured pencils his daughter had been using and, feeling like he was taking an SAS memory test, wrote down everything he could remember on a spare sheet of paper. It all made sense except the one phrase, which suggested Razor had been lifted into the air by an explosion.

Docherty wished Isabel was there, rather than away on business in Buenos Aires. He stared out of the window at the snowcapped Andes, as if he could see through them to where she was.

He read through the message again, and noticed how little had actually been spelt out. The 'bird-watcher' was probably Chris Martinson, the 'wife' presumably Hajrija, 'Barney' the Regimental CO in Hereford. *Detonación levantado*, he thought. An up bang. Bang up. Banged up. Razor had been arrested.

In Guatemala that was not good news. Docherty went through to the other room, rummaged through the desk for his British address book, and cast a despairing glance at his day's work on the computer screen. Maybe he should use this call to tell Barney Davies he was writing his memoirs, he thought. And maybe not.

As he waited for the international operator to make the connection he wondered what the hell Razor and Chris were doing in Guatemala. If Hajrija was there as well it could hardly be on SAS business. He remembered the couple of weeks he and Razor had spent there in 1980, and grimaced. He had not enjoyed dealing with the Guatemalan military, which seemed officered by men with brains, education, culture – and all the moral sense of sharks. The only enjoyable part of the business had been his talks with the leader of the guerrillas, who had gone under the name El Espíritu. That old man had known a thing or too about the military arts, and the other arts as well. And he had been a damned good chess player.

The phone was ringing in Barney Davies's cottage, and

Docherty felt a surge of pleasure at the prospect of talking to his old CO, whatever the circumstances.

A woman answered, and seemed to sigh with resignation when he asked to speak to Lieutenant-Colonel Davies. The CO didn't sound much more welcoming, or at least not until he realized who was calling him.

Docherty told him about the phone message from Guatemala, and offered his translation.

Davies listened, and uttered a short commentary when the Scot was finished: 'Christ almighty, what a fucking mess!'

'I expect you've got people to call,' Docherty said, 'but when you've got a minute it would be nice to know what this is all about.'

'Give me your number,' Davies said, 'I'll call you back later tonight.'

Docherty did so, feeling, not for the first time, an absurd longing for the life he had been glad to leave behind.

Martin Clarke was sipping a between-acts drink at Sadler's Wells, wondering whether to plead extra work and send his wife home in a taxi at the end of the opera, when an employee materialized between them and informed the junior minister he was urgently required on the phone.

Clarke made a helpless gesture to his wife and followed the man downstairs, hoping to God that whatever the problem was it would save him from another hour of ludicrous plotting and overweight warbling. He was shown into the manager's office, where an open phone was waiting on the desk.

'Martin Clarke,' he told the unknown caller.

'Lieutenant-Colonel Davies,' a familiar voice replied. 'Sergeant Wilkinson has been captured,' he said without preamble, 'and I assume you'll want to get your people in Guatemala City on the job right away. If the Guatemalans think we don't know he's been taken . . .'

'How *do* you know?'

Davies explained about the message which had been received via Chile.

'Sounds like some stupid stunt MI6 would pull,' Clarke commented. 'Why didn't whoever it was just ring the embassy?'

'Christ only knows. Does it matter?'

'I suppose not,' Clarke admitted, though he felt far from sympathetic. Shooting a Guatemalan colonel had obviously not been enough for Wilkinson – he had managed to get himself caught into the bargain. The media would have a bloody field day. 'I trust that this business will remain under wraps,' he said.

'If you get your people in Guatemala City moving then maybe it will,' Davies said. 'But if my lad gets tortured or killed because somebody fucks up at your end then I've no doubt the story will be leaked to every newspaper in Fleet Street.'

Clarke managed to keep his temper. 'I don't respond well to threats, Lieutenant-Colonel,' he said coldly. 'And I'm every bit as concerned over Sergeant Wilkinson's well-being as you are,' he added, realizing in the process that it was probably true. If the Guatemalans did torture or kill Wilkinson the Opposition in the House would be queuing up to ask the man who had sent him embarrassing questions.

'I will get back to you in an hour or so,' he told Davies, pressed the disconnecting bar, and punched out another number.

'Get hold of our embassy in Guatemala City,' he told the man on the Foreign Office night duty desk. 'Get them to start pushing the locals about one of our nationals they arrested today in a place called Chichicastenango – no, I don't know how to spell it. His name's Wilkinson . . . yes, the soldier they wanted help from. Then get hold of their embassy here and make the usual requests – treatment according to the law, full access, et cetera et cetera. Firm but not aggressive. And don't talk down to the bastards – they resent it even more than the Arabs . . . Yes, I'm on my way in now.'

That at least solved the problem of his wife, he realized, as the limousine accelerated down Rosebery Avenue in the direction of Holborn. He wondered whether his research assistant would be available for overtime on a Saturday night.

At the Foreign Office he discovered that they had not yet been able to reach the British Embassy in Guatemala City, and that the Guatemalan Ambassador to the Court of St James's was still being sought among the casinos of Mayfair. 'Start trying the other EEC embassies,' Clarke ordered. 'It's about time we found a use for the wretched Europeans.'

When Razor was bundled into the helicopter he more than half expected that the destination would be Guatemala City, where G-2 was probably already furnishing a suite for him in Inquisition-style décor. Contrary to this expectation, the Huey flew south-west for about ten minutes across the jumbled mountains, skirted the western end of a large volcano-surrounded lake, and came down to land in a wide valley flanked with pine forest. Razor briefly noted the approach road winding back in the direction of the lake, walls topped with the familiar glint of his namesake's wire, and several low barracks buildings. There was only one vehicle in sight, and only a few human figures, uniformed or otherwise. It wasn't a military camp, he realized, and, despite the guard towers, it didn't feel like a prison in the usual sense. But it seemed like a very private place, which didn't seem like very good news.

Look on the bright side, he told himself, as they bundled him out of the helicopter. They had fastened his wrists behind his back with wire, but other than that, and much to his surprise, no one had laid a hand on him.

His escort took him down a paved pathway between cinder-block offices, into a one-storey building, and down a long corridor, their boots echoing on the tiled floor. Doors stood open on empty rooms – the place seemed half-abandoned.

One of the guards yanked on his bound wrists, turning him left and propelling him into one of the rooms. The door slammed shut behind him.

As hotels went he wouldn't have given it many stars. Walls and floor were both bare, provided no account was taken of the ominous-looking stains. The only furniture was a plastic bucket, which sat proudly in the river of sunlight streaming in through the single, barred window.

He sat down in the shade, feeling the gravity of his predicament. And not only his – where the hell was Hajrija, and how would she get out of this God-forsaken country now?

He should never have gone down to the town, he told himself. He should never have shot the fucking colonel. He should have argued with the bastard, threatened to expose him.

Cabrera would have killed them both.

Get a grip, he murmured to himself. Good or bad, it was done. He had to concentrate on what lay ahead, had to prepare himself. It might be presumptuous on his part, but he was expecting to be interrogated before he was shot, or whatever it was that they did to colonel-killers in Guatemala. Give them medals was what they ought to do.

He supposed the seriousness of his interrogation would depend on how much his interrogators cared about outside opinion, always assuming they didn't intend disguising the results of their work in something like a car accident. His arrest had been witnessed by several tourists, which might be some help. The problem was, he had a distinct feeling the bastards really were past caring what the world thought. Everyone said they were sadistic psychos, so what did they have to lose by behaving that way?

Razor had to admit he felt scared. It was natural enough. The trick was not to let the fear take you over. He took his mind back to the interrogation which had been part of the selection procedure when he first joined the SAS: those bastards from the Training Wing screaming at him, while their mates beat the hell out of an old mattress in the next room and tried for an Oscar in groans and whimpers. And he had been scared all right, though not scared enough to crack.

In the Gulf War some captured members of the Regiment had gone through the real thing, and most of them had managed to hold out. Razor suddenly remembered the 'fear litany' from *Dune*, one of his favourite books as a teenager. He couldn't recall the actual words, though, or at least only the one line: 'fear is the mind-killer'. He focused on that sentiment until he felt calmer.

Footsteps sounded in the corridor outside, and then the sound of a key in the lock. Osorio appeared in the doorway, and there was another man looking over his shoulder, slender, slightly effeminate, with intelligent eyes. Empty, intelligent eyes.

'Not quite up to English standards,' Osorio said with a smile, looking round. 'This is Lieutenant Goicouria,' he added, introducing the other man. 'He is an interrogator.'

'Nobody's perfect.'

The interrogator didn't seem to have a sense of humour.

Razor stifled an imaginary yawn. The first SAS advice when it came to resisting interrogation was to pretend you were more tired than you were. Interrogators hated interrogatees who slipped prematurely into unconsciousness.

'We have some questions for you,' Osorio said.

Razor said nothing.

'Where is your partner Martinson?' Osorio asked, leaning back against the door jamb and lighting a cigarette. Goicouria simply stared – he was apparently not the sort of interrogator who asked questions.

'I hope he is in Mexico by now.'

'By which route was he travelling?'

'I've no idea. The guerrillas were taking him.'

'And your wife?'

'What about my wife? Do you know where she is?'

'No, but we think you do. You were supposed to meet her in Chichicastenango. Is that not correct?'

'I was supposed to meet a guerrilla who would take me to her.'

'His name?'

'I do not know.'

'Where were you to meet?'

'In the hotel, but I met you instead.'

Osorio looked at him with amusement. 'You are lying,' he said with quiet satisfaction. 'Your friend tells a very different story.'

'Which friend is that?'

'The friend who accompanied you on your journey to Chichicastenango – the Indian we captured in the square at five this morning. He says your wife is in the town and you know where. Is he lying? If so we will have to try more persuasive forms of questioning.'

So Tomás was definitely dead, Razor thought. Osorio didn't even have a name for the man he had killed.

'He is lying,' Razor said. 'Indian speak with forked tongue,' he added poetically, and yawned again.

'Have you heard of the *capucha*?' Goicouria asked. It was the first time he had spoken, and his voice had a slightly rasping quality to it, like velvet dragged across sandpaper.

'Type of coffee, is it?'

Osorio dropped the cigarette and carefully ground it out with his polished boot. He then opened the door and called in the two guards who were waiting outside. They pulled Razor unceremoniously to his feet and hustled him out of the door.

Less than a minute later they were in another room, windowless but twice as large, and with rather more in the way of furniture. There were several upright chairs, one of which was embedded in the bare concrete floor. This one had straps, giving it a superficial resemblance to an electric chair, but the back was open and there were no wires in sight. What looked like a collapsible picnic table stood against one wall, but it seemed lamentably devoid of the ham sandwiches, crisps and jellies Razor remembered from childhood excursions to Epping Forest. In fact, one of the objects on the table looked like a giant condom, and Razor suddenly remembered where he had heard the word *capucha*.

They sat him in the anchored chair, and as one of the guards tied his ankles together the other tightened the strap around his waist. A few feet away Goicouria was waiting, the latex hood in his hands, holding it almost lovingly. When the guard was finished with the strap he was told to fetch a bucket of cold water.

Razor waited, steeling himself for what was to come.

The guard returned all too quickly with the water.

'This is just a demonstration,' Goicouria said, stepping forward to force the *capucha* down over Razor's head. He then tightened the string around the hood's neck, cutting off any access to the outside air, and smashed a fist into Razor's back, forcing him to gulp for whatever air was still inside. The SAS man felt panic rising, and tried to tell himself that they didn't want him dead.

It was getting harder and harder to breathe, almost impossible, and his lungs seemed to be tearing themselves apart in the effort to find air. As his chest seemed bound to explode with the pressure he felt his consciousness begin to waver, the pain to recede, and then the hood was pulled from his head, water splashed in his face, and the pain was back, redoubled in intensity as his lungs clawed for the suddenly available oxygen.

They let him savour the pain for a minute, before Goicouria asked him in a whisper: 'Where is your wife?'

'I don't know,' was Razor's answering rasp.

The hood went on again, and again. Four times in all, before the man appeared in the doorway with the message for Osorio which stopped them.

They half carried him back to the now darkened room, and left him lying on the floor, free to wonder whether he would ever breathe properly again.

Chris and Emelia set out for the south soon after dusk, following the same path which Razor and Tomás had taken only seventy-two hours before. When the confirmation of her brother's death had reached the base camp earlier that day Emelia had insisted on making the journey, and a doubtful Old Man had finally agreed to let her go. She was the only Tzutujil-speaker in the camp, and she knew the way. If the Englishman insisted on following his now arrested partner, then there was no one better to guide him. The Old Man only hoped she wasn't mad enough with grief to throw her life away.

So did Chris, as much for her sake as his own. He saw the grim set of her mouth, the coldness of eyes that had always seemed so full of warmth, and felt like weeping himself, for her, for her brother, for the whole damn country.

He wasn't at all sure he was thinking that clearly himself, but for once in his life he didn't much care. She needed him, Hajrija needed him, Razor needed him. It seemed enough.

The practicalities were harder to judge. Hajrija was being smuggled out of Chichicastenango that night, and taken south to a village near Lake Atitlán, where it was hoped they could join her in three nights' time. There was no word yet on Razor's whereabouts, but the guerrillas were looking, and so, presumably, was London. Chris hoped to God someone found him before it was too late.

It was already too late for Tomás, he thought, as he followed Emelia's diminutive figure down the mountain path. There were no birds singing in the night forest, and even if there had been, he didn't think she would have heard them.

In Hereford it was almost midnight, and Barney Davies was beginning to doubt whether Martin Clarke had ever really intended to call him back. Jean's decision to spend the night at her own home had initially relieved him – he could hardly give her his full attention while all this was going on – but two malts later he was beginning to wonder if he should have been a little more obviously upset that their evening together had been spoiled.

He poured a third, and carried it across to the sound system, where he inserted a CD of late-thirties Billie Holiday and pressed the Shuffle button. The band swung into 'I can't believe that you're in love with me', and just as she took up the melody the telephone finally rang.

'Lieutenant-Colonel Davies? Martin Clarke. I haven't got much to tell you, I'm afraid. The Guatemalan Embassy here has been left in no doubt that we expect Wilkinson to be correctly treated, and we finally managed to get through to our embassy in Guatemala City about an hour ago. They passed on the same message to the Guatemalan Government, who have agreed to let someone from the embassy see your man in the morning.'

'That's excellent,' Davies said, feeling more than a little relieved.

'It's a start,' Clarke agreed, 'but don't expect too much. Our people out there don't have much hope of Wilkinson being released in the near future. If at all. Shooting colonels is not a very popular pastime.'

'I'm sure he had his reasons.'

'Doesn't everyone. His may seem less than adequate to the Guatemalan Government.'

'I understand that. But when all's said and done, they were responsible for arranging the whole business. That must count for something, surely?'

'I doubt it,' Clarke said brutally. 'If you asked a plumber in to fix your washing machine, you'd still be a touch irritated if he murdered your wife.'

Davies had to admit there was logic to that. 'So what's next?' he asked.

'We'll see what the Ambassador has to say after he's talked to all the parties concerned. But I have to tell you: we have zero leverage in Guatemala, and the way the Americans are feeling at the moment they would probably volunteer to join the firing squad.'

'It sounds bad.'

'It is. The way things are right now I'd say there's a better than even chance they'll put your man on trial and shoot him. Anyway, I'll let you know the moment there are any fresh developments.'

Davies sighed and replaced the receiver, just as Billie Holiday started in on 'Gloomy Sunday'. He sipped at the whisky, wondering what options, if any, were open to him.

He was breathing almost naturally now, some four hours after the session with the *capucha*. If it hadn't been for the interruption the session might still be going on, always assuming he would have survived this long.

And they said smoking was bad for your lungs! His smile flickered weakly in the dark room, and again he found himself wondering when they would come back for him.

Think about something else, he told himself. Think about a sunny afternoon at White Hart Lane, preferably in late August, when the perennial dream of winning the League was still precariously intact. Or think about making love in that barge on the Brecon Canal, with the sun going down and . . .

No, he didn't want to think about that. Keep it absurd, like this whole fucking situation. Being tortured by the men the Foreign Office sent him to help. Roaming a country where *Lord of the Rings* and *Dune* seemed less like fantasies than the reality did.

Tomás had known what he fighting for. And, so far as Guatemala went, Razor supposed he did too. His mistake had been finding out when he did, when the only choice lay between a dead colonel and a dead village.

Well, he was damned if he going to come here for another holiday, so his Guatemalan political preferences were probably neither here nor there. But what was he fighting for back home? Peace in Northern Ireland? He had no doubts that the Army had once been needed there, but these days peace seemed to be breaking out all on its own. Hong Kong would soon be gone, and there was hardly room to swing a monkey on Gibraltar. Would the Army end up like its Guatemalan counterpart – stranded at home with nowhere else to go, a heavily armed backup for the police, the ultimate muscle for a government which either would not or could not afford fairness?

He had always thought of the British Army as the best in the world – first equal with the Germans, at any rate – but what did that mean exactly? The best at achieving its objectives? That might be true, but how much was it worth if the objectives were chosen by either idiots or bastards?

Docherty had been fond of saying that it was hard for a soldier to be better than his orders. But not in this case, Razor thought, because in this case his orders had been total crap.

12

The sun would soon be rising on her seventeenth day in Guatemala, Hajrija calculated, keeping her eyes on the *compañero* who was walking ahead of her. It felt more like seventeen weeks, or even months.

Still, it felt good to be out in the open again. The four of them had covered something like twenty-five kilometres since darkness fell, most of them along remote trails through seemingly empty mountains. Their one brush with civilization had been crossing the Pan-American Highway, and as they waited above the road for a suitable space in the traffic she had thought the brightly lit trucks seemed like visitors from another planet.

Since scurrying across the strip of tarmac they had been climbing again, and the path was now angling up towards the last watershed of their journey, a silhouetted ridge-line about a hundred metres above them. They hadn't stopped for quite a while: her three male companions seemed to have finally accepted that she needed no more rest than they did – this *gringa*, she would have told them if she spoke their language, had grown up in mountains not unlike their own.

Unfortunately, this place reminded her of her Bosnian home in more ways than that. Over the last few days she had felt the old despair clawing at her heart again, and this time around the anguish which came with seeing how badly humans could treat each other had been sharpened by her fears for the man she loved, the man whose child she was carrying.

Razor had been taken, and she had no idea where. She didn't know if she was walking away from him or towards him. She didn't even know if he was still alive. And there was nothing to do but keep on walking, keep on hoping.

They were close to the ridge-line now, and minutes later Hajrija found herself gazing at the view from the crest: the shining lake sitting in the vast bowl of mountains beneath the shimmering night sky. And despite the weight of her fears she found the sight still stirred her soul. The star-filled heavens and the vast mirror of water seemed so tranquil, so full of benign certainty.

And, somewhat to her surprise, she saw from their faces that the *compañeros* were experiencing similar feelings to her own. Here in the mountains the Mayan Indians still breathed deeply of the natural world, for where else could they find the sustenance they needed for the struggle against the common enemy?

Chris and Emelia dug in for the day on a wooded slope high above the small town of Chinique, and she announced that she was taking the first watch in a tone which did not invite discussion.

In practical terms it had been a successful night – they had made better than the expected speed, and seen no sign of Army patrols, much less encountered any. But Chris was too worried about his companion's state of mind to feel much satisfaction. Emelia had hardly spoken since their departure, and if it hadn't been for his insistence she would hardly have eaten either. He needed to find a way to let her mourn, or else he feared she would throw her life away, either in some defiant act of sacrifice or out of sheer carelessness.

But lying there in the scrape he could think of nothing to say, nothing to offer or do. How could you comfort someone who had lost each member of her family, one after the other, until only she was left? By telling her that they had died for something noble? What possible goal could be worth such sacrifice?

He crawled across to where she was sitting and took her in his arms. For a moment she beat a tattoo of rage on his back, then carried on mutely sobbing for a minute or more, clinging to him.

Then, abruptly, she pulled herself away, rubbed her tear-stained eyes and said: 'You must sleep – we will need all the strength we have.'

He started to protest, but she was adamant. He lay down again, and the singing of the birds as the sky lightened seemed as cruel as anything he had ever heard.

Woken by the key in the door, Razor looked up to see the two guards entering and feared the worst. They dragged him to his feet and led him down the corridor to the outside world, where the barely risen sun was still battling with the chill of the morning air. There was scarcely time to take in the surroundings before another building loomed, another corridor, and another room. Here the guards removed the wire bindings which had secured his wrists for almost twenty-four hours and then left him, all without saying a word.

He explored his new home. This room, though much the

same size as the one he had just left, boasted not only a mattress but also a small adjoining room complete with flush toilet. The former might be ragged and stained, the latter dry and dusty, but it was the thought that counted. Either his prospects were improving or they were trying to soften him up for another session with the *capucha*.

Just the thought of it seemed to make breathing more difficult.

As if on cue, he heard more footsteps in the corridor outside. The key turned, the door opened, and in came breakfast: a small bowl of chilli, a stack of tortillas and an Atlanta Braves mug brimming with brown liquid which looked like coffee but was probably faking. One of the guards even smiled at him before withdrawing.

Razor ate his way through the food, drank the brown liquid, and did a more thorough security check on his prison. Through the small window in the door he could see an armed guard half asleep on an upright chair in the corridor. The door itself was not particularly solid, but Razor could see no way of breaking it down without alerting the guard. He went across to the window, which was protected by bars and an interior grille. In the distance he could see the coils of razor wire glistening with menace on top of the breeze-block wall.

'Breaking out is hard to-oo-oo do,' he sang softly to himself. He thought of Hajrija and switched songs. 'The best part of breaking out is the making out, ooooh!'

The guard's puzzled face appeared at the window in the door. Razor gave him a friendly wave and lay down on the mattress, wondering what was happening in the world outside. Did anyone other than his hosts know where he was?

It was another two hours before he got his answer. He heard the arrival of the helicopter, and spent five minutes wondering whether it augured well or ill before Ben Manley was ushered into his cell.

Razor felt as if a huge weight had been lifted from his shoulders. He let out a deep sigh of relief, and might even have kissed Manley if the man from the embassy hadn't looked so . . . so fucking English. He was even wearing a suit and tie.

'They seem to be treating you all right,' Manley said, looking round for somewhere to sit and finding nothing. 'By their standards, that is.'

Razor suddenly realized why his room had been changed. 'Last night they put a rubber hood over my head and tightened it until I couldn't breathe,' he said deliberately. 'And when I was nearly unconscious they took it off and threw water on my face. Then they started again,' he added, looking Manley straight in the eye.

The embassy man looked away. He didn't want to deal with this, Razor decided. He works in Guatemala and he doesn't want to know.

'Are you all right now?' Manley asked, still examining the walls. 'No ill effects?'

Razor took a deep breath. 'I'm OK.'

'Good, that's good. Needless to say, we'll deliver the strongest protest we can, but the Guatemalans have already promised London that you'll be treated according to accepted international standards. When did this, er, business take place?'

'Yesterday evening.'

'Ah, well, that must have been before London contacted the locals.'

'That's all right then,' Razor said sarcastically. 'How did you know I was here?'

'Your CO in England got a call from an ex-colleague of yours. Name of Docherty. Someone had phoned him from here, said you'd been arrested and that your wife and Martinson were still free.'

Razor felt another surge of relief. 'Do you know where my wife is?' he asked.

'No idea. According to the Guatemalans both of them have disappeared into thin air. But what I need to hear from you,' Manley went on, taking a notebook from his pocket, 'is your version of what happened last Wednesday.'

With a conscious effort Razor pushed his worries over Hajrija to the back of his mind and tried to give an accurate account of the events up to and including his fatal encounter with Cabrera. But accuracy wasn't going to be enough, he realized, as he watched Manley's face. The man from the embassy had not seen the villages above Zavik, or the dead villages of Guatemala. He hadn't lived with the Kaibiles for a week, or heard the tell-tale scream emerge from the Uspantan barracks. He might be one of Her Majesty's men in Guatemala, but he knew next to nothing about the real situation here.

'I see,' Manley said, when Razor had finished. 'But even if the Guatemalans accepted your story – which they don't, of course – they will argue: "But why didn't you file a protest with the colonel? Why didn't you say you would go to his superiors? Why didn't you even threaten him with the gun, rather than simply shoot him?"'

'It wouldn't have worked . . .' Razor began.

'Perhaps, but why didn't you try?'

Razor held on to his temper with difficulty. 'If I had

done anything else – anything – that village would have been destroyed and all the people in it . . .'

'You can't make yourself responsible for every village on the planet . . .'

'And,' Razor continued, 'once they had destroyed the village they would have had to kill me and Chris. We were potential witnesses. Once I'd fingered their guerrilla leader for them, there was nothing else we could offer them but grief.'

Manley sat there, pen thoughtfully poised. 'You can't prove any of that,' he said finally. 'The Guatemalans deny there was ever any intention to destroy the village, and if there wasn't, then what motive could they have for killing you and Martinson? You see what I mean?'

'I don't give a flying fuck what the Guatemalans think. I know what happened.'

Manley sighed with frustration, as if he was dealing with a particularly obtuse child. 'They also claim that you shot down an unarmed helicopter.'

Razor shrugged his acquiescence.

'Was it unarmed?'

'Probably. It was on a recon mission.'

'Then why?'

'Because if the pilot had managed to report our position we would have had armed helicopters to deal with, and probably troop carriers as well.'

Manley made another note. 'Do you have any idea where Martinson is?' he asked.

'Nope.'

Manley sighed again.

'So what happens next?' Razor asked.

'I don't know. We'll try and get you moved to the capital,

where we can keep a better eye on how you're being treated. The locals don't seem to have decided what they want to do with you yet; they may want to put you on trial, or we may be able to buy you out one way or another. Maybe a promise to keep a lid on the whole business will be enough – it's hard to say at this stage. And there's always Martinson to consider . . .'

'And my wife.'

'Technically she's not our problem. But yes,' he added, seeing the look on Razor's face, 'naturally we have to bear her in mind.' Manley put his notebook back in his pocket. 'Is there anybody you want me to contact?' he asked.

Razor thought for a moment. 'Am I likely to be on the *Nine O'Clock News*?

'Not if we can help it.'

'Then no. If it goes public, I'd like my mother to know I'm OK. But there's no point in worrying her until then.'

'Will do. Anything else?'

'Yeah, ask the warden if I can have some toilet paper.'

In England it was almost five o'clock when Martin Clarke called to give Barney Davies a full report of the conversation. The junior minister seemed more cheerful than usual, but Davies could find little reason for optimism in either the facts or the way in which Clarke downplayed the ill-treatment which had already been meted out.

The only welcome news – which was so predictable that it hardly qualified as news – was that Razor had indeed had a good reason for shooting the Guatemalan colonel.

He asked where exactly the SAS man was being held.

There was a hesitation, and the sound of papers being shuffled. 'A place called San Pedro Norte,' Clarke said at last. 'It's a few miles west of Lake Atitlán. Manley thought it looked like a deserted prison.' The sound of a chuckle. 'But don't get any ideas, Lieutenant-Colonel,' Clarke added. 'This government will not be sanctioning any SAS rescue mission.'

'I realize that,' Davies said obligingly. He knew full well that those days were gone. Maggie Thatcher might have been one of the more obnoxious Prime Ministers in British history, but she had at least been willing to take the odd risk. Her successor had all the gambling instincts of a small-town banker.

After putting the phone down he sat and thought for a few moments, watching the mass of dark-grey cloud looming over the distant Black Mountains. More bloody rain.

Clarke's whole tone had been almost self-congratulatory, he thought. As if the difficult part was over. They had been promised that the SAS man would be treated as well as any prisoner in England, and now the game of diplomatic poker could begin.

Davies looked at his watch, struggled with the arithmetic of time zones, and realized that there was only twenty minutes to spare before the time set aside for a possible call from Guatemala to Chile. He picked up the phone and punched out Docherty's number.

The Scot answered himself.

'It's me,' Davies said. 'I've been talking to the Foreign Office and thinking about what we said yesterday and . . . well, I have a bad feeling about this.' He told Docherty about the call from Clarke, text and sub-text.

'So what can you do?' Docherty asked.

'Not a damn thing, as far as I can see. I can create a stink, but the bastards will just hold their noses. Hell, the way the Government behaves these days one more stink will probably not even get noticed.'

'What about Chris?'

'We've no idea where he is. But that's the main reason I've called you. The people who contacted you must have got your number from Chris or Hajrija . . .'

'I don't know Chris that well, and I don't remember ever giving him this number.'

'Well, it must have been Hajrija then. She may be in contact with Chris by now. They're obviously both in with the guerrillas. Maybe they can do something. This is where Razor is being held – got a pencil?'

Docherty wrote down what Davies told him. 'So you want me to pass this on with our best wishes.'

'It's about all we've got to offer. Tell them to tell Chris not to expect any help from outside. There probably won't be anything one man can do, but that'll be up to him to judge . . .'

'And her,' Docherty reminded him. 'I wouldn't underestimate Hajrija when it comes to a fight, not when Razor's life is at stake.'

Hajrija and the four *compañeros* arrived at the guerrilla camp an hour or so before dawn. She felt completely exhausted, but managed a smile when she saw the man she knew as Mariano coming forward to greet them. At least there would be someone she could communicate with.

He even had news. 'The Englishman Chris is coming here. Maybe tomorrow, maybe next day.'

Hajrija supposed this was good news, but it also made her anxious. With his height and spiky fair hair Chris was even more noticeable than her husband, who had been caught.

'Do you know about the call to Chile?' she asked. 'Can you . . . ?'

'It is all arranged,' Mariano said. 'A man in the City will make the call this evening, and if there is a message for you we will receive it by radio.

The thought that she was connected, however tenuously, with the outside world, made Hajrija feel better.

'And now you need sleep,' Mariano was saying.

A few minutes later she was closing her eyes in a hammock strung between trees, and almost immediately sinking into a deep slumber.

Eleven hours later she woke to find the light already beginning to fade. But she felt better rested than she had for several days, and ravenously hungry. After half falling out of the hammock she went in search of Mariano, and found him sitting on a rock overlooking the lake, eating a tasty-looking stew. Seeing the look in her eyes, he told her to stay there and went to get her a plate.

From the direction of the setting sun, she judged that they were halfway up one of the two volcanoes on the south-eastern side of the lake. Panajachel would be the cluster of brightening lights on the far shore, and the town almost directly below her was Santiago Atitlán. She could see the square where she had rested, and remembered staring up at this very volcano.

Mariano came back with a plate of stew. It was mostly vegetable with just a flavouring of chicken, but after ten hours of walking and eleven of sleep almost anything would have tasted wonderful. He watched with a smile as she devoured it all, wiping up the last drops with the last tortilla.

His face grew more serious as he passed on the message from Chile.

Hearing that Razor was alive and not being mistreated, she closed her eyes and let the relief flood through her body.

'He is being held at San Pedro Norte,' Mariano went on. 'It used to be a prison camp, but now, according to your man in Chile, it is almost empty.' He smiled. 'It is strange, yes, that we hear about the prison next door from a man who is four thousand miles away?'

'It is near here?' Hajrija asked excitedly. 'Where?'

He turned towards the lake. 'Over there, behind San Pedro,' he said, indicating the volcano which rose up beyond the inlet, blocking the view to the west. Maybe twenty-five kilometres as the hawk flies, in the hills beyond San Pedro La Laguna.'

She stared out, picturing Razor in his cell. Maybe he was even watching the same sunset. 'Was that the whole message?' she asked.

'No. The man in Chile says not to expect any help from London.'

Hajrija turned her eyes back to the distant view, and for almost a minute she was silent. 'I need to talk to your leader,' she said quietly.

He smiled. 'That will not be difficult. I am the *comandante* of this unit.'

She supposed she should have realized. 'Then I need to talk with you,' she said, gathering her thoughts. 'Your people have already taken many risks for me,' she began, 'and at least one man has died, and I have no right to ask for more. But I must.' She turned to meet Mariano's gaze. 'Can you find out about this place – how many men there are, what the defences are like? And when the other Englishman arrives here, can you give us a guide to take us there?'

Mariano considered. 'It does not seem likely that there will be so few men that you and your friend . . .'

'The message says it is almost empty,' Hajrija interrupted him.

Mariano raised a hand in acknowledgement. 'That is true.' His face cracked in a smile. 'So we will find out exactly how empty. OK?'

With Manley gone Razor's only human contact was with the guards who brought him food and took him for his daily exercise. He spent most of the Tuesday day-dreaming, and on Wednesday decided to sharpen up his act, setting himself a string of mental and physical exercises. The main danger lay in growing complacent – there was no guarantee that the current benign regime would continue, and if things changed he wanted to be as mentally prepared as was humanly possible.

Chris and Emelia continued their southward journey, walking through the nights and, when granted the cover of mist, deep into the grey light of morning. For Chris it was the strangest trip he had ever taken, a matter of birds singing in empty forests and winds whistling across mountain slopes, of strangers who materialized out of the mist to offer news and guidance, of nights both impenetrable and bursting with stars, of the woman he travelled with, who said nothing and seemed like an angel in the process of turning to stone.

On the upper slopes of the Toliman volcano Hajrija helped with the chores, counted the hours until Chris would be joining her, and looked forward to the return of the two *compas* whom Mariano had sent to investigate the prison camp. This guerrilla unit, the *comandante* had told her, was only about twenty strong, and that only at the best of times. The Army's local depredations had thinned the numbers of the working population, and even those who had joined the guerrillas had to spend time helping on the land. This unit could not afford to be particularly aggressive, and its main purpose was to stay in being until such time as a peace agreement was signed. In the meantime its mere existence acted as a deterrent against the Army's more blatant excesses.

Hearing all this, Hajrija wondered at Mariano's willingness to help her, and wondered still more at the welcoming smiles and unfailing kindness which all the people in the camp continued to demonstrate.

In Hereford Barney Davies watched the rain sweep across the parade ground, conducted the routine business of the day, and waited for news of the negotiations that were apparently underway between the respective governments. He had spent periods like this before, worrying about men he had sent into danger in far-off places, but always in the past there had been the possibility of contact by radio. This time he felt the powerlessness of the complete bystander, and he didn't like it one little bit.

It was just before dawn on the Thursday, with the faintest of glimmers in the eastern sky, when Chris and Emelia reached the crest from which Hajrija and her escort had looked out over Atitlán and its guardian volcanoes.

'That is where my village is,' Emelia said, extending an arm towards the far side of the lake. 'It is called Santiago

Atitlán,' she added, and for the first time in three days Chris could hear emotion in her voice. Glancing sideways at her he thought he could detect a loosening in the facial muscles, and even in the way she held herself. It was as if she had needed the sight of home to let herself feel again.

They dug a scrape just below the tree line, and this time she allowed him to take the first watch. Minutes later she was asleep, her face softening with each passing moment, until he imagined that once again he could see the young woman with whom he had listened to the laughing falcon.

Was he falling in love with her? Or did he just feel a mixture of desire and pity? Whatever his feelings, they seemed somehow inappropriate, both too strong for their current predicament and too weak for the world in which she lived.

The morning went by. He watched the wind slowly disperse the halo-like clouds above the volcanoes and begin to ruffle the glassy, blue-green surface of the lake. Boats began to appear, criss-crossing the lake between the villages on its shore, and around ten o'clock a couple of windsurfers appeared, but there were no signs of a military presence.

It was hard to believe this was a country in which 150,000 men, women and children had been killed by the armed forces in a little over fifteen years. Ten thousand a year, or nearly thirty a day. According to Tomás several hundred victims had been dropped alive into the cones of those three smoking volcanoes which rose up behind the distant shore, beyond the brightly coloured sails of the windsurfers.

Once darkness had fallen Chris and Emelia worked their way down to the lake and began making their way across the fields and tree-covered slopes which lined its eastern shores. It took a little under three hours to reach an observation point above the sprawling village of Santiago Atitlán, and another fifteen minutes before they felt completely confident that no unpleasant surprises were waiting for them in the town below.

The narrow streets were much darker than the hillside, but Emelia led the way through the familiar labyrinth without hesitation, and soon she was softly rapping on a chosen door. A smiling face appeared in the crack, and they were drawn in out of the darkness.

Inside there was light, both the warm glow of burning fir cones and the harsher glare of a bare sixty-watt bulb. There was also a host of people: two men, two women, and more moving children than could easily be counted. The adults seemed to all begin talking at once, in that language that Chris had only previously heard spoken between Emelia and her brother. Every now and then someone would turn to look at him, as he stood there feeling far too big for the room.

After a few minutes Emelia turned to him. 'Gaspar will take us to the camp where your friend is,' she said. 'But on the way I must go to Maximon,' she added, as one of the women pressed what looked like a whisky miniature and a packet of cigarettes into her hand. 'You must come too,' she told Chris. 'It will not be many minutes.'

They set off again through the dark and empty streets, with Gaspar in the lead, Emelia behind him, and Chris bringing up the rear, wondering who the hell Maximon was. It took only a couple of minutes for them to reach their new destination – another one-storey house, larger than most, with yellow light seeping out through the curtained windows. Gaspar knocked on the door, and they were ushered into one of the strangest rooms Chris had ever seen.

The walls and ceiling were almost completely covered with various-coloured paper decorations, and to one side a long table supported a coffin which was liberally appointed with winking Christmas lights. Flowers were strewn across floor and coffin, and tin cans loaded with incense were filling the air with sweet-smelling smoke. In the centre of the bare stone floor there stood or sat – it was hard to tell – a wooden effigy swathed in shawls and scarves. It was only about a metre tall, but both the highly polished boots and the wooden face mask beneath the wide-brimmed hat were life-size, giving the overall impression of a child in adult clothing.

'That is Maximon,' Gaspar told Chris, as he shepherded him towards a long bench that ran along one wall. Emelia had taken a throne-like seat opposite the effigy and was talking to one of the two men who had welcomed them. Both were wearing the same traditional costume – a length of woven cloth wound turban-like around the head, ordinary shirt and tunic, and bermuda-length shorts in woven material of a different pattern. By all rights they ought to look ridiculous, Chris thought, but they didn't.

The second of the two men had already lit around twenty of the candles in front of the effigy, and was now scattering orange flower petals among them. Satisfied with the arrangement, he opened the packet of cigarettes Emelia had brought, wedged a cigarette between the effigy's lips, and lit it. To Chris's surprise the cigarette stayed alight – the effigy obviously had an in-built draught which served to simulate inhalation.

'Death flowers,' Gaspar whispered in Spanish, his finger pointing at the scattered marigold petals. 'They are a prayer for the soul of the departed one.'

The cigarette was now removed, and the opened bottle of brandy applied to the wooden lips, a cloth held beneath them to collect the spillage. The first man was now kneeling in front of the effigy, addressing it with great seriousness, as if he was explaining something. He was the go-between, Chris realized. His job was to speak for Emelia, and to elicit Maximon's blessing or understanding or whatever else it was he was offering in return for the smokes and booze.

And it seemed to be working. In the chair behind her interlocutor, Emelia seemed more at peace, as if a vast weight was slowly being lifted from her shoulders and placed aboard those of the cigarette-puffing, brandy-guzzling effigy.

'Maximon understands,' Gaspar whispered beside him. 'He knows that to free the soul of the dead is also to free the soul of the living.'

Chris was still pondering this when the audience came to an end. Everyone smiled and shook hands, and Gaspar led the way out into the street. Chris had one last glimpse of Maximon, the cigarette burning in the wooden lips, before the door closed behind him. As the threesome made their way up the dark street he tried to make sense of what he had just seen, but his mind couldn't seem to pull it all together. It had been like a bizarre therapy session, a trip back in time, a shuffling of cultures, and all at once.

The journey up the volcano, along paths which wound to and fro across the steep, wooded slopes, took about two hours. For much of the way Emelia talked with Gaspar in their native language, and listening to her voice Chris marvelled at the transformation which the visit to

Maximon had produced. It was as if she had been brought back to life.

They passed the outer sentries at around one-thirty in the morning, and reached the camp itself ten minutes later. One of the figures in olive-green uniforms ran towards Chris and threw her arms around him, tears sparkling in her eyes. Her face looked almost as drawn as it had at their first meeting in the Sarajevo hotel, but this time the cause was more likely to be anxiety than malnutrition. 'Is there any news of him?' Chris asked.

'We know where he is,' Hajrija said. 'And it's not far away – only twenty-five kilometres. It's a prison camp. Some of the *compañeros* have been checking it out for us – they're expected back tonight, any time now.' She filled him in on the events of the last few days, and recounted the message that had come from Hereford via Chile. 'We're his only hope,' she said.

Listening to her, reading the fear behind the excitement, Chris offered a silent prayer that the hope was a realistic one.

He introduced her to Emelia, and the two women spontaneously hugged, as if in recognition of the fact that the sacrificial bond between the one's brother and the other's husband had automatically created a bond between them. Chris was introduced to Mariano and the other *compas* who were present, most of whom seemed even younger than the men and women in the Cuchumatanes.

The food was better in this camp, though, presumably because there were farms nearby. They were halfway through a plate of stew when the two *compas* returned from the reconnaissance mission to San Pedro Norte. The young woman, whose name was Elena, unfolded a map she had drawn of the prison camp, and they all gathered round to examined it by the light of Mariano's pencil torch.

'We watched for two days and two nights, and we talked to the people in San Pedro La Laguna,' she began, pointing out the lakeside village on the map. 'There are only about forty men in the camp – ten or twelve prison guards, four or five administrative staff and twenty-five to thirty soldiers. The only prisoner we saw was the Englishman, but the villagers think there may be two or three more of their people being held there.'

She paused for a moment, then went on to describe the camp and its situation. It was surrounded by a wire-topped wall, and there were guard towers with mounted searchlights at each corner, though only two of these were regularly occupied by guards. There was a single gate in the wall, but this was hardly ever used, since nearly all movement of men and supplies was done by helicopter.

'A hundred *compas* would have no trouble in breaking in through the gate,' her male companion interjected, 'but fifteen minutes later the reinforcements would arrive from other bases and there would be no escape. There are trees near the camp, but the hills all around are mostly bare. If more than ten out of a hundred got back to the volcano it would be a miracle.'

The other *compas* began asking questions, and it was some time before Chris managed to get his own in. 'You said the gate was hardly ever used – so when *is* it used?'

Elena smiled. 'Three mornings a week a truck is driven to San Pedro La Laguna with the soldiers' laundry, and it returns late that afternoon,' she answered.

'It might get you in,' Mariano said, 'but how would you get out?'

'A good question,' Chris murmured. 'But there's one obvious answer . . .'

13

The truck seemed to be looking for the deepest ruts in the track as it climbed the fifteen kilometres from the lakeside village to the prison camp. Chris, one wrist and both ankles strapped to the underside of the chassis, thought the journey gave a new meaning to the phrase 'shaken not stirred', and was reminded of the scene in one of the Bond movies in which the hero had been almost pulled apart on a health-spa rack. When the truck finally jolted to a halt at the gate to the compound, the sense of relief was almost strong enough to obliterate his feelings of apprehension.

A few moments later he heard the whirr of electronic gates opening, and the truck started up again. There was a shouted exchange between cab and gatehouse, and a brief glimpse of booted feet as the driver pulled into the compound. Almost immediately the brake was reapplied, and the truck came to a halt.

He was inside.

The cab door opened, the driver's legs swung down to the ground, and walked around to the back of the truck. Chris had seen the man's chubby face when he first arrived in the lakeside village for the prison laundry, and had heard him flirting with Emelia as Hajrija hurriedly tied three of his own limbs to the truck's chassis.

He was unloading the baskets of laundry now, and making more than enough noise to cover the sound of Chris's breathing. A door opened, a new voice spoke, more boots appeared, and hands reached down for one of the large baskets. The four feet moved away out of sight, and when they returned a minute or so later the driver was telling his friend about a new girl in the village. This time Chris heard the tailgate being pushed up, and the sound of bolts going in, before the hands lifted up the remaining basket. The feet receded again, and a door slammed.

The light was definitely fading now. He hung on, listening to the competing songs of a western wood-pewee and a distant radio. The former seemed more musical, but there wasn't much competition – his time in Colombia had been enough to convince him that Latin American pop music was easily the worst the planet had to offer.

He waited another fifteen minutes, until the risk of disabling himself with cramp seemed greater than the danger of being seen, and then began the job of untying himself. First he released the other wrist, shifted the Uzi around to his front, and slowly lowered his head and shoulders on to the gravel beneath. From this position he could see that the gatehouse was unlit and presumably unmanned, but that the bare ground visible through the gate was now illuminated. He couldn't see the top of the guard tower, but assumed that was where the light was coming from. Away to his right there was the line of one-storey buildings which supposedly housed the prison offices, communications centre and officers' quarters. Two of the windows were lit, but he could see no movement inside.

Pulling himself forward as if he was doing sit-ups, Chris slowly untied his ankles, and gently lowered his whole body to the ground. There he lay motionless for several minutes, watching the buildings which had previously been out of sight behind him, and which according to the guerrilla recon team housed the prison guards. He could hear a faint buzz of conversation coming from inside, but none of the visible windows showed any light.

Five metres separated him from the corner of the building and he crawled rapidly across them, knowing that the bulk of the truck would hide him from any watching eyes in the guard tower. Once beside the building, he pulled himself into a crouch, and began slowly making his way around to its rear. From the next corner he could see the camp football pitch stretching away towards the distant wall, and the fixed lights shining out and down from one of the two unoccupied guard towers.

Hearing the familiar sounds of a football match on TV, he noticed a bluish glow emanating from a couple of the back windows. With any luck the guards would be too engrossed to hear or see anything else.

He moved on past these windows, towards the shelter of the two trees which stood between the large water-tower and the corner of the football pitch. He was now close to the perimeter wall, and about thirty metres from the gate and gatehouse. One of the two occupied guard towers loomed beyond the latter.

He settled down to wait. The sentries were relieved on the hour every three hours, and the next change would be at nine o'clock, but it was the one at midnight which they planned to make use of. Chris pictured Mariano and the two women walking up the track from the lake – they would have covered about five kilometres by now, with another twenty to go. He thought about what he would have to do when the time came, and about his partner sitting in a cell no more than a hundred metres away. He thought about Emelia and the future he couldn't see them having.

The hours went by. The sentry in the guard tower stirred only twice, on both occasions standing up to stretch and light a cigarette before sinking back out of sight. Chris wondered if the man would later appreciate how lucky he had been to draw this particular shift.

At nine o'clock the man's replacement emerged from the other side of the guard quarters, walked across the open space between the gate and the prison offices, and wearily pulled himself up the perpendicular ladder which clung to the supporting structure of the tower. A few words of conversation were barely audible, a louder laugh echoed in the night air, and the guard who had been relieved climbed down the ladder and walked away, yawning as he went.

Chris was just settling down to wait another three hours when a muffled scream sounded from deep inside the camp. As if in reply, someone immediately turned up the volume on the TV in the guard quarters.

He crouched there, knowing it hadn't been Razor screaming, though not at all sure how he knew. Even if it had been there was nothing he could have done on his own, not without wrecking their chances of eventually getting his partner out and away.

He thought he heard the scream again, but it was harder to tell with the TV at such a deafening pitch. He found himself hoping that they kept the volume up.

The minutes stretched out, the night stayed clear. Chris watched the Great Bear slide slowly up into the northern sky, and played word games with himself to pass the time. The TV was still loud enough to mask all other sounds, but as far as he could tell there were few to mask. The lights in the admin block had been turned off, and there was no sign of any movement deeper inside the base. Chris could not see the occupied barracks from where he was, but whatever the soldiers were doing, they weren't taking evening strolls.

At half-past eleven he made his move, working his way along the wall in the direction of the gatehouse. The darkness here would probably have been deep enough on its own, but the contrast with the brightly lit area beyond the wall made it doubly so. Chris had no fear of being seen, and not much of being heard until the noise of the TV abruptly vanished, when even his own breathing seemed to echo in the unearthly silence.

The sentry's head appeared above the parapet, and Chris stopped in his tracks, crouching motionless for a minute and more until the man disappeared again. He inched across in front of the gate and worked his way around the outer wall of the gatehouse until he was almost underneath the guard tower, and only a metre or so from the bottom of the ladder.

It was eleven forty-seven. From where he stood he could see the Guatemalan flag fluttering from its pole in front of the office building. He thought about the quetzal holding its olive branch, and decided a frigate-bird would have been a more appropriate national emblem. They had a habit of poking pelicans' eyes out, and of forcibly drowning gulls in order to steal their catch.

It was exactly eleven fifty-eight when he heard a door slam on the other side of the compound yard, and only a few seconds later when the first cries of the jaguar came echoing out of the distant trees. Emelia was good, Chris thought. Even knowing it had to be her, he found himself wondering if a real cat had put in a surprise appearance.

He heard the guard stir in the tower above, heard the footsteps of his replacement coming across the yard, and took the knife from its sheath. He had killed three men in his career, but all with guns. He had been trained to do what he was about to do, but that was all.

The man came nearer. Twenty metres, ten . . . Chris could hear him breathing, hear the chink of something like a key rattling as he walked. And then the silhouetted figure was in front of him, reaching for the ladder, and Chris was stepping forward, one arm snaking out to smother the mouth as it pulled back the head, the other slicing the blade across the open throat just as the jaguar's cry split the silence.

Chris lowered the dead man to the ground, retrieved his cap and put it on. He started up the ladder, almost letting the knife slip from his blood-drenched hand. He heard the man above him murmur '*Es imposible*', and hesitated for a split-second before putting his head through the hole in the floor. This was the most dangerous moment of all – if the man had time to open fire, then they were probably finished.

Emelia made the noise again, this time drawing it out to cover Chris's emergence on to the platform. As they had hoped, the guard was staring out towards the forest, keen to get a glimpse of Guatemala's most endangered species. '*Dónde está* . . . ?' he began to say, only to feel his head jerked back, glimpse the flash of the blade, know the instant in which the warmth of his life gushed away.

Chris lowered the body into the seat, a collapsible aluminium beach chair with striped plastic upholstery, and fought back the urge to scream. He looked across the camp to the other occupied tower, and saw no indications of alarm. That guard was still sitting in his beach chair. That guard's heart was still pumping blood.

Later, he told himself. If at all.

Three figures in uniform fatigues were running across the sea of light towards the gate. Chris hurried back down the ladder and into the gatehouse, where it didn't take more than a few moments to find the gate controls. He pressed the open button and hoped the hum of the motor wasn't really as loud as it sounded.

Seconds later, with the others all inside, he showed Mariano the controls and pressed the close button. Under the guard tower, Chris gave the *compañero* the guard's cap, and the Guatemalan headed straight up the ladder, whispering '*Buena suerte*' over his shoulder as he went.

The two women were staring at the blood glistening on Chris's hands, arms, face and chest.

'Are you OK?' Hajrija asked. The sight of him had brought it all back. She could almost smell the buildings burning in Sarajevo's old town.

'Yeah,' he replied. He could still feel the blood flooding through his fingers. 'Let's go,' he said.

They advanced across the edge of the yard, and waited a few seconds by the corner of the admin block before slipping on to the darkened veranda. The front doors were unlocked, as they had expected. Inside, a tiled area was separated off from a large office by a long reception counter. Opposite this, doors opened into smaller offices. Directly ahead of them another doorway gave on to a corridor which ran the length of the building. A few metres down, light shone out from under the door of the room they were looking for.

It seemed to be the only light. Chris took a deep breath,

pressed his hand down on the handle, swung the door open and stepped into the room. A soldier was half lying in a chair with his back to the door, his feet up on the radio desk, a comic in his lap. Hearing visitors, he tried to turn his head and take down his feet, but before either action could be completed Chris had rammed the barrel of the Browning into his left ear.

The man's eyes opened wide when he saw the blood all over the gun's owner, and he started pleading, crossing himself frantically as he did so. The sight of the two women seemed to unnerve him even more, and he kept glancing over at them, as if unsure that they were for real.

'Two of your comrades are already dead,' Chris said, raising one bloody hand in proof, 'so we have nothing to lose by killing you. But if you do everything we ask then I give you my word that you'll be OK.'

The man glanced at the two women again, and shuddered. 'Tell me,' he begged, 'what do you want?'

'OK,' Chris said. 'What's the camp commandant's name?'

'Major Toriello, but . . .' He stopped.

'But what?'

'Well, Major Osorio is the ranking officer on base . . .'

Chris smiled. 'OK. I want you to pretend that Major Osorio has just fallen very ill. He has severe pains in the lower abdomen, and it looks like appendicitis. He needs treatment quickly. He needs to be flown to a hospital. Now, who do you call?'

'Divisional headquarters in Chimaltenango. They will send a helicopter for him.'

'And how long will that take to get here?'

'Twenty minutes. Maybe twenty-five. Not much more.'

Chris pulled his sketch map of the base out of his back pocket and spread it out in front of the man. 'Now tell me where we can find the two majors.'

The Guatemalan looked at the map for a few seconds and then pointed a finger at one of the connecting buildings. 'This is where Major Osorio sleeps, but – I don't know – he may still be in the Interrogation Room . . .'

'Which is where?'

The finger pointed.

'And Toriello?'

'The room next to Major Osorio's.'

Chris pulled the Uzi's strap over his head and handed the gun to Hajrija. 'OK?'

She nodded and headed for the door, Emelia close behind her with the Uzi she had taken from the dead sentry.

'Make the call,' Chris told the radio operator as the door closed behind the two women. 'And make it convincing,' he added, perching himself on the edge of the desk, 'unless you really want to die for the sake of a couple of gringos.'

Already he was worrying about Hajrija and Emelia, and wishing once more that one of them had been fluent enough in Spanish to do the job that he was doing.

Hajrija and Emelia set off down the corridor, past a row of apparently empty rooms. The passage turned left, and crossed to another building by means of a covered walkway. Here they heard snoring through a couple of closed doors, including one of the two at the far end of the corridor.

Neither door was locked. The two women co-ordinated their entrances, but only Emelia struck gold, waking Major Toriello by pushing an Uzi barrel into his open mouth. His eyes jerked open, his mouth closed on the cold metal, and he was suddenly very still. 'One sound and I will kill you,' Emelia told him in a whisper, and the look in his eyes said he believed her. 'Now get up,' she said, withdrawing the gun and standing back.

Hajrija appeared in the doorway. 'Osorio's not there,' she said, ignoring the naked Toriello.

'Move,' Emelia told the major, prodding him in the back. They walked back through the silent buildings to the communications room, where they bound the wrists and ankles of both Toriello and the radio operator with lengths of rope they had brought for that purpose. Toriello was also gagged, but the other man was not – they might still need him to talk with the world outside the camp. 'Less than fifteen minutes,' Chris told the two women as they left the office for the second time.

This time they slipped out on to the dark veranda and made their way around the outside of the building to where the lines of barracks stretched away towards the western wall. They walked down the side of the first, and then turned right down the pathless space between the barrack ends, their boots rustling in the dry grass. At the end of the row they stopped and examined the long, low building which stood between them and the helipad. After his morning exercise the previous day, Razor had been returned to this building.

The windows in the end doors showed a dim light.

The two women walked quickly across the space, and Hajrija put a careful eye to the dirty window. Another bare corridor stretched into the distance, regularly spaced doors on either side. About ten metres down, a uniformed guard sat on an upright chair, a sub-machine-gun in his lap. He looked at least half asleep, but Hajrija didn't fancy finding out that he wasn't. One burst of automatic fire and the chances of their getting away would take a nosedive.

It suddenly occurred to her that the man was probably sitting opposite Razor's cell. She took another look through the window and counted five doors, then, gesturing Emelia to follow, edged around the corner of the building and started counting windows. The fifth one along had recently received new steel bars.

She put her hand through them and tapped lightly on the wire grille. Seconds later a familiar face loomed through the mesh, and the feeling of joy almost took her breath away.

Later, she told herself, later. First they had to get him out of there, and to do that they needed to distract the guard. She searched through her English vocabulary for the right words and came up empty. 'Make noise,' she mouthed silently, and when Razor looked bemused, waved both hands in the air and mimed someone shouting. He grinned back at her, raised a thumb in acknowledgement, and then a single finger.

She started counting seconds, and turned to find Emelia smiling at her performance.

They crept back to the doors, feeling hyper-aware of the barracks only thirty metres away, and the more than twenty soldiers who were, hopefully, sleeping in them. Hajrija's mental count had reached fifty-four when they heard Razor rattling his door and calling out to the guard. Seeing the guard get up, she gently pulled the door open, praying that a sudden draught would not give them away.

It didn't. She crept forward, knowing that Emelia was taking aim behind her. If the worst came to the worst there would only be one shot . . .

She was still five metres away when the man suddenly

jerked his head around, and the hand that had been leaning against the wall seemed to twitch towards the sub-machine-gun hanging from his shoulder. Emelia didn't know how she held her finger steady on the trigger, but she did, and Hajrija quickly stepped forward to cover the guard with the Uzi. He looked more stunned than frightened, which she supposed was fair enough. The Guatemalan Army probably didn't get many visits from all-woman guerrilla units.

Emelia moved up to relieve the man of his weapon.

'Open the door,' Hajrija told him.

He obliged, and she pushed him past her grinning husband and into the cell, taking one of the lengths of cloth from her pocket as she did so. 'For gagging him,' she told Razor.

While he did the honours she quickly filled him in on what was supposed to be happening next. 'Osorio is still our best bet for an easy exit,' she said, repeating word for word what Chris had told her. 'Do you know where the Interrogation Room is?'

'Unfortunately yes,' Razor said, putting an arm round her neck and pulling her gently towards him. The smell of her hair was just as he remembered it, and the feel of her lips on his. 'I missed you,' he said, pulling away with a smile and picking up the guard's gun.

The man looked beseechingly up at him.

'Keep nice and quiet and you may live through the night,' Razor told him reassuringly. 'Let's go,' he told the others.

He had done this trip several times now, though since that first occasion they had done him no physical harm. But over the days he had heard the distant screams, seen the fresh stains on the floor, imagined the rest.

Now, approaching the closed door, he heard a soft

moaning noise, and felt the hairs on the back of his hands rising up in protest. It was the sound of someone enduring things that no human being, no living creature, should ever have to endure.

As he stood outside the door he could hear the velvet sneer of Osorio's voice.

He used hand signals to indicate that he would open the door and move quickly to the right. Hajrija should follow him in and move swiftly to the left, leaving Emelia covering the room from the doorway. The two women nodded, and Razor yanked down on the handle, pushed it wide and strode into the room, his eyes taking in the scene, his hands bringing the sub-machine-gun to bear on its prime target.

Romeo Osorio was straddling an upright chair, arms crossed on its high back, smoking a cigarette. His penis was hanging out of his trousers, a drop of semen clinging to its end. On the floor in front of him a naked man was curled up like a foetus, the *capucha* hood loose over his head. As Osorio's head turned to investigate the intrusion his expression went from rage to fear in the blink of an eye.

Lieutenant Goicouria was crouching down on the other side of his victim, his forearms bathed in blood, a thin and bloody blade in his right hand. In his eyes there seemed to be nothing, not even pleasure.

On the table by the wall three fingers had been stood in a row, like trophies. None of them had nails.

There were no other guards, and the only weapon in sight were Osorio's holstered pistol and Goicouria's knife. The twosome had merely been amusing themselves.

For the second time in his life Razor felt an almost overwhelming desire to kill, and Osorio seemed to sense it, flinching at the slight movement of the SAS man's finger on the Uzi's trigger.

'Drop the knife,' Razor said, walking towards Goicouria, and it clattered on to the cement floor.

'The helicopter,' Emelia said from the doorway, and a few moments later everyone else could hear it too.

'You remember how the Nazis used to think of everything,' Razor said brightly. 'Well, so do this bunch.' He nodded towards the stretcher leaning up against one wall. 'Just in case you can't make it back to your cell on your feet.' He yanked the torturer to his feet and almost threw him back against the wall. 'How many other prisoners are there here?'

Goicouria looked at him as if he didn't understand the question.

Razor grabbed the man's right hand, rammed it back against the wall, and drove the blade of the knife through the palm and into the whitewashed plaster. A single high-pitched screech came from the torturer's mouth.

'How many?' Razor asked again, almost hoping the man wouldn't tell him.

'Three. This one and two others. That is all.'

The helicopter seemed to be almost overhead.

The sound of its approach had also reached Chris in the communications room. After gagging the radio operator and dragging him across to the goose-pimpled Toriello, he tied the two men together at the wrist and threw another loop around their necks and a leg of the desk. Turning his attention to the radio, he disabled it as best he could without making too much noise. There were probably others on the base, but there was no point in making life easy for the enemy. '*Adiós*,' he murmured to the four staring eyes, then turned the light out and closed the door behind him.

The drone of the Huey was much louder now, and as Chris emerged from the building he could see it slowly sinking down towards the helipad on the far side of the base. It was another UH-1N, as they had hoped. Enough capacity, enough range, and with any luck it would also be carrying enough fuel.

The guard tower in front of him looked empty, as it was supposed to be – Mariano should have let himself out through the gates at the first sound of the approaching chopper. Chris turned the other way, around the back of the admin block, and broke into a run.

The pilot of the Huey was still a few metres from the tarmac when he saw the two figures emerging from the lighted doorway with a loaded stretcher. It was not going to be an all-nighter, he thought gratefully, and didn't bother to cut the engine on landing. Stepping out to open up the passenger hatch, he found the ugly nose of an Uzi pointing at his stomach.

The army doctor who had accompanied him was receiving a similar greeting on the other side. Both were hustled into the passenger hatch by a young woman in uniform, and after several seconds the penny dropped – these people were not who they were supposed to be.

The stretcher and its apparently unconscious occupant were shoved into the dark space after them, and a male voice told them silence was not only golden – it was also their best chance of surviving the next ten minutes.

* * *

Leaving Hajrija to look after the men in the helicopter, Razor was on his way back to Emelia when the sound of running feet stopped him in his tracks. He stepped into the deeper shadows just as the unmistakable silhouette of his SAS partner jogged around the corner of the building.

Razor blew a single low whistle, and stepped back out of the shadows. The two men shook hands and grinned at each other. Razor led Chris back into the building, explaining the situation as they walked.

'I'll go with Emelia,' Chris said.

They walked back down the corridor to the Interrogation Room, where Emelia was holding a gun on Goicouria as she tried to comfort his latest victim. 'His name is Salvador,' she told them.

Razor took charge of men and Uzi. 'Go and fetch the others,' he told Chris and Emelia.

As they hurried away down the corridor he half dragged the torturer out of the building and across the tarmac, gave him over to Hajrija's loving care, and then went back for Salvador. As he was being carried to the helicopter the tortured man spoke softly and continuously in a language Razor didn't understand.

He gently lowered the man to the floor of the passenger hatch and stood with Hajrija beside the rattling helicopter, her eyes and gun covering the men inside, his looking out across the still oblivious base. He could feel her tension, and could hardly believe how little he was feeling himself. By any objective standards this was a dangerous situation, and yet he felt no sense of danger.

He supposed it was hard to sound a real alarm in a place like this, where screams in the night were part of the aural furniture. Every man on the base would have heard the helicopter – could still hear it – but all of them would be assuming it was someone else's business. G-2's more than likely, and who would want to stick his nose into that?

They would probably have to set off fireworks and start singing 'God Save the Queen' before anyone came to investigate. In places like this people followed orders, and the only man who could give them was lying unconscious in the helicopter behind him.

Still, it was possible to have too much of a good thing. It was probably time to go.

On cue, three figures walked unsteadily out of the distant doorway, Chris and Emelia behind them. Razor turned to the open hatch and ordered the pilot out.

The man sullenly obeyed.

'How much fuel do you have?' Razor asked him, as Chris appeared at his shoulder.

'Almost a full tank.'

'Good. Now my friend here says he knows how to fly one of these, but what he means is he knows how to fly them through a bright blue English sky. Guatemala in the dark may be a little advanced for him, you get me?'

Chris smiled inanely.

'Well, that gives you two choices,' Razor told the pilot. 'One, you can sit in the back with the rest of us and pray, or two, you can fly us where we want to go. Of course, if you choose to be our pilot you'll have to come all the way to Mexico with us, whereas if you opt for economy class we shall have to leave you with the guerrillas.'

The man swallowed once. 'I am your pilot.'

'Then let's go.'

Not much more than a minute later the helicopter was lifting off. As it veered towards the north the only movement in the camp beneath came from the guard in the north-western watch-tower, who seemed to be waving them goodbye.

In the co-pilot's seat Chris was studying the map, and feeling unreasonably disappointed that there was enough fuel for them to reach Mexico. There would be no need to take to the mountains once more, no need of more help from the guerrillas, no reason for he and Emelia to spend any more time together. She and the rescued prisoners would be dropped off at the camp in the Cuchumatanes, along with Osorio and his torturer. They would say goodbye, and that would be that. He would never see her again.

'My brother is in Mexico,' the pilot said suddenly. 'He says Guatemala is fucked.'

'He's probably right,' Chris agreed. But it would also be blessed as long as there were people like her.

In the passenger hatch behind him Razor had securely trussed Osorio and Goicouria, and was now sitting with an arm round his wife, watching Emelia supervise the doctor in his examination of the rescued prisoners. He could not understand a word any of the latter were saying, but there was no mistaking the joy and relief of their liberation.

He felt pretty relieved himself. 'Thanks for coming to pick me up,' he murmured to Hajrija, as if she had just collected him from Hereford station.

She turned to look at him, a smile on her face. 'I didn't want to raise a daughter on my own,' she told him.

Epilogue

Chris parked his Escort by the side of the track, and the three of them clambered out into the mist. The flat crown of the mountain was hidden from view, about four hundred metres above them, a full morning's walk. They started up the path, Chris in the lead, Hajrija behind him, a plastic bag knotted to her belt. Razor brought up the rear.

More than two weeks had passed since their helicopter had touched down on Mexican soil, but in the intervening period all three of them had come to realize that Guatemala was not an easy place to leave behind.

To all outward appearances Chris had settled back into his routine as an SAS instructor, content to see out the weeks which still remained before his official departure from Regiment and Army. He had resumed his helicopter flying lessons and filled out applications for several charity and aid-agency jobs, at least one of which he expected to be offered.

The fact that he found his existence in England flat, safe, almost lifeless, he mostly kept to himself.

Climbing the misty path, he thought about her, as he often did. He wondered what had happened between them, and found that the conventional words seemed even more inadequate than usual. Had he been in love with her? They had known each other only a few days, and yet . . . He smiled at the cliché and yet still felt the power of what it expressed.

He knew he couldn't have stayed, knew she couldn't have left. He accepted it. He had always been good at accepting things, maybe too good. He saw her face frequently in his mind, and every time he heard a bird sing he could see her listening, the way she had that first day in the forest.

Now that the fear of losing Razor had faded, Hajrija's memory was filled with all the people who had helped her – the girl and her family in Panajachel, the old couple and Lara in Chichicastenango, Mariano and the *compas* on the volcano. She had never known such spontaneous friendliness, such a willingness to greet with a smile, such warmth and simple goodness. England had never seemed a friendly place to her, and since their return it had seemed even less so. Now she thought she could detect bitterness behind the coldness, as if the people here sensed that they were missing out on something but didn't quite know what.

She wanted to write something about Guatemala, but what? That being oppressed seemed to be good for the soul? That war was? Was that why she had left Bosnia for England?

As she climbed the path it occurred to her that in previous centuries she could have stumbled on a dead village in these Welsh hills. Not so many centuries had gone by since the English ruling class sent its armies on genocidal rampages through the lands of subservient ethnic groups. But here in 1995 the only bodies they might find would be those of sheep, and the only helicopter gunships looming out of the mist would belong to the army her husband had served for nearly twenty years.

Their baby would grow in peace, in safety. It wouldn't live a life of endless struggle and hardship, wouldn't suffer from malnutrition or have its stomach ripped open by the bayonets of crazed soldiers. All of which was good, and she was grateful for it. But never again would she mistake it for everything.

It was only two months, but already she seemed to be walking differently, Razor thought. Or maybe he was imagining it. He wondered if she should be making this climb, and knew she would only laugh at him if he mentioned it again.

He had a wonderful wife, and he was going to be a father. The rest ought to take care of itself.

But it never did. He wasn't sure if the last month had changed his life, or if it had just set the seal on a process which had been going on for years. His mum had always said that people only understood things when they were ready to. And according to his wife, whose Yugoslav education had included compulsory lessons in Marxist ideology, the old bugger himself had said that problems only become apparent when their solutions become available. Or something like that.

He kept seeing Tomás's questioning face in the dusk, asking him what he was a soldier for.

Barney Davies had been wonderful, but he was only the man who passed the orders down. It was the grey-faced men from the MoD and the Foreign Office and the intelligence services who thought them up. They were the ones who had 'interviewed' him and Chris since their return, the ones who always referred to the guerrillas as 'communists' or 'terrorists', the ones who implied the two of them had gone on a murderous spree, like a couple of armed England supporters lost in the mountains.

By their own lights, they were not unsympathetic. The two SAS men had been simply out of their depth. They had succumbed to stress, to the heat, to their own ignorance – to anything but the call of their consciences.

What did these people know? Absolutely nothing.

So how could he ever trust an order again? He hadn't got a clue.

The mist cleared as they approached the top of the mountain. Just a hill it would have been in Guatemala, but here they could see for miles, south-east to the dark-green expanse of the Forest of Dean, west into the heartlands of Wales. This mountain had once formed part of the border between two estranged cultures, which somehow seemed appropriate.

They took in the panoramic view, not speaking to each other. And then Hajrija untied the knot in the plastic bag, and all three of them reached in a hand. 'For Tomás,' she said, and one by one they cast their handfuls of orange petals to the wind.

Five thousand miles away Emelia awoke, a smile on her face. The poem was lying beneath her chin, where it had fallen in the night. She almost had it memorized now. '*I knew him and still he is there in me . . . I come back to see him, and every day I wait.'*

She sat up and reached for the book which served as her pillow, and replaced the folded piece of paper between the leaves of brightly coloured birds.

SOLDIER X: SAS

OPERATION TAKEAWAY

1

There were many kinds of exile. The old man realized that now. In fact, he wondered whether he had been unfortunate enough to experience them all in the course of his long life. As he ambled along the pavement bordering the busy road, the surface glistening with drizzle, he hunched his shoulders into the motionless cold and found himself thinking of his boyhood. That had been the first one. When he had been very small he had never been able to work out why he was exiled from the company of the other boys in his neighbourhood. Of course, he had heard the rumours of his parents, uncles and aunts, all speaking of Hindus and Muslims, and on holy days he saw how his own family went to pray at a different temple from the one attended by the other people in their street.

A passing lorry sprayed him with a fine film of muddy water as it shot by, heading south for the junction of the M4, which would already be thickening with traffic, even at such an early hour. By 9 a.m. it would have ground to a virtual standstill, clogged like an artery, the flow gradually stiffening to a halt in the moments before his death.

He hated his new country. He still thought of it as new, even though he had left the land of his birth nearly fifty years before. That had been another exile, more obvious than his boyhood solitude but stifling and bitter nonetheless. He looked around at the grey, sullen landscape of concrete, tarmac and red brick. It was barely light, and every house was closed as tight as a fist. Their owners had made pitiful attempts to differentiate their property from the one next door: a glass panel, the colour of woodwork, a cursory stab at flamboyance with a winding pathway. More noticeable, however, were the similarities, apart from the most obvious one of the houses' identical design: a front garden concreted over to provide parking for a clutch of cars; burglar alarms to keep at bay the increasing number of have-nots; and the satellite dish clinging under the miserly eaves like an extraterrestrial orchid, its brainwashing duties long completed but still reflexively cleansing the occupants of original thought.

The bench he usually rested on had been vandalized in the night. He stood before it, surveying the efforts of the mental giant who had spray-painted a swastika and racist slogans across the seat.

'If only I could go home,' he muttered to himself as he read the misspelt words. 'If only I could.'

He tested the paint with one cautious fingertip, and finding it dry, eased himself down, feeling a stab of satisfaction as his buttocks pressed into the swastika. He wondered briefly if the youth had been aware of the symbol's Indian origins. He smiled at the irony and took out a cigarette.

Against the background noise from the motorway he could hear the car alarms starting to go off around the district, each one welcoming its owner with the faithfulness of a dog, bleating an answering toot as a keyring was fired at it. Soon their drivers would be sitting in traffic jams and feeling the tension knot in the solar plexus at the prospect of being late for work.

The old man sat back and drew on his cigarette, glad to be out of it all, yet unable to resist the slightest twinge of regret that his own participation in the conduct of life was at an end. He had never become used to retirement, another one of the many exiles. Had his wife still been alive there might have been some solace in the spread of empty hours that extended from dawn to dusk. But she was dead – yet one more exile that he mentally ticked off on the tally he kept.

A growing roar overhead heralded the approach of the first morning flight into Heathrow. Moments later the fat silver fuselage broke through the low, swirling clouds like a bloated fly, sinking down to settle on a new-found corpse. The old man smiled grimly. He had seen plenty of those in his time. Too many. But that was all such a long time ago. He wondered sometimes if it had been a dream. Nightmare might be a better description.

He watched the plane disappear behind a prim row of houses, its great belly touching down out of sight on the soaking runway. The day had begun pretty much like every other since he had arrived in Britain. Perhaps later on he would go to the temple near his home in Southall, but he never knew whether or not he would actually go inside until he was mounting the steps and walking through the tinsel-adorned entrance hall. More often than not he simply passed by, unable to drum up the courage to face his conscience. He didn't believe in the gods any more. That had died a long time ago, but the temple had proved to be a place of brutally frank reflection and of late he found he preferred the cinema.

When he had finished the cigarette he contemplated smoking another but decided instead to heed his doctor's warning and cut down. By evening he would have finished the packet which had been new when he had got out of bed, unable to sleep, to dress and set off on his walk.

So how would he spend the day? He could go and visit any one of the restaurants, but then his son-in-law would think he was interfering and by midday his daughter would be on the phone, whining at him to give them space. They were so bloody sensitive, the younger generation. They had no concept of respect. All they thought about was themselves and their own selfish fulfilment. Self-sacrifice was an unknown land, and the notion that age had a certain wisdom to offer was as alien as the other planets.

If not the restaurants, what then? He was beginning to regret handing over the management of his little empire to his son-in-law. But he had to admit that the lad had improved their efficiency more than he would have thought possible. He was always spouting the jargon gleaned from the MBA course he had attended after university. 'Total quality management', 'customer care' – stuff like that. In the old man's day it had been enough simply to be the best in the neighbourhood, to crush the opposition by fair means or foul and fill the resulting power vacuum. Now it was all graphs and figures. There didn't seem to be any room for intuition.

He pushed himself off the bench and set off for home. As he walked the drizzle began to harden into rain and he cursed himself for not taking his umbrella. He was a creature of habit and always liked to return by a roundabout route past the cinema, but as he felt the sting of cold water lash against his cheeks he decided to go back the way he had come, taking the shorter path through the park. 'Park' was a grand description for a miserable patch of grass, largely trampled to mud at this time of year. From the far side a narrow path crept between the side of an old Victorian terraced house and a row of fenced-off garages, beyond which a single road cut in front of his own house. He glanced at his watch, trying to shield the glass from the rain. It would take him at least fifteen minutes, enough time to get thoroughly soaked. Perhaps he would go back to bed once he got home. That would solve the problem of what to do with himself. But no. That way lay a quick death. He would take to his bed only when he knew his end was near, and not before.

He approached a row of shops. Built in the early 1960s, they exuded all the charm and grace of an empty cornflakes packet. White wooden boards coated the upper floor and the lettering identifying each of the shops was in stark black plastic, the occasional letter missing. There was a launderette, a newsagent who served also as confectioner and postmaster, a greengrocer, a hairdresser and a chemist, every one of them Indian. It was extraordinary, the old man reflected. If their noble ancestors could see them now and witness what they had become, making their living in such an unpleasant foreign land. They had forsaken the wide, sweeping continent of their forebears, the ancient land of gods and sagas, of princes, fables and legends, to retreat to a dank, miserable corner of the globe that had been civilized for barely a millenium.

The newsagent was winding up his metal blinds and squinted suspiciously at the old man in the gloom.

'You should keep your spectacles on,' the old man called across. 'One day you'll be robbed.'

The newsagent grinned with relief as he recognized the old man's voice. 'You're up early, Mr Sanji.'

'As ever, as ever,' the old man said with a dismissive wave of the hand.

'You should get some sleeping pills from Dr Gupta.'

'Why hasten matters? We'll all be sleeping soon enough, and for as long as any man could wish.'

The newsagent shook his head in bemusement. 'You are always joking, Mr Sanji. Always joking.' He went inside and reappeared seconds later with a paper. 'Do you want to take this with you?' he asked. 'You know what that delivery boy is like. Quite, quite useless. Always late, always idling.'

The old man nodded appreciatively and accepted the paper, glancing briefly at the headlines and then folding it away inside his coat out of the rain. 'Thank you. I expect it's all bad news anyway.'

Chuckling to himself, the newsagent wagged a finger

at him and went inside. A moment later there was the flicker of neon and the inside of the shop was illuminated in the garish whiteness. The old man walked on.

By the time he reached the edge of the park the rain had become too heavy for him to ignore it. For a moment he toyed with the idea of pressing on and accepting the inevitable drenching, but his daughter would scream with horror at the sight of him and then fuss for the rest of the day. His son-in-law would likewise protest, but more from a sense of good manners. In his heart, the old man knew, his son-in-law would be wishing upon him a speedy death by pneumonia. There was no love lost between them. Politeness concealed their mutual hatred.

The entrance porch to an old church provided partial shelter from the rain. The old man squeezed up against the shuttered door and turned up his collar, but the rain slanted in, soaking the toes of his shoes. He turned them in like a pigeon but the water still found them, feasting on the cheap leather until he felt it penetrating to his socks. Strangely, the cold moistness between his toes reminded him of walking barefoot as a boy during the monsoons in the backstreets of Delhi. It was comforting now, knowing that warmth and proper shelter were a short distance away. Not that he had been deprived as a child. But confronted with the poverty of others, he had never felt the security he now took for granted.

Up above, the grey sky was lightening almost imperceptibly. Great swathes of cloud banked and rolled overhead, seeming so close he felt he could reach out and touch them. Another jet loomed out of the sky, the undercarriage down, lights blinking at the wingtips. Inside, he could imagine the passengers tut-tutting at the British weather, peering grimly through the thick windows at the disastrous-looking scene beneath them. The pilot would perhaps have made an attempt at humour and would now be concentrating on the path of lights before him, peeling open as he steadied the aircraft into its lowering approach run, and, perched on their seats, the stewardesses would be touching up lipstick and eye-shadow in readiness for the chorus of farewells by the exit door.

However dark the sky, when he looked back at the surrounding streets the old man felt as if night had fallen again by comparison. It seemed there was not going to be any let-up in the rain and suddenly he felt exasperated at the delay. It was so pointless. So much was pointless these days. He stepped out of the porch and set off as briskly as he could towards the park entrance, darting across the street and passing between the bent railings and the notice warning of the fine for owners who allowed their dogs to foul the pathways. Pointless.

The next instant he thought of his granddaughter and smiled. She at least gave some meaning to his life. She at least would be bright on this dismal, depressing day. But even there all was far from perfect. Her parents had consented to her wishes to be allowed to go to university. The old man had protested. Eli was the delight of his old age, he had said. Her place was at his side. Naturally it had been his son-in-law who had countermanded his order. Theirs was a modern family, he said proudly, not bound by the traditions of the past. Eli would go to university and that was an end to it.

Of course the old man knew that his son-in-law didn't care a jot for his daughter's emancipation. He was simply taking delight in thwarting the old man and depriving him of the only pleasure he had left. But Eli had come to see him and had promised to write at least once a week, and deep down he realized that, however much he resented it, the times had changed. He would be the last one to hold her back. They would see how modern and British his son-in-law was when Eli came back one weekend and announced her own choice of husband. The old man could well imagine the uproar that would create, and then he would be the one to support her decision. Then he would delight in the torment of his son-in-law.

He was about to emerge from the path at the far side of the park when he noticed the car. The windows were clouded with mist and it was impossible to recognize the people inside. He could just make out two figures, both in front. It was some kind of Ford, cheap-looking and obviously an unmarked police car. He smiled to himself. Perhaps his son-in-law had been cooking the books as well as the curry and the Inland Revenue was about to haul him away for interrogation. The old man prayed it would be a long and brutal affair.

More likely, he imagined, it was part of another of the anti-terrorist exercises that the police conducted from time to time on the outskirts of the airport. The idiots had left their windows tightly shut and the engine and heater turned off, until the car looked as though it had just been removed from a giant fridge. They couldn't possibly see through the glass. The buzz and hiss of a radio receiver from inside the car confirmed his suspicion that they were policemen. He sighed and started towards the park exit.

The sound of another engine stopped him. Although he had nothing to fear from the police, having always kept out of trouble, he drew aside into the inadequate cover of the scrawny bush and watched, more out of idle curiosity than anything else. Sure enough, the grubby white Ford Transit that cruised slowly round the corner at the top of the road seemed to be involved in the same exercise. Unlike the car's occupants, the driver of the van had kept the windows clear, and the old man could see the face peering at the houses as if searching for a particular number.

A cold drop of rain found its way down the old man's neck and tumbled down his spine, but the shiver that wriggled through his bones was caused by something altogether different. The van had stopped outside his own house, and through the back of the vehicle he could just see another man leaning over the driver's shoulder. They appeared to be arguing, and behind them he could make out other figures, perhaps half a dozen in all.

He looked anxiously at the unmarked police car again. What was going on? Perhaps he hadn't been so far from the truth about his son-in-law after all. But there was something very wrong, although he couldn't put his finger on it. For a moment he considered crossing the road and going straight indoors, ignoring the police and leaving them to get on with their exercise. But before he could move he heard the rear doors of the van opening and the sound of booted feet jumping to the ground. He watched in horror as the men moved purposefully towards his house and went to the front door, three of them striding down the pathway and the other four or five jogging down the drive. He almost cried out as one of them kicked open the side gate and disappeared towards the kitchen door, which gave on to the back garden.

In the police car the figures didn't move. Then one of them leaned forward and scrubbed a hole in the mist. Through the circle of misted breath the old man could see the surprise on the face and with another bolt of horror he realized that though they were indeed most likely policemen, they were nothing to do with the intruders breaking into his house.

He looked back at the van, where the man next to the driver was stepping on to the road. The engine was still ticking over and the man signalled for the driver to gun the accelerator and prepare for a speedy departure. Until then his face had been turned away from the park, but as the man gave the order to the driver, the old man saw him clearly and his heart missed a beat. There was something about the features that alerted him to the man's lineage. He had hoped to have done with the lot of them but it was obviously not to be. After all these years they had found him at last. Now it would begin all over again.

'Was that you?'

Colin Field grinned sheepishly. 'Sorry. It was that curry last night.'

'Jesus Christ.' Paul Robins screwed up his face and

opened the car window a crack. Instantly a gust of frosty, damp air buffeted its way in, relieving the strain on his nose but reminding him that they had been freezing all night in an unheated vehicle. Reluctantly he closed the window again.

'What a bloody night.' He reached for the glove compartment and hunted around until he found his pack of cigarettes. It was empty. He scrunched it up and tossed it over his shoulder on to the back seat.

'What time do we finish?' Colin asked.

'Don't ask me. Ask that pan-faced git from Hereford. He's supposed to be running the package.'

'Do you reckon he'll give us the run-around again? You know, pretend the exercise has ended and then fuck us off to another task?'

'If he does I'll tell the force they can stick their sodding job. I'll volunteer to go back on the beat and leave special duties to heroes like you.'

Colin nodded sagely. 'Beats me why our own training organization can't run the course. Why do they have to bring in outsiders?'

'Haven't you heard? They's sodding bloody supermen. I guess the boss is hoping some of it'll rub off on us.' He stared hard at Colin, appraising him. 'Some bloody hope.'

'Here, what do you mean?' Colin asked, an expression of confused hurt on his face.

'Nothing.' Paul decided it was best to let it go. They had already had a couple of set-tos during the night and with tempers frayed from lack of sleep he could do without another. Colin eased sideways on his seat cushion and Paul noticed the tell-tale signs. 'Don't you bloody dare!'

'Give us a break. It's either this or I'll have gut-ache for the rest of the day.'

'Make it gut-ache then, but one more of those and you're out in the rain.'

Muttering under his breath Colin sat upright. He looked at his watch. 'Couldn't we call in? Perhaps the ex is over and they've forgotten to tell us.'

Paul laughed. 'Don't be a bigger dick than you already are. Can you imagine Don sodding Headley screwing up like that?'

The radio crackled and a terse message was sent to one of the other teams. Spread in a vast ring around Heathrow, they were taking part in an anti-terrorist exercise that had already been going on for nearly three days. The floor of the car was littered with all the detritus of a stake-out: cigarette packets, hamburger cartons, newspaper reeking of old fish and chips, drink cans, crisp packets, sweet wrappers and heavily thumbed copies of several tabloids, the pages no longer in any sort of order and not one crossword more than a third completed.

Captain Don Headley of the SAS had kept them on the go ever since his initial briefing, and all the teams were longing for the exercise to end. Those who passed were due to proceed to the next stage of training, but Paul and Colin were having serious doubts about their original decision to transfer to the new anti-terrorist squad that was being set up.

'You know what I can't stick?' Colin said after a while.

'What's that?'

'The way Don manages to go without sleep for days on bloody end and still keep his cool.'

He wiped his brow with the back of his hand. 'Me, I feel shagged after one night out.'

Paul grinned. 'He's a right smooth bugger, isn't he? Still, with a little luck he'll sod off back to Hereford soon and leave us in peace.'

The rain lashed against the car window and drummed on the roof. Colin shivered and slid deeper into his leather jacket. The zip was open to the waist and his stomach bulged over his belt. Paul looked at him with distaste.

'In a way it's kind of cosy in here, isn't it?' Colin said, hunting around on the back seat for a paper to read.

'Speak for yourself.' Paul eyed the debris. 'If this is your idea of cosy I can imagine what your house looks like. It explains why your wife left you.'

'Nah, silly cow was worse than I was. You should have seen the kitchen. Looked like a shagging bomb had hit it.'

Paul could well imagine. He had seen the food stains on the walls and ceilings of Colin's office. The man was a walking disaster area.

He rubbed a hole in the breath misting the windscreen. Outside it was starting to lighten. Rain came down vertically, bouncing on the tarmac and rushing in the gutters. He sighed, misting the peep-hole, then looked at his watch for the umpteenth time.

'When do you reckon we'll be ordered to move?' Colin asked.

Paul shrugged. 'Your guess is as good as mine.'

They had been carrying out a series of surveillance tasks in their assigned area, but after their last one they had been directed to their present location to await retasking. It looked a prosperous residential street. The houses were mostly large, with trim hedges, large front gardens and no doubt even larger gardens to the rear.

At the end of the street he saw the large, white shape of a Transit turn towards them. It cruised slowly closer, stopping some thirty yards away. With the water coursing down the windscreen it was impossible to see it distinctly, but he wasn't bothered. It was probably just a plumber or decorator arriving early for a job in one of the houses.

However, the next moment he made out the vague outline of figures bundling from the back of the van and running towards one of the larger houses.

'What do you make of that?'

Colin grunted, not lifting his eyes from the nude in the paper. Her lips were peeled back in a provocative smile, eyes half-closed, breasts thrust out as if someone had just shoved her hard in the small of the back and she was about to topple downstairs.

'Colin, I'm fucking talking to you. Look.'

Reluctantly Colin made his own peep-hole with his sleeve and peered through it at the house. He was just in time to see one of the men kick his way through the side gate.

'Fucking hell!' He dropped the paper. 'It must be

another part of the bloody exercise. That bastard! He sent us here for a break and then hits us with an incident. What the fuck do we do?'

Paul thought for a moment. 'Hang on,' he said, playing for time while he ordered his thoughts. 'They're probably supposed to be terrorists. It'll be a safe house or something.'

'Don't be daft. They wouldn't go bundling in like that, kicking in doors if it was a safe house, would they?'

Paul cursed himself silently. He liked to think of himself as the brighter of the two, but for once Colin was right.

'Then they're probably seizing the house to use as a base for the duration of an attack on the airport.'

'Yeah!' Colin chirped, becoming enthusiastic. All of a sudden their fatigue was forgotten and they sat up and kicked aside the debris littering the floor of the car as they tried to work out how they were expected to react.

'Perhaps they're planning to fire a shoulder-launched anti-aircraft missile from the back garden, or something?' Colin said, his tongue hardly able to keep pace with his ideas.

Paul thought about it and rubbed his chin. 'Could be. We're right under the main flight path all right. Yeah, that's probably it.'

'So what do we do then?' Colin blinked at him, lost for a solution.

'There's too many of them for us to do anything. I reckon we report in and wait for backup.'

'Good thinking. Will you do it or shall I?'

Paul reached for the radio. 'It's my turn. You bogged up the last one.'

He pressed the transmitter switch and spoke slowly and clearly, reporting the incident and requesting support. The message was acknowledged and when he had replaced the handset he sat back with a self-satisfied smile.

It was a couple of minutes before the radio buzzed into life again and the voice of Don Headley rasped into the stagnant air of the car.

'Echo Two, what's all this about a van? Over.'

Paul and Colin swapped grins. 'He's playing dumb,' Colin whispered, as if Don himself were actually in the car.

Paul repeated his report. There was another pause before Don came back and said, 'It's nothing to do with the ex.'

'Yeah, yeah,' Paul crooned easily. 'Look, just log it down that we did the right thing and asked for backup. I know a bunch of terrorists when I see one.'

Don sounded amused. 'If that's the case I suggest you get the hell out of there. I repeat, there are no exercise activities planned in your area for the rest of the day. Out.'

The line went dead. Paul and Colin sat staring at one another.

'Reckon they could be decorators or something? Builders perhaps. They looked fit buggers.'

Paul laughed uneasily. 'They can't be terrorists, can they? Can you imagine it? Here in the middle of bleeding Southall?'

Colin nodded and scrabbled around on the floor for his discarded newspaper.

Suddenly, from inside the house they heard a muffled crack. They stared at each other again, but this time their faces paled.

'Did you hear that?'

'What the fuck was it?'

There was a second crack, and then a third.

'Oh, shit. That's a bloody shooter.'

Colin opened his door and started to pull himself out of the car. Paul snatched at his sleeve and tugged him back.

'Where do you think you're going, Humphrey sodding Bogart? In case you've forgotten, we don't carry firearms.'

'Well, we can't just sit here.'

Paul grabbed at the radio and called the station where the exercise control had been established.

'Get me the guv. And be quick about it!' he snapped.

'He's in a meeting. He told me he was not to be interrupted,' the duty operator replied.

'Listen, you tit, I don't give a fuck. We've got a real incident here. There's shooting in Bramley Road. Tell them to get some armed assistance here on the double. Got that?'

There was a pause before the operator asked nervously, 'This is part of the exercise, right?'

Paul almost slammed the handset against the dashboard in frustration. 'No, it fucking isn't! This is for real. Now do as I say or I'll crawl down the sodding air waves and rip your throat out!'

'So it's not part of the ex?'

Colin swore and started out of the car again.

'No,' Paul persevered with all the self-control he could muster. 'Now pass my message, right?'

'Roger. Out.'

He looked up to see that Colin was almost at the driveway, then quickly got out and rushed to join him. It was only when they were opening the gate that they noticed the man still standing beside the dirty white van. He appeared to be unconcerned by the gunshots from inside the house and when they caught his eyes he smiled pleasantly.

'Hang on, let's ask the geezer what's going on. Maybe it's nothing.'

They went towards him and as they drew near Colin whispered, 'It's a Paki.'

'Brilliant, Watson. Any more deductions?'

The man stepped towards them. 'Can I help you?'

They were taken aback by his Oxford accent.

'Excuse me, sir, but is this your van?'

The man turned round as if to check it was still there. 'Yes,' he said, then, as an afterthought, 'May I enquire who's asking?'

Remembering procedure and feeling suddenly a bit stupid, Paul fumbled in his jacket pocket and produced his identity card. 'Police,' he said.

The man smiled. 'Splendid. How can I help you?'

Becoming impatient, Colin said, 'Was that a gunshot we heard just now?'

The man's eyes widened theatrically. 'A gunshot? I certainly hope not.'

'Well, what was it then?'

'I really couldn't say. I didn't hear anything.' He turned to the driver, who had got out of the van and joined him. In contrast to the two policemen they were both tall, lean and fit.

Paul glanced back at the house. 'Would you come with us, please, sir?'

The man shrugged. 'If you insist, officer.' He said something quickly to the driver in a language that the policemen could not understand.

Keeping the man in front of him, Paul walked down the driveway towards the house. As the front door was shut they veered towards the side gate. 'After you, if you don't mind, sir,' he said. Again the man shrugged politely, still smiling.

A window showed into the kitchen and although the room itself was empty they could hear something being smashed elsewhere in the house. Before they could ask any more questions the man turned and explained, 'We're doing some construction work, you see. A really wealthy fellow, the owner. He wanted all sorts of alterations done.'

Colin relaxed, whispering, 'I thought so. Sodding builders. The boss is going to roast us alive when the heavies turn up and find out. We'll be the laughing-stock of the whole bloody force.'

They reached the back of the house and saw a large, well-kept garden stretching down to a tall hedge at the bottom.

'Come on,' Paul said miserably. 'Let's get this over with.' He turned to the man. 'We'd better check it out if you don't mind.'

For the first time the man's calm smile faltered and a second later it died altogether. His eyes chilled and narrowed and he sighed heavily. 'Of course. I understand. I very much regret the inconvenience to you though.'

Paul chuckled pleasantly. 'It's no bother, sir. Just a peek and then we'll leave you in peace. So as we can say we did our duty.'

'Naturally. Duty,' the man said, his voice low and matter of fact. He seemed to be searching for something in his pocket and when he pulled out a small automatic pistol Paul and Colin stared at it dumbly, the shock not even registering.

'We all have our duty to perform,' the man said. He took a single step backwards, widened his stance and shot Colin in the solar plexus with a rapid double tap. Colin staggered against the wall, his mouth opening and shutting like a fish out of water, and then sank to the floor. Paul watched in mesmerized horror as the smoking muzzle flicked on to its new target. Behind it, the man seemed almost apologetic for what he had just done, and, more particularly, for what he was about to do.

'If only you'd stayed in your car and minded your own business. But you know what they say about curiosity and the cat.'

Paul held out his hand as if ordering a car to stop, as the first of the bullets spat straight through his palm and hammered into his ribcage. He clutched at the wound and his knees gave way.

'You bastard,' he muttered, his words sounding distant and garbled. He didn't seem able to get his tongue around the syllables he had used so often in the past. 'You fucking . . .'

He fell on to his back and stared up at the foul grey sky. Rain stung his face but it was strangely refreshing, a counter to the ache he was just beginning to feel. Suddenly the sky filled with the man's enquiring face looking down at him. Then he saw the muzzle again, lowering, getting monstrously large until he felt its warm metal pushing into his mouth. He tried to speak, to plead, but the cold muzzle was being forced upwards, pressing into the roof of his mouth, the line of the short, hard barrel aiming directly through the slim bone and into the brain.

There were words in his head, something about being so terribly sorry. Wrong place and wrong time. The man's voice was calm as if talking about the weather. The weather. It was a shit-awful day to die, Paul thought, as the pistol flinched at the sudden pressure being applied to the trigger.

2

By the time Don Headley received the news the phones in the ops room were already buzzing with enquiries from the press. At first he couldn't believe what had happened. Reality had broken into the middle of his exercise and two men were dead.

As soon as he could he got away from his desk and drove to Bramley Road. It was mid-morning and the traffic was heavy. On all sides drivers drummed their steering wheels in frustration as the long queues edged slowly forwards. The rain had stopped and a harsh winter light percolated through the thick layers of cloud, muting the colours into one continuous semblance of grey. It was a part of the country Don particularly hated, the dense belt of urban wasteland spread thickly around central London. Successive decades had added to it, pushing it out ever further until towns that had once counted themselves lucky to be outside the city now found themselves being sucked in, not enjoying full membership but rather taken on board as second-class citizens in a dubious club.

Hounslow, Isleworth, Sunbury, Feltham – the names rolled past, each representing an identical sprawl of little red houses and car-packed residential streets. It wasn't so long ago that such roads would have boasted hardly a single vehicle parked at the kerbside, but increasing prosperity had combined with thoughtless marketing by the car manufacturers, whose eyes were solely on profit, and it had resulted in nearly every household owning at least one vehicle. Along either side of every road parked cars were jammed in nose to tail. It struck Don as a case of suicide by self-strangulation on a national scale. No one individual was prepared to sacrifice his car, not even with the prospect looming of the next generation gassing itself. Public transport was overcrowded and stank, so what was the incentive?

For an incentive to work and change a lifestyle it had to produce a more immediate threat. But then with smoking even that hadn't worked, Don reflected as he waited impatiently behind a lorry that was belching obnoxious blue fumes. It was almost possible to predict to a smoker the year in which his habit would bring about his agonizing death, and yet nine times out of ten he would continue. What was the answer? Don was buggered if he knew. Perhaps the species was on track for extinction and it was as simple as that. Self-destruction had replaced self-preservation as the prime motivation in the human psyche, and no one had even noticed. He grinned sardonically. They had probably been too busy watching *Gladiators*.

It was another half hour before he drew up outside the house. A policeman came to his window to wave him on but he produced a pass and was allowed to go in search of a parking space. The curtains in the neighbouring houses twitched as inquisitive eyes followed him out of the car and down the driveway. The couple in the house on the opposite side of the road were less circumspect and stood at their open doorway, mugs of tea in their hands, interested to find their mundane existence disrupted by something as exciting as a murder.

Chief Inspector Rod Chiltern met Don at the front of the house.

'The SOCO's round the back with his lads. Be careful not to touch anything.'

Don scowled at him, resenting the caution. Nevertheless, he was only there as an observer. It was police business and had nothing to do with the SAS. So far.

He followed Chiltern down the narrow path. The first thing he saw when he emerged at the back outside the kitchen door was the body of Colin Field. It was propped up against the wall as if he had just sat down for a rest. His legs were splayed, the scuffed trainers out of sync with the portly figure of their owner. His head was cocked heavily to one side, the eyes open a slit, lips pursed. A trickle of blood had dried to a crack of dark purple running from the corner of his mouth to his chin, but the real sign of damage was the blood on the red brick of the wall, splashed liberally as if a child had flung a can of paint at it.

A couple of yards from him, Paul Robins lay on the crazy-paving terrace. Don noticed the shattered hand and could imagine how Paul had received the wound. The wound in his chest was bad but he judged it had probably not been fatal. That had been reserved for the head shot.

He moved carefully round to the far side.

'Jesus,' he whistled.

Chiltern nodded. 'Not much chance of giving him the kiss of life, is there?' he said.

The explosion of the gun in the confined space of the mouth had blown out most of the teeth, propelling them through the thin wall of the cheeks. But where the bullet had exited through the top and back of the skull there was a gaping hole. It had taken the larger portion of the brain with it and slammed it in a rough fan shape on the paving stones.

'How well did you know them?' Chiltern asked.

Don shrugged. 'Reasonably. They'd been on my course for a while and you get to know the guys quickly that way.'

He was being polite, tempering his opinion because he knew that Chiltern had worked with both the dead men for several years. In truth Don had found them to be a couple of no-hopers, overweight, inefficient, dim-witted and bungling. Just the stupid sods, in fact, to walk straight into the middle of an armed gang without so much as a catapult. But no one deserved to die like this, he thought. Not even these two.

He crouched down beside them and looked around. The scene-of-crime officer had done a thorough sweep and everything that might be needed as evidence was circled with a thin chalk line. Principal among these items were several cartridge cases. Don asked if he might have a closer look at one of them and the SOCO nodded.

'Don't bugger up the prints, and put it back where you found it,' he snapped, busy with a measuring tape, marking the distance from Colin's body to the point where he estimated the firer must have been standing.

Don took a pair of gloves from his pocket and slipped one of them on. Carefully, he picked up the nearest of the cases and examined it. It was 9mm calibre. Powerful enough to silence a full-grown man, especially at almost point-blank range. No wonder Colin had been flung against the wall with such force, he thought.

But there was something unusual about it and a moment later Don realized what it was. He had come across its kind only once before. Several years ago he had been on secondment to the Sultan of Oman's army. The Sultan's quartermaster had done some shopping around on the open market for ammunition in an effort to cut costs. British ammunition had proved the most expensive, and he had finally opted for a batch of Pakistani-made rounds, both 7.62mm and 9mm. They hadn't performed as effectively or as consistently as the British-made ammunition, several of the rounds misfiring and causing stoppages owing to an insufficient charge of powder in the brass case. But they had done the job and Pakistani ammunition had been used a great deal thereafter.

Turning the cartridge case in his fingers, Don was convinced that this was from the same source. He replaced it in its white chalk circle, where it looked as if it was about to be part of some Satanic ceremony.

He voiced his opinion to the SOCO, who grunted and said, 'Right now I couldn't give a stuff. But thanks all the same. I'll get the lads on to it back at the lab. If you're right they'll be able to tell you the exact factory it came from, right down to the postcode.'

Don went into the kitchen, where Chiltern was receiving a report from one of his men. He looked up as Don came in. 'Nice mess, isn't it?'

'That's what happens when you get in the way of a 9mm bullet or two.'

'Well, there's another two dead upstairs,' Chiltern added, shaking his head. 'Right sodding blood-bath this is turning into.'

He led the way into the hall and up the stairs. Everywhere were signs of the intruders' recent presence. Furniture had been overturned, pictures ripped from the walls and ornaments smashed.

'It looks like my own place after the kids have had a party,' Chiltern said, grinning.

They found the next body sprawled on the landing. It was the body of a middle-aged man of Indian appearance. A bullet wound in the back of the left leg indicated that he had been brought down trying to run away from his attackers. Thereafter someone had made a crude attempt at interrogating him. A heavy metal file had been applied to the surfaces of his teeth until they were almost completely rubbed level with the blood-soaked gums.

'That's an old Spetsnaz trick,' Don said in amazement.

'Who?'

'Spetsnaz. Soviet special forces.'

Chiltern winced at the gruesome spectacle. 'What the fuck would they be doing in Southall?'

Don shrugged. 'I don't know, but during the Cold War they sent training teams abroad, just like we did.'

'Passing on their techniques, you mean?'

'Exactly.'

The man's eyes were wide open and staring, bulging out of their sockets with the agony. A cloth had been stuffed at the back of his mouth to prevent him screaming and he had been finished off with a bullet to the back of the head.

'Who was he?' Don asked.

'Just a guy who ran a chain of curry restaurants in the area,' Chiltern replied. 'I've ordered takeaways from them myself. Bloody good they were too.'

'Any idea why anyone would want to do this to him?'

Chiltern shrugged. 'Not a clue.' He smirked. 'Perhaps someone got Delhi belly after his vindaloo.'

Don ignored the wisecrack. 'You said there were a couple of bodies?'

The policeman pointed to an open door. From inside Don could hear the click and whirr of an automatic camera. He stepped over the dead man and went on down the corridor. The bare legs were the first thing he saw, protruding from behind the bed. The police photographer looked up.

'Nasty. Very nasty. It's as clinical as an execution.'

He moved aside to allow Don a clear line of sight to the body. It was a woman. Presumably the man's wife. They seemed to Don to be of a similar age. She was dressed in a bright-blue sari trimmed in gold. Expensive.

He studied the room. It was obviously the home of a well-to-do family.

Unlike her husband's, the woman's eyes were tightly shut; clenched, as if trying to shut out some unpleasantness. One hand was clasped to her throat in shock and the other held a candlestick.

'Looks like she tried to defend herself,' Chiltern said.

A single bullet between the shoulder-blades had thwarted any such attempt, ending her life immediately.

While Chiltern spoke to the SOCO, who had now finished in the garden and climbed up the stairs to start work in the house, Don wandered out on to the landing again and explored the other rooms. There were two bathrooms, a guest bedroom, tastefully decorated but unlived in, and a large room clearly belonging to an older man. There were smashed photograph frames on the floor, and a walking stick snapped in two.

But it was the last room that caught his attention most. Posters hung off the walls, pictures of pop stars and horses. The furnishings were in pinks and pale, gentle shades, and the clothes torn from the ransacked drawers were those of a young woman. More interestingly, there was a single small stain on the carpet close by the door. Don stooped and examined it. The next moment he shouted down the landing to the SOCO.

'I think you'd better take a look at this.'

The SOCO and Chiltern padded down the corridor towards him.

'What is it?'

Don pointed at the stain. 'Looks like blood, if you ask me.'

The SOCO sighed in exasperation. 'Is that all? The whole sodding house is awash with blood, and you raise the alarm over one tiny stain.'

'Yes, but look at the room. Someone's been in here recently.'

'Brilliant! I can tell you're army.' The SOCO shook his head.

But Chiltern saw what Don was getting at. 'Don's right.'

'Thank you,' Don said. 'Have you found the body of a girl yet?'

The SOCO blanched. 'No.'

'Then I suggest you start looking for her because there was a girl in this room less than an hour ago. Look.' He pointed at the dressing table. 'The make-up's open. Don't tell me the intruders wanted to touch up their lipstick.'

'Shit,' Chiltern hissed. 'If they've taken her we could have a hostage crisis on our hands as well as a quadruple murder. What the hell's going on here?' He turned on his heel and marched back to the stairs. 'Don, you come with me. This is police business now. I shouldn't have allowed you in here in the first place. Your assistance and interest are much appreciated, but I'll handle things from now on. Oh, and by the way, I suggest you end that exercise of yours. Reality's got in the way. Thanks for everything, but you can return to Hereford. Send me a report on the guys you think might have passed when you've got a moment to write them up.'

He led Don to the front door and ushered him out into

the front garden. It had started to rain again and as he sauntered back to his car Don turned up the collar of his jacket and hunched his shoulders against the sharp cold. He had seen more than his fair share of action, but the sight of the murders had shocked him. There was something particularly repulsive about the sight of a dead body in an otherwise normal setting. It was bad enough on the battlefield, but in a comfortable house in the middle of suburbia it smacked of the most appalling decay. Two of the men on his course had been butchered in cold blood and in a way he felt responsible for it. They had radioed in to report their sighting of a van and although it had been a police responsibility to dispatch assistance, Don had noticed that there had been little sense of urgency. No one had really believed Paul's message, assuming it to be just another part of the exercise programme. Because of the delay they were dead.

He unlocked the door of his car and got in, turning the key and gunning the accelerator as the engine fired. He glanced at the clock on the dashboard. He could be home in Hereford by teatime. All of a sudden he wanted nothing more than to be out on the motorway and burning up the miles of tarmac between London's dismal outskirts and the fresh air of the Severn estuary, the green hills of Wales beckoning from beyond.

Chiltern had been right. It was a police matter and nothing to do with a soldier. Don's job had simply been to run the exercise and help the police with their anti-terrorist training. What could such an occurrence possibly have to do with him? It was just bad luck that

Colin and Paul had got caught up in the middle of something that was too big for them. They were dumb for getting involved.

Blanking it out of his mind, he headed for the nearest junction of the M4, just east of Heathrow, and threaded his way out into the traffic. The rush hour was tailing to a close but it was always busy on this stretch. Within half an hour, however, the spaces between the cars expanded and soon he had his foot flat on the floor, feeling the miles being eaten up beneath his wheels.

No doubt there would be the usual hearty jokes in the mess when he got back to the barracks. The older he got the more the humour grated. It was all very well when you were young but after a while you started to see that there wasn't much to laugh about in death. Perhaps that was the time to quit.

But as he drove he found his mind flicking back always to the same thing. Not to the bodies of Colin or Paul, the exploded brains on the paving stones and the blood on the wall, nor the body on the landing or in the bedroom, the candlestick clasped pathetically in its small, tight fist. But rather to the empty bedroom with the posters and the untouched make-up jars. Somewhere, if he was right, a young woman had been taken hostage. And although the matter was out of his hands he couldn't shake off the feeling that somehow he hadn't heard the last of it. Somehow he knew that he would be involved with it again.

'Are you sure she can breathe?'

'Don't worry.'

'I'm not worrying,' Ceda Bandram said slowly, glowering over his shoulder at Ali Shaffer, who sat sprawled across the back seat. 'I don't want to arrive only to find that she's suffocated.' He stabbed a finger at Ali. 'You would be held personally responsible. Remember that.'

Ali sniggered and waved a large, nonchalant paw. 'I drilled holes in the underside of the boot. A shame considering the newness of the car, but it couldn't be helped, I suppose. It'll all be charged to the expense account.'

Bandram stared ahead at the slow-moving traffic. Since the events at the house he had changed into a sweatshirt, slacks and moccasins. The van had been dumped in a lock-up garage that had been hired for the purpose and he estimated it would be a good many weeks before it was discovered. By then they would be several thousand miles away.

The team had split up and were now travelling by separate routes and methods of transport to the next rendezvous and the next leg of their onward journey. For himself, Ali and the driver, there had been a waiting BMW and of course he had ensured that the hostage had been brought with him. Every man in the team had been hand-picked but even so he made a habit of never trusting anyone but himself with the most delicate part of any mission.

The only man whom he had not selected was Ali. There was nothing he could do about it, however. Ali had been forced upon him by the boss. He was another relation, although Ceda had never known much about him. But that was the way with families in Pakistan, complex networks of relatives with every so often the discovery of some hidden black sheep. And Ali was such a cupboard skeleton if ever there was one. Ceda had been disgusted with the evident glee with which Ali had conducted the interrogation at the house. It was not that he was squeamish, but there were ways of doing things. One didn't have to enjoy the more unpleasant tasks of the business. Some unfortunate things might always be necessary, but maintaining a sense of propriety kept one separated from the beast. In Ceda's view Ali had crossed that threshold. He glanced back at him again, but Ali was staring happily out of the window humming to himself. His torture of the poor individual at the house seemed to be completely forgotten.

Ceda consoled himself with the thought that there were a great many pitfalls before the team finally reached safety. There would be plenty of opportunities for a fatal accident to befall Ali. Ceda for one would not mourn his loss.

The driver coughed and nodded towards a lay-by. A police car and motorcycle were parked at the roadside, the men scanning the traffic. They had already flagged down two white vans and were attempting to attract the attention of a third. Ceda smiled to himself. He was due to switch vehicles at least once more before the final RV and was confident that even if the police discovered the original van they would be unable to track him in time.

He reached down the side of the seat and pulled out a road map, unfolded it on his lap and began studying the markings he had made earlier. Bored with his humming,

Ali leaned forward, crossing his arms on the back of Ceda's seat and peering over his shoulder to get a look at the map.

'Where to now, cousin?' he asked sarcastically.

'Don't call me that,' Ceda said coolly.

Ali shrugged. 'I thought blood was supposed to be thicker than water?'

'You ought to know. You've seen enough of it.'

'You didn't do so bad yourself, you hypocrite. Dropping those two cops like that.' He shaped hs hand like a gun and put it to Ceda's head, mimicking the shooting. 'Bang, bang. You're dead. Nice work. A bit cold and clinical for my liking, but professional. Uncle would approve.'

'I didn't do it for Uncle's approval. In fact I didn't want to do it at all.'

'Oh no, of course not. I forgot. You're the ex-army officer. Death before dishonour, and all that. I'm sorry.' He sat back with a derisory laugh. 'You're full of shit.'

Ceda gritted his teeth, resisting the urge to go for the gun in his belt. The driver glanced nervously across at him and he relaxed. He was responsible for the whole team, not just for himself. He couldn't afford to lose his temper, and certainly not over a dick-head like Ali.

'Where's the next switch?' the driver asked, keen to divert the conversation away from the rivalry between the two men. It had been evident to most of the team members from the outset but they all knew and trusted Ceda, and were confident that he would see them safely through.

'Not the next service station but the one after that. The

cars have been left in the car park. I've got the registration numbers here.' He patted his breast pocket.

'It seems such a waste just to ditch the car,' the driver added, stroking the dashboard lovingly. 'She's a beauty.'

Ceda smiled. 'That's business. Just be thankful you're not footing the bill.'

Ali perked up from the rear. 'Talking of beauties, how do you intend to transfer the cargo?' He jabbed a thumb at the boot. 'You can't just lift her out in full view of everyone.'

'Don't worry. That's been seen to. The car'll be parked in a nice private spot. No one will see.'

He turned on the radio to cut short any further talk with Ali, pressing the automatic tuning button and watching the digital display purr rapidly through the frequencies. There was some traffic news warning of jams on the M4, and he checked the map to see if it would interfere with their escape.

'Problem?' the driver asked.

'Could be. It's after the next switch. It could have cleared by the time we get there, but it might be wise to make a detour.'

'Won't that confuse the others?'

'It might, but it'll be better than getting stuck in a tailback and waiting for the police to catch up with us. Every extra hour we spend in this miserable country increases the chance that they'll be on to us.'

There was a metallic click from the back of the car and Ceda glanced around to see Ali playing with his pistol.

'Personally I don't care if they do catch up with us,'

Ali said. He aimed down the barrel of his gun. 'Just let them try and take me.' He squeezed the trigger and the hammer clicked shut on an empty chamber.

'Keep that bloody thing out of sight,' Ceda snapped. The traffic was light on the present stretch of road but there was always the chance of another motorist seeing the gun and reporting it to the police.

It was another half an hour before they saw the sign advertising the service station. The driver waited for Ceda's confirmatory signal before indicating and pulling over into the slow lane. Ceda adjusted the wing mirror beside him and checked that they were not being followed. The lane behind was clear. No other car appeared to be coming after them.

The car slowed as the driver worked down through the gears, tracing the white arrows marking the route for cars wanting the main car park. It was moderately busy. Rows of large lorries were drawn up in line and in the other section the only available spaces were the ones farthest from the restaurant and shops. They cruised up and down until Ceda said, 'There it is. The grey Ford.'

'That's a bit of a come-down,' Ali drawled from the back.

Ceda ignored him. 'Park next to it.'

Two orange plastic cones had kept the adjacent space free of cars and as the car slowed, Ceda darted out and moved them, waving the BMW forward until it was close alongside and the driver cut the engine. The boots of the two cars were angled away from the main public areas and were shielded from view by a screen of trees.

Ceda cursed.

'What's the matter?' the driver asked as he got out and stretched, his muscles cramped after the long drive.

'Those idiots who did the recce. They must have come here in the summer. The trees would have been covered in leaves then. Now look at them.'

He was right. The leaves had long since fallen, washed into a brown pulp by prolonged heavy rain, and it was possible to see the shopping area through the bare branches.

'Well, it can't be helped.'

'Do you want us to transfer the girl now?' the driver asked nervously.

'No. We'll wait until the others get here and then do it. I want to have a look around in any case.'

'Good, I'll come with you,' Ali said brightly.

Ceda considered telling him to forget it, but decided not to.

'You stay here,' he ordered the driver. 'If you see any of the others don't make it obvious that we're together.'

'Got it.'

Trying to forget that Ali was beside him, Ceda walked briskly towards the main building. His familiarity with Britain was one of the reasons he had been selected for the mission. In his army days he had been sent for training to Sandhurst and since then he had been back to attend further courses in the country. During those times he had used the opportunity to travel widely. Later, after his resignation, he had worked briefly in Britain, staying with relatives in London and Birmingham. He felt comfortable moving through the rail and road networks, while still maintaining the psychological distance of the visitor. On the present mission that distance was a vital safeguard against carelessness. Familiarity might well breed contempt, but complacency was a far more dangerous by-product.

After a trip to the toilets they went into the concourse and stood for a moment surveying the array of shops and eating places. There was the choice between a sit-down restaurant, a hamburger takeaway bar and a cafeteria. Without asking Ali which one he preferred, Ceda pointed towards the cafeteria and grunted.

They each took a tray and tagged on to the short queue. Plastic-wrapped sandwiches and salads were stacked behind a glass-fronted cabinet, and at the next counter a selection of hot dishes steamed under heat lamps.

'What'll it be, love?' the waitress asked when their turn came.

Ali flashed her a disarming smile. 'The All Day Breakfast looks impossible to resist . . .'

The waitress reached for a plate and started to shovel on bacon and eggs.

'. . . but I'll go for the cottage pie.'

She glared at him and with a heavy sigh tipped the bacon and eggs back in their containers. 'Cottage pie? Are you sure?' she asked, taking a clean plate.

Ali hummed. 'Yeees,' he said slowly. 'I think so.'

He felt a sharp dig in his ribs and looked round to find Ceda staring hard at him.

'Yes, cottage pie,' he said with an air of finality.

In an attempt to placate the waitress Ceda helped himself, bustling Ali along to the till, picking up two coffees on the way. When they had paid and were sitting at a table he leaned across and said threateningly, 'Try that again and I'll shoot you, in public or not.'

'What have I done?' Ali said innocently.

'Drawn attention to yourself, that's what. She'll remember you now, you idiot. If you'd kept your stupid mouth shut you'd be just another customer. But oh no, not you. When the police start asking questions she'll be able to give them a full description of the two of us. Are you satisfied?'

'Don't worry about it. We'll be long gone by then.'

Afraid lest he lose his temper, Ceda started his food, eating more quickly than he would have liked to, feeling as if the eyes of everyone in the place were upon them. This is not good, he thought. This moron could jeopardize the whole team.

The moment he had finished his food he drained his coffee cup and prepared to leave.

'Hang on. I'm not ready yet,' Ali protested.

'I don't give a shit. We're going.'

While they had been eating, Ceda had noticed the rest of the team members arriving in twos and threes. Each group sat alone, acknowledging each other with only the most cursory of glances. When they saw Ceda make a move, they moved too.

Ceda was just making his way out towards the entrance when Ali stopped.

'I need a leak.'

'Again? Be quick about it.'

The other teams walked on past, looking at Ceda with sympathy. There was no love lost between any of them and Ali. Through the glass entrance doors Ceda could see the teams making their way towards their new cars. It would all be over soon, he consoled himself. They would soon be out of the country and in the clear, and as soon as they were back home he would speak to the boss and tell him how the choice of Ali had been a disastrous one.

It was the raised voices that first alerted him to the approach of trouble. From inside the toilets Ceda heard a shout followed by scuffling. He moved rapidly towards the entrance but as he rounded the tiled corner a single gunshot rang out.

The sight that greeted him when he burst through the swing door stopped him in his tracks. A man in the blue overalls of a lorry driver lay sprawled across the floor, blood spreading from his chest across the white lino of the floor. Standing over him, Ali looked up at Ceda. In his right hand he held his pistol, smoke seeping from the muzzle.

'He went for me,' he said simply, as if that explained everything.

Against the far wall, three other men backed away in horror. The door to one of the cubicles opened and a man came out, his face frozen in fear.

'You idiot!' Ceda roared and made a grab for the pistol. But Ali snatched it out of reach, his eyes warning him not to try again.

'He insulted me, I said. No one calls me names and gets away with it.'

Without stopping to listen Ceda spun on his heel and made for the exit. 'Come on,' he shouted at Ali.

In the space of seconds the whole painfully prepared

escape procedure had collapsed about him. The pre-positioned cars, the garage hideaway, the recced routes – everything. All to no avail. Within minutes the police would be on to them. Speed was now their only chance – and even that might not save them.

3

Don Headley swerved on an impulse into the slow lane, carving up a lorry in the process. The driver blew his horn and Don waved an apology as he veered off the motorway and headed up the exit road into the service station. He had been driving for well over an hour and felt in need of a strong coffee. Because of the exercise with the police he had not had a decent night's sleep for several days and his eyes had started to blink shut as the motorway unfurled beneath him, its rhythmic pulse on his tyres soothing his nerves and lulling him into a fatal sleep. He had to wake himself up if he was to make it to Hereford in one piece.

Some way back he had wound down his window, letting the cold air blast in. For a while it had worked, but since he was well used to exposure to the elements even that had eventually been blunted by his fatigue. Now, only a substantial intake of caffeine would do the trick.

It was a service station he had used many times before. He had lost count of the number of times he had made the M4 trip between Wales and London, but over the years he reckoned he must have sampled the delights of every service station along the way. Most of them were pretty rough; various companies had bought them as part of a job lot, stamping each one with its own insipid identity. It had got to the stage where Don preferred to take his own sandwiches and a flask of coffee, and simply sit in the car park by himself before filling up with petrol and pressing on. That morning, however, there had been no time for such preparations, so he turned towards the restaurant and shops and looked for a parking place.

There was the usual assortment of visitors, families with young kids, sales reps in their Fords, Vauxhalls and Rovers, the occasional foreign tourist coping with the difficulties of driving on the left, and a variety of coaches and articulated lorries. An icy wind cut savagely across the car park, sweeping in across the surrounding open fields. He hurriedly wound up his window and shivered, deciding that he would need his jacket once out of the car.

He found a vacant space reasonably close to the buildings, swung his car in and switched off the engine. The car rocked in the stiff breeze that howled along the avenues of vehicles, struggling to get in. When he opened the door the wind grasped at it and tugged it wide. Don stepped out on to the tarmac and turned up his collar, then locked the door and set off towards the main entrance. He had gone only a few yards when he heard a commotion and looked up to see two men pushing their way out of the concourse. In their haste they shouldered aside an elderly couple, almost knocking the man to the floor.

'Bloody impatient bastards,' Don muttered. Everyone was in such a rush these days.

The old man staggered but managed to regain his balance, turning after the men and shaking a wizened fist at them. He shouted something but his words were lost in the wind.

But something else was happening. Through the double glass doors Don could see people throwing themselves to the floor while others scurried for cover. In his half-awake state, the images refused to order themselves in his brain. It failed to register that there was anything untoward about it all. He reached the doors and only then did he hear the shouting.

'He's got a gun!'

'Someone call the police!'

'Get a doctor! There's a man dying in here!'

Suddenly Don's head cleared. He took one look at the chaos inside the concourse and then spun to see where the two men had gone. A large lorry was just pulling to a halt, obscuring his view. He ran around it and scanned the car park. Two cars were tearing away from the service station, but through a thin screen of bare trees he just caught a glimpse of the men ducking into a waiting car. The engine was already turning over, white plumes of exhaust hanging in the cold air, and the next moment the wheels were spinning as it set off.

Don's hand went automatically to his chest and felt the reassuring bulge of the shoulder holster. There might just be time to head them off and get a couple of clear shots at the car before it disappeared past the petrol pumps.

He sprinted past the rows of parked cars. People stared at him in surprise and alarm, unaware of what had just happened in the restaurant area. Someone called out a warning and Don narrowly managed to avoid running headlong into an approaching van. He veered to one side, bouncing off the sides of it and regaining his balance with difficulty. On the far side of the car park he could see the car and its occupants accelerating away. It was heading in the opposite direction to the other two cars. In Don's mind the connection was quickly made. They were all part of the same team. He had seen that the men were Asian and could hardly believe what his instinct told him: that they were the ones from the Bramley Road incident.

However, unlike the two cars that had screamed away towards the exit, the one he was running after was making for a barrier that led out of the rear of the service station on to a minor road. It was a restricted entrance for use by the service-station staff only, and from it access could be gained to the local town and road network. Whoever was in charge of the car obviously had his head screwed on. The other two, by taking to the motorway, were in effect entering a potential trap. The next exit from it was several miles away and by then the police might be able to have a cordon in place. At the very least they would be able to position observers who could report on the cars' direction and progress to enable armed officers to pursue them.

The other car, by taking a back road, was not restricting itself in any such way. It would be able to go in any number of directions and so multiply its chance of escaping.

Don covered the last few yards to the end of one of the rows and as he reached the last parked car he skidded to his knees and drew his 9mm Browning pistol. Holding it in a two-handed combat grip, he steadied himself against the car door and brought the gun into the aim, waiting for his target to appear and enter his sights.

There was the sound of squealing rubber and the car roared into view, the tyres spinning as the driver swung it round towards the barrier. Don waited until he had a clear line of sight and then squeezed off a rapid double tap at the rear window, where he was able to make out the silhouette of a man sitting upright in the centre. He saw the glass frost as his bullets found their mark but the car continued towards the barrier.

He dropped his point of aim to the fuel tank and was about to fire another double tap when something stopped him, freezing his finger on the trigger's fragile second pressure. The image of the girl's room flashed through his mind. If they were indeed the same men from Bramley Road, then they had taken a hostage. Of course it was possible that she was in one of the other two cars, but there was also the chance that she was in this one. The last thing he wanted was to be responsible for the loss of an innocent life. He realized that the most obvious place for the girl would be in the boot, and even if he managed to avoid hitting her and got the fuel tank instead, it was possible that his bullets could start a fire. He couldn't take that risk.

He tried to sight on the tyres but it was no use. In his frustration he fired off another double tap through the rear window in the vague hope that one of his rounds might hit one of the kidnappers.

The next second the bonnet smashed through the

flimsy barrier, splintering the wooden pole and breaking free on to the open road beyond. Don got to his feet and ran after it. As he reached the ruined barrier he tried to aim at the retreating car again but it was too late. He stared after the fast-dwindling target, the frosted rear windscreen now being punched out by the man who had been sitting in the back seat. In the last moments before it disappeared Don glimpsed a face grinning derisively at his failure.

Don cursed, easing off the hammer of his pistol and flicking on the safety-catch. He slid it back into his holster and turned back towards the restaurant. In the distance he heard the sound of a police siren and far down the motorway he saw a blue flashing light.

It suddenly occurred to him that he was probably the only one present who had made the connection between the various cars, recognizing them as all part of the same terrorist gang. The two that had taken the motorway could not have got far. There was still time to go after them.

He ran back to his car, slipped into the driving seat, gunned the accelerator and shot out for the entrance to the motorway. A hitchhiker stood at the roadside thumbing a lift. Don screeched to a halt and when the youngster jogged up to his car, instead of opening the door for him to get in he wound down the window and said, 'There's been a shooting in the service station. There's a police car coming up behind. Wave them down and tell them there are two cars on the motorway heading west and some of the men responsible are in them. Tell them to block the next exit and get a helicopter in the air. Another car crashed out of the back of the car park. Have you got that?'

The youth stared at him dumbstruck. Don repeated, 'Have you got that? I haven't got time to stick around.'

'A shooting?'

'That's it.'

The youth nodded. 'I'll tell them.'

'Good lad.'

Don put his foot down hard and sped away. The cars he was chasing had already pulled away out of sight, so he drew out into the fast lane and put the accelerator to the floor. It felt as though there was a hand in the small of his back pushing him along. He thought briefly of the car that had burst through the barrier. Perhaps he should have chased that one. But no. By the time he could have gone after it the driver could have veered off on to any one of a dozen minor roads. He had a far better chance of catching the cars that had stupidly chosen the motorway.

The road bent into a long, steady curve as it entered a cutting. When it emerged from the far side of the chalk hillsides he had a clear view for several miles ahead. Like a vast fat snake, the tarmac unfolded across the gently undulating countryside and there, way in the distance, he spotted the two cars, one blue and the other red. Both had now slowed to a more normal speed and he assumed that their occupants imagined they were in the clear. After all, it had been the men in the other car who had done the killing at the service station. It was unlikely that anyone had linked them to the shooting. Who could have known that they were all part of the same team?

Don knew. He eased back on the accelerator so as not to arouse their suspicion but continued to steadily close the distance. Mile after mile passed and all the while he drew closer until eventually he was barely three hundred yards behind the rear car. Out in front he could see the blue Honda Accord powering ahead, the red Ford Orion behind it and closer to him. The two cars were separated from each other by about a hundred yards, and Don could see the men in the rear of the Honda turning to exchange hand signals with the driver and front-seat passenger of the Ford. They appeared to be smiling and carefree, and he could make out their cheery waves.

'Enjoy it while it lasts, you murderous bastards,' he said quietly, closing the gap a bit more.

He was almost level with the Ford when in the distance behind him he caught the sound of a police siren.

'Bugger!' he growled.

He looked in the rear-view mirror and saw the blue light of a police car flashing far behind. It was a good couple of miles away and he wondered what on earth the police intended to do from that distance.

'Nice one, lads,' he said. 'You've just warned them you're coming.'

Sure enough, he looked at the Ford and saw the men in the back crane round at the sound of the siren. One of them pointed and said something to the driver, and the next moment the car surged ahead, pulling away fast. But as yet they were unaware of Don's presence and as they accelerated so did he. He knew it would not be long before he was noticed but he had to keep up with them. The driver of the Ford must have flashed his lights to attract the attention of the Honda in front, because the next thing Don saw was the Honda veering away as well. He eased gently up beside the Ford, keeping his eyes fixed on the road and trying not to look suspicious. But the police car was closing steadily and he knew that at any moment the two cars would have to give up all pretence of innocence and make a break for it.

He glanced at his speedometer and saw that the needle was touching ninety. Surely he couldn't escape their notice much longer?

The answer came a second later when the Ford swung across into the middle lane and almost rammed him. Don tugged the steering wheel hard to avoid a collision and almost lost control, as the driver of the Ford had intended. Struggling to keep on the road, he glanced across and saw the men in the Ford staring hard at him.

'Time to forget the pretence, fellas,' he said through gritted teeth, and steered straight towards them.

In response they accelerated, swerving to overtake an articulated lorry. Up in the cab the driver stared at the two cars in amazement and blew his horn as the Ford swung dangerously close to his front bumper.

To Don's horror he saw the rear window of the Ford opening and the next instant a pistol appeared, waving unsteadily in the blast of wind. The firer aimed it in Don's direction and pulled the trigger repeatedly. Over the noise of the engines Don heard the thin cracks of the gunshots and saw the puffs of blue smoke erupt from the muzzle. Although the firing was appallingly inaccurate he knew that there was always the chance of a lucky shot finding its mark. And it wouldn't even have to hit him. At that speed it would only have to rupture a tyre or other vital component to send his car spinning out of control.

He swung the steering wheel to bring himself directly behind the Ford, cutting the pistol's direct line of fire.

'If you want me now you'll have to smash your way through your rear window,' he said.

By now the police car had closed to within thirty yards of Don and the Ford, but to Don's surprise it headed straight for him, the policeman in the front passenger seat waving him to pull over and stop.

'Not me, you stupid fuckers!' he mouthed through the window. 'Them!'

He pointed at the Ford but the policeman ignored him, waving again for him to stop. Don shook his head in exasperation and put his foot full down on the accelerator, aiming straight for the rear of the Ford. Before its driver could react, Don's front bumper rammed into the boot. The car veered to one side and Don watched in satisfaction as the driver fought to regain control.

'Try some of your own medicine, pal.'

He readied himself to take evasive action as he was certain that the gunman would try to hit him again, but it was the police car that reacted first. Believing Don to be the aggressor, the police driver swung towards him, intending to knock him off the road.

'Get away, you arsehole!' Don roared. He stabbed a finger at the Ford again. 'They're the ones you're supposed to be after!'

Once more he surged forward and hit the rear of the Ford, and this time he provoked a reaction. One of the men in the back seat leaned out of the window, the pistol in his fist, and loosed off a couple of rounds at him. Don swerved but one of the bullets punched through his windscreen. A cobweb of cracks fanned out from the neat hole and the bullet buried itself harmlessly in the passenger seat.

He stared across at the police car. 'See what I mean, you gits?'

The policeman blinked back at him in confusion, looking from him to the Ford and back again. Don felt he could almost see the man's brain working.

'That's it,' he muttered as he saw the policeman reach for his radio. 'Who's a clever boy then?'

As the police car reported the gunfire to its control centre, the driver pulled back from the chase.

'Well, that's nice,' Don shouted at them. 'Leave it all to me.'

He looked up to see a sign flash past, announcing the approach of an exit. In the Ford he could see the men engaged in a frantic dispute. The driver clearly wanted to stick to the motorway but the others seemed to be against it. Sure enough, when the exit opened up before them several hundred yards further on, the car swung towards it and shot up the incline. Don followed hard on their heels but the police car was too slow to react and continued on past the exit.

By now the Honda had disappeared. Don had been so involved with chasing the Ford that he had lost sight of it. Nevertheless, he was resolved to catch at least part of the terrorist group. If he could only catch one of them an interrogation might reveal the whereabouts of the rest.

The last glimpse he had of the police car was of its

brake lights stabbing on, smoke burning off the tyres as it screeched to a halt and the driver shot it into reverse to retrace his steps to the exit road. By that time the Ford was at the top of the incline, where a small roundabout forced it to slow down. The driver swung his car into the turn, heading off down the minor road that cut away across country. Keeping as close as he could, Don hoped that it wouldn't be long before the policeman's radio report yielded some help. He didn't particularly want to get involved in a fire-fight with four armed terrorists by himself. It was all he could do simply to track them.

The road stretched away in front, hedges bordering it on either side with farmland beyond. A low mist clung to the barren fields and everywhere looked bleak and desolate. Driving at high speed was more difficult on the narrow road after the expanse of the motorway, but the advantage was that it was more difficult for the men in the Ford to get a clear shot at him. Nevertheless, every so often one of them would give it a go. The shots all went hopelessly wide but it was unnerving all the same.

A cluster of roadside cottages came and went. He was aware of a couple of white, staring faces flashing past before they were out among open fields again. He felt a grudging admiration for the driver of the Ford. The man obviously knew his stuff. It was a long time since Don had done the SAS fast-driving course, but he reckoned that the man in front must have been through some kind of similar training. He appeared to possess all the skills, and it was all Don could do to keep up with him. The slightest lapse in concentration would mean a crash and, at that breakneck speed, instant death.

For a moment he toyed with the idea of trying to get in a couple of shots himself. He realized that the chances of actually hitting anyone or anything were remote, but he might just be able to distract the other driver enough to send him spinning off the road.

He waited until the chase entered a long stretch of straight road with no houses on either side and then wound open his window. Next he reached under his arm for his shoulder holster and drew his Browning. Keeping his left hand on the steering wheel, he put the barrel under its fingers, gripped it tightly and cocked it. Having flicked off the safety-catch, he put his arm out of the window and rested the base of his fist on the car's bodywork. Keeping the car aligned with the Ford in front, he fired off one round after another.

A small hole appeared in the Ford's rear window, then another and another. The car swerved and for a moment Don thought he had achieved his aim, but against all the odds the driver maintained his control on the wheel. In the back, though, he could see that one of the men had slumped across the back seat.

'Gotcha!' he shouted.

He fired again but a second later the hammer clicked on an empty chamber. He cursed. There were several spare clips of ammunition in the glove compartment, so, putting his pistol in his lap, he switched hands on the wheel and reached across to hunt for them. When he had one, he pressed the release button on the side of the butt and popped out the empty magazine, sliding in a fresh one, clicking it home on his knee and then cocking the gun as he had done before.

'A few more ought to do it,' he said out loud.

He steadied his hand out of the window again and continued firing, but the cars were entering a series of bends and for a while he had to use both hands on the wheel, clasping the pistol between his knees, the muzzle pointing down at the floor.

'Don't blow your balls away, Don lad,' he muttered to himself.

The bends were tighter than he had anticipated and he fought to keep the car under control, but at last they pulled clear of them and after another group of houses the cars were once again out on an open stretch of road. He took up his pistol and aimed through the window again.

'This time,' he said, willing himself to concentrate. 'This time.'

The first shot again found the Ford's rear window, and in the front of the car Don thought he saw the driver slump. He closed the distance a little and, sure enough, he saw that the man had removed one hand from the wheel and was clutching at his right shoulder.

'Bingo!'

The Ford started to slow, although in the front seat Don could see the passenger urging the driver on. For a minute or two it gathered speed again, but his bullet had clearly done its job, for the car was now veering all over the road.

'That's it, lad. No need to crash. Just pull over and give yourselves up. Nice and peaceful like.'

Going into a corner too fast, the driver was unable to hold the road. He lost his grip on the wheel and the car careered up a bank and ploughed straight through a thick hedge and into the field beyond. Crows burst into the wintry sky from the surrounding trees, startled by the interruption. Don hit the brake, pumping it gingerly to control his emergency stop. Pulling up on to the side of the bank some thirty or forty yards further on, he pushed open his door and leapt out on to the road, his pistol in his hand. He knew it would be dangerous to go back to the place where the car had entered the field. If any of the men had recovered from the shock they would be expecting him from that direction.

Instead he scanned the hedgerow until he saw a gap beside a tree where he reckoned he would be able to gain access without making too much noise.

He dropped on to his stomach and wriggled up the slope. An old barbed-wire fence threaded its way through the centre of the hedge and he rolled on to his back to work his way underneath the lowest strand. For a moment it snagged on the material of his jacket but he managed to work it free and slithered underneath. The ground on the other side dropped towards the edge of the field, the ploughed earth striped into furrows, hard and bare as iron. He rolled out from behind the cover of the tree, bringing his pistol into the aim as he did so. The Ford sat out in the open, its skid marks visible right back to the hole in the hedge. In the front he could see the driver, slumped over the wheel, unconscious or even dead. Beside him, the passenger had shot through the windscreen and his limp body hung across the bonnet, half in and half out of the car. His arms were splayed and there was blood on his face.

'That'll teach you to wear your seat-belt next time, mate,' Don whispered to himself.

The rear doors were both open and there was no sign of the men who had been in the back. He knew that he had hit one of them, but how badly? And that still left the man's companion unaccounted for as well.

Don's eyes scanned the line of hedgerow. He knew they couldn't have gone far and judged that they must have rolled clear as the car entered the field. Perhaps, once the driver had been hit, they had prepared themselves for just such an eventuality. If so, it had paid off.

As he wriggled out into the field Don caught sight of the men on the far side of the car. They were running towards a large copse, the one man helping his wounded comrade. As they ran, they kept glancing back over their shoulders. The moment he identified them, Don sprang to his feet and sprinted towards the car, keeping it between himself and the fugitives to prevent them from getting a clear line of fire on him. One of the men nevertheless loosed off a couple of wild rounds as soon as he saw Don, but both snapped past him harmlessly, cracking in the air like a whip.

Flinging himself down beside the wrecked car, Don gripped his Browning in a two-handed combat grip and then spun round the side, hunting for his target.

'Stop! Army!' he shouted at the top of his voice.

In response the wounded man half turned and fired again. Don cursed under his breath and rattled off a double tap. It was as though the man had been slammed in the back with a sledgehammer. He hurtled forward, tearing from his companion's helping grip, and sprawled face down on the hard, rutted earth. He moved for a second and then was still.

'Stop!' Don shouted again. But the other man had made good use of the breathing space provided by Don's first shots. Instead of trying to fire back, knowing that Don was behind cover and therefore almost impossible to hit, he sprinted the last few yards towards the copse, zigzagging as he went. Don fired another two double taps, but his bullets all went wide, and the next instant the man disappeared from view, diving through the thick bushes and losing himself among the trees.

To reach the copse, Don decided to take a roundabout route along the hedgerow. To risk crossing the field the way the man had gone was far too dangerous as he could well have been lying in wait. It would be no joke getting caught out in the open without a shred of cover.

There was no sight of the police follow-up and he could only assume that they had taken a wrong turning.

Brilliant, he thought as he darted through the hedge and began to snake along its outer side. They've probably stopped to issue a few parking tickets along the way.

About fifty yards along, the hedge veered towards the copse, leaving only about twenty yards of open space between it and the nearest of the trees.

'That'll do nicely,' he whispered, crouching down when he reached the bend and slipping under the wire. His jacket snagged once again and he made a mental note to lose a few pounds. Better get in some runs, he thought. I've been with the cops too long. All that riding around in patrol cars does sod all for the waistline.

Without pausing he was on his feet the moment he

was through the hedge, and sprinting for the trees. Expecting to be fired at every foot of the way, he zigzagged, but a moment later he pounded through a screen of low-hanging branches and found himself in the copse.

It was gloomy inside. The trees stretched away in every direction and in between them thick bushes and undergrowth sprouted. The floor was a mat of sodden brown leaves and he felt the water soak quickly through the knees of his trousers as he crouched down to lower his profile. He steadied his breathing and listened. After the shots the rural calm had quickly returned. Somewhere far away he could hear a tractor in another field, and overhead a flock of geese screamed raucously as they flew by.

Suddenly he heard the crack of a branch and swung towards the tell-tale sound. He lowered himself on to his stomach and crawled steadily forward, holding his Browning in one hand and using the other to sweep aside the brittle dead branches lest he give his own position away with a similar signal. In the pit of his stomach he could feel the knot of tension curl into a ball, pushing his heart into his mouth until he had to stop and calm himself.

'Steady, lad. You're behaving like some new kid on selection, for God's sake. Get a grip on yourself.'

With his new resolve he moved on, slower than before, forcing himself to relax into the stalk, prepared at any second for a flurry of deadly exchange shots. There was another crack, this time towards the other side of the copse. He frowned, puzzled how the man could have crossed so silently in front of him without being seen.

This bugger's good, he thought. Be careful, Don.

Painfully slowly he closed the gap between them, but as he drew closer he became puzzled. Where he had heard the crack of the twig he could now hear a shuffling. What the fuck's he up to? he thought. Is he digging a sodding trench or something?

But then he was on him. The sound was coming from just beyond the next tree. Drawing his legs up under him, Don rose stealthily from the ground and prepared to rush forward. He took a deep breath, and exhaled. Then one more breath before he burst round the side of the tree. To his astonishment he found himself face to face with a roe deer. For a split second the creature froze, its round, startled eyes fixed on his own, and then it was off, scudding away across the open field beyond the trees, its white tail bobbing furiously as it vaulted over the iron-hard furrows.

Don threw himself to one side, aware that he had just given away his position, furious with himself for having been so stupid. It was a drill he had used a hundred times, rolling twice and coming up in the ready position, but never before had it paid off as it did now.

As he was halfway through the second roll he heard the crack of a gunshot and felt the sting of blown earth on his face. Bullets were ripping into the ground around him and when he came out of the roll, starting to return the fire even as he spun to face his attacker, he caught a fleeting glimpse of the man from the car, partially concealed behind a stout oak.

Don blazed at him, round after round, seeing them impact into the shattered bark until they found their target at last and the man was flung backwards. Without giving him time to recover, Don rushed towards him, his pistol aimed at the prone form. As he rounded the oak he saw the man was still alive.

'Freeze!' he shouted. 'Not one move or I'll drill you!'

The man's gun was a good yard out of reach, cushioned on a bed of leaves, still smoking.

'That's it,' Don said calmly, locking his eyes on the man's. 'There's been enough killing for one day. Don't make me shoot you.'

The man stared back fearlessly. His hands were under him and he seemed to be clutching something to his stomach.

'Show me your hands, mate. Nice and slow like.'

In answer, the man rolled slowly on to his back and Don gaped in horror at the hand-grenade he was cradling against himself. He had already pulled the pin and as Don watched he released the lever. It spun clear with a metallic crack and Don knew that he had only a second or two before the detonator exploded it, rocketing white-hot splinters towards him. Instead of throwing the grenade at Don, however, the man clutched it to his own stomach, simultaneously curling into a ball as if to wrap himself around the deadly object.

For a moment he locked his gaze with Don's. It was a mixture of triumph and anger, without the slightest trace of fear. The next instant Don whirled himself behind the oak, straightening himself taut against the thick trunk as the grenade exploded on the far side, firing out its shards harmlessly into the surrounding undergrowth. But when he looked again, it was to see that the man had been blown almost in two. Where his stomach had been was now only a massive raw wound. He had died instantly.

'Jesus Christ,' Don murmured. 'Who the fuck are these guys?'

It was then that he heard the sound of a police siren, and a moment later the policemen were running across the field towards him.

4

They drove for the best part of two hours before Ceda Bandram indicated a sharp left turn to the driver. In the back of the car Ali sat miserably staring out of the window, watching the countryside roll by. Ceda hadn't said a single word to him since the shooting at the service station and Ali was beginning to wonder if he had gone too far. But what was he supposed to have done? The man had shouldered him aside from the wash-basin and Ali had distinctly heard the racist insult spoken under his breath. He was damned if he was going to let anyone get away with that.

They had heard police sirens as they sped away from the area surrounding the motorway but no one appeared to have followed them. All three of them had kept a careful watch for any sign of a tail but apparently the chase had been confined to the other two cars. Their own road had remained clear. At one point they had seen a police car coming in the opposite direction and they had all tensed themselves for a fight, but the car had sped past, continuing down the road in the direction they had just come. Ali had grinned and made a wisecrack, but Ceda had ignored it.

Studying his map, Ceda let the driver continue straight ahead for a good five miles and then directed him to turn right.

'It's not much further now,' he said.

'What isn't?' Ali asked hopefully. It was true that, as a family member, he could not come to any harm at the hands of Ceda Bandram, but nevertheless he knew that Ceda was not a man to be trifled with. He would undoubtedly have words to say to their uncle and it could even mean that Ali would be barred from further participation in other such missions.

Ceda was concentrating on his map again as if he hadn't heard Ali's question. Rather than repeat it, Ali leaned forward, folding his arm on the back of Ceda's seat.

'Look, Ceda. Do you want an apology? Is that it?'

Instead of answering, Ceda spoke again to the driver, who glanced nervously from him to Ali and back again, terrified lest the tension erupt into violence. That was the last thing they needed. Enough had already gone wrong.

Ali sighed heavily and sank back into his seat, muttering to himself. Clearly there was going to be no rapprochement this side of Pakistan.

The first sign of where they were headed came a few moments later when he looked up and saw a bright-orange windsock fluttering at the end of a tall pole above a line of trees.

'So this is the airfield,' he said. 'A well-kept secret indeed.' He tried to inject a tone of flattery into his voice, although he suspected that Ceda was probably impervious to it. No harm in trying, he thought. The guy can't be totally bloody perfect.

It was a small private airfield, mostly used by light aircraft and gliders. However, as the car rounded a line of hangars that looked as though they dated back to the war they saw ahead of them a small, slim executive jet. Two men paced up and down beside it and when they heard the sound of a car engine they looked up eagerly.

To his immense relief Ceda noticed the Honda parked several yards away. The doors opened and the four men got out and jogged to meet him.

'Pull up over there,' Ceda instructed the driver, indicating a hangar. 'Park the car inside it and tell the other driver to do the same. We're going to need every minute we can get and if it takes the police a while to find our cars, so much the better.'

As he got out of the car he glanced around the airfield. It was virtually deserted. Only beside the entrance gate did a single watchman sit in his booth, idly stirring a mug of tea. In front of him a television screen flickered hypnotically.

'Are the others here?' Ceda asked the other team members as they reached him. He had been alarmed not to see the Ford and the expressions on the men's faces confirmed his fears even before they opened their mouths to speak.

'The police gave chase. Hari left the motorway and that was the last we saw of them. But there was this other bloke.'

'What do you mean?'

The man shook his head. 'I'm not sure who he was,

but he tailed us all the way out of the service station. When the police car turned up I saw him ramming Hari. He followed the Ford off the motorway. I'd swear he was security forces or something.'

'What makes you say that?'

'I don't know. It was just the way he handled his car, the way he drove. He was totally confident. No ordinary man could have acted like that.'

Ceda nodded knowingly, guessing the answer. He described the glimpse he had had of the man he had seen in his rear-view mirror firing at him as they had burst through the barrier gate.

A light dawned on his comrade's face. 'Why yes, that sounds like him, although I couldn't be certain. We were some way ahead.' He looked suddenly worried. 'You don't suppose he could have tailed us all the way from Southall, do you? If so, perhaps they'll be here any minute.'

Ceda waved his hand dismissively, wishing at the same time that he actually felt the confidence he was aping. 'It was probably just a coincidence. If they'd been tailing us we'd have had to deal with a lot more than just one man. He was probably a special forces soldier or armed policeman who just happened to be using the same service station and was lucky enough to be carrying a gun.

He looked all around him. For as far as he could see across the flat landscape the roads were empty. A quick check of his watch confirmed that they were already well past their scheduled departure time. The plan had gone completely to hell and he couldn't afford to delay another minute.

'Everyone on board. You two' – he pointed at his men – 'get the girl. Check she's all right before you carry her aboard. And try to be discreet. Don't let the gateman see what you're doing.'

The driver stared at him in disbelief. 'You're not thinking of leaving before the others arrive, are you?'

'We don't have any choice.' He glared angrily at Ali, who pretended not to have noticed. 'They knew the risks. If they get away from the police they know the contacts who will give them shelter. Because we fucked up the backup team's going to have to be retasked. If our guys get away they can join them.'

The men went to the boot of Ceda's car and opened it. Wide, frightened eyes stared up at them, blinking in the unaccustomed daylight. The girl was gagged with masking tape over her mouth, and her wrists and ankles had been tied with lengths of rope. They hoisted her out, first checking that no one could see. She thrashed and kicked as they carried her the short distance to the waiting plane and bundled her up the steps.

'Where shall we put her?'

Ceda strode across to them and hopped up the steps into the fuselage. 'Strap her into a seat at the rear and stay with her. I don't want her getting loose and giving the game away.'

He smiled at the girl, whose eyes flashed at him angrily. 'As soon as we're airborne I'll untie you and take the gag off, but for now please bear with us. It won't take long.'

She lunged at him with her bound feet and he only just managed to avoid the kick, deftly dodging aside.

As the men carried her into the plane, Ceda's driver came to his side. 'It's too bad about the old man.'

Ali overheard and chipped in, 'You bet it is. Uncle's not going to be very pleased.'

Ceda stiffened his jaw, keeping his fist in check. 'That's not all Uncle's going to be displeased with,' he said woodenly. 'And anyway, even if we did miss old Sanji I've got a plan. The game's got a long way to run. We'll have him yet.'

'I certainly hope so for your sake,' Ali chided.

When the last of the men were on board and the two pilots were starting the engines and running through their pre-flight checks, Ceda and Ali stood on the tarmac by the door and took one last look around in case the other team should suddenly appear. But there was nothing. The countryside was empty of life, barren at the start of winter.

'We'd best be going,' Ali prompted at last.

'OK,' Ceda agreed. He turned to get into the plane, but then, as if as an afterthought, he said, 'Oh yes, there's just one more thing . . .'

His movement was so fast that Ali never saw it coming, the balled fist slicing upwards and crashing into the underside of Ali's jaw. His head whip-cracked back and his body crumpled to the ground. Ali groped blindly, his mind swimming as he struggled on the edges of consciousness. Beside him, he was dimly aware of Ceda crouching down, level with his bleeding face. Through the haze Ali could taste blood and he spat out teeth, hearing them tinkle on the floor.

Ceda grabbed his collar in one large fist and wrenched

his face close to his own until Ali found himself staring into his hard, cold eyes. 'If it was up to me I'd leave you here. Because of you four good men are probably either dead of captured. I trained them myself. Each one of them meant more to me than you do, relative or not.'

He pulled Ali's face even closer until Ali could feel Ceda's spittle on his cheeks. 'Don't you ever cross me again. Don't ever disobey an order. If you do, I'll kill you.'

He threw Ali away and wiped his hands as if trying to remove the stain of something unpleasant. Ali sprawled on the tarmac, trying to get to his knees but failing. As Ceda climbed into the plane one of the men popped his head out to see what was happening. He stared in surprise at the grovelling shape of Ali and at Ceda, who appeared as calm as ever.

'Help him aboard,' Ceda commanded. 'He slipped on the steps.'

When everyone was strapped into their seats, the plane lurched forward and one of the pilots taxied to the end of the runway. Ceda had chosen a place across the aisle from the girl and as the plane hurtled down the runway and lifted into the air he signalled to his men to remove her gag. Through the window he watched the fields and farm buildings shrink in size, the ground rushing past beneath them.

The jet was a slim fourteen-seater and up at the front he could see the pilots at work in the cockpit.

'How the hell do you think you're going to get away with this?'

Ceda looked across at the girl, who was rubbing her lips and cheeks where the gag had been.

He shrugged. 'We already have. Mind you, I'm sorry about our losses.'

She shook her head angrily. 'You must be absolutely mad. The police will stop you before . . .'

Ceda threw back his head and laughed. 'How? With a flying patrol car? A helicopter perhaps?'

'They'll use jet fighters or something. They'll force you down.'

He looked at her with sympathetic eyes. 'You're living in fantasy land, my dear. They don't even know who's in this aircraft. We've filed several different flight plans with the authorities, all false of course. By the time they figure out what happened to us we'll be well out of British airspace. Even if the civil police had some speedy means of liaison with the air force – which they haven't – we'd be over North Africa before they could scramble a fighter aircraft. They wouldn't dare push it that far. Certainly not for you.'

He sat back and relaxed, pleased with himself, although less with the overall planning of the operation than with the punch he had delivered to Ali. It had released the tension wonderfully and he had enjoyed it. He had been dying to see Ali flat on the deck ever since he had been ordered to take him along.

'Mind you, a few years ago in the days of the Cold War they might have been able to give chase. Then they used to keep pairs of fully armed fighters airborne twenty-four hours a day. But not any more.' He leaned back and folded his arms behind his head. 'Nowadays the aircrew sit in nice, comfortable rooms watching the television and drinking coffee. The last thing on their minds is a cross-country chase after some insignificant Indian girl.'

The girl bristled. 'I'm not Indian. I'm a British citizen. I was born here.'

Ceda laughed again and winked at her playfully. 'When did you last look in a mirror? You're as Indian as I am Pakistani.'

She stared at him in amazement. 'I've never heard anything so racist in my whole life! What century do you come from? Certainly not mine.'

'I think I'm going to enjoy our relationship,' Ceda added. He looked at his watch. 'We've got plenty of time to continue this discussion before our arrival.'

A look of doubt crossed her face. 'Our arrival where?'

'Didn't I tell you? Do forgive me. In Pakistan, of course.'

'Pakistan? What the hell are we going there for?' She rounded on him, making full use of the opportunity now that her gag was removed at last. 'And why have you kidnapped me anyway?'

'Yes, I'm sorry about that. It was all a bit of an accident.'

'Was the murder of my parents an accident?'

'We needed information.'

'What could they possibly have told you?' Tears burst from her and she broke into sobs. 'My father ran a restaurant, that's all. Are you from some protection racket?'

Ceda scowled. 'Please don't insult me.'

She was becoming desperate, hunting through her brain for any scrap of information that might give her a clue as to why she was being abducted to Pakistan. The clue was presented to her by Ceda Bandram's innocent-sounding request.

'Tell me about your grandfather.'

'My grandfather? Whatever for?'

Ceda shrugged noncommittally. 'Where was he?'

Eli paused before answering, wondering why on earth they would want to know about him? 'He was out.'

'Obviously. We're not complete fools. Does he still live with you in Bramley Road?'

'Why do you want to know?' she asked, becoming bolder now that she saw her captor wasn't going to treat her as they had treated her parents.

Ceda wagged a finger at her. 'I'm the one who asks the questions. So tell me, does he still live in Bramley Road or has he got some other address?'

She stared at him suspiciously. 'It was him you were after, wasn't it? That was why you killed my father. He wouldn't tell you where my grandfather was.'

'Not at all. He was only too willing to help my associate. He told us every possible location that came into his head. He'd have sold your grandfather down the river if he had been able. We eventually came to the conclusion that he simply didn't know.'

Now it was Eli's turn to laugh. 'You fools. You had the right house all along. My father couldn't tell you because he didn't know. My grandfather has never been able to sleep well. Every morning he gets up before daylight and walks the streets for exercise. Had you waited a bit longer he would probably have walked straight into your hands.'

She saw Ceda blanch. His lips tightened and he turned away quickly. 'It doesn't matter. It's an inconvenience, that's all.' He faced her again. 'A big inconvenience for you, above all. I hope your grandfather is a reasonable man.'

'Let me guess. You're going to hold me to ransom, is that it?'

'Perhaps.' Ceda was beginning to enjoy his exchange with the girl. She had a keen mind and was courageous.

'How much do you intend to ask for me? My family owns a chain of restaurants, but they don't have any disposable cash, if that's what you're after.'

'There are more things to swap a hostage for than just money,' Ceda answered enigmatically.

Down below Eli could see the countryside disappearing below a sea of thickening cloud. The dense whiteness blurred past the window until the plane had been completely enveloped in it and a moment later it burst through into a dazzling blue sky.

'OK,' Eli said at last. 'So you want my grandfather, is that it?'

'Bright, aren't you?'

'Why do you want him?'

Ceda didn't reply. Instead he stared out of the window, signalling by his silence that the conversation was over for now.

* * *

Don had only a relatively short stay in the local police station. Not surprisingly he had been ordered to surrender his gun the moment the police had arrived at the copse and seen the array of bodies.

'I'll tell you straight, Mr Headley,' the inspector said as he stirred his mug of instant coffee in the interview room, 'I take a dim view of cowboys holding their gunfights on my patch as if it's the OK Corral. What the hell did you think you were up to anyway, giving chase like that?'

Don sighed in exasperation. He had been over the story a dozen times already and was becoming impatient. He hadn't slept properly for several nights and had just taken part in a life-or-death struggle with a gang of armed terrorists.

'I've given you the name and phone number of someone who can verify my story,' he said, stifling an immense yawn.

'I'm sorry if I'm boring you, Mr . . .'

'And it's Captain Headley,' Don snapped. 'I've told you that as well.'

'Oh yes, of course,' the inspector sneered. 'You spun my sergeant that SAS crap.' He leaned closer across the table. 'Personally I don't give a shit if you're fucking Superman. I'm going to nail you for your little performance this morning.'

'You'd be better off trying to apprehend the rest of the gang.'

'My patrolmen only reported one car, the one you destroyed.'

'Then who do you think smashed the barrier at the service station?'

'We're checking that out now. I don't intend jumping to conclusions.'

Don shook his head. 'By the time you do the terrorists will be out of the country.' Suddenly he couldn't stand the stupidity any longer. He got to his feet and, planting his fists on the table, leaned towards the inspector, who flinched.

'Look here, pal. Have you rung that sodding number or haven't you?'

Realizing that he wasn't going to get anything more out of Don, the inspector got up and left the room, muttering a brief 'Stay here' as he went.

Don sank into the chair again and crossed his legs. The four walls were completely bare, and apart from the table and the two chairs it was unfurnished. A police constable stood by the door, his hands behind his back, watching Don steadily as if they expected him to make a break for it.

If I was going to, Don thought, that fat git certainly couldn't stop me.

It was a good half hour before there was the sound of footsteps in the corridor and the door opened on the inspector.

'You've got a visitor,' he announced sullenly.

Rod Chiltern stepped through the door-frame. 'Hear you've been busy?'

Don heaved a sigh of relief. 'Rod, thank fuck you're here. These guys have been giving me the third degree.'

'That's not really too surprising considering you've broken almost every rule in the Highway Code, and killed four men as well.'

He stood to one side. 'Come on. Let's get back to London.'

'London? I was hoping to be in Hereford this afternoon.'

Chiltern guffawed. 'How I love that SAS sense of humour.' He glared at Don. 'Get your arse in gear, Headley. We haven't finished with you. I always knew the SAS were soft at heart. It isn't Endex yet.'

As they walked out of the station Don asked, 'What about my pistol?'

'We're keeping it as evidence,' the inspector replied, barely concealing his frustration at losing his prisoner.

'Well, take good care of it. That's army property.'

Leaving his own car in the police pound, Don collapsed into the back of Chiltern's Rover. 'Mind if I get some kip?'

'Please yourself,' Chiltern replied, and a moment later Don was snoring lightly. His sleep was deep but troubled, images of the chase tumbling through his brain. An hour later he awoke with a start to find that they had arrived at their destination. He sat up and rubbed his eyes, peering blearily through the windows. But instead of the police station he had expected to see, he found himself looking at an impressive country house.

The car was parked on a gravel driveway and on either side of the house smooth green lawns stretched away to low-hanging cedars and beeches. Ivy crept up the sides of the house in great enthusiastic swathes, clipped and trimmed around the windows, like a well-kept beard. Don looked behind him. There was no sign of the road. The driveway swept out of sight round a corner, the screen of trees obscuring his view of whatever lay beyond.

'Where's this then? Butlins?'

'Shut it, Don,' Chiltern growled. He switched off the engine and got out, opening the rear door. 'Out.'

Don stepped on to gravel, feeling it crunch beneath his sodden shoes. For one brief moment he considered punching Chiltern in the guts and making a dash for it. But why should he? Surely his instincts were out of place here? He had known Chiltern since the beginning of the exercise and as far as he could tell he was just another regular cop.

'The police officers' rest home?' he said.

'Ha, ha. Very funny. Inside,' Chiltern shot back, jerking his head towards the front door, which was being held open by two anonymous-looking men in grey suits.

Don sized them up. Both were well built but undoubtedly capable of fast movement. Their hair was as trim as the creeper and their eyes narrowed as they followed him inside.

He had seen their kind before. They belonged to the Intelligence service – not the brain section, but the brawn. They were the enforcers and the bodyguards, and Don knew from experience that within their limits they were good. But as regards their broader adaptability, they were much like any other hood – less capable than they thought. They allowed themselves to be flattered by the title 'Intelligence', assuming erroneously that their employers' mental gifts had rubbed off on them. They hadn't, and if push came to shove, Don thought, he could use their self-delusion against them.

The entrance hall was dark and gloomy. Old paintings hung on the walls and two suits of armour flanked the foot of the staircase. Don couldn't help smiling at them, wondering if there were other guards disguised inside. He turned round to face Chiltern.

'Well, what's the game?'

Instead of answering, Chiltern pointed to an open door. 'Wait in there.'

'Listen . . .' Don began.

But Chiltern was already on his way up the stairs.

The room that Chiltern had indicated was a well-stocked library. Books covered the walls and a large leather-topped desk sat in front of a bay window that looked out on to the extensive lawns. There was a phone on the desk and for a moment Don considered trying to call his CO in Hereford. He went across to it and lifted the receiver to check for a dialling tone. There was one.

He was just putting his finger to the first number when there were footsteps in the hall and muffled voices. Quickly he replaced the receiver and moved a yard or two away and stood with arms folded, ready to receive whoever was about to enter.

Only one man came in, his colleague dawdling outside the door for a moment out of Don's vision before moving away to another room and closing the door noisily behind him. The man who confronted Don was every inch the civil servant. His suit was smart but off-the-peg and he wore a shirt that no self-respecting officer would have been seen dead in, the pale blue stripes respectable enough but compromised by the vulgarity of a plain white collar and cuffs.

'Good afternoon,' he said briskly, advancing on Don with one slim white hand outstretched. 'I'm so sorry to have kept you waiting.'

Taken aback by his manner, Don said that it was no trouble. After all, what else had he been planning? Only a couple of days' rest to catch up on sleep and relaxation.

'Now then, about this terrible business,' the man continued, ushering Don to a chair on the subservient side of the desk. 'I hope you don't mind but I'd like to run through it once again.'

'What? But I've already been debriefed by the police.'

'Exactly,' the civil servant said. 'But not by us.'

'And suppose you tell me exactly who you are.'

The man resisted a smile, steepling his fingers in front of him and gazing into the middle distance to present Don with his three-quarters profile. Don presumed that someone had probably once told the fellow that it was his best angle.

'We are part of Intelligence. That is all you need to know. As an officer of the SAS I'm sure you can appreciate our need for discretion.'

'Not particularly,' Don stated bluntly, his hackles rising. 'As an officer of the SAS I would have hoped that I could be taken into your confidence. I mean, we're supposed to be on the same side.'

'Indeed we are,' the man agreed, nodding vigorously. 'But if you don't mind I'd rather not tell you at this point who I represent.'

'OK. We'll play it your way then.' And he began to repeat the details of everything that had happened since the discovery of the bodies at Bramley Road that morning. As he spoke the door opened again and another man brought in a tray of coffee. Don continued with his account as the civil servant poured, sliding Don's cup and saucer over to him with a precise hand.

'You say you gained the impression that the men in the Ford Orion were professionals. What exactly do you mean by that?'

He had been taking copious notes, slipping into shorthand whenever unable to keep up.

Don shrugged. 'Special forces of some kind. Fuck knows whose.'

The man winced at the crudity and scrubbed out his last set of squiggles. Don leaned forward, curious to see what the shorthand for 'Fuck knows' looked like.

'At a pinch I'd say Pakistani.'

'What's that?' the man asked with the air of an innocent. He was a bad actor and Don guessed that he already knew full well the identity of the terrorists.

'It just seemed to all add up. The cartridge case at the house, the method of interrogation and the slickness of the executions, the blokes in the cars . . .'

'What about them?' the man interrupted eagerly.

'Asians,' Don said simply. 'Big buggers, most of them with moustaches.'

'They could have been Iranians or Iraqis.'

'No they couldn't. They weren't scruffy, fat and ugly enough to be Iraqis, and if they'd been Iranians they'd have had a good two days' growth of stubble. They reckon it makes them look macho.'

'And these men?'

'Clean-shaven, well-disciplined military types. At a guess I'd say ex-Pakistani Army.'

'Why ex?'

'If they were still serving we'd have an international incident on our hands instead of this hideaway, hush-hush crap.'

'Maybe we have got an international incident on our hands,' the man said, attempting an air of mystery.

Don smiled cruelly. 'In that case – forgive me for saying so – I wouldn't be being interviewed by a flunkey.'

The man flushed scarlet and Don felt a bolt of satisfaction at having ruffled his feathers at last.

'Right then, Captain Headley,' the man said hurriedly, masking his hurt pride, 'you've been most co-operative.' He shuffled his papers together and slid them into his briefcase.

'Is that all?'

The voice that replied came from behind Don.

'Not quite, I'm afraid.'

Don turned in his chair. A tall, grey-haired, patrician-looking man in his early sixties had silently appeared. 'Thank you, David, that'll be all for now,' he said, addressing the civil servant, who scurried obsequiously from the room.

He gestured to Don to remain in his seat, but instead of sitting down himself he strolled to the window and gazed out at the bleak gardens.

'My name is Sir Anthony Briggs,' he announced as if Don should shiver and quake at the very mention.

'I'm pleased to meet you.'

'If you are then you're a bigger fool than I thought.'

I see, Don thought. First the soft guy and now the hard one. What the fuck's going on here?

As if it was the most natural thing in the world, Sir Anthony said, 'How do you fancy being assigned under my command for a while?'

Don stared at him. He might as well have made some comment about the weather. 'Excuse me?'

'A rather interesting job has cropped up and I believe you're the man to handle it. In fact, you've already thrown yourself in at the deep end by undertaking that heroic chase of yours.' Sir Anthony turned from the window. 'Well?'

Don rubbed his tired eyes, feeling them smart. 'Why is it that somehow I get the feeling that's not a request?'

When Sir Anthony smiled it was like a shark at a feeding frenzy. 'I am glad. You're not so stupid after all. Thank God for small mercies.'

5

High on the glacier the wind cut through the layers of clothing of Ramesh Bandram like a knife. There were a good few miles to go yet before he could count himself out of danger, and on the glacier the threat came not just from natural sources but from human as well. Although it was impossible for anyone to remain in such conditions for any length of time, he well knew that the Indian Army maintained patrols that criss-crossed that part of the frontier with regularity. He had been unfortunate enough to encounter one on his last gun-running trip through the mountains and had narrowly escaped with his life. He had lost the complete shipment of weapons that the Kashmiri rebels so desired and in addition a number of his men had been either killed or captured.

A voice called out from behind and he turned to see that one of the mules had sunk into a drift of soft snow. For once he was glad of the wind, whose howling drowned out the cries of the stricken animal and the encouragement of her handler.

'Get a move on!' he called back, plunging his ice axe into the snow for purchase. He leaned on it heavily, gasping for the air that was pitifully thin at such a high altitude. Other men rushed to the muleteer's aid, the whole cluster thrashing around in the flurries of powdery snow until the mule staggered free of the pure white quagmire and tottered onwards, pulling its handler after it.

Ramesh was almost reluctant to get moving again, but he knew that such a reluctance was the first sign of hypothermia. Pulling his ice axe free, he plunged on up the slope. The crest was invisible, great drifts of snow swirling in the ferocious air currents that had risen all the way from the deep valleys, whipping into a frenzy the higher and thinner they became. He adjusted his goggles. Without them, snow-blindness would set in within minutes. Then the whole landscape would blur into a brilliant haze, and unless treated his sight would be gone for good.

Beyond that cloud of white he knew that the mighty ranges of the Karakoram mountains stretched seemingly into infinity, their towering, snow-capped peaks reaching for the heavens as surely as their few hostile passes reached northwards into China. It was one of the most inhospitable regions on earth, and yet it was where he and his family had carved out their lucrative trade. Ever since the Kashmiri secessionists had embarked upon their armed struggle against the forces of India, Ramesh and his family had made it their business to support them in every way possible. Of course there had always been the struggle, even as far back as the granting of Independence from Britain in 1947. That had been when the seeds of the current trouble had been sown.

It was supposed to have been a time of great joy, the

winning of freedom after centuries of occupation and domination by foreign powers. Instead, Independence had ushered in one of the darkest periods in the history of the whole subcontinent. By dividing the country in two, India and Pakistan, Britain had unwittingly laid the foundations of a struggle that was to cost millions of lives. Before 1947 Ramesh's family had lived in Delhi, owning property throughout the country but especially in Kashmir. At one stroke the British had wiped out years of tradition, and along with millions of other Muslims the Bandrams had been forced to trek north into the nascent state of Pakistan to rebuild their lives as best they could. Their properties in Kashmir had been confiscated by the new Indian state and from a position of wealth they had been driving into penury.

Ramesh bent into the howling wind and laboured up the slope. With every step he pounded out his hatred of all that had happened to his family. He appreciated that comparable tales of misfortune could be told about the millions of Hindus who had been forced to trek in the opposite direction, but it didn't ease the misery of his family's own state to know that others suffered similar torments.

The climb back to prosperity had been as hard and bitterly fought as this very mountain expedition. It had taken its toll on the family, Ramesh's own father dying along the way. It had been his uncle who had pulled the disparate group of blood relatives together and forged the links in the chain that now bound them. The more suitable of the sons had been sent into the army and there had been ample fighting to turn them from refugees into warriors. In the wars with India they had fought with distinction and when the two mighty states had been at peace the regiments had found plenty to occupy them in the frequent skirmishes with tribesmen on the North-West Frontier.

But always at the back of everything Uncle Gilma had been preparing an alternative route to wealth. At first Ramesh had been perturbed when he had discovered the illicit nature of the new family's business interests. The gun-running was excusable. After all, it was directed against the hated state of India. Less easy to come to terms with was the trade in drugs, smuggling and gambling. Nevertheless, for a family thrown into poverty, alternative options were severely limited and Ramesh had soon realized that fact. He had never been particularly religious and so there was little problem of conscience. His brother Ceda had been the one finally to persuade him to leave the army, as he himself had done after a distinguished though short career, and lend his considerable abilities to the furtherance of the family fortunes.

A number of times the family had come dangerously close to conflict with the government, but on each occasion Uncle Gilma had steered a steady course, avoiding exposure of his business interests and even ingratiating himself with those in power. Ramesh had never known whether anyone in the government fully appreciated the extent of the family's activities and was sure that if they ever did they would surely clamp down on them. For now, however, they were left alone to carry on at will, and so it was that

Uncle's most daring scheme was shortly due to come to fruition.

Ramesh knew few of the details. Ceda had been chosen as the one to carry out the core mission. But Ramesh was aware of his own duties and was determined that the family would not find him lacking. Uncle had briefed him on the facts that were necessary for him to complete his own part of the plan and had stated mysteriously that when all the pieces were in place the prize would be greater than any the family had yet won. Indeed, he had said, the whole nation would thank them and reward them for what they had done.

A flurry of snow lashed his face and filled his mouth. He turned his head away and spat to clear it, and that was when he heard the cry from up ahead. Instantly he dropped to his knees, signalling those behind to do likewise. For the journey he had worn ex-army white camouflage overalls on top of his padded jacket and trousers, and as he lowered himself on to his stomach he was grateful for their protection. The driving snow blew over him and blended well with the thick waxed cloth.

'What is it?'

Murap had crawled to his side and peered into the haze to see what had caused the boss to call the halt.

Ramesh shook his head, not taking his eyes off the direction of the crest. 'I don't know, but I heard something.'

'Patrol?'

'Possibly. No one else would be dumb enough to be up here in weather like this.'

For a second the wind dropped and in the pause he

again caught the sound of voices, this time louder than before. He scanned around and saw a line of boulders protruding from the snow about a hundred yards away further up the slope.

'Get the men behind those,' he ordered quickly. 'See if there's somewhere you can hide the mules.'

'Right,' Murap answered. 'Are we going to ambush them or let them pass?'

'That's up to them. Be prepared for a contact.'

Without waiting for further instructions Murap dashed away, waving a series of silent hand signals to the men. The majority of them were ex-forces, and those who weren't had been trained by Ramesh and Ceda themselves until their battle drills were probably better than those of the regular army.

Reaction was instantaneous. The muleteers led their charges as fast as they could in search of downwind cover in the hope that, should any of them bray, the noise would be carried away from the enemy by the wind. Meanwhile the rest of the force headed for the boulders Ramesh had indicated, preparing their weapons as they went. Because of the weather conditions every rifle barrel was covered to prevent moisture getting inside. As they ran the men drew off the sheaths and cocked their weapons. Once at the boulders they sought out the best positions, checking their arcs of fire to ensure they had a clear view of the ground where the enemy was most likely to appear.

Ramesh joined them a moment later. 'No one fire unless I give the order,' he said, keeping his voice low enough for secrecy but pitching it so that it carried along the line.

For himself he selected a gap between two boulders that faced directly into the killing area. Murap crawled to his elbow and said, 'Everyone in position.' He chuckled. 'You know, I think you'd be disappointed if we never had a contact.'

'It keeps us on our toes.'

'Sometimes it puts one or two of us on our backs.'

'Losses in battle are to be expected,' Ramesh replied stoically. 'The trick is to minimize your own while maximizing the enemy's.'

'I'll tell that to the widows. It'll be a great comfort to them.'

Ramesh shrugged. 'The trade keeps them fed while their husbands are alive, and we look after them if their menfolk fail to come back. What more could they ask?'

Murap slapped him on the shoulder. 'That's what I love about you, Ramesh. You're all heart.'

It was some time before they saw the Indian patrol, so much so that Ramesh was starting to wonder if either he'd been mistaken or they had taken another route. Eventually, however, a vague shape materialized out of the white mist and became the figure of a man, leaning into the wind, and behind him, a line of others.

Ramesh tapped Murap, who was busy fiddling with his self-loading rifle. 'Our guests have arrived. Prepare the welcoming committee.'

Murap grinned and slithered on his belly down the line of boulders to ensure that the others were ready. Everyone knew that if it was possible Ramesh would allow the Indian patrol to pass unhindered. The last thing he needed on his back was a follow-up operation. The patrol would undoubtedly be equipped with radios and the moment Ramesh's men opened fire the Indians would send a contact report to their nearest headquarters. Then, as soon as the weather permitted, there would be helicopters in the air searching for them, and on the exposed mountain faces it was often impossible to find cover at short notice. Once they were spotted, other patrols could be guided towards them, entrapping them in a pincer of steel and lead. It had happened only once before and it was not a trap that Ramesh wished to find himself in again.

He hugged the snow, loosening his face mask around his mouth in case he needed to shout out orders and control his men's fire. Fifty yards below him the patrol snaked into the open, traversing the slope with painful care. He estimated it to be of platoon strength, about twenty-five to thirty men in all. The commander was moving close to the front and beside him Ramesh could see two signallers, the long, waving antennas of their radios announcing to all the world that here were priority targets. He glanced sideways and saw that Murap was already on to it, directing the machine-gunner to lay on to the little group and prepare, at Ramesh's signal, to mow them down.

Everything seemed to be going perfectly. At their present speed and direction Ramesh estimated that the patrol would pass out of his way within a further three minutes and that they would head down into the valley he had just left. But the next moment he was cursing softly into his face mask.

With a dramatic motion, the lieutenant held up his hand for a halt. The patrol stopped and Ramesh bit his lip in frustration as he saw that they intended to take a short break. The men gathered in three section groups, and started to spread out groundsheets to sit on while they drank from their vacuum flasks and had a bite to eat.

'Of all the shitty luck,' he growled.

Murap looked at him and shrugged. 'Can't be helped,' he whispered.

Ramesh edged back from the gap in the boulders lest an inquisitive Indian soldier spot him. The snow was still being driven across the slope in flurries, but breaks were appearing in it as the wind lessened. To his horror Ramesh saw one of the Indians get up and start to walk straight towards him.

He can't have seen me, he thought. If that was the case he'd have been running in the opposite direction, or else shooting.

It seemed as though the man intended walking all the way to the boulders, but luckily for Ramesh, halfway there he felt tired, for the snow was deep and at each step he was sinking almost to his knees. So, instead of carrying on, he looked sheepishly back over his shoulder, undid his flies, fumbled through the layers of clothing and began to urinate. The relief on his face could be seen even by the men in the rocks and Ramesh thought it would be a shame to shoot a man caught in such an act. It had somehow converted him from a potential target into a fellow-human.

His task completed, the man refastened his trousers

and turned to rejoin his companions, who had been jeering at him all the while. He hadn't gone more than four labouring paces when the unmistakable bray of a mule carried across the slope from the nearby shallow ravine where the muleteers had taken temporary refuge.

Ramesh stiffened, his eyes fixed on the man's retreating back to see if he had noticed. For a moment it seemed as if he might not have caught it, but then he stopped, cocked his head on one side and listened again. As if in answer the mule brayed again.

'I'll slit that beast's throat myself,' Ramesh murmured. 'And then I'll castrate its handler.'

The man turned to face the boulders, and by now the others in the patrol had heard it too. Ramesh tightened the butt of his SLR into his shoulder, thumb-flicked the safety-catch to the fire setting, and pulled the trigger. In front of him the man jumped in the snow and was flung backwards. As the round hit him in the centre of his chest it looked as if a giant hand had plucked him out of the snow and tossed him casually away. He fell soundlessly, the soft whiteness absorbing his body, but staining a second later with his spreading blood.

The rest of the patrol were on their feet and running. From further down the line of boulders the machine-gun started up. Murap was controlling it well and its fire fell with deadly accuracy to the lieutenant, his signallers and the protection party who were close about him. He had chosen a lousy place for his tea break, Ramesh reflected. Anyone worth their salt would instantly have seen that the boulders provided not only cover from fire but, more importantly –

given the circumstances – cover from the all-pervading blizzard.

Realizing that they were caught in the open, the Indian patrol flung themselves into the snow and started to return fire at their attackers. On either flank some of them tried to work around the edges to see if they could outmanoeuvre Ramesh's party, but Ramesh and Murap had prepared for this and their own flank guards cut them down before they had gone a dozen paces.

It seemed that the lieutenant had been killed by the opening machine-gun burst because the next thing Ramesh heard was the voice of the platoon sergeant rallying his men and trying to instil some sense of order in them once more.

'That's it,' Ramesh found himself saying admiringly. 'Get them sorted out. Return fire and either pull out or counter-attack.'

He remembered an old sergeant in a platoon that he had once commanded on a very similar operation. In that instance they had been caught much as the Indian patrol was now trapped. 'Whatever you do,' the sergeant had shouted afterwards at the young subaltern Ramesh had then been, 'you've got to get out of the killing area. So long as you stay there the enemy calls the shots.'

The strong voice of the Indian sergeant now rose above the noise of battle and Ramesh almost felt like calling off the attack. But not quite.

'Murap! Can you see him? If you can, get the machine-gun on him and shut him up!'

'Wilco!'

A handful of the Indians under the command of a

foolhardy corporal attempted a frontal assault with fixed bayonets. It was brave but doomed to failure. Not one of them covered more than half a dozen yards before being scythed down by rifle and machine-gun fire.

More difficult to counter was a section machine-gun group that managed to withdraw away from the killing area and reach the relative cover of a cluster of snow-covered rocks. At first Ramesh had thought the rocks were just mounds of snow but as soon as his own machine-gun tried to fire at the men, the bullets blasted the snow away, revealing the solid cover beneath.

'What the hell do we do now?' Murap shouted when he saw that the Indians had found a temporary haven.

Ramesh didn't know. As he watched, the Indian machine-gun came into action, laying down an accurate fire on the ambushers. The wind shifted for a moment and on the sudden gust Ramesh heard the voice of the sergeant rallying his men.

'So you made it to the rocks, did you?' he said with a slight, reluctant smile.

Elsewhere across the snow, bodies lay in the limp poses of death, fresh white drifts covering the bloodstains and settling on the uniforms and discarded equipment. Ramesh hunted around for an answer to the problem. So long as the Indian machine-gun remained in action there was no way that he and his men could move. Of course he could always just sit tight and allow the contest to become a waiting game. He had had the time to choose his positions carefully, whereas the sergeant and his surviving soldiers had scrambled into the only sparse cover available. The wind would be considerably worse for him, added to which they had been forced to abandon their packs in the killing area. With the packs had gone their spare clothing and shelters. In such conditions they wouldn't be able to survive for long without them and any attempt to retrieve them would be met with certain death from Ramesh's machine-gun and rifles.

Nevertheless, Ramesh wondered how long he could afford to sit tight waiting for the Indians to freeze to death. If they knew what they were about they would burrow shallow snow-holes and use whatever kit they had to improvise a wind-break. Once out of the wind they could perhaps survive into the night. Could he wait that long? He doubted it. While he didn't think that they had managed to get a message to their headquarters before the signallers had been killed, it was likely that they would have regular reporting times. It was normal practice, especially in such dangerous conditions where an avalanche or crevasse could swallow a complete patrol in a second. All they had to do was miss one such reporting time and their base would send someone out to look for them. Then perhaps the dreaded helicopters would come.

He bit his lip in frustration. He had to act now. He couldn't wait, however much he might want to. Away to the left he could just see that the ground dipped away. If he could make it round there he might be able to creep up on the sergeant's party and surprise them. But what would he do when he got there?

'Hey, Murap,' he called softly. 'Have you got any grenades?'

Murap thought for a second before frowning and saying, 'Yes, but they're on the mules.'

He pointed over his shoulder and Ramesh saw that to reach them he would have to cross a stretch of open ground, at least twenty yards wide, which was swept by the Indian machine-gun. As he was thinking of a solution Murap called back to him.

'We might not have any, but he has.' Ramesh looked to where Murap was pointing and saw the body of the man who had first heard the mule. The snow had almost covered him by now, but hooked on to his belt Ramesh saw the familiar shape of two hand-grenades.

'Brilliant. How the fuck am I supposed to get them?'

'We can cover you from here.'

'I might as well try for the mules.'

Murap shook his head. 'I don't think they can see you from their rocks. Not if you keep close to the ground.'

Ramesh looked and saw that Murap was right. From his position further down the line Murap was able to see that the ground between the Indian sergeant and the body of the dead man rose into a gentle, convex slope. So long as Ramesh crawled in a perfectly straight line and hugged the snow it was unlikely that he would be seen.

He rolled on to one side and undid his belt, then stripped off his harness and shoulder straps. From one of his pouches he took two spare magazines and stuffed them in his pocket. Without the extra encumbrance of the webbing he judged that he had a better chance of making it out and back in one piece.

On the far side of his boulder there was a gap large enough for him to crawl through, and when he had shouldered his way between the two rocks he slithered forward out of cover. Once out on the virgin snow he felt unpleasantly vulnerable. To left and right there was nothing except the bare while expanse, and behind him he could feel the eyes of his men following his progress. He knew that Murap would keep up a steady fire on the Indian position, not increasing the volume as that might alert the sergeant to the fact that something was happening. Then, if he had grenades of his own, he might start to throw them in Ramesh's direction.

Keeping as close to the ground as he could, Ramesh eased slowly forward. His eyes were fixed on the dead body in front of him and on the slight rise behind it that masked him from the Indian machine-gun. Bullets from both sides stung the air inches above his head and at one point he glanced back with a scowl at Murap to warn him and the others to be careful. The last thing he wanted was to have his brains blown out by his own men.

Yard by yard the distance to the body lessened until Ramesh edged himself across the last small stretch of snow and drew level with the man's boots. Pulling himself alongside the body, he got his face alongside the man's belt and was just reaching across for the first of the two grenades when the head tipped his way and the eyes rolled open, fixing him with a deathly stare. Ramesh felt his heart miss a beat with the shock and he only just managed to stop himself crying out. As he stared back in horror the eyes blinked and the man's hand started to move.

Ramesh fumbled desperately for his knife, his fingers, numb with the cold, making hard work of it.

'Damn you,' he rasped, half to himself and half to the Indian. 'You're supposed to be dead.'

He got his knife free and was bringing it up when the man saw the blade and realized that, far from having come to rescue him, Ramesh intended to finish him off. With his last burst of strength he raised his head and cried out, the cry carrying back to his comrades behind the rocks. The next instant it was cut short by Ramesh's knife slamming down into his chest, the blade penetrating all the way to the hilt. His head fell back and the eyes rolled again – this time in death.

But the damage had been done, and the sergeant was alerted to the new threat. Bullets spat in the ground all around Ramesh and he wriggled backwards until protected by the rise in the ground. Even so, the fire was shaving dangerously close.

'If they keep this up they'll cut the bloody top off the hill,' Ramesh thought.

The grenades still hung tantalizingly close on the dead man's belt. As carefully as he could, he stretched up his hand, sliding it alongside the body, and then inched his fingers towards the first of the grenades. It was well fastened to the webbing strap but after a second it came loose and he was able to slip it in his pocket. The other grenade was more difficult as it was obscured by the man's body and Ramesh had to feel for it. At one point as he felt for the touch of the metal his fingers entered the wound that his earlier bullet had caused and he flinched in surprise. He steeled himself to try again and this time he retrieved the grenade.

He moved away from the body, feeling a flood of relief

as the ground dropped steadily beneath him, increasing the degree of cover from the machine-gun that was still hunting for him around the dead body. There was an almost overwhelming temptation to break and run for the safety of the boulders but he knew the urge resulted from fear, and that it was illusory. The moment he showed his head it would be blown wide open by the 7.62mm bullets cracking all about him. So, keeping his nerves on a short rein, he continued back to the boulders, moving as stealthily as on the outward stalk.

Murap was waiting to greet him.

'Well done. I can see you've been a sniper in your day.'

Ramesh rolled on to his back and mopped his brow. Despite the freezing conditions he found that he was sweating, the beads stinging on his face as the wind discovered the rare moisture and stunned it into ice.

'Let's finish this,' he said stonily. 'It's time that machine-gun was silenced.'

'Do you want me or one of the lads to go?' Murap asked.

But Ramesh was already on his way. 'No. This one's mine.'

He resisted the urge to pause for a moment and rest, knowing that were he to do so his muscles would stiffen and the wind would chill him still further. He had to get the business done and get them all off the mountain. It had been bad enough for him, but in some respects it was worse for his men. At least he had been able to keep warm by moving. But they had been forced to lie stationary for some time now and Ramesh could imagine that the weakest and least experienced of them would already be well on the way to frostbite.

The line of boulders petered out some fifty yards to the right in dead ground. Unwilling to risk compromising his position, Ramesh crawled the full distance, arriving at the snow-filled hollow exhausted and gasping. His lungs sucked in the air and he felt the sharp stabs of pain as its dry iciness stung his chest like needles. His throat felt raw and he tightened his mask around his mouth. However, looking about him he judged it safe to run at a crouch for the next bit of the way, before the final crawl, which would take him to within throwing distance of the enemy machine-gun position.

Instead of his cumbersome rifle he had taken a Sterling sub-machine-gun from one of his men. Should anything go wrong with the grenade throw, he would rather rely on the Sterling's rapid rate of fire than on the single-shot capability of his SLR. The SMG's accuracy was poor by comparison but at close quarters a good spread of shot was more important.

Holding it close to his stomach, he ran bent almost double. He had folded the stock, and the weapon sat snugly against him, the curved thirty-round magazine resting on his left forearm as he cradled the underside of the barrel in his left hand and clutched the handgrip and trigger in his right. The safety-catch was off and he had pulled back the cocking handle so that the slightest pressure on the trigger would set it firing.

The ground fell away into a re-entrant and he decided to follow it to its end, which he estimated would bring him to a point roughly in the rear of the Indian position.

However, as he moved, he became aware that the sound of the firing had dropped and that the only shots appeared to be coming from his own men. He slowed his pace, trying to figure out what had happened, when suddenly, round the bend not ten yards in front of him, the whole group of five Indian soldiers appeared at a jog. They had chosen that exact moment to bug out, selecting the same route for their escape that Ramesh had picked for his grenade stalk.

Ramesh swore and dropped to one knee, hugging the SMG firmly. Firing in short, controlled bursts, he directed his jets of 9mm bullets into the oncoming enemy. Taken by surprise, they began to fall as Ramesh raked the re-entrant from side to side with his fire.

Suddenly the hammer clicked mutely on an empty chamber. The man he had borrowed it from had failed to tell him that the magazine was already half expended. One of the Indians saw his chance and hurled himself at Ramesh, who swung with the short, stubby weapon, catching him on the jaw and laying him out flat. But it was the last remaining opponent who presented the real threat. The sergeant had been moving at the rear of his group and, seeing the others fall, had managed to take cover out of Ramesh's line of fire. As Ramesh threw aside the useless SMG and fumbled for his knife, the sergeant dived at him, knocking him to the ground and coming up on top, his own knife raised for the kill.

But Ramesh was no novice at hand-to-hand fighting and brought his knee into the sergeant's side, shouting out to focus the power of his blow. The wind went out of the sergeant and Ramesh thrust him to the side, finding his knife as he did so. There was a clash of steel as he drove down only to meet the sergeant's parrying blow. Both men were on their feet in an instant, circling, each gauging the other, looking for an opening in his opponent's guard.

The sergeant was the first to move, first aiming high and slashing at Ramesh's face and then lunging deeply towards the midriff. But Ramesh had read his intention, seen the desperation in the man's eyes. He knew that his combat subtlety would only extend to a simple feint and thrust, and the moment he was proved correct, he was already halfway into his own spoiling attack, sidestepping, parrying with the heel of one gloved palm and slicing straight into the sergeant's throat. His blade struck home, finding flesh and gristle. The sergeant slumped to his knees, his weapon forgotten as both hands scrabbled at his throat as if he would hold in the air and blood that rushed to escape. It was useless. Ramesh stood back gasping for breath as he watched the sergeant die, toppling over into the snow, dead before his face cushioned itself in the enveloping white softness.

There were voices from behind. Ramesh whirled but it was only Murap and two of the men. Murap whistled in admiration.

'You could have left some for us.'

But Ramesh wasn't in any mood for idle chat. Too many good men had died that day, and they had been delayed in the completion of their task.

'Let's get off this fucking mountain,' he said hoarsely,

thrusting his knife into its sheath. 'We've got work to do.'

'What about the bodies?'

'Leave them,' he answered as he strode back towards the rocks. 'The snow will bury them for us.'

6

Jerry Patel had never ached so much in his whole life. His legs throbbed, his back was a sheet of fire, his arms felt as if they were about to snap, his eyes stung from lack of sleep and his head pounded. Every muscle in his body had been pulled and stretched and tasked beyond the limit of endurance, and yet somehow he was still enduring, still pressing on, still heading for home. The whole decrepit package that was himself was held together by one thing and one thing alone – his will. It was like a determined sea captain, steering his storm-blasted vessel the last miles to harbour, the hold awash, the crew mutinied and gone, the cargo lost. But Jerry was going to make it, or die trying.

The hillside before him went on and on, one false crest after another. As he rounded each supposed summit it was only to realize it had been a mere fold in the ground, with another higher, further, steeper one a few hundred yards beyond. He cursed the land, the weather, himself, goading himself on as if talking to someone else.

'Get your arse in gear, you idle bastard. You lousy wanker, you useless sod, you stupid, pig-ignorant git.'

Anyone listening to him might have been forgiven for

thinking he was a hopeless mental case had they not understood that he always goaded himself like that, driving himself on as if his will marched alongside, integral yet separate, observing, criticizing, urging. It had driven him through the Parachute Regiment's gruelling P Company three years before, and the previous month it had dragged and kicked him successfully through the last hurdle of SAS selection. He had been a little disappointed to learn that, far from being allowed to rest on his laurels, he was expected to go straight out again on an extended exercise with his new squadron, but he supposed that it was all part of the deal. In the SAS, he was fast learning, there never would be any laurels to rest on, not until the Regiment had finished with you and you were back in the mainstream army or pushing up daisies in the cemetery; for Jerry the two amounted to the same thing.

As he struggled over yet another crest a strong wind hit him full in the face, carrying with it a freezing rain that had already soaked him. With the wind, the temperature dropped, and the rain began to turn to ice. It froze up his ammunition pouches and formed icicles on the shoulder straps, adding to the overall weight of his load. The one relief to greet him, however, was the sight of the valley beyond. He had reached the real summit at last and from here on would be able to descend.

He jogged over to a rock and eased down out of the wind to catch his breath and survey the lie of the land. The Brecon Beacons stretched away in every direction, bleak and rugged, their gently flowing contours belying the severity of the climb. Leaning back against the moss-covered rock, he slid to the ground, feeling the weight lift off his shoulders as the rock took the pack. He put back his head and sighed, pulling the straps away from his bruised flesh. A thin coating of ice covered his webbing and the hem of his jacket was stiff with it. He grasped a fistful of the material, feeling it crackle as the ice powdered. Undoing a pocket flap, he took out a tube of boiled sweets and popped one in his mouth, feeling the instantaneous rush of sugar on his tongue, sugar that would soon convert into much-needed energy. Once out of the wind it was surprisingly quiet on the hilltop, the only sound being the patter of driving rain on his pack and on his sodden combats. He took out his waterproofed map and compared it with the landscape below. His Silva compass was in his top-right breast pocket, secured to his jacket by a lanyard looped through the pocket flap's buttonhole. He laid it on the map and aligned the markings on its face with the map's north-south grid lines, twisting the dial until he was able to obtain a bearing from his present position to his destination. When he had it he ascertained his direction to travel for the next leg of the journey, sighting along the body of the compass to see where it pointed. The corner of a forestry block in the far distance marked the approximate spot and he judged that from there he should be able to see the final leg. This would take him to the rendezvous with the transport that would take him back to camp.

Camp. He closed his eyes for a moment and permitted himself the luxury of anticipation. In the corridor outside his room he would drop his pack and webbing, and strip off his wet, filthy combats. Then there would be a long soak in a hot bath, relaxing away the aching muscles and sprains. Afterwards, dressed in clean, warm, dry clothes he would go for a hot meal, perhaps out of camp to a local pub where he could also enjoy a pint or two, finally returning to sleep in a soft, deep bed under an enormous duvet, cocooned until late the next morning, a Sunday, when nothing would be expected of him except attendance at the bar for a few beers with the lads before a huge roast lunch.

The cold rain lashed against his cheeks, startling him awake.

'Fucking idiot,' he muttered bitterly. 'Nearly dozed off, didn't you? You useless piece of trash.' He began to stagger to his feet. 'Where would that have got you? The easiest death in the whole fucking world. They'd have found you in a day or two, frozen solid, so pale they wouldn't know you were a bloody Tandoori until they saw your ID discs and the name Patel.'

He slipped his map away and buttoned up his compass in his top pocket. Tandoori. Some of the guys had called him that during selection and it had stuck. That and other names. Funnily enough he didn't mind them here. In the Paras it had been different. There he'd met the biggest bunch of racists since school and it had been a long time before he had been accepted. In some ways he never had been, but here it was different. The lads were different – everything was. That was why for most of them there could never be any other kind of soldiering after Hereford. When his tour was over he hoped to be able to stay on. If not, he wasn't sure what he would do. He certainly wouldn't want to go back to the Paras and the dreary wasteland of Aldershot and Normandy Barracks.

The downhill going wasn't quite as easy as he had hoped. The ground was largely tussock grass, soft, spongy clumps with bog in between. The options were either to tread from clump to clump or weave around them. The former was fine when you had plentiful reserves of energy but in his present condition all Jerry could do was to slog on blindly, sometimes finding a firm footing on top of the tussocks, but more often than not stumbling into the brown morass that ringed and fed them.

In some respects walking on such difficult terrain demanded greater concentration than ploughing uphill and Jerry found that he had less time for his own thoughts, which was no bad thing. So long as he was busy watching where to put his feet he couldn't moan about how shattered he was. However, once down on the valley floor, the tussocks gave way to firmer ground and he was able to make up some of the lost time.

He came to a broad stream, the water a rich transparent brown from the surrounding peat. It was far from ideal but it would have to do. Down on one knee, he took out his water bottle and refilled it, dropping in a couple of sterilizing tablets. It would taste disgusting, a mixture of peat and chlorine, probably with a hint of sheep's piss to heighten the flavour, but it was all there was. Perhaps if he was lucky he might find a better source near the forestry block, but it was unlikely on the higher ground. For now, this would have to do and it was better to have foul water in your canteen than none at all.

Walking on the level came as an unusual respite from the more customary ascents and descents. For a while he almost began to enjoy himself. The rain continued, though it was not as ferocious as on the summits, but after all, according to one of the earliest pearls of army wisdom he had heard, 'If it's not raining, it's not training.'

God how the army loved its catch-phrases! There was one for every occasion and some folks Jerry had met seemed to be able to go through life uttering little else. They were 'army-barmy'. He could think of other descriptions for them.

His stride had lengthened and he was happy to note that he was covering the ground rapidly. Nevertheless, as soon as he began to climb again he slowed, leaning into the slope and slipping into the old familiar rhythm of the laden hillwalker. One of the unfortunate consequences of being on low ground again was that his destination had disappeared from view. It wasn't a problem as far as keeping direction was concerned; he had his compass bearing for that. But its effect on morale was less than beneficial. Seen from the opposing ridgeline where he had halted, the forestry block didn't look quite so far away, but as he laboured up the hillside he was confronted once again with false crest after false crest, the deceptive folds of marsh and bog that had not been visible from his resting place, now rippling upwards with sadistic inevitability.

Time blurred into a continuum of misery. He tried to switch off his brain and for a while it worked, but always it was the niggling little thoughts that intruded. Would he watch the skiing on TV on Sunday afternoon?

Why were there no black Olympic swimmers and no white heavyweight boxers? Who went round nicking the badges off Volkswagens and what the fuck did they do with them? Did men with pony-tails have a higher or lower IQ than men who wore their baseball caps back to front? When would Cilla chuck the pretence on *Blind Date* and ask the only question everyone wanted answered: 'Did you get laid?'

He was so busy pondering the last question, head bent into his stride, that he almost walked straight into the wire fence bordering the forestry plantation.

'Thank buggery for that,' he wheezed, skirting around the edge until he came to the crown of the hill.

Sure enough, down below on the far side he could just make out the thin, grey ribbon of road and the slight indentation that signified the parking place where the lorry was due in a couple of hours. He leaned on the wire and studied the layout. The area surrounding the road looked barren and empty and if the rain and wind strengthened there would be nowhere there for him to shelter. But the forestry plantation was another matter. So, deciding to take a longer break, he clambered over the fence and pushed through the trees until he found a sheltered hollow beneath some low-hanging branches. It was cosy inside and he slipped off his pack, feeling as if, with the sudden weight loss, he was in danger of floating away like an untethered balloon.

It would probably take him half an hour to reach the pick-up point, so he estimated that he could relax for a good hour. The greatest feat would be not falling asleep and missing the RV altogether. The Regiment would definitely not be impressed. He might have passed selection but he felt as if he was still on probation. He had been particularly depressed when someone had told him that it was a feeling that never passed. The guy had said that you only really relaxed and felt you were 'SAS' when you were out. But when Jerry had passed this on to one of the training sergeants, the man had grunted 'Bollocks'. So what was a new boy supposed to do? Keep his head down and work hard, Jerry had concluded.

He rummaged in the side pouch of his pack and came up with a miniature camping stove. With his knife he dug out a small hole in the soft, needle-covered turf, sufficient to hold the burner, and settled it in. Then, placing a tin mug of water on the tiny blue gas flame, he set about making a brew. The shelter he had chosen kept out the worst of the wind and nearly all of the rain, but the air temperature was still low enough for the water to take an age to boil. When it did, he dropped in a tea bag and stirred the mixture, adding plenty of sugar and a little powdered milk, scrupulously returning the used sachets to his pack for later disposal in camp. The drill had nothing to do with keeping Britain tidy, but everything to do with basic field discipline, since a carelessly discarded piece of litter could lead to the compromise of a patrol.

When the brew was ready he packed away every item of kit and fastened all the loose flaps before settling down with his back against a tree to enjoy his drink. As always he kept his webbing on, his pack close beside him, and his rifle instantly to hand. The first sip of tea sent shock waves of pleasure rippling through him. It was better than alcohol, better than dry clothes, better than sex. Given the circumstances, that is.

The heat penetrated the metal sides of the mug and seeped into his dirt-ingrained hands. The skin was wrinkled from the rain water and it felt wonderful to touch heat, even in such limited quantities. Another sip, and he felt as if he was ready to do the tab all over again. Well, perhaps that was taking things too far. He remembered one of the wartime Chindits saying that whenever you find yourself confronting an insuperable problem, sit down and make a brew, and the problem will miraculously resolve itself. It certainly worked as far as morale problems were concerned. A whole new perspective was put on life and you could set out again on your mission, as if from a new and much more logical starting-point.

All too soon he had drained the mug, and only a grainy residue remained in the bottom. He tipped it out and clapped the mug on to the top of his water bottle, fastening the securing flap over it. The temptation was great just to lean back against the tree and close his eyes for a moment, but he knew that the moment would extend rapidly into a prolonged sleep. In the shelter of the trees it would probably not be fatal, unlike on the exposed hillside, but he would miss his transport, and in some respects that would be just as serious.

He hummed softly to himself for a while, thinking of nothing in particular until he remembered what one of his relatives had said when they heard he had passed the selection for the SAS. They had thought he had chucked in the army to join the Scandinavian airline with the same initials.

'I'm so glad you're out of that bunch,' one uncle had commented with obvious relief, little realizing the hole he was digging for himself. 'I can tell you now that the family has never really been happy with your choice of career.'

There had been an embarrassed silence as the other family members present had signalled frantic warnings behind Jerry's back.

'Yes,' the oblivious relative had continued. 'Both your father and mother have said to me on many an occasion that they felt you could do better for yourself. What with your education and family connections, there could have been a career for you in any number of areas. Accountancy, engineering, law.' He shrugged. 'But the airline business is fine, I am sure. At least it's out of the military! There's an old Chinese saying: You don't use good iron to make nails,' he concluded with a condescending smile.

In the ensuing leaden silence Jerry had looked from his mother to his father and around the room. No one had had the courage to meet his eyes and he had left the house soon afterwards, making the excuse that he was required back at camp.

So that was what they all thought of his chosen path. Wasted potential. They would rather see him sitting behind some desk. Of course, sometimes he felt that way himself, but always he came back to the same conclusion: that he was cut out for something more adventurous. He didn't know where the urge came from, but it was there, and he had to give it expression. The SAS was the perfect means for doing just that and he intended to see it through, wherever it led him..

He looked out through the thick screen of branches and saw that the rain had stopped. A thin winter sunlight was trying without much success to penetrate the heavy clouds. In the tops of the surrounding firs the wind softened from its previous howl to a friendlier if agitated whisper. Jerry stretched out his legs and massaged the muscles through his sodden trousers, kneading the flesh with numb hands. A shudder ran through his body and he checked his watch to see if it was time to press on. The hot bath and change of clothes were beckoning.

He slipped his arms through his pack's straps and eased the load on to his shoulders, juggling the weight until it sat as comfortably as possible. Crawling out from under his cover on hands and knees, he felt the breeze eddying between the tree trunks chill him as it touched his wet clothing. All he wanted now was to be on the transport and bouncing the last miles back to camp.

Once over the wire fence he set off down the far side of the hill, heading for the lay-by, carefully watching his step over the difficult ground yet glancing up every few paces to look at it as if he half expected it to fade from view like the unearthly Welsh equivalent of some desert mirage. But there it was, as hard and real as the tarmac that composed it. Yard by yard the ground separating him from his goal fell away. His pace quickened until he was jogging the final distance. Panting from the exertion, he arrived at last and for the first time in what seemed like an eternity set foot on a metalled road. After the spongy quagmire of the hill country it was as welcoming as a bed with crisp, clean sheets. Right on time, the sound of an engine groaned in the distance and a moment later a Bedford lorry appeared over the rise, gathering speed as it headed down the gentle gradient towards the lay-by. For one horrific second the thought crossed Jerry's mind that perhaps it might continue on past. But no. That only happened on selection. It was the final straw that separated those with unshakeable morale from those without. After a harrowing series of tabs the candidates would arrive at the final RV to be told there was one more to go.

With a squeal of brakes the lorry stopped, the driver peering out of the window as he reversed into the lay-by.

'Sorry about that, mate,' he shouted. 'I almost forgot you'd be here.'

'No problem,' Jerry replied, smiling with relief. Selection was over. He had passed. He was in the SAS now. There would be no more 'sickeners'. 'Don't bother to let down the tailboard. I can climb in over the top,' he said with genuine gratitude in his voice.

A familiar face popped out of the back of the lorry, rubbing sleep from his eyes. 'We here already?'

Jerry looked up to see Sergeant Gavin Steward of the training wing. Steward's eyes lit up when he saw the sodden figure standing at the roadside. 'Tandoori! Good of you to make it.'

Jerry returned the smile a little less certainly. 'Hi, Sarge. Room in there for me?'

'Are you pissed? You didn't really think the crap all stopped with selection, did you?'

Jerry steeled himself for a shock, forcing a smile. 'Fair enough. How many more miles to the PUP?'

'What do you mean, pick-up point? I'll see you back in camp.'

Jerry felt as if his heart had just stopped. 'But that's two days' tabbing, right back the way I've just come!'

'Smart lad,' the sergeant winked. 'You'll go far. Say, about forty miles.'

Jerry waited for Steward to tell him it was just a joke but instead the sergeant rummaged in the lorry and re-emerged with a holdall jammed with radio batteries.

'Oh and by the way, be a good lad and take these for me. You see, I've got my sleeping bag stretched out in here and when we go over a bump they rattle around and wake me up.'

He smiled disarmingly and banged on the side of the lorry to attract the driver's attention. 'Home, James, and don't spare the horses.'

As the lorry started to pull away he shouted back, 'How you doing for rations?'

'They're all gone.'

'Well, there's another lesson for you. Always maintain a reserve. Cheerio.'

The lorry drew out on to the road and accelerated away, a cloud of blue diesel smoke belching from the exhaust. Jerry stood in the lay-by looking after it until it bumped over a rise, rounded a bend and vanished, leaving him feeling suddenly terribly alone. He turned and walked to the edge of the tarmac, and with a heart as heavy as granite he took the first step back on to the spongy grass. He hardly dared raise his eyes to confront the mounting slope that he knew lay before him, the first of many, and as he trudged agonizingly away from the road he felt the clouds close over him and the patter of the cold rain.

7

The old man sat morosely by the window looking out at the bare winter garden. Wherever it was it looked like a hundred other anonymous gardens that sprouted the length and breadth of England. There were the neat flower-beds, now consisting of little more than wet black earth, a paved path winding down to a tool shed just visible between three or four tall firs, a ragged lawn and a plastic washing line strung with dangling beads of rainwater. Where the hell had the police found it?

He had been in the safe house for a week now and the only people he had seen were the two plain-clothes policemen and the one woman who had been assigned to guard him. All three were armed but Mr Sanji knew that if another attempt was made on his life their pathetic array of police revolvers would be of little use against the massed fire-power of his enemies. His only hope lay in the secrecy of his hideaway. He had made several requests for information but for some reason each had been met with polite ignorance. Then he had asked for a solicitor and even this, although noted, had not been acted upon. He was beginning to wonder if he was a fugitive under police protection or a prisoner.

He got up and went through to the kitchen to make himself a cup of coffee. Seated at the kitchen table, two of his minders were playing chess, while the third was in the adjacent room watching television. The senior one of the three looked up as he entered.

'Making a coffee?'

What the fuck does it look like? Mr Sanji thought to himself.

'Yes, do you want one?'

Alec leaned back in his chair and scratched his belly. 'That would be just the job. Dave?'

His companion grunted, his eyes remaining fixed on the board. Mr Sanji noted that most of Dave's chess pieces had been removed from the board and were now arrayed next to Alec's plump white elbow. Alec, on the other hand, appeared to have lost only two pawns and one of his bishops. It wasn't that he was particularly smart – more that Dave was a mental midget when it came to anything more complicated than filling out a parking ticket. Mr Sanji shuddered at the thought of such a man being entrusted with a firearm and, more importantly, Sanji's own life.

The kettle took a few minutes to boil and while he waited Mr Sanji leaned against the worktop and watched the chess game.

'What kind of guns are those?' he asked out of idle curiosity.

'Smith & Wessons. I'd offer to show it to you but it's against regulations.'

Mr Sanji waved his hand. 'I'm not much interested

in guns. Never had any cause to learn about them. Is it difficult to use?'

Alec was clearly unhappy about being distracted from completing the defeat of his companion but shrugged and said, 'Not once you've done the training package. It's a close-range weapon anyway, so all you've really got to do is point it in roughly the right direction and keep pulling the trigger until your man goes down.'

The cursory explanation did little to increase Mr Sanji's confidence in his guards.

When the coffee was made he handed the two policemen their mugs and took his own through to the sitting room. Deep in an armchair, Anne Baron stared mesmerized at the afternoon chat show. Sanji lowered himself on to the sofa.

'Anything interesting?'

He knew the answer before she even opened her mouth. A television addict, Anne seemed to fear that she was missing out on life whenever she was obliged to leave the screen.

'They're talking about the Cones Hotline,' she replied without taking her eyes off the garishly decorated studio set. Two mannequin presenters were conducting a phone-in, their faces concentrated in sincerity as one simpleton after another aired his or her opinion to the nation. Technology had given them the capability of addressing their fellow-man, but no one had stopped to consider whether they had anything worth saying. It was entertainment by reduction to the lowest common denominator, the most primeval semi-human grunt given equal credence and air time alongside the most erudite latterday Socrates. Sanji looked across at Anne, at the dull glaze on her limp face as the images and sounds rotted her from the inside out.

He managed to stand the spectacle for a further three and a half minutes before surrendering all hope of conversation and climbing the stairs dejectedly to his bedroom. A small desk stood under the window and, set in the centre of it, a silver-framed photograph of his granddaughter smiled radiantly into the room. He put down his coffee, sank on to the bed and took the picture in his hands.

'Oh, Eli, why did I ever bring your mother to this terrible country? If only I had gone to Africa or Australia, anywhere but here.' He replaced the photograph, realizing that had he done so then the likelihood was that Eli would not even exist. His daughter wouldn't have married that ridiculous man but someone else instead, and although Sanji might not be in his present predicament, he would never had known the sweet laugh and gentle care of Eli. Life was a strange business, virtually all of it resting on complete chance, and yet no sooner had every random event occurred than it somehow acquired the feeling of destiny. It was deceptive, of course. Seductive even. But quite illusory.

He fluffed up his pillow and lay back on the bed, feeling his head sink back into the soft down. The bed at least was a success story. The house might be drab, his daughter and son-in-law dead, his dear, sweet Eli kidnapped, but the bed was wonderful and, in spite of all his worries, every night he was sleeping like a log.

When he opened his eyes he was startled to find the

room in darkness. For one brief moment he was scared, but when he looked at the luminous hands of his watch he saw that it was some four hours since he had gone up to his bedroom. He obviously hadn't realized how tired he was and had slept the afternoon away.

'What a waste,' he thought bitterly, swinging his legs off the bed and struggling to sit up. But then this whole wretched business was a terrible waste, locked up in the house with three idiots as his only company.

He rubbed his eyes and it was only then that he felt a shiver run down his spine. There was something wrong. It was normal for it to get dark so early at that time of year but the house was fitted with spotlights, ostensibly as part of a normal burglar alarm system although in reality they had more to do with the house's classification as a safe haven. The garden was pitch-dark, however. Ever since he had been there the lights had come on at dusk, and certainly long before their illumination was really needed. But now, as he peered cautiously out of the window, he couldn't even see as far as the fir trees at the bottom of the garden.

He opened his door as silently as he could, went out on to the landing and leaned over the banisters to listen. Through the closed glass-panel door of the sitting room he could hear the noise of the television. Anne was watching cartoons but the room light was off, only the glow from the TV screen flickering through the frosted glass on to the bottom of the stairs.

Sanji was really scared now. He opened his mouth to call out but thought better of it. If there was an intruder in the house the last thing he wanted to do was to alert him to his presence upstairs. But what was he thinking of? This was a safe house. He was under police protection and there were three armed officers downstairs whose sole present purpose in life was to keep him alive. One thought of Alec, Dave and Anne, however, was sufficient to cure him of such a misplaced confidence in his minders.

He crept back into his room and unplugged the bedside lamp, removing the shade and bulb and then, holding it like a club, he started down the stairs. One by one he crept down them, shifting his weight as delicately as a man of his age could. When he reached the bottom he paused to listen, straining his ears to pick up any unnatural sound. But his efforts were thwarted by the blaring racket of the cartoons.

The door knob turned softly in his hand and as the frame inched open he received the full blast of the TV. Tom and Jerry had chosen that precise instant to batter each other and Sanji flinched as if he had been hit himself, almost dropping his lamp. Realizing his error, he cursed himself for being such a coward and went into the room. The armchair where Anne had been sitting was empty except for her gun lying in the middle of the cushion. Sanji stared at it for a moment, wondering whether to pick it up.

It was then that he heard the noise from the kitchen, the scraping of a table leg and a grunt as if someone was shifting something heavy. Like a body, Sanji thought, the goose-pimples rising all over him. After placing his lamp carefully on the floor he retrieved Anne's revolver from the armchair and studied it in the light from the television until he had located the safety-catch and flicked it to the fire position. Then, cranking back the hammer and clutching the grip in both hands as he had seen in the movies, he stepped silently towards the kitchen door. It was ajar and the slightest pressure from the toe of his running shoe swung it soundlessly wide. The glow from the TV screen shone into the darkened room.

Spread face down across the kitchen table, Anne Baron panted, her eyes tightly shut. Her skirt was up over her back and her knickers were gathered around one of her fat splayed ankles. Behind her, and looking equally ridiculous, Dave's fleshy white buttocks convulsed rhythmically against her rump, the business side of him mercifully concealed from view. His trousers had crumpled at his knees and he looked to Sanji like a small boy enjoying a rather unusual piss.

Sanji lowered his revolver, although the thought fleetingly crossed his mind of shooting the pair of them and robbing them of the critical moment. He was just wondering whether he should back away and leave them to their rutting when Anne's eyes half opened and found themselves focusing with difficulty on Sanji's bemused gaze.

'Oh fuck!'

Dave moaned in response, mistaking her exclamation for one of ecstasy caused by his efforts. 'Yes, yes.'

'No, you git. Get off me.'

She bucked her hips to try and shake him off but he was no longer on the same planet. Seeing her dilemma, Sanji tactfully withdrew, pulling the door quietly closed behind him. He went across to the light switch and flicked it on as male cries sounded in the kitchen, followed, embarrassingly rapidly, by the hushed mutter of conferring voices, the one somewhat more breathless than the other.

Sanji gently eased forward the hammer on the revolver lest he fire off his own negligent discharge, and sat down to watch the news which had just begun. As a newscaster recited the day's triumphs, catastrophes and anecdotes, his face shifting gear with each take, ranging through boredom, concern and indulgent mirth respectively, the neon strip-light flickered on in the kitchen. Sanji could imagine the ugliness of its cold mortuary glare shining on the pale, guilty flesh of the two lovers as they rearranged their dress. Sure enough, when the door opened and they filed into the sitting room, it might as well have been the emergence of the living dead.

Without looking at them he asked merrily, 'Anyone making coffee?'

His question went unanswered. Instead Anne mumbled something about make-up and disappeared up to the bathroom while Dave perched on the edge of the armchair and pretended to watch the news. Sanji knew full well that he wasn't the least bit interested in it and it was barely half a minute before he said sheepishly, 'You won't tell Alec, will you?'

Sanji smiled at him, liking the fellow for the first time. 'What's there to tell?'

The relief on Dave's face could have been bottled and sold for a fortune.

'After all,' Sanji continued, 'I'm a man of the world.'

But he was unable to suppress the devil in himself. 'You must love her very much?'

Dave blushed, inspecting his hands as he wrung them and, as Sanji had suspected, he didn't have the balls to deny it.

'Yeah, course. She's a great woman.'

Sanji sighed theatrically, not having had so much fun for ages. 'Ah, the antics of the young. It makes me feel like a youth myself to see such a tender pair of lovebirds.' He leaned forward earnestly, the bit now well and truly between his teeth. 'When do you plan to marry her?'

It was unfortunate that Dave had perched quite so close to the edge of his chair because only the most obvious effort managed to keep him from falling off it. However, deciding that he had been tormented enough, and appreciating that because of the interruption his passion had been rudely accelerated, Sanji relented and drew the baiting to a close by casually mentioning the absence of the spotlights.

For a moment, from the look of consternation that came over Dave, Sanji wondered whether the policeman was trying to get his revenge by unsettling his Indian guest. He spun in his chair, his earlier embarrassment entirely forgotten.

'I assumed you'd turned them off to get a bit of privacy,' Sanji said falteringly.

'No way. I might screw the WPC but I wouldn't tamper with the security system.'

He got quickly out of his chair and drew his revolver from its holster.

'Where is Alec, by the way?' Sanji asked.

'He went out for a pizza.'

'Of course. I forgot it's pizza night tonight.'

Sanji had no sooner finished his sentence than he realized what he had said. The blundering idiots had set a pattern. With only three takeaways nearby it was fish and chips one night, curry the second and pizza the third, in strict rotation, on Alec's insistence. Sanji had suspected that he had never really taken the task seriously, his overriding concern being with the contents of his stomach. The poor fools had no idea who they were dealing with.

Dave made for the light switch and turned it off.

'Where's the remote for the TV?'

'I've got it,' Sanji replied.

'Kill it, will you?'

The picture disappeared, and Sanji sat frozen on the sofa waiting for his eyes to become accustomed to the darkness. After a couple of minutes he was able to make out the figure of Dave standing by the curtain, holding it open a crack and peering out to the front of the house. But the police had chosen the place for its seclusion and it was at the end of an isolated cul-de-sac.

'Shit.' Dave's voice was cold and matter-of-fact.

'What is it?'

'Street lights are all out.'

Sanji's heart was suddenly chilled. He felt his gut heave and for a second he thought he was going to be sick. They had found him again, and this time he knew they would ensure the job was properly done.

'What about Alec?' he tried. 'He should be back at any moment, shouldn't he?'

He could almost hear Dave's mind racing.

'Yes. That's right.'

Neither of them dared voice the thought that entered their minds simultaneously. If they were indeed out there, then Alec would never be returning.

'Couldn't it just be a simple power failure?' Sanji asked.

'It could be. The street light could go out without it affecting the internal power source, but the spots should still be working.'

'Might Alec have turned them off for some reason?'

'No way. At least not without telling us first.'

There was the sound of footsteps padding down the stairs. 'What are you doing standing in the darkness?' Anne said, reaching for the light switch.

'Don't touch that!'

'Why ever not?'

'The external lights are all out.'

'But Alec . . .'

Dave was about to explain their fears when there was a knock at the kitchen door. All three of them stood as stiff as rods. The knock came again, more urgent than before.

'Get down, Mr Sanji,' Anne commanded coolly. 'Keep down until we've sorted this out.'

She and Dave moved through to the kitchen, leaving the door open behind them. In spite of her instructions, Sanji stepped after them, partly from inquisitiveness and partly from fear of being left alone in the darkness.

'Who is it?'

'Who do you think? Open the door.' And then, after a pause, 'It's me, Alec. The pizza's getting cold.'

Dave swapped looks with Anne and glanced accusingly at Sanji as if blaming him for getting them all riled. But as he moved to unbolt the solid back door Sanji hissed, 'Just a moment.'

'What now?'

Sanji wasn't sure. The voice certainly sounded like Alec but there was something not quite right although he couldn't pin it down.

'Ask him about the spotlights.'

Anne gave a long-suffering sigh. 'Do as he says, Dave.'

'Did you turn off the lights?'

Alec's reply came back fast and furious. 'Look, I'm freezing my bollocks off out here. Are you going to open the fucking door or aren't you?'

'That's Alec all right,' Dave grinned.

He started to unfasten the bolts, locks and chains that secured the kitchen door.

'For God's sake hurry, will you?'

Something in the tone of Alec's voice warned Sanji that he had been right to be suspicious. There was a poorly disguised desperation there. It was the voice of a frightened man trying very hard to be brave. Sanji remembered that he still had Anne's revolver and he raised it, bringing it up into an unprofessional aim and pointing it at the two police officers.

'Get away from that door.'

They turned and looked at him, their initial bewilderment swiftly turning to anger. 'What the hell are you playing at? Where did you get that?'

'It's mine,' Anne said guiltily.

Dave scowled at her. 'Great. That's just great.'

'Slide the bolts shut again,' Sanji commanded.

Reluctantly Dave did as he was told. For a moment the door had been secured only by a single lock but as each second passed Sanji watched with satisfaction the defences being put back in place.

'What's up?' Alec's voice again.

Dave coughed in embarrassment. 'We've got a slight problem here. Won't take a minute.'

To his surprise Alec screamed back, 'Open the door now! If you don't they'll kill me!'

Dave reacted faster than Sanji would have thought possible, dropping instantly to the floor and pulling Anne down after him. A second later rounds from a high-velocity rifle pumped through the reinforced door, shaving straight through the empty space where the two police officers had been standing.

Sanji was the last to react, only saved from being hit by being out of the line of fire. But the bullets were now zipping across the kitchen. A shotgun blasted from outside but failed to penetrate the door's solid metal core. There were voices in the garden and Sanji saw Dave mentally counting them.

'Get to the panic button,' he whispered to Anne. She scuttled away on hands and knees to press the button in the sitting room. In the nearest police station an alarm would ring and, recognizing the identity of the safe house, the duty officer would task armed officers to attend immediately.

'How long have we got before help comes?' Sanji called across softly.

Dave shrugged. 'Ten minutes? Fifteen maybe.'

Sanji shook his head. It was hopeless. They could never hold out that long. Their only chance was that the terrorists would realize an alarm had been raised and would want to get clear before reinforcements arrived. But a thought crossed his mind.

'The panic button. How's it connected to the station?'

'It's OK,' Dave reassured him, guessing his fear. 'It can't be cut like a telephone line. It's a radio signal.'

'Radio signals can be jammed.'

'Not this one. It's a special piece of kit. If its frequency's being jammed it automatically scans for another until it gets through and is acknowledged. There's no way they could jam the full spectrum.'

As if to prove his point Anne's head popped round the door and she gave the thumbs up. 'They're on their way.'

'Then all we've go to do is hang on.'

'Easier said than done.'

Dave crawled towards the sitting-room door, and once he was well out of the line of fire he called out for Alec. There was no reply.

'We've got to try and help him,' Anne said.

'He's beyond help now, believe me,' Sanji replied.

To his surprise Dave backed him up. 'He's right. There's nothing we can do for him.'

The front-door bell rang and the three of them jumped. Keeping low, Dave crawled towards the hall, directing Anne to stay and cover the kitchen entrance. Sanji followed him, returning the revolver to Anne before he went. The front door was as solid as the back.

There was a fireproof letter-box but it was made of solid metal, the outer face being the weakest so that any letter bomb would blow harmlessly outwards. To a casual eye the leaded windows were of dimpled glass in mock-Tudor style, but Sanji had been told that only a high-velocity bullet could penetrate them. Hand-grenades would bounce off and all low-velocity rounds would disintegrate on contact.

From outside the front door a voice hailed them.

'David, we want Mr Sanji. We don't want to harm either you or Anne. Just open the door and send him out to us. You have my word that you'll come to no harm.'

Dave looked at Sanji and grinned mischievously. 'Tempting offer, you've got to admit.' But he raised his voice and shouted back, 'You know I can't do that. Why don't you lay down your weapons and give yourself up?'

There was a hoot of laughter from the other side of the door.

'I won't give you another chance . . .'

'Then sod off and don't bother,' Dave snapped back.

Sanji was about to thank him when through the curtained dining-room windows he saw fleeting shapes darting round the side of the house.

'They're trying to attack from another angle,' he warned.

'They can try any bloody angle they like.'

For a while everything went silent. Sanji looked at his watch and saw that at least five minutes had elapsed since Anne had sounded the alarm. He was puzzled.

Surely the terrorists must know that help would be on the way. Even if they reckoned they had sufficient fire-power to shoot their way out, they would know that once contact had been made the police would pour men in until the situation was under control. It would be extremely difficult for the terrorists to break contact and effect a clean getaway.

His questions were answered by a shout from the back garden, followed immediately by the ear-splitting roar of a rocket launcher and the deafening explosion of the munition impacting through the kitchen door.

'Anne!' Dave screamed, forgetting his own safety and getting to his feet. Instantly a hail of high-velocity bullets tore through the front door, threatening to cut him down. Sanji kicked out and hit him behind the knees, knocking him to the floor.

'Stay down!'

Together they scrambled back through the sitting room towards the kitchen. Bullets were now punching through every window, the firers standing as close as they could and aiming down into the rooms, hoping to catch the invisible fugitives on the inside.

'Why don't you shoot back?' Sanji hissed.

'Wouldn't do any bloody good. My bullets would just ricochet off the inside of the windows.'

The inside of the kitchen was an appalling mess. The cupboards had been blown off the walls and every piece of crockery was smashed, splinters littering the debris-strewn floor. The table on which Anne had so recently been splayed had broken in half and the mixer tap at the sink had been torn off so that cold water fountained into the air and spattered in a cascade on to the floor.

Under a layer of dust and debris, Anne lay motionless next to the shattered table. Dave and Sanji crawled to her side and carefully rolled her over to check for a pulse.

'She's still alive.'

'God knows how.'

Sanji glanced up at the door and saw a large, round hole in the centre where the shaped charge of the rocket had driven through. They had only seconds before the terrorists completed the destruction and gained entry to the house.

'Get her into the sitting room. Upstairs if you can,' he said.

He located her revolver and snatched it up. 'Go!'

'You take her. I'll have to stay here to hold them off,' Dave protested.

'I couldn't lift her.'

'But you don't know how to fire that.'

Sanji waved him away. 'It can't be that hard. Now go.'

As Dave half dragged and half carried Anne from the room towards the stairs, Sanji looked up to see a hand-grenade bouncing through the hole and on to the kitchen floor. The handle had gone and as it hit the surface and came to a stop it was spinning like a top. He threw himself into the sitting room and slammed the door the moment it exploded. The door shredded, blown off its hinges by the force of the blast. But it had served its purpose, taking the full force of the explosion and saving Sanji on the other side.

He stuck his head back into the kitchen, gagging on the fumes, to see through the smog a hand sticking through the hole and feeling for the door locks which still held. Bringing his revolver into a wobbly aim, he closed one eye to sight the weapon, then squeezed the trigger. The recoil was not as great as he had expected but the noise was worse, leaving his ears ringing. He had missed, the mark of his bullet a good six inches from the hole, although it had done its job. The hand had gone, its owner not knowing that the gun was being fired by an amateur.

That should give us a few precious seconds, Sanji thought. And every second counted now.

There was a shout from upstairs as Dave called down that they had made it to the top unscathed. Sanji scuttled after them, crouching into a corner as a hail of rounds powered through the front door and fired the length of the hall. But the moment they ceased he was on his feet and pumping up the stairs with the speed of a man thirty years younger.

'Help me with these,' Dave shouted when he reached the landing.

He was manhandling every item of furniture he could find to the top of the stairs and stacking it to form a barricade.

'It might delay them a bit longer.'

Sanji was panting furiously, his heart pounding as he stuffed the revolver in his belt and laid hands on chairs, mattresses, chests of drawers, bedside tables – everything that could be carried by two men.

Suddenly from the kitchen there was a second explosion, different from the first. Dave automatically dropped to the floor in reaction. 'Plastic explosive. They've blown the locks. They'll be inside now.'

As if in confirmation, they heard the sound of booted feet pounding through the downstairs rooms and into the hall.

'At least I can fire back now,' Dave said, and putting the barrel of his revolver through a gap in the barricade he pulled the trigger. There was an answering cry of pain and someone fell heavily. Shouts rang through the ground floor of the house as instructions were barked out.

'What's he saying?'

Sanji strained to listen, but his ears were still ringing with the cacophony of noise. 'Something about going into every room.'

Dave looked puzzled. 'What good will that do? They must know we're all up here.'

They got their answer a moment later when the intruders started to fire up through the ceilings. Although the exterior openings of the house had been reinforced, the internal floors were like those of any other suburban dwelling, a thin mixture of concrete, plaster and wood. To high-velocity bullets they presented little obstacle. In every upstairs room and all along the landing, bullets started to burst through, their lethal potential magnified by the fragments of concrete and wood that they took with them.

'Quick! Into the bedroom!' Dave shouted. It was the largest of the upstairs rooms and therefore the one which would be hardest for the terrorists to cover with fire from below.

Once inside, they flattened themselves against the

walls, watching in terror as hole after hole appeared in the floor, the bullets continuing up through the ceiling. Sanji started to say something but Dave waved him to be quiet, whispering, 'Don't let them hear you. If they get a fix on your position they'll drill the area around you with lead.'

To his horror, as he was pinned against the bedroom wall, Sanji heard the sound of someone coming up the stairs and laying hands on the far side of the barricade to tear it down. His eyes met Dave's, both men acknowledging that if the terrorists got through they were done for.

Dave gripped his revolver in both hands, smiled at Sanji and started towards the door. His steps must have been heard from below because he hadn't gone three paces when a long, unbroken burst of fire shot up through the floorboards at his feet and bracketed him. He spun on the spot and as his face came round Sanji saw that one of the bullets had removed his jaw. The revolver fell to the floor, clattering all the way to the door-frame and his hands came up to the horrific wound. But there was nothing to be done. He sank to his knees and as he toppled forward a second burst found him again, pumping into his chest.

Sanji stared transfixed at the jerking body. So this is it, he thought bitterly. This is how I am to end my days, cornered like some rat. He sank into a ball in the corner, gripped his revolver and aimed it at the bedroom door. The firing from below had stopped now that the terrorists had gained the upper floor. Out on the landing Sanji heard the approach of footsteps. There was a crash as the door to the next room was kicked in, followed by prolonged bursts of firing. Voices, and then more steps, coming closer, approaching, bringing with them death.

8

Anne felt as if she was floating, dimly aware that she had to fight to regain consciousness if she was not to lose it for ever. Above her she could see something whirling. It was slightly out of focus but, try as she might, she couldn't make it any clearer. Then, with one momentous effort, she screwed up her eyes and when she opened them again she saw that she was staring at circular patterns in the plasterwork of a bedroom ceiling.

For a moment she was confused. How had she come to be there? The last thing she remembered was . . . what? The past was a blank, at least the recent past was. Further back she could remember an interview. She was enlisting in the police force. She could remember small-arms training, a run, a passing-out parade. Yes, things were starting to return. She could remember a building, a police station, she thought, and then a briefing, the details of a close-protection job.

With sudden embarrassment she remembered Dave and the kitchen table, and flinched away from the recollection as if there was someone else with her inside her mind who might see her being screwed that way. But she had liked Dave. It wasn't the first time they had

had sex. She couldn't call it lovemaking; she was too truthful for that. The first time had been in a patrol car on a stake-out, the tenseness of the situation adding to the thrill of the act. Then there had been the second morning of the present assignment. Alec had been out and the Indian gentleman had been asleep. It had been early morning and she was in the shower. Dave had been on watch throughout the night and had come in to shave. They had done it there, on the bathroom floor. She had had to bite her lip to keep from making a sound, but it had been great. The best.

She tried to move and winced with sudden pain. What the hell had happened? For an instant she thought it might have been the sex, but this was a very different ache and far less pleasant. With a shock she remembered seeing the Indian staring at her from the kitchen door. It had been terrible. Until then it had been terrific. She saw again the stairs as she padded up them to wash. Dave had laddered her stockings but she hadn't bothered to change them. Who the hell was there to notice in the safe house?

Image by image the past swam back into view. She had gone downstairs and then . . . yes, there had been the question of the lights, Alec's voice, the Indian's caution, and then . . .

She turned her head and a bolt of pain rocketed down the length of her back and legs, reaching to the very soles of her feet. With the vision, however, came the noise, drifting in as if from a far distance. She became aware of the sound of shooting and then of the air around her being alive with fragments of wood, concrete and plaster.

'My God,' she murmured, her syllables slurred so that even she was unable to recognize them. 'They're in the house.'

She realized at once what must have happened and tilted her head towards the door. Someone had carried her into one of the bedrooms. She remembered that there were four bedrooms and she recognized her present location as the smallest one, at the very end of the corridor. Bullets were tearing through the floor, fired from below and someone was coming up the stairs. Anne clenched and unclenched her fingers, relieved to find she could. Slowly she moved them across her body, searching for the wounds. There seemed to be cuts and bruises all over her, but nothing too serious. The shock waves from the rocket exploding in such a confined space must have caused severe concussion. She felt her ears and sure enough there was dried blood there.

She struggled to sit up but it was hopeless, so instead she rolled first on to her side and then her stomach. She knew it would be no use trying to push her body up as all her limbs felt drained of strength, but when she attempted to crawl she found it was just possible to move. Seeing the fire still coming sporadically through the floorboards, she skirted the edge of the room until she reached the door and then eased it open. Peering through the crack, she saw the back of a man disappear into the first of the bedrooms. There was a hail of gunfire and then the crash of furniture and slamming doors as he ransacked the room and cupboards in search of his prey. She ducked out of sight as the man re-emerged but luckily he was looking down at the M16 rifle in his hands, too busy clearing a stoppage and reloading with a fresh magazine, to notice her.

It was then that she heard a noise in the next-door bedroom and instantly guessed that it must be Mr Sanji. If Dave was still alive, she reasoned, she would have heard him firing or at least shouting to try to reason with the terrorists. But there was nothing – only the noise that sounded like someone crawling along the other side of the wall.

Desperately Anne thought whether there was anything she could do. There were several options. She could lie on the floor and play dead. After all, the terrorist would see ample blood on her. But no. His most likely reaction would be to fire a couple of shots into her head at point-blank range to make quite certain.

She could try to hide under the bed or in a cupboard, but she had no sooner thought of it than she rejected the whole idea. This was a terrorist house-clearance operation, not a theatrical farce with the comedians dashing from room to room to avoid being detected. She had already heard him firing into every possible piece of cover in the other room, following it up with a visual search. He would obviously do the same to her room, but she'd rather die in the open than stuffed away in some claustrophobic cupboard.

For a moment she toyed with the idea of trying to escape. Perhaps it would be possible to force one of the security windows open. She smiled sardonically. And what the devil would she do then? Knot the bedsheets together and climb down like an eloping schoolgirl? She couldn't even get to her feet, so jumping down was out of the question, and there was no way she could make it downstairs, where the other terrorists were guarding the exits, waiting for their comrade to complete his mission and rejoin them.

The only other thing she could think of was to tackle the man in some way. She couldn't possibly do it head-on. She would have to catch him completely by surprise and even then she would only get one shot at it.

One shot! With cold dread she realized that she was unarmed. Her revolver was nowhere to be seen. She would have to improvise a weapon from something.

But what if she was successful? There was an unknown number of people downstairs. Nevertheless, her surprise attack on the lone terrorist might just buy enough time for the reinforcements to arrive. They could not be far away now.

She hunted around the room until her eyes fell upon an iron standing inoffensively on a shelf, its flex wrapped tightly round the handle.

'Come here, my beauty,' she whispered. 'Time for a bit of housework.'

Even with the iron firmly in her grasp she still felt little better than defenceless. How was she going to achieve surprise? In her present condition she wasn't capable of any great speed or stealth. The best moment, she reasoned, would be when the terrorist himself was off his guard, and that would be the moment he thought he had got what he wanted. So what was she to do? Wait until he had shot Mr Sanji? Perhaps. But she was uncomfortable with the idea of saving her own skin by sacrificing the life of the man she was supposed to be guarding. However, what if she was able to catch the terrorist at the moment he detected Mr Sanji? He might just pause for a second and perhaps even question him. Yes, that was it.

Taking care not to reveal her presence, she peered through the crack in the door and saw that the terrorist had cleared his weapon and reloaded and was approaching the neighbouring bedroom. Its door was closed and as he reached it he braced himself back against the banisters and prepared to kick it open. Anne shuffled to her knees in readiness. Her head swam and for a couple of seconds her vision blurred, but as she heard the thump of his boot and the splintering of wood, she moved.

The half-dozen paces to the adjoining bedroom were the longest distance she had ever covered, not just because of her injuries, but because she had never killed anyone before. And although she tried to suppress the thought of what she was about to try to do, it chilled her to the bone.

The man's back came slowly into view. He was standing just inside the doorway, his rifle pointing into the room ready to fire from the hip. He was saying something, and with a feeling of triumph Anne realized she had been right. His complete attention was on Sanji's quaking response. The terrorist was ordering him to drop his revolver and as Anne closed the last couple of feet behind him she saw the old man about to comply.

The iron felt surprisingly light in her hand as she swung it up and brought it down with all her remaining might on the crown of the terrorist's head. She had angled it point down and with a sickening crunch she felt it drive into the man's skull. It was as if an unseen puppeteer had cut the strings holding him in play and his body crumpled to the floor, where it lay twitching spasmodically. The thought crossed Anne's mind that perhaps she should wield her terrible weapon again but the tell-tale pool of blood signalled that her immediate task was done, and in any case she doubted she would have been able to muster the strength for a second decisive blow.

A voice called up the stairs.

'He's asking his comrade why it's taking such a long time,' Sanji translated in a whisper.

Anne sank to her knees and retrieved the M16. She had never fired one before but had once used a Heckler & Koch on the indoor range and figured that the mechanism couldn't be all that dissimilar.

'Let them try and get us now,' she threatened weakly, leaning back against the door-frame, the rifle across her lap and pointing down the landing.

Sanji crawled across to her. 'Let me take that. You haven't got the strength.'

But she clung to it doggedly. 'If they come again, use your revolver.' She reached across and picked up Dave's, which was lying nearby. 'Hold this in the other hand and fire them both at once. It doesn't matter if you can't aim properly. They won't know that.'

The voice sounded again, this time more urgent. Sanji paled when he heard another terrorist start up the stairs but now there was another sound, farther away and fainter, but growing louder with every second. It was a police siren.

'About bloody time the cavalry got here,' Anne wheezed.

There was one last shout up the stairs and then they caught sight of a head poking round the corner. Anne squeezed the trigger and to her shock and relief the M16 sprang into life, jarring back in her loose grasp but nevertheless spraying its 5.56mm high-velocity rounds in the right direction. The terrorist cursed and ducked back out of sight. A stream of abuse poured at them from their unseen attackers but the siren was louder than ever now and Sanji and Anne could hear others close by.

A final volley of bullets pocked through the floor-boards, but wild and random, venting the defeated terrorists' frustration rather than claiming the victims they so desired. And then they were gone.

Out in the road there was the sound of a car engine, spinning tyres and a powerful engine accelerating away. A few moments later the sirens were wailing at the end of the street, car doors were slamming and there were footsteps pounding down the driveway. Hearing them, Anne closed her eyes and the rifle slipped from her bloodied hands. The last thing she had seen was Dave's lifeless body in the middle of the bedroom floor. So that was that, Dave and Alec were dead and she herself had escaped the same fate by the narrowest of margins. And what for? The strange little Indian man kneeling concernedly next to her, about whom she had been told virtually nothing.

* * *

The officer in command of the police firearms unit went through the house as the bodies were being taken away and stared in amazement at the damage. He had never seen anything like it.

'It looks like a bloody war zone.'

He turned at the remark from the young constable next to him, and said, 'Did you see what the bastards did to Alec?'

'No?' the youngster queried with morbid interest.

'Well, take my advice and don't.'

'What about Anne?'

'What about her?'

'Will she live?'

The police officer shrugged. 'I only had a quick word with the doc but he seemed to think so. She's a tough one.'

He made his way back to the sitting room, where Mr Sanji was sitting in the armchair, his head in his hands.

'It's all right now, sir.' We've got the situation under control,' he told the old man.

Sanji looked up at him doubtfully. 'Did you catch them?'

The officer quickly busied himself with his holster. 'Erm, not yet.'

'Then how can you say you have the situation under control?'

'We'll get them all right. It's only a matter of time.'

'And so long as they remain at large it's only a matter of time before they get me,' Sanji replied sourly.

The policeman opened his mouth to reassure him but decided to remain silent. He could well be correct after all. There had clearly been a security breach and investigations were already underway to discover the leak.

There were voices in the hall and Chief Inspector Chiltern came in. 'Hello, Ted. Everything OK?'

'Could be better. I was just trying to put Mr Sanji's mind at rest, saying he was safe in our hands.'

Chiltern stared back stony-faced. 'He isn't in our hands any more. There's a car waiting for him outside.' He turned to Sanji. 'Ted will take you to it.'

Sanji looked from one to the other in bewilderment. 'What's going on?'

'Everything will be explained outside, Mr Sanji,' Chiltern replied, not without a trace of bitterness.

Getting the impression that further questioning would prove fruitless, Sanji got shakily to his feet and hobbled after the police officer. As he exited through the front door, he took one last look at the supposed safe house and then went out into the night.

Unlike before, the house was now in a blaze of light. The spotlights had been switched on and in the driveway and road the headlights of cars, vans and ambulances criss-crossed the lawns, while blues and reds flashed on every vehicle roof. However, much to Sanji's surprise, he was led in the other direction, towards the only remaining area of gloom. As he left the glare behind and his eyes became adjusted to the dark, he was able to make out the shapes of three nondescript cars. They were parked in a row, the front and rear cars each appearing to contain four men, and as Sanji walked past the rear car he glanced at the men sitting in it. Even that one restricted view showed him that they were a very different bunch from the Alecs and Daves of the world. All four were lean and could even be described as slight, but from their wiriness he could guess that they were physically very fit. Their eyes were the most noticeable thing about them, alert and wide awake, taking in everything at a glance. Although they were seated in the car, they seemed somehow to be full of energy and Sanji was struck by the impression of an unexploded bomb.

'Who are they?' he asked the police officer.

The man grunted an unintelligible reply from which Sanji deduced that he was none too happy about being required to hand over his charge to someone else. In effect he and his men had been relieved of duty.

The door to the centre car swung open as he approached. Sanji turned to thank the policeman but he was already walking back towards the house.

'Mr Sanji, welcome. Do get in out of the cold.'

The voice was warm and hospitable, but underneath was a formality that signalled a new professionalism. He stooped and lowered himself into the back seat of the car, the driver closing the door after him. All he wanted to do was sleep but he looked to his side to identify his host. The man was well dressed and trim, his greying hair neatly cut but too long to be military. He extended a hand towards Sanji.

'Tony Briggs. We're going to be looking after you from now on. You needn't worry about a thing.'

From the confidence in his voice and from the evidence of the men in the cars with them Sanji felt that for once he could believe this man.

'That's very kind,' he answered, taking the offered

hand and wincing at the hearty grip. 'Forgive my curiosity, but who exactly are you?'

'I represent the Intelligence services and the gentlemen in front and behind are members of the Special Air Service. I expect you've heard of them?'

'The SAS? Yes, of course I have.' He had picked up a book on the famous 22 Regiment after its relief of the Iranian Embassy siege, but had discarded it as propaganda, refusing to believe that any organization could be peopled by such characters. It was so obviously a ruse. However, now that he had glimpsed a handful of men belonging to it he began to wonder whether he had been too hasty in that assumption.

'How is it that you are involved? I mean, wouldn't an increased police guard suffice?'

Sir Anthony smiled indulgently. 'I'm no longer prepared to take that chance. Believe me, you'll be far safer in our hands.'

He reached over the seat and tapped the driver on the shoulder to signal that they should leave. The driver flashed his headlights at the front car and the procession pulled away. Sanji turned to have a last look at the house.

'I'd like to know how Anne Baron progresses, if that's possible.'

'Of course it is.'

'She saved my life, you see. She's a remarkable woman,' Sanji concluded, suppressing the image of her bent over the kitchen table, but only after he had dwelt on it for a few moments.

The little convoy shot away from the district in a very

different manner to the police convoy that had taken him there. Unlike the stolid, steady police procession, the SAS cars sped along, none of them seeming particularly concerned to keep the other cars close by. Now and again Sanji turned to look behind him. On most occasions the rear car was nowhere to be seen, but always, just when he was about to enquire whether they had perhaps become lost, he would glimpse its distant headlights in his driver's rear-view mirror. The lead car was similarly independent, shooting ahead and only once or twice coming into view. Yet even so, Sanji couldn't help feeling more secure than he had done in a very long time. There was no ponderous radio communication, no close tailing, and he began to wonder if contact was maintained telepathically.

He suddenly remembered that one of his questions remained unanswered. 'You haven't told me why British Intelligence is now involved.'

Sir Anthony smiled. 'Why shouldn't we be?'

'Well, after all, I'm a retired restaurant owner whose granddaughter's been kidnapped. What's it got to do with the British government?'

'Look, Mr Sanji. We can play these games if you like, but you and I both know who you are.' He paused. 'Or should I say, who you were.'

Sanji felt himself go cold. 'And who do you think I am?'

'Well, now you are exactly who you say you are, the founder and owner of the excellent Mogul chain of restaurants spread across south London. However, in 1947 – correct me if I'm wrong – you were an Indian government minister in Delhi responsible for the refugee resettlement programme. A minor one, I'll grant you, but nonetheless influential.'

Sanji quickly looked away, staring out of the car window into the dark. The car was streaming along a country road, the trees flashing past in a blur. So it wasn't only the Pakistanis who had found him.

'So what if I was?' he conceded at last.

'Perhaps you should put that to the men chasing you.'

'They never gave me the opportunity.'

Sir Anthony recrossed his long legs with difficulty in the confined space of the car, his hand tapping on his lap. 'We have traced the men who carried out the attack on your house in Southall. They were . . .'

'I know who they were.'

'Then why didn't you tell the police in the first place?'

Sanji closed his eyes and sighed heavily. 'I should have done. I'm sorry. I hoped to be able to avoid all this. I hoped . . .'

'What?'

'Oh, I don't know.' He turned to face Sir Anthony. 'Look, I'm a tired old man who just wants to be left alone. I thought I'd managed it, and then . . . all of this happens. My whole world gets torn apart.'

'Why do you think that is?'

'I don't know.'

Sir Anthony stared at him hard. 'Why do I get the feeling you're not levelling with me? Why would someone in Pakistan want you dead or a prisoner? I can only assume it has something to do with 1947 and the Independence troubles.'

'I don't know, I don't know, I don't know?' Sanji's head was pounding and he felt at the very edge of exhaustion.

He felt a hand patting his. 'All right. I'm sorry, old chap. We'll leave it until tomorrow.'

A thought suddenly crossed Sanji's mind as he watched the countryside speeding past. 'Where are we going?'

'Somewhere that really is safe. Somewhere we can talk and sort all this mess out. I'm no more prepared to have armed terrorists running around the country than you are.'

For a while Sanji dozed, sinking deeper into the seat until a bump in the road woke him. He glanced sideways at Sir Anthony but saw that he was looking out of the window. In the driver's rear-view mirror there was nothing to be seen but a black expanse of night. It surrounded them like some vast land of the dead. And then Sanji heard them, the voices of the countless dead, and he knew that he had to speak. He had kept quiet for too long. He had to unburden himself to someone, and the man next to him seemed as good as anyone.

'Mr Briggs?' he said at last.

Sir Anthony turned. 'Oh, I thought you were asleep.'

Sanji drew in his breath and began. 'I have something to tell you.'

By the time they arrived at Sir Anthony's country retreat, Don was more curious than ever about Mr Sanji. From his first meeting with Sir Anthony he had guessed that the wily old agent knew far more about the case than he was willing to admit to, certainly to Don. He had concluded their meeting by saying that all would soon be revealed.

After that the rest of the team had been assembled and he had been pleasantly surprised to recognize many old friends from Hereford. Once complete, they numbered eight in all, including Don, whom Sir Anthony placed in command. Their first sight of the mysterious Mr Sanji had been when they had gone to the police safe house with Sir Anthony to collect him. He had narrowly escaped death and Sir Anthony was concerned to remove him into their own far safer custody at the earliest opportunity.

The journey went smoothly, Don riding in the front car. His only other brief glimpse of Sanji was when they arrived at the country house and Don went to escort him inside while the other members of the team did a quick scan of the grounds.

Sanji was polite but visibly very tired from his recent ordeal. Don saw him to his room on the second floor, and noticed that Sir Anthony slipped away the moment the cars arrived. Before he disappeared, however, making for his own study, he drew Don aside for a moment and told him that his own CO would be briefing him the next morning.

'Will you be attending as well, sir?'

'No. I have to get back to Whitehall to do some checking. I'll be confirming details for the next phase of the operation with your CO, who will pass them on to you tomorrow. Right now I suggest you get some sleep. Any questions?'

Don had a thousand of them but recognized from Sir Anthony's tone that he had asked Don only out of form, and that he had not the slightest intention of providing him with any answers, at least not there and then. In any case, Don reflected as he watched Sir Anthony march away down the hall, he would prefer to tackle his CO with them. He would be more likely to get a reasonable response from him.

His own room was directly next to Sanji's and the two were linked by a door. A change of clothes for Sanji had been provided by a police team that had brought them from Bramley Road. Don was tempted to have a chat with the old fellow before he went to sleep but no sooner had he knocked on the door and peered round than he heard the sound of snores. Sanji was lying on the bed, still fully dressed, and fast asleep.

Before turning in himself, Don checked with every member of the team that they were all in position. The house was sealed tighter than a drum, with the police providing both an outer cordon and other guards closer in. The role of the SAS troopers was to concentrate on the close protection. If anyone got through the armed police this time, they'd be in for a very nasty surprise. Don had taken the team round every inch of the building and they had spent the day conducting rehearsals in the event of an attack, running through their reactions to every possible combination of assault techniques, so that by the time Mr Sanji was safely in bed they each knew exactly how to react whatever happened.

However, the night passed without incident, as Don had expected. He knew that the terrorist organization would be unlikely to make another attempt on Sanji's life and liberty at such short notice so soon after their last operation. It was also to be hoped that the leak had been discovered and cut, so that no more information would be passed to the terrorists.

The following morning Don was up before first light, having slept for only a few hours. He started by touring the house and when he was satisfied that it was secure he went around the garden and grounds with two of his men.

'What time's the boss coming?' Rob Lindsay asked.

'Nine. He'll be briefing me first and then once I'm happy with the mission I'll sketch out a rough outline plan and then call you all in. I've got a feeling I'm going to need every brain working on this one.'

Rob scratched his head. 'Er, shit, boss. You didn't say I needed to bring it with me.'

'Ha bloody ha.'

When they had completed the clearing patrol, they returned inside and Don went quietly to Sanji's room. The old man was still asleep and Don thought it best to leave him in peace. He could get all the information that he needed from him later.

A cooked breakfast had been laid on in the dining room, and as soon as it was over Don made his way to the library, where he had been told to expect his boss. Sure enough, shortly before nine, a car drew up in the driveway by the front door and a moment later the library door opened and the CO walked in.

'Morning, Don.' Colonel Clive Barrett went briskly to the desk, slapped down his briefcase and opened it, taking out a wad of printed paper, files and maps.

'We've got a lot of ground to cover, so let's get cracking. I ordered coffee on the way in. We're going to need it.'

Don pulled up a chair opposite Barrett. 'I hope you're going to be able to tell me what all this is about, boss.'

'I'll tell you all I know. That Tony Briggs is a tight-lipped bastard. He's hardly given me much background information.' With his papers arrayed in front of him he sat down and paused to catch his breath. 'Right. Here's the mission. You're to go to Pakistan, locate the girl who was kidnapped from Bramley Road, rescue her and bring her back to Britain. Any problems?'

Don felt his mouth drop open. 'Just a few, sir.'

Barrett sat back and smiled. 'It's all right. I've got a bit of information for you.' He pushed a file across the table. 'Read this. It will give you everything we know about the organization we're up against.'

'Is it Pakistani secret service?'

'Good Lord, no. Their government's got nothing at all to do with it. That much we do know. This organization is strictly freelance, though a lot of them are ex-special forces.'

'I gathered as much from the way they handled themselves. What's the op going to be called?'

Barrett grinned. 'How about Operation Takeaway? It seems kind of fitting, given Sanji's business interests and the kidnap of his granddaughter.'

Don groaned. 'If you insist.'

'Thank you for humouring me. Now then, here's what

I propose, although of course the details of the plan will be completely up to you.'

Naturally, Don thought. And when the whole thing turns to rat shit, guess who'll take the rap?

9

For Eli the journey seemed to drag on interminably. Several times the plane landed to refuel, each time at anonymous-looking airstrips. It had obviously all been planned well in advance because people were waiting and the whole procedure was carried out with the minimum of fuss. Although the others on board took each opportunity to walk up and down the tarmac to stretch their legs, she was ordered to stay on the aircraft, closely watched by one of the guards.

After one of the halts, Ceda Bandram handed her a drink that had been included in the pack of supplies and from the writing on the can she saw that they had stopped in Libya. He saw her looking at the Arabic script.

'As you see, we have influential friends,' he told her.

'Influential with whom? Libya's hardly everyone's favourite country, is it?' she answered.

'Only for now. Tomorrow or the next day they'll be back in the fold. Western politicians are the most fickle in the world. The second they see an advantage to be gained from it, they will be wooing even their worst enemies. The only reason they dislike Gaddafi is because he dared to stand up to them.

In the Americans' view that is the worst crime of all.'

Eli decided against pursuing the point. So far Ceda had treated her reasonably and she didn't want to antagonize him. She was certain that she would soon be needing all the help she could get. Far better to appease him, lull him into a feeling that she was just a docile victim. Then, if an opportunity to escape presented itself, she would be ready to seize it. Hopefully, that would be the last thing Ceda and his colleagues would be expecting.

The plane flew on and now that Eli had got her bearings she speculated on its route. From Libya it passed over the southern regions of Egypt before crossing the Red Sea. Then there was a seemingly endless expanse of desert which she was certain must be Saudi Arabia. There was another stop at a desert airstrip and this time she guessed from the dress and features of the people that they were in the Yemen. After that they took off and flew out to sea and for the next few hours she could see that they were over water, the Arabian Sea.

It was the attitude of her fellow-passengers that finally told her that they were nearing the Pakistani coast. Long before land was sighted they were peering through the small, oval windows, and then someone shouted out and pointed eagerly. Ceda leaned over to look and Eli saw a smile crease his lips.

'Who said we wouldn't make it?' he asked triumphantly.

'The game's not over yet.'

'Oh this is no game, my dear. It's far too serious for that.'

Eli resisted the temptation to rise to the bait a second time.

'Anyway who's going to come after you?' Ceda went on. 'The Indian government won't be interested and even if they were there's nothing they could do to help you. They wouldn't dare send troops over the border and risk starting another Indo-Pakistan war. And if the Indian government can't help then the British certainly won't. What are you expecting? The SAS to come storming after us?'

He laughed and added, 'They'd hardly be interested in a single kidnap victim. And even if they did come we'd have a surprise waiting for them when they arrived. As you will see.'

Eli couldn't help wondering what he meant by that. He didn't seem to be afraid of anything.

Down below she could see the brown flatlands and waterways of a river estuary and as if in answer to her enquiry Ceda turned to her and said, 'The Indus. One of the great rivers of the world.'

He stared down at it as the plane followed its course. 'It was along the Indus valley that the first human settlements were established, before Egypt and the Nile even. The Indus, the Tigris and the Euphrates. These were the cradles of civilization. People in the West look down on us now. Few of them realize that our ancestors were living in cities while theirs were still shivering in damp caves. We enjoyed art and culture while they were scratching at cave walls with crude stone implements. And it all began down there,' he said, pointing to the dark, meandering line.

The Indus seemed to go on for ever. Eli rested her head against the seat back and fell asleep, and when she awoke a couple of hours later she looked out of the window and saw that they were still flying along the river's course. Nor had the countryside around it changed. If anything, it was even more barren and when she asked Ceda the reason he answered, 'That's the Thal Desert down below. Pray that we don't have to crash-land here.'

She remembered from her knowledge of the region's geography that if they were crossing the Thal Desert then they were just to the east of the mountainous North-West Frontier Province and most likely en route for Rawalpindi. But when she at last noticed the outlying sprawl that heralded a city of such a size, the plane flew on, only beginning to descend when it was far to the north and the towering blue ranges of the Karakoram mountains were in sight.

'That's Muzaffarabad,' Ceda said, noticing her querying look. 'It's not far now.'

The plane started to lose height shortly afterwards and Eli caught sight of the thin line of a landing strip growing larger with every second. The pilot banked sharply as he dropped down towards it and she was able to get a good look at the surrounding countryside. Everywhere was brown and desolate, the land rising abruptly into bleak, barren hills.

Lining up on the runway, the plane swooped down on to the strip and sped to a halt, turning on the spot before the pilot cut the engines. On board everyone stretched and smiled happily. They were home.

From the edge of the makeshift airfield three old,

battered Land Rovers headed out towards the plane as the crew opened the door and Ali and the others filed out on to firm ground. Ceda helped her out and steered her towards the newest of the vehicles.

'It's a bit of a rough ride from here. We're more likely to make it in one piece if we ride in this one,' he said, playing the charming host.

From the airstrip they drove in convoy into Muzaffarabad, Ceda explaining that they had to pick up supplies.

'Why? Where are we going?' Eli asked.

'Since it's not likely to do you any good to know, I can't see any harm in telling you,' Ceda conceded. 'My uncle owns some land north of here, up close to the Kashmiri border.'

'You mean the Indian border,' she corrected him.

He smiled sourly. 'Kashmir should always have been Pakistani. The British messed things up when they drew up the boundaries in 1947. The entire population is Muslim, after all.'

'It's still Indian territory,' Eli persisted.

'Not for long, if we have our way.'

'What do you mean? Is that why you want my grandfather?'

'Never you mind,' Ceda said abruptly. 'Perhaps my uncle will feel like telling you more.'

Eli was keen to keep the conversation going. Every scrap of information was potentially useful if she was going to get away somehow. 'So tell me about this land your uncle owns. Does he have a house there?'

'A house?' Ceda chuckled. 'You could say that. But why don't you wait and see for yourself?'

I will, Eli thought. But don't expect me to stick around. If you think I'm some helpless woman, then you've got another think coming. The first chance I get I'll be out of here.

The bazaar was a ramshackle affair, and after stacking sack upon sack of provisions in the back of each of the Land Rovers, the convoy set off again, heading north out of the town along the Neelam Road. Once more Eli recalled her knowledge of the region. The River Neelam wound parallel with the border. It was a wild area of thick woodland and mountain and if the Bandrams were involved in some sort of nefarious dealings with the Kashmiris, then it was an ideal location. Pakistani governmental control was far from secure and all manner of bandits and tribespeople carried on lives of smuggling unchanged for centuries.

As she had suspected, the road crossed over rivers and made its way steadily upwards, climbing into pine forests that stretched up the sheer mountainsides. The bridges were rickety affairs and the roads were almost entirely unmade, riddled with potholes and often cracked completely in two by landslides. Whenever they encountered any such obstacle the drivers simply engaged the vehicles' four-wheel drive and skirted around the edges until they were clear.

Even though she was tired beyond belief, Eli fought to keep her eyes open. The scenery was spectacular so it wasn't too hard, but the main reason was to try to lodge in her mind a picture of the ground over which she might have to travel should she be able to effect an escape. She realized that to attempt to cross into India would be all but impossible. The mountains were steep and swept with snow at this time of year. Her best hope was to make her way south and try to find a Pakistani army camp or a police station. Then she would simply have to hope that they were not in league with the Bandrams.

At one point they stopped for a short break beside a river. She was allowed to walk down to the edge and even considered making a break for it. She was confident that if she pretended she wanted to relieve herself they would let her go unaccompanied into the trees. But where would she go from there? No. Now was not the time or the place. She would have to prepare herself first, lay up a secret store of supplies somehow, lull them into a false sense of security, and then, at a time of her own choosing, make her bid for freedom.

She crouched down by the water's edge. It was crystal-clear and cold. The trees whispered in the light breeze and they were so high that the snow crept down almost to their level. Another mile or two and she guessed that they would have entered the snowline proper.

A voice from the Land Rovers hailed her, shouting that they were about to leave. She waved that she was on her way but wet her face first with the icy water. It brought her vividly awake and she gasped with the shock of it.

It was four hours later that the lead vehicle rounded a corner and drew to a halt.

'There we are,' Ceda announced. 'Our destination. Looks a bit like Shangri-La, doesn't it?'

Reluctantly, Eli felt she had to agree, and the prospect

of spending some time there would have been almost pleasant had she not known that the place was to be her prison. But pushing to the fore of her emotions was a sinking dread, for the instant she set eyes on their destination she realized how absurd her notions of escape now were.

It was not so much a house as a hilltop fortress, with walls surrounded on three sides by sheer drops that fell into a tumbling river.

'Legend has it that it was built by Yashman, a brigand, over two centuries ago,' Ceda said proudly. 'Apparently he and later his ancestors held out against the forces of the British Raj until the very end of the nineteenth century, and even then it was only because of treachery that the citadel fell. Some slighted relative betrayed the family to the British and opened the gates one night. It was after a festival and the guards were all drunk. The British stormed in and massacred the lot. Only the leader was taken captive. There was some sort of show trial, after which he was thrown into jail, where he died several years later.'

'And what happend to the disgruntled relative?'

'I'm glad you asked that,' he replied with a sinister grin. 'Another family member caught up with him eventually and slipped a cobra into his bed. But before he did so he had milked most of the beast's poison so that when it bit the traitor it took him several days to die. By the end he was writhing in agony and begging for the release of death.'

Eli stared up at the fortress, watching it grow higher and higher before her as they approached. Her heart sank and for the first time since leaving England she felt truly lost and beyond the reach of help.

'Tell us another, Jerry.'

Jerry Patel paused from his telling of anecdotes from India and sat back in his seat, waiting for the air hostess to set down his meal. From beneath the tin-foil lid of the little tray an aroma was struggling to get out, and when it did Jerry thought it might have been for the better had it failed. He squinted across at Rod's menu.

'What's this supposed to be?'

Rod traced the name with his finger. 'Chicken Madras.' He grinned. 'Up your street, mate. Wog scoff.'

'The Army Catering Corps might think so, but take it from me, this has got nothing to do with what you so politely call wog scoff.'

Rod sniggered. He liked Jerry, even if the lad was the new boy in the team. He enjoyed ribbing him, as did all the lads, but then that was just the way of it. No one meant anything by the name-calling. Everyone had their tag. Rod was a cockney, Geoff a Geordie, Alan a Taff, Tom a West Country yokel, and Jimmie was naturally a Jock. Sergeant Gavin Steward, the archetypal Essex man, had been virtually dragged screaming out of retirement in the Training Wing and Captain Don Headley was the fly-boy in the ointment of the team, a nondescript Home Counties wallah, but good enough for an officer.

Jerry tested his food with the fork and lifted a morsel to his mouth. It wasn't quite as bad as it looked, although his mother would have had a fit at the thought of anyone daring to call it a curry. He looked about him. The British

Airways flight to Delhi was about two-thirds full and all the passengers were busy tucking into their meals before the start of the film. It seemed strange to be going to India. Born in England, he had only been to India once, on holiday with his parents, and even that had been a number of years ago. He could remember visiting a string of relatives, all of whom he had heard of but none of whom he had ever met before. But the overriding memory of that trip had been a sense of dislocation. He felt that he didn't belong there, although in a deeper sense he felt that he did. It was difficult to explain. His cultural roots had become tangled by his parents' emigration to Britain, yet even though they had done everything in their power to integrate him into his adopted country they had at the same time ensured that he absorbed his cultural heritage. He had therefore been taught to speak both Hindi and Urdu, although he counted English as his native tongue, and in Britain he had attended the local Hindu temple with his parents, while learning about Christianity at school.

For a while he had been very confused by the mixture, but in time he had come to accept it. Now, however, he regarded his broad education as a source of strength. The SAS greatly valued language skills and it seemed that he was about to put his own to good use on an operation.

He had been intrigued, as had all the lads in the team, by Captain Headley's briefing. Although their final destination lay over the Pakistani border Captain Headley had decided to conduct the approach to it through India and in particular the province of Kashmir. Jerry had never been to Kashmir before and relished the opportunity to see it for himself. He had read so much about it and as part of his own preparation for the operation he had carried out a thorough map study. He had to admit that he was surprised at the SAS getting involved in such a rescue mission in the first place, but Captain Headley had said that the victim was no ordinary person. Apparently there were higher political reasons why she had to be brought home and for Jerry that was enough. Give me the task, he thought, and that's all I need to know.

He had been longing to tell his parents where he was going but in accordance with SAS security procedures he had kept quiet, even during the weekend visit he had made to his home after the last exercise in Wales. When he had finally staggered back into camp carrying Sergeant Steward's load of batteries he had flopped exhausted into bed and slept for twelve hours. But realizing that he was in danger of wasting his weekend he had driven home and spent a relaxing couple of days with his family. He had taken advantage of the trip home to question his parents surreptitiously about Kashmir and had been happy to glean a number of useful tips from his father.

Now, sitting back in his seat, he listened contentedly to the purring of the engines, consumed by the feeling that he had made it. Instantly he remembered yet again the old adage about not having made it until the Regiment was finished with you, but nevertheless there he was, sitting on the plane, a member of an SAS operational team on his way to a mission. He glanced around at the other passengers, wondering if any of them could possibly feel such happiness or fulfilment. Could any of them guess that he and the men with him were special? Marked out for great deeds? He smiled, pushing away his tray and taking up his coffee instead. Whatever might happen on the mission he knew in his heart that he had already attained an important goal. Even if he were to die in the mountains of Kashmir he had at least achieved something in life.

The airport in Delhi was chaotic and Don Headley almost missed the man from the British High Commission. As India was a member of the Commonwealth it didn't have an embassy, although the High Commission served much the same purpose.

Head bobbing above the crowd of taxi drivers and porters, all of whom were furiously vying for trade, the British official had dressed in the hope of appearing inconspicuous. In consequence he resembled a character from a Humphrey Bogart movie, dressed in a crumpled, sweat-stained linen suit that once upon a time might have been white.

'Captain Headley?' he whispered conspiratorially from behind his hand.

Don stared at him in disbelief. 'Who's asking?'

The man grinned knowingly, as if expecting an exchange of passwords. 'Knowles. Terence. British High Commission.'

He pronounced his identity with great seriousness.

'Headley. Donald. British Army,' Don responded in kind.

Knowles glanced theatrically to left and right, thrilling at the melodrama that had dragged him away from his in-tray. 'Follow me, Captain. Transport is waiting.'

Don looked round at his men, who stood behind him in an amused gaggle.

Prancing on tiptoes like a moorhen, Knowles stepped towards the exit.

'Anyone would think he's looking for trip-wires,' Gavin Steward whispered in Don's ear.

'He's a natural, isn't he? Nice mover.'

Transport consisted of two vans. At a signal from Knowles, the drivers pulled up at the kerb and the SAS team piled in, stacking their kit alongside them.

'Has the hardware arrived?' Don asked.

Knowles tapped the side of his nose with his forefinger. 'Diplomatic bag this morning.'

'That must be some bag,' Rod observed loudly.

'It's a figure of speech,' Knowles explained unnecessarily, missing Rod's exasperated sigh. 'I take it you've brought everything you need with you?'

'Yes,' Don replied. There had been some hasty last-minute packing but they had managed to lay their hands on everything he reckoned they were likely to need. Apart from their packs and equipment, radios, rations and standard kit, they had brought a selection of weapons that would give the team flexibility and fire-power while allowing it to move quickly across difficult terrain. It had been no easy task, but they were confident they had achieved a good balance.

For personal weapons they had a mix of British SA80s, American M16s and Colt Commandos, and German Heckler & Kochs, as well as a variety of pistols ranging from Brownings to Glocks. Then there were the claymore anti-personnel directional mines, plastic explosives and demolitions kit, hand-grenades, 40mm grenade launchers, M72 rocket launchers, and for the fire-support role an American-made light machine-gun. The ammunition for that modest little arsenal would take some carrying and Jerry had started to see the relevance of Sergeant Steward's insistence that the men carry batteries across the Welsh hills as part of the exercise.

The road away from the station was clogged with traffic, but once at their hotel the team entered a world of calm. The men were shown to their rooms and Don called Gavin Steward to his for a chat about the next stage. Once they had managed to persuade Knowles to leave them in peace, they spread out maps on the bed and began. First they confirmed the times for their onward flight north to Srinagar, the capital of Indian Kashmir, and then they ran through the details for the mission thereafter.

Sir Anthony Briggs had obtained clearance from the Indian security forces in the region for the SAS team to be left alone to carry out its mission. They were to approach the border with Pakistan, cross, carry out the rescue mission and return by another route across the mountains. In the event that they were discovered by Pakistani border guards the Indian government would deny all knowledge of the operation and initially the SAS team would try to bluff their way out by saying that they were a British forces mountaineering expedition. But for that to work they would have to be able to dispose of their hardware beforehand. The whole plan was fraught with danger but it was the best that Sir Anthony could come up with.

'Beats me how he can even get the Indians to allow us near Kashmir. They're usually paranoid about security, especially in the border region,' Gavin said.

'It's all down to contacts, I suppose,' Don answered. 'I tried to ask him but he was pretty vague about the whole thing, saying he had dealt through an old friend who owed him a favour.'

'It gets better and better.'

'Yes, but it's not the Pakistani or Indian border guards that I'm worried about. I don't think we'll have too much trouble evading them. The real problem's going to be the break-in to the terrorists' strongpoint.'

Don laid out the satellite photographs that had been supplied of the Bandrams' fortress.

Gavin whistled. 'It's like something out of Kipling.'

'That's because it is.' Don told him the story of the fort's brigand founder and then produced a sketch-map plan of the layout. 'This is as much detail as the Int boys were able to come up with.'

'We'll have to do our own close recce then,' Gavin observed as he studied the sketches.

'Assuming we have time. The weather's worsening by the day. We have to get in, do the business and get back over the mountains before the snow clags in and traps us on the wrong side. If that happens we can expect some embarrassing questions from the Pakistani authorities.'

'If the Bandrams don't get to us first,' Gavin added.

Don slept badly that night, his head spinning with the plans and the dangers of the mission. So when the morning's first light cracked through the curtains he got up and went out to walk the streets before meeting the others for breakfast. The chill in the air surprised him. Somehow he had supposed that Delhi would be hot, but then he remembered Jerry Patel saying something about the cold in winter reaching down to the plains.

He hugged his coat about him and walked through the city, watching the stalls begin to open like the petals of some exotic flower after the iciness of the night. A couple of early beggars tried their luck and found Don an easy touch. One look at their rags was enough to coax a handful of coins out of him. A rickshaw pulled up alongside him and the youth trotting between the shafts tried to persuade him aboard but Don shook his head and lengthened his stride. The youth kept abreast of him, pleading to be allowed to pull Don wherever he chose.

'Look, pal, I'm just out for a walk. Taking the air, OK?'

The youth frowned, not understanding, until at last Don climbed on to the seat and told him in sign language to take him once around the park and then back to the hotel. After all, it was a pretty miserable way to have to earn your living and if he could pass a couple of coins the fellow's way then he would be better able to enjoy his breakfast with a clear conscience.

However, when the rickshaw eventually pulled up outside the hotel foyer Don was embarrassed to see the rest of the team staring at him from the restaurant windows, pointing and jeering.

'Morning, sahib,' Gavin said when Don had paid the

youth and made his way inside to their table. 'Checking out the getaway transport?'

Fits of laughter erupted around the table.

'We could put a pintel mount on the back for a GPMG. Maybe the MOD equipment procurement branch would be interested in the design blueprint. Drop them by parachute behind enemy lines.'

Don helped himself to a bowl of cereal and smiled bravely throughout. 'Sticks and stones,' he muttered through a mouthful of cornflakes.

They didn't see Knowles again until they were at the airport and waiting for their onward flight to Srinagar. There had been a brief meeting with the Defence attaché at the High Commission, who had assured them that their weapons and other kit would be waiting for them on arrival in Kashmir. Then, after a briefing on the current sensitive political situation in the state, they had bundled into their vans and continued on to the airport.

As they were standing waiting for their flight to be called, the public-address system crackled into life and the next instant they were staring at one another thunderstruck.

'This is a call for the members of the SAS. Would the members of the SAS please report to the information centre.'

Don gaped at Gavin, who stared back with a mouth wide open. Around them the rest of the team looked as if they had just come under artillery fire, eyes searching for the nearest cover.

'Knowles,' Don and Gavin said together.

Feeling as though they could rip his head off, they strode rapidly towards the information desk.

'I believe you have a message for us,' Don said self-consciously.

The man behind the desk scrutinized him carefully. 'You are SAS?'

Don realized it was pointless to deny it. 'Yes,' he admitted glumly, feeling the mission crumble about him and wondering what Sir Anthony would have to say when they arrived back at Heathrow the next day. For surely there was no way the mission could go ahead now that it had been so clumsily compromised.

'A Mr Terence Knowles telephoned to wish you luck and say he was sorry he couldn't be here to see you off.'

Don nodded. 'Is that all?'

'That is all.' The man smiled. 'I didn't see your plane on the tarmac.'

'Our plane?' Don asked, puzzled.

Jerry Patel was the first to understand and was at his side instantly. 'No, we're a relief crew,' he stammered. He looked at Don meaningfully. 'Aren't we, Captain? It's an exchange arrangement with BA.'

'An exchange?' Don said, starting to understand. 'Oh yes, sure! An exchange flight crew. We're SAS all right. Scandinavian to a man.'

For the first time Jerry had cause to thank his family for having mistaken the title once before.

'Why, who did you think we were? Members of the Special Air Service?'

The man found this hilarious and shook his head vigorously. 'No, no, no. You could never be that.'

'Why not?' asked Rod, taken aback.

'I mean no offence, but none of you are smart enough to be soldiers of such an illustrious regiment.'

They looked themselves up and down and had to agree with him. Surely such a ragtag bunch of misfits would never have made it through the portals of Hereford.

10

When the time came for Ramesh, Murap and the party to leave for the return journey to Pakistan, the leader of the Kashmiri rebel group turned out his men in a semblance of an honour guard. Each of them was now carrying a brand-new Kalashnikov rifle thanks to Ramesh, and there were RPG7 rocket launchers and medium machine-guns in their secret stashes.

'It is always a pleasure doing business with the Bandrams,' the leader said.

'And it is always a pleasure helping our brothers from across the border,' Ramesh replied diplomatically. The real cause of his pleasure, however, lay in the saddle-bags slung across the mules, the payment for the arms he had supplied. Apart from the gold coinage, there were sacks of opium that would fetch a handsome price on the black market.

With a cheery wave Ramesh led the way out of the compound and up the hillside, aiming for the point where the treeline came nearest to the clutch of farm buildings that served as the rebels' hideaway. Pine forest extended up the hillside and would provide welcome cover for the march over the days to come. He was apprehensive about their extraction from Indian Kashmir as, after their clash with the border troops, they could expect a large number of Indian reinforcements to have flooded the whole area. On previous occasions they had been lucky to make it back at all, and the rumour was that the Indian forces had brought in a new batch of Soviet-made helicopters with a good troop-lift capability.

As they entered the line of the pine trees, he paused and looked back. Far below them the rebel leader had been reduced to a tiny matchstick figure. His arm rose in a farewell salute and then he turned and disappeared into his stronghold. Within days he would be putting his new weaponry to good use against the Indian forces in a series of ambushes and raids. But by then, Ramesh sincerely hoped, he himself and his men would be safely out of the country.

It felt good to be in the shade of the trees. The chilly gloom closed about them like a fist, but protective rather than claustrophobic. In there they would be shielded from the Indian reconnaissance helicopters and only thermal-imaging devices would be able to pinpoint them. Ramesh knew that the Indians had such equipment, but thankfully not in any great numbers.

The path wound upwards for mile after mile. Because of the closed nature of the country he pushed two of the men out in front to act as lead scouts. They trotted off, ready to give instant warning should they spy any elements of the security forces. Murap fell into step beside Ramesh.

'Which route do you intend to use this time?'

Ramesh pondered. He had given the matter considerable thought and although he had settled on one of the passes he was still far from convinced that he had made the correct decision.

'I thought we could try the Tartha Pass.'

Murap tilted his head on one side as he considered the implications. 'Fine. We haven't been that way for some months. It might still be free of snow.'

'It's not the snow I'm worried about. We're equipped to cope with pretty much any weather.'

'Of course,' Murap agreed readily.

'It's a question of gauging where the Indians will concentrate their patrols. Assuming they've found the bodies by now, they've probably deduced which way we were going, so they know we have to return at some time.'

'And you're gambling that they'll choose to put their patrols on the high ridges, thinking we'll take the hardest route back?'

'Exactly. With luck they'll write off the passes as too obvious. At best they might stick a couple of sentries there, and we can cope with those.'

They walked on in silence for a while before Murap said, 'I believe Ceda will be back by the time we get home?'

Ramesh smiled. 'I hope so. It'll be good to see him again. He's been out of the country for too long.'

There was a friendly rivalry between the two brothers but it was never allowed to spill over into hostility. Both excelled in their relevant fields, Ceda preferring political intrigue and Ramesh the nitty-gritty of combat, and over the years each had learned to respect the other. In the special forces they had served alongside each other and had become something of a legend throughout the army. At first it had been a disadvantage when they had left and entered a different kind of service under their uncle. Their fame had caused questions to be asked about their sudden disappearance from the busy social circles in which they had once mixed, but with time people had forgotten and only then had their uncle put them to work.

It was towards evening that they made the first contact with an Indian patrol. They rounded a bend in the track to find the two scouts waiting for them. One of the men put his finger to his lips and waved them into a corner.

'There,' he whispered, pointing ahead to where the trees tumbled down and eventually opened out into a valley. A stream ran along the bottom of it and beside the stream the flames of a small camp-fire could be seen leaping up amid a shower of sparks.

'How many?' Ramesh asked.

The man shrugged. 'I can only see two, but I think there are another two washing down by the river. The ground dips and we can't see them, but when I look through the binoculars I can count four packs around the fire.'

Ramesh looked for the sun. It had already disappeared below the line of peaks and within an hour it would be dark. The moon would not rise until several hours after that, so in sixty minutes they would have complete darkness to cover their crossing of the bare valley. He gave out instructions to the men and ordered Murap to have the mules taken well out of range, adding,

'We don't want to give ourselves away again like before.'

He withdrew into the trees to rest until it was dark enough for them to continue on their way without being seen. After slipping out of his shoulder straps, he settled down beside a rock and checked the magazine on his rifle. Despite the Kalashnikovs that he carried as contraband on almost every gun-running trip, he still preferred his old SLR. It might not be able to put down the volume of fire of the Kalashnikov, but for long-range accuracy it was unparalleled. In the mountains and valleys of Kashmir that was the quality he felt he most required. Fields of fire were wide open and it was often possible to see an enemy several kilometres away. As a smuggler his aim was to keep that enemy as far away as possible, and only the SLR had a real chance of either picking them off or of putting down an accurate harassing fire.

It was almost dark when he was brought fully alert by a familiar sound. Murap was at his side in an instant.

'Helicopter!' he hissed, his face a mask of alarm.

Ramesh's mind swam. Had they been spotted? Perhaps the men in the valley had seen them approaching and reported in to their HQ, requesting reinforcements that were now about to arrive and swamp the area. If so, they would need the darkness to effect an escape.

'Shall I prepare the men to open fire on it as it comes in to land?' Murap asked.

Ramesh hesitated. 'Get them in position but no one's to open fire unless I give the order.'

Murap darted away and within seconds the men had

been deployed in a ragged line, their weapons trained on the valley to their front.

'Get the machine-gun to cover that flat patch to the left of the camp-fire,' Ramesh directed. 'It's an obvious LZ. But remember, no one is to fire except on my order.'

The sound of the approaching helicopter rolled around the valley, making it impossible to tell from which direction it was coming until the very last moment, when it appeared over the far treeline.

'There it is!' Murap said, pointing.

It was a Soviet-built Hip troop-transport helicopter. Ramesh scanned the sky for others. If the Indians had called in reinforcements then they would probably be flying in a company and that would require at least a further two Hips. However, as the seconds passed it seemed that only the one had come.

'What are they up to?' Murap asked. 'Perhaps they reckon they can make do with a platoon?'

'That assumption would be foolish in the extreme after the drubbing we gave them the last time.'

The helicopter swung along the line of the valley, hugging the ground until it was over the camp-fire and the landing zone that Ramesh had predicted.

'They were using the fire as a marker,' Murap said.

However, instead of more troops disembarking, the men by the fire and their two companions doubling up from the riverside, gathered up their packs, weapons and equipment and ran towards the Hip, ducking under the rotor blades and clambering hastily in through the side door. Helping them, an aircrewman hoisted them in, one by one, took a quick look around and then slid the door closed. The engines surged and the helicopter lifted, tilting forward and swinging away along the valley, lifting slowly over the trees and disappearing into the gathering night. The noise of the engine faded away and a moment later Ramesh, Murap and their men were left with the valley, the forest and the surrounding mountains to themselves.

Murap grinned. 'How's that? We've driven them off without a fight! Now we can just walk across.'

Ramesh stared after the helicopter, watching the spot where the darkness had closed about it, swallowing it from view.

'What's the matter?' Murap asked. 'Disappointed we aren't going to have to shoot our way out?'

Ramesh shook his head, smiling uncertainly. 'No, of course not. It's unusual, that's all.'

'What is?'

But Ramesh shook his head, unable to identify the cause of his concern.

'Get the men ready to move. We'll wait for ten minutes to ensure they're not coming back and then we'll be on our way.'

Murap darted away though the trees to collect the men and bring forward the mules, and a few moments later Ramesh heard the familiar jingle of the bridles and harnesses as the animals stepped patiently over the fallen trunks and soft coatings of pine needles.

First Ramesh sent across the two lead scouts, detailing them to check on the area of the earlier fire and the river-bank where the two Indian soldiers had been washing.

Their report came back over their walkie-talkies that the enemy had completely gone.

'Not even their usual piles of rubbish have been left. It looks as if they don't even want anyone to know they were here.'

That's exactly what it is, Ramesh thought suspiciously. But why? Normally they would want smugglers to avoid the passes, driving them into the more difficult terrain of the mountains, where they were more likely to fall victim to avalanches and frostbite. Yet now it was as if a door was being left purposefully open.

A powerful sense of unease filled him as the whole party crossed the valley and entered the forest on the far side, beginning to climb again as they headed for the border with Pakistan, on the other side of the ridge. There again they would have to be watchful, taking care to avoid the Pakistani army patrols. But the greatest danger always lay on the Indian side of the border, for the gun-running traffic was always one-way, feeding the Kashmiri rebels.

All the way up the hillside he wrestled with the fears and doubts, trying to work out why the way had been made easy for them. And if it had not been done for their benefit, then for whose?

Uncle Gilma Bandram sat in the bright room, feeling the fresh, cold air wash over him like a balm. It heightened the feeling of living in an eagle's eyrie, far above the concerns of the world, yet able to swoop down at will, returning with whatever plunder you chose.

He had watched the approach of the convoy from a

distance, having already noted with pleasure how his nephew Ceda had turned an initial disaster into a possible future triumph. The loss of Sanji had come as a blow but the news that Ceda had secured his granddaughter brought swift relief. Perhaps they would be able to do a deal and get their hands on Sanji after all. It was him that Uncle Bandram wanted, him and no other. Anyone who got in the way would have to die.

In preparation for the guarding of his new and unwilling guest, Uncle Bandram had called in manpower from all parts of the family until, by the time the Land Rovers turned the last hairpin bend on the road up to the fortress, the stronghold was a hive of activity. Not since the days of Yashman the brigand had it been so well defended. Even the Pakistani army itself, if it chose, would be hard pushed to take it by storm.

He finished his cup of strong black coffee, throwing the dregs from his high window and watching them diffuse in the darkening air. Six bold strides took him out into the hall and to the top of the steps that ran down to the courtyard. He must be there to greet the young lady. For although she was his hostage and he would not hesitate to have her shot should circumstances dictate, he was a man who enjoyed playing the game of manners, and regularly entertained the very best of company in an ongoing effort to polish his already impeccable social skills.

The large, double front gates stood open on his orders and he placed himself at the foot of the steps as the first of the Land Rovers entered the compound. In the front seat, Ceda sat in a relaxed pose, concealing the inner tension that kept him wound like a spring, ready to explode into action at the drop of a hat. Uncle Bandram smiled warmly at his nephew. It was hard to choose between Ramesh and him. Both had their considerable strengths and few weaknesses, and together they made a formidable pair.

'Welcome,' Uncle Bandram said effusively as one of the guards opened the rear door of the Land Rover and gave Eli a helping hand. 'I trust the journey wasn't too trying?'

In response she glared at him angrily. 'You have my parents killed and then kidnap me, and now you greet me as if I've come willingly!'

He bowed his head in playful acknowledgement of his guilt. 'All very regrettable, I assure you. But you have your grandfather to blame.'

'And how is that? An old man, that's all he is.'

'Only half true, I'm afraid. He might be old, but that most certainly is not all he is.' He sighed heavily, his smile as chill as the night air around them. 'I can see he has told you nothing of his past life, before he emigrated to Britain. Or should I say, before he fled to Britain?'

'You can say what you damned well like,' she spat at him. 'Whatever it is it'll be a pack of lies. He'd never harm a fly. My grandfather's a devout Hindu. He respects life, and always has.'

Ceda took a step forward, noticing the tell-tale twitch at the corner of his uncle's mouth. The girl should indeed be told the truth, but this was neither the place nor the time.

'Uncle, I owe you an apology. I have failed in my mission.'

Uncle Bandram waved aside his nephew's words.

'These things happen. But never fear, we might get Sanji yet.' He turned to Eli. 'In the meantime why don't you show our visitor to her quarters. We are forgetting our manners. She must be cold and tired after her journey.'

Ceda took her by the arm but Eli shook him off. From out of the shadows two old women appeared and moved to either flank of her.

'These ladies will attend to you,' Uncle Bandram said. 'You will find them kind and courteous.' He smiled. 'But don't try to give them the slip. They are local tribeswomen, tied to me by blood. They would kill you as soon as look at you if they had to. And they will if you try to escape.'

When she had gone, Uncle Bandram took Ceda into his study to hear a full account of the mission to Britain, his brow furrowing when Ceda spoke of Ali's lack of self-discipline.

'He was like that as a boy, I remember. I regret my promise to my sister to look after him, but he is family.' He shrugged. 'Still, you have my word I shall not impose him on you again. From now on I will keep him close to me.'

They talked of the second half of Ceda's team – of their deaths and of the backup team's failed attempt on the safe house.

'It seems that we are encountering a lot of bad luck,' Uncle Bandram concluded.

'You get it in every operation,' Ceda tried to console him. 'That man at the motorway service station for instance. I would dearly like to meet him again.' He stared icily out of the dark window. 'I have a score to settle with him.'

The room that Eli was shown into was more comfortable than she had expected. Rugs were scattered about the floor and the coverlet on the large bed was of pure silk. But the first thing she noticed was the window. As soon as the women had left her, locking the door noisily behind them, she ran across to the sill and leaned out to look for a way of escape. The precipitous drop that loomed beneath her almost made her head swim and she staggered back from it quickly lest she lose her balance.

A glance around the room revealed another two windows, but like the first one, neither opened on to anything but a sheer cliff whose base was invisible. She might as well have been locked in an inaccessible tower from a fairy tale.

True to his word, Uncle Bandram had provided sufficient clothes for her. There were trousers, blouses and sweaters, and a warm sheepskin jacket and hat should she venture outside. In the adjoining bathroom there were towels and pyjamas and, feeling suddenly overcome by the stresses of the journey, she decided to run herself a bath.

The water was wonderfully hot and when she had undressed she lay back and allowed it to soothe her aching muscles. It was only then that the despair she had held at bay for so long threatened to break out. Huge tears throbbed in her eyes and she bit her lip so as not to cry out loud. That wouldn't do, she told herself.

She would only find a way out of there if she managed to keep her head. But how? The place seemed impregnable and even if she escaped from the fort she was still miles from any source of help.

When she had dried, she slipped into a skirt and a light cotton blouse and went to the door, being met by the smell of food as she went back into her bedroom. A small trestle table had been set by the bed and on it a tray bore several dishes, varieties of curry, with an accompanying basket of chapattis. She went across to inspect it.

'I doubt it'll be up to the standard of Grandpa's restaurants.'

She spun round at the sound of the man's voice. Ali was sitting on the window-sill, smiling at her coldly.

'How long have you been here?' she asked, glancing at the bathroom door, which she had left ajar.

He followed her eyes and his smile broadened. 'Long enough.'

A thought suddenly occurred to her. 'Does your uncle know you're here.'

'Of course,' he lied. 'It was him who told me to bring you some food.' He got up and sauntered across to her.

'I don't believe you. You took it from the women.' She pointed to the door. 'Get out of here.'

Instead he reached a hand to her hair, running a strand of it between his fingers.

'It's wet. You'll catch your death of cold. Let me dry it for you.'

She tossed her head, flicking away his hand, but as she

tried to turn from him he caught her by the shoulder and spun her round. The next thing she knew his mouth was on hers, his lips pressing into hers, hands holding her by the throat. She writhed in his grasp until he was forced to draw back.

'Keep quiet,' he hissed in her face, 'or I'll . . .'

'Or you'll what? Kill me? I wonder what your uncle would think about that?'

'There are more ways of punishing a girl like you,' he said, his eyes narrowing.

Before she could react he had grabbed her by the arms and flung her on to the bed. She tried to scream but he clamped one hand across her mouth. With the other he tore at the neck of her blouse, the buttons exploding across the silk coverlet.

'I warned you,' he said, his breath coming in gasps. 'Don't struggle or you'll only make it worse for yourself.'

She felt his hand on her leg, caressing, as she thrashed at him with her fists, using her nails to gouge at his face. He cried out, taking his hand from her mouth. She opened it to scream but the next instant he slapped her hard, pinning both her wrists in one tight grasp while his free hand yanked at her skirt.

'Think yourself too good for me, do you? We'll see about that.'

He fumbled with his belt, loosening it as he pressed himself down between her knees. Eli's head was swimming from the force of the blow, but she desperately tried to shake him off her, fighting to retain consciousness and the will to resist.

Suddenly she was aware of a shadow on the periphery of her vision, fleeting and swift, and the next instant she felt Ali's weight being lifted off her. She struggled to sit up, pulling down the hem of her skirt to cover herself, and saw Ali being swung to his feet in the iron grip of Ceda Bandram.

'Thought you'd join her for a little supper, did you?' Ceda said through gritted teeth. His right hand drove into Ali's stomach immediately below the diaphragm, the fingers straight and rigid like a shaft of steel. Eli heard the air go out of Ali's lungs and saw the eyes bulge in his head. But Ceda hadn't finished with him yet.

With Ali's feet barely touching the floor, he held him out by the scruff of the neck with one hand and with the other delivered a short, sharp series of blows. Each blow was directed accurately at a vital point and after every shattering impact Ceda's hand curved or clenched into a new and deadly shape, each one fashioned precisely for its own special task. Forefinger and thumb widened to present the hand's web for a strike at the windpipe, then the hand became a fist, but with the middle knuckle of the middle finger extended for a punch to the solar plexus. Next the hand curled and stiffened into the semblance of an eagle's claw that slapped and clenched tight on Ali's testicles, Ceda using the grip to lift Ali towards the window. Ali opened his mouth to scream but all that escaped was a shrill yelp of agony.

'If you'd wanted some excitement you should have asked me,' Ceda said. 'How's this for stimulation?'

He lowered Ali to the floor and allowed him to achieve a wobbly balance, but the next second he chopped hard down on the collar-bone with the edge of his open left hand. Lastly, with Ali lined up in front of the window that Eli had first seen on entering the room, he clenched his right fist and propelled it into Ali's nose in three ferocious jabs. Blood poured from the man's nostrils, the bone beneath shattered. Ali tottered backwards and sat heavily down on the sill. Ceda took a step forward, swept up his ankles and tipped him backwards out of the window, maintaining his grasp as Ali's last shred of consciousness woke in him the survival instinct. His limbs jerked and he squealed for mercy as Ceda levered him backwards, tipping him head first into the darkness above the sheer drop.

'Ceda!'

Ceda turned at the voice of his uncle.

'Enough!'

Without releasing his grip, Ceda glared out at Ali, enjoying the terror he saw there.

'He deserves to die, Uncle. He has dishonoured the family for the last time.'

'That is for me to decide.'

Uncle Bandram's voice was stern and unflinching and Ceda reluctantly understood that there was no room for negotiation. Slowly he hauled Ali back into the room and let his body slip from his grasp. As he hit the floor Ali retched, bringing up his most recent meal. Ceda glowered down at him in utter disgust.

'Get out of here.'

He placed the toe of his boot under Ali's rump and pushed, sending him sprawling across the floor. Ali scuttled away, flicking a frightened glance at his uncle.

But as he reached the doorway he turned and said, 'I'll get even with you for this, Ceda. You think you're so damn clever, with your military bearing and proud ways. Don't think I don't know what's on your mind.' He glanced at Eli on the edge of the bed. 'I know you want her as much as I do. But you haven't got the balls to take what you want. You never have. That's why you'll always be someone else's lackey.'

'Ali,' Uncle Bandram said softly. 'I wouldn't push your cousin too far. Next time I won't call him off, I promise you. Disgrace me once more and I'll let Ceda have you.'

'Yes, Uncle. OK. We'll leave it for now. But don't expect me to forget.'

He glared at Eli as if lodging the sight of her in his mind for later use. Then he was gone. Uncle Bandram followed him out of the room, calling for the two tribeswomen and instructing them to remain outside Eli's room throughout the night.

Ceda wiped Ali's blood from his hands as he walked towards the door.

'Thank you, Mr Bandram,' Eli called after him.

He turned in surprise. 'I didn't do it for you. I don't like to disappoint a lady, but I was thinking of my family's honour.'

'Honour? But you've kidnapped me!' she said in astonishment.

'Exactly. But that doesn't mean I have to stand by and watch you raped as well. You might temporarily be my prisoner, but you're not going to come to any harm if it can be avoided. And Ali's assault on you could be avoided.'

He continued towards the door. 'I'll have one of the women clean up Ali's mess,' he said over his shoulder, indicating the vomit.

When he had gone and she was once more alone, Eli went to the bathroom and splashed cold water on her face and throat. She found that her hands were shaking, and looked at herself in the mirror.

'Oh Eli, whatever are you going to do now?'

The reflection didn't have an answer. It stared back at her blankly, admitting with the silent passing of each second that she was beyond hope.

11

'So that's about the size of it then.'

Sir Anthony Briggs waved the piece of notepaper at Sanji, who sat dejectedly on the bed.

'They offer the release of the girl if you take the first available plane to Pakistan and hand yourself over to them.'

He waited for Sanji's response but when the old man remained silent, staring morosely at the floor, he went on, 'You'd be committing suicide of course. You can't go.'

'Why not? There's nothing else I can do. I must go.' Sanji got unsteadily to his feet and ambled across to the window. Outside the lawn was being swept by a fine, cold rain. 'I've got nothing else left to lose.'

'Nothing to lose?'

'Don't sound so surprised. I'm an old man, Sir Anthony. My daughter's dead, my business means nothing to me any more, and the person who means more to me than anything or anyone else in the world is in the hands of madmen. If anything happened to my little Eli I could never live with myself. I have to do as they ask.'

Sir Anthony paced the carpet, rubbing his chin in thought. 'I'm afraid it's not as easy as all that.'

'What you do mean?'

'You must realize that if your story comes out it could inflame relations between Pakistan and India and they're tense enough as it is. We've known for a long time that they both possess nuclear weapons and if any conflict erupted into war we are certain they wouldn't hesitate to use them.'

Sanji smiled sadly. 'I think you overestimate my importance. It was all such a long time ago.'

'Not to those who remember.'

'Like Mr Bandram?'

'And there are probably many like him on both sides of the border.'

Sanji shrugged. 'It doesn't alter the fact that I'm at last prepared to offer myself up as a sacrificial lamb, if that's what they want. I've been hiding for long enough. It's time to end the charade.'

Sir Anthony's expression hardened. 'Then there's one other reason for preventing you from going.'

'Which is?' Sanji asked, becoming suspicious. There was a deviousness about the British Intelligence officer that Sanji disliked intensely. It reminded him of the many similar individuals he had been forced to deal with during the Independence movement in 1947.

'The embarrassment caused to my country.' He corrected himself quickly, 'To *our* country, that is. Since you're now a British passport holder.'

Sanji looked into his eyes but saw them only as ball-bearings, devoid of human warmth or feeling. 'We are talking about the life of my granddaughter, a young woman with her life ahead of her. You and I are old men.'

He saw Sir Anthony blanch and added, 'Yes, even you, Sir Anthony. Our lives are behind us. These affairs are just the scrag-ends. We delude ourselves if we think that the world wants anything for us any more. Let us do all we can to help the young to their inheritance. Help me recover my granddaughter, even if it means a few red faces in Whitehall.'

Sir Anthony stalked to the door, coughing to hide his outrage. 'I'm afraid I can't, Mr Sanji. Not after what you've told me. My own research since has confirmed what you said. You may be willing to give up the ghost and throw away your life but I'm still responsible for the security and prestige of this nation. And as long as I am you will remain here and silent.'

He let himself out and although there was no sound of any key turning in the lock Sanji knew that to all intents and purposes he was Sir Anthony's prisoner. The winter rain was now lashing into the swaying trees and looking out at it he realized that he had come to hate the country of his adoption. He sank on to the bed and buried his head in his hands once again, but a new fire had been kindled in his heart. He would not remain silent any longer. Somehow he would confess the errors of the past, even if it was too late to save his beloved Eli. For her there might be no salvation, but at least he would set the record straight and dedicate the bitter truth to her memory.

On another continent, a file of men moved stealthily through the forest gloom. From their fieldcraft it was impossible to guess that none of them had ever operated in the country before. As far as they were concerned, the techniques of soldiering were an international language, adaptable to any land and any situation as required. The moment they were off the beaten track and submerged in the vast Kashmiri mountain forests, the SAS eight-man fighting patrol felt utterly at home. In their case, however, the feeling at home did not in any way herald relaxation. Rather the opposite. It heightened their senses like those of the fox on its night stalk for prey.

The distance between each man was adjusted without thinking, to suit the terrain and the light, the single file expanding or contracting like an accordion so that each man was able to keep easy sight of the individuals in front and behind. Every member of the patrol had been allocated his arc to observe, which, in the event of a contact, would become his primary field of fire. The weapons were distributed throughout the patrol so as to ensure an even balance, the only exception being at the front of the file, where the two lead scouts carried between them enough fire-power to suppress an average infantry company.

Marching third in the patrol, Don surveyed the ground around him, mentally comparing it with the features he had memorized from his extensive map study before setting out. Every so often he slipped the compass from his breast pocket and checked their direction of travel. At each of the short halts, he would move forward to speak to the lead scout, indicating a noticeable feature for him to steer by for the next leg of the march. With such an obvious target to aim for, the scouts were freed from the task of navigation, their full attention being concentrated on their fieldcraft, alert to the slightest sign of another human presence which could mean trouble.

Don, on the other hand, apart from his responsibility for navigation, was constantly considering the options should such a contact occur. As the patrol crossed a valley he would decide what to do if a machine-gun opened up from any one of a number of potential enemy positions. Such mental contingency planning didn't take any particular time. It was ingrained in him and he was constantly slipping easily through the procedure as he marched.

Sergeant Gavin Steward, marching near the rear of the file, had been assigned as check navigator, confirming his boss's compass bearings and map reading and trying desperately to find a fault, but always without success.

Jerry Patel had been detailed to bring up the rear.

'Tail-end Tandoori,' Rod had joked, digging him in the ribs as he passed to take up his own position behind Don. 'We'll send you out for the takeaway when we harbour up for the night. You speak the lingo, after all.'

Jerry was aware, however, that the tail-end position was almost as important as the lead scout's. For if the patrol should pick up an enemy tail the results could be disastrous. An enemy patrol, if sufficiently skilled, could track the SAS team to their night harbour, allow them to start on their drills for establishing the night base and then catch them when they were at their most vulnerable. Don, as commander, would have gone forward with an escort of at least one man to close-recce the potential position, while the remainder of the patrol would cluster in all-round defence to await his return. An attack at such a time would catch the patrol split in two, the commander away from the bulk of his patrol, and no one knowing who was firing at whom. It all boiled down to Jerry's alertness to ensure that any such tracker was detected before he could close up and do the damage.

In such an event the patrol would either go into the contact-rear drill, if the enemy was so close that a fire-fight was imminent; or, if there was a little more time, they would establish a hasty ambush, circling back on their own track to lie in wait and fire on the unwitting enemy – the hunted hunting the hunter.

Jerry's pack was lighter than on his last Welsh exercise, and he derived a grim satisfaction from seeing Gavin Steward stopping every so often to mop his brow. At one point when they closed up for a slightly longer break, he couldn't resist saying, 'Having a spot of bother, Sarge?'

Gavin winked at him. 'Me? A spot of bother? On yer bike.'

It was after they had been moving for a couple of days that they made the first contact with anyone, but rather than a hostile patrol it was an old shepherd close to the border.

The patrol was in the middle of a bare, steep-sided valley and halfway across a slender bridge over a raging torrent, when Gavin raised the alarm. Instantly everyone went into the contact-front drill, closing up as fast as they could to form an extended fire line facing in the direction that Gavin had indicated in his shouted command. However, once they were all on the ground and safely in cover, it became clear that the old man was alone with his flock and presented no threat.

'What the fuck do we do now?' Taff rasped.

'Slot the old bugger, I say,' Geordie replied, only half joking.

'Shut it.' Don studied the ground. The shepherd had obviously seen them but didn't appear to be in any way concerned. He remained sitting on his rock, poking the earth with his gnarled stick.

'Do you reckon he's close enough to see we're not Indian army?' Don asked Gavin.

Gavin weighed it up. 'Doubt it. From his reaction I'd say he's used to seeing patrols in this area.'

'Agreed.' Don looked around for Jerry. 'Time for you to earn your keep. Go and sound him out. Stick to our cover story but don't let him ask too many questions. See what you can get out of him.'

'Wilco, boss.'

As Jerry got up and walked towards the old shepherd Rod asked, 'Shouldn't someone go with him as backup?'

Don grinned. 'You're sounding very caring all of a sudden. Jerry will be flattered to hear you care.'

Rod blushed. 'Just thinking about the drills, boss. Couldn't give a stuff about him myself.'

'Sure, sure,' Don said unconvinced.

Jerry felt suddenly very vulnerable with the thought of the whole battery of SAS weaponry at his back. The old man watched him approach, unimpressed. He was sitting cross-legged on the rock, and as Jerry walked towards him he put his hand inside his jacket. Behind him Jerry heard half a dozen rifle bolts click in readiness to drill the old fellow full of holes, but there was something peaceful about the man and Jerry held up his hand to restrain his comrades. Sure enough, a second later the old man's hand reappeared holding a battered pipe which he proceeded to fill with tobacco from a cloth pouch. He looked up and smiled as Jerry covered the last yards between them.

'Greetings,' Jerry said in Hindi.

'Greetings,' the man replied in Urdu. He was a Kashmiri Muslim but it was obvious from Jerry's appearance that he was Indian. Also, if Jerry was to pass himself off as a member of the security forces he would most likely be a Hindi speaker. However, in an effort to communicate with the local population the Indian forces used Urdu as well, so when he next spoke he used that language, though keeping it rough and ready as befitted an ordinary soldier.

'How many sheep have you got?' he asked pleasantly, looking around the valley.

The man jerked his chin at the flock. 'Just what you see. The grazing's not very good around here, so I'm taking them higher.'

Jerry nodded knowingly. He crouched down in front of the man, judging it to be less confrontational. It could also be interpreted as deferential to the old man's greater age. To Jerry's delight the old man clearly took it as such, smiling at the youth before him like any grandfather upon his family.

'What brings you here?' he asked.

'You know how it is,' Jerry replied. 'Patrolling the frontier and looking for rebels.'

The old shepherd tut-tutted. 'Ah, the rebels. Must there always be men of violence?'

'Our thoughts exactly.'

'Of course,' the shepherd added mischievously, 'you could always go home and leave us alone.'

Jerry chuckled and wagged his finger. 'You know we can't do that. Kashmir is part of India. We love it and its people and want to keep it.'

'Even if its people don't love you? We are Muslim, after all. Wouldn't it make sense for us to join Pakistan?'

'There are many Muslims living happily in India. Why can't you?'

The old man laughed. 'Let us not argue. Will you have some milk?'

He hoisted a goatskin bottle off his shoulder, unplugged the stopper and passed it across. Jerry accepted it doubtfully and held it up, wincing as he tasted the gush of warm, sweet sheep's milk.

'I can see you are a city boy,' the shepherd said as he watched. 'Where do you come from?'

Careful, Jerry thought, ever on his guard. 'Delhi.' It was the one city he had visited with his parents and felt that he could bluff the old man if he had to.

'Ah, that was a Muslim city until 1947. But then all the Muslims were driven out. Many were massacred in the race riots.'

Jerry had heard about the massacres from his father. Countless thousands had died, millions perhaps. No one would ever know the true figure. 'Hindus were killed as well.'

'True,' the shepherd conceded. 'They were terrible times. Many of the perpetrators have never been brought to book.' He held up his hands to heaven. 'But one day they will stand before Allah to account for their evil deeds.'

Thinking it was time to get moving, Jerry said, 'Tell me, have you seen anyone else hereabouts?' He kept his voice as casual and unconcerned as he could.

'No one,' the man said a little too quickly. But then, Jerry thought, he wasn't likely to offer help or information to the Indian security forces voluntarily.

'No other patrols?'

The old man's eyes narrowed. 'Do you not keep track of your own men?'

'Of course. But we've been out for a long time. It's easy to wander into someone else's patch.'

The shepherd looked past Jerry at the prone figures of the SAS patrol. 'Why don't your friends come over here? They could have some milk as well.'

Jerry rolled his eyes conspiratorially, 'It's our commander. He's a real arsehole. Doesn't like to mix with the local population.'

The man nodded sympathetically. 'That's a funny uniform you're wearing,' he said reaching to touch Jerry's combat jacket.

'Yes, it's new. We're paratroopers. Only we've been issued with it so far. Smart, isn't it?'

The shepherd wobbled his head from side to side noncommittally. He looked past Jerry at the patrol. 'I think your commander wants you.'

Jerry turned to see Don waving him back.

'See what I mean? He obviously doesn't like me talking to you.'

'May Allah go with you,' the old man said as Jerry made to leave.

'And peace be with you too, old man,' Jerry replied.

Back at the patrol's fire line, he crouched down beside Don and reported on what the shepherd had said.

'I thought you were going to get a fucking brew on,' Don said.

'You have to show the correct respect for elders out here. He doesn't give a shit about our timetable. If I'd given him the brush-off he'd have known we weren't security forces. They're ordered to do everything they can to appease the locals.'

Giving the shepherd a wide berth, the patrol continued on its way. While Jerry had been talking to him, the members of the patrol had blacked up their faces with cam cream but even so Don didn't want to get too close and risk being recognized as Westerners.

'I still think we should have slotted him,' Geordie said with a backward glance at the lonely figure on the rock.

'That's a real hearts-and-minds philosophy,' Jerry said. 'Very subtle, O wise one.'

'When you've got 'em by the balls the hearts and minds follow,' Geordie countered.

The patrol followed the valley towards its mouth, the ground rising all the time until they were struggling up steep banks of shale.

'According to my calculations, the border should be just two miles on the other side of that ridge,' Don said as they approached the top of the valley. Gavin grunted his agreement and they pressed on.

'Sir Anthony might have been able to pull strings with old friends in the Indian army and have their patrols withdrawn from the area, but we'll still have to give the Pakistanis the slip.'

'I've heard their mountain troops are pretty hot stuff,' Gavin replied. 'Shouldn't we restrict our movement to darkness only?'

Don had already weighed the pros and cons. It was imperative that they get back across the border as soon as possible, spending the minimum amount of time in Pakistan necessary to achieve the mission. On the other hand, if they were compromised by the authorities before reaching the Bandrams' fort then the mission would fail anyway, and the chances of compromise were greatly increased if they moved by day as well as by night. It was unlikely that the Pakistani border patrols were well equipped with night-sights and image-intensifiers, so darkness offered the best chance for a successful infiltration.

He issued his instructions accordingly and when they topped the ridge at the head of the valley and began their descent towards the frontier, Don and Gavin started to look for an LUP where they could lie up until nightfall. They found it a couple of miles further on, in a small cave hidden among an old rockfall, and when sentries had been posted, the rest of the patrol unrolled their sleeping bags and tried to rest.

Before curling up himself, Don crept forward with his binoculars to spy out the lie of the land which they would have to cross later that night. Peering from behind a rock, he laid out his map and compared it with the ground itself, taking a series of bearings to pinpoint his own position. Gavin had already confirmed their location using the patrol's satellite navigational system, which gave them an accurate fix to within ten metres, but Don still liked to keep his old skills well honed. Technical kit could always go wrong or take a bullet through it, and then they would have to fall back on basic compass resection. It was as well to practise the skill while there wasn't the added pressure of necessity.

In this remote part of the mountains there was no form of physical barrier delineating the frontier, but from his map Don worked out that it lay approximately one mile in front of him. The Bandrams' fort was several miles beyond that, so he reckoned that they would be able to reach it that night without too much trouble. With luck there would be enough time left to do a close recce, and then they would have to lie up during the following day in an observation position to observe the various comings and goings of the occupants. That would give them a good chance to pinpoint the defences, locate any sentries and the times they changed stags, ate their meals, went to relieve themselves and so on. With luck he could also establish the whereabouts of Eli herself. He would then be in a position to make his plan of attack. The strike could take place the next night, the idea being that they would infiltrate the fort, effect the rescue and tab across into the relative safety of Indian Kashmir before first light.

Of course they would then have to make the RV with the transport that Sir Anthony had arranged, but so long as his contacts continued to play the game and keep the

Indian patrols out of the way, Don couldn't foresee too many problems.

When he got back to the cave he noted down all he had learned from his brief recce and then tried to sleep. It was strange how relaxed he felt, lying among the rocks, staring up at the clear blue sky overhead. He could hardly believe that he was in Kashmir, about to cross the border into Pakistan. As far as he could tell by looking about him he might as well have been on exercise in Wales. But that was what it was all about. If you got the training right, then the actual operation should feel like an anticlimax. Of course, it never was. Once the lead started flying there was always the added excitement and adrenalin that only ever came with a real mission, but at times like this, on an approach march or in a lying-up or observation position, you should always have the confidence of having been through the drills a hundred times before, knowing them so thoroughly that they were in your very blood and bones.

Before he knew it he was being shaken awake and the blue sky above him had miraculously turned into a deep velvet studded with pinpricks of light.

'What time is it?' he asked, rolling out of his sleeping bag and coming fully alert.

'Nineteen hundred hours, boss.'

He recognized Jerry's gentle voice. He was a good lad, he reflected. He would do the Regiment proud, given time.

As Don rolled up his bag and packed it away, Gavin brought him a brew and some food. All around him the men were preparing to move, their actions disciplined and confident, stemming from thorough training and considerable experience. Each of them had had a distinguished career in a line infantry regiment or the Paras before selection for the SAS and their professionalism made Don almost pity the opponents they were shortly going to confront.

'All ready?' he asked quietly when they were in their patrol formation.

Each of them gave him the thumbs up.

'Move now,' he ordered softly.

For crossing the open ground they shook out into an arrowhead formation, but once at the border they would once again slip effortlessly into single file. As they pulled away from the LUP each man checked his arcs, feeling stiff muscles complain before settling into the rhythm of the march.

A short while later Don turned to the man next to him and whispered, 'The border,' giving the hand signal for single file. The man passed it back, and so on down the line until the patrol had glided effortlessly into the new formation.

They hadn't gone more than a couple of miles when the lead scout dropped soundlessly to the ground, waving the others into cover behind him with the thumbs-down signal for enemy. Don crawled forward. He had assigned Jerry as lead scout in case his language skills were needed. In the event of their running headlong into a Pakistani army patrol it just might be possible, in the confusion of darkness, to pass themselves off as another such patrol.

'Trouble up ahead,' Jerry said quietly as Don came up

beside him. 'I think it's a listening post of half-section strength.'

Don stared into the darkness but could see and hear nothing. In answer to his doubting look, Jerry said, 'One of them just lit a cigarette and the post commander told him to put it out.' He grinned. 'Abuse sounds the same in any language, be it Urdu or Brit.'

'We'll have to skirt around them,' Don said, making a mental note of the position to avoid it on the return journey the next night.

There were two other such contacts before they were clear of the immediate border area and started to see the lights of distant villages and farmsteads. Then, towards the early hours, they entered a region of harsh, rocky landscapes where streams cascaded down from the heights and the skyline showed as a jagged relief of peaks and razor-backed ridges.

Gavin moved forward down the line of the patrol until he reached Don. The moon had risen and in its silvery light Don could see a sheen of perspiration beading the sergeant's face. 'By my reckoning we should be just about there,' he said softly.

'Mine too,' Don agreed. They called a halt, and while the members of the patrol waited in all-round defence, they went forward alone until they came over a slight rise and saw the distant silhouette of the fortress.

'Jesus Christ,' Gavin muttered. 'That nut's going to take some cracking.'

'Let's get a bit closer and look for an LUP. I'll do the close recce myself and take Jerry with me.'

Gavin checked his watch and looked at the eastern

rim of the horizon for any sign of light. 'You haven't got long.'

'I know. If I can just get a look at the other side of it that'll have to do. We can check out the rest from an OP after sunrise.'

They found an LUP within fifteen minutes and once the men were established in it Don ordered Gavin to put out claymores to cover the approaches. 'If the Bandrams' men bump us by mistake I want to make sure we can give them a warm reception.'

He took Jerry to one side and briefed him on the close recce. Both men stripped down to the minimum kit necessary, setting out with little more than belt order and their personal weapons. For the recce, their belt order consisted of spare ammunition, water, emergency rations, sheath knife and survival kit. Maps and compasses were carried in their pockets and Don had a small notebook and pencil to jot down all he gleaned from the recce about the defences and layout of the fort. In a pouch on his belt he carried a Sopolem OB44 night-sight.

Aware that he was now racing against the approaching sun, Don set a ferocious pace. Relieved of the weight of their full packs and webbing, both men felt suddenly liberated and hopped over rocks and streams, covering the distance with ease. Jerry moved several paces behind Don, periodically checking the rear for tails. Every so often they stopped and crouched into cover, Don using his night-sight to scan the fort, jotting down every scrap of information before moving on to the next vantage point.

The view from the far side told him what he needed

to know – that the fort was surrounded by sheer cliffs on three sides. The choices open to them appeared to be either to scale the cliffs the following night, or to attempt an approach along the only track leading in. However, the night-sight revealed a thick belt of mines and wire obstacles covering the slender peninsula that extended towards the fort's front entrance.

'Hope you brought your crampons,' he whispered to Jerry.

Jerry stared in awe at the cliff face and swallowed hard. It was going to be some climb.

They arrived back at the LUP as the sun was brightening the eastern horizon, spreading a heavy line of orange and crimson from rim to rim behind the mountains. As Don crawled in he was challenged quietly for the password, knowing that behind the low, controlled voice of the sentry lay the muzzle of the American M249 Squad Automatic Weapon, a 5.56mm round in the breach, the safety-catch set for automatic fire, and a box magazine packed to bursting clamped beneath.

'Welcome home, boss,' the sentry whispered as Don and Jerry crawled past him and into the LUP. Four of the team were asleep in their sacks while Gavin sat beside his stripped M16 dry-cleaning the working parts for the fire-fights to come.

Don quickly briefed him on all he had gleaned from the short recce. 'I wish we had had more time. I'd like to have been able to take a closer look at the road approach. I don't like ruling it out just because the goons have sown a few mines and strung a bit of wire across it.'

Gavin laughed soundlessly. 'You're just afraid of heights. Admit it.'

'Bollocks.'

When the sun finally appeared, Don crawled forward to the crack between two rocks where Gavin had set up the OP. Perfect, he thought as he looked out at the fort across the valley. Now all we have to do is sit back and watch and wait. With luck, he thought, the Bandrams' men would give away their routine and their positions, and then the next night all they had to do was walk across the valley floor, shin up the rockface, and rescue the princess from her tower. Piece of piss.

12

Ramesh had arrived back at the stronghold with his sense of unease magnified. The return journey had been too simple, without a single Indian patrol being encountered. Such a thing had never happened before and the initial pleasure of the surprise had rapidly turned into a grave suspicion. The military patrols and guards on the Pakistani side of the border appeared to be the same as ever, but it nevertheless left the inexplicable behaviour of the Indian authorities unaccounted for.

He was still puzzling about it when he entered the courtyard and saw Ceda and his uncle standing there to receive him. Ali stood behind them, a huge ripe black eye and a bandaged nose telling of yet another disagreement in his troublesome life. His uncle greeted him but it was Ceda who noticed his disquiet. When he explained the problem Ceda rubbed his chin and suggested that perhaps the Indians were simply changing over the divisions responsible for the sector. If such a hand-over went badly it could often result in a gap in the patrol programme as the outgoing and incoming units shuffled around the district. Ramesh agreed that that was probably what had happened, but all the same he recommended that the guards should be strengthened for the rest of the week.

'The Indians would never dare cross the border,' Ceda answered. 'Our gun-running gets under their skin, but if they were caught in Pakistani territory it could spark a war. They wouldn't dare risk it.'

'Perhaps not, but a small special forces unit might have a shot. A quick in and out.'

Ceda was unconvinced but agreed that there would be no harm in doubling the sentries for a few nights.

Ramesh was interested by the news of the kidnapping of Eli but disappointed that they had failed to get their hands on Sanji himself.

'Don't worry,' Uncle Bandram replied. 'He should know by now that we're prepared to do a swap, and if my information is correct, he'll sacrifice anything to safeguard his granddaughter. Even his life.'

That evening they had a special dinner to celebrate the homecoming of both brothers, and throughout it Ali sat sullenly by himself nursing his swollen face. Murap tried to coax him out of his sulk, but Ali would have none of it.

'What's the matter with him?' Ramesh asked Ceda quietly when the plates were being cleared away and the next course was being laid before them.

Ceda recounted Ali's fit of passion over Eli.

'So she's attractive, this Eli?' Ramesh said, eyeing his brother playfully.

Ceda shrugged. 'For an Indian, I suppose she might be called that. But she's not my type. She's been corrupted by her upbringing in Britain. She has no idea how to behave in front of a man and from the way she dresses, it's not surprising that Ali thought she'd let him have his way.'

Ramesh laughed. 'That's not very enlightened of you.'

'I think I become less enlightened the older I get. Give me a good traditional Pakistani girl any day.'

The next dish arrived, a huge brass platter piled high with rice, mutton and chicken. Ramesh wiped his moustache, happy to be back and enjoying a decent meal instead of facing the hardships of the mountains. But as he ate he relaxed, and as he relaxed, his thoughts went back to the journey over the mountains. Something continued to worry at his peace of mind until he sat back, his appetite gone. He shook his head in dismay and got to his feet.

'Still worrying?' Ceda asked.

'It's no good,' he replied. 'I'm going to have to take a look around.'

Uncle Bandram sat with his face buried in his food, taking little interest in the concerns of his nephew, but Ceda nodded.

'Do you want me to come too?'

He had worked alongside his brother on numerous operations and exercises and knew enough to respect Ramesh's intuitions.

'No, it's OK. You stay here and enjoy your dinner. I won't be long. I'm sure it's nothing, but there's no harm in making sure.'

Don was immensely relieved when he reached the foot of the cliff to find that it was not as sheer and smooth as it had appeared through his binoculars. Lying in his OP earlier in the day he wondered whether they would be physically able to scale it or whether they would be forced to gain access to the stronghold by some other means. However, as he eased into his harness and sought out the first hand and footholds above him, he saw that an ascent would indeed be possible.

Before leaving the OP and moving across the valley floor, the SAS fighting patrol had established a cache for their bergens and extra equipment, each man taking with him only his weapons, ammunition and sufficient kit to carry out the mission. The cache would also serve as an RV after the raid, a place where they would assemble before the tab back to and across the border. Don knew that it would be essential to gather their wits and take stock before starting on the exfiltration phase of the patrol, forcing themselves to ignore whatever hornets' nest their attack had stirred up, so as to retain the initiative and not simply end up fleeing in panic from the surviving enemy.

Don started to climb, the rope around his waist playing out behind him. To left and right of him, the other members of the team started upwards, the patrol climbing in four pairs. His own partner for the ascent was Jerry, and at each leg of the climb Don anchored himself to the rockface and waited for Jerry to come up beside him. So, in a series of caterpillar movements, they made their way painstakingly towards the battlements high above.

It was hard going but the rock itself was firm and dry, providing a wealth of solid holds. Don had often climbed in Wales, as had every member of the team, and for all of them it was second nature. Little by little the ground fell away below, until, looking down, Don could no longer see it in the darkness. The moon had risen and shone on him, lending its welcome light to his efforts. Before setting out he had been careful to secure every item of kit so that his movements were soundless. The slightest noise could betray his presence to the terrorists above and the last place he would want to be caught was splayed out against the rockface. If they were spotted while still climbing they would be completely vulnerable to attack.

When he had been climbing for nearly fifteen minutes he came to a narrow ledge and, checking his position, he saw that he was only a few yards short of the top. He signalled for Jerry to join him and then looked to left and right for the other teams. All of them were visible and he signalled to them that they should gather there in preparation for the final push up to the battlements.

Jerry scaled the rocks quickly and heaved himself up on to the ledge beside Don. Their faces were blackened with cam cream but Don could see the perspiration shining through. Jerry grinned with excitement and gave the thumbs up. Next, Gavin arrived with Rod in tow, and off to the left Taff and Geordie, and Tom and Jimmie.

Pair by pair, Don checked that everyone was set. They were. Steadying his breathing, he was just about to launch himself up the final stretch when directly above them he heard footsteps and the sound of muffled voices. Instantly he reached for the Browning pistol at his belt, leaving his Colt Commando automatic assault rifle slung over his shoulder. He looked at Jerry, who strained to catch what was being said above.

'. . . watch . . . report instantly . . . shoot on sight . . .'

Jerry's eyes widened and he put his mouth to Don's ear to repeat the terse message he had heard.

My impressions from the UK were correct, Don thought as a chill ran through him. These guys know how to handle themselves. It's going to be no pushover.

He holstered his Browning again as the footsteps passed on, and signalled to the team to use knives for as long as possible. They would try to conduct the necessary killing in silence until the alarm was raised and only then resort to the full use of their fire-power. With luck, stealth would get them part of the way through their mission and even when the first shots were exchanged he hoped that surprise would carry them a bit further.

Hand by hand and foot by boot, he edged his way upwards, moving with agonizing slowness. His instincts screamed at him to power up the rockface, leap over the battlements and blaze away at anything that moved, but his training and self-discipline kept them on a tight rein. Doubtless there would be ample opportunity for his instincts to have their way later that night. For now caution was the watchword.

A foot below the battlements, he stopped and listened, trying to locate the nearest sentry. There was nothing. Only the gentle sounds of the night answered him, and somewhere deep inside the fortress the noise of a banquet. He reached up and curled his fingers over the stonework, pulling himself up and vaulting over the top. He landed on a walkway on the other side, his leg muscles taking the impact like springs, cushioning his landing as quietly as if he had come down on sand. His head shot to left and right. There was no one to be seen. Whoever had been speaking earlier had passed on. Two light tugs on the rope brought Jerry up behind him and within the next thirty seconds all the other members of the team hopped over the battlements on to the walkway around him.

Before setting off into the fortress they anchored their ropes to the rockface in readiness for a quick getaway, ensuring that nothing could be seen by anyone walking past the spot. To detect the ropes a sentry would have to lean right over the battlements and stare directly at them.

Don was confident that during the time spent in the OP in the preceding daylight hours he had located the part of the stronghold where Eli was most likely being held captive, and the moment the team was complete he directed Tom and Jimmie to lead off. Behind them he placed himself and Jerry, with Gavin and Rod behind him, and Taff and Geordie bringing up the rear. As they moved, each man traced his assigned arc, the pattern ensuring that every angle could be instantly covered by automatic fire if required. Each man now carried his primary weapon system, the squad light machine-gun being manhandled by Rod in the centre of the formation and therefore able to switch its heavier weight of fire in any direction, forwards or backwards, to right or left.

There was an M206 at both front and rear, the one at the point being carried by Tom and the one at the rear being carried by Geordie. The variant of the basic M16 rifle with a 40mm grenade launcher fitted under the rifle barrel, the M206 was able to provide a fearsome weight and variety of fire, the most flexible weapon system carried by the team. Jimmie carried his Heckler & Koch MP5 sub-machine-gun, the fire selection catch set to automatic, ready to spray anyone who got in his way with its lethal 9mm bullets at a rate of 800 rounds a minute. Taff had opted for the standard British Army-issue SA80 with its automatic capability and 5.56mm rounds. Gavin and Jerry both hefted orthodox M16s, while Don carried his Colt Commando, the shortened version of the M16 that fired the identical 5.56mm bullet but was especially suited to close quarter battle. It was much favoured by commanders who needed a compact weapon to enable them to use radios, maps and compasses with ease while still being able to contribute to the fire-fight when required.

In addition, everyone carried a pistol, but once again the makes varied from man to man as each opted for his own particular favourite, while maintaining a commonality of ammunition wherever possible.

The walkway skirted the outer walls, but within twenty yards of their entry point the patrol encountered the first sentry. Tom was nearing a door when he heard the man clear his throat. Instantly Tom froze, hand-signalling for those behind him to halt. Moving without sound, he handed his M206 to his partner, drew his killing knife and edged forward. When he was right up against the corner of the doorway, he went swiftly into action, swivelling round and grabbing the man, clamping his left hand over the mouth to prevent any warning cry, and at the same time yanking the head back and to the left side, exposing the right side of the neck. Tom arched the sentry back, tipping him off balance and as the man started to go down, he thrust the point of his knife into the gap behind the collar-bone, driving down to sever the artery there.

The sentry convulsed, his arms thrashing wildly, but Tom had him firmly in his grasp and there was nothing the man could do to save himself. When his motions had stopped, Tom lowered the lifeless body silently to the floor, looking around for somewhere to conceal it. Doubtless it would not be long before the man was missed, but if they could make it seem that he had simply strayed from his post rather than been killed, then the patrol would buy valuable extra minutes.

Jimmie now took over the lead, heading down a staircase that led into a courtyard. Three Land Rovers stood in a row and Don inspected them one by one. For a moment he considered the possibility of using them to make their escape, but then rejected the idea. There were limited tracks navigable by vehicle towards the border and to use any one of them would be to telegraph their intentions to the enemy. It would be no difficult task for the terrorists to track and follow them, whereas if the patrol remained on foot they might be moving slower but they would be able to choose any one of dozens of different routes.

'Disable them,' he whispered to Gavin.

While the patrol fanned out to cover him, Gavin worked through each of the three vehicles, opening the bonnet and cutting through every wire in sight. Lastly he removed all three rotary arms and hurled them over the wall. When he had finished he silently closed the bonnets so that to a casual observer they would look as if nothing had been touched.

Several covered alleyways led off the courtyard and, checking his sketch plan, Don indicated to Jimmie the one he thought would take them towards Eli. Jimmie couched the black plastic stock of his MP5 lovingly in the cupped palm of his left hand with his right firmly around the pistol grip. His forefinger was on the trigger and as he moved forward he swept the barrel to left and right in perfect alignment with the direction of his eyesight. It was a technique that he had perfected on the urban CQB ranges at Hereford, where he excelled at snap-shooting – firing by instinct at opportunity targets.

It was a skill he was thankful to have mastered, because suddenly, out of nowhere, two large men came briskly round the corner thirty yards ahead of him. They were deep in conversation, gesticulating with sweeping hand movements, their weapons slung over their shoulders and quite out of reach. The moment they saw the man to their front they froze, mouths wide in astonishment. Jimmie cursed. For a split second he considered rushing them with Tom to silence them with knives, but it was no use. Already they were reacting, hands fumbling for their Kalashnikovs as if in slow motion. Jimmie shook his head, trying to signal them to surrender, but then one of them started to shout a warning, turning to make it carry down the corridor behind him.

Jimmie fired two short, ferocious bursts, switching in between them from one man to the other. Each burst found its target, the clutch of 9mm bullets impacting in a tight group in low centre chest.

'That's done it,' Don said firmly. 'Cat's out of the bag. Move it!'

In a strange way every one of the SAS men felt as though a great weight had been lifted from his shoulders. The need for silence and stealth had now passed and the operation had shifted, in seconds, into a new and higher gear. It was a gear for which they were all well prepared.

Jimmie and Tom darted down the corridor, stepping over the two dead men. Behind them, Jerry quickly stooped and unfastened the top covers of the two Kalashnikovs, thereby disabling them. They were made of thin metal, and after leaning them in the corner of the floor and wall he stamped down on them hard, bending them beyond immediate repair.

'Nice work,' Don said.

'At least that's two weapons in the fort that aren't going to be shooting at us,' Jerry replied, warming to his commander's praise.

Gavin came up behind him. 'Shall I booby them, boss?'

'Why not?'

Gavin grinned and stooped beside the dead men. 'Watch and learn, lad,' he said to Jerry. 'You might have fucked up their weapons, but this is the way to take out a few of their mates as well.'

He took a couple of hand-grenades from his webbing and laid them on the floor. Then, after rolling both bodies on to their stomachs, he placed one grenade under each, gingerly removing the pin but ensuring that the dead man's weight on top of it prevented the handle from flying off.

'There we go. When their mates roll them over to check if they're dead, the handles fly off and the grenades explode, taking another couple of guys with them. Simple but effective.'

The patrol moved away from the courtyard fast, each man sweeping his arc in readiness for another contact. They could hear shouts now, echoing through the rooms and corridors of the stronghold as word spread that something was up and that intruders had breached the defences.

Suddenly there was a cry from the rear and Geordie let rip with his M206, firing the grenade launcher into the middle of a pack of men who appeared in pursuit. The 40mm grenade struck the lead man and exploded, cutting him open but showering the rest of the group with shards of white-hot metal. Geordie switched his finger from the grenade launcher to the automatic rifle's trigger and squeezed off a long burst, raking the falling men as Taff added a burst of his own from the SA80.

As they ran on, Geordie popped open the launcher and dropped out the empty case, slipping in a replacement and clapping the barrel shut.

'Reloaded!' he shouted back to Taff, who had been covering him and now backed away, skipping backwards after the retreating patrol.

They were now running, spinning down seemingly endless corridors and crossing rooms and courtyards.

'Eli!' Don shouted. 'Eli!'

If she could only let them know where she was, he thought, it would save valuable time. Then they could grab her and get the hell out of there. With each passing minute the odds were stacking up against them. For now there was undoubtedly confusion among the enemy. They wouldn't have any idea of the strength or exact whereabouts of the intruders, but that would soon pass as the shock of the assault wore off. Gradually they would establish which areas were still safe, and with that narrowing down would come a picture of the battle. Control would be re-established and blocking positions could be put in, restricting the movement of the SAS patrol and starting to hem it in. Unless they could achieve their aim and get out quickly they would end up boxed in and involved in a battle of attrition – and such a fight they couldn't possibly hope to win.

As they came to every doorway, one of the team would kick it open, searching for any clue as to the girl's whereabouts, but time after time there was nothing but disappointment.

'This place is a sodding rabbit warren,' Gavin barked angrily as he turned back from yet another empty room.

They emerged into another courtyard, larger than the one where they had found and disabled the three Land Rovers, but they hadn't gone half a dozen paces when a burst of machine-gun fire stitched the ground in front of them.

'Take cover!' Tom bellowed, throwing himself into a forward roll and coming up in a kneeling position, firing off the rifle part of his M206 as he sought out the target.

The second he located it, he flicked his finger to the trigger of the grenade launcher, braced himself and fired. The incoming fire had been from a man with a Kalashnikov in a window one floor above the courtyard. Overlooking the space below, it gave him a good view of the SAS patrol, and unless he was taken out Tom knew that he would be able to pin them down until help arrived. But the 40mm grenade was about to do its job.

It popped from the barrel of the M206 and shot through the air, slicing upwards in a neat little arc and in through the window itself. The startled look on the man's face was plain to see, turning halfway to blind panic in the instant before the grenade exploded behind him. His body was catapulted out of the window by the blast, somersaulting with the beautiful grace of an Olympic diver before ploughing head first into the unforgiving paving stones of the courtyard.

'Nice shooting, Tom,' Jerry called.

But Tom was too busy reloading to hear. His full attention was on the drills. For praise might give you a momentary warm glow of pride, but fast and accurate drills kept you alive. Praise was for the new boys.

A flight of steps led up to a platform, on the other side of which Don could see a doorway that seemed to give access to the main living quarters he had spied from the OP.

'That looks like it,' he shouted to Jimmie. 'Take the lead and go for it!'

'Right, boss,' Jimmie acknowledged, darting past Tom, who had completed his reloading drills and was refastening his ammunition pouch.

Jimmie sprang at the steps and hurled himself up them, but halfway up, the stairway darkened and he looked up to see a man blocking his path. Instantly he blazed away with the MP5, but unlike his first victims this man was ready. Pulling back out of the line of fire, the man managed to get clear just in time to avoid being cut down. Armed with a Soviet-made AKR sub-machine-gun, he held the compact little weapon in a pistol grip over the top of the stairs, and squeezed the trigger. The gun shuddered from the savage recoil, spraying the 5.45mm bullets inaccurately in every direction. Jimmie flinched and hugged the sides of the wall, making himself as small as possible so as to reduce his target area.

Seeing him pinned down, Tom took careful aim with his M206 rifle from down below and fired at the blazing AKR. His fourth round struck the wooden stock, shattering and jarring the firer's wrist. There was a cry of pain and the man dropped the weapon and clutched his aching hand.

Jimmie reacted immediately, powering up the steps and throwing himself over the top, spinning as he landed, seeking out the man. He found him shrinking back against the wall and drilled him with a burst from the MP5.

'Clear!' he yelled down the steps, crouching ready to provide covering fire to the others as they pounded up to join him.

But even he couldn't prevent the inevitable first casualty that the patrol then suffered. As Taff closed up, the last man up the staircase, a single shot rang out and he staggered and dropped to one knee.

'I'm hit!' he cried.

Jimmie desperately sought out the sniper but whoever he was he had chosen his position well. Then a second shot rang out and Jimmie saw Taff's head jerk forward as if hit with a baseball bat. He toppled to the floor and rolled back down the steps, coming to rest in a heap at the bottom. His eyes were open, dead.

Before the sniper could conceal himself, Jimmie caught sight of the rifle's muzzle.

'Dragunov,' he muttered, reciting the name of the dreaded Soviet 7.62mm sniper rifle. Equipped with a detachable non-variable x4 scope, it had an effective range of at least 600 metres. Firing from a tower that dominated the courtyard, it had been required to cover barely a third of that distance. Taff hadn't stood a chance.

Jimmie slid out the retractable butt-stock to give himself a more stable shot and tucked it into his shoulder and cheek, before taking quick aim and firing off a double tap at the sniper's location. But the MP5 was a short-range weapon and although as accurate as a rifle up to 100 metres, at anything over that distance its accuracy deteriorated. Jimmie saw his rounds impact on the plaster and brickwork around the muzzle of the Dragunov but the firer was already sighting on a second target, the rest of the patrol on the platform above the Scot.

'Get that fucker someone!' Jimmie shouted as he tried again. 'Line of water barrels, twelve o'clock, fifty yards, Dragunov sniper,' he barked out.

'Got 'im,' Rod's voice rang out.

Jimmie flung himself on his belly and tucked in behind the M249 light machine-gun. The next instant a stream of accurate 5.56mm bullets was pasting the area of the water barrels, snaking closer to the sniper. Suddenly the barrel of the Dragunov twitched and the whole rifle tumbled into view, falling from the wounded man's hands and down into the square.

'Good shooting,' Don shouted.

Instead of staying in cover and nursing his wound, the sniper stupidly broke out and tried to make a run for it. Rod's M249 followed him all the way, finally cutting him down within sight of his escape.

'That's for Taff,' Rod said bitterly.

There were shouts from behind them and as the patrol sprinted across the platform towards the doorway on the far side, a group of men appeared in the courtyard. However, having learnt that the SAS were not to be messed with, they held back, taking cover and trying to pin the patrol down with longer-range fire rather than closing with them in CQB.

'We can't afford to let them delay us,' Gavin said to Don, crawling up beside him as Rod and the others returned fire. 'If we get bogged down in a fire-fight it'll give their mates time to surround us and then we're done for.'

Don thought for a second. 'We'll split in two, each fire team covering the other by bounds. Fire and manoeuvre.'

'Roger.'

In accordance with pre-arranged drills, Gavin took command of the second fire team, which consisted of

Rod with the M249 LMG, Geordie with the M206 rifle and grenade launcher, and himself with his M16. Don continued forward with the lead fire team of himself, Jerry, Jimmie and his MP5 and Tom with the second of the M206s. Both teams were as balanced as possible, each able to provide effective covering fire for the other in the deadly game of leapfrog that now ensued.

While Don led the way off the platform and into the next warren of rooms and corridors, Gavin kept up a steady fire on their pursuers, watching for the moment to order the break-clean from cover. There were at least half a dozen men in the courtyard now and others were joining them by the minute. What was more serious was that they were starting to work their way around the edges. Some form of command was being imposed upon them and, unlike the initial chaotic response, they were becoming a cohesive force instead of a frightened rabble. The clock was ticking and unless the SAS were able to extricate themselves within the next ten to fifteen minutes from the stronghold, the chances were that they would all die there.

It was the thought that was uppermost in Don's mind as he pounded up the steps leading into the new block.

'Go firm here. Prepare to give covering fire.'

His men toppled into cover around him, each settling into position and readying his weapon.

'Jerry, make ready an M72,' Don ordered.

'Wilco, boss.'

Jerry unslung the slender khaki tube from over his shoulder and tore off the end covers. Then, holding the tube in a firm overhand grasp, he snapped it open, and as it telescoped out, almost doubling in length, an eyepiece popped out from the body. Next, with thumb and forefinger he pulled back a small catch to arm the rocket couched inside the disposable fibreglass tubing.

'Ready,' he shouted.

'Try to get that doorway,' he ordered, indicating the main entrance into the courtyard from which yet more men were appearing.

Jerry crawled forward until he could get a bead on it, and, with the tube over his shoulder, he checked that its backblast area was clear and then sighted on his target.

'Firing now,' he said.

The tube was over his right shoulder, his left hand holding the front part of the body, while his right curled over the middle, its fingers on the rubber-capped firing lever. He pressed this down firmly and the rocket exploded into life, firing out of the tube and shooting down towards the door. Jerry looked behind him and saw the black scorch mark of the backblast on the stonework, but the real damage erupted in the courtyard, where the 66mm rocket powered into the concrete above the door-frame and exploded in a shower of falling masonry and metal fragments.

'Now, Gavin!' Don shouted out, ordering the break-clean.

As Gavin's fire team broke from cover, zigzagging back to Don's position, Don's men poured a ferocious stream of lead into the enemy positions, raking them from end to end and keeping their heads down while Gavin, Rod and Geordie sprinted back.

'Last man,' Gavin shouted as he backed past Don, shooting from the hip in short, controlled bursts.

Once through the doorway, Gavin led his team up the stairs, taking the steps three at a time until he found himself in a corridor with only one closed door leading off it.

Without pausing he stood back, bracing himself against the opposite wall, and kicked at the lock with the sole of his boot. The wooden frame shattered and the door fell inwards, landing with a crash on the floor. On the other side of it he saw a bedroom, comfortably appointed, and, from behind the bed's bright coverlet, a frightened pair of eyes peeked out at him. He stared in disbelief.

'Eli?'

The girl rose into view. 'That's me. But who the devil are you?'

'I'm the man with the box of chocolates, love. Time to go.'

13

The moment he heard the firing, Ceda was on his feet.

'Murap, go to the girl. Take two of the men with you. Whatever happens we mustn't let her go.'

At the head of the table Uncle Bandram looked up. 'Who would come all this way for her? Who is it?'

'I don't know, but whoever they are they won't get away with it,' Ceda replied.

He went briskly to his room nearby, buckled on his ammunition belt and took a Kalashnikov from the rack by the door. Ali came in after him, fingering a pistol.

'What about me? Shouldn't I stay here with Uncle?'

Ceda glanced at him with contempt. He picked up another Kalashnikov and tossed it at him. 'You're coming with me. You've wanted to join the family and be accepted for years. Well, now's your chance. Welcome to the heart and hearth of the Bandrams.'

Another burst of gunfire sounded deep in the stronghold, followed by screams.

'Just one thing,' Ceda added cruelly. 'Don't expect these men to be as compliant as the trucker you murdered in Britain.'

To Ceda's delight Ali went pale. Ceda grabbed him

by the scruff of the neck and propelled him out of the room. 'Come on, cousin. You can have the honour of leading the way.'

'But . . . but . . . I . . .'

'No buts. Move!'

He planted his hand in the small of Ali's back and shoved him towards the sound of the firing.

Murap jogged past with his selected men, two large tribesmen armed to the teeth.

'If you see Ramesh, tell him to seal all the exits,' Ceda shouted. 'I'll hunt down the dogs and kill them.'

The first thing he came upon were the bodies of the two men that Jimmie had shot. He was just rounding the corner when he saw another of his men stooping to check them. Something stopped Ceda in his tracks and as he hauled Ali back around the safety of the corner he shouted, 'Don't touch them!'

But it was too late. The man had grabbed the nearest corpse and was rolling it over. Even from his position Ceda heard the metallic click of the grenade lever flying free. His instincts had been right. Neither body had been lying in a natural pose of death, no wounds were visible on their backs and the bloodstains on the ground had been smeared by movement. They had clearly been moved, and an enemy only moved a corpse for one of two reasons – to search it or to booby-trap it. Infiltrators would have little cause to search a dead guard, so the second solution was all that was left.

Ceda winced at the sound of the explosion, magnified in the confined space of the corridor. Dust and debris spiralled along to him and he covered his mouth and nose with one great hand. When he looked there was a third body added to the previous two, only this latest one was lacerated from head to foot by the grenade fragments. Ceda moved cautiously towards it. The second body had not been harmed by the explosion, whose blast had been driven upwards, but Ceda guessed that there would probably be a second grenade under him as well.

'Stand back,' he ordered Ali. 'Over there around the corner. Watch and learn.'

With that, he lay himself carefully along the top of the second corpse, grasped it around the shoulders and rolled backwards, pulling the body on to its side into a position where it fully shielded him from the grenade that he had known would be there. Once again there was the ping of the lever followed by the detonation. When the dust cleared, he got to his feet and surveyed the damage. Ali reappeared sheepishly from around the corner.

'Nice,' Ceda said to himself.

Ali, thinking that the compliment had been intended for him, grinned, but Ceda disabused him of it the next second.

'Nice work, by whoever planted those.' He crouched down and inspected the wounds on the corpses. They were peppered with tiny fragments from a metal coil instead of the larger splinters that an older make of grenade would have inflicted.

'Could be British,' he said thoughtfully.

The bullet wounds in each of the two original corpses were tightly grouped, and clearly 9mm. Ceda nodded knowingly. 'I see,' he said to himself, and his thoughts darted back to the man he remembered from the service station in Britain, the one who had so nearly prevented his escape.

'What is it?' Ali asked, becoming concerned.

Ceda smiled. 'It is a worthy opponent at last.'

They left the scene of the carnage and went in pursuit of the infiltrators, gathering a force of half a dozen men along the way. Ceda barked out orders, sending other men in every direction to seek out the enemy and seal off their escape.

More shots sounded, along with the burst of grenades.

'M206s,' Ceda said with a wry smile, his nose sniffing the air like a badger venturing out of its sett. 'I like these men.'

He broke into a jog, shouting for his men to follow him just as the rocket from Jerry's M72 detonated in the courtyard some way away ahead of him. It was a grizzly picture that greeted him when he arrived. The rocket had brought down part of the stonework above the door-frame and two men beneath it had been virtually decapitated. Their skulls were crushed and their brains lay on the dusty floor about them. Ali took one look and retched.

Someone shouted, 'They're making a break for it!'

Ceda darted forward instantly. 'Keep after them. Don't give them any breathing space. Hound them into the grave!'

But as he stepped into the courtyard he saw a sight that froze him on the spot. To one side a body lay face down in the debris and rubble. In an instant he was kneeling at its side.

'Uncle!'

Gently he rolled Uncle Bandram over. The eyes turned towards him and the lips moved. He put his ear close to the bloodied mouth to catch its words.

'Avenge me, my nephew. Avenge all of us. I had hoped to do it myself, but now it's up to you and Ramesh. Get even with Sanji. Do this for me.'

Ceda fought to hold back his tears. 'You'll live to do it yourself, Uncle,' he said, not really believing his own words.

Gilma Bandram smiled and shook his head, coughing up blood with the effort of speaking. 'No. It's up to you now, Ceda. See to it. See to it.'

His eyes froze and set, the life exhaling from him into the cordite-filled air of the courtyard.

Ceda looked at the men around him. All were staring with disbelief at the body in his arms.

He reached down and closed the eyes, laying his uncle back in the dust and draping his cloak about him, covering the face.

'What are you all staring at? Haven't you seen a corpse before?' he barked at them. He could feel his anger rising now, threatening to blot out reason. He had to fight it, suppress it, transform it into an ice-cold, iron determination. Anger alone had never achieved an aim. It was only as a springboard to other emotions that it could serve a purpose.

Looking up he could just see where the infiltrators were leaving the platform and even in the poor light that shone around the courtyard from the few bulbs he could tell that their movement was that of professional soldiers. His own men were good, but with such an enemy as this trickery and cunning were the best weapons. He would do best to outwit them and outmanoeuvre them. He had to use his advantages rather than allow them to dictate the pace and the course of the fight. Closing with them would obviously result in heavy casualties. They had already proved as much. They were equipped with the most modern of weapons and knew all too well how to use them to maximum effect. But if Ceda could only box them in, force them out into the open, wear them down without closing to close quarters, then he would see just how good they were.

'Ramesh,' he shouted. 'I must speak to Ramesh.'

In response two of his men went away in search of his brother. The others, seeking to avenge the death of Uncle Bandram, surged forward, only to be met by a hail of fire from Don's fire team.

'No, you fools! Can't you see that's exactly what they want. Stay where you are and engage them with fire. I have other plans for our friends.'

In accordance with his instructions, some of the men started to work around the edge of the courtyard, and as soon as they could they reached the other doorways on the far side and disappeared through them, looking for a way round to the rear of the enemy position. Then, a few minutes later, some of the men arrived back with an armful of RPG7s and spare rockets.

'Well done,' Ceda congratulated them. 'A purse full of gold for the man who scores the first kill.'

Instantly the men were in action, fitting the rockets on to the launchers, aiming and firing. The rockets arced across the courtyard and slammed into the stonework around the retreating SAS patrol.

'Reload and fire again!' Ceda shouted.

Another volley followed the first, but this time the SAS had seen the new danger and their automatic weapons spat back at them, bullets hosing the ground until one of the RPG7 firers tumbled over, dead. The man beside him retrieved the weapon and prepared it to fire, aiming for the SAS light machine-gun. His rocket streaked towards its target but instead of the M249 it found in its path the doubled-over figure of Geordie frantically fighting to clear a stoppage from the breech of his M206. The rocket burrowed into the ground at his feet, exploding upwards and lifting him into the air. When Ceda saw the body flung aside like a puppet he cheered and slapped the firer on the back.

'Now another! Give me another!'

But the SAS men had vanished into the building. Ceda cursed and urged his comrades to follow up.

'But remember, don't get too close to them. Like any cornered rat they are at their most dangerous when in a tight corner.'

He was about to follow them himself when a man appeared at his elbow. Ceda turned to him impatiently.

'Yes, what is it?'

The man smiled proudly. 'Ramesh. I have found him.'

'Well? Where is he?'

Something in the man's eyes held Ceda back.

'He says you are to let them escape.'

Ceda stared at him as if he was mad but the

man repeated his refrain, adding, 'Ramesh says to trust him.'

All for going on, Ceda nevertheless paused to consider his brother's enigmatic message. Ramesh had never let him down before. Their mutual trust and support had got the two of them out of a multitude of scrapes in the past, and in his heart he knew that he had no alternative. If Ramesh had discovered the infiltrators' weak point, then Ceda would do well to heed his advice.

Turning to Ali, he shouted, 'Hold the men where they are.'

Ali looked at him questioningly, but Ceda barked back, 'Do as I say! Now!'

While the rest of the patrol sought out the cover of temporary fire positions, Don went quickly into the room to confront Eli.

'We haven't much time. Come with us and stick close to Jerry here.'

He thrust her towards Jerry, who had been briefed to look after her.

'How do you expect to get out of here?' she asked in amazement.

'Don't worry about it. That's my problem. You just keep your head down and do as you're told.' He turned to Gavin. 'You and Jimmie take point. How's Geordie?'

'Dead.'

Don took it in but carried on. 'Jerry, stick with me. Rod and Tom, bring up the rear. You two have got the bulk of the fire-power now. Make full use of it. Give them plenty of stick and keep them off our backs. Any questions? Right. Move!'

Leading the way back to the walkway where the ropes led down the cliff face, Gavin steered a roundabout course that avoided the courtyard, which was now awash with the enemy. By now he had a fair idea of the layout of the stronghold and it was not too difficult a task to find the route back to their entry point. As they went, Rod and Tom burned through their ammunition. They had left a full resupply back with the bergens for the return march, should they need it, but for now they were determined to give the best possible account of themselves.

While Rod hosed down anyone who was stupid enough to show his face, Tom popped off a series of 40mm grenades into the more distant targets, seeking to establish a good spread of fires throughout the complex in the hope of diverting attention away from their flight. In some of the rooms his grenades found plenty of furnishings and bedding to catch alight and within minutes flames were sprouting from several of the windows as the fire spread, unchecked by the fort's inhabitants, who had other concerns.

'We've got to break clean before we dare start down the ropes,' Don said as they neared the walkway.

'I think I've got just the thing,' Gavin replied.

He took a satchel from around his shoulder and darted back and found a narrow archway. Then, crouching down, he opened the satchel and withdrew prepared packs of plastic explosive, which he began to set in place around the overhanging arch and adjoining walls.

'This should take them a bit of time to clear,' he said

as he unreeled the electric cable and wired it into the firing box.

'Take cover, everyone!' he yelled when it was ready, and as soon as the last man was out of sight he pressed the button. An almighty roar filled the air and the ground rocked beneath their feet as if an earthquake was taking place. As the air cleared, Don saw that the archway had disappeared, its place being filled by a pile of rubble that any would-be pursuers would have to burrow through.

'Good work. Now fix up some remote claymores and we'll be on our way,' he said.

Aided by Jimmie, Gavin set up a pair of the devices, laying their cable across the path and drawing them taut to act as trip-wires. In this way, even when their pursuers had managed to get through the rubble they would stumble straight into the next trap, setting off the two-directional anti-personnel mines and releasing the barrage of steel ball-bearings in among them.

'Time to go!' Don commanded.

They set off down the walkway until they came to the point where the ropes had been left. Jimmie skipped over the parapet, found his footing on the outer edge and felt for the ropes.

'Got 'em.'

One by one the men slid over the edge and leaned out into the darkness, Jimmie handing them the ropes. Jerry helped Eli.

'I don't suppose you've ever done any climbing?' he asked hopefully.

'Me? You must be kidding,' she answered, her eyes wide and her voice starting to quake.

He cursed under his breath. 'Might have guessed. Here,' he said, turning his back to her and bending at the knees, 'Hop on. We'll go down piggy-back.'

Eli peered down into the darkness.

'Don't look! Just do as I say.'

She took one look back into the body of the smoking fortress, listening to the shouts, explosions and bursts of gunfire, and did as Jerry had instructed, linking her arms about his neck and clasping on tight.

'Grip me round the waist with your legs, like horse riding. Just don't throttle me, that's all I ask. If you do, we both fall.'

Last over the parapet, Tom scattered a handful of tiny anti-personnel mines the length of the walkway to dissuade anyone from coming too close. It would take some care to clear them in the dark and by that time, he sincerely hoped, the surviving members of the patrol would be safely on the ground.

The descent was considerably smoother than the upwards climb as the ropes had been fixed securely in place and would be abandoned there once the SAS men had made use of them. However, should anyone decide to follow them down, Tom had been instructed to sow a more comprehensive anti-personnel minefield at the bottom, combining it with further claymores and trip-wires.

First to reach the valley floor was Don, and as each man arrived thereafter he directed them into positions of all-round defence until the last member of the patrol was accounted for and they were ready to set off. Shaking out into formation, everyone did a hurried check of weapons and equipment, reloading with full mags, ensuring pouches and webbing were fastened, and taking a quick sip of water from the canteens in readiness for the night tab to the RV, which they knew would be fast and furious.

'All set?' Don said quietly, casting around the patrol and receiving the thumbs up from every man in turn. 'Move now.'

He rose from the ground and the patrol, as one man, rose with him. Jimmie and Tom never heard the bullets that cut them down.

It was as if a hailstorm had been unleashed, but instead of the harmless balls of ice it was lead stinging the air and pock-marking the sand at their feet.

'Ambush!' Don screamed at the top of his voice, hurling himself on to his stomach and firing off a burst from his Colt Commando in the approximate direction of the enemy.

In accordance with standard anti-ambush drills, every man who was still able blazed off a series of bursts, at the same time wriggling backwards into the nearest available cover. Rod got into the rocks first, flicked down the bipod of his M249 and fired a steady stream of lead at each of the enemy's muzzle flashes coming at them from out of the dark. Jerry pushed Eli down beside the buzzing machine-gun and then retrieved Tom's M206, discarding his own M16 and starting to fire off 40mm grenades at every likely position where an enemy might be located.

Don pulled the pins on two white-phosphorus smoke grenades and signalled for Gavin to do the same. Then, when both men were ready, they threw together, achieving a good spread with the four grenades that covered the front within seconds with a thick, noxious blanket of white smoke.

'Move!' Don shouted.

At his command everyone fired off another burst and then broke out, each man running in a different direction with the intention of making his way independently to the RV, where the bergens lay in wait. However, as Jerry was burdened with the extra responsibility for Eli, Don stuck with him, leaving it to Rod and Gavin to peel off to either flank and confuse the enemy as to what was happening.

As Gavin and Rod went, veering in opposite directions, Don could hear them shouting until even he began to believe that a substantial force was counter-attacking the ambushers. He and Jerry on the other hand, held their fire, preferring stealth to mask their withdrawal behind the dense smokescreen. But Don knew that they had little more than seconds before it cleared and then they could expect the enemy to follow up into the killing area to check on the dead and search for survivors.

As Jerry ran, he half pushed and half pulled Eli after him, urging her in whispers to keep quiet and run for her life. Don brought up the rear, sweeping his Colt Commando from side to side, safety switch set to fully automatic, finger on the trigger, ready to blast anything that moved. From further off in the night they continued to hear the sounds of Gavin and Rod, the M16 and M249 replying to the blazing Kalashnikovs, SLRs and GPMGs that seemed to be sprouting from the ground like the spirits of the dead.

They ran for what seemed an age until Eli collapsed gasping on the rock-strewn bed of a dry river.

'That's it. I'm all in,' she gasped. 'I can't run another step. Leave me here and save yourselves.'

Jerry knelt beside her. In the dark she could see him smiling. 'You're just after another piggy-back, aren't you?' he said.

Then he helped her to her feet and she got on to his back again. 'Better take this, boss,' he said, handing the M206 to Don.

They ran on, Jerry hobbling along and Don continuing to provide the cover. When they were well clear of the killing area they stopped and Don took a compass bearing to get a fix on the RV.

'It's about another five hundred yards. Can you manage it?'

'No problem. She's as light as a feather.'

A fresh burst of firing far off on their right indicated that the ambushers were pursuing one of the other two SAS men, and a second later the familiar chatter of the M249 identified the unlucky recipient of this attention as Rod. Jerry and Don swapped glances, both looking away and pressing on as the M249 went suddenly silent after a crescendo of Kalashnikov fire.

It was another fifteen minutes before they arrived at the tumble of rocks where they had stashed the bergens. Jerry set Eli down, stretching and rubbing his aching back muscles and stamping to loosen his joints, which were protesting at the furious pace and the extra load.

'So I was as light as a feather, was I?' Eli smiled.

'Well, almost,' he conceded.

Don dived into the pile of bergens, flinging Jerry's at him and digging out his own.

'Do you want me to set up some claymores?' Jerry asked.

'No way. Gavin could run right into them. I want to kill as many of the terrorists as you do, but not if it puts Gavin at risk.'

When they had sorted out their kit and each had a drink of water, they settled down to wait for five minutes to see if any of the others had made it. Don checked his watch impatiently every few seconds until at last the five minutes were up and they were prepared to go.

'Going without me?'

They looked up in surprise as Gavin tottered into the circle of rocks. He collapsed exhausted on the ground, gasping for breath. Jerry rushed to check him for wounds but Gavin waved him away.

'I'm fine. Just a bit knackered, that's all. But I think Rod bought it.'

'I know. We heard the firing.'

Gavin wiped his face with his neck cloth. 'He was quite close to me at one point and I think that's when they surrounded him. I caught a glimpse of him in the light of some flares they were using. He was standing alone firing from the hip until his box mag emptied. That's when the bastards cut him down.'

'You're sure he was dead?' Don asked.

'Sure. I saw the fucking rounds hit him.'

Don swore and turned away. The mission had been a

bloody disaster. There were only three of them left out of the eight-man team, and although they had rescued the hostage they still had to make it across the border. The enemy were in hot pursuit and it would be daylight in a few hours.

'We'd better get moving,' he said at last. 'I'll take point. Gavin, you bring up the rear, and Jerry, watch over Eli. Here' – he handed back the M206 – 'you're the heavy artillery from now on.'

They all replenished their stocks of ammunition and now that the last man was accounted for Don gave Jerry permission to booby-trap the RV and the unused bergens. He went about it with a will, sowing anti-personnel mines, laying claymores and trip-wires, and placing grenades under the packs and the surrounding rocks, removing the pins and balancing them as Gavin had demonstrated in the stronghold with the bodies.

'There,' Jerry said when he had finished. 'That ought to do it.'

They set off with two hours to spare before first light, blazing a furious trail across country on a simple compass bearing that led straight to the frontier's nearest point. It was unsubtle and even dangerous, but Don reckoned that the priority now was to reach friendly territory by daylight. It was true that they could hide up throughout the next day if they were unable to make it, but that increased the chances of their being found by the terrorists. Also, he didn't know what sort of rapport they had with the local military commanders. He hoped that the two would have nothing to do with each other, but he couldn't rule out the chance that the terrorists might be able to call on reinforcements in the form of army patrols, helicopters, vehicles and tracker dogs.

Eli struggled to keep up, and with reluctance Don eventually decided to slow the pace, judging that they would make better speed with Eli walking by herself than with her being carried by the men in turn. Piggy-back rides were all very well over a short distance, but on a difficult night exfiltration under duress were not to be recommended as an efficient mode of transport.

The ground changed as they marched, switching almost unnoticeably from the barren rock of the fort's surrounding area to the rolling hills and forbidding mountains of the border zone. Every so often they stopped to catch their breath and have a drink of water. At each halt the three men broke open packets of glucose sweets, pushing the succulent capsules into their mouths and drawing on the instant energy. Jerry handed a fistful to Eli.

'Suck one. It goes straight into the bloodstream and feels like a kick in the backside.'

She cautiously popped a capsule in her mouth and felt the sweet crumble the moment it came into contact with her tongue, the glucose washing round her mouth and bringing her wide awake.

'That's terrific,' she enthused, and popped in another.

'Save some for later. We've got a long way to go yet,' Jerry warned.

It wasn't long before Don noticed a lightening of the eastern horizon, and strangely enough it was only then that he realized how exhausted he was. It was not simply from lack of sleep or the physical effort of the attack and then the flight, but more from the stress of high-intensity combat, a tiredness that no amount of training could ever diminish.

Slowly, the razor-thin line of purple brightened and spread, cutting the night in two, pushing the sky up into the heavens once again, locking away its stars for another day and throwing a pale, watery light across the barren lunar landscape. Against this backdrop of mountains and steep forests, valleys and cascading streams, four tiny, stick-like characters clawed their painfully slow way.

Suddenly they heard the noise of the engine. Instantly they were on their bellies, wriggling forward into a ditch that widened and deepened into a dry river-bed. Over the far lip they heard the sound of a vehicle, a jeep, bouncing across country and coming closer.

'Sounds like he's alone,' Don whispered.

'Shall we take him?' Gavin asked.

'Might have to. Let's take a look.'

They crawled forward until they came to a patch of bone-dry scrub grass. Shielding their face behind it they peered cautiously over the top and saw the jeep coming straight at them. Don and Gavin looked questioningly at each other and Don waved Jerry forward with his M206.

'Don't fire unless I give the order. They might not see us.'

Jerry checked that the grenade launcher was loaded and ready, brought the butt into his shoulder and flicked up the sight. But when the jeep was about thirty yards off it skidded to a halt. The dust cleared, the doors opened and four men got out. The tallest of the group spread a map on the bonnet and they launched into a heated debate, pointing at the far valley towards which Don and the others had been heading.

'Looks like they're trying to figure out where the border is,' Don whispered.

Eli had crawled up beside them and stared in terror. 'That must be Ramesh. He's the image of his brother. I'm sure of it.'

'Ramesh Bandram?'

'It must be.'

Thoughts raced through Don's head. Eventually he said to Gavin and Jerry, 'Do you reckon you can pick off the two guys on the left?'

'What are you up to, boss?' Gavin asked suspiciously.

'If we can take a hostage of our own I reckon we might just persuade them to leave us be.' He slid out the retractable butt of his Colt Commando. 'I can take the third guy if you two can tackle his mates.'

Gavin stared in disbelief. 'And what about Bandram? Do you think he's just going to sit there while we slaughter his men around him?'

'Of course not. That's why the moment I've dropped his mate I'm going to bring him down with a wounding shot.'

A sly grin spread across Gavin's face and he checked the sight on his M16. 'At this range I should bloody well hope I could put a round between my target's eyes.'

'Nothing fancy. Just kill him. Don't take any risks.'

When all three men were ready, Don steadied his breathing and sighted on his target.

'On my shot, lads. After the count of three. One . . . two . . . three . . .'

The three shots rang out as one and across the thirty yards of rocky shrub three bodies crumpled around the jeep. Instantly Don switched his point of aim and just as the fourth man understood what had happened he fired again, a single shot that struck home exactly as intended, winging him in the upper arm. Before the wounded man had even hit the ground the three SAS men were up and running, Don heading straight for the jeep in a beeline, the other two swinging out to left and right in an arc. The man Don had shot had left his weapon in the jeep and by the time he had recovered from the shot and started to crawl towards it, Don was closing the last few yards and bringing the still-smoking muzzle of his Colt Commando to bear.

'Don't even think about it,' Don growled, half to himself.

The wounded man lay in the dirt, his wound slight but bleeding a lot.

Don came up in front of him as Gavin and Jerry arrived and checked the others to make sure they were dead.

'What's your name?' Don asked.

Jerry started to translate the question into Urdu but halfway through the man smirked.

'Save your breath. I speak English.' He glared at Jerry with contempt. 'Probably better than you do.'

'So what's your name then?' Don asked again, aiming his Colt Commando at the figure on the ground, his finger tightening on the trigger.

The man tossed back his head, ignoring the pain of his bullet wound.

'I am Ramesh Bandram. And none of you will get out of Pakistan alive.'

14

When Don had dressed Ramesh's wound he hauled him to his feet.

'What about taking the vehicle, boss?' Gavin asked.

'No. It's too visible now that the sun's up. We'll move on foot as planned.'

He stuck the muzzle of his Colt Commando in the small of Ramesh's back and shoved him forward.

'Walk.'

'You don't really think you can get away with this, do you?'

'You'd better hope we do, for your sake.'

'My brother and the rest of the men are right behind us.'

'Then we'll have a nice little reception waiting for them, won't we? Now that you've been kind enough to warn us.'

They set off, Don leading the way with Ramesh, Jerry and Eli walking behind, and Gavin bringing up the rear, keeping a watchful eye on the horizon for any approaching trouble. The border was getting closer by the minute and Don again forced the pace. As he walked,

Ramesh turned his head and asked, 'How much do you know about Sanji?'

Don poked him in the back with his gun. 'Shut up and keep moving.'

But Ramesh wasn't to be silenced. 'You're a professional, I can see that. Your men have fought well. The ones back there died well also. You deserve to know the truth.'

'And I suppose you're going to tell it to me?'

Ramesh laughed. It was the laugh of a man who has long since conquered fear and Don couldn't help respecting his prisoner. 'There are always several versions of any truth, all of them partially wrong and partially right. I suspect your bosses have only allowed you to know the minimum required to do the job.'

If only you knew how right you are, Don thought bitterly.

'I have been a soldier myself. I know how we get used by the hidden men, the faceless ones. They're the soldier's real enemy. They send him to his death for reasons he is never allowed to hear. He just gets the public version, which is little better than an outright lie.'

He turned and winked at Don. 'I can see you know what I mean.'

Gavin called from the back. 'Do you want me to gag him, boss?'

'No,' Don said thoughtfully, and then to Ramesh, 'OK then, let's have it. Give me your version, the truth as you see it. Tell me about Sanji.'

Ramesh glanced back at Eli, ignoring her look of hatred. 'In 1947 Sanji was a minor official in the British administration that was preparing to quit India. As you know, at that time there was no such state as Pakistan, the country was all one, Muslims and Hindus living alongside each other. Then Pakistan was formed as the future homeland for the Muslims and the great treks began. Muslims who had lived in India for generations had to leave their homes and trek north, while Hindus who had lived for millennia in the states that were to become Pakistan travelled south. Some saw it as the only solution to the internal strife of the country that the British had kept together with the might of the army, but others saw it as the greatest disaster to befall us. Gandhi himself thought that, given time, the two religions could co-exist. But it was not to be.'

He paused, the emotion taking hold of him.

'You can hardly blame Sanji for any of that,' Don argued. 'You yourself said that he was only a minor official.'

'Of course I don't blame him for that. Perhaps the great separation had to be. I don't know. But what I do know is that it was the hot summertime, tempers were short and people were desperate. Terrible things started to happen. The killings began. No one knows where or how it started, but within no time at all Hindus and Muslims were killing each other.'

Don felt his flesh crawl as he got a suspicion of what was to come.

'When our dear, nice little Mr Sanji was not working conscientiously in his office, he was doing other things. Abominable, unspeakable things. Secretly, he was the head of an extremist organization that set out, not so much to ensure that the Muslims from his district of Delhi all fled to Pakistan, as to exterminate them *en masse* before they even had a chance of leaving.'

'I don't believe it!' Eli screamed at him, running forward and throwing herself upon him. With his good arm Ramesh thrust her off until Jerry could get control of her. 'He's lying,' she shouted to Don and the others. 'Don't you see it?'

'I said he could say his piece, Eli. I'll see your grandfather has ample opportunity to contradict him,' Don said gently.

Ramesh nodded his thanks and continued. 'He worked as an office clerk for the British by day, and by night he roamed the streets of the Muslim districts at the head of his gang, hunting down innocent women and children and putting them to the sword.'

Behind him Eli was weeping as Jerry walked with one arm around her. Every so often she muttered, 'He's lying. It's all lies. It must be.'

'Among those that he killed was a young married couple. Their name was Bandram.' He turned and looked sadly at Don. 'They were my parents. Ceda and I were only babies. Our Uncle Gilma found us where our mother had hidden us in the family house. He saved us and took us to his home, only to find that Sanji and his gang had been there too. They had killed my uncle's wife and children. Now do you see why we want him? It has taken us all this time to track him down.'

Don's pace slowed and he stared into the harsh light of the morning sky, trying to sift the facts. Ramesh's story had the ring of truth about it. He could feel it in his bones.

'If what you say is true, it's terrible. Yet it doesn't excuse the kidnapping of an innocent girl and it certainly doesn't excuse what your brother did in Britain. That was every bit as barbaric as the things you're accusing Sanji of.'

Ramesh sighed. 'It was never our intention to hurt anyone else. I can only assume that when my brother found himself so close to Sanji and yet saw the prospect of the evil bastard slipping through his fingers, his desperation got the better of him. I know that is no excuse and he will have to pay for it.'

They had come over a rise where the track led between tall, wind-blasted pines. In front of them the ground sloped down towards a broad stream that shone like glass. Ramesh pointed at it.

There. That's what you want. That stream marks the border. On the other side of it is India. Cross that and you're free.'

Suddenly there was a warning shout from the back and Don spun round to see Gavin doubling towards him.

'Trouble. Look.' He pointed back to where two vehicles were hurtling towards them, clouds of dust rising from the wheels.

Don quickly estimated the distance to the border. 'Come on!' he shouted, pushing Ramesh forward and urging the others on. 'Run for it.'

As Gavin ran beside him he panted, 'There's no guarantee Ceda will stop at the stream. They cross it often enough anyway. It probably means fuck all to him.'

'I'm not aiming for the stream. That outcrop of rock just short of it should provide us with good cover. We can fight him off from there. With luck the Pakistani border guards will hear the shooting and come to investigate, and when they do, he'll bugger off and we can nip across. Even if the border means nothing to the Bandrams it bloody well will to the Pakistani authorities.'

They reached the outcrop as the vehicles were screeching to a halt on the crest a hundred yards behind them. Diving into the cover of the rocks and the few trees, Don, Gavin and Jerry turned their weapons on the men pouring out of the jeeps.

'Don't shoot until they do. We'll try and do a deal.'

Ceda was the first to address them. He had found Ramesh's jeep and the three dead men, but as his brother wasn't among them he guessed what had happened. Standing in the open, he hailed Don, demanding that Ramesh be freed.

'Cocky bugger, isn't he?' Gavin said, taking a bead on him, his finger itching on the trigger.

Don stood up and took a step into the open, where Ceda could see him.

'I'll do a deal. I'll let your brother go if you come over here and surrender.'

'Now why the hell would I want to do a thing like that?'

'Because you murdered innocent men in my country.'

'It's war, Mr SAS man. There are always casualties in war.'

'Like your parents? Was that war? Was their death justified?'

Ceda took a step forward, reaching for his gun. 'So Ramesh has told you?'

'Yes.'

'And?'

'And I'm very sorry but your argument's not with the girl nor with us. Nor was it with the men you killed in Britain. So the choice is yours now. Either you give yourself up, or Ramesh comes with us to answer for your crimes.'

Without realizing it Don had inadvertently moved further away from the cover of the rocks and as he finished his last demand, he saw the flash of a gun barrel from behind Ceda, but too late to avoid the bullet that knocked him flying. The next second Gavin was returning fire, the dirt at Ceda's feet kicking in tiny spurts. Gavin cursed his shooting and adjusted his aim, but not before Ceda had flung himself clear.

Behind the vehicles Ceda turned in fury on Ali, the gun still smoking in his hand.

'Who told you to fire?' he screamed at him.

Ali shrugged. 'It was such a clear shot. It was a chance we couldn't afford to miss.'

'Wrong,' Ceda replied evenly, his eyes ice-cold. 'This is the chance we can't afford to miss.'

Ali watched in horror as Ceda brought up the muzzle of his revolver and aimed it straight between his eyes. The finger was tightening on the trigger and he threw himself sideways, flinching from the shot. But Ceda had predicted it and the gun followed the target, only firing when Ali peeked again from behind his cringing arms to see if all was clear. The body flew backwards and lay still. Ceda stared at it without emotion and then spat, his spittle as accurate as his bullet.

On the ground near the rocks, Don rolled on to his stomach, nursing the wound in his side and starting to crawl. A hail of bullets blazed out from Gavin and Jerry, providing just enough suppressive fire to see him back into cover. While Gavin continued to fire single aimed shots, placing them carefully wherever he could see movement, Jerry slid across and examined Don's wound.

'It's not as bad as it looks. Just cut the flesh.'

'That's terrific news, 'cos it feels a fuck of a sight worse,' Don said, wincing as Jerry splashed water on it.

Ramesh shook his head in disgust. 'Barely a hundred yards and Ali couldn't even get that right.'

Gavin reached for the M206 and flicked up the sight, bracing himself to fire the grenade launcher. The small black grenade popped from the barrel and sailed towards one of the jeeps, Gavin holding his breath until he saw it strike the vehicle dead centre. With a huge gout of orange flame the jeep exploded, the fuel tanks igniting and erupting, rocketing parts of the shattered vehicle into the sky.

'Bull's-eye!' Gavin chortled, popping out the smoking empty casing and reloading to engage the second vehicle.

Fortunately for Ceda and his men, they had taken cover away from the jeeps and as they watched the destruction of their transport in horror, they poured a heavy fire down on the SAS patrol in frustrated anger.

Gavin ducked out of the line of fire, the lead stinging and spitting around him and the moment the onslaught eased off he rolled into a firing position again, sighted on the next jeep and squeezed the trigger. Once again the grenade arced through the sky to score a direct hit, the second jeep bursting asunder.

'I'm getting quite good at this,' he said to Don with a wicked grin.

But Don had other problems on his mind. The stream and border were still some way behind them and the open ground was amply covered by Ceda's men. There would be no withdrawal to the relative safety of India before last light, and it was highly questionable whether they could hold out that long. Ceda could sit back, conserve his ammunition and wait for the SAS men to drop their guard or try a break for freedom. They were locked into a stalemate that only an outside agency could break.

It was another hour before such an agency arrived on the scene, and when it did, Don and his men were the most surprised of all.

From the Indian side of the border came the sound of vehicles and moments later a small convoy of four Land Rovers wove their way into the valley at Don's back, making laboriously for the frontier stream. Don took out his binoculars and focused on the lead vehicle.

'I don't fucking believe it,' he muttered.

'What's that?' Gavin asked as he searched for another target for his M206. 'Has the cavalry arrived?'

'If Tony Briggs counts as the cavalry.'

From his hollow where he was being guarded by

Jerry, Ramesh sat up and stared in dismay. 'Did you say Briggs?'

'The one and only Sir Anthony,' Don answered as he watched the Land Rovers draw to a halt across the stream and the occupants debus. Apart from the tall figure of Sir Anthony he could make out half a dozen men in civilian clothes, all Westerners and, from the look of them, Intelligence service. 'Too heavy to be SAS,' he said contemptuously.

But the greatest surprise was when a small, diminutive figure eased out of the rear vehicle.

'Well, well, well. Looks like your grandpa's come to fetch you, Eli,' said Don.

'What?'

'Instantly Eli was at his side, disbelieving until he had handed her the binoculars and showed her where to look.

A slow smile spread across Ramesh's face. 'Now you will be able to ask him if what I said is true.'

'I don't need to,' Eli said defiantly. 'I know my grandfather, and I know it's all lies.'

Don drew her back. 'Unfortunately no one's going to prove anything until we've worked out a way to get over the border. If we try it now Ceda and his chums will cut us to pieces.'

Help came from an unlikely source. No sooner had the party debussed than they advanced right up to the stream and Sir Anthony addressed Ceda Bandram through a loud hailer.

'Mr Bandram, I don't propose to beat about the bush. None of us can afford to spend more time here than necessary. You can expect the Pakistani border guards at your backs at any moment, and I can expect similar rough treatment from the Indians. My contacts have run dry and I've no more favours to call in. You've got something I want, and I've got something you want. We can do a swap.'

In his hideout among the rocks Don stared at Gavin in amazement. 'The bastard's doing a deal! He's going to give them Sanji in return for us.'

Sir Anthony continued. 'It's not my choice.' Don saw him turn briefly to Sanji. 'Mr Sanji has threatened to make everything public unless I allow him to give himself up to you.'

There was a pause while Ceda considered the offer, and after a while he stood up and shouted back, 'All right then. Send him across the river and when I have him I'll let your men go.'

'And the girl.'

'Of course. The girl too.'

Don watched with mounting disquiet as Sanji set out towards the stream. Something wasn't quite right and he didn't like it one little bit. It wasn't like Sir Anthony to give in to terrorists, yet here he was doing a deal with them.

Again the loud hailer crackled into life. 'Captain Headley, move with your men and the girl down to the river now.'

Don gathered up his weapon, wincing at the shot of pain in his side as he moved. He stuck the barrel of his Colt Commando in Ramesh's back. 'Come on. You're coming too.'

'That wasn't part of the deal,' Ramesh protested.

'It's part of my deal. Now move!'

Reluctantly Ramesh got to his feet and with the rest of the group, left the safety of the rocks and walked slowly down towards the river. As they walked, something tugged at Don's mind.

'Tell me,' he asked Ramesh. 'If you know so much about Sanji, how was it that he ended up in Britain so soon after Independence? He was a minor functionary, a man of no influence or status. How come he suddenly disappeared, only to reappear a British citizen who was then able to found a prosperous business?'

Ramesh shrugged. 'He must have had powerful friends.'

'A clerk with powerful friends? I'd say that doesn't quite fit.'

'OK then, it must have been in someone's interest to hush it all up.'

'Perhaps. But whose?' Don asked, directing the question as much at himself as at Ramesh.

On the slope behind them Ceda and his men had emerged from their cover and were moving swiftly down to claim their prize of the hated Mr Sanji.

'Well, he was working for the British.'

'Yes, but there's no way they'd have colluded in any massacres. The British administration did all it could to keep the two factions apart and prevent the bloodshed.'

Ramesh's mind was racing now too, catching Don's thread and tracing it to its terrible end. Something rattled deep in his own mind and the nearer he came to the boundary river the clearer it became.

'Just now you mentioned the name Briggs.'

'Yes. What of it?' Don asked.

Ramesh shook his head as if to clear it. 'I know it sounds stupid, but there was another Briggs, I think. Back in 1947.' He looked up at the sprightly figure of Sir Anthony. 'But it couldn't have been him. Surely. The Briggs I heard of was already old in 1947.'

Don stopped dead in his tracks. 'Another Briggs?'

It was as if Don's hesitation was the trigger. One moment they had been walking towards the river and freedom, the next they were in the centre of a hail of lead. Instinctively Don flung himself to the ground and as he looked up he saw that the men who had accompanied Sir Anthony were no longer standing watch, but were kneeling in fire positions, each man blazing away with an M16.

'Gavin!' Don screamed. But the sergeant had been cut down in the first onslaught.

Jerry crawled forward and wrestled the M206 from the dead man's grasp, shouting, 'What the fuck are they doing? I thought they were on our side?'

Behind him Eli lay flat on the floor screaming in terror. Don glanced up the hillside at their back and saw that Ceda and his party had been targeted as well. Sir Anthony's men had caught the lot of them, Bandrams and SAS, in their lethal ambush. Even Sanji had been scythed down in their murderous fire and now lay on a dry bank of pebbles in midstream, face up and motionless.

Ramesh wriggled up beside Don. 'Give me a gun. For God's sake at least let me defend myself!'

Don drew his Browning and handed it across with its

spare ammunition clips. With his good hand, Ramesh took the pistol and rolled several paces away from Don before coming up and returning fire, using carefully aimed shots despite the incoming torrent from Sir Anthony's men. On the hill behind them Don saw only the prone still form of Ceda Bandram, with several of his men lying lifeless around him. All had been taken by complete surprise in the opening hail of bullets.

Frantically Don searched for a way out. And then he had it.

'Jerry, pass me the last M72 rocket.'

'What's on your mind?'

'Just do it!'

Jerry reached for the khaki tube, snapped it open and armed the rocket. As he handed it over Don said, 'If I don't make it to those rocks we're done for. Put your hands up and surrender.'

Jerry stared at him dumbfounded. 'They won't take a surrender. They'll cut us down.'

'Do as I say. Trust me. I don't think they'll harm the girl. And anyway, they'll kill you if you stay here. It's worth a gamble.'

Jerry looked at him doubtfully but nodded his agreement. He was a soldier and he would obey his commander's order, even if it was the last one he ever received.

Don took hold of the rocket and braced himself to run, fixing his eyes on the far spread of rock that would give him a good shot down the line of vehicles. He gathered his knees under him, took three deep breaths to steady himself, then burst from cover.

'Get some covering fire down!' Jerry shouted, blazing

away with the M206. Ramesh fired off a whole clip, dropping it out and snapping in a replacement to continue.

But Don had set himself a difficult target. It was a long way to the rocks and within a second of leaving his position the Intelligence agents had him in their sights. Bullets bit into the ground all around him. One of them tore at his webbing belt, and another ripped through the sleeve of his jacket. Then the unthinkable happened. Jerry heard a cry of pain, and looking sharply round, he saw Don tumble, fall and come to rest, still a good ten yards from the rocks. His eyes were open and staring, fixed on the river. Eli screamed.

'You bastards!' Jerry shouted, burning through his last clip of ammunition until the firing pin clicked on an empty chamber. He hunted around for more but Gavin's body with its extra ammunition pouches was out of reach and a moment later Ramesh fired off his last round. He turned and looked at Jerry.

'I guess it's time to put your boss's judgement to the test.'

Desperately Jerry tried to think of an alternative, but it was no use. There was none. It was possible that a couple of Ceda's men might still be alive, but they were keeping their heads down and in no mood to risk their lives to save even Ramesh.

'OK then.'

He turned to Eli. 'Got anything white?'

'You can't be serious?'

'Have you got a better idea?'

She dug into her pocket and pulled out a yellow handkerchief. 'Will this do?'

He took it and tied it to the muzzle of the M206. 'Well, here goes.'

Waving the weapon aloft, he shouted down across the river. The firing stopped and the voice of Sir Anthony replied.

'That's more like it. Stand up, all of you, and make your way down to the stream now.'

Jerry started to his feet.

'This is madness,' Eli said, following his lead. 'He'll have us all killed.'

Ramesh was the last to stand and then together the three of them walked slowly down towards the border. As they went, Eli looked at her grandfather's body and started to sob. From behind the row of vehicles Sir Anthony and his men emerged, their M16s levelled at the three individuals now in the open and at their mercy. Slowly the two sides drew together until they were standing on opposite banks of the stream, separated by only a few yards of clear, shallow water.

'So here we all are,' Sir Anthony said pleasantly, a Walther PPK pistol in his fist. Jerry couldn't help thinking how out of character it looked. Sir Anthony would have been much more comfortable wielding a pen, doing his killing from a distance with cunning and deceit as his ammunition.

'We are surrendering to you in good faith,' Jerry said. 'I don't know what game you're playing, and I'm not interested.'

Sir Anthony raised his eyebrows. 'Really? That is good

of you, you miserable little upstart. Who do you think you are to judge me? A bloody squaddie.'

'At least I'm not a traitor. I don't murder people who've put their lives on the line for a mission.'

Sir Anthony feigned a yawn, covering his mouth with the back of his hand. When he had finished he said to his men, 'Kill them,' and turned to walk away.

Jerry braced himself involuntarily for the impact of the bullets in his flesh, every muscle tensing as if that alone could repulse them. But as he did so he saw the expression on Sir Anthony's face change from smug boredom to alarm. He glanced round to see what had caught his attention. Beside the far rocks, Don had risen into a kneeling position. The M72 tube was over his shoulder, his fingers pressing down on the firing button. It was the backblast that Jerry saw first, the cone of flame and smoke erupting from the rear of the tube as the rocket powered out of the front. Then, as the slender warhead streaked across the intervening space, Jerry traced it in horrified fascination, all the way into Sir Anthony's chest, where the nose cone crumpled on his sternum, detonating the charge and blowing him to pieces.

Without thinking, Jerry swung down his M206 and levelled it at the six agents. But all of them had flung themselves to the ground at the blast of the exploding rocket, shielding their faces in their arms, and when they looked up it was to find themselves covered by Jerry's M206 and Don's Colt Commando, little realizing that the two SAS men had not a bullet left between them.

'Stay on the ground!' Don screamed. 'One move and you'll be confetti like Briggs.'

Ramesh waded through the stream and flung away the agents' weapons, keeping one for himself. 'I've got them now,' he shouted back.

With a sigh of relief Don lowered his Colt Commando. He grinned across at Jerry. 'For a moment there I didn't think you were going to surrender like I said.'

Jerry shook his head and started to shake with laughter. 'Surrender! Of all the stupid fucking orders. If I'd only known . . .'

'If I'd told you my plan you wouldn't have been convincing enough for someone as smart as Briggs.'

While Don secured the agents, tying them with rope from the Land Rovers, Ramesh and Jerry checked on the casualties. Back up the hill Ramesh found Murap kneeling over the body of Ceda. His eyes were open and his teeth were set in a grimace of pain.

'He was hit in the first volley of fire and I couldn't get to him,' Murap said weeping.

Ramesh stooped and closed his brother's eyes. One by one the scores were being settled. Sanji was dead, and Ali, and now the British policemen had been avenged with the death of Ceda. He looked out across the rock-strewn ground and saw Gavin's body. Briggs had been slain and with him, Ramesh feared, had died the reason for his betrayal. Why had he tasked the SAS with the mission, only to betray them and have them cut down by his own men? It was a question that Ramesh was no longer interested to ask. With his brother and his uncle dead, he felt more alone than he had ever done in his life.

'Come, Murap. It is time to go home.'

15

The purr of the engines had lulled both Jerry and Eli to sleep. From his seat by the window, Don looked at them and smiled. Their heads had tumbled together and in Jerry's lap their hands were joined. He had to admit that they made a handsome couple.

Outside night was falling, the sun slowly sinking in the west and shooting out orange rays that spanned the entire horizon. It would be a peaceful night, he felt. He himself was longing to sleep but there were too many ghosts that cried out to be laid to rest. Good men had died, and a serious reckoning lay ahead on their return to Britain. Procedures would have to be examined to discover how it was that Briggs had managed to mount the operation without the knowledge of his superiors. And there would undoubtedly be questions from the Indian government about the six British agents found wandering naked near the Pakistani border in Kashmir.

It had been the note found on Sanji that had proved to be the final piece of the puzzle, clarifying Briggs's role in the affair. Eli had found it and Don wondered if she would ever get over her grandfather's confession, which had corroborated everything that Ramesh Bandram had said of him. But more than that, Sanji had written of the other Briggs, the one whose name had sparked a faint memory in Ramesh's mind.

In the dark days of 1947 countless people had died, innocent people of every race and creed. One such had been Vivienne Briggs, the wife of Arthur Briggs, Sanji's boss in the last British administration. She had been caught and murdered in a riot orchestrated by none other than Uncle Gilma Bandram. Arthur Briggs had come to know of Sanji's activities with an extremist terror group of his own, but rather than report him to the authorities, he had concealed the fact, on condition that Sanji's men perform an act of revenge on his behalf. The murders had duly been carried out, and once it was thought that the last of the Bandrams had been accounted for, Arthur left India for the last time. With him went his young son Anthony.

The full story had only been made known to Sir Anthony by accident, during the talk between him and Sanji in the car on the drive away from the safe house. A check of the facts had confirmed the shocking coincidence that had brought the two men together, the ex-terrorist Sanji and the British Intelligence mandarin, their fates inexplicably linked.

Desperate to preserve his father's honour, Sir Anthony had settled on his course of action, blind to the consequences to the innocent members of the SAS team involved. Everyone concerned with the whole shameful business was to have been eliminated, and only Don's cunning and skill had stopped him from getting away with it.

Don pressed the button in his armrest and levered his seat back, stretching out his legs in an effort to relax. They had been good men. Tom and Jimmie, Taff and Geordie, Rod and Gavin, the old hand. They had all done their duty as ordered, carrying out the mission though it had cost them their lives, proving once again that the Regiment could rely on the finest of soldiers whenever the need arose.

He stared out of the window, the sun's last glow quenching itself in the vast expanse of the Arabian Sea. What had made Sanji recant after all those years? he wondered. Perhaps the weight of what he had once done had finally burned into him the guilt that he had managed to suppress all those years before. It had been a great wrong in a time of great wrongs. Crimes had been committed by people on all sides. Perhaps the message was that it would never be in the nature of such an evil to be laid to rest. However strong and resilient the young perpetrator might believe himself to be, however untouched by his crimes, in committing the evil he was unwittingly sowing the seeds of self-destruction in his own heart. Sanji, Uncle Bandram and Ceda, and finally Briggs himself – the seeds had borne their terrible fruit, and the evil come home to rest.

Evil would always beget evil, Don thought. It was only to be hoped that there would always be men good enough and willing to fight it.

SOLDIER Y: SAS

DAYS OF THE DEAD

1

Placida Guzmán shifted her swollen body on the twin bed, trying to ease the cramping pain in her lower abdomen. She was dressed only in T-shirt and knickers, but the erratic swish of the air-conditioner seemed devoid of any power to cool, and the heat of the day still clung damply to her skin.

She manoeuvred herself on to her elbows, wincing at the pain. On the street outside the level of conversation seemed to be rising, and in the distance several sources of music were competing for attention. After a few moments she recognized Selena's voice among the throng.

The patch of sunlight had almost finished its climb up the peeling wall and perhaps a breeze would soon be blowing in from the sea. It would be so nice to go out for a walk on the famous beach, just a simple walk in the sand, just to feel free again.

She sank back on to the bed, knocking a couple of empty laxative packets on to a floor already littered with them, and gently massaged her stomach with her palms. Fifteen months they had been on the island, fifteen months at his beck and call. And the call had come often. He had told her more than once that she was the most beautiful of the five, and it had sounded like a life sentence. She would still be there now if she hadn't got pregnant.

But that was all in the past. Him, the island, the shame. She just had to get through this, and a new life was waiting.

Another wave of pain ran through her body and for a few seconds she had trouble breathing. Where was Victoria? She'd been gone for what seemed like hours. Placida hoped to God her friend hadn't got lost in the strange city. It shouldn't be that difficult to find a drugstore, but something had snapped inside Victoria during one of the nights with Bazua's men, making her behaviour difficult to predict. Sometimes she seemed just like her old self, but at others it was like talking to a small child.

The first thing they should do after this was over was to get help for her. But how and where? On Providencia all the girls had dreamt of going home, but once off the island, once away from him, Placida had found that the thought of returning to Cartagena, to the familiar streets and familiar faces of family and friends, seemed not only unreal but also, in some strange way, the ultimate surrender. It was as if the past could only be buried as a single entity; if she was ever to be happy again the slate had to be wiped completely clean.

She wondered if they would receive the money they had been promised. The man had been angry last night, and she supposed he would be again if nothing had happened, but what else could she do? If he refused to pay them then who could they complain to?

She grimaced, and felt another knot tightening in her gut.

It was almost dark now, and maybe the air was cooler,

but the thought of trying to open the window was too daunting. Victoria could do it when she came back. If she came back.

Where the hell had she got to? Surely the obviousness of her condition would have saved her from being hassled in the street.

Placida thought about the baby growing inside her own belly. For the child's sake she knew she should go back to Cartagena, where her family could certainly offer him or her a better start in life than she could manage on her own. She herself had been happy enough in the house in La Matuna, and the garden with its sweet-smelling hibiscus flowers. Maybe it had been different at the time but she found it hard to remember having a care in the world as she grew up, at least not until Rogello came into her life, and her father's discovery, not that much later, that she was no longer a virgin.

She laughed at the sheer absurdity of it all, and felt something shift inside her. It wasn't a cramp like the others and for one delightful moment she thought it must be the baby's first kick, but then a hot white light seemed to explode inside her, so sweet and so painful, and her heart seemed to thunder in her head. Her back arched once, and as she slumped back down on to the bed the darkness fell across her brain like a swirling black sheet.

A couple of blocks down Miami Beach's Washington Avenue, Victoria Marín was looking in vain for a street sign. It had taken her much longer than she'd expected to find a drugstore and now, clasping the bag containing the new supply of laxatives, she couldn't seem to find the hotel again. The pavements had seemed to suddenly fill up once the sun went down, and with all the non-stop motion and incessant noise she was finding it hard to think.

It had to be that way, she thought, staring hopefully down the neon-drenched street. That building in the distance might be the hotel. It looked white, and its shape seemed familiar.

As she started to walk a hand suddenly grasped her around the waist. 'And how much would you be?' the man asked in Cuban-accented Spanish, his hand working its way up her T-shirt towards a breast.

She stopped and looked at him, tears erupting from her eyes.

His leer gave way to surprise, and then the hand was gone, and she had a fleeting glimpse of his angry face as he turned away. Why was he angry? she wondered. What had she done?

Several people were staring at her, she realized. She hurried on, passing through the aromatic clouds which hung like advertising hoardings outside the restaurants. She was hungry, she thought, and there was only forty cents left in her pocket. They would have to ask the man for some money when he returned that evening.

She reached the building she thought she'd recognized, but even up close she couldn't be sure – they all looked alike, and she hadn't thought to check the name when she went out. But the fat woman behind the reception desk was familiar, and so was the look of contempt she threw Victoria's way.

She thinks we're whores, Victoria thought, and remembered, clear as if it had been yesterday, Marysa shouting at Placida that 'whores got paid', that the five of them were slaves, not whores. 'Slaves have no choice!' she had yelled, eyes glittering with angry tears. 'None of this is our fault! None of it!'

It had been a comforting thought then, and it still was. Victoria started to climb the stairs, taking it slowly. Even though the pellets had all come safely through, her body still felt strange. It was like a country after invaders had been expelled, she thought – it would take time to get back to normal.

She remembered sifting through her shit for the condom-wrapped pellets and shuddered involuntarily, even as her mind thought how strange it was, getting upset about something like that after all they'd been through.

She stopped on a landing, and tried to remember how many flights she'd climbed. Through a window she could see a fat crescent moon setting behind the city, and she stood there for several minutes staring at it, lost in a thoughtless reverie.

Eventually she turned away, and again there were tears in her eyes – these days she couldn't seem to stop crying. But at least she was on the right floor, and it took only a few moments to reach the door with the badly painted number 314.

'I'm back,' she said cheerfully as she walked in, and it was several seconds before her mind accepted the information her eyes were passing on. Placida was lying on her back, one leg raised, its foot twisted inwards. Her eyes were wide open and seemed full of surprise.

Her skin was still warm to the touch, but there was no doubting that she was dead. Victoria sank to her knees, her arms on the bed, like a child about to say her bedtime prayers. This time the tears didn't come, just a soft mewling sound, which seemed to be seeping out of some crack in the night, but which she knew was emanating from her own mouth.

She would never know how long she stayed in that position. The next thing she remembered she was gathering her few things together and, on a sudden impulse, taking Placida's passport as well as her own. She crossed her friend's arms, closed her eyes and mouth, straightened her legs and covered her to the neck with one of the hotel's grimy sheets. Then, after one long and despairing look back from the doorway, she fled the hotel.

Jesús Barbosa walked jauntily across Washington Avenue and through the front door of the Grant Hotel. He was carrying a calfskin briefcase and wearing an open-necked white shirt, freshly pressed cream chinos and a new pair of alligator-skin shoes. A large gold earring in the shape of a fire-breathing dragon hung from one ear, and the smile he offered the fat lady behind the desk reflected, literally, the fifteen hundred dollars he'd just spent on cosmetic dental work. In the words of the last detective who'd found reason to question him, he gave the impression of someone who'd seen one too many *Miami Vice* reruns.

He took the stairs two at a time, hoping that the bitch had finally got herself on the pot. He didn't like making unnecessary journeys, not in heat like this. It was days like these which made him nostalgic for the mountains he had grown up in, where the heat was dry, there was always a breeze and in the evening the temperature dropped more than a couple of degrees. The trouble was, there was nothing to do in those mountains – no music, no cars, not enough women.

Barbosa reached the third floor and walked down the

short corridor to the women's room. Normally he would treat himself to the female mules, but this pair were too obviously pregnant for his taste, though he could see that they'd both been lookers before. He didn't bother to knock on the door, just turned the handle and stepped inside to find the body laid out beneath its shroud.

'Shit!' he muttered angrily, ripping the sheet aside. 'Shit,' he repeated with rather less vehemence, and looked at his watch. He was meeting the *gringa* in an hour and a half, and he didn't want to turn up smelling of corpses. But there was close to half a million dollars' worth of heroin inside this one, and no *puta* was worth that. He sighed, unclipped the mobile from his belt and ordered some transport.

That done, he plucked the six-inch blade from its sheath on his right calf, ripped away the dead girl's clothes, made a rough twelve-inch slit in her abdomen and began searching through her innards for the sixty-nine pellets of heroin that she had swallowed on Providencia.

Half an hour later he had recovered sixty-six, which, with the one that had burst, left two unaccounted for.

It was enough. He wrapped the mutilated body in a sheet, washed his hands and was just looking at his watch when the rap sounded on the door. In the corridor Miguel and Roberto were standing on either side of the small refrigerator, breathing heavily. Once they had carried it into the room he helped them cram the still-flexible body inside – in heat like this rigor mortis took a long time to kick in. Then he followed as they wheezed their way back down to the truck, which was parked in the alley beside the hotel.

They drove off, headed for one of the usual dumping

spots in Dade County, and Barbosa, his briefcase now two pounds heavier, hailed a taxi. With any luck he still had time to store the merchandise and take a shower at his fitness centre before his assignation with the Pamela Anderson look-alike.

It was almost midnight when the cops found Victoria Marín on the moonlit beach. At first they assumed she was helplessly drunk, but there was no smell of liquor on her breath. They searched the canvas shopping bag for drugs but found only two Colombian passports and a few cosmetics. She apparently had no money.

Throughout this process Victoria refused to speak, and it was only by exercising enormous will-power that she refrained from screaming when one of the cops took her arm to lead her to the car.

She couldn't stop herself from crying. She didn't think she ever would.

2

The road arrowed into the distance across the flat Pampas countryside. Farmland stretched away to either side, the farms themselves mostly pinpoints of light on the low horizon. In the vast sky a full moon was playing hide-and-seek with an armada of clouds.

They couldn't be much more than forty kilometres from the outskirts of Buenos Aires, Jamie Docherty reckoned, and soon he would be able to see a red glow in the sky above the highway. He remembered nights as a young man driving back down from Loch Lomond to Glasgow – a close friend had always insisted that the glow was nature's way of warning people that cities were bad for their souls.

Docherty took a glance in the rear-view mirror. Both nine-year-old Marie and seven-year-old Ricardo were fast asleep, which wasn't exactly surprising. Between them, he and Isabel had driven nearly eight hundred kilometres that day, and over four hundred and fifty the day before. The two children had certainly started out hyperactive, but they just hadn't been able to stay the course.

Beside him Isabel was also more than half asleep. She was in her mid-forties, a couple of years younger than he was, but she seemed just as beautiful as the day they had met, more than fifteen years ago.

Docherty smiled to himself as he remembered the first time he'd seen her, striding in through the doors of a hotel in the southern Argentinian town of Rio Gallegos. It had been at the height of the Falklands War – in the immediate aftermath of the landing at San Carlos – and Docherty had been leading one of two four-man SAS patrols which had been secretly airlifted on to the Argentinian mainland for the purpose of observing enemy activity at the Rio Gallegos and Rio Grande airfields. Having done everything which was required of it, his patrol had been on the point of heading for the Chilean hills when a complication arose. Two members of the other patrol had been captured, and there were fears that they would be tortured into revealing the name of MI6's only agent in the area, an Argentinian woman based in Rio Gallegos. So someone had to warn her of the danger.

Docherty had taken the task upon himself, and changed his life in the process. The two of them had ended up escaping together across the mountains and falling in love along the way.

Now here they both were, driving towards Buenos Aires on a warm winter evening. It wasn't the first time they had been across the Andes since setting up home in Chile two years before, but it still felt vaguely akin to putting their heads in the jaws of a lion. Of course, as far as the Argentinian authorities were concerned, Docherty was just a retired English soldier who happened to be married to an Argentinian national. And though his wife had once been exiled for involvement in terrorist activities, that had been long ago, in the time of the 'Dirty War', which nearly everyone but the still-active 'Mothers of the Disappeared' was so keen to put behind them. No one in authority had any inkling that husband and wife had met on Argentinian soil, midway through a military action which had probably helped to swing the Falklands War decisively in Britain's favour.

After Docherty's retirement from the Army they could even have settled in Argentina if they had wanted, but neither of them had. There were too many painful memories for Isabel, and Docherty preferred Chile. There wasn't much to choose between the behaviour of the two armies in recent decades, but he found the people west of the Andes more friendly – more Celtic in spirit than the Anglo-German-oriented Argentinians. The climate was better too, and the mountains, lakes and islands of the south were like Scotland revisited.

Isabel still had friends and relations in her homeland. Her father had died during her exile in England, and her mother had cut all ties, but there were a couple of her father's sisters with whom she still kept in touch and one cousin to whom she had always been close. Rosa lived with her academic husband and three children in a large, rambling house in Recoleta, and it was she who had invited them to the capital. Just for a holiday, she had said, but the two women had known each other a long time and Isabel suspected an ulterior motive. She had told Docherty as much, but neither of them had any idea what it might be.

Maybe she wanted Isabel's help with her elder daughter, who seemed to have inherited her wider family's interest in left-wing politics. The country might be run by a president more interested in cars and women than politics, but the same bastards as always lurked in the shadows.

It could be anything, Docherty thought, as a Mendoza bus blared by in the opposite direction. A holiday was a holiday, and any excuse to take time away from the damn word processor and his wretched memoirs was more than welcome. He'd been working on them on and off for over a year, and on a more or less nine-to-five basis for several months, but he didn't have much more to show for his efforts than a huge pile of handwritten notes. When he tried actually writing it never seemed to come out the way he intended, leaving him to mutter 'you had to be there' at the annoyingly unresponsive screen. And when he had finally managed to put together a coherent chapter on the Bosnian business his publishers in London had come back with a long list of suggestions for alterations, most of which seemed designed to either obviate the risk of Her Majesty's Government taking exception to Docherty's version of events or to encourage Jean-Claude Van Damme to accept the movie part.

Docherty was well aware that a Van Damme movie might make him rich, but the thought of faking his own life story didn't sit too well. If he was going to write the damn thing, he wanted it to tell the truth. He wanted his children to see him as a man who knew he had lived and worked on a moral tightrope, not as some glib action hero pumped up with either Hollywood cynicism or gung-ho fascism. A month had passed since Docherty and Isabel had seen Mel Gibson's Oscar-winning *Braveheart*, and he still felt angry about how bad it was.

Well, at least he didn't have to think about any of that for another week. And the sky was growing red above the highway ahead. He leant over to nudge his wife awake, as she'd asked him to. 'Not far now,' he said.

Isabel yawned and reached for the tube of mints on the dashboard. 'I wonder what Rosa really wants,' she murmured.

In the Colombian city of Cartagena it was almost five-thirty in the afternoon and the lengthening shadows were throwing the crenellated walls of the old fortifications into dramatic relief. Carmen Salcedo, who had just finished her spiel on the era of piratical sackings and let her tour party loose to explore the walls on their own, watched the mostly American tourists happily ambling away, camcorders whirring, cameras poised.

It was certainly a beautiful evening. She stood leaning against one of the abutments, enjoying the blues of sea and sky, the gold-flecked waves and the buildings of the old city glowing in the evening sun. For all its problems – which ranged from drug traffickers through political corruption to air pollution – Cartagena was still a magical city.

Carmen had lived there for all of her twenty-six years. Her parents still lived in the hills behind the city, but she now shared a two-bedroom flat with Pinar, a fellow tour guide. They were going to the cinema that evening, she remembered, and looked at her watch. She should have given her charges twenty minutes, not half an hour.

But it was too late to worry about that now, and so far this group had proved more reliable than most. She walked back across to the bus and found Mariano squinting at a sex comic which he was holding only a few inches away from his eyes.

'Getting short-sighted?' she asked sweetly, making him almost jump out of his seat.

'Don't do that!' he half shouted, glaring at her.

She didn't think he had ever quite forgiven her for turning down the offer of a date, but he was a good driver, and on the streets of Cartagena that was no small matter. 'Sorry,' she said with a smile.

He huffed and puffed, then went back to the comic.

The Pearsons, an American couple in their sixties who had commandeered the front seats of the minibus on day one and, despite several heavy hints, never surrendered them to anyone else, had left a Miami newspaper to guard their precious space. It was almost a week old, but better than nothing, and Carmen sat down to improve her already near-perfect English.

She read the entertainment section first, hoping for a preview of the films which she would be able to see later that year in Cartagena, but they all seemed to be the same old boring hi-tech thrillers. She hadn't heard of any of the bands mentioned in the music section, and if their music bore any relationship to the way they looked in their photographs she doubted if she was missing much.

She ignored the sports section, and was just skipping through the local news when she saw the headline 'COLOMBIAN GIRL KILLED BY DRUGS'. Underneath it the sub-head claimed that 'Traffickers cut her open to reclaim shipment'. Jesus, she thought, and then the two names stopped her in her tracks, and she could suddenly hear her own heart beating. She read the whole paragraph:

'Another girl, whose Colombian passport identified her as Victoria Marín, was taken into custody by police last night. She was carrying a second passport, which enabled police to identify the dead girl as Placida Guzmán, but was either unwilling or unable to further help the Miami Beach PD with their investigation.'

She read on, but there was nothing else, no mention of the other three, no mention of her sister.

'Could you take a picture of us, dear?' someone asked, disturbing her reverie. It was one of the Englishwomen, with her husband hovering behind her. Carmen nodded dumbly, climbed down from the bus, pointed the camera and pressed the button, still in a state of shock.

'Are you all right, dear?' the woman asked, a concerned look on her face.

'Yes, I'm fine,' Carmen replied, smiling. 'It's been a long day.'

'Well, you'll soon be rid of us for the night,' the woman said with a twinkle.

Carmen smiled again, and looked at her watch. Ten minutes more.

They went slowly, but everyone was on time. On the drive back to the hotel she went through the next day's itinerary – they were visiting the nearby Corales del Rosario National Park – and then asked the Pearsons if she could borrow their newspaper for the evening to help brush up her English.

Mr Pearson seemed a bit reluctant, but his wife was only too happy, probably seeing it as a down payment on their continued tenure of the best seats. At the hotel she counted them all out, remembered to re-check the next morning's pick-up time with Mariano, then headed for a phone. Pinar was upset that their evening at the cinema was off, but she could tell from Carmen's voice that something serious had happened. 'I'll tell you later,' Carmen explained, and rang her parents' home. Her mother answered.

'I'm coming up,' Carmen told her. 'I have to talk to you both.'

'But we're going out at eight . . .'

'Just wait for me,' Carmen insisted. 'It's about Marysa.'

'What about her?' her mother asked, sounding almost angry.

'I'll tell you when I get there.'

It was an hour's journey on the bus, maybe even more at that time of day, so she decided on the luxury of a cab, as much for the privacy as the gain in speed. It had seemed the most natural thing in the world to immediately ring her parents, but the tone of her mother's voice had given Carmen cause to wonder. Should she have sat on this information for a few hours, thought about what she wanted to do with it, before putting herself at the mercy of her father's stubbornness and her mother's selfishness? What were they going to say to this? The last time she'd raised the issue with them they'd both been really angry with her, as if somehow it was her fault that their other daughter had been taken from them.

The trouble was, their instinctive approach to anything potentially disturbing was to ignore it, in the hope that it would go away. And it worked for them, or at least it did in the sense that they managed to avoid most of the disturbance which other people called living. But it had never worked for Carmen.

The traffic seemed worse than ever, but shortly after seven the taxi deposited her at the foot of the bougainvillaea-bordered drive. Her parents were fairly rich by legal Colombian standards, her father having inherited the family footwear business. It was the combination of this wealth and the lack of a ransom demand which had eventually convinced them all to accept the police investigator's conclusion that Marysa was dead.

They had likewise assumed that Placida Guzmán and Victoria Marín were dead. And Irma. And Rosalita.

Carmen let herself in through the front door, and a few moments later found her parents putting the finishing touches to their evening's apparel in the enormous bedroom.

'Oh, I wish you wouldn't tie your hair back like that,' were her mother's words of greeting. 'Can't you afford a proper styling?'

'I don't want a proper styling,' Carmen said, running a hand over her severely pinned black mane.

Her mother just looked at her.

Carmen laid the newspaper out in front of her on the dressing table. 'Read that,' she ordered, pointing out the item with a finger.

Her mother sighed and started reading, still fiddling with her earrings as she did so. Then her hand suddenly stilled, leaving the filigree ornament swaying in mid-air. 'Oh, my God,' she said softly.

'What is it?' her husband asked, leaning over her shoulder to read.

'Guzmán and Marín are common names; Carmen's mother said in a small voice, as if she was arguing with herself.

'Not that common,' Carmen said gently. 'And Victoria Marín and Placida Guzmán together – it's too much of a coincidence. It even says that Victoria is twenty-three, which would be right.' She looked at her parents, both of whom seemed to have been suddenly aged by the news. 'Don't you understand?' she said. 'This means there's hope.'

'We understand,' her father said, and the look in his eyes seemed to add: we've lost her once and now we'll get the chance to lose her all over again.

Carmen felt like slapping them both. 'So what are you going to do?' she asked her father abruptly.

He looked at her for a moment. 'Talk to the Chief of Police, I suppose, and get him to contact the police in Miami.'

'Don't you think you should go there yourself? I'll come with you,' she added – his English had never been good.

He shook his head. 'The police in Miami are more likely to listen to a fellow-officer than a Colombian civilian.'

Which might well be true, she thought. 'So will you call now?'

He smiled wryly. 'He won't be in his office.'

'His home then.'

'I don't have his home number, and even if I did . . . Carmen, the newspaper article is a week old. Putting the man's back up to save a few hours is not worth it.'

'And we're going to be late,' his wife added, earrings finally in place.

'You're still going out?'

'What do you expect us to do – spend the evening wringing our hands?' her mother asked.

'No, I suppose not, but . . . You will ring first thing in the morning?'

'I'll go and talk to him in person.'

'Good.' She felt relieved.

'There's food in the kitchen if you want some,' her

mother told her, and once they'd gone she toyed with a plate of warmed-up fish risotto for a while before deciding to head back into town.

On the bus she found her mind running through the events of that fateful August. The five young women, all from good families, all in their last year at college, had taken a picnic a few miles down the coast, in an area which had always hitherto been considered safe. In the early afternoon they had been seen by several other picnickers, as well as joggers and courting couples, but after four o'clock the record of sightings came to an end, and the party had not returned to the college that evening.

No suspicious groups or vehicles had been seen in the area, but when after several days the women had still failed to reappear the assumption had grown that a new guerrilla group must be holding them to ransom. Once two weeks had passed without any demand for money being received, the betting had shifted in favour of either some catastrophic and completely unfathomable accident or what seemed an equally improbable mass rape and murder.

Now it seemed likely that they had been in the hands of drug traffickers all this time. Placida was dead and Victoria was 'unable to help', whatever that might mean. Where were the other three, and what had their lives been like for the last two years?

The answer to the last question was too horrific to contemplate.

Victoria would know, Carmen thought, and she was more likely to talk to a friend than a gringo policeman. If her father didn't get anywhere with his contacts, she decided, then she would go to Miami herself, with or without her parents' blessing, and find out what had happened to Marysa.

Docherty and Isabel didn't discover the reason for Rosa's summons until three days after their arrival in Buenos Aires. On that Tuesday Docherty and Rosa's husband, Giorgio, a second-generation immigrant of Italian descent, had driven to the university, where the media unit's satellite link-up was being put to good use, showing England's final group game against Holland in Euro 96. England outplayed the Dutch and Docherty, a true Scot, duly lamented the Auld Enemy's victory. But as they drove home to Recoleta he had to admit that England seemed to be playing football these days, rather than just kicking it upfield and running after it like headless chickens.

The two men arrived back to find the children running riot in the house while their wives were preparing the ingredients for a barbecue on the patio. Rosa gave the task of igniting the charcoal to Giorgio, collected a bottle of chilled white wine from the fridge and poured glasses for the four of them on the patio table. 'A toast,' she said. 'The future.'

They all drank. Here it comes, Docherty thought.

'Though it's the past I want to talk to you about,' Rosa began carefully. Behind her the evening sun glinted on the waters of the River Plate estuary, and the panorama of Recoleta's famous brightly coloured houses seemed like a child's drawing. 'I have something to ask you – you, Jamie, though of course it concerns Isabel too.' She sighed. 'I don't even know if I should ask you, but I promised I would. And you can always say no.'

His SAS bosses used to say that, Docherty thought.

'Do you remember Gustavo and Eva Macías?' Rosa asked Isabel.

'I don't think so.'

'Gustavo was a close friend of my father. He and his family used to visit us quite often when I was a child.'

'I do remember one friend of your father's,' Isabel said. 'A tall man, stood very straight. He had a beard, I think.'

'That's him. He and Eva had three children – two daughters and one son. The son's name was Guillermo – he was about three years younger than us, I think. I probably didn't pay much attention to him, but I seem to remember he was nice enough.' She took another sip of wine. 'He was arrested by the Army in 1976 – he was a student at the university in Rosario – and never seen again. He wasn't interested in politics, apparently, and no one knows why they took him away.'

'Except the Army,' her husband said drily.

'True. But I'll leave Gustavo and Eva to tell you the details, if you're willing to talk to them.'

'Why now?' Docherty asked. 'After so long.'

'Two reasons, as far as I can see,' Rosa said. 'Are you two aware of what's been going on here the past couple of years? With the Disappeared, I mean.'

'Only vaguely.'

'Well, basically, when Menem became President he made a few noises and sat back to wait for the whole business to just fade away. But it didn't, the Mothers were still at his gates, and then for reasons best known to themselves, a few of the beasts broke ranks and started talking. The old Navy commander not only admitted that up to two thousand people had been dropped in the Atlantic, but even went into details – how those who'd been weakened by torture had to be helped on to the aircraft, and were then given sedatives by Navy doctors before being stripped and thrown out. A little while later the Head of the Armed Forces actually admitted responsibility for human rights abuses in the late 70s and early 80s, although of course no individuals were called to account, and the files have still not been produced.'

'They've probably lost them,' Isabel said scornfully.

'I doubt it,' Giorgio said. 'They may not be very good at fighting other soldiers, but they know how to keep records.'

'The Eichmann syndrome,' Docherty murmured.

'Something like that. A lot of people have claimed that the military kept meticulous records of each and every person they tortured and killed.'

They all sat silent for a few seconds. All these years on, it was still hard to accept the enormity of what had happened.

'Anyway,' Rosa said, the other thing that happened was that the graves started coming to light. A group of young people calling themselves forensic anthropologists have started digging in many of the rumoured locations, and they've already found several mass graves. One of them was outside Rosario, and I think that was what set Gustavo off. From what I can gather, both he and Eva have been busy pretending that they never had a son for most of the past twenty years, but the discovery of that grave . . .' She sighed. 'And then there's the fact that he's dying himself. Some sort of cancer, and I don't think he's expected to last many more months.' She ran a hand through her hair. 'But whatever his reasons – mostly guilt, I suppose – he seems hell bent on making up for lost time. Over the last year – and much to his daughters' annoyance, I might add – he's spent a small fortune trying to find out why Guillermo was arrested and what happened to him. It's become an obsession. He has to know.'

Docherty looked at Isabel, whose face in the shadows seemed drawn with pain, and he knew that she was reliving the traumas of her own arrest and torture, the loss of so many friends. For her sake he wanted to leave the surface of the past undisturbed. 'Death will heal the man's need to know,' he said, the words sounding harsher than he intended.

Isabel looked up at him. 'What does he want from Jamie?' she asked.

'I think he has the name of a man, an Argentinian living in Mexico. I'm not sure, but I think he wants someone to go and talk to this man.'

'Why Jamie?' Isabel persisted.

'Gustavo is convinced this man will not talk to another Argentinian. But Jamie – he is both a foreigner and a soldier, someone both safe and *simpático*, yes? This man might be willing to talk to him, just man to man.'

'Macho to macho,' Docherty murmured.

Rosa rolled her eyes in exasperation.

'We should at least talk to Gustavo,' Isabel interjected.

It was Docherty's turn to look at her. The word 'Mexico' had taken him back to a buried chapter of his own life, one that came before Isabel. 'OK,' he said quietly. 'But no promises.' He knew Isabel still had nightmares about her time in the Naval Mechanical School – he had been shot into wakefulness on enough occasions by her sudden screams – and if it looked like this was going to upset her, there was no way he was touching it.

But there was always the chance it might have the opposite effect, he realized. Maybe something like this would help Isabel to finally exorcize her past.

He was probably grasping at straws, rationalizing his own desire to see Mexico again. Or even worse, just grabbing at any excuse to leave the cursed word processor behind.

The following morning, once Rosa had rung to make certain that Gustavo was well enough to receive them, Isabel and Docherty took the long drive across the city to the Macíases' house in Devoto. 'House' was actually something of a misnomer – 'mansion' would have been a better choice. There was obviously quite a lot left for the daughters to inherit.

Eva Macías, a handsome, white-haired woman in her seventies, greeted them and led them out to the conservatory, where her husband was soaking up the tropical humidity, rather like General Sternwood in the opening chapter of Chandler's *The Big Sleep*. The General had also wanted to know the fate of a missing young man, though in his case the man in question was assumed to be still in the land of the living.

Gustavo Macías was obviously not long for this world himself, but there was still life in the eyes and in the force with which he clenched his gnarled hands. It had taken him a year and a half, he told them, but he now had two names. Major Lazaro Toscono had supervised the operations of the arrest squads in Rosario for all of 1976 and most of 1977. Colonel Angel Bazua had commanded the Army base just outside the city, which served as both detention centre and place of executions, from late 1975 to mid-1978.

Bazua was two years into a five-year prison term for drug trafficking, and would probably be impossible to reach, but Toscono was now an ostensibly legitimate businessman in Mexico City. His business was doubtless a front, but there was nothing to stop anyone knocking on his office door, and Docherty could name his price for doing so. 'Just go and see him,' the old man said. 'Ask him about my son. He will remember. They always remember the names, because they know no other way of telling people apart.'

Docherty looked at Isabel, then at Macías. 'He may just refuse to speak to me, and you will have paid my fare for nothing.'

'When I started this,' the old man said, 'I put half my wealth to one side for Eva – more than she could ever spend. Now money means nothing to me. I will pay you twenty thousand US dollars to make the journey, a hundred thousand if you bring me back the answer. And, of course, any expenses you incur. If you need more, just tell me.'

Docherty was silent for a moment. They didn't exactly need the money, but twenty thousand dollars would certainly come in handy, and all he had to do was travel to a country already etched deep in his heart and ask someone for a consequence-free conversation. It seemed a no-brainer, but . . .

'He'll go,' Isabel answered for him.

Docherty shrugged his acquiescence.

In the car outside, still sweating from their immersion in the conservatory steam bath, Docherty and Isabel sat in silence for a few moments. The quiet street, with its luxurious mansions, perfectly coiffured lawns and ornamental palms, seemed far removed from torture chambers and mass graves, but both knew it for the illusion it was. The torturers might have come from all sections of Argentinian society, but the men who had delivered up their victims had come from streets like this one.

'You're not doing this for my sake, are you?' Isabel asked.

'No. And if this is going to be hard for you I won't do it. We don't need the money that much.'

'I know.' She sighed. 'Sometimes it seems so long ago,' she murmured. And sometimes it seems like yesterday, she thought.

'Some wounds take a long time to heal.'

She grimaced. 'I'll be fine. As long as you look after yourself. You're not in the SAS now. If this pig Toscono refuses to talk to you, that's it.'

'As long as he refuses nicely,' Docherty said with a grin.

She wasn't amused. 'We need you back.'

'Aye,' he said, leaning across and cradling her head in his arms. 'I love you too.'

The 727 from Cartagena touched down in Miami in the middle of the afternoon. Her parents had acquaintances in the city who would happily put her up, but the thought of explaining the reason for her visit to strangers was too daunting, and Carmen had already decided to ignore the list of telephone numbers her mother had written out. The money her father had given her would probably be enough for several nights in a cheap hotel, and if not she had a little of her own to fall back on.

Her parents would be appalled, of course. Carmen knew they hadn't really wanted her to come, though she was far from sure why. They had said they were worried for her – that losing one daughter was bad enough – but they obviously hadn't been worried enough to accompany her. It was hard to believe that they weren't desperate to know what had happened to their other daughter, but . . . Carmen shook her head and turned her attention to the business of disembarkation. She had come. Her parents' feelings – or lack of them – were neither here nor there.

She had changed planes in Miami on all of her three trips to the United States, but the airport had never seemed quite so vast before. Immigration and Customs seemed to take for ever – no doubt flights from Colombia merited special attention. She had half expected the humiliation of a strip-search, but the officials were obviously as tired of the queue as its occupants and she was asked only a few cursory questions, her bag not even opened. With the aid of her guidebook she sought out the elevated Metrorail station just in time to catch an inbound train, and sat watching the sunlight reflect on the looming clutch of windowed towers which marked the city's downtown.

Beneath these towers she had a glimpse of an older and more elegant Miami, but it was getting dark and she had no time to explore. A local woman helped her find the right bus stop for Miami Beach, and when the bus arrived she was amused to see an English-speaking passenger trying, and failing, to communicate with the Spanish-speaking driver. It was like her friend Miguel had said: Florida, California and Texas had been taken from Spain by the gringos, and now the gringos were having to give them back.

The bus drove east across a long causeway, giving Carmen her first views of the Miami which *Miami Vice* had made famous, and sooner than she expected they were driving up through the faded pastel splendours of Miami Beach. She had picked three hotels out of the guidebook, and struck lucky at the first attempt, finding a room that was clean, spacious and cheaper than the book had led her to expect. She showered, changed and sat on the bed, rereading the copy of the report which the Miami police had faxed to Cartagena, and which the local police chief had passed on to her father. The only new fact it contained was the name of the Miami Beach lieutenant in charge of the investigation, and she had an appointment with him the following morning.

There was a small balcony to the room, and she stood out on it for a few minutes, looking down at the busy street, her nose twitching to the aromas of cooking food. She was hungry, she realized, and ten minutes later she was ordering Orange Chicken in a Chinese restaurant recommended by the hotel receptionist. After eating she walked down to the beach, but in the darkness it looked more scary than inviting, so she made her way back to the hotel. She flicked through channels on the TV for a while but then decided it was time for bed, despite the earliness of the hour. She was exhausted, and with any luck tomorrow would turn into a big day.

* * *

She was woken by the barely risen sun shining through the window, and after showering and dressing she made her way down to the empty beach and walked along it, a few feet from the gently breaking waves. She felt apprehensive about her meeting with the American police, but really glad that she had come. Whatever had happened to Marysa, she told herself, life was better than death.

The small Cuban café which she chose for breakfast served the best coffee she had ever tasted, which had to be a good omen.

Back at the hotel she smartened herself up, checked the directions she'd been given and set out for the police station. The walk took ten minutes, and once inside the incongruously modern building she was kept waiting for only a couple of minutes before being shown into Lieutenant Trammell's office. He was a harassed-looking man well into middle age, with an argumentative jaw, big mouth and thinning grey hair. His greeting was warm enough, but he seemed to be having trouble keeping his faded blue eyes open. Fortunately, he was not personally in charge of the case – that honour belonged to Detective José Peña, whose overflowing desk in the squad room was her next port of call.

Detective Peña also seemed harassed, but at least he was looking at her with wide-open eyes. 'Coffee?' he asked, once the introductions had been made and Trammell was back in his office.

'Yes, thank you,' she said.

'Cream and sugar?' He was speaking Spanish now.

'Just one sugar,' she answered in the same language, and examined him as he programmed the machine. He was in his early thirties, she guessed, with short, wavy hair and a face that managed to be both handsome and friendly. The photo of a woman and two children on his desk suggested he was also married.

He presented her with the plastic cup of coffee, and she took a token sip. Pretty good, she thought – in two hours she'd had the best and worst coffee of her life.

'Dreadful, isn't it?' he said with a smile.

'Yes,' she agreed.

They stared at each other for a couple of seconds. 'So what is it you want to know?' he asked.

'Everything,' she said shortly. 'All I know is what was in the newspaper – that Placida was carrying drugs – inside her – and that one of the packets burst and killed her. And that you found out who she was from Victoria . . . How is Victoria?'

He shook his head. 'It's hard to say. I've tried talking to her several times and sometimes she's almost lucid, sometimes she just stares at me as if she can't understand a word I'm saying, sometimes she just can't stop crying.' He looked up at her, and she could see in his eyes that he'd found the experience a more than usually distressing one. 'Whatever they did to her,' he added, 'it wasn't pretty.'

'Where is she now?' Carmen asked.

'She's in a hospital. She's pregnant too,' he added. 'So was Placida Guzmán.'

Carmen bowed her head, then lifted it again. 'Can I see her?'

He shrugged. 'I don't see why not.'

'I want to take her back to Cartagena with me. Her parents are both dead, but she has an aunt who's willing to look after her.'

Peña looked doubtful. 'I don't know when that will be possible,' he said slowly. 'I'm not sure what the legal situation is right now.'

'What do you mean?' she said, both surprised and alarmed.

'She has admitted to bringing in about half a million dollars' worth of heroin,' he said mildly.

Carmen was appalled. 'But she can't have been acting willingly,' she said angrily.

He sighed. 'I know,' he said, 'and I'm on her side. But she and the Guzmán girl had been in Miami for three days before they were found. Even if they had been forced to ingest the drugs there was nothing to stop them telling the officials at the airport what had happened. If they had, both of them would have received immediate medical treatment, and Placida Guzmán would probably still be alive.'

'They were probably too frightened.'

'Probably. And don't quote me on this, but I expect something can be worked out. It should be obvious to anyone that the girl needs help, not a jail cell.'

Carmen took a deep breath. 'Has she said anything about who did this to them? Or where they came from?' And where my sister may still be, she thought.

'Not yet. The plane they arrived on came from Bogotá via Panama City, but there's no record of them getting on at either place. And whenever I've asked her about either place, or anything about the time before she arrived, she just started to cry. She was crying when the uniform found her on the beach,' he added.

'She told you where Placida was?'

'Not exactly. "In the hotel," she said, but she couldn't

remember which one. So we just started with the closest, worked our way outwards, and found the place the next day. Placida wasn't there, but there was a lot of blood and . . .'

He stopped for a moment, and she could see that he was picturing the scene.

'The body was found in a canal about twenty miles away – they hadn't done a very good job of weighting it down.'

'In the hotel room, weren't there any clues to where they'd come from?'

'He'd cleared it out. Jesús, he told them his name was – Victoria remembered that in one of her lucid moments. He was young, Hispanic, medium height – one of a million.'

'What about the passports?' she asked.

'The only stamps were ours. But the passports themselves are probably forged anyway.'

She felt disappointed with the information she had gathered, but could think of nothing else to ask. 'Maybe Victoria will find it easier talking to me,' she said, mostly to bolster her own spirits.

'Did you know her before?'

'Only by sight. My sister was – is, I hope – five years younger than me, and we didn't have the same friends.'

'Well, I'll try and arrange a visit for tomorrow, OK?'

She managed a thin smile of gratitude. 'I have no other reason to be here.'

3

John Dudley took his eyes off the lighted windows of the timber-yard office and turned to his partner. 'Anything?' he asked.

'They just took a corner,' Martin Insley told him from the armchair. 'Seaman caught it.'

'But how's it going?'

'Sounds pretty even so far. But you never know with Spain.'

'He should have given Fowler a game,' Dudley muttered as he put his eye back to the mounted telescope. Through the open window he could hear traces of the match playing on several TV sets, and over the gabled roofs to the south-west he thought he could make out the faint glow in the sky above Wembley Stadium. Everyone in London seemed to be watching the damn game – everyone but him and Insley. If only the damn boat had come in a day later.

It had docked at Tilbury soon after dawn that morning and had begun unloading almost immediately. The four thousand logs of tropical hardwood from Venezuela had been one of the first shipments ashore and after a cursory customs examination the importers had been cleared to reload them on the waiting fleet of trailers. A thorough search would probably have resulted in the seizure of a large haul of Colombian heroin, but the British authorities were hoping for more than drugs to burn. MI5 and the Drugs Squad were eager to break the new and highly ominous distribution link-up between the Colombians and the local Turkish mafia, while MI6 were more interested in the foreign end of the pipeline, and the man who ran it.

The logs had all been delivered to the timber yard in north-east London by mid-afternoon, no small feat considering the state of the capital's traffic, and had been stacked in no apparent order in the open-sided shed. Since then Dudley and Insley had been watching them from the upstairs room of an empty terraced house some seventy yards away.

'We've got another corner,' Insley reported.

Dudley took one last look at the lighted windows, and walked across to grab the proffered earpiece.

'It was a good save,' Insley explained, as they waited for Anderton to take it.

At that moment they were beeped.

'Fuck,' Dudley growled, grabbing the handset.

'The fax is coming in,' a voice told him.

There was a pause, and in the background Dudley could hear the groan of the crowd. They were even listening in the communications room!

'Five names,' the voice said. 'They all look Turkish. Beeper numbers and times. Amounts. Christ, there must be about two tons of the stuff in those logs.'

'Did Six get their source?' Dudley asked out of curiosity.

'Yeah. The one they were expecting.'

'Well, that should cheer the bastards up.'

* * *

In the suite occupied by the British Consulate on the fourth floor of the Swissbank building in Panama City the English contingent were gathered round a borrowed portable, willing the half-time whistle to blow. David Shepreth was probably the least involved of the spectators, and it was with no great reluctance that he deserted the TV to take the incoming message from London. It was brief and to the point, containing nothing more than the source number of the fax which had just been received by the London timber-yard office.

He placed it on the desk in front of him and punched out a number on the phone. Somehow he doubted whether the American Embassy would have closed down for Euro 96.

It hadn't, and a few seconds later he was talking to Neil Sadler, the head of the US Drug Enforcement Agency's Panama Field Office. He didn't know Sadler anything like as well as his opposite number in Mexico City, but they had a relationship of sorts and Shepreth was curious to see what reasons the other man would eventually come up with for refusing his request.

'Hi, David,' the DEA man said cheerfully enough. 'And what can we do for the British Empire today?'

'I need an address to go with a fax number,' Shepreth told him, then read the number off the paper in front of him.

'No problem,' Sadler said. 'It'll probably take me a couple of hours. I'll call you back.'

'Great, thanks,' Shepreth said, and hung up, thinking that anyone who believed the Americans no longer ran Panama was living in a dream. Their only real challenger had been Manuel Noriega – 'Old Pineapple Face' as the media had less than affectionately dubbed him – and the General had been rather too assiduous in promoting his country's number-one industry – the import and export of drugs. Involvement in itself might not have condemned him, but he had compounded his crime by giving Uncle Sam the proverbial finger, and for that he was now languishing in a Florida jail.

He was not exactly missed by his fellow-Panamanians. Like everyone else, the Americans occasionally did the right thing for all the wrong reasons.

Shepreth stood by the window for a few moments, staring out at the square of blue Pacific which filled the space between the two high-rise buildings on the other side of the Via España. As usual a breeze was ruffling the palms which lined the wide avenue; Panama City was not the steamy hell of legend, though in just about every other respect it qualified as a major-league modern dump. The city's business was business, and if Orson Welles had ever done a Central American version of *The Third Man* he could easily have substituted Panama for Switzerland in Harry Lime's famous speech about what makes civilization tick.

The second half had started in the room next door, and Shepreth walked through to join the others. England were not playing half as well as they had against the Dutch, and another Spanish near-miss had the Embassy officials chewing their lips in agitation. Even the two secretaries – both local girls – seemed caught up in the anxiety of the moment. Both of them had lovely legs, Shepreth thought, and wondered why he hadn't noticed before.

He supposed he didn't come to Panama that often, or at

least not lately. Large quantities of cocaine and heroin still passed through the country, but the focus of the drug trade had moved north in the past couple of years, and nowadays Shepreth spent most of his time in Mexico City.

His real employer was MI6, that arm of British Intelligence which dealt with external threats to the security of the United Kingdom. Up until the end of the Cold War its principal occupation had been counter-espionage, but now that spies had either gone the way of the dodo or signed up with one of the corporations for non-political duties, MI6 had been forced into grabbing a share of the war against the unofficial corporations of international crime. These included the Sicilian, Russian, West African and Turkish Mafias, the Chinese Triads, Japanese Yakuza and Colombian drug cartels. With the exception of the Triads, most of these organizations had few soldiers on the ground in the UK itself, and sticking spokes in their collective wheels could only be done on foreign soil.

The other EC intelligence services had a presence in Central America and the Caribbean, but for obvious reasons the principal sharers of Shepreth's patch were the various overlapping American agencies – the US Customs Service, Coast Guard, Drug Enforcement Agency, Justice Department, FBI and CIA. Originally Shepreth's relations with these American agencies had seemed better than those they had with each other, but over the past couple of years this situation had deteriorated somewhat. The Americans' decision to adopt a 'kingpin strategy', whereby all their resources were committed to bringing down a selected few of the biggest drug barons, took little or no account of British and European interests. And when this most-wanted list was finally shared with America's allies it was found to omit the one man the British most wanted included.

It would of course be difficult to put Angel Bazua in prison – he was already in one. It had been specially constructed for him and his 'business associates' on the Colombian island of Providencia, and was said to contain all the comforts of home and a few others besides. Everything that Bazua needed to continue running his billion-dollar business had been thoughtfully provided by the Colombian authorities, from mobile phones and computers to an impressive boardroom table. It was even rumoured that a commodious shelter had been dug beneath the jail, as protection against a bombing raid by competitors.

Elements of the Colombian military and civil administrations were obviously armpit-deep in the necessary corruption, but Bazua himself was not a Colombian – he was an Argentinian. And herein lay the other compelling reason for MI6's interest in him. Bazua had been one of the leading protagonists of the Argentinian Army's 'Dirty War' against its own people, and one of the prime movers behind the attempted liberation of the Malvinas. His son had been killed at Goose Green, further deepening his lifelong hatred of the English, and after the military's reluctant abdication of power he had gone into exile rather than face a potential investigation into his activities during the Dirty War.

By this time the fortune he had accumulated – most of it stolen in one way or another from his hundreds of victims – was considerable, and with the help of old Colombian contacts from his years at the US-sponsored anti-subversion school in Panama, he had bought himself a slice of the Cali drug cartel's international action. In the late 80s, as the star of the Medellín cartel had fallen, his had risen with that of his Cali partners, and even the inconvenience of a prison term had done nothing to slow his enrichment. Most of the returning dollars went into Colombian banks to earn legitimate interest, but Bazua had not forgotten his own country or his hatred, and it was his deepest wish that the two new boats riding at anchor off his Providencia prison would soon be ferrying another invasion force to the Malvinas. Once such a force was ashore the liberal government in Buenos Aires would have no choice but to support the invasion, particularly since it would soon become apparent that this time the British were incapable of transporting a force large enough to dislodge it.

This was not a welcome prospect in London, but British efforts to interest the Americans in action against Bazua had proved ineffective. Washington wouldn't even countenance ganging up on the discredited Samper regime in Bogotá, much less direct action against the centre of operations on Providencia. Bazua was not one of their targeted kingpins, the British were told. There was no real evidence against him. And in any case, there could be no sanctioning of military action on the sovereign territory of Colombia.

This of course was pure bullshit – Grenada and Panama should have been so lucky – but there was no shaking Washington's resolve, even when their own DEA people in the field supported the British. Increasingly, Shepreth and his superiors in London had been left with the feeling that as far as Bazua was concerned the Americans had a hidden agenda.

This idea received further confirmation when Neil Sadler rang back, seconds after the final whistle. The cheerfulness in his voice was gone – now there was an uneasy mixture of resentment and embarrassment.

'No luck, I'm afraid,' the American told him. 'Are you sure this is the right number?' He repeated the one which Shepreth had told him.

'Yes,' the Englishman said, slightly amused by the pantomime.

'Well, it's not listed. Sorry.'

'OK. Thanks for trying,' Shepreth said coolly.

'Any time.'

Shepreth put the phone down. He'd have to check it out in person, which shouldn't be too difficult – the fax machine in question was almost certainly in the office on Calle 35, the one to which he had trailed the freighter captain earlier that month.

He would pay it a visit later, once the Panamanian evening got into its undeniable swing. Then Whitehall would get its t's crossed, and there would be more proof for the Americans to ignore.

In the other room the celebration of a penalty shoot-out win had already begun, and while HM's Consul waxed eloquent about Sheringham's intelligence – 'He thinks before he kicks the ball,' he gushed, slurping his G&T – his number two seemed to be contemplating another goal altogether, his eyes locked on, like heat-seeking missiles, to the valley between the younger secretary's ample breasts.

Victoria looked healthier than Carmen had expected, and very obviously pregnant. If it weren't for the eyes, which seemed to be watching from a great distance, she would have found it hard to believe that the young woman in front of her had gone through a succession of terrible experiences.

The institution in which she was housed seemed more true to type; situated in one of Miami's less salubrious inner suburbs, it felt more like a prison than the hospital it supposedly was. Closed-circuit cameras had watched Carmen all the way to this fourth-floor room, and the nurses all seemed cold-faced and unsmiling. Detective Peña, who had driven her out here in his lunch hour, had warned her it wasn't exactly a rest home, and he'd been right. Victoria's room contained a bed, a basin and a single chair. The door was locked from the outside at all times.

For her part, Victoria eyed this new visitor with more trepidation than warmth. She might look vaguely familiar, but she would probably want to ask questions, like the police detective who had been to see her several times. He'd been quite nice, but she knew he hadn't believed that she couldn't remember anything. And of course he was a man. At least this one was a woman. And maybe she wouldn't stay long – it was so wonderful being alone.

'Victoria, do you remember me?' Carmen asked her, and could tell from the look of alarm that she didn't. 'I'm Carmen, Marysa's sister.'

Tears formed in Victoria's eyes and started rolling down her cheek. She was beginning to think she would dehydrate herself.

'How are you?' Carmen asked. 'How do you feel? Are the people here good to you?'

'Oh yes. They're good to me. They leave me alone.'

Carmen ignored the reproachful look which went with the last statement, and sat down on the bed beside the other woman. 'Do you remember Cartagena?' she asked gently, half expecting the flow of tears to increase. 'The college?'

Victoria gave her a strange look. 'What does it look like?' she asked.

'The college?' Carmen asked, surprised. 'It's a park full of white buildings, with a hill behind it. There . . .'

'Can you see the sea from it?' Victoria asked.

'Yes, you remember . . .'

Victoria shook her head. 'No, but I have dreamt about this place.'

Carmen waited for her to continue but she didn't. 'Do you remember the dream?' she asked.

'Oh yes.'

'What happens?'

Victoria tilted her head to one side, and Carmen could see what Detective Peña had meant about a six-year-old. 'Nothing happens really,' she said. 'I am eating and walking and reading a book and looking at the sea – things like that.'

'Are you alone?'

'No, I have friends. Marysa is there,' she said, and smiled at Carmen, as if she had finally realized who her visitor was.

Carmen took a chance. 'Do you ever dream of going on a picnic?'

Victoria's eyes first widened with surprise and then darkened. 'That's a bad dream. How did you know about it?'

'I don't know. Why don't you tell me about it? Then

maybe it won't seem so bad.' Victoria looked at her – almost hopefully, Carmen thought. 'Tell me what happens,' she said again.

'It's a bad dream,' Victoria repeated. 'We're having a lovely time, swimming and sunbathing and talking. We have some wine and Placida is pouring it into the paper cups and the men come out of the trees and they have guns. We have to go with them in their cars and then the car turns into a plane and we're in the sky above this island, looking down. And the plane comes down to land and the wheels hit the runway and there's a big jolt which wakes me up. It always wake me up, and then I feel better, knowing it's just a dream.'

As if in contradiction of the words, the tears were flowing once more.

Carmen wanted to take the other woman in her arms, but she pressed on relentlessly. 'The island in your dream – is it big?'

'I don't know. It's not small. There's a mountain in the middle and little towns by the sea. It's shaped like an egg. And there's another island – much smaller – at one end, with a bridge between them.'

It was a good description, Carmen thought triumphantly. There couldn't be many islands in the Caribbean which fitted it. Victoria was looking at her expectantly, but Carmen had no idea what she was expecting. 'Do you remember any other dreams?' she asked.

Victoria seemed to retract her limbs, to pull her body closer together. 'Yes, but they are evil dreams.'

'Evil . . . You don't have to tell me if you don't want to.'

Her voice apart, Victoria seemed turned to stone. 'I am with men. They are doing things to me.'

'Who are they?'

'They're his men.'

'Who is he?'

She looked straight at Carmen. 'He told me he was the Angel of Death, but he laughed when he said it.'

'Is he the father of your child?'

It was the wrong question. Victoria shook her head violently, and started crying again. Carmen took her in her arms, held her close, and slowly felt the tension in the younger woman's body begin to lessen.

'Is Marysa in these evil dreams?' Carmen asked after a while.

'Sometimes,' Victoria admitted. 'But I don't want to talk about my dreams any more,' she added.

'All right,' Carmen agreed. She'd thought she was ready to hear the worst, but she'd been wrong. 'So what shall we talk about?' she asked.

'Nothing,' the other woman said. 'Let's just be quiet together.'

And for the next twenty minutes they sat next to each other on the bed, with Victoria's head cradled on Carmen's shoulder. At the end of that time the younger woman made no attempt to deter Carmen from leaving, but she did seem at least slightly pleased by the prospect of another visit the following day.

Carmen had intended to talk to the doctor in charge about Victoria's prospects, but decided to leave that until her next visit – she felt too distressed herself to fight for her sister's friend. Instead she just stumbled out on to the street and started walking, and it was only after a couple of cruising drivers had slowed to offer her remuneration for services to be rendered that she realized what sort of neighbourhood she was in. Luckily a crowded bus stop soon presented itself, and half an hour later she was back downtown. There she walked into the first bar she came to, stonewalled the hopeful greetings of the male clientele and ordered a large tequila.

In a dimly lit booth she thought about what Victoria had told her.

An island. A recognizable island.

Her drink finished, she asked the barman directions to the nearest bookshop. He looked at her blankly, as if the idea of buying a book had not occurred to him before, and she had to be rescued by one of the men she had ignored. He gave her directions to a shop two blocks distant.

She walked down the palm-lined street and found it. An assistant showed her the atlases and hovered beside her until another customer pulled him away. She found the right page, and pushed her finger northwards across the blue Caribbean from the Colombian coast. The first island it reached was San Andrés, the second Providencia – both of them Colombian. The former was long and thin, the latter could have been egg-shaped. She needed a bigger map, and found it in a guidebook to her native country. Providencia was egg-shaped, with a mountain at its heart. And, she noticed triumphantly, there was a small adjoining island at its northern end. A bridge ran between them.

At around a quarter to nine the taxi deposited Shepreth by the sea-front monument to Balboa, and after a few minutes' contemplation of the dark ocean he crossed the busy main road and headed inland up Calle 35. The building he wanted was a couple of hundred metres up on the left – a nondescript modern construction, six storeys of steel and glass. Through the glass doors he could see a liveried guard reading something at his otherwise bare desk.

It was a porn comic – Shepreth had a fleeting glimpse of the usual giantess straddling the usual giant before the guard innocently slipped it under the desk.

'I've got an appointment with someone at Azul Travel,' Shepreth told him. 'My name's Bates,' he added.

The guard picked up his phone to confirm it, and after a few words with someone nodded Shepreth in the direction of the lift. 'Fifth floor,' he said grudgingly, reaching for his comic.

It seemed unlikely that he'd be watching the lighted floor numbers above the lift, but Shepreth went all the way to five just in case. On his way to the stairs he passed the door of the travel agency, with whom he had earlier arranged the necessary appointment. He hoped they would wait at least ten minutes before phoning down to find out what had happened to him.

The office he was interested in was on the third floor. There was no writing on the glass door, and he didn't expect to find a happy bunch of workers inside. Certainly, whoever was renting the space hadn't taken much trouble to protect any contents – the door yielded to Shepreth's lock-picking expertise with almost insulting ease.

The room proved even emptier than he had expected. The fluorescent light revealed no desk, no chairs, no filing cabinets – just a fax machine and a shredder floating on an ocean of burgundy-coloured carpet. 'Snap,' Shepreth murmured as he read the fax's number.

Now all they needed was evidence linking this office with the prison on Providencia. Which wouldn't be easy. Presumably each missive from the island was consigned to the shredder the moment it had been read. He would have to try to set up an intercept of some sort, Americans or no . . .

As if in answer to a prayer the fax clicked into life. Shepreth stood over it, hoping it wouldn't be someone trying to sell Bazua double glazing for his prison.

It wasn't. The fax, emanating from a number which Shepreth recognized as including the prefix for Colombia's two Caribbean islands, contained the usual list of buyers, together with amounts, beeper numbers and instructions for onward transmission to the organization's cell head in northern Mexico. The Americans wouldn't be able to ignore this, Shepreth thought. They would either have to add Bazua to their precious list of kingpins or come up with an honest reason for refusing.

He detached the sheet from the machine, folded it twice and put it in his back pocket, then headed for the door. He listened for a moment before inching it open. The corridor was empty. Relocking the door seemed more difficult than unlocking it had been, and he was still struggling to engage the catch when the lift doors suddenly opened behind him and two men emerged, guns in hand. He had no time to do anything but stare sheepishly at them.

'Looking for Azul Travel?' one of the men asked. He was probably in his mid-thirties, with a pencil moustache and uneven teeth.

The other man, who was younger and wearing tinted glasses above his pitted cheeks, sniggered.

They advanced, one man pushing into the unlocked office while the other kept him covered.

Shepreth just stared at him, willing his mind to keep on working through the fear that was threatening to choke it off. If it didn't his chances of living past midnight were remote. Even if he stayed James Bond-cool they were less than good. The thought plunged him further into shock – in eight years of working for MI6 he had not often found himself at the mercy of people with so little interest in his living and so little fear that they would have to pay for his death.

The one with the moustache pushed Shepreth into the office, closing the door behind himself, and then stood with his gun in the Englishman's ear while his partner did the frisking. This didn't take long. Pitted Cheeks stepped back, shoved Shepreth's automatic into his waistband, unfolded and read the stolen fax, then examined the wallet.

'You're a long way from home, English,' he said in conversational Spanish.

'So are you,' Shepreth replied in the same language, recognizing the man's Colombian accent. He wondered if his voice sounded as brittle to them as it did to him.

'Panama used to be a part of Colombia,' Moustache told him.

'It still is,' his partner said, and both men laughed.

Shepreth said nothing.

'You have probably come to Panama to see the Canal, yes?' Pitted Cheeks asked playfully.

'I've seen it,' Shepreth said.

'Not from underwater,' Moustache said almost perfunctorily, leaving Shepreth with the stomach-sinking realization that the two of them had been through this particular sketch several times before.

Pitted Cheeks, meanwhile, was picking out a number on the phone. 'I need to speak to the Chief,' he said when someone answered, and a few moments later, smiling all the while at Shepreth, he was reporting what had happened. He then listened for a while before signing off and putting the phone back down on the carpet. 'The Chief has a few questions for you,' he said.

Shepreth found himself taking a deep breath of relief.

'But not too many,' Pitted Cheeks added, reading his mind. 'We'll probably still have time to show you the Canal tonight.'

The ludicrous thought flashed through Shepreth's mind that he would never know who won Euro 96. Get a grip, he told himself. This was life and death.

They led him down the deserted stairs and out into an empty alley, and Moustache kept a gun on him while Pitted Cheeks went off, presumably to collect their car. This might be his only chance, Shepreth thought, but really it was no chance at all. Moustache was too far away for a lunge and there was no reason to suppose the Colombian would do anything other than put a bullet in Shepreth's kneecap if he tried. And then he'd never get another chance.

Despite the training, despite what his head told him, it all seemed unreal somehow, standing there so helplessly in an alley in Panama City, with a man who'd more or less promised that he'd never see another dawn. The sounds of the city were all around them, but strangely distant, as if the alley was enclosed in thick but invisible glass.

The Colombians' car bumped its way towards them, shattering the spell.

Pitted Cheeks got out and the two of them discussed whether or not to put him in the boot. They decided against, reasoning that if they knocked him out the questioning might be delayed, but if they didn't he might drum on the lid at the wrong moment. They both clearly enjoyed this discussion – such attention to detail, Shepreth realized, was their proof of professionalism. These men might be lacking in humanity, but not in job satisfaction.

He was ordered into the wide back seat of the car, a black Toyota Camry, and Moustache climbed in beside him, eyes watchful, careful to keep a couple of feet between prisoner and gun.

Pitted Cheeks got in behind the wheel and started the car rolling forward. They turned left out of the alley on to Calle 36 and purred uphill towards Avenida 3, now jostling with people out for their evening stroll through the shopping district. Shepreth thought of lunging for the door, but knew it would be fatal – Moustache's eyes had not left him for a second since they entered the car.

They crossed Avenida 3 and headed up towards the next big crossroads. In ten minutes they might be out of the city altogether, Shepreth thought. If he was going to do anything, it had to be soon. But what? He felt paralysed. Moustache smirked at him, as if he knew exactly what was going on in his prisoner's mind.

As Pitted Cheeks waited to turn right on to the busy Avenida 2 a bus first lurched forward and then abruptly pulled up again as the lights changed. This motion not only fooled Pitted Cheeks, who paused for a second before pulling out, but also a taxi coming up on the blind side of the stalled bus, which was through the red light before the driver had realized his mistake. His emergency stop would have pleased his original instructor, but there was no way he could avoid making contact with the side of the Toyota.

The crash was louder than it felt, and Moustache's gun hardly seemed to waver, but the taxi driver was already out on the street and hundreds of eyes were turned their way. Two of them, Shepreth realized with sudden hope, belonged to a traffic cop who was now walking their way.

Moustache had seen him too, and the gun was now in his pocket, albeit still obviously aimed in Shepreth's direction.

Pitted Cheeks climbed reluctantly out of the Toyota, just as the cop arrived to take charge. As he looked into the car Shepreth deliberately reached for the door handle, opened the door and climbed out on to the street. No bullets gouged into him.

He smiled at the cop and leant against the car's roof for a moment until the man's attention was back on the two drivers. There had to be about two hundred people standing around enjoying the show, and the cop was obviously going to milk the spotlight for all he could. A cacophony of horns was rising from the stranded traffic.

'I'll see you later,' Shepreth told Moustache, and began walking away. Ten steps later he was through the first line of watchers, and looking back he could see that neither of the Colombians was making any attempt to follow him. He walked on along the crowded pavement, his heart thumping in his chest, hardly daring to believe his luck.

From Avenida 2 he took a taxi to his hotel, tipping the driver with a generosity which the man appreciated better than he understood. It took Shepreth three minutes to clear his room and check out; fifteen minutes later he was registering at another hotel under another name, using the alternative identification he carried for such emergencies. He didn't think the Colombians would come looking for him – the risks seemed to outweigh the potential benefits – but he spent most of the night dozing in a chair, fingers wrapped round the butt of his other gun.

4

With an hour-long stopover in Quito, Docherty's journey from Santiago de Chile to Mexico City took just over ten hours. For almost all of the first flight he was able to stare out of his window at the majestic Andes, but most of the second was over water, and the choice of entertainment came down to either Arnie Schwarzenegger or his own thoughts.

Five days had passed since he and Isabel had visited the Macíases in Devoto, two since their return home from Buenos Aires. He had watched out for signs that his wife was regretting her decision to approve the trip, but, natural anxieties apart, there had been none that he could see, and on the eve of his departure, after they'd made love on a bed still strewn with his packing, she had made her feelings clear. 'If it wasn't for the children,' she had told him, 'I'd be coming with you. In fact, there's one voice inside me says I should be going instead of you. These are the people I've been fighting all my life. The people who killed my friends.'

Sitting in the plane, Docherty could see her face on the pillow, the same mingling of determination and anxiety in her dark eyes, and he could remember that moment in the car outside Rio Gallegos in 1982, when the rest of the

SAS patrol had been captured and she'd refused to head for the border alone. 'I could cross ten borders and never leave this war behind,' she had said at the time.

But what was his excuse? Terrible things had been done in Argentina, but the same could be said of many other countries, and though he had more than a vague attachment to old-fashioned notions of justice, Docherty had no desire to take on the mantle of a one-man crusade. The money would be nice, of course, but that wasn't the reason for his presence on this flight either – in fact he wasn't at all sure what his motivation was. He hoped it was more than an older man's attempt to relive his youth. 'But I wouldn't bet money on it,' he murmured to himself.

He shook the doubts aside, and picked up the guide to Mexico City which Isabel had bought for him the previous day. In his two stays there in 1977 he had found the place oppressive, but that was hardly surprising – during the first he had still been crazy with grief and by the time of the second he had the rest of the country to compare it with. In nearly five months of travelling he had fallen in love with Mexico, its people and its churches, its mountains and its beaches.

A part of him had always meant to go back, but another part had feared that for him the country would always be entangled with memories of Chrissie. It was her senseless death on a zebra crossing just six months after their marriage which had driven him abroad in the first place, and fate had decreed that Mexico should be the place which brought him back to life. The life he had given to the SAS and his family, and not necessarily in that order.

He turned his attention to the present. If Gustavo Macías was right, and Lazaro Toscono's business in Mexico City was just a drug-trade front, then he would have to be careful about how he approached the man. It would not do to start hammering on the bastard's front door before he found out what was behind it. As one of his old SAS instructors had put it: a few hours of observation is worth a thousand stun grenades.

It was a pity he had no local contacts – he'd made friends in Mexico, but none in the capital. It suddenly occurred to Docherty that he might be able to pick up some intelligence from the Embassy if he used his contacts in Hereford, but then he remembered that Barney Davies had finally stepped down as SAS CO, and been replaced by someone whom he barely knew.

In any case, he thought, that would be like using a sledgehammer to crack a nut. Or a general to run a country, as they said in Chile.

The plane was losing altitude now, and he spent the next fifteen minutes yawning to unblock his ears, watching as the yellow-browns and greens of the central plateau grew more distinct. Then they were flying down through either thin clouds or dense smog, re-emerging less than a kilometre above an overcrowded multi-lane highway that was snaking its way through shanty-covered hills.

The airport seemed three times as big as he remembered it, but he had no trouble getting through Immigration or Customs. Noticing the Hertz sign, he thought about hiring a car, but decided against it – there was no point in leaving such an obvious trail for an enemy. Instead he fought his way on to the modern Metro, remembering as he did so a recent traveller's comment that its off-peak crowds would pass for a rush hour anywhere else. Two changes and several buffetings later, he emerged from the Zócalo station, no more than a stone's throw away from the great square at the heart of the old city.

This seemed unchanged from nearly twenty years before, and he realized with a grin that he had arrived just in time to witness the six o'clock flag-changing ceremony – one of the world's longest-running farces. The troop of a dozen soldiers was already halfway from the Palacio Nacional to the flagpole in the centre of the square, and by the time Docherty had joined the circle of spectators the drums were echoing, the national colours on their way down. A kind of baroque minuet followed, whereby the huge flag was folded to the size of a small tablecloth and then carried, with stunning reverence, back into the palace.

The crowd was now filtering away, the sun almost gone, its rays touching only the highest reaches of the cathedral on the square's northern side. The sound of more drumming – rhythmic, distinctly unmilitary drumming – was coming from the corner to the right, and he walked across to find a circle of dancers whirling around a single drummer. They looked like Indians, and their speed and agility were amazing.

This was Mexico, Docherty thought. Mayan feet on Spanish stone, the past entwined with the present, drunkenness and death, farce and tragedy. After Chrissie's death everything had seemed grey, but this country kept hitting you in the face with the whole damn palette.

He smiled to himself and resumed walking, heading up Cinco de Mayo towards the hotel he had stayed in nineteen years before. It was still there, but either his standards had risen or the hotel's had dropped, and a cursory look at one room was enough to send him back on to the street. A few yards further on he found one of the places the guidebook recommended. The room he was shown seemed clean and the hotel itself seemed suitably anonymous. He checked in, left his bag in the room and continued on up Cinco de Mayo in search of something to eat.

The old city seemed seedier than he remembered, and not so lively; he supposed a lot of the night-life must have moved to the Zona Rosa a couple of miles to the east, where the streets would doubtless look much like modern streets did everywhere else. No matter, he told himself – he'd get the business with Toscono out of the way and then spend a few days in the real Mexico. He'd take the overnight train to Oaxaca, drink mescal sours in the main square, and see the world spread out beneath his feet on Monte Alban.

Sir Christopher Hanson was only a few minutes late arriving at his club for lunch, but his guest was already there, skimming through one of the hunting magazines with an amused expression on his face.

'These'll be like porn soon,' Manny Salewicz said as he got up, flourishing the magazine.

'What?' Hanson asked, taken aback.

'The way we hear it,' the American said, 'banning blood sports will be the only thing a new Labour government can give its activists which doesn't cost anything. And then the nobility will have to hide magazines like this under their four-posters.'

The MI6 chief smiled despite himself. Since their first meeting a couple of years earlier Salewicz's observations had often had that effect – the CIA man had a refreshing, and sometimes alarming, habit of cutting gleefully through the crap. The last time they'd had lunch together Hanson had been requesting American help for an SBS mission to Azerbaijan, and Salewicz had taken great pleasure in pointing out all the potential pitfalls before agreeing to provide it.

Now, as then, they spent the actual lunch in small talk. Salewicz was fascinated by Euro 96, mainly because the game itself left him completely cold. 'What's so great about a sport where you can't use your hands?' he demanded of Hanson, who could only shrug sympathetically. They then talked about President Clinton's problems with Whitewater, the Queen's with her children, and the Russian election. 'You know what they say about globalization?' Salewicz asked between mouthfuls of roast lamb and mint sauce. 'The only thing worse than its failure would be its success.'

It was only when they were nursing large glasses of port in the members' lounge that Hanson brought up business. 'I want to talk to you about Angel Bazua,' he told the American.

Salewicz raised a quizzical eyebrow.

'In the last week we've connected him to a large heroin shipment,' Hanson went on. He told the American about the timber yard, the hollowed-out logs packed with the stuff, the arrests of the local wholesalers and their Turkish distribution ring. 'We traced the list of buyers back to a fax machine in a Panama City office, and in that office one of our people intercepted an incoming fax from Providencia. There's no room for doubt here,' Hanson said, pulling a file from his briefcase and handing it to the CIA man, 'the trail leads right to Bazua's door. His prison door,' he added with evident disgust.

Salewicz was rifling through the file, playing for time. He'd suspected that Bazua would come up, but his bosses in Washington hadn't given him many cards to play. 'There's no copy of a fax from Providencia here,' he said, looking up.

'It was taken from him.'

The CIA man gave Hanson a hurt look. 'No proof?' he asked.

'He saw it. He'll tell the President he saw it if you like.'

Salewicz shook his head. 'If you want us to get heavy with the Colombians we need real proof, cast-iron, irrefutable, on-paper proof.'

Hanson took a deep breath. 'In there,' he said, indicating the file, 'you'll find documented evidence that Bazua is stockpiling weapons. In a prison! He already has two boats, both of which could transport a couple of hundred men. In Argentina his people are openly advertising for "patriotic soldiers of the motherland".'

'We know. But two boats? Give me a break.'

'When Castro and Guevara set out from Mexico in 1957 they only had eighty men in one boat, and by the time they reached the mountains there were only twelve of them. Who's ruling Cuba now?'

'It's not the same.'

'No, but it's not that different either. We can't afford to leave our garrison on the Falklands for ever, and I wouldn't be at all surprised if a Labour government doesn't bring it home sooner rather than later. A force of highly motivated mercenaries would be hard to dislodge with what's there now, and who knows? – if Bazua picks his moment the government in Buenos Aires may find it easier to back him up than wash their hands of him. The man has to be stopped.'

Salewicz raised both hands in surrender. 'OK, I get it – he's one of the bad guys. But what can we actually do – invade Colombia?'

'You've used special forces against the drug labs on the mainland.'

'Maybe, but not against a prison.'

'It's not a prison – it's a luxury fortress. And if your people don't do something, then I'm afraid we shall have to.'

'All that beef's gone to your head,' Salewicz said jokingly, but he could see that Hanson wasn't amused. The English were certainly in a kick-ass mood these days, what with beef and their goddam football tournament. Even the reference to Cuba had probably been deliberate – all the Europeans were pissed off about Washington trying to tell them who to trade with. 'Look,' he said, 'just hold your horses for a few days. I'll let Langley know how strong your feelings are on this one, OK? I can't promise anything, but . . .' He raised his hands again.

Hanson smiled at him. 'That would be most useful,' he said.

I doubt it, Salewicz thought, taking another sip of port. But maybe he'd find out what his own people's aversion to taking on Bazua was based on, and then convince the Brits accordingly. He certainly couldn't see Washington giving the Brits a green light to go rampaging in the Caribbean.

* * *

Docherty woke up feeling good, without any real idea why. Don't fight it, he told himself, and after winning a long battle with a recalcitrant shower, he felt even better. A café a few doors down supplied a Mexican egg sandwich – complete with avocados, onions and peppers – a papaya shake and coffee, and for the first time in several years he had a hankering for a cigarette. It was the city, he decided. It remembered that he used to smoke.

The streets were a lot fuller than the night before, and not only with milling pedestrians and honking traffic – goods for sale now seemed to cover most of the pavements. He walked back to the hotel intending to call one of the car-hire firms, but decided to ask the receptionist instead. And yes, of course he could get their English guest a car, especially if cash or traveller's cheques were involved. A short phone call to a relative confirmed as much – a brand-new VW Golf would be there in half an hour.

Docherty then spent a couple of minutes with the hotel's city directory, which confirmed the two numbers Gustavo Macías had given him. Toscono's business address was on Balderas, a street running south from the Paseo de la Reforma; his home was in the rich man's suburb of Las Lomas de Chapultepec. Docherty returned the directory to the receptionist, walked out to the bank of public phones he had noticed on his way back from breakfast, and called the home address.

A woman answered, which surprised him. 'Can I speak to Señor Toscono?' he asked.

'He is not here,' she said, and if the tone of her voice was any clue she didn't seem too upset by the fact. 'Who is this?' she asked, as if she'd suddenly remembered the correct procedure.

Docherty hung up and walked back across the street to the hotel. By the time he'd returned from his room the hire car was waiting for him. 'Brand-new' was perhaps something of an exaggeration but at least it started, and the furry breasts hanging alongside the Virgin Mary seemed a typically local touch. He drove west until he reached the Paseo, then turned south down the wide boulevard with its towering palms, over-the-top monuments and modern skyscrapers. One new building which caught his eye looked like a giant Stanley knife, the tip of its blade poised to scratch the low-hanging smog.

In 1977 it had nearly always been possible to see Popocatepetl and Ixtaccihuatl, the two volcanoes which loomed over the city, but Docherty sensed that such clarity was gone for ever. 'Progress,' he murmured to himself.

He followed the Paseo as it swung west along the northern edge of the vast Chapultepec Park, and five minutes later he was entering the suburb from which the park derived its name. 'Hill of the locust' was the translation, he remembered, and the name seemed appropriate enough – the people who lived around here probably hadn't noticed Mexico's economic crisis, much less suffered from it.

Las Lomas de Chapultepec, a few kilometres further out, seemed even richer, and its shady avenues seemed depressingly free of traffic. He was going to stick out like a sore thumb, Docherty thought, not least because nearly every car he saw seemed to be a BMW or a Mercedes.

He found Toscono's house without difficulty and immediately noticed the coils of razor wire interwoven with the tumbling bougainvillaea. Driving on up the hill, he found a small park, and from this relatively innocent vantage-point he was able to get a good idea of the compound's layout and take a sneak shot with his Polaroid. The camera's definition might not be that good, but it was quick, and there was no need to involve a processing firm.

The place didn't look any more inviting on the way down. He had seen no sign of dogs but that didn't mean much; the wire was crossable but the neighbourhood was far too quiet, and probably well watched – in countries like Mexico the police had a clearer idea of who paid their wages. There had to be better ways of getting to Toscono than over that wall.

Docherty drove thoughtfully back into the centre of the city, trying to ignore the rattling noise somewhere beneath him. On the edge of the Zona Rosa he found an outdoor café which put together a passable chicken *torta*, and then sat in La Ciudadela square for an hour or more by way of a siesta. At about three he walked up Balderas to Toscono's office address, which turned out to be a ten-storey glass tower. He waited outside until the lobby receptionist was busy with someone else's query, then walked in and examined the plaques on the wall behind him. As far as he could tell, Malvinas Import-Export was the sole occupant of the fifth floor.

He walked back outside and circled the building, noting the entrance to the underground car park. A car was just going in, and it seemed that the only entry requirement was money. Docherty strolled down Balderas, collected the Golf and drove back to the office building. The man in the booth at the entrance to the underground park took his pesos without even looking up from his newspaper, and he was in.

There were two levels and he examined them both before parking on the upper, along one of the side walls with a good view of the lift doors. Then he settled down to wait, wishing he'd had the sense to bring a magazine or book with them. The car's radio worked after a fashion, but there seemed to be only an unrelenting diet of Latino pop on offer, and he would rather have listened to country music. Well, maybe that was a bit of an exaggeration.

Between four-thirty and five the car park began to empty, and Docherty became worried that only his and Toscono's cars would be left, always assuming that the Argentinian was in his office. After all, he could be at the races, at a casino, or even, to judge from the tone of the woman on the telephone, in the arms of a mistress.

And then there he was – the slightly plump, slightly balding, impeccably dressed man from Gustavo's photograph. The man with him looked and acted like a bodyguard, and as they walked straight towards the Golf, Docherty slowly lowered his head below the level of the dashboard.

He didn't lift it again until he heard the sound of a car starting up. It was the big white BMW about twenty metres to his left, and Toscono himself was in the driving seat, looking pleased with himself. The other man, who was almost a head taller, seemed to be scowling at the world. It was probably something he had picked up at bodyguard school.

Carmen was a few minutes late arriving at the restaurant, but Detective Peña had phoned to say he would be later still. The table he had booked was beside a window, and she sat there with a glass of chilled white wine, thinking about him. In other circumstances, she thought, it was possible that something might have happened between them. Possible but not probable; he might be attracted to her but he was also happily enough married not to act on the attraction.

She had visited Victoria four times now, and each time it had been painful for both of them. Victoria might seem the less affected on the surface, but the fact that she was still hiding in the fiction of dreams suggested a degree of psychological damage which Carmen found almost as distressing as the story which was emerging between the lines of those dreams.

No real names had emerged, either of the people concerned or the place of the girls' imprisonment. 'He' was the 'Angel of Death', the men were 'his men', the island was just that. The details that emerged – the squelch of a water-bed, the stuttering fan, birdsong through a window – seemed rooted in evasion; they were like a condemned man's musings on the beauty of rope.

And yet sometimes there was clarity. 'We all used to play cards in our room,' Victoria suddenly said in one of their sessions. 'I can remember Marysa making a joke about him and we all laughed so much . . .'

Obviously not every moment had been nightmarish, but then they never were. Marysa had always made good jokes, Carmen thought, and found a tear rolling down her own cheek. Seeing Detective Peña zigzagging through the table towards her, she quickly dabbed it away.

'Sorry I'm late,' he said, 'but I've got good news. The charges against Victoria are going to be dropped.'

'That's wonderful!' Carmen said.

'She'll be deported – just formally,' he added, seeing

Carmen's eyes turn angry – 'and your government's already agreed to pick up the tab for everything. You can take her home to Cartagena. That's good news, isn't it?' he asked, noticing that the smile hadn't returned to her face.

She tried to give him one. 'Yes, yes, it has to be. I'm just afraid that my country will not be able to give her the sort of help she needs. I don't know . . .'

The waiter arrived to take their order. 'On expenses,' he said, but she had the feeling he intended paying out of his own pocket. She ordered one of the set lunches – she had never had Vietnamese food before – and another glass of white wine.

'It will take time,' he said, resuming the conversation.

'I know.'

'What will you do next? About your sister and the others, I mean.'

She shrugged. 'I don't know what I can do. What is happening here? Is no one interested in what Victoria has told me?'

'Everything she told you is being passed on to the DEA. But if you're right, and the island she talks about is the one you think it is . . .' It was his turn to shrug. 'It's foreign soil – no US agency could intervene physically. The best they could do would be to make representations to the Colombian government.'

'I understand that,' she said. 'But it's not foreign soil to me,' she added simply.

He almost dropped his chopsticks. 'You're not thinking of going there?'

'I don't know what to do,' she said. 'I don't think you understand what life is like in my country – it is not like here – I can't go to the police and expect that they will prove trustworthy.'

'I know that.'

'Well,' she said, forgetting her food for the moment, 'if I tell the police in Cartagena that I think my sister is a prisoner on Providencia, what will happen? First they will look for reasons not to believe me, and they will say I have only the word of a sick person. If they do believe me and are honest enough to do something about it, I expect there will be queries to Bogotá and the police on Providencia itself. If by some miracle there are honest policemen on the island the only result will be that the kidnappers will have to kill Marysa and the others to hide their crime.'

Peña looked at her with new respect. 'You've thought this through,' he murmured.

'It is not difficult,' she replied, resuming her eating.

'You said your father and the Cartagena police chief are on good terms, so they at least could talk the matter through in private.'

'Maybe,' she agreed. So far she had just passed on the bare outlines of Victoria's story to her parents – giving them the unexpurgated version was going to be a nightmare.

'How big is this island?' Peña asked.

'About twelve kilometres long and six wide.'

'That's a lot of ground to search. And even if you found the place . . .'

'I might be able to take a photograph, get some evidence that no one could talk their way out of.'

She might be right, he thought, but he shuddered to think of her being caught by whoever it was had broken Victoria Marín. 'Talk to your father first,' he urged her.

'I will. But if nothing happens, I can't just leave it. Could you, if it was your brother?'

'No, I suppose I couldn't. But getting myself killed or caught wouldn't help him,' he added.

She smiled ruefully. 'I know.' They looked at each other. 'And thank you for all your help,' she said.

'It's been a pleasure,' he replied, and meant it.

5

Lazaro Toscono left for the city centre shortly before eight o'clock in the morning. As on the previous evening, he was driving himself, the tall bodyguard in the seat beside him. Docherty, who had watched their departure from the small park above the villa, didn't bother to tail the BMW, but simply followed at the snail's pace allowed by the rush-hour traffic. At ten to nine he found a parking space a few blocks from the office building on Balderas, and went in search of somewhere to drink coffee and think through his approach to Toscono. He soon found a pleasant café, its pavement tables shaded from the already bright sun by the branches of a tall eucalyptus.

For a while he sat enjoying his coffee, watching the office latecomers hurrying by. He found it fascinating but not surprising that Toscono worked a nine-to-five day – these days the pull of convention was obviously just as strong for drug traffickers as it was for insurance salesmen. He remembered reading an article about how the Colombian drug lords were all sending their children to the best schools and colleges, then giving themselves up to the government in return for the legalization of their fortunes, which their well-educated children could then use to become legitimate business leaders.

It was all a bit pathetic, somehow.

Docherty had never lost much sleep over the drug trade. As long as there was a demand there would be suppliers – a point so transparently obvious that only the politicians could have missed it. But of course they hadn't really – it was just a lot easier to demonize the suppliers than to work out why the demand kept rising. Drugs had been in use in one form or another for almost as long as fire, from the Native Americans' use of peyote in their ceremonies to Celtic fans' use of lager in theirs, and Docherty, who at times in his life had slipped perilously close to alcoholism, was less inclined than most to see their use as an aberration. People needed to let off steam, relax their own inhibitions, simply have a good time, and there was no doubt that some drugs did the job.

Even so, drugs like heroin didn't do much for the gaiety of nations, and others, like crack and methamphetamine, tended to turn a good proportion of their users into decidedly unpleasant, often dangerous, neighbours. All of which begged the question: why did people want such drugs in the first place? No doubt a hundred people could come up with a hundred different reasons, but as far as Docherty was concerned they all came back to one – this was a world which, for all its surface excitement and technological wizardry, offered less and less to the human heart, and drugs were one of the easiest ways of sidestepping that reality.

Since this process was unlikely to be reversed, and since there seemed little prospect of legalizing soft drugs, Docherty had no problem with locking up the dealers of hard drugs. He just didn't feel that ridding the world of their presence should be a moral crusade – they were crooks, not devils, and in their pursuit of money and influence they probably caused far fewer casualties than their legitimate brethren in the arms trade.

Lazaro Toscono, though, was a different matter. He was not just a drug dealer – he was also a soldier responsible for several thousand civilian deaths. According to conventional wisdom it took two sides to make a 'dirty war', but from what Docherty had read – and what his admittedly biased wife had told him – this had not been the case in Argentina. The military there had not been under any real attack, but had gone about the business of setting up a network of torturers with enthusiasm – child bullies might pull the wings off insects, but these men pulled the limbs of people. And then, unable to accept any responsibility for their actions, they had disposed of the evidence in unmarked graves or the South Atlantic, and left thousands of families like the Macíases in the agony of not knowing what had happened to their siblings and children.

How people lived with themselves after being part of something like that was beyond Docherty's comprehension. He had killed people when his own or a comrade's life was at stake, and he knew what it felt like to be angry enough to want to really hurt someone, but he couldn't begin to understand how a man could countenance the infliction of pain on people he had never met, day in and day out, for years on end.

All of which, he realized, probably put him at something of a disadvantage when it came to dealing with scum like Toscono. What was there to appeal to? Guilt? Making the career move from death squad to drug trafficker hardly suggested a working conscience. Much the same could be said of an appeal to the kindness of Toscono's heart – if he had one, it was presumably available for use only by his nearest and dearest.

The man's sense of honour, perhaps, for military men everywhere, and Latin Americans in particular, often had an exaggerated respect for such notions. If he combined such an appeal with a convincing promise that any revelations would be for the ears of the Macías family only, then maybe Toscono would talk. Docherty doubted it – what was there in it for the drug dealer? – but the only other options were bribery and threats, and despite his desperate desire to know the truth of Guillermo's fate, Gustavo Macías had refused to countenance any payment to those who had taken his son. Docherty had already decided that he would try to scare the shit out of Toscono only when all else had failed.

He drained his cup and got to his feet. The deal with Gustavo required him just to ask, and he had promised Isabel he wouldn't take any real risks. He smiled to himself as he began walking towards the office building – he just knew that he wasn't going to like taking no for an answer from a man like Toscono.

But on this visit he would be polite. It wouldn't have been hard to get hold of a gun – the hotel receptionist would no doubt have a brother or an uncle who just happened to have one for sale – but carrying one into Toscono's den would be asking for trouble. He wouldn't get to see the head honcho without being frisked, and, should they decide for some reason to shoot him, a gun would simplify the task of convincing the local police that they had killed the gringo in self-defence.

He pushed through the glass doors into the air-conditioned lobby and walked confidently up to the attendant. 'I am here to see Señor Toscono on a personal matter,' he said, hoping the Argentinian's curiosity would get the better of him. 'My name is James Docherty, and I have travelled here from Chile to see him.'

So what? the attendant's eyes said, but he picked up the internal phone and relayed the message. 'Fifth floor,' he said briefly, nodding towards the lift.

Docherty walked in, pressed the button, and allowed himself to be carried skyward. So far, so good, he thought. He'd already got further than he'd expected.

The lift doors slid open to reveal a reception area and several doorways leading into the rest of a richly carpeted suite. The waiting bodyguard ran professional hands over Docherty's arms, legs and back, then led him into what looked like a doctor's waiting room. There were several paintings on the wall, all of flowers, and a framed front page of an Argentinian newspaper celebrating the sinking of HMS *Sheffield*, which took Docherty back to the night he'd heard the news himself, pissed half out of his mind in a Glasgow pub.

The door to Toscono's office opened and the bodyguard gestured him in. The man himself was sitting behind his desk in shirtsleeves; through the large window behind him the roofs stretched away towards the fuzzy green line of Chapultepec Park.

'What can I do for you?' Toscono asked as Docherty sat down. He had not offered to shake hands, and his voice was decidedly cool.

'It is a delicate matter,' Docherty began. 'A family matter.'

'You are English, yes?'

'Scottish. And I am married to an Argentinian. This matter has to do with her family,' he went on, stretching the truth somewhat. 'Her uncle had a son, who was a student in Rosario in the late 1970s.'

At the mention of Rosario, Toscono's face seemed to congeal. 'This conversation is over,' he said, getting up.

Docherty remained seated. 'My wife's uncle is dying,' he continued. 'He just wants to know what happened to his son.'

'I expect he died,' Toscono said coldly, his eyes catching the bodyguard's.

Docherty stood up as the man towered over him, and the temptation to take him out was almost overwhelming. But Toscono would probably have a gun in his desk and there were probably other people in the suite, so a demonstration of SAS unarmed-combat skills would be more satisfying than wise. He turned to leave, then stopped at the door. 'Why would you refuse to comfort a dying man?' he asked, but Toscono didn't even bother to look up, the bodyguard grabbed an arm, and a few seconds later he was being bundled into the lift.

'Don't come back,' the man said, speaking for the first time and displaying a row of gold teeth which Docherty could have combed his hair with. He emerged into the lobby and walked out on to the street, telling himself that he'd been wise not to fight back. If he was going to get anything from Toscono he would need to get him alone, and it would be much easier taking out a bodyguard who underestimated him.

He stopped at a convenient bar for a drink and reminded himself that he'd just earned $20,000, but he still felt angry. He told himself it was a childish kind of anger, but that didn't make it go away. He needed to put Toscono on the back-burner and regain his ability to think clearly.

A walk in the park, he thought, and then he remembered one of the things he'd planned to do once his business here was done. In 1977, during his last couple of days in the country, he'd set out to visit two famous houses in the southern suburb of Coyoacán, but both had been closed for refurbishment. He could visit them now, spend a few hours allowing his anger with Toscono to subside, then put his mind to the business of their next meeting. He already knew there'd be one – he might have satisfied the conditions of his deal with Gustavo Macías, but he hadn't satisfied himself.

The thought of driving ten kilometres and back through the capital's traffic was not a pleasant one, so he took the Golf back to the hotel, recovered the guidebook from his room and took the Metro south. A pleasant walk through shaded streets brought him to the last home of the Russian revolutionary Leon Trotsky, whose politics had obviously not prevented him from living in an upmarket neighbourhood. The house itself was not big, but it had a lovely cloistered garden. The rooms had supposedly been left exactly as they were on the day Stalin's agent stuck an ice-pick in Trotsky's skull, and the latter's broken glasses were still lying on the desk where they had fallen.

Docherty found himself wishing his father had been here to see this. The old man, who had been a shop steward on the Clyde most of his life, had often announced his admiration for the man who'd lived and died in this house. If Trotsky rather than Stalin had followed Lenin, he'd been fond of saying, it would all have been different.

Docherty doubted it, but seeing these rooms and the hammer-and-sickle-draped grave in the garden, he felt moved just the same.

After sitting for a while he got up and left, walking the couple of blocks to the Frida Kahlo Museum. She had lived in this house with fellow-Mexican painter Diego Rivera, and both had been friendly with Trotsky. Isabel liked her paintings a lot, and seeing them here in all their vibrancy Docherty could better appreciate why. Looking out into the well-tended back garden he could imagine her, Rivera and Trotsky sitting round the wrought-iron table drinking coffee in the late 30s, lamenting the fact that the rest of the world was sliding inexorably into war.

He ate lunch in an overpriced Coyoacán restaurant, then headed back north on the packed Metro, still wondering what to do about Toscono.

David Shepreth had been back in London only two days but already he felt at a loose end. On impulse he rang his father to suggest a visit, and almost instantly regretted it. His father's words were welcoming enough, but the tone wasn't, and the final 'of course, I'll be watching the football' effectively guaranteed one more evening of non-communication in a relationship already burdened with too many.

Feeling depressed, Shepreth steered the Escort in the direction of Barnsbury and his father's basement flat. The kick-off in the German game had to be imminent but half the fans still seemed to be in central London, or maybe it was just that the whole country had gone mad. As he swerved to avoid one flag-waving pedestrian in Kingsway it occurred to him that it was almost impossible to serve

MI6 in the field and maintain any level of patriotic fervour. If you lived out there in the world it was impossible to ignore the fact that everyone else had a point of view. In these days of international travel only the Americans were still clinging to the childlike belief that theirs was the greatest country on earth – everyone else had grown up and accepted relativity. True, most people were fondest of their own homeland, but that didn't stop them realizing that many other countries had just as much to offer.

As far as MI6 was concerned, this was a two-edged sword. Their agents were working for one country and one country only, but if they were any good at their job they acquired a knowledge of the way the world worked which was completely at odds with any simple notion of 'my country, right or wrong'. The end-result, as Shepreth knew only too well, was a thoroughgoing cynicism, sometimes worn like a badge, at others hidden beneath the mask of a cold professionalism. Everything became impersonal.

And I'm sick of it, he thought, as he waited at the King's Cross lights. He wanted it to be personal. The two goons in Panama with their 'B'-movie dialogue, they hadn't thought of killing him as anything personal, and if he allowed the curtain of his profession's cynicism to close behind him then he was no better than they were – just a player of violent games. Like a Len Deighton, he thought. Game, Set and Match. Hook, Line and Sinker. Egg, Beans and Chips.

Well, he'd already laid an egg in Panama, and Mexico seemed typecast for beans. It only remained to see where he'd cash in his chips.

The thought gave Shepreth his first real smile of the

day, but his father's offhand welcome – they hadn't seen each other for six months – soon put paid to it. The game had already been on for about half an hour, and by some miracle England were a goal up. Shepreth took the other end of the sofa and tried to watch, but soon found his mind beginning to wander. Looking round the room at his father's things from Spain he felt himself drawn, as always, back into the past, to the school holiday visits to his parents in Madrid, which had always promised so much more than they actually delivered. Looking back now it was easy to see that both his parents – his journalist father and highly social mother – had been busy people and that even if either of them had been really interested in their only child, they would have acted little differently. But at the time he had felt alternately abandoned and ignored, and deep down he knew that his life was still ruled by the consequences, that he was torn between conflicting compulsions to hide and to prove his worth to the world.

Why did I come? he asked himself. He tried to take an interest in the game, but found himself wondering once more at how easily his parents had got used to living without each other. His father had taken early retirement and announced that he was returning to England; his mother had said fine, but she would be staying in Spain. Five years later she was still in Madrid and he was still here, and they didn't seem to miss each other at all. Twenty years ago their desire to spend every minute together had caused him to be sent off to boarding school, and now they didn't even bother to call each other.

'How are you doing?' his father asked, and Shepreth noticed that the half-time whistle had been blown.

'OK,' he said. 'How are you?'

His father grinned. 'Pretty good. I've got quite a lot of stuff in the pipeline, and the novel's coming on. Want a beer, glass of wine?' he asked, getting up.

'Beer,' Shepreth said.

By the time his father came back with it the second half was about to start. The old man wasn't as steady on his feet as usual, but he was probably into his fifth or sixth beer by now. There was something vaguely pathetic about him these days. Shepreth thought. He was fifty-seven, but rather than realize the dreams of his youth he seemed to have just carried them through middle age. In his thirties he could often be heard on the radio reporting on events in Spain, and several newspapers had been happy to print his articles, but there had been no advance from that position – he was still writing the odd article, doing the odd piece of translation, talking about the novel which no one else expected would be written. He was a classic under-achiever.

Am I the same? Shepreth asked himself. He lived in hotels, had no real home. His love life was non-existent, his sex life almost so. He was neither enough of a cynic nor enough of a believer to fit in, which didn't augur well for his career prospects.

'Fuck,' his father said, and Shepreth realized that the Germans had equalized. Even he had expected that to happen.

The rest of the game passed slowly by, through the ninety minutes and another non-existent 'golden goal' to the penalty showdown. When Southgate finally missed his father couldn't even manage a curse; he just turned off the TV with a look of disgust and indifferently asked his son if he was staying the night.

Shepreth had meant to, but now he couldn't face it. He felt like screaming at his father, but he simply took his leave and drove back across London to the studio flat which was this year's apology for a home.

Docherty got back to his hotel around five, to find both the receptionist and his room key missing from reception. Perhaps the room was being cleaned, he thought. Perhaps the receptionist was out distributing alms to the poor.

He stealthily climbed the stairs and edged along the corridor towards his room. The door was wide open, and one man in uniform was going through his bag while another leant indolently against the wall smoking a cigarette.

'This is a non-smoker,' Docherty told him as he walked through the door. 'And what the fuck are you doing?' he asked the one elbow deep in his bag.

The arm came out like a shot, but then the policeman remembered who was supposed to be giving the orders. 'Identification,' he demanded, holding out a palm.

Docherty handed over his British passport. The other policeman, he was pleased to see, had ground out his cigarette. Little victories, he told himself.

'You must come with us, Señor Docherty,' the first policeman said, shoving the passport into his tunic pocket.

'Where?' Docherty asked.

'To the police station. It is not far.'

'Why? Am I being arrested?'

'You are required to answer some questions.'

'About what?'

'That will be explained to you at the station.'

The policeman's patience was obviously wearing thin, but Docherty was damned if he was going to get into a car with two armed men he didn't know from Adam. 'I need to see your identification,' he said firmly.

The policeman looked at his partner, shrugged and pulled out a crumpled card.

As Docherty handed it back he said, 'And I want to phone your station to verify that you are who this says you are.'

'We do not have the time for such . . .'

'If I'm not allowed to make that call, you'll have to carry me out,' Docherty said, hoping they wouldn't take him up on it.

They didn't, and he made the call from the empty reception desk downstairs. The two policemen were genuine, for what that was worth in Mexico.

Their car was unmarked, which explained why he hadn't noticed it coming in. One man sat in the back with him while the other broke every rule of the road on their drive to the police station. It was almost dark now and by the time they arrived Docherty had only a vague idea of where he was.

The two men left him in a large, stuffy room and disappeared. He lay down on the long wooden bench lining one wall and stared up at the peeling paint on the ceiling. The fan, having shed one of its four blades, had apparently lost the will to turn.

The minutes went by, then an hour, then two. He could hear feet above his head and the occasional voices of passers-by but not much else. He wondered if they were just wasting his time or deliberately trying to scare him.

Another hour went by. He thought about Isabel and

the children in Santiago – she would be putting them to bed about this time, maybe telling Ricardo a story. He wondered what they'd think if they could see him now.

Still, his only problem so far was thirst. His mouth was as dry as the Mexican dust he'd been swallowing all day, and he was beginning to get a headache. He could no doubt bang on the door and demand water, but in the unlikely event that some was brought it would not be bottled, and he'd rather be thirsty than spend the next week suffering Montezuma's famous revenge.

It was nearly nine o'clock when the door finally opened. Two uniformed men escorted him down one corridor, up a flight of steps and down another corridor, before ushering him into a much better-decorated room than the one he'd just left. Another man in uniform – this one in his forties or early fifties, with a balding head, moustache and rotund frame – was sitting behind a huge desk. 'Sit down, Señor Docherty,' he said in English.

'And who might you be?' Docherty asked.

'I am Lieutenant Colonel Orantes.'

'Police or Army?' Docherty asked. He had considered refusing to answer any questions until he was allowed to contact the British Embassy, but had decided that such a move might needlessly complicate matters. If Orantes was only going to slap him lightly on the wrist . . .

'Federal Police,' Orantes answered. 'It has . . .'

'So why am I here?' Docherty interrupted.

'You don't know?'

'If I did, I wouldn't be asking.'

Orantes raised an eyebrow. 'This morning you visited the offices of Señor Toscono, did you not?'

'I did.'

'Where you threatened him with violence . . .'

'I did not threaten him – he threatened me. I merely asked him about one of his victims in the Dirty War.'

'What happened in Argentina twenty years ago is not the business of the Mexican police. Threats against a prominent citizen – and Señor Toscono is a citizen of this country now – are our business.'

'I made no threats.'

'That is not what he and his employees say.'

'They are lying.'

Orantes smiled. 'And whose word should I take – a prominent Mexican citizen or an Englishman passing through?'

Docherty smiled back. 'I expect you'll believe the man who pays you to.'

Orantes, rather than getting angry, simply laughed. Once his amusement had subsided he fixed Docherty with his eyes, pointed a finger at him and said, 'Do not try to contact Señor Toscono again. If you do, I promise that you will regret it.'

Docherty returned the stare. 'Have you considered a career in films?' he asked.

That did seem to strike home. 'You may go,' Orantes said coldly, breaking eye contact. 'Enjoy your stay in Mexico,' he added sarcastically as the uniformed man led Docherty away.

A minute later he was out on the dark street, and after taking a look in both directions – neither of which seemed particularly inviting – he decided that either was better than standing still. Orantes might be finished with him, or the interview might have been a prelude to something else – like one more unsolved robbery and murder on

Mexico City's mean streets. There was a hint of brighter light in one direction, so he started out that way, upping his pace from a walk to a jog, then a fast trot. It was probably unnecessary, but better to be safe than sorry.

No threatening figures emerged from the shadows, and as he ran the bright glow came slowly into focus. It was the Avenida Mosqueta, which distant memory told him ran past the main railway station.

Feeling relatively safe once more, he walked east, wondering why Toscono had gone to all this trouble. The Argentinian had hardly been ambivalent that morning, so why labour the point? It seemed gratuitous, even insulting, which was maybe the point. Either that or Toscono was an anal retentive who couldn't sleep until he'd covered every conceivable angle.

Outside the station Docherty found a cab. He gave the driver the name of his hotel, but halfway down Tacuba he changed his mind and told the man to drop him off in the Zócalo. There was a small protest demonstration going on in the middle of the square, which reminded him of the Day of the Dead in 1977, when a reproachful cross of flowers and burning candles over fifty metres long had been laid across the stones, pointing straight at the President's door.

In the far corner a drummer was beating out a rhythm, and he walked towards the sound. The dancers were different tonight, but every bit as good. He watched, enjoying the spectacle as his brain worked on the problem of Toscono. When the drum fell silent he realized his mind was made up.

Sir Christopher Hanson switched on his office TV for

the news, but the only thing anyone seemed able to talk about was the wretched football match. He was almost glad that Germany had beaten England – at least now the fever would begin to subside and they could get back to a normal civilized summer of tennis and cricket. But he couldn't quite make the emotional leap – even fifty years after the war it was hard for most people of his generation to wish anything good for the Germans. Only the previous week a bout of insomnia had caused him to watch a film which followed a group of gypsies from pre-war Poland to Auschwitz. These were not crimes that could be forgotten in a hurry.

Would Angel Bazua have enjoyed the Third Reich? Hanson wondered, as he opened the bound printout once more. The light-brown hair and blue eyes suggested possible descent from the early German immigrants to Argentina, but there was no genealogical evidence. Bazua's father, Raul, had been a worker in the Buenos Aires cattle market, his mother, Steffia, a seamstress, but the names and occupations of their parents were unknown.

Bazua's track record suggested a Third Reich-friendly narrow-mindedness, not to mention an appetite for cruelty and pathological patriotism, but on balance Hanson decided the Argentinian would have found the discipline somewhat restrictive.

He read through the file for a second time, making sure he had imbibed all the relevant facts. The fifty-two-year-old Bazua had spent all his childhood years in Buenos Aires; his family, though poor, had never gone hungry, and by some miracle his parents had managed to put enough aside to send the boy to military school. From there he had won a scholarship to a prestigious academy, where he was implicated in a scandal concerning a maimed prostitute. There was no real explanation of how he had weathered this crisis – only a suggestion that blackmail had played a part – but he had graduated with honours a year later, and began the task of working his way up the Army's promotional ladder. He was soon active in extreme right-wing 'clubs' and in 1970–1 he spent a year at the US anti-insurgency school in Panama, where he made friends with like-minded officers from several other Latin American countries. As the war between Left and Right in Argentina escalated in the mid-70s the 'clubs' turned into semi-official death squads, bent on cleansing the nation of all opposition to the ruling coalition of big business and the military. Bazua had been in charge of operations in and around Rosario, a port city with nearly a million inhabitants two hundred and seventy kilometres north-west of the capital.

Some seven thousand people, most of them students or trade unionists, had disappeared during Bazua's reign of terror, but several hundred of those with the richest connections had subsequently turned up, presumably in return for substantial ransoms.

Bazua had not fought in the Falklands War, but his only son – the product of a short-lived marriage from his military academy years – had been killed at Goose Green, further deepening what seemed to have been a life-long hatred of the English. Defeat dealt a huge blow to the prestige of the military, and at the age of thirty-eight he had resigned his commission. Not enough was known about his activities over the next few years, but by the end of the 80s he had relocated to Cartagena on the north Colombian coast and emerged as a major player on the international drug-trafficking stage. He had not challenged the local cartels in the cocaine market, but had, from the beginning, concentrated on the refining, distribution and sale of his adopted country's burgeoning poppy crop. By the mid-90s Colombia had become second only to Burma in heroin production, and Bazua was profiting most from the growth.

He was not untouchable, of course, and by 1993 the need for a scapegoat had caused the Colombians to make a show of imprisoning their only non-indigenous drug baron. A whole new facility had been built on the Caribbean island of Providencia, largely, it seemed, to the chief prisoner's specifications. And the flow of heroin continued unabated. Or almost – the operation in London the previous week had doubtless caused a temporary shortfall in the British capital's supply.

Which would just raise the price and make the bastard a bigger profit on his next shipment, Hanson thought sourly. Some days he felt really nostalgic for the Cold War, and honest enemies.

Why were the Americans being so obstructive? Salewicz had phoned him back the previous evening with a list of rationales and excuses a mile long, but he hadn't even bothered to pretend that he believed any of them. Listen to the subtext, the CIA man had seemed to be saying – sometimes you just can't get what you want, and there's no point in wondering why.

Well, it wasn't good enough. He had given the Americans a chance to explain themselves, make their case, and they hadn't even tried. They might think that would be the end of it, but if Hanson had any say in the matter it wouldn't. Not many things made him angry these days –

apart from his children, of course – but no one was going to finance a second invasion of the Falklands with profits from flooding Britain with heroin. One way or another, Bazua had to be stopped. The question was how.

Hanson stared out of his window. Somewhere in the distance there was shouting – it was probably football supporters. For all he knew, English and German fans were replaying yesterday's game in Trafalgar Square.

On his desk the ancient intercom crackled, as if it was clearing its throat. 'Mr Shepreth is here,' his new secretary announced.

'Send him in,' Hanson replied irritably. She always sounded like a dental receptionist.

Shepreth's tall frame loomed in the doorway. He looked bronzed from his three months in the field, Hanson noticed. 'David, how are you?' he asked.

The old man was in a bad mood, Shepreth thought, as he took the proffered seat. He hoped it had nothing to do with him. 'Fine, thank you,' he answered with more tact than truth. Thanks to his neighbours he had only managed about six hours' sleep in seventy-two. Someone across the street had played loud music for most of the night, and the Americans next door had thoughtfully erected a basketball hoop between the buildings, encouraging their son to bounce his ball through the hours of daylight.

'Good to have you back in one piece,' Hanson murmured, his eyes on the printout he had just rescued from a pile. 'I read your report. Did the Yanks in Panama give you any reason for not coming up with an address for the fax number?'

'I was told they didn't have one.'

'Which was nonsense, I presume?'

'I can't be sure – he might have been telling the truth.'

'But you didn't think so?'

'No,' Shepreth said, trying to recall why he hadn't thought so. 'I don't know Neil Sadler that well, but he sounded embarrassed to me. I don't think he knew why he'd been told to be unhelpful – but he had.'

Hanson leant back in his chair, twirling his pen between his fingers. 'I'm beginning to think this may be one of those stupid internal rivalries the Yanks seem to specialize in,' he said.

Like MI5 and Special Branch, Shepreth thought, but he didn't say so. His boss seemed unusually pent-up today – he couldn't remember him ever calling the Americans 'Yanks' before.

'OK,' Hanson said abruptly. 'I've got a pretty good idea of our current situation. Give me an update on how the Americans are doing in their war with the drug lords.'

'Not very well,' Shepreth said. 'As soon as they knock down one line of kingpins another one springs up. They'd hardly finished slapping themselves on the back for breaking the Medellín cartel when they realized the Cali cartel would probably have done it for them in a couple more years. And since 1992 the Cali people have been taking a beating – quite a few of them are trying to negotiate terms with the Colombian government now – but their old subsidiaries in Panama and Mexico have just struck out on their own. The Mexican traffickers are now the Americans' number-one targets.'

'We're still talking mostly about Peruvian and Bolivian coca, refined in Colombia and then sold on, yes?'

'Mostly. Though the Mexicans are now doing some

refining of their own, and the Colombians have started growing poppies on a grand scale. The shipment we just intercepted was probably grown and refined in Colombia for Bazua's organization to move and distribute. More heroin's going north into the States as well, but at the moment the Americans are more worried by the way the trade in methamphetamines has suddenly taken off. They're just chemicals, so there's no need to grow anything – just get the ingredients to a small lab and cook them up. Thousands of these labs have been springing up all over Mexico.'

Hanson shook his head at the folly of it all. 'And what's the favourite mode of transport these days?' he asked drily.

'It changes from year to year. In the 80s they were sending convoys of planes all the way from Colombia to northern Mexico, but the interception rate got too high for comfort so they switched to small planes hopping their way north via Panama and Guatemala and into southern Mexico – often into territory controlled by insurgents – and from there they'd go north by road. The last bright idea – which was probably Bazua's – was to send jet liners into northern Mexico. They had fake identities painted over the old ones, radar transponders turned off, and they didn't file flight plans. They could carry huge shipments and they were fast enough to outrun anyone that saw them. But it wasn't something they could do too often – or at least not without giving the Americans the proof they wanted that the Colombian authorities were involved. A plane the size of a Caravelle can't take off from a jungle strip.'

'They don't try flying the stuff into the US itself?'

'Not in large quantities. Most of it goes across the

border in containers and trucks, some of it inside human "mules". Each of the main crossover points – Tijuana, Ciudad Juárez, Matamoros – seems to be the personal fiefdom of one organization, and they each have their own links with the suppliers to the south and the distributors across the border. NAFTA – the trade treaty the US and Mexico signed a couple of years ago – has made things a lot easier for the traffickers. The volume of cross-border trade has shot up and there's no way the Americans can search more than one truck in twenty without effectively closing the border down. These days it's easier for the traffickers to get the drugs in than it is for them to get their money out.'

'How are the Americans getting along with the Mexican authorities?'

'Not as well as they'd like us to believe. The Mexicans have too many overlapping agencies, and none of them are completely clean. Traffickers have escaped pursuing Feds with help from an army helicopter. State police have come across Feds trying to bury a damaged jet liner in the desert.' Shepreth smiled ruefully. 'A couple of months ago one state's "policeman of the year" was arrested for trafficking.'

'I imagine the Americans are getting somewhat frustrated.'

'Of course. But the situation's not going to change. The Mexican police and army are paid abysmally, and their earnings on the side just about provide them with a living wage. The country as a whole is probably making about seven billion dollars a year from the drug trade, and it needs every penny of it.'

Hanson had opened the file in front of him. 'It was

the DEA who pushed through the kingpin strategy, wasn't it?'

'Yes,' Shepreth replied, although the question was rhetorical.

'The National Security Council were in agreement, I think,' his boss went on. 'The Pentagon, the Coast Guard and the Customs Service were opposed. Where did the CIA stand?'

This time an answer was called for. 'With the National Security Council, I think,' Shepreth said. 'They usually pride themselves on being above such mundane matters as the drug trade.'

'Hmm. A more centralized DEA means less autonomy for the field offices, right?'

'The head of the field office in Mexico City has complained about nothing else for the last six months.'

'How do you know?' Hanson asked sharply.

'He's a friend,' Shepreth admitted. 'I mean I'm sure he doesn't tell me everything – he's a professional – but I do know he's as frustrated as we are that Bazua's not on the kingpin list. He may not be shifting the same volume through Mexico as some of the others, but he's not that far behind. And as I said, he was apparently the first one to have the idea of using the old jet liners to bring in huge quantities on a single flight. His organization on the ground in Mexico is said to be first-rate, with everyone from cabinet ministers to village cops on the payroll.'

Hanson thought for a moment. 'I want action against Bazua,' he said slowly. 'But the how and the what . . .' He looked up. 'I don't want to move against him until I know why the Americans are so reluctant to. Maybe they do have a good reason, and just can't be bothered to tell us what it is. If so . . . well, a good reason for them may not be a good reason for us – but either way I want to know. So go back to Mexico and see what you can find out. Try and get your DEA friend to tell you why he thinks his bosses are frustrating him.'

'Yes, sir,' Shepreth said. He didn't much like the idea of trading on his friendship with Ted Vaughan, but when all was said and done he knew that the American would love the idea of anyone taking a crack at Angel Bazua.

Carmen looked round the familiar room, but there was no psychological comfort to be had there. She had grown up in this house, and even after moving out she had thought of it as a safe haven from the troubles of the world, but that was not the case any more. Now it was just the place where her parents lived.

They were sitting together on the sofa, not touching or even looking at each other. Carmen had half-expected her father to rant and rage when she told him what she knew but instead of exploding he had seemed to crumple. Both of them had. In half an hour they had seemed to age about ten years.

She had explained about Victoria, trying to cushion the blow by emphasizing how unreliable the woman's testimony might be, but her father had not been fooled. 'You think it's true, don't you?' he had asked, begging her with his eyes to deny it. But she couldn't. The five women had been kidnapped, taken to the island of Providencia, and forced into sexual slavery by a convicted drug baron named Angel Bazua. When two of the women had become pregnant each had been forced to swallow about seventy condom-wrapped pellets of heroin and put on a plane for the United States. The other three were presumably still servicing Bazua and his men in their island prison. And there didn't seem to be a thing they could do about it.

Carmen had then explained to her shell-shocked parents why they couldn't just go to the police. Her father had tried to argue with her, but without a great deal of conviction. What was happening on Providencia might be outrageous, but it could only be happening with the tacit acceptance of law-enforcement agencies on the island. Giving the story to the press would probably get them more attention than an appeal to the police, but the closer they got to exposing Bazua and his cronies the more certain it seemed that he'd simply dispose of the evidence. The three women would just disappear into the sea.

'So what can we do?' her father asked numbly.

'I don't know,' she said. 'I thought about hiring someone – a private detective – but if we can't trust the real police why should we trust a man who works only for money?'

'There must be some honourable men doing that kind of work,' her father said hopefully.

'But how do we find out who they are?' She had been through this conversation more than once with herself, and her conclusion was always the same – the only person she could trust to ask questions on Providencia was herself. She knew it wouldn't be simple or easy – there was no way she was going to rescue her sister from a well-guarded prison – but if she could find out for certain that Marysa was alive that would at least be a start.

'I have to go myself,' she told her parents. An hour ago she would have expected an argument, but now they both just looked at her, fear and hope crowding their faces. 'I'll leave tomorrow,' she said, getting up.

Her father murmured something about paying for everything, but she was already halfway through the door which led out into the sunlit garden. The hammock was swaying gently in the breeze, and the sudden desire to simply lie down and close her eyes was almost overwhelming.

Instead she walked on through the trees, thinking that she would have to try to see Victoria again before she left. The aunt who had met the plane had seemed a kindly person, but Victoria had acted as if she was being abandoned, rather than passed into someone else's care.

Carmen reached the bottom of the garden and stared up at the distant hills, her heart weighed down with sadness, her stomach churning with fear.

6

Docherty sat on his haunches behind the white BMW, his back against the concrete wall. The car was one of only a dozen still awaiting collection in the cavernous car park, and that suited Docherty down to the ground – he didn't want an audience when Toscono came to claim his.

About fifty-five hours had passed since their first meeting, and by this time Toscono had probably forgotten he existed. Docherty had not been idle in the intervening period – he had spent most of the previous day searching out a suitable spot for a private tête-à-tête, and most of the evening shopping for the 9mm Walther PPK which was now stuffed inside his belt. He would have preferred one of the Browning High Powers he was used to, but the dealer he visited in Guadalupe said he hadn't seen one of those for months. Besides, Docherty had gained some experience with the Walther PPK during his first tour of duty in Northern Ireland. The fact that the gun came with a silencer was a big bonus – convincing people that you were prepared to use a gun was so much easier if it looked like no one else would notice.

Docherty tensed as the faint ping announced the opening of the lift doors, but the two men who emerged were not Toscono and his bodyguard. These two walked across his line of vision towards a dark Mercedes, their feet making a slapping sound on the concrete floor. The car's engine burst into life, sounding preternaturally loud in the subterranean space. It purred across the floor, smoothly accelerated up the exit ramp and disappeared from view, just as the lift doors opened again.

This time it was them. Toscono was carrying a briefcase on this occasion, which was all to the good – if he was armed it would slow down his reactions. Docherty's only movement as the footfalls drew nearer was to pull the Walther from his belt. His breathing sounded louder than it should but he knew that was just his imagination.

The slap of their footsteps turned from mono to stereo as the two men walked towards the doors on either side of the car, and the clunking sound told Docherty that Toscono had used his remote. He rose up from his crouch like a well-oiled jack-in-the-box, gun in hand. After a split second's hesitation the bodyguard started for his own weapon, but a perceptible shift in Docherty's aim and the sight of the silencer froze him in mid-motion.

'Both of you – hands on the roof,' the Scot snapped. 'And let the briefcase drop,' he told Toscono.

'You must be mad,' Toscono hissed, but both he and the bodyguard obeyed.

Docherty walked round the car until he was a few feet away from the latter, all the time keeping an eye on the man's boss. 'I can just as easily leave *you* dead on the floor,' he told the bodyguard. 'And if you move a muscle, I will.'

The man's mouth twitched, but he said nothing.

'On your knees,' Docherty told him, and when the man didn't move he pushed the snout of the silencer gently into his back. 'Now or never,' he added.

The man still didn't speak, but a whimper escaped his lips as he lowered himself to the ground. Taking his eyes off Toscono for no more than a second, Docherty crashed the butt of the Walther into the side of the bodyguard's head.

The man slumped forward, banging his forehead against the car door, and ended up curled in a foetal position half under the car. With his foot, Docherty dragged a stray leg out from under the wheel. 'Get in the car,' he told Toscono.

'No,' Toscono said shakily. His eyes were on the distant lift doors – no doubt he was praying they would suddenly disgorge a rescue force.

'Is that your final answer?' Docherty asked, aiming the PPK between the man's eyes and flexing his finger on the trigger.

Toscono got into the car.

Docherty climbed in beside him.

'There were thousands of prisoners at the Rosario base,' Toscono said petulantly. 'I can't remember all the ones I had dealings with, let alone all the others.'

'Shut up and drive,' Docherty told him.

Toscono looked at him.

'Drive,' he repeated.

Toscono drove.

'Smile at the man,' Docherty said as they approached the attendant's booth, but there was no one in it. 'Turn right on the street,' he added.

'Where are we going?' Toscono asked as they emerged on to Balderas.

'Head for the airport,' Docherty told him.

'The airport?'

'Don't worry – you won't be needing your passport,' he said, as the Argentinian slowed the car to join the long queue at the lights. The traffic might turn out to be a problem, Docherty realized – even with the tinted windows shut he didn't fancy holding a gun on Toscono for hours on end in the middle of a grid-locked street.

They crawled up Tacuba, but once past the Zócalo the crush thinned, Toscono was able to keep the car moving at a steady thirty and it seemed as if the worst was over. The Argentinian hadn't said a word since the car park, and his face now seemed set in a mask of cold fury. He had just about recovered from the shock, Docherty guessed, and was now rummaging through his brain for a way out of his predicament.

They turned left on to Puerto Aéreo Boulevard, and were soon passing under the thunderous flight path of an incoming American Airlines jet. 'We're not going into the airport,' Docherty said. 'Take the Texcoco road – it's about a kilometre beyond the entrance.'

Toscono said nothing, just gripped the wheel a bit tighter.

'If you drive into the airport, I shall just leave you dead in the car park and take the next plane out,' Docherty told him.

Toscono's shoulders seemed to sag. 'So where are we going?' he asked as the slip road went by.

'The Texcoco road,' Docherty repeated, and Toscono didn't ask again. They were about a kilometre down that road, the outlying areas of the airport receding to their right, when the small side road came into view. 'Turn off here,' Docherty ordered, and saw the flash of fear in the other man's eyes. 'If I'd just wanted to kill you I could have done it in the car park,' he said.

Toscono pulled the car off the main road and on to a bumpy dirt track which wound through the scrub for about half a kilometre before ending on the rim of a recently excavated crater some two hundred metres square and about thirty metres deep. 'It's for rubbish,' Docherty said drily.

The Argentinian stared out at the vast hole. A plane was taking off a few hundred metres beyond it, but as far as the rest of the world was concerned they might have been on the moon. The highway they'd turned off was an invisible murmur somewhere beyond the thick scrub, the city just a few distant towers beneath the smog.

'Guillermo Macías,' Docherty said softly. 'I want to know what happened.'

Toscono looked at him. He remembered both the name and the boy. Macías had been almost too good-looking, with an angelic face, soft, wavy hair, a colt-like grace. In his mind's eye Toscono could see the pale body on the table, arcing and bouncing under the electricity. It hadn't been necessary – he had offered the boy a way out, only to receive a faceful of spittle for his trouble.

He even remembered why he had been arrested. 'Macías was picked up with several other students,' he said out loud. 'They were found in possession of gummed labels with revolutionary slogans . . .'

'Labels?' Docherty asked incredulously.

'Yes. I was in command of the arrest squad. He was taken to the base for processing, and I don't know what happened to him after that. If he wasn't released I presume he ended up in either a grave or the River Plate.'

Docherty knew Toscono was lying, at least in part – his eyes and mouth seemed to be telling different stories. The gummed label part sounded sick enough to be true, and so did the choice of final resting-places, but Docherty was pretty sure the Argentinian knew more than he was saying about what had happened in between.

Did it matter? Gustavo Macías would at least know why his son had been arrested, and what parents wanted to know the details of how their child had been tortured? He had got what he needed from Toscono.

But not what he wanted. He wasn't even sure what that was, and the reasons he wanted it were no clearer – they might have something to do with old-fashioned right and wrong, or maybe with the fact that Isabel had been tortured by men like this one. At that moment he didn't care.

'That's not enough,' he said softly, as if it was a decision he'd reached reluctantly. He raised the Walther, supporting the wrist of his gun hand on the other, and hoped that an hour under the gun hadn't taken the edge off Toscono's fear.

'I can't tell you any more,' the Argentinian said. His voice was only slightly frayed at the edges, but the eyes were wide with terror.

'Who could?' Docherty asked.

'What do you mean?'

'Give me a name. Who was in command of the camp?'

Toscono thought quickly. Giving this mad Englishman Angel Bazua's name would be safe enough – there was no way anyone could get to *him*. 'Colonel Bazua was in command of the base,' he said.

That at least was the truth, Docherty thought.

'He's in prison in Colombia,' Toscono volunteered.

'I know where he is,' Docherty said coldly. 'What makes you think his memory is any better than yours?'

'It doesn't need . . .' Toscono began, then fell silent.

'This is the last question you'll have to answer,' Docherty told him. 'If I think you're telling the truth you can go and play in that big sandpit out there. If I think you're lying you'll need another couple of kneecaps. Understand?'

Toscono gave him a look of mingled fear and loathing. 'I understand.'

'So why doesn't Colonel Bazua need a memory?'

'Because he has the files,' Toscono said.

'The files?'

'The records of all the prisoners. Not just in Rosario – all the prisoners of the Army.'

Docherty believed him. He looked at his watch. 'It's been lovely talking to you, but I'm going to be late for my plane. So you can go now.' Once Toscono had climbed out he shifted over into the driving seat, put the BMW into reverse and accelerated back up the dirt road in the direction of the highway. By the rim of the crater Toscono had sunk to his knees and seemed to be praying to whatever God would listen.

Shepreth paid his money and paused just inside the doors of the Luz de la Luna, letting his eyes get used to the smoky gloom. A local band was doing a passable job on an old Clifford Brown tune and the jazz club's patrons were listening respectfully, toes and fingers tapping, heads nodding. As he'd expected, Theodore Vaughan was there, sitting alone at a table on the far side of the room, eyes closed in a smiling face. Jazz was the love of the DEA man's life, and this was far and away the best club in Mexico City.

During the two years they'd known each other Ted Vaughan had often brought Shepreth here, and for his part the Englishman had taken the Afro-American to visit some of the lesser-known archaeological gems within easy driving distance of the capital. Both had enjoyed the cross-cultural fertilization, and these days Vaughan could tell his Aztecs from his Toltecs, Shepreth his Mingus from his Monk.

As the pianist went into a solo, Shepreth wended his way through the tables to where his friend was sitting.

Vaughan opened his eyes. 'You're back,' he said, and closed them again.

'I got in last night,' Shepreth told him once the piece was over.

'How was Merry Old England?'

'In mourning. We lost a football match to the Germans,' he explained, seeing the look of incomprehension on Vaughan's face. 'I need something to eat,' he added, looking round for a waiter. The Luz de la Luna might not have had the world's greatest jazz, but the food was excellent. 'And then I need to talk to you,' he told Vaughan.

'Business?'

'Yeah. Off-the-record business, if there is such a thing.'

Vaughan smiled at that. 'After the set?'

'Sure.'

An hour or so later the two men emerged from the club

and into the cool air. It was only just past ten o'clock, and the suburb of San Angel was far from sleeping. One group of teenage boys were honing their skateboarding skills in the parking lot next door, a mixed group of youngsters were talking and laughing outside the cinema just up the road, and in the distance they could hear the strains of the funfair wafting down from the Plaza San Jacinto.

'Have you got your car?' Shepreth asked.

'Yeah, it's over there.'

'Why don't we drive up to the plaza?'

'OK.'

They drove up the hill to find that many of the craft and artwork stalls in the square itself, and most of the fairground rides and freak shows in the adjoining streets, were still open for business. Vaughan found a spot to park the car, paid the local urchins a king's ransom to guard it, and the two of them walked slowly round the square, finally settling on a just-vacated bench close to the fountain. On the seat opposite a young couple were holding hands and staring into each other's eyes.

'Nice,' Vaughan said, lighting a cigarette. No matter how big an Hispanic population the US ended up with, Mexico would still feel a long way from home. He took a drag on the cigarette. 'So how can I help Her Majesty's Secret Service?' he asked playfully.

Shepreth had no desire to beat about the bush. 'You can tell us why your people are so reluctant to go after Angel Bazua.'

Vaughan grimaced. 'Ah, shit,' he murmured. 'Ask me something I know the answer to.'

Shepreth was silent for a moment. 'OK,' he said at last. 'We've got a pretty good idea of how big Bazua's

European operation is. What's his volume of trade with the US like?'

'Big and getting bigger. Top twenty with a bullet. And we think he's recently done a distribution deal with Ignacio Payán in Ciudad Juárez, which would give him a seat at the big boys' table.'

'Which just seems to beg the question,' Shepreth said. 'Why the kid gloves?'

'Like I said, I don't know.' Vaughan hesitated for a moment. 'Off the record, right? I've asked my people in Washington, and they tell me he's in prison, the prison's in Colombia, there are easier fish to fry. All of which may be true, but it still doesn't feel right to me. Most of his organization's here and in Panama, and I can't see any harm in keeping tabs – if we don't, the bastard could have Mexico sewn up without even having to leave his goddam cell.'

Shepreth smiled. 'Do I detect some creative reading of your instructions from Washington? Are you keeping tabs anyway?'

'We're keeping a watch on Payán's people here, and of course that means investigating the people they're in regular contact with.'

'Like Bazua's people?'

Vaughan smiled. 'And I have a question of my own,' he said. 'Does the name James Docherty mean anything to you?'

'No,' Shepreth said without hesitation. 'Should it?'

'He's a fellow-countryman of yours. Ex-SAS, retired to Chile a couple of years ago. Two days ago he met with Bazua's top man here . . .'

'Lazaro Toscono?'

'The same. Docherty paid him a visit. We don't know why, but we do know that later that day some of Toscono's buddies in the police arrested Docherty, accused him of threatening Toscono and warned him to be a good boy in future.'

Shepreth pondered this information. Why would an ex-SAS man be threatening a drug baron?

'So he's not one of yours?' Vaughan asked.

'Not as far as I know,' Shepreth told him. 'Is he still in Mexico City?'

'He was this morning. He checked out of his hotel, took a cab to the post office and never came out again. At least, our guy didn't see him come out. It might have been just carelessness, but he hasn't left the country by plane and he hasn't checked into a new hotel under his own name.'

'You're still looking?' Shepreth asked, amazed as usual by how good the American coverage of the city was. One or other of their agencies must have someone on the payroll in just about every political, legal and military office in the capital, not to mention the various transport and communication agencies.

'Yeah,' Vaughan admitted. 'I'm curious,' he added by way of explanation.

So was Shepreth. It was almost midnight by the time Vaughan dropped him off at the Embassy-owned apartment, and in another couple of hours head office in London would be open for business. His body still seemed to be on English time in any case, and he felt more awake than he had earlier that evening. He made himself some coffee and liberally dosed it with brandy, then turned on the TV. A dubbed version of an old Paul

Newman Western was showing – the one in which he played a white man who'd grown up with the Apaches. When it ended soon after one Shepreth flicked through the channels. One of them was showing a rerun of the England–Germany game.

He switched off the TV, took a shower, then encoded and faxed off his request for information on one James Docherty, ex-SAS. With any luck there would be an answer waiting for him when he woke up.

After ditching the BMW outside a Metro station in the Zona Rosa, Docherty had taken a taxi back to the Old City, collected his bag from the café owner who'd agreed to look after it, and checked into a far from salubrious hotel a couple of streets north of the Zócalo. He registered under the name Kenneth Dalglish, telling the receptionist his passport had been stolen that day. The man looked wounded by this news, but soon cheered up when offered compensation in the form of a ten-dollar bill.

The room looked like it was used for cockroach derbies, but the door seemed sturdy enough, and it would only be for the one night. In any case, Toscono had probably believed him when he said he had a plane to catch – it would have been too wounding for the Argentian's ego to suspect otherwise.

It was almost nine o'clock and Docherty hadn't yet eaten. The market streets north of Tacuba were still full of people, and a stall provided an excellent brace of *enchiladas suizas*, tortillas stuffed with chicken and smothered in sour cream. He could go back to watching the cholesterol later.

After washing the food down with a bottle of Negra Modelo – Mexico's best dark beer – he walked back down towards the Zócalo, keeping his eye out for a public phone. He eventually found one a stone's throw from the cathedral, on the edge of the still-busy square. Arranging a reversed-charges call to Chile was easier than he'd expected, and before a minute was up he could hear the phone ringing in their Santiago flat.

'Yes?' his wife asked briskly.

'It's me.'

The voice had softened. 'Jamie.'

'How's it going?' he asked. 'How are the kids?'

'Fine. Everything's fine. Marie won her race at school.'

'That's great.' He knew how pleased his daughter would be. 'Tell her well done from me.'

'How are you doing?' she asked. 'Have you seen Toscono again?'

'Aye, I have. I had to lean on him a bit, but he was a little more talkative second time around. He told me Guillermo Macías was one of several kids arrested for being in possession of gummed labels with left-wing slogans on them.' There was silence at the other end of the line. 'Are you still there, love?'

'I'm still here. After all this time, the stupidity of it all still takes my breath away.'

'I know what you mean. Anyway, Toscono claims he doesn't know what happened to Guillermo after he was "processed", but he seemed pretty certain the boy ended up in either a mass grave or the River Plate.'

'And?' she asked.

She knew him too well. 'He also told me that his boss, Bazua, has the Army's Dirty War files with him on Providencia.'

'What? All of them?'

'All the Army's. Not the Navy's,' he said gently. His wife and her friends had been tortured at the Navy Mechanical School outside Buenos Aires.

'My God,' she said softly. 'But he's not going to show them to anyone, is he?' she added a moment later. 'And especially not a retired British soldier.'

'He might give me the whole story on Guillermo,' Docherty said hopefully.

'Why would he do that?' his wife wanted to know.

'I don't know. Some of these bastards like to gloat. And if he just admitted to having the files . . . well, the Argentinian press would love the story. They might even get Menem to put some pressure on the Colombian government.'

'Knowing the files were still out there would certainly frighten a lot of people,' she agreed. 'I don't know, Jamie . . . what makes you think he'd agree to see you, or that the Colombians would allow it?'

'They probably wouldn't but . . . it just goes against the grain, leaving the job half done.'

'You've got something for Gustavo, and anything else will probably just hurt him more. Why don't you just come home?'

Docherty sighed. By morning his welcome in Mexico would be overdue, if it wasn't already. 'Aye,' he agreed. 'I'll get a plane to Buenos Aires tomorrow, and go and see Gustavo. I'll call you from there, or from Rosa's.'

'I'll be waiting,' she said, sounding relieved. 'I love you,' she added.

'And I you,' Docherty said. He hung up, wishing he was back in Santiago.

* * *

It was probably the birds rather than the whirr of the machine which woke Shepreth. His watch told him it was only just after six, but despite sleeping for only three hours he felt wide awake. In the main room the customized fax had disgorged three sheets of already decoded material; he took both them and a carton of juice out on to the small balcony, where the sun was making the most of the pre-smog hours.

James Docherty's life and career made interesting reading. He had grown up in Glasgow, the only son of well-known Clydeside shop steward Campbell Docherty ('reference MI5 file 4519/DX', the sender added helpfully). At school he had apparently been clever, serious and unruly – not necessarily in that order – and at the age of sixteen he had joined the Merchant Navy without consulting his family. Two years later, in 1969, he had signed up with the Army. He had passed through SAS selection training at the young age of twenty-two, and had promptly seen service in Arabia. Two years later he had married Christine Jess, but she had been killed in a road accident later the same year.

Docherty had obviously gone off the rails at this point. Reading between the lines, Shepreth guessed that his behaviour had been about to earn him a discharge when someone had shown the sense to grant him extended compassionate leave. The Scot had then spent five months travelling in Mexico.

Could his interest in Toscono date back that far? Shepreth wondered. It didn't seem very likely – the Argentinian had not taken up residence in Mexico until almost a decade later, after the military's fall from power in Buenos Aires. Or could the two men's paths have somehow crossed during the Falklands conflict?

He was letting his imagination race ahead of the facts.

After his wife's death and the long leave of absence Docherty had seen service in Northern Ireland, Yemen and Oman. By 1980 he had risen to the rank of sergeant – the highest an enlisted man could reach – and in that year he had successfully brokered a hostage crisis in Guatemala. Two years later, with the Task Force poised to begin the reconquest of the Falklands, he had led one of two four-man teams inserted into Argentina. Their mission was to keep enemy airfields under observation, and so warn the Task Force of air attacks.

Shepreth took a slug of orange juice. There had always been rumours of SAS activity on the mainland, but this was the first time he'd seen them confirmed in print.

And there'd also been someone working for MI6, he discovered to his surprise. A woman, moreover, an Argentinian exile who had endured torture at the hands of the junta who now ruled her country.

And Docherty had married her.

It was beginning to make sense, Shepreth thought. The SAS man hadn't come to see Toscono about drugs – he'd brought the Argentinian some unfinished business from the Dirty War.

He read on. Through the rest of the 80s Docherty had seen little in the way of active service. He had been an instructor in the SAS Training Wing, and as such had spent several periods on loan to foreign governments which wanted to set up their own élite units. Mostly though, he and his Argentinian wife had lived in Hereford.

She had given birth to two children – a daughter in 1987 and a son in 1989.

Docherty's first retirement in 1993, at the age of forty-two, had been short-lived, for only a few months later he had been recalled to lead a four-man team into Bosnia. One of his SAS colleagues, who also happened to be an old friend, had apparently set himself up as a virtual warlord in the small town where his Bosnian wife had grown up. Docherty and his team had been told to bring him out, but instead of doing so they had reappeared a week later, minus one of their number, with a lorryload of wounded children. Neither the Foreign Office nor the Ministry of Defence had been pleased, but Docherty had claimed all the responsibility for himself and then announced that he was resuming his retirement.

Even that hadn't been the end of his active career – later that same year he and his wife had been members of a tour party taken hostage by Islamic fundamentalists in Central Asia, and both had played a big part in securing their own and the other hostages' survival. Since then they had lived in Chile. She was a travel writer and he was supposed to be writing his memoirs.

Shepreth drained the last of the carton and leant back dangerously in the rickety chair. Whatever it was that Docherty had wanted to ask Toscono, he might also want to ask Bazua. And if he did, then the SAS man might provide another way in, another key to the lock. He wouldn't even need a cover story, because he already had one that was true.

He wanted to talk to Docherty. After reading the MI6 version of his life and career he would have wanted to meet him anyway. Now he just needed Ted Vaughan to find the man.

Only seconds later the phone rang. 'He's staying at the Hotel León on Brasil, under the name Kenneth Dalglish.'

Shepreth laughed. 'I'll go and talk to him,' he said.

7

Having set his travel alarm for six-thirty, Docherty had completed his ablutions and packed by seven. Downstairs the receptionists were changing shift, but neither young man gave him more than a cursory glance – if Toscono had traced his whereabouts they hadn't been told.

He left the hotel and started zigzagging his way south-west through the grid of streets towards a travel agency he had noticed the previous day, hoping it would be open by eight. It was, and he emerged a few minutes later with a booking on the evening flight to Buenos Aires via Lima. The bad news was that it didn't leave until seven, leaving him most of the day to kill.

Breakfast took care of the first half-hour, and a poster on the café wall offered what seemed an excellent suggestion for the time remaining. Docherty had visited the archaeological site of Teotihuacán in 1977, but only two days off the plane from England he had been in no state to appreciate it. It was only an hour away by bus, which would give plenty of time to make his plane. And it would also get him out of the city for the day, making it harder for Toscono to find him.

His mind made up, he walked briskly back to the hotel, where he collected his bag and paid his bill. The receptionist had a shifty look on his face, but there was no one else in the lobby, and no one hanging around too obviously in the street. He set off in the direction of the nearest Metro station.

Shepreth's taxi was just drawing up on the other side of the road when Docherty came through the hotel doorway, bag in hand. The MI6 man passed a five-thousand-peso note to the driver, thinking he would have no difficulty catching Docherty up, but the man took an age rummaging for change. As he glanced up to make sure Docherty was still in view a young Mexican emerged from the hotel and started walking in the same direction. Shepreth wasn't sure why, but he knew the youth was tailing the ex-SAS man.

He joined the procession, keeping about twenty metres behind the Mexican, whose bright-red T-shirt made him easy to follow down the busy pavement. He had read about tails being tailed in thrillers, but never actually witnessed such an arrangement in real life. It felt vaguely farcical somehow, and would be even more so if someone was following him. He glanced around despite himself, and almost tripped over a loose paving stone.

Both Docherty and the youth turned right into República de Chile, confirming Shepreth's suspicions. The Scot, some forty metres ahead, kept disappearing from view in the bustle, but the red T-shirt was an efficient beacon. He followed it down into the Allende Metro station and the three of them stood there on the platform, still some twenty metres apart, waiting for a westbound train. Docherty obviously wasn't heading for the airport.

The three of them changed trains at Hidalgo and again at La Raza, before alighting at the Northern Bus Terminal.

Looking like he knew where he was going, Docherty first put his bag into the left luggage and then walked through to the second-class section of the bus station, where he bought a ticket at the Autobuses Teotihuacán booth. The man was going sightseeing, Shepreth thought. The thought of a few hours at the ruins was appealing enough in itself, but, given the circumstances, felt rather anticlimactic.

The bus was not due to leave for another ten minutes but Docherty had already boarded. Shepreth looked round for the tail – he was involved in an animated conversation on one of the public phones. The MI6 man wondered if he should tell his fellow-countryman that he was being followed and decided against it – he was more likely to learn what was going on by just watching.

The youth was now buying a ticket at the booth. Shepreth joined in the queue behind him and waited his turn. The bus was almost full when he got on, and as he walked towards the back he gave Docherty the traditional half smile of gringo solidarity.

The bus took them out through the rings of the capital's growth, through overcrowded boulevards, industrial wastelands, shanty-covered hills and countryside living on borrowed time. Docherty found it profoundly depressing – the capital seemed like an unstoppable cancer, slowly consuming the country which supported it.

The sight of the great pyramids looming in the distance banished the gloom from his mind. He could remember how on his first visit the sense of excitement had kept bubbling up through the layers of grief, making him feel almost guilty. Now, walking from the parking lot towards the sunken square of the Ciudadela and the small pyramid which covered the Temple of Quetzalcoatl, he felt the same sense of wonder swelling in his chest and wished Isabel was there with him to share it.

He paused at the entrance to the Ciudadela, looking north up the two-thousand-metre causeway which formed the central axis of the ancient city. Teotihuacán was not built high on a mountain, nor deep in some dramatic valley, but there were few more breathtaking sights than this Street of the Dead, arrowing away across the plain to its end beneath the graceful Pyramid of the Moon. To the right of this giant's causeway, more than a kilometre distant, early-bird tourists were crawling insect-like up the massive stairway of the larger Pyramid of the Sun.

Once this had been a city of 200,000 souls, Docherty reflected. It had risen and fallen in the same epoch as the Roman Empire. It had been a ruin when the Aztecs found it.

The Ciudadela seemed overrun by visitors, so he decided to bypass it and head straight up the stone causeway towards those areas of the site the crowds had not yet reached. He ambled slowly northwards, conscious of the sun's heat beating on his head, but exhilarated by the brilliance of the colours all around him. Now that he was out from under the lid of smog which hung over the capital everything seemed brighter, more clearly defined, as if the sharpness of his senses had been turned up a notch.

The Pyramid of the Sun slowly loomed in front of him. He reached the bottom of the steps and started to climb, grateful that he – unlike countless sacrificial victims in the past – would be coming back down. The last time he'd been here archaeologists had just stumbled over a cave deep inside the pyramid which a later Aztec ruler had used to store the flayed skins of his victims.

The climb left him feeling glad he was still in shape, for all around him people were wheezing, massaging thigh muscles, or both. He did a slow circle, taking in the ring of grey hills which surrounded the flat, yellow-green valley, the sparse puffs of white cloud in the wide blue sky, and took a deep breath of satisfaction.

There was a sudden movement behind him, but it was only a couple of children chasing each other along the edge of the platform. As their mother yelled at them – she'd obviously had a real fright – Docherty scolded himself for not being watchful enough.

He walked back down and continued up the causeway towards the Pyramid of the Moon. Not many people had yet percolated to this end of the site, and the high platform's only occupants were a couple of Mexican girls, both of whom seemed more interested in slagging off their boyfriends than enjoying the famous view down the causeway. Docherty supposed it would only be a few years before his daughter Marie started tormenting boys – she already had both the looks and the brains to be a real heartbreaker.

The two girls started down, leaving him alone with his thoughts. The chat he'd had with Toscono was still very much on his mind, and he had to admit he'd enjoyed scaring the bastard. That probably wasn't something to be proud of, but fuck it, the man was a mass murderer and a drug trafficker – he deserved a few clouds in his fucking sky. And as for his boss . . .

The fact that Bazua had escaped payment for his crimes in Argentina didn't sit well with Docherty. The fact that he was still breaking laws with impunity and adding to the sum total of human misery sat even worse. And it wasn't just that people like Bazua had tortured his wife and her friends, though that would have been enough in itself. Docherty had been hooked on the drug of justice from an early age – it was 'the right of the weakest', his father had always said – and at the age of forty-five he still felt the need for an occasional fix.

But not this time, he told himself, as he watched a hawk riding the air currents above the site. This time he was going home.

He looked at his watch – he still had a couple of hours before he needed to take a bus back. Beneath his perch, on the far-right corner of the Plaza de la Luna, sat the restored Palacio del Quetzalpapaloti, possibly the only ruin with a roof in central Mexico. If memory served Docherty well, it offered both shade and beautiful frescos.

He made his way down and ambled around the interior of the palace, marvelling at the decorations. A sign pointed down a flight of stone steps to the remains of an earlier, half-buried building, the Palacio de los Jaguares. He descended the rough stairway into the relative darkness, where a German couple were examining a mural depicting jaguars in feathered head-dresses making music with enormous conchs. After a few moments they left him alone, but his privacy was short-lived, for as he stared at the murals there were more footsteps on the stairway behind him. Four feet appeared, then stopped; a few brief words were exchanged and two of the feet continued on down into the half-buried chamber.

They belonged to a tall, handsome Ladino wearing blue trousers and a cream shirt. He walked forward, as if he too wanted to examine the mural. There was a friendly smile on his face, but his right hand was concealed in his pocket. 'It's beautiful,' he said in Spanish, looking past Docherty at the wall.

'Isn't it?' the Scot murmured. He turned his head back in the direction of the mural, but every muscle in his body was suddenly taut with expectation. This man might be a simple armed robber, but he doubted it. Toscono's set-up was obviously better organized than he'd expected.

The fact that the man hadn't yet produced a weapon suggested he had a knife rather than a gun, so Docherty wasn't surprised when the hand emerged from the pocket and swung viciously towards him, a long blade glinting in the half-light. He stepped aside in one motion, his right hand clamping down on the plunging wrist as his left delivered a karate chop to the side of his assailant's neck. The timing wasn't perfect but the man stumbled on to one knee, giving Docherty the chance to kick him hard in the small of the back. There was a loud grunt, and as the knife span away across the stone floor, the man's partner suddenly appeared on the stairway.

He had apparently given up knives in favour of a silenced automatic. Docherty was still bracing himself for the bullet when the man was suddenly catapulted forward. His head hit the roof above the stairway with a crack that seemed to echo round the chamber, his body slumped to the ground like a sack of cement and his gun did a lazy double somersault in mid-air before dropping on to his crotch.

The first man was raising himself to his knees, apparently oblivious to either his own or his partner's fate. Docherty hit him across the back of the neck this time, hard enough to knock him out. He looked up to find his saviour clambering over the body at the bottom of the stairs. It was the tall young man with the distinctly English look from the bus. 'We'd better get out of here,' Docherty said, and the new arrival nodded.

Upstairs in the Palacio del Quetzalpapaloti they found several tourists wandering round the courtyard, and it would only be a matter of minutes before someone decided to take a look at the jaguars. The two men walked swiftly back outside and headed across the grass towards the northern parking lot some two hundred metres away.

'There's usually some taxis waiting for people who can't be bothered to walk back,' the MI6 man said. 'My name's David Shepreth,' he added.

'I don't suppose I need to introduce myself,' Docherty said drily.

'No,' Shepreth admitted.

'On Her Majesty's Secret Service by any chance?' Docherty asked.

'Something like that.'

They was indeed a line of waiting taxis. 'And how did you manage to appear so conveniently?' Docherty asked as they walked towards the front.

'I followed you from your hotel. Actually I followed your follower.' He stopped ten metres short of the taxi. 'I need to talk to you,' he said, 'but not in a taxi. Any ideas?'

Docherty looked at his watch. 'I need to be at the airport in three hours,' he said. 'And first I have to pick up my stuff at the bus terminal.'

'How about Guadalupe,' Shepreth suggested. 'We can take the taxi there and walk up the hill.'

'Why not,' Docherty agreed, pleasantly surprised. He hadn't often met anyone from Intelligence who'd taken the trouble to find out anything about the culture of the country he or she was working in.

The taxi driver was pleased with their destination too, even after his first outrageous estimate for the fare was pegged back to something less than a minor fortune. As his two passengers settled back into their seats for the forty-five-minute journey he started off down the road which paralleled the ancient causeway.

Now that the immediate crisis was over, Docherty found himself feeling angry with Shepreth for leaving his intervention so late. But after a few minutes of staring out at the passing fields he reluctantly admitted to himself that the anger should be self-directed. He had put himself at risk, and for no other reason than overconfidence. His kids might not have any divine right to a living father, but they should be able to expect something better than this sort of carelessness.

Shepreth, on the other hand, was feeling pleased with himself. He had taken a chance following the youth rather than his fellow-Brit, but it had paid off. The youth had led him to the two *sicarios* and they had led him back to Docherty, who should now be feeling more than a little in his debt.

The taxi picked up speed once it reached the main highway, and soon they were passing through the landscape of denuded hills, rubbish mountains and rusting hulks which characterized the capital's outskirts. The highway arced round the foot of the Virgin's hill and the giant Basilica came into view. The taxi dropped them outside, but the two men had no interest in entering the already crowded church. Instead they threaded their way through the traffic and started climbing in the footsteps of Juan Diego, the Christianized Indian who had started the whole ball rolling in 1531.

He had been happily crossing these slopes when the Virgin appeared to him with a message for the local bishop – a church was needed on this particular hill. Not surprisingly, the bishop proved sceptical, but a few days later the Virgin popped up again in front of Diego, ordering him to gather roses from the crown of the hill. He found the flowers, wrapped them in his cape and took them to the bishop, only to find that the image of the Virgin had become imprinted on the cloth. More than four and a half centuries later the cape still hung in the church below, attracting thousands of pilgrims every day.

Docherty and Shepreth had just reached the first of the small chapels built to commemorate the Virgin's visitations when the Scot broke the silence. 'So what do you want to talk about?' he asked.

Shepreth glanced around. There were pilgrims and tourists both above and below them, but they were about as alone as any two men could hope to be in the world's most populous city. 'We're both interested in Bazua, though presumably for different reasons,' he said.

'Drugs,' Docherty murmured. 'I don't know anything about the bastard's current activities. It's his past I'm interested in.' He hesitated for a moment, but could think of no reason for keeping the truth from Shepreth. 'Friends of friends in Argentina are still trying to find out what happened to their son in the Dirty War,' he explained. 'Bazua was in charge of the local Nazis, and Toscono was in charge of one of the arrest squads.'

'And he refused to talk to you.'

'The first time he did. I saw him again yesterday.'

'Ah,' Shepreth said. He'd been wondering why Toscono had sent his goons after someone whom he'd already ejected from his office. 'And what did he tell you?' he asked.

'He admitted he arrested my friend's son, but denied all knowledge of what happened to him after that. He told me that Bazua could fill in the details. The bastard apparently has a complete set of the Army's records for the period in question, with thousands of names and fates, and probably even a complete list of who got what in the torture chambers.' He smiled grimly. 'There was a lot of German and Italian immigration into Argentina, and someone once said the military inherited the German flair for keeping meticulous records and the Italian flair for battle. For a hundred years every cock-up has been brilliantly documented.'

They walked a few paces in silence.

'So you're on your way home?' Shepreth asked at last.

'Aye,' Docherty said. 'I have a feeling it wouldn't be so easy to arrange a private tête-à-tête with Bazua,' he added wryly.

'A pity,' Shepreth said noncommittally.

'Tell me about the drug angle,' Docherty said.

Shepreth waited until they were past the small crowd which had gathered around another of the chapels, then gave the Scot a brief outline of Bazua's trafficking business on both sides of the Atlantic and the Americans' flat refusal to sanction direct action against him. 'And it's not just the trafficking,' he concluded. 'The bastard's ploughing at least some of his profits into outfitting another invasion of the Falklands.'

'What?' Docherty asked disbelievingly.

'He already has a couple of boats, and his friends in Argentina are enrolling volunteers. The idea's just to establish a presence on the island, dare the British to chuck them off and dare the Argentinian government to abandon them.'

'I thought we still had a fucking great garrison on the island,' Docherty observed.

'It's not as big as people think, and it won't be there indefinitely. Bazua's probably willing to wait a few years.'

'Christ,' Docherty said disgustedly. It wasn't so much the Falkland Islanders he was worried about – though they deserved to be left alone – as the long-suffering people of Argentina. The thought of psychopaths like Bazua riding to power on the backs of a successful invasion brought a taste of bile to his mouth.

And then he remembered a conversation he'd had several years ago with Isabel and a couple of her fellow-exiles. 'The CIA had people in Argentina during the Dirty War,' he said slowly.

Shepreth didn't make the connection.

'Suppose Bazua's records contain evidence of American corruption,' Docherty said.

'It's twenty years ago,' Shepreth said instinctively, but his face was thoughtful.

'Which would give whoever it was plenty of time to climb the career ladder. They might well be in a position to block action against Bazua.'

Shepreth nodded. 'And they probably wouldn't even

have to come up with a reason. Just a hint that Bazua was on the company payroll would be enough.'

They had reached the top of the hill, where the Capilla de las Rosas marked the spot where the miraculous flowers had sprung up. Docherty looked out at the vast city beyond – away to the south-west a plane was gathering height after take-off from the airport. He looked at his watch and turned to Shepreth. 'Time to go,' he told the younger man.

Shepreth didn't seem to hear him. 'What if I could get you in to see Bazua?' he asked.

Carmen stared out of the aeroplane's window at the egg-shaped island below. The sea was a patchwork of blues and greens, with the outline of the surrounding reef clearly visible. Most of the coastline seemed to be rocky, but there were a few sand beaches, and behind these the settlements had grown up. A road circled the island, linking these and leaving the mountainous centre to the flora and fauna. According to her guidebook, Providencia was famous for the variety of its lizards.

She had left Cartagena at ten o'clock that morning, and a good proportion of the intervening five hours had been spent waiting for her connection on the neighbouring island of San Andrés. Most of the other passengers seemed to be foreigners, and once the plane was down she expected a stampede for the tourist office, but in the event only one Japanese couple also needed official help. Listening to the choice of accommodation on offer, Carmen found herself wondering for the umpteenth time what she was doing.

The Cabanas El Paradiso – 'they are pretty wooden cabins by the sea' – sounded nice, especially for only ten thousand pesos, until she started thinking about how vulnerable she would feel alone in a cabin. The Hotel Princesa sounded nice too, and was even cheaper, but she wondered how good the locks would be on the doors of a cheap hotel. In the end she settled for the thrice-as-expensive Dutch Inn, on the dubious grounds that no one ever suspected rich people of criminal intent. Her choice was only about three kilometres to the south, in the hamlet of Aguamansa, and it seemed as if the taxi had hardly had time to get up speed before it was slowing to a halt outside the gabled wooden building.

The receptionist checked her in and showed her up to a large and lovely room, full of old wooden furniture and with windows overlooking the sea. He seemed to give her a strange look as he left her, causing her to wonder how many single young women came to the island. On the plane it had been all couples and groups as far as she could tell.

Well, she wouldn't be spending much time in the discos, always assuming there were any. She looked out of the window at the line of coconut palms waving in the breeze and realized that it was late in the afternoon. There was no point in wasting the last hour or so of light.

She changed into shorts, halter top and sandals, and went back downstairs. As she'd hoped, the hotel had bicycles for the use of its guests, and after checking the tyres and brakes on several machines she picked one out. A minute later she was setting off, somewhat unsteadily, along the coast road towards the next settlement. By the time she reached it her childhood cycling skills had kicked back in, and she was beginning to enjoy the ride.

The road turned inland now, cutting off the south-western corner of the island. It didn't look a likely spot for a prison, but there was no real way of knowing, short of exploring the area on foot. She would do that tomorrow, she told herself, cycling on. There was no shortage of buildings, many of them brightly painted smaller versions of her hotel, more Anglo-Caribbean than Hispanic, but none of them looked in any way official. Behind the ones to the right forested slopes rose up towards the distant peak in the centre, but there were no roads winding up through the trees.

The sea came back into view and she free-wheeled down the slope to where the road took a tight turn along the rim of some cliffs before running into the small but busy settlement of Aguadulce. Here there were many cheap-looking hotels and restaurants, shops advertising motorbikes and snorkelling gear for hire, and a busy dock at one end of the sandy beach. This might have been a better place to stay, she thought. Or not. Was it easier to escape notice in hordes of people or far away from them? There didn't seem to be an obvious answer.

It was getting dark now, but she cycled another kilometre or so beyond the last houses before turning back. By her reckoning she had traversed more than half the circular road since leaving the airport, but had seen nothing which looked anything like a prison. In fact the whole idea was beginning to seem unreal, and as she cycled back towards Aguadulce, intent on dinner, Carmen found herself wondering how many egg-shaped islands there could be in the Caribbean. Had she just jumped to the wrong conclusion? Or had Victoria's mind short-circuited in some strange way? Maybe the girl had spent a childhood holiday here, and memories from that time had become confused with those of the last year.

It was too soon to tell, Carmen told herself sternly. She still had the other half of the road to travel, and there was still the forested centre. There might not be any access by road, but prisons could always be supplied by helicopter, so she would have to keep an eye on the skies. This might be what her American tourists called a wild-goose chase, but if it wasn't, then she was closer to her sister than she had been for over a year.

The Prime Minister looked even more harassed than usual, as well he might. The nation was bored with him, the anti-European crusade in the name of British beef had proved a predictably damp squib, and his own back-benchers were queuing up to stab him in the back. Even England's football team had let him down, evoking memories of 1970 and Harold Wilson's kamikaze election. 'But what exactly are you advocating?' he asked Hanson.

It was late on Sunday evening, and the two men were sitting in shirtsleeves in the PM's private office, discussing the problem of Angel Bazua. Hanson had just finished his summary of the Argentinian's criminal and political activities with a recommendation for action of some sort. 'It's hard to be specific,' he said evasively, 'but I would have thought that at the very least we should aim for the destruction of the two boats. If we could also take out their owner I would be a lot happier.'

The PM grimaced. 'The British government doesn't usually employ assassination as an instrument of foreign policy,' he said mildly.

'Not lately,' Hanson agreed. 'But this is an unusual situation. It sounds ludicrous, but as long as he stays in prison this man is effectively beyond the law. And in the meantime,' he added, looking the PM straight in the eye, 'he poses a clear threat to the security of the realm.'

The PM sighed and examined the bottom of his empty glass. 'Who would you use?' he asked.

'The SAS, probably,' Hanson said, wondering whether he was going to be offered another drink.

But the PM had other things on his mind. 'The Colombians will probably break off relations,' he said gloomily, 'and I'll have the Foreign Office and Trade screaming blue murder at me for halving our market share in Latin America. And as for the Americans . . .' He trailed off. 'I don't think . . .'

'They'll all be angry,' Hanson agreed, 'but not necessarily at us.' He bit the bullet and helped himself from the bottle, then started to tell the PM about Docherty's involvement. 'He has a completely different reason for wanting to see Bazua, but if he does get inside the prison, he should be able to bring some useful information out. He has trained eyes, he's an SAS veteran, and whatever he sees should prove invaluable to an assault force. With good inside information the SAS might be able to do the whole thing incognito. They could even leave a few clues to the real culprits – another drug cartel probably.' Hanson paused, gathering his thoughts. 'If by some chance they are identified, then Docherty would also serve as a pretty good scapegoat. He lives in Chile, he married an ex-communist, and his SAS record offers ample proof that he's a born renegade. With that sort of ammunition we might be able to pass the whole thing off as a private affair, a mercenary operation paid for by nobody-knows-who.'

'We'll hang him out to dry,' the PM murmured.

'The man's a survivor,' Hanson said. He had read Docherty's file that morning, and felt more than a touch of guilt at what he was proposing, but a lot more lives would be ruined if Bazua wasn't stopped. 'He wants to get in to see Bazua, and his chances of coming out again are a lot better if the Colombian government has sanctioned the visit.'

'All right,' the PM said thoughtfully, 'we might fool the Colombians, but surely the Americans have the southern Caribbean under more or less continual surveillance. How are an SAS team going to get in and out without them knowing?'

'They aren't,' Hanson admitted. 'But if we bring them a present they won't be able to go off the deep end.' He explained about the Dirty War records which Bazua allegedly kept on Providencia, and Shepreth's suspicion that they were being used to blackmail high-ranking American Intelligence officials. 'If we can show them how one of their own people has been protecting Bazua then they'll hardly be in a position to complain,' he concluded.

It was a bit thin, but the PM didn't seem to notice. 'So all you want for now is an official request that this man Docherty be allowed access to their prisoner?'

'That's right.'

The PM sighed again. He had the distinct feeling he hadn't heard the last of this business. 'Very well,' he said with a thin smile.

* * *

Docherty ordered another glass of mescal and looked out across Oaxaca's sun-dappled main square. He had been in the south Mexican city for two days now, having taken the overnight train from the capital late in the day of his eventful trip to Teotihuacán. He had been sufficiently intrigued by Shepreth's plan to delay his return home, but it had not seemed a good idea to stay on in Mexico City, where Toscono's goons and probably half the police force would be looking for him.

Oaxaca had been his favourite Mexican town in 1977, and it hadn't changed as much as he'd feared. The town itself was a joy to walk round, the wonderful ruins of Monte Alban were only a hill climb away, and the main square, with its luscious foliage, beautiful cathedral and outdoor restaurants was the perfect place to sit and think. It was at one of these tables, nineteen years before, that Docherty had felt some balance shift inside his soul, as the dominance of his grief felt the first guilt-ridden challenges of a new joy in life.

Ah, Chrissie, he thought now. How different his life would have been if one stupid bastard had known how to drive. He would never have come to Mexico, never acquired the fluency in Spanish which marked him out for the Argentina mission, never met Isabel or adopted this continent so far from his beloved Scotland. It was sobering to think that a split-second decision by a complete stranger could turn your life upside down.

He had phoned Isabel to tell her his change of plan before boarding the train. She had taken the news calmly enough, but he could tell she was worried for him. If Docherty hadn't known that deep in the recesses of his wife's soul there lurked an unassuaged thirst for revenge against Bazua and his cronies, he would have felt a lot guiltier about putting her through the anxiety. As it was, maybe this whole business would complete the process of exorcizing her twenty-year-old demons. Or maybe he was kidding himself and Shepreth's offer had just piqued his curiosity.

He rather liked the young MI6 agent. Shepreth was obviously bright, and unlike most of his colleagues – or at least the ones Docherty had come into contact with – he hadn't immersed himself in self-serving cynicism.

The Scot looked at his watch – punctuality clearly wasn't one of Shepreth's strong suits – then signalled the waiter for a refill, thinking that he should have bought the whole bottle, worm and all. At the table next to his a bunch of English travellers, most of them in their thirties, were telling tales of the six-hour bus ride down to the coast, and he listened in, remembering his own descent of the hair-raising mountain roads in 1977.

The waiter arrived at the same time as Shepreth, who looked like the proverbial cat who'd got the cream. Another glass was requested, and they moved to a more secluded table.

'The government is asking the Colombians to let you in for a chat with Angel,' Shepreth told him.

'Good,' Docherty said. 'And what does it want in return?'

'Your eyes. If you can help us build up a picture of the inside, we'll be better able to judge the feasibility of an assault from outside by your old regiment.'

Docherty's eyes widened slightly. 'That's really on the cards?'

'Looks like it.'

'Any time-scale in mind?'

'The request for the visit was delivered today.' He shrugged. 'The Colombians may sit on it, of course.'

Docherty thought for a moment. 'I think I'd like a good look from the outside before I go in,' he said. 'Do we know where this prison is?'

Shepreth pulled a napkin towards him and drew a rough map of the island. 'It's here,' he said, indicating the location with a cross. 'When I get back to Mexico City I'm going to ask Ted Vaughan if he can sneak out some satellite photos. Don't worry,' he added, seeing the look on Docherty's face, 'I shall tell him to borrow a lot more than the Providencia shots.'

'They would be useful,' Docherty admitted, thinking more of a future SAS operation than his own reconnaissance. He couldn't quite shake the suspicion that there was more to all this than met the eye, although for the moment he couldn't see what it could be. But at least there was no doubting that the joint sponsorship of the British and Colombian governments would make his visit to Bazua's home from home a lot safer than it otherwise might have been.

And safety, he reminded himself, was what family men were supposed to place first on their list of priorities.

8

Carmen woke to her third day on the island feeling decidedly flat. She had ridden round Providencia twice on the previous day, once in each direction, and had seen nothing that might be a prison. She had wandered, with no little trepidation, down each of the two tracks that led into the south-western corner of the island, but found nothing. She had walked up the long path to the three-hundred-metre peak at the island's heart and seen only trees and colourful birds. And as the days had gone by those twin emotions of fear and hope, which had been her constant companions since setting foot on the island, had slowly dissipated.

Sitting outside the Dutch Inn with her breakfast coffee she asked herself how long she should keep looking. Another couple of days at least, but there would soon come a time when one more circuit of the island, staring at the same houses and beaches, would seem utterly pointless. But what else could she do?

Think, she told herself.

Maybe some sort of bluff . . . She had seen the military post outside Aguadulce, and for a few seconds had even thought it could have served as a prison, but it was obviously too small for the sort of set-up Victoria had described. The soldiers, though, would obviously know if there was a prison on the island, and if there was, where it was. If she came up with some story about a friend who had been arrested . . .

It wouldn't help. No one was going to say, oh yes, the prison's down the road – just knock on the gate and they'll let you in.

It suddenly occurred to Carmen that there was no reason why this prison would look like a normal prison. Victoria had always talked about 'him', as if he was the only one that mattered – maybe this was just a house which had been commandeered to hold one man.

But if it was just a house, how could she hope to find it? It would have to be well guarded, of course, probably with a wall or electric fence, but she had seen a dozen sprawling villas which answered to that description.

There had to be more, and a few moments later she realized what. In Miami Detective Peña had been quite certain that this man Bazua was still running his trafficking operations from the prison, and surely that meant he would need sophisticated communications equipment – a tall radio aerial, for example. She remembered seeing one of those, but where had it been?

It took her only a few seconds to remember. The house – a rather lovely one in Spanish colonial style – was on the seaward side of the road about a kilometre north of San Felipe on the island's west coast. In her mind's eye she could see the aerial rising up behind the house.

She gulped down the rest of her coffee, collected her camera and her father's binoculars from her room, and set off once more on the hotel's bike. Less than half an hour later she was passing the gates of the house, taking in the palm-lined drive, the house itself, surrounded by woodland, the silver sheen of the high aerial. There was no guardhouse by the gates, nor any sign of human presence – only a high stucco wall topped with three lines of barbed wire.

About twenty metres beyond the gate – out of sight, she prayed, of any surveillance cameras – she stopped, dismounted and made a pantomime of inspecting her back tyre. She took the hand-pump and started inflating the tyre, making sure to keep her face turned in that direction as her eyes behind the dark glasses examined the hill on the opposite side of the road. It was heavily forested and quite steep, and with any luck she would be able to find a vantage-point which overlooked the house behind her.

Apparently satisfied with her efforts, she climbed back on the bike and resumed her journey. About half a kilometre further on a stream passed under the road in a culvert, and beside it a rough path led up into the trees. That was her way in, she decided. On her way back to the hotel for more jungle-friendly clothes she felt the old knot of hope and fear rising once more in her throat.

Guadencio Santis López was playing eight-ball with one of his bodyguards when Miguel Domínguez tracked him down. As the President of Colombia was currently engaged in lining up a shot his Foreign Minister waited in silence, casting his eye around the newly converted pool room. The last president had used this room of the palace as a TV room and private cinema, watching endless soap operas on an enormous screen far into each night. It had been rumoured that the price of one drug baron's pardon had been the whole of *Dynasty* on video, and that the president himself had given up on his re-election campaign after watching the episode in which Fallon was abducted by aliens.

Pool had to be an improvement, Domínguez thought to himself.

'What is it, Miguel?' the President asked. He had apparently missed his shot.

'I've just had a visit from the British Ambassador,' Domínguez began.

Santis López looked at him in disbelief, as if such an event could justify interrupting his game. 'What did he want?' he asked, his eyes on the table.

'He wanted a personal favour. One of their soldiers – one of their heroes, I gather – is married to an Argentinian woman and he's trying to trace what happened to one of her relations during the Junta years. He wants to talk to Angel Bazua, and the British are asking us to arrange it for him.'

'Bazua's in prison on Providencia, right?'

'If you can call it that. I wish my home was half as comfortable.'

Santis López made a face as the bodyguard sank another ball. 'That was part of the deal.' He glanced across at Domínguez. 'Why are you bothering me with this?' he asked.

Domínguez chose to take the question literally. 'Because it doesn't feel quite right,' he replied. 'The British Ambassador even told me he thought the Americans had been stupid to accuse us of not cooperating with their anti-drug campaign.'

'They were.'

'I know, but . . .'

The bodyguard missed. 'Is there any reason why Bazua should object to seeing this man?' Santis López asked, measuring his next shot.

'My sources say he'll probably consider it entertainment,' Domínguez replied.

'Then give the British what they want,' the President said with a shrug. 'What can we lose?'

Docherty's plane from Oaxaca arrived in Mexico City soon after ten in the morning, and he spent most of the three-hour wait between connections reading an historical novel he'd picked up in a secondhand bookshop. Set in twelfth-century England and featuring monks, sociopathic nobles and obsessive cathedral-builders, it was thoroughly enjoyable.

As there was no direct flight to San Andrés from Mexico, he'd have another, albeit shorter, stopover at the airport outside the Costa Rican capital of San Juan. He'd never been there himself, but unfortunately he remembered Isabel's account of landing there. Apparently, the approach to the airport in question was down a deep valley where the crosswinds were fierce enough to turn even a large airliner into a flying see-saw.

It wasn't a very exciting prospect, and as the plane began to board he almost found himself hoping that Shepreth had finally graduated from mere unpunctuality to complete non-appearance.

The MI6 man arrived a few moments later, brandishing a large envelope. 'Copies of the photos,' he told Docherty. 'You should probably destroy them before you get to San Andrés.'

'I'll eat them on the plane,' Docherty said with a straight face.

Shepreth didn't seem to hear him. 'The Colombians have agreed to your visit,' he said. 'You're to present yourself to the military post on the island – it's just outside Aguadulce – at ten a.m. on Friday morning.' He looked at the Scot. 'I think that's it.'

'When are you coming over?' Docherty asked him.

'Tomorrow. Providencia's a small place and I didn't think it would be such a good idea for us both to arrive on the same day. I'll meet you on or near the dock at eight tomorrow evening, OK?'

'Aye,' Docherty said. He was pleased the Colombians had agreed to the visit and given him the chance to see a devil in the flesh.

Carmen reached back to scratch her right calf, wondering what had bitten her this time. As far as she knew, there were no poisonous reptiles on the island, but there were certainly plenty of biting insects. She had now spent most of two days lying face down on the ground, peering over a rotting fallen tree at the compound below.

She had no cast-iron evidence to show for it, but she was certain that this was the prison in which Victoria had been held captive. For one thing, the house had twice received visits from the military – on the first occasion it had been a lone officer in a jeep, on the second two other officers in a car. For another, there was the layout, which was more than twice as extensive as it appeared from the road. Behind the two-storey main house, facing each other across an open space, there were two barrack-shaped single-storey buildings, each about thirty metres long. In the space between them there seemed to be a swimming pool. Carmen couldn't actually see it, but the shimmering reflections on one of the gutters certainly suggested the presence of water.

In front of the house there was a short, palm-lined drive, which ended in a turning circle beside a double garage. The high stucco wall which fronted the road did not extend around the entire circumference – from the corner of the property which Carmen could see a high wire fence ran off through the trees in the direction of the sea. Unusually for a prison, the overhanging coils of razor wire had been arranged to keep people out rather than in.

Beyond the buildings and the probable swimming pool she thought she could see the beginning of a path, which would presumably lead down through the trees to the nearby shore.

But nobody had used it since she started watching, and nobody had conveniently appeared in a window. The previous afternoon, soon after the arrival of the two officers, she had heard shouts and what sounded like a bouncing ball, and for a few seconds a figure had come into view close to the beginning of the distant path. He had probably been collecting a stray basketball, but she hadn't actually seen a ball.

A couple of hours later, with darkness beginning to fall, she had had a fleeting glimpse of someone's head above the roofline, and though she couldn't put her finger on exactly why, she had been convinced that it was a woman. But there had been no time to take a picture – she would have needed a continually rolling camcorder to catch either of the human sightings.

A higher position might provide a view of the space

between the buildings, but above her the slope of the hill flattened out for quite a way before resuming its climb. She had tried shinning up a couple of the trees, but in both cases it had proved a difficult, noisy and overly visible activity, and had offered nothing more than a better view of the surrounding foliage.

She needed better binoculars, she decided, or maybe just some old-fashioned luck. As another member of the insect kingdom drilled her ankle for blood she told herself not to get discouraged. If she stuck at it long enough she was bound to see something.

Docherty walked past the entrance to Bazua's place of detention, noting the electronically operated gates and the lens of the surveillance camera peeping out through the palm fronds. A few minutes later he reached the spot from which the path led up through the trees and, after a few moments' hesitation, started up it. He had decided that morning that there was really no need for the recce he had mentioned to Shepreth, but the path was there for the taking, so why not satisfy his own curiosity?

The going was easy enough for the first hundred metres or so, but then the path abruptly petered out, as if it had realized there was nowhere to go. This didn't surprise Docherty, but the discovery a few minutes later of a reasonably new bicycle did. The cyclist had dragged his machine a good thirty metres through the undergrowth before leaving it under some trailing fronds, which suggested an unusually determined attempt at concealment.

There was a metal tag attached to the handlebars claiming ownership on behalf of the Dutch Inn, Providencia.

Docherty squatted down, then rubbed some of the damp

soil between his hands and applied a few streaks to his face. It wasn't an SAS make-up kit, but it would have to do.

The trail of the cyclist wasn't hard to follow through the heavy undergrowth. The footprints themselves suggested a small man, and the direction in which they headed implied an interest similar to Docherty's own. He moved forward as silently as the terrain allowed, remembering his days at the SAS Jungle Training School in Brunei almost a quarter of a century ago. 'I can hear you, Docherty!' the instructor had screamed, 'you sound like fucking Pan's People!'

What happened to them? Docherty wondered. He supposed most of them were grandmothers by now, which was a depressing thought.

He could catch glimpses of the road now, way below and to his right. And then he saw her.

She was about forty metres further down the shallow slope, just behind what looked like the rim of a ridge. Docherty steadied himself and trained the collapsible telescope on her. She was lying on her front, studying the view ahead with her own binoculars over a fallen tree. He couldn't see her face, but she had shiny black hair beyond shoulder length, a trim waist, nicely rounded behind and long legs. She was wearing a black, long-sleeved shirt, blue jeans and black boots. There was a camera on the ground beside her, but it didn't seem to be fitted with a telephoto lens.

'What the hell?' he murmured to himself. Why would a young woman be watching Bazua's prison?

He took his eyes away from the woman before her sixth sense had time to register his presence, and wondered what to do. She seemed to have the best spot, but he could hardly amble up and ask her to give him a turn. And there was no real need for him to examine the compound below – not yet at any rate. He obviously needed to talk to her, but this was neither the time nor the place, as she might well panic if he suddenly appeared out of nowhere, and for all he knew she was cradling a gun to her breast. He might not hear the shot but someone down the compound would.

He looked at her again. She was scratching her leg, and Docherty wondered if she knew how much insects loved rotting tree-trunks. In fact she seemed generally fidgety – like most people she was probably not used to holding her body in one position for any length of time.

It would also soon be getting dark, and he could see no sign of any night-vision equipment. She would probably be leaving soon.

He made his way back through the forest, descended the path and started walking south along the road. As he passed the gates of the prison compound he wondered whether she was watching him through her binoculars and hoped that she'd had the sense to use some sort of veil across the glass to eliminate tell-tale reflections.

In San Felipe he asked a friendly local about the Dutch Inn and discovered that it was an expensive hotel on the island's southern shore. Assuming that she'd choose the shortest route back, he walked on to Aguadulce, where an open-air bar offered both a drink and an ideal observation point.

She cycled through about forty-five minutes later, shocking him with a first sight of her face. In profile she looked stunningly like a young Isabel. It wasn't just the features, though the arrangement of the cheek-bones, the generous lips and dark eyes were all reminiscent of his wife – it was the intense look on her face, the seriousness of purpose, which reminded him of his first hours with Isabel, caught up in the throes of war at the other end of the continent.

He watched her cycle past the hotels and shops until she and the bicycle were just a spot in the distance. It was almost six o'clock, which gave him a couple of hours before his meeting with Shepreth.

The shop which rented out motorbikes was only a stone's throw away, and still open for business. A few minutes later he was cruising along the seaside road on a 250cc Yamaha, not quite Steve McQueen in *The Great Escape*, but close enough.

The Dutch Inn was a beautiful old building, standing between the road and a palm-lined beach. He hadn't yet worked out how he was going to ask for a woman whose name he didn't know without getting shown the door, but in the end there was no need, for as he propped up the Yamaha in the rear parking lot she emerged from a back entrance with a tall drink in hand and walked across to one of the empty tables which overlooked the beach. She had changed into shorts and a red halter top.

He walked inside, discovered to his amazement that the bar served draught Guinness, and carried a pint out to her table.

'May I join you?' he asked in Spanish.

She gave him the surprised look of someone deep in thought, and before she could say no Docherty sat down. Up close the resemblance was still striking, though perhaps not in a purely physical way. Now it was the sorrow-filled eyes which reminded him of Isabel, gazing out through the grimly held mask of determination. This woman had seen tragedy, and logic suggested that Angel Bazua had been the man responsible.

'I saw you watching Bazua's house,' he said softly.

She stiffened, not knowing what to do. Should she get up and walk away? Or run?

'I think we are on the same side,' he added, and allowed himself a smile.

She felt instinctively that he was telling the truth, but what did her instincts know? 'Who are you?' she asked. It was the first question that came into her head.

'My name's Jamie Docherty,' he said without hesitation. 'I'm British, but I'm married to an Argentinian, and we live in Chile. Do you know about the Dirty War in Argentina?'

'Yes, of course.' Was he going to give her a history lesson?

'My wife was one of the victims. One of the luckier ones – she was tortured, but instead of killing her they sent her into exile. She still has friends from those days, and one old man who's dying has become obsessed with the need to find out what happened to his son. He hired me to talk to the arresting officer, who now lives in Mexico City. I did that, and he claimed that only his boss would know the details of what happened to a particular prisoner. His boss is Colonel Bazua. I'm going in to talk to him tomorrow morning.'

Carmen was getting over the shock, but was still having trouble grasping hold of what had been said. He had confirmed that it was Bazua's house – that was the first thing. And he had said he was on the same side, which might mean nothing but could mean everything – ever since her first talk with Victoria she had felt the weight of having to do it all alone. And he was going into the prison tomorrow. There had to be some way he could find out about Marysa.

Docherty waited and watched, knowing that it had been a shock to her, hoping that she would trust him. When she did speak it was his turn to be shocked.

'I think my sister is a prisoner in that house,' she said slowly. 'And two other women. They all disappeared more than a year ago, five of them, and until three weeks ago everyone thought they were dead.' She told him about the newspaper on the bus and her trip to Miami, the talks with Victoria and what she'd learned of Bazua's drug operation from Detective Peña, the realization that she could not risk asking for help from the Colombian authorities.

Docherty listened in silence, his sense of rage stirring deep within.

'Maybe when you are in the house,' she said, 'you will see my sister or one of the others – I have photographs in my room – and then I will have proof to take to someone.' She looked at him imploringly.

'If they are there,' Docherty said gently, 'I doubt if I will be allowed to see them. If the British government hadn't asked the Colombians to allow my visit I doubt whether I'd have got my nose in the door, and I don't think they'll be giving me a guided tour of the establishment. Of course I'll keep my eyes open,' he added, seeing her look of despair. 'I can even ask the bastard what he does for female company. But . . .' He hesitated for a moment, as the implications of her story sunk in. The presence of innocent women inside the compound would be a complicating factor if it came to direct action. And the woman she'd brought back from Miami would have precious knowledge of the layout.

Of course he couldn't tell the woman any of this – such a clear breach of security would give Shepreth and his people kittens.

But if tomorrow came and went and he had nothing to tell her, then what would she do? She didn't seem the type to just give up, but she was an amateur, so she'd either get caught watching the house and end up sharing Bazua's bed with her sister, or she'd manage to kick up an enormous stink and focus every mother's son's attention on Bazua's home from home. Even if the suits in Whitehall weren't scared off, the bastards in the prison would be on maximum alert.

No, he decided, they'd be better off bringing her on board.

His watch said twenty to eight. 'I'd like you to meet someone,' he told her, draining the last of the Guinness.

'Who?' she asked, suspicious again.

'His name's David Shepreth, which reminds me – I still don't know yours.'

'I am Carmen Salcedo,' she said.

'Pleased to meet you. Shepreth works for the British government, and they don't like Bazua because he's flooding London with heroin and spending his profits on outfitting a fleet to retake the Malvinas . . .'

She couldn't help the smile which crossed her face. 'I'm sorry,' she said.

'It is kind of ironic,' Docherty admitted. 'But a friend in need . . . If London's willing to shake the tree we may get the chance to catch our apples.'

She understood what he meant immediately. 'The enemy of my enemy is my friend,' she murmured.

'Unless he's a Rangers supporter,' Docherty added. 'Ah, never mind . . . My friend's waiting for me in Aguadulce, and that splendid machine over there is waiting to transport us.'

She looked at it doubtfully, but didn't really need persuading. The feel of her strong young body pressing into his back was somewhat disconcerting to Docherty, yet reminding himself that he was old enough to be her father didn't seem to make much difference. His mother had always said that men never really got past their teens – it was just that their bodies led women to believe they had.

The look on Shepreth's face as they walked towards his perch on the dock probably had nothing to do with her age. 'Just tell him what you told me,' Docherty said to her, and she did, walking along the dark beach between the two men. The stars were bright above, the ocean stretched away to the distant horizon and Aguadulce's single thoroughfare was alive with light, noise and the smell of cooking food. Every now and then they would hear the whisper of couples elsewhere on the beach, and on one occasion the less ambivalent sound of lovemaking.

As Carmen told her story, Docherty occasionally glanced across at Shepreth and was gratified to see what looked like genuine sympathy in the younger man's eyes. Not that the shorts and halter top didn't help.

There was also a hint of uncertainty in the MI6 man's expression, and Docherty guessed that Shepreth was having trouble deciding how much he should now tell the woman. On impulse the Scot decided to force the other man's hand. 'If the government OK's direct action,' he said bluntly, 'then I think Carmen should talk to her friend Victoria again.'

'Direct action?' she asked, looking from one man to the other.

'It's a real possibility,' Shepreth admitted, giving Docherty a glance that was half reproach and half gratitude. 'But first our friend here has to beard the lion in his den.'

The following morning Docherty slowly walked the two hundred metres which separated his hotel from the island's military post, still wondering how he was going to present himself to Bazua. He was not expecting the Argentinian to offer him any details of Guillermo Macías's fate, and he doubted if he'd get far beyond the front door of the prison, but with any luck this would not be the end of the business, and there was always something to learn from any confrontation.

Anger seemed a likely tool. The official nature of the visit surely offered Docherty some protection, and if he could provoke Bazua into losing his temper the consequences might be more illuminating than dangerous. It was a theory, at any rate.

He reached the military post, which amounted to no more than a couple of one-storey pre-fabricated buildings in a walled compound situated between the road and the sea, and was shown into the OC's office. Captain Sonoma was outwardly polite, but there was also an air of genuine curiosity in the man's eyes, as if he already knew more about his guest than he was supposed to. He fitted the description of one of the officers whom Carmen had seen visiting the prison, and had probably learnt about the business with Toscono from Bazua himself.

Outside an empty jeep was now waiting, and as he climbed in Docherty took one last look round. Judging from what he'd seen so far, he put the post's strength at no more than twenty men. There was one UH-1H Iroquois helicopter standing on the pad, apparently ready for use, and another standing off to the side, minus its engine and tail rotor. Beyond them he could see a sleek-looking patrol boat tied up at the jetty.

Sonoma himself drove the jeep, greeting many of the locals with a smile or a gesture and keeping to a reasonable speed on the mostly empty road. He opened and closed the electronic gates with a remote control and finally came to a halt right outside the front door, where two young soldiers who hadn't been there the previous day were standing guard. At least they were trying to make it look a little more like a prison, Docherty thought.

He followed Sonoma in through the wide wooden doors and gained a glimpse of a courtyard beyond as he was ushered in through another doorway to the right. If he hadn't already known of the other buildings and recreation area from the American satellite photographs, he would have remained in ignorance of their existence.

The room he entered had the feel of a stage set. The wall coverings and curtains suggested an old-fashioned reception room, the table with its opposing chairs a setting for interrogations. They had tried to make it look like a prison visitor's room, he realized.

Sonoma indicated that Docherty should take the seat on the far side of the table, then sat down on an elegant-looking Spanish chair beside the door. They waited in silence for five minutes, then another five. The captain was clearly getting irritated but he made no move to find out what was causing the hold-up.

And then the scream sounded. It was muffled by walls and distance, and there was only the one, but Docherty was pretty sure it had come from a woman.

'One of the prisoners,' Sonoma explained. 'We have mental cases here.'

'Women?' Docherty asked in a neutral tone.

Sonoma hesitated for only a second. 'No, there are no women here,' he said.

Docherty was still deciding whether or not to let this go when Bazua walked in through the door, closely followed by two soldiers bearing automatic rifles. The fiction did not extend to the prisoner's clothes, which looked like the usual Club Mediterranean casual wear. The Argentinian didn't seem any older than he had in Shepreth's photograph. There seemed to be hardly an ounce of excess fat on the bronzed limbs, his muscle tone seemed excellent for a man in his early fifties and the light brown hair, though greying at the edges, was showing no obvious sign of thinning. Prison life obviously suited him.

He sat down and looked at Docherty, vague amusement in his eyes.

Docherty returned the stare. It would have been nice to see some of the corruption on the surface – a hint of dissipation in the mouth, a touch of evil in the eyes – but the man just looked like a happy thug. And he was going to tell Docherty sweet fuck all.

He owed it to Gustavo to ask.

'Señor Bazua,' he began, with at least a trace of civility.

'I am working for a fellow-countryman of yours named Gustavo Macías,' he went on, in a tone which suggested that as far as he was concerned this was no more than a job. 'His son disappeared after being arrested in Rosario in November 1976, when you were the Officer Commanding the local Army base. I have spoken to the arresting officer, whose name you probably remember' – Docherty allowed himself a slight smile – 'and he informed me that you are in possession of the relevant records.'

Bazua's smile was an ad for expensive American dentistry. 'I have never heard of any such records,' he said. 'And if I had, what possible reason would I have for sharing some information with an enemy of my country?'

Docherty looked at him. 'Common humanity?' he asked ironically. The eyes were a give-away, he thought. They weren't empty – they were cruel. This was not a man for whom killing meant nothing – this was a man who actually got off on it. Power was an opportunity for sadism.

'You will pay for what you did to Toscono,' the Argentinian was saying.

Docherty grunted. 'He was easy. A weak link in your organization, I'd say. Maybe you should employ more Colombians – they don't seem to scare quite so easily.' He gave Captain Sonoma a smile.

'You were in the Falklands,' Bazua said. There was a definite chill in his voice now.

Docherty thought about saying he'd been at Goose Green, but the news that the man on the other side of the desk might have killed his son could really trip Bazua over the edge, and the Scot didn't want to end up as the victim of a hard-to-credit accident. 'I've got nothing against Argentinian soldiers,' he said. 'The Argentinian Army's really brave when it comes to fastening electrodes or making people eat their own shit, but none of the real soldiers ever join the Army. As a matter of fact,' he went on conversationally, 'one of the twentieth century's greatest soldiers was an Argie.'

Bazua just stared at him.

'Che Guevara,' Docherty explained with a smile. 'Heard of him? Of course, he actually did some fighting, put himself at risk.'

'Why did you come here?' Bazua asked in a poisonous monotone.

'To ask you about Guillermo Macías. You refused to tell me anything.'

Bazua was on his feet. 'Get me out of here,' he said coldly.

'I think it's up to Captain Sonoma to decide when the interview is over,' Docherty suggested.

'It is over,' Sonoma said, as Bazua disappeared through the doorway, minus his escort.

'This must be one of those prisons where the accent is all on rehabilitation,' Docherty murmured to himself.

Captain Sonoma didn't say a word on the drive back to Aguadulce, and when they reached Docherty's hotel – which he hadn't mentioned – he just sat there, staring resolutely ahead, waiting for the Scot to jump out.

'Thanks for your help, Captain,' Docherty said cheerfully. 'I will make sure my government lets your government know how much your efforts are appreciated.'

'Thank you, Señor,' Sonoma said through gritted teeth, and let in the clutch.

Docherty smiled to himself and went in search of a drink. At least he hadn't been thrown off the island.

Two hours later he was halfway up the path to El Pico, where he had arranged to meet Shepreth and Carmen. The forest had grown more patchy as he ascended, and there had already been several spectacular views of the eastern coastline below.

He paused at the next one, as much to enjoy the view as to check that no one was following him. There had been no sign of anyone on the road, and this was the third time he'd broken his journey up the mountain, but it always paid to make sure. The three of them had chosen El Pico as a meeting place precisely because they didn't want to be seen together.

A young American couple in hippie-ish attire went down the path, but no one else seemed to be coming up. Docherty resumed the climb, and half an hour later he was at the summit. A German couple he had seen at breakfast that morning were standing together on one side of the flat peak, Shepreth and Carmen on the other. Docherty nodded at both couples and sat down on a convenient rock to enjoy the view.

When the Germans obligingly departed a few minutes later, Carmen almost ran across to Docherty. 'Did you see anything?' she asked excitedly, and Docherty hated being the one to dim the light of hope in her eyes.

'No,' he said. 'But I heard a woman's voice. It was raised, so it was hard to tell at first . . .'

'She was shouting?'

'Aye,' Docherty lied. 'The Army captain who took me

in said it was a man, one of the prisoners, but he was lying. I'm sure it was a woman.'

'What did you see?' Shepreth asked.

'Hardly anything. They'd rigged up the first room inside the front doors as an interview room, and Bazua was brought to see me there.' He gave them the gist of the conversation. 'I got him angry, but it didn't help. All in all, I think I got more out of visiting the military post. There's no more than twenty men based there, and they seem to have only one working helicopter at the moment.'

'Yeah, but how many more men are there inside the prison?' Shepreth wanted to know.

Docherty shrugged. 'I doubt if there's any soldiers stationed there permanently – they'd probably ruin the social ambience. No, I reckon it's just him and his *sicarios* – probably no more than a dozen in all. I mean, it's obvious he's not expecting to be attacked, or at least not from the land or the sea. I'd guess his main fear is a bombing run by one of the other cartels, so he's probably got an air-raid shelter in there somewhere.' Docherty smiled. 'If it wasn't for the women and the records I'd be recommending that our boys try dropping a few.'

'But . . .' Carmen began, thoroughly alarmed.

'As it is,' Docherty went on, 'we'll have to go in on the ground, which means knowing the layout inside out. We've got the aerial photographs, which should . . .'

'I had a talk with a few of the locals this morning,' Shepreth interrupted him, 'and it seems that nearly all the building work on this island is done by a firm in Cartagena – Sánchez Construcción.'

'They are the biggest firm in the city,' Carmen said.

'So they should have the architect's plans of Bazua's prison,' Shepreth concluded.

'It's worth a shot,' Docherty agreed. 'And while you're there Carmen could try talking to her friend again.'

'I can try,' she said, without much enthusiasm.

'You should get off the island yourself,' Shepreth told him.

Docherty shook his head. 'It'll look kind of suspicious if I leave and then come back. And anyway, I don't think Bazua will risk having a go at me on Providencia – it'd look a bit obvious.'

9

Carmen and Shepreth managed to get seats on that evening's flight from San Andrés to Cartagena. They neither sat together nor acknowledged each other on either the short hop across to San Andrés or the hour-long trip south to the mainland, which they shared with a strange mixture of Colombians on business and gringo travellers leap-frogging past Panama on their way from Central to South America. At Cartagena airport they went through a pantomime of running into each other, then took a taxi together to her flat.

As Carmen had hoped, this was one of the weekends which Pinar spent in Bogotá with a tour group. It wasn't the possible lack of room which had worried her – Shepreth could easily sleep on the sofa in their living room – but the avalanche of questions which his presence would have precipitated. It had been a long time since she'd invited a man back to her home.

He hadn't wanted to come, of course, and had argued that it would be safer for her if he stayed in a hotel. She had talked him out of it, fearing that having got her away from Providencia he might just leave her high and dry.

The fridge was low on supplies, but there were enough vegetables for a stir-fry, which they ate in front of the

TV. Both were conscious of the fact that they'd been thrown together by circumstance rather than choice, and felt somewhat awkward because of it. It was not much past ten when Carmen announced that she was tired enough for bed, and wished him goodnight. She lay down, intending to get her thoughts in order, but the next thing she knew it was morning and there was no sign of him in the flat.

A few angry moments later she noticed that his bag was still there. She'd just finished showering and dressing when he returned with a bag full of pastries for breakfast. 'It's a lovely day,' he said.

They sat out on the small balcony, eating the pastries and drinking coffee, enjoying the sunshine and the slight breeze blowing up from the sea. A month ago Carmen would have taken such simple pleasures for granted, but now she found herself treasuring each minute.

'You're going to call Victoria's aunt?' Shepreth asked, breaking the spell.

'Yes, I'll do it now,' Carmen said, getting up.

The aunt, whose name was Elena Marín, answered the phone almost immediately, as if she'd been sitting with a hand poised over the receiver. Carmen asked how Victoria was, and after a short pause Elena replied that she was no worse. 'Are you coming to see her?' she asked hopefully.

'This morning, if that's all right?'

'Oh yes. That would be wonderful.'

Carmen went back out on to the balcony and told Shepreth, who said, 'While you're seeing Victoria I'll take a look at Sánchez Construcción.'

Ten minutes later the taxi arrived to take Carmen out to Elena's house on the outskirts of the city. She hadn't earned any wages for several weeks now, and she'd intended taking the bus, but Shepreth had insisted on giving her the fare. Later that day she would have to see her parents, but she hadn't yet worked out what she was going to tell them. Her father wouldn't keep financing trips to Providencia without a good explanation – he'd be too worried that she would do something stupid.

Elena's house, though quite small, stood in almost a hectare of land. After greeting Carmen at the door, Elena led her through to the kitchen, from whose window they could both see Victoria. She was sitting with her back to one of several large trees just behind the house, staring into space.

'She spends hours like that,' Elena explained. 'She cries a lot, which I suppose is understandable, though it almost breaks my heart.'

'What did the specialist say?' Carmen asked.

'Not much. He recommended psychotherapy and gave me the name of a man here in Cartagena, but Victoria refused to talk to him.'

'I'd have thought a woman therapist would have been better,' Carmen said, surprised.

'I know. I talked to this man, and I don't think he believed the story we agreed on.'

'Hell,' Carmen murmured. They'd tried to re-create the circumstances of Victoria's ordeal in a different setting, because anything connecting her to Providencia and Bazua might get her killed.

'You know,' Elena said after a few moments, 'the terrible thing is, when she's not crying she actually seems quite happy.'

Maybe, Carmen thought, but it seemed like an amnesiac's kind of happiness. Shepreth had offered her a photo of Bazua to show Victoria, and she had brought it with her just in case, but the young woman in the garden didn't seem in any state to take a shock like that. As she stepped out through the kitchen door Carmen came to the sudden realization that before Victoria's healing could begin Marysa and the others would need to return.

'Hello,' she said from a distance, not wanting to give the woman a shock.

Victoria looked startled anyway.

'Remember me?' Carmen asked.

'Of course,' Victoria said, wrapping both arms around her knees and pulling them towards her chin. 'You're the one who brought me home.'

Shepreth strolled round the old part of the city for the best part of an hour before heading towards the head office of Sánchez Construcción. Carmen had already known where it was, because the firm's move into one of the oldest and most beautiful houses in the walled city had been big news a couple of years earlier. They had apparently had two reasons for doing a no-expenses-spared restoration job on the sixteenth-century house – the eldest of the Sánchez brothers was a history buff in his spare time and his two younger siblings were eager for the lucrative government contracts which similar jobs would provide.

The classic two-storey Castilian villa was in the heart of the old city, right next door to the San Ignacio church. It had an interior courtyard, and through the intricate wrought-iron gates Shepreth could see a riot of vegetation and hear what sounded like a fountain. There were no obvious signs of an alarm system, though, which was somewhat surprising.

Or maybe not, Shepreth thought, walking on before his loitering became noticeable. If the building was used only for office work and impressing clients then there was unlikely to be anything worth stealing on the premises.

The same could not be said of the next house in the row, which housed the City Museum. There was likely to be all-night surveillance in one form or another.

He walked on to the end of the street, spent a few minutes staring at the sea, then started back. There was no way he could go in over the iron fence facing the street, for even if the latter was, by some miracle, empty, there were too many overlooking windows. Entry via the museum would just double the risk of tripping an alarm. It had to be either the rear wall or the church.

The rear wall, he discovered, stood above a six-metre drop. Below it was a busy road, and beyond that the sea.

It had to be the church. The building itself stood about thirty metres back from the road, at the centre of a large paved area. Several large trees kept most of this in shade, and a dozen or more adults were chatting on the scattered iron benches while their children chased each other around the two circular fountains. Shepreth slowly circumnavigated the church, enjoying the age-old simplicity of its design and surreptitiously studying the wall which separated its grounds from the offices of Sánchez Construcción. It was only about two metres high, and in one place a bench had been placed right underneath it. Getting over would be no problem, but getting over unseen might be. Latin Americans loved spending evenings sitting out in places like this, and since it was Saturday there'd be a Midnight Mass.

He walked back to the flat, thinking about Carmen. It was a long time since he'd felt so attracted to someone, but he didn't really know anything about her. She'd told him she was a tour guide, and that she worked here in Cartagena, mostly for several foreign tour companies. She lived with a female friend and didn't apparently have a boyfriend, which would have been more surprising if he hadn't known about the abduction of her sister. Something like that might well have forced her in on herself.

She was obviously brave, stubborn and loyal. But was she clever, kind, naturally curious? Did she have a sense of humour? He couldn't remember ever hearing her laugh, but considering the circumstances that wasn't very surprising.

He let himself into the flat with the spare key she'd given him, set up and turned on the coffee machine, then stepped out on to the balcony just in time to see her paying the taxi driver. She looked up, saw him and smiled.

He had known this woman less than forty-eight hours, but it was hard to think of anyone he had felt so connected to.

'How was it?' he asked as she came into the kitchen.

'Sad,' she said. 'And not very useful. There was just one thing which might help – she went through the usual list of things like the water-bed and the fan and the birds singing and this time she added something – she kept talking about the moon filling the window. Which suggests an east-facing window. If she was in Bazua's bedroom . . .' She looked at Shepreth. 'I know it's really thin.'

'You never know,' he said.

'So how did you get on?'

'You remember the house?'

'Yes.'

'Well, the only way in seems to be over the wall by the church. If I can get over that without being seen . . .'

'You'll need a diversion,' she said.

It was a little after ten and the grounds surrounding the church were far more densely populated than they had been during the day. The two fountains were the preserve of the younger teenagers, the benches reserved for their paired-off elder brothers and sisters. On the pathway from the street to the open doors of the church several beggars were waiting for alms from the midnight congregation. Every so often a military patrol would ride past in a jeep. According to Carmen they followed a regular route around the walled city through the night, mostly to protect tourists who couldn't resist the spell of the narrow streets by moonlight.

The two of them had been sitting on the bench by the wall for about an hour now, since bribing the previous occupants to leave. 'Any minute now,' Shepreth said looking at his watch, and at that moment they could hear the jeep coming up the street. It drove slowly by, the driver waving at a group of girls while his companions smiled, their cradled sub-machine-guns pointing at the sky.

As the jeep disappeared from view Carmen got to her feet and started across the rough paving stones towards the opposite corner of the grounds. Shepreth had enjoyed the last hour, sitting close together and sharing family histories, and as he watched her walk gracefully away a pang of desire shot through his loins.

He watched her light a cigarette, stop by the litter bin as if she was searching for something in the plastic bag, then drop the bag in. He looked at his watch. About two minutes, she had said. When she was a kid she and her friends had done this all the time. And since the home-made fuses had never let them down they'd never been caught.

She disappeared behind the church on her way back round. Half a minute went by. A minute. She was only about ten metres away when the firecrackers went off in the litter bin, jerking every head towards them. Shepreth had been expecting it, and even he felt a momentary pull.

No one was looking their way. He put one foot on the top of the bench and rolled himself over the wall, almost in the same motion. Leaping over a wall without knowing what was on the other side was rather unnerving, but he landed in nothing more dangerous than a bush. He squatted there for a moment, letting his eyes get used to the darkness and listening out for any sign that his arrival had been noticed. On the other side of the wall the string of firecrackers exhausted itself, and he found he could hear the waves crashing against the rocks a hundred metres away.

Satisfied, he headed towards the back of the darkened house. The sudden sound of a distant police siren caused his stride to falter for an instant, before his brain reassured his nerves that it couldn't have anything to do with him.

It crossed his mind that the last time he'd broken into an office he'd nearly ended up in the Panama Canal. Which wasn't a pleasant thought.

Breaking into this one was easier than expected. He had no difficulty springing open the shutters on one of the rear windows, and the sash windows themselves weren't even properly fastened. A few seconds later he was examining a typical board room with his pencil torch.

The door was locked, but no match for his steel 'credit card'. He edged out into the courtyard, which was mostly in darkness – the setting half moon was casting its silver spell on only the uppermost leaves of the various ornamental palms and the apex of the fountain. There was no sign of any human occupancy.

He started working his way round the ground floor, unlocking and where possible relocking each door in turn. In one of the rooms facing the street he found what he was looking for – a mountainous map cabinet with some forty drawers. After checking that the shutters were as lightproof as possible, he checked under P for Providencia. Nothing. Rather less hopefully, he tried B for Bazua. Nothing there either. He was just about to start going through the whole cabinet from top to bottom when another idea occurred to him.

He looked under 'M' for Ministry of the Interior, but eventually found it under 'I'. The Sánchez brothers had obviously done a lot of work for the government, most of it in Cartagena, from schools to military barracks, police posts to waste-disposal depots. And they had also built both a military post and a correction centre on Providencia. Shepreth spread the two sheets out on the floor. The correction centre plan not only included interior diagrams for the two buildings familiar from the satellite photographs, but also placed the two new constructions within the context of the site.

He was still rolling up the two sheets when he saw the photocopier. It would certainly be much better to leave the originals here, because if their absence was noticed and Bazua informed, he wouldn't need a brain transplant to figure out why they'd been stolen. But could he risk the light?

Who dares wins, he thought, remembering the SAS motto. His watch told him he had another ten minutes before the patrol went by.

He switched on the machine and when it had warmed up he folded the plan in two, put it in place and lowered the lid. If he'd been wearing a jacket he could have used it to cover the machine, but he wasn't. So he draped himself across it instead, rather like someone trying to X-ray their own stomach.

A faint light flared twice in the dark room. He stood up and went through the process again for the other half of the diagram. And then twice more for the military post. There were no cries from the street, no police sirens. He pulled out his shirt, stuffed the copies into his waistband and tucked the shirt back in.

He put the diagrams back, switched off the copier and made his way back round the ghostly courtyard to the room through which he'd entered. He relocked the door from the inside and went out through the window, pulling the sash down and then, with some difficulty, refastening the shutters from the outside. As he approached the wall he heard voices on the other side.

Shepreth had been gone only a couple of minutes when they appeared in front of her. She couldn't remember either of their names, but the faces were familiar from her school days.

'Remember us?' the older-looking one asked. He seemed more than a little the worse for drink.

'No,' she said coldly.

'I'm Ramón,' he said, sitting down beside her and stretching both arms along the back of the seat. 'And this is my brother Paolo.'

The younger man sat down on her other side, pulled out a packet of American cigarettes and offered her one.'

'I don't smoke,' she said. 'And if you don't mind, I'd like to be alone.'

Paolo actually started to get up, but thought better of the idea when he saw that his brother had no such intentions.

'A beautiful woman should not be alone on a night like this,' Ramón said sarcastically. 'Why are you so unfriendly?'

'I'm waiting for my boyfriend,' she told him.

'He is late?'

'I was early.'

'I don't think he's coming. Why don't you come for a walk with us?'

She gave him a scornful look. 'Why would I want to do that?'

'Because we can show you a good time. Go to a club maybe, or a party. Wherever we go it'll be better than hanging out in a churchyard.' He let his hand rest lightly on her shoulder. 'How about it?'

She brushed the hand away, and turned round to face him. 'No,' she said. 'Understand that? It's really simple. N-o. No. I do not want to go anywhere with you. I do want you to leave me alone.'

Ramón sighed. 'This boyfriend must be a real superman. I think we have to stay and see someone like that, just so that we know how to improve ourselves. Don't you think so, Paolo?'

Having arrived on the other side of the wall in the middle of this conversation, Shepreth's initial irritation soon turned to anger. The prospect of climbing back over and banging the two young men's heads together was an appealing one, but he was quite sure Carmen could take care of herself, and there had to be more prudent courses of action open to him.

He walked across to the wall which bordered the museum's grounds. There had been no sign of armed guards on the street in front of it, and it was possible that the building's alarm system was considered defence enough. In which case, he could use the grounds as an escape route.

He was raising himself up to take a look across the wall when there was a rushing sound from the other side, and a slavering mouth full of very sharp teeth materialized not much more than a metre from his face. He dropped back to the ground, his heart suddenly thumping at about five times its usual rate, just as the dog began barking up a storm on the other side of the wall.

In the distance a human voice was asking the dog what the trouble was.

'Shit!' Shepreth murmured to himself. The street had become his best chance.

He hurried down the side of the Sánchez Construcción villa and stopped at the corner for a look. The dog was still barking next door, but there didn't seem to be anyone out in front of the museum. Most of the street was out of sight from where he stood, and the chances of it being empty seemed somewhat remote. His watch told him the patrol would be passing in less than two minutes. The odds didn't look too good, but they were only going to get worse.

He ran for the wrought-iron gates, which seemed to offer the easiest climb, and concentrated on getting over them, not even looking up and down the street until he dropped to the pavement outside. About a hundred metres away a couple were walking towards him, but they seemed engrossed in each other. In the opposite direction a taxi had just pulled up outside the gates to the church grounds, but it was facing away. He was just congratulating himself on getting away with it when a shout came from behind him. Two armed guards had emerged from the museum and were walking towards him, sub-machine-guns at the ready.

Hearing the dog bark, Carmen put two and two together. Shepreth must have realized he couldn't rejoin her in the way he planned and sought another way out. She hoped he'd seen or heard the dog before crossing the other wall.

If he had, what would he do? There was no back way out, so it would have to be the front. She stood up abruptly and walked away from the bench, hoping that the bastards wouldn't follow her.

They did of course.

'If you don't leave me alone, I'll get a policeman,' she half shouted over her shoulder.

'We're doing nothing,' Ramón shouted back, but the footfalls seemed to die away slightly.

She reached the gates and turned into the street just in time to see Shepreth halted by the guard's shout.

'David,' she yelled, turning his head once more, and ran towards him with outstretched arms. As they embraced like long-lost lovers, she saw over his shoulder that the guards were still coming forward. She freed herself from the embrace, glanced quickly back down the street and strode towards the approaching guards. 'See those two boys,' she shouted angrily, pointing back at the hovering Ramón and Paolo. 'They have been harassing me. I want them arrested.'

'That is not our business, Señorita,' the first man said.

'It should be the business of every man to protect innocent women,' she said haughtily. 'Come, my darling,' she said, taking Shepreth by the arm. 'We will be late.'

The following evening Docherty was lying on his hotel bed, Walkman on his chest, listening to soul singer O.V. Wright lament a wrong verdict by 'the jury of lurve'. He had spent a reasonably relaxing weekend, walking and swimming by day, reading and sleeping by night. He had really wanted to talk to Isabel, but there was every chance that the call would be monitored, and Bazua's reach certainly extended to Chile. Carmen had promised to ring his wife from Cartagena, so Isabel would know that he was all right, but he still missed the sound of her voice.

A police officer had joined him at his table during breakfast that morning. He said that he was from the local station in Santa Isabel, and that he was obliged to ask Docherty some questions.

Actually there was only one – what the hell was Docherty still doing on Providencia?

'Taking a holiday,' the Scot had told him. 'I was hired to come here and talk to Angel Bazua, as I'm sure you know. And now that I've talked to him, I'm spending some of the money. You have a beautiful island here.'

The man had departed happily enough, though whether Bazua would be satisfied was something else again.

Lying there listening to O.V. Wright, he found it hard to believe in happy endings, but then who wanted to listen to the Osmonds?

There was a tap on the door. Docherty swung himself off the bed and walked silently across to the door. 'Who is it?' he asked, taking care to keep behind the jamb.

'It's me,' Shepreth said.

Docherty opened the door.

'I moved in down the corridor,' the MI6 man told him. 'Carmen's there now.'

Docherty followed the younger man to his room, which looked practically identical to his own. Carmen was standing with her back to the curtained window, looking happier than she had three days before.

'Did you talk to Isabel?' he asked.

'Yes. She's fine, the children are fine. She sends her love. I told her more or less everything and . . .' She hesitated.

'And she sounded worried,' Docherty suggested.

'Yes, she did. But she didn't say anything, just that you should be careful.'

'Aye,' said Docherty. There was no way round that one. 'So what have you got?' he asked the two of them.

Shepreth produced the architect's drawings with a flourish, and laid them out on the bed.

'You didn't have any trouble, then?' Docherty asked as he examined the plans.

Shepreth told him the story of the break-in, stressing the role Carmen's quick thinking had played in their getting away with it, and Docherty saw the look that passed between them. If they weren't lovers already, they soon would be.

'These were worth the risk,' he said shortly.

'And Carmen may have got something from Victoria Marín,' Shepreth said.

She explained about the moon-filled window, half expecting to see an incredulous expression on Docherty's face.

'This room or that one,' he said, finger jabbing at the plan. 'There's two obvious ways this could be done,' he went on. 'Assuming the SAS get the job, we could bring in a troop – that's sixteen men. The Royal Navy could bring them within range, but there's nowhere to put a helicopter down inside the compound, so if we want to catch Bazua by surprise – and for the sake of the women and the records I think we do – then they'd have to come in by boat. I don't know how sophisticated Colombia's defences are – not very, I expect – but I don't think there's much chance a Royal Navy boat would get past American surveillance. And since they can't be told what we're doing there's a good chance they'll alert the Colombians. And we don't want their air force turning up.'

'Maybe the Navy could come up with a cover story for the Americans,' Shepreth suggested.

'Maybe,' Docherty said, without much conviction.

'What's the alternative?' Carmen asked him.

'More stealth, less men,' Docherty said. 'Assemble a

four-man patrol here on the island and bring them in one by one. With surprise more or less guaranteed, I don't think the five of us would have too much trouble.'

'I have a feeling someone might point out you're no longer on active service,' Shepreth said, remembering Docherty's record.

'So I'm an on-site consultant,' the Scot said.

'And anyway there'll be six of us,' Shepreth said with a smile.

'Seven,' Carmen reminded him.

Later that night Docherty lay awake in bed, trying to remember how many of *The Magnificent Seven* had survived. Had Horst Buchholz been one of the three who rode away, or had they already left him behind in the village? He had been one of the three, Docherty decided, which meant four had died. He could remember them all – Coburn's knife dropping from his fingers, Robert Vaughan's fingers scraping down the wall, the gold-happy one whose name no one ever remembered. But most of all he remembered the children putting flowers on Charles Bronson's grave.

He didn't want Maria and Ricardo doing that, not until they were well into middle age.

10

The sun was barely over the horizon, the fields sparkling with dew in the early-morning light, as Lieutenant Colonel Timothy Greaves drove south from Hereford towards the Severn Bridge and the M4. There were shorter routes to London, but he had always loved this road through the Forest of Dean, and the meeting in Whitehall didn't start until eleven.

Of course, he could have saved himself the drive by arranging a flight to RAF Northolt, but in these days of military economy it was considered somewhat extravagant to use the RAF as a personal taxi service. And in any case who could think in a helicopter?

Greaves was not exactly looking forward to the meeting, but there were butterflies of excitement in his stomach nevertheless. It was nearly a year now since he had succeeded Barney Davies as the Officer Commanding 22 SAS, and he had spent quite a lot of that time waiting for the chance to play his part in one of those special operations which punctuated the history – the legend, almost – of the Regiment. They didn't happen very often, and when they did they were as likely to take place outside the public eye as in it.

The subject of that day's meeting would not be offered

as grist for headlines, and that fact gave rise to a certain ambivalence in Greaves's mind. He would have to ask his men to risk their lives in the awareness that they would be unacknowledged in success and quite possibly disowned in failure. Several such missions had been carried out in Barney Davies's time, and Greaves knew that his predecessor's pride in their success had been more than a little tinged with bitterness. Too many men had died unrecognized.

Sergeant Jamie Docherty had been involved in several of those operations, including one of the most dramatic, the insertion of a four-man patrol into Bosnia. He was newly retired when the need arose, but had been reinstated for the duration of the mission.

Greaves had read through Docherty's file the previous evening and wondered. No other regiment in the British Army – probably no other regiment in the world – would have persevered with someone like Docherty when he went so comprehensively off the rails after his wife's death. And just about any other regiment would have court-martialled him for wilful disregard of orders at some point in his career. Yet there seemed no doubt that he'd been a brilliant soldier, at least insofar as the SAS defined the breed. His record in action showed that he'd frequently been better than his orders.

Greaves himself had seen precious little action since the capture of South Georgia and the reconquest of West Falkland. Then there had been training stints in a couple of African countries and a couple of mind-numbing tours in Northern Ireland. He shook his head, as if to dislodge the thought that soon he'd be sending more men into that murderously futile mess.

But first the joys of Colombia, he told himself, as he passed the midpoint on the swaying Severn Bridge. The river below seemed choppier than usual, despite the clear blue sky overhead.

His thoughts returned to the morning's meeting, the exact purpose of which seemed far from clear. During their telephone conversation the previous day Sir Christopher Hanson had implied that it was both a rubber-stamping exercise and a ritual sharing of responsibility, but Greaves had learnt to take anything Intelligence said with about a ton of salt. He feared a concerted attempt to impose political restraints on his military freedom of manoeuvre, and knew that he would have to resist any such pre-emptive tying of his men's hands.

In his written submission to the Prime Minister he had offered two possible courses of action, both loosely based on the suggestions emanating from Providencia. Hanson's man Shepreth was supposedly the source of these, but Greaves thought he could see Docherty's fingerprints all over them. He was also pretty certain that the politicians would refuse to sanction the larger-scale plan – no matter how it was dressed up, the dispatch of a full SAS troop sounded too much like an invasion.

But four men out of uniform could be inserted in secrecy, and once the job was done they could be passed off as mercenaries in the employ of a rival cartel. Admittedly there wasn't much chance of weapon supply or bodily extraction without the Americans taking notice – it was surprising any sunlight still reached the ground with all the surveillance planes and satellites that littered the skies above the Caribbean – but risk-free options seemed remarkably thin on the ground.

If the politicians asked for certainty he'd tell them there wasn't any, but that he certainly wouldn't bet against his men getting the job done as discreetly as was humanly possible.

The Prime Minister was already seated at the head of the rectangular walnut table when Greaves entered the room. This was not the first meeting he had attended in Whitehall, but it was his first view of the famous Conference Room B, which turned out to be stunningly ordinary.

There were six seats around the table. A man with thin, greying hair and piercing blue eyes sat facing the PM. Seeing Greaves, he got up and offered his hand, introducing himself as Christopher Hanson. There were two men on the other side of the table, one of whom Greaves knew, one he had frequently seen on *Newsnight* and *Question Time*. The former was Douglas Minchey, a junior minister at the Ministry of Defence, the latter Martin Clarke, who held an equivalent rank at the Foreign Office and was also rumoured to be a possible challenger for the Party leadership. They both nodded greetings, Minchey with a smile, Clarke with a frown that would have curdled milk.

The Foreign Office would hate this, Greaves thought as he sat down. The chair next to him was apparently spare.

The PM cleared his throat – nervously, it seemed to Greaves. 'Sir Christopher, if you could bring us all up to speed . . .'

Hanson obliged. Without once consulting his notes he told the story of MI6's increasing interest in Angel Bazua's twin career as drug smuggler and bankroller of

Argentinian irredentism. He described the various and vain British attempts to interest the Americans in action against Bazua, and went through the events of the past few weeks – the accidental involvement of an ex-SAS man, his discovery of the Argentinian's possession of certain Dirty War records and the possible explanation of American behaviour which that suggested, the decision to ask the SAS proper to consider operational options.

The PM asked Greaves to outline what those were.

He was about to do so when the Foreign Office minister intervened.

'With respect, Prime Minister,' Clarke began, 'wouldn't it make more sense to discuss the potential consequences of any such action before we get down to specifics?'

'I think we're all aware that our relations with both Colombia and Washington could be seriously affected,' the PM said. 'And once we've heard what is possible we should have a better idea of how to minimize the potential damage,' he added dismissively, turning his attention back to the SAS CO.

Greaves outlined the two options he had submitted, on impulse stressing the purely military advantages of the larger-scale assault. He was conscious that when it came to playing politics he was an amateur among seasoned pros, but he was hoping that giving the Foreign Office something to shoot down would make them more inclined to let the smaller insertion go through. Out of the corner of his eye he could see a smile on Hanson's face, as if the MI6 man knew exactly what was going on.

'Which do you recommend?' the PM asked when he had finished. He still seemed nervous to Greaves.

'If we send in the larger force we can be pretty certain

of achieving our immediate objectives – the destruction of Bazua and his boats. But the element of surprise won't be so great, there'll be more casualties and it will be impossible to conceal the operation from the Americans. The second option relies more on the skills of a few men, but as long as we solve the weapons supply problem the operation will be effectively over before anyone else knows about it. And if by then we have the means to mollify the Americans, then the Colombians will find it hard to prove our involvement.'

Clarke was not having any of it. 'The first option is clearly out of the question,' he said. 'A cynic might think that it had been conjured up just to make the second option look more reasonable. Either way, we'll be sending British soldiers on to the soil of a sovereign nation to blow up boats and kill people.' He locked eyes with the Prime Minister. 'Are we really going to sanction the use of the SAS to assassinate a drug baron?'

'Well, they can hardly bring him home,' the PM said coldly.

'If you really have moral qualms about this operation,' Hanson told the FO minister, 'I think you should save them for a more suitable occasion. Bazua is a mass murderer, drug dealer and worse.'

'And since when has MI6 set itself up as the moral guardian of the New World Order?' Clarke asked sarcastically.

'Gentlemen!' the PM admonished them. Greaves was expecting him to side with his minister, but he didn't. 'I would obviously prefer to work with our allies in this matter, but that seems to be the one option which is definitely denied us. And with all due respect to the

Foreign Office's real concerns, I don't believe we can let the fear of American disapproval deter us from the pursuit of crucial British interests. I want those boats destroyed and I want this man brought to book.'

There was a glitter in his eyes as he enunciated the last sentence, and Greaves suddenly thought he understood why the man had seemed nervous before – it was because he had decided on a course of action which seemed completely out of character. But why? Greaves wondered. Was it the drugs that enraged him, the thought of another war or just Bazua's character? Was there anything there to undermine life-long habits of caution? No, he decided, and then he understood. The man was on his last legs politically and he knew it – there was no need to hedge any more. Like those beyond the age of responsibility he could do whatever he felt like doing. Taking on Bazua was like a last hurrah for seventeen years of Tory rule.

'So are we all agreed on the smaller-scale option?' the PM was saying.

There were nods from around the table, an almost infinitesimal twitch of the neck in Clarke's case.

Now Greaves knew why the meeting had been called. The PM had needed Clarke's metaphorical signature next to his own, just in case everything went wrong.

The SAS CO took the quicker route home, and despite stopping off for a late lunch in Witney was back in his office at the Stirling Lines Regimental HQ of 22 SAS by a quarter past four. He felt physically tired after seven hours of driving in one day, but mentally refreshed by the distance he had put between himself and Whitehall. The meeting in Conference Room B had left him feeling manipulated and none too respectfully inclined towards his political masters.

It had also left the Regiment with a job to do.

Once he was behind his desk, Greaves's first action was to order two cups of tea, his second to summon Major Jimmy Bourne, the long-time head of the Regiment's Counter Revolutionary Warfare Wing. The planned action against Bazua didn't come within the CRW Wing's purview, but before his retirement Barney Davies had recommended Bourne to Greaves as the best available source of personnel information and general advice, and on more than one occasion during the past year the new CO had been grateful for the tip.

'So we've been given the green light?' Bourne asked before he was even through the door.

'Plan B,' Greaves told him, indicating the waiting cup of tea.

'Good,' Bourne said, shovelling sugars into the dark-brown brew.

Greaves stopped counting after three. 'So who shall we send?'

'I've been thinking about that,' Bourne said, testing his tea for sweetness. 'It'll have to be one of our best, or Jamie Docherty will walk all over him.'

Greaves smiled despite himself. 'Does the bastard really expect a consultant's fee?'

Bourne grinned. 'That was a joke,' he said. 'But he'll bloody well expect to be consulted. I think we should give the job to my senior sergeant.'

'Wynwood, right?'

'Yep.'

'He just got married, didn't he?' There had been a

photograph in the local paper which Greaves had found amusing – the bulky Welshman with the big grin and mass of dark, curly hair, the diminutive bride looking demure and serious enough for life in a convent.

'That was a couple of months ago,' Bourne said. 'A great bash,' he added wistfully. 'Anyway, he knows Colombia.'

'I know.' Wynwood had been one of two advisers sent by Her Majesty's Government to help train the Colombian Special Forces Anti-Narcotics Unit in the early 90s. After his partner and a prominent local politician had been kidnapped by the drug-dealing Amarales family, Wynwood had taken charge of the four-man patrol sent in to execute a rescue. The team had proved successful but not in the way intended, and had ended up having to walk across a mountain range to escape pursuit. Even then, two of their number had died at the hands of the Amaraleses' *sicarios*. 'The Colombians might remember him,' Greaves thought out loud.

'The name maybe, but we can change that. He's brilliant in the field, he speaks fluent Spanish and he'll get on with Docherty.'

'OK, I'm sold, he's the PC. What about the others?'

'Why not get Wynwood in here?' Bourne asked.

Greaves hesitated – even after a year back he was still not fully attuned to the Regiment's uniquely democratic ways – but only for a moment. 'Why not?' he agreed.

Joss Wynwood was just getting into his car, having decided to trim the odd half-hour off his working day. He and Sarah were going out for a meal with her elder sister and brother-in-law that evening and he wanted some time with his wife before they went. They could do a jigsaw together, or take a shower together, or . . .

It was his sister-in-law's thirty-eighth birthday, and he'd be thirty-nine himself in a couple of weeks. Next year he'd be forty. He had used to worry about getting older, but not since meeting Sarah.

He was just moving towards the gates, midway through fastening his seat-belt, when the trooper appeared in the side window, running along beside him and tapping on the glass. He rolled the window down and slowed the car to a crawl, letting the trooper slow to a walk as he delivered his message. The news that the CO wanted to see him made him feel like a schoolboy caught skiving off school early.

'Any idea what it's about?' he asked optimistically.

'Not a clue, Sarge,' the trooper told him with a grin.

Wynwood parked the car and walked thoughtfully across the parade ground towards the CO's office. The sky in the west was beginning to fill with clouds, which usually meant overnight rain. With any luck he wouldn't have to water the garden.

He knocked on the door and heard the CO's 'come in'. Wynwood hadn't had that much to do with Greaves since his appointment the previous year, but like most of the Regiment he'd been pleasantly surprised by the ease of the transition. Barney Davies had been a much-loved and respected figure, and so far Greaves didn't seem that much of a comedown.

It wasn't just the CO waiting for him inside – Jimmy Bourne was there as well. Maybe the CRW Wing was being abolished. He took the seat next to his immediate superior and prepared to be enlightened.

'There's another cup of tea on the way,' Greaves said by way of preamble. 'We've been given a job to do,' he continued, and proceeded to outline what it was.

Wynwood listened, feeling initially torn between wanting to go and not wanting to leave his current happiness behind. But as the CO, with occasional help from Bourne, sketched out the prospective operation, the Welshman's two decades of professional commitment reasserted themselves. The job itself seemed straightforward enough; the only obvious problem was weapons supply. The actual assault should present no real difficulties, as long as it was properly planned and executed. And as for the getaway, Bourne had apparently spent most of the morning confirming that a chopper from the Caymans could be customized to collect the team from just outside the twelve-mile limit.

'We think you're the best man to lead the team,' Greaves told him.

'Thank you, boss,' Wynwood said automatically. He had just seen the new film of *Mission: Impossible* and half expected to be handed a self-destructing tape. 'Who else have you chosen?' he asked.

'No one yet,' Bourne said. 'You're here to help us pick the names out of a hat.'

Terry Stoneham left the car by the wooden gate, not really caring whether he was infringing on a farmer's right to move his livestock, and started up the public footpath, kicking stones as he went. Every time he saw the kid a great bundle of conflicting emotions seemed to knock him sideways, and as usual he found himself wondering why he was putting himself through it all. Mark was Jane and Don's child in every way that counted. It might have been his sperm which fertilized the egg, but Don had been the one at the birth, the one who had watched the first walk and heard the first word. He was the one the kid called Dada.

He kicked another stone, with slightly less vicious intent.

Jane had asked him to let go, stand back, give up the kid. All his friends in the Regiment thought he was just digging himself a hole to be miserable in. Even his parents had told him to think about what was best for the boy, and God only knew how much they wanted a grandchild.

But he couldn't bring himself to do it. He didn't know if it was a real attachment or pure stubbornness, just as he still didn't know whether he'd really loved Jane or only thought he did.

His early life had not prepared him for this. In a world of broken families and free-wheeling angst his parents had loved each other and him – just about the only thing he'd been deprived of was a sense of deprivation. He'd been a happy baby, a happy child, a happy youth and a happy grown-up, right up to that moment when his pregnant wife had told him about her lover.

But that was two years ago, he told himself as he reached the top of the hill. Just before the hostage crisis in Samarkand which he and Rob Brierley had sorted out with a little help from the locals. Well, quite a lot of help actually. He had really fancied Nurhan, the woman in charge – in vain, unfortunately – but at least the fancying had helped dull the pain of his ex-wife's betrayal. He had noticed today that he no longer found Jane in the slightest bit sexy. He had given up on her, so why couldn't he give up on a kid he only saw for a couple of hours each week, a kid moreover who didn't really seem to know who the occasional visitor was?

He thought he'd make a good father one day, but then Don already seemed to be one, and an art teacher was less likely to get killed than an SAS sergeant, even one who seemed permanently stationed in a classroom full of smart-arse trainees.

Stoneham smiled to himself and ran a hand through his straw-coloured hair. 'Ah, what the fuck,' he murmured to himself and gazed out at the fuzzy line of the distant Black Mountains. Maybe he could get a security job with Princess Di, entrance her with his ready wit and manly body, and get a cut of the millions Charlie had lobbed in her direction.

He laughed and looked at his watch – he had a class in half an hour.

There was no irate farmer waiting by the gate and the traffic was kind, so he made it with three minutes to spare. The trainees were full of enthusiasm and long on naïve questions, and by the end of the class he felt old for his thirty-four years. Still, he'd outlived Jesus, he thought, as he headed for the canteen and a possibly life-threatening meal. He was only ten metres from the doors, and could almost smell the spotted dick, when the adjutant collared him. The CO wanted to see him at eight the following morning, and he should cancel his classes for the coming fortnight.

At twenty to eight the next morning the 'Twins' were mopping up the last of their fried eggs with slices of white bread. Both accent and appearance offered proof positive that there was no blood relationship between Corporals Sam Blackman and Charles McCall. The Liverpudlian 'Blackie' had dark hair and an almost gangling frame, the Glaswegian 'Bonnie' ginger hair and a riot of freckles, but since their simultaneous badging in 1990 the pair had seemed virtually inseparable. They were now in the last stretch of their second three-year term in the SAS and had no intention of missing out on a third.

But shit happened, as the Americans said, and on this particular morning they were anxiously wondering why the CO had developed this sudden yearning to see their pretty faces.

'It can't be about that fight you got us into, can it?' Blackie asked plaintively.

'Which one?'

'In the Slug & Pellet.'

'It was you got us into that one, staring at that tart's tits.'

'It was you asked if they were real. That was what really set her boyfriend off.'

'Yeah, yeah,' Bonnie agreed, remembering the breasts in question.

'Anyway, that was two weeks ago,' Blackie said. 'He'd have had us in before now.'

'So what did we do last weekend?'

'We went to that party in Ludlow.'

'We crashed that party in Ludlow,' Bonnie corrected him. 'And you tried to go swimming in the punch-bowl.' He sighed. 'But let's look on the bright side. He doesn't want to tear us off a strip – he wants to tell us what a great job we've been doing. Or maybe there's a job waiting for us, and we can get out of fucking Hereford for a while.

Give the women a chance to miss us. You know, build up expectations for when we return.'

'Yeah, right. An all-expenses-paid fortnight in sunny Belfast.'

'It could be another HAHO drop on to the mountain above the bad guy's lair,' Bonnie said reminiscently. He and Blackie had been part of the back-up troop parachuted into Colombia in 1990. They had been on the ground no more than a couple of hours, but just about every minute, not to mention the preceding hour-long drop, was etched in the memories of the two men.

'Christ, I hope so,' Blackie murmured.

'Or they could send us after that Bosnian Serb – what's his name? – the one they want for the war crimes.'

'Karadzic.'

'Yeah, that's him. Well, someone's got to arrest the bastard, haven't they?'

Blackie shrugged. 'It'd be a change.'

'Those Bosnian women won't know what hit 'em.'

'Your sledgehammer wit, you mean?'

Bonnie grinned. 'You're just jealous. That new barmaid at the Pig's Head thought I should go professional.'

'She was winding you up.'

'No chance. I think I'm in there this weekend.'

'If you're not in Bosnia,' Blackie said, looking at the canteen clock. 'I think it's time we got our orders from Jimmy.'

They gulped down the last of the sludge-like coffee and started across the parade ground in the direction of the CO's office. In the distance the unmistakable figure of Senior Staff Sergeant Wynwood was coming towards them. 'Christ, maybe we are going back to fucking Colombia,' Blackie muttered.

'Change of venue, lads,' said Wynwood. 'It's the Kremlin for us.'

'So what's it about, boss?' Bonnie asked innocently.

'All will be revealed shortly,' Wynwood told him. 'As the actress said to the bishop.'

'I bet that made his cassock bulge,' Blackie murmured.

In the briefing room they found the CO, Jimmy Bourne and Terry Stoneham already waiting. The mounted water-buffalo's head, a forty-year-old souvenir of the Regiment's time in Malaya, gazed moodily down at the assembly. As they took their seats, Bonnie and Blackie noticed the large-scale map of the Caribbean draped across the easel.

Bourne started the ball rolling with a brief biographical sketch of Bazua and his activities. Stoneham, Bonnie and Blackie, who were hearing of the man for the first time, looked suitably angered by his presence on the planet. The involvement of Jamie Docherty – a famous SAS old boy – was greeted with interest.

'Can we call him Grandad?' Bonnie wanted to know.

'If you want to end up feeding the sharks,' Wynwood told him.

'Right,' Bourne said, leaning towards the map. 'Now for the interesting bit. You four are off to the delightful Colombian island of Providencia.' He tapped a point in the Caribbean which seemed closer to Central America than Colombia, then folded the sheet back to reveal a smaller-scale map of the island itself. 'Wynwood and Stoneham will arrive tomorrow afternoon, Blackman and McCall will spend a day on the adjoining island of San Andrés – an uneventful day, I should stress – and then move over to Providencia the following day. That night – preferably that night – you will break into Bazua's home and sink his boats.' He did a round of the four faces. 'All clear so far?'

'Not really,' Blackie said. 'Why do we need to break into his house to sink his boats? They're not in the swimming pool, are they?'

Bourne grinned. 'We didn't want to make it too simple in case you got bored. For one thing your chances of escape will increase about a hundredfold if you destroy Bazua's communications with the outside world. For another, Bazua has something the Intelligence boys want to get their hands on – he has military records from the 70s Dirty War in Argentina.'

'Most 70s records are crap,' Bonnie murmured.

'Why do they want them?' Stoneham asked.

Bourne looked at Greaves, who nodded. 'They may find out that Bazua has an important friend in American Intelligence,' he told them.

'What about Bazua?' Stoneham asked. 'Do our masters want him dead or alive?'

Bourne looked at Greaves again.

'We don't want him brought out,' the CO said. 'The government couldn't put him on trial without admitting that British troops had snatched him from Colombian soil.' He paused, looking almost embarrassed, Wynwood thought. 'I've been put in a difficult position,' Greaves went on, 'which I'm afraid means that you're in one too. MI6 want this man dead, and they will also be involved in this operation – they already have a man on the island. I can't say that I'd shed too many tears if Bazua gets killed, but I have been given no orders for his assassination. So I'm afraid you're going to have to play it by ear.' He paused again. 'And there's another complication. There are several women on the premises – we don't know how many. Five were kidnapped on the mainland a year or so ago and taken to the island, and as far as we know three of them are still there. They're Bazua's prisoners – slaves virtually. And there may be more than three.'

'Christ,' Stoneham said, 'are we supposed to bring them out with us?'

Greaves sighed. 'If you can. I think that's another decision that can only be taken when the time comes. As far as Her Majesty's Government is concerned the important thing is to get in and out without leaving any British fingerprints, and as far as I'm concerned the number-one priority is getting you all back in one piece. Working within those parameters . . .' He shrugged. 'But to get back to where we were. Shepreth – that's the MI6 man – will have the primary responsibility for grabbing the records and taking care of Bazua; you will take out the boats and assist him in whatever other ways are necessary. Is that clear?' he asked, thinking it was anything but.

The objectives were diverse, the chain of command confused, and there'd be no chance of a rescue if things went badly wrong.

But if the men in front of him shared his doubts, there was no sign of it on their faces. All four of them had an expectant gleam in their eyes, like kids who'd been promised an adventure in the woods.

'We'll clarify as we go along,' Wynwood said.

* * *

On Providencia the days were passing slowly. Shepreth and Carmen were seeing a lot of each other – it seemed safer to pretend that they were strangers enjoying a holiday romance than unattached loners with no apparent agenda, and if Shepreth had had his wish they would have been doing more than pretending. In Cartagena he had begun to hope that she reciprocated some of his feelings, but since their return to the island she had retreated back inside herself. Shepreth hoped it was the proximity of her sister rather than second thoughts about him which had caused the change.

He had not tried to keep her in the dark about the imminent operation, telling himself that she would be needed to reassure the women once they were released. Which might well be true, but it wasn't the real reason he was wilfully ignoring every security regulation in the book. He was emotionally involved, and pleased about it. He had a personal stake, and he liked it that way. He couldn't see any reason why his professional obligations should come into conflict with his personal loyalties but if they did then he'd follow his conscience. And if that cost him his job, then the hell with it. He wanted Carmen, but that was only the half of it. He wanted to feel better about himself.

For her part, Carmen was only too aware of Shepreth's more basic urges, and at times the temptation to respond was almost irresistible. But she didn't let herself. It would have been more than a betrayal of her sister – it would have been wrong for her and Shepreth too. She liked him, and she could already imagine falling in love with him, but she couldn't shake the feeling that jumping into bed with him in the middle of all this would cause either or both of them to emotionally short-circuit.

When it was over . . . well, then she'd be more ready to trust her own feelings and to believe that his interest was more than an awkward blend of lust and sympathy. In the meantime she tried not to let herself think about what might be going on in the house on the other side of the island, and not to let impatience rule her days.

She was not the only one eager for action. Docherty was once good at waiting, but age had made him more impatient, and he missed his wife. He liked both Shepreth and Carmen, but apart from hurried meetings in the hotel room, he had no contact with them. He liked Providencia, but he'd finished his book and the three tapes he'd bought for the Walkman were wearing out. He'd walked just about every path on the island by the Tuesday, and he'd never been one for just lying on a beach.

When Shepreth delivered the news of the SAS team's imminent arrival he breathed a deep sigh of relief, but later that evening he noticed that the age-old mix of fear and excitement had acquired a new ingredient – guilt. He had always thought that there had to be things worth risking his life for, but the older he got the fewer they seemed to be, and he wasn't completely sure that Angel Bazua was one of them.

Or that Isabel would think he was.

11

Providencia was a small island, making secret meetings hard to arrange. If the four of them were seen gathering in one of the more secluded spots then suspicions were likely to be aroused, and on balance Docherty reckoned that a meeting in one of the small settlements, in full view of the locals, carried the lesser risk. So he and Shepreth first 'bumped into each other' in the bar of an Aguadulce hotel, then 'just happened to wind up in conversation' with two fellow-countrymen who had just arrived from San José.

Joss Wynwood and Terry Stoneham both looked fit, Docherty thought. In fact, almost too fit for the travellers they were supposed to be. He had met them both before, but they were from a later SAS generation, and he didn't know either of them that well. He had spent more time with Stoneham, particularly in the days following the Samarkand hijack business, but he was also well aware of Wynwood's reputation and pleased to see that the Welshman had been chosen to lead the SAS team.

After about ten minutes of innocent male chatter about football, women and the local beer, Wynwood quietly wondered whether this might not be the best place to talk.

Docherty took one last look round the room. There didn't seem to be anyone in earshot, and in any case the people they most needed to worry about would have a hard job understanding English, particularly the Welsh and Scottish versions spoken by Wynwood and himself. And talking here would certainly look potentially less suspicious than hiding in a hotel room or wandering down to the beach together in the dark. 'Aye,' he decided. 'Why not?'

'The other two will be here tomorrow,' Wynwood told Docherty and Shepreth. 'Blackman and McCall – do you know them?'

Docherty shook his head.

'They're full of bullshit, but I'm told they're reliable when it counts,' Wynwood said. 'Terry and I will hire a boat in the morning and go for a ride. After dark we'll be picking up the you-know-what, which we'll need to stash somehow – I don't fancy leaving the stuff in the boat for twenty-four hours.'

Docherty thought for a moment. 'On the hill above the target,' he suggested. 'We can dig a scrape in the trees.'

'Sounds good. Have you taken a look at the seaward side yet?'

'I have,' Shepreth said. 'We took one of the tour boats which circle the island. It kept much further out from the shore in that sector, but I got a reasonably good look through the glasses. There were a couple of men on the dock with SMGs – Uzis, I think – but they didn't look like they were expecting trouble. The wire fence follows the shoreline by the way, just inside the trees, and there's a gate by the dock.'

'Electrified, I presume,' Wynwood said.

'Nope,' Docherty told him.

'Christ, they're making it easy for us.'

Docherty shrugged. 'Not many people break into prisons,' he said.

'I suppose not,' Wynwood muttered. 'What's our best estimate of enemy strength?'

'We don't really have one,' Docherty admitted. 'There's no way of seeing right into the compound, and however many people there are in there, they never seem to leave. Carmen watched the place for two days. She saw four officers visit, but nobody else went in or out.'

'Sounds like a social club,' Wynwood commented.

'It is one.'

'Sounds like a brothel,' Stoneham observed.

'It's that too,' Docherty said, 'only I don't think the women are getting paid. One of them's Carmen's sister, by the way.'

'Ah,' Wynwood said. That hadn't been in the briefing.

'That's why she's here,' Docherty explained. 'What are your orders about the women? What are the rules of engagement, come to that?'

Wynwood smiled. 'I don't think there are any.' He looked at Shepreth. 'But MI6 is supposed to be taking out Comrade Bazua.'

'Are they indeed?' Docherty asked.

'If possible,' Shepreth said curtly. 'The records are more important. Without them, Bazua's days will be numbered in any case.'

'And the women?' Docherty asked again.

'We'll take 'em with us if we can,' Wynwood said. 'If there's twenty of them, they won't all fit in the boat.'

'Carmen will have to come in with us,' Shepreth said.

'She'll be able to reassure the other women, and we may need help from them.'

Wynwood grimaced. 'Makes sense,' he agreed.

'You were complaining that it sounded too easy,' Docherty reminded him.

Next morning Wynwood and Stoneham walked down to the dock in Aguadulce and took their time picking out a boat for hire. Since it was the low season the choice wasn't great, but there was one sturdy-looking eight-metre boat which looked more than adequate. It was fitted out for deep-sea fishing and reminded Wynwood of Humphrey Bogart's boat in *To Have and Have Not*. Now all he had to do was train Stoneham to walk like Walter Brennan and find himself a Lauren Bacall.

Not that he needed one. For a few seconds he let Sarah swim round his mind, and could hardly believe how much he missed her.

Stoneham, meanwhile, was negotiating with the boat's owner, an English-speaking West Indian sporting a Boston Red Sox baseball cap. He was initially reluctant to let them have the boat without a chaperone, but once Wynwood had demonstrated that he could handle the boat, knew what a reef was and was prepared to pay twice what the boat was worth for a week's hire, the objections seemed to melt away. 'But no drugs!' was his parting shot. 'Just girls,' Wynwood agreed. 'And a small arsenal,' Stoneham added under his breath.

They spent the morning circling the island at a leisurely pace, getting used to the boat and stopping on two occasions to make use of the snorkelling equipment they had also hired. It was the second time in a year that

Wynwood had enjoyed the beauties of the reef – in the previous autumn he had honeymooned on the similarly named island of Providenciales in the Turks and Caicos Islands, where his old SAS comrade Worrell Franklin ran a clinic with his Gambian wife.

Soon after two they passed the target's dock for the second time, and as on the previous occasion there were two men on guard. This time they were both smoking, and Wynwood was sure he could detect the smell of marijuana across the water. The dope was probably a first line of defence against the Latino pop which was pouring from their boom box, but if things got really bad they could always shoot themselves with the Uzis that were leaning against one of the concrete capstans.

Half an hour later the two SAS men docked the boat at Santa Isabel and washed down a delicious lunch of fresh lobsters with tolerable local beer. Stoneham leaned back in his chair, belched and announced that a soldier's life was sometimes hard to bear.

Wynwood was glad his companion had cheered up – on the flight from RAF Brize Norton he had seemed almost suicidal.

They got back to the boat with about three hours of daylight remaining, and Wynwood steered them away from the island on a north-north-west heading. An hour and a half later they reached the prearranged spot. Stoneham decided to try his hand with a fishing rod, something he had never tried before, and after a while he realized why. Wynwood collected a beer from their cooler and watched the sun going down over the empty sea, thinking about Sarah and how lucky he was.

* * *

'Nice place,' Bonnie McCall said, surveying the activity on Avenida Colombia. He and Blackie Blackman were sitting on the wall between the beach and the road, watching the ebb and flow of San Andrés Town's night-life. The other side of the Avenida was lined with busy hotels, and the smell of frying fish made Blackie feel almost nostalgic for Blackpool.

'Pity we can't make the most of it,' he said, as their eyes swivelled to follow two nubile locals. One of the girls said something in Spanish, the other glanced over her shoulder, and both giggled.

'We promised the boss we'd be good,' Bonnie said in a tone of mock anguish.

Neither man said anything for a couple of minutes; they just sat there listening to the swish of the waves behind them and the confused rhythms of competing discos further up the road.

'It's all a bit unreal, isn't it?' Blackie said after a while.

'Yeah. I was just thinking that I should have told my folks we were off on a jaunt. I didn't want them to worry, but if I don't beat the clock they're going to get a hell of a shock.'

'Nah,' Bonnie said. 'What's the point of worrying them and *then* giving them a shock?'

'Yeah, maybe.'

'Yeah, well. So should we have another pint, do you think?'

Blackie shook his head. 'No, let's be really good. I've got a feeling we may be needing all our brain cells tomorrow.'

* * *

It was two minutes to eight when Wynwood heard the plane in the distance, and soon he could see it – a growing black speck in the star-filled sky to the north. It was a Cessna of the type most frequently used by drug smugglers, and had been chosen for that very reason. Why should the American operatives in their AWACS and satellite-tracking rooms take more than a passing interest in a smuggler's plane heading south *towards* Colombia?

The Cessna was almost overhead now, and first one, then a second, parachute appeared, pale white in the moonlight, drifting slowly down. The first of the crates hit the water with a mute splash some two hundred metres away, the second moments later not half that distance from the boat. Stoneham engaged the engine and began chugging towards it.

A few minutes later both crates had been manhandled on to the deck. The two men disengaged the parachute lines, knotted the material around rocks Wynwood had collected for that purpose on the beach at Santa Isabel, and threw them overboard. They then turned their attention to the crates' contents. Inside the first, tightly wrapped in waterproof oilskin sacks, were six Heckler & Koch MP5SD silenced sub-machine-guns and a supply of C3 plastic explosive with detonators, fuses and electronic timing devices. Inside the other, similarly wrapped, were six Browning High Power 9mm pistols, two PRC 319 satellite radios, six Davies CT100 microphone/receiver sets, six lightweight Bristol Type 18 armoured jackets, six pairs of Passive Night Goggles (PNGs), one nightscope, a dozen stun grenades and a flotation bladder with a small bottle of carbon dioxide.

'Where's the Chieftain tank?' Stoneham asked.

'They always forget something,' Wynwood muttered. 'You start sorting this lot out while I get us headed in the right direction.'

Stoneham unwrapped everything and started sorting it into two piles. In one he placed two of the MP5s, handguns, CT100 sets, armoured jackets, half the explosives and one of the PRC 319s. This pile was then carefully rewrapped in the waterproof oilskins and attached to the flotation bladder. He then turned to the other pile, packing everything but the PRC 319 into the bergen backpacks which had previously held their clothes and personal effects. That done, he took over the helm, leaving Wynwood free to align the satellite radio's antennae and type the single word 'received' on the miniature keyboard. A little while later he received an equally terse reply from Grand Cayman, nearly six hundred kilometres to the north: 'acknowledged'.

For the next hour they sat mostly in silence, watching the hump-shaped island slowly loom larger. There were a few clouds in the western sky now, but the almost full moon hung suspended among the stars to the east. Passing the scattered lights of Santa Isabel and Pueblo Viejo to port, they moved in towards the island's western coastline a kilometre or so to the north of the target's dock. A torch blinked twice on the rocky shore, and for a moment Wynwood found himself wondering how many boats had surreptitiously edged their way in towards Caribbean shores over the past five hundred years.

Docherty and Shepreth, both knee deep in the gentle swell, took charge of the loaded bergens and vanished back into the darkness as Stoneham headed the boat back out towards the open sea. After drawing a wide semicircle around Bazua's dock he headed the boat in towards another cove that they had scouted earlier that day. This one was surrounded by mangroves, and after inflating the flotation bladder with carbon dioxide Wynwood clambered down into the water and attached it to a convenient root. The buoyancy had been calculated just right for the weight, holding the bundle a foot or so beneath the surface.

He climbed wearily back on board and Stoneham headed down the coast to Aguadulce, where, to his surprise, the boat's owner seemed to be waiting for them. As they pulled in to the dock he walked to and fro, apparently checking the boat for signs of major damage. Finding none, he seemed reassured. 'Catch anything?' he asked, as Wynwood leapt out to tie her up.

'Threw 'em back,' the Welshman replied.

By this time Docherty and Shepreth had reached the hiding-place on the hill. They had felt exposed walking down the road, but only two cars had passed them, both driven by local West Indians. The second had stopped to offer them a lift, exhaling ganja fumes through his wide smile.

Docherty had dug the scrape earlier that day, so now all they needed to do was drop in the bergens and cover everything with the already made roof of cut branches and large leaves. 'You go first,' he told Shepreth when they were done. The MI6 man nodded and slipped off through the trees. He had a knack of moving quietly, the Scot thought.

The slight sounds faded away, leaving only the breeze in the foliage above, the occasional chirp of a night bird, and the sound of his own heart. Way above him the upper branches of the trees were swathed in the light of the moon.

He squatted on his haunches, remembering the desert mountains of Oman, the bare hills of southern Argentina, the snow-filled valleys of central Bosnia. What a life, he thought. He wouldn't have swapped it for the world.

On the other side of the island Carmen was sitting at her favourite table outside the Dutch Inn, staring out at the darkened sea. She knew what was supposed to be happening that evening, and she had tried to picture the different scenes in her mind, but her subconscious kept pushing her forward twenty-four hours to the moment of truth.

She had resisted being left out, but now, in the privacy of her own thoughts, she could admit how terrified she was. In Cartagena it had all seemed like a game, but now it all seemed real again, and she was worried that she might let Shepreth and Docherty down.

She should do something to take her mind off it, she thought. But what? She was hardly in the mood for dancing, and going for a walk at night seemed like asking for trouble. She could always go to bed, but she knew that her chances of getting to sleep were slim. Tomorrow was probably going to be the most exciting day of her life – she would either rescue her sister or end up sharing her prison.

The idea made her shiver.

She thought about the Englishmen. They seemed confident enough, but for all she knew they were hopelessly outmatched. Bazua would hardly have lasted as long as he had if he'd been a pushover.

12

Blackie and Bonnie came over on the early-afternoon shuttle from San Andrés, took a pick-up around the island to Aguadulce and spent an idle half-hour lounging in the bar of the Hotel Princesa. At three o'clock Wynwood passed through the bar, but made no attempt to talk to them – the sign that everything was still going according to plan. A few minutes later the two young men walked back outside, where they shook hands and parted like recent acquaintances. Blackie walked down the beach towards the dock, leaving Bonnie waiting by the side of the road for a pick-up going north.

The Glaswegian had to wait only ten minutes, and the journey up to Puerto Viejo took less than that. He walked down the dirt track to what the guidebook claimed was the island's cheapest hotel, paid for a room, dumped his bag and went out again, walking north around the rim of Santa Catalina Bay to Santa Isabel, where he ate an early lobster supper at the same restaurant Wynwood and Stoneham had used the day before.

After watching the sun sink into the bay over a couple of Cokes he started walking slowly back to his hotel, reaching it just before eight. He took a vigorous shower, laid himself out on the bed of his spartan room and stared at the patterns of peeling paint on the ceiling. At £2.50 a night the place was a steal.

At ten he turned the light off, waited a few minutes, then slipped out of the door. There was music spilling out of an open doorway across the yard, and a couple on a bench above the beach seemed to have their tongues in a knot, but no one looked his way as he turned the corner of the building and hurried up the dirt track to the main road. There was a light on in the two-storey shop at the intersection but it went out as he approached.

He took the road south, still walking briskly. The moon was rising in the east, and for a while he could see its light scattered across the sea to his right, but then the road cut inland, running almost like a tunnel through the tropical woodland. He walked on, trying to calculate the distance. The path was supposed to be slightly over a kilometre from the shop, and just as he began to think that he must have walked that far, there it was, winding up alongside the stream into the darkness of the forest. He took the prescribed fifty paces and gave a faint whistle.

There was an answering whistle, and a few moments later Wynwood emerged out of the darkness. The Welshman was already kitted up, his face beneath the PNGs artistically streaked with camouflage cream, a CT100 unit fastened to his collar, an MP5SD cradled in his arms. He gave Bonnie a pair of PNGs and gestured him to follow, and for the next few minutes they threaded their way along an invisible path through the dense foliage. Several times Bonnie felt the brush of unknown entities on his face and offered up several silent prayers to the effect that any poisonous spiders or snakes on the island had already been endangered out of existence.

There was another faint whistle from Wynwood, an echo up ahead, and in the green glow of the PNGs Bonnie could see three other figures sitting on the forest floor. One was a wiry-looking, short-haired man with a half-amused expression on his face, the second a taller man of not much more than Bonnie's own age, the third . . . was a woman. Like everyone else she had darkened her face with make-up, but unlike the others she wasn't wearing body armour.

'Get kitted up,' Wynwood told him.

'Yes, boss,' Bonnie said, and did as he was told, wondering who the woman was. By the time he had finished there were still nearly two hours of boredom to enjoy before they moved off down the hill.

Stoneham had casually picked up Blackie from his dock-side vantage-point soon after four, introduced him to the boat's owner as a fellow-Brit that he'd just met, and offered him a few hours of fishing. Blackie had been suitably thrilled, and, pantomime over, they had taken the boat a couple of miles offshore, where they watched the sun go down and argued over whether Sheringham or Fowler should be partnering Shearer in England's attack in the '98 World Cup.

Once the sun had gone down they moved lazily north, heading in to shore to collect the weapons bag from among the mangrove roots. They then rode at anchor for a while, as Stoneham put together several explosive devices.

By ten-thirty they were off Aguadulce again, eating sandwiches and taking turns observing the small military post through the nightscope. As on the two preceding nights, there was virtually no visible activity – just a single uniformed sentry sitting in an upright chair at the landward end of the protruding dock and one window showing light in the command building. There was no sign of anyone aboard the patrol boat which was tied up on one side of the jetty.

At eleven-forty the light went out, and at midnight the sentry was relieved. His replacement walked down to the end of the dock and back before settling into the already warmed seat.

Two minutes later Blackie lowered himself over the side of the boat and began swimming towards the shore, the waterproof pouches containing the two bombs strapped across his chest. The water was warm, he was a good swimmer and as far as he could tell there weren't any sharks closing in for the kill.

As he approached the jetty the patrol boat came between him and the sentry's line of sight. He worked his way round to the stern, where he fastened the first of the two explosive devices to the rudder-propeller assembly which lay just beneath the surface. He then carefully inched through the water to a position beneath the landward end of the dock and looked at his watch. There were two minutes to wait. He hung there in the water, one arm wrapped around a jetty support.

Stoneham started the engine right on cue, and there was an almost imperceptible rise in the decibel level as he brought it in towards the dock. The sentry heard the boat too, if he hadn't already noticed it with his eyes. There was a scraping sound as he got up from his chair, and then the creak of boots on wooden boards. He yelled something in Spanish – something along the lines of 'You can't dock here, you fucking idiot!' – and there was an obsequious reply from Stoneham, requesting further directions. Blackie pulled himself out of the water and on to the jetty. Twenty metres to his right the sentry was standing there gesticulating, his back turned toward the base. Blackie took the five steps necessary to get him through the gate and sank to his haunches. He could hardly believe that something so obvious could have worked, and he felt grateful that he hadn't had to cut the sentry's throat. Or at least not yet.

The compound seemed deserted. It was even less well lit than the dock, with three of the four floodlights either off or broken, and two bare light bulbs shining forlornly above the doors to the two main buildings. Behind him the conversation was still going on, the sentry sounding increasingly exasperated with this stupid gringo God had pushed in his direction.

Blackie moved towards the helicopter pad, checking the fence to his right for possible ways out. He found several. Over the years the sea had eaten away at the foundation and in several places the bottom of the fence simply lifted like a flap. It looked like the sentry was going to see another dawn.

After securing the second explosive to the underside of the helicopter's nose cone, Blackie scuttled back to the fence and slipped underneath it. The rocks below were slippery, but the sentry was still standing with his back to the shore, watching Stoneham turn the boat around. Blackie slid into the water and began swimming after it. Five minutes later he was clambering over the side.

They headed out to sea, not turning north until they were some three kilometres from land and the lights of Aguadulce were strung like a necklace beneath the silhouette of the hills beyond. Almost immediately they turned back towards the shore, and soon after twelve-thirty they were lying about two hundred metres off the coast and about twice that distance south of the target dock. The two boats earmarked for Bazua's Falklands invasion were drifting at anchor some fifty metres offshore.

They were now within CT100 range of the others.

'The charges are set,' Stoneham reported to Wynwood, and as he said the words his ears picked up the sound of a plane. 'What the fuck?' he murmured to himself – there were no night flights to or from the island.

'It's up there,' Blackie told him, pointing. 'It's a big plane, an airliner.'

'It's a Caravelle,' Stoneham said, half to himself and half to Wynwood. 'It's coming in to land at the airport.'

'That explains it,' Shepreth whispered to the others.

Fifteen minutes earlier four men had emerged from the house below, clambered into the Cadillac which one of them had collected from the garage and disappeared in the direction of Santa Isabel. None of the departees had been in uniform, which seemed to suggest they were Bazua's men.

'The Caravelle must be *en route* from Colombia to Mexico,' Shepreth went on. 'Probably with about five million dollars' worth of heroin on board. Bazua's boys will be making sure nothing leaves the plane while it's refuelling.'

'Sounds reasonable,' Wynwood murmured. He did some mental arithmetic. It would take them ten to fifteen minutes to reach the airport, the same to get back, and the jet would probably be on the ground for at least half an hour. Say an hour in total. The poor bastards were going to miss the party.

He took a quick glance at the others, all of whom looked as tense as he felt, and gave the signal for go.

They worked their way back to the path and descended it in single file. A car went by on the road below, its headlights flaring green through the PNGs and the noise of its engine slowly fading to the north, leaving them with only the sounds of the breeze and the burbling stream.

Reaching the moonlit strip of road, they broke into a steady trot, ears and eyes alert for the sound of traffic, ready to dive back into the shadows of the trees. A hundred metres later they turned off, clambering across the crumbling wall of the property next door to their target. The large house that loomed away to their right was in no better shape than the wall, but would doubtless make some developer a fortune in the future.

It was Docherty who had scouted this route and he was in the lead now, working his way through the overgrown garden and adjacent woodland to the fence which surrounded Bazua's luxury prison. As Bonnie went to work with the wire-cutters, the others squatted down to wait. By Wynwood's watch it was twelve forty-eight.

The seconds ticked by, punctuated by the click of the cutters. Shepreth shared a nervous smile with Carmen, and resisted the temptation to reopen the earlier argument about the body armour. She was right – provided she kept out of the way as she'd promised, he would be the one who needed it.

Carmen was grateful for the smile. She felt scared, and would have been more so if it hadn't all seemed so unreal.

Here she was squatting by a wire fence in the middle of the night with a bunch of gringos, her face covered with gunk, a gun tucked under her belt. She had never fired one in her life.

The click of the wire-cutters had stopped. Bonnie lifted the flap and beckoned to the others.

Wynwood examined his watch again. 'We're going through the fence,' he said softly into the microphone.

'Acknowledged,' Stoneham murmured in all their ear-pieces.

'Remember,' Wynwood reminded the others. 'Don't speak any English if you can help it.'

They squirmed through the hole one by one and headed on through the forest, Wynwood in the lead, followed by Bonnie, Docherty, Shepreth and finally Carmen. In the distance a thin wash of green light seemed to be filtering through the trees, but it was impossible to tell whether it was man-made or a trick of the moon.

They had only about two hundred metres to travel, but it seemed a long time before the first rectangular shadow appeared in front of them. This was the northernmost of the two specially constructed buildings which extended in a westerly direction behind the main house, on either side of the swimming pool. There were only a few narrow windows visible, and none of these showed any illumination, but a faint green glow above the roof suggested a light source in the open courtyard beyond.

It was now twelve fifty-seven. The column split into two groups, with Wynwood and Bonnie moving to the left and the others to the right, heading for opposite ends of the building in front of them.

The threesome didn't have so far to go. Docherty

took off his PNGs and inched an eye round the first corner. There was no one visible, and no light from the end window, which they were hoping was the one that Victoria Marín had seen filled by the moon. The only other east-facing window was in the building on the other side of the pool, and the satellite photos had shown a basketball hoop on that end wall.

It was twelve fifty-eight. Shepreth had ushered Carmen into the nearby trees, and was now employing the same hopeful gestures dog owners use when trying to persuade their animals to stay. Docherty advanced along the end wall and put an eye round the next corner.

To his left a faint yellow glow filled the distant doorway to the main house, but no lights showed in any of the windows. During their various stints on watch over the past week Carmen and Docherty had never seen any signs of life in this part of the compound, and the current plan of attack was based on the assumption that it was unoccupied.

The two buildings on the other side of the swimming pool were definitely in use, and thin lines of brightness around the central windows and doors of one indicated that the communications room was still operational. Both the room to its right and the small building to its left – which they had guessed contained a back-up generator – were in darkness.

There were no outside lights burning, but the pool's underwater lights were on, casting a shimmering blue glow over the whole courtyard.

A dull thump sounded in the far distance, then another. If he hadn't known better Docherty would have assumed there was a fireworks party in Aguadulce. His watch told him it was exactly one o'clock.

As Shepreth appeared at his shoulder, Wynwood and Bonnie came into view away to the left, carefully skirting the back of the villa. The young Glaswegian took up a position from which he could cover both the gate through to the interior courtyard and the doors facing the communications room. Wynwood was about twenty metres away from the latter when its door suddenly swung open and a man strode out. He saw the SAS man coming towards him, took in the gun and camouflaged face, and opened his mouth, either as a prelude to shouting or simply to gape with surprise. Wynwood's MP5 spat fire, throwing the man back, and there was the sound of something breaking in the room behind him.

Docherty had already started forwards along the front of the other building, and as the first *sicario* went down he opened the first door and tossed in the stun grenade, then pulled it shut once more. The thunderclap seemed to rattle the window, and a line of light flashed in the gap beneath the door. He stepped quickly in across the threshold and dropped to one knee, MP5 at the ready, but it took only a second for his senses to conclude that the room was empty.

'Shit,' he murmured. So much for moons in the window.

On the other side of the swimming pool Wynwood had reached the communications room door at a run, which was just as well, as another of Bazua's men was halfway to his feet, gun in hand. Wynwood put a triple tap through his upper trunk, spinning him back and round across the chair he'd been sitting in. Man and chair collapsed in a heap, taking the floor fan with them.

This ended up on the dead man's face, whirring at the ceiling.

Wynwood's eyes scoured the room. There was a sophisticated array of radio equipment, plus the usual telephone and fax, but there was no sign of any records – no computer, no filing cabinets, no leather briefcase with the words 'Dirty War' embossed in gold.

Docherty and Shepreth were only a few metres from the next door when it burst open, disgorging two men, both dressed only in shorts. As one fired his Uzi from the hip in the general direction of the communications room the other took off at a run for the far end of the swimming pool. Bonnie ducked back inside the doorway, which gave Docherty a safe shot at the man with the Uzi, whose body was propelled forward into the pool, where its impact on the water made a resounding splash and caused shivers of blue light to dance wildly over all the walls.

The other man was past the end of the pool now, and had almost reached the shelter of the main villa, when Bonnie cut him down. The Colombian's gun seemed to keep firing as it cartwheeled out of his hand and glass cascaded down from broken windows in the main house.

Four down, Docherty thought, but where the fuck was Bazua?

The sound of running feet made him spin round, just as the two guards from the dock emerged out of the trees to his right. Shepreth opened up first, and one man went down, but the other turned tail and ran, spraying bullets behind him as SAS fire zipped through the foliage to either side.

It was like a shooting gallery, Docherty thought. But where were the fucking prizes?

There were more doors to open – the one leading into the room with the basketball hoop outside, which Wynwood was now moving towards, and the last two on this side of the pool. The first of these, the one from which the two *sicarios* had burst, opened into a dormitory of sorts, with several beds, posters of naked women with their legs invitingly spread, a large TV. There was even a pool table, but Bazua wasn't cowering underneath it.

For Carmen, the last couple of minutes had been endless. She had heard gunfire, explosions, a splash, breaking glass, and for all she knew her English allies had all been killed by Bazua's men. Her mind told her this was unlikely and that she should stay where she was, but apparently neither her heart nor her feet agreed, because a couple of seconds later she found herself tentatively extending her head round the corner of the building.

She gasped at the scene in front of her, the bodies littering the courtyard, another floating in the pool. But none of them, she realized with a leap of her heart, were dressed like the Englishmen. Two of these were walking along the far side of the pool, and as she turned her head Docherty and Shepreth emerged from a door further down the near side. They were alive . . .

And then she saw the door open in the far corner, the figure in silhouette, head looking this way and that, gun in hand.

'*Atención*,' she screamed.

Docherty spun round, saw her standing there and followed the direction of her outstretched arm. The door which they had assumed led only to the back-up generator was open, and there was a flicker of shadow on the inner wall as someone disappeared inside.

'I'll take it,' Docherty yelled in Spanish, forgetting he was wearing a microphone and almost deafening the others. 'You take the last room,' he yelled over his shoulder at Shepreth, and didn't bother to wait for the MI6 man's agreement. Skirting the end of the swimming pool at a run, he almost skidded to a halt by the side of the open doorway. A quick glance inside revealed both the expected generator and a flight of steps leading down into the bowels of the earth.

He started down the steps, forcing himself to take it slowly and carefully. At the bottom of the steps corridors ran off to both left and right, and he took the former, which led directly into a luxurious suite of rooms.

Docherty took them one by one, rerunning the old 'Killing House' training like a mental video, refusing to let impatience and his strong intuition that the rooms were empty lead him into a fatal mistake. The largest room boasted a huge round bed and not much else. Another good-sized room contained two tan leather sofas, a TV and a sound system; a third served as a small office. There was a swish-looking bathroom and toilet. At the corridor's end there was a room containing six bunk-beds.

They were all empty.

And then the sound of a distant shot echoed in the enclosed space.

Moments after hearing their bombs go off in the Aguadulce military post three kilometres to the south, Stoneham and Blackie had slipped into the shallow water and started towards the dock. On the way they heard the Uzi bursts, and were not surprised to find that the guards had abandoned their position. 'We're on the path,' Stoneham told Wynwood, just as another burst of automatic fire split the night.

'One headed your way, Terry,' Wynwood said in his ear.

The two SAS men headed carefully up the dark path, counting on the PNGs to give them the edge.

They had been walking only a few seconds when they heard the man coming towards them, and a few moments later they could see him. Both men stepped behind convenient trees, and Stoneham spent several valuable seconds trying but failing to remember the Spanish for 'stop'.

'Stop, you bastard,' he screamed in English, but the Colombian's only answer was to tighten his finger on the Uzi's trigger and keep running, presumably in the hope that the spray of bullets would act like a shield. It didn't. The two MP5s almost cut him in half at the chest, his mouth gushed blood, and he was dead before he hit the ground.

'One down,' Stoneham reported in.

'Come on in,' Wynwood told him. He and Bonnie had just checked the remaining room, which had turned out to be the prison armoury, containing, in Wynwood's rough estimation, well over a million pounds' worth of brand-new weapons and equipment.

In the basement Docherty regained the bottom of the steps in time to greet the descending Shepreth and Carmen.

'Look after her,' Docherty told the MI6 man curtly,

without pausing in his stride. The corridor ran straight ahead of him into the distance, and he guessed with a sinking heart that it had been designed as an escape route. Forty metres later he reached another flight of steps, and realized that he'd been right. As he started ascending, a car's engine burst into life, and he knew that Bazua was gone.

The steps emerged into the garage, and as he ran out through the open door headlights swept past the gates and on to the road. He heard the others coming up the stairs and turned, and it was then that he saw the woman's body. She had on only a T-shirt, and her face had been all but destroyed by the bullet. She'd broken free of Bazua's grasp, Docherty guessed, and the bastard had just shot her in the back of the head. 'The fucker's escaped,' he said into the microphone, disgust in his voice.

He looked up to see Carmen falter in her stride, the guilty relief in her eyes as she realized it wasn't her sister.

'It's Irma,' she said, as if she was talking to herself.

Docherty looked at his watch. Six minutes had passed since the bombs had gone off in the Aguadulce military post, and they couldn't count on many more before the local authorities put in an appearance.

Carmen had other ideas. 'We can go after him,' she said, pointing to the other car standing there.

'No we can't,' Docherty told her, and she looked as though she'd been slapped.

'But . . .'

'He's heading for the airport,' Docherty said, remembering which way the car had turned outside the gate. 'Even if we could catch him there's no way we could get off the island, not now. The locals are probably on their way already.'

'He's right,' Shepreth agreed.

The look on Carmen's face clawed at Docherty's heart. 'We'll get the bastard,' he told her. 'It just won't be today.' He didn't add that Bazua might well dump the other two women the first chance he got.

'You promise you'll carry on?' she asked fiercely, gazing from one face to the other as if determined to catch them in a lie.

'Aye,' Docherty said, looking her straight in the eye. 'Now let's get going.'

They retraced their path down the tunnel and as Shepreth searched through the small office Carmen wandered round the room with the bunk-beds, staring at the various pieces of women's clothing, the magazines, the cosmetics by the mirror. She looked about fifteen, Docherty thought.

'Only two beds have been slept in,' she said suddenly.

She was right. He put an arm round her shoulder, meaning to pull her gently away, and at that moment his eyes caught sight of the painting on the wall in the main bedroom. A Spanish woman was sitting at an open stone window, and the space itself was filled by the moon.

'That means there were only two women here,' Carmen said, a hint of hysteria in her voice.

'Maybe,' Docherty agreed. 'Or maybe one was with Bazua,' he added gently.

She gave him a look that was half hope, half heartbreak.

'There's nothing here,' Shepreth said behind them. 'He must have taken the records with him.'

'Then let's go,' Docherty said, propelling Carmen towards the corridor and steps.

'Victoria told me he was like a worm that burrowed,' she said, 'but I just thought she was talking about sex. If I had . . .'

'Forget about ifs,' he told her. 'They're only there to keep us humble,' he murmured.

In the compound outside Bonnie was keeping watch while Wynwood placed the charges in the armoury. The body in the pool was floating happily on its back. Another day of the dead, Docherty thought.

Wynwood emerged a few moments later, having lit the five-minute fuses. 'There's enough weapons to mount another Falklands invasion in there,' he told Docherty. 'But no luck with the records,' he guessed, noticing that both Shepreth and the Scot were empty-handed. He shrugged. 'Well, let's get the fuck out of here. Terry and Blackie are planting the charges on the boats.'

It was twelve minutes past one.

They headed up the path in single file, with Docherty bringing up the rear. He was just thinking that the five minutes must be up when he heard a tooting horn from the direction of the villa – the local military had arrived at the gates and were demanding entry. There was another toot, longer this time, and then, as if in response, a yellow flash lit the sky. It was instantly followed by the sharp rip of the first explosion. That was the communications room, Docherty guessed, and the fuller-throated roar of the next detonation proved him right.

They reached the dock just as Stoneham and Blackie returned from fixing their charges, and with all seven of them on board Wynwood headed the boat north at its maximum speed of about fifteen knots. If the commandant of the military post in Aguadulce had instantly asked his superiors on San Andrés for help a helicopter could be arriving at any minute, but Wynwood wasn't expecting any such quickness of thought or independence of action. The commandant wouldn't have wanted to involve outsiders without clearing it with his real boss, but he would only now be discovering that Bazua had flown the coop, and it would take him a few minutes to realize that he had been left in an impossible position. At that point he might cut his losses and ring either San Andrés or the mainland.

If he did, Wynwood reckoned, they had about fifteen minutes in which to lose themselves on the open sea before a search got underway.

They had travelled about a kilometre when the first charge went off behind them. Wynwood looked back to see the second jagged flash erupt against the dark background of the coastline, and then a third, a fourth, a fifth, a sixth. Stoneham and Blackie had done a thorough job on Bazua's navy.

He looked round at the others. There were grins of relief on the two younger men's faces, but on Stoneham's and Docherty's he saw a reflection of his own sombre realization that their mission had been a partial failure. Then he told himself that meant it had also been a partial success. They had destroyed the bastard's boats and his weapons stash, they had driven him out of his safe haven, at least for the moment, and all without suffering a single casualty, which had to be worth something. Bazua would find it hard to replace what he'd lost. Acquiring new and sophisticated military equipment was never simple, even when money was no object, and governments willing to let drug barons run their organizations from prison were, mercifully, thin on the ground. No doubt the man had friends in Mexico, but they wouldn't be as powerful as the ones he'd made in Colombia. And next time he might not be so lucky.

But it wouldn't be the SAS who got the bastard. And Wynwood couldn't help finding that hugely disappointing.

A few metres behind him, sitting in the boat's stern, Docherty's thoughts had been moving in much the same direction. His script, though, had a different ending – even without the promise to Carmen he would probably still have considered Bazua unfinished business, and with it there was no room for doubt.

He looked round for her, and saw that her head was cradled in Shepreth's shoulder.

'Boss,' Blackie said suddenly, and everyone turned to follow the direction in which he was pointing, certain that the Colombian military was in hot pursuit.

They had forgotten the Caravelle, which was climbing into the sky above the diminishing hump of Providencia. It seemed to pass directly over their heads before veering away in the general direction of Mexico.

'Where's a terrorist bomb when you need one?' Bonnie asked no one in particular, as the Caravelle vanished among the stars.

Shepreth walked forward to talk to Wynwood. 'I need to let some people know about that plane,' he said.

'People where?' the Welshman asked him. 'We've only got Grand Cayman listening in.'

'They can pass the message.'

'OK. Terry, take the helm, will you.'

Stoneham obliged, and Wynwood set up the PRC 319 on the cabin roof, typing in the message as Shepreth dictated.

By the time he'd finished they were more than halfway out of Colombian waters, and as the remaining kilometres slipped by the eyes of the team were more or less permanently focused on the southern horizon. Even though an attack from the air seemed unlikely, a fast patrol boat could still try to take them into custody.

But neither aircraft nor boat loomed in the south, and Stoneham had no sooner announced that they were in international waters than a moving speck appeared in the northern sky. As this swiftly grew into the expected Mk 3 Sea King they made ready to leave the boat. The pilot hovered overhead as the rope ladder was lowered, and one by one they clambered up it, leaving the empty craft bobbing happily on the swell below. As the pilot turned the helicopter back towards the north another member of the crew poured mugs of tea from a giant Thermos.

13

The day had dawned a dull grey in London, and it had been raining on and off ever since. The perfect weather for his mood, Sir Christopher Hanson thought, as he threaded his way through the maze behind Whitehall in the direction of the Prime Minister's back door. He had been up all night anxiously waiting for news from the Caribbean, and still hadn't shaken the feeling of disappointment which had eventually accompanied it.

Of course the night hadn't been a dead loss – there had been achievements too, and it was these which he planned on stressing in his report to the PM. Hanson thought about opening with 'Well, there's good news and there's bad news – which would you like first?', but he knew that all he'd get from his audience would be a stony look. It was hard to believe these days, but the man had possessed a sense of humour when he came into office.

It was only seven a.m. but the PM was already at work in his private den. He gestured Hanson to a chair and pushed aside whatever he was working on with ill-concealed irritation. The MI6 chief found himself wondering whether a Labour government really would make his life more difficult, as all his subordinates expected.

'They're back on Grand Cayman,' he said, sitting down. 'No casualties.'

The PM looked confused for a moment, then comprehension dawned. 'Good,' he said. 'And the Argentinian?'

'He escaped,' Hanson said flatly. 'Probably to Mexico.'

The PM grimaced.

'But they destroyed his base, his ships and his armoury,' Hanson went on, exaggerating only slightly. 'It'll take him a long time to recover.'

The PM didn't look mollified. 'How did he get away?' he asked.

'I'm not sure. There'll be a full debriefing as soon as the men arrive back here. I thought it would be wise to get them away from the . . .'

'The scene of the crime,' the PM suggested drily. 'Yes, you're probably right.'

'I do know that an illegal flight landed on the island in the middle of their operation, which was something that no one could have foreseen.'

The PM scratched his forehead. 'I don't suppose they got their hands on the military records?' he asked.

'I'm afraid not. He must have taken them with him.'

'If they exist. So we've got nothing to show the Americans?'

'No,' Hanson admitted. 'But I'm told the team didn't leave any fingerprints behind them, so we could at least try feigning ignorance. Just play dumb, as the Americans would say.'

The PM made a scornful-sounding noise. 'They may not have left any fingerprints but I'll bet the sky was lit up for miles around. And what are the chances the Americans didn't track the helicopter back to the Caymans?'

'Smugglers use the Caymans. And we may have been lucky – the Yanks aren't omniscient. Maybe just this once their operator didn't notice the blip on the screen.'

'You're grabbing at straws, Christopher,' the PM said. 'I think I'd rather go with your earlier suggestion than simply deny all knowledge. Washington won't believe a word of it, but they might buy the idea that the attack was mounted by a renegade ex-SAS man.'

'There's still the flight to Grand Cayman,' Hanson said.

'This man – I've forgotten his name . . .'

'Docherty.'

'He could have got hold of a helicopter on the black market, couldn't he?'

'Probably, but . . .' Hanson paused. He had spent the last couple of hours thinking about how to pursue Bazua, and had come to the conclusion that in Mexico the only real help he could offer Shepreth was Jamie Docherty. Neither the Americans nor the local authorities could be used for obvious reasons, and the chances of getting the PM to sanction another SAS operation on the North American mainland were non-existent. 'If the worst comes to the worst,' he said, 'then we can throw him to the Americans, but I'm sure you'll agree that the optimal outcome for everybody – remains the elimination of Bazua and the seizure of his records. And I think Docherty can still be useful in that regard. He knows Mexico.'

The PM shook his head, but there was a thin smile on his face. 'And what do we tell the Americans in the meantime?'

'Tell them you don't know what happened but that you're determined to get to the bottom of it. Imply that some of our people may have taken matters into their own hands. He should understand that – his own people are doing it all the time.'

The rap on the door woke Docherty, and there was a moment of disorientation before he remembered where he was. They had landed in a secluded corner of the empty airport soon after five, and a minibus had driven them not much more than a kilometre to the hotel, where he had just about managed to set Isabel's mind at rest, and bless the fact that he was no longer in command of anyone, before collapsing on to the soft bed. Wynwood and Shepreth had no doubt been up for hours, reporting back to their superiors in the UK.

It was Wynwood at the door, and by the look of his red-ringed eyes he hadn't had any sleep.

'What time is it?' Docherty asked between yawns.

'Nearly nine. Yes, I know,' he added in response to Docherty's look of reproach, 'but we're off in about half an hour. Fancy a cup of coffee before we go?'

'Sure,' Docherty said. He had not only come to admire the big Welsh lunk over the past few days – he had grown to like him too.

He reached for his only pair of trousers, thinking that some of his increasingly hard-earned fee from Gustavo Macías would have to be spent on another set of clothes. Downstairs the hotel restaurant was still serving breakfast, but the two men just ordered coffees and took them out to one of the gaily coloured metal tables which sat beneath the palms around the empty pool. As they lowered themselves gingerly into the metal chairs a couple of buses full of tourists swept past on their way to the airport.

'They're not wasting much time bringing you home,' Docherty observed.

'No,' Wynwood agreed. 'The other three are pretty pissed off – they were hoping for at least a couple of days on the beach.'

'But you weren't?'

'I've just got married,' Wynwood said, as if that explained it.

Remembering the first few weeks of his marriage to Isabel, Docherty guessed it did. 'Congratulations,' he said.

Wynwood smiled. 'So what'll you do now?' he asked.

Docherty shrugged. 'God knows. Or Shep does.'

'I wish we could have finished it,' Wynwood said.

'Aye,' Docherty agreed, thinking about Carmen. 'But then think how happy we'd have made the bastard's competitors.'

Wynwood grinned. 'So tell me – is there life after the SAS?'

It was phrased like a joke, but Docherty knew it was a serious question – one he'd asked himself often enough before his retirement. 'Aye, there is. And a family helps. But it's hard at first. I think if you've been doing something long enough, retirement usually is.'

'Yeah,' Wynwood agreed, thinking of his dad, who still got up wanting to go down the pit, even though the nearest working one was now a couple of hundred miles away.

'Any idea what you're going to do when the time comes?' Docherty asked.

'None,' Wynwood replied cheerfully. Over the Scot's shoulder he could see Blackie and Bonnie ogling one of the chambermaids in the foyer, and a few seconds later

Stoneham appeared in the doorway. 'The car's here, boss,' he said, walking towards them. 'Good to work with you,' he told Docherty, extending a hand.

'Likewise,' Docherty said, taking it. 'Give my love to Hereford,' he told them both, and a couple of minutes later he watched as their car disappeared in the direction of the airport. They'd sleep all the way home, he thought, and when they got there everything would seem a bit unreal for the next few weeks. They were the SAS – they did things other people thought only happened in films. A picture of the Brecon Beacons filled his mind's eye, and then his old CO's face on that night in the Glasgow pub when he'd asked Docherty to go and look for John Reeve in Bosnia. He could see the Dame lying beside the lorry, the wonder of death in his eyes, and he could hear Razor mixing proverbs in the scrape above the airbase at Rio Gallegos. There was no fool like a friend in need.

He missed it all right. But he wouldn't have given up the life he had now to get it back, even if he could.

It was still only nine-thirty, but he felt wide awake now, and decidedly hungry. The hotel served up the sort of English breakfast which reminded him of his childhood – the holy trinity of bacon, eggs and toast, his dad had used to call it – and which Isabel was reluctant to sanction at home. He was on his second cup of coffee when Carmen appeared in the doorway, eyes blinking in the strong sunlight.

She was also wearing yesterday's fighting clothes, and they didn't look any better on her than his did on him. Her eyes looked more subdued than tired, and they sat in silence for several moments waiting for her coffee to arrive.

When it did she tore open two sachets of sugar and stirred them in. 'I want to say something,' she said without looking up. 'Yesterday . . . when you promised to keep looking – I know that you had to say that or . . .' She looked up. 'I can't hold you to that promise. You have a life of your own to live.'

He smiled. 'Thanks,' he said. 'But if it's at all possible I intend to keep looking. The problem is, I'm just a private citizen these days – I don't have the resources we'll probably need to trace Bazua's movements.'

'I know,' she said with a sigh. 'Neither do I.'

Assistant Secretary of State Calvin Stahoviak had come in to Foggy Bottom that morning expecting nothing more than a chance to catch up on his paperwork. Instead he was listening to a crisis call from John Holzman, the US Ambassador in Bogotá.

'You know people who start spraying you with saliva when they get really mad?' Holzman was asking him. 'Well, Domínguez is one of those. By the time he'd finished I felt like I'd been caught in the rain. But this is serious,' he went on, hearing Stahoviak's grunt of amusement, 'and they really are pissed with us. Their goddam honour has been insulted. At the moment they're just venting, but unless they get some real satisfaction we're in for trouble. Just lodging a protest isn't going to cut it this time.'

'What will?' Stahoviak asked. He was wondering which particular bunch of morons in either Intelligence or the military was responsible for sticking a hornet up Bogotá's backside.

'The sight of heads rolling,' Holzman said. 'And if you

want really happy people then mount them on stakes and mail them to the Presidential Palace.'

'Shit,' Stahoviak murmured, more to himself than the ambassador. 'I'll get back to you, John,' he said, and resumed eating the chocolate croissant he had picked up *en route* from home. The accompanying frappuccino had seemed like a good idea on the sweltering street, but in the chronically over-air-conditioned State Department offices it almost made him shiver.

He sipped at it nevertheless, wondering how the Colombians might express their anger. There were the old diplomatic stand-bys of course, like rabble-rousing among the other Latin American countries at the OAS or the UN, but with Colombia there was also the added problem of never knowing quite who you were dealing with. Official government, cartels, guerrillas – they all seemed willing to help each other out when it came to sticking knives in poor old Uncle Sam.

He finished the croissant, reached for the phone, and spent the next hour tracking down the guilty party, only to find that it was the fucking Brits.

Stahoviak felt almost as intrigued as angered by this piece of information. What in God's name did they think they were doing shooting up islands in America's backyard? 'Are you one hundred per cent certain?' he asked his source at the Customs Service.

'Yep. Our AWACS tracked their chopper from the Caymans to a point just north of Providencia – consistent with a pick-up from a boat – and then back again.'

'So what did they want on Providencia?'

'Probably Angel Bazua.' The Customs man explained

who Bazua was, and why the British in particular had a grudge against him.

'Did they get him?' Stahoviak asked.

'No idea. But the AWACS tracked another flight – a large jet this time – which left Providencia for northern Mexico at around the same time. Bazua could have been on that.'

'OK, thanks,' Stahoviak said, and hung up. The Brits might have a good reason for running amok on Providencia, but that was neither here nor there. This was American turf, and they didn't get to play on it without an invitation. Someone would have to do some tough talking, and it might as well be the President.

He asked his secretary to connect him to the White House.

Carmen and Docherty were still sitting in the chairs by the pool when Shepreth found them. From the look of suppressed excitement on the younger man's face, the Scot guessed it was good news. Maybe Bazua's plane had crashed.

'We're still on the case,' Shepreth said.

'We?' Docherty asked.

'Ah,' Shepreth said, smiling. 'I've been asked to put a proposition to you. Her Majesty's Government would like to offer you a twenty-grand consultancy fee. For assistance in the field.'

Docherty's surprise was short-lived. After all, who else did they have available? They needed people with military experience when it came to taking on the private armies of the drug barons, and while they might get away with using the regulars on an isolated island like Providencia, the Mexican interior would be a very different kettle of fish. And if things went wrong he would be the scapegoat on the spot.

He saw that Carmen was waiting anxiously for his reply, and fought back the temptation to refuse the bastards' money. If he did they'd probably spend it all on raising cabinet ministers' salaries. 'So when do we leave?' he asked.

Shepreth looked at his watch. 'I'm off in half an hour – the quick way, via Miami. But since Bazua has probably told our American Mr X about your visit it seemed wiser to book you and Carmen via Honduras. There's a plane to La Ceiba at four this afternoon, and from there you can pick up a connection to Tegucigalpa. It'll give you both time to pick up some clothes,' he added with a smile. 'The tickets will be waiting for you at the Islena Airlines desk. You OK for money?'

'Aye,' Docherty said – he still had a wad of Gustavo Macías's traveller's cheques burning a hole in his back pocket. 'I'll phone your flat first thing tomorrow morning.'

Shepreth got up, hovered for a moment as if uncertain whether to give Carmen a goodbye kiss, then just placed a hand lightly on her shoulder before turning and striding off.

'He's sweet on you,' Docherty observed.

'I know,' she said noncommittally, but there was pleasure in her eyes.

In London it was almost five in the evening, and the sun was making a last-ditch attempt to put in an appearance. The Prime Minister took a deep breath and picked up the receiver. 'Bill,' he said, as if the call was a pleasant surprise.

'John,' the voice on the other end began, the southern US twang adding a layer of amiability to his tone, 'I suppose you can guess the reason for this call.'

There didn't seem much point in simply feigning ignorance – that would just put the President's back up. 'I hear there's been some excitement in the Caribbean,' the Prime Minister said mildly.

'And is the British government claiming responsibility?' the President asked, both irritation and amusement in his voice.

'As of this moment,' the PM said carefully, 'the official position of the British government is to deny any involvement in the events which took place last night.'

The President sighed audibly. 'OK,' he said. 'But would you like to tell me – off the record – just what the hell is going on?'

'I'd be delighted. Angel Bazua has been using his so-called prison as a base for both drug trafficking and other activities hostile to the interests of the British Crown. We have made repeated requests for American cooperation in confronting the Colombian government and all have been refused.'

'The DEA tells me he falls just outside their top ten of major-league players, and our policy, as you know . . .'

'Our information differs,' the PM said, as gently as he could manage. It was time to bite the bullet, as his audience would no doubt say. 'And we think we know why it differs,' he went on. 'We believe that Bazua has an American protector – or even protectors – someone highly placed in one of your agencies responsible for combating the cartels. And once we had realized that this man or men existed . . .' He let the words hang for a second. 'Well, I'm sure you'll understand that we had no choice but to act unilaterally.'

There was silence on the other end.

'Mr President?'

'You don't know the identity of this man? Or men?'

'No, but I can send you everything we have which points to his existence.'

'Thank you. I'll look into it.'

'And I shall start an investigation into the possibility that British forces' equipment was illegally used in a raid against this Colombian island. And I shall tell the Colombians that if we indeed find that this has occurred, then we will build them a prison to replace the one that was destroyed. I'm sure prison design is much the same the world over.'

The President couldn't resist a guffaw. 'I'll be getting back to you, John,' he said, and hung up.

A few moments later he was on the phone to Langley, thinking that if there was one thing he didn't need right now it was a goddam Intelligence scandal. Not with the election less than four months away.

Shepreth spent most of his two flights, not to mention the one-hour stopover in Miami, thinking about Carmen. He had got used to her being there, a thought that rather frightened him, particularly since he was far from sure that she reciprocated his feelings. Sometimes he was convinced that her emotions were so overloaded by worry for her sister that she didn't really see him at all, or at least not as anything more than someone to help her find Marysa.

His plane touched down in the Mexican capital soon after six. He took a taxi to his flat, asked the driver to wait while he showered and changed, then directed him to San Angel and the Luz de la Luna. Arriving between sets, he found Ted Vaughan alone at his usual table, drinking in the Mingus record that was playing on the sound system.

Vaughan raised both eyebrows when he saw Shepreth. 'I'm not sure I should be seen with you,' he said, 'but since I can't wait to hear all the fucking details of your people's latest brainstorm, I suppose I'll have to be.'

'I'll tell you everything,' Shepreth promised, 'but not here. Fancy another drive up the hill?'

'Sure,' Vaughan said, getting up and draining his glass. 'I was just about to leave anyway – I've got an interdepartmental briefing in a couple of hours. I only came down here to get a fix of the real world before listening to those turkeys talk.' He glanced sideways at Shepreth. 'You ever think you're in the wrong job?'

'A little more with each passing day,' the Englishman said as they reached the street. The same group of youths as last time seemed to be practising with their skateboards. Maybe they never went home.

'I think I've reached th[...]tainty stage,' Vaughan said.

As they got in[...] car Shepreth was thinking that he had neve[...] his friend sound quite so jaded. He knew th[...] kid Vaughan had seen his family torn a[...] crack epidemic, and he guessed that if the [...]an didn't feel he was making a difference in the [...] against drugs then the job would have little appeal. Vaughan wasn't someone who liked playing games. He was clever, but he worked from the heart.

They drove up to the Plaza San Jacinto, and Vaughan found a parking space on a nearby side-street. As they strolled round the noisy square Shepreth filled the American in on everything that had happened since their last meeting – from Docherty's discovery that Bazua had the Argentinian Army's Dirty War files to the raid on Providencia early that morning.

Vaughan was not happy to hear that Bazua might have an American protector. 'You don't have a shred of proof,' he argued, but his tone lacked conviction.

'We don't,' Shepreth agreed, 'but it's the only thing that makes sense.'

'Shit,' Vaughan said, as much in sorrow as in anger. He shook his head. 'It sure would explain a lot,' he murmured.

'Do you know where Bazua is now?' Shepreth asked.

'We've got a pretty good idea. The Caravelle was seen coming in to land on a dry lake bed in south-western Chihuahua. We'd already tipped off the Mexican Feds after your message came through, but this place is in the middle of nowhere – it's still Indian country, for Chrissake – and they still had about twenty miles to go when they met the bad guys in a conv[illegible] coming the other way. A bunch of Ignacio Payán's men, comp[illegible] with a local police escort. There was a stand-off, but the r[illegible] had only about a third as many men, and they backed do[illegible]

'Was Bazua with the bad guys?'

'If he got on the plane in Providencia [illegible] been. The Feds found it empty, and there wer[illegible] have [illegible]er roads out of there.'

'Were there any women?'

'No one mentioned any.'

Shepreth hoped that was all it was. He didn't think it was possible to throw someone out of a pressurized jetliner, but then for all they knew Bazua had left the women behind on Providencia. 'So where does this Payán hang out?' he asked the American.

'Would you believe a monastery?' Vaughan said. 'Name of Ixmíala. It's one of the ones the Spanish built in the first fifty years they were here. You know the kind: half monastery, half fortress.'

'I know,' Shepreth said. He'd visited a few during his off-duty explorations of the Mexican countryside. 'I'll need the precise location,' he told Vaughan.

'You're still after the bastard then?'

'Yep. And a satellite photo of the monastery wouldn't go amiss.'

'I'll do what I can,' Vaughan promised him. He flashed his even teeth in a smile. 'If you're right, and some bastard in Washington is keeping the rain off Bazua's head, then I want to be one of the first to know his name.'

Soon after ten the following morning Shepreth, Docherty and Carmen were gathered round the map which the MI6 man had spread across the Scot's hotel bed. 'The DEA think he's holed up here,' Shepreth said, pointing to a spot in the mountains some thirty kilometres west of the small Chihuahua town of Norogachic. 'He somehow persuaded the local state government to sell him one of the old fortress monasteries. It's in the mountains, and accessible only by dirt road or helicopter.'

'Tarahumara country,' Docherty murmured reminiscently. He had a vague memory of the name, but couldn't picture the town. What he remembered were mountains that glowed in the sunset, clear rivers running through canyons deeper than Arizona's most famous tourist attraction, and a people who had so far been spared the two-edged sword of progress. It had been like visiting the world when it was young.

'You've been there?' Carmen asked, surprised.

'Aye. I spent about six weeks there twenty years ago. Did a lot of hiking in the mountains. It's a beautiful place.'

'I don't suppose you've got any contacts in the area?' Shepreth asked hopefully.

Docherty shrugged. 'It was twenty years ago,' he said again, 'but who knows? Most of the time I was there I stayed with one Indian family, and I don't suppose they've moved very far. It's an enclosed world.'

'Not any longer,' Shepreth said drily. 'The drug people have moved into the area in a big way over the last five years. And not just to establish secluded stopovers for stuff heading north – they've got the Tarahumara into the poppy-growing business.'

'There's hardly any decent soil in those mountains,' Docherty said. 'They probably need the money to feed their children.'

'A few of them may be making money,' Shepreth said, 'but some are getting killed, and a lot more are getting beaten up. According to Vaughan it's like the Wild West revisited.'

'That's a shame,' Docherty said.

Shepreth was examining the map again. 'Where exactly did you stay?' he asked.

'I was based in a village near Batopilas,' Docherty said, pointing it out. 'That's where the family lived.'

'It's almost next door,' Shepreth said.

'It's about seventy-five miles away by dirt track,' Docherty corrected him. 'Or a two-day hike across the mountains.' The Tarahumara were famous for their walking, he remembered. Some of their young men could give the SAS a run for their money across the Brecon Beacons.

'Why would this drug lord want to live somewhere like this?' Carmen wanted to know.

'He's also got a big villa in Ciudad Juárez,' Shepreth told her. 'We don't know how much of the year he spends in the monastery.'

'He probably likes hunting,' Docherty murmured, and looked up from the map. 'It's not a small area, but the Tarahumara are – or were – a tight-knit community, and someone in Batopilas will know what's happening in Norogachic. I'll get up there and nose around – with any luck the Torreses will still be there.' Paco, the teenage son with whom he had spent a week hiking in the wilderness, would be over forty by now. 'I think you two should head for Divisadero,' he went on, pointing it out on the map. 'It's on the Copper Canyon Railway, just above the Copper Canyon itself. They were building a couple of swanky hotels when I was there, and you can enjoy the view for a couple of days while I do all the work. I'll get in touch when I have something.'

'Sounds reasonable,' Shepreth said, his dislike of the enforced inaction more than offset by the thought of the company he would be keeping.

'OK then,' Docherty said, 'seconds out, round two. And I expect I'll be needing a handgun,' he added as an afterthought.

14

As the small plane touched down on the runway at Hidalgo del Parral the mountains to the west were silhouetted against the deep-red sky. Docherty descended the rickety steps and headed across the tarmac towards the taxi rank, where several welcoming smiles were competing for the right to fleece the gringo. The lucky winner drove him straight to the town's best hotel, sorely disappointed by the Scot's ability to remark in fluent Spanish that he'd noticed the faulty meter.

After eating an excellent *comida corrida* at a nearby restaurant Docherty took a stroll round the town centre. Hidalgo del Parral was famous for being the site of Pancho Villa's assassination, and the habit of violence seemed to have lived on in the groups of surly-looking youths who watched him walk by, pursuing him with menacing murmurs of '*Gringo*!' But then he didn't suppose there was much else in the way of entertainment on offer.

Soon after dawn next morning he walked down to the bus station, where a red-eyed driver pointed him in the direction of the pick-up point for those heading west into the Sierra Tarahumara. Half an hour later he was sharing a wooden bench in the back of a four-wheel-drive Dodge pick-up with a mixed bag of Mexican farmers and forestry workers. They took on more passengers in the old mining town of San Francisco del Oro, and then, on a rapidly deteriorating road, began slowly climbing into the mountains. About eight dusty, bone-rattling hours later, Docherty stepped gingerly down on to the square at Batopilas, a small town surrounded by soaring canyon walls. His body might be aching, but he felt that familiar intoxication of the spirit which only the world's high places seemed to conjure up.

He bought and consumed a couple of *empanadas* on a bench in front of the old adobe church, then went in search of transport for the last few kilometres to Uruáchic. A forestry official answered his thumb, and an hour later he was being dropped off in another smaller square in another smaller canyon. The village had changed little in twenty years, though there were more shiny pick-ups in evidence, not to mention electricity pylons. Docherty walked down to the store which the Torres family had run, and ducked in through the low doorway. It took a few seconds for his eyes to get used to the dark, but there it all was – the worn leather saddles hanging from the wooden beams, the ubiquitous crates of Coca-Cola, the hessian sacks full of maize and beans.

He realized the man behind the counter was staring at him. A second later, they recognized each other.

'Jaime!'

'Paco!'

The two men hugged, and stared at each other some more. The lithe teenager with whom Docherty had gone hiking in the mountains had not put on much weight, but his face was gaunter, and his dark eyes seemed more hooded than before. 'Come,' Paco said in Spanish, 'we'll go to my house. It is time to close anyway.'

He insisted on carrying Docherty's bag as they walked the couple of hundred metres to the farmhouse on the outskirts of the village. Paco's mother, Juanita, was a Tarahumara, but his father, Fidel, was half-Mexican, and they had inherited the house from the Mexican side of his family. The outbuilding where Docherty had slept for several weeks was still standing, dwarfed by the canyon wall behind it.

Juanita and Fidel were sitting out on the porch, enjoying the last hour of sunshine before shadows filled the canyon. They looked old now, though they were probably only in their early sixties, and it took both of them a while to recognize Docherty. When they did, huge smiles creased their leathery faces.

Another woman was standing in the doorway. 'This is my wife Siniya,' Paco said, and the woman shook his hand, curiosity in her large, dark eyes. 'You will eat with us?' she said in halting Spanish, reminding Docherty that a lot of the Tarahumara spoke only their own language.

'I'd be honoured,' he said.

'And then the two of us will go walking in the mountains,' Paco insisted, before he saw the reproachful look in his wife's eyes. 'Or perhaps not,' he added, and everyone laughed.

Three children joined them at the huge table inside. His two eldest sons, Paco explained, were both married and living in Batopilas. He asked Docherty whether he was married, and was clearly pleased with the answer. No doubt he remembered that the Scot had been lugging around a broken heart the last time they met.

Between mouthfuls of bean stew and the local maize beer the adults swapped stories of the past twenty years, while the younger children stared at Docherty through saucer-like eyes. It was not until afterwards, when Paco and Docherty were alone on the porch with second bottles of Tesquina, that the question came up of what had brought Docherty back to Uruáchic. 'It is wonderful to see you again,' Paco said, 'but there is a seriousness in your eyes, my friend. I do not think you have come to the Sierra for a holiday.'

Docherty grunted. 'I wish I had,' he said. 'But first, tell me what is happening to the Tarahumara. I have a friend who tells me that there has been trouble here in the last few years.'

Paco shook his head, but not in denial. 'Much trouble,' he agreed. 'It is the drugs, of course, or the people who deal in them, and it has been going on for a long time now. The men first came with the packets of seeds, and they promised ten times more for a single crop than anyone could earn from corn or beans.' He shrugged. 'Some people planted the seeds,' he said, 'and at first they made a lot of money. Each year that the rains failed a few more would decide to grow the marijuana or the poppies, because otherwise they were afraid their families would starve. But they did not get rich – the buyers offered less and less for each crop, and if anyone refused then men with guns would visit them. They have frightened teachers away from several schools and they stopped the building of a clinic.' He stood up. 'Come, I want to show you something.'

They walked down the empty street towards the dimly lit centre of the village. Paco opened the wooden door of the small adobe church and went in, lighting a candle from the supply inside the door. He walked to one side and held it up to the wall, which Docherty could see was pock-marked by bullet holes, and then held it above the deeply stained wooden floorboards in the aisle. 'There was a meeting here six months ago, a meeting of farmers to discuss how they could fight back against the drug people. And in the middle of it three men walked in with guns and opened fire. Four of the farmers were killed, and many more injured.'

'What did the police do?' Docherty asked.

'Nothing.'

'And the state government, the *Federales*.'

Paco shook his head. 'They make noise about stopping the drugs, but that is mostly for the *Nortamericanos*.' He smiled. 'They spray the crops, pretending they are killing them, but they are spraying water.'

'The drug people – do they have one leader?'

'In this area it is a man named Ignacio Payán. He has a fortress in the mountains near Norogachic.'

Docherty felt both satisfaction and a twinge of guilt. 'I have business with this man,' he began, and Paco's face dropped. 'He has kidnapped a woman, the sister of my friend. And he is protecting a man named Angel Bazua, who killed many of my wife's friends.'

Paco was smiling again. 'You are still a warrior, yes?' he said.

'Old habits die hard,' Docherty admitted. 'I need to get into this fortress and get the woman back. I will also kill Bazua and Payán if I can.'

'All by yourself?'

'Another man is waiting with my friend in Creel, but that is all.'

'These are vicious men,' Paco said, looking down at the bloodstained floor. 'I have a cousin in Norogachi,' he said. 'He has been trying to organize people against Payán for several years, and though they have run his truck off the road and given him several beatings he refuses to accept defeat.'

'I'd like to meet him,' Docherty said.

On the same day that the Scot had taken his flight to Hidalgo del Parral, Carmen and Shepreth had flown further north, to the larger city of Chihuahua, and early next morning they boarded the Vista Tren for their five-hour journey to Creel on the famous Copper Canyon Railway. The train was predictably full of tourists, most of whom were travelling all the way to Los Mochis on the Pacific coast, but the two of them made no attempt to socialize. Carmen just stared out of the window at the green ranching country and distant mountains, while Shepreth read a novel he had found in his hotel room the previous night.

At first sight Creel looked like a set for a Hollywood Western – streets of log cabins complete with ranchers and Indians, a trading store and a Jesuit mission. The bank, post office and hotels looked a little more modern, and the forest managers in their gleaming new pick-ups looked as if they'd strayed into the picture by accident. The Nuevo looked like the best hotel on offer, and after taking two rooms they wandered round the town, ate dinner and went to bed.

There was still no word from Docherty the following morning, and Shepreth managed to persuade Carmen that going on one of the organized minibus trips to an impressive waterfall would be better than sitting around waiting. Through the first hour of the four-hour journey she felt as listless as the day before, but gradually the brightness of the colours and the clarity of the mountain air revived her spirits, awakening a feeling in her chest and stomach which she eventually recognized as simple happiness. This realization brought guilt in its wake – how could she feel happy when she knew what Marysa was going through? – but deep down in her soul Carmen knew that at that moment there was nothing more she could be doing.

The Basaseachic Falls, which their guide proudly announced were the highest in North America, were certainly beautiful, but as Carmen stared at the tumbling shroud of water she felt something more than mere wonder. The Falls were like a reaffirmation. The water fell and fell, and life went on.

That same morning Paco took Docherty into Batopilas and found him a lift to Norogachi. The road up the canyon was in no better state than it had been the day before, and the bottoms of the passengers in the back of the pick-up rarely spent more than a few consecutive seconds on the wooden benches. Docherty found such physical preoccupations almost a relief – he had woken that morning with thoughts of an old Western on his mind and had instantly realized why. In the film, which he remembered from his schooldays, John Wayne had spent years looking for a niece who had been captured by Indians. And when he had finally found the grown-up girl his first inclination had been to kill her, because her years as an Apache squaw had turned her into one of them.

What had happened to Carmen's sister? Docherty wondered. Could anyone come all the way back from where she had been?

The pick-up reached Norogachic just before eleven. He recognized it now – the two barrack-like buildings sandwiching the adobe church with its corrugated-iron roof, the convent school and the small hospital. If he walked a little further down the road he would be able to see the Copper Canyon stretching and deepening into the distance.

He walked the other way, following the directions Paco had given him to a small adobe house near the river. As he walked towards the door two men emerged, one of them cradling an AK47 in his arms.

Docherty stopped. 'I would like to see Manolo Torres,' he said, reaching slowly into his pocket. 'I have a letter of introduction from his cousin.'

The one without the gun came forward to take it, then disappeared inside the house. A few moments later another man emerged, gesturing Docherty forward. 'I am Manolo,' he said. He had the same mouth as Paco, but his nose was sharper, the eyes even darker. And he looked more wary, which probably wasn't surprising.

He led Docherty through to the yard behind the house, stopping on the way to pour his guest a cup of coffee from the pot on the stove. A long bench stood up against the house and a few feet away an antique typewriter sat on a collapsible metal table. On the other side of the yard two women were sitting outside an outhouse, rolling ground corn into tortilla balls.

'I remember your first visit,' Manolo said conversationally. 'I was only about ten.'

He didn't have the full use of his left arm, Docherty noticed, and wondered if that was a consequence of the beatings he had received. 'Your family treated me very well,' he said, conscious of how inadequate the words sounded.

Manolo nodded. 'So what do you want from me?' he asked. 'Paco says you are an enemy of Payán, and that you need help, but help with what?'

Docherty began at the beginning.

The minibus got back to Creel just before dark, and after showering off the dust Carmen and Shepreth walked down the main street in search of somewhere nice to eat. Although it had been a gruelling day neither felt tired, and both were aware that they felt easier with the other, as if some invisible bridge had been crossed. In the restaurant they worked their way through a bottle of wine and talked about everything but the reason they were here in the mountains of northern Mexico, only realizing that the establishment was closing when the proprietor started stacking chairs on the other tables.

Not wanting the evening to end, they walked to the empty station, where the risen moon was reflecting in the rails. She took his arm as they walked down the dusty platform, and as they turned by the signal she stopped him and looked up into his eyes.

He leant down to kiss her, gently at first, and then, as their tongues entwined, with mounting passion.

He cradled her face in his hands and looked into her eyes. Like a little boy seeking reassurance, she thought, but there was kindness there too, and desire. She took one of his hands and placed it over her left breast, so he could feel the hardening of her nipple, and they kissed again. 'I don't want to sleep alone tonight,' she told him.

'That makes two of us.'

They walked back across the square, fighting and losing the temptation to run as they reached the main street. They rushed in through the hotel doors like a whirlwind, laughing their way up the stairs and clawing most of each other's clothes off before he realized they'd forgotten to shut the door.

That done, they stood there embracing each other's nakedness for a minute and more before lying down together, kissing and feeling each other's excitement mount. As he finally entered her, Carmen had a sudden vision of her sister's face, but when she opened her eyes to his all she saw was the mirror of her own desire.

Shortly after darkness filled the canyon two young Tarahumara arrived with the horses. Docherty, who had not ridden for more than a decade, mounted his with some trepidation, but the animal greeted him with nothing more fearsome than a stamping of the front foot. Manolo, who had abandoned his jeans for a more traditional-looking loincloth, looked as if he'd been born in the saddle.

They rode west down the canyon, keeping to the southern side of the swift-flowing river. The dirt track on the far bank would have allowed a faster pace, but Manolo was wary of meeting a four-wheel drive full of either Payán's men or the local police. If anything went wrong he didn't want anyone to know he'd been out.

After about an hour they left the canyon floor, turning up a long and gently sloping cleft which brought them out on to a moonlit rim about five hundred metres above the barely visible river. Another valley, steeper this time, led them up to a dry and broken plateau, and in a niche among the rocks Manolo made a fire and heated up maize coffee to wash down their tortillas. As they sat eating, the Tarahumara, his face thrown into stark relief by the firelight, recounted the story of his people's struggle with Payán and the authorities. He didn't glorify his own role; in fact he seemed genuinely amused by the fact that he had become a living symbol of the resistance. And he made no attempt to hide his feeling that they were fighting a losing battle.

Which feeling, Docherty thought, probably explained why the man was taking a chance on helping him. If the gringo proved to be a superman, then they would all benefit, and if he proved a damp squib, then the Tarahumara would be no worse off than they had been before he arrived.

It was just gone eleven when they put out the fire, checked that the horses were secure and started across the broken plateau on foot. The moon was high now, spreading its light across a vast panorama of mountains, and for the best part of an hour Docherty followed Manolo across the rocky landscape, clambering in and out of deep clefts in the rock, striding across stone slopes which time had worn as smooth as a marble floor.

They were heading down a dry stream bed towards a group of stunted trees when Manolo suddenly stopped, so that Docherty almost banged into him. Over the other man's shoulder he had a fleeting glimpse of something slithering away into the rocks. 'We are almost there,' Manolo said softly, as if that were the reason he had halted, and a couple of minutes later they were looking out across the head of a deep valley. Almost directly in front of them the crenellated walls of the Ixmíala fortress monastery glowed in the moonlight.

Their view of the walled compound was from the side. On the right, nestling against the head of the valley, were two buildings, the church rising up behind the two-storey living quarters. A wide flight of steps led down from the front of both buildings to a large open space, and an arched gateway in the wall to the left disgorged a dirt track which disappeared into the darkness of the valley beyond.

Two four-wheel drives and an R44 Astro helicopter were parked on the open ground which fronted the monastery buildings; this space, Docherty remembered, was called an atrium. The stub of stone in the middle would once have supported a cross, and the broken towers at each corner of the wall were what remained of the chapels. Atriums were intended for the use of overflow services, though how the local clergy ever expected to fill a church in a place like this was beyond him.

He indicated to Manolo that he wanted to move left, for a better view of the front of the buildings. The Indian nodded, and led the way.

Docherty's intentions were purely professional, but he couldn't help spending a few seconds admiring the front of the church. The details of the carved door and stone columns were hidden by distance and darkness, but the gabled belfry, with its seven bells still hanging in the seven arches high above the door, possessed the sort of simply beauty which he had always loved.

Almost reluctantly he trained the SAS nightscope on the building which stood to the right of the church. There was an open chapel at the front, and the glow of light was visible through an open door in its inner wall. As he watched, several figures suddenly walked into that glow, almost eclipsing it. There were four of them, all men, all in uniform.

'The local *Federales*,' Manolo sneered.

They climbed into one of the pick-ups, which reversed before speeding off down the valley road in a moonlit cloud of dust. Docherty directed the nightscope back towards the interior of the building and kept his eye on the inner glow for several minutes. No one extinguished it by shutting doors, and soon the lights were going out on the second floor.

Manolo put words to what the Scot was thinking. 'There would be no trouble getting in,' he said. 'We have sometimes thought about such an attack ourselves. But where would we run to afterwards? We have to live in this land.'

Docherty didn't, but then getting away from it didn't look much easier. As the two of them walked back across the plateau, reclaimed their horses and rode back down to the canyon, he went through their options. There didn't seem many to choose from.

Shepreth and Carmen emerged from the hotel room at about nine, both wondering what had hit them. They had spent more of the night making love than sleeping, but it wasn't just that – neither he nor she had ever been gripped by such a desperate passion. It might be wonderful – it was wonderful – but it also felt almost unreal, and that feeling was exacerbated by the receptionist's news that there was a message from a Señor Docherty.

'Arriving early afternoon,' was all it said.

They had breakfast, stared at each other for a while, then went back to bed.

They came back downstairs soon after noon, and Shepreth called up Vaughan from the booth in the lobby. 'I'm in the Nuevo Hotel in Creel,' he warned the American. Privacy was not guaranteed on calls originating anywhere in the Sierra Tarahumara.

'Your client also seems to be in Chihuahua,' Vaughan told him. 'According to my head office he's trying to do a deal with them, a cross-border deal. Know what I mean?'

Shepreth guessed that Bazua was trying to buy immunity with the Dirty War files. 'And are your people interested?' he asked.

'Hard to say,' Vaughan told him. 'But if you want to make a deal with him yourself I wouldn't waste any time.'

'Right. Thanks, Ted.' Shepreth hung up the phone, feeling worried. If Bazua dealt his way across the border then MI6's hopes of getting hold of the Dirty War records would disappear. And there was also a very good chance that he would consider any current female companions surplus to requirements.

'Bad news?' Carmen asked, appearing beside him.

He had just finished telling her what Vaughan had told him when Docherty came through the hotel doorway. The Scot looked rather dusty, having spent the last four hours bouncing north on the mail bus from Batopilas.

They went upstairs to Shepreth's room, which didn't look as if it had been slept in. And there was also a subtle change in the way his two partners were looking at each other, Docherty realized. As Shepreth told him the news from Mexico City he grinned at the two of them, feeling pleased for them both.

'We can go in tomorrow night,' he said when the MI6 man was finished, and went through what he'd discovered over the previous couple of days about the Tarahumara situation in general and Payán's fortress in particular. 'They won't take part in any assault,' he said, referring to the Indians, 'and with good reason – their people would bear the consequences. Unlike us, they haven't got another home to run to. But they'll help us with intelligence – Manolo is talking to some of the women who are driven up to do Payán's cleaning and laundry – and they'll lend us horses. Can you two ride?'

They both could. Shepreth had learned during a short and boring posting in the Middle East, Carmen during family visits to an uncle's ranch in the Magdalena Valley.

'Does that mean your sister can ride too?' Docherty asked her.

'Better than me.'

Shepreth was spreading out his map of the area. 'Where are we riding to?' he asked pointedly.

Docherty didn't answer right away. 'There's no problem getting in,' he began, 'but there's only one road out of the valley and not many more out of the area. Even if we got a good jump on them I don't reckon much of our chances of getting out of the state. And to get a good jump we'd have to either find and kill everyone in the place or find and destroy every means of communication they have – radio, mobile phones, whatever. Which doesn't seem very realistic.'

He looked from one face to the other. 'The alternative is an hour's walk across the mountains to where the horses will be waiting, and then an eighty-kilometre ride down the Copper Canyon to Divisadero here.' He pointed it out on the map.

'The train?' Shepreth said doubtfully. 'We'd be on board the damn thing for about seven hours, and even then we'd only have got as far as Chihuahua.'

'Aye,' Docherty admitted, 'but that's one of the things in its favour – no one'll be expecting us to just jump aboard a train that's headed for the state capital.'

'What's the other?' Carmen asked.

'The train will be full of tourists. If all they see tomorrow night is a couple of gringos, then they're going to have a much harder job picking us out from a train full of tourists than they would in a stolen pick-up. The Mexican police can't arrest a whole trainload of gringos.'

'That makes sense,' Shepreth admitted.

'Where do we go from Chihuahua?' Carmen asked.

'North, I suppose,' Docherty said. 'But let's get within striking distance before we worry about that one.'

15

Docherty landed on his toes and immediately sank to his haunches, his eyes scouring the fortress monastery's compound. The façade of the church rose above him, the gable belfry silhouetted against the stars, while away to his right the Astro helicopter and a Dodge pick-up stood almost side by side in the middle of the stone-paved atrium.

Shepreth dropped down beside him, and the two men slipped across the ten metres that separated them from the wooden doors of the church. As Docherty had feared, they were bolted from the inside. The sentry would have to be taken out.

Half an hour ago he had been sitting smoking a cigarette just inside the open chapel, not more than twenty metres from where they now stood. He was tempted by the thought of just walking round the corner, trusting that surprise would immobilize the man for the necessary few seconds, but only for a moment. Surprised people were hard to predict, and this one was carrying a noisy-looking Uzi.

Docherty and Shepreth were carrying silenced Browning High Powers and wearing borrowed AK47s slung across their backs. The Scot gestured what he wanted the MI6 man to do, and Shepreth obliged, first taking himself round the corner of the church façade furthest from the sentry and then starting to tap the stone with the butt of his Browning.

It was not a threatening noise, but it was food for the curious. Docherty heard the chair scrape back, the boots on stone, and waited in the doorway of the church.

Perhaps the man was careful not to walk too close to the façade, or perhaps he wasn't thinking about it one way or the other, but he was way beyond the reach of an outflung arm when he passed the doorway, and Docherty had no choice but to take him out with the gun. The Browning coughed twice, the silhouetted head jerked and the body concertinaed on to the flagstones, muffling the rattle of the Uzi which fell beneath it.

Docherty waited a few seconds but heard nothing, and went to drag the body into the church doorway, where it sat like a gruesome Guy Fawkes. He then inched his way along the façade for a view of the open chapel. The guard's seat was empty and a packet of cigarettes lay beside it on the floor.

Shepreth was back at his shoulder now. The two of them moved silently across the chapel and the adjoining empty room to the doorway which led into the inner courtyard or cloister. According to the intelligence Manolo had gathered from those who had visited or worked there, between four and six men habitually occupied the three rooms on the opposite side of the cloister from the church. Payán's room were almost directly above where they now stood, with windows facing out across the atrium and the valley below. His recent guest had also been given a room on the first floor, on the southern side of the cloister, above the rooms occupied by Payán's men. The woman – and there was only one – had the room next to Bazua's.

The cloister itself was dark, but there was a light on in one of the downstairs rooms, which hadn't been the case half an hour before.

Shit, Docherty thought. The light could mean anything from a change of sentries to an unexpected crap. There didn't seem much point in investigating, or at least not until they had finished their business on the second floor. Following his mental map, Docherty led Shepreth towards the nearest of the two flights of stairs.

As the two men emerged on to the upper veranda they could hear talking below them, which meant that at least two of Payán's men were awake.

The door to Bazua's room was slightly ajar, allowing a shaft of moonlight to illuminate the empty bed. Shepreth slipped inside, leaving Docherty to keep watch, and took out his pencil torch. There wasn't much to look at – only a bed, a washstand with a bowl of water, an open suitcase on the floor. He knelt down beside the latter and was wading through the clothes when he noticed the rectangular bulge in the lid pocket. He pulled the zip open, extracted the heavy ledger and shone the torch on a random page: '. . . *from 180 to 220 volts, two sessions with the submarine* . . .'

'I've got them,' he whispered to Docherty, undoing the buttons of his shirt so that he could carry the ledger inside it.

And after that things began to go rather quickly.

They were heading for the woman's room, and still about ten metres from the door, when it suddenly opened. A tall man stepped out, his nakedness exposed by the light shining out of the door, his half-erect penis sticking out in front of him like a miniature battering ram. He walked across to the edge of the veranda, where he stretched his arms above his head before dropping his hands on to the wooden rail.

Both Docherty and Shepreth recognized the man from Vaughan's photographs – it was Ignacio Payán.

The Mexican's face twitched in their direction, as if he had suddenly become aware that he was being watched, and his mouth was still opening when the two Brownings sent four bullets through his upper torso. He tottered for a moment, then collapsed on to the wooden floor with a loud thump, cutting off the conversation below.

Shepreth had already resumed his stride towards the woman's room, but he was still six metres away when Marysa Salcedo appeared in the doorway with Angel Bazua's forearm locked around her neck and what looked like a table fork pressed against her throat. They were both naked.

Shepreth stopped in his tracks about two metres ahead of Docherty.

'I'll kill her,' Bazua said, then shouted for help.

The odds could only get worse. Hoping Bazua wouldn't catch the movement in the shadows until it was too late, Docherty raised the Browning and fired, taking off the Argentinian's right ear in a spray of blood. The hand with the fork recoiled, jerking Marysa's head sideways and giving the Scot a clear second shot.

He sent it through Bazua's right eye, just as an answering shout came up from below.

Shepreth ran forward as Marysa was dragged down by the dead hand around her neck. She pulled herself violently away and then started pawing at his back in what looked like a paroxysm of grief.

Shepreth reached her side and pulled her gently away. Bazua's bare back was oozing blood from the cuts she had gouged with her nails.

'We've come to take you away,' he said in Spanish, half conscious of running feet below. 'Your sister Carmen's outside waiting for you,' he added.

At the word 'Carmen' she turned her face towards his as if she couldn't believe it. 'Carmen is here?' she asked.

'Yes,' Shepreth told her. She was as beautiful as her sister, he thought, but there hardly seemed room for anything but fear in her eyes.

Docherty emerged from the room with a handful of clothes just as feet sounded on the front stairs. As he scooped the naked woman up in his arms and half ran with her towards the other end of the building, Shepreth brought his AK47 into position and fired off a burst in the direction of the charging shadows on the stairs.

In the other stairwell Docherty was helping Marysa into her clothes, but hardly noticing what a lovely body she had. 'I can manage,' she told him curtly, and he realized that he'd been stupid to assume that Victoria Marín's psychological escape route would also be hers. Whatever arrangements Carmen's sister had made with herself for the sake of sanity, they obviously hadn't included a flight into dreamland.

'I'm ready,' she said.

Docherty indicated that Shepreth and Marysa should go first, and as the MI6 man led the woman down the stairs the Scot fired a last burst down the length of the veranda with his own AK47.

At the bottom of the stairs Shepreth found there was only one way out, and that led into the open cloister. He hesitated a second, saw no one on the far side, then grabbed Marysa's hand and made a dash for the door which led into the church. Finding it shut but mercifully unlocked, he heaved open the heavy wooden door, bundled her through and stepped in after her, just as bullets ricocheted around the stone columns to his left.

Docherty was still in the other doorway. The flash from the guns told him Payán's men were in the far corner of the cloister, and that to reach the outside world they would have to cross his line of fire. 'I'll keep the bastards busy,' he yelled to Shepreth. 'Get her over the wall and come back in through the open chapel.'

'OK,' Shepreth shouted back, just as the Scot opened up with a murderous burst from the AK47. He grabbed Marysa's hand and hurried her through the empty church. There were no seats, no pulpit – only a wide stone floor dappled by the silver moonlight from the windows.

Reaching the front door, he removed the long wooden bolt and gingerly pulled open one door. Docherty was still firing repeated bursts across the cloister next door, and if any of Payán's men had made it through to the atrium Shepreth couldn't hear or see them. He ran for the wall, one hand ready with the Browning, the other pulling Marysa after him. 'Carmen!' he shouted.

'I'm here,' came a hopeful voice from beyond the wall.

'Your sister's coming over,' he told her, cupping his hands like a stirrup to help her up on to the top of the wall. The moment her foot had left his hand he was heading back towards the buildings at a run, only slowing slightly as he turned the corner towards the entrance to the open chapel.

They were only about five metres apart when they saw each other, and their fingers must have clenched on the triggers at exactly the same moment. For the longest split second of his life Shepreth stared down the barrel of the Mexican's gun, then a hammer seemed to hit him on the chest, knocking him his back on to the edge of the steps. I'm dead, he thought, but the stars were still shining above him.

And then he realized that Bazua's ledger had saved him.

He stumbled to his feet and started forward again, a little more cautiously this time, his hand shaking slightly from the shock. The man he had killed was face down on the flagstones, arms by his side, as if waiting for a massage.

Shepreth walked carefully through the open chapel to the doorway which led on to the cloister, and inched an eye around the jamb. Three of Payán's men were sheltering behind the old stone columns, one firing, the other two reloading. He aimed at the former's legs and the man dropped with a squeal. The other two made a dive for the shelter of the nearest room. 'Clear,' he yelled to Docherty, and watched the distant figure of the Scot scurry along behind the far columns and disappear into the open door of the church. One more burst of fire into the relevant room and Shepreth abandoned the cloister, running back out through the open chapel.

Docherty was waiting in front of the church, slamming another magazine into his AK47. 'Go,' he told Shepreth, turning the gun on first the helicopter and then the pick-up.

The explosion of the helicopter's fuel tank almost knocked Shepreth off his feet as he ran for the wall; the boom from the pick-up was almost anticlimactic in comparison. He clambered over to find the two women waiting, Carmen's anxiety dissolving into a huge smile as he appeared. A moment later Docherty was jumping down beside him, urging everyone up the slope which the three of them had descended not half an hour before.

As they climbed the path the whole head of the valley seemed lit by the burning vehicles below, but no figures emerged into the atrium. Payán's men no longer had their leader to make their decisions for them, and his right-hand men in Chihuahua and Ciudad Juárez were a long way from the action. Docherty reckoned that their chances of reaching the border had improved considerably in the last half-hour.

Getting across it was another matter. If there was an American name inside the ledger Shepreth was carrying, then that American would soon be pulling out all the stops to recover it. One of his agents at the border crossing perhaps, obeying orders he didn't understand. 'Could you come this way, sir? I'm afraid we'll have to look after these records for you . . . A possible threat to national security . . .'

And that was an optimistic reading – Mr X would no doubt prefer that they were killed. Docherty kept walking, half of his mind celebrating their success, the other half searching for ways to make it stick.

A few metres behind him Carmen was also counting blessings and curses. Her whole being seemed to be almost quivering with relief that her sister was alive, that Shepreth hadn't been badly injured or killed, that they were on their way. But it had taken only a few seconds for her to realize that her sister was not the same person she had been a year ago. Of course she hadn't really expected that she would be, but she couldn't help hoping . . . Now only time would tell how serious the damage was, and the sense of heartbreak which that provoked seemed so at odds with the happiness which kept bubbling through her whenever she thought about Shep.

He was bringing up the rear, still a little in shock from that moment when he thought his life was over. The bullet had caught a corner of the ledger – another couple of inches down or to the right and he wouldn't have been walking anywhere.

They were ascending the dry stream bed now, and the fires in the valley below were no longer visible. The moon was riding high in the centre of a shimmering universe, the shadowy mountains stretching away, and the thought crossed Shepreth's mind that it wasn't the sort of place from which you took a taxi home.

For the next hour Docherty navigated their way across the broken plateau towards the niche in the rocks where he and Manolo had waited two nights before. There they rejoined the Tarahumara, along with one of his young disciples, their backpacks and the six horses.

Docherty returned the AK47 to its rightful owner. 'Payán is dead,' he told Manolo.

The Indian's lips creased in a smile. 'And the man you were looking for?'

'He is dead too.'

Manolo nodded gravely, then gave a wan smile.

They mounted the horses. Despite Carmen's assurance Docherty was half expecting problems with Marysa, but the opposite seemed the case. Once in the saddle she seemed more animated than before and more at ease with her mount than Docherty was with his.

The six of them made the long descent in single file, reaching the canyon floor soon after two-thirty. Even with the benefit of the hidden moon the trail was almost invisible to the naked eye, and for the next few hours they were totally dependent on Manolo's knowledge of the canyon. They were still about eight kilometres from the station at Divisadero when the first rays of light began working their way down the eastern canyon wall, and Manolo led them out of the main canyon and up a narrow wooded cleft past a succession of small waterfalls.

'The walk to the station is all uphill and sometimes steep,' he told Docherty. 'It will take the women at least two hours.'

The Scot did a quick calculation. The train was due at ten past one, but it was unlikely to be less than half an hour late. They didn't want to be hanging around the station for too long but then they could hardly afford to miss it. 'We'll be here for about five hours,' he told the others, adding that they should try to get some sleep if they could. Which of course was easier said than done. His own brain seemed determined to watch endless reruns of the night's events, so he just lay there with his eyes open, head on the backpack, staring up at the kaleidoscope of colours on the soaring canyon wall.

The next thing he knew, Manolo was shaking him awake with the news that it was almost eleven o'clock. He woke the others, and wished he'd been more careful with Marysa, whose eyes sprang open with an expression he wished he hadn't seen. Then they closed again and she pursed her lips, as if she was trying to squeeze something from her memory.

Ten minutes later they were ready to go. Docherty thanked Manolo and asked him to give his goodbyes to Paco. 'Tell him I will bring my family to meet his,' he said, hoping it would be possible.

The walk to Divisadero took less than the expected two hours but it was hard work just the same. They arrived at the station looking like one more group of exhausted gringo backpackers, and were duly set upon by the sellers of Indian trinkets and Mexican snacks. There was no sign of Payán's men, either uniformed or otherwise. If a search was underway – and it was hard to believe that it wouldn't be – then it hadn't yet reached here.

Docherty bought a couple of *burritos* and sat down to eat them, his eyes scanning the station area. He was pleased to see that there were several other gringos waiting for the train – a couple who looked and sounded like Germans, two obviously American young women and a lone male with the Australian flag plastered across his backpack.

The minutes ticked by, and eventually the train arrived – a line of dirty green coaches pulled by a blue diesel. Apparently it stopped for fifteen minutes at Divisadero, during which time the tourists were expected to gape at the canyon below, take photographs and buy souvenirs. The four of them watched out of the window, expecting at any moment to hear the whirr of an approaching helicopter above the idling hum of the diesel.

The train eventually clanked out of the station. Docherty bought their tickets to Chihuahua and surveyed the other occupants of the first-class carriage, at least half of whom were gringos. He caught one of the men smiling at him, and realized it was a smile of envy from another middle-aged man, one who hadn't got a woman as gorgeous as Marysa sitting next to him.

Creel was the train's next stop, and if any station in the mountains was being watched then that would be the one. It seemed to take an age to reach, but when they finally pulled in alongside the crowded platform there was no line of men waiting with guns. There were two uniformed policemen standing beside the doorway to the station building, but their wholehearted attention was almost immediately claimed by the two American women who had got on at Divisadero, and who were now asking for directions.

In the seat behind, Carmen and Shepreth were both remembering their first kiss on this very platform, three long nights ago.

The train resumed its journey, following a succession of winding valleys down from the mountains. Docherty's mind continued to race with unverifiable assumptions and unanswerable questions. No one had seen Carmen, so their pursuers were probably looking for two gringos and one woman. Did they have any photographs, either of Marysa or himself? He could just imagine Bazua taking humiliating shots of women, and it was hard to believe that someone hadn't taken his own picture on Providencia. But maybe he was just being pessimistic. Maybe there was no pursuit.

As they neared the small town of Cuauhtémoc he wondered whether it would be safer to leave the train rather than go on to Chihuahua. No, he decided. They would probably be the only gringos getting off there, and at Chihuahua their fellow-tourists would serve as camouflage. They would stay on board.

The sun went down behind the train, and the last hour of the journey was travelled in almost complete darkness. They stepped down on to Chihuahua's single platform fearing the worst, but another pair of uniformed policemen did nothing more threatening than ogle the gringo women, and during the taxi ride to the city centre they could all feel the tension beginning to drain from their bodies.

The main square was full of life, and there the taxi driver dropped them off at a car-hire firm that was just about to close for the day. They wanted an early start to visit the ruins at Casa Grande, Shepreth told the reluctant proprietor, and once a sizeable bonus had changed hands the man was able to appreciate their urgency. Five minutes later they were on the way out of the city in a dark-blue Nissan Cherry, with only three hundred and fifty kilometres of modern highway between them and the border town of Ciudad Juárez. For the next three hours Docherty and Shepreth took turns at the wheel, and as they sped along the straight and frequently empty two-lane road the Scot began to feel more optimistic.

That feeling took a bit of a dent when the lights of the state police car brightened in their rear-view mirror. As it passed them the officer in the passenger seat stared across, turned to say something to the driver, then gave Shepreth the signal to stop.

'Shit!' the two men murmured in stereo. Glancing in the back, Docherty saw that the two women were awake again. He took the Browning from the dashboard compartment and pushed it into his belt beneath the hanging shirt.

The two Mexican policemen climbed out of their car and walked carefully back towards the Nissan, each with one hand on the butt of his holstered gun.

'*Buenas noches*,' Shepreth said.

'*Buenas noches*,' one of the men replied curtly, as he did a round of the faces. 'Passports,' he demanded.

Docherty groaned inwardly – Marysa wouldn't have one. He handed the nearest man his own, reckoning that it would be better if the cops had their hands full when he pulled the Browning on them, but at that moment Carmen cheerfully produced two passports from the pouch she wore around her neck.

Docherty hardly had time to feel relieved before another problem reared its head – did the Mexicans know they were looking for Colombian women? Would Bazua have bothered to advertise the fact? Would Payán's men have known? As the Scot's fingers inched towards the butt of the Browning once more his mind wrestled with the various options. Should they take their own car or the police car? They could lock the two officers in the boot of one of them . . .

The Mexican was still studying Carmen's passport. Now, Docherty thought, but at that moment bright lights flashed in the rear-view mirror.

The car was going fast, and as it went by they had a brief glimpse of young American males, a brief sonic deluge from their car stereo. The Mexican stared after the vanishing tail-lights, a frown on his face, and almost absent-mindedly handed back the passport. A few moments later he and his partner were in pursuit.

The four of them just sat there for a moment.

'How come you had Marysa's passport?' Docherty

asked, still staring through the windscreen at the disappearing police car.

'I've had it all the time,' she told him. 'I wanted a picture of her to show people on Providencia.'

They resumed their journey, and some fifteen minutes later they passed the policemen and the American youths, one of whom seemed to be counting out dollar bills. Forty-five minutes after that they were entering the outskirts of Ciudad Juárez, eyes peeled for a suitable-looking motel. The border was now only a few kilometres away but Docherty had no intention of attempting a crossing until he was certain that all the other options looked worse. As things stood at the moment there were people in authority on both sides of the Rio Grande who had a vested interest in stopping them.

They chose a mid-priced motel, and after they had been given the keys to two of its rooms by a sleepy-looking girl of about twelve, Shepreth phoned Vaughan at his apartment in Mexico City. 'Just get over the border,' the DEA man told him. 'My friends in Washington tell me the President already has a private investigation going – it's just a matter of time.'

Shepreth explained that they might run into problems if they just presented themselves at Mexican emigration.

'It seems like about ten million people have managed to get across without presenting themselves to anybody,' Vaughan murmured. 'OK, just sit tight,' he added, rather more sympathetically. 'I'll see what I can arrange.'

Shepreth told the others what Vaughan had told him.

'We could go through the tunnel,' Marysa said.

They all looked at her.

'Angel was boasting about his escape from the island,'

she said quietly, 'and his friend – the pig you shot – he told him about a tunnel he has built under the border, right under the Rio Grande.'

'Did he say where it was?' Docherty asked.

'Not exactly. But he has a bottling plant – for Mexican beer, yes? – and he said the noise of the machinery covered up the noise of the digging.'

Docherty reached for the telephone directories on the washstand. As far as he could work out there were only four bottling plants in Ciudad Juárez, and only one of them – according to the city map they had already borrowed from the girl in reception – was within stone-throwing distance of the river.

'Now?' Shepreth asked him.

'Why not?' the Scot said.

They all climbed back into the car, and Docherty drove them towards the centre of the town. It was a quarter to one in the morning, but small groups of men seemed to be loitering on every corner of the ugly modern streets, looking like they'd been hired by some spendthrift movie mogul to create a restless, almost ominous atmosphere. The main square showed more activity, but the hustlers were too busy to notice them and the whores turned away when they noticed the women in the back seat.

Payán's bottling plant was another kilometre to the west, one of several industrial premises which lay between the wide road and the glorified concrete drainage channel which went by the name of the Rio Grande. There was a light shining through the open door in the loading dock as they went past, but no sign of a night shift in progress. The high wire gates were closed.

A few hundred metres further up the road Docherty

turned the Nissan round and stopped for a moment. There was probably a way in from one of the adjoining premises, but he was still wondering what to do with the other three while he investigated when a Toyota Land Cruiser purred by.

He watched as it slowed and came to a halt, either at the gates of the bottling plant or somewhere very close by. He turned off his own lights and moved the Nissan forward, pulling up behind the other vehicle just as the gates swung open.

'Ready?' he asked Shepreth, and followed the Toyota in.

As he drew up behind it a man on the loading dock glanced in their direction, then gave the men in the Toyota an enquiring look. They obviously had no idea what he was asking them, because neither of them looked round until their questioner's hands shot up in the air, and by that time Docherty's Browning was waiting to invite them out of the cab and into the factory.

Once everyone was inside, the loading-dock door shut behind them, Shepreth and Carmen held guns on the three men while Docherty went to make sure that the rest of the building was empty. He came back a few minutes later with a ball of wire and the news that it was.

The sight of the wire made the Mexican night guard talkative. 'Do you know who you are messing with?' he asked them contemptuously. 'Payán – that is who. He will roast your balls over a slow fire for this.'

'I doubt it,' Docherty told him mildly. 'We killed him yesterday.'

The man started to laugh, but the look on his companions' faces put a stop to that. They were now frightened.

'Where is the tunnel?' Docherty asked them briskly.

'We don't know,' one of them said. 'We have just come from Chihuahua. He will know,' he added, indicating the night guard.

'Well?' Docherty asked.

'I know nothing about a tunnel,' the man said sullenly.

Docherty walked over to him, grabbed his belt with one hand and thrust the barrel of the Browning down inside it with the other. 'Where is the tunnel?' he asked again.

'I show you,' the man said breathlessly.

It was under one of the storage rooms which lined one wall of the main building. A concrete slab floor on steel rollers slid aside to reveal a shaft about thirty metres deep. Aluminium ladder-like stairs were provided for humans, winches for the bundles of cocaine, heroin and whatever other contraband came this way.

The night guard obligingly turned on the lights and Docherty went down. In the chamber at the bottom there was a neatly stacked mountain of plastic bags containing enough drugs to relaunch the American 60s. Facing this yet-to-be-realized fortune was a large opening in the wall. Docherty flicked one of the switches beside it and the lights came on, illuminating a concrete-reinforced tunnel some two metres high and one metre wide which stretched away into the distance. He flicked the other and heard the hum of air-conditioning. Well, he thought, you couldn't expect smugglers to raise a sweat.

'Send 'em down,' he shouted up to Shepreth, and the three Mexicans descended the stairs. Once Shepreth had joined him Docherty fastened the three men's wrists and ankles with wire. They wouldn't have much trouble getting free once their captors were gone, but by then it wouldn't matter. As the other three started down the tunnel he cast a wistful look back at the hoard of drugs, thinking that it would have been nice to wash them down a drain. Unfortunately it would also have taken most of the night.

The tunnel, which proved to be about a kilometre in length, ended in another chamber at the bottom of another shaft. Docherty climbed the metal stairs and listened for signs of life above. Hearing none, he pulled the switch which rolled back the concrete slab and climbed out into a warehouse full of shoeboxes. He called down the all-clear and went in search of the outside world.

A single bolted door led him out on to one of El Paso's darker streets.

The other three emerged, and all four of them started walking towards the better-lit street in the distance. The neon signs of several hotels appeared above the rooftops, and they were just nearing the crossroads when a police car cruised into view. Docherty instinctively put his arm around Marysa's neck, knowing without looking that Shepreth had done the same with Carmen. Marysa flinched and then stiffened at his touch, but she didn't pull away, and after one lingering stare at the late-night revellers the cop drove on. Two minutes later they were bribing a night receptionist to give them rooms.

Docherty was woken by the sun streaming in through the crack which he had deliberately left in the curtains. Shepreth was still asleep in the other bed, snoring slightly.

The Scot lay there for a moment, then got up and gently

prised open the connecting door. In the adjoining room the two sisters were sleeping like spoons, Carmen's left arm wrapped protectively around Marysa's waist. They looked like young girls, a picture of innocence.

He had heard Carmen and Shepreth on the balcony in the middle of the night. They had been whispering at first, but then there had been silence for a while, and finally the ecstatic breathing of lovemaking, her muted cry, his muted groan. Docherty could remember a handful of occasions in his adult life when he had been an unseen witness to others' pleasure, but this time he had taken a strange delight in the sounds. This was love he was listening to, not just sex.

He had no idea what would happen to the two of them. They came from different worlds – Shep had the worst job in the world for relationships, Carmen a sister who would be needing more attention than most children. Maybe he was turning into a romantic in his old age, or maybe he was just seeing his younger self and Isabel reflected in their mirror, but Docherty found himself believing that they would a find a way to be together.

It was almost seven-thirty. He took a shower and then woke Shepreth, who looked groggily up at him. 'You're on guard,' he told the MI6 man, picking up Bazua's ledger from the top of the TV and letting himself out of the room.

The hotel still seemed half asleep, but the rest of El Paso was already well into its stride. Docherty walked across the palm-lined square thinking that the town looked more Mexican than American, and nothing like the place described in the Marty Robbins record he'd bought in 1959.

The office supply store was just opening as he reached

it, allowing him the choice of the six copier machines in the window. There were almost five hundred sheets in Bazua's ledger, which meant that he would be turning them for the best part of two hours.

As the copier whirred and the bright light slid to and fro he stood there, turning the pages on automatic, thinking about Guillermo Macías, whose name he had found under the date of his arrest. Toscono had not lied about the reason for that – the boy had been picked up with a group of others and charged with 'spreading malicious propaganda'. For five weeks he had been repeatedly hung by the wrists and given high-voltage shocks with electric cattle prods, for no other reason than the warped pleasure of his captors. On Christmas Eve he had been one of seven dropped from a helicopter into the River Plate, his wrists bound with wire.

To judge from many of the other entries he had been one of the luckier ones, but Docherty didn't imagine the boy's parents would see it like that.

He thought about the five young women who had been kidnapped into slavery more than a year before. Marysa had told them that Rosalita had killed herself after only a few weeks on the island, but had so far refused to say anything more about the long ordeal. Placida and Irma were also dead, Victoria and Marysa damaged in ways he couldn't begin to comprehend. He asked himself how his fellow-men could behave in such a way and got no answer.

The machine whirred on, and eventually the entire ledger had been copied. He packed it into a box provided by the store and then made three additional copies of the two pages which detailed the involvement of two named

American Intelligence operatives – there was no mention of which agency they worked for – in the extended torture and gang-raping of four female student prisoners at the Rosario army base in early 1977.

After making three copies of the covering letter he had composed in the early hours of the morning he gathered everything together and headed for the post office. Half an hour later the box was on its way to his own address in Chile and the three envelopes were travelling express to the *New York Times*, the *Guardian* and the German magazine *Der Spiegel.*

He re-emerged into the sunlight with the original ledger and dodged his way through the busy traffic to the centre of the square. It was still only ten o'clock, and on impulse he bought a coffee from the kiosk and sat in the shade to drink it. The people, like the town, were mostly Mexican, and he sat there watching as they went about their daily business. Maybe it was the sunshine, the riot of colours, but now, as in 1977, he found these people so full of life.

Maybe that was why they needed their Days of the Dead – yearly reminders that life was also hard and cruel.

Docherty didn't think he needed the health warning any more. Maybe this time the good guys had emerged relatively unscathed, but there had been enough times in the past when that hadn't been the case, and he had his doubts whether either of the surviving women would ever be the same again.

But then even the bad guys had souls.

Docherty looked up at the pure blue sky, sighed and got back to his feet. He had seen enough days of the dead. He was ready to write the fucking memoirs.